Horsewater

Gary James Daynes

Boxing Hare Publishing

www.boxingharepublishing.com

All of the characters in this book are fictitious and any resemblance to actual persons, living or dead, is purely coincidental. The names, incidents, dialogue and opinions expressed are products of the authors imagination and are not to be construed as real in any form and are not the views or opinions of the author or publisher.

First published in 2024 by Boxing Hare Publishing Ltd
www.boxingharepublishing.com

ISBN: 978-1-9995916-3-2

A CIP Catalogue record of this book is available
from the British Library

Set in Garamond 11
Cover artwork and design by © Gary Daynes 2024
Book design by Boxing Hare Publishing Ltd

For Bert - 'Beezer the Geezer' - a brave & wise 'true gent.'
A great character and gentle giant, sadly missed.

And to all of my other Equine Friends, whose beautiful company I've been blessed to enjoy for so many years and who've all helped bring me such fun, joy, wonder, excitement, fear and variety to my life.
Along with much pain, sadness and poverty!

But I wouldn't change a thing. Thanks to you all.

Especially dedicated to:

Tirus - St. Swithin / Bonzo / The Old Man

Fred - High Flyer / Frednee Bear

Goldie - Berkeley's Fools Gold / P.J. / Ploppy Joe

Splodgie - Casanova / Midnight Madness / The Old Codger

Meg - Little Meg

Samson - The Colonel / Snorky / Samuel Joseph the Horse

Cirrus - Silver Cirrus / Lady Petunia

Tess - Contessa / Scarey Marey / Plodski Mare

Bert - Horizontal Herbert / Beezer the Geezer / Mr. B

Bonnie - The Moo / Barney Rubble / Lady Griswold / Trollop

Ted - Oakheart Pilgrim / Uncle Ted / Lord Chumley / Chumbo

Thanks also to Bunny - for the first days of independent riding.
Finn - for some great days out in the field.
Rosie - for that amazing jump with the Bloodhounds!
Balmacara - for a memorable and amazing experience and for safely getting me around Fakenham Racecourse (We didn't lose!)
Bronte - Beautiful girl and so glad you made it back home.
Spider - Naughty but Nice Chap - Gone too early.
To Mitzy (first ride), Tango & Meshach from Cringleford and Salvo, Lulu and Irish from my time at Stoneleigh. All great memories - Great horses.
And all those many other horses who I have been blessed to ride and meet.

See the back for details of all my equine family and their lives.

The European Brown Hare
(Lepus europaeus)

This page is dedicated to these stunning and grand creatures who grace our fields and whose preservation should be encouraged by all to enjoy their beauty forever. Such a joy to see racing across grassland and open fields.

Non-native to the UK originally, they are thought to have been introduced in Roman times or even earlier - 2000BC. What did the Roman's ever do!

Hares are most common in the UK on open farmland, grassland or woodland edges and live in scrapes or 'forms', which are shallow depressions in the ground or grass. They will dip down and flatten their ears when seen.

Golden-brown, with a pale belly and white tail, hares are larger, more athletic and slimmer than rabbits, with distinct black-tipped ears and long legs and stunning big yellow / black eyes.

With those long and powerful legs Hares can reach speeds of up to 45mph, being the UK's fastest land mammal. You won't catch one!

The much admired sight of 'Boxing Hares' seen in the early spring; where it is in fact unreceptive females fending off amorous males, is synonymous with the saying of the 'Mad March Hare'.

The gestation period for Hares is about 42 - 44 days, and they have litters of two to three, called Leverets. They are born in grass-lined nests, called Forms.

Hares live on average about 4 years in the wild, but can live up to 12 years in captivity. Being a very athletic, open-space animal, they are not good pets!

Iceni Queen Boudica was believed to have consulted the entrails of a hare as a sign of her victory against the Romans in AD 61; hares rapidly being established by then.

The Hare, a symbol of regeneration, fertility and forms of magic, has long been associated with Pagan rituals and is famous for being associated with the moon, and hence the 'Moon Gazing' Hare is linked with many superstitions.

The Ancient Egyptian's worshipped a Hare goddess known as Unut or Wenut - 'The Swift One.' - Very apt.

Admire and enjoy these beautiful animals, more especially when you gaze at the star constellation Lepus, just at the base or feet of Orion The Hunter.

The Hare

'The patience of the hunter is always greater than that of the prey'

Trespassers Will Be Eaten - *Slowly*

Prologue

The Hunting Act 2004 received Royal asset on
18th November 2004.

It became English Law on 18th February 2005.

Hunting with hounds - as practised by nobility and all for hundreds of years - was banned in England.

Hunts vowed to adapt and continue hunting. But also wait.

The Conservative party vowed it would repeal the act.

The Labour Prime Minister resigned in 2007.

The 'prudent' Labour Chancellor became the new
Prime Minister & took over office in Downing Street.

But it was a short-lived poisoned chalice.
The World's finances were in a mess.
Credit Crunch, Broken Banks, Economic Downturn
and Recession followed. Bad times for government.

A General Election was rapidly held.

The Labour Government was brought down and the shortest serving Prime Minister resigned.

A landslide Conservative Government was elected.
The new Prime Minister was a former keen Hunter.

The Conservative's kept their promise.

In 2008 The Hunting Act 2004 was repealed.

Tally Ho!

25 Years Earlier...

The young boy stirred within the bed. Raising his head, he stared into the gloom, noting the curtain move. A whining draught blew through the aged box-sash timber windows. No moon lit the interior of the silent bedroom, and any streetlights devoid in the depths of the darkened countryside.

On the landing a floorboard creaked. A heavy foot.

Instinctively, the boy awoke fully. His eyes widened.

Head raised from the pillow, ears straining for the source of the sound, he tilted his head, scanning the shadows, his senses alert.

Another soft creek. Near his half-opened bedroom door.

A gentle thump. A muffled voice. Deep within the house. Downstairs.

The boy rose fully, pushing aside the sheets. Small feet hung over the bed edge. The room was damp, the air chilly. He sensed a figure softly approach the bedroom door, then a large dark form framed the doorway.

The boy tensed, drawing a soft breath as the object passed through the half-opened door, sliding silently against the doorframe and into the room. He froze as the figure drifted like a ghost towards his bed, before squatting down.

"Chris?" came an enquiring whisper in the dark.

"Yes dad?" the boy queried, his tone equally hushed.

"Someone's downstairs. Prowlers. They shouldn't be here. I'm going to look. Stay up here with mum. Don't move!"

The whispered order in the dark was firm, strong, but reassuring.

Alert young eyes watched with nervous excitement as the shadowy image exited the room as silently as it'd entered. The boy rose from the warm bed, the chill air prickling his skin. His heart pounded, half fear, half excitement.

A creak indicated his father's progress along the dark landing.

Something thumped heavily downstairs in the lounge.

Then voices. Unwelcome voices. Strangers.

His father's orders ignored, the boy rose quietly from the bed. Dressed in candy-striped cotton pyjamas, his bare feet carefully settled upon the smooth linoleum flooring. Tiptoeing, he padded softly over the cold surface towards the partially open doorway. Easing open the old timber door, he looked to his left, wide eyes gazing down the dark narrow landing.

The blurred silhouette of his father could be seen moving steadily ahead in the gloom, now cautiously approaching the top of the stairs.

"Get back in your room!" A voice hissed from behind.

The boy gasped, jumping and spinning on his haunches.

"What's going on mum?" he whispered to the figure.

She did not answer, as their heads turned in unison to see the vanishing blur of a father and husband disappear from sight, moving into the dark stairwell.

"Dad thinks we've a burglar. Maybe two. He's going downstairs to look."

The gentle voice of his mother whispered calmly in the gloom.

"And get back in your room to wait." She added firmly. "Now!"

The boy ignored her, clutching the doorframe, the figures tentatively poised, ears pricked, heads tilted, both listening for sound, whilst sensing movement.

Suddenly yellow torchlight flashed up the stairwell. Erratically waved, the bright beam sent obscure silhouettes dancing upon the stairwell wall and landing ceiling above. Both mother and son stared at the images in equal horror and fear, observing silently the brief, but weird macabre lightshow.

Muffled shouts. Loud crashing. Curses.

Bright flash. Deafening roar.

A shotgun blast. Then a deadly hush.

"John, John!" The woman's scream in the gloom broke the quiet.

Silence responded.

The boy froze, gripping tight to the doorframe as his mother's outline raced past and down the landing. Her bare feet padded on the wooden floor like damp slaps, as her ghostly image reached the stairwell, then was weirdly illuminated from a torch beam shone up from below. Staring in shock, his mother's ghoulish form disappeared down the stairwell, her tense voice still calling, almost screaming, then breaking into a painful cry. "John! Oh no!"

A mother's scream, then unknown male voices echoed up the stairwell, to break the boy's temporary trance and spur him into movement. He released his hold on the door and dashed along the landing, reaching the empty stairwell, down which moments earlier both of his parents had disappeared.

Fear flooded through him as he looked down the dark staircase. At the bottom, eerily illuminated from behind by swirling torches and dancing shadows, his mother's shadowy face appeared, staring up at him in terror.

"Run Chris! Run and hide!" She screamed up at the boy from the base of the stairs, tear filled eyes and horror etched upon her face. From the top of the stairs the boy's small arms reached out as his mother began to run up the staircase, her face etched with terror, one futile hand stretching out.

She made it up five treads.

A face appeared behind the boy's mother.

The stern face of a man. A stranger.

Looking beyond his mother's fearful face, the boy's eyes focussed upon the image of the man. A shotgun lay in the man's hands.

The boy stared at both man and gun.

Gun barrels rose swiftly, levelling at his mother's back.

She made it onto the seventh tread.

From the landing the boy reached out with both arms.

A tear dripped from the boy's knowing eyes.

Momentarily his gaze united with his mother. Union.

As she rose onto the eighth tread, without hesitation, the man's index finger curled firmly around the second trigger. Squeeze.

"Hide Chris!" She cried. "Strangers. They shouldn't be here!"

Those were her last words, lost in a deafening roar as the gun erupted.

Shotgun pellets tore into her back, disintegrating her spine, ripping onward through her stomach, spraying the boy in a shower of blood, flesh and bone.

The helpless boy watched his mother's lifeless body fall.

It slid back down the treads, her jaw thumping upon each tread in a series of juddering thuds. Blood smeared upon the white-painted boards as the lifeless carcass came to rest in a tattered, foetal-shaped heap at the base of the stairs.

In the gloom the blood-covered face of the boy gazed down. He stared emotionless, eyes glaring, gaze fixed upon the face of his parent's assassin.

Two pairs of eyes met each other, both cold and cursing.

The orphan. The killer.

"Sorry son. You've seen me," came the gruff, cold voice.

The man's hands shuffled around the stock and without moving his gaze, the killer expertly flicked the top lever, opening the shotgun. Two empty cartridge cases ejected, rattling to the floor with a gentle clatter. Instantly two fresh blue cartridges were slid into the chambers. The killer's eyes remained focused at all time on the motionless boy, who silently stared down at the man below.

Gun closed, the man pulled the weapon firmly into his shoulder and levelled the barrels, the aim deliberate. A brass bead centred upon the boy's pale face.

The unmoving boy looked down, cold eyes focused upon the dark holes of the barrels, then drifted down towards the man's index finger.

He gazed intently, watching it touch the first trigger, curl around the thin metal blade, then watched unmoving as it was squeezed.

The deafening blast roared up the stairwell and for a split second a vibrant orange flash illuminated the narrow white-plastered walls. Then darkness returned as pellets tore upwards, ripping into the wall at the top of the stairwell, kicking out a plume of thick dust and debris.

The boy's head disappeared. Gone.

"Fucking little bastard!" the gunman bellowed.

"What the hell's going on? A fresh voice joined the gunman.

"Missed him! The little shit." The gunman cursed.

Upstairs a door slammed.

The new man looked curiously on at his gun-wielding colleague.

"Oh my god! Why did you have to go and shoot her?"

The new voice spoke with concern, observing the bloody body of the woman lying at the base of the stairs. A gaping dark-red hole had been punched clean through her body.

"Now we're for it. You twat!" He yelled at the killer. "Two dead. Not good."

"She saw me," returned the first voice gruffly. "What was I to do? So did the little shit up there. We've got to kill him as well. All of them. Let's go."

"You what? A kid? You ain't trying to kill a kid I hope?"

The second man's voice responded with a nervous quiver.

"No way man, that's bad. I don't do kids. Not me."

He glanced at his compatriot warily, the gun menacing in his hands.

"It's easier to kill the lot," the gunman began justifying. "No witnesses. The bloke came down with a gun. He deserved it. That's self-defence. Then the woman ran at me. She probably had a hidden knife or scissors. Who knows? Self defence. Anyway, she saw me too. So has the kid now. We're in shit street big time. What's one more? It's easier to kill the lot. No witnesses. Then torch the gaff. I ain't doing any more bird for anyone. We'll both get life no matter how many die. One or three," the gunman coldly stated.

"We? What 'we' is this Dick? You killed them, not me. I was just getting the silverware and other posh goodies. I ain't gonna help you kill no kid," cried the second voice. "Killing kids? That's criminal!"

"You ain't got to kill anyone, chicken shit, I will. Just keep getting the good stuff. I'll sort the little bastard out. Then we can burn the place down, get out of here and no one will know it was us."

The second man shook his head, unsure, unwilling, but also compliant; intimidated by his brutal, gun-wielding colleague, whom he knew too well.

Waving torches, the pair regarded the tattered body of the woman at the base of the stairs, laying only yards away from her husband. His spread-eagled form lay upon the quarry stone floor of the lounge, fresh pooling blood glinting like black treacle in the torch glow. The gunman moved forward, carefully stepping over the woman's body and proceeded cautiously up the stairs, shotgun held before him, poised and ready. Upon passing the woman's body, he turned his torch, flashing its beam at his companion. He stood motionless, staring at the two corpses, shaking his head in disbelief.

"Get the rest of the stuff!" he bellowed, "Quickly, before anyone else comes. I'll soon get this matter finished. And keep your bleeding gloves on! Move!"

The other man reluctantly dissolved into the gloom of the darkened lounge, muttering. His torch waved wildly about, casting bizarre shadows around the rough-plastered walls of the old farmhouse, as he searched for more booty.

The shotgun-wielding killer proceeded up the stairs, carefully placing each step upon the treads, one at a time. The torch, wedged between left hand and shotgun stock, waved erratically before him with each cautious step, the beam illuminating the blood-spattered stairwell. Reaching the landing, finger upon the trigger, he spun around, swinging the gun and torch into the gloom.

The torch illuminated a dark narrow landing, which suddenly became dimly backlit from a glow emanating up the stairwell, as a light downstairs in the lounge had seemingly been switched on. To free his hands, the gunman dropped the torch, the low light now radiating up the stairs being sufficient.

In the gloom, the gunman made out three doors set on the right side of the landing, with one door directly at the end facing him. All the aged timber doors were closed. Straightening his back and snorting, preparing himself for action, the gunman cautiously advanced down the landing. Upon reaching the first bedroom door, he pressed his back against the wall. Standing adjacent to the door, he spun around, faced the door, and in one swift movement, kicked it open. He fell through the opening doorway, whilst one handed, he swung the shotgun into the darkened room. His free hand felt for a light switch.

The room illuminated.

The man squinted. An exposed light bulb glowed, hung on a simple cable. It illuminated a spare room, with a bare wooden floor and boxes neatly stacked along the back wall. The man's experienced eyes scanned the empty interior.

Moments later he sent the room back into darkness, then proceeded back onto the landing and stepping three strides sideways, stood beside the door of the next room. Again he violently kicked the door, the force causing it to swing back into him. His shoulder stopped the movement of the loose door and turning sideways, he fumbled for the light switch along the wall.

The room illuminated.

Again skilful eyes scanned the bedroom. A single bed stood against the far wall, mixed with an array of furniture. The small room was full of toys, games and associated boxes, all neatly stacked. A number of brightly coloured rosettes were proudly displayed at the base of the bed. The man advanced into the room, a small plastic horse crunching under his uncaring foot. He moved toward the empty wooden-framed bed, his actions deliberate, face an over-confident smirk. A cream sheet and grey blanket hung down low from the bed to the floor, seemingly purposely positioned, almost as if to cover the open space beneath. He smiled. Reaching the bed, he lowered his body and slowly lifted the sheet with one hand, the other pushing the shotgun barrels under the seemingly empty bed space, finger poised on the trigger.

He peered underneath the bed.

A pair of eyes stared back.

"Got ya!"

His finger tensed on the trigger. Then paused.

He signed, then thrust an arm beneath the bed, roughly grasping at a small head, pulling the small body clear from underneath the bed.

The large teddy bear hauled from under the bed was tossed across the floor with contempt, the gunman cursing. He returned to his feet and headed toward a tall mahogany wardrobe set against the far wall. Pointing the barrels before him with one hand, levelling them at waist height, he pulled at the left door with his free hand. His eyes focussed upon a pair of small black riding boots, toes pointing towards him, a long coat hung conveniently above. He smiled, jabbing the barrels into the jacket, expecting soft tissue and a yelp, but was disappointed with empty clothes and wooden thud from the wardrobe.

He pulled open the remaining door, only to reveal more child's clothing, the bottom of the wardrobe filled with numerous pairs of children's shoes and boots, all stacked neatly in pairs. He slammed the wardrobe doors shut and scanned the remainder of the room, noting horse posters, more rosettes and a couple of trophies, set upon a small bookshelf stacked with books.

But no child. Dejected, he headed back towards the landing.

Flicking off the bedroom light, he shut the bedroom door behind him, eyes blinking as he re-entered the dark landing.

The landing illuminated.

A sudden orange flash. Blinding.

A roaring blast. Deafening

Flash and roar. Over in a second.

But the effects were eternal.

The brief orange flash vanished and the roar subsided.

Lead pellets tore into the left side of the intruder's pelvis and upper leg. The metal beads continued their journey, tearing remorselessly through the man's body, ripping into groin and bladder and blasting away his genitals. The man's jeans instantly soaked in a foul mix of urine and blood. The blast forced the gunman backwards. He fell heavily onto what was left of his torn and tattered buttocks, dropping his own shotgun, his senses in disarray. Shock and awe.

He sat with no sense of pain due to the shattered spine base. Slumping against the wall, he became aware of hot fluid squirting onto the floor before him, but was unaware of the source. His ruptured femoral artery freely leaked away his life with each vibrant red spurt. Two minutes of life left. Not long.

In the gloom, the eerie outline of the child slowly appeared.

A .410 shotgun was grasped firmly in both hands.

The butt protruded beneath his armpit, the gun too big.

One of the two barrels released a plume of light smoke.

The boy advanced, casually looking down at the gunman.

Losing vast quantities of blood, the original spurt had reduced to a gush. Sticky dark liquid pooled about where the man's groin had been, forming a black puddle. The defeated gunman slowly raised his head, bewildered and deep in shock, life fading, he staring silently as the boy approached.

The boy closed in, his face inches from the unwanted guest. His gentle image was pale, ghostly, almost glowing in the gloom. His skin smelt of fresh soap.

"You shouldn't be here," the boy whispered gently.

Casually, he simply stepped over the dying man, but slid the intruder's fallen gun away from reach with his small foot. Just in case.

Silently he moved along the landing. Stopping at the top of the stairs, he peered cautiously around the corner of the stairwell and gazed down.

A voice boomed out from the lounge area below.

"Was that it Dick? Did you get him? Is the little bugger dead?"

Silence greeted the enquirer in the lounge.

"What the hell are you doing?" the man yelled, concern in his voice as he moved towards the base of the stairs. "Dick! Dick? What are you doing?"

Silence responded.

There was a simple answer.

Dick was dying.

In thirty seconds he'd be dead. Gone.

His colleague looked warily up the dark, empty stairwell, and then down at the bloody form lying at the foot of the stairs and then within the lounge. He shook his head, regarding the bag filled with the evening's booty, then again at the two tattered bodies, which minutes earlier had been the small boy's parents. It had cost then their lives. He swallowed and shook his head as the iron-like acrid stench of blood and sweet smell of cordite filled the air.

Dick! Answer me, you tosser! If not I'm getting the hell out of here now and leaving you to take all of the shit! You can burn the place down."

The now frantic voice hollered once more up the silent, semi-illuminated stairwell, the top landing in eerie darkness, no sound coming down.

"Dick! What the fuck are you doing up there? Answer me."

Silence returned down the gloomy stairwell.

Dick wasn't doing anything. He was dead.

Half out of curiosity and half out of some strange criminal loyalty, the man edged forward and put a careful foot on the base of the stairs. He eased up the first tread, then stepped up another tread, now standing over the woman's body, averting his eyes from the mess beneath him. The tread creaked as he pressed his body against the wall, sliding past the woman's lifeless form, moving quickly up the next few treads. Red streaks smeared behind him as his back brushed against the blood-splattered wall. Cautious of the silence, he carefully dropped down onto all fours, crouching his body down low as he approached the top of the stairs, his face inches from the landing floor.

Slowly he peered around the stairwell corner, blinking eyes adjusting to the gloom, as he stared into the darkness of the landing.

Two black steel circles were thrust into his face.

He froze where he lay.

The steel circles were warm against his skin.

He snorted heavily. The scent of cordite was fresh.

Attached at the other end of the shotgun was a young boy.

His expression was blank - lifeless.

"Don't shoot me kid," the distraught voice squealed.

The boy remained silent, gun unwavering.

"I had nothing to do with this. It's all Dick's idea. His fault. Honest! I'm innocent. Just let me go. Yes? Don't shoot me. Please!"

The man's eyes flicked from gun barrels to boy's face.

Pressed hard against the man's nose, the barrels squeezed his ruddy flesh.

The man gulped, now wanting the toilet.

"You shouldn't be here." The boy spoke in a soft whisper.

His manner was nonchalant. His gaze lost.

"I know," the man replied, wincing. "I'm sorry."

The boy simply shrugged his shoulders.

"Bye."

A flash and roar.

The man's face exploded, disappearing with half his skull.

The blast forced the boy back. He fell onto the landing floor with a bump, the smoking shotgun resting in his lap.

There he sat in silence, in the darkness. Alone.

Dry eyes stared at the gaping, bloody hole in the wall.

The strangers had all gone.

Good.

'They shouldn't have been there.'

Chapter 1

If you go down to the woods today you're sure of a big surprise....

'Trespassers Will Be Eaten' the sign boldly declared. Bright headlights illuminated the intimidating warning, before sending the hand painted sign back into darkness, the white beams revealing the gloomy woodland track.

The male driver smiled, just as he'd done months earlier when first seeing the sign, unsure then if a joke or for real. The headlights of the silver Mercedes Coupe drifted away from the warning sign and as the driver switched to sidelights, it sent a soft glow around the vehicle in the pitch black, as it slowly crept deeper into the wood, the large engine merely ticking over.

The narrow dirt track twisted through the woods, the firm dark earth barely visible in the dim light. At a T-junction, the track split into two, separated by a large beech tree and clump of brambles. The car deviated left, the chosen route short, finally ending at the base of some dense bushes.

The driver always parked in this same tight spot. Secluded to the sides by various tall bushes, brambles and mixed saplings, with taller trees and dense holly bushes to the front, it was almost the perfect hidden parking space. Set within the large, empty wood, it was well out of sight from anyone foolish enough to travel along the narrow woodland track, day or night.

The car stopped, engine shutting off, lights cancelling.

Silence encompassed the vehicle.

It was 6.30pm, but already dark. Heavy cloud blanketed any glow of the full moon. The tips of overhanging branches softly tapped and rubbed against the car roof and bonnet, gently stirred by a chill, early November wind. The passenger in the car grinned at the driver, her hand reaching across the gear stick to touch the top of his thigh. For a few seconds the occupants remained still and silent, as if waiting for some command to move. Both smiled.

Then with no words spoken, as if a well-practised routine, the pair both began removing their jackets and shoes. They clambered onto the cramped rear seats of the vehicle, their ghostly figures obscured by already steamy, dark windows. The man reclined on the soft cream leather, raising his legs onto the door rest, as the woman crawled atop, sniggering, pulling him close, tongue kissing him long and deep. Four eager hands explored two excited bodies.

Pete Jenkins was keen to get on, but for other reasons.

He'd promised his wife he wouldn't be late home.

Shepherd's pie for tea. Again. Most likely burnt. Again.

His marriage had been on the rocks for years. Many years.

Wife Jill suspected affairs, but never found proof.

Maybe she didn't want to. Too much to lose. Pretend it was nothing.

However, things were now getting complicated. Difficult. Not as planned.
Somehow life was never simple for Pete. Never as planned. Self inflicted.
Debbie, with dangerously sharp fingernails, was now eagerly removing Pete's underpants and trousers in a well-practised singular movement, She was the one getting a bit too serious. Talk of 'divorce' and of 'settling down,' had been muted by her. Not something Pete wanted. Definitely not with Debbie.
Other than sex, the pair had little in common. Debbie had no other interests, except for eating chocolate and enjoying the expensive clothes and shoes Pete bought her. And at twenty-two, she was twenty years Pete's junior. A great shag, but and at times he felt it. Debbie was very demanding. In many ways.
Temp work led Debbie to Pete's insurance company.
Fluttering eyelids and a short skirt led Pete to Debbie.
From then of Debbie simply led the way. All the way.
Neither party had been shy coming forward. Open wide.
Pete had Debbie on his desk within two weeks of arriving.
Or was it the other way around? Pete was never quite sure.
That was six months ago. Things moved fast and furious.
'I wonder what Jill's doing?' Pete mussed, sighing softly whilst stroking Debbie's already busy bobbing head fully hardened him. *'Who cares!'*
Debbie removed her face from his groin, a string of semi-transparent fluid attached to her lips, and kissed him hard. Pete's eager hands fumbled with Debbie's cotton blouse. Three buttons were quickly undone and his hands moved inside, feeling her small warm breasts restrained by her tight lacy bra. He fumbled with the front fastening, until with a wiggle, the catch released. Out fell two perfectly round breasts, like grapefruits, freed from a restraint. He drew her forward, kissing her throat, then moved down to the space between her breastbone. Debbie arched her back, willingly offering a breast with a cupped hand, pushing the soft flesh against Pete's mouth. He drew hard, nuzzling upon an acorn-shaped nipple. Debbie sighed, then released a deeper appreciative moan as Pete's hand went South.
Momentarily Pete thought of Jill at home again, cooking his tea. Whatever Jill had burnt for tea could wait. Pete already had his mouth full.
Moments later, stripped down, the pair were in full swing.
Debbie's lace thong had been removed and lay discarded in the floor-well of the car. Secretly she hoped Jill might discover it and ask serious questions of Pete, whom she sat astride and was deep inside. Grunting and groaning, bodies firmly conjoined, the pair thrust away as best each could in the confines of the luxury sports coupe. Various items of clothing lay discarded about the car, Pete naked all bar his socks, Debbie in just her blouse for some warmth. Pete's hands were inside her top, holding tightly onto her breasts, both for support and encouragement. Debbie smiled. She enjoyed having sex with Pete. That said she enjoyed having sex with most men.
But Pete was special and all part of what Debbie had planned for an age.

Basically uneducated after leaving school, Debbie soon tired of shop assistant jobs and casual work. Long boring hours for little pay. She'd left home at seventeen, living with a variety of boyfriends, soon learning that it certainly sometimes paid to do nothing and just 'lay-on your back.' It allowed her to live rent-free for a few more months with an irate boyfriend, who'd finally tire of her lazy manner and demanding needs and then want her out.

At five foot six, she had an athletic body, and put it to good use. Attractive, with a thick mass of long auburn hair; which she proudly claimed didn't come from a bottle, she had a pretty face, with a neat nose and slightly pronounced cheekbones, almost giving her an East European look. Her deep brown eyes, when fluttered over by her thick dark eyelashes, quickly melted many a man's heart. Doing the occasional 'temp' work in offices to pay the bills, she soon discovered many older managers found her naturally attractive. There'd been the odd fling with a couple of old duffers, but nothing serious. It usually meant being called back for another contract, and the older men liked to treat her; taking her out for meals, hotel breaks and buying the odd nice gift.

Despite her natural good looks, she seemed unable to keep a steady boyfriend. Mostly she admitted because she was plain lazy and didn't basically want to do anything. She loved children, having always wanted a big family and would be quite happy suckling a baby all day, whilst eating chocolates and watching scandals, 'soaps' and chat shows on TV all day.

Unfortunately, the class of boyfriend she usually attracted lived in a shared house or a grubby bed-sit, and struggled to pay for those. A freeloading, chocolate-eating nanny to a child they didn't want was not most boyfriends idea of their younger 'Live today, Die tomorrow' lifestyle. Any 'young executives' she met at various offices nearly all lived with their 'mummy' and were both waiting for the Dream Girl, with a stable job and education, to pop into their lives. Not a 'loose temp', who'd sleep with anyone.

Morally wrong or not, she knew by scoring with a top businessman, married or not, it'd be a sure way to escape the almost pre-ordained repeat drudgery of her council estate childhood. She'd sworn to herself she'd never end up in a 'boiled cabbage' stinking council house, with a 'piss-head' abusive husband, just like her mother. She'd long decided, that whatever it took, she'd have it all and a little bit more, whilst still doing nothing. No matter what it took.

Enter Pete. Debbie's dream ticket. She wanted Pete and all he offered her financially. Also he wasn't too bad looking for an older man. A cross between a Hollywood B-lister and well-groomed Premier League footballer. Maybe.

But importantly, Pete was weak when it came to women, despite all of his cocky salesman's bravado. He saw women as another sale; never resisting a chance to 'source the lead' then 'close the deal'. He'd closed the deal on Debbie easily. But then she'd made sure of that. She'd been guaranteed.

Pete was an easy target. Putty in her long 'French nail' hands.

Debbie had it worked out. Everything carefully schemed. She hoped.

So far it was all going to plan. Well, sort of……. Maybe. A few issues.
The sooner Pete told his 'drippy bitch of a wife' Jill about her and their affair, the better it'd be. Well at least for Debbie. She was jealous of Jill, who happily drove about in the flash 3 series BMW paid for from Pete's fat commissions, whilst doing nothing all day. Other than undertaking voluntary work at a local charity helping disabled children. It appears she either couldn't or didn't want children of her own. Something to do with a tight uterus. Tight cow more like. Pete claimed the pair never 'did it' and that Jill was a prude and frigid.
Pete kept delaying telling Jill. Making excuses. But soon he'd have to tell her.
Something had happened. No exit now for Pete. The door was closing.
Pete earned enough to pay off Jill and his current home, as well as buy the new luxury house Debbie wanted. And car. A 5 Series BMW. In black.
She'd already selected their future home on the new estate. And car.
Pete hadn't seen either. He had no idea. But Debbie had been around 'their new house' twice with the estate agent. Soon it'd all be theirs. Car to follow.
They usually met after work, going to country pubs, staying at the occasional hotel, or making out in the office. When in a hurry it'd be the back of Pete's car. Like now. They usually came to a remote place in woods on Thursday evenings, having done so for a month or two. It was their own private joke. 'The Thursday Night Shag Site,' it was laughingly called. Deep in some creepy woods, down a track, off a back road, in some small remote village, the name of which Debbie had no idea, nor cared. It could be anywhere or the Moon.
Pete apparently discovered the place 'cold calling' late in the summer. Said it was the perfect spot. Debbie wondered if Pete always knew of the place and had brought other women and office girls out there. But she didn't care.
Back in the summer it was fun to 'do it' outdoors.
Windows open, soft breeze and twittering bird song.
Now it was dark and getting cold. The fun had gone.
She couldn't carry on much longer shagging in the back of a car, in the freezing countryside. Also things had changed.
Pete's mood had changed too. Woman's intuition.
Debbie sensed he might ditch her. And worse, not ever tell Jill.
But soon Pete would have to tell Jill about her. Very soon.
Something had happened. Something serious. Important.
Pete never wore condoms, preferring the 'natural feel' of firm flesh, within moist tissue. Assumption on Pete's part, when asked if she was 'on the pill' the first time he'd gone inside her and already deposited his load. A bit too late to ask really. It'd neither been confirmed nor denied by a giggling, eager Debbie, who'd told Pete: "You've nothing to worry about." Not much. Liar.
Assumption has often been stated as being: 'The Mother of all Fuck-ups.'
Also it would seem the 'Mother' of many babies.
Debbie wasn't on the pill. Never had been. Never would. Ho-hum.
Her period was three weeks late. She was always regular.

It'd certainly get a reaction when she told Pete she was expecting his child.
'Wonder if he wants a boy or girl? Both? Twins ran in her family.'
But not yet. Patience. She'd wait. Until it was definite by at least three or four months. Then it'd be too late to react. Whatever Pete decided, and however he reacted, she'd have him under her thumb - at least financially - forever.
She may have even told Jill herself by then. Or better.
Perhaps she'd send her a copy of the first scan photo.
The message 'Guess Whose?' scribbled across the bottom.
That'd certainly provoke a response. Like a bin-bag full of Pete's clothes dumped on the doorstep. But her thoughts returned to the now, as Pete's thrusting body began to tense, as she knew he was about to come inside her. She moved for support, his thrusting harder, the palm of her hand brushing the condensation-covered window clear. Something outside moved.
"Ooh!" Debbie jumped, eyes focussed on the window.
She tensed, their conjoined hip thrusts momentarily ceased.
Debbie stared, eyes transfixed on the black glass.
An object slithered up past the window.
Pete eased up, sensing Debbie's sudden tension and her motion easing.
"What's up? Is something wrong?" he enquired, trying to raise his head.
"A big snake just slithered past the window!"
Debbie's tone seemed more confused than concerned.
"You what?" Pete was also confused, but more annoyed by the delay.
"It just slithered past the window. Big snake. I'm sure. Long and dark."
Pete ignored her and began rocking his hips again, squeezing her breasts for encouragement. She wiped the cold condensation-covered glass with a free hand, peering into the dark, seeing nothing but black and water drops.
With that there was a small thud upon the bodywork.
Pete tensed, trying to turn his head in the confined space.
A rattle and scratching sound to the car roof followed.
Pete and Debbie froze, both nervously spinning their heads about in various directions; eyes wide, ears alert, tensions high, their pulses thumped.
Another thud, rattle and more gentle scratching sounds.
"It's simply the bloody trees and wind!" Pete sighed. "Stupid us!"
Debbie giggled, unsure, but the pair instantly relaxed, the tension subsiding.
She sighed, turned away from the window and gazed back down at Pete.
"Snake? In these woods?" Pete said, then laughed loudly.
"The only snake around here is this mighty python. And right now it's deep inside your beautiful moist pussy. And it's just about to spit its poison!"
The pair laughed loudly, all concern suddenly gone.
Debbie began to rock gently and Pete smiled. His thoughts returning to quickly finishing off Debbie, driving home, and consuming Jill's burnt dinner.

Chapter 2

Watch and pray, that ye enter not into temptation......

Bible - Matthew 26:41

The vehicle was being watched. Monitored. Closely.
Each time in the same spot. Thursday evenings. Regular.
Details noted. Car followed. All recorded.
Like clockwork. Perfectly positioned each time.
Routine. Regime. Predictable. Careless. Fatal.
The vehicle gently rocked, the movements observed.
Sounds came from within. Laughter.
Time for action. All as planned. In detail.
Now it begins. But also it ends.
Beneath the vehicle something stirred. New movement.
Long and thin. Carefully drawn along by unseen hands.
The rope slithered. Then rose up. High into the darkness.
High up above the car, lost in the gloom and swaying branches, something hung down, offering only a dull glint. A large metal ring.
The rope magically rose on up towards the ring above.
Tethered to the thin rope, a thicker strap. Strong. Unyielding.
It willingly followed, securely tied to the thinner rope.
Up it rose. Swiftly. Silently. Just as planned.
Rising high, the thick black strap rose, swaying slightly.
A gentle thud. It brushed upon the car's metalwork.
'*Shit!*' - In the darkness eyes widened. A breath was held.
Sound and motion within the car ceased. And outside too.
A hand on glass. Porthole of condensation cleared.
A disfigured face through blackened glass. Muffled voices.
The strap hung. Motionless. All movement paused.
Breath held. Keen eyes in darkness watched. Patience.
Laughter. Fresh movement. Noises. Rocking car.
Breath exhaled. Heavy sigh. Tension eased. Back to work.
Gloved hands swiftly resumed their dutiful tasks.
Various straps continued their planned journeys.
A smile in the darkness. Satisfied.
Job done. Phase one complete. All as planned.
Time for action.
Game on!

Chapter 3

I looked, but there was no one to help......

Bible - Isaiah 63:5

Pete was close to ejaculating when he heard the engine roar. Totally lost in that key moment, his mind fluttered, and he was unsure of the sudden noise. Debbie however seemed less concerned, snorting softly with each deep hip thrust, also close to climaxing, pressing her groin harder onto Pete's hips.

Pete was in that strange state when sex overtakes all; the only aim being to complete, at all costs, the full act of copulation. Subconsciously he sensed danger, however, his conscious mind, namely being aware of Debbie's thrusts and sighs, told him to ignore it all. At least until he'd come. Then worry.

It wasn't long. Pete grasped at Debbie's breasts, groaning loudly as nature took its course. Debbie tensed enjoyably at the new stimulus of Pete's rough grasp and harder thrusts, close to climaxing herself, but also now aware of a loud engine roaring nearby. She also chose to ignore it. Pleasure over Pain.

'Was it a car? Maybe Jill had followed them? Cool! That'd be fun!'

In the darkness Debbie mused at the possibilities, with a wicked smile.

The thought that Jill could be watching outside excited her further.

A few more thrusts and she'd also be done. Make this a good one.

'Where are you Jill? Watching? Maybe listening in? Perhaps you want to join in too, to make it a three-some. I don't mind. Your too late Jill, Pete's all mine. We're a family now!'

For Pete, the moment of intense pleasure was over. Gone. Done.

He was back to normality and becoming concerned. Very concerned.

'What was the source of the roaring engine outside? It sounded close. Very close. And loud. Very loud. Too loud and close. Had Jill followed them? Shit! Time for some excuses.'

Debbie's body tensing, hips twisting, groans deepening and firm hands upon his chest, broke his thought. She twisted roughly about Pete's hips as deadly fingernails dug into his body, before emitting several cries of pleasure.

Pete's body shook, seemingly along with the entire car, but also at Debbie's frantic bodily motions and somewhat exaggerated cries. He could never work out if it was all genuine or slightly theatrical and done solely for his benefit. He didn't care. Debbie seemed to sense he enjoyed her loud vocal climax; it making him feel he'd serviced her well. Jill, if she ever made any sound at all, emitted a soft sigh or grunt, then simply turned away to quickly fall asleep.

Debbie's cries were mixed with a series of hip-breaking, breath-taking thrusts against Pete's waist. Her nails racked across him and the whole climatic event finally ended with Debbie's sweaty body collapsing upon an exhausted Pete, her mass of hair falling across his face, almost suffocating him.

Then the earth moved.

Shaking violently, the car rocked, then lurched sideward, almost as if rising. Debbie fell heavily across a panicking Pete. Suffocated by her mass of hair, and pinned down by her body, he was unsure what was happening. He tried to push her forcibly away, wondering why the car was suddenly moving, almost floating, as if lifted up and rocked by huge unseen waves.

"Wow! I don't know about the earth moving, I'm sure I felt the car move!" Debbie exclaimed, laughing loudly, still in the after-throws of her orgasm.

"You did feel the car move, you stupid cow!" yelled Pete. "Get off me!"

His mood had changed. The moment of pleasure over. Fear had set in as the car slewed heavily, as if swinging in space, the nauseous motion like that of a fairground ride. The pair were thrown sideways, conjoined bodies tangled. Pete, desperate to discover the cause, was unable to move. He remained firmly squashed beneath Debbie's moist straddling hips and her sweaty sticky body. Coming to her senses, suddenly frightened, Debbie clung tight to Pete. The car violently tipped forward, the rear lifting up, tipping them against the backs of the front seat. Outside, the engine noise intensified, the deafening roar of a large diesel unit close by now reverberating through the car body.

"What going on Pete?" Debbie cried out in the gloom, her head spinning within the car, gazing at steamy windows. "Do something Pete! I'm scared."

Pete frantically tried to straighten himself, ignoring Debbie's pointless cries, but he couldn't move. Her body still lay firmly planted on top of his, and worse, she was tightly holding onto his body for both comfort and support.

The car lurched back violently, tipping up almost forty-five degrees, throwing Debbie sideways. Pete finally partially freed himself, now able to move his arms, but not his legs. Debbie's moist crotch was now seated upon them, her neat buttocks painfully pressing down upon his ankles, trapping him again.

"Wipe the bloody window!" Pete yelled, the engine roar outside deafening, vibrating against the swinging car. Crashing sounds all about the car, and worse, against the bodywork, only added to the intense noise and mayhem.

Debbie wiped the condensation off the window, revealing only blackness outside, still ignoring Pete's plea to move. Hands cupped to her face, pressing against the cold damp glass, she peered out into the gloom beyond the car.

She screamed, instinctively jumping back at some vision outside, crushing Pete's ankle further with her hips and legs. He winced painfully.

"Branches and stuff are crashing past the car. The trees are moving!" Debbie whimpered, now almost in tears. "What is happening? Is it an earthquake?"

"What? Trees moving? They can't be. We're not moving. Are we?"

Pete exclaimed loudly, confused, but also very worried. He roughly pulled his legs free of Debbie's buttocks, turning in the confined space, then spun about to face the window. Wiping the cold black glass, he looked outside.

A large tree branch crashed past the dark window.

Pete reeled back, eyes wide, his face etched in horror.

"Holy shit!" he cried. "What the fuck is happening?"

Pete felt ill, his heart sinking with a sense of helplessness; no longer in control and confused. Regrets of going with Debbie now flooded through him like raw sewage. He should have stayed at home with Jill.

Boring Jill. Nice Jill. Reliable Jill. Her burnt food wasn't all that bad. Well, maybe...

Ear-piercing metallic sounds screamed from the vehicle, the whole structure violently juddering. Pete winced, wondering what was happening to his car. The vehicle swung heavily again, spinning about its central axis. Pete grasped the seats as Debbie fell back onto him, but he instantly pushed her away, so the pair were finally seated within the back of the car, free from each other.

A loud dull thud. Creaking steel. A body panel crumpling.

Pete shuddered. This wasn't good. It was bad. Sickening.

'What would Jill say about the beautiful car? She adores it. Oh shit! Maybe T-Cut out any scratches before she sees it. It might not be too bad in daylight and just need a touch-up.'

Pete lifted a thumb to his nervous lips, thinking, nibbling the flesh as another deafening crash echoed within the car. Pete let out a long, heavy sigh.

"What's happening?" Debbie yelled, as a heavy thump resounded about them, rocking the car. It woke Pete from his frantic thoughts of T-Cut, Jill and home, the place he wanted to be. Jill's Burnt Shepherd's Pie any day.

"Seems like something has grabbed the car and is dragging it through the trees in the woods," Pete replied, trying to explain. "That's all it can be."

"What?" exclaimed Debbie. "You don't think we've been attacked by a dinosaur do you? Or maybe a big dragon?" Debbie stared at him in horror.

Pete stared in the dark, eyes narrowing, shaking his head in total disbelief at Debbie's dumb and ignorant reply, wondering why he was with her. He knew.

The car rocked and swung. Hard and deep scratching sounds along the body resonated painfully through the car, hurting the incumbent's ears.

It'd need more than T-Cut and bit of Turtle wax now. Maybe a full valet and re-spray?

"What's happening to my fucking car?" a distraught Pete screamed aloud, the true dilemma becoming clear. "And what the hell is Jill going to say?"

Debbie's head swung to face Pete, her eyes cold and cursing.

The word 'Jill' drew her attention, opening a raw wound.

"Jill? Jill! We're dying, being eaten by a dragon, and all you can think about is your frigid slut of a wife. Fuck Jill! It's probably her fault," yelled Debbie.

Pete stared into the dark. Whatever happened from here, they were finished. History. No more cheating. Well at least not with her. Dumb selfish bitch.

"Just open the door or window Pete and get me out of this car! Now! I want to go home!" Debbie was crying. Pete felt a pang of guilt. Only just.

"These back windows don't open," replied Pete, lunging over the central console and falling into the front passenger seat, finally free of Debbie.

Tree branches cracked around, each rocking the car. The sound of heavy scratching, mixed with the roar of a large diesel engine and violent shaking of the vehicle, all helped confuse their senses and make the occupants feel sick.

"We need to open the front windows or the doors to see what is happening!"

Pete grabbed the handle and pushed the door. The lock clicked, but the large door of the Coupe wouldn't budge. He pushed harder, bashing his shoulder against the door, but an invisible force outside seemingly held it closed. Face sweating, anger surging and desperate, he wiped the damp glass with his hand, pressing his face to the surface. A dark, two-inch wide vertical strap appeared to lie firmly against the door and window. 'The snake.' And the answer.

"Something's holding the door shut. It's that snake thing you said you saw," Pete called out as if to explain. "It's some sort of heavy rope or strap."

"Pete, do something. Get us out of here. I'm scared," whimpered Debbie. "I don't want to die. Not here, not with our baby. Pete, I'm pregnant."

A silence - if it was possible amongst the infernal noise and turmoil raging on in the crazy world outside - seemingly hung in the air. A pin maybe dropped.

Debbie's words sank into Pete's head. Instantly.

One word alone from the sentence numbed his senses.

'Pregnant?'

The word had a unique quality, invoking many differing emotions.

Joy. Happiness. Fulfilment. Pleasure. Expectation. Fear. Concern. Worry. Dread. Panic. Horror. Terror. Of all the words to choose, 'Terror' struck Pete as being the best. Shear terror. Maybe even horror. Intense terror and horror.

"Don't be so bloody stupid," Pete said unconvincingly as a reply.

He wasn't sure if his cold response concerned Debbie's comment on their survival chances, or her personal maternal status. Maybe both.

The blood in Pete's neck pumped intensely, his face flushing hotter than minutes earlier whilst he'd enjoyably been in union with Debbie; an act he now suddenly regretted, along with every other time he'd been inside her.

The shock hit home. Hard. *Pregnant?* Pregnant! Baby? *No!*

She couldn't be. *Could she?* He was really in the shit now. Deep shit.

Stuff the car and a few scratches. They could be polished out and repaired.

A baby was for life, not just for Christmas.

'What would Jill say? A baby. His baby. Their baby.'

Would that make Jill a Stepmother? Or maybe an Aunt. As well as a divorcee.

Another loud bang and violent shake brought him back, with thoughts of immediate survival than babies. Debbie and her baby were secondary. Settling into the drivers seat, Pete fumbled for the ignition key. He clicked it forward a turn, grabbing the light-switch. Magically the headlights illuminated.

Two beams of white light cut into the gloom.

Pete stared out through the windscreen in disbelief.

The dirt track and bushes where they'd parked up had all gone.

Vanished. The trees and familiar dense holly bushes were no more.

The car had been transported. Moved. But worse. Much worse. Staring in amazement out through the windscreen into the illuminated gloom beyond, a strange whirl of foliage swirled past the car within the darkness. Leaves, branches and mixed debris all moved past, as if caught up in a tornado.

More bizarrely, as Pete stared at the mayhem in silence, there appeared to be no ground beneath the vehicle. It had gone. Pete's eyes widened, looking down in shear terror. They were floating. Seemingly hanging in the air.

He pressed the window switch, the sheet of glass lowering with a soft whine. In blew cold night air, along with the full deafening roar from outside. Pete pushed his head through the window, squeezing past the 'snake' that clung tightly to the door. Wincing against the sudden rush of chilling air and noise, he looked about in the gloom, noticing the black 'snake' or nylon lifting strap. A series of these appeared to pass under the car, then stretch over the roof, to form in a 'vee' shape high above the car roof, disappearing into the darkness and raging mayhem. In the dim light he could make out the darkened ground rushing beneath the hovering car, branches and assorted debris falling away.

Horror pulsed through him. The car was at least ten feet off the ground and hurtling backwards. His heart sank, realising what was happening, as bizarre and unreal as it seemed. Turning his head, forcing his shoulders out through the gap, he looked back in order to determine what had lifted the car into the air and was now seemingly dragging it through the deep and dark woods.

Pete felt a sudden whack as a branch crashed into his head. Snapping as it dragged across his face, wailed out loudly. The branch cut his ear and slashed his face, creating a deep long gash. He retracted his head, grabbing the 'snake,' shaking it violently, venting anger and pain. But the strap didn't move, being firm and as taut as steel, although having a soft texture. Pete now understood.

"It's a lifting sling! Your snake's a fucking lifting sling!"

He yelled to Debbie in the back, who was now redressing, donning Pete's shirt, her own top lost somewhere within the car. He shook his bloody head seeing her apparent lack of concern to their dilemma in his moment of panic.

Only a woman could think like that. Maybe only a 'Debbie.'

Blood streamed from his cut face, on down his neck and to his bare chest. Warm and sticky, it dripped into his lap. The blood would stain the seats.

That'd never come out. The car was ruined. *What would Jill say?*

He felt nauseous, from a mix of pain and shock, and slumped heavily into the rocking driver's seat. For once he'd been defeated and had lost control.

Suddenly the movement eased and the ear-splitting noise subsided.

The change was dramatic. Gone were the infernal sounds. Now an ominous silence resounded, broken only by the creaking lifting slings as the car gently swayed, seemingly in time with the loud tick of the out of sight diesel engine.

"We've been lifted up by a mobile crane," Pete reported to a silent, staring Debbie who didn't seem to listen, his tone now much calmer, trying to clearly explain the situation. "Then it's dragged us off through the woods."

Debbie simply blinked, face ashen. She didn't understand or care.

"And I think we're in deep shit. Really deep shit!"

Chapter 4

Fear has many eyes and can see things underground.

Miquel de Cervantes

Debbie cast Pete a frown, then promptly dismissed him, fumbling in the back of the car. She was retrieving clothing; placing them close to her face to determine onto which anatomical part the item belonged. Pete paused, staring at Debbie, shaking his head, his contempt growing and all care now gone.

With only the tick of the idling engine and creak of slings above the swaying car to break the silence, Pete looked out the windscreen, still amazed at what had just occurred. Nauseously, the headlights flicked up and down, as the car gently rocked back and forth, like a ferrous wheel car in the breeze. In their sway the bright beams of the headlights intermittently picked out dark ground and shrubs below, before tilting up, and illuminating dark thinning treetops.

Back and forth the car rocked, Pete briefly mesmerised by the action, still unsure of what was really happening or why. Each arc slowly decreased until the creaking and rocking eased and the car levelled out, the headlights then bizarrely focussed on the eerie dark treetops. Silently the pair sat in the car.

Pete dumbstruck; thinking, worrying. Debbie fumbling; dressing, vacant.

The sky above suddenly grew lightener, as the heavy dark clouds thinned, revealing a previously hidden full moon. The glow softly illuminated the surrounding area with a strange palette of black, grey and silver hues. Pete looked out at the looming silhouettes of trees, some thirty feet away, then down to the dark ground, about fifteen feet below, head shaking. It was all strangely eerie and unwelcome. Scanning the surroundings, it appeared the car had come to rest in the middle of a small clearing, hanging within its centre.

In silence they sat, for what seemed an age, but in reality was only a few seconds. Debbie had done up three of the buttons on Pete's shirt, enough to cover her breasts. She couldn't find her blouse and decided Pete's shirt would suffice. She now fumbled with the buckle on one of her ankle-strap sandals. Pete had bought Debbie the designer five-inch high-heels only last week as another special gift. He liked them, telling her they made her look sexy as she strutted about in them around the office, her buttocks wiggling.

Debbie liked them because they were expensive. Top Designer Brand.

"What's going on? Where are we?" Debbie whispered, raising her head over the seat, scanning the dark treetops, then looking at Pete for an answer.

"We've been lifted up by a crane and dragged through the woods," Pete replied, also in a whisper. "God knows how or why he's done it. Bastard!"

"Who? What are you talking about?" Debbie interrupted, confused, her voice becoming concerned that Pete knew something. "Who has done is this?"

Pete ignored her, lost in his own thoughts and deeper worries.

"The bastard's somehow wrapped a lifting sling around the car then lifted us up with a mobile crane," Pete said knowingly, but felt it was beyond Debbie.

"If this is a joke, I don't find it funny. Is this to do with that bitch Jill? I bet it is. Fucking cow! I want to go home. Open the door and get out. I'm scared."

In the gloom Pete stared at Debbie, shaking his head.

'How did I ever get into such a mess?' But sadly Pete knew the answer.

"I can't open the door. There's a lifting strap jamming it shut. I can only just squeeze my head through the window. And it's got nothing to do with Jill." Pete said defensively. "So leave her out of it. It's someone else. Tosser!"

"Who? I want to get out. I'm scared Pete. Find out what he wants. And tell him I'm pregnant. Ask him if that fucking bitch Jill put him up to it."

Debbie turned away, eyes scanning the floor, looking for her second shoe.

"That *fucking bitch Jill,* as you call her, is my wife," Pete responded with venom, glaring at Debbie in the silver gloom, his true feelings being vented.

"Pity you forgot about that a few moments ago when you happily had five inches of your body firmly inside me." Debbie's reply was equally as vicious and cold, just like the chilling air now seemingly creeping around them.

Pete disregarded Debbie, his contempt growing, turning instead to peer out the window. He pushed his head past the sling, wincing as his torn ear caught on the doorframe. The cold night air hit him like a slap as he surveyed the silvery-grey of the moonlit clearing. The cloud thinned out further and the moon seemingly brightened, the darkened outline of charcoal trees standing stark amongst a mix of graphite and greys now visible. The small movement within the car caused the vehicle to rock. Debbie cursed, fumbling with the ankle strap of the second shoe, just retrieved from beneath the driver's seat.

Pete turned as best he could and looked down towards where the idling diesel engine emitted its rattle, but could see no shape or movement.

"What do you want?" he yelled into the dark, towards the unseen operator of the loud ticking machine in the gloom. "We're sorry for trespassing. We didn't know this was private property. Please let us down and we'll leave."

Silence responded.

The cloud thinned further, the clearing turning a bright silver-white, the moon above glowing brightly, although cold and hazy. Pete stared into the trees, now clearly making out the dark silhouette of what appeared to be an agricultural forklift about twenty feet away, its long boom reaching high into the clearing. He followed the outline of the boom, soaring high above the car, where it was attached to the lifting straps which supported the car. His eyes followed those straps down from a hook, which descended towards the roof of the car. Here they separated, one strap disappearing over the opposite side of the car and the other running past his head until it vanished beneath the car, running underneath, then joining the opposing strap. Pete nodded.

It was as he'd thought. Someone had somehow managed to attach lifting slings to the underside of the car, raise it up, then drag it hundreds of yards backward through the woods. Now they'd been left stranded, suspended ten to twenty feet above the ground, the car smashed to pieces. *But why?*

A wave of nausea washed over him. *'What kind of sick bastard would do this?'*

Pete really didn't want to know. Instead he thought of Jill. At home in the warm, preparing his burnt meal. With added ash. Slippers set beside his chair, as always. She was probably wondering where he was. *Maybe she knew.*

He missed Jill. He missed his slippers. But sadly not the burnt food.

Pete's mind returned to the current dilemma. And more. Debbie's comment.

'Pregnant. Baby! Debbie wasn't pregnant - was she? What a nightmare! God please no!'

He wished even more that he was at home with boring old Jill, He sipping a glass of Jack Daniels and reading the newspaper. Jill watching a soap. Bliss.

'Debbie, pregnant? No! It's a lie. She's on the pill. She said so. Didn't she? Isn't she?'

Pete felt his bowels loosen and new sweat break out. Double deep shit.

A gentle sway of the car brought Pete back to reality, realising his current predicament needed resolving first. He swallowed hard, instinctively feeling something was not right. Far from it. This was way beyond being a sick joke.

This was serious. Deadly serious. Deadly.

Continuing to gaze down, Pete could only determine black beneath the car. He stared harder. This area appeared a darker shade than the surrounding silvery-grey of the woodland clearing. He flicked his head back and forth.

'Was this possible? Maybe a moon-shadow, cast by the car?'

Pete was puzzled.

There was darkness and there was darkness.

But the area below the car was dark. Really dark. Too dark.

Pete scanned the ground beneath, then looked over to the clearing.

The clearing was coloured a silvery-grey with varying shadows.

The ground beneath the car was just dark. Black. Pitch black.

There was something wrong. Seriously wrong.

Looking away, Pete could make out a definite mixed shade of dark grey for the ground around the clearing, interspersed with small patches of irregular shaped black objects, which were obviously bushes and plants. The dark outline of trees forming the clearing also appeared to have a sense of form, depth, colour and texture, and were all random shapes and black or grey.

However, the area directly below the car appeared to have no depth or colour, being a regular rectangular shape and simply black. Pete was puzzled.

It couldn't be the car's shadow, as it appeared larger than the car, with clearly defined sharp edges and the moon glow was at an angle. *What the hell was it?*

The ticking of the big diesel engine suddenly ceased and Pete's attention returned to the forklift as the clearing was sent into silence, but for the soft creaking of the straining lifting slings. Pete and Debbie held their breaths.

A gentle squeak came from the hidden forklift, followed by a distinct clunk, as it seemed the cab door was closed. Pete tensed, sensing movement below, then he saw a silhouetted figure move past the front of the forklift.

"Please put us down. We're sorry for being here and won't tell the police," Pete called out loudly to the silent and unseen stranger below.

"We didn't mean to trespass. We were simply lost. Let us go and we'll forget it all. We'll say nothing. Put us down. Please!" Pete begged to the darkness.

Debbie's face suddenly appeared in the gap beside Pete's.

"Help! Help us someone!" She screamed out blindly into space and loud. "There's a fucking madman down here! Put us down you fucking wanker!"

Pete scowled, shaking his head, pushing Debbie firmly back inside the car.

"Shut up you stupid cow," Pete cursed, glaring hard at Debbie in the gloom. "We need to negotiate. That'll really help, calling him a wanker! You idiot!"

Suddenly the thin cloud cover above broke fully and pure silver moonlight streamed into the car via the sunroof. It illuminated the interior with a dull silver-grey glow, also fully lighting the clearing below with a mix of shadows.

Debbie gazed up through the sunroof, clearly seeing the distinctive 'Vee' shape of the lifting slings, with the hook and telescopic boom of the large agricultural forklift soaring high over their heads and into the night sky above.

Dark clouds, driven by the wind, rolled back over the moon, returning the car and the woodland clearing back into deep shadow and dark grey tones.

Beside the cab, the figure moved. A gentle whining noise began emanating from the forklift and the car juddered. Then almost barely noticeable, it began slowly moving. It was a gentle rock, but told Pete all he needed to know.

They were being lowered.

Pete felt the movement, and a wave of euphoria washing through, as Debbie moved within the middle of the car, her hands reaching up to the sunroof. He ignored her, sensing the slow steady decent of the car, relief flowing, knowing there'd soon be an end to this drama and all going well, he'd be able talk his way out of the issue. He'd negotiate a deal. Then go home. Somehow.

"We're being lowered!" Pete exclaimed, ignoring Debbie's actions behind him, pushing his head back through the gap in the side window to see clearly what was happening. The thinning clouds above cleared once more, blown on a brisk breeze, casting bright moonlight once more across the clearing.

But not to the ground underneath the car. Nothing.

The area beneath the car remained black. Pitch black.

Pete looked hard at the earth below.

It remained totally featureless.

His eyes flicked to one side.

The ground of the clearing held a dull graphite tone.

Substance. Structure.

His eyes flicked back to the pitch-black square below.

Featureless. Empty. Nothing. *Nothing?*

His mind whirled in a confused state, as slowly but steadily the car descended and the square of black ground beneath them grew ever closer.

It was as if there was no ground below them. Nothing.

Only an empty space. A void.

Like a hole. *A hole?*

Pete became aware of a whirring now within the car. Debbie brushed roughly against him and then appeared to crouch in the centre of the car. He ignored her, focussing intently on the ground, the horrifying realisation now dawning.

Pete now knew why the ground below seemed so dark.

It was simple. There wasn't any.

"There isn't any earth below," he whispered to himself. "Oh no!"

Terror raced through him, his unseen face etched in fear.

He turned to Debbie, her back now turned away from him, trying to get her to realise their dire situation but she seemed focussed on her own task.

"Hole! It's a fucking great hole!" Pete yelled frantically.

Debbie hovered within the centre of the car, seemingly unfazed.

"My god! We're going to be buried alive!" Pete almost screamed.

Debbie was strangely cool, crouching in the back, oblivious to Pete's desperate cries and growing panic, her hands pressed up against the roof.

"Buried! Inside my beautiful car. Fucking hell! What'll Jill say?"

Pete was becoming frantic. "We've got to get out. Quick!"

Debbie didn't need telling. She'd planned her course of action and had wound back the electric sunroof. She now stood upright in the middle of the car, ready to make her exit, her body passing through the opening sunroof.

Realising what she'd done, and seeing his chance to escape too, Pete pushed at Debbie's bare buttocks, now fully in his face, only partly covered by his best shirt. He pushed his hands hard against the firm flesh, which only minutes earlier he'd been caressing, trying to force her into the chill night air.

"Get out. Get out! Quick, you stupid bitch! Hurry. We've got to get out!" Pete cried, all gentlemanly demeanour gone, pressing hard at her body.

Debbie lifted herself through the sunroof, ignoring Pete's frantic cries below and his hands grappling upon her bare buttocks and legs. She touched the damp car roof outside, her high-heeled feet struggling to find purchase on the top of the car seats. Suddenly the car jolted violently, abruptly tilting forward, the rear of the vehicle hitting the edge of the hole. The action unbalanced Debbie and her left foot slipped, sending the long thin heel of her shoe flying out. The pencil-thin steel stiletto heel tip caught Pete full in the face, punching a hole clean through his top lip and cracking a front tooth.

He squealed in agony, grasping at his face, as a fresh jolt of new intense pain tore through his already aching head. It sent him crashing backwards, tumbling down into the car, towards the dashboard, his head cracking the windscreen. Spinning around, as he landed heavily in the driver's seat, he clutched his bloody face and raised his aching head to look outside.

Pete looked on in awe at the sight before him.
The headlights illuminated a dull screen of brown.
Slowly, a solid wall of soil passed before the car's bonnet.
The car was entering the hole.
And Pete was already in the ground.
He was being buried alive!
His stomach went queasy, all energy lost.
This was no sick joke.
This was just sick.
He sat and stared, as layers of soil slowly drifted past.
A strange earthy darkness enveloped the vehicle, which was descending front first into the hole, the car sinking deeper, tipping Pete forward in the seat.
Hands pressing onto the dashboard, he stared out in disbelief.
The headlights, reflecting back off the wall of soil, sent back a diffused amber glow throughout the car's interior. Roots and stones could clearly be seen.
Pete's fear-filled eyes gazed at the wall of earth before him.
A distressed, whimper broke from his bloody lips.
"Buried alive."
What on earth would Jill say?

Chapter 5

Look before you leap – Look after number one.

Proverbs 311 / 310

Debbie had pulled herself through the sunroof and was sitting upon the rim of the car roof, her legs hanging inside. The cold damp steel roof instantly numbed her buttocks. In one continuous movement she swung her legs out, knelt up and then stood fully onto the car's roof. Her high heels slipped ungainly on the tilting car roof, so Debbie grasped at the lifting slings above her head to steady herself. In the gloom she became aware of the reason for Pete's panic. The car was beginning to disappear into a large hole, dug in a clearing within the woods. However, the position was slightly out, and the rear of the car had caught on the lip of the hole. This was causing the front end to slowly tip forward, the submerged headlights dimly illuminating the rim of the massive square hole in a strange orange glow. The car was sinking nose-first into the soil like a miniature Titanic, disappearing into a glowing, earthy brown sea. A wave of panic hit Debbie, realisation of the seriousness of Pete's screaming words hitting home. *'We're being burying alive!'*

Debbie could hear Pete's frantic cries from inside the car beneath her, as she steadied herself, her heels slipping again on the damp roof of the tilting car. She grasped tight onto the soft, yet strong lifting slings, maintaining her balance with her slipping high-heels, and looking down, regarded the hole, then the car. The ground had drawn level with the angled roof, the wedged boot section now all that prevented the car from being completely buried.

Debbie had to make a split second decision.

Stay and help Pete, now frantically clawing at the edge of the sunroof.

Or jump, and simply save herself.

Decision time.

Stay and help - or jump and run?

No choice. Debbie jumped.

As the ground drew level with the descending car roof, Debbie released her grasp on the sling and leapt, propelling herself clear of the vehicle. Rolling onto the damp earth, she rose, twisting to look behind, just in time to see the car jolt sharply. The bank of earth beneath the boot collapsed and the car suddenly levelled off. The roof was now at ground level, gently swinging back and forth, as the hole collapsed further and the car fully disappeared.

Debbie shuddered, gazing at the eerie sight.

'Where was Pete?'

A muffled cry answered her question.

"Debbie! Help me. Please!" Pete called feebly from the hole, yelling out from the open sunroof, now out of sight. The cars buried lights illuminated the pit in a strange up-lit golden glow. The hole appeared like an orange volcanic fissure, the car itself no longer visible, only the lifting sling, taut above, still connected to the forklift boom and the light-beams within.

Debbie felt sick. She gazed in bewilderment, squatting and hugging herself within the clearing, ten feet from the hole. Then there was a jolt as the lifting sling went slack as the forklift boom levelled off and came to rest about six feet above the ground. The car was now trapped, buried deep inside the hole.

And so was Pete.

The hydraulic whirring and heavy chug from the diesel engine stopped and the area turning deadly silent. Debbie gazed in a frozen state of awe and shock just as the clouds thinned, bathing the clearing once more in bright, cold moonlight. Debbie began shaking, both through fear and involuntarily due to her semi-naked state. Her pale, bare skin and white shirt-clad body glowed like a ghostly phosphorous image within the black and silver gloom.

Then something moved near the forklift. A person.

And it headed straight towards her and the hole.

Debbie froze in terror, her eyes locked on the dark figure silently advancing twenty feet away, approaching the opposite side of the hole. The assailant's unseen eyes seemingly bored through her, causing her to shiver harder.

Standing ghostlike within the clearing Debbie stared at the silent attacker who was moving swiftly and at ease towards the hole and car roof.

She thought of Pete, still trapped inside the car.

Poor Pete.

She should help him.

She certainly should.

She thought of going over to the car to help.

Thought about it.

Momentarily.

Debbie was off.

Rising up and turning sharply to run, her high-heels dug firmly into the soft soil, gripping like miniature anchors, causing her to stumble, her body catching upon a tangle of vicious brambles. The savage and unforgiving thorns dug deep into her bare legs and dragged her down. She let out a scream, frantically fighting to free herself, Pete's loose shirt snagging upon more thorns, ensnared her further. Looking back over her shoulder, the dark figure steadily approached the edge of the pit and paused. A bubble of snot blew from Debbie's nose as she desperately tore at the brambles, tears of terror now flowing. She pulled at the shirt, then looked back again, not wanting to, but the action instinctive. In horror she saw the silent tormentor step into the hole, reducing in height, now standing upon the car roof.

Debbie whimpered, tearing frantically at the bramble ensnared shirt, ripping a portion off to free herself. Then she was suddenly clear of the grasping brambles, but stumbled, falling into a forward roll, but onto open ground. Standing upright, she turned once more, fearing her pursuer would be upon her. But he remained in the middle of the hole, standing upon the roof, the scene illuminated in an eerie orange glow. Casually the attacker reached up to the top of the boom, and removed a heavy shackle from the lifting straps, these shackles dropping with a heavy dull thud upon the car roof.

Debbie let out a feeble cry upon seeing the straps drop, knowing the car was now stuck in the deep hole, along with Pete, now trapped inside.

The assailant turned to chillingly glare across the ground at Debbie.

Debbie felt ice flow through her veins. Never in her life had she been more afraid than now. Or felt more alone.

Pete's muffled cry suddenly flowed from within the hole, rising up through the sunroof, breaking the tense silence.

"Deb's! Help me get out. Please! Help me!"

Debbie's heart pounded, knowing this was no practical joke or prank, simply designed to scare the pair of them, Jill's fault or not. This was for real.

The person on Pete's car roof, now coldly glaring at her from the pit, was planning to bury them both alive. He clearly wanted to kill them both.

Kill Pete. And kill her too!

But who, and why? Did Pete know them?

In those seconds, as she froze in terror, staring at the moonlight horror before her, the questions freely flowed.

Was it somehow connected to Jill? It had to be that jealous old bitch!

Debbie felt deep down Jill was behind it all.

A jealous woman's natural instincts.

'Maybe she'd hired a Hit-man to kill them for the insurance. That'd be somewhat ironic.'

Suddenly her line of thought was broken as Pete's head rose from the sunroof. His torso swiftly followed, rising strangely within the middle of the hole like some ghoul rising up from a freshly dug, over-sized grave.

It was.

This was to be Pete and Debbie's grave.

Unmarked.

Pete's rising upper torso turned as his shoulders rose free and clear from the car's sunroof. As did his head, gazing across the pit towards Debbie. Standing on the seat backs, he began lifting himself up fully, now the car had settled.

The silver moonlight illuminated two bodies.

One upon the car roof. One half rising out of the car.

Pete looked towards Debbie. He smiled. A bloody grin.

Debbie looked at Pete - then behind him. She winced.

The figure, unseen by Pete and towering over him on the car roof, looked down at the half man rising at his feet, then glanced towards her. Cold eyes.

Through the silvery glow, Debbie saw Pete's cheesy smile look her way, his face mixed with black streaks of flowing blood to disfigure his face.

"I've made it," Pete cried, almost joyfully. "I'm free! Help me out!"

Debbie shook her head, wanting to cry. Her eyes were fixed upon the figure behind him, still unseen by Pete. Her throat seized up, body quivering.

Tears began welling, but no sound or bodily movements were forthcoming.

The towering figure upon the roof adjusted his position, the shackle, firmly gripped, was drawn back and poised to strike. Debbie knew what'd follow.

"Pete. Look out!" Debbie screamed. "Behind you!" She added, lifting her arm, pointing towards the unseen person standing directly behind Pete.

As Debbie screamed, Pete instinctively turned his body, his head swinging, then looking up, suddenly aware of the dark figure standing above him.

But he was too slow.

His body, trapped within the sunroof and stressed from the ordeal, and mind bewildered and confused, offered little chance of an easy escape. Pete turned, the person towering above now clearly visible in the bright moonlight.

"You!" Pete cried out, looking up in stark horror.

The large shackle swung with full force into Pete's face.

Pete's left cheekbone split in two, face concaving inwards. The force threw his body to the right, head crashing heavily onto the car roof. Bright lights flew through Pete's dazzled head, as the sickening metallic taste of blood began to pour into his mouth. Choking, he tried to come to terms with the situation, but had only three seconds to respond. Not long enough.

The next blow of the shackle smashed Pete's head into the car roof.

Pete's unresponsive torso lay caught in the rim of the sunroof, his arms limply flayed out before him on the roof. Across the pit, Debbie gazed on.

Fight, flight or freeze. Debbie had options.

Senses numb, mind and body in shock, Debbie selected.

Debbie chose freeze.

The attacker looked across at Debbie, then down at Pete's body, standing tall and erect, as if proud of his night's work. Debbie even sensed he smiled.

A heavy boot stamped forcefully onto Pete's bloody head. Job done.

Pete's unresponsive body slid back as the flaying steel-capped foot continued repeatedly kicked Pete's torso, driving his now motionless form back through the sunroof and into the car. Lifeless, Pete fell in a crumpled heap inside the vehicle, his body sliding and settling naturally upon the rear seats.

Through the rear windows, where moments earlier a giggling Debbie had peered out from, Pete's glazed and lifeless eyes stared blindly at the earthen walls of his glass and steel coffin, set within its tranquil woodland grave.

Blood poured from his shattered head, down his body then soaked into the fabric of the once immaculate seats of his beautiful car.

What on earth would Jill say?

Chapter 6

Fear lent wings to his feet.

Virgil

Debbie gazed in disbelief at what had so brutally unfolded before her. This wasn't some form of petty revenge by Jill; this went deeper. As she saw Pete's head brutally smashed in by the iron shackle, and his limp body callously kicked back into the car, she knew one thing for certain. She was next.

Debbie had used up 'Freeze' as a choice.

She now had two options left.

Fight or Flight.

No option.

She pulled herself up off the dirt and frantically scrambled over the tangled undergrowth and brambles. Thorns ripped her flesh and her heels sank into the soft soil, wringing her ankles, but she ignored all the fresh pain and blindly ran. At that point the clouds parted and the moon above gracefully lit the woods before her, as if to kindly assist in her travels, but also casting a confusing mix of silver and black shadows. Debbie crashed through deep undergrowth, terrified to look back, fearful of the figure she was sure would be following. She ran on, dashing carelessly through bushes and vegetation, pushing aside tree branches, desperate to escape the horror behind her in the clearing. Suddenly she stumbled over a hidden log, her body flying through the air. Passing over dry dead bracken, she felt herself crash heavily down onto firm soil. Scrambling up, winded, her hands appeared to touch dry dusty ground and her feet no longer sank in as she fully righted herself. Either side of her she noted undergrowth forming a natural waist-high barrier, with a range of taller, well-established trees set behind. Somehow, in her frantic panic, she'd stumbled onto a four-foot wide dirt track and potential escape.

She steadied herself and turned her head left to right, having no clue where the clearing lay, as a mix of darkness and sliver glow surrounded her. There were no sounds, so instinctively turned in any direction she felt took her away from the clearing and onto safety. Walking a few strides, as her feet gained greater purchase, she then accelerated into a steady jog, running on just the toes of her shoes along the narrow, but clear moonlit track. She headed off, unaware of her direction, but not caring, so long as she was moving, and hopefully getting away from the clearing, and Pete's brutal killer. However, after only a short distance her lungs burnt, as the initial adrenaline burst subsided and reality, trauma and shock all kicked in. But on she continued, now in a light jog, breath heavy, running down the gloomy wooded track.

How close was her hunter? Did he know where she'd gone? And where was she?

Debbie was too afraid to want the answers to the questions she asked herself, but instinctively turned her head to look back down the track, as her lightly pounding legs continuing propelling her forward along the twisting track.

Her eyes widened in relief at the sight behind her.

No one was pursuing her. She was alone.

Nothing but the moonlit track and silhouettes of the trees she'd just passed on the track followed in the silver gloom. Easing up, she sighed inwardly, relieved, somehow expecting to see a dark figure sprinting behind, ready to strike her down. There was no one there. Nothing bar moonlight and trees.

She'd escaped. *'Escaped.'*

The words ran through Debbie's head like a warm tonic. Unconsciously she slowed down, hope flowing through her, the ache of her lungs and limbs now suddenly noticeable, as painful lactic acid flowed into her joints. She turned her head back around, looking ahead once more down the silvery track.

Debbie screamed. A large black silhouette loomed before her.

Momentum propelled her straight into its grasping limbs.

Within seconds Debbie was within it's firm grip.

Debbie let out a gasp of breath, all air knocked from her, as a small prickly conifer tree enveloped her body. The branches of a small Spruce spread like encompassing arms across the track from which she'd slightly deviated. Sharp needles on rough stems snagged her shirt, stabbing into flesh as a rebuke for her inconsideration to crash into its flexible form. Her momentum sent her clean through the small, soft branches, careering her body back onto the track, falling in a forward roll, the thump taking her wind. Stunned, grasping for air, Debbie scrambled back up, briefly regaining her breath and composure. Scanning the track, before continuing on, she looked only ahead, her pace now noticeably slower and laboured. Debbie had never been into any form of keep-fit, simply preferring lots of regular sex to keep trim. Her lungs ached and legs burnt, feeling heavy, and she felt unable to run any more, needing to rest, catch her breath, and decide how to proceed.

The moonlit silhouette of a large tree appeared ahead, set slightly off the track on a sharp bend. Upon passing it, she quickly sidestepped, turned around and placed her body hard against the tree trunk. The coarse bark scratched her skin through the thin, sweat-dampened cotton of Pete's shirt.

Spinning her head around, she gazed up the dim track.

Her breath roared like a steam train as her body tried to desperately take in much needed oxygen. She cupped her hands over her mouth in a vain attempt to silence the wheezing and hide the mist emitting from her mouth.

Cautiously, Debbie peered around the tree, looking down back along the track along which she'd just blindly run. She gazed intently into the gloom

Nothing save the trees and shrubs she'd just passed lining each side broke the empty glow showed along the moonlit track.

She was alone.

Standing still, breath heavy, she took in the events of the last few minutes to plan her next step. It was unreal, as if watching a bizarre film, the scenes into which she'd fallen. But this was no movie. Pete had really been murdered.

By who and why? Did he know his killer?

Debbie's mind raced with thoughts. But one burnt deep.

The killer would have buried both of us alive! Why?

Poor Pete. He was dead. And she'd run off and left him. Guilt over her inaction washed over her in waves and a flurry of thoughts screamed through her mind, as her eyes remained fixed on the track. Emotions begin to well up, rising from deep within as she began to sob, tears rolling down her face as she openly wept, her body shaking through cold and raw emotion.

'Crack.'

A twig snapped.

In the quiet of the woods, it sounded like a gunshot.

Instinctively Debbie tensed, self control and natural fear easing the sobbing, her breathing suddenly relaxing as she stared at the track and became silent. A dirt-covered hand smeared away the fresh tears, as her eyes focussed ahead, pressing her shaking body closer to the tree, peering into the gloom, listening.

Another sharp crack.

In the silence of the woods the sound was deafening.

Movement. Soft footsteps. Near to her position.

Getting closer. Much closer. Too close. *Shit!*

Debbie was sure the sounds were nearby, but then realised they were actually much further down the track, most likely back along the way from where she'd just run. Fresh fear swelled within her as she realised she was not free and away, but being hunted. In a heightened state of natural survival alertness, she now became aware of her surroundings and absorbed the scene.

The large tree onto which she hung had behind it an array of large evergreen bushes. Unknown to Debbie these were long-established Rhododendron. With heavily leafed, long sweeping limbs, these large plants offered good naturally deep cover, with open space to hide beneath the main base area.

Her mind worked quick, and squatting down, she moved away from the tree. Dropping onto her knees, she crept backwards underneath the long spreading arms of the tall, gangly shrub. The soil beneath was dry, as crouching low, she quickly moved into the centre of the plant. Cautious of each slow movement, aware of each soft snap or rustle, she shuffled backwards, until she lay almost flat within it, ten feet from the large tree she'd rested upon moments ago.

Before her, in a clear line, the moonlight illuminated the large tree, but more importantly, the track. Her eyes slowly grew accustomed to the soft glow and her night-vision improved as she relaxed. Beyond the moon, stars began to twinkle brightly as the sky cleared from grey cloud to a blanket of dark black. But then the temperature began to rapidly drop and she immediately became aware of Pete's sweat-damp shirt now cooling upon her wet back.

Pressing her body low onto the dry vegetation beneath the sweeping Rhododendron she stared at the silhouetted trees and shrubs lining the track, watching and waiting. She knew it was simply a matter of time before the thing she feared arrived. But with her breath easing, and now feeling more secure and safe within her hideout, Debbie began to make a plan of action for survival and escape. However, she didn't have any clue where she was, or even what village they were near. Nor did she know how far away the road was from these woods they'd driven into before parking up. It was all a blur.

What the hell did Pete say this village was called? God only knows. Death-ville!

She'd never cared where they were, even when they were going to a remote village pub. It didn't matter, so long as she had a nice meal, lots to drink, a fancy pressie and a good shag after. Who cared where it was?

Now she had to plan a way out of this mess and survive. But from where?

Her body shuddered as the chilling air began to bite. She shivered and then began to involuntarily shake, as her teeth intermittently chattered. But her eyes remained fixed upon the track, her mind planning what to do next.

She'd wait a while, see if Pete's killer passed, let him go by and then slowly retrace her steps back to the clearing. The crane must have left tracks and a mass of debris through the woods. She'd find them, trace the track back out the woods, onto the main road, then hail down a passing car. Someone would call the police, who'd hunt down Pete's killer and end this nightmare. Easy.

Debbie nodded, pleased with her positive, clever thinking and simplistic plan. She was a survivor, and hadn't gotten to where she was in life by not scheming and planning. However, as her sweating body began to cool, with only Pete's torn shirt to cover her body and her 'sexy heels' upon her feet, she began to shudder involuntarily. Then her teeth loudly chattered. Conscious of the sound, she placed her finger in-between, trying to deaden the machine-gun-like sound resonating in her skull, as her whole body now shook.

She cursed, realising her mobile phone was somewhere inside Pete's car, and now deep in the ground within a dark wood, the location of which she had no idea. Alone and helpless and now begin to badly feel the cold, she peered at the tiny gold dial on the cocktail watch Pete had bought her, but struggled to make out the time. All she could determine in the shelter of the bush was a silvery glint on her exposed grey arm and it too was already becoming cold.

How long would she have to wait? Minutes? Hours? The whole night?

She'd heard of people sometimes dying from exposure after wandering out all night when fully clothed. And here she was, almost naked. She'd surely die of exposure if she stayed out all in the woods too long. But she must wait.

Another fresh wave of panic and doubt ran through her mind.

Find a way out of the woods now, or try to stay put? Which?

The cracking of a twig nearby answered her question.

Debbie's entire body froze. The shaking stopped.

Someone was on the track.

Debbie's head rose, ears cocked. They were close. Very close. Too close.

On the track, alongside the large tree by which she'd stood moments ago, the silhouette of a person eerily appeared in the moonlight. Their movements were slow and cautious. One step at a time; each footfall carefully placed.

The silhouette appeared to cock its head, listening with each step; prowling like a hunter seeking out its prey.

It was a hunter. And Debbie the quarry.

The outline was so clear on the track, a wave of panic swept through Debbie.

If I can see him so clearly, he must be able to see me too.

Dread pumped through her. This was the end.

She lay on her belly, trapped beneath a large plant; easy pickings should her hunter suddenly launch an attack. Fresh fear and dread flowed through her. She'd had it. But the hunter appeared to be searching, head visibly turning from side to side, listening intently and seemingly unaware anyone was hiding under the bushes yards away. Debbie could clearly see the figure openly on the bright, moonlit track, drifting step by step down the track, then pausing; illuminated in a dark ghostly grey like pewter. No facial features could be determined, but the bodily silhouette was clear and defined in the moonlight.

The hunter paused, head cocked. Listening.

Suddenly unseen eyes turned towards Debbie.

Debbie swallowed hard, closing her own eyes.

This was it. All over.

Her natural instinct was to scramble away. To get up and run, then dash off through the undergrowth, hoping she could out run and lose her pursuer or somehow find safety. She now wished she'd loosened one of her shoes, so she could smash it into his face, and gouge an eye out with one of the pencil-thin 'Sexy Heels.' Anything to try to defend herself and wreak revenge on her attacker and enable her to escape. But she hadn't. The slender designer shoes remained firmly secure to her now mucky feet, which lay tucked behind her.

Regrets. The story of her life.

The hunter stood motionless, perfectly still. Listening. Looking.

Level with her position, the figure stood, only a few yards away.

Had she been seen or heard? Maybe. But then again, maybe not.

The attacker was standing, ears cocked, listening intently. Her body shivered and the finger clamped in her mouth slipped. The sound of rapid chattering teeth followed. Debbie's eyes widened in terror as the burst of machine gun fire roared loudly through the woods. The deafening sound ripped through Debbie's head, shattering the night's silence, making her wince in horror.

She thrust the finger back into her mouth, biting hard. Silence.

The hunter didn't move, body fixed, save for a sharp turn of head, eyes fully focussed in Debbie's direction. She winced; uncertainty sweeping through, sure her teeth chattering had now given away her secret position.

Unseen eyes stared motionless into the gloom, their attention seemingly set upon the area behind the large shrub under which Debbie lay.

Debbie's heart raced. The killer knew she was here. She was certain.

This was it. Game over. Wait for it. Wait for the blow.

The moonlit figure stood stationary, gazing into the dark, eyes fixed firmly upon the bush. Clearly visible, hanging from their hand was a long thin bar. End curved viciously upwards, the moonlight reflected off the weapon in a dull glint. It was a Crowbar. Just like the one her brother had often used when she was younger; visiting and entering houses he didn't own, then emptying the contents, before he got three years inside for aggravated burglary.

He knows you're here. And he is going to kill you! It's the end.

Debbie gazed at the figure, then closed her eyes, tightening her slackening bladder, praying for a miracle or swift death. First option preferred.

Head smashed in with crowbar. Body thrown into the hole with Pete.

The inevitable thought of her end raced through her head.

Poor Pete. Poor me. I don't want to be buried in a pit with Pete.

Debbie wanted to cry, to escape, or do anything. But not die. Not yet.

Not here, not under a bush. Head smashed in, and her once beautiful body torn, tattered and no doubt violated; before being discarded forever into an unknown grave in an unknown wood. Not how she'd planned her happy life.

The figure stood unmoving, absorbing the night sounds, seemingly waiting.

A rustle broke the dark silence.

Debbie's eyes flicked sideways, head stationary.

The predator's head turned sharply too, legs fixed, but upper body rotating.

The hunter's unseen eyes focussed upon the track.

Both hunter and quarry faced the same direction. Movement.

A point in darkness, several yards further along the track.

Four eyes, set in two frozen faces, both stared into the gloom.

Something else was moving through the woods.

Debbie was not alone.

The hunter listened intently, unmoving, patiently waiting.

Another bush along the track clearly rustled.

Then a twig snapped.

The predator's feet silently rotated on their balls, to line up the body. Taking a cautious step forward, the dark form advanced one step along the track. Then one more. The figure paused, listening, head cocked, ears focussed.

On another step, pausing, keen ears intently listening into the night.

Briskly, but silently, the eerie silhouette stepped away, one careful step at a time, until disappearing into the silver haze along the track, to leave in Debbie's line of sight only the outline of the large tree.

She finally breathed. Softly. Her hunter was gone. For now.

The moonlit track before her was now clear and the cold, black sky and silence returned, as her pulse decreased. For once Debbie felt the tension ease down a notch. Just one. Then the thoughts raced through her mind.

She'd not been seen. She was sure. If not, he'd have raced forward towards her and struck her there and then. But he'd missed her. Decision time.

Wait or run? Live or die. Make your decision. Now!

On cue, Debbie's body began to involuntarily shake, as the brief adrenaline rush faded. Her question was answered. The trembling returned, highlighting the true state of her rapidly chilling body core temperature, as the night rapidly grew colder. The finger popped from her mouth again, the pneumatic drill of chattering teeth once more resounded, as her body shook in unison.

She had to move, whether her pursuer was waiting for her or not.

Already she could feel the cold setting into her bare, torn legs, which now ached. If she didn't move soon she'd get stiff and cramped and she'd never be able escape in a hurry if her pursuer returned and found her laying deep within her hideout. Or worse, she'd die overnight of hypothermia.

A fresh wave of hope ran through her. There was no choice. She would survive this ordeal. Flight and Freeze had been used up. But now she'd consider Fight as an option if she now met her pursuer. And she'd fight hard.

Debbie decided she'd move and now was the time. *But which way?*

Left, back the way she'd come and towards the clearing, where the car lay, to then retrace her journey into the woods? Or right, down to the track, the way her pursuer had just vanished? Options. The choice of direction was obvious.

She'd head back along the track from where she'd just run. But then to where? Debbie felt she should go back to the clearing, and check out the car, to see if Pete was still alive and needed help. But she didn't dare.

She hated the sight of blood - especially her own. It'd be more sensible to leave Pete within the car in the clearing, just for now, until she could find some help. Then she'd come back to him, with the police. It made sense.

They'd help Pete and get the mad man who'd done all this.

That's if Pete was still alive. He might be. But Debbie knew that was unlikely.

She shuddered at the thought, knowing in reality it was now all about saving herself and not worrying about Pete, and why she shouldn't waste any time.

Remembering how she'd stumbled onto the track, Debbie decided she'd head back along that small track. That would possibly link up to the main dirt track they'd driven on to enter the woods. She'd walk quietly through the woods, listening as she went, until she found a way out. Then onto a house or road, where she'd hail someone and get help. Plan sorted. Feeling invigorated, although still apprehensive, Debbie paused. Hearing nothing, the woods silent, she gently rose onto all fours. Her limbs were already aching, but the shivering eased as she crawled forward a stride at a time from her darkened hide. As she moved, the twigs beneath her cracked and snapped, sounding like exploding cannon shells in the silence, as she eased forward.

Panicking at the noise she crawled faster, the fear of making too much noise overcoming stealth, until she cleared the spread of the Rhododendron and reached the edge of the track. Rising up fully, tottering slightly, she pressed herself against the rough bark and strange safety of the large tree. Panting from the effort, her eyes frantically scanned the silver glowing track ahead.

Her eyes flitted from side to side. Nothing moved.

The moonlit track was deserted and silent. Empty.

It was quiet, but seemed too quiet. Debbie's pulse raced.

Silently by the tree Debbie stood, her head bobbing either side of the trunk, listening intently for the sound of twigs cracking or bushes rustling, in case her hunter moved back along the track towards her and raced in for the kill.

But silence flowed through the woods, broken only by Debbie's softly controlled breath and heavy thud of her beating heart within.

'Go!' The words flashed into Debbie's mind and her body responded. She moved fully out onto the track, walking on tiptoes, trying to prevent the thin heels of her shoes from digging into the soil, but also adding speed. The white shirt and her bare flesh appeared to glow, as her moonlit form reflected stark in the gloom. After a few steps she stopped, and in a crouched position beside a bush, listened with keen ears, hoping she'd hear nothing. Silence.

Like a glowing phosphorous ghost in the moonlight, she rose fully and tiptoed further along the track, listening intently all the time, as she softly and swiftly moved. Once more she stopped, bobbed down, turned her head around and listened. Her senses were on full alert, heart pumping, adrenaline flowing, but her breathing controlled and now she also felt in control.

Nothing followed behind or appeared ahead on the track.

Just a welcomed solitude and silence filled the woods.

She sighed and moved further on along the track, this time moving several strides before pausing and squatting. Again silence and the chill darkness of the night were her only companions. Her slow, individual strides soon increased, as bouncing on her toes, like a cat, she swiftly trotted along the track. Glancing back and forth, her senses alive, she'd pause every five or ten paces to quickly glance over her shoulder, to observe a clear, moonlight track behind. Continuing in this manner she jogged around a bend in the track, glancing behind as she turned. An empty silver track followed.

Trotting on more confidently, head flicking forward, her shocked eyes suddenly focussed upon an object ahead. A black form, set slightly off the track. Stark and clear, it stood before her. Debbie's blood turned to ice.

She stopped dead within the track, shoes flicking up dirt as her heels dropped and she stalled, almost tripping herself up as all forward movement ceased.

Her eyes widened in horror.

The hunter was there. Waiting for her.

Debbie's heart thumped, terror gripping her body, as she absorbed the dark image before her, its long arms reaching out, waiting to grab her.

Then instantly her blood thawed and she relaxed, releasing a soft sigh, almost embarrassed by her own false fear. Her lips formed a brief smile, unseen within the darkness, as she recognised the true identity of the form.

It was a tree. 'That' bloody tree! Debbie cursed herself inwardly.

She recalled the small spruce tree, set slightly off the track, into which she'd crashed painfully earlier, as she blindly ran down the track. She recalled its fine branches, almost human-like, reaching out across the track to grab at her.

Standing in the moonlight, she shook her head in mock defiance at the small conifer standing in the silvery-gloom ahead on the track. That bloody tree!

Debbie's confidence was growing. A tree! She wasn't afraid of a tree.

She was a survivor and would get out of this alive, knowing she should not fear every shadow, but had to be bold, though also cautious and careful if she was to survive. The object ahead was only a tree. It could not hurt her.

With renewed confidence she jogged on towards the tree, brushing defiantly against the spindly, grasping branches, which temptingly reached out across the track. Debbie almost challenged them to grab her as she ran by.

They did.

Firm hands grasped Debbie's arm.

A vice-like grip abruptly pulled at her, grabbing her arm, then threw her off balance in one swift action. Debbie gasped in horror, her high-heeled feet stumbling and collapsing, as she fell down onto the track. Arm still gripped, she was pulled back up, body twisted and thrown against a large tree on the opposite side of the track, the air knocked from her, as shock took hold.

From behind the small conifer, illuminated by silver moonlight, but hidden within the limbs of the small Spruce tree, her hunter boldly emerged.

The foreboding spectre stepped towards Debbie.

Debbie stared in shock; body and brain frozen in disbelief and terror as firm hands held both her arms tight, then pressed her body hard against the tree.

Debbie sighed, then whimpered. She'd failed. Again.

A scream began to bellow from deep within, but was choked into silence by a leather-clad hand. Releasing an arm, it forcefully closed her jaw. It clamped her mouth with immense strength, pushing her head back roughly against the tree, the hunter's body pressing hard against hers and the trunk of the tree.

Debbie whimpered, gazing into the face before her.

Cold eyes, empty like the moon, stared back.

"You shouldn't be here." A voice spoke calmly.

The eyes were fixed, expression frozen. As if dead.

'I'm sorry,' Debbie blinked silently, a tear flowing.

A silent pause followed. Eyes met eyes.

The hand on her jaw released its grasp. Debbie breathed. *'Release? Freedom?'*

But the free hand reached only down, to then rise up. Debbie's eyes followed the movement of the arm, seeing the hand drifting up towards the moon.

A black hook was outlined. The crowbar - like her brother's - was held aloft.

The dark shape, stark and vivid, contrasted against the silver orb above.
For a split second Debbie gazed longingly at the moon high above.
Cold and stark, it was her witness, but she knew not her saviour.
Hot liquid flowed from between Debbie's legs, splashing down onto her neat knees in a hot stream. It trickled on downward to her slim ankles, running over the straps on her sexy heels, over her small feet and into the soil.
The shoes were ruined.
What would Pete say?
"You shouldn't be here," the voice repeated softly.
"I know," answered Debbie. "I'm Sorry."
Debbie sensed she saw a nonchalant shrug.
She may have been wrong.
It didn't matter.
The arm swung down.
Debbie's head opened like a melon.
The crack of her splitting skull echoed through the woods.
Then silence.
The strangers had gone.

Chapter 7

Do not walk through time without leaving evidence of your passage.

The lifeless eyes gazed from the back of the truck. Glazed over with the grey mist of death, they stared sightless at the three figures curiously regarding the owner's still form with a series of inquisitive nodding heads.

"Found her this morning in one of the barns."

A gruff, emotionless, local-accented voice grunted.

Two other heads simply nodded, seemingly unconcerned.

"Okay at eight thirty last night when I checked the barn. So she must have died sometime later on in the evening. Shame. She was a beauty."

"Do you know how she died?" A warmer voice replied, the accent, seemingly more accustomed to the Southwest, appeared foreign to the current company.

"Can't be sure," the gruff voice returned. "A bastard fox made a right mess as well. Bitten right through her belly. Pulled out half her guts. Lovely mess to greet you first thing and clean up. And I ain't even had me brekkies yet!"

A couple of hearty chuckles joined the jolly quip.

"That's why you let us to hunt on your land Jack," a third voice responded. The tone was firm, authorative, with a distinguished public school edge.

"So we can control the bloody vermin doing such needless damage."

The three figures moved in closer, gazing upon the bloody, motionless form without any form of reaction to the bloody mess. Despite the chill of the morning, the corpse already smelt strongly of death.

"I'll get the winch and drag her out," chirped the man with the Southwest accent. He walked off towards a small white painted out-building, near to where the lorry was parked. The other two men turned away from the body and began discussing milk quotas. More important gossip. The Southwest man emerged, reeling out a length of steel cable with a small hook-end and dragged it towards the legs of the corpse lying in the back of the truck.

"She was a pretty looking lass," he casually commented, pulling slack from the cable, bringing the hook closer to the body. "Any idea how old was she?"

"Only seven. Not a bad lass and a bloody good milker too. Always produced nice calves too. One did well at the last show. Nice stock. Think she possibly had an 'eart attack and dropped dead. What you reckon Martin?"

"Maybe," replied Martin, the man with the winch and Southwest accent. He lifted the cow's thick rubbery lips to look at the gums. They were a very pale pink, almost white, and their colour didn't change as he pressed his thumb into the hard gum. He shrugged his shoulders in a nonchalant manner.

"Bit hard to tell. The fox has already bitten into her belly and spilt all the blood. Maybe. There are no other signs and she doesn't appear sweaty."

"My youngest lad's cleaning the mess up. None too pleased I can tell you." Jack Barlow replied with a chuckle and grin. "Get the lazy beggar used to doing some work for a change. Some proper hard, dirty work."

"I can let you know better how she died when I cut her open and see what her heart looks like," replied Martin. "Or quickly do it now and tell you if you're desperate to find out to sort your paperwork out."

"Nar, don't worry," Jack Barlow, the dairy farmer, replied casually.

"I can sort the paperwork out later. Just wanted to get her out of the barn. Mess and stink was spooking all of the other ladies. They were becoming distressed. Don't want to reduce their milk yield!"

Both spectators watched as Martin wrapped the stout steel cable around the dead cow's front hooves, forming it into a loop with the clip-hook and pulled it tight around the pasterns. He walked off to the out-building. Moments later a gentle whirring sound was heard and it took up the slack in the cable. As the cable grew more taut, the front legs of the cow began to extend, lifting up together. The muddy hooves rose, almost in a final praying motion, then with a jolt, the heavy form of the cow began to slowly move out of the back of the lorry and slide down the ramp at the rear of the truck. Suddenly the sound of hounds baying came from behind the outbuildings. They'd smelt fresh blood.

"Thank you for bringing her to us Jack," the distinguished voice of Reginald Hornchurch, Master of the Shoteton Harriers, eloquently spoke. "It's very much appreciated. Not many take the time or trouble."

"Thought it'd save you a bit of diesel and Martin some time in not having to come out yourself," said Jack Barlow, owner of the cow.

"I know how the Hunt can do with saving every penny. And Martin's usually run off his feet this time of year, especially with hunting 'avin only just started proper. Trying my bit to help and save everyone time and money."

"Bloody good of you to think like that Jack. Wish a few more would help like you. It helps bond us farmers and hunters together. You're a good chap."

Reginald Hornchurch, known simply as 'Reggie' replied diplomatically. Standing at five foot ten, he was extremely strong and fit, despite the stocky, slightly over-weight appearance. With a typical farmer's rosy-cheeked face, which was always tanned, he had small tufts of white hair fringing a bald strip. Despite his age of fifty-four, Reggie maintained a boyish complexion, making him ageless and charming, especially to the ladies, which he used to its full benefit. His fourth wife, Elizabeth, would vouch for that. But not openly.

"Well Jack, we'll be seeing you in few weeks to sort out your meet," Reggie continued, as the cow began to slide unceremoniously down the rear ramp, its guts dragging along behind it in a brown and purple, stinking tubular mess.

"Dirty bastards," Reggie sneered, regarding the mess almost with contempt. "Let's hope we can get the Charlie that did this in a couple of weeks. That'll teach it. Be one less fox to worry about. Then we'll do the same to him!"

The cow's body reached the end of the ramp and was then dragged a short distance across the grit and dirt of the yard, sliding on up a small concrete ramp and then on into the floor of the out-building. Martin Catchpole - Huntsman for the Shoteton Harriers - released the electric winch button and the cow's movement stopped, its taut legs then dropping to the concrete floor. Hanging on the doorframe, he turned to face the two chatting men.

"Best be getting back," spoke Jack Barlow turning towards the blood stained ramp, his ruddy face crinkling up, nodding towards the Huntsman.

"Do you want me to run a hose over that for you?" asked Martin.

"No. Thanks Martin. Kind to offer, but I'll get me boy to hose the whole lot out properly when I get it back. Give him something else to do."

Jack bid farewell to both men and got into the truck cab. Reggie stood back watching, hands set inside the green quilted jacket, removing one to wave a fond goodbye, as white exhaust smoke puffed and the truck trundled away. A hand waved a salute from the driver's window, as the truck moved down the tree-lined gravel drive, past the paddocks, and then disappeared into woods.

"Bloody good of him to save us a trip," spoke Reggie, watching the truck.

"Yes Sir," replied Martin. "Very useful, saved me a trip and more so, this carcass is good feeding for the hounds. Bit of a mess though. Bleeding foxes!"

Martin Catchpole was the Huntsman for the Shoteton Harriers. It was one of the few jobs, outside the military, government office, or royal institutions, where members of the public, and more so their employees, were spoken to with a degree of rank or status - usually Sir or Ma'am. Hunts retained this air.

Reginald Hornchurch was the Master of the Shoteton Harriers, and as such, Martin worked for the Hunt and indirectly for Reggie. As Reggie was 'Master of the Hunt,' he was formally referred to as 'Master' or 'Sir.' Often less formally as 'Boss' by Martin, usually when in the field, but depending on who was present and also that of Reggie's mood. His mood could switch from jovial to foul in the blink of an eye. Friends and farmers socially called Reginald - 'Reggie' - but behind his back was also known as 'Horny,' due to his renowned promiscuous nature and infidelity. He was on his fourth wife.

Martin was classed as a 'Hunt Servant', being an employee of the hunt. As the Huntsman, Martin's job was varied. Professional horseman, slaughter man, butcher, tanner, dog trainer, kennel keeper, amateur vet, game-keeper, painter, builder, driver, negotiator, odd job man, gardener, grounds man, entertainer and of course, first and foremost - hunter. It was a unique job, and Martin could count himself as only one of a small number of such spread about the country and who worked directly for the remaining hunts.

Reggie had come over to 'The Kennels' that morning to check out final details with Martin for Saturday's Hunt Meet and confirm the fields they could hunt on and those they had to avoid, at all costs. Whilst being a unique and historic institution, part of the service the hunt provided was the disposal of 'fallen stock.' This was farm livestock dying from 'unnatural causes.'

The meat from un-slaughtered animals could not generally enter the human food chain. The hunt thus provided an economical way for farmers to dispose of such large carcasses, whilst building a bond with the farmers and thus in exchange, gaining land upon which it could hunt. It also provided the hunt kennels with cheap meat for the ravenous pack of over forty hounds, housed at a country house and kennels, own by the hunt, known as The Kennels.

Martin Catchpole, now in his third season, enjoyed his work and the strange, yet thoroughly enjoyable and unique lifestyle being a Huntsman brought. He was an excellent horseman, having ridden since young, where he'd learnt to ride the family horse, kept on his father's small holding. He joined the army at a naïve sixteen, then after basic infantry training, he got his ultimate wish and joined The Kings Troop Royal Horse Artillery. When applying for his chosen regiment, his ability to ride put him well above the other applicants. After training, he worked his way up to riding with the troop and onto what he'd always dreamed of, taking part in the thrilling gun carriage displays in the summer at the local county shows, which travelled all over the country.

He moved through the non-commissioned ranks and rode at the front, on the lead horse in a string of three, guiding it swiftly through the zigzag of high-speed carriages and horses, keeping the audience breathless. Also trained in sword work, he enjoyed amazing audiences with displays of his skill; such as chopping melons perched on poles clean in half, as he joyfully galloped past on a bay charger. It was a great life. Although stationed at St. John's Wood in the middle of London, he travelled all over the country for a wide range of shows, displays and military tattoos, as well as the various ceremonial royal duties around London. It was a great life and one he enjoyed fully.

He was twenty-six when he met Sharon in a beer tent at the Royal Show at Kenilworth. She was the daughter of a local farmer and also rode. That evening he sneaked out from the unit's tent to meet Sharon for a date in the nearby pub. After a great evening, they kept in touch by letter for two years, seeing each other whenever time permitted or Martin had leave, both riding out at Sharon father's farm. The excitement of the displays began to lose its zest for Martin, and the long winters, with the boring daily chores in London began to get to him. He longed for more, as well as a stable relationship with Sharon. She flatly refused to move to London, but enjoyed Martin's company, love of horses and easy nature. Defence spending cuts gave Martin the chance to leave; more importantly with the MOD offering a pay-off and pension to quit, so he did. They decided to find a job working with horses and spent the first summer together in Surrey, looking after a string of polo ponies for a multi-millionaire businessman. As autumn proceeded, and the polo season finished, so did their equine jobs. They then moved onto a riding school, enjoying teaching and schooling horses, living a simple, but enjoyable life. They snuggled up in a caravan on site through the winter, until the spring arrived, with warm weather but unwelcome news and another fresh challenge.

Bank officials appeared, looking to take the place over from the hotfooted, bankrupt owners. They'd vanished a few weeks earlier, owing the bank, and the now Mr & Mrs Catchpole, a lot of money. Martin and Sharon were wise and had the sense to hide a selection of the best horses, along with the yard's horsebox, as the bank came along to see what they'd just repossessed.

The horses were swiftly sold, and the horsebox swiftly vanished too, along with Martin and Sharon, it becoming Martin and Sharon's mobile home. They enjoyed their semi-nomadic existence for a while, parking up the horsebox in lay-bys or travelling around various riding establishments looking for casual work as it was offered. But they longed for a more stable location, an income and horses to ride; something the pair deeply missed and longed for.

As summer approached, they returned to the polo playing millionaire for another frantic season preparing and training the array of horses he owned, earning extra money using the horsebox for deliveries, when not working.

However, as the summer drew on and autumn and the cold threatened, along with immanent unemployment and homelessness once more from the Granny-flat at the millionaire's farm, they answered an ad' in Horse & Hound for a Huntsman in a small Norfolk Hunt, unaware of what it really entailed.

Martin had hunted a few times when he was a child, as had Sharon, but he knew nothing of the complex nature of the Hunt itself and especially looking after many hounds and all it entailed and the politics of The Hunt.

He answered the advertisement, and was offered an interview straight away. The pair drove to Norfolk and Martin met the Hunt's Master; the rather pompous, yet agreeable and jovial Reggie Hornchurch, whom he liked at once, having a military manner. He was then grilled on what he knew about horses, hounds and hunting in general by the pretentious Hunt Committee.

Consisting of a number of aging farmers and rich young businessmen, he had a brief interview. Here it was clear Martin knew lots about horses, but little on the other two subjects, namely Hunting. To his amazement they swiftly offered Martin the position of Huntsman and Sharon as Second Whipper-In.

Reggie told them to consider the offer before deciding and then look around 'The Kennels,' which would be their home. Set deep within woodland, this small country house, with kennel yard housing forty hounds, was a property The Hunt owned and was where the Huntsman would live free of charge.

Martin remembered the excitement they felt driving to The Kennels for the first time to view their potential new home. Careful not to scrape the sides of the horsebox on the heavily wooded track leading in from the quiet road, the place held a magical appeal. The 'Trespassers Will Be Eaten' sign boldly on display at the entrance had raised their eyebrows. They'd glanced warily at each other then laughed loudly, wondering what they were letting themselves in for. They later learnt it was an 'in house' joke with all members of the Shoteton Harriers, where many hunt members or followers displayed identical signs to their own property entrances as a humorous and yet dark warning.

As the woodland track opened out, it revealed the white painted, late Victorian house, including the low roofed kennel block, various work sheds and out-buildings, with neat post and rail paddocks sweeping around. In the bright late summer sun, a strange tingle ran through them both. They turned and faced each other, both smiling, knowing they must accept the position, it feeling perfect for them. Martin at once became the official Huntsman for the Shoteton Harriers, with Sharon 'Second Whipping-In.'

The salary was poor. He slaved in the winter, with long hours in the freezing cold and pouring rain. Yet they received beautiful, free accommodation, the opportunity to ride some great horses provided by The Hunt, and rode over wonderful ground many never got the opportunity to see. As a benefit, other than maintaining the property and rearing hound puppies, they had most of the summer off. Martin and Sharon moved into The Kennels in late August, just in time for the 'Cubbing' meets. These were the traditional early morning hunt meets where horses and hounds were trained and gained fitness, along with riders and their horses, many rested through the summer months.

Reggie, and the Shoteton's amateur Whipper-In, John, were a great help in the first few months, guiding Martin and Sharon through what was required. As was Steve Harrison, The Shoteton Field Master. He led the riders over a mix of terrain, following the hounds, and seemed a very cheeky, likeable rogue. It was a trait seeming to run through many members of the Shoteton.

Martin, with his military background and discipline rapidly learnt the ropes and all the etiquette, routine and behaviour expected from such an established institution and tradition, with Sharon also becoming a keen part of the team.

It was only later they learnt why they'd been taken on so willingly. The previous Huntsman had gone down for eighteen months for sheep rustling. Thus the Shoteton Harriers were facing the rapidly approaching new season without a Huntsman and Kennel man. Desperate, the inexperienced, yet keen Martin got the position by default. Hence Sharon became Second Whipper-In for the first season, and their relationship with the hunt members grew strongly and quickly, as Martin learnt the personalities and nature of the key members of the hunt and Reggie's varied mood swings, which changed daily.

The mounted field became great friends in the winter, with them all riding out two times a week, but then seemed to mysteriously vanish in the summer months. This was except for when they met for the various social functions organised by the Hunt Supporters Club at key hunting events, such as the Puppy Show and other key social occasions run by various hunt supporters.

Reggie, Steve, local farmers, and various riders, along with the notorious Hunt Committee - made up from many of the former group - rapidly accepted Martin and Sharon into their fold, making them feel genuinely and perfectly at home, as they quickly settled in. The pair loved the whole experience, which was seen more as a dedicated way of life, rather than a job.

Now they were into their fourth season and hunting for 'real' was permitted after the political changes, with no longer a need to 'pretend' they were drag hunting, after the disastrous Hunting Act had finally been repealed.

It surprised Martin what he'd learnt in a short space of time. Despite being brought up on his father's smallholding, working mostly with fruit and vegetables, other than horses, he knew little else, especially about hounds. He never dreamed years later he'd find himself killing, skinning, disembowelling, bleeding and carving up a wide range of livestock. Then feeding huge chunks of that freshly cut flesh to a pack of ravenous, yet loyal hounds. Now it all seemed second nature and he thoroughly enjoyed the unusual occupation, despite some of the sights it brought, and the tough lifestyle he endured.

His job involved looking after the forty plus hounds kept at the kennels, which he cared for like his children. It was sad when his favourite hounds had to be destroyed, due to either injury, or old age at around the age of seven, because their useful life as a hunting hound was over. Tradition and hunt policy deemed they'd be put down at an early age; a controversial point, often made much of by non-hunting people. But most of the time Martin took it all in his stride, becoming harder and more accustomed with each season.

It sometimes worried Martin he'd become desensitised by it all, somehow enjoying carving into pieces a once living animal without a second thought, and watching eagerly as the keen hounds tore away at the flesh, gazing on in wonder as the hounds bolted down huge chunks of meat in minutes.

Deep down, he knew he somehow enjoyed the brutality of it all, and would often stand smiling, watching intently at the hounds tore into the raw flesh. With this morning's cow, kindly provided by the dairy farmer Jack Barlow; after finding it dead in a barn on his farm, he now had another casualty to bleed, disembowel, skin, carve up and feed to the ravenous hounds. But it was all in a days work for the Hunter, and he wouldn't swap it with anyone.

"I'll leave you to it for now," Reggie spoke with a nod, checking his watch. "I'm off to see Steve. Things to discuss. I might pop in on the way back to check on Chatty if I get time. Let me know how she is. Hopefully okay."

Chatty was a very good bitch hound who'd badly torn a pad a few days back, and was a personal favourite of Reggie's. He knew the hounds was in safe hands with Martin, but he took great pride in his hounds, thoroughly enjoyed their company, and would often spent time at the kennels alone with them.

"Okay sir," replied Martin, his head down, calling from the small out building known as the Cutting Room, already grasping at a large, razor-sharp knife, ready to slice into the cow's flesh and trim out the filthy hanging innards.

"I'll try and find out what killed his girl so Jack can complete the various forms for the Ministry and get back in touch with him. Bye!"

Reggie raised his hand in a casual farewell as he walked off, knowing Martin was best left alone, then disappeared, climbing into his Range Rover.

Moments later the sound of Reggie's dark Range Rover started up and the powerful V8 engine roared. It then crunched upon the stones along the drive of the kennels, as it slowly headed off and out towards the wooded track.

Martin noticed the Cutting Room grow darker. Someone had silently entered the back doorway from the courtyard that linked onto the large kennel block.

"Hullo luv," he spoke, before turning. When he raised his head, the shapely silhouette of Sharon framed an entrance leading from the Cutting Room and on into a small courtyard, then on further into the main whitewashed house.

"Gawd what a stink," the woman spoke with a distinct 'Brummie' drawl. "I've just made you all a nice cuppa, but now see Reggie and Jack have both gone. Typical. And I got the best biscuits out too. What a waste."

Martin eagerly eyed a small tray held in Sharon's hands, upon which sat three mugs and an assortment of fine quality biscuits.

"I could certainly do with one. I'll come inside out of the cold and sort this poor cow out later. Poor cow, get it!" Martin tittered, proud of the joke.

Sharon simply shook her head. She'd long given up on Martin's silly quirks and corny jokes and turned with a toss of her head and a grin.

"Those biscuits look very nice," Martin quipped, catching Sharon up as she turned away and nipping at her buttocks. "Mine are the chocolate ones."

"You're rationed to three, you fat bastard. You'll need a new Scarlet if you put on any more weight." Sharon replied, skilfully moving her hips from Martin's grasp with a wiggle, as the pair approached the house doorway.

"Yeah, but it's still early in the season. This is my summer fat to see me through the harsh winter months. I'll be as skinny as a rake by the time March comes. Best I have a few more biscuits now to build up my strength."

With a smile, the pair disappeared into the farmhouse, ready to consume the pile of tea and biscuits. The sound of baying hounds, ever hungry and naturally keen to hunt, followed behind them as the door closed.

The hounds could smell fresh blood and wanted feeding too.

Chapter 8

The best way to solve any problem is to remove its cause.

Martin Luther King Jr.

Steve Harrison wasn't a happy man. He had a problem. He recalled an old saying: *'There's no such thing as a problem, merely an opportunity to find a solution.'*

He pondered the positive thought, willing it to work or resolve the situation, but sighed heavily. Dejected, he slumped back into his chair, rubbing his chin.

No. He definitely had a problem. A big problem.

Steve Harrison was the Shoteton Harriers Field Master. He ran a business from his small farm, primarily buying and selling equestrian products; stocking everything from whips to gates, saddles to horseboxes, as well as offering hay, straw and a varying range of farm equipment. In fact anything you could need in the agricultural or equestrian world. And more.

Now it seemed he also sold tractors. Dodgy tractors. Very dodgy.

An excellent, hard riding horseman, he was a much harder businessman and even worse husband. He liked the ladies and they liked him. He'd ridden when young, stopping briefly when in his teens, but returned when he met, then married, his horse-mad, now ex-wife, Isabelle. It was a sore subject.

He'd made his small fortune the hard way. Whilst working as a Sales Rep' for an agricultural machinery company, he'd seen some opportunities for himself, so slowly bought the odd piece of old farm machinery at local markets to sell on. Slowly his sales skills paid off, using his natural cheek and charm, and he quickly became known as the 'go to' person for many agricultural items. This brought him into contact with a number of local farmers who were involved in hunting, and this was how he met 'Izzy.' The pair instantly hit it off.

From a well-established competitive 'horsey' family, who were hard and took no prisoners, Isabelle Johnson had been into every aspect of the equestrian world all her life. She'd competed at all levels; from racing around at local gymkhanas, to serious high-level three-day eventing. After a frantic, whirlwind relationship, the horse-mad Izzy soon got Steve back into riding and introduced him to the world of hunting. Here the feisty, yet enigmatic pair, became rather notorious on the hunting field. Partly for Steve's flirtatious, fun-loving and cheeky nature, but also for Izzy's no-holds-barred temper, taking no nonsense from anyone. The pair settled in together at Steve's small farm and livery yard. Then with Izzy's drive and ambition, they developed a business together selling various equestrian products. Steve set up a small mail order saddlery business for Izzy to run, initially as a hobby, but which soon expanded into a mobile tack shop. When Izzy wasn't riding and Steve had a spare moment, the pair sold at various local gymkhanas and horse shows.

They rapidly moved into mail order, then sold online and things blossomed. Steve soon found himself spending more time involved with his own affairs and Izzy's business than working for his main employer. Steve's natural good looks, charming but cheeky nature and 'gift of the gab' made the business boom and he began buying and selling anything local farmers or horse owners wanted. He gave up his full-time job and the pair became as good as business partners as they had been bed partners.

But that was a few years ago, before Izzy's well-publicised dramatic departure; from both his life, bed and business. As great as their relationship was, Steve always had trouble turning down any 'sales opportunity;' no matter who was flashing their cash, eyelashes or their knickers. Usually all of them.

This weakness was to be Steve and Izzy's downfall.

The pair made the Sunday papers after Izzy came home unexpectedly early from a cancelled eventing competition. She found Steve in their bedroom carrying out 'Market Research' on a new range of whips with their two young grooms. The youngest of the girls had been tied to the bed and received the full vent of Izzy's anger when she burst into the bedroom, to rudely interrupt the playful threesome's 'test procedure' of whips and other leather goods.

'Mrs Whiplash' and 'Three-in-the Bed Hunter' were some of the headlines. Various tabloids printed details of the cheating huntsman's bedroom activities, involving the two young grooms. What added fuel, and much interest to the news story, were the actions of his violent, embittered wife.

She'd severely beaten the youngest groom, still secured to the bed, testing the whip out across her exposed buttocks, back and legs. A few seconds earlier she'd chased Steve around the bedroom, almost removing his manhood in the process with a well-aimed swipe of the lethally thin schooling whip.

The older groom had managed to escape by jumping out a bedroom window, breaking an ankle in the fall. She hobbled off to call for help, leaving her younger colleague to receive the full vent of Izzy's lethal whip-lashing rage.

Ever the gentleman, Steve hid in a wardrobe for safety, until the screams and cries for help of his young groom were too much and he burst out, knocking Izzy unconscious with one punch. Things could never go back from there.

Steve tried to pay off the grooms to keep them quiet, but the younger one's injuries were too great and her parents pressed charges. The police became involved, and it was curtains for Izzy, who was charged with serious assault.

An accompanying photo, taken outside the courtroom on the day of the trial, of Izzy's bitter face and her clenched fist smashing straight into an over-cocky photographer's lens, became legendary; almost winning the cameraman a Pulitzer Prize. Six months in prison broke Izzy and their relationship.

Steve's foolish cheating had ended everything in tears, regret, and saw the break up of his business and marriage. Steve looked after Izzy's two horses whilst she was in prison, but lost all ambition and interest in their business, especially the equestrian side in which Izzy had excelled.

He no longer sold at shows and generally looked after the day to day business end at the farm and the few liveries they had, preferring to 'wheel and deal' with larger ticket items, such as 4 x 4's, horse boxes and trailers, having a part-time girl undertaking the small amount of work on the Internet and some mail order sales and doing all the boring admin work Izzy enjoyed.

He still bought and sold anything he thought could make a profit, including the current item that now gave him his latest problem. An almost new tractor. He'd bought it cheap - very cheap - from a local farmer he'd known for years, and like many, he'd fallen on hard times. Very hard times. The farmer had gone bust and was due to have the bailiffs come around any day.

They wanted the farm's listed assets to sell on to pay debts.

He'd sold Steve the tractor for cash. At a very low price.

It seemed far too good to be true. And it was.

Unbeknown to Steve it was not legitimately the farmers to sell on, being one of the farms assets, which the bank wanted back as payment for the huge debts incurred. The bailiffs were keenly looking, but first they had to find it.

Cash firmly in hand, the farmer was keeping quiet about the tractor's whereabouts, as that of his own. He'd gone. Vanished a few nights previously, with his wife, two sheep dogs, and whatever belongings would fit into suitcases and their also hotly financed 4 x 4 Jeep and livestock trailer.

The only problem Steve had now was what to do with the big lump of multi-horse-powered steel and rubber. An incredible piece of kit, but technically not his to own or sell on. Hence the problem. He'd hoped to sell it on quick, but this now seemed out of the question, unless he could change its identity or find someone equally as dodgy to take it off his hands. Not too hard.

Unfortunately, unlike cars, there weren't many tractors written off, so it would not be a simple case of giving it a re-spray, changing the VIN plates and selling it on via a dodgy auction. As he had with cars. All he could hope was to lease it to a contractor and get some return on his now dubious investment. This meant he might have to store it over the winter if he couldn't shift it, and he was missing the money, something Steve never liked.

He always hated to lose out on a deal, or the opportunity to bed a young lady; two of Steve's greatest attributes, yet also his greatest weakness.

He stood rubbing his short-cut strawberry-blond hair, pondering, when providence seemed to arrive. It appeared in the shape of a dark Range Rover from the top woods. Steve eyed the approaching vehicle and the dust it kicked up, knowing it could be one of the many local farmers, a hunt member or another horsey person looking for a deal, the prestigious off-road 4 x 4 being for many their vehicle of choice. It trundled down the twisting track, along the loose gravel of the driveway and on into the farm, parking on the open yard, where an array of lorries, trailers and farm equipment stood. The Rover pulled alongside an almost identical coloured Rover belonging to Steve and drew to a halt. Steve at once recognised vehicle and smiling driver.

Reginald Hornchurch exited the Rover, met by a grinning Steve; the welcome warm and genuine and happy smile returned.

"Reggie! Good morning Sir. And how are you?"

Steve greeted him with a firm handshake and arm slap.

"Good Morning Stephen, I'm fine. You seem very well." Reggie replied in his distinctive gruffness, his eyes already scanning the yard, noticing a large green and yellow object standing proudly before him. His eyes glinted.

"I say, looks like you've got yourself a John Deere. Bloody good piece of equipment. Where on earth did you pick that up? It looks fairly new. I assume it's yours. Not stolen I hope?" Reggie grinned wickedly at his friend.

Steve grinned. "A Seven seven three zero. A fine example. Like new. Why not take a look?" Steve replied, a twinkle in his eye, now in Salesman mode.

Reggie stepped forward and expertly eyed the monster. He playfully rubbed his chin, but his interest was genuine. He touched the big front tyre.

"Been looking at the new TR's Very expensive though. This is nice."

Steve saw the interest and selling signs. He moved in.

"TR's? Save your money Reggie. This has got air con', Sat-Nav', and all the works; it's half the price and as good as new. One-ninety horse power. Can't decide whether to lease it out for contract hire or sell on. Picked it up quite reasonably. Looking for a quick return on my investment. Wouldn't happen to know anyone who might be interested in her would you?" Steve smiled.

"Umm," Reggie replied, grinning widely, knowing Steve Harrison too well, appearing to think hard, but already scheming and doing the sums.

"Was due to replace my main tractor next summer. Would have preferred something new though, for tax purposes. I still could. However, it depends on what you're asking for this beats and what deal we can do. Let's talk."

The twinkle in Reggie's eyes matched that of Steve's and was one of the reasons why the pair got on so well in all manner of dealings.

"She's not nicked I hope!" Reggie finished with a guffaw, slapping Steve's shoulder. He almost choked, but knew Reggie knew that it could be.

"As if Reggie!" Steve replied with a smirk, recovering and trying his best not to blush too brightly, although he did. "Okay, I admit it. It is nicked. I stole it this morning from your North Farm. Don't you recognise it?"

"Ah-ha! Well now you mention it…" Reggie replied laughing, playfully punching his fellow hunter. "Hard work pulling a plough with a horse!"

"How about we discuss how little you'll let me take it off your hands for over a cup of tea. I've also got some details to run over for the Cole's meet."

"Yes the Cole's meet. Great ground to ride over. He puts on a fine spread," Steve responded, thoughts drifting. "One of Izzy's old favourites."

Reggie eyed his hunting colleague with all-knowing eyes.

"Yes. Wonder what cronies she'll bring along with her this week?"

"No doubt that skinny pratt Pearson," Steve replied, his tone distant. "What a tosser! He really hates me. I can't think why! What have I done to him?"

"Well considering you rode over his chum and nearly killed him, I think that gives Pearson good grounds to dislike you!" Reggie laughed. "Anti idiots."

"I simply lost control of Samson. Horses are unpredictable animals. An accident. The courts agreed. He shouldn't have been there on private land."

Steve grinned wickedly to Reggie, who chuckled, shaking his head, recalling clearly a key incident last year where a anti-hunt supporter at their meet was trampled by Steve's horse Samson, and put in hospital with serious injuries.

"Any way Reggie, enough talk about stupid Antis, let's get down to the real business in hand," Steve said, patting Reggie's back. "Tea. Strong and white, like my horses. Irish Breakfast, Assam, Earl Grey or Tetley's – What'll it be?"

The two smiling men wandered off towards a Portacabin, which served as Steve's office, to enjoy an early round of Assam. There, Steve extolled to Reggie all the pleasures life would bring to him if he acquired the tractor from him at a knock-down bargain price. Both men were keen on a deal and Steve Harrison beamed, welcoming the opportunity of a sale, or at least the opportunity to get some money back. With a bit of profit.

Perhaps the day wasn't so bad after all.

'Problem? What problem! Remove the problem - Solution found.'

After an hour of intense negotiating, followed by half an hour of discussion on the forthcoming hunt meet, Reggie had a new tractor, and details of the meet at the Cole's farm had been resolved and sorted.

And it had only cost Steve three cups of best quality Assam. A great result.

As Reggie left Steve standing outside the Portacabin, he bid farewell with a hearty wave and wandered over to his Rover. Steve dashed back inside and rapidly began making some discrete phone calls to various associates in the trade, to organise changing the identity of the offending tractor.

Problem solved. Almost.

Reggie set off and left the open area of Steve's farm, and drove onto the dirt track, which meandered through the small woods bordering the edge and led to and from Steve's property, before connecting onto the main road. Tapping the steering wheel, deep in thought, he too had problems to solve.

Keen hunter's eyes instinctively scanned the deep woods and tracks as he slowly passed through, noticing birds and wildlife flit about, all lost in their own worlds. Each had their own concerns and survival problems. People it seemed were no different. Only their problems were often of their own making. As were his. As he approached the section of woodland track where it met the road, he passed the very familiar sign he'd seen so many times.

'Trespassers will be Eaten'.

Something hit him. A thought.

He braked hard, abruptly stopping the two tons of vehicle. It skidded for a few inches upon the dry track before halting with a jolt.

He turned his head around to glance back at the sign more clearly.

Reggie's face broke into a grin.

Into his mind came the idea.
It was perfect.
In a flash it provided the answer.
Clear. Flawless. Like crystal.
Reggie grinned.
He'd seen the sign on countless occasions too and from The Kennels, and back and forth to Steve's, never really taking any notice, the words simply a Shoteton joke. Indeed he saw identical copies of the sign every single day at his own farm, where he had them posted at the main entrance and along the numerous tracks covering his vast acres and assorted farms. Numerous copies of the same sign were posted at a variety of other local farms, mostly at the entrances to members who rode out with the Shoteton Hunt.
It was an almost trademark sign, displayed at the entrance to the properties; displaying a degree of malice intent, but also a common bond, designed to keep away unwanted visitors, but with dark humour related to the hunt.
The sign sparked within him the solution to a problem.
It had been a long-standing problem.
The problem needed resolving.
The cause needed to be removed.
A chill shuddered through Reggie's body.
The idea was so perfect it was frightening.
He found himself grinning at its simplicity.
Then chuckling loudly.
He eased the Rover forward, nodding silently to himself.
Problem identified. Solution established.
Cause removed. Problem solved.
As he pulled away from the dirt of the woodland driveway and onto the dark tarmac of the country road, he'd made up his mind. It concerned a problem that'd been troubling him for a long while. But now he had the answer.
The solution he'd suddenly discovered amused him and he was soon merrily laughing to himself as he drove along. A large finger pressed a CD into the Rover's music system and La Treviata boomed from the powerful speakers, as he gunned the Rover's big engine and roared up the road.
He began singing joyfully. Or as best he could.
Today, the mood-swinging Reggie was a happy man.
'Problem? What problem!'

Chapter 9

By heaven, he echoes me, as if there were some monster in his thought too hideous to be shown.

William Shakespeare - Othello

Gravel crunched noisily to the side of the house and a large engine roared by. Chris Turner moved quickly within his house and peered out of a narrow window to investigate. A white police Land Rover rolled past the house and stopped abruptly in the large yard, spitting gravel from beneath its wheels. Pulse racing, Chris steely regarding the unwelcome and uninvited intruder. Especially 'one of them.' Stretching out a hand, he grabbed a well-faded wax jacket, the forearms worn to a pale yellow. On his legs were cream jodhpurs, along with a pair of green 'Hunter' Wellingtons, the side buckles having long since fallen off. He moved swiftly for his stocky five foot seven frame and from the window scanned the yard and vast areas beyond, as if searching for something or someone else, then glared at the solitary Rover, as its single occupant opened the door. A nerve in his neck twitched as he moved to the wooden, split stable door leading out into the yard. A massively built Black and Tan Doberman, lying asleep on an old blanket beside an Aga cooker, stirred. Alert, but reluctant to leave the cosy bed, he sensed his owner's tension and rose fully, feeling obliged to show some willing and earn his keep.

"Quiet Max! You stay there. No eating anyone!" Chris spoke quietly, a single finger raised mockingly to his lips. "I wonder what the pigs want?"

Chris advanced slowly to the door, closing the bottom section, ensuring the Doberman remained inside. The dog happily returned silently to its bed, seemingly uncaring of any intruders. Chris was in the yard and advancing towards the Land Rover just as the driver exited the vehicle, eyes firmly fixed upon the policeman, who adjusted his leather tool belt, as if ready for action.

It was a crisp morning, but the early November sun warmed the air enough to take away any initial chill. Grey clouds drifted high in the blue sky and it had threatened to be a nice day. Now someone looked set to ruin it.

"Morning," Chris offered, approaching the unwelcome visitor, almost as a question than a polite greeting, striding forward with purpose.

"Ah, Good Morning Sir," replied the policeman. A tall, burly man in his early thirties, he would pass as an England rugby player, with his rough good looks and a heavy, yet fit-looking build. Short-cropped blonde hair framed bright blue, slightly piggy eyes, which peered from his pale face as if squinting.

He instantly reminded Chris of an image from a book 'The Three Little Pigs' that he'd read when younger. His thoughts flicked for a second to his parents. Something stirred. Deep memories returned, then were quickly pushed away.

His mind returned to the present and the uninvited guest. Chris reluctantly shook the policeman's offered hand, noting smooth skin and no rings.
"Good morning Sir, I'm PC Roger Burton," the policeman introduced with a sour, fake and sickly smile. "I've been transferred up to this region and I'm getting to know the area and slowly making contact with all the locals."
'Locals?' Chris considered bitterly, instantly disliking the policeman.
'Who does he think he is? A missionary in Africa? Is he going to convert me?'
"New to these foreign and forbidding parts then are you?" enquired Chris, his tone almost derogatory and condescending, his expression matching.
The Constable missed the point, eagerly looking past him, instead eyeing up the stables and large white-painted farmhouse, taking in everything.
"Yes," the policeman finally replied, turning back and realising he'd been asked a question, but unaware of the snide remark, his attention elsewhere.
"Moved up here from Essex two weeks ago. Just finding my feet."
Chris nodded silently, his head tilting forward, keen eyes looking down at the constable's large shiny boots. He grinned to himself, before looking up and stared directly at the Constable, his expression suddenly cold and impassive.
Burton missed the silent humour, but seemed pleased by his quiet, attentive audience, although unsure of him. He continued speaking regardless.
Chris listened, or appeared to, but his thoughts were also elsewhere.
"Bit strange all this countryside. Can't get used to the quiet and lack of any real action," he continued, as if justifying his reasons for being on the farm.
"Its big news here if a sheep goes missing. City guy myself. I enjoy the real action. Had to move on though. Personal reasons. Women. You know."
Chris stood unresponsive, eyes fixed hard upon the policeman.
"Split up with the Missus," PC Burton continued talking, too freely, almost into space. "Thought moving away from the city would be a fresh start. Trouble is I'm big city born and bred. This is a bit of a culture shock you could say. Nothing but cow shit and small roads. Slow moving and too quiet."
Chris simply stared, not responding, his expression blank.
Burton suddenly became aware of his silent, unresponsive audience. Feeling uncomfortable, he realised he'd said too much, as was often his habit. Burton paused. Face flushed, pale cheeks glowing, he looked about the farm.
"Didn't even know this place existed until yesterday," Burton said, changing tact. "I've driven past a few times looking and missed it. Well hidden."
"Good. That's how I like it," replied Chris curtly. "Out of sight and mind."
His gaze was cold and hard, like his tone. He stood firmly, hands in his jacket pockets, unmoving, staring at the policeman, who shuffled uneasily. Feeling uncomfortable, his eyes darted about, looking for something to discuss.
"You keep horses I take it?" the policeman continued, gazing at the long row of stables running in a line behind him, a couple of equine heads looking curiously his way, trying to make fresh conversation, but losing badly.

Chris slowly turned his head towards the long row of stables behind the policeman and regarded them as if for the first time ever. They stretched up beyond the house some fifty feet, turning to form an 'L' shaped yard. A number of equine heads protruded out of the half doors. Beyond lay a series of neat post and rail fenced paddocks, separated by a series of dirt tracks, stretching uphill, then disappearing up into a vast woodland in the distance.

Chris slowly scanned the length of the stables, as if he had only just noticed they were all there. He noticed the policeman's gaze followed his, then slowly he turned back, to face the young policeman with a blank expression.

"No. I keep large pigs," he replied coldly, with no emotion.

The policeman's face went blank and his piggy eyes squinted slightly, glazing over as he tried to internalise the information slowly dissolving in his brain. Inside the gears churned over. He looked over his shoulder to see a big bay horse looking at him over a stable door, its head nodding up and down, lips flapping freely, as if sharing a private joke with the owner. He got it.

Burton turned back to face the horseman, his face flushing red, noting the horseman's face break into a grin, the harsh words sinking in.

"You nearly had me there for a minute," the policeman laughed nervously, blushing brightly, but burning inside, wanting to punch the horseman.

"Hmm. Yes, it looks like I did." The grin waned and Chris' face was set back like steel, but his eyes twinkled. "My little joke." But it wasn't.

Burton smiled uncomfortably, like the victim of a practical joke, which he was; feeling obliged to laugh, when really just wanting to smash in the pranksters face into a pulp. That would have pleased him. Very much.

Chris grinned, sensing a point won over the nosey policeman. "I run a livery yard, as well as training and breaking in horses." He proudly announced.

"Must be hard work," the policeman replied, nodding, looking back at the stables, trying to show an interest, break the ice and regain some control.

"No, I just sit on my arse most of the day."

Chris' humorous response was deliberately dry and blunt, as was he.

The Constable chuckled, as he got what he hoped was another joke more swiftly, beginning to understand the annoying arrogant bastard before him.

Silence then hung in the air like a lingering frost.

Chris's expression returned to a cold and unsmiling gaze.

Burton felt uncomfortable, as was intended. Although the horseman was much smaller in stature, his aura seemed to tower over the policeman, the horseman's presence almost like a dark threatening thundercloud. It was.

The policeman recovered some composure and then continued in a different, more familiar role and manner, that of inquisitor, taking back control.

"Sorry, but I didn't get your name Sir. Mister….?"

"That's 'cos I didn't tell you."

Burton glared, disbelieving the rude response and lack of reply.

The horseman paused, as if considering the matter. "Turner. Chris Turner."

Burton nodded, as if now happy with a positive and cooperative response.
"Nice place you have here. Is there a Missus Turner?" he enquired, now confident in his role of interrogator and feeling back in control.
"No," Chris replied bluntly. "Just me. I live alone, with my horses."
The rude and curt reply shook Burton momentarily, but then he recalled how uncooperative most of the other local farmers and landowners were whom he'd recently met when touring the area. Nearly all were rude and defensive. This horseman seemed no different, but definitely had a colder edge.
"Well you must certainly get lots of attractive ladies around all these horses. Tight white jodhpurs, whips, spurs and all that, you know!" The policeman quipped with a chuckle, in a male-bonding manner, winking playfully.
An expressionless pause followed before Chris responded calmly.
"Loads," Chris answered. "Unfortunately any around here are either married or bat for the other team. I'm happy as I am. Have you finished? I'm busy."
The manner the statement was delivered took Burton back. The horseman's expression was cold. He glared at the policeman, all conversation ended.
Burton had seen enough for the minute. His instincts told him Mr Turner was not all he appeared to be. However, what he appeared to be, he could not quite work out. Yet. He decided to deliver his pre-prepared speech and leave.
"Well, as mentioned, I'm in the area to get myself known to you locals."
Burton turned to face the horseman with a sickly smile.
"So you've already said. And? Hurry up, I'm busy." Chris responded.
Burton flushed at the horseman's blunt interruption.
"Just to let you know if you see anything suspicious or need any help, don't hesitate to ask for me personally. I'm PC Roger Burton, your local contact, based at North Walsingham. We're here to provide support to the local rural population and try to combat rural crime." Burton finished, drawing back his broad shoulders, pleased with his brief speech and relieved to get it out.
"Well thank you Cunt-stable," Chris replied, with a deliberate pause.
The words were drawn out and made the P.C. turn.
He was about to comment, but the horseman continued.
"I'll bare that in mind. And should I see any rogues, bandits, highwaymen, sheep shaggers or similar baddies about these parts, I'll put down my shotgun, call off the posse and get straight on the phone to you chaps instead. Then wait for five hours for you to simply tell me to fill in some forms instead."
Burton was stunned, now boiling up inside. Tensing up, instinctively ready to strike, he was for once unsure how to respond. He sensed deep hatred and bitterness, with no hint of humour in the horseman's comment, only vitriol.
'Did he really just call me Cunt-stable?' thought Burton, still unsure what he'd heard or how to act. *'Or was it his accent?'* Either way, he didn't dare ask.
He looked hard at the unmoving, unblushing and calm horseman.
Burton knew he should react, but felt uneasy and unsure.
"I take it you don't much care for the police?" He finally asked.

"You'd be totally correct," Chris replied bluntly.

"Any reason why?" enquired Burton, now back on home ground.

"I'm sure you'll find out soon enough. As a policeman. Are we done?"

Chris looked away from the unwanted intruder, turning his body sideward, as if dismissing the guest, his attention and gaze drifting up the dirt track to the fields stretching beyond. A woodpecker tapped in the distant woods, its hollow rat-a-tat breaking the morning's silence. The horseman listened.

Burton's eyes followed the horseman's gaze, head instinctively drifting with the turn of the smaller man, to see the neat post and rail paddocks with horses grazing and vast spread of mature woodland set beyond, from where the hidden woodpecker lay tapping away. His attention was brought back at once by the swift movement of the horseman's head, his body turning.

Remaining silent, Chris looked straight into the face of the uncomfortable policeman before him, but who was blushing. Neither spoke, only stared.

Burton felt that for once he had found a match. For now.

"Is that it? Finished?" Chris asked bluntly. "Or are you going to arrest me?"

Burton flushed even brighter, unsure how to respond to the arrogance.

"Only trying my best to help the local community. But I guess you're busy and so I won't keep you any longer. Thank you for your time, and good-day."

Burton issued the response through gritted teeth. Realising he wasn't wanted, he smiled nervously and silently stepped back towards his Rover, deciding any further conversation was pointless. He opened the door, climbed in and started the engine. The horseman remained stationary as Burton slowly turned the vehicle around in the yard. He then paused the Land Rover beside the horseman, whose hands were still set firmly within his faded wax-jacket pockets, silently watching. Burton wound down the window, gazing down the yard and up at the dirt track leading up to the woods beyond the paddocks.

"Can I get out that way?" the PC enquired, ever curious. Ever nosey.

"No, it just leads to the woods. No one else lives here. Just me. You have to go back the way you came in through the woods on the main track. Farewell."

Burton recalled the route through the wooded track then decided to add a final comment to try to break the ice and win over the rude, ignorant, in-bred.

"By the way, I like your entrance sign. Noticed it as I entered the woods on the way in. 'Trespassers will be eaten.' Very funny. I hope its not true."

"Maybe it is, maybe it isn't." Chris replied, his face for the first time breaking into a slight grin. "Strangers make cheap dog food. Lots of protein."

Then he abruptly turned, walking away, gravel flicking from his heels as he headed back towards the house, finally coldly dismissing the policeman.

Burton watched in disbelief at the arrogance of the rude little man, cursing silently at the heathen yokel as he pressed on the accelerator, set to leave and head back into the back woods. The police vehicle moved off through the yard and then disappeared around the corner it'd entered, crunching upon gravel until it moved onto the dirt of the main wooded track and away.

"Wanker," Chris exclaimed loudly, walking back towards the house. He lent over the lower part of the stable door, picking up a bunch of car keys, which lay upon a dresser. Max immediately sprang up at the sound of the rattling keys, jumping up and placing his feet on the top of the bottom door section, sensing a chance for a trip or a new adventure after his nap.

"No boy. I'll only be a minute. Stay here and guard the place. Don't eat too many baddies. If you have to attack them, suck slowly and don't chew!"

Patting the dog on the head, he jogged out of the house, turned left in the yard and around the corner into another smaller courtyard on the opposite side of the house. Here stood a black Range Rover. Jumping in, he quickly gunned the V8 engine into life and followed on after the police vehicle. As he turned into the first part of the woodland track, he slowed up, not wishing to close up too quickly onto the police vehicle, which was somewhere ahead.

Although early November, most trees still jealously clung onto their leaves, not wanting to give them up to the ever growing blanket of red, yellow and brown debris beginning to cover the ground beneath. This natural cover, along with the mix of bushes, conifers, hollies and green brambles, making up the ground cover of the dense woods, provided sufficient cover to hide Chris' large dark Rover as he moved cautiously along the twisting dirt track.

As Chris slowly passed the numerous small tracks drifting off the main one into other parts of the woods, he peered down at the ground. He was looking for any tell-tale tyre tracks which might indicate the policeman had gone astray and driven off, exploring down any of the numerous tracks which led into various parts of the vast and encompassing woods. But he saw none.

He continued on through the woods, attentively scanning the undergrowth and track ahead, checking the policeman had left and not decided to nose around. To his delight, as he began turning the last bend before the final straight section of woodland track, he saw the brake lights of the white police vehicle in the gloom ahead. The vehicle and unwelcome guest was preparing to leave and appeared to be waiting to pull out directly onto the main road.

Chris braked hard, stopping the large 4 x 4 and quickly pushed the Rover's gear lever into 'R' causing the huge vehicle to judder slightly, before it slowly drifted backwards, gliding under a large tree. He braked and held back just enough to able him to see the bright red brake lights of the police car.

For a few seconds the brake lights of the police vehicle remained on, the bright red orbs glowing within the shade of the trees like the bloodshot eyes of a dragon, seemingly peering into the woods, searching for a fresh victim.

The lights went out and the white police Land Rover pulled forward, turning right out into the main road and then promptly vanished, being obscured by the branches of trees and the high mixed hedges, which fringed the outside of the woods and helped to keep the property of 'Horsewater' so well hidden.

The intruder had gone. Chris sighed.

Unknown to Chris, the driver of the police vehicle had instinctively looked back into the rear view mirror just before he pulled out. It was natural for the policeman. And he'd seen something. Something lurking behind him.

It was the front of a dark Range Rover. Sitting, waiting and seemingly hiding back in the woods. And it'd followed him through the woods.

'Was it the arrogant horseman's vehicle? It must be.' The policeman mused.

He'd find out after a vehicle check for the farm, but was already convinced the silhouette of the vehicle hiding in the trees must belong to the horseman.

'Why had he followed me out?' the policeman wondered. *'Hiding something?'*

As he pulled away, the Land Rover moving onto the tarmac of the country road, Roger Burton thought hard, already disliking the small horseman and knew he warranted further investigation. Feeling very uneasy, policeman or not, he instinctively sensed the strange horseman had something to hide.

A trip to the local Pub tonight, The Bell, might provide some background on this strange character. He'd been there a couple of times to get a feel for his new beat. It wasn't too bad. And a few free beers for some of the weird locals usually provided more background information than any police record.

Not everything was on a police file.

Local people knew tales and stories about local people.

He'd soon discover what secrets the horseman hid.

As he thought more of the strange situation he found himself in, he began to wish he'd not left the city, as he considered his first two weeks on his new rural beat. What a bunch of rude bastards these country people were.

Perhaps this guy wasn't so odd after all. He seemed to match all of the other obnoxious, rude and deliberately awkward farmers and other weird 'locals' he'd met over the last few weeks. Most were highly secretive and guarded.

'Give me a drugged-up yob with a broken bottle in his hand any day. At least you knew his true evil intentions.' Burton mused back to much happier times.

'Not like these weird bumpkins. All probably shagging each other and their livestock.'

Rounding the first corner from the woodland entrance his thoughts returned to the present, as a black Ford car drove past, slightly erratically. Driven by a very attractive dark-haired woman in her late twenties, the car drifted slightly across his section of road, causing him to brake and swerve. Bright clear eyes, with a hint of mischief, set in a tanned, rounded face, beamed back at him, almost as an apology. Burton eased up, returning the dark haired stunner his best smarmy grin and also slightly mocking head shake as a gentle rebuke.

'Perhaps the countryside isn't so bad after all.'

Watching in his mirrors, he noted her indicator flash, as she turned off the road and into the woodland track he'd just pulled out. The attractive female driver had entered Horsewater, heading towards the arrogant horseman.

'Married or a dyke?' Neither, Burton mussed with hope.

Very interesting, he thought. Very interesting indeed.

He pushed his foot hard on the accelerator with renewed vigour, heading to meet and greet his next 'local' victim. God help them and also him.

The Bell it'd be tonight, to meet more 'Locals' but also learn about Mr Turner and all of his lovely mares. Purely for research purposes, of course.

Perhaps he should buy himself a horse, he considered, with the image of the gorgeous woman now on her way to see the arrogant horseman still fresh.

In the black Ford, Tracey Johnson pulled into the wooded drive with relief. She always smiled sweetly at the police, just in case they ever stopped her for speeding, which was highly likely with how she drove. Tracey didn't recognise the local policeman she'd just passed though, from the brief erratic glimpse. He seemed nice, although he did seem to have piggy eyes, she noted.

As she proceeded into the woodland track, she caught sight of the rear of Chris's black Range Rover moving slightly ahead of her, seemingly having just turned around in one of the many twisting woodland tracks, but now heading back to the farm. She pressed her foot harder to catch him up, being careful not to bottom-out her little car on the many potholes that lay along the long, winding woodland track. But the Range Rover moved along more easily over the rough terrain, leaving her smaller car struggling to catch up.

Tracey was excited, yet apprehensive at the same time. She wanted to speak seriously with Chris, knowing that if she was to achieve the outcome she dearly wanted, she'd have to play Chris very carefully. Something never easy.

She swung her car out of the woods and onto the short section of track that led to the clearing where Chris' house and stable yard sat to form the farm and woodland estate simply known as Horsewater. As down to earth as she was, Tracey never got over the feeling of travelling through a strange portal to another land each time she came out of the dark woods and into the beauty of Chris' farm. The big white house sat within a wide clearing, with the large stable block, various barns and the bright paddocks set about, almost as if hidden from the rest of the world by the massive sprawling and encompassing woodland, all helping to make it such a special place for horse owners.

Moments later the black Ford parked on a hard-standing near to the house. Chris, heading towards a stable, turned around and paused, silently regarding the driver, who stood beside the black car. The Doberman, wandering across the yard with Chris, now had its attention firmly set upon the woman.

"Go Max! Kill!" Chris barked the order, pointing harshly at the woman.

The Doberman responding instantly with a vigorous sprint.

"Morning Chris. Good Morning Max!" Tracey called, smiling as she squatted down, then spread out her arms as the vicious black and tan killer raced on towards her, sliding to a halt, his short stump of a tail wiggling vigorously.

Tracey wrapped her arms around the excitable dog, kissing his long black nose, then rose fully, the Doberman now bouncing at her heels, as she slowly walked across the yard towards Chris. He turned in the yard, smiled and headed back over towards to her, Max trotting fondly alongside.

"Any trouble Chris?" Tracey enquired cautiously. "I passed a police car."

"Nothing to worry about Tracey. Just a nosey pig being too friendly, doing a routine visit and snooping around. Introducing himself. Tosser!"

Tracey was long aware of Chris's thoughts on the police. She smiled.

She stood level in height with Chris and had a good figure, with curves in the right places, shown off by tight Navy jodhpurs and a lightly quilted cream-coloured waistcoat, although she would typically complain she was 'a bit fat.'

"Well I hope your visitor hasn't put you in a bad mood," she spoke, a glint in her wide brown eyes. Her long flowing dark hair and well-tanned face gave her the look of a classic gypsy 'Carmen' and caught the attention of most men. Chris paused, looking hard at Tracey, whom he knew only too well, his face breaking into an embarrassed grin. He knew she was after something.

"You want something I take it?" He chuckled, blushing.

"Am I really that predictable?" Tracey cheekily laughed, tilting her head.

"Yes!" Chris grinned, face glowing brightly as he shook his head.

Tracey looked down and smiled at the Doberman, patting his smooth black coat, the dog's massive tongue hanging down, panting appreciatively.

"Well Max, I need to ask your daddy a very big favour!"

She kissed Max's nose and then temptingly looked up.

Tracey regarded Chris, her brown eyes twinkling.

"You will say yes, won't you? Please!"

Chris sighed, head shaking. "What now?"

Chapter 10

It is happy for you that you possess the power of flattery with delicacy.

Jane Austen - Pride & Prejudice

"Let me feed my hungry beast first," responded Tracey, as she looked down the yard at a big chestnut coloured horse, annoyingly banging a hoof against the stable door. "Then I'll grab some coffees and we can have a cosy chat!" She teasingly fluttered her eyelashes at Chris, who simply shook his head.

"Come and find me when you're done," he called, walking away, grinning. "And I'll see how many times I have to say no before I finally give in!"

Tracy beamed a smile and strolled down towards the stable block. A big chestnut horse thrusts its head over its stable door in the yard and whinnied loudly, kicking once again at the bottom of the door, the timber shaking.

"Mummy's now coming my little baby," she called to the agitated equine, as she disappeared into an open stable which served as a feed room. After a few seconds of rummaging, followed by various bangs and crashes, she emerged holding a flat black rubber bucket filled with feed. The horse became more agitated, bashing the door harder and pressing against it with his chest, but eased back as she approached the door with a gently waving hand.

"Don't be so impatient you big bully," Tracey said, opening the stable door, placing the feed on the floor and leaving, letting the horse finally enjoy his breakfast. Chris appeared from another stable on her right, making her jump.

"You're running late today. He's been getting grumpier by the minute. Must have a clock in there," said Chris, smiling, moving closer.

"I've got today off," Tracey replied with a sigh. "I'm going to ride later. I've had a couple of things turn up, hence why I need to speak. Is now good?"

"Never is a good time, so you'd better talk as I walk. You know my patience levels with most things range from zero to nil. I'm currently mid-way."

He then proceeded to walk over towards a small lean-to shelter, where an assortment of wheelbarrows stood. Tracey followed him over.

"I've got a big favour to ask." She felt herself flush slightly as Chris turned round and looked at her expressionless. Tracey knew he could be mean but fair, unless you were a horse. Horses came first. He was always nice to horses.

"I know Tim and Nicky leave in two weeks time, well, have you promised their stable to anyone yet?" Tracey gave Chris her best sad look and pout.

"No, not yet, as such," he replied. "Been tied up with a lot of things, but as you know I have a list as long as my arm. There was someone I know from way back I was going to call this week. Jennifer. New horse called Ted. Why?" Chris tilted his head slightly, waiting, as an all- knowing smirk appeared.

It was very rare for anyone to leave Chris's yard, but Tim and Nicky, a young couple who kept a horse with Chris in part livery, were leaving. Tim worked for an insurance company in the city and had been promoted to Divisional manager. It meant they'd have to move to Sheffield, but for fifteen thousand a year extra, plus company car and bonuses, it was something the career focussed couple had leapt at. Chris always had a long list of people keen to come to his yard; half-written, half-mental. It was a mix of his quiet, good nature, his excellent way with horses, free help and advice, along with the fact that he was one of the best teachers and breakers of horses around which made him so popular. It also helped that he was heavily into hunting and freely took people along in his horsebox. Mixed with the great off-road riding, it made his yard, Horsewater, one of the most sort-after liveries in the area.

Tracey smiled sweetly, her speech well prepared.

"Well, my cousin has just split up from her partner. He's a cheating scumbag. They're separating and she's keen to return back home here, to live with her parents for a while. That's my aunt. Only one problem. A big one. She's got to move her horse too and asked if I knew of anywhere she could possibly keep it. I told her I knew of the best livery yard in the world - Yours!"

"Flattery will get you everywhere," Chris replied with a slightly embarrassed flush, but also knew she was right, with some amazing woodland rides.

Tracey continued, now she thought she was on a roll. "I know you have a long waiting list, and I shouldn't twist your arm or beg, but I am. And she is my cousin. Blood! Her horse is great too, and best of all, she is gorgeous!"

Chris sniggered, glowing even brighter, his head shaking whilst grinning.

"Do you mean the horse or your cousin is gorgeous?" Chris replied. "I hope it's the horse. I hate ugly horses. None permitted in my yard!"

"They're both stunning, Tracey replied with a beaming smile, laying it on thick and heavy. "My cousin. And of course her stunning horse too. Penny."

Chris chuckled, face glowing, looking down in serious thought.

"What should I tell her? Can she come and look around? You can meet her and then decide?" Tracey continued, hoping pester-power would win.

"Well I've not actually promised the place to anyone yet," Chris answered. "But I did mention it to Nigel on the hunt the other day. He's keen to come here, but only I think so I can take him to every hunt meet. And he likes all you women here. And I know Jennifer wants to come and get me to help her with her new horse Ted. But I haven't told either anything definite yet."

He paused for a few moments, regaining his composure.

Tracey paused, for once remaining silent, adding pressure, watching Chris.

"Okay then, but only as it's you, and you're an annoying pain in the arse!" he finally replied, looking playfully at her. "You can ask her to come and have a look around, I'll meet her, and then decide. But I'm not promising anything. She may not want to come here herself. When can she come for a look?"

Tracey paused, but only briefly, already knowing her response and game plan.

"I told her we're going to the Cole's meet this Saturday and she said she might like to follow," Tracey responded, almost bouncing with excitement.

"She's never been out hunting before, but would probably love it. I hope so. I said she could follow us to see what happens, as she has no idea. She's got a strange notion it's a bunch of mad posh folk racing about the countryside on horseback with a bunch of dogs, ripping apart cute fluffy little animals."

"Sounds like a good description to me!" Chris answered with a dry smile. "And usually whilst half-pissed! Did you mention that part to her?"

"Well that definitely describes me!" Tracey pushed Chris in the arm.

Chris playfully fell to one side before straightening himself with a grin, wondering what he'd let himself in for, but knowing Tracey, had a good idea.

"That's great," Tracey squealed. "I'll let her know and bring her down on Saturday. She's staying with her mum for a few days to look for somewhere to stay locally. She's moving from Leicester and has a house to find too. It's all a big mess. New house and new stables. I can't wait to tell her. It's so exciting!"

Chris paused, placing his hand under his chin, thinking.

"I don't know what sort of house she's looking for," he added, "but old Pete Jackson's got one of his cottages in Woodheath just become vacant. One of his tractor drivers lived there. Moved out to look after his mum, I believe. He doesn't charge much for rent, but it depends if that is the type of thing she's looking for. It's a bit rough and down-to-earth, but is a home. She'd probably prefer something modern in the middle of Norwich, I assume?"

"I don't think she's too bothered. She's an artist and would probably like living in a cottage in Woodheath. I'll ask her and if she's interested, you can let me have any details." Tracey almost skipped off back towards the stable.

"Thank you so much Chris. You won't regret it, honest!"

"By the way," Chris called, hearing his phone ring and heading back towards the house, Max at his side. "What's her name and what is the horse like?"

"Anna. That's my cousin, not the horse. Anastasia is her proper name, but she hates it. Too posh she reckons," Tracey explained. "Just call her Anna. Her horse is a lovely mare called Penny. She's a fifteen three Bay Dutch Warmblood. About nine years old, I think. You'll love them both."

Chris nodded, raising his eyebrows, slightly apprehensive at the thought.

He didn't like strangers, but trusted Tracey's judgement of her cousin. He wandered off, leaving an excited Tracey talking merrily to her horse.

"Right then Fred, let's get you sorted. Maybe in a few weeks time you'll be going out with your new mate Penny, if uncle Chris stays in a good mood."

She then planted a kiss on the pink and white end of his brown nose.

Chapter 11

Who could deceive a lover?

Virgil

Not far from Horsewater, over at Wroxingham Hall, things weren't well. Lord Burlingham was in a foul mood, stomping around the Drawing Room, dressed in the finest olive green tweed plus-fours and matching jacket. At fifty-five, he looked and acted every part the typical English country gent; which he actually was. Tall and slender, with a slight Roman nose, his rosy complexion bore thread veins to his sunken cheeks. Tufts of grey hair protruded from the sides of a flat tweed cap, which covered a bald strip. It was always worn, except it seemed in bed. The cap was a part of his eccentric nature, along with many other strange habits 'His Lordship' demanded.

The high ceiling of the room was decorated with gilt cornices and ornate architraves. Numerous original oils hung on the walls, showing various past generations and custodians of Wroxingham Hall; either posing solemnly in their finest garments, performing some heroic act whilst brandishing a sword, or proudly seated on horseback. Or a mix of them all. Genuine period furniture was positioned purposefully around the large, naturally well-lit room, with small rugs positioned upon the original wax-polished beech floor.

"What the blazes do you mean, you haven't got time?" Lord Burlingham screamed. "Haven't got time! You do bugger all as it is. Bone-idle! And lazy. Be bloody different if it meant poncing around on a horse or working out at that bloody health club of yours. You're a bloody lazy cow Virginia!"

Lady Virginia Burlingham was unfazed and dodged the torrent of abuse like a pro-fighter ducking blows. Twenty years his junior, they'd been married for three years and Virginia was used to his frustrated outbursts and tirades.

"Look darling, you know I'd love to help out at this weekend's shoot, and usually I do," Virginia explained in her most patronising and compassionate, yet false, voice. "But I always hunt on Saturdays, as you know. And I'm surprised you won't join me. That's very poor. It's the Cole's meet this weekend. One of the best. And we don't want to fall out with them by not attending, do we darling? Then I've got an important dressage test on Sunday, which I've got to go to early, as it is a qualifier for the championship."

She tilted her elegant head, as if to better explain her busy social calendar to a non-listening, non-compliant recipient who stomped about the room.

"But this is an important shoot, with some old business associates attending. I want you there! What the hell does it look like if my own wife isn't there with me at the peg, or can't be bothered to help out with lunch?" he retorted.

Lord Burlingham marched back and forth, past a red hand-woven tapestry, glancing towards his beautiful wife. She lay semi-reclined on a Chesterfield Chaise-lounge, slim body barely covered by a silk nightgown in peach.

"I'm got to check on Marmaduke this afternoon at Chris Turner's. But first I'm off to the health club shortly for my work out and a quick tanning session. You don't want me going all white and flabby, and ending up looking like those foreign potato-pickers you employ in your fields, do you darling? It could so easily happen. Think, this body would then be ruined forever."

Her tone changed and she shuffled on the chaise-lounge, to reveal a long slim, tanned leg. Just for good measure she tossed her long brunette hair, for it to fall in a wave beside her, displaying her elegant neck. From a small round face, long lashes flutter over deep brown, soft, appealing eyes. She pouted.

"Well for how much I get to see your bloody body lately it'd make no odds!"

Skilfully not biting the venomous comment, she fired back equally hard.

"But you're always busy yourself darling, managing the farms or sorting out business in London. We don't ever get time together. My bedroom door is always open, as you know. But you're the one who's always dashing about."

"That's 'cos I have to do everything around here myself! I'd probably be better off living with one of those bloody awful foreign spud pickers. At least I'd get to see her doing some proper work, rather then lazing about on a bloody horse," he replied, face red and voice pitch rising, as he continued.

"Sometimes I'm convinced you're seeing someone else. You're never here, always avoid me or you've got a headache. It'd be curtains if I ever found you were seeing someone else. You'd both be for it," he roared, red-faced, glaring.

"How dare you Bertie darling. That's a very hurtful thing to say. How do I know you're not seeing someone else? I often wonder, with you sneaking off in the evenings. But I never ask what you do or where you go. And you have many close lady friends who always seem to be calling just as I'm going out. You could be seeing one of those fat-arsed spud pickers for all I know."

Virginia hoped her bronzed face did not flush too red as her husband looked at her deeply for a few seconds, before he turned away, flustered, to gaze back out of the window, across the perfect green lawns, manicured rose garden, over the Ha-ha and the vast parkland beyond, lost in his own deep thoughts.

"You could have a peep now if you want darling," Virginia spoke in a soft, low tone, head tilted. With that, in a slow seductive manner, she rose to her full lean height. A long slender, well-tanned leg seductively extended from the peach-coloured silk day coat, which covered her matching all-tanned body.

Lord Burlingham missed the remark, such was his blind fury, but caught the reflected vision of her rising in the windowpane, through which he gazed. He turned his head, and then spun his body around, staring in stunned silence.

Virginia stood before the chaise-lounge, untying the silk belt securing the gown about her slim waist. Lord Burlingham simply stood silent, transfixed like a hedgehog caught in headlamps, just about to be flattened. He was.

He felt a sudden bulging in his tweed trousers as the belt was carelessly removed then flirtingly tossed towards him, landing a few feet away. Virginia's silk gown flapped open, aided by other leg movement. He caught a brief glimpse of the perfectly trimmed tuft of hair seated above the slit between her thighs and beneath her perfect flat stomach. He gazed on fully, jaw dropping, transfixed upon the vision, like a drooling schoolboy seeing his first pin-up.

Virginia grasped the fronts of her silk gown and opened it up, pulling it back over her shoulders, to reveal the full beauty of her lean, tanned body. She let the gown drop off her shoulders to the floor, pushing it aside with a slim, small foot. Her neat breasts were firm and pert, after many vigorous workouts and personal massages at the gym. She cocked her head slightly to one side, pouting her lips gently towards the silent man before her, breaking the silence.

"Well, are all these work-outs at the gym all worth it darling?" she said, running a hand provocatively up the inside of her thighs, the fingers brushing past the small tuft of dark pubic hair, then on past the small diamond in her pierced navel. Her hand moved further up to her breasts, softly cupping one and caressing the dark, acorn-hard nipple with a rotating forefinger.

Lord Burlingham stared, feeling a growing dampness in his tweed trousers.

"Why yes darling, well worth it all. You're beautiful," he said as he stepped forward, seemingly entranced, then regaining some form of composure.

"A bloody lazy hussy, but a beautiful lazy hussy! Stuff those spud pickers!"

As he got to within two feet she stretched out a slender arm and stopped him abruptly with the flat of her hand, pressing it firmly against his chest, gazing all powerfully at him. Lord Burlingham remained frozen, no longer in control, putty in his beautiful wife's skilfully manipulating hands. Like dough.

With one hand still set upon his chest, the other moved down towards his pitched tweed plus-fours. The button fly fasteners were almost wrenched open and a hand moved inside. A fumble inside was followed by a deep sigh.

Virginia Burlingham vanished from her husband's sight, bobbing down.

Squatted before him, she quickly enveloped him with her lips, drawing hard on his firm member, her hand squeezing his testicles. He let out a soft sigh and gently placed his hands on her now slowly rocking head, looking out through the large French windows, out at the parkland and beauty beyond.

"Beautiful dear, bloody beautiful! You wonderful hussy!"

Twenty minutes later Lord Burlingham strutted boldly across those same lawns, heading towards his gamekeeper, Mike Hawthorn, who turned off the engine of the quad-bike he sat astride, awaiting an earful of bellowed orders.

"Bloody wonderful morning," Lord Burlingham bellowed with vigour, as he marched towards him; bounce in his stride and smile set firmly upon his face.

"Why yes sir, it is indeed a very lovely morning. I was going up to Drakes wood to check the partridges," he replied, surprised by his boss's good nature.

"Mind if I jump on the back of that thing then old chap? I'll come with you and check on them too," he asked. "It's a wonderful day. Simply wonderful."

Mike Hawthorn moved the shotgun and canvas bag that lay across the back of the quad onto the front rack and Lord Burlingham climbed onboard, as if twenty years younger. As the quad-bike set off across the grass an electric blue Audi TT convertible crunched along the back drive. The horn tooted and a slim, tanned arm waved vigorously at the two figures setting off on the quad bike, both turning their heads, but knowing who it was.

Lord Burlingham waved back as Mike gazed on, grinning to himself.

"It certainly is a wonderful morning sir," he retorted with a smirk.

As the Audi turned to the main drive, and out of sight of the quad-bike riders, Virginia lowered the window and spat out a huge spray of mouthwash.

"Bloody disgusting," she said to herself, wiping the corners of her mouth with a tissue, careful not to smudge her fresh pink lipstick. She pressed the accelerator of the Audi and gravel spewed out from the tyres. The car hurtled off, a mix of designer sportswear and riding clothes seated on the back seat.

But secretly Virginia was concerned as she drove off.

'Did Bertie really know what was going on?'

He was slow, set in his ways, but definitely not stupid.

Maybe he'd seen her at some point, or heard rumours.

Possibly he was testing her out this morning. Highly possible.

Hopefully she'd put aside any doubts, but would have to be more careful in the future how she acted and what she said and did. Much more careful.

Things were getting serious.

Very serious.

And she had a lot to lose. Everything - and more.

There could be serious consequences. For everyone.

Foot pressed hard, the Audi accelerated along the long driveway, with vast grassland set either side, stretching out to the expansive woods, which in turn linked up with the smaller estate of Horsewater, owned by Chris Turner. Pressing a button on the dashboard, music blasted out across the parkland. Reaching the gatehouse, where Wroxingham Hall met a country road and the outside world, she glanced in the mirror at a sign set back within the entrance.

'Wroxingham Hall - Trespassers with be Eaten.'

The ornate notice boldly proclaimed its threat in neat black lettering upon a white background. Virginia Burlingham stared at the mirrored image of the stark notice and flushed red, suddenly aware of its threat.

She swallowed hard, knowing its true potential meaning.

Things were getting dangerous.

From here on, she'd proceed with great care.

Great care indeed.

Chapter 12

Happiness in marriage is entirely a matter of chance.

Jane Austen - Pride & Prejudice

A few miles away, Reginald Hornchurch was heading home to The Grange in an unnaturally buoyant mood. He turned off the country road and headed onto the track leading to his farm, coming in the back way, passing the black and white painted sign set boldly upon a stout oak post at the entrance. With a beaming grin and chuckle he noted the 'Trespassers Will Be Eaten' wording. He shook his head in amusement, as though he'd never seen the sign before in his life, rather than every day. A small hedge lined the track on the left, with a rustic post and rail fence on the right, forming the boundary of a small paddock. Two large bay horses, clad in bright blue turn-out rugs, had their heads fixed downward, grazing. They deliberately ignored the clicking sound made by Reggie, as he leaned out of the Range Rover window, slowly driving along the dirt driveway, proudly admiring his homebred 'children'.

The Grange, a large, whitewashed manor house, had been in the Hornchurch family for generations, and had changed little from the original classical Georgian style. As well as covering the several acres making up the main house, estate gardens and out buildings, it also included over two thousand acres of mixed agricultural farmland and cottages. The driveway Reggie drove along brought him round to the back of the house, where a mixture of old white painted stone walled buildings, barns, stables and newer Dutch barns lay almost hidden from view from the main grand entrance. Reggie parked in front of a barn containing various tractors and farming equipment. Getting out the vehicle he looked towards a farm worker clad in dark green overalls, walking over towards a row of cowsheds situated over in a far corner.

He glanced around upon hearing the Range Rover stop and saw Reggie get out. He looked over and nodded, somewhat reluctantly and cautiously.

"Morning George, hope all is well," hollered Reggie in an unusually friendly manner, waving his hand high. "It's a great day!"

"Morning Mister Hornchurch," the farm worker replied. "I'm off to get more silage to take to the dairy herd," he added, as if needing to explain his lack of action, expecting a rebuke or unnecessary order to be barked back.

Reggie replied with a smile, nod and a simple 'thumbs up,' then moved off through the array of whitewashed walls towards the back of the main house. The house was classic Georgian, square and symmetrical in style, the main house entrance, seldom used, faced out onto a large paddock, in which a magnificent cedar tree stood centrally, being several hundred years old.

Reggie went in through the back-way, via a small porch, leading into a utility room area, which opened up into the main kitchen. Apart from the modern kitchen units and utensils, the layout was classical in style, including the obligatory Aga and bleached wooden Butchers Block standing centrally in the wide-open space of the kitchen. The unstained, natural oak wood doors, the high ceilings and white walls gave it a light and homely feeling, despite its generous size and classical farmhouse kitchen appeal. A pot bubbled away on the Aga, warming the room and filling the air with the smell of home cooking.

A Wire-haired German Pointer silently greeted him, rising up from the comfort of its deep bed by the Aga, offering its paw as a welcome. Reggie shook the dog's paw, smiled, then gave the dog a hearty pat, rubbed its harsh coat and patting its head. He left the dog, which returned to its silent guard duties and, with heavy sigh, lay back down and promptly fell back asleep.

Reggie proceeded straight on towards the door opposite that which he'd entered, which in turn opened out into a half wood-panelled hallway, the walls decorated with a variety of original hunting prints and local landscapes in oil, with brass wall mounted wall lights set along its length.

He proceeded along at a hearty pace and then entered a wide-open lounge. Once more, apart from a wide-screen TV set in one far corner, and various obligatory items of modern electrical equipment, the long rectangular room was furnished in a traditional period style. Upon a dark, polished wood floor lay numerous brightly coloured rugs, strategically positioned about various settees, chairs and small tables, all perfectly set within the room. A woman sat upon a deep green two-seater settee watching the TV with her back towards the door where Reggie entered. She didn't bother to turn upon hearing the heavy thud of feet on polished boards, ignoring the person who'd entered.

"What have you been up to dear," Reggie asked politely, after a few silent seconds, standing a few feet behind the settee and staring at the back of the woman's long, elegant neck. Still she did turn or warmly acknowledge his presence, but simply replied in a monotone, almost explanatory manner.

"Rode Trojan earlier. He's fine. Now getting dinner ready. About to do some lunch, but I didn't know where you were. Do you want anything?"

She spoke without feeling or respect, in a matter of fact way. Although the accent was not common, it was not one of class either. She continued to gaze at the TV as she spoke, as if the new arrival to the room was not welcome.

Reggie felt his blood begin to boil and usual anger rise.

How the hell did he ever get into this situation? - He knew.

He forced himself to smile, even though the woman could not see his face nor his controlled bitterness and anger, but knew he *should* be nice.

"If you're going to make some lunch, then I'd love to join you. I've had a busy morning myself," he replied, his tone warm, but clearly forced.

The woman turned with a frown, not expecting any form of civil reply. A torrent of abuse was usual in private, the nice approach reserved for public.

However, today Reggie beamed happily down at his wife, who looked back at him slightly puzzled. Maybe he'd just sacked a farm worker. Maybe two.

She rose from the settee and glancing at her husband with a brief fake smile, passed him and headed into the kitchen. Reggie turned around and followed her along the route he'd just taken. Elizabeth wore cream jodhpurs, which hugged her legs and slender figure well. For a woman in her mid forties, she still had a very good body, not that Reggie ever got to see or feel much of it nowadays. On top she wore a navy sweatshirt, over which fell her light-brown hair. A few rogue grey hairs appeared through from the last time it had been coloured, and which she seemed unworried and uncaring.

"What do you want Reg?" she repeated upon entering the kitchen, Reggie unclear whether she meant just for lunch or from life in general.

"Whatever you're making will be fine," he replied as politely as he could.

Slightly puzzled by her husband's unusually nice manner, she wondered what was going on in his scheming mind. They'd separated earlier that morning in a blazing row. About nothing, as normal, and he'd stormed out on her. Usually he'd sulk about for days, not speaking, or even just vanishing, often staying in one of the keeper's cottages on the estate. Now he'd come back for lunch as if nothing had happened. Hence, why she was puzzled and also concerned.

Elizabeth Hornchurch was forty-six and had been married to Reginald Hornchurch for four years. It was her second marriage and Reggie's fourth. That should have been the warning sign when she'd fallen under his charms after meeting him an Opening Hunt Meet five years ago. He was Master and had spotted her at the meet, riding in a paddock. He'd wasted no time in offering her a glass of cherry brandy and at once began chatting. At that time he was in the process of settling the divorce of his third wife, Lady Tabatha.

An attractive and fine upstanding woman of title, whose family owned more land than Reggie, the marriage to Lady Tabatha had seemed a convenient match; more akin to a marriage of princes and princess in Tudor times than modern reality. They'd been unhappily married for about four years before Lady Tabatha decided to leave Reggie for their groom. The groom in question was an attractive twenty-five year old Swedish girl called Ingrid, whom Reggie had previously been trying unsuccessfully to bed himself for a whole year.

He knew why she'd rejected all his best advances when he discovered Lady Tabatha and the groom Ingrid in the tack room, playfully rubbing saddle soap over each other's breasts. His offer to join in had been forcefully rejected.

He sacked Ingrid on the spot, but she left in Lady Tabatha's BMW coupe, unfortunately for Reggie with it being driven by his now soon-to-be Ex-wife, and a handful of luggage the pair had hastily thrown together. Lady Tabatha sent a man around to collect the rest of her belongings, as well as to drop off a divorce letter. It caused great sensation within the local social circles, and Reggie disappeared for the summer, until the smirks and gossip had subsided.

Luckily for Reggie, Tabatha's title came with her parent's land, which was far greater than that which Reggie owned. The reason the divorce got messy, and made the gutter press, was due to Reggie trying to claim on Lady Tabatha's family estates. In the end they decided Reggie would keep what he had, and Tabatha and Ingrid would settle together in a cottage on one of her parents vast farms in Suffolk and that would be the end of the sordid mess.

Elizabeth had herself been divorced for seven years when Reggie charmed her. She'd ridden on and off since she was a child, bought a horse after her divorce and begun hunting again with a friend who had tried to her to get out a bit more to socialise. She worked part-time at that time as a legal secretary for a firm of solicitors in Norwich and began hunting as much as she could afford that winter, being reliant upon her friend taking her in her box.

It wasn't long before Reggie was offering to pick up her horse for her, and then she began seeing him seriously. She was wowed by his lifestyle, the land and at first his fine gentlemanly manners. But she soon realised he had a furious temper, which frightened her the first time she heard him tear to pieces a farm labourer who'd accidentally hit a barn with a tractor.

She'd missed male companionship, and although when they first made love it was nothing to write home about; just a short burst of grunts and groans, she enjoyed his company, the protection he offered and the lifestyle, knowing he was a rich farmer with vast amounts of land. After a short courtship, they married within ten months of their first meeting and she soon got into the role of becoming a country lady, despite her urban upbringing.

At first the relationship worked well, and she accepted his fits of rage and fury, mixed with bouts of gentlemanly politeness, hearty laughter and strong sexual nature. But as with all relationships the honeymoon period soon ended.

After a couple of years the thrill of the lifestyle wore off and she saw the true spiteful and spoilt nature of her rich, land-owning farmer husband. It was also at that period she realised his sexual attentions also had a habit to wander elsewhere and what she offered him were the basics. He needed more.

She could only guess at the real reasons for his occasional disappearances to London on business, or visits to the long established family accountants. These were in addition to the solitary visits to country fairs, hunting events, weekend shoots away at various friend's estates or other manly country pursuits, where he told her, 'she needn't come along if she didn't want to.'

So she took the hint and didn't, staying at home alone with the horses.

Whereas at first she'd followed him everywhere, as the relationship lulled, and he went away more often without her, she had no doubts that he was seeing other women. With whom she did not know, but it obvious that he was getting his real sexual enjoyment and fulfilment elsewhere. It didn't bother her greatly, as she'd never been wowed by Reggie in that department, nor needed it herself, but she did miss the warmth and affection, and true love, she'd hoped a man might bring into her often lonely life.

It was about a year ago she began considering having an affair herself. Their relationship had faded to almost zero on the sexual front, Elizabeth freezing at the very thought of Reggie touching her. Yet she still had a woman's basic needs, yearning to be loved and cared for by a tender true loving man.

She'd met a male companion, who was at first a genuine friend. But then it developed. The smiles, nods and small-talk of a certain gentleman she met regularly, become advanced. Then, before she knew it, things happened, and she'd meet her newfound lover whenever it was safe for them both.

Elizabeth knew Reggie would go ballistic if he ever found out she had the audacity to cheat on him, despite it being okay for him. Elizabeth feared him greatly, such was his bitter temper and mean nature, but this didn't stop her from seeing her man. If anything, secretly it added spice by having an affair.

She didn't know where the relationship would eventually go, despite their joint genuine deep affection, and didn't dare ask her lover the question, as he was known to Reggie and mixed within their varied social country circle.

He was not financially in any position to support Elizabeth, and as she had no source of income of her own, the pair knew Reggie would throw her out and fight tooth and nail to prevent her getting anything of his land or money in courts, or maybe worse. Elizabeth knew if he proved she'd been adulterous, he would have a good case against her and leave her penniless.

Reggie could afford good solicitors and mixed with such people in Lodge Meetings. She couldn't afford anything. He'd see she was landed with a crippling legal bill and destroy the pair, simply out of spite. She also feared deep down what else he might do, as did her lover, both knowing his temper.

For now their affair was simply that. A common bond, which brought then both genuine love and affection. The longer Reggie didn't know, or have any suspicions, the easier her life, even if she was living on dangerous ground.

However, it was at times like this, when all of a sudden Reggie became his old gentlemanly, polite and warm self; the one who'd first charmed her, she became worried and suspicious. One reason was a feeling of guilt, in that she felt perhaps she was at fault. Had she been a better wife in some ways, he would possibly not have strayed, and neither would she. But it was a lie.

Despite knowing about Reggie's wayward sexual habits, she still saw her cheating with her lover as being disloyal, and something unnatural to her. But then the other side of her told her his kindness was just a front, and Reggie would always cheat, despite whom he was married to and what they offered.

Thus she sensed this sudden act of kindness only meant he was plotting, or seeing someone himself, and her natural survival sense made her more wary.

"I'll make a Ploughman's" she said, looking into the well-stocked refrigerator. "I've got some of that local pickle you like," she added trying to please.

"That would be lovely. I'll open a bottle of Hock. Do you want me to help or just get out of your hair?" Reggie offered, fair too politely to be real.

"You go into the lounge and I'll bring it through when it's all ready. There are some letters here in the rack you can go through beforehand," she replied, promptly passing him the mail in a hope to get him out of her kitchen, where he looked as much at home as a large turd in a small goldfish bowl.

"Okay dear," he replied, pecking her on the cheek, making her wince.

"I'll take the wine through and pour you a glass."

Elizabeth Hornchurch was puzzled.

She'd not seen Reggie in such a good mood for years.

Whatever the cause, she knew she'd better make the most of the moment, as it probably wouldn't last, and he'd soon be back to normal.

Maybe his latest mistress had dumped him and he was feeling vulnerable.

Or he'd just bought a piece of land in a cheating deal.

Something strange had happened. *But what?*

Reggie definitely wasn't his normal self.

He was happy. Nice. Well almost.

Something was wrong. But what?

Reggie was never nice and happy.

That was worrying.

Very worrying.

Chapter 13

Mere innocent flirtation, not quite adultery, but adulteration.

Lord Byron

Tracey rode down the track that led back to the yard from the paddocks and main woods after her long hack out. Passing the ménage, Chris was riding a large grey horse. The muscular horse was cantering sedately in a neat, almost perfect circle. She drew on Fred' reins and paused for a few seconds to watch the amazing control he had over the powerful horse. She'd have liked to sit and watch, but knew Chris hated spectators when schooling, so she smiled sweetly, and giving Fred a gentle tap with her heels, rode on. She wanted to stay in his good books for the next few weeks. Such was his concentration, Chris seemingly didn't acknowledge Tracey. If he did, no smile was returned. Nothing unusual there, she thought, with an inner chuckle.

As she entered the yard and prepared to dismount a bright blue Audi convertible roared into the yard, pulling up straight outside the house, rather than on the hard standing where everyone else parked. Tracey looked at the car as she jumped off Fred, at once recognising the driver.

"Morning Lady Burlingham," Tracey called over, being overly polite.

"Oh, hello," the elegant, slim woman replied in an accent that could have split a walnut. She wore tight yellow jodhpurs, tucked neatly over the top the latest suede riding trainers, although neither looked as if they'd ever been in contact with a horse or saddle. On top she wore a tight fitting, bright green wool lambs sweater, which enhanced her size eight waist and surgically lifted breasts. It offered enough warmth to keep out the cold, and a degree of dignity, should it get too cold that a couple of things stick out. Not that it would have bothered her; especially the way she regularly hung around Chris.

"If you are looking for Chris he's riding in the ménage," Tracey continued in her best fake posh voice. She would have normally called it 'the school,' but a more distinguished accent seemed to unknowingly creep into her speech and manners whenever she spoke with Lady Burlingham or certain others.

"I believe he's schooling your big grey. Looking very smart!"

"Oh, thank you very much," Lady Burlingham replied with a exaggerated flutter of her spider-like eyelashes. With a swift spin of her slender ankles, she turned and headed off towards the ménage, her neat firm buttocks wiggling.

Lady Virginia Burlingham was one of those women who seemed ageless. She was obviously over thirty, but how much over thirty was anyone's guess. She had a figure most anorexic teenagers would dream of, kept in trim by riding and her personal physical trainer at the gym, which rumour had it got very personal and physical, to help her work off those last few extra pounds.

Regular tanning sessions, both under the sun bed at home and the real one in the Mediterranean, kept her skin coffee brown all year round, all helped by expensive moisturisers. A top hairdresser kept her long brunette hair perfect, which all helped her from externally ageing too soon.

If the saying, 'A woman is as old as the man she feels,' was true, Lady Burlingham wouldn't be Lord Burlingham's age, but instead should be about twenty-one. Allegedly, she also had the sexual appetite to go with such an age.

As she strode majestically towards the ménage, the string of her thong could just be seen through the bright yellow material hugging her tight buttocks. Tracey looked down at the slight Muffin-top that hung over the top of her jodhpurs, and squeezed at the small pockets of lard attached to her hips.

"It's not fair!" she muttered to the horse, watching the perfectly-shaped, long yellow legs vanish out of sight and quickly returned Fred to his stable.

Keen to listen, she sneaked out and then along the front of the stables.

"Chris darling, he looks beautiful," Tracey heard as Lady Burlingham approached Chris in the Ménage, still working the grey horse hard. He looked over and pulled it back from a collected canter into a walk and looked down.

"Oh Marmaduke, you look lovely!" Virginia continued as Chris and the horse approached the stained timber rail and he moved towards the horse's smitten owner. She stood on the lower rail, firm breasts provocatively leaning over.

"Can mummy give you a nice big kiss?" Virginia grinned wickedly up at Chris, as the grey horse approached and shook its head, almost in reply.

"And what about Uncle Chris. Would he like one too?"

Chris blushed, looking down, but grinned widely.

"Thanks for the offer, but he can have my share."

"He doesn't know what he's missing, does he darling," she said cheekily, looking up at Chris with a huge smile, giving the horse a hearty hug.

Virginia, accustomed to Chris's playful rejections, ignored the rebuff and planted a bright red lipstick kiss mark on the horse's dark grey muzzle. It wiggled its nose in reply, shaking its head, flecks of foam flicking off the bright bit in its mouth. Chris steadied the horse, pulling it still again.

Then in a slightly quieter tone Virginia continued.

"He looks marvellous Chris. You've done such a wonderful job, as ever. I'd expect nothing else. I was passing by and thought I'd just drop in to see you."

"It's not me. He's got it in him and it's a matter of getting it out and toning up key muscles. Like I'm sure you do at the gym. Hence your fine curves," Chris replied, trying to hide the glint in his eye and slight curl in his lips.

Virginia raised her eyebrows and smiled back broadly.

"Cheeky man! You'd be amazed at what muscles I've got Chris and what I can do with them. If only you'd let me show you!"

Chris chuckled, his face red, then leapt out the saddle. Taking the reins he patted the large grey horse then walked it along the timber rails, over towards to an entrance gap in the ménage. Virginia followed around the outside.

"When will you be coming to collect him, or do you want me to drop him off for you?" Chris enquired, as he met Virginia at the gateway, she sliding the single timber rail across to let the pair out. "I'm hunting on Saturday, at the Cole's meet, as I know you are too, so I can bring him over on Sunday or later sometime next week. Whatever suits you. When is your first event?"

"Well I've got a few lined up. The first one is Thursday week, but it's nothing special, so I'll use that as a trial run only. I wish you could come over and watch Chris. Will you please? Tell me where I'm going wrong and all that."

She tilted her head and stared longingly for added effect.

Chris smiled and rubbed his chin, thinking about his own plans.

Virginia's face was inches from his, their bond and friendship obvious.

Out of the corner of her eyes, the quick-witted Virginia thought she noticed someone watching from the side of the stable block, then duck back. She had no doubts it was the woman whom she'd met moments ago, and guessed she was spying on the pair, and looking for some tasty gossip to spread.

What Virginia Burlingham keen eyes and quick wits however didn't notice was the person in dark green camouflage clothing, carefully observing the pair from beside a large oak, set back within the back woods in the far distance.

High-power binoculars focussed upon the couple, watching intently.

"I'll see if I can make it and would love to help. But Virginia, you're a better dressage rider than I'll ever be," he replied genuinely. "I simply sort out the horses and leave the experts like you to do the rest. If I'm not busy I'll come."

"Please do Chris. You really must. I know it's all in the leg and hip action," Virginia replied jokingly, then began thrusting her crotch back and forth in quick succession towards Chris's legs, wrapping an arm around his waist and rubbing her slim yellow-clad legs up and down against his thigh.

Chris playfully pulled away, skilfully guiding the big grey horse between them, blushing brightly as he suddenly caught sight of Tracey wheeling a barrow across the yard, glancing curiously at the pair. Wide eyed and in shock, her head went down. Virginia released Chris's hand and laughed out loudly.

"That'll give your girls something to talk about Chris!"

He simply shook his head, and like naughty children, the playful pair chuckled, noting Tracy's blushing red face, pretending she'd seen nothing.

However, in the distant woods, the actions of the playful pair weren't missed.

These were coldly noted by the silent observer.

Chapter 14

He that wants money, means and content, is without three good friends

William Shakespeare - As You Like It

Later that same evening, at their Norwich home, Gavin and Dawn Davis had been arguing. Again. Gavin had returned home from his office job to find the latest credit card bill. He knew something was wrong when he found the TV off and the dinning room table lit with candles. Dawn was smiling like a kitten that'd shit somewhere it shouldn't. She was over him like a rash; too chatty and overly nice, and it wasn't until Gavin had changed from his suit into more comfortable jogging bottoms and T-shirt, and went into the kitchen to see what meal she was preparing, he spotted the bill on the pin-board. It was £200 over what he'd calculated they'd already overspent for that month.

That was why Dawn was being so nice; wearing special perfume and short silk pyjamas in pink, enabling easy access. Gavin could read her like a book.

Cook a nice meal, have a good shag and then all your bills and worries simply evaporate. Life was as easy as that. At least in Dawn's world it seemed.

Despite the warm welcome, kind words, good food and open invitation of a pleasurable evening of wanton lust, once he'd seen the bill he had only one thing on his mind. Instantly he flew into a panic, wondering how the hell he was going to pay the additional amount, when he couldn't even afford the first. And no amount of shagging in pink silk would pay that bill. Unless you worked the streets. He openly told her he couldn't afford the latest bill.

Money, despite never seeming to have any, was a taboo subject between them, and hence often not discussed. Any money they ever had went on ensuring their two horses were fed and their liveries paid. It was the only interest they shared, and all that kept the pair together. Their two horses were almost like the children they didn't have and probably never would. Both through financial constraints and also physical ones - on Dawn's side.

Gavin simply paid what he could, when he could, by juggling the various bills with his basic fixed salary and cutting costs, usually to his own detriment. Dawn was hardly ever involved in finances, other than their spending. Usually she didn't dare ask, always assuming Gavin would find money from the 'Magic Money Tree' at the bottom of the garden every month to pay the next bill that appeared. But not this time. Someone had taken an axe to that tree.

That was only the start. After his outburst on how they'd pay the bill, he mentioned he had worries about employer; a large insurance company in Norwich, who might be laying off staff. Dawn began to blame Gavin for not appreciating her and all she did with the horses each day, and went on to explain how she'd gone out of her way to make tonight a special evening, and how he'd ruined it all by talk of money and bills. It was a usual Dawn ploy.

Ever the meek, mild and soft-hearted one, Gavin felt guilty about the trouble Dawn had gone through, yet still knew they were already seriously in debt. The horses always came first, and anything else would be given up to ensure their bills were paid. But it was getting harder. The hole they were in was large and Gavin had just been given a bigger shovel. He had to stop digging.

The pair sat at the table, the candlelight reflecting off Dawn's lightly tanned skin and dark, bob-cut hair. She was attractive, which was also a saving grace, but sadly lacked any real education, and clung to Gavin for all support. Gavin had tried to enjoy the smoked salmon fillets, served in a dill sauce with new potatoes, fresh peas and all washed down with an expensive bottle of Asti, which he disliked, it being too sweet. Mentally adding up the cost, he sighed. He'd have been happy with a fish-finger sandwich and glass of cheap Shiraz.

But between each forced mouthful, where Dawn spoke only of what she'd done all day, who she'd seen at the yard, and how hard tea was to cook, Gavin sank inwardly. Then Dawn mentioned the hunt meet at the weekend.

It was the 'Big One' they simply couldn't miss. The Coles.

But not for Gavin. It meant spending more money they didn't have. He'd completely forgotten and told her they could not go and they'd have to call it off. Then it started. Dawn was insistent they were both going, as she'd spent all day cleaning the best tack and getting the kit ready. In addition, it was one of the most important meets of the early season. Everyone attended Ernie Cole's meet, where the hosts laid on a huge spread and served Champagne cocktails. It was a must. And they were going, no matter. Full stop.

Gavin had given up in despair, tried to enjoy the meal, but the atmosphere was ruined and he munched painfully through each mouthful with a heavy heart, his mind elsewhere. He glanced up at Dawn in silence, also sulking and munching, her heart in the evening gone too. In a way he felt sympathy, but also knew inside it was what she really craved. He couldn't carry on like this, living a life of lies and deceit, but also of forced poverty and unhappiness.

He was not happy. Truthfully he hadn't truly been happy with Dawn for years, if ever. She just fell into his lap at the wrong time it seemed.

Now she was simply a habit. A convenient routine.

But she was not his true love.

That person was elsewhere.

But out of reach. For now.

He glanced at Dawn, his eyes lifeless, watching her chase a rogue pea around the plate her fork. Quietly, without any fuss, he rose, almost un-noticed by a pea-chasing Dawn, her focus on her plate, and drifted off out into the hall, then from sight. Dawn seemed unaware of his actions, or assumed he was going to the bathroom, which he did. But then he went to the bedroom, quickly changed and without warning was in the hall and out if the door.

Car keys and jacket in hand, the door clicked shut behind him.

He had to get out. To breath fresh air and think.

Importantly, he had to get away to see someone. He needed to speak with the only person who could help and only understood him.

That person wasn't Dawn. Never had been. Never would.

As soon as Dawn heard the door click and the V8 engine roar outside she dropped the fork and dashed from the table on into the hall and opened the front door peering out into the gloom, dressed only in her short silk pyjamas.

"Where are you going?" She hollered, unwilling to step out bare-footed onto the wet drive or into the cold night air. "Don't go Gavin! I'm sorry!"

Gavin didn't hear, and if he had, he chose to not respond, as the car left the driveway. Turning the wheel he flicked the lights on then sped off, leaving Dawn dismayed on the doorstep. Head shaking, tears rolling down her face she closed the door, slumping in the hallway, sobbing deeply, wondering what she could do to save their already fragile and delicate failing relationship.

They'd met four years earlier, when Gavin was twenty-seven. He'd moved his newly acquired horse to the livery yard where Dawn, three years his junior, also kept her horse. Neither had been in any long-term relationships, Gavin having worked overseas with an oil company for a few years, making good money, before returning to his birthplace and enjoying the fruits of his labour. Here he took up horse riding again, something he'd first done when younger on his cousin's farm, but now deciding to buy and keep his own horse.

Dawn was shorter than Gavin, and although not fat, always struggled with her weight. Mildly attractive, with a 'Pixie' cut dark brown hair, it made her more striking then she would be otherwise. Gavin had no 'film star' looks, but his quiet, polite manner and natural caring attitude had been seized upon by Dawn. As a hollow person, who needed attention and support, she saw Gavin as such a provider. His interest in horses was a rarity, as was being single, so as soon as he arrived at the livery yard where Dawn kept her horse, a number of the girls flashed their eyelashes, but Dawn made her interests apparent.

Introvert, Gavin welcomed any attention, never being one to chase the ladies, he was happy to accept anything and soon they rode out. A romance quickly blossomed and their common interest in horses helped, with Gavin being the far braver and better rider of the pair, which Dawn happily accepted. Before long they were buying an over-priced new house together and seemingly playing at happy families, enjoying each others company and the excitement of living together, as well as the shared interest of horses and then hunting.

Then Dawn lost her job at the factory. She'd only worked there briefly, seemingly to help them get the mortgage. From then on, she found it difficult to maintain a steady job. A poor education, lack of interest and a general lazy attitude soon transpired. In addition, it seemed she preferred spending most of her time at the yard, doing the horses and 'yacking' to the girls, rather than get a paying job to help. She told Gavin she worked hard doing the horses each day, but it didn't help bring in much needed money and Dawn seemed oblivious to his repeated cries that they were struggling with their bills.

Gavin worked hard to ensure the bills were paid, and Dawn had on and off jobs, but never stayed for more than a few weeks at each one, either being fired or simply deciding she wouldn't go in any more because she didn't like the place or the people. Or they didn't like her. Probably it was both.

The income had gone down, but the bills always rose; their lifestyle and commitments seeming to outpace Gavin's poor salary. His savings had long been eaten up by trips out and treats for the pair in the early days, when life had been fun, but now they were slowly and surely spiralling down into ever increasing debt. A new credit card was acquired to transfer the debt from the first, only to add more pain. Then another, and so on. But the capital wasn't reducing. Whenever money was mentioned, Dawn would fly into a rage and accuse Gavin of no longer loving her, making her feel guilty and blaming her for all of their problems. She'd get a temporary job to show willing, but usually pack it in again within a few weeks, and then it'd start over again.

That night, as Gavin had sat gazing at the over-priced diner, stabbing rolling peas by the candlelight with an ever-sinking heart, he knew something must change. And soon. He dreaded the thought of the expense for the weekend's hunt meet, despite knowing who'd also be there and the secret pleasure it'd bring, no matter how brief any liaison might be. But as much as he wanted the company of that person, in any brief moment he might get when Dawn wasn't clinging to him, his logical mind told him it also meant more expense, with the cap to pay and cost of the fuel for the Range Rover. His heart was a mix of logic and desire, knowing what he really wanted he could not have.

It was at this point that he knew he had to get out and speak with the only person who knew him and fully understood, despite the huge risk it involved. And so he'd left, despite knowing Dawn would be in tears, and that he'd get a torrent of abuse when he returned, followed by Dawn forgiving him, and throwing herself at him, desperate to keep him, not matter what.

As he drove into the dark of the night he began pondering ways in which he could get out of the terrible situation he now found himself in with Dawn.

He had to sort this mess out once and for all.

There were options, but they were all messy.

A number of people would be hurt. Badly.

And that included Dawn.

But it was a price he'd accept.

Dawn would have to go.

Whatever it took.

Good or bad.

Chapter 15

Perfume is a story in odour, sometimes poetry in memory.

Jean-Claude Ellena - Perfumer

The barn door emitted a long creak as the woman gingerly entered the large gloomy interior, the odours of hay and straw heavy. She nervously peered about in the dim glow, the barn softly lit from the singular dust-covered fluorescent tube strung on rusty chains in the roof area from the high timber beams, the old oak work having supported the building for hundreds of years.

The odour of straw and hay was mixed with that of a stronger perfume; a lemony scent. The unusual smell made the woman's nostrils twitch, yet smile at once upon it's immediate recognition. She knew the owner of the scent.

It is claimed that smell is the main sense most linked with memory.

This scent held only good, pleasurable memories.

The woman carefully walked forward into the interior of the barn, emitting a gentle, inward drawn 'twit' whistle, not unlike that of a female Tawny owl.

Silence followed.

She stood momentarily, ears trained, head tilted sideward.

Further into the vast barn the woman stepped, moving towards a stack of straw bales, cautiously looking about in the low light, nervous of someone or something unknown. Again she let out the owl-like whistle, expecting a reply.

Silence followed.

She raised her arm, glancing at it to check her watch.

A 'tut' was released from her mouth. She was late.

Was she too late, she wondered. She hoped not.

She stood centrally within the ancient barn, close to the straw bales, hands on hips, skilful eyes and ears searching. No sound, other than a soft muted whine of the wind outside emanated from within the building.

Nothing. The barn was empty.

Suddenly a man's body dropped down before her.

She instantly jumped back, gasping, raising her arms to strike the figure.

Her heart pounded and adrenaline poured through her body, nature instinctively preparing her for fright, then flight or fight.

"Boo!" the figure exclaimed, standing fully upright.

"You bastard," the woman gasped, catching her breath, lowering her arm and then relaxing slightly. "Don't ever do that again. You utter, utter bastard!"

A smile crossed her face in the gloom and she playfully punched the man's chest with the bottom of her raised fist. He smiled too.

He reached out and tenderly touched her arms, steadying her body.

"Did you think I wasn't coming?" the man said as the woman regained her composure and smiled, the man gently drawing their bodies together.

"I could smell your aftershave as I came into the barn, so I knew you'd been here, but knew I was late and thought maybe you'd gone," she replied.

"Is it that strong? I wouldn't do as a poacher then!" the man replied with a chuckle, as if it was a personal joke between the pair, both grinning broadly.

"I can smell your scent on my body after we make love. It seems so strange but it's lovely and makes me remember you later. My only worry is if it lingers on my skin or clothing. What if he smells it?" the woman replied, now being held gently within the arms of the man she loved, enjoying the soft embrace.

"I can usually taste your kiss on my lips hours later. It's lovely," the man responded, looking softly at the woman. "But sweetheart, don't worry about my scent on you. I doubt he could smell a fox if it farted straight in his face!"

The pair burst out laughing then drew their heads close together, the mirth subsiding as their lips met. They fondly kissed, silencing each other, strong arms pulling both their bodies firmly together. The man, slightly taller than the woman, and of medium, athletic build, playfully scooped up the slender woman in his arms. She giggled as he lifted her up, placing an arm around his neck, playfully kissing him on his cheek as he carried her off through the barn, over to where some low lying bales of straw formed a natural platform. On top of the rough straw bed had already been thrown a wool blanket.

She raised her eyebrows appreciatively, her face breaking into a broad smile, as the man lay the woman down onto the blanket. She turned to face him, head momentarily rested upon a supporting palm, as he stood beside her. The man swiftly clambered up onto the straw platform with an athletic leap and began kissing her neck and chest. She giggled, stroking his face.

"How long have we got?" he enquired, pausing for breath.

"Sadly, only about an hour," the woman replied.

"I just wish we could be together longer," the man sighed. "For always. If only I had the resources. We could tell everyone and not be so secretive."

"Yes I know, and don't worry darling. I love you as you are, no matter what."

With that they kissed. Hands touched faces, caressed necks, before moving across their bodies. Then tenderly they began to undress each other.

But the lovers were not alone.

Through a gap in the barn's ancient brickwork a silent figure watched.

Blood pumped with a resounding thump. Rage, fury and jealousy grew, as it leered enviously at the naked bodies writhing pleasurably inside the barn.

Slowly it drew a long thin knife from inside its jacket pocket.

A rough finger ran along its keen bright edge. Deadly sharp.

The figure raised its head, breathing deeply, inhaling the odours.

A scent from inside drifted on the night's breeze.

And it was one that would be remembered.

Chapter 16

For many are called, but few are chosen.

Bible – Matthew – 22:14

The chill night air blew drizzle along the dark streets, its damp breath soaking all it touched. A broken drainpipe intermittently spat water from its cracked bottom, bursts splattering onto the green-stained concrete, before spilling into the gutter. Two women stood huddled beneath a lamppost, the black walls of the nearby derelict building absorbing the dim light like a sponge.

The pair paced back and forth upon their small patch of jealously guarded territory, keen eyes ever-watchful. Stamping high-heels clattered like hooves, skilfully avoiding irregular cascades of cold water. The first women tugged at a red leather jacket, drawing it close to her slim body, pulling it tight over a scant white vest top. The garment barely covered her firm breasts and provided little warmth, the excuse for a jacket opening as soon as the grip on the lapels were released. A short denim skirt barely covered her buttocks, the cotton damp sticking to her pale skin. Her slender, well-shaped legs were also bare, perched upon five-inch high patent red stilettos.

A dark Range Rover passed by on the opposite side of the road, bringing no attention, other than an experienced glance from both women. Headlights cut through the dark and drizzle as it passed on, seemingly just another car mixing with the occasional passing traffic. The area was not popular, unless you were looking for a short cut or were out for business. Special business.

The second woman, dressed in a mix of black lace beneath denim, atop a black leather skirt, cursed. Stamping her black suede high-heels, she glanced at 'Red,' sighing again, before scanning the dark empty road. The women barely spoke, exchanging the odd word or nod, their eyes always on the traffic.

An engine roared, drawing close beside the pair, causing them to turn. The dark Rover had reappeared. It abruptly stopped beside the lamppost and the passenger side window, in dark-tinted glass, descended with a soft whine.

The two women stared, attention on car and occupant.

Business. But 'Friend or foe?'

The 'Old Bill' used all sorts of vehicles these days and tried all types of tricks. You could trust no one. Police or punter. All were evil and crooked.

But instinctively they knew, and seeing the single male driver lean towards the open window, scanning the women with an expert eye, the pair eagerly displayed themselves like fine produce in a delicatessen's shop window.

Hips kinked, breasts thrust forward, and legs extended out in heels, the cold and damp of the chill November night was momentarily forgotten.

This was money. And time for action.

'Red's' leather jacket opened, the hand 'accidentally' slipping, revealing pert grapefruit-round breasts set within damp white cotton, the cold nipples firm.

Her 'Black' partner's equally useless short denim jacket opened too, revealing smaller, but equally neat breasts, set tight within a black stretch lace bodice. Beneath a hip-hugging strip of black leather, technically a skirt, which sat upon long legs in black suede high-heels, the smooth, damp skin well tanned.

Tonight's menu was revealed to the prospective diner.

Red leather on damp white cotton, with a strip of denim, set upon rare meat upon a stack of Patent red heels? Or Denim, over black lace with a slice of leather and tanned fresh meat, well presented on a tower of fine black suede?

Black or Red?

The Rover driver scanned the menu intently with an expert eye; like a Cordon Bleu chef, eyeing each woman. The pair on offer gazed eagerly at the customer, preparing to take the driver's order. But what would he select?

The order was placed with a silent, pointing finger.

Black. She was to be tonight's feast.

Red stepped back, crest-fallen, tugging at the useless red leather jacket, the cold biting once more, now seemingly harder.

'Black,' slightly taller and more slender than 'Red,' swaggered forward as the winner, her black suede high heels clicking on the damp pavement. She leant into the Range Rover window, spoke for a few seconds, then removed a piece of chewing gum, throwing it onto the pavement in an exaggerated gesture. Pulling the large door open, she climbed into the large vehicle, settling into the big leather seat. Closing the door, she extended her arm through the open window, waving farewell to the dejected figure in red leather. Her arm swiftly retracted back in as the dark glass moved up automatically, closing out the cold night and sealing the women within. The big V8 engine roared and the vehicle with its new occupant returned to the darkness from whence it came.

The pick-up had taken thirty seconds.

All as planned by the confident driver.

The male driver spoke no more the entire journey. Pleased to be out of the cold and wet, the woman in black and denim sat back in the tall deep seats of the Rover, enjoying the silence and warmth, stretching out, feeling the heater blowing warm air upon her long, damp legs and wet suede-covered feet.

She peered ahead out the wide windscreen as the brightly-lit city streets turned into orange-hued suburbs and then those in turned into dark unlit country roads. For twenty minutes they travelled in silence, the vehicle's dark interior warm and pleasant, until the vehicle slowly pulled off the small country road and headed down a pitch-dark dirt track, the ground uneven.

A white sign with black writing flitted past, momentarily caught in the lights, before sinking back into the gloom. The woman cast a glance, noting the strange wording. Momentary a wave of concern passed through as she absorbed the information, then instead smiled, as if seeing a funny dark joke.

The lights punched through the darkness and drizzle, the wiper blades squeaking upon the screen as the big 4 x 4 rocked slightly, moving along an unmade track. Finally the vehicle stopped at a white building, with soft lights already glowing inside. The man exited the vehicle and beckoned the woman out the Rover as he walked towards the front doorway of a white-painted house. The woman slammed shut the car door and scurried quickly behind.

Her heels crunched upon gravel as she dashed to the door, not wishing to get wet again after the warm journey had dried her out. The gentleman client kindly opened the door and held it open as she ducked past and entered the house. Inside, the woman quickly scanned the contents with an experienced eye and at once was impressed. This wasn't a grubby bed-sit, two-bit hovel or cheap, stained bed hotel. This was a home, where the man lived. Maybe alone, or maybe with an unsatisfying frigid wife. Good furniture, various ornaments, period pictures of country scenes upon the walls, and a photos of horses set upon a dresser. But strangely no people, or centrepiece wedding photo of the 'happy couple' hung in view. Also, in the soft light, she saw the man clearly for the first time since casting a glance at him in the gloom of the car.

And he pleasantly surprised her too. The man wasn't her usual casual punter; being one she imagined wouldn't need her services, although she knew they varied considerably. She'd had many a good-looking married man in the past, whose wife wasn't supplying the 'required goods' or who wanted something else 'a bit special' which the wife wouldn't provide. Maybe this guy was the same. Although she'd long given up caring, it was nice not having someone too revolting, and not stinking of booze and fags grunting in your face, as they bashed away for their few seconds of pleasure. The comfort of a large warm house and a clean, fresh, soft bed was always better than having your arse or face bashed against the damp brickwork of a dark back alley.

She smiled at the man. She could get to like him. Possibly.

He returned her curious stare with an expressionless gaze, as if transparent or made of glass. That worried her, sensing no fear or emotion.

"Nice 'ouse mate. Live her all alone do yer?" she asked with a local accent, breaking the ice, trying to learn more. She gazed at him with a smile.

The man failed to answer the question, but responded with a curt gesture of a head nod for her to follow. They walked through a kitchen area, set out in a neat traditional country style. The man pressed a light switch and opened a smallish wooden door, set within an old timber frame. The hinges were big and black, the door white, both clean, freshly painted and well maintained.

The door was pulled open and she automatically stepped forward, peering down and into the opening offered by the man's extended hand. She instinctively stepped forward, then, looking through the door, her gaze immediately drifted downwards. Before her were a series of stone steps leading into what appeared to be a brightly-lit cellar. She hesitated, looking back at the man who silently nodded, steering her through the opening.

She walked forward, stepping onto the first two steps, the heels of her shoes clattering loudly on the bare, well worn stone, echoing in the room below. Faltering, slightly worried, she peered ahead, trying to look into the cellar, but a bright un-shaded bare bulb blinded her, preventing her from seeing further. The man closed in behind, pulling the door shut and pressing her forward with his legs, forcing her further down into the cellar a further two steps.

"Eaah! I ain't going in there," she said, forcing herself back against the man. "There are probably spiders, cobwebs and creepy-crawlies down there."

"No there aren't," the man replied, his tone soft, yet strong and spoken with a firm sense of authority. "And yes you are going down there. Now!"

With that he pushed her forward, shoes slipping on the smooth stone steps. The man caught her as she stumbled, lifting her bodily, carrying her forward the next few steps. The woman began to struggle, but could feel the man's strength as he lifted her, his arms wrapped around hers and her body. Flaying feet floated above the steps as he carried her forward the remaining flight. At the bottom he gently placed her down, her heels clattering on a stone floor as she righted herself and spun around, glaring coldly at the man before her.

He seemed unfazed, looking back at her with no emotion.

The air below in the cellar was warm and musty, but the walls clean, freshly painted and the surprisingly tidy, with boxes neatly stacked upon a number of benches. Importantly to the woman, it was devoid of any cobwebs, and no spiders or creepy-crawlies were lurking. At least none she could see.

The man sensed her apprehension and doubt from the nervous glance.

"You've nothing to worry about and you'll do what you are being paid for," the man said firmly, gently guiding into the centre of the cellar with the palm of his hand pressing against her back. She spun around to look at him angrily, disliking the strange situation, a mix of fear and hatred, but also intrigue.

"You know what I'm paying you for," the man said, nodding to confirm their verbal agreement, "Do that and you'll be alright. Nothing else. Honest."

He looked purposefully towards the far wall, where a series of old wooden beams, seemingly bracing the old building above, formed a large 'X' shape. Painted in gloss black, they were stark against the whitewashed plastered wall. Attached to the top and bottom of the 'X' were soft leather buckled straps.

The woman followed the man's gaze, suddenly becoming aware, the fear and uncertainty growing more evident in her eyes as her eyes took in everything.

There were four leather straps. Two top, two bottom.

Wrists and ankles ties.

For restraining someone - upright.

"Look mate, you said kinky. A bit of bondage, but that is pushing it," she said nervously. Then thought of her 'habit' and the money she owed from her last load. She didn't want another beating from them. Bastards. She owed a week's rent too. "I'll do it," she said. "But it'll cost double what I said. If not, you can fuck off and I'm out of here. You can go and wank yourself off."

She glared coldly at the unmoving man, who simply shrugged his shoulders. He pulled out a wallet, handing over a handful of notes, which she checked and promptly thrust into the top pocket of her denim jacket. She looked towards at the 'X' beam, back at the man, and then grinned widely.

"Nothing too rough mate," she said, some relief returning to her voice. "And not too tight. I know what you lot can be like. I don't want any chafe marks."

With that she slowly strolled towards the wooden beams, her heels clicking, buttocks swaggering in the tiny black leather skirt that clung tight to her trim thighs. Her long bare legs beneath were shapely, but looked paler in the bright white light of the cellar and showed off several dark bruises. She touched the aged beams, her hands drifting slowly over the rough texture, but surprising smoothness of the old timber, her confidence in the situation now growing. Cheekily she slapped the black woodwork hard and turned to grin at the man.

Her heart leapt and she physically jumped.

To her surprise, the man was already directly behind her.

She gasped, the man standing silently only feet away, moving seemingly unheard upon and over the cold stone flagstones as he'd follow her.

He stared hard and silently, as if absorbing her image, taking in the details of her attractive, heart-shaped face, framed in a short cut, dyed auburn hair. She looked several years older than her true twenty-five years. Time on the streets, mixed with drug abuse had added lines and years. She felt her stomach flutter, such was his strong and silent presence. The man was domineering, exciting, sensual, yet also slightly dangerous, but in a good way. And she like it.

The man reached for her bleached Denim jacket and carefully peeled it off, sliding it from her fine shoulders like a gentleman. He stepped to one side and gently placed it on a nearby bench. It revealed a skimpy, black, stretch lace top, through which her firm but small breasts rose, the dark nipples firm.

The man gently slid his hands across the stretched lace, the back of his hand skimming across a presented breast, almost teasingly. The woman grinned, genuinely excited, as his hand drifted across her waist and to the short, hip-hugging, black leather skirt. The same gentle hand glided across the smooth fabric before reaching the top of her bare thigh. Slowly his fingers moved up and around, exploring hidden treasures. His face was inches from hers, but no emotion was displayed as soft, stroking and probing fingers rustling within a tiny patch of bristling hair, identifying to the man she wore no underwear.

The woman felt an internal pleasant squeal of anticipation, almost keen and willing to proceed, enjoying the man's gentle, teasing touch. He stepped back to regard his purchase, the woman pleased for once someone was admiring her beautiful face and well-toned body, rather than just treating it merely as a piece of warm living meat in which to inject some of their bodily fluids. This was going to be more then two minutes up an alley in the rain with a stinking drunk. Or equally worse, a long, sweaty 'grunt-a-thon' in a car, with a fat slob who couldn't get it off. This was going to be good. A quality customer.

The man reached over and carefully gripped her wrist, guiding it towards the timber and straps. She turned to face him, pressing her back to the cold wall. "Keep your shoes on," he spoke softly. "I like them. Nice heels!"

The woman smiled, genuinely, glad he was opening up and admired her.

Still holding her wrist, he raised it up to the leather strap, quickly fastening her wrist to it, the woman offering no resistance, just smirking playfully. He repeated the action with the second wrist, which too was willingly offered.

Then reaching down, he slowly moved her first leg, still with her shoes on, gently gripping her slim ankles, guiding her leg over to the strap, where he fastened the soft, well-oiled leather. Moving her leg voluntarily, spreading open her legs, the man repeated the action with the other ankle.

The woman was now securely strapped to the solid old wooden 'X' beams by well-oiled, old leather straps, still fully clothed, in the tight black lace top, short leather skirt and standing high in her black suede stiletto heels.

The man stepped back, eyes wide, and the first time, displaying any signs of pleasure or enjoyment, with a smile crossing his face. The woman smiled back, firmly secured to the timbers, but the straps not too tight or painful.

"By the way. My name's Lesley," she announced, trying to build a bond.

The man didn't seem to care, nodding silently to simply acknowledge she'd spoken and he'd heard, as he stepped back for the wall and blankly stared.

Slowly he removed his clothes, as if in no hurry nor being embarrassed, it all being part of the experience. Firstly his shoes and socks, then his fleece top and T-shirt, followed by his jeans and then seemingly without any care, his pants. All were placed in a neat pile on the long timber bench alongside her jacket. He then stood completely naked, looking silently at the woman.

She looked down at his waist and raised her eyebrows. Smiling, impressed with what she saw, she flicked her tongue out teasingly, wanting what he had to offer inside. The man slowly moved forward, drawing level with another old wooden bench set against the wall. He glanced at the bench, then looked at the woman, his face breaking into a sheepish grin. The woman looked back, enjoying the excitement; a mix of fear and sexual anticipation stirring, it bringing her alive for once. It had been an age since she'd actually wanted sex, other than it being a means to feed her habit, as well as her stomach.

Now she felt herself moisten and looked at the man, now firm and hard like rock. She desperately wanted him inside her, invitingly wriggling her hips.

The man paused by a bench, his grin broadening, breaking into a chuckle.

The woman laughed. The man laughed too.

"Do you want it in you?" The man teased almost childlike.

"Oh yes," she replied, her tongue moving across her lips.

"Are you sure?" The man tittered, looking down at his massive erection, a hand playfully rising to his face, pretending to hide a sheepish a grin.

"Yes! Stick it in me. Hard!"

The man laughed - loudly. Too loud.

She laughed too, but only briefly. Then she stopped.
The man was laughing at the woman, not with her.
This wasn't what she wanted. Something was wrong.
Fear began to replace lust. Desire turning to terror.
She looked at the man, herself no longer smiling, but now staring at the man with fear filled eyes, and wondering what she'd let herself into.
'What was he laughing at?'
Then the man also stopped laughing, pulling away a cloth lying on the bench, revealing something hidden beneath. The woman's eyes flicked sideward.
A large knife.
The long blade glinted bright in the white cellar light.
Her eyes fixed upon the blade and instantly tried to move a foot, and then an arm. She pulled each limb, writhing and twisting her torso as best she could. But no strap moved. Still standing in her heels, body firmly secured in the upright 'crucifix' position to the wooden beams, being fully restrained by the soft leather straps she'd willingly let the man secure her with, she cursed.
She was well and truly trapped. Fool!
Seemingly unaware of his visitor, the man lifted the knife, firmly clasping the black wood and brass-pinned handle. He lovingly admiring the steel weapon, running a cautious finger along the fine edge, ignoring the whimpering cries now emanating from the woman firmly strapped to the far wall.
Then his gaze turned fully to the woman.
"We need to cut those clothes off," he whispered.
Tears began to run down her face.
She shook her head, a plea of 'No' silently uttered.
He smiled, chuckling once more.
A deep, dark chuckle. Pure evil.
The naked man walked forward, glinting blade thrust out before him, the deadly knife erect, like him, the tool firm in his hand and ready for work.
Pressing the blade firmly against the woman's belly, he teasingly moved the sharp tip over her body, gently sliding it between leather, lace and skin.
Softly, the blade pushed inwards.
Then it sliced.
The man smiled.
Screams bounced off the freshly painted cellar walls.

Chapter 17

And I saw, and behold a white horse:
And he that sat on him had a bow: and a crown was given unto him: and he went forth conquering, and to conquer

Revelation - 6:2

Saturday morning was dry but chilly. The early light a mix of grey clouds hued in soft yellow and pink, set upon a pale sapphire sky with a light frost slowly leaving the ground. The small Nissan 4 x 4 pulled off the side road and into darker surroundings, heading onto a woodland dirt track, trundling past a 'Trespassers will be Eaten' sign. The pale light broke through the trees, some still retaining leaves, but many others becoming stark and bare, their cast leaves now laying scattered carelessly along the dirt track. Three bodies, bundled up in fleeces, peered out the vehicle's windscreen, the driver looking long and hard at the sign with some concern. She raised her eyebrows, turning with a silent questioning look, to face the woman sitting in the back seat.

"Chris's little joke. Helps keep out strangers," said Tracey, leaning over.

"It looks grim and bleak as you drive in with all the trees bare, but the great thing is you're miles from any roads, so the horses are safe from anyone fiddling with them, and there are loads of woodland tracks to ride around, as well as a small cross-country course and the ménage. It's really great here!"

The driver and elderly female front passenger looked at the seemingly depthless woods, intently absorbing the surroundings. The ground beneath the trees was a mixed carpet of green, yellow, brown and orange leaf litter, with bright green clumps of brambles, hollies other evergreen shrubs and bushes fighting through and between the various trees filling the woods. Odd leaves, like brown snow, gently fluttered down and around the vehicle, as it slowly, but steadily drove along the woodland track. As the vehicle turned the final corner of the woods and headed down the straight section of track into the clearing and the yard, Tracey could see the driver's expression change.

"And don't be put off if Chris in a grump. Everyone's normally flustered and in a rush on a hunt day, especially Chris. So smile sweetly, say little and don't for god's sake get in his way. He's nice really, deep down. Well, sometimes!"

The 4 x 4 broke free of the woods, out into the clearing, pulling up onto the hard standing just away from the house and stable block, parking next to a number of vehicles. The three women got out and began to walk towards the stables when Chris appeared, stomping over from the house. He glanced sideways, smiled at the figures without looking, then instinctively turned away.

He headed on, but then stopped, his head spinning around to regard the three figures slowly approaching. There he stood, staring at the central figure.

For several seconds her image alone sucked into his vision like a bizarre shot from a movie, with everything else about him out of focus. Suddenly realising he was staring at only one figure, he blushed and changed his focus onto the remainder of the group walking towards him, and now only ten feet away.

But his eyes seemed to naturally drift back onto the taller central figure, whom in turn smiled nervously back. Tracey spoke first, taking her hands out of her fleece and pointing at various bodies now standing beside her.

"Chris, this is Anna and her mum, Joyce. My aunt. Anna and Joyce, Chris."

"Pleasure to meet you both," said Chris taking the older woman's hand first and giving it a quick firm shake. He then turned to directly face Anna in the centre of the group, a slight grin crossing his face, but quickly subdued.

Anna stood before Chris and he immediately noticed her height and how elegant and proud she stood. She appeared taller than him by about three inches, her fine, slim build and long legs exaggerating her height. She had long, straight golden-brown hair, which had a slight red tint, accentuated more so in the soft early light. Her hair framed her pale, but flawless face, with a neat fringe, cut just above her slightly arched, thin eyebrows. She wore only a small amount of make-up around her eyes, and her beautifully shaped lips bore a light plum-coloured lipstick. Her nose was delightfully small and her slightly pronounced cheeks rose as she nervously grinned, displaying a set of perfect white teeth, as her face broke into a huge natural smile. Although wrapped in a thick grey fleece, he could see she had a slim, yet athletic body, and the navy jodhpurs showed off her long, attractive legs. She was stunning.

Chris extended his right arm and took Anna's delicate hand, with its long, fine fingers and short, unvarnished nails. Gently shaking it, he looked directly at her bright eyes. They were a beautiful grey-blue colour and reminded Chris of the sea on a winter's day. For several seconds they held him transfixed, as he gazed up into them. He stood staring, soaking in the image, entranced by the grey eyes, until her face flushed and turning her head slightly, she diverted his gaze. He blushed, aware he had been gazing too long and looked over to the older woman. She shared some of Anna's beauty, however, age had loosened her face, but she still shared Anna's elegant style and fine looks.

"It's great to meet you Anna, and you too Joyce. I can give you a quick look around the yard now, or Tracey can show you everything. She's probably told you all about the yard. And also told you that I'm normally flustered, grumpy, moody and busy on hunt mornings. If not on most days. Mister Grumpy!"

Anna smiled again, tilting her head slightly provocatively, glancing at Tracey with a grin, then spoke for the first time. Her voice was soft and gentle, tone slow and deliberate, the accent educated, but with a slight Northern edge.

"Tracey has told me only good things about you and your wonderful yard. And how it is the best in the area. I'm pleased you could see me today."

Chris grinned, eyeing the smirking Tracey, then looked back at Anna.

"What do you do for a living, sell double glazing? You clearly know how to charm someone!" Chris joked, smiling, his face flushing as he looked down.

Anna simply returned the bashful smile as the whole group chuckled.

"If you want to get on Chris," Tracey began, "I'll show Anna around, if you don't mind. She's going to follow today and be my groom, helping me with Fred. That way you can get on and we hopefully won't get in your way."

"Okay Tracey, that sounds fine," replied Chris. "But don't show her the bad bits. Or those big rats! We don't want to put her off." Turning back to Anna, he continued. "Are you planning to follow the hunt all day? I hope so."

"Yes, although I don't know what to expect," Anna replied, looking at Tracey for support. She just grinned, as Chris continued on freely.

"Great. You'll love it, hopefully. I'll then have a little chat when we return to see what you think of everything and when you want to move Penny over. Assuming of course you'd want her to come here. I understand you may want me to collect her too, which I am more than happy to do. No problem."

"Thank you, that would be wonderful," Anna replied, her heart racing at the sudden thought of an offer, if she'd heard correctly. She glanced at Tracey.

Chris smiled at the three, nodded politely, then turned abruptly away and walked back over towards the stable he'd originally been heading towards.

The three woman all excitedly looked at each other, then in a huddle quickly moved over to the feed room to get Fred's breakfast. Also making sure Chris and no one else moving about the yard was in earshot before anyone spoke. It was Tracey who broke the silence, excitement clearly obvious in her voice.

"You bleeding jammy cow! He's as good as said you can move Penny in straight away. He fancies the pants off you. Wow! Did you see his tongue nearly on the floor as he gazed at you? I thought you'd tread on it. I've never seen him smitten like that before. Amazing. He's usually so grumpy. We'd often thought he was a bit funny. What do you think? Do you fancy him?"

"Tracey!" Anna cut in, trying to save the embarrassment before her mother, "I've only just got rid of Bruce. I don't want another man right away!"

"Well I fancy him rotten!" Joyce surprisingly cut in. "Small, but nice. I Wish I was twenty years younger and had a horse. He's got a nice tight bum too!"

"Mother!" Anna exclaimed. "How dare you! Well now you mention it, his bum is rather nice. Not that I was looking of course. Just hearsay!"

The three women giggled as they moved towards Fred's stable, the door banging as he called for his breakfast, which was duly served. As Fred ate, Tracey quickly showed Anna the main parts of the yard and where her stable would be if she decided to move Penny. Anna examined the simple but ample timber stable, but seemed uncaring, her attention and focus on the busy yard.

Various bodies flitted about, mixed with a variety of differing equine heads appearing over stable doors, many whining. An array of sounds, from slamming doors to crashing wheelbarrows filled the air. Returning to Fred's stable, they groomed the horse between them, with Joyce watching on.

On a number of occasions Chris strutted back and forth across the yard, Anna, with a degree of caution, noting the Doberman dashing about from stable to stable, sniffing everything. Tracey called Max over, introduced him to Anna, and who after coaxing the large dog instantly gained a new friend.

Chris seemed to be constantly dashing around. Anna glanced towards him, feeling a tingle trying to catch his eye. He smiled back on one occasion, but then appeared to ignore her and take no further notice, focussing on with his never-ending, multitude of jobs. Anna felt a slight disappointment at first, like a girl at a disco trying to catch the eye of a possible prize date for the evening, but to no avail, then realised she was hoping for too much far too soon.

Although having been around Anna and Penny on many occasions, Joyce was fascinated by the frantic activity in the yard, as half a dozen horse owners prepared their mounts for a day out hunting, all something new to her.

Fred was tacked up and Tracey declared ready to load. Anna was surprised to see all of the horses travelled fully tacked up. It was something strange to her and totally against everything she'd ever been taught or learnt about horses.

"Once you get to the meet the horses get so excited you can't always tack them up," Tracy explained to a keen audience of two. "Also it saves time after having some nibbles. You just drop the back, unload and jump on board!"

When everything had subsided slightly, Chris walked over to the group. He'd somehow changed into his hunting gear. He wore a bright yellow hunting shirt, with crisp white stock, held in place by a huge gold pin, with a cream check waistcoat and clean white jodhpurs. Other than the suede boots on his feet, he looked like he could have come off the set of a period drama. Anna noted he had shiny black leather riding boots and a big heavy black hunting coat hung up in the lorry, ready to be adorned when finally at the meet.

Chris smiled at them all and then looked professionally at Tracey.

"Ready?" It seemed more like an order than question, it all regimented.

"Yes, whenever you want to load up," she replied firmly, shocking Anna.

Turning to Anna, Chris looked deep into her eyes, for a second too long.

"If you follow my box and Julie's trailer you won't get lost. When we get to the meet come and grab a drink and food and meet some hunt members. But be warned, they are not quite all the gentlemen they may try to appear!"

The words drifting off as enchanted, Anna gazed back, amazed by it all.

"Are you travelling with me in the lorry, or with Anna?" Chris asked.

"With Anna of course," Tracey replied cheekily, tilting her head at Chris.

"Then I can teach her all about hunting, and also talk to her about you!"

Chris blushed, and with a toss of his head, walked away with a big grin.

A few minutes later the sound of a large diesel engine erupted from behind one of the many barns, and standing outside the stable, Anna watched Chris's big seven-horse lorry reverse into the centre of the yard. It was a mix of white and blue, and bore an artist image of a white horse leaping down the side.

Jumping out the cab, two other women from the yard were already dropping the large tailgate at the back. For the yard, it was a normal set the routine, and everyone appeared to know their own roles and act automatically.

Chris's grey, Cirrus went on first. A 16hh flea-bitten grey, she'd turned almost white with age, but had the odd fleck to her coat. An ex-steeplechaser, who was extremely bold, she'd jump over or through almost anything she was shown. Chris led his mare up, tying her in place within the lorry, to be automatically followed an attractive young woman in her early twenties.

Sally, Chris' groom, was short, with a slim hourglass figure and natural bright blond hair, cut in a 'bob.' She led her horse, Goldie, and tied him up beside Cirrus. The old grey ignored the new companion, too busy tearing into a hay net hung beside her. Goldie whinnied, furtively turning to look out the rear, awaiting his next companion, but also knowing what was to come.

A 15.2hh chestnut Anglo-Arab gelding, Goldie was a bit mad, but a very popular horse around the yard, once belonging to Chris. Sally was also slightly mad, so the two naturally made a good partnership. Sally worked part-time for Chris as his occasional groom, looking after some of his liveries and helped whenever she could. She also worked for her parents, who ran a local potato farm, mostly doing admin and paperwork. Working for Chris mixed a bit of pleasure with business, although everyone knew that was as far as it went between the pair, with Sally engaged to a local guy she'd known since school.

Tracey prepared to lead Fred from his stable, seemingly knowing the running order of how the horses were loaded into the big lorry and that she'd soon be ready to load the ever-excited horse. Anna passed her the headcollar, as Joyce watched on, amazed by it all; stunned by the sound of clattering hoofs mixing with the clunks of stable latches being opened and doors slamming shut.

A solid black cob, with large white blaze appeared from a stable further along from where the group watched on. Led by Carol, a short, slightly over-weight woman in her fifties, she casually led the 15hh black cob mare called Tess, who slowly plodded along and up the ramp, both seemingly with no cares.

Carol, Anna learnt, was a rather strange and quiet woman, who although not unfriendly, kept her own company. Because of this she came over as being slightly stuffy. She lived alone; her husband dying of liver cancer three years earlier and ran her dead husband's bookshop in the city. Of neat appearance, with short, slightly spiky brown hair, and deep brown eyes, she had a pale complexion set upon slightly solid, square features. She'd kept her horse in livery with Chris for many years, and often went out for long rides alone, occasionally being seen riding on the land of Wroxingham Hall, which bordered onto Chris' vast Horsewater estate, often meeting Lord Burlingham.

Seeing Carol move the black cob slowly forward and up into the rear of the large horse lorry, it prompted Tracey, and without any words spoken, she flicked the bolt on Fred's stable door and led out the excitable 16hh light bay gelding out into the yard, followed by an equally silent Anna and Joyce.

Fred eagerly totted forward, skilfully pulled back by Tracey, aided it seemed by numerous four-letter word based rebukes. Joyce turned with a grin to look at Anna, who simply smiled, shaking her head. She knew her cousin well.

Fred trotted across the yard and ran up the rear lorry ramp, almost dragging Tracey with him. She checked him back and turned him sideways to stand alongside Tess. The black mare grizzled at her new companion, the backward pointing ears enough warning for Fred to know his place. Anna had carried a small haynet from the stable and passed it up to Tracey, who in turn tied it in place, the excitably gelding relaxing now that he had something to eat.

A woman, dressed in full hunting gear, stood watching the activity from the opposite side of the yard, but in particular seemed to look long and hard at Anna. She sensed the woman's stare and turned about to look at her, smiling almost in a submissive manner. Luckily the woman smiled back.

Tracey, standing at the end of the large lorry, called over to the woman.

"Are you taking your own box again Julie?" She pointed at a Land Rover.

"Yes. You know Bonnie. You can close the back up if Chris is happy."

Tracey nodded and jumped down the side of the lorry and bent down to grab the rear ramp. Sally appeared at the other side and with little effort, the large rear ramp swung up and in place with a gentle thud. The two women secured the latches, sealing the four excitable horses, all munching on hay, inside.

"This is Julie," Tracey introduced, stepping over to Anna and the woman now standing beside her. Julie was forty-six and very much an independent woman. She enjoyed hunting, but liked to be able to come away from a meet whenever she wanted, and hence often travelled separately to most meets.

She stood about five foot six inches, with neatly cut, brunette hair, which was highlighted to give her a slightly younger look. She had eyes of a dark grey-blue, which shone like dark gemstones in a light, naturally tanned face.

"Which horse is yours?" enquired Anna, her eyes scanning the stables and a number of curious equine heads, all eagerly watching the comings and goings within the busy yard over their doors, seemingly waiting to be chosen.

"The coloured mare," Julie indicated with a nod. To which, and as if on cue, a beautiful, fine light-brown head turned to look in its owners direction.

"Wow! She looks lovely," Anna commented. "Can I go and see her?"

"No!" The response was firm and hard. "No, please don't!"

Anna raised her eyebrows, the harsh comment shocking.

"Don't worry Anna," Tracey intervened. "She's a bitch!"

Anna looked at Tracey, then at Julie, slightly unsure of whom she meant.

"No, not her!" Tracey grinned, looking at Julie with a wide grin. "Although she can be a bitch too! We mean her horse, Bonnie. Bitch with a capital B."

"It's true," smiled Julie. "She may look nice and pretty, but she's absolutely evil and will bite you really bad without any warning. She's a total cow!"

"A bit like you Julie!" Tracey joked, playfully pushing the older woman in the arm, then hugging her warmly, both woman genuinely smiling.

"She's right. If you do come here, be warned. Bonnie is the most evil horse in the yard. If any I've ever met. Brilliant to ride, but only Julie and Chris can handle her. She's a total nightmare. Crazy but nice in some strange way."

Anna looked over at the coloured mare, whose beautiful and graceful fine head gazed seemingly lovingly over the door. Almost tempting her it seemed.

"Bonnie all is not as she appears. A bit like Horsewater." Julie uttered softly.

Anna was stunned by the comment and about to enquire further, when Chris appeared. All turned like well-trained troops facing their commanding officer.

"Are we all set ladies?" Chris asked, but again it seemed almost an order.

The two woman nodded positively. "Then let's move 'em out!"

An assortment of well-dressed woman suddenly scurried about and Julie turned back towards Bonnie's stable, as Chris politely nodded towards Anna and then turned away. Sally followed on, as did Carol, leaving the three woman looking over towards the coloured mare in the nearby stable.

"Do you need a hand?" Anna enquired, trying her best to show willing and be helpful, but also suddenly curious by this new woman, Julie.

"My Rover and trailer are around the side. Bonnie is ready and I'll lead her into the trailer, but if you want to close the ramp, it'd be much appreciated. I'm used to loading her on my own. But please don't try and pat her."

"No, because she'll kill you," Tracey quipped, glancing at the 'sweet' equine. "Actually, don't even look at her, or you might turn into stone! Medusa!"

Julie shook her head at Tracey, and smiled at Anna, who immediately felt genuine and natural warmth from Julie, but was amazed by their characters.

"I'll introduce you to some hunt people when we get to the meet and maybe when you move here we can go out for hack. I'll show you around the farm."

Julie's comments, unlike her scowling horse, seemed warm and caring.

Anna felt warmed and genuine friendship, thanked her and agreed she'd take her up on the offer, as Bonnie was loaded with no issues and nobody bitten.

"That's assuming Chris will let me come," Anna added with a rueful grin.

Julie smiled back as she checked the trailer and moved towards the Rover attached at the front. Opening the vehicle door, she looked long at Anna.

"I don't think you'll have any worries there. It would seem Chris has already decided you're to be one of his ladies, from how he looks at you."

She finished off with a wink then climbed inside, closing the Rover door and fired up the engine, leaving Anna slightly shell-shocked, but also curious.

As people moved about, finishing off and ready to go to the hunt, Anna gazed silently about the yard, wondering what other secrets Horsewater held.

Very soon she'd learn. And her life would change forever.

Chapter 18

A gold rush is what happens when a line of chorus girls spot a man with a bank roll.

Mae West

Anna remained curious of Julie's comment as everyone finished and scurried about the yard, like a military unit about to set out on a dangerous patrol; people moving off to their respective vehicles, ensuring everything in the yard was closed up or collected and tidied up as needed. Tracey called to Anna to grab the tack box outside the stable, as she wandered back over to her 4 x 4. Joyce had already headed for the vehicle and all three clambered inside.

"What did Julie mean?" Anna enquired to Tracey, sitting beside her.

"Not all as it seems and 'One of Chris' Ladies?" She looked curious.

Tracey simply giggled, as Anna fired up the engine and watched the vehicles in the yard, awaiting movement. Joyce was already settling snugly down in the back, ever quietly curious and inquisitive, watching all the activity outside.

"It's one of those things with Chris. He like the company of ladies, but doesn't, at the same time, if you know what I mean. Hence he's a bachelor."

Anna's puzzled expression displayed her level of understanding.

"Chris only has women in his yard. He dislikes men. He'll happily chat to women and train their horses, but doesn't have a girlfriend. He's not your typical 'Bloke' or a guy you often meet at some yards who fancy themselves.

"Does he bat for the other team?" It had to be Joyce who asked the obvious blunt question from the back. "Is he one of them? You know, a bit funny?"

Tracey almost choked with laughter and turned to face Joyce, whose face also broke into a wide grin. Anna joined in with the chuckles, although didn't know why, such was the infectious nature of her mother's naïve comment.

"No, but that said he's not your typical man. We've often said if Chris was a woman, he'd probably be a lesbian. He loves the company of woman and seemingly dislikes men. He just likes his horses too much. They come first."

"So does he not have any wife or girlfriend?" Anna enquired.

"No. Not at least anyone we've ever seen. He's very private, despite having us all technically wandering about his home every day of the year."

"Has he never been married or had a serious partner? There must be a stack of women who'd go out of their way to have a share what he has here. It's a stunning place and financially it must be worth a fortune. Not that I'm a gold-digger and planning to become Missus Turner," Anna joked. "Give me time!"

"You've no chance Anna. I think many have tried, but all have failed. Chris isn't stupid, and doesn't seem to need the company. Many a gold-digger has left very disappointed. He's more likely to marry a horse. Maybe Bonnie!"

"Well he's a bit short, and besides, I've had enough of men for the moment. Bruce still keeps trying to contact me, but I've told him to stop. I'd simply be happy to get the chance to bring Pen here. Do you think he'll let me?"

"Who knows, but I think he's smitten. Even Julie agrees, and she's a wise old sage and known Chris for years. But Chris is a complex character."

Tracey stared into space, thinking deep, before speaking further.

"I've know him for years. He'll go out of his way to help you, but if anyone crosses him, it's fatal. You sense he'd get even somehow. That said, he can be great fun and is absolutely brilliant with horses. But I think you're okay."

Anna stared out the window for a few seconds, watching Chris dash across the yard with the Doberman following close by, moments later to be shut up in the house. Chris ran back, turned around to scan the yard, raising a hand to wave at someone unseen, then jumped into the lorry cab along with Sally and Carol. The three women in the Nissan simply watched in silence, as the lorry was fired into life and slowly eased forward. Julie pulled her Land Rover and trailer in ahead of Anna's vehicle, to sit in behind the big lorry, which slowly moved forward. Anna followed on behind the small convoy, which began heading out the yard and into the woods they had driven through earlier.

"How far is it to the meet?" enquired Anna, looking down at her fuel gauge, which was just over half full, suddenly wishing she'd fuelled up more.

"Only about fifteen miles," Tracey replied. You'll have plenty of gas, so don't worry. However, you can use a bit up following all day. You should be okay."

"What exactly will we do by following?" Anna enquired, still unsure.

"It depends how involved you want to get," Tracey began to explain.

"Basically we follow the riders along the roadsides and watch the action, and you're there to support the hunt in general. But also people will point out to the Huntsman where the hares may have gone if they see it cross a road or help people on or off the horses, or if they fall. It's great fun and I often follow for a few hours even if I'm not hunting, just for the social side of it."

"Fall off?" Anna grimaced. "No one mentioned it was dangerous! Perhaps I'll stick to my dressage or occasional showjumping," she joked.

"Anything involved with horses is dangerous, as well you know. Expensive, dangerous, but amazing fun," Tracey beamed. "You should get one Auntie!"

"I hope I don't see any poor foxes get torn up," replied Joyce, not totally convinced by the hunting idea and unsure why she was there, other than as support for Anna. "I like foxes. Cute and cuddly. When not killing chickens."

Tracey raised her eyebrows, "Well, we hunt with Harriers, which are smaller hounds than Foxhounds and basically they only chase hares. Supposedly." Tracey said, trying to allay her Aunt's fears. "They will chase a fox if they get onto one, or even occasionally deer, although we shouldn't and the Huntsmen get the hounds off straight away. But it's rare we get a fox."

Anna looked on fascinated, as Tracey continued speaking and they headed on out of the woods and into the village. Joyce liked hares too. Big rabbits.

"You do occasionally see a hare caught, but it's not that often, as the hounds are so fast that it's over in seconds. I don't like seeing animals getting hurt or killed, and I like hares. Very nice animals. But I must admit it's the excitement of the chase most people really enjoy. Most who ride out really don't want to see anything killed, hence why we used to drag-hunt. But live hunting is much more frantic and unpredictable. Mad! That's what adds the extra buzz. And you get to gallop over some great ground you wouldn't usually get to see."

The conversation paused slightly, Anna focussing on the track as the small convey headed on through the woods, Chris's large lorry ahead rolling slightly on the uneven track, the top brushing against the trees and scattering brown leaf confetti onto the track and passing over the roof of the vehicles. Anna listened on intently to Tracey, whilst watching the vehicles move.

"Harriers are faster than foxhounds. That makes it more fun but dangerous. It's fucking brilliant! Oops, sorry Auntie Joyce! I forgot you were back there!"

Tracey chuckled, and Joyce simply smirked. She was long used to her niece's foul mouth from numerous family get-togethers and parties, when she often got drunk and her free-flowing mouth spouted Karaoke songs or profanities.

"You'll have to have a go when you move down, Anna. I assume that you are going to come? Please say yes. We'll have great fun together, along with all the others from the yard. I think you will get on really well with Chris."

"He hasn't actually said I can bring Penny here yet," began Anna cautiously.

"The yard looks nice, stables and ménage are great and the riding super, so I'd love to move here, but didn't you say he'd promised it to someone else?"

"Anna, the way he looked at you today, and what he's said, you are as good as in. Just make sure you don't say you hate hunting at the end of the day or perhaps he might change his mind. But I don't think that would even stop him. I bet he fancies you something wicked. You lucky cow! I knew it would have to be you if he ever fell for anyone. He seemed to really like you, which is strange for Chris. He usually hates everyone, anything new or strangers."

"Should I buy a new hat?" Joyce joked. "Do you get a title marrying into such land? That might make me a Lady! And your dad would be a Lord!"

"Mother!" Anna glared in the mirror, but with a smile, head shaking.

"I'd love to come here with Penny, but men, and Chris, are off the table."

Anna grimaced, wondering if the man she'd suddenly found herself attracted towards would turn out to be as disappointing as the other man in her life.

The talking subsided and the small convey safely exited the woods and trundled on, picking up speed on the back roads, passing through numerous small villages, then touched the main road for a short while. As they did Anna noticed another small, but very smart lorry box in her mirror, moving quickly on in behind them, driven by a singular woman, catching up the convey.

Anna spotted it in her mirror and told the others. "We've got a tail!"

Tracey turned around and instantly identified the bright blue lorry box, with its distinctive number plate. She smiled, clearly recognising the driver.

"Lady Burlingham. I didn't think she'd miss this meet, Tracey declared."

"Who's she?" enquired Anna, curiously looking in the rear view mirror at the attractive woman behind the wheel of the equally attractive horse box.

"She's stunning and got a smart horse box. Nice number plate too. VB 4500. Suppose she's loaded too?" Anna's voice held a hint of envy.

"Should be VD 4 500," responded Tracey harshly. "For the number of men she's probably given it to. Posh rich cow!"

Anna looked surprised at Tracey's cold and curt response.

"She's married to Lord Burlingham. He's rich, but is much older than her. Gold-digging cow! They live at Wroxingham Hall. It joins onto Chris' land via the back woods. Huge estate. She's also got the hots for Chris something wicked. Always calling into the yard. He does a lot of work for her horses."

Anna's eyes flicked up into the rear view mirror, her gaze somewhat too long, absorbing the woman's soft features before flicking back to the road.

"Saw her at the yard earlier on in the week," Tracey began to recollect.

"Thrusting her crotch at Chris. He simply laughed. She's probably giving him one, along with all of her other boyfriends. People reckon she's at it like a rabbit and Lord Burlingham doesn't have a clue, or just doesn't care."

Both Anna and Joyce both raised their eyebrows at the new information.

"Is that all you horsey people ever do?" Joyce laughed. "Get up to it with each other in the hay barns! I should have bought a horse a long while ago. No wonder you don't want to give Penny up Anna. You're all sex mad!"

"Mum!" Anna exclaimed, this time more bitterly. Her face glowed red, as a raw nerve was exposed. "I wasn't the one shagging my secretary, remember!"

Joyce blushed and silently looked out the window, realising she'd made a wrong comment, with Anna's soon to be Ex-husband, Bruce. His infidelities, and inability to keep his pants up, were the cause of Anna and he separating, and why she was moving away from Leicester with her beloved horse Penny.

With that they all suddenly fell silent as Tracey gazed silently ahead, not wanting to ruin things further and thinking of the busy day to come and Joyce sat watching the countryside pass by, hoping no rabbits would die.

Anna, boiling with a mix of emotions, looked into the rear view mirror.

VB4500 had closed up behind her 4 x 4.

And the driver was clearly gorgeous.

Anna eyed up the potential competition.

Chapter 19

The best political weapon is the weapon of terror.
Cruelty commands respect. Men may hate us.
But we don't ask for their love; only their fear.

Heinrich Himmler

A face gazed up from the black water of the ditch, the blank eyes staring skywards. The image was shattered by a stream of dark yellow urine, the creator watching his reflection vanish into an array of frothing bubbles, formed in the dark, putrid ditch water. He increased the pressure on his bladder, hips playfully gyrating for added dramatic, visual impact. Relieved.

A battered blue Ford hatchback sat parked up on the grass verge nearby, seemingly alone in the sparse countryside, but about two hundred yards from a large farm entrance. Dave Pearson, the car owner, raised the hood on his German army-surplus Flecktarn parka, worn to fend off the early morning chill, blowing from the open fields. Leaning on the rust-spotted car bonnet, he raised a pair of small binoculars to his bloodshot eyes, intently scanning the farm entrance, before swinging around to scan the single-track road heading toward the farm. Wet, bright green sugar beet tops stood out stark and glaring against the deep brown soil of the wide-open and flat fields.

He ignored the younger man urinating into the ditch, who was now walking back towards him, adjusting his flies, as in the distance, and approaching at speed, a small lorry appeared. He'd already watched a mix of lorry boxes and horse trailers, towed by various four wheel drive vehicles, intermittently pass them on the road, to then head on in through the entrance of the farm.

The next vehicle rapidly approached and duly passed, with Pearson leering menacingly at the two occupants; an aged male driver and younger female passenger. Pearson audibly tutted and shook his head as they passed, with the vehicle's occupants purposefully ignoring the two scruffy men on the road.

Dave Pearson's urinating cohort, having finished his much needed bodily function, scrambled over and joined him, also leaning on the car bonnet.

"That's better. Can't beat a good piss. This cold's terrible."

Dave ignored his colleague, and gazing ahead, spoke like a military leader.

"The bastards are slowly pouring in. Like flies round shit. Scum, all of them."

In his mind he was a commander, watching rival troops form up before him, both sides preparing for battle. This was his own personal campaign.

"This is going to be a big field. The scum seem to like it here and it always draws a larger than usual group. Blood-lusting filth!"

Guy Simpson, the man from the ditch, squinted in the low early November sunlight towards the collection of farm buildings nearby, watched by Pearson.

The main collection of out-buildings, including the old red brick farmhouse, were partially obscured by the brown and orange leaves clinging to the row of Oak and Ash trees surrounding the main plot of the farm, along with a mix of Holly and Copper-Beech hedging. Only the entrance gates gave a clue as to the direction onto which all the vehicles were heading within the farm.

"What's the plan Dave?" Guy enquired naively, but with enthusiasm, looking towards the farm. "Dash inside and give 'em all a good kick'in?

Guy was new to the 'Anti' game and unsure why he was standing freezing cold on a country road early on a chilly Saturday morning in November, alongside a potential psychopath he didn't really know. Last night he'd somehow been convinced to further the 'animal welfare' cause. Secretly he didn't care, but assumed it could be a bit of a laugh, chasing 'Toffs' on horseback across fields and verbally, if not physically, abusing all of them.

That appealed to Guy, along with going to raves, drinking, smoking dope, and picking up like-minded girls. Watching a farm was boring. And cold!

"The actual meet, when they mount up, is eleven thirty," began Dave, in a schoolmaster tone to a lowly pupil. "That's when they set off. They usually meet up earlier, like now, and then stroll off to a barn or house. Here they gorge themselves senseless on food they don't really need and which could feed the starving in a Third-World country. They then get pissed up on cherry brandy, port, sherry, whisky, Brasso, agricultural diesel or anything seemingly alcoholic they can find, all of which could power a generator in Africa."

"Wow! Lucky bastards!" Quipped Guy, his eyes widening with excitement at the sound of free food and alcohol. And lots of it. Stuff the Third World.

"Sounds like fun. No wonder they do it! Perhaps we should go steal some horses and join them!" Guy spoke eagerly, still unsure why he was there.

Dave's cold glare brought colour to Guy's cold face. The unrelenting stare caused him to shuffle uncomfortably away from the steady, steel-eyed gaze.

Dave worried Guy. Everyone said Dave Pearson was 'A bit of a Nutter.'

Guy felt now it was true. He feared he'd be quite at home running an SS extermination camp, if his left wing idealistic views didn't conflict with his militant tendencies. It'd no doubt be acceptable to Pearson if the incumbents were 'Toffs' or anyone he considered better off than him, which was generally most people at large, including the 'Poor Third-World Bastards' he spouted so freely about trying to help, seemingly along with all of the world's wildlife.

"Then they mount up," Dave continued to explain, ignoring the ignorant and unwelcome interruption, "and the wanker in the red coat makes a patronising speech to the stupid farmer who lets them gallop all over his land. The tosser with the dogs then lets them all off, so the vicious pack of hounds can roam across the fields and go everywhere they feel fit, including into peoples private gardens. Here these savage dogs see what innocent creatures they can chase and murder, with the arseholes on horseback all happily cheering. Wankers! And all supposedly in the name of sport and entertainment. That's hunting."

Guy watched awestruck, wondering if he should get Dave a soapbox to stand upon. Maybe he should also consider growing a short nasal moustache.

"Meanwhile, the stuck-up twats on horseback gallop about, getting pissed, cheering each time something dies, and riding into anyone who has the nerve or courage to stand up against them. That's it. Hunting. A bunch of rich stuck up twats with nothing better to do, all half-pissed, galloping about the countryside on horses they don't care about. Then slaughtering loads of innocent animals, by using a bunch of under-fed, starving dogs that they then kill off when aged six or seven. That's hunting, and they all call it a sport."

Bewildered, Guy looked at Dave. He could understand the underlying hatred to the cruel activity, but wondered if deep down there was another reason for the hatred, and was still unsure as to why he was actually there himself.

Dave ignored Guy's questioning gaze, now fully into his military commander and political reformer mode, grateful for an attentive audience of one.

"In a way it's bit like military manoeuvres. For both sides. How they plan their hunt and how we intercept them. Do you know anything about military tactics?" Dave looked casually at Guy. He looked back, shaking his head.

"I imagine they'll head out of that drive, cross the road, turn right towards us and put the hounds into that beet field opposite. They'll see if they can flush anything out for an early kill, to keep the bloodthirsty punters happy. You usually get a few hares holed up in sugar beet. That's why I think they'll sweep through it early on. So we'll need to be ready and prepared to stop them."

Dave pointed towards a field of green leaves, indicating to Guy what sugar beet was, just in case he didn't know; which wasn't far from the truth. Bright and shiny in the low morning sunlight, they still held a melting frosty dew.

Guy thumped his gloved hands together and stamped his boots, trying to circulate his blood, having no real interest in sugar beet, only thinking of the sweet sugar he'd loved to have put in a in a cup of steaming hot tea instead.

"We'll head along the road behind them," Dave added. "Cut up along the opposite side and try to get in with the hounds or in front before they have a chance to get started. They hate that. Flush out the hares first. Great tactic."

Dave chuckled, Guy unsure if it was to him, himself or just madness.

"But we'll see what Izzy says when she gets here. She knows the land very well, although she'll probably agree with my plans. Where on earth is she?"

Guy regarded Dave curiously, noting his gaze drifted dreamily as he'd mentioned Izzy. Guy couldn't wait to see Izzy either. He'd heard so much.

"Wish it'd warm up a bit," said Guy, now far more concerned with his body temperature than chasing any 'Toffs' and saving stupid hares. "I'm freezing."

"You'll soon warm up when we get running. Whatever you do though, don't get in front of any of those fucking horses. Some off these bastards will mow you down without thinking. They'll deliberately ride at you. Not good. Nasty mess. I've seen some bad shit in my time," Dave muttered, almost to himself, his eyes drifting off again, as if thinking or recalling a specific event. He was.

Guy looked hard at Dave, taking in his cold blue eyes, set within the gaunt, pale face. With the close-cropped blond hair, set upon a tall, skinny frame, Dave Pearson looked like a Russian Gulag reject. But Dave's words hit home.
'Dangerous? Nasty mess! Run over? No one mentioned this serious stuff. Shit!'
Guy just wanted to hurl abuse or maybe punch some old Port-quaffing Toff. Have a laugh whilst chasing about. Something to boast about in the pub. But not get hurt. Guy realised he'd better get some more in-depth knowledge.
"So the main idea is to keep their dogs away from any rabbits or foxes and generally stop them from killing anything, so we ruin their fun. Also to harass and hurl abuse at the drunken old toffs as they ride past on the horses?"
Guy enquired, trying his best to show some interest and get clarification.
"But not to get in the way of any of the big horses or we'll get hurt?"
Dave nodded slowly, glad Guy vaguely understood, but doubted he really did. He hoped so, but didn't really care. Izzy would sort things out.
Guy was just 'Cannon Fodder' to make up the numbers. Expendable.
There for today, but unlikely to stay the course. Not like Izzy. She was a true Anti, just as he was. There were few of them, but they fought the cause.
Guy now wished he'd taken up the offer to go around Trudy's last night after they'd left the pub'. She'd said he could stay over. Word had it that she went like a steam train in a tunnel after smoking a bit of dope. Guy had kept some resin just for the occasion, but Dave had somehow persuaded him to leave the pub early and doss over at his bed-sit overnight. He'd told him it'd be an experience he'd never forget, and it'd give him real 'street-cred' with Trudy.
The down side was they'd have to make an early start in order to follow the hounds from the kennels and establish the hunt location, often kept secret. A few pints and some Pernod's, and with further chat from some of the other occasional Anti's in their group, Dave had excitedly persuaded a gullible Guy.
Thus he'd stupidly turned down Trudy, thinking this would be fun. Fool!
But now he regretted it. Deeply. His mind drifted to what could have been.
He'd probably be lying in the warmth of Trudy's flat, nuzzling up to her little white tits and shaven pussy, instead of freezing his nuts off in a wet field with a psychotic animal rights nutter, discussing sugar beet and military tactics.
Dave, listening to Guy was ready to correct and educate his pupil further.
"They chase hares, not rabbits. European Brown Hare. Lepus europaeus to be exact. More sport supposedly, as a hare can run at forty miles an hour. It gives the hare a chance. And this lot rarely get onto a fox. Also the dogs are called hounds. Harriers actually. Smaller and faster than the Fox Hounds you usually see out hunting. This bunch only hunt endangered Brown Hares. Wicked fuckers!" Dave almost spat out the final words, with deep venom.
"But yes, basically the main idea is to stop the hounds getting to any hares, disrupt the flow of the hunt and cause as much grief as you can. Best to follow whatever Izzy or me do. Izzy will guide you. She's one of the best and knows how to annoy them. But don't get too mouthy or violent though."

"Why not?" enquired Guy, again somewhat puzzled. "Why don't we just push them all off their horses and kick the fuck out of them when they fall on the ground. Only a bunch of pompous old duffers, I assume. Easy pickings and that'd teach the cruel bastards a real lesson!" Guy booted at a clump of weeds as an aggressive gesture, but there really wasn't any heart in it.

Dave glared at him, just as a parent would an unruly child.

'Idiot. Why had he recruited him? Useless! Ignorant twat!'

"Because we're animal rights protestors. Professionals. Not simply common hooligans or thugs!" Dave responded curtly at the blushing Guy, shaking his head and tutting. "And besides which, there are more of them than us. A lot more! Also, they are not all old, and they ride fucking great horses, carry whips and they are not afraid of beating you with them. Also, they also have lots of followers on foot and in cars to support them. This unruly crowd watch them all and watch us too. They would kill us all if we even tried!"

Guy flushed crimson, his face warming. He'd been told.

A surge of fear and resentment passed through him. This was war.

He gazed silently across the fields of green and brown, noting the trees in the distance, their brightly coloured leaves occasionally drifting down, caught in the slowly growing, but weak sunlight. His feet were numb and hands tingled.

What the hell had he let himself in for?

Next Saturday it'd be Trudy's warm flat for sure.

He wouldn't be standing in a freezing cold field, gazing over frosty, wet sugar beet, beside an absolute nutter. Next Saturday morning his head would be resting upon Trudy's notorious 'Bee-sting' tits and Dave could go and shove his endangered brown hares hard up somewhere dark and moist.

If he needed a hand, or a boot, Guy would willingly offer!

Chapter 20

It is discouraging how many people are shocked by honesty and how few by deceit.

Noel Coward

Still standing by the ditch, Guy was saved further berating or embarrassment from his dictatorial comrade by the roar of a large lorry, moving fast along the road behind them, their attention previously being focussed on the farm.

"Hello, here comes trouble," said Dave turning swiftly as a bright yellow lorry with green lightening-flash stripe decal appeared at speed. Hurtling down the country road, in the direction of the farm, the lorry appeared to weave at the last minute straight at them, scuffing the edge of the verge.

The two spectators leapt onto the grass bank, just as the vehicle missed them and their car by inches. The lorry left a cloud of grit and dust in its wake, blowing up into the Anti's faces, the back draft sucking them off the verge.

"Fucking Wanker!" screamed Dave at the back of the lorry, now standing in the middle of the road, fists angrily shaking. "I'll kill you Harrison, you tosser! Kill you!" he yelled, contradicting his lecture on being a peaceful protestor.

Guy stared at Dave, bemused, then looked off at the speeding truck.

An arm with a solitary raised middle finger appeared from the side window, rising up, before disappearing as the lorry braked and pulled into the farm.

"Who the fuck was that mad idiot?" enquired Guy, dusting himself down, still shaken, gazing at the lorry as it disappeared. "What a total wanker!"

"A perfect description Guy," replied Dave, nodding as added confirmation. "That Total Wanker was Steve Harrison. Izzy's ex-hubby. A complete and utter wanker to be correct, and one of the main reasons why we are here."

"Izzy used to be married to him?" Guy replied in disbelief. "Wow!"

Again he now wondered if this 'Anti' activity was more than a way of venting jealousy at people with more money than they had. Perhaps it was personal.

"Definitely don't get in his way out there," Dave began, venom in his voice, breaking Guy's thought. "Bastard! He will run you over and kill you."

Guy stared, keen to learn more, but with concerns rising by the minute.

"He's the bastard who rode over Midge. Broke his arm, leg and three ribs. And it never went to court. An accident! The bastard galloped straight over the poor sod. I was there. He rode straight at him, smiling! Not nice. Midge had no chance. He lay screaming in agony as Harrison just rode off laughing."

Guy looked at Dave, wondering what the hell he'd let himself in for. He'd heard about the incident with Midge. It'd made the local press and even TV. He recalled watching some flash guy leaving court, sticking two fingers up at a camera and laughing. It must have been Harrison. It was all clear now.

He didn't know what happened after but heard Midge began concentrating on handing out anti-vivisection leaflets in the city instead. Seemingly safer.

As Guy stood by the ditch, lost in thoughts, contemplating the life expectancy of the average Anti, another small convoy headed towards them, but driving more sedately. A large lorry led the way, followed by a Land Rover and trailer, a solitary 4 x 4 and then another smaller lorry box.

Dave and Guy mounted the verge and stood back, just in case, as the convey passed by at a sensible speed, the drivers glancing toward those standing on the verge, who in turn regarded them all back with malice. Anna glanced at the two men as she passed, half out of curiosity and half concern, as Tracey had only just begun to warn her about the annoying Anti's. Trouble. Big time.

"Who were that lot?" asked Guy, as the convey disappear into the farm driveway in an orderly manner and dispersed. He had his eyes on one person.

"I recognise the first lorry; he's usually out a lot. As is the lorry at the rear. She's a right posh bitch. Lady Summit. Don't know the others. They're all the same. Posh twats, all out to kill innocent wild animals. Wankers. All of them."

"I fancied the slim bird with the long blond hair driving the jeep. Think she was eyeing me up. She gave me a long stare," said Guy, Anna's image fresh.

Dave glared. "They're all evil bastards. The women are stuck up sluts who'll only open their legs if you own a farm or string of racehorses. Whores!"

Guy now sensed this was all a very personal campaign and unrelated to animal welfare. Pearson would probably pester members of a Morris Dancing club if they were doing something he objected to, or had more than him.

"How will I recognise the mad bloke in the yellow lorry when he's riding on his horse? You know, Izzy's hubby? They all look the same. Posh toffs!"

"Ex. He's no longer her husband. Ex-husband. And thank goodness too. They're divorced. Izzy is now single." Dave firmly corrected. "Harrison rides a big black horse. Built like a brick shit house. Evil looking fucker."

"What, Harrison or the horse?" enquired Guy, puzzled.

"The horse is a big black, evil-looking fucker. Harrison is a ponce, with an all year suntan. A smarmy twat! Don't know what Izzy ever saw in him, other than his money. She's much better off without him. Best thing she ever did was to leave him and swap sides. Izzy is a wonderful woman. Brilliant!"

Dave's vision drifted, as if recalling all of Izzy's glory.

Guy stared at Dave and now understood the deep anger.

Dave checked his watch. It was 11.15am and only three other vehicles had pulled into the farm in the last few minutes of silence. Guy noticed Dave looking into the distance, searching the skyline, now appearing flustered.

"Is Izzy actually coming today? I thought she'd have been here by now."

Guy dared to make the enquiring comment, sensing the cause of Dave's skyline searching and constant watch checking was for her alone.

"She said she'd be here early," Dave replied. "But who knows after she left with that flash twat last night. I warned her not to, as we had an early start."

Guy sensed real jealousy flowing from Pearson with regards to Izzy.

"I sometimes have doubts. She's out chasing this lot, fighting our cause, but still picks up stuck-up rich twats!" Dave continued, seemingly speaking aloud.

"She obviously can't give up the rich life," returned Guy, his face then flushing, wondering if he'd said too much and spoken the truth out of line.

Dave regarded Guy with respect, nodding in silent agreement. "Maybe."

For another five minutes they waited, Dave peering through the binoculars for any movement in the farm, where the odd figure could be seen flitting about from building to vehicle. He was becoming clearly agitated by Izzy's delay, more frequently scanning the countryside with his binoculars. Suddenly he noted the flash of sunlight striking off a windscreen in the distance. The glint moved swiftly across the country, then steadily a bright green Toyota RAV 4 appeared, bouncing up the verge, to stop behind Dave's rusting hulk.

At once the stoop in Dave's figure went and he became erect, almost military in his manner. Shoulders back, he was on parade. The pair noted two images in the front of the car through the windscreen, curious as to the other body.

"Don't tell me she's brought the twat from last night?" Dave spat out the words, seeing an obscure outline in the passenger's seat. "That's all I need!"

Both doors of the 4 x 4 opened almost together and Izzy bounced onto the verge with a spring, wearing a black baseball cap. From the back hung her long blonde ponytail. As Dave stepped towards her, he quickly but carefully eyed her up, feeling the quivering inside he always felt each time they met.

She wore brown suede hiking boots, into which where tucked tight, figure hugging black leggings. On top she wore a dark green fleece, tied tight at the waist, showing off her flat stomach and also revealing her neat, tight buttocks, which sat atop her long, slender legs. She looked past Dave, ignoring him, not even offering any form of greeting, her gaze instead drifting towards the farm.

"Ernie Cole's farm," she muttered, seemingly to herself rather than anyone. "Always put on a great meet did Ernie. Good old chap. Great riding."

A twinkle in her eyes and a slight wry smile gave Dave, who stood looking at her face, an inkling of where she truly wished she was right now. And it obviously wasn't beside him. Her gaze drifted back to Dave and he looked down, the vision of Izzy with cherry brandy, nibbling fruitcake and swapping horse stories, evaporating. Rising his head, puffing his chest, he smiled at her.

For today she was all his. And his to enjoy. And he would - in full.

Isabelle Harrison was a strange character. She was naturally beautiful, being tall and slim, yet with the correct curves in the right places. Naturally blond hair fell down in waves, but was today was tied up, hanging out the back of her baseball cap, which was almost her trademark and could be seen flapping about across the fields like a Palomino's tail. She had a heart-shaped face, with healthy complexion set with sapphire blue eyes. Her nose was small and neat, but her lips a little thin, this the only flaw in a perfect face and matching body.

To Dave she was pure beauty itself. He adored her, flaws and all.

Izzy could, and did frequently, melt a man's heart at a hundred yards with just one wink from her large blue eyes. A brilliant, natural horsewoman and former keen hunter, she'd had a happy and eventful life with her ex-husband Steve Harrison. That was until the incident with Steve and the two young grooms, which changed both of their lives forever. From the day of the whipping, where Izzy left the farm and filed for a quick divorce, she suddenly becoming an instant, over-night 'Anti'. Many people claimed it was simply out of revenge, and an easy way of getting back at Steve, but also that deep down inside she was still as keen as ever about hunting, and by becoming an 'Anti' gave her a means to keep in touch with the sport she enjoyed and also to be around Steve, who it was thought she still secretly loved.

To the rest of the Anti's and the local League Against Cruel Sports section, she was something of a hero. She was classed as the complete hunter who had now 'Seen the Light' and jumped ship over to their camp, recognising the errors of her ways and now repenting, being keen and active Anti.

The hunts however despised her, although many members still held a degree of respect for her as a past horsewoman and hunter. However, she knew too many of the hunts darker secrets, often kept from the public eyes. Also, she knew all the meet locations and ground they covered and so had great insight as to where the Huntsmen would guide the hounds over the varying ground.

Izzy turned to Dave, looking at him for the first time, smiling mildly.

"Morning Dave, bit nippy. This is Wendy. She's very kindly come out to give us support," she said pointing at a young girl who'd exited the passenger side of the RAV and who now stood silent, looking both nervous and cold.

Dave and Guy had failed to see her, so intent were they on gazing at Izzy. Guy took his eyes off Izzy for the first time and looked over towards Wendy.

She was petite and had a frail appearance, but also some charm. A navy blue wool hat covered most of her head, leaving a small, round, pale face, from which peered two bright green, timid-looking eyes. She wore a similar colour fleece, which seemed to drown her tiny frame, supported upon black jogging bottoms and black training shoes. She shuddered, rubbing her gloves and hugging herself warm, clearly not someone used the outdoors.

Guy had met Izzy briefly a few times before and heard lots more about her. She was gorgeous, with a presence that sets some from others. Izzy certainly had class and more. He knew Izzy was well out of his league, but Guy's attention was drawn to Wendy, whom he thought was cute. Very cute.

He immediately stepped over to the shy recruit, stretching out a welcoming hand, smiling a toothy grin, his hidden tail now firmly wagging.

"Hi, I'm Guy," he said, extending a hand. A small green wool glove was wrapped inside his as he vigorously shook her hand. Izzy glanced at the new couple, now gazing and chatting happily to each other, instantly hitting it off.

She grinned broadly, raising her eyebrows to Dave. 'Young love.'

Dave gazed at Izzy, wishing she would treat him in such a manner.

"How big a field is there Dave?" Izzy asked in a professional tone, breaking the 'lovers' glance, as they all turned her way. She was looking intently over at the farm, remembering some happier days, but knew her job for today.

"A lot," Dave replied. "We followed the hounds from the kennels at about ten o'clock and since then we've seen about thirty boxes or various vehicles with trailers enter the farm, as well as the usual stream of followers and hangers-on in various cars. It seems like it will be quite a large field."

"I'm not surprised," replied Izzy. Her eyes sparkling. "It's Ernie Cole's meet. He always put on a brilliant spread, with champagne cocktails, punch, and all the works. The riding here is brilliant. Looks like they're in for a good day."

Dave regarded her with a cautious look, before Izzy spoke on.

"So let's try and spoil it and ruin their day!" She grinned wickedly.

Dave's face for once broke into a smile, a fist clenched.

"Yes! Let's go and fuck up their day big time! Bring it on! Fuck them all!"

Izzy ignored Dave's sudden burst of over-exuberant vigour and venom.

"I thought we were supposed to have a few more join us today," Izzy asked, looking at Dave. "Glenda and Peter called me early this morning to say they couldn't come, Peter's arthritis playing up it seems. But I had my doubts when they said they'd come. They are happy to pass out leaflets, but neither are up for any fieldwork. Weren't you going to get another car full?"

She saw Dave tense up and purse his lips, knowing she'd hit a nerve.

"Typical all bull-shit and no balls," Dave replied. "A no show by that bunch too. Probably still in bed and then they'll nurse a hangover. It's just us today."

Izzy simply shrugged her shoulders as if she didn't care. It was a familiar task trying to get people to chase around a cold wet field, for a cause many were happy to shout about, but not put into real action, and with the risk of death!

Standing silently, her gaze drifted. A thousand yard stare recalled many happy past meets at 'Good Old' Ernie's. Images of yapping hounds, excited sweating horses, with the smell of leather, all stirred by copious alcohol were recalled. The anticipation, then mix of excitement and fear as the horses raced off.

For a brief moment those memories raced through her veins once more.

She sighed inwardly. Good days. Bad days. Her former life.

God, she could murder a cherry brandy. Bring back the good days!

Silently Dave stared at Izzy's side profile, enjoying the view, but wondering what thoughts ran through the beautiful head he so much loved.

One day he hoped he would find out.

One day he would.

Izzy spun around to look at Dave and nodded.

'Game on!'

Chapter 21

And I looked and behold a pale horse:
And his name that sat upon him was Death and Hell followed with him.

Revelation - 6:8

Inside Ernie Cole's farm, Anna parked her 4 x 4 next to Chris' box. Getting out she saw a flurry of bewildering activity, with horseboxes of various sizes, trailers and 4 x 4's everywhere. A variety of people dressed in a mix of riding clothes, country tweeds or bright coloured fleeces mingled about the farm.

Anna's party of three, led by Tracey, stepped over to Chris's lorry. Julie, who'd parked her Land Rover and trailer alongside Anna's vehicle, joined them. Bonnie bashed at the floor of the trailer for attention, causing it to rock violently, but was reprimanded by Julie and then promptly stopped.

Carol and Sally busied themselves, talking with Chris, checking the horses in the lorry, and generally organising items, before joining the group.

"Let's go and get a bite to eat, shall we?" Chris asked the women, now all standing together. All nodded eagerly. Although unsure, Anna felt a pang of nervous excitement as the group headed toward the farm, moving into a low roofed barn under which stood a mass of bodies feasting and drinking.

Anna scanned the vast timber-framed barn, with dusty aged timber side panelling, upon which hung an array of farming implements. Many tools had not been moved or used in years, evident by the rust and piles of dormant dust. A collection of chains, rope and other items joined the tools, but also in one corner sat some modern tractor attachments, showing the barn would usually be part of a functioning farm. Light streamed in through gaps in the red Pantile roof, where massive cobwebs, covered in black dust, hung high in the open timber beams, packed out in various places with lengths of reed.

As Anna's focus returned to the array of trestle tables, adorned with food and drink, Sally and Carol made excuses and peeled away, Anna watching the pair approach a distinguished looking gentleman in a tweed jacket, who gave them both a peck on the cheek and warmly hugged Carol. The remaining group, prompted by an eager Tracey, entered the central area around the barn, which was humming with people. Numerous nods and polite hello's came their way and suddenly an outstretched arm detained Chris as he drifted by.

Anna could not believe her eyes. Numerous trestle tables, covered in crisp white tablecloths lay stretched before them, upon which, set on the finest china crockery, every type of buffet food imaginable. At one end of the tables stood a table brimming with various bottles of alcohol, along with a separate table stacked with orange juice, brandy and champagne other bottles. The spread was better than the buffets at many weddings Anna had attended.

Tracey and Julie needed no invitation and walked boldly up to the drinks table. Anna and Joyce timidly followed. An elderly, yet elegant lady, dressed in fine Tweed stood behind the drinks table and smiled sweetly at them.
"Would you like a Bucks Fizz? Or maybe a Champagne Cocktail? You can have both if you want Tracey!" The old woman's eyes twinkled wickedly.
Tracey's eyes bulged with excitement at the thought and eagerly accepted the cocktail option, first, watching like a child at Christmas as the Brandy and Champagne were mixed, poured onto a singular sugar cube in a cocktail glass.
Julie smiled at the lady and accepted a Buck's Fizz, already happily sipping as Anna and Joyce joined her, both looking in pleasant surprise at the host.
"Good Morning Mrs Cole. Excellent spread as ever," Julie said between sips, then took two further glasses of the sparkling liquid, passed them to a slightly bewildered Anna and Joyce. "Here you are!" Julie smiled.
"Oh my god!" replied Anna, had reaching out, then pausing. "I'd love to, but at eleven in the morning? You must be kidding. And I've got to drive too."
She paused, looking at the grinning face of Julie, then Tracey, who'd already downed her cocktail and was eagerly scanning the bottles on another table.
"Oh, what the hell!" she conceded, happily accepting. Joyce accepted her glass without hesitation, taking a refreshing gulp. Anna took a delicate sip, eyes widening with delight. The ladies all gratefully thanked their smiling host, and with glasses in hand, headed towards the tables covered in food.
"Doesn't everyone gets drunk?" enquired Anna, following Julie over to the tables laden with food, the drink tingling and already hitting home.
"Yes!" Tracey exclaimed. "That's half the fun. It sounds really bad, but I've gone out half pissed some days. You wonder how you stay on the horses!"
Julie laughed loudly, nodding in agreement, punching playfully Tracey's arm, amused by the shocked expression and disbelieving shake of Anna's head.
The group of ladies delicately picked their way through an array of food fit for any wedding feast. Before them lay sandwiches, quiches, salmon strips, sausage rolls, crisps, chicken legs, fruitcake and an array of sliced cold meats, all lain out on fine china, and set upon the series of tables for all to enjoy.
Anna looked around at the wide selection of people enjoying the feast, drinks and jovial company. All were dressed in a wide range of elegant, traditional hunting and country dress. Anna sensed she'd gone back a hundred years. It was an amazing and pleasant experience and one she was pleased to enjoy.
As Tracey and Julie chatted, Anna scanned the various faces around the barn and tables. They varied from young, rosy-cheeked children drinking what she hoped was Cherryade, to old women, some of whom looked like they must be over seventy, yet who were still dressed up for riding. There were a few handsome young men, some in riding gear, others in country clothing, who she noticed glanced her way more than just once. Some older, portlier men glanced her way, touching their caps politely when they spotted her looking.

"I feel I've travelled back in time," Anna said to Tracey, who was taking it all in her stride, now drinking a small plastic cup filled with a deep red liquid, to join the Champagne Cocktail and Buck's Fizz, which had already disappeared.

"Yes, that's one of the great things about hunting," Tracey replied, nodding as a reply between bites upon a cheese and pickle sandwich. "It's part of the tradition. Everyone is so polite and friendly, although some of the older men can get too friendly sometimes, if they've had too much of this!" She raised the small glass, its diminishing deep red contents having the desired effect.

"Where did you get that?" Julie enquired, upon seeing the dark red spirit in her hand. She followed Tracey's nod, spotting the bottles of Cherry Brandy and proceeded to grab a small glass herself. Joyce looked on in amazement, then realising that she wasn't driving, joined them in grabbing some glasses of the sweet red liquid, much enjoyed by Hunters. Anna put on a pretend sulk, knowing she'd be over the limit if she drunk any more, so helped herself to a big chunk of homemade iced fruitcake as a form of consolation.

As the woman chatted, Tracey and Julie discreetly pointed out who various people within the hunt were, much to the curious, yet keen interest of Anna.

Julie seemed to know everyone, and Anna immediately feeling at home with the older woman, enjoying the warm banter and her polite yet unforced company, sensing a bond growing. The effects of the alcohol swiftly worked on Tracey. A string of expletives, which wasn't uncommon, began to flow, as she merrily chatted and laughed, much to the amusement of Julie. She was used to Tracey, but her actions seemingly shocked her Aunt and quieter, rather embarrassed cousin. Shortly Julie apologised and left their company crossing the barn to begin chatting to a short, middle-aged, plump woman.

Anna gazed around at the various people enjoying the free banquet laid on for all, selecting a mushroom Vol-au-Vent, whilst Joyce and Tracey continued to devour even more sandwiches. Julie chatted to the plump woman, then both turned to look in Anna's direction. The woman had dark hair and very dark brown eyes and laughed happily with Julie. The pair then proceeded back over to the gorging group of women, as Tracey reached for a fourth drink and a handful of crisps. Julie introduced the shorter woman to Anna.

"Anna this is Suzie. Suzie, Anna," Julie pointed back and forth to the respective woman, who in turn politely smiled, Anna unsure was happening.

"Anna's moving to Chris's yard and going to start hunting with us soon," Julie explained, as if everything was already decided. "Anna, do you mind taking Suzie in your car? She's following today but only has a small car. It may get stuck down some of the muddier tracks. Also she knows all of the roads and routes, as well as everyone in the hunt, so she'll soon be able to explain to you what is going on and what you should and shouldn't do. Do you mind?"

Julie and Suzie looked at Anna, awaiting a response, as Tracey ate on.

Anna was surprised at Julie's open manner, but immediately agreed, deciding it'd be much better to have someone experienced showing them about.

She was beginning to warm to Julie and liked her open, friendly and genuine nature and how she'd welcomed her so easily to the hunt, and also how everyone seemed to assume she was going to Chris' yard without question.

Chris appeared from where he'd been chatting, grabbing a glass of cherry brandy and a brown bread tuna sandwich, then stood quietly beside the chatting ladies. Suzie smiled, stepped forward and greeted him with a peck on his cheek, to which he openly blushed, but grinned, asking of her horse.

An attractive, elegant lady, dressed in a figure hugging, expertly tailored black hunting jacket and banana coloured jodhpurs approached. Ignoring everyone, she stepped straight up to Chris and stood unashamedly beside him, prodding his arm for attention. He turned to acknowledge her with a wide smile.

Anna glared at the beautiful woman, recognising her at once as the driver of the lorry that had followed them. She merely glanced at Anna as if she was transparent then looked away, turning to face Chris direct, touching his hand.

Anna instinctively disliked her. Julie smirked, seeing Anna's jealous glare.

"Chris sweetie," said Virginia Burlingham eloquently. "I've been looking for you since you arrived. I hope you haven't been avoiding me. Naughty man!" She spoke with a seductive grin, then lowered her tone, but Anna heard.

"We have to talk. Now. In private. Quickly. Lets go ! Follow me."

Chris, blushed, smiled and led away by Virginia, the pair discretely moved to a corner of the barn, away from anyone, and began chatting quietly.

Anna, curious and naturally inquisitive, tried to listen or lip-read, however, Tracey was constantly talking about various horses, as the volume of her voice seemed to increase with each fresh swig of cherry brandy. Anna cocked her head towards Chris and Virginia, trying to avoid looking as if she was eaves-dropping, but caught a couple of words which made her blood curdle.

"Don't let Bertie find out!" Anna overheard Virginia say slightly louder.

A hand placed upon her arm made her jump, and drew her attention away. She turned to see Julie speaking. Worried she may have been caught out, she turned her attention to Julie, but was still intrigued by the secret conversation.

After a few moments, the pair separated and Chris moved across the barn. Virginia strolled past Anna without a glance, heading straight out of the barn, her poise perfect, walking tall and with a seductive swagger as if on a cat-walk. No trace of fat was visible upon her pert, firm lemon-clad buttock cheeks or upon her slim, sculptured waist. Anna already hated her.

From the corner of her eye she caught someone looking at her. She turned, cheeks glowing red to see a smiling Julie keenly watch her.

"Don't worry about her," she said with a grin, appearing to read easily Anna's thoughts. "Do you want another drink or something else to eat?"

"Not if I ever hope to look like that!" Anna quipped.

Both women burst out laughing, to amused and curious looks from Joyce and an apparently already half-cut Tracey, who'd been chatting to Suzie.

Anna furtively sought out Chris, slightly disappointed he did not seen to have time for her, hoping she could speak with him; to learn something about him, and importantly, find out if he'd let her bring Penny. But he was elusive.

Slowly the people began to drift away from the tables, and Chris, appearing from nowhere, rejoined them. He made a gesture to Tracey and Julie as Sally and Carol also suddenly reappeared, having left their two gentleman guests.

"Should we be getting on board?" Sally enquired, it's nearly time.

"Yes, I think we'd better," replied Chris, looking around the slowly dispersing room, then at the whole group, who agreed and started to drift off.

Tracey wobbled, hanging onto Suzie for support, who in turn loudly laughed. Julie made one last dive at a plate of cheese sandwiches, picking up three, thrusting them into Anna's hands, who blushed, hoping no one was watching.

"Hold onto these a mo'," Julie said and quickly grabbed another plastic glass of cherry brandy. She came back and took one of the sandwiches, grinning at Anna and Joyce. "You eat the others, I'm watching my weight," she joked.

Anna smiled and passed the sandwiches onto her mother. She puffed out, feigning being full, but still promptly took them, whilst carrying a glass of sherry in the other hand she'd managed to find. Joyce was enjoying Hunting.

The group strolled back to the lorries, where upon seeing their owners return, the horses beginning to get agitated, either whinnying or bashing the side of the horse box. Everyone went back into automatic mode, busying about, even the rapidly sobering Tracey. Hats were grabbed, along with gloves and other key items, and Chris' lorry was rapidly unloaded of horses.

Anna was amazed at how swiftly the group changed from a crowd of half-drunk, laughing and feasting girls, out on a Hen-night, to serious mounted riders. She held an excited Fred, who spun back and forth, as Tracey nimbly mounted, then was about to offer to help Chris, only to find he was already on board his mount Cirrus, and tightening his girth. The grey mare stood impeccably still and he gazed down at Anna, smiling and giving her any real attention for the first time since arriving at the meet. Anna was pleased to receive it and somewhat nervously gazed up at Chris, about to speak.

"Can you give me a hand, if you don't mind, please," Julie yelled, interrupting Anna's moment to talk with her host, as she heaved herself into the saddle.

"But don't touch Bonnie or she'll bite!" With a nod, she gestured to Anna, who understood and obligingly handed her hunting whip and the beaker of cherry brandy. The highly-strung, excitable coloured mare swung sideways, then back and forth, as somehow, one-handed, Julie managed to control the horse, whilst guzzling down the liquid, before passing Anna the empty glass.

"God I needed that! Steady up you grumpy old moo!" Julie pulled the reins.

Anna grinned, seeing how Julie and her horse appeared in a strange way to be the perfect match; both eccentric. She turned back around to look for Chris, but he'd moved away from the lorries, drifting off, seemingly as elusive and reclusive as ever, until she noticed a man pull alongside him and chat.

"Would you mind giving me a leg up?" a voice called. Anna turned to see Carol holding her black Cob, Tess. She'd hardly seen or spoken to Carol.

The stunning black mare, bearing a white blaze, had the characteristic cob features she loved; notably 'the head of a Duchess and bottom of a Cook.' Carol, slightly over-weight, bobbed up two times, as Anna gripped the older woman's chubby leg and almost threw her into the saddle. Carol puffed and thanked her as she landed, then adjusted her girth, as Anna held the reins.

"She's beautiful," said Anna genuinely looking at the black mare, giving the relaxed horse a gentle slap on the neck and then began tickling her nose

"Beautiful, but lazy!" Carol joked with a smile. "Like some hunt members!"

Anna chuckled, but noticed Carol's gaze drift across the paddock, where a number of mounted riders were entering together. One of these had to be Virginia Burlingham. Anna gazed at Carol, to see the usually happy woman glaring, almost bitterly at the stunning 'Lady' who trotted by, oblivious to all.

Anna sensed some bitterness towards the younger woman as Carol rode off, nodding a thank to Anna, before chatting to an older gent on a big Bay.

Sally, seemingly as elusive and solitary as Chris, and hence possibly why the pair worked so well together, had mounted her gelding Goldie unaided and sat waiting patiently near the box. Once all were securely mounted, the group rode off into the paddock, where the other mounted riders had all headed.

Suzie appeared from behind another lorry, trotting over to join Anna and Joyce, and the new threesome wandered on behind the horses and onto the paddock, where the rest of the mounted field were all assembling.

Anna had never seen anything like it in her life. She'd been to many horse events, and was used to seeing large numbers of horses, however, the scene before her reminded her of the many old hunting prints she'd seen hanging on the walls of country homes, antique shops or often at car boot sales.

Horses in all shapes, sizes and colours, were everywhere, along with a mix of smartly attired riders. Children in neat tweed jackets sat upon platted ponies, some with lead-reins attached to concerned mothers, dressed equally smart in Navy jackets with golden-pinned stocks. Others, looking barely old enough to control a horse, sat boldly alone upon their ponies, or happily trotted around in groups, merrily chatting. The lady riders were elegantly dressed in various navy, black or mixed tweed jackets, with the men mostly in set in black, heavy wool, hunting coats, but the occasional gent was set in a neat tweed.

Some wore scarlet, and Anna become transfixed on one gentleman attired in red who sat upon a large grey horse and clearly stood out from the rest. He casually rode amongst the mounted field, white-thong hunting whip in his rein hand, green hunting cap raised in his free hand to the various ladies he passed. His red cheeks glowed like Santa Claus' on Christmas morning. He caught Anna's stare, stopped his horse, and looking in her direction smiled.

"Good Morning ladies," Reggie boomed out at Anna and Joyce.

The pair stood dumbstruck for a few seconds, unsure how to react, both going bright red, before simply smiling and returning the greeting.

"Morning Suzie. Not joining us today?" he added, looking sideways with a smile at Anna's newfound acquaintance, whom he clearly knew.

"Not today sir," replied Suzie. "Poor Charlie's a bit lame. Nothing serious. Resting him and hope to be out soon. I'm following today. Great field."

Reggie nodded knowingly, turning his attention back towards Anna.

"I've not seen you two beauties before. Fresh blood! And will we be seeing you fine ladies out riding with us soon? I do hope so," he continued, his eyes twinkling with devilment, moving from Anna to Joyce, his grey mount still.

Joyce blushed, then replied nervously but proud, pointing to Anna.

"Well you won't see me on horse back, I'm a bit too old for all that, but you might see my daughter, Anna. She's moving her horse down to Chris Turner's yard and hopes to be riding out with you very soon. Don't you love?"

Anna blushed and winced inside, wanting to curl up along with her already turning toes; her presumptuous mother as ever naively embarrassing her.

She hoped Chris wasn't within earshot, and furtively glanced about, happy to see he was missing as ever, not sure he would offer her a place at his yard.

"Daughter? I thought you two were sisters!" Reggie cheekily declared, beaming brightly. "And in my book you're never too old for anything!"

He winked at Joyce, who blushed even brighter and he turned to Anna.

"I'll certainly look forward to seeing you out with us very soon then," he said, looking directly at Anna, who blushed. Reggie's power and magnetism, along with his eye for attractive woman, was unashamedly on display.

Reggie thanked them, raised his cap again and rode on to greet more riders.

"That was Reggie, or Reginald Hornchurch to be correct. Our Hunt Master. Basically he's the big boss," said Suzie quietly, smiling at the two dumbstruck women, watching him ride around the paddock like a mighty warrior.

"He can be really nice, especially if you're attractive! Until you do something wrong hunting. Or if you happen to be married to him. Then he can be a total bastard. Brilliant horseman though. He's okay really, but just be warned."

"Oh, he's married. What a shame!" said Joyce, playfully looking despondent. "I'm out of luck then. I was just about to buy a horse." She chuckled.

"Mother! You're already married, remember? I'll tell dad!" Anna exclaimed.

"That's his wife over there," Suzie explained, grinning at Joyce. "Number four I think. I've lost count. Do you really want to be number five?"

The pair discreetly looked towards where Suzie indicated, Joyce smirking.

Elizabeth Hornchurch, who sat elegantly upon a fine dark bay mare, was chatting to two other ladies on similar mounts, but watching her husband.

"Doesn't stop him allegedly playing the field," continued Suzie smirking. "That's why he's called 'Horny.' But only behind his back. Elizabeth must know he cheats. But she can do nothing, unless she wants to lose everything."

"I think he's a grand gentleman. I've never had a man raise his hat before," Joyce, replied proudly, adding "Your father's never raised his hat to me. Not even when wearing one of his baseball caps. I'll insist he does from now on!"

An amused Anna shook her head, smiling at her mother with a huge grin and began looking about amongst the forty plus horses for Tracey, Chris and Julie, who were mingling about within a sea of elegant horses drifting about. She then spotted the trio, who were slowly heading back over towards them.

Tracey spoke first as she approached, half-pissed, Fred strutting about.

"I see you've met Reggie," she said smiling widely at Anna. "No doubt he fancies you. You'll be wife number five Anna. Beheaded wasn't it?"

Even tipsy Tracey seemed capable of recalling the fate of Henry VIII's wives.

"Actually I think he was after mum," replied Anna with a grin. "Good job you can't ride, isn't it mum? If not it'll be your head on the block!"

"I've decided to start having lessons next week," Joyce joked. "Then I'll be racing about with all you lot. Maybe. But I'll kill him off before he does me!"

They all smiled as Julie pulled Bonnie up next to Tracey, but standing away.

"When will you be off?" Anna asked excitedly, looking at Julie.

"Soon. Martin has just let the hounds out," she replied. "Over there. Look!"

With that Anna watched as a stream of hounds of various colours, but mostly a mix of cream, black and tan, poured out across the edges of the paddock, middling with horses and nosing at every new scent in their path. The large array of weaving hounds amused Anna, each appearing to have its own unique character, yet each a key element within the whole team.

Martin, the Huntsman, immaculately turned out in scarlet and seated upon his large black Irish-Draught cross Thoroughbred gelding, Bert, hurried after a few drifting hounds, flicking the tail of a white-thong hunting whip, calling out different hounds names as some began to go astray from the pack.

Chris pulled Cirrus up and smiled down at the women, Joyce more amused by the sight of the hounds. Anna stepped forward to pat Chris' grey mare.

"Gorgeous," she said, deliberately gazing up at Chris rather than the mare as she spoke, their eyes meeting and unmoving. Chris blushed, smiled, then broke eye contact as Reggie's voice boomed out. All of the mounted riders turned their horses and people on foot moved about to face him. Martin expertly brought the hounds to heel in a loose pack around Bert's hooves.

Reggie sat upon his large grey mount, his bright scarlet jacket stark against the almost pure white coat of the horse upon which he sat. He oozed power, respect and a degree of fear, as all gazed at him, no one daring to speak. Reggie's voice, clear and authoritative, loudly barked out various instructions for the day, warning all of where they could and couldn't ride. He warmly thanked the Cole family for hosting the meet, their amazing generosity, and splendid hospitality, as ever, before formally introducing Steve Harrison as the Field Master for the day, the rider in charge of the Mounted Field.

Anna had noticed the man Reggie introduced riding a round the paddock, seated upon a huge black horse, laughing and joking, mostly with woman. He too looked very grand and handsome, but with a cheeky, over-confident air she recognised all too well. Tracey had already warned her about Steve.

With a nod from Reggie, Martin blew on his hunting horn, the tone sending a strange tingle through Anna's chest. Flicking the thong of his hunting whip, Martin moved Bert forward and in turn set the hounds off, leading them out through a gateway and down the farm driveway they'd driven up earlier. Reggie followed closely behind the hounds, but Steve Harrison held back with the riders, giving Reggie and Martin a minute to clear the farm entrance, and then pushed on behind, leading the mass of riders who filed in behind.

"Looks like were off," Tracey squealed, spinning around upon a bouncing Fred, turning in the direction of the disappearing hounds and slowly moving group of horses, calling back to Anna. "Have fun!"

Chris looked down, smiling at the ladies, focussing his eyes upon Anna for a second longer than required, before nodding politely, then he turned his keen grey mare away, trotting off towards the main group, joining the pack.

"See you in a while. I hope! Look after them Suzie and don't get them lost!" Julie yelled out, being tossed about on an excited Bonnie, waving them bye with a big smile, as Bonnie spun sideways and dragged Julie off to join her compatriots, all rapidly heading in a chaotic bunch towards the farm gateway.

"Okay, its time to go," spoke Suzie to the pair. "Lets quickly get in your car and move off or we'll lose them. Hope you're sober, this could get hairy!"

Suzie's comment drew some concern from Anna wondered what she'd let herself in for, but a wide grin from Joyce, who found it all exciting.

So far everything had gone well and the day was as she'd hoped.

The people were warm, welcoming and great fun.

What could possibly go wrong?

Lots.

Chapter 22

Know thy self, know thy enemy.
A thousand battles, a thousand victories.

Sun Tzu

Izzy's memories of past hunt meets snapped back to the present at the sight of a green Land Rover appearing at the end of the farm track, which then sped off away from them. It was one of Ernie Cole's workers, who led the car followers. It told Izzy the field were setting off, some of the followers already setting off behind the lead vehicle, keen to get ahead of the mounted field.

"Looks like they're off!" she announced loudly, turning the Anti's heads.

Seconds later a collection of black, tan and cream hounds poured down the driveway, like a living mottled carpet, scattering about out onto the road.

"Here we go," yelled Dave excitedly, springing into life and breaking up the small talk between Guy and Wendy. The pair suddenly remembered why they were standing in a cold wet field as a magnificent grey horse and huge black horse appeared, with distinctive red-scarlet jacketed figures seated atop each.

"I see Martin's on Bert today," continued Izzy aloud to herself, looking at the stunning and bold 17hh black horse, with a slight 'Roman' nose. Izzy, still lost in her own world, was coming back to life, recalling days when she'd ridden. A smile spread across her face at the sight of the frantic hounds mingling about on the road, sniffing at the verge and inside the ditch for any scent.

"Game on!" screamed Dave, jumping up the bank, raising binoculars to his eyes to look for the rest of the riders, which could just be seen on the track.

"Hopefully they'll head down here and we can follow, then quite easily along the road and then the beet, where can get in amongst them," said Izzy.

Approaching the road, Martin spotted the figures as the hounds milled in the sugar beet field ahead of him. Antis - as was expected. But worse - Izzy.

"Sir!" he hollered to Reggie. "Looks like we've got company."

He raised his whip, pointing it down the road. Reggie could see the two cars and four figures perched on the grass verge, who in turn gazed back at the advancing group of horses and hounds now pouring down the drive.

"Yes, so I can see. Looks like Steve's ex-Missus and her smelly friends again. No doubt that repulsive, skinny bastard there. Keep the hounds together. We don't want them catching anything nasty, should they bite him!"

Both men grinned, each hating the notorious Pearson.

"Yes Sir," replied Martin, wishing the anti's would just leave them alone for once in a while. They'd approached the end of the drive and all thirty-seven hounds were beginning to fan out onto the sugar beet field opposite the farm entrance, sniffing and searching, but awaiting Martin's command.

"Martin," yelled Reggie. "Don't go right as planned. Track left up the road at a good trot for a mile. We'll go around Yew Tree Wood then come back here later. That'll give the tossers a good run. See how fit our anti friends are!"

Martin grinned at the smiling Reggie, nodding in acknowledgement, calling the hounds, turning them left and then breaking into a trot. Reggie followed on, cracking his hunting whip to move on a few idle, sniffing hounds.

The four antis were a hundred yards from the farm entrance, proceeding at a steady walk towards the drive. Izzy knew the routine and expected the hounds to turn in towards them and search the beet for an early hare and chase. However, she saw Martin and Reggie suddenly break into a trot, turning away.

"Bastards!" exclaimed Izzy, with the other jogging antis behind her.

Martin glanced back at the four anti's, who'd just run past the end of the driveway. The remainder of the mounted field, led by Steve, were about to exit. The antis glanced at the mass of horses and rising bodies heading for them, but continued their pursuit after the lead hunters and hounds.

The antis, led by Izzy, caught up with Reggie and Martin, and gazed at the hounds, spilling out between the two fields, along the road and grass verges.

"Morning Martin," yelled a puffing Izzy, as she began jogging alongside him and Bert. "See you are both looking as sexy as ever," she smiled cheekily.

Martin flushed, grinned and simply touched the peak of his cap with his whip in a polite, yet silent gesture. Aware of his position, he turned away, cracking the whip at the hounds, whilst using a bit more leg to push on his mount, trying to ignore Izzy and look professional before an annoyed Reggie.

"Good Morning Miss Harrison. Come to grace us with your presence?" Reggie called, voice booming, peering down at Izzy from his mount Samson.

"Morning Reg," Izzy replied with a fake, patronising smile, knowing he hated the shortened, common version of his name. "Yes, we're going to see if we can piss up your day and save some poor hares from your needless slaughter."

"Tut, Tut! Such language! Your manners have certainly gone downhill since Steve decided to rid you from his life. I hope you all have a very tiring and wasted day. Farewell and good day!" Reggie responded with a wicked grin, but also touched his cap, then kicked on his horse, proceeding past Izzy.

Izzy replied with a single fingered salute behind his back, as he trotted off.

Dave, jogging a few feet away, caught the banter, feeling a mixed sense of jealousy and anger at Izzy's playful actions. "Which way should we head?"

"It's obvious the bastards are going to try and out-run us this morning."

Izzy turned to see the whole of the mounted field of about forty riders now pouring up the road, advancing at a fast trot. She stopped and stepped up onto the verge, letting Dave and the two newfound lovers catch up.

"Let's just let this lot go past," began Izzy, "I think they might be doing a full circle to lose us, and will come back here, but I'm not too sure. Just wait."

She re-gained some breath and Dave stood with hands on hips, regarding with contempt the rapidly advancing group of pompous horses and riders.

"I'm not sure what the crafty sods are up to today, so may be best to get one of the cars. Lets' see for a few minutes when the field comes," Izzy added.

Dave nodded as the mounted field filled the road, three or four abreast. Leading them, positioned centrally within the road like General, sat Steve Harrison, astride Casanova. A large black horse, foam was already flying from the bit, as he powered towards them. Steve beamed at the figures standing on the verge as he approached, looking directly at Izzy, his eyes twinkling.

Izzy scowled back as best she could without smiling, although inwardly felt the usual stab of bitter jealousy, knowing she wasn't riding out alongside him.

"Good morning darling." Steve hollered with a smile. "Wonderful crisp day. Care to hop on board Casanova and make a three-some for old time's sake? It'd save wearing out those lovely legs of yours! You look hot!" He grinned.

Steve now level, trotted past on the massive horse. The ex-couple peered at each other, as Steve puckered his lips and blew out a kiss as he passed.

"Go screw yourself Steve," Izzy yelled, glaring falsely, her face suppressing a smile, aware of Dave's burning eyes close behind. "You'd better look after Casanova," she added. "He's a good horse. Was one of the best. Make sure you don't fuck him up, like you do with most of the things in your life!"

As he passed, Steve turned in the saddle. Looking back, he cheekily grinned.

"You know I treat my horses just like my women dear!" He hollered with a full hearty laugh. "Ride them hard and then give them a jolly good whipping!"

Steve turned around to face the road and hounds ahead, then disappeared from Izzy's view, lost in a mass of horses and bobbing riders flowing on behind. The various coloured horses and smartly-clad riders filled the narrow road, the clattering hooves and puffing horses, mixed with riders chatter and the clank of colliding stirrups, all added to the frenzy of sight and sound.

Izzy flushed and scowled at the passing field as they rode by, some politely ignoring her, eyes focussed ahead, others glancing down in disgust. However, many others smiled or nodded, knowing her from past days and still friends.

Chris, riding on the outside of the pack, caught her eye as he approached and smiled, having known and respected her for years. He nodded politely.

"Morning Chris, see you've got Cirrus out," Izzy called as he approached on his grey mare, Izzy's smile genuine. "And you're looking as smart as ever!"

"Morning Izzy, thank you," Chris replied with a blush, then grinned. "She's going as good as ever, just like when you used to event her. Good days."

Tracey and Julie, riding aside Chris, looked straight ahead, ignoring Izzy. Tracey, head still buzzing from too much drink, bit her tongue, wanting to make a sarcastic comment, but thought and knew better, and knew Chris still respected Izzy. His reply was quickly lost as he and the other riders swiftly trotting on by, before he was lost from view in the mass of trotting horses, their hooves clattering noisily along the road. In less than a minute, all forty horses and their smartly dressed, bobbing riders, had passed, leaving only white scuffmarks on the black tarmac as evidence of their presence.

"We'll wait to see which way they head, but I think we need to grab a car," spoke Dave after the horses had all passed, trying to gain some control, uncomfortable with how he'd seen Izzy and Steve exchange grinning glances.

"I'll go and get my car if you want," Dave continued, feeling they may get left behind and wanting a decision made and some action taken, sensing he was the only truly serious Anti out, noting Guy and Wendy tittering together.

"Okay Dave," Izzy agreed, seeing the horses rapidly move away and hearing the sound of various vehicles, driven by the car followers, rapidly approaching from behind. "Run back and grab your car. Catch us up on the way."

With that Dave clambered up the bank and ran across the field, heading back towards where their two cars were parked. He scowled venomously at the car followers, who were now exiting the farm drive and proceeding up the road.

They shook their heads in disgust at the anti as he ran straight across the field, carelessly damaging the sugar beet leaves as he tried unsuccessfully to run between the wet glistening tops of the root crop. The flotilla of 4 x 4's and other mud splattered vehicles, including Anna's, proceeded slowly up the single-track road, a few hundred yards behind the now disappearing horses.

"We'll keep going and Dave can catch us up," Izzy called to Guy and Wendy. "I think they are going to do a quick full circle, try to lose us, and then come straight back on this field whilst we're still running about trying to find them. But we can't be too sure, so lets go on ahead, just in case I'm wrong."

It was a common trick of Martin and Reggie's. In order to lose any anti's, they would often change the planned route at the last second, which in this case was originally to hunt directly onto the sugar beet fields opposite Ernie Cole's farm. They would trot off for several miles, often in a circle, and attempt to wear down or lose the anti's, before returning back to where they originally intended to hunt, hopefully without any antis to interfere with them.

Izzy was sure this was their tactic today and knew they could come straight back within ten minutes. However, they could alternatively hunt a totally different piece of land and return back here on the homeward leg. Either way, she dare not risk losing the mounted field as it could take an age to find.

It always amazed her how easy it was to lose forty horses and riders and a pack of forty baying hounds. But it was. It sounds ludicrous to those who've never hunted, but was very easy, especially if the hounds are in full flight and the riders move off and into a wood, past a hedge, or ride at speed over a rise in the land and onto another field where there are no roads nearby.

She had often lost contact with the mounted field and pack herself, both as a rider when out on a slow horse, and again as an anti. Often the saving grace to locate them is the call of the hounds or Martin's horn blaring across the countryside as guidance. Hence why Dave went back for the car, whilst they carried on in pursuit as best they could. At worst, she could track the scuffed hoof prints on the tarmac or soil and try to guess where they might head, with Izzy's knowledge of the area in general and where they could hunt.

Izzy had hoped more would be out today to help them, expecting at least five other supporters to join them and make up the numbers and thus cover more ground. But as usual, they'd been let down last minute. Not all of their anti companions were as keen as Izzy or Dave. It took a lot to get up from your bed on a chilly Saturday morning, to then run about the cold countryside.

The mounted field moved quickly down the road, vanishing, being obscured by the high banks of the narrow twisting lane. Although she knew Ernie Cole's land well, and the usual places Martin and Reggie would hunt, she also knew there was a lot of land to hunt, including a number of woods. If they lost sight of the mounted field early, they could be playing catch up all day.

Izzy heard the engines of the main group of car followers growling behind, likewise keeping in touch with the riders, to ensure they too didn't lose track. She moved to the side of the road along with her two colleagues, as the first few cars cautiously passed, faces scowling, then followed by a fleet of others.

Joyce, sitting in the front of the car with Anna saw the jogging figures ahead, unsure who they were, but soon guessed from their conversations.

"Don't run them over," Joyce spoke, seeing Dave dashing across the field. "They all look very aggressive." She turned to look at Anna, who was pensive. Suzie, seated in the back, was leaning forward, her face a beaming smile.

Dave, jogging across the beet field, scowled at the car followers, coldly eyeing each of them up with his usual disgust. 'Pathetic,' he mused, then recognised the attractive blond woman 4 x 4 driver from earlier look at him nervously. He glared hard, just as his foot hit a massive beet top, causing him to trip.

"Oh that's Izzy!" Suzie suddenly announced from the rear of Anna's car, smirking at Dave's misfortune. Her grinning face drifted away from Dave and back to the long-haired anti running further ahead in the road. Anna regarded Suzie in the mirror, as she looked excitedly, but nervously, at the three antis, now drawing level with their slow moving car. Anna half watched the road, and half watched the antis, of whom she'd heard dreadful stories, as she also tried to keep close to the vehicle ahead. The three figures, jogging along the edge of the road, drew closer, with Anna ever wary of their presence.

Seated behind her, Suzie suddenly wound her window down and leant out.

"Yo, Izzy dude!" she called, hanging out of the window. "What're you doing you old bag? Get out the bloody way! Get oof mee land!"

Anna and Joyce froze as Suzie waved out of the window, apparently yelling insults at the tall blond anti who looked towards Anna's car with steel eyes.

Anna clenched her buttocks, wondering what on earth their new acquaintance in the back was doing; seemingly openly inviting trouble from the three antis running ahead. Joyce swung around to stare nervously at Anna, who looked at Suzie in the mirror with fixed eyes, waiting for serious trouble.

The blond anti, Anna now knew as Izzy, turned around. She gazed coldly at the approaching car and especially rear passenger, hanging out of the window.

"You look out of puff. Too much shagging you old cow!" Suzie hollered.

The bonnet of the 4 x 4 was now level with the antis. Anna tensed up, waiting for her windscreen to be smashed by a flint or the doors kicked in.

"Do you want a lift?" Suzie called, now level with the tall blond anti.

"Suzie, Hi!" Izzy happily replied, peering down towards the window, smiling broadly and greeting the shouting person in the rear like a friend. She was.

"I'd love a lift, but think I might get you and your friends into trouble!"

Izzy and Suzie chuckled, as Anna eased the car up slightly, enabling the two woman to chat, realising that Suzie clearly knew the Anti, called Izzy, well.

"Unfortunately I think you're right. Especially as this is Anna's first meet. She's our driver," Suzie announced, pointing at Anna. "I don't think she dares upset Reggie, nor wants to get banned from the Shoteton by associating with the likes of you, before she even started hunting." Suzie chuckled.

Izzy looked in at the driver of the vehicle, who glanced sideways, nervously smiling back at the blond anti, unsure how to react. Anna noticed her stunning looks and long pigtail hanging from behind her baseball cap.

Anna caught Izzy's eyes and a strange feeling passed between them. She flicked her eyes back to the road, then back at Izzy, and felt a connection.

For some reason she was sure somehow their paths would strangely cross.

A shudder ran down her spine as she absorbed Izzy's features, she in turn, with a steely gaze, weighed up Anna, almost ignoring Joyce. The blonde Anti, although seemingly friendly, looked a force to be reckoned with. Anna smiled vainly, and to her surprise, Izzy nodded and respectfully smiled back. Then, half an eye on the road, she looked away, still jogging alongside Anna's slow moving vehicle, turning her attention back towards Suzie in the rear window.

"Are you still at John's yard?" Izzy asked, Anna noticing the cars piling up behind her and the gap ahead growing, slowly losing touch with the vehicles.

"Yes. You'll have to come and visit. John won't mind. You know him, laid-back as ever." Suzie called back, Izzy disappearing, raising her hand, waving at her old friend, as Anna gently pressed on the accelerator and moved away.

"I will," Izzy called loudly as the other vehicles now slowly passed, obscuring Anna's 4 x 4 from her view as they rounded a high-banked bend in the road.

"Who on earth was that", enquired Anna as she suddenly sped forward in order to catch up to the other stream of vehicles ahead, secretly glad to be clear of the antis and any potential trouble, although all had seemed well.

"Izzy. Isabelle actually, to be posh. She used to be Isabelle Harrison. Our Field Master Steve's former wife." Suzie began to explain. "He's the flash guy riding the big black horse at the front. Casanova. Very apt! Izzy used to hunt with us. Great rider, but she's now an anti. Shame really. I used to ride with her all the time. Great fun and we got on really well together. Still do, but we don't see too much of each other now. Pity what happened between her and Steve, as secretly I think they both still really love each other. Great pair."

Joyce, intrigued by the brief conversation, and always one for gossip, turned in her seat and faced her newfound friend and asked Suzie to fully explain.

Suzie happily began to tell the familiar and now famous tale of how Izzy caught Steve in bed with his two grooms and about their subsequent bitter separation after all of the press coverage and prison. Anna, half watching the road, cocked her ear, and listened both shocked and amused to the tale Suzie them told so beautifully about Steve and Izzy; and in full graphic detail.

Joyce chuckled, even more convinced horsey people were simply sex mad.

Anna regained contact with the other car followers just ahead and the stream of vehicles snaked along the road, getting closer behind the mounted field, all of whom were moving ahead at a good pace, with Reggie, Martin and all of the excitable hounds moving fifty yards ahead of the pack of riders, some drifting into the margins and edges of the fields, noses to the ground.

Meanwhile, Suzie began recanting further torrid tales about hunting and its dubious participants, to Joyce's' keen ears and grinning face, whilst inwardly Anna was reeling with shock, wondering what she'd become involved in.

Further back down the road, and heavily panting, Izzy, Guy and Wendy realised they were fighting a losing battle. The mounted field had trotted off at pace for about half a mile and then hit some stubble and cantered off, the whole pack disappearing past some hedges, to be lost from sight. The rest of the car followers had passed the three jogging anti's and sped off in pursuit of the other cars and the mounted field and pack of hounds, which had quickly covered a great deal of ground, exactly as Martin seemingly planned.

Luckily Izzy knew Ernie Cole's land well and the area's they would hunt. She decided to call a halt and all three of them squatted down by the side of the road to regain their breath and wait for Dave to arrive with his car, hoping the battered wreck would actually start. Their faces flushed, Guy and Wendy chattered, whilst Izzy scanned the horizon for Dave's car or a rampaging pack of hounds and thundering horses, knowing anything could happen when hunting; in that a rogue hare could turn and bring the whole pack back to them in seconds. But the countryside went quiet and as they paused, their pulses eased and the initial wave of excitement and disappointment passed.

Izzy recalled Steve. It was with the usual mix of excitement and jealousy.

She silently peered down at the damp grass, lost in her thoughts recalling his grinning face and joking words when the sound of an old chugging engine appeared to disturb her. Dave, in the car, leered over the dashboard as he drove his battered Ford up the road to pick them up, raising a hand to wave.

Izzy sighed inwardly, but them smiled and waved back, as best as she could.

She called over to the two new lovers to gain their attention, a smile on her own face, recalling when she was so happy. So long ago it seemed.

Rising up, scanning the land in the distance, she moved towards Dave's car.

She was only just warming up and was ready for a good day.

Finger-crossed it wouldn't disappoint.

But it would.

Chapter 23

Victory is reserved for those who are willing to pay the price.

Sun Tzu

After their initial burst to lose the Antis, the mounted field moved onto a field of drilled winter wheat, the small bright green shoots just beginning to show through, adding colour to the damp chocolate brown soil. Steve led the now steaming pack of horses down the side of the field, keeping close to the edges and small grass headland, so as to not damage the crop. The soil was soft, making the going slow, before crossing a grass headland and moving onto another identical field that ran parallel with the road. Fifty yards ahead, moving diagonally straight across the middle of the field, striking and bold in their bright red jackets, rode Reggie and Martin. The hounds, trotting a few yards ahead, noses to the ground, searched for any scent. The privilege of being the Huntsman and Master, and the fact there was only the pair of them, permitted them to ride wherever they wanted to search their quarry.

Martin looked across the field, seeing numerous car followers parked up along the road, the occasional body propped up upon a bonnet, but no one running on foot. He yelled over to Reggie, riding twenty yards to his right.

"Seems we've lost our company, for the time being. Too fast for them!"

Reggie nodded. "Lets hope it stays that way. Head over onto that field," he indicated with his whip. "We can get in a few more fields and hopefully get onto a scent. Put something up for some entertainment before the bastards suss out where we are heading," he added. Martin nodded to acknowledge, then flicked the thong of his whip at a straggling hound to encourage it on.

"Izzy isn't daft. She'll quickly find us on Ernie's land." Martin replied.

Upon reaching the end of the wide field they tracked right, their mounts effortlessly leaping over a small ditch separating the fields, it bringing them into the middle of a field of un-ploughed stubble. The hounds followed and leapt the shallow ditch, some of the younger hounds stopping momentarily for a quick drink, lapping up the stagnant but refreshing water, before being yelled at by an impatient Martin, keen to get them moving on and working.

Meanwhile the mounted field, led by Steve, and following a field behind, with a wood to their rear, headed along the edge of the drill, until they too reached the ditch. Steve pointed Casanova at the three-foot wide gap and squeezed his ankles, his mount easily hopping across and landing safely onto the opposing stubble field without a second thought. Steve noted Martin and Reggie ahead, some two hundred yards away on the left-hand side, so trotted away to his right, aiming to bring the mounted field around on the opposite flack.

One by one the riders followed Steve, their horses leaping the small ditch, and all landing safely onto the stubble the other side. Each rider then excitedly pushed their mounts on, enjoying any excuse for a canter across the brief piece of stubble to catch up to Steve, who in turn headed towards the bottom of the field at a gentle canter, to draw parallel with Martin and Reggie.

The large rectangular-shaped un-ploughed field of stubble was flanked on the right and the bottom by a dense mixed deciduous wood, some trees retaining their fading yellow and brown leaves, but many trees were already stark and bare, providing a dense backdrop to the field. At the end of the field, a glossy black crow, pecking at the soil, noted the fast approaching intruders, as the hounds scuttled about to one side and Steve moved at speed on the woodland edge. With a few swift beats of its wings, the crow rose, swiftly flanked sideways, to disappear amongst the trees, resting on a tall branch, to silently observe. As more riders approached the ditch separating the two fields, many began to bunch up, as some horses refused, blocking progress. Their frantic riders kicked and cajoled their mounts, flapping reins and making numerous clicking sounds, often accompanied by the occasional severe slap of a whip.

All were desperate to swiftly get over the small obstacle, both to save face and embarrassment before their fellow more capable riders, but importantly, to not lose the fast moving field. Those luckily clearing the ditch made their way over onto the stubble, racing on towards Steve, the ground firm but giving, the push on an excuse for an early canter, as many riders quickly followed on behind Steve and Casanova. His massive hooves kicked up huge divots, the clods flying past several riders faces as they closed in behind.

From the roadside, the car followers noted the change of ground and pulled over to the side of the road, excitedly watching the mix of horses and hounds fanning out across the distant field and canter across the unploughed stubble.

Anna, following behind a Range Rover pulled her Nissan onto the small piece of verge and quickly exited the vehicle, looking on in awe at the mass of horses thundering across open country, along with a few stragglers still trying to cross the ditch. Suzie jumped out and stood alongside her, soaking up the image, sadly wishing her horse was sound and could be amongst them. Joyce decided to stay inside the warmth of the car to watch, confused by it all. Anna gazed at the riders jumping the small ditch, itching to be out amongst them.

She could see Steve riding ahead and leading the way on the far side, the dark wood a backdrop to the bright red jacket, his huge black horse blending in the scene. Looking through the crowd she tried to make out Tracey, Chris and the others, scanning the blur of horses and riders. Chris on Cirrus was easy to see, despite several other greys being ridden out, the white coats of the horses bright against the dark woods. She then spotted Julie close behind, Bonnie easy to see in her mix of brown and white, then Tracey on Fred, all clearing the ditch together with ease, happily cantering across the stubble, appearing to be laughing, their faces beaming with excitement, pushing on their mounts.

Steve and the first wave of riders had slowed to a trot, drawing level with Martin and the hounds on the far side and now approaching the end of the field, the large ancient woods towering about them. The remaining riders cantered down to catch up, many pulling hard on their reins to stop.

Watching, Anna's heart felt heavy, yearning to be out there onboard Penny; to be part of something traditional, yet also dangerous and exciting. She suddenly felt eyes looking at her and turned her head to see Suzie staring, her round face smiling at Anna. Anna blushed as Suzie grinned.

"You wish you were out there, don't you?" she said knowingly. "I do."

Suzie's own gaze drifted longingly across the field, like a lover looking out to sea, remembering someone lost in a storm, her gazing matching Anna's.

"Yes," replied Anna, gazing onwards. "I've never hunted, but it looks great. So natural, so free, and such fun. But obviously dangerous. I'd poo myself!"

"I doubt you would," said Suzie with a chuckle, her eyes following the horses. I wish I was out there. Once you've ridden out, it's terrible watching. Good fun, but never the same. You're always itching to be out there. It's the adrenaline buzz. Very addictive. You'll have to ensure you ride out when you move your horse to Chris's yard. He's a great and will look after you."

"Thank you," Anna replied, touched by the kindness. "I just hope he'll have me at his yard. Everyone seems to assume so, but he must have a list of other people first. I'd love to go to Horsewater, but I can't assume anything."

"Oh I think you're fairly safe," Suzie replied, smiling, as if knowing a secret."

The sound of hounds breaking into a high-pitched yelp drew their attention back to the field, as the hounds streamed in unison over the stubble, heading back the way they'd come, but running parallel to the road. Reggie and Martin turned their mounts on a sixpence and thundered on behind. With reins held high in one hand, kicking hard, Martin lifted the hunting horn to his lips and with his other hand blew hard. The horn's haunting blare drifted over the field, the sound raising the hairs on Anna's neck, her eyes widening.

"They're on!" yelled Suzie excitedly. "Look, just there at the front of the hounds, you can see the hare. A small brown dot but coming here. Get on!"

Anna looked at the fast-moving hounds, unsure what she was watching, seeing only a mass of changing colour, then she scanned the rough ground slightly ahead of the hounds. Suddenly she saw a large brown ball of fur skipping nibbling across the stubble, seemingly only a few yards in front of the lead hounds and heading in a straight line towards the other far end of the field and grass headland, the hounds closing in. Instantly the hare changed course, jinking sharp left, throwing off the lead hounds, one hound trying to turn too quickly rolling over on the stubble with a whimper, another too.

The slower hounds arced left in eager pursuit, closely followed by Martin and Reggie, now racing at full gallop, huge clumps of soil being thrown up from the hooves of Bert and Samson, the black and grey horses a stark contrast.

Steve and the mounted field turned and closed in, racing in a line across the stubble, but still fifty yards behind Martin. Some riders frantically hauled on the reins, trying to control their excited mounts, also in full gallop, threatening to overtake Steve; which is a hunting sin, but usually forgivable with Steve.

On the hare raced, three hundred yards away, heading straight towards the road, the small ditch and field of drill all that separated it from the group of roadside spectators. Most had exited their vehicles upon hearing the blare of the horn, knowing what it meant. Others noted the sudden excitement and opened car doors to see, including Joyce, who looked on strangely fascinated, noticing the hare race ahead of the hounds, silently willing it to escape.

The hare reached the ditch and flew over it in one bound, but with two hounds close on its tail. The hounds faltered slightly, one stumbling and sliding into the murky waters with a resounding splash and yelp, the second and several others close behind, covering the ditch in an easy leap and on.

The hare continued on, now moving across the second part of drilled wheat, over which Martin and Reggie had ridden only a few minutes earlier. The hare headed straight for the road and collection of parked vehicles lining the verge, the occupants of which looked on in awe at the amazing sight before them of life and death speed. The hare seemed blind to the hounds presence, its focus on the safety of the field of sugar beet opposite, separated only by the road.

In silent awe the crowd watched as Reggie and Martin hammered their horses in hot pursuit behind the hounds, the hare still well ahead and clear of the ditch, towards which Martin and Reggie returned once more. Martin blew once more on his horn, reins in hand, face red, standing upright in the stirrups, heels kicking at Bert's flanks, as the ditch approached. Bert leapt clean over, landing deep in the soft soil of the drill opposite, heavily dipping his nose, but was skilfully recovered one-handed by Martin, who hauled up on the reins, then with a kick, pushed the massive horse onward.

Reggie followed on some ten yards behind, more cautious, his mount Samson taking the ditch with a steadier leap, landing safely on the opposite side. Reggie turned in his saddle, hollering an instruction across to Steve, who was closing in too, with about thirty galloping horses and riders in hot pursuit.

Steve hauled on Casanova's reins, pulling up yards from the ditch, the massive horse blowing hard as he dug his hooves into the soil. Foam sprayed from its black mouth as it gyrated on its hocks, reluctant to stop, but he did.

Steve raised his hand, the mounted field behind seemingly all knowing what to do, pulling frantically at keen horses, many of which also spun on their hocks to turn, instinctively wanting to join the chase, but all now restrained.

Stopping in a line before the ditch, they watched as the hare raced on across the drill, and then on at speed towards the road. The brown ball of fur skipped through the green shoots of winter wheat, with tiny sprays of loose soil thrown up from its long, but nibble feet, the stream of hounds close behind, the hare's massive ears flicking back, large eyes aware of its pursuer.

Anna's senses buzzed as she watched silently with Suzie beside her, a natural, almost primeval hunting instinct flowing through them, as they and the many others spread along the roadside, watched the battle of one against many.

The action was mixed with the sound of the wailing horn and cry of forty baying hounds, all rapidly approaching the road. Anna felt a mix of shock, awe and excitement combined in a strange manner, where inward she willed the hare to win, as the hounds appeared to close in on their dashing quarry.

Then the hare seemed to change gear, and without effort, put on an extra spurt, racing away from the lead hound, accelerating at speed and moving swiftly over the soil, the hounds flooding on behind and yelps growing louder as they tried to close in. But the hare was well ahead, and moving quicker, now only a hundred yards from the road, where the spectators excitement rose and loud hearty cheers began to rise from the former silent observers.

Unseen, a battered Ford Fiesta zoomed along the road and raced past the car followers, heavily screeching to a halt in the middle of the road. The doors flew open and Izzy leapt out, followed by Dave, who over-dramatically, in TV Cop style, slid over the bonnet of the car to join her at the verge. The road followers turned momentarily to regard the new spectators with bitter disgust, before ignoring them and switching their attention back to the chase before them, the hare and hounds only fifty yards away and closing very fast.

Izzy instantly assessed the situation. Her experienced eyes scanned the field, taking everything in, looking at hunters, hounds and hare, then swiftly at the field of wet, glistening sugar beet behind them. Her face broke into a smile.

Exiting from the back seats, Guy and Wendy clambered slowly out the car, their senses alert, now ready for some real action, waiting for orders.

"Leave it. Let it run!" yelled Izzy, seeing Dave about to run into the field to intercept both the hare and hounds. He turned momentarily to question her.

It was a common, if dangerous trick of the antis. They'd often intervene between the hounds, quarry and even the horses, by jumping forward towards the hare and hounds when they were on a run, or cut in-between. The hare would often run past, or jink wildly off course, and the hounds become distracted by the waving and yelling of the humans; whom they obeyed. Even when in full flight, it being the way Martin maintained such control.

However, it was this fate that befell Midge. He'd leapt out in front of a pack chasing a hare, but a bit too late. Steve Harrison was close the pack of hounds and 'unable to stop in time.' So simply rode straight over the top of Midge.

'Accidentally,' of course, the Field Master sadly claimed in court, full of fake remorse, whilst Midge's battered body was still recovering, heavily bandaged.

Dave scowled at Izzy upon hearing her cry at stopping his potential act of heroism before their new recruits and more importantly, before the whole field. Unsure of her reasoning, he accepted as a loyal, subservient Lieutenant, but in reality wanted to be the Captain. Maybe even a General. One day.

"Let it run on," Izzy repeated, seeing Dave's doubting and ever-shifty stare. "It'll clear this field and cross over. They can't hunt the land opposite." She spun around as she spoke, pointing to the beet field on the opposing side.

"It's Mike Adam's land. He hates Reggie! No hunting there!" Izzy yelled.

Dave scanned the scene, about to comment, but remained silent with the hare only yards from them. She was right, as she always seemed to be.

Reggie and Martin thundered across the drilled field, hounds streaming well ahead in full cry, Martin blowing on his horn, but a different tune.

Steve turned and now led the mounted field across the bottom edge of the stubble on the opposite side of the drilled field, moving tangentially to Reggie and Martin, in a vain hope some of the road followers might scare the hare back towards them onto their field, so they in turn could bring it back around into the path of the hounds, knowing all too well what Izzy already knew.

Steve was ever the master tactician, but today was too late and out of luck.

True to what Izzy said, the hare ran straight out of the field of drill, mounting the small grass verge, ignored the bemused group of on-lookers within the followers and ran unhindered straight across the road. None of the followers tried to stop its progress, sensing the sport, and the athletic brown beast was gone in a second, running on into the beet field opposite, disappearing into a mass of wet dark green leaves, only a brief clatter of the leaves flapping a clue.

Anna looked on in silent awe, surprised at the size of the hare as it passed by her in a flash, but yards away. In that moment she absorbed the brightness of its coat; a mix of black and soft yellow tinges, it's large black-tipped ears, and most stunningly, in that brief moment, absorbed the image of its huge eyes - a startling yellow and brown. Joyce watched too and smiled, cheering inside.

Within seconds the lead hounds began pouring across the road, a number running straight on into the beet field, yelping and still pursuing their quarry. Martin, behind, frantically blew upon his horn again to recall the hounds.

Now was the anti's time and moment of glory. Izzy and Dave leapt forward, frantically waving arms and calling at the pack of hounds, distracting them. Confused, and with the scent lost, most of the hounds suddenly stopped in the road, leaping about excitedly at the attention. A small number ran on into the beet, following the hare, but the chase was over and the pack broken up.

Guy looked on puzzled, seeing some hounds running on into the beet field, still searching for the hare, unsure what he and Wendy should do. Keen to be part of the action, he joined Izzy and Dave, waving his arms vainly at the mud-splattered hounds, some of which playfully leapt amongst them. Wendy was a bit more hesitant, wary of the wet, dirty and smelly pack around her.

"I thought you said they couldn't hunt on there?" Guy yelled to Izzy above her calls to the hounds. Izzy was too busy to reply, caught up in the noise and chaos of about twenty-five hounds racing about the road, looking for some guidance. But seconds later Martin answered Guy's question to Izzy.

Martin, well ahead of Reggie, clattered onto the road, Bert's shoes skidding on the black tarmac, leaving white scuff marks. Martin blew hard on his horn, this tone different to that of a few moments ago. With a sweaty Bert clattering about on the narrow road, he yelled loudly between blasts on his horn, calling the few loose, hare-chasing hounds back to him. Reggie, red-faced, joined him on the road, moving along, slightly away from the cars, clearly annoyed.

But neither hunter moving forward onto the land onto which the hare had fled and a few hounds had strayed. The scarlet-clad pair remained solidly on the road and within the boundaries they knew they could hunt, not daring to enter the field out of a mix of hunting respect and fear of the owner.

Amazingly, the hounds within the beet, responding to the horn, stopped their advance and somewhat reluctantly began moving about near the edge of the field, before returning to the hunters. Martin hollered and continued blowing, until the entire pack had rejoined them. Here, the pack of damp, muddy and sweaty hounds milled around Bert's hooves, sniffing at the new scents discovered around the roadside, including the road followers and antis.

Izzy looked at Guy and grinned. He smiled back, amazed by the scene.

"They've never been allowed to hunt that land," Izzy proclaimed proudly. "So I knew they'd have to blow up for the hounds to come back once the hare crossed over and entered safe ground. One nil to us I think. Result."

"Looks like you lost that one Reg!" Izzy yelled playfully over to Reggie, who turned away, ignoring her. Red-faced and scowling he called at various hound.

"Antis one, Wankers nil!" Dave joyously proclaimed even louder.

Reggie bitterly dismissed them, all earlier humour gone. He turned his mount Samson around and called abruptly to Martin, as the pair of hunters muttered quietly about their next move. With the hounds closely bunched together around them, eager noses sniffing at the verge edges, the pair guided the pack along the road and back up towards a field entrance where Steve was bringing his group out from the freshly drilled wheat and about the join them.

Anna looked on in awe at the scene, amazed at the skill with which Martin collected all the hounds together so quickly. One moment forty hounds were racing wildly across a field in full pursuit of their quarry and then moments later the pack of hounds were collected about him, moving in an orderly pack up the road; sniffing and seemingly unconcerned, as if nothing had happened.

The group of anti's stood proudly on the road, watching defiantly as the defeated army of horses and hounds retreated, proceeding along the road, a sense of loss and bitter defeat written upon their faces. Martin and Reggie's voices were subdued, but all knew the day was young and they'd soon be ready to find another hare to chase, and next time, hopefully be victorious.

The antis, especially Dave, smugly regarded the road followers now returning to their vehicles with a satisfied scowl, safe in the knowledge that at least one more hare would be around for another day. Some glared silently at him.

Izzy looked at the group of car followers, who gazed back at her group with mixed feelings. Many with anger, bitter at their cocky and disruptive nature, with the majority simply trying to ignore them. Even Suzie in this instance changed her demeanour and ignored Izzy. Most drivers returned to their warm vehicles, and away from their enemy's gloating gaze. Stationary, Anna's gaze along the narrow road seemingly met Izzy's. She looked straight back at Anna, expressionless, the look deep; either a strange bond or future conflict seemingly building between the pair, neither knowing which or why or when.

Anna turned, breaking the contact, and returned to her car. As the cars began to move away, Anna followed suit, no one speaking, until Joyce spoke up.

"Well that was exciting. Great fun. But I'm glad that rabbit escaped!"

Anna and Suzie roared with laughter, as Anna turned and grinned broadly at her mother as they drove away, following the stream of vehicles before her, unsure where they were heading or what the rest of the day would bring.

For another hour, the time was mixed with periods of watching events from a distance, as hounds and riders milled about from field to field; sometimes at a walk, other times at a canter or full gallop. Or they'd drive about, gazing at empty fields and distant woodlands, trying to find the pack. In these times, where the whole mounted field and forty hounds vanished, the only hint they were about would be the distant sound of Martin's horn, or the tell-tale sign of horseshoe markings in field entrances or scuff marks on the road.

When they caught sight of them all they'd watch the hunt move onto a new field, the hounds search out their quarry, with the mounted field following.

Occasionally a hare would appear and the hounds give chase, speaking loudly with excited yelps, as they raced seemingly over or through almost anything, steadfast in the instinctive pursuit of their quarry. But the clever hares seemed to be one step ahead, always managing to escape, and at times the hare appeared to almost play with the hounds; suddenly putting on an extra spurt or changing direction, just as it seemed it'd be caught by the lead hounds.

Suzie was great company, knowing the area well, and guided Anna along countless roads or farm tracks, although usually they followed other vehicles following, the numbers of which noticeably waned after about an hour.

Behind the hounds at all times were Reggie and Martin, urging them with horns when in pursuit or off track, or cracking whips when at a walk, to move the pack along and keep order. For short periods they'd lose all the hounds completely, as the pack raced off into various fields or woods, the Whipper-In's racing about to catch up the lost hounds and bring the pack together.

The mounted field, skilfully led by Steve, followed at a distance; either behind the pack, on a flank or even on an adjoining field, in case a hare was set up and ran through. Often the riders would be seen heading off at lightening speed down a field, road or track, trying to anticipate where the hounds would end up, planning to cut off the route of their quarry and steer it back towards the hounds, the red-faced and excited riders happily following Steve.

Each time the mounted field moved off and out of sight, the car followers would leap into their vehicles and chase in hot pursuit, trying to work out which way the hunt would go next; following wherever actually possible, often down dirt tracks. Travel was dependant on the type of vehicle driven or the driver's bravery or stupidity. Several 4 x 4's went off road, mud spraying from behind their vehicles, Anna enjoying a few such scary moments herself, much to Suzie's joy and Joyce's horror, telling her 'not to damage her car!'

Sometimes the followers would meet the mud-splattered mounted field head on, sweating horses pouring down tight country lanes, passing dangerously close to the cars. Anna winced each time a rider's boot and stirrup missed the car body or the mirrors by inches, as the walked, trotted or even cantered past, with seemingly scant concern to who or what else was about.

Hooves would slide on roads, sparks flying from shoes. The occasional rider would fall, the loose horse collected by anyone close and the rider safely reunited. The pace was frantic and seemingly chaotic, but the rider's faces as they passed, always displayed smiles of pure excitement and enjoyment.

Anna looked on in amazement, as the riders seemed to break every rule in the 'Riding School Handbook.' She'd been taught to ride 'properly' by good instructors and everything these riders undertook seemingly broke all of these rules. But this displayed how good the riders were and also how fit and controlled the horses and riders were too. But Anna also began to appreciate the wonderful sight of horses and hounds working together in unison, guided by Martin and Reggie; she was enchanted at how smoothly the pack of hounds responded so willingly to the pair with each simple command.

For some riders the pace was too great, or their horses, or indeed their own bodies, too old or not fit enough to cope with the frantic pace, dangerous ground or heavy going. These small groups or pairs of riders would often be seen drifting away from the main pack, chatting as they walked along, then trotting along at various points to meet up with the main pack, as the group zigzagged from one field to the other, the riders seemingly aware of where they'd meet up again, or unconcerned, just enjoying the company of those around and the great ground over which they could freely ride.

Anna gazed in envy at the brightly coloured, although now mud-splattered riders and dirty, sweating horses, each time they passed. Seeing the smiles on their muddy faces, enjoying the cheeky comments from Tracey, brief waves from Julie, and polite nods from Chris as they passed, Anna would have given anything to have joined them, and knew from then on she wanted to hunt.

Chapter 24

If you know yourself but not the enemy,
for every victory gained you will also suffer a defeat.

Sun Tzu

For the rest of the day Izzy and her small group of anti's were in and around the car followers or mixing with the mounted field, indirectly plaguing the riders who'd ride on and pretend they weren't there, and ignore them, even when they caught up and ran right alongside. Occasionally the anti's became completely separated from the mounted field, as the horses hurtled off, Izzy's group standing no chance of keeping up. But with her knowledge of the land and all the tracks and by-roads, usually within a short time, they would suddenly re-appear before Martin and Reggie, annoyingly mingling with the hounds on the fields, or moving alongside Steve and the mounted field.

They did not directly attack or verbally abuse the riders, but would call to the hounds, or simply appear on a track or stand silently alongside, annoying and pestering the hunters, who mostly viewed them with a deep bitter contempt.

Anna was surprised at how everyone seemed to simply ignore the antis most of the time. She'd been expecting direct, aggressive confrontation, abuse or even violence. But they appeared simply to annoy with their almost silent and persistent presence. They caused no direct trouble, despite even running with the hounds in the fields, where opportunity permitted. They'd often walk behind the hounds, anticipating any actions, trying to befriend the hounds and generally frustrating Martin and Reggie, before the pair moved the hounds on, where the ground allowed. For most of the time they said little, but it was the silent, passive approach that worked. Additionally, they all carried recorders and camera's, in case they were ever abused.

The members of the hunt knew this and hence the general reluctance to take direct violent action, which many, including a number of car followers, would have liked. Steve seemed less tolerant. On occasions, when the mounted field met with the antis, he'd cast the odd cheeky glance, or make the occasional playful comment at Izzy, but to the other three antis, he was very respect.

If on a track or road, he'd ride directly at them, especially Pearson, whom Anna too had noted as a more militant member, and immediately disliked.

She'd also noted, carefully watching it all, that there appeared to be genuine hatred between these two. Steve would almost seek out Dave Pearson, and the anti likewise. He'd often directly attempt to annoy Steve more than any other rider, although Dave also appeared fearful and cautious of Steve and his black mount Casanova. And rightly so. Despite the name, Casanova was a massive and very intimidating horse, especially when ridden hard by Steve.

Anna often found herself watching the actions of the anti's more than the riders, their actions intriguing. The two young and clearly novice antis seemed out of their depths, looking to Izzy and Dave for guidance all the time, with Pearson barking out instructions to where they should go. Of the four antis, Izzy was the one who seem to worry her, but she could not work out why.

Suzie was a fountain of knowledge and explained to Anna that the number of antis varied weekly. Some weeks the Shoteton hunted unbothered, with no antis present at all. On other occasions they'd muster larger numbers, often a dozen, and could be a real and sometimes aggressive nuisance, completely ruining a days hunting. To Anna, who was learning fast, it seemed the sole purpose of the antis was to simply distract the hounds, deliberately spoiling any chases, should they get onto a hare. So far they'd had limited success.

The riders, although mud-splattered, wet and tired, were always smiling whenever Anna met up with them. Any pause or break also appeared to be an excuse for someone to pull out a hipflask, which was eagerly passed around.

She'd caught Chris' eye on a few occasions and his smile had warmed her, adding encouragement to her desperately wanting to move Penny to his yard; more so now, so she could enjoy this newfound world. Tracey was as mad as ever, often racing past at speed and hollering playfully to Anna and Joyce, or sipping from a hip-flask whenever they stopped, often joined by the others.

Breaks where the field and road followers could get to meet up were sporadic and varied, sometimes lasting for a few seconds, other times for ten or more minutes, when on open areas, where they could all watch the hounds.

It was getting late in the day, the hazy sun dropping low in the greying sky, as the mounted field stopped for what might be the final well-earned rest. A number of riders had already left, drifting away, and the mounted field was beginning to thin, as less fit horses, or equally less-fit and tired riders, slowly retired and returned to the farm and boxes for an early day and return home.

Izzy's group had been temporarily lost, not seen for some time, losing touch after the field had a put in a series of long runs across some fields of set-aside. As they paused, the remaining few car followers watched the mounted field move onto a bare, flat and empty field, with no banks or ditches bordering the edges. The field dropped down on one side to a small road, upon which the half a dozen still keen road followers, including Anna, had parked up.

With a chance to have a final chat, a number of riders drifted across the field to meet up and speak with the followers by the road, exchanging sips from a variety of rapidly emptying hipflasks. Whilst chatting, eyes also watched Martin and Reggie work the hounds across the bare, fallow field. Steve, although laughing and chatting, was as ever watchful carefully for any movement on the field or any change in action or response of the hounds.

Tracey, Chris and Julie rode slowly over towards Anna's car and all three climbed out to meet them, and began speaking, asking how they were enjoying the day. Anna's beaming face was a simple and perfect response.

Chris' eyes twinkled seeing her happy, the smile on his mud-spattered face broad as he spoke directly to her, one of only a few opportunities it seemed he'd had all day. Tracey, also mud-spattered, was still full of excitement, Anna unsure if it was fuelled by adrenaline, alcohol, both, or just her nature.

A series of red-cheeked, mud-covered riders, their horses steaming, milled around. The smell of warm, sweaty horses reminded Anna why she enjoyed the sport so much, despite non-horsey people never understanding why horse owners were oblivious to the long-lingering foul stench they seemed to carry.

Whilst chatting to the group, Anna noted Lady Burlingham was still out, seated a few yards away. Amazingly, despite her mount being covered in a crispy dark foam and mud spray, she herself remained spotless, all bar for a few minor mud spots on her jodhpurs. Anna found her eyes flitting from her to Chris, before noting a red-faced, smiling Julie carefully watch her actions.

Whilst listening and talking, Chris maintained a watchful eye on Reggie and Martin still working the hounds in the middle of the stubble field. Anna also enjoyed the sight of the sniffing hounds, guided skilfully by Martin and Reggie across the barren field, their red jackets stark in the low light. Suddenly Chris caught sight of a hare rising and running from its form, unseen by others. The ball of fur set off at speed at an angle from where the hounds roamed, unseen by both hounds and hunters, but not by the eagle-eyed and alert Chris.

He hollered loudly to Martin two hundred yards away. The cry switched Martin's attention from the hounds to Chris then instantly in the direction of Chris' raised pointing whip, which indicated a fast-moving brown object.

Anna almost leapt as Chris' voice boomed out surprisingly loud over her. He immediately broke off the conversation, turned Cirrus and cantered towards where the majority of the mounted field stood, including an alert Steve.

Reggie and Martin spotted the rapidly moving brown shape scuttling across the field and Martin blew up on the horn, instantly drawing the hound's attention. The mud-covered hounds, reacting to the horn, and now using sight rather than scent, spotted their quarry and set off in rapid pursuit.

Steve, alerted by Chris, quickly mustered the mounted field, hollering loudly. A small number of riders were thrown about by their excited mounts, trying to pocket still open hipflasks as their horses prepared to join their racing fellow equines, long before the riders were even prepared. Chris, moving at speed on Cirrus, closed in alongside Steve, cantering with him on a flank, the two seemingly aiming to cut off the hare's run before it made it to the road.

The hare moved across the field at speed, having now broken into its second gear, and its turn of speed still surprising Anna. She held her breath, watching intently as it raced across the open ground, the hounds following some fifty yards behind; their howling calls exciting, the blare of Martin's horn intense. The sight and sounds were primeval and yet strangely exciting to Anna, despite her earlier pity for the hare; the sight reminding her of a historic cavalry charge, as the mounted field raced to catch up with Steve and Chris.

Unexpectedly, the Anti's appeared, this time on foot, running around a bend in the high-hedged road behind them. Jogging on, unsure where the hunt was due to the quiet, their attention was drawn by the sudden commotion ahead.
Turning, they were met by a mass of horses and hounds pouring across the wide open field before them, the yelps, now audible, telling Izzy the hounds were 'on' their quarry. The horn was reinforcement, but as yet, she could see no hare, the sight and sound of horse and hounds charging directly across a field towards them thrilling her inwardly, her pulse thumping. *'Good old days!'*
The hounds and mounted field, all chasing the hare, headed towards the end of the open field, and also now the four antis. Martin and Reggie rode hard behind the pursuing hounds, the mounted field rapidly approaching on their left flank. Such was the sight of the activity, confusion and their speed across the ground, the antis all failed to spot the small brown hare racing at the front of the pack of hounds and running straight at them, their eyes on the riders.
Dave looked across the road behind, over at the next field, assuming a hare had run on and crossed the road already, and that the mounted field, now less than two hundred yards away and approaching at speed were still in pursuit.
Izzy automatically followed Dave's gaze, all four antis confused by the events unexpectedly and rapidly happening before them, trying to determine where the hare had run and establish how they could intervene without being ridden over by the approaching horses. Dave and Izzy, their backs to the charging group, continued to look toward the opposite field. Guy and Wendy however, both stunned by the spectacle, looked on ahead in awe at the sight before them, as twenty plus horses, and around forty hounds, all charged directly towards them; the unique experience both exciting and deadly frightening.
Guy looked at his new-found love, squeezing her hand as he registered fear in her wide eyes, keen to show her strength and leadership, despite the shock.
The hounds were a hundred yards away and rapidly closing when suddenly Guy spotted the mottled brown hare skipping across the stubble, only just ahead of the hounds, which in turn were now only about fifty yards away, but directly in front of them, the hounds closing in fast. Possibly too fast.
Having seen Izzy and Dave scare off the hounds earlier in the day, by waving his hands and yelling at the hounds, Guy thought in an instant he would use his initiative. It'd show Dave he was just as good and keen an Anti as him, despite being cold and pissed-off. However, for Guy, it would prove fatal.
With Dave and Izzy's attention firmly upon the field behind, convinced the hare had crossed the road, releasing Wendy's hand, Guy steeped away and ran into the field. Arms raised high, yelling and waving frantically, he ran straight towards the hounds and approaching horses, to let the hare run free. Wendy, all fear gone; upon seeing her newfound hero charge bravely towards their sworn enemy, she too joined Guy in the field, rushing forward, yelling, hands high. By the time Izzy and Dave heard the yells from their newest recruits, turned around and realised what was going on, it was too late. Far too late.

The two youngsters bravely ran toward the rapidly advancing lines of horse and hound, the thud of hooves audible, the hare between them, all closing in.
The hare, content in its natural form of flight, knew its land well and that the hounds were behind it. But also it knew it had a good lead, more speed within it's legs, and was easily proceeding towards the next field, where a hedge and wood bordered the boundary, providing the natural safe cover it sought.
Ears pressed hard against its back, its long legs pumping with the sound of thunder and death crying behind, and with the sight of the fresh field ahead, the hare prepared to speed up, knowing it could move much faster if needed.
But how quickly things change.
Suddenly two fast-moving objects appeared. Screeching humans.
Blocking the hare's naturally escape route. Panic.
The hare's yellowy-brown eyes flipped sideways. Horses thundered along its alternative flight path. Close behind, calling for blood, ran the hounds.
The screaming humans directly before it were the closest threat.
Secondly were the horses. Third, the hounds, which it could out-run.
Uncertainty ran through its usually quick instinctive quick mind. Confusion.
The hare stopped, flattening its body for a split second, losing momentum.
It spun around, away from the humans, but on into the path of the hounds.
Mistake. Big mistake. Fatal mistake.
Within seconds, due to its hesitation and confused state, the hounds were upon it. The hare jinked to dash sideways at the last second, in one last valiant escape bid, but for once it was too slow and the advantage was lost.
The lead hound's yapping mouth tore at one of the hare's back legs, snapping at it in full flight. The teeth locked in deep, tearing the limb clean off as the hound's speed and momentum thundering on, flipped the hare over into the dirt of the field and into the mass of hounds. The first high-pitched screams of the hare were drown by the combined yelps of the other snapping hounds, mixed with Izzy's cry of horror, as looking at the scene, she realised what had suddenly happened. Within seconds a multitude of savage mouths dived onto the flimsy carcass of the hare, tearing at the once beautiful creature, instantly turning the creature into a pile of bloody fur pieces and splintered bones.
Izzy raised her clenched fists to her head, screaming out loud in bitter rage.
"No! No! No! You fucking stupid bastards!" she screamed.
The curse was clearly aimed towards Guy and Wendy, who pair stood silent and dumbstruck, looking on in terror, just feet from the gorging, bloody faced hounds, who still fought; tearing at the splitting, ripping hare's pelt.
Wendy burst into tears as Reggie and Martin pulled their steaming, snorting horses up beside the excited hounds, tattered corpse and stunned antis. Some of the hounds were now rolling in the blood of the hare, spreading dark red over their muddy coats, as Guy stretched out his arms and hugged a distraught, shaking, tear-strewn Wendy, the sight of the kill too much for her.

Izzy stood silently gazing as the mass of riders she knew so well drew to a halt before the bloody and victorious hounds. Martin pulled out his horn, blowing out a triumphant 'Kill' for all to hear, his face going purple with the sustained effort. Reggie, seated beside on Samson, grinned broadly, looking at the distraught Anti's standing only a few feet away, relishing their success.

"Own goal!" he hollered to Martin, for all to hear. His smile was wide.

Wendy and Guy hugged each other in tears.

Izzy and Dave stared in stunned and bitter silence.

Reggie looked smugly towards Izzy, bitterness returned in her eyes.

"One all I think Miss Harrison!" His voice boomed out, smiling coldly, his pleasure obvious as he then turned about to greet the mounted field who were all thundering to a halt behind him, their riders cheeks aglow.

Dave could no longer control himself. He marched up to Guy, who was still hugging the sobbing Wendy, and gripping his shoulder, he roughly spun the novice anti around, causing him to release Wendy, who fell onto the ground.

"You fucking stupid twat!" Dave yelled directly into Guy's face.

Guy was stunned by the explosive action and rebuke and looked down at the whimpering and distraught Wendy, about to offer her a hand up.

"What the hell did you do that for?" Dave continued, ignoring Wendy. "You should have let the hare run, then cut in between the hounds. Idiot! You just killed that hare. Stupid, murdering Pratt!" Spittle flew from Dave's mouth.

Guy had had enough of this mad bastard for one day. He abruptly shrugged free his shoulder from Dave's grip, stepped back two paces, released Wendy from his grip and swung his fist out at Dave's head with a wild flying strike.

The action was so unexpected it caught Dave unawares.

It was not a powerful punch, landing on his temple, but enough to knock Dave sideways, causing him to stumble, and for his feet to slide on the muddy soil. Losing his balance, he fell over onto the field, landing on his backside.

A huge roar came up from a number of the mounted field, led by a joyous Steve, his loud booming laugh filling the air, as he raised a fist. He was heartily joined by a roaring and red-faced Reggie, now even more joy filled at witnessing the open bust-up of the self-warring anti's they despised.

Dave picked himself up, glaring at Steve, as Guy grabbed Wendy's muddied hand. He pulled her back up and the pair stepped away a few paces, Guy drawing Wendy close to his body, the pair surveying Antis and Hunters alike.

"You can go and stick your precious hare's up your arse!" Guy yelled at Dave, who'd been joined by a stern and silent Izzy, her eyes cast downward.

"Sod the lot of you! You're like a bunch of squabbling kids," Guy continued, turning to face the entire field, as well as Dave and Izzy.

"It's just a big game for all of you. None of you really give a toss about any animals being saved or killed. It means nothing to any of you. All pointless, other than who wins a point against the other. It's a big cruel game."

Everyone, even the normal chirpy Steve, remained silent. Staring. Unmoving.

The horses and hounds seemed to fall silent too, as all the creatures standing upon the field regarded Guy. And they all knew he'd spoken the truth.

Silently he turned; watched by everyone in the field or roadside, leading Wendy by her small hand, the pair moved solemnly across the stubble then onto the road and past the hedges, to slowly walk home, wherever that was.

At that moment it seemed the entire countryside fell silent, as an array of consciences were briefly and painfully touched as they watched the pair go.

Izzy sighed heavily and grabbed at Dave's sleeve, helping him to his feet and then turned, preparing to exit the field. She avoided eye contact with any of the hunters, all still silently looking at the shattered figures vanishing around the bend in the road, Guy's words still ringing truthfully within their minds.

Dave pulled his arm abruptly away from Izzy, turned and stepped forward, looked at Reggie and Martin, then swung around to face Steve, who sat only a few yards away on Casanova. His eyes bore into Steve, the Field Master's usual laughing and tanned face serious for once, staring back at the Anti.

"You Wankers think you're so fucking clever," he yelled. "You tossers! But I'll get you bastards back one day. Just wait! Especially you, Harrison!"

Steve stared coldly at the Anti he hated, his finger damningly pointed towards him. But he kept quiet, a usual cheeky quip and comment not worthy now.

With that Dave spun around, turning his back on the silent crowd. Izzy turned too and walked close by, not daring to look back. For once ashamed, she muttered to a bitter and rage-filled Dave that they'd better call it a day.

The pair got onto the road and headed back to where they'd parked the car moments earlier, but what now after the events seemed a lifetime ago. Luckily it was in the opposite direction to where Guy and Wendy had headed.

"Okay," began Steve after a few seconds of silence, trying to break up the sudden gloomy atmosphere which had pervaded to riders, horses and hounds.

"Let's move on then. Where to next Sir?" Steve said looking over to Reggie, hoping for some leadership. It quickly came, Reggie smiling once again.

"Proceed onto the next field Martin," Reggie said boldly. "Good kill, now move the field on. At least we won't have any more trouble from that rabble."

"Yes Sir," Martin acknowledged, touching his whip to his peak, then pulling sideways on Bert's reins, he whipped the hounds away from the kill site.

The mounted field sat watching the two anti's walk away, then turned their attention to the bloody-faced hounds around Bert's hooves moving away.

With Steve leading off, the rest of the mounted field all slowly rode on, at least knowing they were free of any annoyance from the anti's for the rest of the now dying day, as short as that'd be. Some riders were somewhat shaken by the grim truth, brutally and so unexpectedly thrown in their faces by their enemy. Each rider was seemingly lost in their own thoughts, Guy words for most painfully true. Few who hunted really enjoyed a kill.

But no one enjoyed being told about it so coldly either.

The truth hurt.

Anna had watched it all unfold with a sense of horror and stood in stunned silence. Even though she was a hundred yards from the incident, she'd seen it all happen so clearly and felt sadness for the death of the hare.

Silently, inwardly she blamed Chris for calling up and setting the hounds off onto the hare only he'd initially spotted. The usually chirpy Suzie stood beside her, silent for once, as the pair solemnly returned back to the vehicle in which Joyce sat, she too feeling sad about the incident she'd just witnessed.

She liked hares. And rabbits. They were cute.

They all silently settled into the 4 x 4, lost in their own thoughts, but each feeling in a way the hare was unlucky to die in such a strange way.

All felt it should have lived. Somehow it was simply unjust and not sporting.

It was this strange feeling that took over Anna for a while as they slowly drove on in silence, following the field, still watching the hounds, but the excitement of the day lost. Whilst it seemed great fun to chase these beautiful animals about the countryside with a pack of spectacular, colourful hounds, in turn being chased by stunning horses, with elegantly clothed riders; the scene traditional and picturesque. However, when an animal actually died, everyone seemed filled with a touch of sadness and regret, despite initially going out with such knowledge and the intent of killing. Despite the thrill and excitement of the chase she'd witnessed all day, it was a feeling Anna knew she'd always find hard to fully understand and completely accept if she hunted, never enjoying the brutality of the kill. It was not an uncommon, and one usually shared by most hunters, openly or most often, secretly.

The chase was the excitement they all sought.

The kill an unfortunate end result.

However, not everyone shared those thoughts.

Some within the Shoteton held darker secrets.

Much darker. And crueller.

For some they too enjoyed the chase.

But also, for some, the kill was the ultimate thrill.

And something they truly enjoyed.

Chapter 25

Laughing faces do not mean that there is absence of sorrow. But it means that they have the ability to deal with it.

William Shakespeare -

As the day wore on, one by one, or in pair's, horses and riders grew tired, and making their polite apologies, began to peel away from the field, drifting back to Ernie Cole's farm for a well-earned rest and return to normality.

Anna had found the whole day incredible, despite the unfortunate death of the hare souring the day; indirectly caused by the Anti, who was supposed to be its saviour. As she'd watched the horses thunder past, either through fields of stubble or pounding through sugar beet, the beet tops exploding under the hooves, Anna wished she was onboard Penny, riding alongside Tracey and Chris, sharing smiles and feeling the danger and excitement for real.

Suzie looked at Anna, who gazed at the remaining horses in the now fading watery-grey light, the chill beginning to set in too, the day clearly over.

"Do you still wish you were out there?" Suzie enquired, knowing the answer.

Anna's beaming smile and nod a positive silent response to the question.

It was around 3.00pm, beginning to get colder and the sky darken to a leaden grey when the remainder of the field began the steady trek back to the farm. Tracey trotted over and met up with Anna parked up on a verge and told her they were now heading back. Chris, splattered with mud, had a rugged look seated upon Cirrus, who, rather than grey, was now a muddy-brown colour from her chest and belly backwards. Julie's face was peppered with mud spots, as was her once immaculate navy jacket, but all were smiling, although obviously tired. Suzie told Anna to drive back to the farm ahead the riders, so they could help un-tack and refresh the horses when they returned.

When they arrived at the farm, they saw urns of hot tea and pots of steaming coffee laid out, along with remains of the earlier buffet, but with further fresh cake and biscuits. Anna noted a huge fruit cake with eager eyes.

Some riders who'd returned early were already enjoying a quick refreshment before heading off, including Lady Burlingham, whom Anna noted left a short while earlier, but alone. Anna eyed her steely, watching her delicately nibble upon a biscuit like a timid mouse. She looked immaculate, beautiful, and seemingly untouched by the cold, mud or the rigours of the long day.

Anna had seen her numerous times throughout the day riding alongside Chris, the pair laughing, whilst also seemingly flirting with a number of riders, including Steve. Despite clearly being well-liked, pleasant, yet posh, Anna instantly disliked Virginia, although she didn't know why. Jealousy?

Certainly not, she falsely convinced herself. Beautiful Rich Posh Bitch!

When the remaining mud splattered field returned with the hounds, led by a weary Reggie and Martin, all the riders ensured their steaming horses were quickly washed down, legs checked, given water, rugged up, travel boots wrapped around wet legs, and then put on their respective boxes and trailers for a well-deserved rest and a hearty munch on a fresh full hay net.

Martin attended to the now tired and filthy hounds, which milled around at the base to their lorry, after ensuring they too had a long drink. He expertly ran an eye over them all, looking for any injuries and checking the pads on a number for any stone cuts, to ensure all were well and they were not lame.

Tired, but happy, everyone went back to the barn for tea. Carol and Sally came over to chat, having seemingly been no more than fleeting images on horseback all day it seemed to Anna, stopping for the odd roadside chat.

They politely and genuinely asked what she thought of the day, encouraged by her happy and positive reply, smiling back. A tired and weary Chris, who was rather quiet, joined the group and smiled briefly at Anna before disappearing yet again. Suzie thanked Anna and Joyce for their company and them spoke with Julie, whom she clearly knew well and went off with her and Bonnie. Anna tried her best to help with any of the horses, and helped Tracey put away Fred, who was clearly tired. Julie returned and joined Tracey and Anna, guiding them into the barn. Joyce happy to join them for refreshments.

In the barn, with those remaining, much of the talk was of the anti's bust-up. Reggie, Martin and Steve could be overheard laughing loudly about the incident in a corner of the barn, joined by Ernie Cole and some others.

As she grabbed herself and Joyce some fruitcake, Anna noticed Steve glance her way a couple of times. His looks and beaming smile were obviously appealing, and with the absence of Chris, not unwelcome by a grinning Anna.

Riders, laden with cake and warm beverages drifted over to various members of the Cole family and thanked their hosts as they left and also Reggie, Martin and Steve, for providing a good day's sport, shaking hands or polite pecks on cheeks as deemed appropriate by or for the various parties concerned.

Chris appeared from whatever unknown task he'd been undertaking, calling to his weary party for them to leave, the light failing fast and chill growing. All agreed, including Tracey and Julie, who with a giggle were robbing chunks of fruit cake off a nearby table and wrapping it in napkins, much to Anna's shaking head but wide grin, increased further when her mum joined them.

Steve, who'd not seen Joyce and Anna earlier, looked long and hard at Anna as they all approached the key huntsmen, led by Chris. She felt her skin flush, but also her lips instinctively rise in a cheeking, flirtatious smile, upon seeing Steve's intense gaze drift from her, over to Chris, then back again.

"Good day I hope Chris?" He boomed out. "Great call on that hare."

Chris nodded as acknowledgement, although somewhat forlornly.

"Pity it turned out how it did. But that's how things go. Shit happens."

The three huntsmen nodded. It was obvious Steve's attention was elsewhere. Reggie's crafty gaze followed Steve's, towards Chris' new female friends.
"And where have you been hiding this pair of beautiful young fillies, Chris?" Steve asked excitedly. "Are they a stunning new addition to your stables?"
Chris simply chuckled, glowing red as usual, flipping from Anna and Joyce.
"I spotted these ladies earlier today," Reggie quipped. "First dibs Steve. They are mine! Sister's as I recall," he chuckled, winking at Joyce who grinned back, turning her head in a bashful manner, but for once enjoying the banter.
"Steve, please meet Anna and her mother Joyce," Chris announced formally. "Anna and Joyce, this is our very capable Field Master, Steve Harrison. But note I didn't say gentleman. Excellent horseman, terrible man!" Chris grinned.
With a nonchalant chuckle, and jokingly feigning to punch Chris, Steve stepped forward and gave Joyce a peck on her cheek. He then unashamedly grabbed Anna, lifting her off the ground, giving her a peck on both cheeks. Anna was stunned as he drew her firm against his body then warmly hugged her, before releasing a blushing, astonished, yet smiling and breathless Anna.
"Oh no! Should I go and buy a hat?" roared Tracey, winking at Steve.
The group all heartedly laughed, aware of Steve's magnetism with women. Both Anna and Joyce seemed star-struck and bashful, the pair blushing and giggling with the attention; like two young girls at a prom night, although Chris clearly shrank away, leaving the giggling woman with their new admirer.
"I certainly hope we'll be seeing you out again soon!" Steve winked at Anna with a big grin. "Maybe on horseback. I take it you ride… well!"
Anna beamed back. "I certainly do ride, and well too! I hope I might be out soon as well," she replied, her heart fluttering, as Tracey and Julie looked on.
"How come I never get a kiss from you Steve?" quipped Tracey, smiling.
With that Steve plunged forward and grabbed hold, playfully grappling her and jokingly pretending to snog her, before releasing her from his grip.
Tracey roared with laughter as Martin and Reggie simply shook their heads, long aware of Steve's playful antics and also that of most of the riders.
Tracey, as loud and as bubbly as ever, introduced Anna to the Huntsmen, explaining her situation in full detail, much to Anna's real embarrassment. Chris stood alongside, quiet and seemingly pensive, Anna catching his look. Inwardly she was concerned everyone assumed she'd be moving to Chris' yard, when he'd shown little interest in her all day or even made her an offer.
Steve smiled broadly, unashamedly eyeing up Anna and admiring her looks.
"Well if you move to Chris' yard and ride out with us, I'll certainly keep an eye on you. Chris would be a fool to not invite you. I look forward to it!"
After a few more happy exchanges, Julie also getting a kiss and hug from a happy Steve, they said their farewells and wandered back to the respective vehicles. Chris appeared rather solemn as they walked back, but Anna was still glowing over Steve's kiss and last comment, being quietly teased by her mum as they walked to the vehicles about Steve being her 'new man.'

The cold of the day was setting in, and all were now tired and ready to get equally weary horses back home. After returning to the vehicles, checking everything was safe, they prepared for the steady journey back home.

The poor, watery-grey light of the short, early winter day rapidly faded, and it was very soon dark and gloomy. With headlights on, the small convey made its way back through the dark country lanes, woods and on into Chris's yard.

The lights were on in the yard when they returned and a bouncing Max chased across the yard to meet Chris. He was happily greeted, but the group knew there was still much to do, and the weary figures quickly unloaded the tired horses, returning them to warm stables with feed and hay. They then proceeded to put away an array of damp equipment and muddy tack, laying items out to dry later in the large and slightly forbidding tack room.

Anna busied herself, helping Tracey with Fred and then Julie with Tess, keen to be seen to assist where she could. She kept glancing over towards Chris, who was busy himself, brushing off and then rugging up a tired Cirrus.

He appeared engrossed in his own tasks and to Anna, seemed to have almost forgotten she was there. Worse, Anna thought, her stomach fluttering, he was deliberately ignoring her. Maybe he'd decided not to offer her and Penny a stable and was putting off the decision until the last moment.

With a deep snort, she decided to bite the bullet and find out what he'd decided; hoping for the best, but preparing for the worst. Seeing him head back up the rear ramp of the massive lorry, she seized the initiative, grabbed a wheelbarrow and broom, and headed for the back of Chris' horsebox.

"Do you want me to help clean it out," she offered boldly.

Chris paused, looking at her in the glow of the yard lights, now the darkness had set upon them fully. He was caught for a few seconds by the glimmer on her face and stood silently absorbing her image as she smiled up nervously.

"Well Anna, I was going to ask to have quick word." His tone was cold, seemingly tired and weary, his expression down; almost reluctant and shy.

Anna prepared herself for the worst, expecting a negative response from Chris, wondering where else she could find to stable Penny and get far away for her annoying husband Bruce. If it was local to the area, she could still hunt out with the Shoteton, but she'd miss Tracey's exciting daily company, and ideally wanted to be Horsewater with the strangely alluring Mister Turner.

She looked impassively at Chris, eyes weary, his smart mud-spattered hunting jacket replaced by a tatty wax jacket, with a warm dark blue fleece beneath.

"I meant to ask if you'd decided whether you want move Penny to the yard or not?" His tone was cold and direct; almost a question to her than request.

Anna tilted her head, unsure she'd heard correct. *Was it a question or an invite?*

"Well, if you want me to come?" Anna enquired, still equally unsure.

"I could wish for nothing better. That's if you want to?" Chris enquired.

He said it almost as an embarrassed, begging question, as if she might refuse.

It stunned Anna, catching her off guard. It seemed he was unsure if she wanted to move to Horsewater, rather then the other way around.

Anna's face broke into a huge beaming smile, showing her teeth in full.

"I'd love to move Penny here. I couldn't think of anything better too. That'd be wonderful. Thank you so much!" Anna almost wanting to hug him, feeling herself bounce up and down on the balls of her feet at the base of the ramp.

Chris' face broke into a huge grin, lighting up his previous sad expression.

"She's still in Leicester, isn't he?" Chris enquired further, Anna impressed he'd remembered where Penny was currently. "Do you need her collected?"

"Tracey did say you possibly might be able to collect her," Anna responded almost apologetically, but grasping the potential opportunity of what seemed to be an open offer. "But only if it's okay and you don't mind. It's a way off."

"It won't be a problem picking Penny up and I'd be more than happy to. I pick up and drop off horses all of the time, all across the country. It'll have to be a weekday though. Let me know a day which best suits. Early start too!"

"Wow! Thanks. As soon as possible please, if you don't mind," replied Anna nervously, not believing her luck, still bouncing inside and out at the offers.

"Any chance of next week sometime?" Anna wasn't letting go of the chance.

"How about Wednesday?" Chris offered promptly, knowing his diary.

Anna's mind whirled and quickly excusing herself from Chris, ran across the yard towards Tracey. Her long, agile legs carried her the distance in a few strides, where she spoke with Tracey to confirm some details with her.

"Wednesday is fine," replied an excited Anna upon a swift return, this time stepping up the rear ramp. "Tracey said she'll come to give a hand, if you don't mind. She'll also have a nose around my old yard then, no doubt!"

"No problem," Chris confirmed with a nod. "I'll see you here Wednesday, when Tracey normally comes down to put out Fred. We'll set off early. Give Tracey the details over the next few days, so I know where I am heading. Also, tell her to bring some of her best Brie and Cranberry sandwiches!"

Anna sprung on her toes, bouncing excitedly, then reached forward and gave Chris a gentle hug. He seemed surprised by the sudden contact, his body initially tensing at Anna's gentle grasp, but relaxed slightly, his face flushing, but smiling. Anna flushed too, releasing him, aware Chris was obviously less flamboyant and more private person than her. As the pair stood momentarily regarding each other, a sudden uneasiness running over them, Chris added.

"Tracey also said you need somewhere local to stay? I don't want to sound pushy, but know of a local cottage up for rent. Nothing special, but its close."

Anna looked on intently as he continued, stunned by his help and generosity.

"It's called Pear Tree Cottage. Bit tatty, but the best thing is it's only up the road. You don't have to take it up, but I thought it might help. Old chap farmer owns it. Tenant moved on. Just give him a call. I mentioned you, so it won't be unexpected. I've known him for years. My parents knew him...."

He paused, as if thinking and broke off the thought, staring silently at Anna.

Anna looked shocked at the open warmth of someone whom she'd been told could be empty, cold and distant now being so helpful to a total stranger.

"Why thanks. Thank you very much. If you let me have the details I will give him a call as soon as possible and arrange to have a look. Thank you so much. You don't know how happy I am. This is great! I'm so excited!"

"Well, I'm sure you and Penny will be very happy here," Chris said somewhat formally, gently shaking Anna's slender gloved hand. He gazed momentarily into her grey eyes, both their faces flushing, gently holding her fingers a while longer, before letting go. She smiled broadly back through the gloom of the horsebox, enchanted by the strange horseman, as well as the amazing day should been through and the new world she seemed to have entered.

"You don't have to worry about cleaning out the box. Thanks for offering. Me and Sally will do it tomorrow. I'm knackered and just want to get in!"

Chris looked at her deeply, blushed, then turned silently away, walking briskly down the ramp. As he reached the bottom of the ramp he smiled back.

"I've just got a few calls to make inside. I'll pass the cottage details onto Tracey. If I don't see you anymore tonight before you leave, I'll see you early Wednesday morning. Sharp! Goodnight. It's been wonderful meeting you."

Raising a hand, he moved into the darkness, then stomped on over towards the big white house, Max at his heels, leaving Anna lost in her own world.

Standing on the rear of the lorry, she suddenly felt many eyes upon her and turned. Tracey and Joyce stood cheekily smiling from the orange glow of the nearby stable block, silently watching on, but cheekily waving, their happy expressions a mix of amusement and curiosity. But they seemed to know.

Anna gave a thumbs-up and jogged over towards them to give them the exciting news, unable to recall being as happy for many years.

She was sure the move to Horsewater would be life changing.

It would. She would not be wrong.

But little would she know why.

Chapter 26

O, beware, my lord, of jealousy! It is the green-eyed monster which doth mock the meat it feeds on.

William Shakespeare - Othello

Dave Pearson stared out into the darkness, his reflected image on the single pane of grimy glass ghostly. A hollow vision reflecting a hollow man.

It had not been a good day. In fact one of the worst.

Every time he tried his best to impress Izzy, something happened.

It always turned to shit. Never anything good.

Today had been no different. No, today had been worse.

He'd been humiliated, before her very eyes.

Pearson shook his head, still recalling the events.

Defeat and anger boiling, simmering in a sweaty, dirty shell.

And worse. He recalled Steve Harrison's face.

The tosser staring down at him from his evil black horse.

Laughing, mocking, as he lay defeated in the muddy field.

Bastard! He'd pay one day. Soon. Very soon. In full.

'What on earth had Izzy ever seen in that stupid, pathetic man?'

His eyes flittered around the single room bed-sit. The furniture consisted of a wardrobe, leaning over like the famous Tower of Pisa and seemingly in danger of collapse. It matched a chest of drawers; same style, including the same dangerous angle of tilt. The items wouldn't have looked out of place in an early Sixties sit-com, set in the Thirties. A variety of objects, lost in the gloom, lay discarded upon the floor like detritus. The bare bulb strained to illuminate their hiding places. Maybe it was best it didn't. Something moved.

A stack of well-thumbed books, magazines and pamphlets lay in a corner, where a triangular dark patch overlooked the predominantly left-wing reading material. The bed he sat upon creaked, the bedclothes lined with dirt at the creases and being the only ones, were never unchanged. Breadcrumbs from consumed Vegan cheese rolls, lay scattered at his dirt covered, bare feet.

He should wash, but the stupid bitch from the other room had used all of the hot water for the night. So only ice-cold water flowed into the solitary bath of the shared-by-five bathroom. The scum-line, long since engrained into the aged enamel like a Plimsoll line, was a guide of how deep to fill with water.

Dave sniffed at his bare feet. They stunk. Black lines of filth edged his long fungal toenails and dirt engrained the hard skin. He picked at a lump of skin, which fell from his heel, then flicked it onto the floor. It disappeared amongst the dirt that consumed the threadbare carpet. He considered washing his feet, but decided they'd have to remain as they were until tomorrow. Maybe.

His vision drifted to the only window and he rose to stare out at the dark slate roofs of the houses opposite. Then towards the street, a hundred feet away, the dimly lit and damp pavements, matching the poor neighbourhood.

An occasional vehicle passed by on the quiet road, usually drawing slowly up to the kerb. The occupants would speak to the numerous women who stood by the dim lampposts, pausing briefly, before moving off, usually with a fresh occupant inside, the street empty once more until replaced by another.

He looked hard as a new vehicle caught his attention.

It was a dark Range Rover.

He moved a step closer and pressed his body against the lukewarm radiator which ran in front of the large window, resting his fingertips upon the peeling paintwork on the window board. Thin, un-drawn curtains hung either side of the aging original box-sash windows. Dave rarely drew them, his room in the Victorian building high and the dust falling from them making him sneeze on the rare occasions he felt he needed any total interment privacy.

He gazed down at the world of filth and corruption that surrounded him.

Drug dealers and Whores. All of them. And worse.

Filthy, stinking whores. Selling their bodies to any bastard who'd give money to provide somewhere to inject their reproductive bodily fluids. Bastards!

An image of Izzy momentarily flitted into his mind, then Steve Harrison, both doing things he could only dream of, before being replaced by the image of the two scantily clad women outside, now stood beside the Range Rover.

This was interesting for once. The sluts were arguing about something.

Two women, both in their twenties, both wearing only enough material to cover the key parts of their flesh, were speaking to the unseen driver of the environment polluting gas-guzzling Rover. And they were not happy.

One of the women, barely dressed in black, stormed away from the Rover, throwing her hands in the air, screaming abuse. Her friend, hugging her, also yelled at the car driver. Both were not happy to see the potential customer.

Dave gazed on, half entertained, half curious, wondering what kind of conversations people like that engaged in and what world they lived in.

And what did those whores do for their customers?

He could only muse. And maybe dream. If only.

The other woman, clad in a red leather jacket and little else, returned to the vehicle. She appeared to be hurling abuse at the driver, who hadn't moved away, obviously made of strong stuff or possibly involved with the women.

Dave wished he was closer, so he could hear, but the window, long painted shut, wouldn't open, sealing him into his airless, stinking box of filth.

A figure appeared from the shadows. Someone new. Interesting.

Dave gazed on intently. Action. He enjoyed trouble. Better than T.V.

The big man, hidden deep within the shadows, both by skin tone and choice of dark clothing, suddenly appeared like a massive black-hole, highlighted in the dim light of the singular lamp post around which they stood.

The heavy-set black man lumbered up to the Range Rover, pulling the women in Red away, and began speaking to the driver of the vehicle. Fingers wagged and the black man's head kept turning back and forth to look at the two women huddled in the shadows, then back and forth at the driver.

The black man, stretched out an arm, pointing a finger into the shadows from which he'd emerged and the woman in red stepped sideways, looking back into the gloom. The pimp moved, his speed surprising Dave for his size, momentarily disappearing into the shadows, before re-appearing with the woman in black attached to his hand. Pulling hard at her wrist, the woman in black's high-heeled feet scuttled across the pavement, then stumbling, was tossed towards the Rover, the woman falling to her knees. The woman in red stepped forward, leaning down to help her colleague, but the pimp pushed her aside, grasping the woman in black himself, lifting her bodily from the damp pavement and almost throwing her into the Range Rover.

No sooner was the door closed did the vehicle speed off, moving along the quiet street. The woman in red stared coldly at the disappearing vehicle, her friend inside, before her 'guardian' shoved her back into the darkness.

Dave shook his head, amazed at how some men treated women; abusing the warm and delicate flesh placed before them and not respecting their beauty.

An image of Steve Harrison, then Izzy flitted into his mind once more.

He bitterly shook his head. A Classic case.

A man who had it all, including a beautiful wife most men would worship. But he'd simply blown it all away. Uncaring and irresponsible. Wanting more.

Not Dave. He wouldn't have. Never with Izzy.

He would have worshipped her. He'd have given her everything.

It highlighted even more what a despicable person Steve Harrison was.

And highlighted even more why he needed to be put in his place. And would.

Dave sighed heavily as he skulked back onto the bed, looking towards the leaning chest of drawers, upon which sat a small TV set, a battered aerial atop.

He knew there was little of interest to him on any channel, so it remained off. He spun around, to look at the area of wall on the hidden side of the leaning wardrobe. Rising from the bed, he slowly walked towards over the darkened area, reaching out, touching something on the wall, almost hidden from view.

His fingers glided over a news article pinned to the wall.

Dave stared at it for the umpteenth time, absorbing the image.

Izzy's face loomed out at him.

The newspaper article had Izzy's distinctive face and long blond hair. With her left arm outstretched, palm raised directly at the intrusive photographer, she was trying to shield her face from the intruding camera. Her right hand, hidden, was clenched into a fist by her side, about to hit the same reporter.

The image was taken seconds before she floored the photo-journalist, on the way to the court hearing. The expression on her face was not her best.

Bitter, angry and full of rage. But it was Izzy. Perfectly.

The heading 'Horny Hunter's Wife Nicked' was printed boldly above a double page spread, where the full details of the trial and background details were printed for all to see, read and wonder. For a few days. It made news.

Dave's attention switched to another press cutting. This showed a better image of Izzy, being taken when caught off-guard by a hidden cameraman.

This time she bore a bright smile on her glowing face, the characteristic blond ponytail hanging through a dark baseball cap, this heading different.

'Horny Hunter's Wife Becomes Anti.'

Dave touched the paper, running his fingers just above the image. His finger hovered, cautious not to smug any of the precious newsprint.

He flicked his eyes once more, this time focussing upon another image.

This was a colour photograph, taken by an amateur.

It was a good photograph though, showing Izzy in the countryside, smiling naturally, and dressed in her characteristic black leggings and hiking boots.

She stood alongside a number of other people, including Dave.

But he stood three people away from her. He'd always regretted that.

The photo' was taken quickly, with no time to line up, by another Anti.

Somehow he'd been pushed and moved away from Izzy. As ever.

He'd wanted to be photographed standing beside her. Bodies touching.

In his rightful place, right where he belonged. Beside her.

The place where he should and would be. Soon.

Everyone in the photo, taken last winter in a beet field by a senior member of the League Against Blood Sports, was looking straight at the camera.

All were happily smiling, grinning, and cheering - except one person - Dave.

He was looking sideways at Izzy.

Dave touched the photo, pursed his lips, and blew a kiss at the central figure with flowing blond hair. He smiled. He sensed the photo smiled back.

His eyes drifted to another series of photos, he'd taken. A series of images, supposedly of the hunt, but all of which had Izzy within them at some point.

A horse racing past, with a snarling huntsman, but with Izzy standing nearby. Various horses leaping a hedge, but with Izzy staring awestruck. A huntsman yelling at a group of anti's, but with Izzy standing alongside looking on.

Then he stared at his most precious photo.

Izzy staring straight at the camera. Dave's camera.

It was one of a few times she'd let him photograph her.

He'd asked one morning as they were waiting, and cheekily she'd posed for. With a field of muddy stubble as the backdrop, one hand was posed on her hip and her slim waist on display, with long legs below, slightly spread out.

But importantly, she bore a beaming beautiful smile.

A genuine smile. Just for him.

He absorbed the image, soaking in all of her natural beauty and softness of her pure skin. But still his stomach ached and he yearned for more.

He sighed heavily and moved his gaze along the wall. Anger flowed.

His eyes flicked onto another image, once more taken by himself.
It was of Steve Harrison.
The snug, cocky face loomed out across the room. Bastard!
Dave snarled, bitterness boiling like bile to be spewed from a sick stomach.
A large knife appeared in Dave's hand.
Massive. Old and worn, but still deadly.
The Great War army bayonet was bought from a car boot sale years ago.
Its long blued-steel blade was razor sharp - Dave ensured so - and the pitted hardwood handle, still strong and solid, the rivets good and firm.
Dave had often mused whether the bayonet had ever been thrust into anyone's soft and yielding flesh or jammed into hard bone; wondering if the weapon had expended life and considered what devastation it had wreaked.
He hoped it had. And lots.
And all deserving.
'Bang!'
The bayonet smashed into the wall.
Driven hard into the photograph, the tip split Steve Harrison's face in half.
The ancient yet deadly bayonet wobbled within the image and wall.
Dave gazed in awe, smiling at the sight.
"Soon," he whispered softly. "Very soon."

Chapter 27

A journey of a thousand miles begins with a single step.

Lao Tzu / Confucius – Dao De Jing

The yard lights illuminated the stables in a soft orange glow, contrasted with areas of deep dark shadow, as Tracey and Anna pulled into Chris' yard early on the Wednesday morning. Julie's car was parked up on the hard standing and a full barrow stood outside Bonnie's empty stable, already mucked out. Julie worked at the local hospital, Tracey explained, and was nearly always the first to arrive and turn out, rain or shine. Other owners arrived at the yard at differing times, with Sally and Chris doing any full liveries or a required.

Julie greeted Anna and Tracey, smiling as ever as the exited the vehicle.

"I hope it goes well today. Once Penny's settled in must go out for a hack."

Anna smiled and thanked her, feeling the same genuine warmth she'd sensed when they'd first met. Julie, busy as ever strolled by and they carried on into the yard, Tracey stopping at Fred's stable, but Anna, feeling bold and excited to be back at Chris' yard, continued on to Cirrus' stable, where she could see Chris rugging-up the grey. She peered over the door, just as Chris turned, jumping slightly, their faces only a few feet apart. She gave him her best grin.

"Hi," said Anna nervously, seeing the unsmiling, slightly cold glaring reply. "Sorry to make you jump. We're here, obviously! Do you need a hand with anything?" She flashed her teeth in a wide grin, trying to break the ice.

"Oh Hi. No thanks, I'm fine," he replied somewhat bluntly. "Give me about thirty minutes and I'll be ready to go. You can help Tracey with Fred and get Penny's stable ready. I'm a bit set in my own ways and have my own routine."

With that, and no further niceties, he unbolted the door and lead the grey out towards the paddocks, turning his back on Anna without a second look.

Anna felt flattened, hoping he'd be overjoyed to see her, after the warmth she'd felt on Saturday, but knew she was expecting too much too soon.

She knew inside she fancied him, although she'd met him only once, plus the fact he was smaller than her, and knowing he could be moody. But despite all those negative points seemingly against him, she sensed there was something else about Chris. Something strange and unseen that seem to draw her to him.

Chemistry. That was the word used. And she felt it. Strange as it was.

But what chance would she have? It seemed he could pick any rich woman he wanted; not that he himself was poor from the land he owned. And from the way Lady Burlingham hung around him, he already had someone very much interested in him, even if she was married to the neighbouring Lord.

But then he also appeared to be a confirmed bachelor. Tracey had clearly told her that, and there had never been any serious potential 'Missus Turner'.

He certainly didn't 'Bat for the other Team,' as she eloquently put it; enjoying the company of women and seemingly not that of men, but no one had any knowledge of any long-term female partners. Chris, it'd been decided, was wedded to his horses. Also being shy, it seems he let few people close within his tight world. It was possibly this inaccessibleness which added extra allure.

Having only just extricated herself from the grasp of her former partner, Bruce, as much as she'd have liked some attention from Chris, she was happy to start a new phase in her life too, and conceded she should be happy he'd let her bring Penny to his yard and simply be happy with that alone. So with a slight glum feeling of rejection, hands thrust deep into her jacket pockets and feeling a little down, she went back to see if she could help Tracey.

Tracey was changing Fred's rugs. He was not too pleased, as he was trying to eat his breakfast at the same time as Tracey was putting on his turn-out rug.

"Chris in a grump?" a voice enquired from somewhere beneath Fred's belly.

"Yes. How did you know?" Anna replied curious, looking for her cousin.

"Always is in the morning. Miserable sod and very moody. Even he will tell you that. He has set routines and likes to be left alone in the morning to get done and do his own thing in his own order. Wait until he's mucked out and had a cuppa. Then he'll be back to normal." Tracey replied knowingly.

"So what is normal like then," asked the ever-curious Anna.

"Quiet, moody and grumpy!" laughed Tracey.

Anna shook her head, grinning as Tracey appeared and secured Fred's front rug straps, weaving past his head and then moved over towards the door.

"He can be the warmest, friendliest person going, and do anything for you. He has a great dark sense of humour, but he's also very inward; quite shy and closes himself down. And hard work to speak with sometimes, unless it's horses. Hence why he appears moody. So don't get too many big ideas."

Anna flushed slightly, her cousin knowing her well. Too well it seemed.

"He may disappoint if you try to dive in with both feet. Sorry to bring you down to earth. Many have thought the same about him, as you possibly have. A good-looking, rich, single horseman. Perfect husband material. But not."

Tracey gave Anna a knowing frown and shrug over the stable door.

"Just don't try and get too close. You won't. No one I know has ever penetrated that hard exterior. Not even me. And yes, I tried too, once. You'd have to be very special." Tracey looked genuinely saddened towards her cousin, for once being strangely serious. With that, Tracey untied the empty net and passed it onto a sad-faced Anna. "Fill that! Please!"

Anna sighed, but smiled. "I'll make myself useful and then go and get Penny's new stable ready for her return. At least that'll cheer me up."

Hay net in hand, she strolled off to the hay barn, her dreams battered, but not destroyed. She consoled that at least she had a great new home for Penny, and that was more than she could have dreamed of just less than a week ago.

Once the chores were done, with Tracey assisting, Penny's stable was made ready. The fresh bedding almost glowed golden, the smell of new straw refreshing. A plump haynet, hung in the corner and a large tub of water complimented the setting. Anna stood proudly surveying, hands on hips.

Chris passed by a couple of times, smiling as he led out horses, followed by a happily waving Sally, who appeared and wished them a safe journey, before also busying herself with various tasks, and happily chatting with Chris.

They waited by the tack room, making general conversation and discussing the journey until Chris finally appeared, dressed in jeans and a fleece, in what seemed a slightly more pleasant mood, now with a real smile on his face.

"Okay then ladies, all set?" Chris asked, his eyes wide and looking eager.

Both nodded, Tracey grinning insanely, Anna smiling nervously.

"Let's go and pick up Penny," he said with a smile, which did little to cheer up the now increasingly nervous Anna. "I hope you brought some of your best sarnies Tracey?" he commented. "She makes the best selection going."

He looked at Anna, and again she felt a strange, warm connection.

"Brie and Cranberry for you Chris. In a French baguette."

"My favourite!" Chris exclaimed, Anna, surprised by his sudden warm and happy expression. "I should marry you!" Chris smiled wide and brightly.

"Yes, but you'll have to get in a long line," Tracey laughed loudly.

"How about Anna? She's single now. And I'm sure she's up for it! If you marry her, it'd make you my Cousin-in-law, or summit. I'll buy a hat!"

Anna winced, flushing a bright red, matching a bashful Chris' facial colour and embarrassed expression. He looked down but quickly quipped back.

"But we've only just met. We should wait at least two weeks. And then I'd need to announce our formal engagement in The Times. Let's see shall we?"

"I won't buy a new hat just yet," laughed Tracey. "Just a baseball cap."

With the atmosphere relaxed, blushing faces reducing in colour, the girls grabbed their bags, complete with snacks. They headed for Chris's lorry with a sense of childlike excitement and climbed inside, ready for their journey.

The big truck roared into life and rocked as it slowly moved out of the yard, winding its way through the woods, carefully missing the tree branches, which seem to provide just enough clearance for the lorry roof. All three sat in the cab, with Tracey nearest Chris and Anna beside the window, quiet and deep in thought. They sat in silence for a while, until they got clear of the farm and began to pass through the village, heading for the main roads and the start of their long journey. Tracey began to chat, mostly about horses, whilst Chris concentrated on guiding the big lorry through the country lanes, eventually moving onto the dual carriageway system. Chris then relaxed, made the odd comment, but mostly listened to Anna and Tracey's conversation. Slowly he began talking, and Anna found herself grinning across Tracey towards Chris, as she became used to his dry, blunt, but very quick wit. As he slowly opened up, she found him more talkative and charming and enjoying his company.

The early morning light revealed a clear sky. Thin cirrus clouds, hued with pink and grey, hung high in the distant pale blue sky. The sun would still be an hour before rising fully and a gentle yellow and white glow appeared on the far wide horizon, indicating its intended point of arrival.

The miles turned over and the countryside slowly changed. They passed through small villages with fields separated by hedges, woods or copses. Then as they moved further west, out of Norfolk, the fields became broader and wider, with fewer hedges, until they reached the Fens. Flat, borderless and seemingly lifeless, with no break to the horizon except for the occasional piece of machinery, lone farmhouse, barn, drainage ditch or track to break up the bleak and dull landscape, the black, but highly fertile fields stretched out for miles in a never-ending panorama. The sun, now slowly rising, threw an orange hue across the low Fenland fields, bathing everything in a tangerine glow. The low sun made the occupants of the lorry cab squint for a short period, until rising sufficient to change into a watery-yellow, the rising angle of light becoming less blinding. Onwards, westward, they steadily travelled.

The subject of Penny had been mentioned a couple of times by Tracey and Chris had made the odd comment. As the two women finished mentioning some of the showjumping and dressage events Anna had competed on with Penny back in Leicester, Chris broached his first personal question.

"If you don't mind me asking, why are you moving back to Norfolk?" he asked direct. "You've been away a while. What made you want to return?"

As soon as he'd asked the obvious question, an embarrassed silence followed. Anna and Tracey regarded each other with raised eyebrows and silent stares.

Chris flushed, realising he'd made a mistake, recalling Tracey mentioning that it was something to do with 'man problems' when she'd first discussed Anna, and suddenly realised the answer was obviously too personal and painful.

Anna looked at Tracey for an answer, who in turn just looked to the blushing Chris. She answered for Anna, to save her cousin further embarrassment.

"Man problems. You know. Personal stuff," Tracey said. "Ex-hubby stuff."

"Oh, sorry for asking." Chris flushed, looking straight at the road ahead.

"Actually," Anna, butted in, feeling she should explain fully and honestly.

"You may as well know. I am in the process of getting a divorce; finding out my husband had been having an affair with his mad bitch of a secretary for over a year. I decided to move back to Norfolk, where I was born, to start fresh. I haven't lived here for over fifteen years. My family still do, including my mum, who you met the other day. I've decided to return to my roots."

Chris nodded to acknowledge her open response, sensing she was inwardly glad to tell him, despite it being painful, and an embarrassing admission.

"I'm looking forward to starting a new and fresh life back in Norfolk," Anna announced and felt relief as she noticed Chris' expression change, the initial red leaving his cheeks as he seemed more relaxed and confident towards her.

"And you so much again for helping this all happen. It's really appreciated."

Chris simply nodded as an acknowledgement, seemingly to relax fully.

"Sorry for asking and prying, but it was just a general question. I forgot Tracey mentioned something when she first spoke about you to me. Thanks for telling me so openly. It can't be easy and must be painful breaking up."

"Actually, I think Bruce is a complete tosser!" Tracey boldly announced, looking direct at a red-faced Anna, who seemed shocked by her cousin's frank, if not honest admission. "She's best shot of him to be honest Chris. He's a Pratt! None of us ever liked him. Smarmy, flash git! A prize wanker!"

Anna put a hand to her mouth, as if in shock, wide-eyed, but her face slowly breaking into a massive grin, amused by Tracey's honesty, shaking her head.

"Well I'm sorry Anna, but he is a complete tosser. Let's be honest," Tracey continued, speaking freely, now she'd opened her mouth, as was her way.

"He treated you like shit for years, but you simply couldn't see any wrong. We all could. Whenever we met him at parties, we wondered what you saw in the pretentious twat, other than being a hunk. But you seemed to be totally besotted. He was an arsehole, who thought he was God's gift to everything."

Anna's red face cracked, as she burst out laughing, hitting her cousin's arm and catching her breath between heavy sniggers, her cheeks glowing bright.

"Well thanks for that vote of confidence on Bruce!" Anna managed to say in-between her roaring fits of laughter. "Perhaps you should have told me that a few years ago. Then I may well have left him a long time ago. Yes, Bruce can be a bit of a pratt." Anna said, chuckling. "No, I take that back. He is a pratt!

Chris grinned, then burst out laughing too, amused by the two women's open and frank comments and their now infectious laughter.

It was the first time Anna had seen him laugh. Tracey and Anna both rejoined him, seeing the blunt and humorous truth behind Tracey's comment, the lorry cab now filled with laughter as the three occupants relaxed further.

"What do you do for a living?" Chris asked, the laughter easing. "If that isn't personal and likely to cause more embarrassment," he added with a wry smile.

"I'm a freelance graphic designer," Anna began, with an air of confidence.

"I design artwork for a range of customers. Mostly the advertising industry. Artwork, packaging and stuff like that, but I also so do magazines and books. I'm working on the cover for a potential best-seller," Anna said proudly.

"Well I am impressed," replied Chris, nodding, his eyes twinkling, taking his gaze off the road for a few seconds, looking past Tracey and directly at Anna. Their eyes met and once more Anna felt a strange connection.

Anna smiled back and again sensed a natural warmth from this strange man, whom she so much wanted to learn more about. But he seemed to have an invisible barrier around him, preventing anyone getting too close. Yet. Anna saw it as a challenge and was determined she'd get through, if she could.

The conversation waxed and waned, mostly about horses past and present, and the three joyfully shared Tracey's 'highly-acclaimed' - and justly so - sandwiches as they drove, all washed down with bottles of soft fruit drink.

The countryside varied, becoming undulating hills as they approached the beautiful countryside around Rutland then onto the Leicestershire borders. The entire landscape opened up around them, revealing miles of gentle rolling hills, dotted with copses and separated by brush hedges spreading for miles.

"Beautiful countryside," Chris exclaimed as they rounded a small brow in the road, throwing the view out before them. "Best hunting country in Britain."

"Have you ever hunted here?" enquired Anna, sensing passion in his voice and how his eyes scanned. "You seem very keen on this area of the country."

"Yes," he replied. "Only a few times, some years back now. A huntsman from another meet invited me. Wonderful country, made for hunting. Great!"

The three silently reviewed the beautiful countryside, with a landscape which could not be imitated elsewhere, making this part of England some of the most picturesque and the best hunting land around, and also being the historic home to some of the biggest and best known hunts in the country.

Chris eyes gazed over the landscape and he seemed lost in distant memories, remaining silent for the final part of the journey, until the open countryside slowly changed to mixed urban developments, the countryside fading as they approached the outskirts of Leicester and he asked Anna for directions.

"Six Hills is where Penny is stabled," she said and began to guide him around the outskirts of Leicester; a city she'd come to know well, but which now held bad memories. It was as she was directing Chris over a roundabout that she first thought she saw the car. It was one she knew well. Very well.

The image caused her to stop in mid-sentence, her head spinning around, eyes set upon the vehicle, but it was soon lost from sight by traffic.

Both Chris and Tracey looked at her for a second as she paused, noticing some form of apprehension or concern cross her face as her head searched. Chris concentrated on the busy roads, but Tracey looked hard at Anna, who was seemingly lost in some deep thought, gazing back out the side window.

"Okay?" Tracey enquired, sensing some uneasiness. "Everything alright?"

Somewhat nervously Anna simply nodded, unconvincingly confirming she was, then continued speaking, but with a knot in her belly, making her feel uneasy for the first time that day. Tracey sensed something wasn't right too.

"Are you okay? Last minute regrets?" Tracey quietly spoke to Anna, worried by her sudden mood change, her face now pale and anxious.

"No, it's definitely not that," Anna answered. "I'm fine really, don't worry. It's nothing. Something I thought saw, but I was wrong. It's nothing, really."

Tracey was not convinced, sensing Anna's sudden apprehension.

"I thought I saw something or someone back there, but I think I was wrong. Don't worry about me, probably just my imagination. I'm being silly. We'll soon have Penny safely away. I can't wait," Anna replied nervously, feeling she should explain, but afraid to admit to what she feared she really saw.

She vainly smiled, giving further directions to Chris, in a hope to change the atmosphere and also reassure herself. Soon Penny would be onboard.

The lorry, still guided by Anna, drifted out of Leicester and then onto a series of smaller country lanes, finally passing a collection of stone-built houses, before turning off the road and pulling into a large farm entrance.

Anna pointed to Chris where to park the big lorry, and as soon as it was stationary, they all jumped out, glad to be able to stretch their bodies and move their tired, stiff limbs. It'd been a long journey but they arrived safely.

Surveying the scene before them Chris was immediately impressed. The farmhouse, built of a yellow local stone, with various barns and traditional stable yard, was clearly immaculate. They were swiftly greeted by a Labrador, appearing from nowhere, which sniffed them all and jumped up Anna.

"Hello Betty!" Anna exclaimed, affectionately stroking the excited dog who leapt about, then greeting the others. "I'm going to miss you girlie."

"And we'll miss you and Penny too," said a woman, suddenly appearing from within one of the side barns, slowly walking forward, smiling warmly.

"Hi Jan," said Anna, turning to greet the lady walking towards them with a bright smile. She was of medium height and build, with a slightly weather beaten, naturally tanned face, which despite being attractive, showed the woman's true age of late forties. Her brown bob haircut was flecked with grey and no attempt had been made to cover it up. Jan stepped towards Anna and openly hugged her, who naturally returned the affectionate greeting.

"Jan, this is my cousin Tracey. Please excuse her if she swears. Or spits! Possibly both at the same time! And this is Chris. Penny is moving to his yard in Norfolk and he has so kindly agreed to collect her for me. He's my angel."

Jan looked at Chris with an admiring glance, then at Anna, smiling, raising her eyebrows and smirking. Anna, caught the meaning, blushed and looked away, trying not to grin, hoping it'd been missed by Chris, which it was.

They all greeted each other with handshakes and after Anna proudly showed them around the yard with Jan, she introduced Penny to Chris. He seemed impressed by the horse, casting a quick professional eye over the mare, who nuzzled Anna, pleased to see her owner after several days absence.

Jan invited them into the farmhouse for refreshing cups of tea and slices of freshly baked cake, which were heartily consumed. After a short chat, knowing they had a long return journey back, and were keen to get on, they returned to the yard to prepare Penny for her long journey home.

Jan too was busy and made her apologises for not being able to see them off, as she too had to rush off, with an appointment into Leicester. However she patted Penny, wished them luck for the future, promised to visit them all, and after a short, tearful hug, waved them all a fond farewell. She zoomed off in her 4 x 4 pick-up truck, leaving the happy threesome to load up Penny.

Chris moved the lorry around into the yard, dropping the back, whilst Anna and Tracey saw to booting and rugging up Penny. Tracey and Chris loaded up all of Penny's tack, rugs and associated paraphernalia, gathered from the tack room and barns and placed it in the area at the front of the lorry.

Tracey shook her head at the mass of rugs and tack Anna had collected which needed to be loaded, but knew only too well that it was often the way with 'horsey' people. She had a multitude of rugs for Fred, but only used two.
Anna had a quick dash around the stables and paddocks, to say goodbye to a few of her favourite horses, before having one final look over the paddock gate to scan the yard and fields she'd happily called home for many years, with a mixed feeling of sadness, but also excitement for a new adventure.
Keen to get on, Tracey led Penny out of the stable and proceeded to lead her towards the lorry as Anna said her final farewell. She turned back to join Tracey at the base of the lorry, where she was holding Penny. Chris, standing in the back of the lorry, at the top of the ramp, was preparing to tie Penny up once she was led up. Everything was ready and all Penny had to do was walk up the ramp and she'd soon be off to her new home. Chris gazed down at Anna from the back of the lorry. Their eyes locked, the pair smiling.
Suddenly Anna's eyes moved away from his face.
Drifting beyond the lorry, eyes widening, her smile rapidly vanished.
Within a heartbeat her look turned into one of utter terror and fear.
Chris looked down at her, slightly puzzled, wondering what had caused the immediate change in Anna's expression. Just then he heard the roar of a car engine pulling up close and stopping alongside to the lorry.
Anna and Tracey froze in their tracks, holding tightly to Penny.
The pair stared beyond the lorry. Their look was one of combined shock.
Anna put her hands to her head as a car door slammed shut.
With a look of despair and total disbelief, tears began rolling.
She'd been correct with her earlier suspicion in Leicester, after seeing the car pass by at speed and recognising the driver, as their eyes connected.
She'd hoped he'd the driver had not recognised her.
But Anna was wrong.
Or that he'd have dismissed the passing glimpse, not really expecting to see Anna back in Leicester so soon, or certainly not seated in the front of a lorry.
But Anna was again wrong.
The man had recognised Anna. Instantly.
Turning his car around, he'd then followed, at a distance.
He'd taken his time. But then he was in no hurry.
The man knew exactly where the lorry would be heading.
And why.
Fate once more had been cruel to Anna.
She stood shattered, staring at the man before her.
It was Bruce.

Chapter 28

First they ignore you, then they laugh at you,
then they fight you, then you win.

Mahatma Gandhi

"Where the hell are you taking that thing?" A man's voice boomed along the side of the horsebox. "Put it back. That stupid creature is going nowhere!"

Chris, unseen in the back of the lorry, and until then unaware of the cause of Anna's look of horror, peered around the side of the horsebox, holding onto the side partition and awaiting Penny. Unseen to him, an Audi A6 estate car had parked past the front of the lorry, from which a man had climbed out.

The man, just over six-foot tall, of athletic build and smartly dressed, stormed along the side of the lorry. His attention was on Anna and Tracey, still holding onto the now nervous Penny. Chris, still unseen by the man, peered around from the side of the lorry, curious, but as yet, not concerned.

The man was good looking, with a solid jaw line, neat nose and square, but attractive features. Well groomed, swept-back light brown hair, gave him the appearance of a typical male model in his late thirties. One who'd not look out of place modelling men's suits or underwear in a mail order catalogue. Dressed in a navy suit, with bright red tie and crisp white shirt, the man appeared out of place amongst the dirt of a stable yard and working farm.

As he stomped alongside the lorry, he fleetingly glanced up, noticing Chris. But the man's brown eyes dismissed the smaller man standing on the lorry, regarding him as insignificant. Instead, he proceeded straight towards the two women holding the horse at the base of the lorry. That was his focus.

"What the hell do you think you're you doing Snooks?" he asked Anna aggressively, stomping towards her, reaching out for the horse.

An evident look of anger and fear crossed Anna's face. She pulled back.

"You can't take the horse. That thing is staying here. And so are you. You're moving back home. Now! Let's go. Stop being stupid. You're staying here!"

The man stopped just a few feet from Anna, then turned to regard Tracey as if she was excrement on the street, upon which he didn't want to tread.

"Bruce, I told you I was taking Penny. We agreed. She's going. Now."

Anna spoke in a nervous tone, showing fear; horse and handler instinctively stepping backwards. "I'm not coming back," she continued, voice breaking.

"I've told you countless times. I don't care if you've finished with that floozy Lucy or not. We're finished. I'm starting fresh. Leave me and Penny alone!"

"Yes, fuck off Bruce," added Tracey, boldly stepping forward, still holding onto Penny, who was shuffling about, sensing the tension about her.

Bruce regarded Tracey as someone might a slug, but she continued.

"You had your chance, but decided you'd rather shag that stupid slut of a secretary instead. Now piss off and let Anna take Penny away. Clear off!"

Bruce regarded Tracey with total contempt, sneering at her and Anna.

"Why don't you piss off yourself and let go of that stupid horse. It doesn't even belong to you," Bruce said with venom, who pulled Penny further away.

"The only time I ever see your bloody face is when there's a marriage or death in the family. Then your family think they're going to get a free piss up or something for nothing. Now get out of my way, you common cow!"

Bruce finished, glaring at Tracey, then stepped forward to grab at the horse, causing Penny to re-coil back, clattering on the concrete, dragging Tracey.

Anna lunged and grabbed at Bruce's hand, now clutching the leadrope on Penny's headcollar. All three now hung onto the rope, as Anna yelled at Bruce to leave them alone, Penny became frightened, nostrils flaring, head lifting.

No one saw where Chris came from, but Bruce felt a prod in the base of his ribs, making him wince and dip in one nervous reaction, releasing his grip.

"Who the hell are you?" Bruce said angrily, turning to face the small man who now stood beside him. Towering above Chris, Bruce leered at him, then turned to face Anna. "Ha ha! Have you started dating pygmies now Snooks!"

Bruce sneered at Anna, now almost in tears, before turning back to glare mockingly at Chris, eyeing him up, seeing before him only someone smaller.

"And who the hell are you, her new bleeding boyfriend? What happened? Did you shrink in the wash? Ha ha!" Bruce glared at Chris, who stared back.

"No, I'm not her boyfriend," began Chris in a calm, clear and uncomfortably cold manner, his eyes set upon Bruce, unmoving. "I've been hired to collect this horse. Which I will. You're scaring it, so please get out of my way, let me do my job and load the horse. Go away. You shouldn't be here."

Bruce could not believe what he'd just heard. He looked at Chris, first in surprise, then grinned, feeling superior. However, as the small man remained motionless and impassive, a strange feeling of doubt passed through his lower belly, making him tighten up at the smaller man's lack of fear or concern.

"And what are you going to do about it, short-arse?" Bruce said aggressively, trying to build up his confidence, stepping back, his face inches from Chris'.

"Stop you if necessary. But I think you are intelligent enough to allow us to proceed and not cause trouble. Please move aside and let me load the horse."

Chris replied quietly, but with confidence, showing no emotion, his body stationary and face unmoving, seemingly having no fear of the bigger man.

Anna and Tracey stared in silence. Even Penny seemingly looked on.

Bruce regarded Chris, weighing up the small man, assessing if it was bluff or genuine boldness. His smile vanished for a second, realising the small horseman was actually serious, knowing a lot of jockeys were fearless. He looked over to Anna in a sneering leer, as ever over-confident in himself.

"Well you can't take the horse," Bruce said arrogantly. "The horse isn't Anna's property to take. It's part of our joint assets. To be sold off. Meat!"

Bruce leered at the now tearful Anna, who was hugging Tracey for support. She shook her head in disbelief at her horrible, arrogant husband.

"And what money we get, after it's made into dog food, will be divided when the divorce goes through. The horse is to be sold and the money split. Or should we just split the horse in half now and have a bit each. I'll go and get a chainsaw. Half each. Unless you want to rethink Snooks? Ha, ha!"

"Don't call me Snooks," replied Anna, sobbing. "You know I hate it. And don't talk about Penny like that. That's why I hate you. You can't even stand horses. You don't know one end from the other. You never come and watch me at shows, visit at the yard or give me any bit of attention. Everything has to be focussed upon your needs. You are totally selfish. Leave me in peace."

Bruce ignored Anna and turned his gaze back to Chris, glaring at him.

A smug, overly confident grin swept across Bruce's face.

"So I'll ask you again Pygmy, what the hell do you think you are going to do about it? This horse is my property. Are you going to stop me taking it?"

Chris was unfazed and regarded the man before him.

"Actually I've just bought the horse off Anna, so it now belongs to me," he began calmly. "I'll give you your half of the money when it's safely delivered back to my farm. How does that grab you? Will a cheque do? I can mail it to you wherever you like. Where should I send it? Mister Twat of Arseville?"

Bruce was floored by the comment and stood staring, dumbfounded, his blood beginning to boil. Anna and Tracey looked on stunned, a hand rising to Tracey's mouth in an effort to hide a grin. Desperately she wanted to laugh.

"Who's is this little shit?" Bruce said, turning to Anna, shaking his head.

"Bastard! I'll teach you!" He stepped forward, drawing back his fist.

Before the blow was even delivered, Chris moved like a cat and side-stepped Bruce's well-published failing punch. Continuing the fluid sideward motion, Chris delivered a single, jabbing punch straight into Bruce's floating rib.

The big man stood still for a second, like a tree with its base cut through.

He stared blankly at Chris, unsure for a second what had happened. Then the pain and instant lack of oxygen took over. He let out a gasp, falling to his knees, clutching his side. Fighting for air, the pain registered in his body.

Chris ignored Bruce as he collapsed onto his knees, gasping for air and then tipped forward onto all fours. Calmly he walked over to the two stunned women and the nervous horse, which he gently patted, taking the rope.

Silent, the pair looked down at Bruce, then at their hero with Penny.

"Right then, let's get Penny on board shall we?" Chris spoke calmly.

The two women regarded the crumpled figure of Bruce, now going purple, as Chris calmly led Penny away, speaking quietly and towards the ramp. Like a perfect lady, Penny went up first time, the ramp clattering noisily underfoot. Chris swiftly tied her in place, whilst Tracey swiftly followed on up with a haynet, busying herself in the lorry, pretending the wheezing figure of Bruce; still kneeling on the floor, didn't exist, although she peered down to check.

Anna stood in the yard and looked silently at the form of the one-time husband she had loved and worshipped, but no longer. She despised him; such was his betrayal. Bruce slowly began to regain his breath and rise up.

"You couldn't let me go peacefully could you?" Anna said to the beaten figure before her. The anger welled up in her; eyes streaming, fists clenched.

"I'm surprised you even remembered where I kept Penny, as you took so little interest all the time we were together." Anna wept, but felt her strength and bitterness growing. "You never came to the yard or watched me ride at any shows, instead moaning about work. Yet now you take a sudden interest? You just had to mess up one more bit of my life, didn't you? Ten years I've put up with your shit, moving from one home to another; losing touch with my friends, just to satisfy your career moves. Whilst just being a slave to you, doing all your housework and fetching you beer and pot noodles in bed!"

She caught her breath, venting bitter emotions long held back.

"I've finally learnt my lesson. I don't love you and haven't for years. You betrayed me with that slut Lucy. Good luck to you both. She's a nutter! Leave Penny and me alone to make a new start. Is that clear? We're finished!"

Sobbing heavily, Anna stormed past the silent figure of Bruce as he slowly rose and coldly stared at the three figures pampering and securing the horse in the back of the lorry. They climbed down the ramp, all ignoring Bruce.

Tracey led Anna around to the front of the lorry, putting a comforting arm around her shoulders, neither turning to look back at the defeated man. Chris also turned his back to his new enemy, but knelt down to raise the tailboard, firmly securing it in place on both sides. Bruce, clutching his side stood looking on, trying to regain both breath and some dignity. Chris turned as he'd finished and looked direct at Bruce. Without speaking he dismissed him and turned, walking away down the side of the lorry and climbed into the cab.

"All set?" he enquired casually to the two women as he climbed inside, both hugging each other, Anna now in the centre of the seat and closest to Chris. The pair simply nodded as a response and the lorry was started up with a hearty roar, put into gear and began to slowly ease forward, passing Bruce's parked Audi, then moved clear of the yard and out through the farm gates.

Chris glanced in the lorry's large wing mirrors to see a defiant man glaring coldly at the back of the lorry, before then slowly walking back to his vehicle.

"Sorry for all of that, and thank you," spoke Anna, her red eyes looking sideways towards Chris, sniffing, her nose red. He simply grinned.

"No worries. Shit happens! Now to get back home safely."

"I told you Bruce was an arsehole!" Tracey exclaimed. "An extra-large one!"

The two ladies chuckled and Anna momentarily gently touched Chris' hand as a thank you. He flinched at first but then smiled, placed his on top as a warm gesture, before she withdrew it and fumbled for a tissue.

"My mascara will run!" she joked with a gentle sniffle, looking in the mirror. "Bloody men! I'll stick to horses from now on. Much less demanding."

With the tension eased, the three settled in the cab, staring out the big screen. Each was lost in their own thoughts as the lorry headed onto the country lanes, returning back the way it'd come, and taking Penny to her new home.

As he slowly drove down the country lanes from Jan's farm, Chris glanced in the lorry's mirrors, looking behind, as Anna and Tracey both sat quiet and subdued. It wasn't long before Chris saw behind him what he was expecting.

Sitting back some distance, trying to keep out of sight and ducking behind hedges in corners was an Audi estate. Slowly, with deliberate intent, Chris headed along the narrow roads, furtively glancing in his mirrors, whilst watching the road ahead. They travelled for another mile, the Audi some way back, but still behind and clearly following discretely. However, another car had pulled in behind the slow Audi, slowly forcing it to move faster and thus ever closer to Chris' lorry, which it was reluctantly doing, until the Audi was almost directly behind the lorry. As the road ahead narrowed, with trees overhanging above, Chris manoeuvred the lorry into the middle of the road, as if to avoid the branches and gently applied the brakes, stopping the lorry.

The woman looked at Chris puzzled as he quickly began to get out the cab.

"Just want to check the back's done up properly," he said casually jumping down onto the road. "Be back in s few seconds. Stay put. No worries."

He was gone from the cab in a flash, the women looking at each other, but doing as instructed and now free from Chris, naturally began chatting.

Bruce saw the horsebox ahead stop, and being pushed from behind by the car following, its elderly driver appearing impatient, he reluctantly stopped the Audi only a few feet from the back of the now stationary horse lorry. The gentleman driver behind Bruce appeared curious, wondering what was going on ahead, his view of the road blocked by the back of the lorry and the slow moving Audi which in turn had been forced to stop in the middle of the road.

Bruce too wondered what was happening, his view of the world simply the rear of the large lorry, with the wording 'Horses' before him, screened with hedges and over-hanging trees either side. The car behind blocked him in, so he could not reverse. He huffed, annoyed he'd now be seen and his plan to secretly follow the horsebox and Anna back to Norfolk had been blown.

Suddenly the horseman appeared from the lorry cab, moving down the side and towards the rear of the lorry, as if to head his way. Bruce peered out the windscreen intently, curious as to what was going on, and wondering if something was wrong with the lorry. The horseman paused, quickly reaching into one of the side locker on the lorry and removed an object.

Bruce craned his neck to look at what he'd retrieved.

Then stared in horror.

It was a massive hunting knife.

Fear seized Bruce as he saw the horseman grin widely.

Knife held low to his side, so only Bruce could see it, he advanced.

Bruce froze. Fight, flight or urinate?

Bruce's eyes flicked up into the rear-view mirror, looking for a way to reverse back, but the car behind blocked all movement. Focusing on the horseman, Bruce began to panic, seeing him advance towards his car, the jagged edge of the huge blade hanging low and glinting dull. He glanced back in the mirror, noting the patient elderly driver behind, chatting away to a woman passenger, seemingly unaware of the approaching knife-wielding madman.

Confusion raced through Bruce's mind as he realised he was trapped.

He fumbled for the seat belt catch, but in his panic his thumb slipped and it would not release. He tugged frantically at the black webbing. Too late.

The horseman was level with the front of the car, the knife massive in his hand. Instinctively Bruce hit the central locking button, all doors locking with a resounding and comforting thud, cocooning him inside his glass and steel shell, as his new adversary stood inches away, beside the driver's door.

Bruce turned to see the horseman smiling at him through the window.

The horseman's eyes stared at him, cold and empty.

Fear raced through Bruce.

He knew dangerous men when he saw them.

And this man was dangerous. Very dangerous.

He swallowed, staring silently at the leering mad-man outside.

Suddenly the horseman's hand rose, the massive knife blade clear and deadly.

It drew level with the window. The blade was huge and heavy.

Bruce closed his eyes, the blade's impact a gentle thud.

A hot flow of urine filled Bruce's lap. Bladder released, it poured through his trousers, seeping onwards and into the Audi's seat. Sensing another small jolt, and hearing a hiss, he cautiously opened an eye, wondering what'd happened.

Where had he been stabbed, and why did he felt no pain? Bruce mused.

Why hadn't he heard the glass shatter as the knife hammered through and smashed fatally into his skull? The thoughts raced through Bruce's mind.

Maybe he was already dead. So swift and fatal was the blow. Was he dead?

Bruce, both eyes open, turned his head to see he was alive and the horseman still outside. But he'd moved, and was now on the passenger's side of the car.

Another thud, and the car rocked once more, as another swift stab from the deadly knife tore open the other front tyre. Air rushed from that tyre to match the first one, the front of the car now slowly sinking down both sides.

Bruce's fear changed to anger, realising what the small guy had done, as he looked down at the seat-belt buckle, which now released as he pressed firmly.

He prepared to exit the vehicle and take the horseman on.

Then the horseman returned to the driver's side window.

Bruce paused, and went to grab the door handle. Then he felt the damp warmth between his legs and looked down at the seat, suddenly aware of what he'd done. His face flushed, and he shook his head, a mixture of fear and embarrassment flooding through, confusing his usually quick mind.

He wanted to cry for the first time in years, his mind in a whirl for once, unsure of how to act; hating the fear and not being in power or control.

'Bastard!' He screamed internally. But he was scared. No sound came out.

A shadow loomed over, the light fading, as he became aware of the presence of the horseman standing before him, peering into the driver's side window.

His eyes were dead, his facial expression emotionless.

Bruce eyed the serrated-bladed hunting knife in the horseman's hand, raised menacingly close, separated by only a thin membrane of fragile clear glass.

Bruce looked at the horseman. The horseman stared back.

Silently, with a wagging finger, he motioned for Bruce to wind down the window. Bruce froze, fearful of what would happen, but with a greater fear of what might happen for disobeying the order.

He touched the window button gently, his finger shaking.

The switch responded with a soft click.

Chill air entered as the glass lowered an inch.

He looked up slightly, cautiously raising his ear to listen, whilst half watching the knife, expecting the steel blade to smash through the glass and plunge into his skull, splitting it in half like an axe cleaving a block of soft firewood.

Wincing, he waiting for the sound of glass shattering and for the impact of the blade as it hammered into his head.

Instead a gentle voice pierced his skull.

It spoke softly through the small gap in the window.

"Leave Anna alone. For good. And don't try to follow us. Goodbye."

Bruce waited for a few seconds, the silence palpable, realising his eyes were closed. Opening his eyes, as though in a bizarre dream, he watched with relief to see the horseman walk away as swiftly as he'd appeared, moving alongside the lorry, pausing at the side locker, before then climbing back into the cab.

Moments the lorry pulled forward, disappearing around the wooded bend in the tight road ahead, vanishing from sight, leaving a shaken man sitting in the now cold, damp, acrid smelling seat of the car. Bruce sighed.

A figure appeared, big and large at the driver's window.

Bruce leapt sideways, shaking. With terror stark in his eyes he cowered away from the person standing at the window. He looked up at the vision.

"I say old chap?" An elderly gentleman enquired through the gap in the window, clad in tweed jacket and cap. "Are you going to move your car?"

Pressing his finger fully on the window button, the Audi's glass lowered with a whir. The old man looked in at the shaken, sodden Bruce. "Oh I say, looks like you've split a drink. Can you move your car please? My wife has to get to her W.I. meeting. She's presenting her prize-winning Victoria sponge cake."

Bruce stared silently at the vacant old man, who appeared confused at his lack of response, then glanced at the front of the car, noticing the flat tyre.

"Oh I see, you've got a puncture. How unfortunate. Must be why you stopped. We'll have to drive past. I hope you get it fixed okay. So long."

The old man returned to his car and carefully pulled past the stationary Audi, brushing against the hedge to pass. The elderly couple waved happily at the stationary figure sitting in the Audi as they passed.

Bruce looked blankly out the windscreen, his face a sheet of white alabaster.

Back in the lorry, Tracey and Anna were unaware of what occurred, such was the speed of the incident, it taking less than a minute. Chris made no mention of Bruce as they slowly drove back, but carefully checked his mirrors.

The journey home was more sober, with an air of gloom, despite the happiness Anna should have felt knowing Penny was on her way to a new home. Checked a few times by Anna and Tracey, Penny travelled well.

The day moved on, with the sun dropping in the sky, as the miles were eaten up beneath the rolling wheels of the horsebox, as it dutifully cruised along. The land once more changed from the rolling green hills of Leicestershire to the wide-open spaces of the Fens, then to the hedged flat fields of Norfolk.

It was getting dark again as they arrived back in the yard. Julie was magically back there, almost as if she'd never left, getting Tess in. Chris' part-time groom Sally was seeing to the liveries, as well as Chris's own horses, the yard as busy as ever. Once the lorry stopped, the three climbed out, stretched their legs and lowered the back, to the curious eyes of Julie and Sally peering in.

Untied, a proud Anna slowly led Penny down the ramp, as she excitedly looked about. Anna did well to control her, as whinnying, she spun about, taking in the sights. But Anna guided the inquisitive horse into the new stable, and Tracey quickly pulled the door shut. Penny charged forward, calling to her new neighbours, snorting loudly, and taking in the new scents and sounds.

Tracey and Anna laughed, finally at ease and relieved to be safely back. Chris wandered over, smiling, pleased to see them all excited but safely home.

"Welcome to your new home Penny," Anna said, smiling.

Chris patted the excitable horse's neck, as she strode forward.

"Thank you so much for getting her for me Chris, and for helping out today with Bruce. Sorry about him and all that shit. What an idiot!"

"No problem. It was a pleasure. I think you will both fit in very well here," Chris smiled, giving Penny another pat. "Welcome to your new home."

Anna reached out and stretched her long arms around Chris, gently hugging him. He tensed, surprised by the action, but then relaxed as he looked into her grey eyes. "Thank you Chris. I really mean it. You've been an angel."

Tracey looked on across the yard, a broad smile set upon her face.

"No worries," Chris replied, as Anna released him and he wandered back to the lorry. He turned to look at Anna with a smile, their eyes connecting.

It'd been a long day, but Anna was sure she and Penny would be happy in their new home. Her new life and freedom beckoned. Life started now.

She was now totally free of Bruce.

He was history. *Wasn't he?*

Chapter 29

Morning has broken like the first morning,
blackbird has spoken, like the first bird.

Eleanor Farjeon

Anna woke early, well before the alarm. Unable to sleep, a whirl of thoughts had unsettled her all night. Whilst she appreciated the temporary hospitality of her parent's home, by lodging back in her old bedroom, as well as bringing back enjoyable childhood memories, she couldn't help feeling like an intruder. It also didn't help that Anna was a lark, always rising early, whereas her parents weren't even aware there were two Five O'clock's in a full day. In addition, she was now a mature woman, who'd previously enjoyed her freedom, and now longed to get back to having a place of her own.

She'd briefly seen the small quaint cottage Chris had put her onto and spoken with the owner. As it was vacant, she was going for a full look later today. All going well, and no rats, she'd soon have a place of her own. It seemed as if fate was for once rolling her some good dice. Or so she hoped.

Rising and dressing quietly, she tip-toed down into the kitchen of her parent's large house and made herself a coffee. As it cooled, she checked the clock. She didn't want to arrive at the yard too early to appear paranoid, but not too late to appear slack and uncaring. Drumming her nails on the kitchen table, dressed in jodhpurs and a long-sleeved top, she re-checked the clock again. Five minutes had passed. Conceding to the pangs of fear, donning her wellies from the conservatory, she grabbed her thick fleece, bag and car keys, and left half the warm coffee on the table. Heading out into the gloom, the street lights illuminating the quiet estate in a pale orange hue, she quietly closed the back door and headed for her 4 x 4 parked in the large driveway.

It was still dark as she drove to Horsewater, with a mix of excitement and apprehension swirling inside. Chris hadn't rung last night, so she could only hope all was well with Penny and she'd settled in well to her new home.

Anna looked nervously about the woods as she drove off the country lane and turned into Horsewater. She grinned at the 'Trespassers ….' warning sign at the entrance; the same sign she'd first thought cold, dark and disturbing.

But now she was now beginning to understand the owner's dark humour.

The trees of the woods were dark and eerie, the sensation strange to drive through alone for the first time, but it also added to the thrill of a fresh start to her life. As she drove along the long, twisting woodland track, the branches of the trees appeared to reach out at her 4 x 4 and try to ensnare her.

For a fleeting second she thought of Bruce, and saw his hands grasping out the get her; to clasp at her and take her back to the life of drudgery she'd left.

She shook her head, feeling bold. Bruce was history. All over and gone. Horsewater was the future. Whatever that might be. She was starting anew. The new cottage, not far away, would hopefully be her new home. Penny would settle in at Horsewater and an exciting new phase of her life, with new friends, possibly within hunting, would begin. Also, she couldn't help but feel drawn towards the short, moody, strange, but somehow alluring horseman. But was it simply the rebound. A need for company? Time would tell.

As she emerged through the trees into the clearing around Chris' yard, the lights were already ablaze, with Julie's Land Rover parked in what seemed to be its permanent place. She checked her watch. It was six-thirty, with the first light barely breaking the horizon in a dull grey-blue glow.

"Hi," a voice called over as she exited her vehicle, turning. "You're early."

Anna smiled to see Chris wandering over towards her, the Doberman close by his thigh, its eyes set upon her. Anna looked cautiously at Max, having met him only a couple of times, but always slightly intimidated by the big dog. Chris appeared to sense her caution and sent Max away, the obedient dog trotting back to the house from which they'd emerged, happy to be inside.

"He's obedient," Anna quipped, nodding toward the disappearing dog.

"Just like his owner," Chris smiled. "Also, he can't bear to leave his bed by the Aga. He looks evil, but is as soft as poo really. Again, just like his owner."

"I couldn't sleep last night, worrying. Is she okay?" Anna enquired nervously, looking across towards the stable, walking across the yard with Chris.

"No problems," Chris responded. "Checked her just before Midnight and she'd eaten most of her net out and was already down asleep. Long journey. She was up early when Julie arrived and seems fine, whinnying happily over the stable door. Penny that is, not Julie. Although I do wonder about her!"

Anna grinned, beginning to get a sense of Chris' strange humour and also of those in the yard. Tracey she knew well, but Julie seemed as equally mad.

"I'm so pleased," replied Anna, the stress visually venting from her body. "Thank you again for everything you did yesterday." She looked long at Chris, who blushed in the dim light. "It was really appreciated. Ex-hubby and all."

"No worries," he replied. "Glad I was of use. And he wasn't a problem."

"Hmm, yes, Bruce. Typical of him." Anna blushed. "Pain in the arse. But then he is an arsehole too. Anyway, a fresh start. This is for you by the way."

She pulled out a bottle of red wine from her bag, thrusting it into Chris' hands, his expression surprised. "I hope you like red. An extra thank you."

Anna blushed, looking at Chris' appreciative smiling face, reading the label.

"I'm very grateful, and you really didn't have to," he said, admiring the label in the soft yellow light. "Thank you. It's very nice. Shiraz. I love red wine."

"And if you need a hand drinking it, then I'm your man!" Anna quipped.

"I doubt that very much. Man I mean," he grinned, cheekily scanning Anna's curves with a nod. "But I may take you up on the offer. Only if joined with good company, a lump of cheese and a big bowl of cheese and onion crisps."

Anna's face glowed at the possible invitation, wincing after she'd made the comment, unsure if she'd pushed things too far, too soon, but felt warmed.

"Don't let Tracey see it," she added. "Red is fatal for her!"

"Any alcohol is deadly to her," laughed Chris, knowingly. "And others!"

Anna felt relaxed as the pair headed side by side towards Penny's stable, who promptly appeared with a whinny, her eyes bright and alert.

"Sounds like she's also pleased to see you this morning," Chris added.

The fine bay head, highlighted by a prominent diamond-shaped star on her forehead, rose high above the door. Anna patted her neck, and kissed her muzzle, aware from the side of her vision Chris was intently watching.

"She's a stunning looking lady." Chris smiled.

"That's why she's called Lady Penelope. A real lady, just like her owner!"

Chris shook his head and Anna laughed. "She's very showy in the ring. And can be a bit of a tart and show off. But I'm afraid, that's not like her owner!"

"Oh, now I'm disappointed," Chris chuckled, then flushed red, seeing Anna's embarrassed but appreciative grin at their growing playful banter.

The pair admired the striking bay mare over the door, both silent for a few seconds, lost in their own thoughts. Anna cast a glance towards Chris, standing only a few feet away. Chris looked into Anna's grey eyes, seemingly lost for a moment, staring intently, before suddenly looking down.

"I forgot to ask where you're living. At your parent's house didn't Tracey say? Was Pear Tree Cottage any good? I know it's a bit tatty, but..."

"No, it's wonderful. I had a quick look and should be going back today with my mum to check it properly. If it's all good, and the rats aren't too big or aggressive, I'll be renting. It needs some decorating, but it's a traditional old cottage in the country, and just up the road. Perfect. Thank you again."

Chris raised his eyebrows and nodded positively, happy he'd helped.

"Excellent news. It's a quaint little place. Needs a lick of paint. I've know Pear Tree Cottage and its owner Jeff since I was a kid. He used to be friends with my….." Chris paused and failed to finish the sentence, looking own.

Anna had been informed by Tracey of Chris' past, his childhood, and what happened to his parents. She'd been warned it was an area not to encroach.

Anna heeded the warning well and looked away, down towards the paddocks to break the silence, then turned back to face him as Penny barged the door.

"It needs decorating, but dad knows some people and all going well, I'll be getting some old furniture off mum and Tracey and soon moving in properly. I'll be sorting it out over the weekend. At least I'll only be about a mile away."

"Welcome neighbour! I'll bring you a cake or pie!" Chris joked. "I'll also be able to pop in and borrow a cup of sugar or a bag of sugar beet if needed."

"You can pop in and have a cup of tea. Or better still, maybe bring that bottle with you!" Anna winced as soon as she'd spoken, wondering if she'd pushed it too far, noting the embarrassed look and subtle glow to Chris' face.

"I will, once you've settled in." His response was polite, but non-committal, but he turned to look at her, Anna feeling a warmth churning within.

"Hello!" a voice announced, breaking the moment. "How is she doing?"

"Hi Julie. I'm doing very well!" Anna joked, knowing she meant the horse. "And Penny's settled in well too, all thanks to her new Uncle Chris."

"He'll always help you settle in, won't you Chris?" Julie quipped, winking at Chris, who simply smiled back. "Like a shoehorn in a loose slipper!"

Chris shook his head and Anna grinned as the three gazed across at Penny, who was unfazed by the new attention, enjoying having the back of an ear rubbed by Anna, as Julie patted her neck. Chris suddenly glanced at his watch.

"Must get on. Lots to do. Good to see she's settled in. Sorry, I have to dash."

With that Chris was gone. Anna watched him strut across the yard, once more a feeling unsure of him and his strange nature and mannerisms.

Julie watched her with a smile, Anna suddenly aware of the attentive gaze, as red-faced, she turned to face her new friend. The pair glanced at Chris.

"You'll get used to Chris, but never understand him," Julie began quietly, although Chris had moved away. "Great guy. Always busy and works non-stop. But unique. And with an armour-plated shell no one will penetrate."

"He's very nice and I appreciate what he's done. I'm just glad to be here."

Anna spoke warmly, looking down, absorbing her own thoughts, but also Julie's words, but thinking deeper. Julie looked at Anna, sensing she may be happy, but knew like many before her, she definitely wanted more.

"Anyway, enough man talk, lets get down to real business. When are we going to ride out? You need to explore Horsewater and its mysteries!"

"I can't wait," Anna replied. "I'll give Penny a few days to settle in before riding. Then it's the weekend. Are you all out hunting again this Saturday?"

"Not this weekend. I don't hunt every week, nor does Chris. It's at a meet some distance away and is one that isn't that good. Lots of roads and boring."

"How about Sunday?" I'm supposed to be decorating and sorting out my potential new home over the weekend, so Sunday morning would be ideal, if you're free. Tracey should be about. We can all go out. Be warned though!"

"That's a date," confirmed Julie. "Sounds great. You'll be amazed where you can ride here. I'll see you about, but look forward to Sunday. Must dash!"

With that Julie patted Anna's arm, rubbed Penny's muzzle and jogged off towards her car, checking her watch as she ran. Anna's new friend seemed always busy and in a hurry, not unlike Chris. It was a common aspect of horse owners, who Anna knew only too well herself, worked hard to keep them.

Anna wandered away and looked around the floodlit yard. Chris was busying himself in a stable further along, and she now knew better than to annoy him further, so resigned herself to the job of turning out Penny. However, she was slightly reluctant to turn her out too early into a new paddock in the dark, so decided to spend some time sorting out her kit from yesterday, sorting out rugs, her feed and then in pampering her best friend for a while first.

Going into the large tackroom, formed from a set of stables and part of an old barn combined, it provided a secure storage area. The odours of stale and damp rugs, oiled and old leather, horse feed, coffee and hay all permeated the air; the 'horsey' smell unique to a tack room, but it did have a cosy feel.

She wandered to the area set aside for her equipment, typically towards the back area where it was darker and the smell of old rugs was thick and heavy, but it suited Anna. The space was generous and permitted her to store her various rugs, along with a saddle rack for her tack, with space below to place her grooming kit in a wooden trunk and all the other paraphernalia associated with horse ownership. Along the middle wall, near the door, a small kitchen area had been created, with a sink, rusty fridge and a couple of old kitchen cupboards to store items. An ancient battered timber table sat nearby, with a series of rings marks etched into the wooden surface, around which were positioned numerous chairs; from modern plastic seats in bright orange, possibly liberated from a village hall or school, to old timber ladder-backs, formerly part of a grand dining suite, but now serving a more lowly purpose.

Various dust-covered rosettes hung on the wall near the sink; once treasured trophies of memorable events, along with a large blackboard, upon which were scribbled various messages. Anna noticed one, which made her smirk.

'Wed' - Anna and Lady Penelope Arrive. Be nice to her or else! - Tracey.'

Noting the kettle set beside the sink and a vast array of mugs, many with horsey images or logos upon them, she smiled, and made a mental note to get herself a mug of her own. Along with various pots, containing tea, coffee sugar stood an old tin, marked in black marker-pen; 'Biscuits - One at a time!'

Anna grinned to herself again, making another mental note to bring a packet of biscuits to break the ice and also to ensure she brought some good coffee.

Suddenly Sally appeared in the doorway, moved over to another section of the tackroom and turned, as if noticing a stranger within. She smiled warmly at Anna, but carried on with her task, seemingly unfazed by her, as if she was already part of the furniture. Without malice, but busy, she turned and spoke.

"Oh hello. I see Penny's settled in well. I thought she would. Lovely horse."

Anna was about to reply, but with that she was gone, a handful of equipment hastily grabbed. Anna realised she was not being rude, but had her own work to do about the yard and seemed to follow in Chris' footsteps. Rooting about in her various tack boxes, she dug out Penny's brushes and turn-out rug, ready to turn her out after giving her a good grooming whilst she waited.

Anna knew Penny would most likely roll in mud straight away once turned out, but the brushing would be as therapeutic for Anna as it was for Penny, and give her time to recall the chaotic series of events which had taken place following her decision to move back home to her place of birth.

She now had Penny in a new yard, leaving behind Jan and the friends she'd made at Six Hills over the last few years. It was a place she'd been happy at, and reluctant to leave. But she hadn't expected things to happen so quickly.

But Bruce had changed it all. Selfish, arrogant Bruce. 'Typical Bruce.'

He'd destroyed her life and all she'd held true, despite giving everything she could to the self-centred and conceited man for years; following his career about the country, so he could get everything he wanted, and much more.

And he'd decided he certainly needed more than Anna could offer.

Seemingly in certain areas. Anna felt her blood boil and herself 'inadequate.'

Lucy, his 'loose' slapper of a secretary, had happily supplied those services.

But Anna had always had doubts of indiscretions with Bruce.

Lucy probably wasn't the first and certainly wouldn't be the last place where Bruce's 'old tug-boat' would find a port to harbour on a stormy evening.

But Bruce was history. Out of her life. Gone.

It was now time to start fresh, to see what new joys or sorrow, life would bring and time for a new adventure. Horsewater, along with Tracey, Chris and the strange riders associated with the Shoteton Harriers looked to provide it.

As she groomed an appreciative bay mare, being left alone as others busied around the yard, it gave her time to reflect on the past, wondering what may have gone wrong and what lessons, if any should could learn.

Whatever happened fro here on, she was determined to make fresh plans for a brighter future, and maybe find a new and genuinely loving partner. With that she gave the warm, and now shiny horse a big comforting hug.

At around seven-thirty, a familiar head with bright smiling face appeared.

"I see you've both survived the night," joked Tracey. "She's looking shiny. Pity she'll be covered in shit in just a few minutes, when she rolls in the mud!"

Anna laughed, knowing Tracey was right, but welcomed the friendly face.

She left Penny to help Tracey with Fred, following her to the paddocks, where Tracey showed her the paddock Penny would be turned out into.

The early morning gloom had lifted and despite being chilly, it looked like it'd be a mild, dry day as Anna surveyed the row of green paddocks, set within the sprawl of mature sweeping woodland on all sides. Crows cawed high above the tall woods in the distance and Anna felt a pang of excitement.

Chris appeared to be keeping a deliberate distance whilst he busied himself along with Sally, but Anna noticed continuous glances in her direction, often smiling. Finally, when all was set, Anna led Penny out, smartly wrapped up in a blue hooded turn-out rug, being joined by an equally excited Tracey. As soon as Chris heard the clop of hooves in the yard he stopped mucking out and moved over to join them, wandering with them out of the yard and down towards the array of paddocks, neatly divided by timber post and rail fencing, topped with white electric fencing, the gentle 'tick' a reminder not to touch.

"Hope she turns out okay," Anna spoke cautiously, the bay mare's head high, looking about her at the other excited horses, her diamond star flashing.

"She'll be okay. Probably have a chase around for a few minutes, geed-up by the other horses, but will soon settle down. Don't worry." Chris offered.

"I'd be worried! I think she's going to trash that new rug!" Tracey laughed.

Tracey's quip, as ever cheered everyone up, as they steadily moved down the track. A number of horses, already turned out, trotted across their paddocks to witness the new arrival. Penny grew taller, trotting on tip-toes, challenging Anna to restrain her, as she noted Chris' cautious look. But Anna knew her horse well, and despite the prancing nature knew she was still in control.

"Are you okay?" Chris enquired. Anna simply grinned, rather nervously.

Chris had allocated a small paddock close to the stables for Penny to graze for a few days. Usually reserved for sick or lame horses, she'd stat there until she was settled. Then he'd move her along into the main paddock area within the vast clearing, set within the huge woodland to create the lush paddocks.

Chris opened the gate to the paddock as Anna led in Penny, who beginning to strut quicker as she saw the field and new neighbours. As soon as she was inside the paddock, and Chris and Tracey had hastily shut the gate, Anna released her headcollar. Snorting loudly, Penny strutted over to the far rail, before turning, trotting up and down the fence line for a few seconds, looking about, then promptly put her head down to taste the new grass. Two nibbles later she raised her head, bright eyes looking about and released a whinny, in response to a call from another horse several paddocks away. Head back down, she took another mouthful of grass, then continued eating. The three spectators watched for a few more minutes, but all the mare did was eat.

"Well that was an anti-climax," Anna announced, part relieved, but part disappointed, expecting chaos but hoping for peace. "But in a way good!"

Chris simply shrugged his shoulders. "That's horses for you. Never do what you expect. I'll keep an eye on her. Any problems, I'll call you."

Anna thanked Chris and once again they parted, as did Tracey, who had to dash off to work. Anna proceeded to muck out the stable, and prepare everything for later. Chris was busy as ever, and a number of other liveries came, including Carol, the older woman who owned the black mare Tess.

She seemed nice and worldly-wise and spoke briefly to Anna, the pair watching Penny from afar. She declared she was riding and swiftly brushed and tacked up her black cob, then rode off through the yard, down the track past Penny and disappeared off into the distance and towards the woods.

Anna stood watching the pair from the yard for a few moments as they vanished into woods, absorbing the beautiful surroundings of Horsewater, hoping she too would soon be out exploring the deep woods and more.

She gazed at the paddock one more time to see the bay mare unfazed, head down and happily eating and noted Chris watching from the yard, seeing her look his way, a simple raised arm and thumbs up giving her reassurance.

Anna returned the wave and headed back towards her 4 x 4 just as she heard the sound of a large rumble through the woods. A smart black Range Rover rolled into the yard, parking alongside Anna's car. Chris moved straight over.

Totally disregarding Anna, Virginia Burlingham leapt out, then strutted majestically across the yard as if she owned the place. Maybe she did.

Anna enviously watched cream jodhpurs, so tight it appeared she was naked from the waist down, display a perfect rear. Stunning sculptured legs, set within a pair of brown leather long boots, strutted as if on a Cat-walk. On top Virginia wore a skin tight, lambs wool sweater in baby pink, showing off her smooth lines and neat figure, and importantly, her perfect firm boobs.

Anna felt her blood boil, unsure why, as she enviously watched the perfect female specimen stomp across the yard, but felt justified when she spoke.

"Chris sweetie!" Virginia announced aloud, breaking into a delightful jog and running up to Chris, arms spread out as if they'd been apart for years.

"Ginny!" Chris announced, seemingly unaware of Anna, catching Virginia and lifting her up, hugging her warmly, then pecking each delicate cheeks.

"Where's the Audi?" he enquired, looking over at the Rover, then seemed to notice Anna watching him. He visibly looked away, turning Ginny to him.

"It's got a perishing puncture. So I've stolen Bertie's Rover. He won't need it. Doing something on the estate today and has the old Land Rover."

Side-by-side the pair walked down the yard, Chris seemingly oblivious to Anna. Insult was added further as Max trotted from the house and across to Virginia, muzzling his glossy black head under her hand. She affectionately rubbed his ears, completing the happy threesome, as the group wandered off, deep in conversation, heading around the back of the stables to the ménage.

It seemed everyone liked Virginia - except Anna!

Puffing her cheeks she climbed into her 4 x 4 and looked across the yard as she fired up the engine, watching as Chris and his friend disappear from view.

But Anna wasn't the only one watching.

Someone else was intently watching too.

Within the woods, across from the paddocks, someone on horseback.

A glint of light reflecting off small field binoculars revealed their location.

But the clue was missed by all, as eager eyes, jostled by the horse beneath them, watched the distant couple, mentally recording the activities.

But the rider failed to see another watcher.

Hidden deeper within the woods was someone else.

This silent observer had also noticed everything.

Horse and rider within the woods.

Chris and his flirtatious visitor at the yard.

Along with the attractive tall woman in the yard.

The second watcher had seen all.

And this keen observer made detailed notes.

Chapter 30

Better a thousand enemies outside the house than one inside.

Proverbs

The following day Chris was in a stable preparing to tack up his showjumper, Saint Swithin. A chestnut gelding, with distinct Roman nose, Tracey had told Anna the bolshy horse was famous for having less patience than Chris, and that he'd bite anyone at the first chance, so to be wary. That said, he wasn't as evil as Bonnie. For his credit, he was a brilliant showjumper, and Chris adored him, being one of only a few people who could handle or ride the horse.

The sound of a large diesel engine growling into the yard drew his attention. It was mid-morning, and most of the liveries had been and gone, although Anna was about still accustoming herself to Horsewater and Chris.

Chris peered over the stable door to see a white police Land Rover. Tutting audibly, and glancing from side to side, he quickly opened the stable door, ready to intercept the unwelcome driver. Saint Swithin, arrogantly barged at the door, but Chris knowing the horse only too well, shooed him back inside. The Land Rover door opened just as Anna was returning from the muckheap. Curious, she turned to look at the tall policeman who'd climbed out.

Grinning broadly at Anna, he adjusted his tool belt, hiding his small belly.

"Morning madam," he said, smiling widely and lifting his chest, eyes flicking up and down Anna's slim body. "Haven't seen you in these parts before. I'm certainly sure I'd have remembered you if I had. Fine start to the day."

He looked long at Anna, eyes moving from her feet to her face, then back, stopping halfway. Anna returned the smile to the good-looking policeman, but felt slightly uneasy by his intent piggy eyes. The pair stood in silence.

"Did you want something," Chris suddenly enquired from behind, his tone abrupt. Both Anna and the policeman turned, Anna surprised at his manner.

"Good morning. It's Burton. We met a week or so ago you may remember."

The policeman glanced at Chris, then back at Anna, who stood looking at the two figures. Curious, she immediately sensed friction between the two men.

"Wondered if I could have a few words. Just a routine enquiry about a local matter, you know." He looked back at Chris, his tone cold, businesslike.

Chris blushed and glanced at Anna. She caught Chris' look, sensing this was a private call, and duly smiled at both men, nodding. Wheelbarrow in hand, she was about to return to Penny's stable, which she was mucking out.

"Would you mind just keeping an eye on him for me please Anna?" Chris called. "He's tacked up and I don't want him catching his reins. Be careful though, as he can be a bolshy bastard. I think he'll like you. But take no shit!"

"Certainly Chris," replied Anna, "No problem. I'll smile nicely at him!"

Anna wandered over to the stable, where the Chestnut was getting agitated, then cautiously pushed the horse back to enter the stable, carefully patting his neck to try to appease him. He calmed down, but eyed Anna warily. Ever the typically curious woman, whilst holding the reins, Anna cocked her ear sideways to listen from inside the stable, just able to hear the policeman.

"Fine day," the policeman opened, in a loud Cockney voice.

"What do you want?" Chris asked the policeman bluntly.

In the stable, Anna raised her eyes, shocked at his rude and cold manner.

Burton blushed at the blatant rudeness and lack of expected respect, then composed himself, now used to such a tone from most of the local farmers.

"Just a routine enquiry sir. Do you know a Peter Jenkins or a Debbie Ward?"

Chris's face remained emotionless. "No. Should I?" He stared coldly.

"Well it is all just routine really," the policeman continued, his tone relaxed, but Chris knew the questions had hidden intent. "Missing person enquiry."

Burton scanned Chris' face, looking for any sign of emotion; touching of the face or lips, loss of eye contact or turning away. The horseman didn't react.

"Sorry, am I missing something?" Chris asked, agitation in his voice.

"As I said, just routine. They've probably run off with each other. Seems the most likely answer. So you've never heard of, or met a Peter Jenkins sir?"

The policeman asked again, this time his tone more serious, his gaze fixing upon Chris' unmoving face. It was clear he had something up his sleeve.

Anna listened intently, gently patting Saint Swithin and rubbing his neck, so he'd remained quiet and she could her more, his hooves rustling the straw, obscuring the odd word. She was naturally curious about the policeman's visit, wondering if Chris was in trouble. She was also shocked at his rudeness and lack of respect to the policeman, who if anything, seemed uneasy in the horseman's presence, as though he feared Chris, rather than the reverse.

"Not that I recall," replied Chris cautiously, noticing the policeman's change in tone. "The name means nothing to me. But then I meet loads of people."

"Oh," replied the policeman, in a cocky, controlled manner. "It seems Mister Jenkins had your farm details written down in his works appointment diary."

He looked at Chris with a tilted head, pausing for dramatic effect, like a TV Cop', but the horseman remained unmoved, and simply checked his watch.

"Peter Jenkins noted down as having visited you about five months ago. An insurance cold call I believe. It may have been nothing, as he visited quite a few farms in the area that week. But it included yours. Don't worry sir, I'll be visiting the others later as a matter of routine to check them out too sir. So I don't want you to think I'm just picking on you in particular Mister Turner."

Chris flushed for the first time, the bitterness boiling toward the policeman.

Burton looked smug, noticing the subtle change in skin tone. Result.

"Your name and address were on the list under my area to check out. And for some strange reason, your details stuck in my mind. Can't think why!" He finished the statement, looking confidently at the horseman. Too confidently.

"Did it now? I wonder why you might recall my name in particular?" Chris responded coldly, but remained impassive, his eyes cold, steady, unmoving.

The policeman gazed back smugly, but also clearly uncomfortable.

"So you're telling me you've never met a Mister Pete Jenkins? He made a rather rude note about you in his diary, it seems sir. Wouldn't do for me to repeat what he wrote. It seems you weren't very welcoming. Far from it."

The policeman almost grinned at the horseman.

Chris' face flushed, obvious anger boiling within. He stepped forward.

"I have lots of visitors. Some are friends whom I openly invite and welcome. A lot are uninvited, annoying Wankers! Unwelcome people who shouldn't be here, but who still come." He paused for a few seconds, looking firmly at the policeman, ensuring he knew he'd been added to that side of the list.

"He may well have come here trying to sell me something I don't need, but I don't recall his name. He was nothing. Insignificant. I have leaves and rubbish blow through my yard, but I don't remember each piece. What has it got to do with me if he did visit me months ago?" Chris asked coldly, his stare fixed hard on the uncomfortable policeman, who knew fully where he stood.

Anna was becoming more curious, excitement flowing at the tone, yet feeling guilty for listening in on a private conversation. She could not believe how rude and calm Chris was. Then she smiled, almost laughing, feeling from his replies she was beginning to better understand the no-nonsense horseman.

"He and his secretary vanished at the same time," Burton went on, about to add some details. "One evening. Neither returned home. Mister Jenkins was married. His wife is upset. Very concerned. And no money has come out of either of their bank accounts. Usually when lovers vanish, they drain their bank accounts beforehand or spend cash or cards as they travel. No credit cards have been used and they haven't gone abroad. They both seem to have vanished from the face of the earth. Disappeared. People are concerned."

The policeman paused, looking at Chris for a warm, concerned reaction.

The horseman was unmoved. He stood coldly regarding the policeman, his expression seemingly one of boredom and agitation, than of any concern.

"Additionally Mister Jenkins mobile phone record, and that of Miss Ward, were both recorded as being within a three mile radius of these parts on the evening they both disappeared. It seems there's a digital blackspot nearby, so we can't pinpoint where the mobile phone signals died or their journeys ended. But nothing has been recorded on either phone since. Very strange."

Chris remained impassive, unresponsive, simply staring blankly, then spoke.

"Perhaps they were running off and threw their phones away nearby in a ditch as they drove off, exactly so they couldn't be traced by busy-bodies and they could make a new start? I would if I wanted to suddenly disappear."

Burton stared at Chris' as if absorbing the idea, as though it was something he'd not considered. Or maybe he had but didn't want it as an answer.

"Maybe," the Policeman conceded with no commitment. "Good point."

The two men stood regarding each other. Unseen, Anna continued to listen, the brash Chestnut horse beside her seemingly at ease, the occasional mint slipped into his mouth appearing to greatly assist the usual impatience.

"The car was a silver Mercedes coupe," Burton continued. "Quite a distinct car. Easy to recognise. But the car also hasn't been seen since that night either by any police force or cameras. I take it you don't recall the car or haven't seen it about? Their disappearance isn't being investigated as suspicious. Not yet. Double missing person at present. Mister Jenkins wife is very upset."

Burton emphasised the word 'upset' as he stood awaiting feedback.

It had no effect. Chris looked unconcerned. "And?"

The policeman faltered at the uncaring, blunt response.

"We're enquiring if you've seen the car in the area or know anything that could help. Have you seen any strange cars on your farm lately?"

"Yes," came the stern response. "A white Land Rover with blue light on top. It keeps coming here uninvited. Driven by someone most unwelcome."

Chris stared at the policeman, who looked back coldly, unsure if the man before him was serious, or it was some form of local dark humour.

Anna was nudged for another mint, pushed against the stable door, the bolt clunking noisily as the top of her body appeared over the door, face blushing. The policeman looked towards the stable, to see Anna peering over the stable door. Her long, bright hair caught his attentive eye, along with the head and neck of the bright chestnut horse, now becoming as impatient as his owner.

Anna quickly pushed the horse back, disappearing, her unseen face flushing brightly, wondering if Chris knew she'd heard anything, or even if he cared.

Chris caught the policeman's glance, turning to see an empty stable door, but sensed Anna was listening to them. But he didn't seem to care.

"Is that it then?" asked Chris bluntly, turning back to face the policeman. "Anything else? I've got work to do." Chris stared at the unwanted guest.

Burton felt uncomfortable in the horseman's presence, but this time was determined to get one over on the arrogant and rude horseman.

He nodded towards the stable. "Very nice looking lady. Gorgeous in fact," he said with a cocky grin. "Which sort is she then? Married or a lesbian?"

Chris eyed him steely, pausing for a second, then recalled their last conversation. He glanced back towards the stable, where on cue Anna's head and smiling face appeared again, followed by an impatient chestnut gelding.

He turned, then replied, his face breaking into a grin for the first time.

"Married. Husband is about your height and build. I met him only a few days ago. Charming chap. You'd probably get on well with him." Chris grinned.

Burton sensed he was missing a private joke and knew he was beaten once more, but decided to put in a final attack; the blow he'd been keeping back and couldn't wait to deliver. He smiled at Chris, his look slimy and smarmy.

"Sorry about the other week, when I first came and visited you." He paused, building up, trying his best to draw in the horseman for a reaction.

"I didn't know about your past when I first visited. The tragic incident with your parents and issues you had when younger. I do apologise if I came over too strong. I didn't know about your past record then. But I do now."

Burton stared hard, and emphasised the word 'record,' the letter 'd' hanging in the air; almost reverberating. 'Record.' 'Criminal Record' he wanted to say.

He waited for a response, lips raised slightly, as if about to smirk, but he controlled his features well. As nothing came back he continued speaking.

"If we, in your local police force, can help you in any way, to offer you reassurance in any rural affairs or farm security, just give us a call. Anytime."

Chris went ashen, shaking inwardly. Face full of hatred and anger, the emotions burning deep in his belly, he held it in check; but not enough for the policeman to register. But Chris quickly recomposed himself, the colour returning; unseen clenched fists quickly opening, the blood returning.

He glared at the policeman for a few seconds, the dislike and hatred shared between them apparent in their stares, before Chris finally spoke.

"Goodbye then. Message received. You can leave now. I've got work to do."

He turned on his heels and with no further comment headed towards the stable, leaving the dumbstruck policeman standing alone in the yard, Burton once more looking at the back of the arrogant and fearless horseman.

'Tosser,' Burton mouthed at the horseman's back, standing dumbfounded.

He was tempted to yell after the horseman, call him back and question him further, but something prevented him. A secret fear within him, to which he did not want to admit to, that held him back. Or maybe something else.

He stood watching the horseman approach the stable. As he did, the tall, attractive woman looked out and carefully opened the door for the horseman, who joined her inside. Anna glanced coldly at the policeman over the door, swiftly closing the stable door behind Chris, casting one final, now slightly curious look at the policeman, as Chris moved inside and over to his horse.

"Lucky bastard!" Burton muttered walking away, recording Anna's image.

He climbed back into the Land Rover and gunned the engine into life.

"Lucky, lying bastard," he said aloud in the vehicle, smirking as he turned the Land Rover around, catching sight of a dark Range Rover parked at the rear of the big house, again taking note. He drove out the yard, back up into the woods and away, not welcoming the task of interrogating more rude 'locals'.

"Who was that?" Anna enquired naturally, as Chris stood inside the stable, obviously unhappy, cheeks flushed, standing beside her and Saint Swithin.

"No one important. Just an annoying pig nosing about, as they tend to do. Asking stupid questions, as they tend to do. But doing nothing to solve real crimes, as they don't do. You probably realise I hate the police. Arseholes!"

Anna looked at him slightly shocked; embarrassed now she'd asked the question and wondering if Chris knew that she'd overheard nearly all of the conversation. She felt a burst of guilt at having listened into the policeman's questions and wondered if Chris did really did know anything. Or cared.

He was a hard person to work out, even though she'd only known him a short time, but felt an invisible barrier prevented anyone from getting close, exactly as Tracey had warned. She looked at Chris, feeling slightly uneasy at the sudden closeness with which she now found herself with him in the confined stable, with just him and a bolchy Chestnut horse for company.

The feeling wasn't unpleasant, but quite the opposite, with a warm electricity passing between. The sensation was like two shy teenagers meeting at a disco, but neither knowing what to say or do, only a horse separating them both.

Chris broke the silence, his look almost bashful and his face flushing.

"Sorry for you getting involved. I meant to ask you, have you managed to sort anything out with Jeff's cottage at the weekend. Was it any good?"

He grabbed a hoof-pick from a tack box and began lifting the horse's hoof, to find Anna had already cleaned them. He smiled and nodded a thank you.

"It's a lovely place," Anna replied happily. "I've agreed to take it on and will be moving in. I need to sort out some furniture and decorate a few parts, but otherwise it's great. I'm really pleased with it and also very happy here too."

She was genuinely excited, the incident of the last few minutes now washed from her mind with mention of the cottage, which was to be her new home. The strange warmth she felt from Chris made her want to hug him.

"You have been an angel to me lately. I don't know how I would have sorted everything out. It seems like fate has played its part and helped me meet you," she said looking across the back of the chestnut horse directly at him.

Chris blushed, but was hidden slightly by the horse moving.

"Yes it does," he quietly replied, Anna sensing he wanted to say more.

"Happy to help." He paused, then shocked her. "Do you want to hunt next weekend? I've space on the box if you want to join us. There's no pressure."

"Oh my god, yes please! That would be great. Penny is already very fit. Yes. I'd love to come, but you know I've never hunted before. Do I need to be a hunt member?" she asked, her voice becoming excited at the thought.

"No, no worries. You can come as a visitor and just pay a cap. I'll phone our secretary Shirley and tell her you'll be coming with me as my guest. I'll sort it all out. You'll love it I'm sure. It's a bit hairy though, as you saw."

"Will you be taking him?" Anna enquired, patting the stocky chestnut horse, who'd grown accustom to her and hadn't tried to bite her, yet.

"No chance!" exclaimed Chris. "He's far too valuable. I wouldn't risk him."

He saw the look on Anna's face at the comment, as though her horse and others weren't as valuable as the arrogant, yet lovable chestnut showjumper.

"Sorry," he continued. "I don't mean it like that. All horses are valuable and I take care of them all. But they have their roles and what they are best at. He is a Grade B showjumper and I'm afraid he is not worth the risk or danger to take hunting. He is worth a lot of money as a showjumper. Also it'd mess up all of his training if he thought he could simply gallop about all day, even though he would," Chris explained, hoping he'd not belittled Anna's horse.

"For a lot of horses hunting is a brilliant and natural way to spice them up," he continued. "It allows them to run free, naturally with a herd. The horses absolutely love it. But for others, it ruins the years of training put in for a particular discipline. So no, sadly he won't be going, although he did go Stag Hunting on Exmoor with his previous owners. Went like a stag too I heard!"

He gave the chestnut a hearty slap, then checked the tack and girth. With no further comment, he grabbed the reins and lead him out of the stable.

"Thanks for keeping an eye on him. I look forward to riding out with you at the hunt. We'll have to ride out around the farm when I get a spare moment. I know you'll be riding around with Tracey very soon, but I'll show you the back woods and a few other tracks around the farm. It'll be a fast ride!"

"I'd love that," Anna said excited. "I'll look forward to it, and I'll keep you to that, provided I survive the hunt meet first! That will be so exciting!"

Chris smiled. "You'll be fine. You can ride alongside me. I'll take care of you. Tracey manages to stay on board, and she's usually three-parts drunk!"

With that Chris whipped down the stirrups and leapt straight into the saddle. The arrogant chestnut swished his tail as they trotted away. Anna admired the pair, watching until they disappeared towards the ménage, then wandered back to finish off mucking out with fresh vigour, excited at the thought of hunting, and now wanting to tell Tracey her exciting news.

The thoughts of the policeman's visit had vanished.

But were tucked away in her memory.

They'd be recalled at a later date.

Then Anna would wish she'd never overheard the conversation.

And importantly, mention of the name Peter Jenkins.

Chapter 31

I for one venerate a petticoat.

Lord Byron

"Bruce, sweetie, why are you packing?" the woman enquired, her concern overly expressed, voice pathetic; like a poor local stage actor in rehearsal.

"I told you. I'm going away. Business," the man replied bluntly. "Off first thing tomorrow. Important work. As mention, I've got to sort out a branch."

"Oh sweetie, do you have to? I'll miss you. Where are you going again?"

The woman put on an exaggerated pout, tilting her head for extra effect.

"Ipswich. The branch has problems. Total mess as you'd expect from yokels. Sorry Lucy, it's important. I'll be gone a week." He spoke with authority.

"Oh darling, I know what you do is important, as are you. Hence why I love your power, but must you go?" Lucy wrapped her arms around Bruce's neck.

Bruce feigned a smile, pecking Lucy on the lips.

She looked deep into his eyes. Very deep. Too deep.

"Where is Ipswich again?" Lucy enquired. "Near the east coast isn't it? That big lump sticking out in the sea. Isn't that where your ex-wife has just gone?"

Bruce paused, realising Lucy wasn't as stupid as she often looked. But he already knew that. "No, that's Norwich. It's further north and more yokel."

"They sound similar," Lucy commented, pecking Bruce's nose with her lips; eye contact strong. "Full of farmers. Sheep and pigs. Maybe even chickens."

"Norwich is in Norfolk. Ipswich is in Suffolk. About fifty miles apart," Bruce duly explained. "However, both are still about fifty years behind the rest of the world. I don't even know if they have electricity yet. Probably not."

Lucy might have been clever in a crafty and conniving way, but she wasn't bright enough to get Bruce's joke. She persevered for her own reasons.

"Do you have to go tomorrow? I was hoping we could have a duvet weekend. I wanted to play Doctors and Nurses. Again. You like that. And I've got a new outfit! It's extra saucy." Lucy raised her eyebrows.

'Not another Nurses outfit!' Bruce sighed inwardly. Outwardly he smiled.

Lucy fluttered her long false eyelashes, searching for an appropriate response from her puppet, pulling another string. Bruce feigned looking glum, as if he'd miss something special, but had his own plan and agenda.

"Oh dear. Too bad. Another time." He kissed her nose.

"No worries, I'll put it on now!" Lucy chuckled. "Wait!"

Before Bruce could respond Lucy was gone, disappearing from the main bedroom, dashing off into the spare bedroom, before then moving on into the bathroom, the door slamming shut. Bruce sighed, running his hands through his hair, wondering what Lucy was doing. He was becoming bored.

Bruce grabbed a mix of clothing, finding himself holding a T-shirt Anna had bought. He lifted it up and stared long and hard at the simple item of clothing. Then he pressed it to his face, as if absorbing a lost perfume or faded memory. The images of him wearing the shirt with Anna raced back.

Good times, before he let his cock run away and usually strong self-discipline and focussed energy lapse. But then he could never resist a pair of fluttering lashes, nor a pair of legs spread open before him on an office desk. Lucy.

'How the hell did it ever get to this?' He mussed, but knew.

Lucy might provide all he needed sexually, but so had Anna to a degree.

Nothing special, just basic and boring, but it had served his needs.

If only he'd taken a bit more notice of her and that stupid horse she doted on, then maybe things wouldn't have become so bad.

But horses were boring. Stupid creatures. They bit, kicked and farted.

They weren't as interesting as football or watching porn movies.

It was all so boring, watching someone trotting about on a dumb creature whilst clad in some fancy outfit. Although Anna's long legs in her tight jods' had always given him the horn. Then there was the expense of keeping the hay-munching, continuously shitting, ignorant creature. They cost loads.

Anna could never see how she spent almost as much on her horse in a year as he could spend on a week long luxury holiday in the Canary Islands.

Ridiculous. Waste of money.

It was one of the things that'd caused so many arguments. His lack of interest, the constant complaint of the costs and her lack of attention to him.

Although that said, Anna did always pay her way for the horse and never asked him for money. And generally, contributed more than ample financially to their coffers to pay bills and save a bit, unlike the current incumbent.

He stared at the bathroom door, shaking his head. Lucy. Liability.

She'd lost her latest temp job. Again. What a useless cow!

Except in the bedroom department. There she excelled.

Lucy had been fired for incompetence from the accounts practice where she'd met Bruce, despite him trying his best to get the company to retain her.

His position became unstable when the true reason he was so keen to maintain her services was discovered. This being the 'overtime' the pair were undertaking in the office at night. CCTV had captured some very good clear images, which could have made good money on certain dubious websites.

Bruce only kept his job because he knew too many of the company's dirty financial secrets. That was all. He wasn't that good. But Lucy had to go.

By this time Anna had also discovered their relationship, the history of it all, and finally left, deciding to move back home to her old home of Norwich.

'What a stupid mistake!' Bruce cursed himself for the countless time for being drawn into Lucy's clever web of deceit, as the sound of running water and heavy thumping noises resounded from within the bathroom.

'What the hell is she doing in there? Changing the toilet cistern?'

Bruce never thought he'd tire of sex, Anna and him always being fairly active, even if she was a little prude and boring and didn't give him anything special.

But Lucy was draining. The first few role-playing games were great fun and exciting, something different. However, Lucy's imagination seemed to focus solely on playing at Doctors and Nurses and Teachers and Naughty Pupils.

Sometimes a weird combination of both, which Bruce still didn't understand.

Fun at first, the joke. 'Wow, that's a big thermometer, should it go in there?' initially amusing. But no more. The games were boring and wearing thin.

Sex was great with Lucy, but that was it. Nothing else.

No discussion on the latest news, controversial politic events or anything mildly intellectually stimulating. Lucy thought 'Intellectual Conversation' was either a heavy-metal rock band or some form of birth control.

Bruce looked at the T-shirt once more. Memories of Anna wearing it and nothing more than a grin made him smile. The memories of her pert nipples pressing through the fabric and tuft of hair below the waist atop the gorgeous long legs aroused him. He'd shagged Anna in that T-shirt.

No. They'd made love in that T-shirt. It was different.

'I wonder what Anna is doing now and whose arms she's laying in?'

He sighed heavily at the thought. Hopefully he'd soon find out.

The bathroom door burst open, jolting Bruce back to the present day with an unhealthy shock as he spun around. A vision in a short white PVC dress, with strategically positioned red crosses upon the breasts, stood before him.

The white dress, or what there was in skin-tight PVC, finished just below the crotch. White fishnet stockings, set within five-inch high red stiletto heels continued the ensemble. A nurse's hat, pinned to Lucy's long blond mane completed a bizarre image. Bruce was unsure if he was aroused by the sight or frightened. Whatever, it brought him back to earth with a heavy thump.

His jaw dropped and his cock naturally rose, but still he felt deflated.

He scanned the image framing the door; one arm raised, a leg slightly cocked, the fish-netted thighs teasingly rubbing together. Inwardly Bruce sighed, despite any external appearances, such as the evident rise of the appendage to the front of the cotton shorts, happily noted by a watchful Lucy.

"What do you think sweetheart?" Lucy pouted seductively.

'Trollop. Slut. Whore.' Bruce contemplated a suitable genuine reply.

"Wow! Stunning. What else can I say?" Lots it'd seem. But he didn't.

Lucy fluttered her long dark lashes and sauntered over to Bruce, exaggerating her stride in the high heels. She paused before an now attentive Bruce, who gazed at Lucy's perfectly formed, ample breasts; one of her best assets, which were somehow impossibly restrained within the short, skin-tight white PVC dress, the buttons straining. Naturally Bruce wanted to help them escape.

"Oh Doctor," Lucy spoke, the voice tone that of a delinquent ten-year-old.

"I've got this terrible pain in my chest. Do you think you can take a look and give me some relief?" She thrust her chest towards Bruce's now open mouth.

Playfully, Lucy tore back one of the red crosses on the breast of the dress and an erect nipple appeared; dark brown like a ripe acorn. Forcing it towards him, it threatened to take out Bruce's eye as she squatted down before him. Her hands reaching down to his groin, her sharp nails making him tense up.

"My, what a big thermometer," Lucy said in a saucy voice, claws fondling his manhood, pulling it to her. "I've got a fever and need my temperature taken."

Bruce groaned inwardly at the pun. 'I didn't see that coming.'

He drew on her nipple, as expected, but now also willingly.

"I think you should take my temperature doctor. Now. I'm feeling hot. So very, very hot! I need my medicine. I need that thermometer in me. Now!"

Lucy spun around, nipple flicking free from Bruce's mouth as she turned, then presented her exposed buttocks and squatted down onto his thighs. A wiggle, quick fumble with her claws and nature took its course.

Bruce forgot all about Anna once more, as he took the nurse's temperature. His own dramatically rose, along with his blood pressure, as he gripped Lucy's hips, pushing himself hard and home, much to an appreciative Lucy, who let out an exaggerated moan as he went inside her fully. Totally consumed once more, Bruce's hands slid up the front of Lucy's plastic dress, and roughly pulled open a button. Lucy's breasts breathed a sigh of relief, erupting out the dress and falling into his hands, appreciatively squeezed hard.

Lucy sat deep into Bruce's lap, wriggling her neat buttocks harder, beginning to groan heavily. Her hands gripped Bruce's, dragging them away from her breasts then guiding them down between her legs for the best sensual effect.

"Oh doctor! You're such a naughty boy!" Lucy giggled.

Bruce made little response, other than a heavy sigh, rocking away.

"I hope you'll remember what a bad nurse I've been when you're all alone down there in Ipswich sucking on sugar beet. I'll need to be severely punished once more when you return home. You'd better think of me."

Bruce simply grunted as a suitable reply. He was close to erupting.

Kissing the back of Lucy's neck, hips thrusting hard out against her buttocks, out of need, anger and frustration, he made the most of her body.

Releasing his tension with a series of deep groans, he replied.

"Of course I'll think of you when I'm away, you naughty girl!"

Lucy sighed heavily, happy, still thrusting, but her needs unsatisfied.

Bruce sighed too, but hoping it'd soon all be over.

After which he'd concentrate on his trip. He had lots to do.

Then, when he was in Norwich, Lucy would be the last thing on his mind.

Chapter 32

Beauty is only skin deep,
and the world is full of thin-skinned people.

Richard Armour

Anna was ready for her first ride at Horsewater. She'd be accompanied by Tracey and Julie, both having the day off, and welcoming the chance to show Anna round. Chris had flitted about the yard, speaking occasionally, but as Anna was becoming to learn, he focused solely upon his work most of the time, attending to the yard, and wasn't one for idle chatter, with anyone.

The seemingly never ending tasks involved with running a large yard, with a number of full liveries, as well as running what Anna was quickly learning was a large, predominantly woodland farm and small estate, along with the other business concerns he undertook, such as horse transport, that being without riding a multitude of horses for other clients in the area, meant he was constantly flitting about the yard, with little time for anyone else in his life.

She could now see where he got the reputation of being moody, mostly due to the hard work he undertook. In odd moments he'd briefly chat, and show a warm, generous and dark-humoured side, but not for long. He'd then soon be back to work in some form. However, he always had a smile for Anna, which she sensed, rightly, wrongly, or possibly in hope, was more than casual.

Although he got on well with all the woman at the yard, she sensed he was both shy and also rather awkward with people in general, and simply didn't enjoy their company. Not like horses. With these he'd spend an age, quietly talking, and even laughing to them, as though were his drinking buddies.

He seemed to have a magical touch with anything equine, horses responding accordingly, and spent more time with them than any human in the yard.

He'd driven off earlier on an errand, leaving the girls to prepare for their ride, again promising Anna he'd ride out with her one day. It was a promise Anna was going to ensure he kept. Unlike the invitation to possibly share the bottle of red wine, which as yet had been unfulfilled and seemed even more distant.

Carol suddenly arrived, dashing over to the small group, always in a fluster.

"Do you mind if I join? I don't want to impose." The older woman enquired, curiously regarding Anna. "Didn't think I'd get the time, but I have."

"Certainly not Carol. You and Tess may have a calming influence on Anna and Penny. I think she's a bit wary of us and thinks we're a bit mad!"

"Well Tess hardly gets out of second gear," laughed Carol. "So if you don't mind a slow and sensible ride, it'd be great fun. I'll be quick to tack her up."

The four women dispersed, each busy preparing their own mounts. Anna groomed Penny and before long had her tacked up, her excitement growing.

Bringing her out of the stable tacked up for the first time, she proudly stood in the yard, waiting for the others. Julie was next, leading her grouchy, skewbald Standard-bred, Bonnie, closely followed by Tracy, with a bright and alert Fred. Carol pushed open her door, to almost drag out her mount. The three woman looked on, smiling at the reluctant black Cob, nicknamed Plod.

"She's a bit like an oil tanker," joked Carol. "It takes a while to get her going, then about a mile to stop her!" The three onlookers chuckled warmly.

The woman mounted up, checked girths and then headed by Julie, followed by Tracey, then Anna, and with Carol typically at the rear, they slowly headed out the yard. The group rode down to where the Ménage was situated, riding on past along a track, which passed a paddock and some wasteland, before heading on up into the woods. Anna had briefly strolled around the paddocks and areas near the yard on her own in the few days she'd been at Horsewater, but so far hadn't ventured further along the tracks and on up into the woods. As they approached the towering woods, with the dark shadows the mass of trees cast, it all seemed to hold a magical, childlike attraction for Anna.

"How many acres of land does Chris own?" Anna enquired, as they rode along a wide track, trees either side, the track heading into the woods.

"Several hundred acres of woods, plus all the grazing and land around the yard, which I think is another fifty acres or so. Maybe more. Also some hay fields set within glades in the woods. And then also there are some small bits of arable land that he rents to various tenant farmers and which border onto parts of the Wroxingham Hall estate. It's big. No-one really knows."

"Isn't Wroxingham Hall where Lady Burlingham lives?" Anna asked, her curiosity pricked at the name, and keen to learn more of her perceived 'rival.'

"Yes," replied Julie. "Their estate is even bigger. It stretches for miles!"

"Lucky bastards! How the other half live!" Tracy joked.

"But Bertie works very hard to maintain the estate." Carol suddenly spoke up from behind, all turning towards the rear, to see her now blushing face.

"Carol is a good friend with Lord Burlingham, aren't you?" Julie announced calmly, smiling long and casting a knowing glance at a red-faced Carol.

She looked away, fussing at Tess' mane to divert the attention.

"How did Chris get his land?" Anna enquired, keen to know more about the horseman, but not want to be too nosey. "Was it from his parents?"

"Yes, from what I know. His grandparents had more land I believe, but some went to Lord Burlingham, for some money reason. Chris inherited all of this when just twelve. It was put in trust and he lived with an uncle for a while."

"Yes after that dreadful incident." Carol spoke again. "Chris' parents and Bertie's family, I mean Lord Burlingham, go back years. They've always been very close families," spoke Carol, correcting herself upon seeing Julie's grin.

"As I told you," chirped in Tracey, "Chris' family were all killed by burglars when he was young. Horrible incident. It made headline news at the time."

Anna felt sympathy for Chris. "That's sad. No wonder his dislikes strangers."

Everyone went silent for a few moments, as if reflecting the ruined life of a young child, despite having such abundance since, yet always loneliness.

"Enough of this gloom. Let's get cantering!" Tracey announced with her usual vigour. "Straight bit coming up! Brace, brace, brace!"

With that she pushed on Fred, Julie responding easily with Bonnie, Penny instantly breaking into canter upon seeing his fellow equines move into third gear. Carol required some encouragement with her heels upon the lazy Cob.

"Where are we going!" yelled Anna, closing in behind her two friends ahead, the trees tall and large, but well set back from the track, which was wide and relatively straight. The short stretch of firm, brown compacted dirt had leaves scattering across, the track an obvious favourite run with the riders.

"Follow us. Just a quick canter in the trees," Julie yelled, turning her head to see Anna smile broadly, tightening the reins on Penny, the bay mare's mane flowing back. Anna was excited once more to be riding, more so fast and on unknown ground. She in turn turned to see the wide white face of Carol's black Cob Tess thundering on behind her, her rider also happily smiling.

As the track narrowed and trees became closer set, with sweeping branches, Julie and Tracey pulled up, their mounts appearing to know instinctively the exact place to return to trot. Tess needed no second pull, but Anna's transition on Penny was less swift, the excited Dutch warm-blood wanting to continue on, Anna pulling hard. But Anna won the battle and the group moved from canter into a quick trot, back down into a walk, before settling back into the saddles, both horses and riders gaining breath and relaxing.

"That was great!" squealed Anna, grinning widely. "Great start to warm up."

"Wait until we get onto the long tracks with the jumps!" Tracy replied. "That'll really test you both out!" She smiled at a now nervous faced Anna.

"Not me," quipped Carol. "Tess and jumps don't mix! We'll skip those!"

The party continued riding through the woods for another twenty minutes, moving from walk into trot and then the occasional canter where a track widened. The woods varied from massive aged deciduous oaks, to towering ash, silver birches and beeches, with areas of newly planted pines, larch and spruce, the tracks seemingly endless, her guides appearing to know each route well. Occasionally they'd come upon a glade, the change from dark woods to bright open sky and green grass refreshing. Some tracks bordered Chris' property, defined by wire fencing, where arable land edged along the tree boundaries, before returning back to the seclusion of the woods. Reaching a long track, breaking into another glade used for growing hay, the gap between the trees was wide enough for them to ride alongside and all talk freely.

"You keep mentioning your former partner in unfavourable terms," enquired a curious Julie to Anna. "What's he like? If you don't mind me asking."

Anna and Tracey looked at each other, Tracey's face breaking into a smirk, knowing how cheeky Julie was. Anna winced, looking at Tracey, wondering what was obscenities were about to flow from her cousin's sewer-like mouth.

"A lovely man!" Tracey declared. "Wonderful. Anna's stupid leaving him."

Anna laughed loudly, shaking her head and smirking at her cousin.

Julie looked unsure, curiously regarding the two women. "Really?"

"No! He's a complete tosser!" Tracey announced proudly, no longer able to restrain herself. "Self-conscious, pretentious twat. Thinks he's God's gift and considers no one other than himself. Anna did well to be shot of him. Dick!"

Anna momentarily looked genuinely hurt at the honest, blunt opinion.

"He's not that bad. We were together for ten years," she offered.

"That I do find truly amazing," said Tracey. "Anyone else would've left him after one year. But that's only 'cos you're too easy going and blind to all of his cheating ways. He was a wanker. We all thought so. And you know it too."

Anna remained silent, absorbing the brutal comments, but inwardly aware they were true as she'd admitted herself. "I suppose you're right."

"No suppose about it. He dragged you all around the country, and off to Amsterdam for a year. And all just to promote himself and his career. He didn't give you a second thought. Never did." Tracey took a breath.

"You couldn't see beyond the lifestyle, his charm and stunning good looks."

"Good looking, ambitious and rich. You never mentioned that. Sounds the perfect man for me! What does he do for a living?" Julie enquired.

"Financial Director for a big construction company. Chartered accountant." Anna was surprised how proud she still appeared to be of Bruce's job status.

"Very impressive," said Julie. "Rich and fancy! Can I have his number?"

"We weren't that rich, just comfortable, but I worked too for myself. But yes, he is still good looking though." Anna admitted bashfully. "Handsome!"

"And doesn't he know it!" proclaimed Tracey rather loudly and in full vent.

"He's a bleeding poser! Ponce. He thinks he should have been a model."

Julie grinned. "Tell me more! He's getting better by the minute. And let me have his phone number. I'm in there now he's free. Only kidding!"

"Well he's like a cross between Brad Pitt and Matt Damon," Anna somewhat proudly announced, her face flushing bright at her own description.

"In his dreams!" Tracey barked, shaking her head. "Brad Pitt-ish. But only on a very good day. Or so he'd hope. And if the wind was blowing right!"

"I definitely want his number!" joked Julie. "Rich, brains and Brad Pitt. And you left him? Are you totally stupid?" She grinned playfully at Anna.

Anna looked at Julie, her facing glowing, understanding the witty banter, but inside knew more about Bruce. Much more. Carol, still behind, just grinned.

"But you do get a package deal with Bruce. Like his sulks, mood swings, selfish 'Me me me' attitude, and his rude, arrogant nature. That's without his disgusting personal habits!" Anna announced with a wide smile.

"Aah! You've seen the light," smiled Tracey. "Spill the beans oh enlightened cousin! Julie needs the full truth before she gets on the phone and becomes his next wife!" The group of woman all chuckled, but looked at Anna.

"He chews his toenails! I can't believe now how I ever put up with that. And lazy. Does nothing about the house, and wants you to fetch him cans of beer to drink in bed whilst watching TV. Along with Pot Noodles!" Anna smiled.

"Pot Noodles in bed!" Julie laughed, face wincing as if she'd eaten a lemon. "The toenail chewing I can accept, even I do that. But Pot Noodles in bed? That alone is grounds for divorce! Ask any good solicitor!"

"No, the grounds for divorce are him shagging his stupid slut of a secretary," Anna stated in a sudden bitter tone. "Stupid cow took photos of them playing 'Doctors and Nurses' and amazingly posted them online. That's how I found out! Looked like a porno mag' cover. Strangely I got an anonymous message."

"That's without the other infidelities you didn't know about," Tracey added.

Anna regarded her hard. "There probably were," she then agreed with a sigh.

"I've always had doubts about him," Tracey continued. "At Jenny's wedding a few years ago, he chatted up one of my friends. Over her like a rash. You were dancing I think. But he saw me watching him. That why he hates me."

"Perhaps you knew inside, but didn't want to admit it" Julie added seriously.

"Yes, I probably did," Anna admitted, regarding Julie, the horses moving sedately beneath them, making the talk somewhat therapeutic in nature.

Carol at the rear remained quiet, deep in thought, almost reflective, or maybe possibly observant. Absorbing all, Anna noted the quiet, more mature of the group had said little. "What about you Carol, are you married?"

"I'm afraid my husband died three years ago. Cancer."

Anna winced inwardly, realising she shouldn't have asked.

Carol noticed the flush of her face and downcast eyes.

"Don't worry about raising it. These things happen. It's been a few years and you have to move on. I have. But he was a nice chap. A true gentleman and was good friends with Lord Burlingham. We both were. And I am still."

The fun from moments earlier seemed to have lulled and the four remained silent. Then Tracey perked up seeing the woodland track ahead widen.

"We're supposed to be having a fun ride out, not a miserable therapy session. Let's drop Bruce talk. Come on, time for another canter. A good one!"

They moved into what seemed to be their set formation, with Fred in front, Anna tucked in behind Julie's anti-social coloured mare; a tail swish informing Penny she'd strayed too close, and Carol on the reluctant, but ever-faithful Tess, who was forever bringing up the rear, where she seemed happiest.

At a reasonably steady pace they cantered on, moving from the glade back into the woods, twisting and turning along the tracks, occasionally ducking or dodging a low branch, Anna's whoops of joy evidence of her enjoyment. The group eased up once more, re-gaining their breath and control of their horses.

The wide track turned back into denser woods, but Anna sensed they were heading back toward the farm, the horses all now at walk, regaining breath and composure. As they approached another minor junction, Anna was surprised to see bright white and red PVC tape strung across a track.

"What's that?" she enquired, puzzled to see such a bright and obscure thing deep in the dense woods, assuming they could simply ride anywhere.

"Chris sometimes closes off some tracks. They might be cutting some trees, or there are big loose branches or he's doing some other work. Who knows."

Anna looked through the trees, suddenly spotting a bright yellow agricultural vehicle parked within a glade. "What's that digger doing there?" Anna asked.

"Who knows? Tree cutting or planting, drain digging or something else," Tracey replied. "Chris is always busy or has some Contractors coming in."

"You do need to be wary," added Julie. "Although if they're felling any trees or doing some big work in the woods he'll usually warn us all to stay clear."

Anna surveyed the vast array of the woods, still amazed at her luck to be able to keep Penny at such a great location. The tracks and riding at Horsewater were a horse rider's dream, the owner equally as nice, or so Anna hoped.

"This is a great place. Absolutely amazing. Thank you so much Tracey for getting me a place here for Penny. I really appreciated it and can't believe it."

"No problems Cous'. I'm glad you're happy and think you'll fit in perfectly."

"It's wonderful I couldn't be happier," Anna proclaimed with a smile.

The riders spent another ten minutes showing Anna other tracks and trails around the farm, before deciding to make their way back, Tracey explaining they'd only covering part of the estate, and how some parts of the woods linked directly with Lord Burlingham's estate, although couldn't ride there.

Carol, seemingly an expert any thing related to Lord Burlingham, his estate and Wroxingham Hall, added some details, which further intrigued Anna.

"What's the score between her and Chris?" Anna asked openly, assuming it was common knowledge. "I saw her the other day over Chris like a rash."

Carol's face glowed red and a moment of tense silence followed.

"Don't even go there!" Tracey sounded serious for once, head shaking.

"Don't go where? Are they having a fling?" Anna asked bluntly, some of her cousin's bravado wearing off onto her, before she noticed the silent and guarded response and felt own her face burn, assuming she'd said too much.

"They are just good friends," Julie stated. "That's it!"

"Very good friends!" Tracey added with a wry smile.

Carol remained silent, her stony face showing evident disdain.

Knowing how she felt when she'd discovered Bruce was cheating on her, Anna felt sympathy for Lord Burlingham, although she didn't know him.

"Well as much as I like Chris, I'm not impressed if they're cheating," said Anna, jealousy and anger now clearly shown. "I know what its like and wouldn't think much of Chris if he was knocking off her. I appreciate he's single, and can do what he wants, but she is married," Anna announced freely.

"Virginia should appreciate what she has. A huge posh estate, and lots of money no doubt. I know she's gorgeous, so I could understand her fancying Chris and having an affair with him, especially if Lord Burlingham is old."

Carol's face seemed set to explode; Tracy and Julie for once also seemed shocked by Anna's cold, blunt statement, and free thoughts and opinion.

"I don't think is anything in it," Julie said, trying to defuse the situation. "I've never seen them do anything other than show a real and keen interest in horses. They really are just friends. She plays about and puts it on I'm sure for fun, but it all seems playful teasing. They could almost be related. Sort of."

"I must admit I've also never seen anything serious," Tracey added, for once serious, defending Chris. "They're good friends; almost as brother and sister."

"He's definitely not funny I assume?" Anna enquired; mouth in free-flow.

"He certainly doesn't bat for the opposition, although we did often wonder. Rumour has it he vanished with some young woman at the Hunt Ball after drinking a bit too much. Both came back a while later red-faced and smiling."

"I think he's shy and introvert and just puts up barriers with some people," Julie added. "He likes you though. A lot. That much is clearly obvious."

"Do you really think so?" Anna blushed, somewhat taken aback.

"The way he looks at you. And how he acts around you. Classic shy Chris."

Anna was pleasantly surprised by Julie's blunt and open comment.

"Yes, I agree. He definitely fancies you. You jammy cow!" Tracey added. "He's asked me lots about you on the quiet! But I've been coy, for once."

Anna's look was one of real shock, but delighted surprise. Inwardly she felt a warm childlike flutter, as if waiting to be asked out on a first date.

"Strange, but nice," she added. "I do fancy him though. But he ignores me!"

"He ignores everyone if a horse is about. They come first. Horses, Max, the birds around the farm, then anything else. Just play him cool," advised Julie. "If it's going to happen, it will. Don't push it. He likes his own company."

Tracey turned around on Fred, her smile a big cheesy grin.

"I'm not going to buy a hat quite yet, but might pencil a date in my diary for a late summer wedding! Will it be white? Ivory, or maybe slush-coloured?"

The woman all roared with laughter, as Anna shook her head, face glowing red, but excitedly absorbed the information. For once she was unsure how to respond and not fully convinced, but the positive comments were welcome.

However, she was sure that if anything were to ever happen between them, there'd be no third woman hiding in the background.

No 'Lusty Lucy' as she'd painfully discovered with Bruce.

They'd only be two people in their relationship.

Virginia would have to go. For definite.

But that was a long way off. A dream away.

At present she was happy to simply be at Horsewater.

However, if she could pull Chris, it'd be a true bonus.

Inwardly Anna smiled at the possibility.

Only time would tell. And she was patient.

Chapter 33

In trust I have found treason.

Elizabeth I

The PAACE meeting took place monthly, usually at an old Quaker church in the centre of Norwich. Two elderly spinster sisters had set up 'People Against Animal Cruelty and Exploitation' over twenty years earlier, horrified by vivisection and animal cruelty aspects relevant at the time, including the once infamous smoking beagles and more. The founders had long since departed from the world, and PAACE had been taken over by a mix of followers, some genuine animal lovers, others extreme left-wing ideologists.

They included rebellious tattooed youths with multiple body piercings, lost for a real identity as yet, to super-hysterical Vegans, who constituted as evil anyone associated with touching a living creature and potentially causing it harm by looking upon its form, or even worse, treading upon its shadow.

PAACE was also where the local anti-hunt protestors met to discuss and arrange future campaigns against local hunts and try to recruit further devotees. They received advice, backing and much needed financial support from some of the larger anti-blood sport organisations and other donors.

This evenings meeting was a special occasion. An under-cover officer of one such major group was to give a speech on hunting, presenting a slide show on artificial earths. The event had been publicised with a few column inches in a local paper, and leaflets handed out at the weekend, the organisers hopeful it'd be well attended, and attract some fresh faces to support their just cause.

Dave Pearson was one of those involved, and hoped the event would be a success. After being shown up in front of Izzy, he was hoping tonight his light would shine bright again. He'd helped organise various aspects of the event and prepare the hall and adjoining annexe. It was filled with numerous stalls, displaying a range of Green Issues, including vegetarian, spiritualism, holistic health and animal rights information, with items for sale to raise money; from T-shirts, to health food snacks, and small self-publications.

The crowds had slowly begun to drift into the meeting place, milling around, chatting, flicking through leaflets, or buying the occasional Tofu pasty. Most were familiar faces, people who campaigned for a wide range of Green, New Age, or assorted animal rights issues. Not only hunting, but including animal experimentation and science campaigns. Others enjoyed the companionship of like-minded people, who dreamed of world peace, such places attracted.

Izzy looked towards Pearson, who was briefly attending to a stall whilst the stallholder went to relieve himself, He seemed to be taking an age and Pearson was clearly becoming agitated, constantly checking his watch.

He wanted to mingle, especially with the main speaker, who he was keen to impress, rather than give out leaflets, sell meat-free pies or chat to geriatrics concerned about the welfare of stray kittens. He was above that and felt he should be working under-cover. Like his brother did for larger organisations.

He wanted to be out in the field, doing real surveillance work, which he was good at. Hiding. Watching. Recording. Getting cold and dirty, but making notes, anything to show to the ignorant general public what hunting scum were really like. That's what he enjoyed and how he saw his role in life.

Izzy wandered over to the stall, scanning the literature with mixed thoughts. Some was pure propaganda and lies, some cold honest truth no hunter could explain or justify. And she felt she should know, having seen both sides.

"Looks like we've got a good crowd tonight," she said looking up at Dave, being polite and trying to make small talk. She found it hard speaking with Dave, aware there was more to him than met the eye. Something hidden lurked within; such as lifting a large stone, to see something crawl away you didn't want to find. Inwardly he always made her shudder, like watching a spider crawl around the ceiling, wondering if at some point it'd fall onto you.

Dave looked at Izzy, heart fluttering, as it always did whenever he saw her. He gazed silently at her for just too long for it to be polite or comfortable.

"Yes. Very good crowd," he begun proudly, as if he was the sole reason to draw them in. "Let's hope we can recruit some more keen people to join us in the fields. So many talk the talk, but do little else, and don't walk the fields."

He paused for dramatic effect, looking long at Izzy, keen to make a point. She'd already got it and wasn't impressed. But she politely nodded back.

"We need to get back out there and make a real show of strength. We can't let that scum think they've won. It was embarrassing. We should be stronger."

He was trying not to be direct, but she knew he was referring to the recent incident. Other than having an argument at the time as they'd walked off, the event had been brushed under the carpet and not mentioned since.

"Yes," agreed Izzy, but only kidding herself, knowing it was unlikely they'd recruit anyone worthwhile tonight. People might care about animal issues, and attend small events in a warm hall in the dry. But getting someone to rise early on a Saturday morning, then run around a muddy field in the freezing cold for five hours, wasn't everyone's idea of action. People liked to complain, vainly offer support and buy a badge, but then do little else. It was the way sadly.

"We have to discuss plans for Boxing Day after the meeting. That's the next big one we really need to hit." Izzy spoke freely; Dave looked on intently.

"Forget any other meets. Boxing Day. That's where we need to hit hard. Get as many as possible in the market square, with banners and placards. Have the local media involved. I'll call the TV station, although they usually attend. They always like to promote any trouble, as it makes good footage over Christmas. Then get a good number in the field, to cause as much disruption as possible. We need to make a big show and totally spoil their special day."

Dave felt happier Izzy was talking aggressively. He'd wondered if she might pack it all in after the hare incident with Guy and Wendy. He was unsure why he had these doubts about Izzy's loyalty, but they always bugged him inside.

"Great," replied a happier and freshly inspired Dave. He smiled. Sort of.

"We'll make sure we mention it at the talk and get a few together afterwards to see who'll do what and sort out timings. Maybe we can get some of our less-able bodied colleagues out, showing real support for once, even if waving a placard at a TV camera." Dave spoke with passion and felt he was back on track with Izzy, ready for a fresh fight with the evil hunting establishment as a whole, but primarily the Shoteton. And importantly, with Steve Harrison.

From across the room a familiar voice called. Both looked up and Izzy saw a tall, slim woman with pale complexion wave at her. Izzy made her excuses to Dave and wandered over to the skeletal-form-of a-woman called Mary, who began chatting excitedly. Dave watched intently, especially Izzy.

He knew the woman to be a keen animal rights supporter, and strict Vegan, but one who never joined them out in the fields to protest against hunting, although totally truly opposed. 'Too dangerous and violent,' she'd often state, preferring more peaceful campaigns against animal experimentation.

She was the typical supporter he didn't want on board. In addition, she looked so frail, he doubted she could run ten yards across a beet field, let alone survive a day out in the wet, with horses thundering past at speed; ridden by drunken aggressive posh arsehole snobs, all out to kill you at the first chance. She'd be wedged in a horse's hoof if she went out, needing a hoof-pick to remove what was left. A good meal wouldn't hurt her, Dave mused, noting the wafer-thin body and lack of shape. Not like Izzy's curves, he considered fondly, watching her perfect form drift away with 'Skeletor.'

Eyes set upon his dream, he failed to see the figure move in front of his stall, studiously scanning the various leaflets. The man stood there perusing.

Dave suddenly became aware of a presence and looked at the figure before him, who was showing particular interest in the anti-foxhunting information. The man had his head down, closely scanning photographs of local hunts, closely examining the photographs in which the riders and their horses could be clearly seen, their cheering but evil faces saluting the death of a poor fox.

Dave looked at the top of the man's head for a few seconds, letting him absorb the barbaric scenes of a young fox being torn apart by blood-covered, half-starved savage hounds, before speaking firmly.

"Barbaric isn't it?" Dave said, half as a statement, half as a leading question, hoping for an agreeable positive reply. Dave knew his stuff.

The guy opposite did not reply, but simply raised his head.

He stared blankly at Dave, as if he'd not heard him or it was spoken in a foreign language. Either way, he didn't seem to care, but instead the man appeared to be absorbing Dave's image, sucking him in, and paused for a few seconds, before simply nodding, his gaze cold, hard and unmoving.

Dave shivered. It felt as though someone had just walked over his grave. Maybe they had. He just didn't know were it was located, yet.

The man was in his early thirties, lightly tanned, with short-cropped brown hair, cut in a military style, but not extreme. He was the same height as Dave, but stockier and certainly well-fed, something unusual for the matchstick thin, pale Zombie-life forms who tended to frequent the PAACE meetings.

He was fit, hard and capable of handling himself. Certainly no Hollywood model, with something of a brutal look, but he held an edge. He'd clearly seem much in life and seemingly hadn't been too phased by all it'd delivered.

The thing that really hit Dave were the man's eyes.

They were dark brown. Very dark. Almost black. Lifeless.

For a second Dave stared straight back, hypnotised by their glare, feeling himself being sucked into the dark empty pits. It was as if he had no eyes. Only empty sockets, passing straight through into his head. Dave tried to remember where he'd seen eyes like that before. Then it came to him.

They were like the lifeless eyes of a shark. Dead eyes.

Dave knew instantly this was a hard man, one not to mess with and immediately feared him, but was also curious. The man moved his stare from Dave, almost as if releasing him from his trance; almost permitting him to move, which he did willingly. Moving around the stand, Pearson stood boldly alongside the strange, intriguing person, who still had not spoken.

"Hi, Dave Pearson," he said, a long, thin hand being extended.

The stranger looked at Dave's offered hand, as though he was unsure what it was, or if he actually wanted to touch it. Maybe the owner had Leprosy.

The man slowly moved his head, raised his eyes and then grabbed Pearson's offered hand with a speed and firmness that surprised Dave, almost making him jump with the action. The grip was firm. Very firm. Too firm. Powerful.

Dave winced as his knobbly fingers were crushed, arm shaken in the socket, before happily released. He attempted a smile, fingers numb, all pain hidden.

"Hello," came the stranger's blunt reply. The voice had no accent, but had authority. "Some interesting material. Very interesting. Good stuff."

"Have you been to one of our meetings before?" asked Dave, trying to be friendly, break the ice, yet curiously enquiring at the same time.

"No," came the swift reply. The stranger offered no more.

Dave felt flustered, wanting to open up the stranger, sensing something.

'Don't ask a closed question,' he thought, remembering something he'd been told long ago by a one-time friend to try to chat up women. Unsuccessfully.

This person intrigued him. Yet also worried him. Dave was excited.

Like a dark room, which had to be entered to discover the contents, but also knowing that entering the darkness could lead to one's tragic downfall.

Dave had to know more. He'd enter that room, and try to find the switch.

He braced himself, pulling his skinny shoulders back, then spoke again.

"What made you come here tonight then?" asked Dave, confident he'd get the stranger talking with his change to an open question and fresh approach.

"Ad' in the paper," the man replied abruptly, shooting Dave down with his reply, offering no more information and looking down once more. He picked up a leaflet and thumbed it, before putting it back down, as if uninterested.

'Waste of space,' thought Dave, squinting coldly.

Dave had had enough, and was relieved, as John, the actual stallholder finally returned. He shuffled sideways, about to make his excuses to the stranger and leave when the stranger spoke to him. His words sent Dave's pulse racing.

"What are the names of the local hunts around here?" he asked, his tone still blunt, looking straight at Dave. "I'm interested."

Dave felt more was to come. This guy wasn't some no-action tree-hugger. He meant business. However, what that 'business' was, Dave was unsure.

"I'm interested in learning about them and all their members," he continued, then paused, tension purposefully building. "Is there much activity?"

Dave ignored John, who was about to respond and dived straight in, keen to retain the attention of the strange man who clearly had deeper thoughts.

"There are four main packs. The Shoteton Harriers, The North Norfolk Foxhounds, South Norfolk Harriers and Lynn Foxhounds." Dave announced proudly, knowing all the packs in detail. He paused, awaiting a response.

The man simply stared, as if mentally noting it all. Maybe he already knew.

"Are you interested in hunting?" Dave enquired, the question deliberate, his pulse racing. "We have a details on them all. Some more so than others."

'Be patient.' He smiled, awaiting a response. The man was taking it in.

"When do they meet?" The man's cold reply did not answer Dave's leading question, but simply asked more. "The Shoteton. They seem the most local."

Dave was getting excited, but unnerved by the hard stranger's questions.

"Mostly on Tuesday, Thursday and Saturdays, depending on the hunts. They vary slightly. The Shoteton are indeed the closest. Are you possibly interested in looking to help us disrupt them? We're always keen for any new help."

Dave enquired cautiously, but directly, hoping the guy wasn't about to ask for the hunt secretary's number, to then book a day's hunting out with the opposition. The excitement was almost evident in Dave's voice, sensing he may have a new and physically able recruit. He didn't want to lose this lead.

The stranger silently looked at him, long enough to make Dave feel very uncomfortable. Briefly Dave wondered if the guy was from 'the opposition' and actually belonged to a hunt. It would not be the first time members of hunts had infiltrated their meetings, in some cases, quite openly. On one occasion husband and wife members of the Shoteton had sat through a whole meeting, despite being openly recognised straight away by Dave and Izzy.

The man was doing research for the Hunts' Newsletter and wanted to see the views of the opposing side. The pair had taken a lot of barracking after the talk, with brutal questions, but they stood strong and defended themselves.

Secretly Dave had admired them at the time for having the 'balls' to turn up to such a meeting, risk being discovered, and then defend their side of the battle. It took guts. Even if he viewed them with disgust, as staunch hunters.
There was always hope they could change their views.
Izzy was such an example. She'd changed. *Hadn't she?*
The stranger regarded Dave and his offer for support, but his eyes indicated no sign of emotion or flicker within as to how he was going to respond.
"I may be interested in helping you out. In some form or the other," he replied coldly but with strength and authority, looking deep into Dave's eyes.
"I'll listen to your talk, make my mind up, then maybe we can speak after. Are about all evening?" The man was slowly opening up and exciting Dave.
"Oh yes, I'll be about. All night." Dave said eagerly. "I'm the main organiser. Please come and speak to me after. I'll be happy to discuss any thoughts."
With that the stranger turned and walked off toward the main meeting room, leaving Dave dumbstruck, watching him swagger away, slapping the leaflets he'd picked up against his leg. John, the stallholder looked into Dave's ashen face, now vacantly gazing towards the empty main hall door, through which the stranger had just passed to take a seat within the main hall for the talk.
"Yoo Hoo. Dave?" John called in an effeminate voice, waving his hand across his face, seeing no eye movement only a vacant stare. Then Dave looked at John, flinching as he went to touch him, shuffling away, as if John carried a contagious disease. Maybe he did. Dave hated male physical contact.
"You okay Dave? Wakey, wakey, sweetie," John continued. "Do you need a cup of strong Camomile? You look like you've just seen a ghost."
Dave shook his head, still in a daze, staring into space. Then turned to John.
"No," he finally spoke. "Not a ghost. Much worse."
The meeting went well. About fifty people of all ages turned up and the talk by the undercover officer predominately showed a series of 'artificial earths' constructed to maintain fox numbers in key hunts around the country. These were the same key hunt areas claiming foxes were pests and the simple reason they were hunted was to get rid of them. A major contradiction it was argued, as the artificial earths attracted the foxes into the area and thus encouraged them to breed larger litters and on it all went. Then the mounted hunts killed the newly created fresh 'stock' of foxes or pests, as they now legally could.
The talk was well presented, with lots of genuine evidence by some serious investigators, but with a heavy anti-hunt bias and emphasis on cruelty.
Dave had hoped he might get to sit near Izzy, but he'd been asked to move some tables and when he finally made it into the meeting room, found she'd made it there before him. She was seated with Mary and another paper-thin and equally white, but strangely attractive woman. He, for his sins, became sandwiched between a tall thin woman, whom he knew was a lesbian and fancied Izzy, and a lecherous old man, who took in stray dogs, and Dave suspected only came to the meetings simply to prey on younger members.

Making excuses, Dave moved away and instead found a seat on its own, near the back of the hall. It turned out to be a good position and enabled him to watch the meeting, but scan the key people within the room, including Izzy.

But the spot meant he could also closely watch someone more important.

Throughout the talk Dave kept a close eye on the stranger he'd met earlier, who it seemed deliberately sat alone too, in a corner part of the high ceiling, former Georgian chapel reading room. It appeared he was strategically seated so he could see most of the people attending too. Dave eyed him carefully, watching as the talk went on, so he could see the expressions on the man's face as cruel aspects of hunting, experimentation, vivisection, puppy farms, intensive farming and all other aspects of animal cruelty were discussed and debated, often with graphic recollections, photographs or images.

Dave looked for any reactions. But there were none.

After the various talks, a number of the audience asked questions, but the stranger remained silent, simply looking and listening, seemingly absorbing it all. On a couple of occasions he looked over at Dave, clearly aware that he was being watched too, but took no interested. Dave smiled at the man.

Still his expression did not change. And he didn't respond.

When the questions had finished, the chairman of the meeting thanked their guest presenter. The crowds left the meeting room and went back into the lobby area for informal chats, more Tofu pasties and tasteless hot herbal tea. Dave wanted or needed neither, and rose to catch the stranger, keen to speak with him. He needn't have bothered. He walked straight over towards Dave.

"Very good talk. I take it you and your friends primarily sab hunt meets?"

He asked bluntly and directly to Dave, staring coldly at him.

Dave flushed slightly at being asked the question so openly, but inwardly felt a rush, both from pride of what he did and at the possibility of recruiting a new member. It was hard to get people out in the fields, many being too old and unfit, unable to dash across fields all day. Others were too nervous, wary or afraid of direct confrontation with the hunters, preferring quiet lobbying, having blind faith in the government changing the laws back again.

This man was hard. Maybe ex-military. Someone who could hold their own and not to mess with. He'd be a great recruit. Tough. Taking no shit. Perfect.

Steve Harrison's smarmy image flicked into his mind. A vision of the stranger's boot heel stamping into his face flashed before him. Perfect recruit.

Dave approached the man, hand extended, wanting to welcome the stranger on board. He was met with an instant ice-cold glare, the dark eyes flicking down to the offered, offending hand. Dave removed it, face flushing red.

"Perhaps I can get you a cup of tea. Only herbal on offer I'm afraid. Mint or Camomile? I can explain the main hunts, their members, when we go out and what we do. Whatever you want." Dave said excitedly, rubbing his hands.

"Mint tea is fine. I love it." The man seemed to relax. He even smiled.

Dave smiled back, amazed at the stranger's sudden change.

Dave extended an arm to guide his new best mate towards the food area. He casually followed. "Sorry, I didn't get your name," Dave dared to enquire.

"Adam Yates," the man replied calmly, then added more, now opening up. "I'd be interested to learn about the local hunts. The Shoteton in particular. I've heard of them. Also any key hunt people. It's these I have an interest in. I can possibly help you out. Cause some trouble. Maybe close them down."

Dave's eyes widened. He felt he'd met his soul mate and glowed inwardly.

The pair wandered towards the tea stall, the excitement in Dave flowing. Izzy eyed them cautiously from afar and he caught her curious glance. Excusing himself from Adam, he dashed over, keen to tell her of his new recruit.

"Izzy, I've got a chap over here, Adam. He's interested in joining us. Possibly sabbing. Come and meet him when you get a moment. He seems hard and ruthless. I have a strange feeling about him. I think he's just what we need."

Izzy looked over at the stranger, who stared back, his dead eyes meeting hers, burning through the back of her head. His expression remained unchanged, not mellowing or smiling joyfully, as was usual with most men upon meeting Izzy, often keen to chat her up, in a vain hope to get her into bed.

Instead he stared. Detached. The look calm, calculating and unemotional.

This man was a professional. *But at what?*

Izzy shuddered inwardly, sensing trouble. She'd seen eyes like that before in the past. Often in something which was dead. And they usually spelt danger.

"Okay, sounds good. I'll join you, but after I've sorted a few things out," she replied, making any excuse to delay, unwilling to be in the company of either.

"Great, I look forward to it. He seems a bit strange, but I think he's going to be good for us," Dave replied excitedly, and wandered back to Adam.

Izzy stared at his back, worryingly noting a fresh spring in his step.

She watched the two men walk off, now deep in conversation, an unpleasant feeling passing over her, once again doubting Dave's judgement.

Izzy sensed only bad vibes, sensing the stranger had his own secret itinerary.

And if so, it could only bring trouble to them.

As well as those in the Shoteton.

Only time would tell if she was right or not.

Chapter 34

Pleasure is found first in anticipation, later in memory.

Gustave Flaubert

On Saturday morning Penny sensed a difference in Anna, instinctively aware of an air of excitement within her owner, whickering as Anna gently nipped her black muzzle giving it a playful tweak, followed by a pat on the neck.

"Mummy's got a surprise for you today," Anna joked, face beaming with joy. "You've got to be good. Mummy's taking you out hunting with Uncle Chris."

Only concerned about not having been fed, the horse pushed hard against the firmly closed lower door, kicking her forefoot for attention. Anna ignored her, walking towards the tackroom. Under her baggy navy jogging bottoms her clean, crisp beige jodhpurs hugged her legs tightly like a second skin. She didn't dare expose them to the grime of the yard or Penny as she groomed her; until they were finally ready to set off. Anna was keen to look her best.

The cold crisp morning was dry and clear, the blue-white sky, from which the stars were only just fading, had a pink, wintry tint. The forecast was for a dry, but bitterly cold day. With an hour to go before the sun was even due to start to rise, Anna knew it was going to be a long day. Her nose dripped and ears tingling with the chill, but the excitement warmed her inside.

Anna had hardly seen Chris to speak to, only catching glimpses as he scuttled about the yard. He was busy with the yard in general and in preparing Cirrus, Anna herself was busy ensuring Penny looked her best to worry too much, everyone with their own concerns, including Tracey, who'd said a polite morning greeting, but disappeared, busy with preparing Fred for a long day.

Penny was groomed, tacked up with everything checked and double-checked, and so Anna moved along the stable block to peep into Fred's stable. Late as ever, and slightly flustered as ever, Tracey politely told Anna she didn't need a hand when offered, and so Anna moved off, with some free time to spare.

To ease her nerves, which tingled like a child on Christmas morning, Anna wandered along the track to the schooling paddock and fields, which led up the gentle hill, rising towards the massive back woods far in the distance.

The woods swept around the top fields in one mass of never-ending trees, the branches rapidly becoming stark in the early winter landscape, creating a dark spreading backdrop, which cut short the slowly lightening horizon.

She stood looking up at a swirl of rooks that suddenly appeared above the field, gazing in wonder as around a fifty or more of the large black birds formed a huge mottled black and blue blanket in the sky above her. They swirled around in what appeared to be a disorganised melee, but was organised, until slowly they peeled away into four distinct groups, each spiralling upwards and away from the other group in twisting formations.

Anna watched, mesmerised, then as strangely as the flocks appeared, they vanished, drifting away, one lone rook remaining and moving over the back woods, where it could be seen perching, silhouetted dark on a high treetop.

"Fascinating aren't they?" said Chris from beside her.

Anna physically jumped, unaware he was stood beside her, spinning around.

"Yes, they are," she replied nervously, catching her breath, heart pounding, surprised, yet warmed by his unexpected and unseen presence.

"Are they rooks or crows? I never know the difference," she added, trying to hide her nerves; a strange gentle panic set in, unaware he was there.

"They're rooks. Slightly smaller than crows, with whitish beaks. And they have baggy trousers. Easy to remember. Rooks live in rookeries, crows live on their own. Very sociable, clever birds with their own communities. It is said they sort out their own laws and deal out there own punishments. Best way."

Anna turned, smiling, warmed by his knowledge and strange charm, but felt almost fearful of his unknown side, which held its own intriguing fascinating.

"Most live far off in the back woods as a large colony and come out in groups early on, scavenging for food or planning where to feed for the day."

He turned to face her, noticing her intense gaze, then suddenly stopped, face flushing and nerves returning. The familiar shields Anna knew of went up.

Then turned, gazing back towards the woods, his birds and his comfort.

Anna smiled, knowing he also sensed electricity between them, building like a thunderstorm. Chris shuffled then looked bashfully, almost like a teenager.

"Are you and Penny all ready to go?" He was back on his own ground.

"Yes," Anna replied, butterflies leaping in her belly at the thought of the forthcoming day. "Nervous and yet excited. As ready as we will ever be."

"Don't be nervous," Chris smiled reassuringly. "It's not as bad as you may think. Well actually, maybe it is! Possibly even worse!" he joked.

He saw Anna's look of nervous shock, then smiled even brighter.

"Tracey, Julie and me will all look after you. And if they can stay on board, so can you. You'll be fine after a drink. Come on then, we're ready to load up."

With that, Anna and Chris drifted back to the yard side-by-side, until reaching the yard. As Sally and Carol were not going out today, Julie had taken up the offer to go with Chris, especially as she'd also agreed to help look after Anna, and so would be staying all day. The horses were swiftly removed from the stables, then loaded up, just as Anna had seen before. Once secure and tied, the lorry rear was shut up. Chris was left to drive alone, which Julie had reassured Anna he didn't mind and actually preferred, as he clambered into the cab, and the three excited woman all jumped into Julie's Land Rover to follow Chris's close behind for the fifteen miles to the meet.

There had been a light frost and the roads were still icy in places, especially the narrow lanes where the sun missed, making the journey slow, although there was no hard frost in the ground. The journey gave the women a chance to have a good chat about how Anna was settling in and at her new cottage.

When they arrived at the farm where the meet was being held, they parked up in a paddock at the back of a small farm, and quickly joined up with Chris. They checked the horses in the back of the lorry, who were all fine, and still munching on haynets, before going off to enjoy the hospitality provided.

The meet was nowhere as elaborate as the one Anna had first attended at Ernie Cole's a few weeks previous. Even so, as they wandered inside a barn, Anna was excited by the array of food and drink kindly provided by the hosts.

A selection of sandwiches, cold meats and cake greeted them, set on tables covered in a mix of clothes. In addition there was a table with the obligatory mixed bottles of alcohol, but sadly no champagne cocktails this time.

As with the last meet, an array of smartly dressed people milled about, politely eating, whilst socialising in small groups, washing it all down with a mix of sherry, port, cherry brandy or orange squash for the various children.

Anna glanced around, recognising a few familiar faces from the last meet, along with some new faces she'd not seen before. Tracey passed her a plastic tumbler of cherry brandy, which she happily accepted and gulped down, now having a taste for the potent red liquid. The sweet liqueur both warmed her throat and belly, but also rushed to her head, relaxing her with a gentle tingle. They began making general conversation and as with the last meet, Chris was accosted by several people, who pulled him aside for a chat or word of advice.

Amongst these, seemingly as no surprise to Anna, was Virginia Burlingham. She appeared to plague Chris at the first chance, the pair quietly speaking in a corner of the barn, much to Anna's annoyance. She'd hoped to spend some time at the meet with him over a drink and some food. But to no avail.

The bitter wind cut through them and she was glad of the crisp white stock wrapped tightly around her neck, secured by a large gold pin Tracey had leant her. As usual, her cousin seemingly chatted as much as she drunk and ate.

They did not spend long eating, due to the cold wind, which blew relentlessly into the barn, turning their cheeks red and making their noses drip. Anna noted Julie sank three large tumblers of cherry brandy, followed by a handful of sandwiches, joined in quantity by a mirthful Tracey. Anna could never work out if she was drunk, such was her usual state of merriment. Anna decided to join in with her two companions, giving up any hope a some quiet socialising with Chris, who was now chatting to a red-faced man in his sixties.

Anna found herself reaching for more alcohol, unsure if she was drinking port or cherry brandy, or both, but not caring. Grabbing fresh tumblers of Cherry Brandy, and more sandwiches as they left the barn, the trio giggled like young girls on a hen-night, as they returned to the lorry to attend the horses.

"Oh my god! I feel half pissed," a smiling Anna whispered to Julie as they wandered back, bashing against her, feeling light-headed, her ears buzzing.

"So do I!" Julie whispered, tottering beside her. "But I don't care. Best way to go hunting. You'll fear nothing! And if you fall off, feel nothing!"

She grinned broadly, as jogging from the barn, Chris joined them. Seeing Anna swaying, her grin as wide as ever, he cast her a sly, concerned but rueful grin. He playfully tutted and shook his head at Julie and Tracey, aware of their bad influences and drinking habits from many years of their acquaintance.

"Are you okay?" he quietly asked, moving beside Anna. "Can you stand!"

She stared at him, leant on his shoulder for support, then holding a sandwich about before her, viciously took a bite, wickedly grinning at Chris.

"I'll be fine with you beside me sweet-heart," she stuttered, them flushed bright red, suddenly aware of what she'd said with her mouth liberated.

Julie roared with laughter and Chris simply smiled, his face flushing red too, but made no attempt to remove Anna from his body, as she rested her head on his shoulder, put her arm around him. and looked at him with puppy eyes.

Tracey laughed loudly, staring at the conjoined couple, shaking her head.

"I best buy a hat!" Julie added. "And book a church. And you two a room!"

The whole group laughed loudly, and were joined by Tracey and Julie linking arms either side of Anna and Chris, the foursome strolling back in the cold.

The group made their way back to the horsebox, and regrettably Anna released Chris from her clutches. He appeared unfazed and genuinely smiled as she slowly came to her senses, and hoped she hadn't be too open or loud.

Chris seemed to switch back to the professional horseman mode, and Anna, quickly sobering after the first hit of alcohol, realised what she was doing.

They sorted out their tack and personal items and swiftly unloaded the horses. Anna quickly mounted Penny, who was held by Tracey, the horse becoming excited by the new surroundings and large number of strange horses milling around. Anna tried to settle her down, with a mix of fear and excitement coursing through, eased by the alcohol still dulling her senses. She glanced over to the lorry, where Chris stood on the ramp looking towards her, a big smile on his face. Anna smiled back, only to have Penny spin her around and face a pair of elegant bays trotting past the back of the boxes, their lady riders clad in matching dark blue jackets and yellow breeches.

They looked at Anna as though she was a child, with no control. Tightening the reins, and keen not to hit the deck and make a total fool of herself, she turned Penny back around, only to see Chris had vanished and Tracey was beginning to walk towards the back of lorry, ready to lead out Fred.

"Are you sure you'll be okay getting on Fred?" Anna called, keen to help and not feel a burden, although secretly knowing she could do little on Penny.

"Yes, don't worry. He's an angel," she replied. "Been there, seen it, done it and he's even bought the T-shirt – well, the saddle cloth. Thanks anyway. You just try to steady Penny and keep her relaxed. Walk round the paddock."

Julie, who'd already mounted Bonnie, pulled up beside Anna.

"They're going to release the hounds. Penny will most likely go nuts as they mill about, so make sure you turn to face them. They tend to run between the horses legs but cause no issues. Don't let her kick any. Please!"

Anna recalled her first meet, where she'd watched with her mum and winced at the thought of all the hounds freely roaming around the horses. Now she was in that very situation. Then, as if by magic, a stream of motley coloured beige, tan and black hounds poured across the paddock. Their noses rubbed along the ground as they darted everywhere, weaving between horses, boxes and people on foot, who had now also begun gathering in the paddock.

Anna looked on at the hounds as they skirted the edge of the paddock, their noses sniffing out every strange scent in the grass and feet skipping about in the cold, still slightly frosty grass. Martin would call out names, as unruly hounds dared to stray, only to at once to rejoin the pack when called.

Sharon, riding a fine dark bay horse, and acting as Whipper-In, helped Martin round up the hounds, flicking her hunting whip with a sharp crack. Penny jogged around, eyes fixed firmly on the patrolling pack of hounds, keeping Bonnie close by for support, aided by a sensible and suddenly sober Julie.

"It's amazing how he knows all their names and how they all respond," Anna commented, looking at Martin, impressed at how he controlled the hounds.

"Yes, they are very well trained," Julie agreed. "And they all respond to their own names. The huntsman, that's Martin, knows them all individually. They've got over fifty hounds at the kennels. Yet he knows them all. Treats them like his kids. He's a great hunter and brilliant rider. Nice guy too."

Julie nodded politely as an elegantly dressed elderly lady with a toothy smile, seated upon an immaculate, light chestnut horse approached the pair. A leather 'bum-bag' was secured to her waist and she held an almost regal air.

"Good Morning ladies. And what a glorious day it is too, despite that biting chill wind," she announced in a natural, well-spoken, flowing manner.

"It is indeed a beautiful day," replied Julie, who was normally polite, but seemingly forced her accent more acutely when replying to the lady.

"This is Anna. It's her first hunt today. She is Chris' guest."

Anna blushed, nodding respectfully, unsure how to reply.

The lady smiled broadly at Anna, who blushed a deeper red, as if she knew something secret. The lady was around sixty years old, yet had the slim fresh features of someone who'd had a fine lifestyle. She wore only a hint of make-up and her erect posture and air gave her a regal look. Her thin, pinkish lips forced back slightly protruding teeth. Greying, once brown hair, was neatly held in place by a hair net, in turn covered by a dark green hunting cap.

"Anna, this is Lady Carter. She's the hunt secretary." Julie proclaimed in her finest voice as an introduction, even sweeping her hand.

"Just call me Shirley," replied Lady Carter, genuinely. "I do so hate titles and formalities. I'm simply here to enjoy the riding. And I want your money!"

Anna smiled nervously. "Good morning. It looks like it's going to be a great day, although cold. I hope I survive the day. It's mine and Penny's first meet."

"You'll be okay. She looks fine. Stunning mare. Dutch-warm blood?"

Anna nodded enthusiastically, instantly impressed.

Lady Carter had a dignified air, and would haven't have been out of place in an Edwardian TV drama set in a country estate, her manner and dress making her appear to belong to that era, not today's fast-paced, rat-race society.
"I've moved back to Norfolk and I'm keeping her at Chris Turners yard," Anna added proudly, wanting to add more about herself and Penny.
"Oh, the untouchable Mr Turner," quipped Lady Carter, in a jovial manner, her wise eyes scanning Anna's face. "Ah, so you're his new lady. He rung me to say someone would be joining him. A stunning lady he told me. And didn't lie! So glad you came. Chris is excellent with horses, but hates humans!" She continued with a smile and chuckle, her teeth breaking through her grin.
"Some humans are exempt though!" Julie chipped in laughing, seeing Lady Carter's wise and probing gaze towards a blushing Anna. "But not many!"
"Yes he's broken many a horse and also many a single ladies heart. Mine too!" Julie joked, knowing Chris was still over by the horse box with Tracey.
"If only I was ten years younger. Damn!" Julie added, shaking a pretend fist.
Anna and Lady Carter grinned at the shared joke.
"How about you my dear. Smitten by Mister Mysterious yet?" Lady Carter questioned, grinning inanely, her wise, brown, intelligent eyes peering hard into Anna's face, as if seeking a reaction, but knowing the answer already.
Anna went scarlet at the brutally open question, feeling her neck burning under the hunting stock, as she knew the answer, and also sensed the wise lady beside her did too. She just grinned as a silent response.
Lady Carter's grin broadened, with her horse-like teeth protruding between her thin pink lips. She let out a deep and hearty un-lady-like chuckle, to leave the question verbally unanswered and saving Anna any need for a response.
"Well ladies, bad news. I need your money. It's cap time! Hand it over!"
"Chris has our caps," Julie answered almost at once. "He's over by the box, just about to get on Cirrus I believe. He's the rich one!"
"No problems. I'll get them off him," Lady Carter replied, ever happy to collect money for the hunt from anyone. "Nice to see a good turn out and some fresh faces. We certainly need them. Thank you for coming Anna and I hope to see you about in the field. Have a very good day. I know you will."
"Thank you Shirley, we will," replied Julie as Lady Carter nodded and turned her horse away, heading toward the box, in search of Chris and money.
"She's nice. I thought as a Lady she'd be stuck up, like the other I know," Anna said to Julie, suddenly realising how bitchy the comment sounded. Julie simply grinned and remained silent as they began to walk around the perimeter of the paddock, Penny still looking nervously toward the hounds as they milled about, but more horses began to fill the paddock, giving Penny something else to look at, and also seemingly ease her, as if she was at a show.
"You'd be surprised actually," began Julie. "Most of this lot have more land and money than they know what to do with, yet they are as nice as pie if you talk to them politely. Some can be a bit 'up their own arse' but most are nice."

The paddock was filling up with a wide range of horses, from fine thoroughbreds to heavy cobs, in varying colours; from gloss black to pure white greys. Anna watched cautiously as people rode by, glancing at their horses; first with a keen eye, and then at the rider and their turn out. She hoped Penny and herself looked respectable. Likewise the dress code varied, from a range of tweed jackets; worn by both men and woman, to dark navy or black hunting coats, again worn by both sexes. All though appeared to come from another era, their manners polite and dignified and all politely nodding a greeting or raising a whip to their cap as a form of recognition.

"Look out, that's The Master. Reginald Hornchurch," proclaimed Julie, nodding toward Reggie. Anna looked to where Julie indicated, as slowly he regally rode through the mass of horses toward them. "He's the big boss."

Anna nodded. "Yes, I met him the last time. When I followed with Suzie."

"Oh yes, I remember," replied Julie. "He was smitten by your mum as I recall. And you too. He likes his ladies. Any age. Dead or alive! No offence!"

Tracey trotted over to join the pair and they turned to face her just as Reggie passed then pulled up, touching the peek of his dark green hunting cap.

"Good morning ladies," he exclaimed loudly, pulling up his massive grey horse Samson, who then stood solid still. "A fine threesome if ever I did see."

"Good morning Sir," Tracey replied in such a tone that it shocked Anna. She was more used to a stream of obscene profanities flowing; not the word 'Sir.'

"I believe I met you following on foot?" enquired Reggie, looking direct at Anna, face beaming, rosy cheeks glowing. "I never forget a pretty face!"

Anna blushed, her face burning up, aware of Reggie's intent gaze.

"Yes you did. Nice to meet you again. I'm glad to be on board, although nervous. My first time," Anna replied, noting her tone suddenly posher too.

"It's wonderful seeing you. I hope you enjoy your day," Reggie replied with a nod, then touching his cap, moved on towards another group, calling cheerfully. All three women watched Reggie go, before Anna spoke first.

"It's like going back in time a hundred years. Everyone is so calm, polite and respectful. Even you didn't swear Tracey. Blimey!"

"I know, it's great isn't it!" replied Tracey in her more familiar, casual manner, as Fred jostled about beneath her. "That's what's nice, and is something those who want to ban hunting again never see. Hunting folk are some of the nicest people you could meet. But they're seen as the idle rich, all charging about the countryside. 'The unspeakable chasing the uneatable.' Antis and bored Townies who know nothing of the true countryside jealously resent us, when they should get off their fat arses and try it themselves."

Julie nodded in agreement with the strangely sober and diplomatic Tracey, as the three women watched Reggie ride on, then politely chat to Chris, who was seemingly trying his best to rejoin them, but being stopped by everyone.

"I think he fancies you," piped in Julie, looking at Anna, the comment out of the blue following Tracey's rant. Anna regarded her with some confusion.

"Who?" exclaimed Anna, flushing bright again, her eyes focusing on Reggie and then Chris, unsure who she meant. Julie missed the point and continued speaking, still looking over to the two men seated upon grey horses..

"Mind you, he fancies most women. That's why he's called Horny."

Julie noticed Anna's glowing cheeks and focus upon Chris.

She grinned widely, suddenly understanding what she'd missed.

"Reggie I meant," she added, laughing, seeing Anna look down sheepishly. "He clearly fancies you. But you never know about the other one too!"

Anna looked up, her face glowing, smiling and then jokingly responded.

"Perhaps he'll ask me to marry him and move into his massive farm. Reggie that is," she added, seeing Julie's eyes widen. "A bit old for my taste though!"

"Which farm would you like, he's got four spread around these parts," said Julie. "Mind you, he'd have to get rid of his wife Elizabeth first, and give her two of them. That could be a problem. Unless of course he kills her off!"

"Perhaps he's a Mormon and could marry all three of us, as well as keep Elizabeth. He'd have four wives. We could then have a farm each. It would be a fun honeymoon night," giggled Tracey, then flushed red herself.

They all laughed, as Anna looked about the paddock, watching Martin group the hounds, looking for someone she'd much rather spend a honeymoon with than a lecherous old man, be he the owner of four large farms or not.

She anxiously watched Chris with Reggie, hoping he'd be about for when they set off. With that Chris left Reggie, walking towards the group, nodding politely to various riders who passed him, before joining the group of ladies.

"Sorry for the delay. People. They won't leave me alone! Everyone okay?" he enquired, specifically looking at Anna. "Are you okay?"

Cirrus stood bolt upright, looking towards the hounds on the far side.

"Yes, I'm fine. She looks wonderful," Anna replied, admiring both horse and Chris together, her eyes lingering. Chris didn't miss the long look and blushed. Anna looked away and down at her mount, patting the bay's neck.

"Penny is still on her toes, but calmed down a lot. Thinks she's at a show."

"Whatever you do, don't for gods sake go in front of the hounds on the field or charge past the Field Master. That's him over there, Steve. You met when you followed. I'm amazed he hasn't ridden over to greet you yet. He will."

Anna glanced towards the magnificently scarlet jacketed figure of Steve Harrison, smiling, remembering his hug and cheeky kiss. He seemed to be deep in conversion with a man in a tweed jacket, set upon a black horse, and laughing openly with two ladies seated on bays beside him, Steve seemingly unaware of Anna even being there. She turned her attention back to Chris, absorbing all he said, keen to not mess up and let him or herself down.

"Steve's very easy going and won't tell you off too much, but it's a matter of hunting etiquette. However, Reggie will scream out without a second thought. Also don't let Penny kick or stand on a hound for god's sake! Or Martin and Reggie will both crucify you!" Chris politely but firmly and nervously lectured.

Anna already knew, but nodded politely to Chris to acknowledge, noting he seemed as concerned about her and Penny, and how they would cope, as she did herself. It was both reassuring and worrying, for she didn't want to let anyone down. She could have done with another cherry brandy, or two.

"Let's move towards the hounds," he announced. "They're about to set off and you don't want to get left behind. Anna, you had best ride alongside me."

The four rode over towards the group of riders who'd formed around Reggie and Martin, with Steve sitting to one side of the group, smiling widely. All looked stunning in their scarlet jackets and green hats, with silver hares on the green velvet collars. Anna sat entranced, Penny beneath for once still.

Her eyes scanned the wide range of riders, all attentive to their leader, as Reggie gave a brief speech, similar to before, thanking their hosts, explaining about the ground they'd hunt and then wished everyone a good day.

With a starling blast of the horn from Martin, fully waking Anna's senses, the hounds streamed out across the paddock and off down the grass track they'd driven up, pouring out onto the road, with Reggie and Martin behind.

They were off. Anna felt a weight in her stomach move as she trotted off, proud to be alongside Chris, smiling across to him, he returning the smile. She patted Penny, then firmly grasped the reins as they surged forward, almost running into a bay horse before her. Her stirrups clunked against Chris' and nervously she looked to him, never having ridden so closely packed to so many horses before, losing count at thirty bobbing heads.

All around her a sea of multi-coloured horses moved as one, their riders clad in black, navy and tweed jackets, faces all smiles, all rising up and down, the excitement building within her, the chill air now hot. She turned around in the saddle to smile broadly at Tracey and Julie riding close behind her. They beamed back with wide cheeky grins, Tracey playfully sticking out her tongue.

A nervous Anna wondered what her first day out hunting would bring.

Chapter 35

Every great move forward in your life begins with a leap of faith, a step into the unknown.

Brian Tracy

The bright red jackets of Reggie and Martin aboard their respective mounts pursued the hounds out the driveway at a fast trot, closely followed by Steve, leading the mass of riders who followed behind, making up the mounted field. All poured into the neck of the track from the paddock where they'd congregated, Julie and Tracey falling in tight behind Chris and Anna. As they moved onto the track, Penny's eyes grew with excitement, the proximity of thirty plus unknown horses awakening a natural instinct to charge with a herd. Chris and Anna's stirrups clanked together, and their boots rubbed, as they joined the throng proceeding at a fast trot down the narrow farm driveway.

Anna turned, looking anxiously at Chris. He looked back, with a broad grin.

"Okay?" he asked quietly, Anna simply nodding, hands set tight on Penny's reins, smiling back, the butterflies in her stomach stopping all speech. At the bottom of the track they joined the road and turned left onto a tarmac road, chasing after the leading huntsmen and the pack of fleeing hounds.

Cars, belonging to followers, were strewn along the verges, along with the odd unfortunate local out for a drive, forced to move over and park up as the ungainly mass of hounds, horses and humans poured down the centre of the road. Sparks flew off horses shoes, as the pack moved at pace, leaving behind the familiar white scuffmarks on the black tarmac road Anna had followed.

Anna glanced around the sides of the roads, looking for Izzy or any other Anti's who might be about, ready to yell abuse or pester them as she'd seen before, but was relieved to see none present yet. She breathed a welcome sigh.

The mass of horses and riders moved at a fast trot for about a mile, quickly covering ground, Penny already puffing, mostly through the excitement, as the hounds, directed by Martin and Reggie, were guided through an opening in a side hedge. Led by Steve a few yards behind, the mounted field followed, moving onto an unploughed rotting stubble field and down a hedgerow.

Reggie and Martin rode across the middle, the hounds cast before them, sniffing and searching in a tight group for a scent line. The remainder of the field, guided by Steve, moved in single file beside the hedge, forming a long column along the headland, the soil firm underfoot. Anna followed Chris, with a string of horses ahead; as they rode in line, with Tracey holding a snorting Fred close behind. The line of horses ahead stopped, and Anna pulled firmly on the reins to turn Penny to the right, now facing into the field.

Martin and Reggie drew the hounds, looking for a line for the hounds to run.

"Good. Keep her steady and always face the hounds," Anna heard Chris whisper, noting Chris' flea-bitten grey Cirrus standing stationary beneath him rock solid, her manners impeccable, a true hunting lady of many years. Fred and Bonnie, set beside Anna, had also turned sideways, as simultaneously both Julie and Tracey looked across towards Anna, their faces beaming. Tracey nodded to check Anna was okay. A smiling face confirmed she was, although a nervous stomach betrayed her true feelings of fear and excitement.

Soon the whole field were turned, facing inwards, like an ancient cavalry line, set and ready to charge, all riders intently watching the two bright red jackets in the centre of the field follow the pack of hounds which scuttled ahead.

Anna's stomach fluttered with the adrenaline rush, despite only sitting on a horse in a field. Inwardly she preyed Penny wouldn't misbehave and be the first to break the line of patient horses, or worse, rear up and dump her, to embarrass her and Chris. But for now, she too was being a perfect hunter.

"They're going to draw this field. If the hounds pick up a scent line or hare, upon Steve's command we'll gallop forward. It may draw a blank. Whatever, just follow me!" Chris whispered, it seemingly etiquette to quietly watch the hounds, although she noticed some in the line were openly chatting.

Anna smiled nervously and excited, still unsure what Chris was talking about or what to do, other than follow his lead. Then the sound of high pitched yelping and baying emitted from the pack of hounds and their heads rose.

Anna's ears and head pricked up at the noise. She turned quickly to look at Chris. But his focus was on the hounds. Anna in turn looked out across the field to see the hounds were chasing off at speed, the lead hound ahead, the pack moving towards the left of the field, as a small dark shape moved quickly before the pack. A hare. The two red jackets of Martin and Reggie set off in gallop behind the pursuing pack. The horn was raised to Martin's lips, reins in other hand, as he sounded 'Full on.' The haunting wail of the horn resonated across the field, as the pair thundered across in pursuit of hounds and hare.

"Here we go!" Chris yelled, whether to himself, Cirrus or Anna she was unsure, but he sounded excited, his cool reserve gone and all barriers down. Anna liked this Chris and felt her own nerves ease, but excitement grow.

She was unsure if anyone gave the command, or who moved first, but a stream of horses began pouring out from the neat stationary line it'd formed along the hedge, to suddenly flood across the field, all horses in full charge.

Anna turned to see the back of Tracey's dark jacket as Fred had already taken off, her legs kicking his flanks. Julie needed no encouragement and followed on just behind on an excitable Bonnie, the pair several lengths ahead. Anna glanced at Chris, to see him still beside her, face beaming, as she sat deep into the saddle, feeling Penny fight within her hands. Chris, hands held high, held back the prancing, impatient Cirrus, who shuffled on her hocks, ready to rear.

"Go!" he yelled, smiling widely and with a mad glint. Anna willingly obeyed, dropped the rein contact and Penny leapt forward, clearing the ground.

The bay mare lurched excitedly, stumbling, before regaining her footing, then began charging across the yielding dark brown field of rotting stubble. Anna felt the power beneath her, as Penny's legs thundered away, and she embraced the surge, as her breath was momentarily taken, looking ahead at the mass of charging horses. The form of Cirrus came charging alongside, also at full gallop, Chris drawing the grey mare close to, only yards away from Penny.

"Are you all right?" Chris yelled across, his face a massive smile, wind-tears streaming in his eyes, voice only just reaching Anna through the roar of wind and the thunder of hooves. Divots of mud flew about like cannon shells.

"Yes! Bloody brilliant!" she called back, smiling broadly, almost unable to hear herself due to the wind and sound of thirty charging horses. A variety of mud divots, clods and stones, kicked up by the horses ahead, flew past and Anna ducked instinctively as debris flew past, her eyes streaming as the chill wind cut into her cheeks. Chris guided Cirrus away slightly, but Anna sensed he was keeping a close watch on her, just in case. But she didn't mind.

The mass of horses charged on towards the place where the pack of hounds had reached a hedge at the far end of the field. Still hot on the hare's scent, they were proceeding to jump, crawl or find their way through the obstacle, in pursuit of the now rapidly vanishing hare. The two huntsman followed on.

Anna could make out Fred and Bonnie about twenty yards ahead, rapidly approaching the same hedge at the end of the field, as horses began to weaved across the ground at various angles. Some were pulled back, others charging past and off in all manner of direction or turning circles, as riders struggled to maintain control. Penny was on autopilot and thundered over the ground, oblivious to Anna, who began heaving on the reins, looking down at the field rushing past below, hoping no rabbit hole or large flint appeared as she raced across the unploughed field. Suddenly a loose horse appeared, one of the fine bays she'd seen earlier, the rider nowhere in sight. Anna now began to get worried, sensing she'd totally lost control of Penny.

She also became terrifyingly aware they were rapidly approaching the end of the field, where a mass of horses were slowing down or pulling up at the hedge. Someone had bravely. or unintentionally crashed through; one making a horse-sized opening. Other horses ducked and weaved, then an elderly gentleman in tweed flew over the hedge, his horse remained the other side. Seemingly stunned by the lack of rider, it began to turn away, but only momentarily, as a quick-witted Steve grabbed the reins. In the melee, he called over the hedge, as a red-faced, and mud-covered gent promptly appeared, laughing loudly, joined by a grinning Steve. He quickly passed over the reins of the excited horse to its recovering rider and checked the rest of the field. With no time to waste, aware he should be leading, Steve and his mount Casanova boldly jumped through the hedge, where an increasing number of horses and riders were trying likewise, seemingly unaware of the small, unseen ditch the other side of the hedge, it being the cause of many of the refusals.

Other riders, more wary or sensible, including Julie on Bonnie, along with some slower stray hounds, had moved to the left side of the hedge at pace, heading down towards a natural opening further along, where the two fields joined. However, the detour meant possibly losing contact with Steve, the main part of the mounted field, and the hounds, most of which were still in pursuit of the rapidly vanishing hare, somewhere in the woods and beyond.

Anna saw Fred leap the hedge and ditch in one great bound, Tracey staying on board with ease; experience, alcohol and no brains being Anna's reasoning why Tracey feared nothing. Julie and Bonnie had long since vanished from sight going the alternative route. These chaotic events happened in a whirling flash before Anna, as further back on board Penny, witnessing mayhem all around and ahead, she became aware she was herself running out of field.

She tried to recover control over Penny, giving a couple of sharp pulls on the reins. But worryingly, felt no response. Onwards Penny pounded, as Anna pulled frantically on the reins. Hedge, ditch and panicking horses were rapidly approaching, all too fast. Anna cursed, panic coursing through her pounding heart as fast and hard as Penny's hooves. Several hard jabs on the reins, and much yelling seemed to awaken the blindly galloping horse, oblivious to the fearful jockey onboard. Glancing sideways, Anna suddenly became aware of a large white object pulling alongside her, then moving slightly ahead. It was Chris on the Cirrus, galloping hard. He yelled over, his face serious.

She glanced at him, fear clear in her eyes, tears streaming from the wind. Sitting deep into the saddle, being bounced about a few strides, she planted herself hard into the soft leather and hauled firmly on the reins, pulling back several times, using all of her back and arm muscles as Chris had called.

Penny suddenly became aware of the bit being pulled almost into her neck and eased up, just as Cirrus pulled across their path, steering her slightly off course and back in a long loop in the field, clearing them on the immediate danger as they made a huge wide circle. Penny bounced down in rapid transitions, from gallop to canter, then trot as they looped around in control, then quickly settled into a walk, once more facing the hedge several yards away, where a mass of horses were fighting for a place through the gap or deciding to race off the longer route where Julie had vanished on Bonnie.

Anna breathed heavily, sweat streaming down her back, her heart pounding. She smiled a 'Thanks' across to Chris, who smiled back, spots of mud on his face and hat. She looked at him for guidance, as the horses around the gap thinned and they both appeared to be approaching the front and the hedge. Decision time. Jump the obstacle or turn away. More horses were thundering up behind, so they had little time to consider their options. Do or die.

"Which way should we go?" she enquired nervously to Chris, his face red, but knowing the way she wanted to go. Inwardly, the challenge of the ditch excited and tempted her. And also she wanted to impress, but was also wary.

"Straight through if you're game," replied Chris, grinning. "Penny will easily jump that hedge and the ditch. It looks more scary than it is," he continued. "Go on! You can both do it. Don't think, just instinctively jump!"
"Yes, but will I still be board!" Anna replied unsure, her stomach fluttering.
"Follow me through as I go. Just kick hard and sit deep. Penny will naturally follow. Trust me. Go for it!" Chris urged her confidently. With that Chris and Cirrus moved ahead, pushed through and leapt the small ditch and hedge in one bound. Psyched up, along with hearty encouragement from Chris flying over, Anna kicked on the slightly hesitant Penny, pushing her reins hard. With a swift firm dig from Anna's heels, Penny leapt forward, propelling the pair across the small hedge and ditch in one great bound, clearing it by three feet. Anna's body flung forward in the saddle as she landed, her head hitting Penny's neck, gently winding her, as she collected the horse back and moved across to Chris, who sat smiling widely onboard Cirrus in the new field.
"Ha, Ha," she roared loudly. "That was brilliant! Thank you!"
"Said you could do it. Well done both of you." Chris said, pushing Cirrus towards Anna and reaching across, giving Penny a pat on the neck, as another horse appeared over the ditch, landing only a few feet away from them.
"We best clear the area," advised Chris, seeing more horses about to cross. "Try not to lose the field. Martin and Reggie are already a field away."
Anna looked across the new field to see galloping horses racing away before them. The pair needed no encouragement, and continued their charge across the field of set-aside, the rotting undergrowth smashing under the clattering hooves, as they cantered at a steady pace, trying to catch the rest of chasing field, with Steve almost vanishing from sight, Tracey being close by his side.
Chris rode slightly ahead and looked around, his face one of pride and joy. Anna smiled back, her heart pounding with excitement just as a large divot, thrown up from Cirrus' hoof, flew up and hit her hat peak, exploding over her face. Chris laughed loudly as Anna shook her dirt-covered head.
"You bastard!" she yelled playfully, as she too burst out laughing, dusting her hat with a sweep of her glove, understanding the dangerous banter.
As was the way with hunting, the charge across the new field was short-lived and the main part of the mounted field who'd cleared the hedge and ditch, had gathered up in the bottom corner of the field alongside a smiling Steve.
The hounds, Reggie and Martin had vanished, then Bert's hooves were heard clattering down an adjoining road, as Martin tried to re-group and gather the hounds, the hare lost. Reggie following on, also chasing loose hounds.
Steve was now gathering the growing group of red-faced riders together, and began guiding them toward an opening in the headland and out onto the tarmac road Martin and Reggie had cantered down in pursuit of the hounds.
The riders trotted on after Steve, and as Chris and Anna approached, they saw Tracey in the group of horses near the gateway, her face red and breath puffing, but ready to move on with the main front runners beside Steve.

"You made it safely over the ditch," hollered Julie as she approached, joining them from a side track, where she and a number of riders had taken the safer, but slightly longer route, rather than leap the hedge. Out of breath and red-faced, Anna just nodded, hauling up the excited, now sweating and steaming Penny, as she joined the happy group of riders, all quickly recovering.

"They both did very well," Chris announced between breaths looking proudly over to Anna, who grinned. The smiling faces, and growing bond was not missed by a red-faced Tracey, who seated upon a sweaty Fred grinned cheekily at her cousin. She nodded to the mud-covered hat.

"I can thank him for that!" Anna laughed towards Chris. "Bastard!"

The group of four trotted down the road together, with Chris slightly ahead, as an excited Anna recalled the thrilling experience of crossing her first hedge and ditch to Tracey and Julie, the adrenaline still flowing. They both grinned.

As the group of happy friends trotted down the tree lined, tarmac road, flurries of small, crisp leaves blew ahead of them. To Anna, they appeared like groups of small carefree children scuttling off to play. She smiled at the weird thought, and felt herself and Penny chasing the leaves; but the leave always seemed to keep just one step ahead, or were blown into the verges as she caught them, disappearing amongst the brown piles, only to have fresh leaves take their place and continue the strange chase. Fun and childish, Anna could not remember being so happy and carefree for years, and all the worries and concerns of the past months blew away, just like the chased brown leaves.

She looked at the bobbing figures happily trotting around her, Chris and Tracey just ahead and turned to look at Julie, just behind her right shoulder.

"Are you glad you came?" Julie asked, seeing Anna's beaming smile.

Anna just nodded for a reply, the massive smile telling all, the noise of the hooves clattering on the road making it hard to reply without shouting.

It was in this happy mood and with such great company that Anna continued on through the day. One moment riding slowly along country roads, dirt tracks, or field edges, laughing or chatting with the close group, to seconds later find herself galloping madly across a barren field, chasing the pack.

The bitter Easterly wind kept the temperature low all day, and faces, toes and hands cold. At one point they moved onto a field of frozen mud, resembling sheets of dirty brown glass. The field of maize had long been cut down, but where the ground had become waterlogged, the water froze into thin, opaque ice sheets in low parts of the field. As the riders moved across, each sheet deafeningly shattered like plate glass beneath the horse's hooves. Anna winced each time a sheet of ice exploded beneath Penny, revealing a pool of oozing brown liquid mud from below, flowing out like strange alien blood.

But despite the bitter cold, she had not known such happiness in years.

Chapter 36

Where jealousy is the jailer, many break the prison,
it opening more ways to wickedness than it stoppeth;
so that where it findeth one, it maketh them dishonest.

Thomas Fuller

The day continued in a similar fashion for several hours. They'd walk down small country roads, sometimes still covered in frost, trot with care on drilled headlands, and then thunder across fields of unploughed stubble or set-aside, chasing the hounds full on. Other times they'd stand in groups for small periods, often at the corners of fields, waiting for Martin & Reggie to draw the hounds across a field, only to draw a blank, the scent seemingly poor on this dry chilly day. As they chattered and tried to keep warm the groups would share much needed swigs of various alcoholic tipples from hip flasks and chat to the car followers, just as when Anna followed. The pace varied and at some points Anna found herself at the front of the field, close behind the chatty and cheeky Steve Harrison, who made playful banter and cheeky quips to an amused Anna, as he dashed about all day leading the Mounted Field.

Sometimes she rode alongside Chris, then as they galloped off, the pace or ground varying, he would on occasions disappear, leaving her to her own means, appearing to have confidence in her and knowing Julie or Tracey were nearby. Then Chris would reappear from a headland or wood and rejoin them, strangely appearing as if from nowhere, Anna unaware of where he'd been, and Chris never offering explanation when Anna curiously enquired.

Many of the mounted field would want to chat to him, despite his notorious anti-social nature. And as much as Anna wanted to be part of Chris' world too, it was evident he had his own life, and seemed shrouded in some secrecy.

To her relief Anna noticed Lady Burlingham appeared to keep her distance from Chris on this day, and had been less flirtatious and cheeky. Tracey then informed her that the elderly gentleman, who'd ridden alongside her most of the day, was in fact her husband, Lord Burlingham. Hence why she appeared to be on her very best behaviour this day. He was clearly older than her, but was a good rider, most often at the front of the pack on an athletic light bay, and seemingly constantly chatting and joking with Steve. Tracey informed her that he'd been in the cavalry when younger and was an excellent horseman, something he and his younger wife did hold in common, if not their ages.

On one occasion, where Anna was towards the rear with Julie, she saw Chris chatting with Lord Burlingham. Virginia kept a low profile, although chatted and laughed with Chris; she was far less as open and clinging to Chris. In fact, her attention today seemed drawn more toward another rider, and not Chris.

It was a strange set up, with everyone knowing everyone else and meeting up in small groups and chatting on and off. At one point a car appeared and Julie thundered off to happily meet the driver, which turned out to be Carol.

The pair chatted as Anna trotted over to join them. Carol added she was driving by and thought she'd briefly see what was happening. However, her focus seemed to be upon certain riders milling about the field. Her face broke into a beaming smile as Lord Burlingham thundered over to warmly greet her, leaving behind a red-faced Virginia. The varying on-off relationships were too confusing for Anna, who simply recognised the numerous bonds, or not, like the typical connections formed in any club, group or organisation.

The hunt members were possibly closer as a group due to the fact they were all keen and able riders, but also the various persecutions they frequently found themselves under by a wide range of the general public. One of these, the Antis' Anna had feared would emerge and create havoc and ruin her day.

But they strangely never appeared; leaving the hunt to move freely about the land they'd been allocated without hindrance or intimidation for once.

Tracey kept a watchful eye on her cousin, but would often thunder off, her roars of laughter drifting across the fields as she'd joke playfully with Steve, who was obviously attracted to her, but then attracted to most of the female riders. Other times during the day she'd be near to the back of the field, riding with her and Julie, losing sight of the leading pack, mixing with other slower riders and chatting to Anna. Julie would introduce to Anna the various riders, and tip her off as to who they were, what they were like, and who was supposedly having an affair with whom; a common thing it seemed with members of The Shoteton. She liked Julie and felt a common bond growing as they chatted about all sorts, Bruce often coming into the conversation.

Anna was amazed at how easy it was to lose over thirty horses, but frequently did, ensuring she did not push Penny too hard on her first day, and Julie ever cautious with her soured-face mount, who grizzled at Penny all day.

As well as losing touch with the horses, Anna was equally surprised just how easy it was losing over thirty hounds, and two gentlemen clad in bright scarlet.

Most of the time Reggie and Martin were nowhere to be seen, only the haunting sound of the horn blowing up somewhere in the distance, indicating their location, as the pair tried to collect up and re-group the wayward pack of hounds who were several fields, a road or a dense wood away from them.

But in all, cold and chilling wind put aside, Anna loved the day and being a hunter for the first time; joining an elite and unique group of horse riders. For her the day was too short, and as they headed home, only fifteen riders made it back to the farm with the hounds, Anna proud to be one of them. Riding back with a mud-spattered Chris beside her, smiling proudly, she smugly noticed Lady Burlingham and her husband had both left. She knew she'd physically taxed Penny, but also that she was a fit horse, however, Anna was determined to stay the day and make the most of such a great opportunity.

She was fascinated when Martin 'blew for home' on the horn and how the hounds magically grouped together, the tight pack moving together as one pack down the road with Martin and Reggie behind, with not one hound attempting to break the tight group they formed. The remainder of the field rode close behind the two huntsmen, led by Steve, as all headed for home.

They made it through the farm gates and back over to the lorries and with cold, damp and aching limbs, dismounted, stretching various bodily parts to regain full movement. They checked the damp, mud-strewn and now tired horses for any cuts or sores, and un-tacked them, ensuring all had water, before rugging and then loading them up in Chris boxes. Here the horses relaxed, tucking into fresh haynets with much vigour. Cold, mud-splattered and equally tired, but still very happy, the group of four then slowly wandered back into the barn where they'd started out from hours earlier for drinks.

Once again the sight thrilled Anna, as the hosts had lain on a warming tea to welcome everyone returning. Urns of tea and coffee were set on trestle tables once more, accompanied with stacks of biscuits, scones and fruit cake.

Julie and Tracey, never shy, dived into the fruitcake, before grabbing a cup of tea each. Chris, the gentleman, passed a cup of steaming dark-brown tea to Anna, who gratefully received it with a twinkling eye and gentle smile.

The party drifted off towards the main group, where Martin and Reggie were chatting to a vibrant Steve, who was happily discussing some details of the day to a pair of elderly ladies, both dressed in dark green tweed and donning headscarves, all seemingly enchanted by the dashing, stunning Field Master.

A ruddy-faced man in a wax jacket, with check-shirt covered belly hanging over some well-worn cherry-red trousers, laughed heartily with Reggie. His spindly wife, with wispy grey hair stood alongside, looking on intently too.

Julie and Tracey, knowing the hosting pair, moved over and thanked the couple, to be joined by Chris and Anna, who also heartily thanked their hosts and all shook the hands of Reggie and Martin for giving them a great day.

Reggie, never missing an opportunity, stepped forward and gave Anna, Tracey and Julie a peck on their cheeks. The woman all blushed, especially so Anna, suddenly noticing a red-faced woman standing beside Reggie, who she knew was his wife, Elizabeth. She glared at Reggie, not an innocent warm gesture, but harshly, as if there was some deep-seated bitterness within.

Upon seeing the ladies receive their kisses, Steve Harrison set down his cup of tea, excused himself from his guests and leapt over towards the group.

"I can't let you beautiful ladies get away without a kiss," he yelled, openly grabbing at Tracey and jokingly pulling her too him and squeezing her tight. She punched him playfully in the arm, as he released her, then pecked Tracey's and Julie offered cheeks. The pair stepped back and Steve stared at Anna, his grin spreading widely as he clearly recognised her from the day.

"Where on earth did you find this beauty, Chris?" he called out. "She's got to be wedding bells material. Sorry, I'm assuming you're not married!"

Anna smiled and blushed, but noticing Chris blush a deeper red as he stepped back, shrugging his shoulders and grinning as Steve moved forward towards Anna. "Best horses and best ladies, that's our mysterious Chris."

Anna turned to glance at a red-faced, silent Chris, but also felt her own face flush, naturally attracted to the gregarious Field Master, who grabbed at Anna's hands, then drew her into his body. Holding her close, giving her a hug, he pecked her on both cheeks, looking into her grey eyes with a cheeky, knowing smile. Chris shuffled, smiling vainly, but looking uncomfortable.

"I hope we'll be seeing you out again soon. Anna, isn't it?" Steve asked, gazing intently at her. "I never forget a pretty name. Nor a very pretty face."

Anna blushed, tilting her head provocatively and smiled cheekily.

"Well you may, or you may not. Who knows?" She replied coyly naturally teasing a man she found attractive. "You'll just have to wait and see!"

Steve Harrison roared with laughter, grabbed her hands, still looking deeply, then raising one hand to his lips, kissed the top of her palm, before releasing her from his grasp. His eyes twinkled, as he looked long at her smiling face.

Anna felt her stomach swirl like she'd not know for ages.

"I love your attitude Anna," Steve chuckled. "Brilliant! I look forward to seeing you out again. Very soon, I hope. Chris, I hope she comes out again!"

Anna smiled back, still blushing, feeling a warm rush within. Since leaving Bruce, he was the first man to truly charm her. She felt attracted to Chris, but couldn't explain why; being aloof and mysterious, whether deliberate or not. He seemed to draw her in one minute, then push her away the next. Give her attention, then ignore her. But Steve oozed genuine 'smarm and charm.'

It was what woman were naturally attracted to, even if Steve had danger written all over him. But why shouldn't she accept Steve's cheeky advances and enjoy his attention? She was now free and single and he was handsome.

Behind her she felt several sets of eyes boring into her.

Julie and Tracey's faces were set with broad grins.

Chris stared solemnly; eyes set, but face decidedly down.

The group stepped away with a nod and Steve waved a fond goodnight to them, as did Reggie, Martin, and Sharon, who'd been whipping-in all day.

They walked away, smiling widely, except for Chris, who looked somewhat dejected and stayed silent as they all returned to the vehicles, clearly tired. Here the horses were quickly checked and then the engines fired up. The still chatting and giggling ladies clambered into Julie's Land Rover and a lone Chris returned to his lorry and proceeded to lead the way back to Horsewater in the growing gloom that had descended, in both the light and also in mood.

As they headed back to the stables, the woman chattered about the exciting events of the day, with Tracey and Julie laughing about Steve, but warning Anna about his past sexual exploits and his 'fast and loose' reputation with woman. Anna remained coy, simply enjoying the thought of some attention from Steve and was also excited about going out at the next hunt meet.

"Why didn't we see any anti's out today?" asked Anna, curious as to their absence as they drove off. "I thought they'd be out, but glad they weren't."

"I don't know," Julie replied. "They don't always come out, but they might be keeping a low profile after the incident with those two having a fight over that hare the other week. Or they're simply harvesting their crop of Tofu."

"I'm glad they weren't out. Tossers spoil it," added Tracy. "Today was good, for a change. Anyway, don't bad-mouth Tofu. I quite like it in Soy sauce."

"Tofu tastes like cardboard. Yucky shit!" replied Julie. "We don't get Antis out every week," Julie continued. "There are only a few who come out regularly, Izzy and her skinny side-kick friend mostly. I think they swap from hunt to hunt as well, although Izzy and that horrible skinny git, who hangs after her, generally pester us. I feel Izzy has her own agenda, as Steve's ex."

Anna looked at Julie, having met Izzy, but with the strange sense about her.

"I used to like Izzy," added Tracey. "Great fun, before she turned rogue. Now she's a pain in the arse. Probably out Christmas shopping," she grinned.

They slowly returned to the yard in the dark, the dark sky, indicating another chilly night. Apart from being cold and tired, Anna concluded it had been a very good day, and one she would long remember, for many happy reasons.

However, none of the tired but happily chatting and joking occupants of the Rover, nor Chris, deep in his own thoughts, spotted the estate car drive past them in the dark. It was just another car passing tired people in the dark.

But it wasn't. The occupants of the vehicles should have been more vigilant.

Its headlights and the gloom obscured the identity of the car and driver.

Just before the turning into Horsewater, the driver swung his head around.

Chris' horsebox and Julie's Rover turned into the entrance of Horsewater.

They noticed nothing as they drove through the gloom of the dark woods.

However, the car driver didn't fail to miss the vehicles or importantly, the occupants. In fact he'd been going out of his way all day to try to find them.

Both Chris and Julie's group failed to notice the car abruptly brake, turn around in the road, and then watch as the small convey disappeared down into the wooded track, heading back to the safety and warmth of Horsewater.

The driver of the Audi sat some yards from the entrance to the woods, white smoke drifting from the exhaust, but headlights momentarily switched off. The driver could not believe his luck at seeing the same horsebox and driver he'd vowed to find and seek revenge upon from the incident in Leicester.

Bruce smiled. The 'God of Information' had indeed been on his side.

That 'God' had been by an old policeman friend, who owed him a big favour from long back, where Bruce had provided him a false alibi to save his arse.

His old policeman friend was cautious in providing the full details, knowing Bruce of old and not totally trusting him, despite knowing he'd saved his own marriage when Bruce lied about where he'd been late one night.

And it wasn't on duty. Leastwise, not with the police, but more so his lover.

The policeman knew he'd be in serious trouble if anything happened, hence why he'd only given Bruce the name of a small village in Norfolk where the horsebox he'd enquired about 'might be located.' Bruce had claimed his wife wanted to buy the horsebox, having seen it parked at a horse show, falling in love with it, but not knowing who owned it. Bruce had told his policeman friend he'd buy his wife the horsebox as a surprise birthday present, if he only knew exactly where it was located. Norfolk was a very large county.

His old policeman friend wasn't stupid. But did owe him a big favour.

He'd informed Bruce all he could disclose was that it was owned by someone in the small village of Salheath. He'd have to find the exact place himself.

That was all Bruce needed. He'd been driving about the small village all day, hunting, but had missed the hidden entrance. And now he'd found his quarry.

He'd been lucky seeing it pass; even more so watching it sneak back into its dark, wooded hideout. Better still, with the arrogant pigmy driving it.

But then he was always lucky. As everyone always told him.

Luck, however, he recalled was when 'preparation meets opportunity.'

Seeing Anna and her newly found friends following on behind in the Land Rover had been the cherry on the top of the cake. A perfect result.

It however both excited and enraged him.

He now knew where she kept that annoying horse.

That was a result. That excited him.

But Anna also appeared happy. Without him.

That was what enraged him. She should be sad.

But at least she wasn't in the lorry cab with the pygmy troll.

That was something positive to accept.

Bruce considered that maybe the small man slept under a bridge and feasted on passing goats as they trotted over. Or was that Trolls?

Who cared. Trolls, dwarfs. They were all the same to him.

Bruce smiled, knowing it had been a good day for all.

A very good day indeed. Result.

Now it was time for action.

Chapter 37

His promises were, as he then was, mighty;
but his performance, as he in now, are nothing.

Henry VIII - William Shakespeare

At The Kennels, a few days later, Sharon was excited. She was preparing for her 'girls night out.' A pre-Christmas party with a number of women from the hunt, along with a couple of local farmers wives, for a regular social gathering.

Martin was outside in the kennels, busy as ever seeing to the hounds needs. Sharon stood before the mirror holding up a different top in each hand, deciding which best suited the black trousers she was planning to wear. She shook her head, deciding neither, both too adventurous for her. Dropping them on the bed, she opened the wardrobe and pulled out her favourite beige trousers and brown top, the ones she always wore and felt comfortable in. She paused for a second, looking deeply into the mirror, staring at the person before her. Focussing in on her face, she examined the fine wrinkles; the laughter lines and crows feet, which were slowly becoming permanent fixtures, rather than appearing when she smiled. Dressed only in her white lace knickers, she looked at her outline sideways on. Her small belly hung slightly over the waistband. She lifted it up and drew her stomach in, but the skin still fell down in a small fold. She looked further up. Her breasts had always been a good point and were still full and rounded, but they too were beginning to get a bit too flabby and starting to sag. It was all going South!

She and Martin had always had a fairly good sex life, with the occasional on and off period, but generally it was good. But at the moment they seemed to be in an 'off' period, but not through her wanting. It was Martin who seemed had become less interested in her at the moment. She was not getting any younger, but neither was he, so it was probably natural. The winter months took their toll on Martin, being non-stop busy; organising and attending hunt meets and seeing to the constant needs of the fifty plus hounds in their charge, let along all of the butchering of dead-stock to feed them. It was a tiring time, and little wonder Martin had less interest in his wife.

But it was the small changes she'd noticed. In bed she'd provocatively thrust her buttocks towards him; a sure sign in the past for him to make a grab, as she was 'up for it.' But he'd just lain there frozen, or simply turned away.

Sharon wondered if maybe he was seeing someone else. He'd never strayed before, and she assumed he was loyal, but was still a potentially 'good catch' and many women in the hunt liked him; openly chatted and flirted with him. But there were other things. He'd hinted about wanting to try 'other things' with her a while back, but she was reluctant to do them. Too kinky for her.

He'd only playfully hinted, but it'd made her wonder and a bit afraid at the time. She was not a complete prude, but it made her curious about Martin, and how his needs may be potentially changing as she grew older, and less attractive, and also realising how distant he was becoming lately. But none of that would solve the ever-growing waistline, sagging flesh and indecision on clothing. She sighed, grabbed her usual bra, and then rechecked her watch.

Sharon was looking forward to the evening, especially at seeing Helen, who acted as an amateur Whipper-In for the Shoteton and often helped out at the kennels, always taking on young puppy hounds for exercising. She heard a door shut downstairs and then footsteps on the old wooden stairs, their hollow sound resonating along the landing floor, just as she was slipping her feet into her usual, 'boring' low-heeled black leather shoes. She took a quick look in the mirror. Safe, boring and predictable. That seemed to be Sharon.

Martin came into the bedroom, looked at Sharon's image in the mirror, and raised his eyebrows with a smile. "You look nice sweetheart," he said as he slid passed her, playfully grabbing her buttocks with a gentle tweak, putting paid to the Sharon's doubts from a few minutes earlier.

"Are you driving tonight?" Martin added casually.

"Yes," replied Sharon, looking in the mirror, not really catching what he said, still unsure of her bland clothing and if she should change again.

Martin looked concerned, his face flushing. "But I thought you said you were going in Helen's car?" but not looking at her, fumbling in a drawer.

"What? I mean no. No I'm not driving. Helen's picking me up," she replied, now listening. "It's her turn to drive this time. And she'll be here soon."

Martin smiled, turned from the drawer, kissed her neck, then quickly left the room and drifted back downstairs. The sound of the TV downstairs came on as Sharon pulled out a pair of high-heeled black suede shoes. Martin had chosen them one day when out shopping together in Norwich. They were not usually her thing, being too high, but he'd convinced her she looked good in them. She'd only ever worn them once, as they were too high. She slid her feet into them and tottered before the mirror. They were far sexier than her usual low heels, highlighting her fine ankles, but she felt awkward and ungainly in them, had to walk like a model and even felt a bit of a slut. When she'd previously worn them to a Hunt Ball they'd hurt her feet like hell and quickly came off when she started dancing. She'd have preferred wellies.

Looking into the mirror, admiring the extra height and shape they provided to her legs, she already felt her feet ache. He thought for a second, looked at herself once more, before flicking them off and slid back into her old favourite 'flats' regarding the discarded shoes. "Another time," she muttered, carefully putting the suede high heels back into the bottom of the wardrobe.

Sharon finally changed into the original clothes she'd selected, then went down into the small lounge, filled with photo's of past equestrian events.

The walls were adorned with rosettes and unique hunting memorabilia collected by Martin, giving the place a genuine old world, yet homely feel.
Martin looked up at her as she entered, then back at the TV, without commenting. She stood silently framing the doorway for a few seconds, hoping he'd notice her and make another comment about her appearance.
"I'll be off in a moment dear," Sharon said, trying to gain his attention.
"Have you got anything special planned for tonight?" She asked.
"Oh sorry love," said Martin, diverting his attention from the TV, getting up. "You look very nice," he replied, without actually looking. "I'm staying in. Watching TV. I'll have a beer, then check the hounds. It's been a long day."
With that a car horn tooted outside. Both heads spun, unaware of the car.
"That'll be Helen," Sharon said, without looking out the curtained windows. "We're running late. I'd better dash. Don't eat too many cookies tubby!"
Martin smiled and rising, gave her a peck on the cheek. "Have a good night and don't drink too much." He smiled genuinely and she kissed him back.
"Any ideas what time you'll be back?" Martin enquired. "I may be up, but it depends on how late you'll be, so I might turn in. I won't bolt the door,"
"Just before midnight, I think," she replied, dashing to the door, waving a hand as the door shut. "See you. I've got to dash. Be good!"
With that Martin smiled and waved at the closing door. He returned to the settee and sat down with a sigh, pressing the TV remote, and listened to the sound of crunching gravel and the fading engine roar of Helen's car leaving.
Seconds later he was up, head cocked, dashing through the hallway to look out of the window, watching Helen's car tail-lights vanish along the darkened drive, out of his line of sight, moving off into the woods. Sharon was gone.
Martin dashed upstairs, racing into the bedroom, throwing off his old jeans and sweatshirt. Stripping down naked, he moved into the bathroom and quickly washed, before returning to the bedroom, where he donned some smart, yet casual clothes. He looked in the full-length mirror, the image of Sharon still fresh within as he regarded himself, a pang of guilt passing through him. But not for long. A passing thought of Sharon was all he had, as he turned and grabbed his jacket, heading back down the aged wooden stairs.
In the kitchen he collected his keys and went outside. Walking out past the kennel block and into the drive area, he breathed a lungful of fresh crisp, cool air, now ready for the evening, but momentarily listened to the night.
The hounds in the nearby kennels howled briefly upon hearing the door shut, instinctively knowing it was Martin and food, but went silent as he made his way over towards one of the out buildings where a dark Range Rover stood.
As he walked up to it, senses keen, he heard a sound.
The sound was unique and unusual. In the woods.
Martin cocked his head, listening hard, and again heard it.
The sound of laughter.

He cocked his head, scanning, as taught in the military, and looked away in the distance, in the direction from where the sound emanated, honing in onto a certain point in the distant and all encompassing, distant dark woods.

Moving into the barn, he clambered into the Rover and fired the big engine into life. Lights off, the large 4 x 4 rumbled out of the barn, moving alongside the house on the gravel track. Window down, Martin listened intently.

In the woods he heard further sounds.

Strangers - perhaps.

He cursed at the annoyance.

He too had been also looking forward to a good night out.

A very good night.

But first he had to check out the noise.

Hopefully it wouldn't take long.

In darkness, the Range Rover slowly moved along the dirt track. It's lights off, the big vehicle moved on into the woods, following in darkness the unseen trail set by Sharon and Helen only ten minutes earlier.

Head out of the open window, he listened intently.

Martin was back out hunting.

Chapter 38

If one tells the truth, one is sure, sooner or later, to be found out.

Oscar Wilde

Steve Harrison looked at the clock, shook his head and swore. He was going to be late if he wasn't quick. He'd been doing paperwork and checking his ever worrying bank statements. Things weren't good and he needed some extra finances, somehow. He had some ideas, but as ever, they weren't totally kosher. He sighed, aware the time had slipped away from him yet again.

He took a slurp of his now cold cup of tea, grimacing at the taste and left the cup as he rose up from his chair within his Portacabin office. He grabbed his green fleece from a hook and picked up the car keys lying on his desk. Steeping over to a nearby table, he threw a number of items into a small black rucksack, gazing inside to double-check he had everything he needed.

Locking the Portacabin office door behind him, he strode purposefully across the wide open yard with the rucksack full of parts, walking over to the dark Range Rover sitting before him. Pausing momentarily he gazed into the gloomy dark sky, with no lights showing for miles around. Tranquillity.

He had a busy night ahead and smiled at the thought of what was to come.

It excited him and kept him alive.

A still, quiet but chill winter's night, it was the type he loved, where a certain buzz hung in the air. The atmosphere almost had an expectancy something could and would happen. He stood in the open yard for a few seconds, scanning the area, sniffing the chill night air like a fox looking for its prey.

But something was wrong.

His natural hunting senses were working.

A sensation like electricity passed through him.

He looked towards the farmhouse, considering returning to its safety, or to perhaps check all was secure within. Long and hard he thought and listened.

Then he heard it again.

A noise. In the distance. Unique.

Something his subconscious had noticed before but he hadn't.

He paused, scanning the dark open yard, squinting into the gloom, looking at the mass of varied junk and vehicles that littered the place, providing potential hiding places for anything and everything that may want to lurk.

Steve's farm was a good place to lose things.

Many things had vanished in the past. All sorts.

But something was out there. Hidden.

Watching him. He was sure.

Steve's senses were on edge. His skin prickled.

He cocked his head, eyes scanning the dark woods in the distance.

It was late, and so was he now, but that meant nothing.

Time was irrelevant to those who hunted him. And many did.

That sound once more. Clear and definite.

It was there. In the distance. In the woods.

He looked, turning towards where he thought the noise emanated, peering sightless out into the darkness and woods beyond.

He checked his watch and bit at his lip. Time was going.

Thoughts raced through his mind. Decision made.

He clambered into the dark Range Rover and gunned the big engine, which roared appreciatively. The bright lights flicked into life, illuminating the yard area and revealing little beyond the usual items, as Steve expected.

He pressed the accelerator and the powerful engine propelled him along the dirt track and up on into the surrounding woods.

Ploughing through the darkness of the trees, the bright light beams scanned the woods and countryside, searching for a possible source of the noise.

As the Rover raced on through the woods, Steve tutted and shook his head.

Tonight he had more important things to concern him.

But for now, he must find the prowler in the woods.

Then deal with them appropriately. And decisively.

Chapter 39

When one is in love, one always begins by deceiving one's self; and one always ends up deceiving others.

Oscar Wilde

That same evening Elizabeth Hornchurch stood beside an oak dresser in the kitchen of The Grange, staring down at her Christmas shopping list, having tidied up the crockery from dinner. Reggie wandered in, his heavy footfalls at once ominous upon the aged wooden floor. Ignoring him, she continuing to look down at the list she was preparing. Reggie had not been good company over the dinner of lamb chops and mixed veg' she'd prepared. Moody and self-contained, Elizabeth had tried to make conversation, but he was sour and bitter, and she received only curt responses. He'd complained about issues on one of the farms, with a sugar beet problem, which would cost him money. Big money. It was all details Elizabeth had little care for and ate on in silence.

As he now entered the kitchen, Reggie was skulking about as normal.

"I've got to pop out. Discuss the Boxing Day meet with Martin and Steve," he announced bluntly as if he needed to justify himself. He never did.

Elizabeth stopped writing and looked up, knowing he was lying. She could always tell when Reggie was lying. If he was going to do what he'd just said, he would have simply gone and done the errand without any explanation.

By explaining, it meant he was covering himself up with lies. Fool!

It was all silly. Elizabeth knew Reggie far too well. But she didn't care.

He'd strangely been different the last few weeks. He still flew into the odd tirade and rage, but had begun to apologise if he did. Something was up.

It was as if he felt guilty and sensed he needed to justify his what was doing.

But it was all pointless. Elizabeth knew Reggie was scheming. But at what?

Perhaps he was genuinely trying to change. Unlikely, but maybe.

She looked at him for a few seconds, staring direct into his cold eyes, the silence between them cutting. He looked away first. She flushed inwardly.

Yes, he was lying. Nothing had changed. Same old Reggie.

And things would never change. Unless she did something.

Soon she would. She had a plan. For once she was in control.

Elizabeth composed herself, hoping she wouldn't sound as false as Reggie.

"Actually, I've got to pop out too. I need see Jane about a few arrangements for over Christmas, so I'll be going out too. In just a few minutes."

She felt she'd lied much more convincingly than Reggie.

There was a hollow stillness in the air. The scene like a game of human chess, each trying to catch the other out as they planned their next deceitful move.

So far Elizabeth was winning. Either that or Reggie simply no longer cared.

"That's fine," Reggie lied, face red, breaking the silence. "I don't know how long I will be. May stop off at The Hare and Hounds on the way back. See if Mister Crawford is there and have a quick drink. He's usually about and I have something I need to discuss with him about his future hunt meet."

"Okay dear," replied Elizabeth smiling, trying to appear to care, but hoping she didn't over-egg the fakeness. "Don't drink too much. There's a new policeman about Jane said. Got piggy eyes. Not very nice. Pulled someone over last week for drink driving when coming from The Bell. Watch out."

Reggie nodded in response, either as confirmation of the information or as a silent thank you. He'd heard about the new copper too. A nosey bastard.

"I shouldn't be too long and was just about to leave actually, Jane hasn't got too long to spare, so you will have to lock up and let Jager out for wee. Bye."

With that Elizabeth turned, picked up her bag from the dresser, stepped up to a bentwood coat stand and grabbed a wool shooting jacket. She moved over to Reggie, seemingly examining in detail the label on a bottle of wine, and pecked him on the cheek. He was surprised by the swift and unusual action and before he could respond, Elizabeth turned and was bustling out the kitchen through the back doorway, leaving Reggie standing dumbstruck.

Reggie watched as Elizabeth disappeared, glowing red with anger, slamming the wine bottle down at the sound of the door closing and cursed loudly.

"Bloody woman. Who the hell does she think she is playing with?" He cursed aloud to the kitchen wall. "The bloody bitch! She'll pay for this. Dearly."

He wandered into a the utility room, where a pair of yellow eyes gazed up. He rubbed the mottled brown head of Jager, his German Wire-haired Pointer and stepping forward to let him out into the yard, where the hunting dog trotted off, sniffing. Meanwhile, Reggie wasted no time and busied himself, letting his rage subside and gathered the items he needed for his evening.

A few minutes later he called the dog, who obediently trotted back through the door in silence to settle back in his warm bed beside an old boiler. Reggie checked the main front door and placed a screen over the log fire, which was burning low in the hearth and followed the tracks Elizabeth had made a short time earlier out to the main back door. It led into the courtyard at the back and various white-painted outbuildings. The bright walls appeared to glow in the subdued light, ghostly highlighting Reggie as he strutted across the grey flagstones, out through a small gateway before reaching his Range Rover. As unlocked the vehicle's door he heard a distinct sound far off in the distance.

He cocked his head, listening intently; sure he'd heard something.

There is was again. Somewhere in the distance.

Clear and obvious. Was it the sound of laughter?

The land around The Grange was vast, being a mix of arable fields and mature woodland. Some of the land also adjoined his main neighbours, those being Lord Burlingham and his Wroxingham Hall estate, Chris Turner's Horsewater and even parts of Steve Harrison's much smaller property.

They were good neighbours to have, even if some neighbouring properties were in some cases set some miles apart. But these neighbours were trusting, loyal and like-minded and all members of the Shoteton. All good men.
The kennels were not too far away either, directly adjoining Reggie's estate to the north and actually part of his farm. Martin was loyal and trusting too.
Very loyal and totally trustworthy. Dependable. In all matters.
Long ago, well before Reggie or his recent relative's days, the entire estate, including The Kennels, Chris' Turner's Horsewater estate, and even Steve's smaller property, had all been part of one huge estate. It'd stretched out to Wroxingham Hall, where the current Lord Burlingham and his carefree and attractive young wife Virginia now lived. But a distant relative of the current Lord Burlingham - long since passed away - had wagered poorly on a business venture, and lost a lot of his land in a somewhat dubious deal. It thus split the one-time, massive, sprawling estate into several farms and plots, which in turn had been divided to some degree to form the current local farms and estates.
The history interested Reggie, and he was aware distant fate had been kind, giving him through time, luck and birthright his own massive playing field, where he could do as he pleased, when he wanted and no one could stop him.
Reggie loved it. He embraced the independence it brought and the enormous sense of power and control it gave him over many and all that went with it.
Reggie liked power. Being in control of everything.
He also knew he would never relinquish any of the land.
To no one. Never. Ever.
He'd been lucky with Lady Tabitha. Very lucky.
Then so had she. Very lucky. She knew it as well.
Hence why she'd asked for nothing. She could have received worse.
He hoped he'd learnt from his mistakes too. Lesson learnt.
Elizabeth would never divorce him. She wouldn't dare. If she did, she'd leave with what she came with. Nothing. Or maybe even less. Just her life.
Maybe should wouldn't even leave with that. Who knew?
But hopefully matters wouldn't ever come to that.
Elizabeth knew the rules and what she could expect.
Lost in his thoughts, Reggie sighed, checking his watch.
Then he heard the sound once more. More clearly.
It was nearby. It needed investigating. At once.
Reggie's hunter instincts bristled with fresh excitement.
He loved danger, the thrill of the chase. And more especially - The Kill.
He rechecked his watch, knew he had time, and fired up the Rover engine.
Slowly the vehicle crept forward into the darkness.
Reggie smiled. He was off hunting again.

Chapter 40

Better suffer for the truth, than prosper in a falsehood.

Proverb

Dawn Davis was unhappy. Gavin was late coming home. Again.

He'd always been reliable in the past, regular as clockwork, as with everything in life, but not lately. He had changed. Things had changed. Why?

When asked, Gavin blamed it on the new management at work, pushing him to reach targets and complete workloads, with inadequate staff. Typical.

He was staying late at meetings and becoming stressed before coming home. He'd even been forced to go away on more business trips, as well as often visiting the company late in the evening to check on the night shift.

She knew they needed the money and couldn't afford for Gavin to lose his prestigious job, and all it entailed, but it was becoming too much for her.

They'd argued over it several times, Dawn telling him he should stand up to the management, but with Gavin storming off each time, as usual in a huff, moaning that she didn't understand. But it always came down to money.

Dawn spending it, and Gavin earning it, but having none left. Only bills.

She'd not been suspicious at first, and always fully trusted him never to cheat.

But things changed. Now she had her doubts. Suspicions. Something wrong.

There was something else. Not just money worries seemingly troubling him.

They'd always had money troubles. As long as they'd been together and had horses, their lifestyle always ran away with them and income never caught up.

There was something else these days though which seemed to plague his conscience. Gavin was always loyal, but also very private. Maybe secretive.

She was becoming convinced he was possibly having an affair.

Things had definitely changed lately. In many ways.

It was only a woman's instinct something was wrong.

She had no proof, and didn't want to look for any. Yet.

But he no longer wanted to touch her. Anywhere.

And he looked at her differently too. Through her, rather than at her.

He'd look at her as though she was made of glass, or as if he was assessing her, comparing her with someone else. Someone better.

And he had become increasingly distant and withdrawn.

Her moaning and complaining at him over petty issues possibly didn't help.

She'd vowed she'd try to change and also look for a job. That'd help matters financially and ease the pressure. She'd start looking later next week. Maybe.

Most of all though, deep down, she found it hard to believe he'd have an affair. It was almost beyond him. Gavin didn't have the nerve.

Gavin lacked confidence with women, being quiet and shy, and even incapable of finding anyone else. Dawn had ensured that didn't happen over the years, by putting him down; telling him he was nothing special. Lucky to have her and lowering his self-esteem. Dawn never complimented him on his looks, and told him repeatedly he was lucky to even have anyone.

He seemed to agree. Why wouldn't he? She was right.

If he was having an affair, the real question was with whom?

That was what Dawn needed to know. Who on earth could it be?

It had to be someone from work, as she never let him out of her sight and kept a tight rein on where he could go and whom he could possibly see.

He had no other social life. Other than horses and hunting.

He didn't need anything else. Dawn and the horses were all his life.

Gavin hardly ever talked about work and most of his colleagues were male. They hardly had any secretaries any more, as everyone typed their own reports. If it was a woman from work, it'd be a bet she made the first moves.

Gavin wouldn't. He was far too shy. It was Dawn who'd made the first moves on him when he arrived at her yard. She wasn't going to let any of the other little bitches at the yard then get their claws into him when he arrived.

Maybe she was simply being silly. Maybe not. But something was wrong.

With a heavy sigh, she looked at the clock again. Five minutes had passed since she last looked at the dial, but to Dawn it seemed like an age.

She decided she'd give him another five minutes then ring him on his mobile again. She'd already left two messages asking where he was.

He always moaned about her running up the phone bill, so she was hesitant to call him, and he wasn't really late. She simply felt something was wrong.

Importantly, she was feeling down and needed him with her. She was lonely.

It seemed ironic sometimes that he worried about her spending a few pennies on making a phone call to him, to check that he was okay, yet he would occasionally drive to work in the Range Rover, like he had today. It cost a small fortune in petrol to run, rather than use the smaller Peugeot.

Dawn drummed her fingers on the table, glanced at her watch, then the clock, then at the empty table. She began to wonder if she cared too much for him and stifled him. Perhaps she should let him have a more breathing space.

But why should she? She wanted him for herself and needed him around her.

Simply to be there. All the time. She needed the company.

That was what she really wanted, although she'd never admit it.

She didn't love him, not really, not for Gavin as himself.

It was something she'd known that for years.

There was no real emotional connection. Simply a need.

Like an addition. She simply wanted his companionship.

But she'd not give him up for someone else to have.

He was too good a catch to let someone else take from her.

It made her boil inside, thinking someone else may be getting his attention; attention that belonged solely to her. No one else. Just her.

But Gavin would never cheat on her. Never.

She hoped. Fingers crossed.

Perhaps he'd had an accident. Maybe that was the reason.

Biting her lip, she glanced at the clock once more.

She'd give him fifteen minutes, and then ring again.

Maybe ten. Be patient.

No. Five minutes.

And then she'd call.

No. She'd call again. Now.

'Where the hell was he?'

Chapter 41

Hell is empty and all the devils are here.

The Tempest - William Shakespeare

The figure turned at the top of the stairs, gun held firm, the barrels swinging down the long, unlit landing. Eyes searched the gloomy interior.

Numerous doors ran off along the side. One at the end.

But the prowler knew the correct door to choose.

He'd been here before. Many times. Watching. Waiting.

A floorboard creaked, but onward the silhouette moved.

Undeterred. Proceeding with purpose, the figure strode forward.

Silently and unseen, knowing its final destination. It was there.

The bedroom door opened, not cautiously, but with force.

With the door violently swinging back, crashing against the wall, the figure marched forward in the dark and up to the bed where a body lay sleeping.

A finger moved onto the trigger of the shotgun, barrels thrust hard at the shape lying in the bed, pressed firmly against their head.

Chris turned his head, eyes wide open, but unafraid.

In the dark he stared unemotional, at the person before him - as if waiting.

The barrels rested against Chris' head; steel hard and cold.

Chris looked impassively at his assassin, a faceless figure.

Finger squeezed, hammer clicked, gun fired. Boom!

The explosion roared through Chris's head.

A bright flash. Deafening roar. Then silence.

Chris awoke in a sweat, panting, fighting for breath.

Bed sheets thrown off, he rose, searching the dark room.

His hand reached down, grabbing the small but deadly sawn-off .410 shotgun, hidden, but strategically placed under the bed.

But the room was empty. It always was. Every time.

He ran a hand through his hair, carefully replacing the gun.

Sitting up he stared into the darkness, ears cocked, listening.

Something was wrong. Instinct told him.

He sensed it as he looked at the glowing red digits of the clock on the dresser opposite. The evening was still early. He'd lain upon the bed earlier, just for a quick rest, but it being a long and tiring day. Then fallen asleep.

How long had he lain there? Who knew. But whatever, it was too long.

Now fully awake, he peered through the bedroom window, wiping a porthole shape into the condensation, to check all was okay.

But it wasn't. The dream was a warning.

It always was. He took note.

The film of water left behind by Chris' sweeping hand distorted the dark images of the yard outside. A cloudy night, with no trace of wind, the bare branches of the tall trees nearby stood like dark sentinels.

The yard appeared empty, with the single head of a restless horse hanging over a stable door, the others resting, eating hay or sleeping.

He should not have fallen asleep. Undisciplined.

Things still had to be done. Important things. As ever.

But he'd had a rest to consider those matters.

Max, his silent and ever-present guardian padded up the stairs upon hearing his master. His toenails clunked heavy on the bare wood. After a reassuring pat on his sleek black head and rub of his tan muzzle, he silently followed Chris back down the darkened staircase and into the kitchen.

With no lights on, he walked freely about the house in the half-light. The gentle warmth of the Aga filled the room as he quietly unlocked and opened the door. Max went forward eagerly to get a whiff of the night air that blew into the kitchen, but Chris pushed the dog back with his leg as he grabbed the wax jacket hanging near the door and slowly opened it wider. Max forced past his leg and ran into the yard, sniffing silently, exploring unseen scents and unheard sounds, then cocked his leg up the corner of the nearest stable.

Chris stepped forward and stood silently by the door. Pulling in deep breaths of cool night air, the hair on the back of his neck prickled. As he suppressed a shudder, he cocked his head, listening intently at the silence around him.

He sensing something rather than heard it.

Turning his head, he scanned the distant woods, listening.

But all was quiet. Or so it seemed. But maybe not.

Checking his watch, he called Max back to the house, ushered the dog inside, threw him a pig ear treat and closed the door, grabbing the Range Rover keys.

Then he heard it. Clear and definite.

He turned his head towards the woods.

Again the sound came, slightly muffled by the distance and the depth of the woods through which it'd travelled, but it was clear and distinct.

Chris listened intently once more.

Again he heard the noise. No doubts.

He checked his watch, shaking his head.

This he didn't need. He had things to do. Important things.

Looking up to the night sky, with keys in hand, he moved over to the Range Rover and climbed inside. With a roar of the massive engine, the unlit vehicle raced out of the yard and slowly disappeared off into the dark woods.

There were intruders in Horsewater.

And they shouldn't be there.

Chapter 42

In secret we met, in silence I grieve, that thy heart could forget, thy spirit deceive. If I should meet thee after long years, how should I greet thee? With silence and tears.

Lord Byron

It was a dark at Wroxingham Hall, as Mike Hawthorn wandered cautiously about the rear garden area. He was easily spotted by Virginia Burlingham, but luckily he didn't appear to see her. She was relieved the Gamekeeper hadn't seen her. But then as it was her home, so she knew the best places to hide.

She hated sneaking about the Hall and all of its grounds, especially at night, acting as if it wasn't her own home. But she had no choice.

She'd received a call. Urgent, they'd said. The caller was anxious to meet, as briefly as that might be. She'd warned them she dare not be long, as guests were arriving for dinner and it was more than her sham of a marriage was worth to make excuses to go out that night. But when the call came through, she knew she had to meet up to comfort them, if only for a short time.

They'd been there for her in the past, and she'd be there for them. Always. Fate had linked them together and they'd always be there for each other in some way, despite the risks and danger they both knew and what it meant.

Mike luckily didn't spot Virginia, who was wrapped up in a heavy woollen, green tweed jacket and dark leggings and knew how to deftly skirt around the ancient walls of the hall unseen. Mike seemed to have his own worries.

He was wandering from one of the side buildings, furtively looking about, impatiently waiting for someone to arrive. He cocked his head, listening.

Virginia looked on curiously, and although keen to keep her rendezvous, watched him intently, puzzled by his actions, wondering what he was doing near the hall, when he should have left the estate and be back in his cottage.

His job, amongst many, was to look after the estate and this included game keeping. But for some reason, tonight he seemed to be on edge. Usually he had free rein to wander the estate and access to all of the buildings, day or night, so his current cautious and suspicious manner intrigued Virginia.

She could have called to him, or quietly walked over and spoken, asking him what he was up to. However, she didn't dare give away her own location, or cause questions to be asked later where she herself was going in the dark.

It would have got back to Bertie. And he already had enough suspicions.

Virginia watched Mike walk over to a series of white washed buildings set at the back of the hall, which were originally a massive stable block. In the old days these buildings stabled around ten shires, in the period when they were used to work the land around the hall, long before tractors.

The other stable block around the back of the hall, towards which Virginia was trying to sneak unseen, was used to house her horses, as well as Bertie's.

The converted stable block, where Mike dithered about, housed assorted smaller farming equipment and tools, along with a couple of quad-bikes, also a Land Rover and an old Range Rover, often used for shooting parties.

These were older vehicles Bertie kept for use about the estate, instead of trading in; ever frugal with money, knowing too well his ancestors had been less so. Mike occasionally used the old Range Rover to drive shooting party guests about the estate. Usually he used the quads or the Land Rover on the estate for the real muddy jobs. From her vantage point Virginia watched him cautiously, intrigued why he was now fiddling around near the Range Rover.

She checked her watch and cursed, knowing she'd miss her rendezvous if Mike didn't hurry up and get out of the way. The person she was to meet wouldn't have long either and she'd told them the same.

They'd have to be quick or Bertie would be back and notice she'd gone.

Then she heard the sound.

It was somewhere in the distance, maybe in the woods, but clear.

Mike appeared to hear it too. He looked about, cocking his head, trying to establish where it came from on the estate. Far off in the woods, maybe.

Then it came again. Both hidden people hearing it simultaneously.

Virginia was curious, sensing Mike may have heard the sound previously, and hence his stalling around the Rover. Then Mike opened the Rover door and hopped inside. The massive engine roared into life and the white reversing lights illuminated the painted courtyard, causing Virginia to duck back behind the wall, lest she become illuminated and he see her in the mirror. The Rover turned and slowly driven through the ornate stone archway entrance at the bottom of the courtyard, then out towards the woods on the estate.

'Where on earth was Mike going at this time in the evening?'

The thought puzzled Virginia, but she had her own worries and was relieved by Mike's sudden departure, it making her flight path to the stable block safer. She waited until the roar of the Rover faded away, and then cautiously looked around once more, to ensure her path was clear, still puzzled as to the origin of the sound, and thought perhaps Mike was going off to investigate.

She knew him well, and liked him, being warm, kind and compassionate man. But his loyalties were set firmly with Bertie, who provided both his wages and a home on the estate. She knew if Mike had seen her, he would have reported it to Bertie. With her own issues at the forefront again, pleased to be free, she ignored the incident and quietly moved on towards the main stable block.

Tonight, no one must know she was meeting her lover.

The briefest of flickers from a torch beneath a massive Rhododendron bush, set slightly back from the stable block, caught her attention. In May and June, the beautiful purple-flowering bush, was one of many hundreds of the grand bushes scattered around the entire estate, being established generations ago.

Although a foreign import, the tall spidery waxy-green leafed bushes, with their stunning array of bright flowers, were something of which Bertie was particularly proud. Especially in the spring, when in full bloom, as their brightness filled the woods with a vibrant mix of pink, purple and red flowers.

The torch flash indicated they were there. Waiting

Virginia smiled, her heart leaping.

At last they'd have a few precious minutes together and she could calm their fears. Virginia jogged into the stable block and flicked on the main light, squinting at the brightness as the lights illuminated the stables. They would not have been out of place in a period drama. A central corridor, in original cobbles, ran between two opposing rows of panelled and sweeping barred stables. They dated back to Victorian times, and other than the odd lick of cream paint every twenty years, and black to the bars, were almost unchanged.

Heavy cast iron hayracks sat in the corners of each stable, with ornate rings, set on heavy cast bosses in the middle of the wooden panelled stables. The doors were of heavy wood and barred, as were the half fronts, permitting the horses to see each other across the corridor. The sides of the stable were high panels at the back, sweeping down in an ornate curve, the sides again being bared, allowing the horses to see thro', but not bite. There were thirty stables in total, fifteen each side of the corridor, but now the ornate block only held eleven horses. The days when the entire block would be filled with a mix of riding and carriage horses for the hall's residents were long gone.

Virginia went up to Bronte, a retired bay mare, wiggling her fingers through the bars. The mare stretched her neck forward, it clicking due to old age and stiffness, but she didn't move her legs, just nuzzled her muzzle against Virginia's twitching fingers, the horse appreciating the itch and attention.

"Lucky girl. You can do that to me if you want."

Virginia jumped, surprised someone unseen was hiding so close behind.

Her face broke into a smile as the hidden visitor emerged fully.

"Ginny, thanks for seeing me. Sorry to put you out," they spoke softly. "I just needed to see you for a few minutes. Things are terrible at the moment."

Virginia stretched out her arms and flung herself upon her lover, who in turn grabbed her trim waist, spun her around and kissed her fondly, their tongue tip skipping over her fine lips. She opened her mouth, responding fully as the pair joined up, kissing long, deep and passionately, all frustration vented.

"I can't stay long, but I wanted to see you. Just to hold you close for a few minutes," Virginia said, breaking off their kiss, but holding her lover close.

"Bertie's popped out. Seeing someone about the next hunt meet. Reggie, or Steve I think. Possibly both of them. Then going to The Kennels. I can't recall. However, he'll be back in about forty minutes. Then I've got a dinner party to sort out. The Hurlingham's are coming around. Bloody snobs!"

Virginia spoke in her finest accent, and then smirked when she realised.

The pair just held hands and grinned, eyes engaging, both knowing.

Virginia saw the reaction of her comment and they both laughed, each realising what she'd said and laid her head onto upon the supportive shoulder.

"God I love you," they said, somewhat sad and sorrowful. "I just wish we could be together, but you know our situations. We both do. And I'm afraid what he may happen to you if Bertie finds out. He'd never understand."

"Maybe not. Maybe he would. I never know with Bertie. He's strange too."

Virginia looked at the person before her, who she'd fallen in love with many years earlier. But a series of tragic twists of fate had not allowed them to share their lives together. Then once more, they'd met up again through another strange twist of fate, and found their love for each other had never died.

Now they were both trapped in their own worlds, which they both hated, but endured, knowing the possible serious repercussions for each if their true love was known. The genuine love for each other was seemingly forbidden.

They hugged each other again and kissed fondly, hands gently caressing the other's necks and cheeks. As their lips broke contact, they continued hugging tightly, each lost in their own deep painful thoughts and desperate needs.

"Why did you need to see me tonight?" Virginia enquired with no malice.

"Usual worries. And I think they suspect. It all seems to be getting to me, more so with Christmas coming. I also realised we probably won't get to see each other properly until Boxing Day. Even then it'll be brief, as you know on such a day. I wanted to see you, hug you, kiss you and tell you I love you."

Virginia cocked her head and looked deep into their eyes.

"You are so romantic. That's why I love you. And you know I'll always look after you. I always have, and will. I just wish we could finally be together."

Virginia wandered over towards another stable with an exaggerated provocative swagger, where a light bay horse with a prominent white star on his head moved forward. Her lover stood watching for a few seconds, then followed, hugging her from behind, tight to her buttocks; arms wrapped about her waist, lips kissing her neck, hands then moving up to her breasts.

"Who is that?" they enquired. "I've not seen him before."

"This is Spider," replied Virginia. "One of Bertie's. Nice chap. But bites!"

"I don't think I've seen him out on this one."

"No, you probably haven't. He's semi-retired too. Bad back. Bertie only occasionally rides him around the estate. Bertie should ride more. He was in the Blues and Royals Cavalry regiment when younger. Used to be a brilliant rider. Still is really, if he wanted to, although rides much less these days. He had a nasty fall some years back out stag hunting on Exmoor and only rides occasionally, as you know. More interested in his shooting parties now."

"He looks a lovely horse," they spoke, admiring the beautiful horse.

"He is a grand chap, but can be cheeky and a bit nippy. So watch out. Bertie won't let me ride him. Says I've too many of my own and I'll break him!"

Virginia giggled and then sighed, her seemingly perfect world clearly not.

Her lover squeezed her firmly from behind, kissing her neck.

"He did say he may ride out Boxing Day now," Virginia continued. "It'll be a bit of a bummer for us if he does. I was hoping he wouldn't come, being too focused upon his shoots over Christmas. I think he feels he needs to do more to please me, as I think he's also noticed the changes in me too lately."

"I hope he doesn't come out. It'd be great if we could meet up on Boxing Day. Maybe sneak off again, just like before. Try and talk him out of coming."

Arms hugging her tight, Virginia spun around, the pair's lips meeting again. After a long embrace Virginia broke free. With her hand extended, she stepped playfully along the corridor; eyes twinkling, smile wide and teasing.

"I was looking at the empty stable next to Meg's," she said, bright eyes flicking invitingly to a stable beside one where a small black driving pony, which Bertie occasional drove around the estate, lay resting.

The two lovers smiled as the small black pony, who, always inquisitive, rose up with a stretch and moved to the front of the stable Virginia stretched over to hug the small eleven hands pony, who could only just see over the door

"She's a great driving pony. Lovely nature. But has foot problems. Don't all ponies? Bless her. Bertie occasionally drives her out on some shoots for fun."

Virginia patted the pony, looking once more into the empty stable beside her.

"I've got about thirty minutes before Bertie gets back and we prepare for dinner. If you're up to it! I'm sure Little Meg won't tell anyone." Virginia grinned at the pony, then at her lover, taking their hands and guiding them.

A smile provided the silent answer as they followed to the stable door, Virginia's hands grabbed their waistband, her nimble leg raised, wrapping around their back, pulling them closer, dragging them close against her body.

They kissed again, hands drifting across willing bodies, fingers sliding into waistbands, moving down. Gentle sighs responded. A seeking hand gently moved inside Virginia's jacket, fingers caressing a soft breast and firm nipple.

"Beautiful," a soft voice spoke. "Perfect shape and size. I love your breasts!"

"So do I," Virginia spoke with a sigh. "They cost enough!"

The pair giggled like children, lying in the enveloping stable bedding, hands swiftly removing clothing, as probing fingers explored intimate body parts.

A curious but silent Meg watched the lovers entwine.

Unknown to all, someone else had also seen them enter the stables.

They now stood hidden, watching the pair fondly kiss and undress.

And then they listened to the sounds of pleasure.

Like Meg, they saw all; missed nothing.

Chapter 43

Words have no power to impress the mind,
without the exquisite horror of their reality.

Edgar Allen Poe

The streets of Norwich were quiet that night. In particular the area where Sarah and Chantelle stood. All very quiet. A big football match was on the television and it was amazing how that would affect trade.

Sarah and Chantelle were not doing well. Business was poor. Money in need.

Chantelle had performed 'hand relief' on a guy earlier and Sarah had only just turned up. It always amazed Chantelle why it was called 'hand relief.' It was a wank. Purely and simple, a wank. No need to add any advertising glamour.

It amazed her more so men actually paid someone good money to do it for them, when they had two good hands themselves. Seemed a complete waste of time to her, but she was more than happy to take £30 off a guy to do it.

Sarah was in a state. She'd not had her fix and was getting jittery. She needed money quickly to get some gear off Tony. He'd long given up letting her have any credit or to pay for it in kind. She couldn't interest him that way anymore. Tony preferred real money. That paid for his own habit. He could get a shag anytime he wanted from any of the other girls who he supplied.

The pair hoped someone would come along soon. Good money.

Then the Range Rover appeared. Wish answered.

Chantelle eyed it suspiciously and hung back, as Sarah freely moved forward.

She began to look in horror at the car and the driver, recognising them from the time when Lesley had got in one similar. Very similar. But was it them?

Chantelle remembered that night clearly, but Sarah was already leaning in the open passenger window, talking trade, when the horror hit Chantelle.

"Sarah," she whispered loudly, moving up behind, but was drowned out by the rumble of the idling big V8 engine. She called again and tottered forward in her heels as Sarah was opening the big vehicle door, about to get inside.

"Sarah. No! Don't go with him," she hollered, grabbing at the door. But Sarah had climbed into the warm interior and settling into the seat. Chantelle hung onto the large door and pulled it open, looking past Sarah, at the driver.

He glared back, expression depicting both annoyance and embarrassment.

Chantelle stared hard. 'Could he be the same person who'd taken Lesley?'

For a second Chantelle paused and was now unsure. He didn't look the type. But often they never did. Doubt entered her mind for a few seconds.

"What's the matter?" Sarah asked, annoyed. "He's okay. I'm desperate for money. He's paying me twice the going rate. I'm not turning that down," she said, wrenching the door from Chantelle's hand, smiling back at the man.

A mix of anger and fear boiled within Chantelle, as she looked at Sarah with steely eyes thorough the open window. Sarah, a sudden feeling of guilt passing through at how she'd treated her friend, smiled back at Chantelle.
"Don't worry, I'll be okay," she said through the window with a grim smile.
With that she disappeared from Chantelle's view, as the dark-tinted window automatically glided up and closed her off from her friend. The big engine of the 4 x 4 roared and the vehicle moved off, disappearing into the dark streets.
Chantelle shuddered, moving back into the shelter of the doorway where moments earlier they'd both been standing discussing the hardship of life.
But now Chantelle stood alone and cold. As ever. Seemingly her life.
A wave of foreboding, doubt and sadness washed over her.
She looked down at the green-stained pavement. Life was shit. Real shit!
'Why hadn't Sarah listened to her? The fool!' But then she understood.
Chantelle thought of Lesley and the time she'd got into a similar vehicle.
Did they never learn? Were they all helpless idiots. Maybe they were.
She decided she'd had enough for one night and turning, started walking. Just then a car pulled alongside. Instinctively Chantelle stopped, glancing over as the small saloon car, turning as the passenger window wound down.
"Are you looking for business love?" the driver called, somewhat meekly.
Chantelle paused and composed herself, stepped forward, and peered inside the car. A man in his sixties stared back. Sad, nervous and lonely eyes gazed at her, flicking down to her tight neat breasts. A tongue licked lips.
He could be a copper, but would have to be well past retirement age.
Most coppers these days packed it in at fifty to take their pensions.
This old chap, unless an actor and made up, was a proper punter.
"Yes. What are you looking for?" she asked.
"Hand relief. Do you do that love?"
Chantelle grinned to herself.
"No problem mate. My speciality. That'll be thirty quid. Okay?"
The man eagerly nodded, like a panting old dog seeing a new bone.
"Bunch of Wankers out tonight," she muttered to herself with a smile.
Eagerly, with the clatter of heels, she stepped forward, climbing into the car.
The car was warm, dry and tidy, but had a whiff of damp dog. Ho-hum.
Off they drove, seemingly unseen, Chantelle happy for another easy pay-off.
But hidden from view, two people watched it all. Intently.
One from high up; staring down in disgust.
He shook his head.
The other watched with deeper intent, making notes.
People and cars. Times and places.
All noted down, for future use.
It was important.
A successful evening for all, it seemed.

Chapter 44

In the middle of the journey of our life, I came to myself in a dark wood, where the direct way was lost.

Divine Comedy - Dante

Most people are unaware of how sound travels at night. When the general hum of background noise, mostly traffic, but even the chatter of birds and insects has subsided, the countryside can be an incredibly quiet place at night.

Sound, especially high-pitched noise, will travel for miles. Any good soldier, poacher or burglar knows it is better to talk in a low murmur, rather than a high-pitched whisper. The three youths, seated in a car within a woods that night, neither knew this fact, nor if they did, simply didn't really care.

The leader of this group, and owner of the car in which they sat, was Barry Wilkins. Seventeen, he'd just bought his first car. And he was trying best to impress his friends. The 'new' car was an old Peugeot hatchback and he'd spent all afternoon polishing the weary red paintwork and tinkering with the engine, desperate to get an additional couple of horsepower from the already knackered leaky engine. To further impress all, he'd stolen some of his older brother's cannabis earlier in the day, enough for two shared roll-ups.

Barry was from a neighbouring village; living in the middle of a row of eight council houses built in the fifties for farm workers, and set away from the main part of the village. With the decline of the farming industry, the houses became part of the area's Social Housing, housing local 'problem' families.

Barry's conspirators that night were Kevin Patterson and Neil Smith, both from another small neighbouring village a few miles away. Kevin was also seventeen and Neil was the baby, being only sixteen. They'd originally met at school, and typical with small villages, kept in touch socially, meeting up when bored; which was often, and usually looking for illegal kicks or trouble.

That night they'd been cruising in Barry's car, stopping off at a number of friends houses to show off his 'new wheels,' before Barry decided they'd finish the night off with a rip around a local wood. This'd display his driving skills and the hatchback's rallying potential; both of which were limited to none. Smoking the joints he'd made up had made him forget the hours spent earlier on the polished paintwork, but added to the encouraged bravado.

They'd smoked the first joint quickly. Then the second hit non-smoker Neil like a slap from a piece of fresh haddock caught today by a Norfolk trawler.

He laughed and whooped loudly, as Barry tried his best to spin the small car around in a 360-degree 'Do-nut' on the soft wet leaves that littered the many small tracks leading into the massive woods into which they had driven.

The group of lads inside the car whooped and laughed with no inhibitions.

"Shut yer mouth up yer twat," hollered Barry, through the laughter and loud engine roar. "Screaming like a girl! And anyway, someone will hear you."

"Why? Who's going to get us, Dracula?" chuckled Neil, grinning insanely.

"No," replied Barry. "The mad fucker who lives here. He kills people and eats them. True. My brother said so. He knew someone who'd been eaten."

All three roared out laughing as the car spun once more on the loose soil.

"You're all fucking stoned," laughed Kevin, turning to speak to Neil, seated in the rear, leaning forward onto the back of the front seats. Both laughed loudly, Barry joining them, looking round temporarily at the hysterical pair.

The jolt and thud was minor, but brought the car to a stall, throwing all three inside the car forward as the car stopped. The noise ceased and heads turned.

"What the fuck," yelled Barry, turning to see a small tree before the bonnet, the headlight beams flooding into the darkness of the surrounding woods.

"You've hit a tree! You knob!" roared Neil hysterically, joined by Kevin.

"Oh shit! I bet it's bent the fucking bonnet," Barry whined with regret, recovering instantly from the former euphoria as he opened the door to climb out; becoming tangled within the seat belt and fell head first out the door into the dark undergrowth that seemed to engulf and swallow up the small car.

The two occupants inside fell about in louder fits of laughter as they watched their concerned driver disappear into the darkness, vanishing completely from view, leaving only the open door and letting in chill air and darkness.

After a few seconds Barry did not re-appear, as the pair inside stared out of the open door into the darkness beyond. The glow from the headlights lit the woods ahead in orange, but there remained neither sight nor sound of Barry, either beside or in front of the car. The roars of laughter subsided to titters, then after the vanishing body had not risen to stand beside the door, the laughter began to ease to a chill silence. Kevin was the first to show concern at the sudden disappearance of his friend, leaning towards the open car door.

"Baz. Baz! Where are you? Oi Baz, are you alright?" Kevin called.

"Yeah, come on. Get back in. Don't be a wanker," Neil added. "We ain't getting out to help you mate. Not in these woods. Something might eat us!"

Neil finished with a chuckle, Kevin laughing loudly to join the mirth.

But there was no response, only silence, Barry, somewhere outside the car.

A stillness hung in the car, neither of them moving for what seemed like an age, but wasn't, as both teenagers tensed up, sensing something was wrong.

Neither was brave enough to venture out the car to see what had happened to their friend, although concerned. In the darkened interior, wide-eyed and afraid, the two youths regarded each other, wondering where their driver was.

Suddenly a gentle scraping sound was heard on the outside of the passenger's front door. Both Kevin and Neil turned swiftly around, their attention focussed, eyes moving away from the open driver's door towards the source of the scratching sound, only inches from where Kevin sat in the back.

He tensed up, instinctively leaning away from the closed door.

A distorted face pressed against the rear, side window.

Neil's scream rang through Kevin's skull. He threw himself across the back seat, arms flaying, trying to reach the front seat. Kevin automatically leapt away from the face too, hitting the central gear lever.

The passenger's door was thrown violently open.

A dark figure lurched in towards them.

"Aaagh!" Barry screamed, loosely grabbing at Kevin, before flaying his arms widely about like a demented Zombie towards an ashen-faced, wincing Neil.

"Ha, Ha! You should have seen your fucking faces!"

An ecstatic Barry roared, as he fell in hysterics into the car, laying upon a writhing Kevin. He in turn pulled himself up, nursing a bruised buttock where he'd hit it on the hand brake and pushed away the still laughing Barry.

"Stupid fucker. We thought you'd been eaten!" said Kevin.

As soon as he'd spoken the words, he realised how silly it sounded.

All three roared back into laughter at the thought.

As the laughter subsided, Barry spoke more seriously.

"You guy's had better get out and help give me a push. The front valance is stuck on an old tree stump. Jammed. We ain't going anywhere soon."

Kevin fell out of the door, still giggling. Neil tipped the seat forward and clambered out to join him, the three crashing about in the dark undergrowth.

"I've got to have a slash," Neil said and staggered into the darkness.

Kevin moved to the front of the car with Barry.

"Come on Neil, stop pissing and give us a shove!" Barry yelled, seeing his friend vanish into the gloom. "I'll get in, start it up and put it in reverse. You push," Barry instructed, as he proceeded to get back into the car.

"Hold on, I'm busting for this piss, then I'll help you push it," Neil replied, gazing off into the dark. "What are those lights down there?"

No one heard his question through the sound of the engine revving, as he stood in the black of the woods, making decorative urine patterns into space.

He strolled over to the car, which Barry was revving up and Kevin was pushing at the front end with half effort. Neil put his head in the passenger's door, grinned at Barry and repeated his question, pointing over his shoulder.

"What are those lights? Coming up there through the woods?"

Barry took his foot off the accelerator and followed Neil's hand, the interior light slightly diffusing his night vision. He squinted to look out the back.

"Fuck me!" Barry yelled, tone serious. "It's the bastard who lives here. Quick! Let's get out of here!" With that Barry, thinking fast, turned off the cars headlights, plunging the car and the surrounding woods into darkness.

"Give Kevin a hand to push!" he yelled to Neil. "Hurry up! Push it!"

Neil, blinking in the gloom, sobering up and sensing an emergency, lumbered towards the front of the car and told Kevin what was happening. They looked at the rapidly approaching headlights cutting swiftly through the darkness.

Both swore and began pushing the car with increased effort.

Barry put his head out the window and yelled. "Lift it up, don't just push!"
He looked at the headlights now slowing in their approach through the dark woods, seemingly unsure of exactly where the previous bright car lights in the gloom had gone, now Barry had switched them off. He felt smug and clever at his quick thinking as he revved the car, knowing anyone looking for the car would now hear the engine noise. The car shook and he preyed it'd move, his two friends in the darkness outside pushing hard, their images ghostly.
With a big heave the car lurched backwards, causing both Kevin and Neil to fall forward away from the car and crash into the wet leaves and dirt of the woods. The car zoomed backward, then spun around, the rising pair laughing.
"Quick. Get in!" yelled Barry, no longer amused, sensing he had seconds to get back onto the track, then away, before his pursuer located them and they were caught. The pair playfully fought each other to get in, as they grasped at the door handle, before climbing in together. Neil being the slightly smaller, clambered over the seated Kevin and threw himself onto the back seat.
"My lovely car's going to be a fucking mess. Look at it!" Barry moaned as he cranked the steering wheel around, pushed the car into first gear and headed towards where the lights had been racing through the now pitch-black woods.
"Where have they gone?" queried Kevin, winding down the window for a better look and to listen. "I can't hear anything. Where is it? It's gone!"
"I bet they're listening for our engine," said Neil calmly.
"Who gives a shit, lets get the hell out of here," said Barry, realising he was right. He flicked the lights onto full-beam, revved the engine, slipped the clutch and swung the car back onto the side track they'd driven down earlier.
Foot down hard, soil flaying out behind from the spinning wheels, he headed back for the main track, which led into the woods from the main road. The car lurched from side to side and had moved fifty yards along the track, headlights cutting a swathe of white through the darkness, when Neil yelled.
"I can see the bastard. Look! To the left of us. He's racing us man! Wow! Look at the vehicle close in. This is brilliant! He's trying to ram us. Ha, ha!"
Barry and Kevin, more sober, looked worryingly to their left, to see the vehicle's bright lights hurtling through the trees, just as Neil had said.
It was moving fast. Very fast. Too fast. It'd soon catch them or overtake.
"Oh shit!" yelled Barry. "He's coming up a side track and is going to try and cut us off at the main track junction. Then we'll be trapped. Bastard!"
He gunned the little car as hard as he could, the back end sliding back and forth along the slippery surface. In the gloom he could make out a wall of trees, which meant the track junction was just ahead. He knew the vehicle wasn't too far away the glow of its lights flitting off the trees towards where he was heading. Not daring to take his eyes off of the track he called out.
"Where is it now?" Barry spoke in a serious monotone.
"You don't want to know," whimpered Kevin, looking at the lights rounding the track, about to broadside them. "Close. Very close. Maybe too close!"

"He's going to get us. Ha, ha! Then eat us!" Neil sat in the back, laughing,
"Fuck off you stupid twat!" roared Barry, as he hit the track junction and swung the back end of the car tightly around, compensating for the swing with the skill any rally driver would be proud. Neil in the back was thrown from one side of the seat to the other, laughing loudly, then bashed his head.
Kevin hung onto the doorframe, a mix of fear and excitement surging through, as the full glow of the chasing vehicle's headlights filled the car.
"Oh my god, he's going to hit us!" he yelled, the interior of the car brightly lit as the pursuers headlamps burnt into the back of the little car, only feet away.
"Fuck me he's close," said Neil, squinting at the glowing orbs close behind, his laughter stopping. He lifted himself up, peering out the back window at the four bright, blinding orbs, illuminating the entire car and woods ahead.
Barry didn't dare look back or even in the mirror, which he'd tipped down to keep the lights from dazzling him, but skilfully kept the car hurtling down the main dirt track, looking for the way out, onto the road and to safety.
"Stop, Barry!" yelled Kevin, his voice breaking. "This isn't funny anymore. We'll die. Stop and tell him we're sorry. Maybe he'll understand."
"Don't talk like a twat," Barry growled, ignoring Kevin's desperate plea. "He'll crush us this close if I stop. Anyway, he'll leave us alone as soon as we hit the main road. He's a typical farmer. Git orf mee land!"
Neil chuckled at Barry's farmer accent. Kevin sat terrified, seat belt in hand.
"Once we get out of here we will be safe," Barry repeated, reassuring himself.
The noise was deafening as the two vehicles hurtled along the wooded track; both from Barry's screaming engine, the rumble of suspicion on the rough ground, and the roar of the large 4 x 4 engine in close pursuit behind them.
Barry drove with all the skill he'd practised on his games console, concentrating hard, noting ahead a faint funnel of slightly brighter light, as the arch of trees leading out onto the main road appeared. Not daring to reduce his speed, or assume victory, Barry kept his foot down hard and prayed nothing was coming along the main road. He approached the end of the woods at full speed, the lights behind dropping back slightly, the driver of the 4 x 4 obviously less brave or not so stupid, braking slightly nearer the exit.
As Barry's car hit the main road, he swung the steering wheel sharply one-handed, whilst momentarily pulling the hand brake hard with the other. The result was a perfect ninety-degree hand brake turn. It caused the car to rock violently, tipping sideways and throwing the occupants against the doors. The screaming tyres left dark rubber skid marks on the road, before the forward motion of the car helped regain it's composure. Only as the car righted itself did Barry released the handbrake and gun the little car, pressing his foot hard down and change gear. The vehicle hurtled along the road as Barry grabbed at the rear-view mirror, pushing it back into place to look behind.
"Is he behind us?" he yelled, seeing nothing, breathing slightly heavy, the tension easing. "Can anyone see him? Where is the bastard?"

Neil, who'd been smashed against the rear windows, clutched his head with both hands, mumbling. Kevin, stunned in the passenger seat, stared blankly. He shook himself back into life with Barry's question and looked back out of the windows, moving his head from side to side. Darkness followed them.
"We've lost him, I think." he said unsure, then re-looked.
"Yes! Thank fuck for that. Nothing. You've lost him."
Kevin spoke with a sense of triumph coming through.
"Ace driving Bazzer. Phew man! That was bloody close."
Barry relaxed in his seat and eased off the accelerator. A sense of pride flowed through him at his skilful driving, but also a great sense of relief. Then he let out a loud whoop of exhilaration, releasing his tension, raising a fist.
"Some driving or what man! Move over Colin McRae!"
Kevin, now recovering, slapped hands with Barry and began laughing, the relief of escape flooding over them. He took a deep breath.
"I don't know about your driving, my head hurts. I hit it!" grumbled Neil.
"Shut up moaning," replied Kevin, his tone happier. "You're lucky we even got out of this. If not, and he caught us, he'd have eaten your head!"
All three laughed as Barry eased the car down to a sensible speed.
As Kevin spoke he turned, grinning at Neil slumped in the back, then looked beyond him and out of the back window into the gloom.
A large dark shadow appeared to be following the car.
Kevin stretched his neck, focusing past a confused Neil, his eyes set beyond the dark glass and upon the looming object. It was big and moving fast.
"What the fuck is that?" he queried, staring out the back.
"What?" replied Barry, looking into his dark mirror, seeing nothing behind, only darkness, the back of Kevin's bobbing head and Neil's grinning face.
"Neil, look out of the back window. Quickly!" Kevin yelled.
Neil sat upright, rubbed his head then peered out at the road behind.
The cloud was clearing slightly and the hedgerows dropping down in height to show open road behind, the dark woods now a long way back.
A large black form sat ten yards behind them.
Neil's stomach sank.
It was the 4 x 4 without any lights on.
And it was right behind them.
Moving fast and closing in.
"The bastard's still behind us!" Barry cried.
In silence, Kevin stared in terror.
"Oh no!" Neil yelled. "We're going to be eaten!"

Chapter 45

When you fear a foe, fear crushes your strength;
and this weakness gives strength to your opponents.

William Shakespeare

Barry glanced up into his mirror, but saw nothing. However, from the tone of Neil's raised voice and Kevin's obvious concern, he needed no further confirmation. He pressed the accelerator hard and the car responded. As he felt the power kick in, the vehicle behind switched on its lights, illumining the smaller car. The sudden brightness blinded Barry and he tipped the mirror, before focussing on the road ahead. Neil and Kevin both shielded their eyes from the bright headlights closing in on their car, as Barry skilfully drove his car along the country lane, the 4 x4 very close behind and keeping pace.

The two cars hurtled on through the dark countryside, nose to tail, passing through a sleeping village with a loud roar, weaving swiftly together through the twisting roads, with an occasional squeal of tyres, racing past houses and parked cars until heading back out into darkness of the open country again.

Barry glanced intermittently in the mirror, but the pursuing vehicle clung close behind, keeping only a few yards away, it's bright lights obscuring either the shape or type of vehicle from Barry and his passengers, but it was big.

The fun had turned to fright inside the silent car. Barry threw the nimble little car about the country roads, seeking out twisting bends to try to gain a small gap of several seconds on the lumbering giant following behind him.

He knew the area well and was a quick thinker. Just ahead he knew there was a T-junction with high field banks either side. He hoped that if he could make it down to the junction just ahead and unseen, it might be enough to throw his tail off sufficiently for him to get the small lead he needed to then escape.

As the junction approached he was ready. Eyes flicking up, he checked the mirror to see the big car was now one corner behind, the headlights about to come around the sharp bend. Using the hand brake and avoiding the foot brake, he flipped off his headlights and simultaneously hurled the car sharp right, turning abruptly down the right hand junction. The tyres screeched as the car skidded violently, the rear end and left wheel hitting the bank on the other side, before bouncing back into the middle of the road, with the car continuing it's forward momentum down the new side road in total darkness.

Shaken from side to side, Kevin and Neil sat silent in the back, eyes wide.

Barry, slowing slightly and driving into the gloom ahead, glanced up into the mirror, as his car continued down the darkened road. Eyes set firm in the mirror, he counted four seconds before the bright lights of his pursuer in the 4 x 4 flew past the junction and onwards past the road he'd just turned off.

Its large bright beams cut across the gloomy low countryside away to their left side and onwards, racing into the dark countryside in the wrong direction.

"Yes!" Barry yelled, punching the wheel, his attention on the headlights moving away behind him. "Lost the bastard. Am I good or what?"

All three glanced over at the bright lights shining across the field to their left, appearing to slow, the driver realising its quarry was lost. They all cheered in triumph, slapping their hands, gloating at the enemy they had just deceived.

They'd escaped their hunter. For now.

And onward their darkened car moved. Unseen. By everything.

The roe deer didn't see the dark mass approach either.

It'd begun to cautiously cross the strip of hard black ground separating the two stubble fields. The deer didn't expect to meet a darkened car that night.

Barry didn't expect to meet a strolling deer either. Snap!

He only became aware of the deer as he turned to look at the road ahead.

Then he saw it, fully, as an unexpected object hit the bonnet.

The front of the car chopped off the deer's back legs, as it's shattered body hurtled up the bonnet, a bloody mess sliding on, to stop on the windscreen that it smashed. There it lay; dying eyes gazing in at equally stunned faces.

Barry instantly slammed on the brakes, the flash of bright red lighting up the countryside behind, highlighting to anyone who might care their location.

It was all that was needed.

The hunter had seen the flash of red.

A red glow also lit up behind the hunter's vehicle.

"What the fuck is that?" yelled Kevin. He stared at the mass of fur and blood splayed across the windscreen. The deer's now lifeless eyes gazing in at him.

"It's a fucking deer. Where the hell did that come from?" screamed Barry "Get that thing off my car!" He turned his attention from the mess on the windscreen, past Kevin and on through the side window to the dark fields.

The two passengers either ignored him or didn't hear. Both sat within the stationary car, staring at the dead deer peering in through the windscreen.

"I ain't touching that thing," said Kevin, wincing.

"Neither me," added Neil. "I'm a vegetarian. Well, I am now."

"Where's that bastard gone?" yelled Barry, awakening everyone's senses to the next possible crisis. "Where the fuck did he go?" Barry hollered, seeing no sweeping headlights, his attention on more serious matters, knowing that the big 4 x 4 was not now racing away across the countryside as he'd hoped.

"The car? Where is it? It's vanished. And someone move that deer!"

Kevin turned his eyes and looked to his left, back across the darkened fields, now following Barry's searching gaze. But he too could see only dark fields, silhouettes of hedges or the occasional tree. No car lights as they expected.

"Yes, where the hell did he go?" questioned Kevin, now realising in full what Barry meant and his new concerns. "Where the hell is that car?"

"Behind us!" yelled Neil.

Through the rear window he saw the dark form approach, its lights out, but hurtling up behind again, this time moving very fast and looking to ram them.

"Shit! He's going to ram us!" Neil screamed, just to clarify the details.

Without even looking, Barry put his foot hard on the accelerator and roared blindly down the dark road. He fumbled for the light switch, found it and the road ahead lit up, but in a smeared vision of red, with the deer's blood spread over the windscreen. He flicked the window-wiper lever, but the wiper arms moved only a few inches before thudding into the deer. He raised his neck to peer through a clear gap in the top corner of the screen, past the prone body of the deer, pointing the car as best he could down the centre of the road. The car picked up speed, swerving around the twisting country lanes, Barry tilting his head to see the road. Frantically he looked in the mirror and yelled.

"Where's the bastard now?"

"You don't want to know!" hollered Neil.

Kevin turned to look out the back and at the big black vehicle behind them, its lights still off but seemingly able to keep level. He breathed hard.

"He's right on our arse and closing in. Go quicker Barry! Hurry!"

Suddenly the chasing vehicle's lights came on in full beam, just as Barry took another look in the mirror. Wrong choice. The glare blinded him.

For a second, seeing only white, he lost concentration. Long enough for him to miss the sharp bend in the road. By the time he'd blinked and looked back out of the small gap in the windscreen, trying to clear his eyes, it was too late.

Careening across the width of the narrow road, the car mounted the bank.

The oak tree had stood in its spot for over two hundred years.

It was not going to move for anyone or any object.

Not even for half a ton of sheet metal and plastic car.

The front end of the car crumpled against the unyielding tree and the engine mountings sheered off. Momentum pushed the boiling hot block on through the dashboard. It travelled back into Barry legs, smashing both femurs.

The shattered long leg bones tore through his femoral arteries.

He would have been dead within two minutes due to massive blood loss if the engine hadn't carried on into his body. It crushed his rib cage, rupturing his liver. Fatal. The shock and trauma, and his body's natural reflexes, caused him to pass out instantly. Barry would never wake.

Neil, sitting in the back, felt his whole body lift up. He was flying!

He sailed past the slowly crushing form of Barry and passed clean through the crashing window screen. The force caused him to fly over the bonnet, past the deer, and clear of the vehicle. Until his head compacted against the oak tree's unyielding trunk and rock hard bark. Then he stopped.

His skull fractured and neck compounded into his spine by six inches, killing him instantly. His limp form crashed back down from the oak tree and onto the bonnet, his blank face staring lifelessly at the deer lying beside him.

Kevin was the lucky one. He was still alive. For the moment.

He'd been looking out the passenger window when the car had left the road, leaning hard against the door. By chance the door had popped open as the front end of the car crumpled and the side panels deformed, springing open the door against which he leant, and through which he was cleanly thrown. Unfortunately he left the best part of his right hand in the torn remains of the door as he was ejected out sideways. But who needed fingers? Not Kevin. His collarbone snapped and right tibia shattered as his flaying body hit the tarmac. Grinding along the rough surface, his jeans tore through to the skin below as he slid along the road face down, the rough gritted surface grating his kneecaps and what was left of his hands like fresh Parmesan cheese.

He lay on the tarmac several feet from the now still car, dazed and confused. The sound of the hissing engine, pouring its boiling contents into Barry's smashed and lifeless body, broke the silence of the night. Semi-concussed and in searing agony, Kevin tried to raise himself. But his smashed body and various broken bones refused to support his weight and he fell back down.

Turning his head, he looked over at the mangled remains of the steaming wreck. Formerly, and for a short period, Barry's pride and joy. But no more.

"Bazzer. Neil. Where are you guys?"

His weak cry was met with silence. And a pair of feet.

Turning his head forward, he painfully raised his face, slowly looking up.

A darkened figure hovered over. Silhouetted in the night sky, it peered down, silently observing the form at its feet; like an entomologist does a bug.

"Help me please!" Kevin cried, in desperation and pain.

Silence replied.

"I'm sorry. You've got to help us." Kevin spluttered.

The silent figure momentarily glanced sideward, then gazed back down.

"My friends are in the car. Hurt bad. I wasn't driving. It was Barry. His idea. Not mine. I didn't even want to go in the car. Help me!" implored Kevin.

Still the person stood above him, silent, head turning once more, seemingly regarding the wrecked car, then casually it gazed back down at Kevin.

The feet turned around and the dark form silently moved off. Shuffling away, they disappearing out of Kevin's limited line of sight.

"Where are going? Don't leave me. Help us you wanker!" Kevin yelled.

He began to cry dry tears, sensing the person was leaving. He didn't want to be left alone, with his friends dying or dead. Not on a shitty country road.

As Kevin moved, adjusting his body to see where they had gone, a shot of pain tore through his left leg, causing him to let out a yell, as the fractured bone cut through flesh. He bit his lip, peering at the rear of Barry's shattered car then over towards the 4 x 4, which he could now just see. Here he could hear noises, movement, as if someone was sifting within a car boot.

The person was still here. Getting something from the back of the 4 x 4.

They hadn't left him. Maybe they were trying to find a first-aid kit.

What a hero. Not a Wanker. They might even get help. Thank you.

A wave of euphoria swept over Kevin as the silent stranger was obviously looking in the car boot for something, probably to help him and his mates.

Maybe they knew Neil or Barry were trapped, and in a worse state than him, but still okay. Perhaps they were going to help them first. What a saviour!

But Kevin was unaware that Neil and Barry were already dead.

Another shot of pain pulsed through as he tried to move and see the back of the 4 x 4 better. It was a Range Rover, but its lights were switched off, all the road and countryside in darkness. The only light came from Barry's car.

Only one rear light glowed a gentle red, and with one headlight smashed, the other emitted just a dull orange glow, it being embedded in the embankment.

With the sound of soft footsteps on tarmac, the figure reappeared.

Kevin raised his head to see a small green container in their hand.

A first aid kit thought Kevin, as the darkened form stood over him.

"Thank you," Kevin muttered. "I hurt all over."

The splash of liquid made him yell in shock. Poured from the container, it washed over his body and cut face, stinging his open and bloody wounds.

"Whoa!" he yelled. "Don't soak me. I need help, not a wash!"

Still the liquid flowed, stinging painfully as it began to soak into his clothes.

Then the smell hit him. A very familiar smell.

The stench of the fumes rising off the liquid took away Kevin's breath.

Then fear raced through his mind.

He recognised the pungent, suffocating odour of the stinging liquid.

Petrol.

"What are you doing?" He cried. "Help me!"

The figure ignored him and moved to the back of the smashed car, carefully pouring quantities of the stinking liquid over the back of the car and through the passenger door. More was poured liberally over Barry's shattered and bloody corpse, before the figure calmly moved to the front, past Neil's form on the bonnet, and more petrol was emptied out. Then they disappeared.

Fear overtook Kevin and a surge of adrenaline washed through. Wriggling, he frantically tried to pull his body away from the now petrol stinking car.

But then the person's booted legs reappeared before him.

Shuffling around, Kevin's futile movement ceased.

A stout leather boot had trodden upon Kevin's broken ankle.

Kevin screamed. The foot was pressed down hard.

Then harder. Seemingly for fun. Or punishment. Or both.

Silently the figure above looked down at the whimpering form.

"Help me! Help me you bastard!" yelled Kevin. "Please!"

They did so, happily complying, by removing their foot.

"You shouldn't have been there." The voice spoke soft and calmly.

The leather booted feet stepped back a stride, then a well-aimed toe engaged with Kevin's face. His nose broke and the force of the kick caused his body to roll back and fall over towards the car. Kevin cried out with new pain.

Instinctively curling into the foetal position, he waited for the next blow, as blood poured into his mouth from the smashed nasal bone and he began to choke on the mix of blood and petrol fumes rising off his body.

But no further kicks followed. They walked away. Briefly.

Then they returned. Walking with purpose.

Kevin never saw the match.

It was casually flicked onto his petrol soaked jacket.

But he heard the strange 'Whumf' sound. And he knew.

The fumes instantly ignited and his body was engulfed in a fireball.

An orange glow illuminated all around. A bright orb in the dark countryside.

Kevin felt the heat of the flames as the petrol on his body ignited, and as the water within his skin began to boil. As his skin burnt, adrenaline flooded his torch-like body and he rose, pulling himself to his feet, his senses oblivious to all pain, as burning muscles contracted and the fat within his skin ignited.

He fought the flames licking at his face with melting hands, his singed hair gluing to his peeling, burning scalp. The skin blistered instantly into giant wheals, before the heat crisped the flesh into brown crackling, pulling the limbs taut, twisting and disfiguring them. Sucking in the searing heat, gasping for breath, the hot flames burnt his throat and lungs and melted his eyes.

Kevin staggered, now dying, falling towards the car. Flames, leaping from his body, ignited the petrol poured on the wrecked car and the two bodies, which moments earlier had been his best friends. The force of the explosion, as the car ignited, blew Kevin's torch-like body back across the narrow road.

His flaming form lay in the road, violently shuddering, the once pink flesh turning a crisp brown; the skin tightening and contracting the muscles within the limbs of the once human form, snapping the tinder-dry bones.

The figure, silhouetted against the bright orange glow, which illuminated the night sky and dark empty countryside, stood back to watch the inferno.

Momentarily it seemingly admired the clever craftwork.

But also ensured all about were dead.

Then, brushing down their clothes, they climbed into the former pursuit vehicle. With it's lights still off, the Range Rover was carefully reversed back down the road, until finding a gap in a field, it was turned around.

With a last casual, but satisfied glance, the driver steadily drove the darkened vehicle away, slowly back the way it'd come. Only when it hit the outskirts of the village it had passed through earlier were the headlights switched on.

In the distance, a bright orange glow lit up the night sky.

And a gentle smell, not unlike roast pork, filled the air.

Chapter 46

Necessity hath no law.

Oliver Cromwell

P.C. Burton strode into The Bell at Salheath like he owned the two-hundred year old public house. He was due to start a night shift later, having the day off, and decided before yet another evening of boredom, he'd catch up some local gossip and drove his beloved Mazda MX5. He loved the red sports car, especially in the summer months. With the roof down, he'd eye up all of the women strolling along the streets in their short skirts, cropped tops and high heels, some returning his looks and wolf-whistles. That was back in the city, in the warm summer months. But now it was December, cold, chilly and he was stuck in Country-bumpkin Carrot-chew'in Land with only muddy lanes.

There were few women for him to show off himself and his car; other than old women in headscarves, wrapped in wax-jackets and strutting around in mud-covered green wellies. Or horsey people. No high-heels and mini skirts.

The added cold weather, muddy narrow roads, filled with potholes and cow shit made the car lose its usual urban charm. Joan, his soon to be ex-wife, always claimed he loved the car more than her, as he lovingly polished it each weekend. He never used to answer. But the car always got a kiss. She didn't.

Burton first visited The Bell soon after being given his new beat, and found it a pleasant establishment, genuinely getting on with the cagey barman, Jeff. Occasionally he called in for a singular, legal pint and chat, to build up some rapport, and also in the vain hope he might actually meet an attractive single local woman, who hadn't been created by interbreeding goats with dwarfs.

This early evening, as he opened the heavy timber door and strolled into the large bar, he noted a reasonable mix of people. A few were usual locals he recognised, as well as some he assumed had driven in from Norwich, making it a hospitable and busy public house in such a quiet part of the countryside.

He'd seen a couple of regulars well over the legal drink-drive limit a few times and had considered nicking them one night when on a late shift. Most likely he'd wait until he was having a bad week and then get someone else to nick them, for a few extra brownie points. It was always good press to nick drink-drivers, and it did your credibility wonders with the hierarchy. But not tonight. They could crash into a ditch and die for all he cared. Just so long as he wasn't on that shift later to help clear up the mess or get involved.

As he entered the bar the usual glancing heads turned to see who'd entered their almost sacred land. Many immediately turned away to resume their drinking and chatting when Burton was recognised by those who knew him.

The barman noticed the large policeman and smiled, whilst wincing inside.
"Is this an official raid Roger, or you just being social? If that's possible."
The man behind the bar asked, his eyes flitting sideward to a regular.
"No Jeff, this is an official raid and I must ask everyone to leave the premises immediately." Burton grinned sickly. "Especially that young lady over there, who's going to have to leave with me and take down everything I say."
Burton continued with what he considered his best off-duty policeman joke, glancing towards a couple of young women in the corner he'd noted with a skilful eye as soon as he'd entered. The pair of women both grinned back bashfully, giggling, before turning away and laughing into their drinks.
"And you're suppose to be a copper? God help us all," the barman replied, smiling but shaking his head. "What'll it be then?"
"A pint of your finest bull semen please." Burton replied with a Cheshire cat wide grin. "That's what you country folk drink around here, isn't it?"
The barman shook his head again and two young lads close to the bar looked at the policeman in enchanted amusement, but also with some caution.
"I've got Stout. Will that do instead?" Jeff enquired, ready to pour a pint of what he knew Burton usually drunk. "Similar, but won't fertilise you. I hope."
"That'll be lovely. Along with information," the policeman replied quieter, leaning forward over the bar. Burton's eyes glinted at the now blushing Jeff.
The barman went a bright red, looking cautiously sideways as he pulled the pint, waiting for the head to form, then recovered his composure, asserted loudly, so no one would think him a local snitch, should they have overheard.
"We've got plenty of information for foreign tourists. Are you lost again sir?"
Burton remained silent, smiling over-confidently, knowing the score as the barman passed over the pint of black liquid with white top, eyes fixed.
"Well," began Burton, drawing a mouthful of the black, creamy liquid, wiping the froth from his rubbery lips. "I visited a chap called Chris Turner a few times. Runs a riding school or something. Stables. Lots of horses and lots very attractive ladies. The place is set deep in some woods not far away. Horsewater. Strange name, but this is Norfolk. He seems very wary of strangers and the police. Or maybe it was just me he disliked. Understandable. But he's weirder than the rest of you strange lot around these parts. And that's saying something. Do you know anything about him? Just curious."
Burton added a chuckle and smile to the dry witty comments he'd made.
Two older men standing to one side overheard and turned around to face the policeman. They regarded him silently, to be joined by two other older men, who'd been playing darts, but who suddenly stopped throwing at the mention of Chris's name. The group all stood silently staring. The policeman looked around, wondering what he'd said wrong and if he was about to be lynched
"I thought you'd been informed about our Mister Turner, you being a copper and all that," said Jeff, breaking the silence and seeing the old faces staring. "Bit of local folk law what happened. And he's also something of a hero."

His silent audience listened on, waiting for Jeff to continue, which he did. "Still I suppose it's history now, but you may have only read your biased police reports not heard everything that happened properly."
He paused and turned to face the group, intently watching.
"How longs it been Jack?" he enquired, looking at one of the older men of the group. Burton's head following the barman's gaze, to see a wizened gent.
"Must be well over twenty years now," the man replied, looking down into his beer, as if recalling. "Maybe more. Times flies. Like rooks and crows."
All five men stood silently by the bar, gazing at the policeman, who spun his head around from each staring face, wondering what they were all privy to.
"What really happened then," Burton answered, puzzled by the silent stares and wanting to know more than he did already. "Is anyone going to tell me?"
"Well it was a long time ago," Jeff began in a slow, methodical tone, but with practiced ease and pace; his audience intently listening like children.
"Must be over twenty years ago now, but basically the story goes like this…."
Burton sat seemingly spellbound, listening to the story of Chris Turner, as told by the locals of Salheath, not the police. It was more entertaining than the proper police report of the incident he'd already read, but didn't reveal. It contained all the finer detail, but none of the charm the barman offered.
"That's basically it," finished the barman. "Killed them. Both. Bang! Bang!"
Burton turned his head to see a silenced pub, everyone inside listening.
"Watched burglars kill his own parents, then he shot the two burglars stone cold dead himself. Cold-blooded. And well done to him. Proper justice."
Burton already knew.
He'd also read the psychological reports.
That's what worried him.
"He was about twelve at the time," Jeff added. "Poor little sod. Completely acquitted of murder after. And rightly so. Bastard burglars. Both got what they deserved. Too young to stand trial and because of the circumstances, it was deemed self-defence and nothing was ever done. Happened in the very house you probably visited." The barman stared cold and hard at Burton.
"Chris loves horses, hates people," the older man added. "His dad did too. Good chap. Mister Turner hates strangers. But he especially hates the police."
Burton looked at the barman, waiting for more. It came.
"Your lot were blamed for not patrolling the area enough at the time, despite numerous warnings by other locals that burglars were seen in the area, such as by the neighbours. The younger Lord Burlingham, as he was at the time, at Wroxingham Hall, had been broken-in months earlier. Typically nothing was done by the police then, despite evidence. All the crimes were linked to the same two men who were killed. Chris did us all a favour. He's a good man."
The group nodded and Burton sensed he was on his own. Vulnerable.
"If your lot had done your job, it'd never happened," someone added.

The comment by one of the older drinkers was met with various muttered agreements, nodding heads, and a red face from Burton. All stared at him.
He wondered for a moment if he was about to be dragged out the back and thrown down a well. Or maybe eaten. That'd seem more fitting he felt.
The group of avid listeners were obvious fans of the cold-hearted horseman and seemingly stood in full support of similar vigilante actions, as he'd sensed on visits to the numerous local farms, where he'd received a cold response.
Now he felt he knew why. It was a strange area. But he was in Norfolk.
"You were lucky he didn't shoot you!" An aged voice spoke out.
Burton turned to look at a smiling wizened gentleman.
The old man simply stared, but with a wise, uncaring grin on his face.
The barman and locals all laughed heartedly.
But Burton didn't.
He stood white faced, taking a long gulp of his stout.
His thoughts were elsewhere.

Chapter 47

Where the good and the bad and the worst
and the best have gone to their eternal rest.

Edgar Allan Poe

It'd been a long and boring night for P.C. Roger Burton at South Washam police station. He'd enjoyed the evenings back in London. Always something happening and some excitement. There would always be a local gang-fight, an exciting armed robbery, burglary, drug bust or now and again, a juicy murder.

But in 'Snoozeville,' other than stopping a suspected drink driver - usually a farmer - attending a barn fire, settling a domestic dispute, or trying in futile to find a long-gone suspected poacher, who'd disappeared across a field or into a wood, nothing exciting or dangerous ever happened. It was boring. Usually.

He'd begun his shift at mid-night, after his visit earlier to The Bell. It was now 5.00am and he was looking forward to finishing at 8.00am.

Out of boredom, he'd spent the last hour re-checking the missing person request once more. It was the insurance salesman and secretary who'd both vanished at the same time. Pure coincidence? Hardly. But interesting.

It was an obvious moonlight flit, but something about the thing bugged him. He'd questioned the horseman, as his farm had been noted down as a cold call in the appointment diary. But he'd denied it, or claimed he couldn't remember the event. 'Arrogant Tosser' was written beside the name in the appointment diary, which was apt. Words must have been exchanged, so it annoyed him greatly that the horseman claimed to not recall the meeting.

There was something about the horseman he didn't like or trust, beside the fact he'd killed two men in cold blood when a child, and never did time.

His instincts told him there was more to this strange guy, who had a yard full of horses and very attractive women, and he wanted to know what it was, but already knew a great deal about the strange Mister Turner from others.

That said, it seemed he wasn't the only strange person around these parts.

He'd questioned several farmers and people locally recorded as being called upon by the salesman. And most had also lied about ever knowingly meeting him too, despite notes being made against all of their names and addresses.

Pompous Farmer. Dodgy Tractor Dealer. Slaughter man. Rude Arsehole.

None of the notes on any of these people, and other calls in the locality, were hardly complimentary; most rude and insisting he left their land - at once.

None where any better than the horseman, but it was the veil of local secrecy between them all which he found both annoying and suspicious.

His mind was eased by a call from the main switchboard, looking for a local unit to attend, his response monotone, until he heard the full report.

"Accident, just outside Woodswick? Multiple causalities. Great. I mean, okay. Other services responding. We'll assist. I'm on my way," he said out loud. He slapped his hands together, yelling to his companion, dozing in a chair.

"Bill, Bill. Wake up you tosser! We've got a call. An RTA near Woodswick. Ambulance there and also fire have been called and are on the way. They need a couple of locals to close off the scene. Great! I'm off. I'll radio details through when I get there and you can follow. At last, some fucking action!"

Bill remained laid back in the seat, coat over his head, simply a grunt of acknowledgement from him as Burton dashed outside to the Land Rover.

It only took ten minutes to get to Woodswick, but then another five to find the actual location, which he did with the aid of a local man. Another farm worker. He was wandering up the road, expecting the emergency services, and keeping an eye out for them. The man was the brother of the tractor driver who'd found the mess, and had reported the accident. More in-bred farmers.

Word had passed quickly by the locals. Maybe by pigeon. Or rats. Who knew.

Burton was surprised to be first at the scene, but could hear sirens wailing in the distance. If they had the same issues finding the location as he did, it'd be a few minutes before they arrived. Not that there was anything they could do.

The wreck was still smouldering as Burton approached, although the heat and main fire had long died out. Still dark, the first sign of morning light breaking across the wide-open fields, it gave the whole scene a weird, almost eerie atmosphere - like a film set - as the image began to appear clearly.

He'd seen a few road traffic accidents working in London; mostly drunks or petty car thieves, but as his headlights illuminated the scene of carnage, this mess appeared to be one of the best, or worst, depending on your viewpoint.

The shell of a car was against the trunk of a large oak tree, the top part of bark burnt from the fire, but otherwise unscathed. Its bare branches were too high to be caught by the brief but intense fire. The scene stunk of something.

A tractor was parked nearby on the high grass bank that separated the fields from the road. A thin, ashen-faced man in green overalls stood beside it, deliberately standing several yards from the wreck. Burton parked up next to the red and silver tractor and got out. Putting on his cap, he adjusted his belt.

"Morning officer," the man said in a local accent, but subordinate manner.

"Good morning sir," replied Burton, loving the sense of authority offered.

"I take it you found the vehicle sir and made the call?"

"Yes. 'Bout arf an hour ago. There's bodies inside. And one on road too. I ain't touched nuffint tho.' Nasty mess. Not good. Probably local lads I think."

Burton quickly translated and followed the man's finger towards a charcoal log in the road. He at first quizzed the man's assumption it was a body, then feeling his stomach rise, realised it was indeed what had hours earlier been a living human, but was now something which resembled a discarded hog-roast.

Burton knew this was serious. But also an opportunity for him to shine.

His thoughts raced to it being a possible local drugs deal that'd gone wrong.

"Have you touched anything at all sir?" Burton began, trying to work out what to do next, and how best not to look so white in front of the relatively calm farm worker, now he realised there was another 'hog-roast' inside.

"No. I stopped when I saw the wreck, got out and wandered over to see what it actually was. Looks like there could be three or four of them. Hard to tell what's really what. Couple of burnt lumps on the bonnet. And there's one inside, as well as the one on the road. Got back in me tractor and phoned your lot. Then I came back here in case someone came. I called me brother and told him to keep an eye out for anyone like you, but I ain't touched nuffint," he repeated in a broad Norfolk drawl, his gaze drifting to the wreck.

"Very well sir, you've done well. If you'd like to stay there please," Burton replied and wandered over to the scene of what smelt like a mass barbecue.

As he closed in Burton sniffed the air once more. Pork. It smelt of pork.

For a second he wondered if that's what humans actually tasted like.

No, he re-thought. Probably chicken. Everything tastes like chicken.

As he advanced towards the burnt log, its form became apparent, and he looked somewhat grimly at the twisted figure outstretched on the ground. Its entire body was crisped, yet still showed the signs of having once been that of a living human. It had one visible arm and hand outstretched, but badly contorted; reaching out, as if trying to grasp out at something, or someone.

He carefully stepped past the blackened body, not looking at it too closely and approached the remains of the car. He shone his torch into the wreckage and could see more clearly the damage done to the tree and car, the latter being the loser; now a mix of burnt material and scorched buckled steel.

A body, only partly burnt, lay on the bonnet. The upper half, being lightly grilled, was still partially identifiable, although blackened. It reminded Burton of grilled sardines he'd eaten in Portugal on the seafront at Albufeira when on holiday with Joan, the fish's glazed eyes staring up from the plate, dead and sightless. Like those of the body on the bonnet. He'd never eat them again.

This was not good. Kids. There was another burnt form beside the one on the bonnet and yet another one inside. His heart began to beat fast and a cold sweat broke out on his brow, despite the chill of the grey, gloomy morning.

No one liked finding dead kids. It wasn't right. Old people dying, in any form, was acceptable. They'd had their life. And besides which, fewer people usually cared. Kids had parents who didn't usually expect to bury them. Often they also had brothers and sisters, who expected them to grow up and become aunts and uncles. Not simply become a memorial stone engraving.

Next to the kid on the bonnet, whose legs protruded into the car, appeared a smaller body, almost burnt beyond any recognition. But it looked too long legged to be human, but may have been. Maybe it was a pet dog, flung out of the windscreen with the crash. It was hard to determine fully, and Burton didn't scan it all too closely in fear of embarrassing himself throwing up.

Inside the car was the worst mess. It was what finally made Burton turn away, run across the road and throw up in the field opposite, but luckily not spoiling any evidence. The tractor driver looked at him sympathetically.

The burnt corpse, face blackened and almost skeletal, sat erringly upright with empty eye sockets. Its teeth grinned insanely back at Burton in a chilling leer; the body seated in the metal meshed framework of what was the car seat. The blackened engine block lay on the body where its legs should have been, its crisped arms, held tightly onto the engine block, almost as if for support.

Once he'd recovered his composure, Burton strolled back to his car, making his apologises to the farm worker, before radioing through the details and requesting urgent assistance to cordon off the road to preserve the scene.

As he waited for the additional teams to arrive, the sound of their sirens growing, he wandered about the road, half in order to regain his composure, but also to see what might have caused the accident. The early dawn light began to rise over the fields through the thin blanket of pink cloud.

He noted skid marks on the road, but several hundred yards from the scene of the accident. There were seemingly none at the actual scene. As he glanced back at the car, a thought hit him. He wandered back to the tractor driver, now standing with his arms folded, looking bored and cold.

"Anyone missing a dog around here?" Burton enquired.

The man shrugged. "Dun know," he replied. "Why?"

"I think that might be a dog on the bonnet. Perhaps they hit it, carried on down the road, then swerved and hit the tree. Car ignited and killed them all," explained Burton, as much to himself as to his listener, then stood silent.

"Could well be a deer. Get a lot them around here. The local hunt often gets onto them by accident. And a lot of people poach 'em. Good eating. So I've heard. Not that I would," he added, quietening down, suddenly not wanting to show too great a knowledge on the subject of local deer poaching.

"Umm, that could be what it is. I think it had little hooves. Looks like three bodies. Tragic. Do you think they could be local?" enquired Burton.

"Blast I hope not," replied the driver, wondering if his own son had been in bed when he'd left home earlier. "Could be. Hard to tell by what's left of the car. Don't recognise it. Didn't really think about it until you said that."

Burton took the man's details and was about to let him go as he heard the siren of the ambulance passing through the village. The tractor driver began to turn the big vehicle around in the nearby field entrance, where Burton was seeing him back. Suddenly he abruptly yelled, shouting above the noise and waving his arms at the driver to stop. The big vehicle stopped with a judder.

"Whoa! Stop there. Don't go back. Did you turn around in here earlier?" he hollered in the cab, above the chugging noise of the large diesel engine.

"No. After I saw the wreck I simply parked up on the bank where it's been all along, until you came, until now," explained the nervous tractor driver.

"Well don't come back any further. It looks like a car has been in this field entrance already in the last few hours. They've stopped then turned around."

The tractor driver, in his high canopy, looked behind him. Tyre marks.

"You're right there boy," he added. "Looks like a car has turned in this field entrance. A 4 x 4 by the size of those wheels. Do you reckon someone could have seen the accident and gone off to report it? I didn't see anyone."

"I don't know," replied Burton listening to the tractor driver, taking in the possible explanation, but already thinking of other potential reasons.

"We'll have to see. Thanks for you help." Burton replied with a nod, patting the big tractor door. "We'll be contacting you and get a full statement."

With that the tractor moved on back towards the village, riding up the grass bank to allow the ambulance to pass, and then picked up the driver's brother, who been patiently waiting along the road, but was now keen to get away too.

The early light was beginning to hit the scene as the two ambulance crew got out wandering over to Burton; seeing the burnt out shell, expressions grim.

"Any causalities?" asked the Paramedic, already checking and knowing.

"Looks like three. All dead I'm afraid. Burnt to death. Not a pretty sight."

Burton slowly walked back to the wreck with more composure, now he'd accepted the sight and grown accustomed to the lifeless, blackened figures.

"Any other cars involved?" enquired the second paramedic, shaking his head.

"It doesn't appear so. Certainly nothing I can see in the immediate area. Think they were travelling at speed, possibly missed the bend; going by those skid marks, then they hit a deer, before crashing into the tree. I think that is the burnt lump on the bonnet. There are quite a few deer about these parts," Burton said firmly, feeling authoritative with his newfound knowledge.

The ambulance crew could see that there was nothing for them to do and they remained until a fire engine came minutes later to check the car was safe. Then the entire road was cordoned off as a whole series of vehicles came and went. Details of the vehicle were radioed in to find the owner, to then begin the grim task of informing relatives. In this case it appeared to be parents.

With only a few weeks before Christmas, it would be especially unwelcome news, with presents already bought, or even wrapped, never be opened.

It wasn't long before the identities to the bodies were known. As mother's stirred and made breakfast, to discover the household was a person light.

By midday the police had all three names and Burton was glad he'd been relieved of duty, so he did not have the grieving parents to deal with. As hard as he was, it was never easy telling a wailing relative someone they loved was never coming back. Worse still, explaining their loved one was barbecued.

Driving back, as an old green Land Rover passed him, he began to think more about the incident. The rogue tyres tracks in the field plagued him.

Tired and mentally fatigued, he made a mental note, then returned to his flat in Norwich, showered, threw off his clothes and fell fast asleep on the bed.

Chapter 48

I am not like other people. I am burning in hell.
The hell of myself.

Charles Bukowski

"Bit of a mess down the road," began Martin, speaking to Sharon.

"I was exercising the hounds on the common when I saw ambulances and police cars all moving about. Busy. Spoke with Pete Hawkins. Reckons there's been a nasty accident. Car fire. Seems bad. Couple of people dead."

"Oh dear. I wonder what happened?" asked Sharon, half curious.

"Don't know," continued Martin. "When I spoke with Pete, he claims he often hears cars racing through the village at night. Wonders if they were joy riders. Possibly a stolen car. This one is burnt out. Possibly young kids in it."

"Oh my god," said Sharon. "That sounds terrible. Did you hear anything last night when I was out?" enquired Sharon. "I wonder what happened?"

"No, I didn't hear anything around here. I stayed in all night. Had a beer and watched a bit of TV, then read and was in bed when you rolled in late. All quiet when I checked the hounds at eleven. Did you or Helen see anything?" replied the huntsman, deflecting away any further questions.

"Not when Helen picked me up," Sharon replied. "Too busy chatting, and to be honest I don't remember too much about even coming home," she said with a grin. "I'll have to call Helen to see if she saw anything driving home."

"No, you flopped into bed and went out like a light from what I recall," replied Martin, picking up his fresh mug of tea.

"Wonder what happened," Sharon asked again, but with little care.

"What do you want for breakfast? We've plenty of bacon," she added with a smile, changing the conversation. "Your favourite."

Martin grinned back, rubbing his stomach.

"That'll do nicely love. I like the smell of grilled pork in the morning."

Chapter 49

In hell there is no other punishment than to begin over and over again the tasks left unfinished in your lifetime.

Andre Gide

"Hear about all those kids who got toasted last night?" Reggie asked Steve. The pair were sharing an early glass of port in Steve's Portacabin office.

Morning was too early for Port for some, but not Steve and Reggie. Never.

Reggie had driven over, glad to get away from The Grange and Elizabeth, although she strangely seemed to be in a happy mood. But not with him.

"Caught something on the local radio. Then a couple of my men mentioned it. You know how quick word goes around. And without using pigeons!"

Steve smiled, getting a familiar joke. "What happened? Do you know?"

"We think the little bastards stole a car, got drunk and piled into a tree. Good old oak as well. Hope its not damaged. It's been there hundreds of years. If the bark's been torched, it'll might die. Took out a deer on the way it seems. Bastards! Possibly caused the accident. Serves the little shits a lesson!"

Steve looked at Reggie, considering his reaction. "Not a very nice way to go. And they're someone's kids. Especially horrible just before Christmas," he commented, his tone compassionate. "Waste of presents!" The pair chuckled.

"Yes, I suppose you're right," Reggie eased. "Kids annoy me these days. I had some trespassing in my woods a while back, and had to get rid of them. Bloody nuisance trespassers. Shoot them all, I would. Shouldn't be there."

"I totally agree," said Steve, nodding. "I've dispatched a fair number from here in my time. I can't stand the bastards roaming about, spying on you, or trying to steal things. I'd be the first to shoot them and bury them in the woods. But that sounds a nasty incident. Kids is kids. They're not poachers."

Reggie appeared to succumb, another glass of the fine Late Vintage Port offered by Steve helping to relax the pair, as they discussed important matters.

"Any way, enough grim talk. The Mitchell's meet. What are we going to do?"

"Yes indeed Reggie. Problems, problems. No solutions."

They then discussed the land they could hunt and landowners they'd need to contact, but also a whole range of issues. There was always so much to do, and so little time to do it in. The story of their lives. Busy people.

As they discussed the details, it was clear to Steve something clearly niggling Reggie. He was not in a good mood. Not even after a couple of early Port's.

Steve on the other hand was happy. Very happy.

He'd had a good night. A very good night indeed.

Chapter 50

If love be blind, it best agrees with night.

Romeo & Juliet - William Shakespeare

Dawn straightened Gavin's tie, as he prepared for work, adjusting it around the collar of the crisp white shirt she'd ironed last night. She hung her arms loosely around his neck, looked at him, gazing dreamily into his eyes, then kissed him on the lips. A tender peck. She waited for a reaction.

He looked at her blankly, seemed to realise where he was, and with whom, then smiled and quickly kissed her back. But with no emotion.

She pulled him closer, kissing him long, her tongue flicking across his lips. He was slow, and almost reluctant to respond, but then kissed her back fully.

Dawn's sigh was a sign of appreciation. And relief. She was happy. For now.

They broke free from their kiss and she looked at him longingly.

He still had that distant look in his eyes.

"Last night was great," she said grinning. "You took a long time coming, but that made it good. It was lovely. Must do it for longer more often."

Gavin flushed, and then tried to look away. Dawn eyes still twinkled.

"No need to be embarrassed. It makes it better for me. Sorry I molested you when you came home. I just couldn't resist it," she said kissing him again.

"I was so worried when you came in so late. I was concerned something had happened. Turned out to be a very special night after all though, didn't it?"

Gavin blushed again as he pecked her on the lips, wanting to get away, but trying to not make it look too obvious, words seemingly failing him today.

Someone else was in his thoughts that morning.

On in the background, the TV had a round up of local news. Gavin broke free of her embrace, turning his attention to the news, listening intently to the report of an accident involving three youths in a village just outside Norwich.

Dawn noted his keen attention and they both listened to the brief details.

"How horrible," Dawn began. "But probably racing like idiots. Pratt's. Almost serves them right if they were, although that's a bit mean. Not good for the parents. Hope no one else was involved. Some people just drive off."

Gavin blushed, looking away from the TV in silence, his eyes cast down.

He checked at his watch again, deep in thought, his mind elsewhere.

"Must go love. I'll call. Won't be late tonight, honest."

"Don't mind if you are, if it means we get another night like last night!"

With that he was gone, picking up the keys to the Peugeot, pushing away the Range Rover keys, almost with contempt.

Chapter 51

A false witness will not go unpunished,
and whoever pours out lies will not go free.

Proverbs – 19:5

"Elizabeth!" cried Virginia. "I didn't expect to see you here. What a pleasant surprise. Did you want Bertie? Or are you breaking into our stables?"

Elizabeth Hornchurch froze, and then turned around, as if taken by surprise. She was walking around the back of the old stable block at Wroxingham Hall, heading towards the small workshop where Mike Hawthorn worked.

"Oh, hello Virginia," Elizabeth said, face glowing, wearing a look of shock, but quickly recovering, seeing the grinning face, realising Virginia was joking.

"I was passing by on a errand and decided to drop off a few Christmas cards. Bit early I know for some, but it saves postage. And I was in the area."

"Thank you very much," said Virginia, taking the large white envelope on top, noticing another, in a red envelope left in her hand below. Elizabeth deftly moved it sideward, but knew Virginia was too smart, and her keen eyes had already seen the name on the front of it. She smiled. Clever cow.

"We've got Mike a card too. This one. I was about to drop his off in his workshop and hand it too him. Do you know if he's about?" she enquired.

Virginia gazed at Elizabeth, the corners of her mouth set to curl, when Mike and Bertie walked around the corner of the building together, both with broken shotguns in their arms. Two men regarded two women, both showing surprise. One more so than the other. Smiles crossed all their faces.

"Lizzy!" Bertie joyfully called, walking up to her and kissing each cheek. "How the devil are you? And how's that old bastard Reggie?" He grinned.

Elizabeth flushed, her eyes flitting sideward momentarily, embarrassed.

"We're both fine. Same old Reggie, as you know and aptly describe. And yourselves?" she replied, looking across at Mike, who sheepishly smiled back.

"I'm not too bad." Bertie replied. "Actually I've never felt better. I'm going to hunt this Boxing Day. Virginia has inspired me to get out more, and I'm going to ride out on my old chestnut, Spider, for the first time in an age."

Virginia appeared to force a smile; more like a grimace. Or bad wind.

"That'll be wonderful Bertie," Elizabeth falsely replied too.

"Reggie will be pleased. We need as much ridden support as possible for the Boxing Day meet. It's such an important meet, as he always tell me."

"It will be the first time I've ridden out on Boxing Day at Windford in many years. I can't wait!" he replied, looking at Virginia, who looked away.

Elizabeth looked at Mike and stretched out her hand. The pair smiled.

"This is for you Mike. From me and Reggie. Happy early Christmas."

Mike looked a bit embarrassed at first, until he fully heard what she said. Their hands linked momentarily, the red envelope and card held between, before Elizabeth released her grip, seemingly somewhat reluctantly.

"Thank you." he replied. "I'll have to pop yours round later. In a few days or so. I'm terrible. I always busy leave mine until the last minute."

"Did you hear about that terrible accident up the road?" Elizabeth said, breaking the silence. All three looked on, apparently unaware, heads shaking.

"Car accident. Seems to be quite bad," she continued. "Three or four people killed, along with a pet dog, so I believe. Nasty. A whole family I think. Seems they took the bend wrong and hit a tree. Car burst into flames. Horrible."

"Gosh!" exclaimed Virginia "That's awful. Isn't it Bertie?"

"Terrible tragedy," replied Bertie in a matter of fact tone; genuinely shocked.

All four then stood in silence, regarding each other, unsure what to say next.

"If you find out who they were, we should send them our condolences, especially if they're local. I hope not. I certainly didn't hear anything last night. We were both here all night. Dinner with the Hurlingham's. Very nice couple. He's in finance. How about you Mike. Were you about at all last night?"

"No. I left off after checking the partridges. I was in all night, watching the local football match. Good game. I didn't hear anything."

Virginia looked at Mike long and hard, knowing the truth.

'Lair, liar pants on….' She broke off the chilling thought.

Mike gazed back at Virginia, his cold look unsettling.

Elizabeth looked at Mike, blushing, then glanced at Bertie.

Virginia also looked at Bertie, knowing he'd returned late from his trip. Very late. Almost ruining their dinner party. Where had he been? No one asked.

But he was very flustered and red-faced when he returned. From where?

Bertie glanced at Virginia, seeing her curious, probing look and turned away.

The four liars regarded each other. And each knew the other was lying.

"You'll have to come in for a quick coffee Lizzie. I wouldn't hear otherwise. Virginia makes a fine Latte," Bertie spoke, breaking the momentary silence.

"You too Mike. You always enjoy a good cup of coffee. Join us."

"Thank you, but I'm covered in mud. And must get on," Mike replied politely, raising the card to Elizabeth. "Thank you. I'll ensure I get a card back to you. Hopefully I'll also see you out on Boxing Day at Windford?"

"You will. And I'm certainly looking forward to it," she replied with a smile.

Elizabeth made her farewell to Mike, who headed towards his workshop.

She looked back toward the old stable block where Mike had stood, but he was gone. Leaves blew across the empty yard. From inside the white building, watchful eyes peered from the aged, brittle glass, where dusty cobwebs clung.

Someone knew the truth about last night's cruel events.

Maybe they all did. For they all had their own secrets to hide.

Chapter 52

I am all in a sea of wonders. I doubt; I fear;
I think strange things which I dare not confess to my own soul.
God keep me, if only for the sake of those dear to me.

Bram Stoker - Dracula

Since moving Penny to Horsewater Anna had been busy, frantically working to get a host of work completed before the traditional Christmas shutdown for companies or any New Year deadlines. She'd ridden Penny in the school a few times, when not working, but still hadn't really explored the farm, other than for the one hack out with Tracey Julie and Carol. Worse, since the hunt meet, she'd only seen Chris intermittently in the mornings, dashing about, and wondered if he'd taken offence at Steve Harrison's open advance, or was simply being the 'Chris Turner' everyone had warned her about. Elusive.

However, she put all of her doubts to bed, when dashing past in the yard, about to pick up a horse for someone, Chris called over and arranged a day to finally ride out together and show her around the estate properly. So for the first time, she'd hopefully get to know Horsewater, and owner, a bit better.

Today was the day and she had a mix of emotions running through her. Deep down she kept telling herself that it was only a hack out with the man who owned the impressive yard and estate where she kept her horse. But somehow she felt that there was more to it. She certainly hoped there could.

She'd donned her smartest cream jodhpurs; the ones usually reserved for shows, the material clinging to every aspect of her legs and displaying her neat bottom beautifully. Even more so in a white thong. She ensured she arrived at the yard in good time, also wearing a little more make-up then she'd normally wear to ride out, and saw Sally pottering about doing some of the liveries.

She'd never really worked Sally out. An attractive girl, who seemed set in her own little world, she simply did her own thing, almost on autopilot and hardly spoke with Chris and merely smiled and nodded to others. When she did speak with Chris, it was like an old married couple, who knew what each wanted and needed and got on. They simply did what had to be done, spoke little, accepted the other being there, and had a good working relationship.

As much as she was attracted to Chris, Anna felt no threat by the attractive Sally, who was engaged to a local man who worked for his parent's business.

From experience, Anna knew that meant nothing. She'd known of a good friend back in Leicester who'd been married for twenty years. She'd never strayed or been tempted and was totally loyal. However, she met a man completely by chance, who too had been married for many years, and who'd also never considered cheating. Within six months of first meeting, they'd both ditched their life-long partners and were now happily living together.

Anna approached Sally as she looked for Chris. "Hi Sally," Anna began, "Have you seen Chris? He seems to have vanished once again. Like magic."

"Hello Anna. I think he's indoors. I heard the phone go and he nipped inside. I doubt he'll be long. You're riding out with us today aren't you?"

The words instantly deflated Anna. 'Us.' Plural, as in more than two.

Anna had dumbly hoped it'd be a quiet and intimate ride alone with Chris.

Now, as much as she liked Sally as a fun person, she'd have the company of his one loyal companion. Some potential date. Damn! She cursed, but smiled.

Maybe it was deliberate, Chris wanting Sally as chaperone.

Anna kept her composure and smiled, trying to find a positive aspect.

"Yes, that's right," she replied slightly disheartened. "I just wondered whether to tack Penny up yet or wait," she said making an excuse, enthusiasm waning.

"You might as well get ready. I'm not actually riding out with you. I've got to nip back home and help dad on the farm. We've got a big order to get out for Christmas. I'm now getting Tirus ready, so as soon as he comes out, he can jump onboard. Then I'll be off. I know he's looking forward to riding out."

"Tirus?" enquired Anna. "Which horse is that?"

"I mean Saint Swithin. He's also called Tirus or sometimes Bonzo. Saint Swithin is his posh show name. Tirus is his stable name. All very confusing. Don't ask. A long story. Sometimes he gets called much worse! He's riding out on him. So good luck. He's mad. The horse. Well also maybe Chris too!"

Anna's heart was lifted by the words and beamed openly. Sally then watched, slightly puzzled, as the strange woman skipped over towards Penny's stable.

Anna got down to work with the brush and groomed Penny to within an inch of her life, so she sparkled as best she could in her clipped winter coat. Then nipping to the tackroom, with Chris still seemingly nowhere in sight, she returned and began to put on the tack she'd cleaned especially last night.

She'd just finished adjusting Penny's girth as Sally's blond bob and smiling face appeared over the door, making her jump, such was her concentration.

"Chris is now going to get Tirus out. He was on the phone. He's in a bit of a grump this morning, but that's nothing new. It's usual. Just ignore him!"

Anna raised her eyebrows and grinned, as Sally opened the stable door for her and Anna led Penny out, the pair looking National Show level ready.

"You both look very smart for a hack. Have a good ride and stay on board!"

Sally waved as she wandered off across the yard and over towards her car.

Anna led Penny over to the mounting block and got on board, looking around the yard for Chris. At that moment he appeared from the stable and led Saint Swithin out of his stable, whipped down the stirrups and promptly leapt straight onto the stout chestnut horse from the ground.

Anna smiled, silently impressed and rode over to him, her face beaming.

"Good morning! I've been waiting for this day."

Chris smiled back, somewhat sheepishly and embarrassed.

"Morning. So you're ready for the grand tour?"

Anna beamed back, like a teenager on her first date, trying not to stare.

"Certainly. I can't wait," she almost giggled. "Lead the way, Oh Master!"

Chris shook his head and chuckled as the pair joined up in the yard with broad grins and headed out off the yard, both in silence, but hearts racing.

They rode up past the schooling paddock, where Anna had spent most of her time since arriving, and then up on towards the paddocks and the woods beyond, where she'd ridden out previously. At first they rode side by side, neither speaking, but both admiring the horses turned out in the paddocks, who excitedly trotted up to the fence to see them walk past. Penny rose up a few inches, her stride shorting and elevating, but she behaved, where as Tirus seemed unfazed, being the alpha-male of the whole yard and had done it all.

The ever-present rooks wheeled above them in the grey, cloudy sky, which rose above the distant bare treetops towards which they headed. Silently they both watched, Anna fascinated by the birds and knowing Chris was too.

As they began to head towards the woods, Anna broke the silence first.

"How long have you lived here?" she asked warily, knowing the answer, but wanting to break the ice, if not she feared they'd ride without speaking all day.

"All my life. I was born here. So thirty five years," came his simple reply.

He did not elaborate or return a question, simply looking at the trees.

Anna fell silent again. She was happy, but felt awkward.

When they'd hunted he hadn't spoken greatly, communication being mostly facial gestures, quick comments, or witty jokes. But she'd still felt quite close to him and sensed he'd been attracted to her. But now things were awkward

During the few weeks she'd been at his yard, their paths had crossed, but he'd always seemed busy; either schooling horses or dashing in and out in his Range Rover, or the horsebox, collecting or transporting horses for people.

She had not really had much time to chat on a personal level or even the odd passing comment. He never joined the girls gossiping in the tack room, when they huddled around for a cup of coffee before setting out on a hack or doing some schooling, and everything he did around the yard was regimented, set to strict timetables and routines and very business-like. But he still had an aura.

Anna had been hoping their ride out would help bring them closer, and she'd learn more about him, still attracted to him, despite his grumpy and introvert nature. She felt he was deeply shy and that inside there was a genuinely nice man looking to give and receive love, despite his often gloomy nature.

There was also a very daring question she'd been hoping to ask him, and now wondered why she'd bothered considering it, feeling very apprehensive and almost reluctant to go ahead with it. They were heading towards the opening of the woods, when as if he was reading her thoughts, he spoke out.

"Sorry if I am a bit quiet this morning. I didn't have a good night last night and I've had lots to do today. I tend to be rather set in my ways, regimented, and also quiet first thing and not overly chatty, so I'll apologise in advance if I appear a bit of a grump and not good company," Chris said, smiling weakly.

Anna looked at him admiringly for his frank honesty and smiled broadly, then chuckled. He returned her smile, his main form of communication.
"I've ridden a few tracks with Julie, but I thought the woods were spooky. I've not been here on my own. The Boogie Man might eat me!" she joked.
Chris grinned and nodded firmly, as if confirmation the 'Man' may well do.
"She also warned me of certain parts that we couldn't ride in. Preservation areas or where you're doing tree work with contractors or loose branches?" She hoped her new line of approach, less personal, would open Chris up.
He looked at her for a few seconds, as if weighing her up before answering.
"There's nothing to be scared of in the woods. Well, except maybe for the Hobgoblins, Trolls and Orks, who lurk in some of the darkest, most secret hidden parts," he said with a broad grin. "And then of course the Zombies!"
Anna got the dark joke; seeing him smile, happy he was warming up.
"Yes, there are lots of tracks you can ride on, some I'd prefer you didn't. Most of those are fenced off in some form, or I'll tell you, so it's fairly clear which they are. I'm lucky to have so much woodland. It's beautiful in the spring when the trees break into leaf and the bluebells are vibrant. Then the woods are particularly wonderful," he replied dreamingly. "But they are also a crop, and so need management, which takes up my time which no one sees."
Anna looked at him long, realising how at one he was with his surroundings, beginning to understand him more and why he was so busy and flustered.
He caught her stare and blushed; his other main form of communication Anna was learning. With that he turned off the main track and onto a smaller, well-used one, highlighted by the hoof prints from previous excursions.
"Fancy a quick canter?" he asked, his tone changing, becoming excited.
Anna looked nervously ahead at the maze of trees, branches sweeping across and smiled, simply nodding apprehensively. With that he was off.
The chestnut needed no further encouragement, roaring off along the track, instinctively knowing where he was heading. Anna was more cautious, as Penny broke into canter and closely followed her new companion, clinging onto his heels. Anna hoped Tirus' rider knew where he was going and wasn't planning on making any sudden stops, as she felt Penny wouldn't oblige.
She was too close to him to be hit in the face by the mud and leaves the horse threw up, but continuously ducked under the occasional low branch, which suddenly came upon them as they wove around the twisting track.
Penny was loving it, and Anna fought to keep a tight hold so she didn't get too close to Tirus, or worse, overtake, having no idea where she was heading. Suddenly a few yards ahead, on a straight section of track, a large fallen beech tree lay. Anna looked ahead of Chris at the imposing log and wondered if they were going to stop or not. The answer was not. He was heading for it.
Chris looked around at Anna, smiling broadly and yelled through the noise.
"She jumps doesn't she?" he called, almost as a knowing statement, rather than a question, which had options. "I hope so! Hold tight and just kick!"

Anna had no time to reply, only to see Chris point Tirus at the tree trunk. He flew over it like a true professional, jumping only enough to clear the tips of his shoes, landing perfectly on the opposite side. Even before he landed Chris was turning his face with a grin, to watch Anna, approaching at speed.

The tree approached rapidly and Anna tensed up, her pulse increasing from the frantic pace, as another surge of adrenaline pumped into her system. She checked Penny as she approached, who leapt cleanly over the big trunk, Anna feeling as though she'd flown for a few seconds, as Penny landed safely the other side of the track, Anna tipping forward but recovering. She breathed again and steadied Penny up, upon seeing Chris hauling on Tirus' reins, pulling hard at the mad red horse. She did likewise on Penny and within a few strides they'd returned both horses back to a steady trot and then transitioned back down into a walk. Both horses blew out, their nostrils flaring widely.

Anna was puffing too and patted Penny on the neck, excitement flowing through her. Chris was hardly fazed and simply turned around smiling, his cheeks slightly red, the same colour as his mount, but smiled widely.

"That cleared the tubes," he said grinning, seeing how out of breathe Anna was. She just nodded, her smile beaming, the happiest she'd been in a while.

They steadied the horses into a quiet walk and turning around in the saddle to face Anna, the conversation began to flow. They began talking about past horses, always an easy conversation piece for horse owners and Anna quickly learnt Chris would skip anything personal, so did not ask anything directly related to him or more importantly his past, not involving horses.

Other than being somewhat moody, she felt he was happy, and very much appreciated his life and never appeared to want for company; wherever he sought it out or people simply needed him. But Anna knew already he was not selfish, and appeared genuinely giving, but certainly disliked strangers.

In turn he asked about her life and how she had come to move to Leicester. He seemed careful to skirt around the subject of Bruce, aware it was a delicate subject, but he came into the conversation frequently and it turned out Chris was a very good listener. Anna realised he was better at listening than talking, and seemed to prefer to do this, with Anna preferring the other.

They walked through the woods and Chris showed Anna tracks she could ride down and others she shouldn't, and pointed out specific old trees he'd known all his life, the woods seemingly holding a deep meaning to him.

They had another thrilling canter, almost as if he was testing out Anna's nerve and riding ability, as they weaved through more trees and jumped a couple of smaller obstacles on the track. Chris seemed to be slowly opening up to Anna and she felt that he was warming to her, although she sensed he was very defensive and almost put up a protective wall to stop her getting in too deep when she asked some questions. She wondered if it was his shyness or some deeper fear, worry, feeling or emotion he wanted hidden away.

He still appeared to have a dark, humorous side. An unknown aspect that intrigued Anna rather than frightened her. Their conversation got onto the subject of Christmas, which was where Anna had hoped they might get onto.

"What do you do for Christmas?" she asked casually, but with purpose, feeling more open with her questioning. "Do you do anything special?"

Chris paused, thinking deep, as if accessing the question in depth and its potential meaning and connotations, before finally answering.

"Nothing different to any other day of the year. Horses still need to be done. And they don't seem to know or care it's Christmas. None of them have ever bought me present! They must be Atheists!" He smiled at his dark humour.

"The full liveries need to be done as normal, and more so, with other people going away. And I have my own to. So nothing special. It's another day, but usually more busy. I'm not really a Christmas person. How about you?"

"Normally I'd be flitting across country between Bruce or my parents, and life would be chaotic. As well as doing Penny, unless Jan did her. So she would be like you, taking on other people's work. Lot's of racing about and no joy. Usually end up in an argument, with Bruce getting his way," she began to answer. "But this year I will simply be at my mum's for Christmas lunch."

Anna chatted freely; keen to see Chris was still attentive, the horses walking.

"Mum's got quite a big house. We have one or two relatives come around. Tracey is coming around too with her other-half. Would you like to join us?"

She amazed herself at how naturally the casual lunch offer came out.

It almost sounded natural and unplanned. A pleasant passing remark.

However, Anna had planned and rehearsed the question in various forms for a whole day. Each time she'd rehearsed, her stomach felt like a goldfish was swimming around inside, fluttering about inside; being unsure of the tone, wording and manner in which to ask, hoping she didn't sound too pushy.

Now the seemingly casual question, an invite to join her for Christmas lunch, had simply fallen from her lips, almost as if never planned.

Anna tensed up, waiting. Had he even heard her offer?

The silence that followed seemed almost endless.

The only sound was the clop of hooves on hardened dirt.

Anna felt her face go red, and then could hear her heart pounding.

Chris paused before replying, the longer the couple rode in silence, with only the squeak of leather and gentle clop of hooves to break the silence, the less confident Anna became of a positive response and internally she squirmed.

Chris looked over to Anna; face a brighter red then his normal embarrassed look, as if unsure how to reply without offending a new friend. Just a friend.

It was obvious he was frantically thinking of a response, Anna sensed, but most likely looking for a way to politely say no and make a host of excuses.

She winced, knowing she'd been too forward, too soon. As ever.

Finally he raised his head, looked at her eye to eye and spoke.

Anna felt a knife slicing through the tension.

"Thank you. It's a lovely offer, and very kind of you, but I wouldn't want to intrude on your special day. Besides, you and your family hardly know me."

"All the more reason to find out more about you!"

Anna was stunned by her own reply; the natural chirpy response flooring him, leaving him smirking, but in silence, again thinking hard and deep.

Anna now felt embarrassed for him and was about to offer a way out; sensing she'd put Chris in a tight situation and ruined the chance of any future relationship developing; blighting the brief friendship that'd grown.

She'd blown it. Gotten too clever, too soon. Typical Anna.

He was going to say no. She knew it. And she'd been warned.

The Untouchable Mister Turner. And now she'd tried to grab him.

By Tracey, Julie, and even Lady Carter. They all knew. They told her.

Did she ever listen? No. She knew best. But didn't.

A rush of panic swept her body, and she felt she should apologise.

As she went to speak Chris beat her to it.

Ducking to avoid a branch, Chris looked her in the face.

"Okay then. Yes. But if you really don't mind. Yes, I'd love to come."

He replied firmly, without hesitation, actually smiling.

Anna's heart leapt and her face split in half with the smile.

"However, there are complications and Quid pro quo's attached. I have to do the entire yard that day, as Sally has the day off. And I'll need to be back mid afternoon to get them all in. So once lunch is over, I'll be clock-watching, if you don't mind. But yes, I'd love to share Christmas lunch with you."

Anna was shocked, expecting a rebuff. Instead she now realised his time spent to reply was working out the logistics of what he'd do with the horses.

She was totally speechless, her beaming smile, with teeth and all, the perfect response; such was her joy, especially at how he'd replied.

"That's brilliant. Thank you!" She almost squealed, then tried to remain cool.

"I'll happily come down Christmas morning and give you a hand with the horses and all the chores. Likewise in the afternoon. How does that sound?"

She'd thought that might be the case when she planned her endeavour.

The excitement surged through Anna, her stomach fluttering.

Chris simply nodded as a response, seemingly working things out too.

"It's a deal then, but if you really don't mind." he replied.

"I couldn't think of a better way to spend Christmas." Anna was still excited.

"You'd better ask you mum first," Chris added cautiously. "To check it will be okay with her having me as a guest".

"Don't worry, I already have," Anna said with a grin. "She's already got a larger turkey, extra vegetables and a nut loaf, just in case you're a Vegan!"

Chris laughed, shaking his head, realising he'd been set up, but happy he had.

He kicked Tirus into a gentle canter and began to playfully race away down a twisting track, weaving between trees, leaving Anna behind a stride.

"You cheeky bugger!" he called back to Anna. "But thanks!"

Anna smiled broadly, kicking Penny into life, quickly moving forward and catching up, thundering on behind for a few strides, until she caught him up and drew alongside on a wider section of track, then they eased back.

Dropping back to a walk, the colour in their faces returning, along with their breath, Chris began talking more freely. He seemed to have dropped his guard slightly now the ice was broken and asked a bit more about the arrangements for the day. He then told her what he needed to do around the yard and when he needed to be back, slightly apprehensive, but seemingly a detailed planner.

They agreed the various arrangements, which seemed to put Chris at ease.

He admitted it'd be the first Christmas away from the farm for years, the last time being spent with Virginia and Bertie Burlingham. Lord Burlingham, as well as being his neighbour, was also a long time family friend for many years it seemed, and hence also Virginia, who he referred to simply as Ginny.

Anna winced at the very mention of Lady Burlingham's first name by Chris, and the open and fond nature he spoke about her. However, Anna felt she'd won an inner victory at tempting Chris to her mum's for Christmas and possibly away from the clutching claws of Lady Virginia Burlingham.

For this Christmas Day, Chris Turner would be all hers. Or so she hoped.

They returned to the yard to find Tracey bustling about. She'd known about Anna's ride with Chris, and even though she wasn't working, had deliberately waited until later before turning up. That way Chris wouldn't invite her out on the hack out with them and ruin the opportunity. The pair had it all planned.

When the two happy riders came into the yard, side-by-side, with stirrups clanking, Tracey sensed a growing bond and wandered straight up to them; smiling broadly, full of excitement, she forget she was part of the conspiracy.

She'd told Anna to ensure Chris knew she'd be there too, as he'd known Tracey for years and might feel it was more of a gesture of kindness between the two women, rather than an all-out blatant date with just Anna alone.

Tracey stepped up to the pair as they dismounted in the yard, taking the reins for Chris as he leapt off Tirus. But her mind was on other matters.

"Did you hear about the accident the other day Chris," Tracey asked.

"Yes, briefly. Bertie called me when it happened. But I've heard no more since. Too busy as usual. Do they know who they are yet?" he enquired.

"Yes. All local I believe. Next village. Or at least one of them. Those rough council houses we pass, although where exactly they all come from I don't know yet. You might know them, or their parents." Tracey continued.

Chris seemed uninterested and was walking away, leading a sweaty Tirus back to his stable, now back in moody 'Yard Mode.' Anna stood holding Penny.

"It's the parents I pity. And with just a few weeks before Christmas," she said, thinking deep. "Drink and drugs I'd heard. What a waste of life."

"Lets hope that it's a lesson to other kids not to mess about in cars," Chris spoke cold and bluntly as he led Tirus back to the stable, leaving the two girls to chatter and deliberate the causes and consequences of the crash.

Closing the stable door, Chris called over to Anna as she walked past with Penny, leading her to the stable, his face momentarily returning to a smile.

"Thanks for the great ride, your lovely company, and for you know what." He spoke somewhat cagily, with a coy smile and a rare twinkle to his eyes.

He looked at Anna warily, then over at Tracey, who stood in the yard with a grin, unsure if Tracey should know about the invitation, as he smiled at Anna.

Anna simply nodded, smiled, then winked, almost as a silent, secretive reply.

"No Chris, thank you. You've made my day. You really have."

Tracey suddenly remembered the planned Christmas lunch question and forgot about the local victims of the car crash she'd heard from a neighbour.

"Oh, I forgot. How did it go?" she asked in a whisper as she moved over to join Anna at Penny's stable, the pair almost dashing inside.

"Yes! He's coming," Anna replied happily, spirits instantly lifted.

Tracey shook her head, amazed he'd accepted Anna's offer.

"No! I don't believe it. You jammy cow! Wow. Wait until I tell Julie!"

"I'll tell you all about it and what we did on our ride when I've turned Penny out. You can give me a hand. It was great ride by the way. Fantastic day."

With that the pair untacked Penny and Anna began to quietly fill Tracey in on the events. Both women were enthralled by the thought of Chris coming over for Christmas, and spoke in an excited whisper, lest he should hear.

The two giggling children spoke in quiet tittering tones and didn't stop until they watched Penny chase off in her paddock and promptly roll in mud.

Chris had returned to being his usual moody self and after turning out Tirus, quickly sorted out some things in the barn, then disappeared once more.

Anna watched him vanish off in the Rover without another word.

She hoped it wasn't regrets about agreeing to Christmas Lunch.

But once again his brief sparkle had gone.

Would she ever be able to fully charm the Untouchable Mister Turner?

Time would tell.

Chapter 53

Before you embark on a journey of revenge,
begin by digging two graves.

Confucius

Dave Pearson's battered Fiesta was parked in a secluded lay-by, half a mile away on a country lane. The journey on foot to the entrance of the woods had taken him no more than ten minutes at a gentle jog, Pearson ducking into the cover of the hedges along the verges twice as cars passed; he unseen.

He paused at the opening to the woods, the drizzle annoying; both for deadening all sound, but also for soaking all it touched. However, it was also beneficial to his needs, when added to the darkness, ensuring only the foolish or brave were out in such conditions. Pearson considered himself the latter.

The primeval fear of the night was natural, harking back to an ancient time when uneducated people believed bad things lurked in the dark.

Bad things that committed evil. Nothing had changed.

Looking from side to side down the quiet empty country road, he cautiously stepped into the woods, the ground underfoot soft but firm, from constant vehicle movements. Damp leaves squashed like wet cotton under his hiking boots and large heavy drops fell from the trees onto his head, adding to the annoyance and cold. Moving forward a few yards, he stopped; turning to look back out at the circle of grey indicating the way back to the road he'd come.

Then onwards he strode, into the intense dark where he headed, the change in levels of grey and black noticeable. Breathing deep, and knowing the need of his cause, he turned his back to the light and proceeded cautiously into the dark. His eyes adjusted, making out the black outline of trees, the track a black line within the grey trees, guiding his way with no need for a torch; the edges of the track defined, holding some shape and form in the gloom.

Used to walking in the dark, he was soon striding confidently along the woodland track, feeling proud and strong as he proceeded, moving deeper into the depths of the woods, knowing his goal. Cautious, he'd intermittently would stop, turn around, listen and move his head, checking for sounds, to ensure no one equal to or as skilled at night walking as him, were behind.

He was good, but always knew he may not be alone.

Many he sought also hunted, in a variety of ways.

And he could easily be their quarry.

The trees opened out at a junction within the woods, providing the traveller with a option for direction. Pearson knew where to go. Further along, the track widened, the trees being sparser and undergrowth reduced in the winter.

After a short time, before him another circle of light began to emerge, indicating the track had reached an exit from the woods. Steadying his pace, and moving carefully to the edge of the track, he skirted to the side, settling beside a small tree, kneeling down and gripping the trunk. His destination.

Before him lay a clearing, with paddocks and clearly defined white buildings some distance away. Their features were hidden in the gloom; shapes dimly visible, but various lights provided guidance to their form and exact location.

Pearson shuffled down onto his haunches, his heart thumping, a mix of fear and excitement flowing. He loved this aspect of his craft, knowing what he wanted to do. It took great courage to even think about doing what he was now actually doing and get this far. It was dangerous.

He sat within the damp undergrowth, beginning to settle down, ignoring the cold, damp and darkness. This was what he did best. Wait and watch.

A twig cracked a few yards behind him.

His head spun around. A shot of adrenaline automatically pumped through his body and his heart rate increased, his senses being doubly alert.

Scanning the darkness and the source of the sound, he stared into the gloom of the woods behind. Purposefully he held his breath, slowly regulating it, his senses alert, eyes and ears searching out the area of the noise. Nothing.

Instinctively he spun his head back toward the clearing and buildings, as an illuminated rectangular of light appeared, set within one of the buildings. Within the distant light of the open door the silhouette of a person appeared. Pearson looked on intently, watching the rectangle of light fade as the person exiting the house closed the door and moved away from the house.

Action. Activity. Someone was moving about down there.

Two sudden cracks. Twenty yards away. Clear. Distinct.

Pearson's head spun in the direction of the sound.

Someone was moving inside the woods too. And behind him.

Pearson's blood pumped, nostrils flared, heart raced furiously as he spun his head back around, to stare sightless into the darkness of the woods.

His eyes and ears scanned, trying to suck in any sound, shape or movement.

Another crack. Small. Then another, defined and heavier.

'Fuck me! There's someone else in the woods. And close!'

Pearson's breath became heavy, but he regulated it, as he furtively scanned the dark woods behind him, seeing and hearing nothing.

Instinct once more urged him to look back down into the clearing.

The distant silhouette, back-lit, stood gazing up towards the woods.

'Shit! They must have heard something. Double-shit!'

Pearson's whole body froze. Then he wanted to urinate.

'Had the person heard something too? Maybe the other person? Not good.'

Pearson spun his head around, crouching lower along the tree trunk, hoping he didn't break the sky-line and present a shape to whoever was also stalking in the woods behind him with an identifiable position. Maybe it was a trap.

Head moving cautiously from side to side, he scanned the interior of the woods with both eyes and ears, but heard nothing.

Then he saw the shape. Clear and distinct. A human form.

Standing boldly and clearly upon the track down which he'd walked.

Pearson's heart and mind went into overdrive.

'Who the hell is that? Why are they here? Are they following me?'

He felt himself drop lower, momentarily losing sight of the stationary, silent dark form, clearly standing on the track; looking and listening, just like him.

'Were they looking for him. Or the person in the clearing?'

Pearson dare not answer the question.

Bright lights suddenly flashed up from the clearing.

The roar of a large engine broke the silence of the evening.

Pearson's gaze turned to the clearing as the vehicle moved, headlights cutting into the gloom and heading towards the woods. Ten feet from the edge of the track, on the forward edge of the woods, he knew he was clearly visible to anyone driving up the track, especially with the aid of full beam headlights.

'Stay put or run and hide? Think. Quick! Action.'

The sound of heavy crashing through the undergrowth behind, coming from where he'd seen the person stand moments ago, and now seemingly fleeing too, provided him with another option. Freeze with terror and panic.

Pearson's body went rigid as he looked into the woods, scanning the dark to determine any defined shape of the person now fleeing; but he saw nothing.

Aware of the rapid movement of the vehicle, its beams hitting the forward edge of the woods and already casting a yellow glow to the woods, Pearson knew he had to act, and act quick. Just as the other person behind him had.

The headlight glow increased and the engine growled like a hungry beast.

'Duck and hide. Now! Go!'

Pearson obeyed his own command, diving into the soaking wet undergrowth, hoping his dark green jacket and low profile, set away from the track, would not be spotted. He only had a few seconds to find the answer, as the dark Range Rover appeared, roaring from the clearing and into the woods.

Holding his breath, Pearson forced his body into a small ball as the vehicle raced by, roaring on into the woods like a mythical dragon seeking out a gallant knight set out to slay it. Him. He wanted to raise his head, to look at the driver as he raced by, but knew he must remain hidden and unmoving.

The vehicle roared past, cutting a wave of light through the dark woods, sending a glowing orange beacon before it. Pearson did then raise his head, eyes scanning the gloom for the signs of his fellow night stalker, but he could see nothing save for the red taillights of the now disappearing Rover.

The deep roar and bright red lights enveloped the woods, then the swathe of orange light before the vehicle rapidly diminished as the Rover swiftly moved on through the woods, then exited them where he'd entered. Its engine roar died off as it moved onto the distant road, returning the woods to silence.

Pearson sighed heavily, now unsure how to proceed, the purpose of his well planned and careful mission destroyed, not now sure if he was even alone.

For thirty minutes he sat beside the tree, unmoving, the drizzle blown into the woods from the clearing soaking him through and causing him to shiver.

Hearing no more from the woods, other than the drip of rain, odd tree creak, or gentle rustling sound of creatures moving in the undergrowth, but nothing as heavy as his earlier stalker, he assumed he was truly alone in the woods.

He checked his watch, the luminous dial dimly showing he'd wasted too much time. Cautiously he rose, breaking the skyline, his cold and aching limbs painful, but slowly coming into life. As he moved back onto the track, gazing into the gloom, his ears were tuned for any sound. His eyes scanned the dark of the woods before him, searching for any irregular shape or movement, wary of either the return of the Rover, or of meeting his fellow night-stalker.

'Who the hell would be out in these conditions?' Pearson perused.

But really he didn't want to know. Let alone meet them.

For fifteen minutes he moved slowly along the track, 'ghost-walking' as silently as any special-forces expert could have achieved. Then before him, the exit to the woods appeared, its dim arch of grey light most welcome.

Slowly and cautiously Pearson moved out onto the road, audibly sighing, relieved to feel firm tarmac under his feet and see night sky above his head, rather, for once, than a canopy of trees, despite the rain the sky released.

In the distance he heard a distinctive roar. The sound of the Rover returning.

Lights cut across the countryside, heading straight back towards him.

He froze, the distant headlights turning about the twisting road, but clearly back towards his current exposed position, the roar of the engine increasing.

Pearson scanned his options.

Thick dense Blackthorn hedge to one side. Ditch to the other.

He had no choice.

As the lights suddenly drew level, threatening to illuminate him and reveal his unwelcome presence, he threw himself into the ditch; just as the headlights swung around the corner, illuminating the place he'd stood seconds earlier.

Pearson slid down the side of the ditch, rolling into the stinking contents, his breath gasping upon contact with the ice-cold water. The Rover raced by above, back into the woods, like the evil dragon returning to its lair.

As the engine roar subsided, soaked and stinking, Pearson clambered out of the ditch. Cursing loudly, fist shaking, his anger burnt deeper.

It hadn't been a good night. Not at all. But there'd be other times.

Revenge was sweet. And also patient.

But he also held a question.

'Who the hell was the other stalker?'

Chapter 54

Liar liar pants on fire!

William Blake

"Where are you Bruce? I need to know. We need to talk. Now!"

Bruce froze upon hearing the familiar voice on his mobile. 'Shit!'

Now was not a good time to speak. Definitely not now. If ever.

He'd instinctively taken the call without checking the caller I.D. just as he was leaving the pub.' As he now glanced at the phone, the number displayed wasn't one he recognised. The caller's original number had been barred.

The caller had changed their phone number to catch him out. Clever bastard!

The woman on Bruce's arm teasingly stuck her tongue into his free ear.

He squirmed, playfully pushing her away, raising a finger to his lips. The high-heeled, tottering blond beauty grinned, swaying like a gale-swept tree in danger of falling, but raised a corresponding finger to her full red lips too.

"Sorry sweetheart, but I've just left a long group meeting. Very busy."

His female companion lurched forward and playfully grabbed at his crotch, pushing him against the damp wall, her hands going inside his jeans.

They'd had a meeting all right. And would be having another very soon.

Bruce tried to concentrate upon the caller, but was interrupted by the woman before him, her hands everywhere, pressing her body against his, her hands clinging onto him for support, before suddenly she vanished from view.

"You what sweetie? I can't hear you properly. They don't have a good signal down her in Ipswich. Yokels. They don't even have phones or electricity. They communicate with two hollowed-out potatoes and a bit of tight string."

Bruce felt a hand grasp at his groin, fingers fumbling. The sharp fingernails extracting his manhood were in danger of circumcising him. He glanced down to see the blonde hair of the woman he'd been drinking all night with in the local Norwich pub, close to his waist. He knew where this would end.

His attention turned the anxious caller. Or he attempted to, anxious himself.

"What do you want Lucy? Is everything okay back there in Leicester?"

He felt his jeans slide down from his waist and cold night chill upon the tops of his legs. Warm hands and a warmer face promptly replaced the cold air.

He winced with pleasure, shielding the mouthpiece of the phone.

"You called the Ipswich office and they told you I'm in Norwich? Oh, I see."

He cursed inwardly. 'Bastards! Double bastards.'

Bruce winced and sighed heavily. But not just from being found out, and his secret discovered, but due to his manhood entering the warm moist mouth of the woman crouched at his waist, whose name he could not even recall.

Blond, slim, horny, dumb and drunk, was all he needed to know.

He arched his back slightly, moving it away from the cold, damp brick wall, and in doing so forced himself deeper into the warm, enveloping mouth of his new companion, the pleasure increasing, trying his best to restrain himself.

"Yes, I am in Norwich now. But only for a few days to sort out their mess too. It's all linked. Both branches. I forgot to mention it. It's not important."

He began to explain, but his words were cut short as the woman below gave his testicles a squeeze in order to finally gain his full attention. It worked.

"No I'm not with that 'Fucking Bitch' as you aptly call her. There's no need to get upset or aggressive. Yes, I know and agree she's a 'Skinny Ugly Whore.' I can tell you're upset, but there's no need to be or to get violent. Again."

The action below was becoming heavy; just like the call.

"Well, that's a bit of a strong thing to say about her, and you can't really do that to someone. It's illegal. You'll do time. A long stretch for something like that. Maybe life. But don't worry I haven't spoken with her. Honest."

The activity below was becoming intense, followed by a harder squeeze of his reproductive glands, causing Bruce to wince and almost drop the phone.

"Sorry Lucy, I'm in the middle of something important right now."

Bruce sighed heavily, biting his lip, trying to keep control.

"I'll have to call you tomorrow. Something's come up."

Chapter 55

Don't blame people for disappointing you.
Blame yourself for expecting too much.

Unknown

A mile from where Bruce was having his encounter with the unknown but willing blond, his mobile now switched off, Chantelle met up with Sarah.

The pair stood beneath the usual dripping drainpipe and Chantelle was clearly relieved to see her friend, although Sarah could not work out why.

It'd been a few days, and at first Chantelle was apprehensive to mention anything, knowing how Sarah could be on occasions; also, she didn't want to make herself look too concerned. In addition, she didn't want Sarah to think she may be trying to steal a customer. Chantelle, being tall, slim and naturally blond, was much more attractive then Sarah. She was smaller, and although she still had a nice figure, didn't have the extra height and fine legs Chantelle was blessed with, and most men found very attractive. Also Sarah had wavy brunette hair. Chantelle was blond. 'Gentlemen prefer blondes.' It was true.

Most of the time Sarah was relaxed, and so long as they were paying, she was more open to any customers 'special needs.' More so than Chantelle, who openly admitted she wouldn't do some certain things simply for the money. Luckily she didn't need to. Her looks brought her some regular, good-paying decent clients. However, Sarah would do almost anything to feed her habit.

Perhaps Chantelle had been wrong about Lesley or had a different client, but with a similar looking vehicle. There were so many, and lots of their clients drove flash 4 x 4's, many being living in the country. They seemed to have lonely, quiet home lives, but highly active sex lives. And usually lots of money.

She broached the subject with Sarah gently, as a cold wind blew around their legs, the drizzle chilling adding to the overall chilled and depressed feeling.

"How'd the guy with the dark Rover go? The one I was worried about?"

Sarah eyed her suspiciously, seemingly thinking, and then recalling.

"Oh yes, him. Good. Horny guy. Why?" Her tone became defensive.

"I just wondered," Chantelle replied cagily. "Lesley picked up a similar guy a few weeks back. Remember? I was a bit worried he may be a bit dangerous."

Sarah knew about Lesley and what happened. She shuffled her heels, blew into her hands, eyes scanning the streets, trying to delay a response, thinking hard, trying to hide the truth as she looked cautiously at Chantelle.

"No, couldn't have been him. This guy was very good. A bit kinky, but nothing serious. Paid me double as well. I would have done it for free."

Chantelle was not convinced, but nodded to acknowledge.

"Hope he might be a regular. I could do with some," Sarah added smugly.

Before Chantelle could reply a police car cruised past on the opposite side of the road, slowing down as the driver saw the two women by the drainpipe.

"Oh shit, that's it I'm off," spoke Sarah without a second thought and turned away to head down the side street. Chantelle didn't need another word. She separated from her partner, heading straight off in the opposite direction.

"Bastards! See you later. Take care," Chantelle called as she marched along the pavement, turning down an alley, which cut deeper into an older part of Norwich. Trotting on her toes, stiletto heels occasionally clattering on the old cobbles, she was down the alley and out of sight before the police car pulled up to the side of the pavement, the drizzle and gloom obscuring her image.

The policeman grinned, seeing the two fleeing women, with nothing he could do. The two women had technically committed no offence. But he'd at least moved them along, keeping the streets of Norwich cleaner and safer for a few more hours, and thus done his bit. He'd earned his money. Maybe. Also it was cold and raining. The police car was warm and dry. And there was paperwork and forms to fill in. He wasn't getting out of his warm dry car to chase anyone in this weather; not even Jack the Ripper. He drove on.

As Chantelle tottered along the damp cold streets, she sighed, knowing it'd be another quiet and penniless night. But it was time to head home and get back in the warmth. She simply needed to get herself a few more good-paying regular clients. Money men. Or maybe a rich husband. Highly unlikely.

She had considered getting out of the game for good. But how else could she earn a living? She had no education, other than natural survival wits, learnt from living on the streets. Who'd pay her for the limited talents she had?

Such men were few and far between. Rocking horse poo.

What chance did she ever have of finding one? None.

Deep in thought, she passed such a well-dressed man, who had a blond, slim woman, not dissimilar to herself hanging off his arm. He was a hunk. A real catch. Maybe a model. Catalogue stuff. Maybe men's underwear. Or socks.

Jealously Chantelle regarded the woman holding onto the man, all smiles and giggles. She was clearly drunk and hardly able to walk in high-heels, her legs moving haphazardly like those of a concussed baby giraffe.

Bruce glanced at Chantelle, cocking her a crafty wink.

Chantelle simply grinned at the hunk and sighed.

Clearly it'd been a good night for some.

But not a good night for others.

There was always hope.

Things might get better.

Maybe.

Chapter 56

Better to fight for something, than live for nothing.

General George S. Patton

It'd been almost a week since the tragic car accident and life moved on. At least for some, but not for those who'd just lost children, and who wouldn't be able to celebrate Christmas with those who were now sadly gone.

P.C. Roger Burton was not having a good time either. He'd only had a few hours sleep when Joan, his ex-wife-to-be, had called on the phone about the divorce. Again. He wished the annoying bitch would just leave him alone.

Why couldn't a hole in the ground open up and swallow her? Maybe it could.

A new motorway bridge. He knew such people. Sadly, it was illegal. Pity.

As well as bleating on about what she wanted, or needed, she'd also finished off by adding she had a new boyfriend. An Italian businessman. Into leather-goods she'd boasted; whatever the hell that meant. Certainly not bondage, as Joan was too much of a prude. He'd suggested it one night, and she'd said a definite no. Said he was a weird pervert and needed to see a head doctor.

Joan proudly announced her new Italian Gelding was taking her to Naples for the Christmas period. He had a villa. Hot-tub as well. Lovely!

Burton cursed. Did he really need to know that? Shit-stirring bitch!

He'd managed just a few hours sleep before going back in. They were short staffed due to a 'flu outbreak. More like a 'Christmas shopping bug' outbreak.

The low, pale yellow afternoon sun was just fading and the chill setting in. He was due to re-interview the tractor driver who'd found the boys bodies. All three victims had been officially identified and named, but no cause yet. Locally it'd been big news, and even been on the national news. Burton had hoped he might get his face on the TV, but the Chief Constable had made his own bullshit speech about the terrible tragedy, and it was all kept brief.

Everyone was convinced the three lads were simply racing about. Reckless. Most likely on their own, driving too fast, when they'd hit the deer.

They'd lost control and the car had hit the tree. Boom! Fuel tank burst.

Evidence of THC in the bloodstream from smoking cannabis, and some traces of alcohol had not helped with any support, despite their young ages.

Another sad case of youths, alcohol, drugs and fast cars, the Chief Constable had stated sadly. Maybe lessons to learn, he added in a dull monotone pitch.

No one had any doubts the accident was caused by youthful stupidity.

Except maybe Burton. There were issues on how the car caught fire so easily, although it was accepted the impact was severe enough to rupture the fuel lines, then ignite on the hot engine block, or possibly the occupants cigarettes.

A melted, empty fuel can, blown free from the car, appeared to have been in the rear of the car and had added to the ignition, causing the severe burning of the youth thrown clear. It seems he burnt alive. Unlike the others.

Full forensic tests still had to be undertaken to close off the case formally, but as there were few other clues, no witnesses, and no evidence of any other vehicles seemingly being involved, it was highly unlikely anyone would pursue it further. Most people's minds were now on Christmas. It would wait.

The skid marks at the junction before the crash were considered to be where the boys had turned the corner too fast. This possibly led to the car being out of control when it consequently hit the deer and then the tree. Simple answer.

No one else was going to waste any serious time looking for theories that weren't there, with budgets being tight and overtime currently being stopped.

The unsolved prostitute murder earlier in the year had cost the division a lot of time and money, with no clear result. So a tragic, but simple RTA, caused by three stoned youths, was going to be wrapped up as soon as possible.

The media had a good session, blaming bored local louts reeking havoc on quiet country lanes, endangering life, by racing about in fast cars whilst drunk or stoned. Various community leaders asked for more local services and cash.

But it'd all soon die down with Christmas now so near.

As Burton drove through Salheath he was in that state of mind where driving is almost automatic, mind on many things, and he was only half aware of the road ahead. It was only after he'd driven over them, then recognised the opening into the woods opposite, he realised where he was. A revelation hit him and automatically pressing his foot upon the brake, he abruptly stopped.

The honking car horn behind caused him to swiftly look up into his mirror. It was only then he noticed a car immediately behind, almost crashing into his vehicle, swerving past, to avoid a collision. He blew out in relief as an irate little old lady drove alongside, glaring and waving an angry fist at him.

PC Burton looked at her in amazement as she passed, the old woman's head shaking, saying something he wouldn't have understood, even if he'd heard it.

He smiled to himself, shaking his own head at the old woman's gall.

This time looking in the rear-view mirror, he reversed the police vehicle back, slowly, to check what he'd half seen and had so caught his attention.

He stared at the road in front of him. Skid marks.

They were distinct and clear. Fresh rubber skid marks.

Sweeping from the opening in the woods and out onto the road.

A vehicle must have been travelling at speed to create them.

And recently. Within a few days maybe.

What made him smile was where they came from.

Chris Turner's Farm. Horsewater.

Someone had come out of the woodland entrance in a hurry, skidding on exit, and leaving a large amount of their vehicle's rubber on the road. Why?

Interesting. Very interesting. His smile broadened.

Now was a good time to visit that yard again. And question Mister Turner.

But fate as ever decided otherwise. A call came through. "Disturbance at Witherswick. Violent assault in progress. Any cars in the area please respond."

The skid marks could wait. A bit of aggro,' was right up Burton's street.

Perhaps the country beat wasn't so boring after all. Real action. A fight!

He radioed through he was less than five minutes away. On went the siren and blue flashing lights and was off; roaring the Land Rover along the country lanes like a rally driver or maybe a bored, drunken, local lout. Both similar.

He soon found the eight council houses, located on a lane surrounded by wide open arable fields. Burton knew them from when he'd had cause to visit one of the occupants before, also for aggressive behaviour, whilst drunk.

The vision before him was indeed a 'Violent Assault,' as radioed through.

He'd assumed whilst travelling to the scene that the disturbance would be over with by the time he got there. Maybe two locals were arguing over a piece of sugar beet, or a mouldy potato for their evening meal. With fresh rat.

Most fights or domestic violence are very short lived, lasting for only a few blows, with much swearing and not much else. It is only professional fighters who can fight for any long period, without either dropping from serious injury, exhaustion or concussion. As he pulled up, Burton noted the two men in the front garden of one house were not doing too bad a job at showing how prize-fighting should be done, and still exchanging blows like pro's.

The larger built of the two men had the fatter one in a headlock, and was proceeding to smash his head against a wheelie-bin. The fatter man was tearing frantically at the taller one, grasping at an already shredded T-shirt, looking for some form of purchase and something to grip other than skin.

Without any hesitation, and always ready to join in a fight, or even provoke one, Burton bumped the Rover up the verge, threw open the door and was out of the vehicle in seconds. His tool-belt already on, he went pounding up the pavement, flick baton already drawn and raised in his hand.

Unseen by him, a screaming woman suddenly appeared from no where. She yelled at Burton not to hurt her husband, and waved a plastic broom at him, threatening to insert it somewhere physically inside the policeman, without any anaesthetic. Burton was amazed for a split second at her speed and actions, but more so for her aggressive comment and proposed action.

'What the hell was the other guy now doing?' he thought.

Burton countered a deft strike to his head from the woman's flaying broom with his baton, shattering the handle and sending it flying from her hands and across the unkempt garden, instantly frightening the woman. She stepped back swiftly into the safety of a doorway, slamming the door, suddenly not wanting any more action, nor any protection to her delicate husband.

"Okay you guys, break this up please!" Burton yelled at the two wrestlers.

The side of the wheelie-bin split open with the impact of the fat guy's head hitting it, tearing open the fat mans ear, warm blood spraying over Burton.

Both men ignored Burton's cry and continued wrestling each other, with the wheelie-bin now somehow joining the fracas, being attached to a head, or arm, with rubbish, or potential food, cascading everywhere around them all.

Burton sidestepped the aggressive wheelie-bin, dodged the two burly men rolling about on the front lawn in rubbish and torn clothes, and quickly took stock on how to act; being half-tempted to let the pair kill each other.

Decision made, stepping back, Burton pulled out his CS spray and sprayed it direct into the faces of the two men. He remembered he should have shouted a warning first, so for good measure did so, but only after; as both men quickly released each other, frantically rubbed their painfully stinging faces.

Once the melee died down, the broom woman came outside with water to rinse the stinging spray from the men's eyes, and the full story became clear.

Patrick Smith, the bigger guy, had been on a drinking binge. He'd then gone to the house of Brian Wilkins, father of Barry Wilkins. Both were parents of the boys who'd died in the car crash. Patrick Smith had kicked in the front door, blaming the other for his son's death, as he was driving and thus at fault. The fight began in the lounge. Wilkins wife phoned the police after her husband rammed Smith's head into their tropical fish tank; glass, fish and water filling the lounge. The incident continued with varying blows, destruction of furniture, and thus spiralled out into the front garden.

Both men now sat on the cold muddy patch of ground, which made for a front garden, bleeding and in torn clothing. However, instead of raining insults and blows, the men now sat in the mud hugging each other, both in tears, along with former broom-wielding wife, all weeping uncontrollably.

It was a sight Burton had never seen before and made even him emotional. He loaded the crying hulk of Patrick Smith into his car and the back-up car, driven by Bill, took away the still weeping Barry Wilkins. Molly Wilkins was left behind, to clear up the mess and try to retrieve the now dying fish.

The light was fading rapidly as Burton drove back through Salheath and the cold setting in fast, with the sky a dark grey with a subtle pink hue. Snow was forecast, and even a City-slicker like Burton could tell that it was coming.

Once again he drove past the skid marks outside Chris Turner's farm, and glanced down at them. He looked in the rear view mirror at the shaken form of Patrick Smith, face bloody, weeping eyes red. A beaten man in many ways.

"Don't worry Mr Smith, I'll find out what happened to your son. If there's anything suspicious, or anyone else involved, I'll catch them. My promise."

In the back seat, Patrick Smith looked at Burton, wary of the policeman and unsure what he'd heard. He had no reply, but nodded an acknowledgement.

Tiny wisps of snow, like dying moths, began to blow gently past the windscreen and headlights of Burton's Rover. He cursed silently.

The snow was indeed coming.

Chapter 57

Suspense is worse than disappointment.

Robert Burns

No one from the yard was hunting the week before Christmas, the fresh fall of snow not helping matters and resulting in the meet being cancelled again, as had been the previous meet, due to the poor weather. It happened quite frequently, especially if the ground was hard, frost potentially injuring the hound's feet, as well as being too slippery for the horses. Fog another reason for calling off hunt meets. Losing forty hounds in thick fog was not amusing.

The fresh snow they'd had overnight was nothing heavy, just a light, powdery covering, but it had been blowing in from the East in brief snow showers for the last week, usually melting during the day, and any flurries didn't last long. But it was enough covering to cause disruption to a part of the country where although the winters were cold, snow was still a novelty, but also a nuisance.

Chris was busy as ever; tending to matters about the yard, the estate in general, and whatever he seemed to do, dashing about from place to place, never seemingly resting, more so everywhere frozen or snow-covered.

His and Anna's paths crossed at the yard, but other than a shy, cheeky grin, and the occasional conversation regarding horses, he'd shown little attention, and they'd had no chance for another long chat or even spoke of anything related to Christmas day. Anna hoped it was all okay and even still on.

Anna still couldn't work out if it was nerves, shyness or that he simply didn't care. She was so used to Bruce, who was over people like a rash. Intense and full on, ensuring he was at the centre of everything, and everyone knew it.

But Chris was distant and insular. Once again Anna knew she was hoping for too much from him, and seeing things that weren't there, now beginning to understand what so many had said about him. No wonder he was single.

She realised he'd only accepted the Christmas lunch invitation as a matter of being polite, and not her hand in marriage. And it was also probably because Tracey was there too, that he'd agreed. It was obvious he had a soft spot for Tracey, but more so as a long-term friend, as well as knowing she'd been engaged to her partner for years, although he had no interest in horses either.

Chris talked to Anna of them both riding out again, which was encouraging, but bad weather, busy workloads and life in general had prevented everything from happening, so she could only see what Christmas day would bring.

That final week before Christmas everyone had either had gone Christmas shopping, or were saving their horses for the Boxing Day meet. Anna had hoped go out for a hack with Julie and Tracey again, however, the poor weather yet again was not on their side and seemingly conspired against them.

There had been a heavy frost and light covering of snow to stop them riding any hard tracks or on any of the roads, but she hoped they might get to ride out past the paddocks and on into some parts of the woods, as the tracks were soft and the tree covering would keep things within clear. She loved riding in the snow and wanted to see the snowy woods in stark contrast.

The cold spell and overnight snow had turned the roads coming through the village into potential death traps once more, with a layer of thin ice setting in, made worse with the flurries of light snow settling on top and compacting.

It covered up road markings, and more. Much more.

Anna had arrived at the yard as normal, waved at a busy Chris, who simply smiled and nodded. She went into the tack room, made a cup of coffee, then sat on an ottoman, listening to Tracey and Carol talking about Christmas.

The tack room was warm and cosy, despite smelling of damp, wet leather, sweaty horses and fresh coffee. It was scattered with bridle hooks and saddle racks, on which sat rows of tack, along with boxes brimming with brushes and countless pots of strange ointments and sprays to treat almost any equine ailment; past, present or yet unknown. Rugs in all colours, scented with horse sweat, were scattered about, or hung from a set of racks to the rear; the area so gloomy few ever dared to venture that deep alone or without a gas-mask. Everything added to the unique aroma only horse owners fully understand, or can physically accept, without wearing a full HazMat suit and respirator.

Fresh biscuits and cake mixed with the aromas. Carol insisted upon drinking only percolated coffee, and had her own brewing system in the corner, just for her, which filled the room with steam and a coffee aroma. Not horses.

The others used instant coffee; simply for speed, a large jar always seated upon the sink unit, beside a battered, yet well-used kettle. This would never pass any electrical safety or environmental health checks and even bugs were scared of it. Numerous mugs, many without handles, or with cracks that defied their liquid-retaining capabilities, were scattered on the worktop.

Anna had ensured she'd brought her own new mug, and also brought a fresh packet of biscuits each week, which were secured in an old toffee tin. Only the naughty and greedy ever took a biscuit; which was all of them.

Playful scorns of shame were issued when someone took two, which was often, and hence why the tin was always being refilled with a variety of treats.

Julie came bustling in, stomped a light covering of snow off her feet, and began speaking, moving over to the sink area to make a strong cup of coffee.

"Are we going to venture out in this snow then?"

"I'm game if you are," said Tracey. Anna smiled and nodded approvingly.

"Let's get our snow-shoes on!"

"Well I'm not going out. Too cold for me and too slippery for Tess," said Carol, always seemingly looking for an excuse not to ride.

"I'd better tell Chris that a few of us are riding out. Just in case he's in the woods. I'll pop over and let him know." Tracey called.

"Don't bother. I just saw him nip out as I came in. Dashing off in the Rover to pick something up. Maybe your Pressie Anna!" Julie grinned.

Tracey stood by the sink, tipping out her coffee dregs, face beaming.

"Did you know Chris is going around Anna's mums for Christmas lunch?" she announced jokingly, like a brash schoolgirl. "That's almost a date. Well it must be in Chris' books. Maybe he'll ask for your hand there too! But don't worry, I'll be there too, just to ensure there's no naughtiness."

Everyone turned to look at Anna, who flushed a deep red.

"And as he's going around, he'll have to buy you a present. I'd bet that's where he's going now. I wonder what he'll get you." Tracey grinned at Anna.

Anna playfully glared back, her face glowing, shrugging her shoulders, and seeing all the enquiring faces set upon her enjoying the playful banter.

"Sexy underwear!" Julie joked. "Black or white Anna?"

"Anna doesn't wear any, do you? She's all natural!" Tracey teased.

She shook her head, throwing a copy of a horse magazine at her cousin, who ducked to avoid the missile, which scuttled off into the dark area.

The woman all laughed, seeing Anna embarrassed, but still smiling.

"Actually, I prefer Electric Blue," Anna quipped. "Just like me!"

Chapter 58

The devil took him to a high peak and showed him
all the kingdoms of the world and their glory.
And all this I will give to you, if you fall down and worship me.

Matthew 4:8 / 4:9

Roger Burton drove through Salheath one last time in his Mazda MR5 that morning, as he was about to head back to London to spend Christmas with his parents. He was happy to get away from the smell of clean air, mixed with pig shit and sugar beet, and inhale fresh smog and diesel fumes instead.

And get to see some good old friends. He also loved his mum's super huge Christmas lunches, which she prepared with all the trimmings and more. He especially loved her bacon wrapped sausages and homemade stuffing. He'd not had a proper good roast in an age. Not since Joan left. The thought of the steaming gravy and Yorkshire puddings and thick slices of turkey made his mouth water as he looked around at the bleak bare countryside all about him.

The weather was cold and dry with the back roads icy and the brief flurries of blown snow staying in sheltered areas. Here it clung in lumps and patches, especially in areas where the weak winter sunlight hadn't reached; usually where trees or hedges had sheltered the ground and the frost had remained.

This is what'd happened to the area of road outside Chris Turner's property, which still held an interest for Burton. He'd parked up and now looked at the stretch of road outside the entrance. It was still covered in a layer of ice and snow. Burton knelt down to look at the compacted frozen water and wiped at it with his leather glove. He cursed as his hand glided over the hard slippery surface, knowing its secret was held below. Hidden, but there. Hearing a loud engine roar on the road behind him he rose up and swiftly spun around.

Spinning, almost slipping on the ice, he turned to see a dark Range Rover roaring down the road towards him at speed. Heading straight towards him, and his sports car, Burton stared at the Rover and at Chris Turner's face.

The large 4 x 4 loomed straight before him. Terror set in his eyes, Burton saw Turner smiling. The Rover encompassed all his vision, taking over his world, dwarfing him as the massive vehicle powered towards him at speed.

Burton looked on as it smashed into his beloved Mazda. Onwards it continued, like an unstoppable tank on a destructive journey, all viewed as if in slow motion, crushing the flimsy Mazda before it. The sliding chassis smashed into his body, crushing him. The rupturing steel tore apart his body, like a peeled orange, spreading his flesh and blood over the icy road like a giant spatula; turning the light snow and frost covering of the dark tarmac into subtle hues of red, pink and orange, not unlike a deep winter sunset.

Burton's secret now lay hidden forever beneath his torn and bloody body, spread across the pink ice-covered road, crushed beneath his beloved MX5.

Blinking, Burton then noted Turner had seen the man before him, kneeling on the frosty road ahead of his parked sports car and had carefully applied the brakes, ensuring the Rover didn't skid on the ice, clearly cursing the stupidity of the person before him, whom he recognised as the annoying policeman.

Chris saw the policeman and for a few seconds had other thoughts. Choices. Options. Maybe life-changing ones, for both parties; but didn't take them.

The Rover slowed down as it approached the off-duty policeman's sports car, with plenty of room to spare. Just. But Chris made the policeman sweat.

Standing at the Mazda's bonnet, Burton shuddered and awoke himself.

He stared at the driver; the terrible thought that'd just run through his mind drifting away like a morning dream. Lost and gone. Was it a premonition?

Burton didn't believe in such shit. Or tried to convince himself he didn't.

Or was it a dark feeling he had about this strange man, who now peered at him from behind the windscreen of the killer vehicle, curiously looking at the pale-faced policeman. The Rover slowly edged forward alongside the Mazda, moving towards the entrance into the woods, then stopped alongside Burton, who stared red-faced at the driver. The passenger side window lowered and Chris Turner stretched across the wide seats to peer out at the red-faced policeman, a curious and unusual grin spreading across the horseman's face.

"Lost something?" Chris called out bluntly. He looked down at the stretch of road Burton had been examining, smiling upon seeing the ice and snow.

"A rather dangerous place to park up. Problems? I nearly hit you."

Burton looked flustered, thinking fast. "Yes, I mean no. Good bit of driving on your part. I shouldn't be in the road on a bend. Silly of me. I thought I'd got a puncture. Can't tell on these icy roads with low-profiles." He replied, unconvincingly, then wondering why he was apologising to the man he hated.

Chris looked at him coldly, with no reaction or emotion.

"Finished for Christmas have you?" Chris asked more politely, but as if also to establish why Burton was outside his property entrance in plain clothes.

Burton was fighting for answers; trying to appear in control. It was difficult.

"Yes, I'm off for a few days. Back to work on Boxing Day. Going home to London to spend Christmas with my parents," he replied, trying to sound natural. "What about you? Will you be having a big family Christmas?"

Burton suddenly realised the error of what he'd said, but then secretly enjoyed the thought of the horseman unable to enjoy a nice family Christmas.

Chris flushed, taking in the harsh meaning of what had been said, rightly or wrongly, then recovered, the crude comment washing over him.

"I'll be having Christmas at home with my horses. But they annoyingly can't pull crackers! Mind you, I may then get a few of the girls over in the evening and have one of our wild all-night Christmas orgies. Maybe get a few of the horses involved too. Who knows! Enjoy yours. Merry Christmas!"

He grinned at the policeman as the tinted window rose up and the horseman vanished from Burton's view. The Rover moved on into the entrance, to then disappear into the dark, consuming woods. Burton shook his head, watching the vehicle vanish, stunned by the horseman's cool and brazen attitude.

"Cocky bastard!" Burton cursed, shaking his head, glaring into the woods. "And a Merry Fucking Christmas to you! Tosser!"

He glanced down at the frozen road, knowing what potentially lay beneath and how condemning it could be. Questions could at least be asked.

He smiled, knowing the ice would soon be gone. And that he'd be back.

Turning, Burton climbed into the Mazda and slowly pulled forward on the icy road, until he was clear of the opening and road bend. He then put his foot down, keen to get away and begin his well-deserved break. He'd only gone a few yards on into the village when he realised he was going too fast and hit an icy patch as he approached yet another of the many twisting bends.

Foot on the brake, wheels locking, the sports car began to slew sideways. The rear drifted straight across the corner of the bend and onto the other side of the road, hitting the grass bank opposite with a gentle thud. Burton cursed.

Coming around the corner at that very moment was a small car, the driver being the same old lady he'd met a few days previous in the patrol car. The woman braked at the sight of the car before her. It slid momentarily, but she managed to steer out of the skid, and onto the wrong side of the road at the last second, avoiding the Mazda. Burton looked on in horror as he saw the old lady's car appear, then sighed as it luckily missed his car by inches.

A furious fist flew up at him from the old lady; shaken wildly once more, her face one of outrage as she hit the horn and cursed. Shaking her head and tutting loudly, she carried on driving, leaving the red-faced policeman.

Carefully, checking the road, he got out the Mazda to see what damage he'd done to his precious car, now embedded against the earth bank.

He saw the damage. Minor and merely cosmetic, but still annoying.

Sighing heavily, his breath misty, he looked up at the sky.

'Happy Christmas P.C. Burton.' He thought the seasonal message

Head shaking, he now couldn't wait for Christmas to end.

Bring on Boxing Day.

But maybe he wouldn't have been so keen.

Not if he knew what was coming.

Chapter 59

Silent night, Holy night, All is calm, All is bright....

Franz Xaver Gruber

The Boxing Day Meet, by tradition, is the key hunting meet of the year for most hunts; and historically held at a focal point within a town or village square, rather than private land or estates, or at a public house or upon fields

Lately, due to the issues regarding the hunting ban and protests, it'd become an important day for hunts to use as propaganda and media exercise. Mostly to boost public opinion, for traditionalists keen to uphold the practice, and to counter increasing anti-hunt demonstrators attempting to disrupt the hunts.

The Boxing Day hunt meet held great traditional meaning, and until mad 'politically correctness' took over, winter hunting scenes were common images on Christmas cards. Nowadays, people seemingly just prefer Robins.

However it is seen, on both sides of the hunting debate the Boxing Day meet is a major event, and one where each side attempts to ensure they have full and solid support. For the hunts it is a time to maintain the tradition for the large numbers of general public who turn out to support this unique day; who for many, it is part of their Christmas celebrations. It is a showpiece event to many supporters, who'll only ever see a hunt meet one day a year and want to witness the unique spectacle of horses and hounds together in a town centre; upholding an age-old tradition, so close to being lost and show the sport is still thriving in a changing environment, despite being under a spotlight.

For the anti-hunt brigade it's a time to demonstrate the barbaric nature of the sport. Their followers are usually a mix of people, whose key aim is usually to disruption and the end to what they regard as a pointless evil activity.

Hence, when on Boxing Day, the battle lines are clearly drawn, both sides aiming to make their presence clearly known, with ugly scenes often resulting.

Because of this deep friction, and propensity for violence, the media embrace the Boxing Day meets with wide open arms, sending out TV crews and as many photographers from local papers as they can, wanting the best cover.

None would openly admit they were looking for the best fight scenes or images of bitter rivalry, just as no one would admit they enjoyed watching a car race, only in the hope there was a massive crash, but that no one gets hurt.

This Boxing Day meet was no different and the Shoteton Hunt were meeting up in their traditional venue of Windford. A small Norfolk market town, here they'd form up in the historic and picturesque market square, usually to great support by many locals, before setting off. Then they'd hunt the land and fields nearby, just as they'd done so for many years before the ban, and now more even more keenly since it's reprieve and the Hunt's true revival again.

They usually had a good number of the general public watching, but as ever, they'd requested through the various members, for as many ridden members to attend, as well as car and foot followers, to give their hearty vocal support.

Reggie, Steve and Lady Carter, as Hunt Secretary, had all been on the phone over the past week, contacting people who regularly or occasionally hunted with the Shoteton, to encourage and cajole them into attending this meet. Some less able, but keen supporters would turn out with their mount, only in order to sit on the horse in the Market Square and then take it back home.

This year they hoped to have fifty riders, which for the Shoteton was a good and would mean the square was packed. The phones had rung right up until Christmas Eve, by which time most people either had other thoughts on their mind, or it was considered impolite to intrude. All concerned were hopeful this year it was going to be an excellent Boxing Day meet, and one they would remember for many years to come. It would. It'd go down in history.

On the other side of the hunting debate, at PAACE, similar plans were afoot with its supporters were called too, getting set for one of their key days too.

Dave Pearson was ensuring as many supporters as possible would be giving up their Boxing Day lay-in to come out and protest and support the cause. This year he had some new support, which was making him buzz inside.

He'd been speaking regularly to Adam Yates.

Adam was his new 'best buddy.' Or so he hoped.

Adam had promised Dave strong support. Very strong. And lots of it.

Dave had also been on the phone to Izzy, ensuring she'd be out for Boxing Day too. He doubted she'd miss it, but had had limited contact with her since the last PAACE meeting, and hadn't met with her face-to-face since then.

That didn't mean he hadn't seen her, or didn't know what she was doing; simply that he'd not spoken to her directly. But he'd seen her. Often.

She simply hadn't spotted him. He'd made sure of that. He was too good.

Izzy had her usual life to live, and had been busy with workloads and other events to attend. But when he finally got to speak, and discussed arrangement, she needed no encouragement. It still made Dave wonder how Izzy could swap from enjoying the hunting lifestyle so much, to suddenly being so against it. Or so she professed. Especially the Boxing Day meet. It was such an important date in the hunting calendar, that few missed it. Either side.

He still wondered if she secretly wished she was there; proudly mounted on a fine horse, drinking her 'stirrup cup' before the crowds of onlookers, with Steve by her side, laughing and joking with the other stuck-up scum.

He stopped thinking. The thought of Steve Harrison, let alone being with her, the pair happily riding out and laughing, made his blood boil furiously.

Dave was unsure whether to tell Izzy what he had planned, knowing she had strong views on any 'heavy' protests against the hunt, or being too aggressive towards them. Using violent behaviour was not acceptable in any form to her.

Disrupt, pester and annoy. But to what avail? Kick heads instead. Better!

Dave again wondered if this was because she secretly liked the members of the hunt, respected them, and didn't wish to see any real harm come to any of them. Or whether she did truly believe in peaceful and non-violent action, but firm, active protesting. In his opinion all who hunted were scum. Filth!

Viable and legitimate targets for any attack, so long as it solved the issue.

He'd decided he'd not tell Izzy about the extra support hopefully coming this year. If indeed they all came, they'd bring something the Shoteton had never seen before. It'd wake them up. No more than they all deserved. And long overdue. And he had have Adam Yates to thank. Whoever the hell he was.

The Essex and Herts.' Hunt had strangely abandoned their meet this year. They traditionally met up in the centre of Ofley, but due to a row with the new labour council, which had taken over since the last election, it'd voted to not permit the Hunt's presence in the town centre, under local enforcement measures. Instead, the hunt would meet on a large private estate owned by one of the Joint Masters and only invited guests would be permitted to attend. They had good security and plenty of farm workers to keep guard. Bastards!

Adam Yates knew of this and apparently, much to Dave's excitement, knew of a number of the 'Essex Boys,' as they were affectionately known. They were a group of aggressive Anti's who frequently sabotaged and annoyed the Essex and Herts.' Hunt. They were also linked to an anti-vivisection group and were well organised, but also highly aggressive. They were often written about in the media for personally attacking scientist's families in their homes.

They made Dave and Izzy's antics look like a group of Morris Dancers taking on an armoured unit of the Waffen SS with back-up! Unleash hell. Please!

Adam Yates, still really unknown to Dave, seemingly had good contacts. And lots of them. He knew of a number of these characters, and worse it seems.

Dave was still unclear what Adam actually did for a living; having tried to find out, but he didn't care. After the initial meeting, he'd persuaded Dave he could encourage a few carloads of 'Hard-core Anti's' to come up to Windford for the Shoteton meet, instead of going to the abandoned meet at Ofley.

They wouldn't lose their Boxing Day fun, and Dave would benefit from the chaos. All winners. Adam would organise and finalise details, stating all the mob needed was petrol and booze money. Adam had seemingly supplied it.

It was with this feeling of anticipated excitement, yet unknown danger, which buzzed around Dave Pearson that Christmas Eve as he finally went off Christmas shopping for his mum's present. Difficult with limited funds, but she was easily pleased. Very easily. Pound Store. But he had other issues.

He couldn't decide if he should buy Izzy a surprise present or not. Problems.

It'd be an excuse to give her something, not just for Christmas as such, but to offer it as a 'thank you' for all her help during the year. She could then read into the gift any true reasons or emotional feeling he may have for her herself.

Dave hated Christmas, simply because he had no money, but also he couldn't think what to get her, and how she might respond. Problems indeed!

He decided he'd buy a box of chocolates, but wouldn't buy her a card.

They used up valuable timber resources, even if from re-cycled paper, and were pure commercialisation. Besides, he wasn't sure what to write inside.

The thought of Christmas Day at his parents wasn't too exciting either. He'd have to endure his mum's greasy gravy and raw potatoes, and always insisted he ate Turkey, despite his protests about being vegetarian. He'd eat it, purely in to keep the peace, but also secretly because he liked it. He never bought meat himself. As no one he knew would know he'd ever eaten it, it didn't really matter if he lapsed just this once. After all it was Christmas. Just once!

His brother would be missing again. But that was seemingly permitted.

He did 'Real Conservation Work,' his parents would always boast, and was usually abroad somewhere working undercover for a big organisation.

Dave both admired his brother, but was also bitterly jealous of him too.

His brother had the life he wanted. Bastard! Clever, lucky bastard!

He worked for various worldwide environmental charities, carrying out undercover investigations and surveillance work. It was serious stuff. Highly dangerous, and he could be anywhere from a Brazilian rain forest, to a fur factory in Canada. He'd take film and photos, and collate information for various organisations. He was good at what he did, and Dave respected and worshipped him, but also wished he could do such work himself.

Many times his brother had spoken with him, and said he'd look into getting an opening for Dave. But it never happened. Too many complications.

Dave had a criminal record for possession of cannabis. Numerous times.

It didn't help, prohibiting travel to some foreign countries. His brother was clean. A leading light. Dave was the part of the family who'd failed to shine.

In his parents opinion he was merely a candle. His brother a bright torch.

But he'd endure Christmas Day and maybe get to speak with his brother via a satellite phone. Possibly in a jungle, a desert, or onboard an anti-whaling ship.

He'd be anywhere rather than at home, eating water-pumped turkey and dry packet stuffing, all washed down with extra-greasy gravy. Yummy! Not.

His dad would go on about football, get pissed up on stout, tell crude jokes and then fart all day; stinking the house out with the smell of rotten sprouts.

He was not looking forward to it, but he would endure it.

Boxing Day was what he was really looking forward to.

Maybe an event he could boast about to his brother.

Dave felt it'd be a day to remember. For a long time.

He wouldn't be wrong.

It would be a day he'd remember.

Forever.

Chapter 60

Meekness is to be strong and able to do harm,
but restrained and gentle.

Matthew 5:5 - Bible

'Where the fuck are you?' began the text message.

Bruce wished he hadn't checked his bleeping phone.

'Xmas Day tomorrow. I'm here alone in my Sexy Santa outfit. Why aren't you here? I've got you a Special Pressie. Very Special!'

Bruce winced, wondering what the hell to do. Shit!

He knew it was cruel and mean not being back in Leicester with Lucy, but he had better things to do. He'd never been one for Christmas, but had planned to see his parents in Leeds and was now travelling there, as annoying as it was.

He'd then dash straight back down to Norfolk for Boxing Day.

He had plans for the Feast of St. Stephen. Big plans.

Wasting time with Lucy, dressed as Sexy Santa or not, didn't fit his plans. She'd have to wait, and so would Santa, sexy or not. He hadn't even bought her anything either. Nor would he. As far as he was concerned she was history. Hopefully the lack of Christmas attention might make her see sense.

'Are you with that fucking skinny bitch? Dead Whore!'

Bruce winced as he checked the next spiteful text message.

Anna wasn't a skinny bitch. She was tall, slim, with great legs. Stunningly beautiful, had a great bum and gorgeous grapefruit-sized tits.

He felt himself harden at the memory. He loved to kiss the small scar she had on her buttock, caused by a dog-bite when she was a child. Beautiful arse.

God what an idiot I've been. A total Pratt. Bruce thought long and hard.

But there was still time to put things right. He and Anna were meant to be together. It was so clear and he'd convince her. He'd win her back. He always did. But get Christmas over first. Then get her away from that dwarf.

The phone bleeped again. Bruce sighed, carefully checking the mobile cradled in his lap, his attention deviating on the road up to Leeds.

He didn't recognise the number. Had Lucy switched phones?

'Other night was great. Really good. Hot! FYI You may need pharmacist before they close for Xmas. Rash. Itchy. See you soon - Jenny. XXX.'

Bruce was curious. Jenny? Who the hell was Jenny?

He searched his head, assuming it was a wrongly sent text.

Memories of the blow-job and quick shag behind the pub, then another longer one in the back of his Audi estate flooded back.

Oh yes. That was Jenny. He must have been pissed too.

Had he really give her his number? Idiot. He was really getting slack.

Nice bird, great tits with long legs. Good face. But no brain. Loser. Also no future. What did she want from him. A new house?

He re-read the message, his face flushing. Rash? Itchy? Oh shit!

The phone bleeped again. His sigh was heavier.

Hopefully not Jenny again, wanting a date over Christmas. Or cream.

It wasn't Jenny. Nor Santa. It was Satan.

'I'm going to find that bitch and kill her. Happy Xmas!'

Bruce regarded the mobile with wide eyes and swallowed.

It was from Lucy again. Who else.

Which 'bitch' did she mean? Anna or Jenny?

Bruce swallowed hard. He didn't want to know. But did.

With a firm press of his thumb the mobile was switched off and thrown onto the Audi's backseat with his overnight holdall.

A nice serving of his mum's Christmas Pub and big dollop of Brandy Cream tomorrow would put everything right. Along with some large single malts with dad. Aberlour. His favourite whisky. It'd all then be forgotten.

Then a long snooze as soon as The Queen began chatting.

No offence Ma'am.

He smiled at the thought, his attention fully on the road.

After Christmas everything would be back to normal.

Lucy would be gone. History. Forgotten.

Who? He smiled.

Anna would be back in his arms. And his bed.

Just where she belonged.

Everything would be sorted.

No problems. He hoped.

Chapter 61

Twas the night before Christmas, when all through the house, not a creature was stirring, not even a mouse.

Clement Clarke Moore

It was chilly in the yard on Christmas Eve, a stiff breeze blowing loose hay and straw, which collected at the base of the stables. However, as is typical, warmer weather was due to blow in overnight for Christmas Day, and the snow would probably be gone before dawn. Therefore, apart from a few sheltered places, once again, it wouldn't be a proper white Christmas. Grey.

Anna was huddled up in a fleece jacket, ready to hang Penny's haynet when she spotted Chris wander across the yard. Like most of Christmas Eve, he'd been busy all day and it was the first real time she'd had to see or speak with him and nervously approached, hoping all was well still as he'd said little.

"Still okay for tomorrow?" she enquired apprehensively, hoping the answer was still yes. If not, there'd be a lot of disappointed people, primarily her.

"Certainly. I'm looking forward to it," he said eagerly, smiling, looking long at Anna, as if absorbing her grey eyes. "Sorry I haven't had time to speak. And so long as you're still okay to help in the morning. Please let me know if it's a problem or if you need anything from me." Chris sounded apprehensive.

"No problems at all. I can't wait either. I'll be ready, bright and early. It'll add to the fun. I feel like a ten-year old!" Anna raised her hands together, clasping them almost childlike and grinned at Chris excitedly, her eyes twinkling.

He blushed back, as if unsure of how to reply, his emotions hidden.

The pair stood in silence for a few seconds and Anna suddenly hoped he'd open up more tomorrow. He was evidently shy and awkward with woman, but she hoped he wouldn't be a crashing bore. Knowing how welcoming her dad was, and the fact her mum was also smitten, she doubted he'd have five minutes of peace. Then she knew her grandmother would be there too.

That was where the danger lay. She was as clever and wily as any old fox, and could instantly work people out. It was a great strait to have; however, when mixed with a mind that had little conciseness, and a loose mouth, it was a dangerous combination. Anna hoped her grandmother wouldn't see in Chris something hidden, and then embarrassingly announce it aloud to the world.

Tracey was bad enough. And with that, as if reading her thoughts, her car arrived, pulling up the door flying open. She stepped out, striding boldly across the yard she openly winked at Chris. He grinned back cheekily.

"All set for tomorrow?" she asked, stepping toward the pair; timing perfect. "I hope you've got your best clothes dry-cleaned. No wellies or horse shit allowed at my aunt's! Morning suits and Top Hats only! And wash too!"

Chris chuckled, smiling broadly, knowing Tracey's cheeky banter.

"I've ordered extra mistletoe. Should be enough to cover the whole house, so you'll not get away without having a snog."

Chris glanced warily at Anna, who in turn looked steely at Tracey.

"Not for her stupid. For me! I haven't had a kiss off you since that Hunt Ball and few years' back. Remember? I can't forget it. Never washed since!"

Chris glowed red, glanced at Anna, then looked down, head shaking.

Anna blushed, and then glanced at the pair, wondering what secret history the pair might harbour. Lots possibly. But then maybe nothing.

Tracey regarded Anna, cheekily tapping her nose with an extended finger.

"Our secret is safe Chris. Beside, you were too drunk to remember. But I still have the psychological scars. And also a few physical ones too if I look hard enough. I've a huge scar on my chest; where you stole my heart!"

Anna burst out laughing and a red-faced Chris simply grinned wider.

"Have you been drinking?" Anna asked her free-spirited cousin. "I hope not, especially if you're driving, and with that new creepy copper nicking people."

"Fat chance of that. I'm just high on Christmas spirit. You know me. I love the special day. I hope the happy fat man brings me lots of expensive goodies. I'm sober today, however, tomorrow I'll probably be pissed. Not that you'll notice any difference. So watch out Chris, I'll be after you! You can pour your brandy sauce over my Christmas puddings any day. Just name the place!"

With that Chris could take no more, burst out laughing and shook his head, walking away from the two women and towards the barn. He had work to do.

Anna playfully punched her cousin's arm and dragged her towards the tack room, before she did any further damage.

"I look forward to seeing you first thing. Nice and early!" Chris called, raising a hand, just before disappearing into the barn. "I'll have the kettle on."

"Are you excited?" Tracey asked seriously, but with a squeal. "I am."

Anna simply nodded. "Yes, but nervous too. For both of us. Him and me."

"I still can't believe you got him to come. He rarely goes out socially, except to a few key events for the Hunt," Tracey whispered, looking at the barn.

"Do you think I'm reading too much into it all?" enquired Anna, anxiously.

"Who knows cousin," replied Tracey. "I'd just enjoy the day, act natural and see what happens. All I know is that if you've got him to leave his house, then you must have something he likes. Maybe that neat arse and those long legs!"

Anna chuckled and playfully pulled down the peak of Tracy's baseball cap.

"Time for a quick cuppa. Then home to get my wrapping finished."

"I hope you bought me something big and very expensive," Tracey chuckled. "I only accept designer brands. Along with the original receipt and bag!"

"I got your present from the Pound Shop. Half price!" Anna grinned.

"Well so long as you've bought Fred some carrots, I'm happy. Let's hope tomorrow brings us all much joy and happiness. Put that kettle on!"

Chapter 62

Somewhere over the rainbow, way up high,
there's a land that I heard of ....

Harold Arlen / Yip Harburg

Dawn was settling down with a large glass of Chianti and cheese twists, as she prepared to watch The Wizard of Oz on TV for the umpteenth time. It was one of her favourite movies and always warmed her spirits. She was in a good mood and couldn't wait for Christmas Day tomorrow. One sleep left.

She'd bought Gavin a number of special presents, even though he'd told her not to bother getting him anything this year, as he wasn't buying her anything.

They'd agreed they needed to save money, wouldn't buy presents, and maybe get something each in the New Year when things were reduced. Sensible.

Dawn had agreed, but still decided to buy him a few secret presents.

She'd put them on the new credit card she hadn't told him about.

There were only a few items. Nice treats. Special. Like Gavin.

Just a few hundred pounds worth. Not too much.

She'd worry about paying it off in the New Year. Maybe.

Dawn was determined to make up for what had been a bad year for them.

She knew she'd not helped matters. They'd gone down hill rapidly over the last year, but she couldn't really work out why. She wasn't the easiest person to live with, a little demanding, but was grateful for all Gavin did. Her mood swings, tantrums and dependency, didn't help. And Gavin had to work so hard to keep them afloat. And he did work hard and often late.

She knew she should do more for him. And she tried. Sometimes.

Gavin always forgave her and would always be around.

He was always dependable. Although he had a few faults, like all men.

Predictable and dependable were his key points. That's what she needed.

Despite what she put him through, he'd always be there for her. That was why she wanted him. And needed him. Like oxygen and water.

He came into the lounge with a bottle of 'Christmas Beer' Dawn had bought him specially, when a mobile phone bleeped, indicating a text message.

She looked up at him. He looked at her.

Dawn got up and checked her mobile phone.

"It isn't mine. It must be yours," she said.

Gavin looked unconcerned, rarely getting text messages. He waited a few seconds then got up and casually, yet discreetly, and checked the phone, which was set upon the side unit beside a small table lamp. Dawn looked on curious, knowing Gavin hardly received text messages or any mobile calls.

Gavin felt uncomfortable, knowing Dawn was looking at him, feeling a little uneasy, but externally displayed nothing. Or tried too. Not very well.

"It's from Dave at work. Wishing everyone a Happy Christmas and plenty of beer! Daft bugger. Probably out and already half cut," he said with a chuckle, after scrolling through the message and seeing Dawn watch him closely.

"That's nice of him," Dawn replied, no longer concerned, munching a cheese twist, and turned to watch the TV ready for her favourite movie.

"Come and sit beside me Gav'. Wizard of Oz. Our favourite. I love the scarecrow. He's so sweet. Like you. You remind me of him."

Gavin winced and uneasily sat beside her on the 'not-yet-paid-for' sofa. The first payments were due in February. Less that two months away. Worrying.

He sat somewhat uncomfortably for a while, munching awkwardly on flaky cheese twists he didn't want, before making his excuses and getting up to go to the bathroom. Dawn, eyes on the TV, paid no attention as he left, unknown to her, taking his mobile phone with him, hidden within his pocket.

Once in the toilet, checking Dawn hadn't followed him and was genuinely engrossed in 'Oz, he quickly sent his own reply to the earlier text message.

The text message finished;

.... Happy Xmas 2. Love U Sweetheart - Gav XXX.

The messages, sent and received, were deleted. As agreed.

He returned to the sofa, upon which Dawn was curled.

She smiled at him, wrapping an arm around his leg as he reluctantly sat close beside her. Then he endured the film he also hated.

He wasn't the Scarecrow. He had no brain. Gavin did.

Gavin was the Tin Man. No heart.

Leastwise, not for Dawn.

Maybe he was also part Lion. No courage.

For now. But he was getting stronger.

The dangerous text message had at least made him happier.

It would now make Christmas more bearable. Just.

Chapter 63

We wish you a Merry Christmas.....

Christmas Carol

Reggie had invited Martin and Sharon to The Grange for a quick Christmas Eve drink or two. Or maybe more. It was a tradition he liked to uphold, helping to keep the bond with his Huntsman, which was already strong.

Sharon in turn never missed an opportunity to have a free Cherry Brandy or five, especially at the expense of Reggie. In addition, it gave her a chance to chat with Elizabeth; a rarity, unless speaking out hunting, when usually things were frantic, and Sharon was chasing about fields, whipping-in the hounds.

The woman could now talk shop. Important stuff. Horses.

Elizabeth didn't go out often, usually staying at home, but enjoyed the odd social night with other hunt members. Reggie however appeared to do what he wanted, whenever he wanted. Sharon felt a degree of pity for Elizabeth.

Almost simultaneously, three mobile phones bleeped, denoting they'd all received a text message. The occupants of the room all regarded each other with amusement. Reggie's head flicked between his two guests and Elizabeth.

His phone sat silent in the kitchen. He glanced about at the three bodies.

"Blasted phones! No peace, even on Christmas Eve." Reggie cursed.

"It's only because no one texts you," Elizabeth responded to her annoyed husband, his cold glance enough rebuke for her to realise she'd spoken out of tune, even if Sharon sniggered and Martin had a grin on his face.

A red-faced Reggie falsely chuckled, trying to make light of the sore matter.

Sharon openly looked at her phone first. She smiled.

"Helen. Wishing me a Happy Christmas. And says I've got to go out with her after Boxing Day. Girl's Christmas night. Yes!"

Martin glanced at his phone, his face red, but he remained quiet.

Sharon, seated opposite on a green baize Edwardian style chair, looked at him curiously. "And yours?" she enquired curiously. "Secret admirer?"

Martin's cheeks flushed as red as Reggie's when in a rage, then he smiled, chuckling as he looked towards Sharon. "Mum, getting all modern. Wishing me a happy Christmas. Text messages! She'll be getting a computer next!"

All heads silently turned towards Elizabeth, whose eyes nervously flitted from face to face, but tried to avoid Reggie's cold and burning glare.

The three eagerly sat looking on, drinks in hands, curious smiles on their faces, awaiting the name of the secret texter to Elizabeth.

"It's from Bertie," Elizabeth announced, placing the phone close to her side. "And Ginny. I mean, Virginia. Both wishing us all a happy Christmas."

Elizabeth felt her cheeks glow. She wasn't a good liar.

And she knew Reggie knew. He glared silently at her.

"Anyway Reggie. How about opening another bottle of Cherry Brandy?" Sharon slurred the words, but added a chuckle; breaking the sudden unease that had settled in. "This bottle must have a hole in it, as it's all gone."

"The only hole in is at the top," Martin chipped in. "And its contents have somehow gone mostly down your neck!"

Reggie chuckled and rose with a smile to fetch a fresh bottle to refresh everyone's glasses. As he rose and wandered over towards the drinks cabinet, unseen by Reggie, Elizabeth quickly deleted her text message.

Glasses refreshed, Reggie raised his and made a toast.

"To all of you. Good health and a Merry Christmas."

The soothing red liquid was heartily swallowed.

"And here's looking forward to a memorable Boxing Day Meet!"

All four happily nodded in agreement.

It would indeed be memorable.

Chapter 64

Life is a great disappointment.

Oscar Wilde

Dave Pearson received a text message too that Christmas Eve night, as he strolled alone through the quiet streets of Norwich; a gift-wrapped present for Izzy under his arm. He stopped beneath a dim streetlight to read the message, then smiled and nodded to himself.

This alone had made his Christmas. Maybe.

It was the confirmation for which he'd been waiting.

Adam Yates. His new best mate. Maybe.

The news wasn't as good as he'd hoped, but it still made him smile and walk on with increased vigour. The message confirmed the number of Anti's Adam was bringing, or that he'd encouraged to come to Windford on Boxing Day.

Not as many as Adam had hoped, but still a good number extra. Action!

He smiled to himself as he headed towards Izzy's flat, located by the river, in an up-market section of Norwich. It still amazed him how she could swap between the differing lifestyles, and also where she got her money.

He knew she had a sales or marketing position in a posh company, using the experience from when she worked for herself. He knew who the company was, and Izzy's office too, but he never asked fully what she did for a living.

He wouldn't dare. And besides, he deemed it to be rude.

As he headed up to the new block Dave breathed onto his hand to check how badly his breath stunk. Not good. He flipped a small mint in his mouth, then adjusted his best combat jacket, as he pressed the bottom door buzzer.

No one answered. He waited and pressed again.

Still no answer came from the intercom for Izzy's flat that permitted access to the entrance lobby through the electronically operated door lock.

He felt the lead weight of disappointment build in his belly, pulling down harder as he looked at the present for Izzy tucked under his arm.

Just then a resident excused himself from behind, wanting to gain access to his own flat. The man input the code into the digital door lock and moving past Pearson, entered the block. Dave waited a few seconds for the man to enter the lobby area, watching the entrance door slowly swing shut, before carefully thrusting his foot in the bottom of the door, jamming it open. He allowed the man to clear the lobby and disappear up the internal stairs, before flicking the door fully open with his toe. He grasped the leaf, pushed it fully open and entered the exclusive building. He was in. So simple really.

Slowly heading up the stairwell, excitement building within, he moved up two flights of stairs to then proudly stand outside the door to Izzy's flat.

A slight tingle ran through him, now being so close to where she lived. He'd seen it from a distance many times, and watched her from across the way through the apartment windows on numerous occasions; but he'd never actually stood outside her door. He'd never dared, nor had reason, until now.

He adjusted his combat jacket and pressed the doorbell. Again no reply.

Cautiously he put his ear to the door, listening intently.

Nothing could be heard inside. 'Damn! She's out.'

Harder still he pressed his ear to the double-glazed glass.

"Can I help you?" came a slightly feminine male voice.

Dave leapt, turning to see the source of the voice.

It was from behind. His heart thundered as he span round to see a man standing in the door of the flat opposite staring coldly at Dave.

In his early forties, with balding hair, dark square-framed glasses, his skin was pale, almost white. Overweight, he had a curious and pompous appearance, and reminded Dave of a Witchetty Grub. He was probably a Bank Manager.

The pink fur slippers did nothing for him. Not good.

"I was looking for Izzy," mumbled Pearson, cautiously.

The man silently regarded Pearson, scanning him intently.

"I don't think Isabelle is about at the moment. Out."

His manner was forthright, but also worrying. Creepy.

Alarms rang in Dave's head. Homosexual Bank Manager.

"Left with some guy earlier today. After lunch I recall. Muscular chap. Quite nice looking and well fit. Well I thought so. He'd do for me!"

The man raised his eyebrows and grinned, tittering effeminately.

His eyes once more ran upon Pearson's body. Worryingly.

Dave felt the small knife in his pocket slide into his hand.

He'd have happily slid it across the man's flabby gut.

"I can take the present for you and pass it onto her when I see her next, if you want. Probably tomorrow morning. She usually goes for a run. Every day. Regular. Very fit. If you like that sort of thing."

Dave knew. He'd seen Izzy go out in her running gear. Many times.

The man smiled a sickly, dangerous smile. His eyes ran up and down Dave once more, absorbing his image, as he looked at him intently, before staring.

Dave felt warning bells rattle loud. He pulled himself more upright, coughed to clear his voice, and tried to sound more masculine.

"No, that's okay," he said, trying to add a degree forcefulness to his tone.

"I'll give it to her another time. I see her regularly. I must go. Things to do."

"Shame," replied the vile creature. "What a waste."

Dave regarded him coldly. The hidden knife was now firm in hand.

For a moment the pair stood in silence.

Dave thought of slicing the man's face off, but knew there were cameras in the lobby. It wasn't worth it. Also it wouldn't bring him any closer to Izzy.

It'd be a bad move, although most likely highly enjoyable.

"I'll be seeing her in two days time. I'll give it to her then," Dave replied firmly and turned abruptly, dismissing the fat man, heading back for the stairs.

The fat man sighed; tutted loudly, shrugged his shoulders and then shuffled his pink slippers back inside, closing the door.

Dave scuttled down the stairs, entering the chill night air and looked up at the sky, cursing at life and all of the shit it seemingly brought him.

The streetlights obscured most of the stars, which were slowly being covered by a fine blanket of warm cloud drifting over with warmer weather.

He regarded the gift-wrapped present in his hands, and then tore away the decorative paper. Opening the expensive box of chocolates, he began shoving several in his mouth, as he headed back towards his damp, lonely bed-sit.

For him it wasn't such a good night after all.

Christmas?

Bah! Humbug!

Chapter 65

Twinkle, twinkle little star, how I wonder what you are!

Jane Taylor

It wasn't only Santa Claus who was busy Christmas Eve. Out in the darkness, alone on a country lane, someone was busy resolving a potential problem.

It'd been there a few days, and the owner of the problem was aware of its possible implications. It needed resolving. Certain people were clever.

They had all types of scientific data, details and testing equipment, and could discover such hidden secrets. Unless such secrets were destroyed or removed.

Such was the operation. Using a combination of petrol, sand, salt and various brooms, along with cunning and hard work, the issue would be eliminated.

It wasn't an easy task, but was helped with most people being indoors, preparing for the big day tomorrow. Thus, the roads were all deserted.

But it was an important job. One that had to be done. Tonight.

The brief orange glow of flame and small plumes of black smoke, as petrol burnt upon tarmac, swiftly drifted unseen into the night sky. Momentarily it lit up the dark depths of the countryside, before rapidly dying down to darkness.

Once completed, it left the person smiling. Job done. Result.

High up in that sky the stars shone bright, although cloud was set to drift in, bringing warm weather, and so the brief spell of snow would rapidly go.

Hence the importance of the job and urgency to complete tonight.

Above rose the mighty constellation of Orion. The Hunter.

The three stars of Orion's Belt shone bright, pointing as always from East to West, with the stars from his sword pointing down to the lesser known constellation of Lepus, The Hare, which sat at the great hunter's feet.

Pausing, they regarded the stars, which made a fitting pair of constellations. Orion - The Hunter. Lepus - The Hare. A perfect match.

Admiring them, the observer once again spoke their silent prayers.

Just as they did every night. To remember those gone, but never forgotten.

And to give thanks for surviving another day.

Orion watched over, until the task was complete.

Then light clouds magically began to drift across, as if the great hunter was drawing curtains on the evening's work; no longer needing to keep watch on his fellow hunter. They could now retire safely for the evening, knowing the deed had been done and their secret was safe. As were they. Once more.

Task completed, they returned to the warmth of their home, closing their own curtains, and began preparing for a big and important day tomorrow.

For some it had been a very good night.

Chapter 66

Every traveller has a home of his own,
and he learns to appreciate it the more from his wanderings.

A Christmas Carol – Charles Dickens

Chris woke earlier than normal on Christmas morning with a strange feeling of excitement he'd not known in many years. He rose from his bed, stretched and looked out the side window and into the yard. In true English Christmas style, a warm front had moved in over night, the temperature had risen a few degrees, and all the remaining snow had melted and there was no frost.

No picture-perfect 'White Christmas' everyone dreams of, but instead, it promised to be a mild, sunny day. Autumnal almost. Good British weather!

Donning his smelly 'mucking out' clothes, he headed down to the kitchen, automatically switched on the kettle, to be met by a yawning, stretching Max, only now, somewhat reluctantly, rising from beside the warm AGA.

"Happy Christmas," he muttered with a smile, patting the glossy black and tan head. Opening the door, he let Max run off into the dark yard to explore, the automatic security lights lighting the way as he dashed about, urinating up the stables. Maybe Max would find a fresh policeman lurking somewhere to eat for Christmas lunch, Chris humorously thought, his spirits high.

Taking the freshly made mug of coffee with him, he went out into the yard, glancing at the numerous stable doors, with still snoozing horses within, opened up the tack room and began to mix the horse's feed. It wasn't long before he heard the sound of a vehicle coming into the yard. He checked his watch. It was only 5.15am. Anna was early, very early, which was good.

Chris looked out the tack room and saw Anna appear from the darkness, strolling down through the illuminated yard towards the stables, Max jogging up to her, his black stump of a tail wiggling. As he approached she gave Max his second Christmas head pat of the day, it being warmly received.

"Happy Christmas," Anna called to Chris, beaming brightly, despite looking slightly tired. Her face seemed more lined than normal and small puffy bags lay beneath her eyes, giving them a sleepy appearance. In a small way it made her look more vulnerable, childlike, and even more appealing. Chris gazed at her somewhat dreamingly and Anna appreciated the long look, smiling back.

"Good morning," he replied. "Ditto Happy Christmas and all that stuff."

They both paused, regarding each other, as if wondering what they should do or say next. The pair simply ended up embarrassingly smirking at each other.

Anna desperately wanted to give, and then hopefully receive, a Christmas kiss. However, she thought it too bold and up front to ask, especially knowing how bashful and retiring Chris could be, so blushed and gently looked away.

"I'll get Penny sorted first, then help you, if that is okay," she said. "Once she is out of the way I won't be fussing after her. Then it'll be all work."

Chris stood momentarily silently looking and thinking, before replying.

"That'll be fine. You do realise I very much appreciate you doing all of this for me and helping out. And especially for inviting me over for lunch."

Anna blushed in the dark, the subtle lights of the yard hiding her tone.

"My pleasure. It's just a pity I'm not at my best first thing, looks or mind. I'm not a Lark. Still half asleep I think. I'm more of a owl-type person."

"Well you're a fine looking Owl to me," replied Chris with a grin, looking away sheepishly after he'd spoken. "I'll be getting on then. Come and find me when you've got Penny sorted and we can see what needs to be done."

"If I need anything, I'll give you a hoot!" Anna quipped with a chuckle.

With that Chris walked off grinning, leaving Anna to wander to the tack room, where she flicked on the kettle, ready for a brew. She quickly sorted out Penny's breakfast, fed her and rugged up as the horse eagerly ate, despite it being slightly earlier than usual. Anna turned her out in the dark paddock, the air surprisingly mild and welcome, after the cold snap. Penny wandered off, sniffing the ground, somewhat unaccustomed to the earlier start.

Chris had already turned out two livery horses, so Penny was not alone. Anna quickly mucked out the stable, re-laid it, filled haynets and water buckets, so it was completely ready for when she returned later that evening and was done.

She wandered across the yard to find Chris mucking out one of the liveries.

"How can I help? I'm at your service, ready and waiting!" she quipped.

Chris looked up with a smirk, long-handled fork in hand.

"Grab your tools and do next door if you don't mind. It'd be a great help."

"No problem, Squire," Anna joked, touching the peak of her baseball cap. "That's why I'm here. But don't beat me too hard me Lord. It is Christmas!"

She noticed Chris chuckle and smiled to herself, pleased he understood her childish sense of humour, as she went off to get the barrow, tools she'd used for Penny and quickly began mucking out the stable next to Chris.

Anna felt she should make conversation through the partition dividing the two stables, but he seemed content working away silently next door, and was slightly dubious about disturbing him. Then Chris surprisingly spoke, asking her about any favourite past horses, riding and general horsey chit-chat.

Anna was amused by his warm, chatty nature, and hoped it'd bode well for the day. It wasn't long before he'd finished the stable and looked in the Anna's stable, who was also close to finishing off, the pair working hard.

"What's next Boss?" she jokingly asked, looking up, when both of their attentions was caught by a vehicle coming into the yard. Julie emerged, bright and early in the gloom, and wandered down the yard laden with a large bag.

"Good morning and Merry Christmas," she called, seeing Anna's head appear. Chris' head popped out of the neighbouring stable and he grinned.

"Hi Chris. Happy Christmas to you too. Two busy bees. Good to see!"

He smiled and nodded, Anna stepping out into the yard, fork in hand, then joined at her side by Chris, the pair looking like a couple. Almost.

"I have a pressie each for you two," Julie announced, pulling out two smallish gift-wrapped presents. "Nothing special. And I've kept the receipts!"

"I bet it's the same as last year, but in a different colour!" Chris grinned, as though he knew he'd get something from Julie. "It'll be great! As usual."

"I've put all of your presents in the tack room," he said, unusually smiling for such an early morning. "Same old stuff and no receipts! Like it or sell it!"

It amused Anna to think Chris appeared to buy presents for everyone at the yard; not something she expected, but indicated he was obviously kind.

Anna blushed upon receiving her present from Julie, glad now she'd bought some emergency presents for the various people at the yard, just in case.

"I've got yours in my car." Anna informed her. "I'll go and get it for you." With that she headed off towards her car and Julie eagerly followed. Then when out of earshot, grinning from ear to ear, Julie whispered to Anna.

"I hope today goes well. Wish I could be there. It'll be great for Chris to get out and I am hoping for good news tomorrow. Perhaps I should buy a hat!"

Anna blushed. "Well I hope he enjoys it too. I won't expect too much. It will just be nice to give him some company for this one special day."

She opened her car and placed Julie's present inside and gave Julie hers in exchange. Both women smiled knowingly, then walked back towards the stables, chatting about anything other than Chris, knowing he'd likely hear.

Julie quickly busied herself with Bonnie, putting out the anti-social horse, mucking out and relaying the bed, so all was ready for later, before saying her farewells and chasing off to prepare her own festivities with her own family.

Tracey also appeared not long after, racing about frantically in her usual disarray to sort out Fred and joked with Anna about being Chris's slave and reporting him to the authorities. She teased him about getting him beneath the mistletoe, then confirmed details on seeing her later at Anna's mums.

Then she too was swiftly gone, everyone lost in their own worlds on that one special day with much to do. A few others came and went; all watching Chris and Anna undertake the various yard duties usually performed by Chris and Sally, all offering Christmas wishes, and some pecking Chris on the cheek. Presents were exchanged and the yard had a general happy feel to it, although most people dashed in and out. Anna had never seen Chris smile so much.

Anna was surprised how well she and Chris worked together; she mostly turning out the various horses whose owners could not come down, or full liveries, with Chris mucking out and doing the harder, more physical work. Anna would fetch bales of straw or shavings on the large wheelbarrow, or fill haynets and buckets, and the pair working like a well-drilled team with little chatter. She could now better understand why Chris was usually so flustered, moody and spoke little in the mornings when she was at the yard, with so much to do, quite often on his own. Perhaps he wasn't such a grump!

Anna had curiously peeped inside the tackroom earlier, when Chris briefly vanished, and saw an array of identical presents laid out on the small table in the middle. A number of people who'd arrived and then left had taken their presents, as only a few remained, and as she returned to make a much-needed cuppa, she eagerly scanned for one with her name upon it. After a quick look, she felt downhearted when she couldn't find one. Then a shadow appeared in the doorway, making her jump and spin round, such was her keen attention.

"I've got your present indoors," Chris announced, almost appearing to read her thoughts, his eyes twinkling, lips curling into a grin at her shocked look. "I was going to give it to you at your mum's, unless you want it now?"

Anna blushed, almost embarrassed at being caught peeking at the presents; like a naught child on Christmas Eve, then smiled, staring straight at him.

"I have something for you too," she replied, grinning. "Something special."

Chris smiled back, hanging on the doorframe, and for a second they stood gazing at each other, like the day Anna had first come to the yard and their eyes had first met. He looked away, blushing, eyes cast down, before adding.

"I've also got your mum a little something." He spoke almost apologetically as if to break the atmosphere. "I hope she won't mind? Just a small gift."

"That's very kind. She'll love whatever you've got her." Anna blushed too.

"A ton of horse muck! Fresh from the yard trailer," he proudly announced with a grin, his eyes sparkling. "I'll drop it off in her driveway tomorrow."

Anna looked stunned, her mouth dropping, then smiled and laughed.

She jokingly swiped at him with a tea cloth, Chris ducking, then he dashed out the tackroom, chased by a laughing Anna, to almost run straight into a bewildered and startled Carol, who caught him in her arms, shaking her head.

"Children, do behave!" she joked. "Or you'll get no sweets or presents!"

A red-faced Chris looked into the smiling face of Carol holding onto him, as Anna stumbled out of the tackroom; tea cloth in hand, lunging forward, she was about to strike at Chris, then stalled, her bright red face glowing brightly.

"Wasp!" Anna announced, staring at Carol. "Big one! Christmas wasp!"

Chris blushed, freeing himself from Carol's grasp and sheepishly regarded Anna, who in turn looked down as though being rebuked by a Head Teacher.

"Well I'm glad to see you aren't getting on very well," Carol joked, regarding the pair like young teenage lovers; head shaking, but with a big genuine smile. "By the way, Happy Christmas! But it looks it already is for you two!"

The chuckling pair separated, Anna going back into the tackroom with Carol to make tea, Chris going to muck out and hide; something he was seemingly good at. Carol spoke briefly, curiously watching the pair as she pottered about the yard and swiftly did Tess, seemingly with no time for chatter today.

She then quietly, but seemingly proudly, informed the pair she was dining with Lord and Lady Burlingham; it being the first time the pair had entered Anna's thoughts, and Ginny's name had even been mentioned that day.

Chris smiled, knowingly, and Anna wondered what everyone else knew.

Anna and Chris returned to business, doing the remainder of the horses, casting the odd glance or grin at each other, but both mostly now keen on getting the tasks finished, so that they could both set off. Finally all the chores were done and most people had come and gone quickly about the yard, no one dithering, so they could enjoy the rest of the day with their families.

The weak winter sun, screened by thin cloud, had risen, and now cast a subtle yellow hue over the yard, as everything had been completed, and their hard work was finished. Anna suddenly felt nervous and apprehensive, almost out of place, knowing it'd now be time for them both to go around to her mum's for the 'Big Day,' whatever that may transpire to be. They'd agreed days earlier they'd both travel in one of Chris' cars, so he'd be free to travel back to the yard urgently if needed. If all went okay, Anna would travel back with him after lunch to help him get the horses in, then she'd drive back to her mum's for the evening in her own car, it left at the yard. All planned.

"I'm going to pop in, wash and change quickly. I don't think these stinking clothes are suitable. Do you want to come in the house and wait?" Chris asked cautiously, almost with a degree of reluctance and apprehension.

Anna nodded, strangely having never been inside Chris' farmhouse before.

"If you don't mind, or I can wait in the tack-room. I'm not bothered. I've brought some clean clothes to change into at my mum's. I'll wait wherever you want me to. I'm easy. Well, not like that! But give me a few drinks!"

Chris grinned at the joke, then indicated for her to follow him over to the house. Anna felt equally nervous, although she didn't know why. Even when she agreed to come to Chris's yard, it'd all been very informal and he'd briefly spoken with her in the tackroom, discussing the costs and various basic rules.

With a nervous excitably stomach, she wandered towards the white painted farmhouse, walking alongside Chris, almost shoulder to shoulder and pace for pace, noticing how much smaller than her he was as they walked together.

Even though it was only by a few inches, she glanced sideward, and then found herself almost stooping to compensate for the height difference. Chris didn't seem to notice and stomped ahead, got to the door and opened it. Max ran out to greet him and the new stranger, unusually so close to his master's territory. He sniffed Anna before confirming the identity of the intruder.

Chris beckoned Anna inside the house, and upon passing through the stable door, she was immediately impressed with the homely nature of the kitchen. For a single male, especially one who'd spent all his life working with horses and usually covered in dust, wearing scruffy clothes, it was clean and tidy, and a very respectable and well-kept home. She was at once impressed.

Chris led her on into the typical farmhouse kitchen, which had dark exposed beams to the white painted ceiling and walls and a traditional cast-iron Aga set within a brick chimneybreast, to which Max settled beside. Chris offered her a seat at a large pine table, on which sat an old mug, half filled with a cold coffee, alongside a selection of well-thumbed equestrian magazines.

"Would you like a drink?" he enquired. "The other mugs are clean!"
"No, I'm fine," she replied nervously, but chuckled. He silently nodded, then disappeared through an open doorway beyond the large kitchen.
"I'll wash and change, if you don't mind waiting?" he said, poking his head back through the doorway from what was a lounge. "I'll be quick!"
Anna simply replied with a smile, as Max moved, skulking around; as if on guard duty, then lay prone in the doorway between the kitchen and lounge, looking up at Anna. She felt uncomfortable with the massive but passive black guard dog almost laying siege, his eyes upon her, as she casually looked around the large and homely kitchen. It was clean and tidy, but showed signs of being lived in, with items laying about and boots cast about near the Aga. She heard sounds of movement upstairs and assumed the stairway was set further along, possibly leading off the lounge, into which Chris had gone.
Her eyes curiously flitting about, noticing a small white and black painted wooden door near the lounge door. It was old, but solid, the hinges original black wrought steel. She wondered where the door led, assuming it went into a cupboard, or maybe down into a cellar, like most old farmhouses had.
Curious of the thought of a house with a cellar, and what secrets it may hold, it both intrigued and spooked her at the same time. She found herself gently tapping her heel on the kitchen floor, hoping for a hollow sound to follow.
Max's ears pricked up at her discrete foot tapping action.
Anna paused, noticing Max's keen, unwanted attention.
The floor felt hard, but Anna could not determine if it was solid or not.
It could be stone or wood, and the cellar may not run beneath her, but it still held a child-like curiosity. The thought grabbed her more, wanting a result.
She thumped a bit hard with the heel of her Jodhpur boot.
Max sat upright, eyes fixed at her, looking slightly threatening.
Anna saw the dog's actions and ceased her tapping, feeling apprehensive and growing unsure of Max, who'd normally scare the hell out of anyone.
She also wondered if Chris might have heard her too. That too was scary.
It wouldn't do their relationship any good if Chris thought she was snooping about his house at the first chance. She also didn't want to be Christmas lunch for Max, as he stared hard and cold. Maybe he'd eat her in the yard.
Anna smiled weakly at the dog, and also to herself, her curiosity settled.
The floor had sounded hollow. There was a cellar beneath her. Cool!
What dark secrets may lie hidden away below in the dark cellar, she pondered. Buried intruders, nuns or vintage wine? Maybe all. She grinned.
Her vivid curiosity was then drawn to the wall between the apparent cellar door and Aga, as a couple of framed photos, seemingly of Chris on horseback were proudly hung. Intrigued, and bored waiting, she rose from her chair.
Max, still lying down, head between paws, softly growled; eyes flicking up.
Anna froze, glanced at the grumbling black dog, smiled, then cautiously eased back into her chair. Max went quiet. Message understood. Chris was clever.

Still curious, despite the huge hint from the grumbling dog, Anna slowly stretched forward. She shuffled her bottom upon the chair a few inches, as if settling, until she was merely perched upon the chair's edge. Her eyes were half set upon the attentive guardian; who permitted such movement, and half on the latest thing to grab her attention. Sliding her feet, she managed to sneak forward and cast a look at the largest photo, set proudly on the dresser.

It was of Chris, leaping over a huge cross-country water jump fence, seated upon a large Bay. She didn't recognise the horse, but glanced at the image of the person standing beside the fence, cheering him on. A very familiar face.

Virginia Burlingham. As clear as day. Fist raised, cheering on her man.

She stared long at the photo, hackles up more than Max's.

What place did she hold in Chris' life? Anna wished she knew.

Sounds above and the thud on timber stairs warned Anna of movement and she shuffled back into her seat and lifting up a random magazine, just as Chris appeared in the doorway, smiling broadly. Laying the unread magazine back down, she looked admiringly at the blushing man stood before her. He was dressed in black trousers and neat blue cotton shirt, but no tie. She smiled.

It seemed strange seeing him dressed so smartly, Anna only usually seeing him wandering around the yard in scruffy clothes, or in full hunting dress.

"You look smart. Very smart!" she politely stated, making him blush redder, before he stepped fully into the room. "I thought you were someone else!"

"Should we take my smart Rover or my shitty, mud-covered one?" Chris asked, seemingly genuinely, as if it was down to Anna to choose the vehicle.

"You've got two Rover's?" she curiously enquired, face smiling.

Chris simply grinned back. "Maybe I have more than two! Who knows?"

Anna looked at him puzzled, shook her head, then chuckled.

"It has to be the posh Rover. You're going to meet my dad!"

Chris nodded in agreement, grabbed a set of keys from a pile, then reaching into a pot, gave Max a pat and a host of treats. The big black dog shuffled down beside the Aga and began munching as Chris guided Anna outside.

He locked the farmhouse door as Anna jogged over to her car to get her bag and belongings then locked it up. She wandered back to Chris in the yard and followed him, heading for a small barn at the rear of the farmhouse. Here another black Range Rover lay deep inside and out of general view. This one was new and shiny, his usual 'run-about' Rover still parked beside the house and being the one she usually saw him race about in, to and from the yard.

Anna chuckled, further surprised by this strange man with so many mysteries as he fired the remote locking and opened the passenger door for Anna. She silently nodded a 'thank you,' as he politely closed the door behind her, then moved around to the driver's side and placed a large bag on the back seat.

Anna grinned somewhat sheepishly, surprised at his sudden charm.

"Will Max be okay on his own?" she enquired, it feeling strange seeing the yard empty of people and leaving him alone. "Seems sad leaving him today."

"He's okay and in the best place. He's a great guard dog and companion, but bone idle to be truthful. He's an Aga fan and will happily snooze all day, Christmas or not. And he's an Atheist! To him it's just another day to snooze and maybe eat the odd stranger who might pass by. As he usually does."

Anna grinned, enjoying Chris' strange, dark humour.

"Okay, then, lets go. Christmas lunch and alcohol awaits!"

They headed out the yard and through the woods without speaking further. As they approached the opening in the woods, where it met the road junction, Chris paused, seemingly looking long at the small piece of clear road ahead.

"Good to see the snow has melted," he said, smiling to himself. "Just what we need for tomorrow. No ice, so it's certain the meet will be on. Great."

Anna noticed his focus and looked out at the road ahead too.

"It looks like the road's been gritted?" Anna asked almost as a question.

"Yes, the Council often do it, as it's a dangerous bend on this corner."

Anna simply nodded and thought no more, but noticed Chris smile.

"Typical Council though. A bit too late. Or maybe not."

With a big grin he carefully pulled the Rover out the entrance to Horsewater and out onto the roadway. As they moved away Chris glanced back into the mirror, smiled once more, before gently accelerating away.

"I think it's going to be a great Christmas," he spoke softly to Anna.

She simply smiled back a warm feeling inside.

"Very good indeed!"

Chapter 67

Christmas isn't a season. It's a feeling.

Edna Ferber

They hardly spoke until they'd passed through the village and then began to make casual talk. Their conversation slowly picked up, horses and hunting the common theme, and chatted freely on those subjects. Chris drove into the outskirts of Norwich, then Anna guided him to where her parents lived. Chris knew the area vaguely, it being an older part of the city, with larger period houses; set back set back, with big gardens. 'Millionaires Row,' he recalled.

"Just down there," indicated Anna, directing Chris down a tree-lined avenue of prestigious properties, where Anna's parents house was situated.

"Nice area," Chris commented quietly, smiling at Anna. "Very nice!"

She blushed and smiled back, knowing exactly what he meant.

"Yes, it is a bit posh! But I'm not. And neither are my parents. You've met mum. They just happen to have done well. Or my dad did. Quite a successful businessman. Humble beginnings, did well, then bought a nice big house."

"Blimey! It's bigger and better than my house," joked Chris.

"Yes, it is nice, but they don't own half of Norfolk!" Anna replied.

Chris chuckled at the comment, casting her a playful, wicked look.

"Neither do I, really. Only a few woods and some other properties. Bertie and Reggie are the real big local landowners. They do own most of Norfolk!"

Anna nodded to acknowledge, realising she didn't want to either embarrass or impress, but followed on to explain her past and her parents success.

"Dad had a double-glazing business and it did quite well. Actually, very well. He sold it all up a few years back, but it was really successful. He worked hard when I was a kid. Very hard." Anna explained. "Don't laugh, someone has to sell windows. And they're not all cowboys. Sometimes they leave the horses at home, and they don't all wear spurs!" Anna joked, slightly embarrassed.

Chris smiled at her candid humour as she continued.

"They're both retired now, though Dad does some consultancy work for the company who bought his business. Keeps him busy." Anna added.

"Part of the deal really when he sold up, so as to get an income, not that they need it really. He just likes to be busy and keep his finger in his big pie."

She saw Chris looking at her curiously, casting her a coy look and grinned.

"They're not that rich," she flustered, getting embarrassed. "Just a little bit!"

Chris smirked, secretly impressed and assured, knowing some background.

"Good job I didn't bring the beat up Rover and brought my smarter one," he joked. "If not your parents servants wouldn't let me park it on the drive!"

Anna grinned wickedly and playfully slapped his arm, before indicating where he should park on the long drive, in which there were already six other cars parked. They got out and Chris retrieved a large carrier bag from the back, then somewhat apprehensively, followed Anna towards the big front door.

It was a typical detached Georgian town house, symmetrically set out with original timber large sash windows either side an inset stone doorway. Anna walked straight up to the door and opened it without pressing the old brass and ivory doorbell. Chris timidly followed her into a large central hallway, where Anna dropped her bag, then carried on past one room on their left, and moved directly into what appeared to be a large, square-roomed lounge.

"Yo! Chris dude! How's it hanging?" A familiar voice yelled, as an already tipsy Tracey staggered over, wearing a very short blue dress and dangerously high black heels. Before Chris knew it Tracey had a sprig of mistletoe hung over his head and had planted a quick kiss on his lips. He blushed scarlet and smiled, then quickly looked around the room at all the eyes now upon him, and then towards Anna, almost puppy-like, to seek out help and support.

Tracey moved up to Anna and thrust the mistletoe into her hand.

"Your go Cus'. Give him a big 'un! Suck his face off! That's if you haven't already had a big snog down at the stables! Bet you have! Naughty, naughty!"

Anna shook her head, face glowing bright, as she glanced at a red-faced Chris, then at the mistletoe held beside her. She cast a steely and stern look at a giggling Tracey who took another slug of the champagne in her hand.

Anna eyed her cautiously, realising Chris's embarrassed look and tried to shoo her away, but she refused to move, giggling and smiling at them.

Chris moved sideways and gave Anna a quick peck on the cheek.

It was so unexpected Anna was surprised and turned around, realising it was actually Chris' who'd kissed her cheek. She grinned widely, seeing his smiling face, as a huge round of applause erupted, and a cheer from Tracey, followed.

Joyce came over to save the pair any further embarrassment, knowing how annoying, yet fun her niece could be. Tracey, happy the pair had kissed, moved back to her partner, who was regarding her cousin's new boyfriend.

"Happy Christmas!" Joyce said. "I'm so pleased you could come," she added, turning to Chris. "I'll get you both a glass of champagne. Is that okay?"

Chris nodded eagerly, as did Anna, who stood close beside him.

Joyce saw he had a bag in his hand, and realising what was in it, politely asked if she wanted to take it from him.

"Yes, please do. There's a present there for you and your husband. Sorry, but I don't know his name. Also one for Anna too. Hers is the big one."

He offered the bag and Joyce wandered off, leaving the two alone, as they watched her place its contents beneath a large natural Christmas tree in the far corner, decorated in a mix of gold and red decorations, its lights flickering, and an array of brightly coloured presents spread wide around its base.

Tracey watched her aunt place the presents down and raised a glass to Anna.

Anna grinned and saw Tracey wink, Anna glad for once she'd momentarily left them in peace. Chris looked around and quickly counted eight people in the high ceiling room, which was decorated in a modern manner and strewn with Christmas trimmings and cards. Anna noticed him looking about the room, and at the faces, so quickly ran through the list of relatives who made up the assembled crowd, as well as Tracey and her long-suffering fiancé.

Chris noticed an old lady, seated in a high-backed chair in the corner, regarding him with a long stare. Their eyes met and he and she both smiled.

Joyce arrived with two flutes of champagne and they both politely clinked their glasses together, looking into each other's eyes for a few seconds over the rims, before looking away and each taking a good gulp of drink.

"Where's dad?" enquired Anna to her mum, who'd noticed their long lingering looks, and the closeness in which they stood beside each other.

"You know your father," she replied. "Kitchen. Playing at being Head Chef and Commander-in-Chief. He'll be through soon. I told him you arrived."

With that a tall, well-built man, with short-cut white hair; looking like retired Royal Marine, strolled into the room, with a navy apron tied about his waist. He wandered towards Anna, stretched out his arms and gave her a huge hug, almost lifting her off the floor. "Happy Crimble! Missed you first thing."

He turned to Chris, towering above him in both height and build and gazed down at him for a few seconds, seemingly sucking in everything in one look.

"You must be Chris. Unless she's picked up a stranger! I've heard a lot about you from these two. Good stuff. Pleased to meet you," he said stretching out his hand, giving Chris's hand a firm shake, looking at him equally hard.

Anna introduced Chris to her dad, Alan, and they briefly made small talk, before Alan excused himself, muttering 'sprouts' and dashed back into the kitchen, Joyce following on to assist and prevent a disaster. Anna excused herself too; spoke quietly to Tracey, who looked across as Chris with a smile.

"I'm going to nip upstairs and change. So you don't feel out of place, Tracey is coming to chat with you. Don't take too much notice though, as she's half pissed already," explained Anna, looking towards her cousin, who began to waddle over to them both, with her fiancé attached for physical support.

"Don't worry, I've seen her drunk many times. Nothing new. I'll see you in a few minutes," he replied, feeling a bit uncomfortable, but smirked at Tracey.

As Tracey joined Chris, Anna nipped out of the room. The conversation covered the usual yard talk, although Chris spoke also with her fiancé; who was quietly spoken and humble. Ten minutes later Anna re-appeared.

Chris stared long at the dramatic change in appearance. She'd made up her face, wearing slightly more than she at stables, and wore a long, tight-fitting black dress with a delicate gold floral print. The dress clung to her slim body, at which Chris couldn't help but stare. She wore heels, which when she stood beside Chris accentuated the height difference quite considerably. She blushed as she saw him look up at her, obviously admiring her looks, but with a grin.

"You brush up well after a good grooming," Chris quietly joked, and Anna gently elbowed him, the cheeky gesture not missed by a grinning Tracey.

"I hope Tracey's been behaving," Anna said, seeing her cousin read too much into their relaxed body language and the cheeky contact between them.

"Of course I have Cus'. I've been a very good boy, haven't I Chris," Tracey slurred, to Anna's chagrin. "I'm always a good boy, except when I'm not!"

Chris laughed and shook his head. Seeing a drunken Tracey was nothing new. Her fiancé seemed oblivious and unconcerned by her state, clearly used to it. Almost ignoring her, he starting to chat to Chris about football. A subject he knew little about, he politely listened, making the odd comment to show some interest. Anna and Tracey discussed their respective nail polishes.

Tracey introduced her parents to Chris and they then chatted to him about horses, mostly racing it seemed, but a subject he was happier to talk about.

Joyce wandered through and announced lunch was about to be served. It all seemed formal, and momentarily Chris did wonder if Anna's parents had servants, as everyone filed from the lounge into an adjoining dining room.

Before them lay a very large dining table of polished hard wood, laid out with silver salvers and cutlery and the finest china crockery. Joyce pointed out each person's place setting; denoted by a delightful hand-written place card. Thankfully for Chris, he was seated between Anna and Tracey; Chris knowing Anna would have wanted it as such, but also opposite the old lady he'd seen, who was Anna's nanny. She was slightly smaller than Chris, and had a pale and wrinkled appearance, but bright blue, almost piecing eyes. They held a twinkle and unique wisdom; clearly gathered through the years of experience they'd witnessed. As they seated Chris felt her look bore into him, searching, as though able to read his thoughts. But her smile was warm and honest.

However, he knew at once she was possibly going to be trouble.

Anna whispered an apology to him for the formal nature, but Chris smiled, and whispered how impressed he was. Alan brought in the food, centrepiece being a huge turkey, looking more like a small ostrich, along with a gammon joint - or half a pig - and a wide variety of vegetables in tureens and dishes.

Alan carved the turkey and plates and tureens were soon passed around. Once the food was placed on the plates, and people began eating, a gentle banter began. Tracey was as vocal as ever, her fiancé simply shaking his head, but her mum and dad, sitting almost diagonally opposite to Chris, appeared equally as noisy. However, the boisterous banter and chatter ensured that it was far from a stuffy atmosphere, but a very happy and jolly occasion.

Anna glanced sideways at Chris who smiled, and slid his hand across her leg and into her hand, gently gripping her fingers and giving it a gentle squeeze.

She blushed, then gently squeezed his hand as acknowledgement, surprised, but deeply warmed by the intimate gesture.

So far it had been a great Christmas Day.

Chapter 68

I will honour Christmas in my heart,
and try to keep it all the year......

A Christmas Carol – Charles Dickens

When Anna's nanny spoke direct Chris, just as he was munching on a perfect roast potato, it seemed to silence the whole table in one strike. Everyone fell silent and seemed to listening intently to the simple cutting question.

Even Tracey sat in stunned silence, a fork-full of food hovering mid-flight before her open mouth; everything stalling in time as Anna's nanny spoke.

"How do you feel about the hounds being destroyed so young in their life?"

She asked the question in a direct, matter of fact tone. Like a journalist.

Chris paused from eating and looked either side, as if to ensure she'd actually addressed him; as until then, the old lady had remained silent and simply ate.

"Nanna, I don't think Chris wants to talk about hunting. Not over Christmas lunch," Anna said, intervening and blushing crimson. She frowned hard.

The old woman remained silent, her sapphire blue eyes never leaving Chris's face since she'd caught his eyes and asked the question. He smiled back.

"No, that's okay Anna," Chris said, it seeming strange him using her name. "I don't mind answering, if it's okay to discuss such things up the table?"

He looked at all of the faces now regarding him, as if for approval, stopping at the head of the table with Alan. He too shook his head, smiling at the smaller man whom he immediately began to respect and admire; having the courage and politeness to ask permission to answer the question so boldly.

"Do you mean the fact most hounds are destroyed before they reach the age of seven?" Chris asked, as if to confirm he'd understood the question fully.

The old woman simply nodded, a wry, clever smile crossing her thin lips.

Chris began to speak, aware a table of diners now looking intently at him.

"I must admit I personally feel it cruel that a hunt will destroy hounds when they become what is deemed too old and no longer fit for the job for which they have been bred. However, a hunt is a business to a degree. If it retained its old hounds, it would soon run out of space to keep them and it'd cost a fortune to feed them all, as well as the space needed. It'd help if they could be re-homed, but they are a pack animal, who often find it hard to adapt to normal social life. Sometimes a couple are re-settled to large country homes. I suppose it is too much trouble really for the hunts to find new homes for them all, although I know some do. There's a big enough problem re-homing all of the stray domestic dogs on the streets already. My dog Max was a rescue dog. So to answer you question, no I don't like the thought, but sadly accept its part of hunting," explained Chris, looking directly at the old woman.

She smiled knowingly, seemingly satisfied by the reply. The remainder of the table all sat stunned, silently impressed by the direct and honest answer.

"I didn't know they killed off all the hounds!" Tracey suddenly exclaimed. "Poor little sods. That's sad. No wonder I never recognise any!"

"The reason you probably never recognise one hound from the next is 'cos you're usually half-cut!" Anna quipped with a grin, the comment met with a roar of laughter around the table and a playful punch from Tracey

Chris smiled, shrugging his shoulders and blushed as he looked at Anna, caught between the two women, the atmosphere relaxing, but all listening.

Chris quickly fired a question straight back to Anna's nanny.

"You seem quite knowledgeable. Have you ever hunted? Or are you a secret Anti? I haven't seen you running about the fields chasing us!" Chris' broad grin ensured everyone knew he was joking and Anna was amazed at his dry and direct humour. The old woman smiled even broader, before answering.

"I've ridden out a few seasons in my earlier days. And been to many a Hunt Ball. They were wild affairs! But that was a long time ago. Before you were born. In the days of coal and steam my lad!" She chuckled playfully.

Chris smiled back with a wide grin, impressed by her dark side and coyness.

"I never knew you'd hunted Nanna," proclaimed Anna. "You sneak!"

She looked at her grandmother shocked, and then at her mother, almost for acknowledgement that the old lady hadn't finally lost her marbles and was trying to wind up Chris. Joyce simply shrugged her shoulders, as if to acknowledge she knew nothing of her mothers seemingly secret past either.

"It was a long time ago. Well before I met your granddad and obviously well before I had your mum. Everyone rode horses in those days. Wheels hadn't been invented. And we lived in caves!" She grinned, seeing chuckling faces.

"But yes, I used to ride out for a few years when I courted a country lad. Didn't come to anything. He went off with some posh girl. Had money. I hadn't thought about it until Joyce said you were bringing a horse man friend who hunted, and it brought back good memories," she casually explained.

Heads turned about the table, all seemingly surprised by the revelation, Joyce looking at her mother in a new light and Alan amazed at the family secrets.

"Anyway, it's nice to meet you." She then turned her attention to Anna.

"And I'm glad you've dumped Bruce in exchange for this one. Much better. I never did like him. Stupid, big-headed, Pratt! What an arsehole he is!"

Tracey roared out laughing, spitting a huge piece of potato across the table, as Alan and Joyce momentarily looked at her mother in embarrassed wonder. Then they too laughed loudly, nodding in agreement at the comment. Anna blushed crimson, before joining in the laughter roaring around the table.

The ice had been broken and Chris and Anna's nanny began to swap old hunting tales as the food was enjoyed by all in great surroundings. Then Alan presented a large Christmas pudding in grand style; the blue and purple flickering flames of the burning brandy bringing a hearty cheer all round.

Anna sat and listened on as Chris and her nanny chatted. Adding snippets herself, she was fascinated and happy at how they seem to hit if off so well.

She was more surprised at how the 'quiet, moody and grumpy' Chris openly chatted, and amazed her grandmother or mum had never mentioned her hunting days to Anna before. Her grandmother had hardly spoken to Bruce, who always seemed above himself and treated her nanny like a second-class citizen, no longer of any use to society and thus not worth talking to or about. Thus it seemed she enjoyed the natural, easy and honest manner of Chris' who accepted her fully for who she was; a knowledgeable and fun old lady.

After the meal was finished they retired to the lounge in fine spirits, where it seemed the tradition in Anna's parent's house was to have a relatively early lunch and then exchange and open up the main presents, having only opened a few small presents in the morning. Anna sat on a chair and Chris on the floor close next to her, his arm resting on the side of the chair beside Anna.

Then, with eager faces all gazing towards the tree, a strange silence settled amongst them as the presents were distributed. Joyce was the main dealer, as Alan serviced any drinks needs. She passed Anna a few gifts that were under the tree and then two onto Chris; one from her and Alan and another being from Anna. Chris openly blushed at receiving one from Anna's parents and was doubly glad he'd now he'd bought them both a gift.

Presents were opened around them and everyone showed off the gifts they'd received with excitable chatter. Tracey sat the other side of Anna and the pair giggled like children as they regarded various presents, including ones from people at the yard. But most of the time, Anna and Chris seemed to be locked in their own private world, unaware of the people around them.

Anna felt great warmth coming from him, and found herself repeatedly glancing his way, her stomach fluttering. He seemed to instinctively move closer, putting an arm on the rest of the chair, only a few inches away from her hand. She desperately wanted to touch his fingers, but resisted, unsure of Chris's reaction to such a move, and also fully aware of the many eyes watching them, especially her nanny. She sat close to the Christmas tree, with a large sherry, but kept looking at the pair like a hawk, a soft grin on her face.

Chris took the present from Anna's parents. It was a bottle, but its shape gave it away immediately. He grinned as he began to open it and spoke as the pair looked at him. "I think you'd better open my present to you now."

They looked puzzled, until Alan passed Joyce the exact same shape and sized present as they'd passed to Chris. Both opened the large bottles of cherry brandy at the same time and laughed heartily, the pair now understanding.

"I knew you liked it after you followed on the first meet," said Chris. "So I thought I'd buy you a bottle drink at home as a memento."

"Well I know you love it too," replied Joyce, "having seen you drink lots, so thought it would top up your hip-flask. Don't give any to Tracey!"

They thanked each other across the room and Alan and Joyce smiled back, then regarded each other warmly. Chris sensed a loving couple opposite.

Anna reached the present from Chris, just as he was about to open the one from her. They both cautiously opened the presents at the same time. Chris had bought Anna a large 'Coffee Table' sized book on showjumping, for which she was extremely grateful. She felt quite emotional at the trouble and expense he'd gone to buy what she knew was an expensive book; more so considering the short time she'd known him. Tracey smirked, and mockingly stuck out her tongue to Chris. He'd bought her a box of fine chocolates, and bottle of wine; it being almost the same identical gift he'd bought everyone and left in the tackroom. He had also bought her a bottle of champagne as a special treat, but seemingly nothing as grand or personal as Anna's book.

Tracey was secretly glad Anna and Chris appeared to be getting on so well, but only hoped it wouldn't end in tears for her cousin, who seemed smitten.

Anna whispered a 'Thank you' to him and began flicking through the large book at once, with masses of photos, and detailed diagrams of how to approach jumps. She wanted to hug or kiss him, but knew it was not the time nor place and also that relationship was supposed to be simply as friends, although most within the room could see it differently and she felt so too.

She placed the book down and looked on as Chris carefully inspected the small present Anna had given him. It had been beautifully wrapped in gold paper, with a red bow and trimmings. Anna was pleased Chris took time to admire the time and effort she'd taken to wrap even the smallest of presents, before he opened the small package. Her heart fluttered as he slowly began to reveal a small white box. Inside the white box was a red velvet case, which Chris slid out. He opened the velvet covered case to reveal a gold Stock Pin, in the shape of a hunting whip, but with a centralised hare's head as a detail.

Chris stared in silence, looking in great detail at the very personal gift.

Anna suddenly worried if it was too personal, or came across as too 'pushy.' They'd only known each other a few weeks, nothing had happened, and she hoped he'd not read too much into the rather intimate and personal gift she now presented him with. She thought she'd better explain further.

"I saw it in an antique shop and thought I had to get it for you. It seems unique. A one off. Is it okay? Please say if not. I've got the receipt!"

Chris simply turned and stared, a broad, genuine smile crossing his face.

"It's brilliant," he whispered. "Absolutely stunning. You really shouldn't have, but I love it. It is great. Thank you so much. I'll wear it tomorrow."

Anna flushed red, but beamed a smile, her heart fluttering as he reached over and touched her hand, and gave it a gentle squeeze, causing Anna to nearly drop her book. Chris took his hand back as she scrambled to recover the falling book, then realised half the room were looking at them both, in particular, Anna's nanny. She eyed them from across the room with a merry twinkle and thin-lipped grin, which knew Chris had noticed, by winking.

Tracey suddenly brought Anna back to reality, excitedly waving a pair of bright fluorescent pink wellie socks in her face, which her fiancé had bought.
"Aren't these great? Fab!" She squealed. "You'll see me comin' for miles! "
"We can normally hear you first," Chris dryly commented, to everyone's amusement and laughs. Tracey simply stuck out her tongue, then kissed her fiancé to thank him. He simply shrugged his shoulders and then laughed.
Once the presents had been opened and wrappings discarded, trays of nuts and tins of chocolates were passed around, along with more drink. Chris and Anna abstained, knowing they'd both have to drive soon in some form, the reality of keeping horses meaning they both had to keep very sober heads.
The time had flown by and it wasn't long before Chris was looking at the large ornate French mantle clock, which regularly chimed with a startling 'ping' on the quarter, making him jump each time. Also, outside, in the ornate garden, through the large sash windows, he could see the fading light, and knew he and Anna would have to return to the yard to do all of the horses.
Chris cast Anna a cautious look, not wishing to be rude. She caught the look, and reading his thoughts announced to the crowd that she and Chris would have to leave and jokingly 'do some work.' Anna went off to change into her 'yard' clothes, before returning. They said their thanks and farewells to all and agreed that as Tracey was now almost unconscious, they'd do Fred for her.
She slurred a thank you too them, her fiancé laughingly, shaking his head.
He was well used to her drinking habits, as was Chris, who its seemed always did Fred for her on most Christmas Day's. Tracey was sober enough to cast Anna an exaggerated wink, as she stood swaying in the doorway, as the pair prepared to leave Chris said a warm farewell to Anna's nanny, who kissed him on both cheek as he bent down, the pair now the best of friends.
"I'll be seeing more of you I hope young man," she said, winking at him as he rose, then cast a smile at Anna. He silently smiled back and gently nodded.
Anna's parents saw them to the door, but as Anna was coming back, wished Chris a good evening and told him he was more than welcome to return with Anna if he wanted to for more drinks or a buffet supper. He thanked them, but explained he'd be fine and had things to at the farm, as well as check on the horses. Also, he needed to ensure everything was ready for Boxing Day.
They finally escaped, and Anna's parents waved goodbye as the pair climbed into the Rover and drove off, Anna waving a hand out of the window.
The atmosphere in the car was quiet but warm, almost like when lovers have made love and lie happily and silently within each other's arms; enjoying the warmth that emanates from each other, with no more words needed.
When Anna did speak, it was brief and answered all.
"Have you had a good day? I hope so. I have."
"I've had a wonderful day. Thank you so much."
Chris reached across the wide console of the Rover and touched her hand. She smiled, and held it until they arrived back at the yard of Horsewater.

Passing through the woods, now in increasing darkness, the dark canopy enclosed them in a strange, dark enveloping hue, which they both welcomed.
Once they arrived back at the yard, the romance was over and it was back into 'business mode' for the pair, knowing all the hard work to be done.
Chris let out a happy and bounding Max, who sniffed Anna, before dashing off towards a barn and urinating up the corner. He vanished briefly, no doubt emptying the other end, before then returning to the kitchen and his Aga.
Life was hard for Max. Eat, urinate, poo, sleep. Repeat. Then repeat again.
The pair hurried around, undertaking the various tasks. Anna brought Penny in and gave Chris a hand with the various other horses and retrieved Fred, who was sent to bed with a kiss from his absent drunken mum via Anna.
Chris had to bring in the anti-social Bonnie, who other than Julie, was the only person on the yard the horse was permitted near her, unless she was biting them. Chris brought in together his equally moody chestnut Saint Swithin and Cirrus, whilst Anna fetched Goldie for Sally, having a well deserved day off and was no doubt by now partially drunk. Anna fussed the gentile Anglo-Arab, who Anna decided was far too attractive to be a gelding.
Tess, Carol's cob, was in when they arrived, the black mare watching the frantic activity whilst munching clumps of hay in her big lips. Carol, no doubt sober, had brought her beloved Cob in earlier and was now enjoying her Christmas either alone, with friends, or at Wroxingham Hall. Who knew?
Anna and Chris worked well together, and before long they had a yard-full of horses, who's usual owners were either drunk, temporarily morbidly-obese, or simply miles away visiting relatives. Unaware, their horses were safely in their stables, rugs changed, eating feed, with full water and hay and ready for bed; all oblivious what a frantic and busy day it'd been for those attending to them.
A couple of liveries came and went, thanking Chris for his present and discretely asking about their day; mostly just being polite, and offering little interest. Most were in too much of a hurry; keen to get back in the warmth and back to more eating and drinking. Finally everything had been completed and Anna stood looking at Chris, the magical sound of contented horses gently ripping into hay-nets being the only noise to be heard. It was now dark, with the bright yellow yard lights casting deep shadows in even darker places. A slight chill beginning to settle in, as the sweat on the pair's old clothing cooled, and they now regarded each other, finally taking a well-needed breath.
"I've had a great day. Thank you for your gift. It is wonderful," Chris spoke; suddenly returning to the shy, bashful person Anna had begun to know.
"And thanks for lunch with your lovely family too. They are all great."
"It has been wonderful," replied Anna, warmly. "Thank you for coming and making it so enjoyable. It's been great, but now it seems horrible to leave you on your own. You know you can come back to mum's if you want, and you're clearly more than welcome. By everyone. There is still lots of food to eat!"
Both parties grinned, seemingly at the thought of even more food.

Anna looked at him longingly, a sense of sadness and sorrow appearing in her face, knowing she didn't want the day to end either; desperate not to see the magic which had grown all day simply disappear as darkness fell.

Chris smiled back. "I couldn't have wished for a better day. It's genuinely been great. I'm used to being on my own, so it isn't a problem, honest. But I'll see you again in a few hours for the Boxing Day meet. We've got a big day ahead of us and we'll all need our sleep. Me definitively!"

"That's true, and I'm looking forward to it. Wouldn't want to miss it. At least you've met a few more of my family. Tracey wasn't sick, my dad didn't punch you and more amazingly, my Nan seems to like you. That's a first!"

"That has to be a result then. All of the boxes ticked."

Anna grinned at Chris, who chuckled bashfully.

"I'll go back to my mum's then," Anna replied, reluctant to move or wanting something else to happen. "And I'll make sure I'm back at the cottage sober and in good time, so I can get ready for tomorrow. I don't know how Tracey will cope, but no doubt she will. Tomorrow should be a day to remember."

"I hope so," replied Chris, the conversation dying, as they looked at each other, scanning their faces, knowing what each wanted, but none daring to act. Uncomfortably they stood, bashfully staring, the distance between them too great for any action to be natural and not telegraphed to the other before it was done, but neither having the courage to make the required move.

Then Chris made the first move. But away from Anna.

He turned sideways, as though to turn away, then spun back, as if to say a final goodnight. Seeing him about to go, Anna pounced. Before he realised it, she'd covered the uncomfortable distance and was directly before him.

She craned her neck forward, aimed at his lips and fired a quick peck, hoping it'd hit its target and not embarrassingly miss. The kiss was short and sweet, but landed fully on his lips. It was so quick it seemingly shocked Chris, who didn't have time to react. Anna, just as quickly after the peck, dropped back a step and moved away from Chris, then blushed, seeing his shocked face.

"Happy Christmas. It's been a great day," she whispered, blushing.

Chris suddenly leant forward, gripping her fingers gently with his hands, then drawing her towards him, pecked Anna fully on the lips too. He then eased back a step, but still holding her hands and gazing into her face.

"I don't know why, but I've been wanting to do that since I first met you," he announced, boldly, but somewhat sheepishly, his face glowing.

"Then why the hell didn't you!" Anna was as bold as ever and beaming.

She dived forward, grabbed Chris tight and kissed him fully, pressing his body tight and close to hers, their lips contacting before breaking free.

The pair giggled, still holding hands, their chilled noses rubbing softly against each, enjoying the moment of warmth and closeness. He pecked her on the lips again, then playfully kissed the tip of her nose. Anna giggled.

"I'd better let you go," he spoke. "Not that I want to. Now go. Please!"

Anna nodded knowingly, despite her own reluctance and wanting more. However, she then pecked him softly on the lips once more.

"Sadly, I don't want to go, but know I must. It's been a perfect day. However, until tomorrow," she said. "I can't wait to see you then."

With that she turned, her face burning up, as Chris stood staring at her back, admiring the view as she walked up the yard, his heart pounding, as did hers. She turned, somewhat teasingly half way, and waved with her hand at her waist. Chris raised his hand fully, and turned back to the house, and stood by the door, which he'd half opened, still watching as Anna got into her car.

Max met him at the door, reluctantly rising to see the fuss, his long black nose appearing through the gap, as Chris stroked his head and smiled.

Anna fired up her car, flicked on the lights and was warmed to see Chris still standing by the door; Max's face peering through the gap, as the pair watched her drive away. He raised his hand and smiled, and she cheekily raised her hands to her lips and blew a kiss as she drove past the house. Chris smirked.

The lights of her 4 x 4 cut through the darkened woods, and for the first time since she'd arrived at Horsewater, she drove happily through the gloom of the dense and encompassing trees with no fears, smiling like a Cheshire cat; merrily singing along with the Christmas carol playing on the radio.

It'd been a great day. For once it seemed as if there was no evil in the world.

Only joy, love and hope for peace; just as the carol announced.

Tomorrow though would be another day.

Christmas Day and all it's joy would be gone.

Evil would prevail once more.

It always did.

Chapter 69

Good King Wenceslas looked out,
on the Feast of Stephen, .

John Mason Neale

Chris' lorry drove steadily into the car park in the market town of Windford, to join many others assembling for the Boxing Day Meet. The small car park, at the rear of a library, had been allocated by the Council for the hunt and its followers to park the lorries, as was the long-standing tradition. He had five horses on board. Anna was following in her 4 x 4 and pulled alongside the lorry. Julie was bringing her Land Rover and trailer with Bonnie onboard, parking beside them as usual. Anna got out with Carol and Tracey, who were her passengers. Carol had chatted happily about her meal at Wroxingham Hall with Bertie and Virginia, whilst Tracey remained strangely silent, seeming to wince every time the jolly Carol mentioned quaffing food or Vintage Port.

Anna knew Tracey would perk up once she had more alcohol and food inside, mixed with adrenaline from a charging Fred set firmly beneath her. As they exited the vehicle, Anna surveyed the scene in wonder and amazement.

The small car park was swamped with lorries, cars with trailers, horses, and different people chatting away; most donned in country tweeds adorned with tinsel or an obligatory dog at foot. She was shocked to see so many horses, people, dogs and vehicles jammed into such a small area, but the whole thing seemed organised and natural, with everyone knowing what to do.

Joyce, who'd driven to Windford alone and was looking out for them, saw them arrive in convey and walked over. Alan had stayed at home, seeing to their relatives and preparing lunch. Now an 'avid hunt supporter,' Joyce, had come to absorb the tradition, see the hunt off, and also meet Chris again.

Anna was amazed at how many horseboxes and trailers were there already, and it was beginning to get difficult to park, despite the size of the market town's large car park. Chris however seemed un-phased, and Sally, who'd ridden down with him in the cab as ever, seemingly took it all in her stride.

They quickly moved into action and the horses were swiftly unloaded, already tacked up and ready to get on board, simply needing their girths tightened. Julie pointed out to Anna that they'd mount up in the car park and then ride into the Market Square as a group, before setting off. Anna could already hear lots of noise and activity further on within the town, just beyond the row of buildings where they were located, which then formed the market square.

She'd become slightly accustomed to hunting now, despite having only been out a couple of times, but the thought of meeting up in a busy town square, with hundreds of spectators watching her every move, was a bit concerning.

This, with any noise from any Anti's, worried her slightly and she felt a buzz of nervous anticipation. Penny was also visibly excited by the event, on her toes, and clattering around the car park, as she was swiftly unloaded, taking in the strange environment and close proximity of so many new horses. Joyce looked on in wonder as the group quickly mounted, and before she knew it, they were all ready to set off, with nearly fifty horses clattering about in the car park; riders chatting to people, or others nervously waiting to set off.

Getting the horses ready earlier at the yard had all happened in a rush, and neither Anna nor Chris had had much time to speak to each other, after the previous exciting day. They'd exchanged quiet, cheeky smiles, but such was the hive of activity and number of people dashing about the yard, sorting out horses, ensuring they looked pristine, and everyone had everything organised; neither managed to say more than a few words. Any small talk was related to horses, preparing for the meet, or Tracey telling everyone how ill she felt. But before long, everything was sorted and they were off, driving to Windford.

Now, seated nervously upon Penny, Anna looked at Chris onboard Cirrus. She'd typically managed to poop bright green slop down her gleaming white back legs, met with a head shake from Chris. He asked Anna if she was okay, then drew alongside, seeing her concerned look. They then posed somewhat embarrassed for a quick photo, as requested by Joyce. She happily smiled at the pair, and clicked away various shots, as Cirrus nibbled at Penny's ear.

Tracey had woken up slightly and cheekily grinned, seeing her aunt taking photos of the 'Happy Couple.' She jokingly pointed to her left hand and the third finger. Anna shook her head, glancing sideward, but Chris luckily missed the gesture, as Gavin and Dawn then rode over to speak with him. Riding their pair of almost identical Grey's, they were joined by an elderly man, all politely asking Chris how his Christmas went as they all drew alongside.

When Anna heard him emit the words 'Fantastic' she smiled, proud to be beside him, but was then nudged apart by Tracey and Carol, as the pair pulled up on Fred and Tess. Julie was keeping the anti-social Bonnie away on a quieter section of the car park, and Anna glanced at her, smiling to ensure she was okay. A tip from her whip and big grin confirmed Julie was certainly fine.

Penny seemed to settle down, despite the jostling of various horses bustling about in the confined space, added to by a smiling and laughing Sally on an excitable Goldie, who unintentionally pulled in alongside Chris. This pushed Anna further away from him and she found herself beside a rotund old gentleman on a stunning Bay. He began speaking to her about Christmas pudding and eating too much. She glanced at his belly and quietly agreed.

Steve, Reggie, Martin and Sharon, joined by her friend Helen; who was acting as Whipper-in, all stood proudly in a corner area of the car park, along with Shirley, the Hunt Secretary. Their red jackets looked stunning in the low December sunlight. Martin had released the hounds, and was expertly keeping them tightly together in that same corner area of the car park.

When all the riders were mounted, Anna roughly counted about fifty. They all moved over towards where a group were collecting and Joyce left them, wandering off to get a position in the Market Square to watch them ride in.

The assembled horses jigged about in the car park until Steve's voice bellowed out, calling them to form up together for a pre-meet discussion. He looked extremely smart in his bright red jacket and seated upon Casanova, his huge black horse, who looked as immaculately turned out as ever. As Steve called the riders together, Chris ensured he was beside Anna, making excuses as he weaved Cirrus through the throng, jostling past various horses, nodding to the riders, to pull in alongside her. She glanced at him sheepishly, glad he was there, and the pair moved towards the red jackets, joined by a cavalry of horses in all shapes, colours and sizes. Tracey bustled over, pulling up on the other side of Anna, nudging Fred in. Before them, Steve, Martin and Reggie proudly sat, admiring their legion of praetorians, the hounds at their hooves.

"How are you feeling?" Chris whispered across to Anna.

"Okay, I think. Bit nervous to be honest," Anna replied. "So many horses."

"Don't worry. Stick with Tracey and me and you'd be okay."

"Yeah. Keep with us Cus and we'll see you're all right," chirped in Tracey.

Chris chuckled, and she smiled, it being the first time they'd had together since last night. Cirrus shuffled and pushed towards Penny, Anna and Chris' stirrups clunking together; it appearing even their mounts knew something.

"Good Morning and thank you for turning out this fine Boxing Day," Steve announced, drawing Anna's attention. "I hope you've all recovered enough!"

Anna glanced at Tracey, and shook her head, grinning. Tracey smirked.

More riders closed in to hear what Steve had to say. Anna turned in her saddle and saw Julie seated behind her on Bonnie, set back slightly, with Carol and Sally lost out of sight somewhere amongst the mass of shuffling horses.

Happy most riders were within earshot, and could hear, Steve continued.

"We will ride into the square now and have a quick drink and piece of cake, before setting out. Please be on your best behaviour, as today we are on show to the public. They've come here to see us uphold a long-term tradition, which is our honour to do. There are quite a few anti's about, but we don't expect any real trouble, just the usual noise, chants and foul verbal abuse."

Anna felt herself tense up, suddenly feeling as if she was about to enter battle, and wondering what she'd let herself in for. She glanced at Chris, who seemed to sense her concern, but simply smiled and mouthed 'Don't worry.'

"Please ignore any comments," Steve continued. "Either general or personal and do not react to any intimidation. We have many supporters in the crowd, and a large police presence here today as well, both here in the town, and who will also be following for a while. They are on our side - supposedly!"

He grinned, smirking at the array of chuckling faces, many who laughed.

"Have a great day, take care as ever, enjoy it and stay out of trouble. Let's show everyone how well disciplined the Shoteton are. Thank you. Let's go!"

With that he turned Casanova around and nodded to Reggie, who in turn spoke to Martin. He blew on the horn, and with Sharon and Helen whipping-in, they moved the hounds on past the horses and out of the car park in an orderly manner. Several hounds ran off, sniffing the parked vehicle wheels or nosing up at unsuspecting pedestrians, many who stopped to pat them.

Chris ushered Anna on, along with Tracey and Julie. Forming a tight pack of four and they fell in with the other fifty horses assembled in the car park.

Steadily the mass of horses moved across the car park and onto an adjoining road. Here the sound of their shoes clattering on tarmac roared loudly, accompanied by the clunk of stirrups clashing as the riders moved on in mass.

"Try and keep close to us," said Julie, pulling alongside her as they headed for the Market Square. "Penny might get a bit excited if she loses sight of her new found friends and there'll be lot of noise and confusion in the square."

Anna simply nodded as acknowledgement, her stomach fluttering. Ahead she could see a large group of people as the road entered the town square.

They rode up a single lane street, ancient whitewashed black timber-framed buildings tight either side. The upper-storeys overhung towards them, giving a greater feeling of being enclosed and confined, and the neatly rounded black beam-ends had split with age. The sound of fifty sets of clattering hooves echoing back off the walls was almost deafening, but Anna felt she was part of history; for centuries the timber beam ends having witnessed many horses pass beneath them, long before cars had ever arrived and changed the world.

As they rode into the square Anna's head was filled with the sound only a mass of chattering and chanting people can create, being amazed to see such a large crowd gathered. Before her, in the market square, stood several hundred people many rows deep, lining the pavements and roads wherever she looked.

The group rode on and found themselves in a naturally formed corral, with buildings on three sides, forming the large open, market square. Lined on all sides were people, from young to old, along with police officers, bright in their fluorescent jackets, keeping a cautious look out for any potential trouble.

The scene washed over her and at first she was unable to pick out any specific faces in the crowd, such were the numbers, all appearing to be a blur, as she looked around, keen to try and see her mum's face amongst the many.

Anna was amazed by the mass of people and noises. She looked toward Chris, being separated from her by a big bay horse ridden by an elderly man, pushing into Penny from her side, who in turn was being buffeted by more horses pushing into the square from the car park as more piled into a small and confined area. This jostling pushed Anna and Penny further away from Chris and deeper into the thronging and flowing crowd of horses.

"I do apologise," the old gent said to Anna with a tip of his bowler hat, before buffeting his way along some other horses as a fine grey horse pulled in beside her, ridden by a young woman who smiled meekly and shook her head as an apology at the chaos. And further away Chris seemed to drift.

Anna smiled nervously, but found herself being pushed across the square by more horses still flowing in, moving closer towards the crowd on one side of the square. Chris and Cirrus had disappeared completely in a sea of horses, with Penny, sensing Anna's tension, becoming anxious, shuffling about in the continuous movement and rotation of jostling horses. They continued to flow into the tight confines of the square, within which they were contained.

Another bay pushed in on her other side, the lady rider looking as distressed as Anna, pulling her reins, trying to control her excited mount. Anna looked across the mass of moving horses to see Julie moving towards her on Bonnie. She pushed her way through like a plough, but was then stopped in her tracks by more horses drifting in front of her, before finally making it over to her.

"Are you okay?" Julie asked. "You look a bit worried."

Anna smiled nervously, reassured by the sight of Julie.

"Yes. Well, no, actually I'm not. I'm shitting myself! It's a unnerving seeing so many horses and being so close to all these people. I keep wondering if Penny will tread on anyone, kick out or rear up. It's chaos," she explained.

"Yes, it can be a bit scary. That lot don't help," Julie said, looking towards the Anti's at one end of the square, waving their placards and chanting loudly. "Animal lovers my arse. They don't care they're scaring the hell out of the horses, so long as they shout loudly to try to make their pathetic point heard."

More horses entered the square and Anna frantically searched for Chris or Tracey. She couldn't see Tracey, but caught sight of the familiar grey with Chris on board, half way across the square. He caught her eye and shrugged his shoulders; surrounded by jostling horses, and seated beside an elderly lady.

Anna and Julie were pushed closer to the crowds, formed up behind safety barriers at the kerb, until things settled and Anna managed to ease up, most of the horses having entered the market square and beginning to find a space.

Penny, seemingly reassured to have Bonnie beside her, was more at ease than Anna could have hoped, but she was pleased to have Julie beside her. She scanned the crowds lining the sides of the square, looking for her mum.

The faces and heads were a blur as she searched, now seeing the Anti's.

"Hi Snooks," someone spoke. "Happy Christmas."

Anna froze, the hairs on her neck prickling.

She instantly recognised the man's voice in the crowd behind her.

Anna hoped she was mistaken, but turned around in the saddle to scan the faces behind and identify the source of the familiar comment.

Her blood froze and she hoped was wrong.

But Anna knew from the voice she wasn't.

She turned Penny around fully to look at the crowd lined up behind her.

Directly before her stood a smiling Bruce.

Chapter 70

I think that God, in creating man,
somewhat overestimated his ability.

Oscar Wilde

Bruce stood before her grinning, as ever in his smug, overly-cocky manner.

"What the hell are you doing here?" Anna asked abruptly, flushing and furtively looking to see if Chris was nearby. For once she hoped he wasn't, then noticed he'd become trapped centrally within the main group of riders in the square; several horses deep away, various people chatting to him as ever.

Anna looked at Bruce, in a manner that would've turned any mortal instantly into a pillar of salt or stone.

But not Bruce.

He'd long since told everyone he was like a Greek God.

Maybe he was. Immortal. Or so he thought.

Anna couldn't decide if it was a good or bad thing Chris wasn't seated beside her. Probably not she very quickly decided.

"I thought I'd come and see you off," Bruce said casually. He grinned.

"And wish you a Happy Christmas, seeing as you weren't about for me yesterday. Did you have a nice day yesterday at your mums? Was your pigmy boyfriend there with you? Or did you just both have a cosy day at his farm?"

Bruce spoke sarcastically, with a smug, all-knowing grin, his eyes narrowing, but cautiously looking about the riders, as if to see if Chris was nearby.

"How dare you follow me here. You stupid pathetic bastard Bruce!"

Anna hissed the words hard and direct. A couple standing beside winced, realising they were in the middle of a potential domestic, but unable to move.

"Piss off and leave me alone!" Anna's face flushed, as did the faces of the people either side of Bruce, aware of the bitter confrontation about to kick off between the elegant lady rider and the cocky man before her in the crowd.

Anna began to worry if Bruce had followed her yesterday, or was simply guessing she'd be at her mum's; as she did every year. Either way, she was shocked and horrified to see him stand before her. More especially so as he never ever bothered in the past to watch her at any other horsey event.

She became agitated and looked for a way to get Penny away from the edge of the crowd, where they seemed to be penned in by the mass of horses in the square ahead, and fenced-in people standing on the edges of the pavements.

Julie heard Anna's comments to someone in the crowd and immediately sensed something was wrong, noting Anna scowling at someone harshly.

"Julie, this is Bruce, my horrible ex-husband-to-be." Anna announced.

Bruce flushed, and then grinned as he looked up at a woman on a horse.

"Pleased to meet you. Are all of Anna's new friends as stunning as you?" Bruce responded, smiling at Julie with his usual over-confident smugness.

Julie simply grinned back, shaking her head in disbelief at his corny nature.

She regarded Bruce and was naturally impressed by his appearance. He was good-looking, but her views were tainted, as she'd already heard about him. Also, she'd known enough smug, cocky men herself to read Bruce like a book. Although never married, she'd had various long-term relationships, and even an affair herself at one time for several years with a married man. But strangely for her, she'd never found her perfect partner. Nor cared to, preferring her single lifestyle and the freedom to do as she pleased.

Bruce had all of the warning signs of the kind of man who might be fun for a few dates, but would soon become domineering or a cheat. Probably both.

Anna almost smiled at Bruce's cheeky comment to Julie, his quick wit being an aspect she'd previously liked in him. But she forced herself to look away, so he didn't catch her amused look and read something else wrongly into it.

Deep down she felt contempt and anger for his intrusion on her special day, although secretly inside she also couldn't help but admire his determination in hunting her down, and finding her in Windford. It indicated he had feelings.

Questions flew through her mind in lightening speed as to how he'd found her, knew where she kept Penny and that she'd be here today. All the worrying thoughts passed through her mind as she looked for a way to escape from this part of the crowded square, away from Bruce, and back to Chris.

Anna scanned the crowd of people, looking to find her mum amongst them. She knew the sight of her mum might scare off Bruce, as she'd soon tell him her thoughts and where to go. She was also now glad her dad wasn't there. He took no prisoners, and would have flattened Bruce out cold on sight.

She caught a glimpse of her mum, way off over in the far corner of the square where they'd originally ridden in. Waving a solitary arm, she smiled upon seeing Anna catch sight of her. The reins held in one hand, Anna beckoned her mum forward with her free hand, to indicate for her to come on through the crowd. But she shrugged her shoulders, to indicate she could not move about the square, it being as packed-in people as was the central area with all the horses and riders. She sighed, swung her vision round, then suddenly a face within the crowd of people caught Anna's attention. 'Her?'

Anna glanced at the image at the woman standing within a shop-front, partly hidden, seemingly only a few metres away from her mother. They hid up, as if deliberately not wanting to be seen. But Anna had spotted her.

She was dressed casually, and in her hands held a long-lens camera, as did many spectators. As soon as she saw Anna look her way, and realised she'd been seen, the woman disappeared, ducking down and off into the crowd.

For the second time today Anna's blood froze at the sight.

'But was it really her? Why on earth was she here too?'

Bruce spoke again, flipping Anna's attention back to the present danger and shaking one worrying thought in her life over to another. Possibly worse.

"Come on Sweet. I'm sorry for all of the shit I've caused. We can discuss it. Stop this messing about. Come home. I'm in a hotel. Pop over. Let's talk."

Bruce gazed up at Anna, his face set with a sympathetic, yet coy grin. Anna looked down contemptuously. At one time she would have simply caved in like a typical quaking wench; but now she had new strength and vigour.

"I want you to come back to Leicester with me. You can bring the nag back too. Jan will take her back. I've asked her already. She's looking forward to it and the stable is reserved for you and that thing. Let's stop playing games."

Anna's face glowed and was set to explode, discovering Bruce had obviously spoken with Jan and arrogantly made arrangements with her for Anna to move 'that thing' - namely Penny - back to Leicester. No way.

The assumption and typical arrogant nature of Bruce's action made her boil, and the enraged expression was not missed by Julie, sensing the bitterness.

She moved Bonnie forward, the coloured horse's head close to Bruce.

"Bruce, isn't it?" Julie enquired in a low tone, head tilting slightly seductively. "I like your ski jacket. Very nice. Fits you well. In all the right places. Snug. Shows off your muscles. And they colour suits you. Very smart. I like it all!"

She giggled and Bruce actually blushed, then ruffled his shoulders, absorbing the compliment like a sponge. Anna cast Julie a slightly puzzled look, wondering why she was encouraging Bruce, seeing his face glow and brighten.

"I understand you like horses? I love men who like horses. Usually sensitive and passionate." Julie continued in a manner Anna had never heard before. "Would you like to pat mine? Bonnie. Bonnie by name, bonnie by nature."

Bruce confidently stepped towards the barrier as Julie edged Bonnie forward, the mare's head extended over the steel safety barrier toward her new friend. Bruce raised a hand to pat the coloured mare, proud to show his horse skills.

"What a lovely horse," he proclaimed, head turned, smirking at Anna.

Instantly Bonnie's ears flattened, nostrils expanded, and her head flew out; her teeth flying forward at lightening speed, bit hard into Bruce's forearm.

Julie instinctively pulled the aggressive mare's head back, as a howling Bruce clattered to the pavement; right hand clasping the left arm Bonnie had bitten.

The people around Bruce all separated, as if Moses' had appeared with his staff, gasping in shock at the man who'd been attacked and now collapsed.

Bruce rolled about in agony, yelling and cursing, Bonnie's bite hard and deep.

"I'm very sorry sir!" Julie proclaimed. "Wrong aftershave. She didn't like it!"

With that she expertly spun Bonnie around and kicking hard, and with no concern for the other horses around her, pushed a space before her. Like an equine plough, she bustled away the horses in her path, face set with a huge smirk. A gap opening ahead, she turned around to look at Anna, indicating with a flick of her head for her to follow. Anna half turned, smiled and then looked down at the crest-fallen figure of Bruce, being helped to his feet.

"I'll never come back to you. You're history Bruce," Anna stated, calling to him as he rose from the ground. "And don't follow me. I have a new life."

Concerned by his plight, two old women brushed him down, sweeping dust off his smart ski jacket, much to his deep embarrassment and flustering.

With that Anna kicked Penny on into the gap Julie and Bonnie had created, to see Chris on Cirrus buffeting his way through the horses over towards them as she joined Julie, the threesome now all well away from the barriers.

"Are you all okay?" Chris enquired with concern, his head scanning the crowd, realising something had happened from the people's shocked reaction and having seen Bonnie lunge forward and Penny dangerously spin around.

"Yes Chris, all okay. Nothing to worry about," Julie spoke. "Typical Bonnie!"

"Thank you," Anna added, looking red-faced at Julie, trying to hide her glow.

"We were getting penned in and then a man tried to touch Bonnie. Well you know her! She didn't like him very much. And I can't say I can blame her!"

Julie grinned at their private joke, missed by Chris, but absorbed by Anna with a smirk. He turned Cirrus in the crowd, nodding for the pair to follow.

Anna furtively looked about to see what'd happened to Bruce, but an elderly gentleman now stood in the place at the front where Bruce had been moments earlier, seemingly having completely disappeared from the crowd.

The threesome formed up on the other side of the square, and Joyce then appeared directly before them, having made it carefully through the crowd. The group pushed further forward through the now calming group of horses to meet her, most riders settling down and now enjoying a drink and cake.

They now all stood proudly before a smiling Joyce. Camera poised, she began taking photos. Anna typically blushed, but was pleased her mum got her and Chris in together, along with shots of her saviour's; Julie and Bonnie. Never one to miss out, Tracey even managed to magically appear and get in on the action, bustling in on Fred, glass of port already in hand - as to be expected.

If Anna appeared apprehensive on any of the photos, her eyes seemingly focused anywhere other than directly on her mother, it was because she was cautiously looking about the square for Bruce to appear and spoil everything.

Or possibly the woman she'd also seen. Or maybe thought she'd seen.

Both unwanted parties seemed to have vanished.

But both were definitely unwelcome and worrying.

Anna relaxed slightly now Chris was beside her and things began to settle down and the horses eased up, as everyone found a space to stand. Various foot followers wandered through the horses, passing glasses of Port and cake up to the riders. Chris took two glasses and carefully handed Anna one.

Anna gulped the red liquid in two swigs. The Port hit home and warmed her.

With a sigh and a smile to Chris, she felt she was now ready for anything.

Almost anything.

Chapter 71

Unrequited love does not die; it's only beaten down to a secret place where it hides, curled and wounded.

Shakespeare

On the other side of the market square the antis were noisily waved placards. Dave stood next to Adam Yates, who was on his mobile phone, talking to his 'associates.' They'd managed to get lost en-route and would possibly miss the start of the meet. Adam, not from the area, was trying to guide them in, with Dave's assistance. Norfolk's roads were notoriously bad to navigate, and they were currently on a country lane looking at an old windmill across marshland. Not much use, but worrying, as they shouldn't have been that far away.

Izzy had watched Dave talking with Adam, who she greatly distrusted. She sidled over as Adam drifted off. "What's going on with you new best buddy?"

"He's got some additional support coming from Essex. A bit heavy."

Dave admitted for the first time with a sly, all-knowing grin. He'd kept the secret inside him for so long, he was itching to tell Izzy. He smiled, hoping she would share his excitement and be impressed.

Clearly she didn't and wasn't. Instead she sighed, shook her head in disgust, and cast a sideward glance at the dubious Adam, chatting away on his mobile.

"Dave, we don't want a rent-a-mob coming and causing us trouble, do we? And who is he? Adam Who? I don't trust him. And why should we do that?"

"It's time they learnt. Why not?" enquired Dave, dejected by her reaction.

"Because they'll come here, cause massive trouble for us, and no doubt lots of damage, then piss off back to their neck of the woods. I know these people better than you. Reggie has farm workers who do whatever he instructs. No questions asked. It'll leave us with the shit to sort out next time we go out. We're the ones who'll get the grief off this lot next time out. Not your new mate and chums. They'll be long gone. The hunt accepts us at the minute, but could cause real trouble if they really wanted. We have to play this carefully."

"Play Izzy?" Dave spoke with a degree of anger; bitterness in his tone.

"I don't consider this a game. For me it is a cause. Lets take real action!"

Izzy wondered what was eating Dave, other than his deflated ego, but could suspect. She knew she had to approach him from a different angle.

"Look at him over there. That's James. He used to play rugby for Norfolk. Posh, but tough. He could pick you up and use you as an arse-wipe!"

Izzy pointed over to the burly figure of James; a heavily built man, seated upon a massive Irish-draught-cross. He was another keen hunt member, and on the committee. Currently he was chuckling away to his best mates Steve and Reggie, glass of port in hand, his cheeks matched the drink in colour.

Dave simply didn't care. To him those who hunted were all 'stuck-up scum' and should be barracked and antagonised to drive some sense into them, and show them up as the evil murderers they were. As well as Posh Bastards!

He looked at Izzy slightly puzzled, it obvious their causes were not the same, but point in case, the 'Posh' James was a typical rich 'Hunter' whom he hated.

Izzy looked at Adam, still speaking on his mobile but wandering back over to the pair, his face expressionless; something else she didn't trust in him.

Although she wasn't vain, Izzy was used to most men's jaws dropping when they saw her. Then they stared longingly at her, determining what part of her anatomy they wanted to explore, before trying to sweet-talk her into bed.

Adam Yates hadn't. To him she was nothing. Not even a cog in a very small mechanism. Hence he wasted no time on her. Everything about him appeared calm, calculated and professional; as if part of some larger, secret plan.

"The cavalry should be here in fifteen minutes," Adam said, looking at Izzy and then away and to Dave, as Izzy blankly ignored him. Adam didn't flinch or colour up, seemingly emotionless and uncaring of Izzy's contribution.

"Oh good," said Dave, rather thinly, now trying to show some interest, even though he knew he'd made a mistake by getting Adam heavily involved.

"How about getting some chants going and more placards spread around the square," Adam suggested, taking control. "Let's get some noise and action!"

With that Adam pulled out from his rucksack a large, high-quality camera and small video camera. Izzy curiously looked at the professional equipment, but Dave, oblivious, eagerly followed Adam as he wandered into the crowd.

Izzy knew if Adam Yates were an insect, he'd bear bright yellow and black stripes. He'd also probably have a big deadly stinger coming out of his arse. She ignored him and wandered off to see Mary, the skinny girl she'd chatted with previously at the last PAACE meeting. Mary wore a vile multi-coloured, hand-knitted wool hat her lesbian girlfriend had knitted for her as a Christmas present. It was horrible and Izzy tried not to smirk looking at it perched upon Mary's skinny head. It reminded her of a heavy woollen tea cosy her nanny used many years ago to keep her favourite pot warm. She'd always hated it.

"I love your hat," Izzy politely lied, grimacing inside, but smiling externally.

"Thank you. It's great! Made from recycled wool," Mary proudly announced. "Recovered from landfills. I'll get Jean to knit you one," Mary beamed.

Inwardly Izzy winced, wanting to puke, but nodded enthusiastically.

Izzy turned towards the hunt members, glancing at Steve, smartly dressed in his finest hunting clothes, boldly seated upon a well-brushed Casanova. Steve caught Izzy's longing look, missing nothing, and raised his glass of Port in salute and grinned wickedly. Izzy blushed and looked away sheepishly.

"Come on Dave, let's get these placards sorted and raise the volume a bit," said Adam. He lead Dave off, as he looked over his shoulder at Izzy, not missing anything it seemed, before the pair vanished into the crowd of Anti's.

The placard holders were moved further around the square and Dave and Adam began chanting: 'Shame on you' in unison, getting more Anti's to join in, but without a great deal of real enthusiasm. Adam eagerly took photos.

Sitting on Casanova, Steve heard the weak chants and whispered something to James; a local hotelier and businessman, who chuckled and his big round jolly face broke into a huge smile, nodding in acknowledgement. He hunted regularly, organised many social functions for the Shoteton, and was well respected within the hunt. Watched by James, Steve shuffled Casanova closer to the main group of anti's, who were chanting and cupped his hand to his ear, as to gesture that he couldn't hear them; laughing loudly, joined by James.

His action was met with a chorus of exaggerated jeers and boo's from the anti's, to which he simply turned Casanova away and chuckled openly to the burly James. Sitting next to James was Gavin, on his grey Duke. Although quieter, he was good friends with both Steve and James, and laughed at Steve's gesture, looking at the group of anti's with a mixed feeling of both disgust and pity. Dawn sat primly next to him on her grey horse, Poppet.

"Don't get involved Gavin," Dawn whispered seriously across to Gavin, worried he could invite trouble with James and Steve. He looked at her cold.

"Don't be silly, what do you think they are going to do?" he answered coolly, the mild effect of the glass of Port seemingly increasing his bravery.

"Come over here and punch your head in!" Dawn replied.

Gavin blushed at her harsh, blunt, but honest reply, knowing she was right. He was not the bravest in the world, regardless of how many ports drunk.

"Hippie scumbags." Dawn muttered, looking at the anti's with equal disgust. "They all want to get off their arses and get a job. Lazy, idle, tree-huggers."

Gavin eyed her curiously, his face breaking into a grin at the thought of her comment. Dawn didn't work, never wanted to, yet pre-judged the antis simply because of their views and antics, automatically considering them lazy.

They probably all worked harder than she had ever done in her entire life.

Rising in his stirrups, he looked over the heads of the horses to see Elizabeth sitting some distance away, next to Lady Burlingham. Both looked his way, tipping whips and smiling back, one more so than the other. He smirked.

Dawn didn't miss the look and tried to see who Gavin was smiling at so warmly. As she scanned the faces, she could catch no-ones eye, except Reggie, who was looking her way, strangely staring intently. His expression was not warm, until someone beside him spoke, then a false smile was spread.

Lord Burlingham was out, as promised, enjoying the day and good company and sat beside Virginia, Reggie, Lady Carter and Carol. Mike Hawthorn stood on foot at his side, as always seemed to be his way and position. However, he also seemed to have his attention focussed elsewhere. On someone else. He was smiling at a rider seated within the crowd, whilst scanning the others. Also, in addition to keeping a wary eye on the antis and any dubious activity, acting as Bertie and Virginia's unofficial bodyguard and loyal protector.

The anti's were still heckling Steve, but with years of practise he ignored them, until one Anti in the crowd caught his eye and his face instantly lit up.
"Happy Christmas my darling," Steve called to Izzy, blowing her a kiss.
"I missed you yesterday at lunch. I waited. You should have popped in. I still have your pressie in my lorry if you want to come and get it after the meet. I'll give you it now, if you want." He grinned, all heads turning to look at Izzy.
She went crimson, stopping in her tracks along with Mary, who was shocked. To her it was simply typical of the blood-lusting male perverts who hunted. They should all have their wicked dicks cut off, then fed to hounds, so they couldn't fertilise any more poor women with their evil and corruptible seed.
Izzy glared at Steve, thinking of something apt to say, but her heart was fluttering, as it always did when she saw him, and she simply blushed.
"Piss off! I hope you've eaten too much Christmas pud and get gut rot," she replied loudly and with venom, much to the loud laughter of all the Anti's.
Steve responded with a laugh and blew her another kiss. Without thinking, Izzy jokingly imitated she caught it, then pretended to throw it to the ground and stamp on it. The simple action made Steve's grin vanish and face blush.
It was something the pair jokingly did for fun in the days they were together.
She still remembered, Steve thought, staring long and hard at the 'Anti.'
Izzy blushed too after she'd acted instinctively; realising nothing had changed between the pair. Simply time and a bad choice of roads at life's T-Junctions.
She looked at Steve, long and hard, face red, eyes connecting. Momentarily they both silently remembered the good days. Izzy looking at Steve for a few seconds too long, before she turned away, to disappear into the crowd.
Dave, talking with Adam, stopped and witnessed the incident. In full.
He stood gazing at Steve Harrison, who for a few seconds looked solemn, gazing vacantly across the bustling square to the empty space where Izzy had been, before someone beside him spoke and he recovered his composure.
Dave suppressed the dark rage welling inside, causing him to shake, then refocused his attention on Adam and what he was saying. He listened, but his mind was elsewhere, and wanted one thing. Blood. Steve Harrison's blood.
Glaring at the vile man before him, he knew their time would come. Today.
Then he looked at the array of scum he despised, all drinking an evil toast.
Once everyone had drunk their stirrup cup or three, and the gossiping had subsided, a general hush seem to fall over the entire square. Even the antis fell silent to listen to the speech they all knew was to come. All heads turned in.
Reggie stood in his stirrups and in his finest voice spoke to the assembled crowd, both to riders and those standing in the crowds, enjoying the glory. He thanked them for their support on this great day and how the tradition would long carry on, despite outside pressures and attempts to again repeal the law.
Reggie raised his hunting cap to finish and salute, as hearty applause rang out and he returned back into the saddle. Breath regained, he smiled across to Martin and Steve, who nodded approvingly. They were ready to go. Game on!

The applause of the spectators was suddenly drown out a small chorus of boos and jeers by the antis, now fired up by Dave, Adam and also Izzy. Mary, standing beside her; an unwanted affectionate arm looped through Izzy's, screamed a shrill noise, not unlike cat being run over. It made Izzy wince.

The riders seated within the market square, proud to again reclaim years of tradition, ignored all the jeers and abuse, but also knew they were now about to move off. Preparing, they returned the empty glasses, adjusted girths and said farewells to others, in anticipation of the day's forthcoming events.

Izzy scanned the faces of the placard waving group, many of whom would now simply disperse and return home. Maybe to enjoy a piece of nut-loaf, factory-farmed turkey sandwich, piece of gammon or sausage roll; to continue their Boxing Day with friends and family, but feeling they'd done their bit.

Just like the spectators; watching on in support of the hunt, standing around the market square in a mix of warm country clothing or 'Sunday Best.' For many this was their 'Boxing Day Treat' and made up part of their festivities. Whether they truly supported the activities of those mounted, or believed they were upholding a great tradition was questionable too. But each side felt it'd done its part to support or deride an activity on which opinions varied.

Izzy knew it would now be down to the few loyal followers who'd get out in the fields to harass the hunt and do the real work. She was happy they had a more out today, including some who could actually move unaided; without needing a disability scooter or care-worker in tow. It made it easier to cover the wide areas of land the hunt would draw today, but also sometimes it made it more difficult to control the groups, with people not fully understanding what to do or feeling they 'knew best.' As recently happened. Also, many naïve activists didn't fully understand the potential dangers associated with the activity. It wasn't safe. Horses killed people. Often. Accidentally, or not.

As they wandered off, Mary clung onto Izzy's arm like a limpet and Izzy worried for her safety if things ever turned nasty and got out of hand; which luckily they hadn't. Yet. What had happened to Adam Yates 'Rent a Mob' Anna was unsure, and she didn't want to ask and possibly stir up trouble.

Perhaps it was some sort of bravado on his or Dave's part, or the people had let him down, as so many did, especially the day after Christmas, when many had over-indulged. She could only hope they wouldn't show up and their usual group, plus a few new recruits, would be with them today to follow the hunt. Izzy didn't want any trouble today and luckily Dave had been keeping away from her, sticking with Adam, but had cast her wary looks all morning.

Martin blew loudly on the horn, to the joy of those watching who let a light cheer, then followed by boos. Then he and Reggie led the hounds out of the square, closely followed by Sharon and Helen, who'd fallen in behind and were whipping-in any hounds who were reluctant to leave the square or ran off to nuzzle someone in the crowd, attracting their unwelcome attention.

Many spectators in the crowd loved to call over or pat the hounds, thinking they were cute and cuddly. Some were, but they had a job to undertake. It greatly annoyed Reggie, Martin and Sharon, although they feigned smiles to any person in the crowd patting the hound, before they'd sharply flick the thong of the whip, call its name and swiftly moved the hound on. They knew the hounds were there to do a job. It was simple. Kill. Hunt and kill.

The hounds and leading four riders set off down a side street, the people in this area stepping onto the pavement. The police, from past experience and much previous planning, ensured the antis were kept on the opposing side of the square and they all strangely obliged. Thus, they couldn't hinder any progress of the hunt moving out of the square, or get into any danger by jumping in front of the horses and causing real issues or harm to riders.

This was the kind of stunt Izzy feared Adam's followers might be planning, or worse, trying to cause havoc in the market square for maximum publicity. But thankfully they hadn't appeared, and in reality, despite the protests, the event was well practised by the local council and police. Everything continued calmly as it had for many years, with all sides strangely knowing the rules.

Steve left a small gap as the hounds and lead four rode off, then promptly fell in behind, raising his hand for all to follow on. Accompanying him close by were Lady Carter, James, Elizabeth, Bertie and around fifty other riders.

Gavin and Dawn slipped in behind the lead pack, and although more quieter and reserved than the boisterous Steve or hearty James, Gavin was good friends with the pair, and often rode alongside them. As his horse Duke would go almost anywhere, Steve often used Gavin as a 'pathfinder,' to find tracks or routes through woods; a fact Dawn enjoyed and relished, now proudly riding out in the front group. She looked at the people watching them ride past from the pavements, and proudly at herself in the shop windows.

Checking her reflection in the glass shop fronts, an image in the dark glass of a rider close behind her caught her eye. Turning in her saddle, Dawn almost jumped at the sight of the woman rider. Lady Burlingham.

She was riding right behind Gavin, for some reason having seemingly been separated for from her husband, Bertie, who rode ahead beside Steve.

Dawn feigned a smile and received an equally false, feeble smile in reply.

'Stuck-up, rich cow' Dawn thought. She didn't like Virginia.

Virginia didn't like Dawn. But she kept her feelings closed.

Anna prepared to join the departing group of riders she could see swiftly heading off down the side street, and said a nervous, but smiling 'Goodbye' to her mum, who proudly stood on the pavement, waving. Chris grinned. Tracey jokingly stuck out her tongue to Joyce as she took more photos. Julie playfully prodded Tracey with her whip to get the happy bunch moving, as from nowhere, Goldie's elegant head and Tess' large form fell in beside Julie and Tracey. Sally and Carol both appeared from the main crowd, where they'd been chatting. Thus, the group of six from Horsewater were now all together.

Their group settled in with the main pack, now riding out of the square and down the side street, where the group broke into a trot. The mass of horses moved down the narrow historic street, and the noisy clatter of hooves resonating off the walls of shops and neat townhouses was almost deafening. Anna was on the pavement side, with Chris on her right. She smiled at him, her heart fluttering now they were off, but also relieved to be out of the confines of the square. As they advanced down the side street, still lined with many followers and others simply out for a stroll, she scanned the crowds, proud to be part of the tradition and see so many happily smiling and waving.

She smiled back gently at the various happy faces. Then froze.

There on the side street just ahead clearly stood Bruce.

With his usual cocky grin, he stood smiling.

She glanced furtively at Chris, then back at Bruce as they rapidly approached and almost drew level where he stood; her eyes wide in anger, but also fearful.

Bruce raised his hand, waving sarcastically towards her.

Chris spotted Anna's glance, followed her fearful gaze to the left and saw Bruce standing on the street. He glared long and hard, the bitterness evident.

Bruce stared back at the rider of the pale horse; somehow confident he could do nothing within the crowds and mass of horses. Then Bruce seemingly recognised Julie and the unique coloured horse that had bitten him, moving rapidly close behind Anna, with Tracey on her right, glaring at Bruce.

"I'm going to sue you. And that vicious nag! Assault!" Bruce hollered.

"Good luck," replied a smiling Julie, turning in her saddle. "I'm a lawyer!"

Sally and Carol, riding behind Julie and Tracey, caught the harsh exchanges, and Sally glanced back at the tall, attractive man standing on the pavement, clutching his arm. He caught her long glance and winked with a head nod.

"Wow! He's a bit of alright! What a hunk!" Sally proclaimed to Carol then Julie, turning in her saddle to smile back at Bruce. "Do you know him Julie?"

"Do not go there!" Tracey exclaimed. "Do not go there. First class tosser!"

Sally looked at her curiously, turning once more, but Bruce's image was now lost by the mass of horses trotting behind them and the fast pace.

"Anna's ex." Julie stated. "And besides, you're engaged. Cheating old hussy!"

Sally absorbed Julie's comments and embarrassingly flushed, but then broke into her familiar child-like chuckle. She winced as she saw Anna turn around, unsure if she was looking at her, or to check if her ex-husband was gone.

"Don't let that idiot spoil your day," Tracey offered, for once remaining quiet and seeing Anna's red face and worried look. "Forget him. Just enjoy today."

Anna looked ahead, wondering how long this would go on, but also felt embarrassed. She glanced at Chris, knowing he was now looking at her.

"Are you okay?" Chris enquired warmly, then reached across with his left hand, Cirrus' reins in his right, and gently touched her gloved hands, both gripped tightly upon the reins as they trotted along together.

"Yes, thank you," she sighed, looking at him, relaxing. "I am now."

Behind them Tracey silently nudged Julie, the pair looking quietly at each other with big grins, watching intently as Chris removed his hand and their knees bumped and stirrups clunked against each other as they closely rode on.

Anna switched her mind from Bruce to the thought of controlling Penny within the mass of horses, which were now rampaging down the widening street, riding four or five abreast in places and filling the whole road, which had been closed off by the police. Far ahead she could see the stream of hounds flowing down the street and the red jackets of Reggie and Martin.

The sight within a modern town centre looking unreal but she was proud to be part of it as the pace picked up slightly and the narrow streets turned to wider modern roads, the riders happy to be free of the confines of the town.

They moved through out of the town and past many local homes, where people stood at doors, many with wreaths upon them or bright decorations adorning the houses. They stood in front gardens and waved at the riders as they passed, or held children up at decorated windows, all to see the hunt ride past, the riders happily waving back and some, such a Bertie, tipping hats.

Anna was touched by the friendly nature of most of the local residents; keen to come out and watch them pass. She thought they might have been against the hunt, due to the inconvenience and disturbance it brought the town; along with the fact they had over forty hounds and fifty horses, trotting noisily past their house and disrupted their town square for a few hours each year.

However, the opposite seemed to apply, and the locals seemingly embraced the intrusion of the hunt for the one special day; welcoming the tradition returning and being maintained after it'd been banned for a couple of years.

Anna glowed inside, happy to be part of such a unique part of the country's heritage, despite all those who still tried to ban it, and was proud to be riding out with such great new friends, wondering how quickly her life had changed.

It was seemingly one of life's T-junction moments.

Anna had looked at the signpost and turned.

She could only hope she'd taken the correct turning.

Time would tell.

For now, she could only enjoy the moment.

She hoped the special day would be memorable.

It certainly would.

Very memorable.

Chapter 72

Everything has beauty, but not everyone sees it.

Confucius

Before long they were riding out into open countryside and territory more familiar with hunting, rather than the unnatural streets and tight confines of a market town. They moved off the road and onto a field of set-aside land and slowly spread out. Anna looked back and was amazed to see a convey of cars of all description following. She was used to a few cars following, and had followed herself with several other cars on her first time down to Chris's yard, but this large number of vehicles surprised her. The stream of cars seemed to disappear down the road, around a curve, and then on out of sight.

Anna tried frantically to see if her mum's car had made it out of the town and managed to follow her. She said she'd follow for a short time, knowing she had to get back home and prepare a late lunch. Anna would like to have waved to her mum, so she could proudly see her out hunting for real.

More importantly, she was also cautiously looking for Bruce's Audi estate. She furtively scanned the road, without making it too obvious; looking for both vehicles, but it was almost impossible to determine either amongst the wide range of vehicles that snaked along the road as far as could be seen.

Martin and Reggie took the hounds to cover the first field and the mounted field fell in line behind Steve. Chris kept close to Anna, the feeling from yesterday still strong within them. He'd occasionally look over and smiled, she returning it likewise, each silently grinning, the glances not missed by Julie and Tracey, nor a curious Sally and Carol, who could only easily guess.

From the onset the pace was fast and the hounds got onto many hares, although soon lost them, their pace too fast and the ground too poor or scent not good enough for the hounds. Despite the recent snow and cold weather, the ground was good and firm underfoot, with the horses all going well, but the scent line was poor for the hounds to keep onto anything for a period.

As the pace eased and groups spread, riding down a farm track, James found himself beside Chris and Anna, and unashamedly admired her elegant looks.

"Where the hell have you been hiding this stunning lady?" James asked Chris, cheekily winking at Anna. "Chained up in your cellar with all those others?"

Chris blushed, but raised a finger to his lips, turning his head to both sides, as to check in an over-dramatic fashion that no one was listening.

"Shh! She doesn't know about any of them! We need to keep that a secret," Chris whispered far too loudly, then grinned wickedly at Anna, who raised her eyebrows and smiled, beginning to understand his darker sense of humour.

James chuckled loudly, rocking about in his saddle with laughter.

"I picked the locks on my shackles and escaped!" Anna declared, as the two men chuckled again at Anna's equally quick and witty comment.
"James, this is Anna. Anna, this is James." Chris formally introduced the pair. "Ignore him and anything he says. It's all lies. Mostly. But some may be true."
James grinned, gazing appreciatively at Anna, already liking her humour.
"She's been out a couple of times," Chris added, "but mostly when you've been sunning yourself abroad or busy making more money. No doubt to add to the rest," Chris jokingly replied, knowing James well. He simply smiled.
"I hope you'll be coming with him to the Burn's Night Ball," enquired James after a few strides; forthright and straightforward, as was his no-fuss manner. "I'd love to see you there. Very much so. I'll take you there myself if he doesn't ask you. But I'd better warn the wife. That might a bit of a problem!"
Anna looked at Chris puzzled, unsure how to reply, totally unaware of any Hunt Ball, as no one had mentioned it, but knew how much she'd love to go.
Chris flushed, then stated simply. "I hope there'll be quite a few of us coming from my yard this year. I've been meaning to sort out numbers and book a table with you, but I've been busy. Tracey usually sorts this out, but you know her. Probably forgot and leaving to the last minute. She doesn't a party. I'm sure Anna would love to come with the others, wouldn't you?"
Anna liked Chris' coy reply and somewhat hidden 'group' invitation.
She smiled back at Chris somewhat over-exaggerated, and warmly at James.
"I'd love to come. You'll have to give me details," she replied direct to James, but glanced at Chris. "And check with our wife. Unless Chris asks me!"
"It's only a month away. I'm surprised Chris hasn't asked you personally. Not very good if you ask me. But he is a cad!" replied James, grinning at Chris.
"He's obviously got so many to choose from he hasn't decided which one to take yet. Maybe he'll select one of those wenches he keeps in the cellar!"
Anna chuckled, but was suddenly unsure of James' comments about women in Chris' cellar, remembering only yesterday when Max growled. But she enjoyed the jovial company and banter, feeling more relaxed in his presence.
"You never know, I may become all modern and ask Chris myself, instead of waiting for a 'wench' to grab him," she exclaimed, making Chris go crimson.
"You've got a great one here," James roared with laughter, slapping a big paw on Chris' back, making his tip forward and Cirrus almost jump at the action.
"I'll make sure I seat you two near me on the top table, then I can keep an eye on you. I sense trouble from you two! I'll give you some details when we get back. And you can make sure Chris brings you, or he's in big trouble!"
Anna smiled, instantly liking the rotund, but very happy James, who touched his hat peak, kicked the flacks of his big horse, and trotted off ahead of them, moving up towards Steve, to give him a heart slap on the back too.
"I should have mentioned the Ball," an embarrassed Chris said quietly to Anna as they watched James ride away, the pair now riding side by side and alone once more. "Busy. I forgot! It's been a busy time. Not for a month."

Anna was unconcerned, but liked how Chris now appeared embarrassed and seemed to be apologising for not asking her out to a ball; it almost assumed he would. That said, until yesterday, there'd been no reason why he should.

She turned her head to scan the bleak open countryside around them, the double-rutted farm track cut within a beet field lined with hedges the only features, noting some riders ahead and some behind, enjoying the solitude.

"I thought Tracey had mentioned it to you. "Chris continued to mumble. "It's her sort of thing. She usually gets a list and books with James. It's a good night. Late January. I go, although just really for the Hunt. It can get rowdy!"

"Well, Mister Chris Turner, will you do me the honours of being my date for your hunt ball?" Anna spoke confidently, but her glowing face betraying the false bravado. Chris blushed, but smiled back, looking deep into her eyes.

"I accept your invitation Ma'am and will be delighted to accompany you." Chris' face glowed, but he clearly enjoyed the banter and Anna's boldness. "I'll send my man around with a carriage to collect you. Dress is formal."

Anna tittered, now enjoying and understanding Chris' humour, then playfully punched his arm, the pair smiling. Anna was about to reach across and grab his hand, and felt bold enough to lean across and kiss him, but was unsure if it was too soon. Instead, now in silence, she turned her head to look down the long, muddy track ahead of then, with open ploughed fields either side. The countryside was bleak and empty, but their spirits were high and full.

Aware they were lagging behind the main group, a few hundred yards ahead, they prepared to kick on when the clatter of hooves could be heard from behind. Both turned simultaneously to see an elegant grey horse approach.

Sadly for Anna an equally, or better, elegant rider sat upon it. Anna winced upon seeing the unwelcome intruder, about to ruin her romantic moment.

"Chris, sweetie! Happy Christmas!" Virginia Burlingham announced in an exaggerated manner, pulling her mount up to a trot, then a walk. Drawing level she pulled alongside Chris on his clear side, causing Cirrus to nudge into Penny, who in turn moved over, pushing Anna onto the edge of the track and the rough headland, Penny stumbling. Anna glared across Chris to Virginia, who was oblivious as ever to her. She smiled at Chris, then grabbed his hand.

"I haven't had a chance to wish you Happy Christmas," she spoke softly, looking into his eyes. "I must give you a kiss. I was going to call you yesterday but we had a few around at the hall. Before you know it I've had too much Pud' and Port, and I'm snoozing it off in a chair. All too quickly the day's gone. You could have come around. I did invite you. Bertie loves to see you."

"Yes, I know, and it was very kind of you to invite me, but I was at Anna's." Chris stated somewhat proudly. His face glowed seeing Virginia's strange grin.

She glanced across at Anna, but said nothing, noticing the steely gaze Anna returned back, sadly without any Christmas spirit; only sharp daggers.

"That's nice," was all she replied, dismissing the point. And the daggers.

She smiled at Anna, as one would to a fond pet about to be destroyed.

Her knees knocked with Chris and stirrups clattered as their horses jostled on the track, pushing Penny further into the headland and field. Anna glared.

Virginia seemed oblivious and uncaring. "Anyway, I can't give you your usual Christmas kiss, as it's too late. So this will have to be your Boxing Day kiss."

With that she removed a hand from her reins, kissed the soft brown leather fingers of her glove, stretched out her arm, then gently pressed her fingers against Chris' cheek. Her finger remained on his face for what seemed an age, as Chris glowed red. As did Anna, shocked at the open and brazen flirtatious act. Then, just as quick, Virginia regained her reins, kicked her mount into a canter, and thundered off. A few strides out she turned around with a cheeky grin. Rising up in her saddle she blew a kiss and teasingly lifted and pushed out her perfect backside. "Toodle-pip and Happy Christmas!" she hollered.

Anna's face matched that of Chris; both matching the Port drunk earlier, as they regarded Virginia's rear end with differing views. She faced forward and cantered down the track toward the main group riding ahead of them all.

Anna stared silently at Chris, her look one of shock and amazement.

Chris simply looked at Anna, shrugged his shoulders, grinned and sniggered.

"Don't worry about Ginny," he added. "It's just how she is. It's nothing. Really. We've known each other for ages. We're really just very good friends."

Anna glared, noticing his embarrassment and wasn't about to get into a full-blown 'domestic' after exchanging one sneaky Christmas kiss, and there was nothing 'official' between them. But she wondered what'd gone on between the pair, now disliking 'Lady Sluttington-Whore' even more. If possible.

Trying his best to drop the incident, Chris suggested they catch up with the main pack, so broke into a quick trot. The banter and chat vanished as they moved on and joined the main group. Luckily Tracey, Sally and Julie were amongst these and the usual chatter and jokes began. Tracey offered Anna her hip-flask, and unusually she took a huge double swig. She needed it.

The incident was forgotten and the day went by swiftly, with the mounted field moving across the country quickly, covering a lot of land, as is common with hare hunting. They encountered various ditches; a common aspect of hunting with the Shoteton it seemed, most wide, deep and water-filled. But Anna soon became accustomed to jumping them, and when encouraged by a smiling Chris beside her, and trusting Penny, she soon lost all her fears.

They rode through woods, often jumping out of them and into fields, or into them from fields, several times leaping into unknown woods through small or thin hedges and even over ditches. It was often in these cases where Steve would send Gavin through ahead on his ever-reliable mount Duke. He'd make a path or find a route if the woods were dense, so the field could follow.

It was a challenging but enjoyable day for a novice like Anna, but Penny was fit, the ground generally good, and both horse and rider fully enjoyed it; always encouraged by an eager Chris and teased by taunting Tracey and Julie.

Anna spoke with Steve a few times during the day when the field stood and waited for the hounds, and although he made the expected cheeky comment, he eased back and seemed to know, possibly tipped off by James, that she was with Chris and 'Out of Bounds,' and respectfully didn't push matters.

Despite the large number of Antis in the market square, few were seen on the fields. Possibly due to the fast pace and masses of foot followers early on blocking the roads. When a few did arrive on the scene, they'd usually arrive only in time to see the riders disappear into dense woods or race off across another field in a canter and then lose them, to start the search again.

For the Anti's it was a poor day playing catch-up. Not want Dave planned.

Anna caught sight of her mum briefly early on, parked within a line of cars, waving at her from near an unploughed stumble field. Anna acknowledged her wave by raising a hand, but it was typically as they headed off into a dense wood. It was the first and last she saw of her, knowing she had to return home for lunch. However, she was glad she'd turned out, had the experience in the market square, and met had Chris, whom she knew her mum liked.

The pace kept up for a couple of hours and once again Anna, Chris, Tracey, Julie and a couple of other riders had dropped back from the fast moving front of the field. They knew they could soon catch up, but momentarily rested their horses on the edge of a wood. The car followers had dropped off too, although many loyal supporters still kept watch from the roadside.

As the roads were less congested, Izzy and her varied crew of antis could now be seen more often racing about in their cars, dashing about the country lanes, trying to locate Steve and the main pack, along with the hounds.

But what Anna was hoping she wouldn't see, and she'd secretly kept a quiet look out for all day, sadly did appear in the early afternoon. An Audi estate.

A chill ran down her spine when she caught sight of the distinctive sports version of the large estate car. It was Bruce's Audi and he sat within.

She glanced at Chris, who was joking with Julie and sat turned facing away from the road. He'd not seen the vehicles on the nearby road, nor luckily had Tracey, again turned away, playfully prodding Chris with her whip.

Anna furtively looked toward the cars moving slowly down the small lane, then turned to join the conversation, but it didn't hold her attention. She glanced back at the road, noting Bruce's Audi was behind a Land Rover, which stopped on a low headland, hindering his progress. Anna thought the driver of the Land Rover was Lord Burlingham's gamekeeper. He appeared to be keeping an eye on his employers, having followed them closely all day.

Bruce went to drive past the Rover via the opposite embankment when a familiar battered Ford, with Steve's ex-wife inside, raced past both vehicles. It caused Bruce to brake hard and curse. Anna noticed the exchange of cold glances between Bruce and the occupants of the Ford, but then turned her attention back to Chris and her small group as someone spoke. Thankfully, Chris hadn't seen the Ford race past, or more importantly, recognised Bruce.

Three other riders rode up towards Anna's group and nodded politely as they rode past and moved on to join the main field further along the edge of a small wood. Seizing the opportunity, and with a swift glance towards Bruce's car, Anna suggested they also move on too. Lucky for her, all agreed.

The antis had parked their Ford just off the road a few yards past Bruce's car, half on the low embankment and were now disembarking, looking up towards Chris' group. Bruce looked at the four protestors with strange curiosity.

Unaware of the potential disaster to unfold from the roadside if they'd remained, following Anna's suggestion, the group moved on, focussing on the field and wood to their side, where the hounds had entered. Anna breathed a sigh of relief as they all disappeared round a bend in the tree line, and out of sight, no one else aware of what lay on the road behind them. With a final glance, she was pleased to see no screaming antis or Bruce running on behind.

Anna hoped Bruce had simply come to Windford out of curiosity, or maybe to try to speak with her in an attempt to try to talk her around, as was his way. But the fact he was still following, worried her greatly. But he was arrogant.

Anna didn't dare mention anything to Tracey, it only being luck she and Julie were chatting and hence luckily missed seeing Bruce or recognising his car.

If so, she knew a confrontation between Tracey and Bruce was sure to have resulted. However, despite moving off, Anna now had the constant worry and niggling doubts, that Bruce might, and probably would, show up again.

She was sure he would. But when? Who knew.

Bruce had seen Anna and was also sure he'd see her again.

And soon. In fact he could almost guarantee it.

As the small group of riders rode off, Bruce considered his options, noticing the battered silver car parked before him, wondering who the hell they were and how they fitted into the hunting game. They didn't look like the usual bunch of 'Posh Toff's' driving in smart 4 x 4's or similar country people.

Bruce regarded the group in the battered Ford, then suddenly realised who they were, assuming that they were antis. He'd noticed the rows of placards, wielded by hippies, cat-loving old single-women, neurotic anti-vivisectionists and pale flesh and bone Vegans in the market square; but he'd taken no real notice or interest in the people he considered stupid hippy tree-huggers.

He'd only been interested in finding Anna within the crowd of stuck-up horse riders and hoped he could speak with her. Then convince her, as he was sure he would, to return back to Leicester with him, and into his bed.

He hadn't expected the massive cheering and jeering crowds in the town square, and then worse, to be attacked by a maniac horse and embarrassed before hundreds of people. Humiliating. If he could somehow get revenge on the cocky bitch riding the vicious 'Apache' horse, he would. He'd thought little of the antis until now and had no interest in their course or concerns.

However, the woman in the passenger seated suddenly grabbed his attention.

A dark baseball cap sat upon her head, hiding part of her face, but a mane of golden hair hung out the back. She was seemingly berating the driver, and as she turned sideways, Bruce noted a very attractive and intelligent face.
The driver, seemingly oblivious to Bruce, clambered out of the car, speaking loudly into a cheap mobile phone. The remainder of the car's occupants, including a skinny woman with some weird knitted object placed upon her head, all clambered out. They scanned the woods and road about them.
Then, one of the Anti's noticed a car parked close by.
Bruce looked at Izzy.
Izzy looked at Bruce.
Bruce cocked one eyebrow and smiled. Typical Bruce.
Izzy grinned back; smitten, but then turned her attention back to Dave.
He stood by the open driver's door, dramatically leaning against the roof, speaking on his mobile to Adam, shaking his head, yelling loudly.
"Where the hell are all these extra people you promised? This is shit!"
Dave raised his eyebrows and shook his head to Izzy who simply tutted, and then turned to speak with Mary, aware of someone else looking at her.
Then she caught wind of Dave's conversation. Chillingly she listened.
"They're actually in the area. Looking for us? Are you sure? Excellent news, Adam. Yes, I know it's been chaotic. The pace has been really fast and we've struggled to make contact all day ourselves. And we now the country. Where are we? Just up from the small junction we passed each other earlier. Near a small wood. We'll stay put. We're parked up in front of a flash Audi estate with a ponce inside. And there is a green Land Rover nearby. See you soon!"
"They're coming!" Dave spoke excitedly to Izzy. "The cavalry. Yes!"
She regarded Dave with fresh concern, shaking her head.
"Now we'll see some real action!" Dave was excited. "Game on!"
He scanned the road, looking for the cavalry to arrive.
But Izzy's attention was on something else.
The cheeky Audi driver, playfully waving at her.

Chapter 73

My foe outstretched beneath a tree....

The Poison Tree – William Blake

Chris' group soon joined up with the main field, closing in to see the pack now at work. Anna enjoyed watching the hounds spread out across the field, with Martin and Reggie close behind, their jackets stark and bright against the dull brown of the surrounding fields and the backdrop of the skeletal woods, set in a stark dark brown, faded green and grey backdrop. Bleak, gloomy.

The image of Bruce had gone, but was not forgotten. Sadly.

The pace was fast, and the mounted field soon begun to stretch out, very few riders and horses able to maintain the chaotic and hectic pace of the few front riders. But as ever, Steve was there, keeping in touch with the hounds and always followed by a few hardened riders and fit horses. They moved quickly on and the hounds drifted back onto a stubble field, which in turn led onto a dense and dark wood; one they'd previously been through early on in the day.

Blowing up, Martin went in rapid pursuit of the hounds, kicking on Bert, in order to maintain contact with them as they chased a new hare, which had appeared on the edge of the field as soon as they'd begun to cover it. Reggie pushed on Samson, thundering alongside, following Martin and the hounds directly across the field towards the small dense wood they'd been in earlier.

Sharon and Helen, the Whipper-In's, had long vanished, going off in search of stray hounds, which had been lost from the last hare two fields back.

Steve noticed Martin and Reggie's actions and knew the land well. Guessing where they might come out, he led the straggling mounted field back towards the small dense wood, made up mostly of Larch to drain the poor damp soil.

Gavin had lost Dawn at some point long back, her mount Poppet slow and unstable on the softer ground, and Dawn not the most confident rider. She always moaned at Gavin upon their return, that often he'd left her. However, anytime he caught up with her she was usually casually following behind, in no hurry to move on, and chatting to someone else who had a slow horse.

However, as usual, he was going well on Duke, his grey ex-steeplechaser and keeping in touch with the front, riding close to Steve, almost like his trusted lieutenant. Behind him rode James, Lady Carter, Virginia, Elizabeth and three younger riders, all who'd done well to keep up with them all on ponies.

On the road the few car followers who were left; many given up and gone back home for turkey sandwiches, were lucky to be in the heat of the action for once, as they now watched Reggie and Martin chase across the field.

Unfortunately so too were the anti's, now hollering loud and watching the unfolding action. As was a bemused Bruce, seated in his car and curious.

Steve had noticed Dave Pearson's car arrive with Izzy inside, and also some other vehicles, including Mike Hawthorn's, all parked up nearby. Hence why he was also keen to clear the area and move everything on. He'd been around the block too many times to fall for any tricks from Izzy or the scum with which she now sadly associated. They'd been lucky to avoid them for most of the day, and he didn't want the day spoilt by giving them any sport now.

Suddenly a second hare appeared before Martin and Reggie, confusing the hounds just as they'd almost reached the edge of the field. It split the pack of hounds as the two hares ran in different directions, both going towards the woods at opposite ends, scattering the hounds as they blindly followed within the dark confines. Martin blew up, hollowing at the 'speaking' hounds within, all howling and yelping excitedly from differing ends of the compact wood.

"We'll have to go in and get them," hollered Reggie, cursing loudly, knowing he'd lost Sharon and Helen a field or two away and the wood was thick.

"Yes sir, looks that way," replied Martin. "Bastards! Typical shit!"

"Nothing is ever easy. Less get them back," Reggie replied stolidly.

Martin jumped instinctively into the woods, with ease clearing the small ditch separating the field from the wood. Reggie followed on, disappearing into the dark wood with an elegant leap, Samson flying through twigs with a crack.

The couple could be heard blowing up and hollering, as they called for the hounds to re-group, cracking their whips within the dense wood. The whips retorts sounded like pistol shots, deep inside the wood and lost from view.

Steve saw where Martin and Reggie had gone into the woods, and knowing the land well, led the few riders immediately with him alongside a hedge, up the side of the adjoining field and then into an opening into the next small wood further down. This wood in turn linked onto the main one, where the hounds had entered from the adjoining field. Inside, Martin's horn blowing and Reggie's hollering could be heard, as the pair hoped to collect the hounds, re-group, and then head back out onto the open fields again. Woods were never good news for Harriers, which were a fast-paced, open field hound.

Chris' group, riding further back, saw where Steve lead riders and followed on at a walk, pleased to now almost be back in touch with the main pack and technically where they should be, riding with the Field Master. Glancing back, he noticed a couple of other stragglers slowly catching up, including, Dawn, Sally, Carol and a few others whom he recognised. They paused to let them catch them up, so they could all then re-group within the woods with Steve.

The woods Steve entered, ahead of the other two groups, were a mix of Larches, evergreens and deciduous, densely planted together, giving a dark and gloomy appearance and permitting very little light within. The inside of the woods revealed two tracks, one going in deep, and the other skirting around the edge of the woods. The ground inside the woods was soft, peaty and wet, almost boggy in places, despite the densely packed trees, which had probably been planted so close together in a hope to help dry up the land.

A pale cream blanket of fallen and slowly rotting pine needles carpeted the floor in a subtle beige, mixed with patches of dark exposed peat underfoot, where the ground had been disturbed or became boggy, or where the horses hooves kicked up dark divots as they slowly walked. Steve headed off along the latter track, with Gavin, like a trusted wingman, by his side. Hounds could be heard deep within the side woods, with Reggie and Martin still calling to them. Steve and Gavin, followed closely by James and Lady Carter, moved deeper down the track, the rest of the few riders following, including, Lady Burlingham, who was chatting to Elizabeth, and the three younger riders.

To Steve's amazement, two hares ran in front of them, dashing through the unfamiliar dense woods and over the track from the edge of the woods, going deeper into the gloom, the area seemingly rife with hares, which obviously knew the area well. Steve raised his hand and halted the small group, as both he and Gavin noticed one of the hares did not appear to move from the track and run deeper into the woods, like the others had, but instead appeared to remain on the edge of the track, pulling frantically at its head, gently thrashing about, almost as if stuck or strangely restrained. Which it was.

Curiously, Steve and Gavin looked on at the poor animal, unsure why such a fast beast both respected wasn't moving, but frantically trying to free itself.

Seemingly unable to move away from the inquisitive humans seated upon horses now looking down upon it, the hare's yellow-eye gazed back. Gavin spoke first, breaking the eerie silence between the pair as they looked on.

"Is that hare caught in a snare?" he questioned openly and clearly.

"Yes, that was what I thought," Steve answered mournful. "I wasn't too sure, but unfortunately it looks like it is." He stared sadly at the creature he chased.

Gavin looked down at the stricken animal, as James and Lady Carter, pulling up behind, gazed on silently too, all now coming to a halt.

"Not really sport, is it?" Steve added. "Should be free. A far hunting chance."

"That's what I thought," replied Gavin. "I know were out here to get them as such, but that really is not the way it should be. No chance this way."

Before he could say more, Gavin was off Duke, passing Steve the reins, and striding across the ground, wandered over to the distressed hare.

"That's a good chap Gavin," said Steve realising what was on his mind too, having considered the same option, but being more reluctant to act.

"Try and release it from the snare, then let the poor thing free," he called.

Lady Carter, James and Elizabeth, along with three young riders and Virginia had pulled up behind, and all curiously watched on.

"Mind it doesn't bite Gavin." Elizabeth said, offering some advice. "They've also give one hell of a kick. Those legs take no prisoners! Take care."

Gavin paused, grinned, then looked at her cautiously, casting an eye toward the other members of the small group now watching. Smiling at them, and seemingly not aware of any danger from the hare until he'd begun to advance towards the thrashing creature, he now wished he'd not known more.

Who'd set up the snare in woods was unknown and never would be.

It could have been a poacher or a gamekeeper. Either or neither.

No one ever came forward. Nor would. They'd dare not.

Even though it became the catalyst for the string of tragic events to rapidly follow, it was forgotten after the incident subsided and the incident recalled.

The long, brass picture-wire snare was attached to a rusty angle-iron stake, driven deep into the soft ground, and set just off the track, the loop hooked up onto a low twig to raise the wire at hare neck height. It'd worked perfectly.

Gavin slowly approached the hare, which was struggling violently. He'd seen countless hares running about out through many seasons of hunting, touched stuffed ones and even carried a few dead ones, always surprised by their size and weight. They were big animals, as was this one. But all usually dead.

However, this hare was very much alive and wanted to remain so.

As Gavin approached, it leapt about wildly, the snare pulling harder against its neck as it threw itself about to avoid Gavin's grasp. Weaving about, hands flaying, he tried desperately to grab it, but the hare writhed about, leaping from his gloved hands each time he made contact and attempted to grip and hold the powerful, frantic animal which saw him as a natural killer.

Steve and James chuckled, mildly amused by Gavin's desperate struggle, both half wanting the hare to have a sporting chance to get away, but also aware of the fact that if the Anti's saw the snared animal in Gavin's hands, it'd give them fuel to their claims of cruelty, unaware the opposite was the case.

Lady Carter and Elizabeth looked on silently, hoping for a good outcome; along with Virginia, who remained quiet too, but watched on intently. She was seated beside the three young riders; all looking on in amazement, unsure if this was a regular thing when hunting, quietly muttering to themselves.

James shouted encouragement to Gavin, whose mind was set on the task at hand, still trying to grab the frantically wriggling hare, which continued to slip from his grasp each time he took hold, such was its weight and strength.

The small group looked on, focussed on the man and the hare; all willing the hare freedom, and hoping Gavin would come out unscathed too.

Gavin made another attempt to grasp at the hare, but it lurched sideward and he stumbled onto the damp peat soil. Rising back up, gazing into the loose cover and the dead bracken, movement caught his attention.

Something in the undergrowth was watching him.

Dark eyes and a black nose, set within a pale face.

Gavin gazed at the face in horror.

A hound was approaching.

Chapter 74

I have been all things unholy. If God can work through me,
he can work through anyone.

St. Francis of Assisi

The hound was a single stray harrier, lost from the main pack, and slowly moved through the woods. Head down, it had drifted through the dense undergrowth of the wood, attracted by the scent of the various hares passing, and also the voices of the riders within, following an unknown instinct. Whatever the attraction, it heard Gavin's movements, drawing it in further.

Then saw the frantic hare. Instinct rewarded.

Eyes alert, head held high up above dead nettles, brambles and thick undergrowth, it trotted forward and on towards Gavin and it's quarry.

Gavin caught sight of the hound just as it lunged at the hare.

This time he caught the hare as it leapt almost vertically, jumping away from the hound and straight into the safety of Gavin's welcoming hands. Although squatting down, to reduce the tension of the long snare, he firmly grasped the writhing brown fur body and held it close to him. Its long black-tipped ears brushed against his face with velvet softness and for a second Gavin could only admire its beauty and strength and doubt why he hunted them.

Beside him, mud covered and inquisitive, nose erect, stood the hound.

Its instinctive aim was simple. The kill the creature Gavin held.

A yellow and brown eye looked deeply into his Gavin's as he held the petrified animal close to his hunting coat, whilst frantically trying to loosen the snare from around the hare's neck. At the same time he was trying to shield the heavy, wriggling hare from the hound, now at his feet and nuzzling at both him and the hare. For what seemed like an age, but was only a few seconds, he tried to juggle between protecting the hare from the hound, but also desperately trying to release the snare from its neck; the task made harder by the probing hound beside him, whom Gavin repeatedly tried to shoo away

From the corner of his eye he spotted another hound approaching, then one more, as the stray hounds naturally began to reform back as a pack. Steve, fully aware of what was happening, yelled at the two new hounds to leave, loudly cracking his hunting whip in their direction as best he could with the low tree branches about. But Gavin was under a lower hanging tree, down a slight incline off the track and out of reach of Steve, high up on Casanova. In addition, Steve still had hold of Duke, who stood patiently alongside him.

Further hounds began to drift through the woods, being flushed out of the opposing woods by Martin and Reggie, but also naturally drawn towards the hare, as the next newly arriving hound began to slowly close in on the first.

The first hound, at Gavin's feet, pushed its muzzle up toward the dangling legs of the hare, nipping with its jaws and trying to grab at the big hairy feet. Gavin swung his body around, shielding the hare and began to gently kick out at the hound with a flaying leg, whilst trying to keep his balance, not helped by the heavy, wriggling hare. Clutching the writhing hare high enough up to be clear of the hound, he was still trying to free the long snare, pulling at the iron stake, in the hope that it might move, frantically aware that more hounds were heading into the woods all the time and then onto him.

James cracked his whip too and moved forward a few steps in an attempt to keep the hounds away from Gavin, as the two hounds moved in. Lady Carter joined him. Steve stood holding Duke, aware a disaster was seconds away.

From his low position off the track, Gavin peered out through the trees, onto the field and beyond. He could see a line of car followers parked up, their drivers exiting the vehicles and looking over towards the woods where he stood, seemingly curious as to why a group had halted in the woods.

Worse, he could also see a group of anti's leaving their vehicle and begin to stride purposefully across the field and also head towards the wood, curiously looking towards the small group sat within, but importantly for them, at long last they were no in touch with both the hounds and mounted field.

More riders began coming up the side of the field, moving along the edge of the wood, then slowly began to enter the wood where he and Steve's had originally. Other riders too, separated in the earlier dashes, were taking a slower approach, drifting across the field from the opposing wood, also curiously looking towards the group milling around within the woods, but also keen to re-group with Steve, their Field Master, and the lead horses.

Gavin knew that before long, what would have been a quiet and discrete job, that only himself, Steve and a handful of riders would have known about, was now in danger of become an incident in full view of the entire mounted field, a small group of car followers, but worst of all, a pack of angry Anti's.

Gavin began to panic, knowing that both hounds and Anti's; along with rest of the field, would be near him within a minute and so had to move quickly.

"Can you get the snare off Gavin?" called a desperate Steve, himself only too aware of the potentially dangerous situation that was beginning to unfold.

"It won't keep still," yelled a concerned Gavin. The hare still squirmed and leapt about in his hands and he did his best to keep it pressed against his chest and keep at bay the three hounds now nosing about at his waist.

Then the first hound leapt at him, grabbing at the hares leg. Gavin pushed it away with his own leg, desperate not to loose his grip on the hare, which squirmed upwards. Strangely, it was the break he needed, enabling him to get a firm grip on the writhing animal. He hugged the hare tight with his left arm, relaxed the grip of his right, and holding the hare close, managed to release the wire from around the hare's neck. Finally the hare was free.

But it did not yet have its freedom.

Gavin was now in a worse predicament. He had the hare freely within his hands, held tight to his body, but was now surrounded by about half a dozen keen and eager hounds. He stared at the sight before him, shaking his head.

The small pack of hounds, growing in numbers, seeing their natural foe feet away, and tantalising held so easily before them, began pushing in on Gavin.

Panic was evident in the hare's beady yellow eyes, which never left Gavin's face, but for once sensed its captor was in a way also potentially its saviour.

Gavin fought to keep the hounds at bay, as Steve, James and Lady Carter tried to help, cracking their whips and calling over at the increasing number of hounds, which began to flood into the woods. These were drawn instinctively or being driven into this section of the wood by Martin and Reggie from the far field, totally unaware of what was occurring, trying to regroup the pack.

Gavin looked about him to see a growing mass of curious bobbing heads with dark, keen and intent eyes, all focussing in on him, each hound naturally drawing the other over. He felt as if he were an island in a sea of sharks.

The hare was a lone castaway stranded upon that island. However, the tide of hounds was rapidly rising. At any moment the safe haven would submerge into the depths and that lone castaway, the hare, would be consumed.

Death seemed to easily flow forward, as the wave of hounds eagerly lapping at the islands shores increased, ready to claim their lone victim.

Gavin felt despair for the hare he'd tried to save and looked towards Steve. He returned an equally hopeless look, seeing Gavin now almost completely surround by about twenty plus hounds, still desperately clutching the hare.

Martin's voice could then be heard approaching, calling at the other hounds he and Reggie were leading, half of which now almost surrounded Gavin, several jumping up, trying to get at the huddled form secure in his arms.

"What's going on?" Martin hollered to Steve, sensing something wasn't right, seeing him standing holding a spare horse, then took in full the predicament.

Looking out through the woods and across the field, the four advancing anti's, peering into the woods, could also clearly see a hunter standing within, rising up above a mass mottled cream, black and tan pack of harriers.

Then, as they advanced forward, things became clearer. A lone figure stood openly holding a hare, it's velvet brown coat stark against his black jacket.

To them it appeared as if a hunter had caught a hare and was openly baiting a pack of hounds; far from knowing the truth was exactly the totally opposite.

Gavin could suddenly hear the cries from the anti's as they began to run across the field; mixed with the yells from Martin, James and Steve, all still attempting to control the hounds, which were now baying at Gavin and the hare, pawing at him, their muddied paws sharp as they clawed at his legs.

He thought desperately what to do, in serious danger of being knocked over by the mass of hounds now leaping and pawing at him, all desperate to get to the hare, which he firmly held to his body. He considered his options.

And they were limited. Very limited.

He had the hare free of the snare, but now there were about thirty hounds in a large circle jostling about him. Those at his feet were desperately trying to jump up at the frightened creature held tight and protectively within Gavin's grasp; all ready to tear it to pieces within seconds of its expected release.

What on earth could he do? Wide-eyed, he looked at Steve for help.

"Throw it clear of the hounds," Steve hollered. "It's your only hope. The hounds might get it, but at least it'll give it a sporting chance to run clear. Raise it up high and throw it as far as you can. But quickly!"

Gavin looked on in desperation, unsure where he could safely throw the hare, being surrounded by a sea of cream, tan and black heads, all looking intently in towards him with no clear safe haven to throw the poor animal.

He heard shouts coming from the field just outside the woods, and then the thunder of hooves, as the remainder of the mounted field came riding around near the front of the woods to join the melee. Others closed in behind Steve from the track in the wood, to suddenly witness the strange incident.

Still the hounds nuzzled, pushing their noses up Gavin's jacket, trying to tug at the hare's legs. It wriggled within Gavin's arms, seeing the horror about, trying to save itself. Desperate to save the hares life, if at all possible, Gavin lifted the hare up high, in both hands, careful not to stumble and fall as he was jostled by the mass of hounds moving in and around his legs.

Several jumped up, almost knocking him over as he raised the hare above his head, almost like a ritualistic act; ready to throw the hare clear of the hounds.

Christmas, an aptly named young bitch hound, was lighter in weight than the other hounds and almost white in colour. She was a favourite of many, simply because she was so easy to recognise, friendly and also rather cheeky.

On this day she was decidedly mud coloured, with a hint of white. She saw the hare lifted high, and the opportunity to grasp the animal seemingly being offered before her, and sprung forward. Leaping up and bouncing off the back of another hound beside her, she leapt straight at Gavin's raised hand and caught the hare fully in the flanks. Her jaws clamped shut as she fell.

Sharp teeth crunched deep into the hare's side, cracking the poor animals thin ribs, she momentarily hung, swinging from Gavin's solid grip.

He looked on terrified at the swinging hound, bit hard into his precious hare, it in turn screaming high above him in a mournful screech.

The weight and momentum of holding up both hare and hound, along with the force Christmas had leapt at Gavin was too much. He collapsed, dropping hare and hound together, both disappearing into the ravishing mouths.

The sea of hounds consumed Gavin and the hare.

Chapter 75

Character is revealed when pressure is applied.

Henry Ford

A loud cry of "No" broke out close by as Gavin turned and saw Dave Pearson running towards him. He recognised the skinny Anti who'd harassed them on many occasions and who now stood only metres away, separated by only a covering of bare branches and scrub within the woods and the massive sea of leaping hounds surrounding him. Numerous faces appeared, including Izzy, who everyone knew from year's back, but also some fresh Anti faces.

This new group of Anti's looked decidedly aggressive and were running up to the woods behind the lead group of Pearson and Izzy, which included a very skinny woman who appeared to be wearing a tea cosy upon her head.

Mostly clad in black, three of the new group of Anti's were the 'Essex Boys,' the other being Adam. But he stood aside, with a number of cameras around his neck or in his hands. Near to Adam, peering through the woods, now with Mary at her side, stood Izzy. She looked on silently, staring firmly through the tree branches. Not at Gavin, but at Steve, almost in disbelief at the incident.

Steve, a natural hunter, spotted the rampaging group of antis, some of whom he recognised, others he didn't. But he recognised his former wife's chilling stare and knew her abstinence from the melee meant she sensed trouble.

Stranded amongst the sea of hounds, Gavin rose fully, a look of horror and defeat upon his face as he stared at the hounds, tugging and pulling at the hare he'd hoped to save, but now in vain. The hare's pelt was ripped and torn, and its fine bones cracked, as snapping, bloody jaws all fought for a piece. Etched in Gavin's memory, the hare still regarded him. It's bright brown and yellow eyes never leaving his memory, as though forever cursing him for his intended act of kindness, which had gone so drastically wrong. He'd failed.

It was a burly, shaven-headed, black-clad anti, standing by Dave within the woods, striding forward like an angry Viking, who made the first move.

"You fucking evil bastard," he yelled, as he charged head first at Gavin, who was still surrounded by the pack of hounds, and now busy tugging and tearing away at any remnant of the hare, their lips and muzzles red and bloody.

The first anti waded through the mass of hounds, kicking and flaying at them with heavy boots, as he aimed straight for Gavin, who seemed unaware of everything else now going on around him, only seeing the hare's final stare.

"Leave my babies alone you stinking bastard!" Martin yelled. Positioned away, near the wood's edge, he saw it all and kicked Bert on. He pushed the big horse on towards the hounds and the rampaging anti; cracking his whip hard, trying to deter the anti approaching Gavin, and also protect his hounds.

Gavin was no street fighter and looked on bewildered as the burly, black-clad anti ploughed through the mass of surrounding hounds and was upon him in seconds. The anti grabbed Gavin's collar, pulling his face close to his.

He yelped in shock, the anti's foul and putrid breath warm and sickly.

The head-butt was swift and well practised. Gavin flew back with the force of the blow, stumbling and crashing onto the soft woodland soil and falling back amongst the mass of jostling hounds, hands reaching up. He vanished.

"No! Gavin, my sweet! Leave him alone, you fucking filthy piece of shit!"

A woman's common screeching voice cried out through the woods.

All heads spun about the woods to identify the source of the strange voice.

Suddenly a grey horse broke free from the ranks of riders within the woods.

They all looked on in bewilderment; their amazement was intensified as they watched Virginia - Lady Burlingham - charge forth, screaming foul-mouthed abuse and obscenities at the anti and aiming her horse directly towards him.

Everyone looked on in astonishment upon hearing Virginia's yell, the voice and usual character not one and the same. Or so they thought. Wrongly.

"Hold on Gav'!" Virginia screamed more. "I'll get that fucker!"

She'd silently watched the whole incident unfold, since entering the woods from the track and quietly seen it all. From when Gavin had dismounted and onwards; watching the tragic series of events unfold, knowing he'd tried so hard to vainly save the poor hare. And she could keep quiet no more.

The anti's attack on the man she loved was more than anyone could take.

Virginia knew Bertie was close behind; somewhere on the track within the woods, but she now no longer cared. It had long been over. He was no fool

She knew their marriage was a sham. And so did Bertie.

Kicking on her horse, she bursting through the crowd of riders, including Elizabeth and James, dashing past Steve and onto the pack of hounds, now being moved on by an equally shocked Martin, who also was heading towards the anti. Martin paused and stared in amazement at the charging form of Lady Burlingham, as unknown profanities still flowed freely from her mouth.

Gavin regained his composure upon seeing the advancing form of his guardian angel and true love of years, seated upon her valiant white charger.

Reinvigorated, he stood up and took a swing at the Anti. He was lucky. The anti was distracted by Virginia's shout and speed, fearing the horse may trample him. Gavin's blow hit him clean on the temple, just as he turned his head. It sent the anti straight down, falling into the remaining hounds.

Still being called and whipped by Martin, the hounds ignored this new obstacle, and jumped over his thrashing body of the collapsing anti, making him scream loudly as the hounds claws and rough pads scratched at his face.

Virginia smiled at Gavin, proud of his heroic action, as he was her; charging to his rescue. She rode up to him grinning, dispersing the hounds about her horse's feet and uncaring, almost trampling the Anti. She dismounted and took a battered but smiling Gavin in her arms, warmly holding him tight.

Adam and Dave were just entering the woods, closely followed by Izzy, along with the other two aggressive 'Essex Boys.' They'd arrived far too late, getting lost, but were keen to get into some action. For them the day so far being a washout, and in addition, they'd been paid well by Adam for trouble.

On seeing their colleague fall into the hounds, and hearing his cry, all except Izzy thought the hounds were mauling him. Another 'Essex Boy' boldly dashed through the woods, ran around the hounds and straight up to the woman holding a grey horse and comforting a man who'd decked his mate. Coming up on Virginia's blind side, as she gazed at Gavin, the anti pulled out a length of cut down broom handle, which he'd had slipped up his sleeve. He skilfully slid it down and into his hand and raised it, ready to strike hard.

"You fucking stuck-up bitch!" the Anti screamed, flaying the stick at Virginia.

"Ginny, look out! Behind you!" Gavin screamed and she turned instantly.

Virginia saw the Anti's raised stick and countered the strike with her hunting crop like a skilled swordsman, swiping the stick away and unbalancing her attacker. Enraged, the Anti regained his footing and turned, ready to strike again. But this time Gavin rose and charged around the front of Ginny's horse, pulled at the reins and reached the Anti just as he made the strike; this one crashing down upon Ginny's shoulder, sending her crashing to the floor.

Gavin came up behind the Anti and punched him hard in the kidney. Seeing Virginia fall down, a furious Gavin pounded two more swift blows into the Anti, but this time into the back of his head; hard knuckles connecting with delicate neck bones. The anti collapsed, clutching the back of his head and kidneys, dropping the cosh and falling to the ground stunned and in pain. Gavin rushed around to the opposite side of the horse and bent down, to see the fallen form of Virginia lying equally dazed on the ground, but rising up.

"Ginny! Ginny, my love, are you okay?" he screamed, pulling her too him.

As he reached her, also grabbing the horse's reins, she pulled herself up from the bracken into which she'd fallen, slowly sitting upright, getting a breath.

"I'm okay Gav', but what about you? I thought he was going to seriously hurt you. I hope you're okay. Did he hurt you Gav'? Are you sure?"

Gavin nodded positively and the two sat in the bracken, affectionately hugging each other, lost in their own private world. Both were oblivious to the activities going on about them, and the stunned looks of the mounted onlookers, including that of Bertie and Dawn who both stared on in silence.

Bertie, red-faced, sat in the woods, surrounded by the crowd of on-looking riders who'd witnessed the incident and looked on, shocked at the affection shown by the two. Dawn, unseen by Gavin sat outside the woods in the field, coldly watching, now knowing in full what she'd long feared, but had not wanted to believe. Resolutely she pulled Poppet away and slowly rode off. Unseen tears welled up in her eyes as she rode away alone, quietly sobbing.

Things moved quickly and simultaneously, as Gavin and Virginia embraced each other, no longer caring that their long secret affair was out in the open.

Dave Pearson came racing through the woods. But he had a different target. Leaping through the dead bracken and undergrowth, and screaming wildly, he headed straight towards Steve, who up until then had done nothing wrong.

"You fucking murderous bastard!" he yelled, careening through the undergrowth with open rage and hatred, looking for an easy target and vent.

Casanova, beneath Steve, saw the screaming angry man hurtle towards them and although usually stable, nervously shuffled back. Unwillingly, but fearing he'd lose complete control, Steve released Duke, who he'd still held onto for Gavin, calling over to anyone in the woods to catch the now loose horse.

Steve looked at the enraged man who charged at him, full of bitter anger and venom. Izzy came crashing through the trees too, a few metres back, but a more cautious Mary stood watching in shock from the edge of the woods.

Adam Yates had quietly followed the first group of antis into the woods, but stepped back from the rampaging, screaming mob, squatting beside a large beech tree, taking in everything, and also numerous photos of the incidents.

Unnoticed, as commotion ran through the woods, he pulled out a digital camcorder, enjoying all he witnessed with a seemingly professional air. Quietly he sat by the tree, happily recording all the sounds and images in the woods, smiling broadly, keen eyes glistening, enjoying every minute.

All was just as planned. Good. A result. Maybe it could get even better.

The Anti beneath the hounds pulled himself up, kicking a couple to clear his way. Martin, fuming, watched with anger and fought through the low sweeping branches to protect his 'children,' whom the Anti was freely kicking.

"You Wanker!" Martin hollered at the anti, who's German Army surplus boots lashed out at the hounds around his feet, their blood stained mouths still chomping at pieces of what remained of the unfortunate hare.

Kicked on by spurred heels, Bert crashed through the undergrowth. Martin's first swipe of his whip missed the anti's head by inches, as half stumbling, the pointed horn end of the crop swung past the anti's head with a whoosh.

But so quick was Martin's counter-swipe, from many years of sword practise, that this time the horned end caught the anti full in the face, smashing into his nose, breaking it with a deafening a earth-shattering crack. He fell heavily.

The Anti screamed in agony, clutching his now bent nose, as bright red blood began pouring down his face. Dropping to his knees, he put his hands down for support as he fell. But sadly for him this was just as Martin pushed on Bert. The hooves of the large black horse crashed forward, onto his hands, and crushed the fingers of the anti's outstretched hands into the soft soil, but still broke them all. The Anti's new screams were lost amongst the numerous other yells and cries resonating from all parts of wood as a riot seemingly broke out. A brutal kick from Martin to the already smashed face of the Anti, as he pushed Bert on, was enough to finish him. He rolled about on the woodland floor, broken fingers clutching a shattered face in total agony.

Martin cruelly looked at his victim, chuckled, and simply moved Bert on.

As numerous screaming bodies flew about within the confines of the woods, various frightened horses began to dash into each other; rearing up, spinning on their heels and dragging riders into the low sweeping branches of the trees.
Steve seeing Pearson charge at him, hollered for everyone to calm down, but it was futile and carnage reigned all around, to which he was responsible.
One of the younger children's ponies reared up, and the young girl fell off, the pony promptly fleeing in terror deep into the woods, peat divots flying up through the air as it thundered off. The young girl cried, from both the shock of the fall, but also the loss of her mount. A second pony, stable companion of the first, bolted in pursuit of its companion; the terror stricken and screaming young rider holding on for dear life as it ran off. The panicking pony weaved dangerously through the woods in order to catch its companion.
Lady Carter, watching the events in horror, cantered on through the woods after the two ponies, skilfully ducking under the low branches, following the sounds of the young girl's screams, to hopefully locate her within the woods.
The events happened simultaneously, with Adam, hidden beside the tree, struggling to record it all, whilst taking key photographs of each new event.
His smile grew wider as each fresh disaster unfolded, to his joy.
From the roadside, the car followers heard the various screams and yells too, and aware of what may be happening, various people ran towards the woods.
As the sounds from the first fight concerning Gavin ran through the air, they quickly streamed across the field toward the woods as fast as they could run.
Unseen by all, one of the police vehicles allocated to monitor the events that day was also driving along the same road. The policemen inside the vehicle, keen and alert, suddenly noticed hoards of people running into a small wood.
Many, along with horses and riders, were screaming and yelling. Chaos.
Without needing to be first-class detectives, which neither were, the two local policemen knew something was afoot upon seeing the melee before them.
The police car stopped and the two male officers gazed at the mob.
Back to work. The short Christmas break was over.
One smiled. The other looked apprehensive.
One was always up for a fight. The other not.
First out the door, P.C. Burton was back.
Action at last. Hopefully trouble.
Game on!

Chapter 76

The course of true love never did run smooth.

William Shakespeare

Reggie, deeper within the adjoining wood, and separated from Martin by some distance, had been rounding up a few rogue hounds after the two hares had split the pack. Upon hearing the commotion and first screams and yells from the adjoining wood, he knew there was trouble, and fought his way through the low branches and scrub of the wood onboard Samson. Urgently, he pushed the grey horse forward through the dense undergrowth; with the few hounds he'd collected up together sniffing at his hooves.

A veteran of many campaigns, Reggie knew the yells most likely meant trouble with anti's. He'd been surprised they'd not seen more throughout the day, noting the large crowd in Windford. However, being Boxing Day, and a landmark day for both sides, he'd expected trouble in some form. But he knew Martin and Steve could handle most things, and the likes of James, an ex-rugby player, never took any trouble. He feared what he may meet.

He arrived in the section of woods where everything was happening, just as the third hired 'Essex Boy' yob came crashing through the woods to assist his fallen comrades. Also armed with a small bat, he flayed it wildly at anyone or anything that got in his way. The bat struck James hard on the knees, and the burly man winced as a second blow was aimed higher. James swiftly turned his horse to avoid the strike, but in doing so, spinning his massive mount on its hocks to avoid the blow, it sadly revealed Elizabeth seated behind him.

She was also fighting to control her frightened horse, it nervously shuffling, trying to move sideways; but she was trapped beside a tree and various other horses which had subsequently closed in behind the original small group.

The anti lunged wildly with the bat, flaying blindly into the space now created by James, not caring who or what he hit. They were all scum in his mind, and besides, he'd been paid good money to cause 'real trouble.' Double bonus.

The length of wood made contact with Elizabeth's horse's neck. Frightened, rather than injured or pained, the horse reared, tipping Elizabeth backwards. Then it promptly spun, ducked beneath the low branches, and cantered off.

Elizabeth fell heavily onto the ground, winded, dazed and shocked. The anti continued forward. Baton raised, seeing an easy target laying on the ground. Man, woman or child, he didn't care, so angered was he upon seeing his comrades fall. With a bitter grin set upon his face, bat raised, Elizabeth looked up in terror at the black clad youth stood over, about to viciously strike at her.

"No!" She screamed, fear in her eyes, arm instinctively raised to protect herself, waiting for the crashing blow of the baton to fall upon her.

But it never came. Instead the anti crumpled before her. Like a felled tree.

"Lizzie!" A man's voice had cried out close by, followed by the sound of feet crashing through the undergrowth. Then the anti fell beside her, a second before she'd heard a familiar voice from someone she loved, call out to her.

"Piece of shit. How dare you harm her. Scum!" The familiar voice cursed.

The fist of Mike Hawthorn flew straight back into the face of the anti, his arm disappearing within the black hood, only reappearing as the anti's head flew backwards, accompanied by his collapsing, flaying body. With the heavy cheek breaking punch, the anti fell onto the dirt, to lay beside a gasping Elizabeth. She turned sideways, to see blood pouring from the battered anti's mouth, as a pair of strong hands gently raised her wheezing body upward.

Mike Hawthorn had been following and seen the whole episode erupt from the roadside. He'd run across the field and through the woods, just in time to see Elizabeth attacked. Now he cradled the woman he loved in his arms.

"Are you okay?" Mike asked, supporting her head, brushing dirt from her face with a gentle hand; fondly kissing her forehead before who gazed on.

Elizabeth wheezed, but managed to regain her breath and nodded, smiling.

"I knew you'd come to help me Mike. Thank you," she croaked with a tear. "That's why I love you so much. Always there when I need help."

Kneeling on the soft bed of pine needles and peat, Mike cradled her head in his arms, gently brushing pine needles from her jacket, then looked up and across the scene of mayhem around him, to see the riders staring on in shock.

Reggie's glare, sitting from afar in the woods, said it all.

He remained silent, seated upon his mighty grey, his thousand-yard stare, as if lost in his own thoughts. But the bitterness in his eyes said it all.

Then he looked away, ignoring the pair with hatred and contempt, seemingly now more concerned with finding the hounds. He yelled at Martin, checking if he was okay, asking if any hounds had been injured in the scene of chaos.

Mike looked away from Reggie and turned his attention to Elizabeth. He whispered something to her as she turned her head to see the figure of Reggie ride away, off through the woods, but turned to bitterly glance their way.

She flushed scarlet, seeing his mean, cold expression, then burst into tears.

The couple tenderly hugged each other, seated amongst the dead bracken and pine needles that littered the area, as mayhem continued amongst the remainder of the mounted field, followers and anti's who were still standing.

The first anti who'd attacked Gavin scrambled up, and upon seeing the mess of his two fellow warriors, turned back toward his attacker. Ready to get even, seeing the man who'd killed the hare now with the woman who'd struck him, he wanted revenge. However, he didn't count for the sharp eyes or tenacious unknown upbringing of Virginia. The anti ran on, but Virginia spotted him. She stepped forward and flicked out her hunting crop, lashing it out wickedly in one swift movement. The leather thong caught the anti hard around the face. He screamed as it cut into his cheek and then wrapped around his head.

With a harsh yank of the whip by Virginia; like something from an adventure movie, the sharp jerk spun the anti's head sideward, his body following in circles, to crumple back down onto his knees, his face bleeding and smarting.
"Come and have another go you fucking wanker! Have a go. Tosser!"
It was Virginia who hollered loudly into the face of the battered and defeated Anti, standing boldly before him like an Amazonian Princess. She screamed loudly, in a voice far from that of any 'Lady' or anyone knew, but instead more reminiscent of someone brought up hard on an inner-city council estate.
This was indeed where she came from. And where she'd first fell in love with Gavin, nearly twenty years earlier, when they were both dirty-faced children.
Here they'd run together along the dark and dangerous back streets, causing trouble, but also taking none; 'Ginny' always being tougher than gentle Gavin. Back then they were young and not ready for the turmoil life can bring. Teenage lovers from when they'd fist met at school, they'd sadly they drifted off to live separate and vastly different lives. Only to strangely meet again one day whilst out hunting, instantly remembering their true love for each other.
But then they were both married, and in love-less relationships they wanted to leave, but knew they both couldn't or shouldn't, needing time or an excuse.
Now they had that excuse. And no longer cared, everyone knowing the truth.
Bertie looked on red-faced, then disappeared from sight with a small number of riders, who'd either no nerves, or thought better of becoming involved in such a fracas. A number looked on at Bertie, leaving his wife in such straits, without comment, face scarlet; a mix of anger and embarrassment.
But few knew their real lives and the true state of his marriage. In many ways.
Carol, riding beside Bertie, placed a comforting hand upon his.
He gripped hers back and smiled warmly at his friend. And secret lover.
Although everything happened at once and in a blur, it all seemed to pause for a few moments as the initial incidents with the anti's and riders took place.
However, Dave Pearson stood on the edge of the tree line.
Now was his turn and his time.
He stared intently at one rider seated within the woods.
Steve Harrison.
Eyes connecting, he screamed at his sworn enemy.
He was ready for his fight.
Game on!

Chapter 77

We shall never surrender!

Winston S. Churchill

Dave glared at Steve, but as he stood in the woods, Steve's focus of attention flipped as events changed; from Gavin and Virginia, then Elizabeth and Mike. He then watched as Reggie eerily moved off along with Martin, taking the hounds with him, saying nothing, but his chilling face speaking volumes.

As things subsided, he focussed on the bloody, stunned and battered anti's littered within the woods. He was also aware of the bolting ponies, and how Lady Carter had ridden off to find them, along with the screaming anti's still dashing in and out of the woods, along with road followers shouting and numerous riders all now appearing to witness carnage and confusion.

As Field Master, the mounted field were his responsibility, and for the few seconds he sat upon Casanova, his mind in a whirl at the mayhem, his quick mind for once unsure what to do and how to react. This wasn't in the book.

However, his attention became fully engaged in a new direction, when he heard the words 'Evil Tosser!' screamed his way. With Casanova stationary, he turned his head to see the skinny anti and Izzy both staring in his direction.

"Dave, leave him, he's not worth it," he heard Izzy beg, as she saw a furious Dave advancing forward. Steve looked contemptuously at the advancing anti.

Glancing sideways into the woods, Dave could see his battered cohorts, old and new, and knew this battle with his sworn enemy had been a long time coming. Steve in turn disliked the skinny Anti, but to him, he was simply an annoying idiot, who followed Izzy about and clearly had his sights on her.

To Steve the Anti was nothing. Simply an annoyance and pest. Similar to a persistent fly you'd repeatedly wave away, before finally swatting it flat.

But for Dave it was personal. Very personal. For Dave, it was everything.

Izzy stepped forward and reached out to touch Dave's shoulder, but he shrugged her hand away and stomped forward through the woods, heading on toward Steve. Her attention was momentarily drawn to Lady Burlingham, standing in the woods with her horse. She glared bitterly at Izzy, as if about to come over to her and cause further trouble. From what Izzy had just witnessed, she wouldn't have been surprised if she did. But Virginia looked away, her attention now set upon her newly declared love, the pair hugging.

Izzy's attention returned to Steve, who seated upon a motionless Casanova looked toward her, almost with a look of sadness. But as Steve saw Dave advance on him, Izzy noticed a glint appear in her former husband's eye.

"You poncey piece of shit!" hollered Dave to Steve, who casually looked back at the advancing Anti like he was something he'd find in a blocked toilet.

Dave stomped through dead bracken, the brown stems cracking underfoot, and swept some low tree Larch branches to one side, moving with purpose towards his enemy. Steve glanced about, noting the confusion of riders, followers and anti's scattered within the confines of the wood, and involved in their own trials, battles or incidents. He now had his own to address.

Steve kicked Casanova towards Dave in a brave attempt to intimidate and scare off the advancing Anti. Casanova was a big horse and in any normal circumstances Dave would have been nervous of the beast and offered more respect, especially knowing Steve had mown down one of his friends before.

Today was different. Dave was keen to impress, and full of hatred and bitterness. Thus any fear within was washed over by his bid to get revenge on the man astride the big horse before him and show himself to Adam and the other stricken antis. As he moved forward, Dave's eyes fell upon a large fallen branch that lay near the trunk of a tree. Reaching down, he picked it up, and in one swift action, brought it up, swinging it towards horse and rider.

Steve spotted the action and anticipated the movement early on, noticing the Anti glance at the large branch, sensing what he'd do. Thus he hauled on the reins just in time to check Casanova's progress and then turn him sideward.

The swinging branch flew past the horse's head, who then reared, rising up on his hind legs, hooves wildly flaying, but kicked forward by Steve to counter the action and bring Casanova back onto all four feet. Incensed with anger at the blatant attack, and with a jab of spurs, Steve pushed Casanova forward again. Then in one action, he drew forth his hunting whip, and swept it down in a lethal return counter-blow, straight towards the anti's head.

Dave was quick and side stepped the blow, countering the whip strike with the middle of the branch, then followed through, swinging the piece of wood at Steve as passed. The rotting branch hit Steve on his back and although hurting, carried with it simply momentum, rather than hard striking force. The half rotten branch shattered into many small fragments upon impact, and the moss and lichen upon it left a huge green mark across Steve's red jacket.

The impact and noise spooked Casanova, which tipped Steve forward and off balance, causing him to lose his right stirrup. He hauled up Casanova, trying to regain control in the confines of the woods with other riders moving clear of the now spinning horse and rider, and enraged, branch-wielding anti.

Dave's effort at swinging the branch in turn swung him around and he found himself looking towards the front of the big horse, which drew alongside him.

He then found his left arm against the horse's saddle and Steve's free hanging leg, out of the stirrup. Unsure of how tight a saddle might fit, Dave grabbed at the stirrup leather with his left-hand, pulling hard, trying to dislodge Steve, with the intention of dragging him off his saddle. But the girth was tight and didn't move. Steve glanced down at the Anti beside him, just as Dave slipped his hand inside the loop of the empty stirrup leather, to pull hard, determined to unseat the 'Knight' before him and fight him on the ground on his terms.

Steve regained his balance and put his foot hard back into the freely dangling stirrup. As he did so, Steve felt the Anti's hand inside his loose stirrup leather and pressed down hard with his boot. The loop of leather tightened like a vice upon Dave's arm, clamping him firmly to Steve and Casanova's side. Foolish.

"I wouldn't have put my hand in there. Not one of your better decisions!"

Steve spoke softly to the Anti, with a grin, then pushed on Casanova.

Dave realised the folly of his action. He tried to free his arm, but the tension on the iron-like leather, along with the extra pressure Steve was now exerting with his calf muscle, pressing hard down into the stirrup, were far too great.

The heavy leather clamped onto the anti's wrist, burning the skin, even through the combat jacket. His arm twisted as the horse moved, involuntarily dragging him along and across the woodland floor. Casanova, egged on by Steve, began to strut forward, involuntarily dragging Dave along with him.

Steve looked down at the entrapped Anti and smiled.

Dave glared up, his face changing from scarlet to white anger.

He spat up at Steve, the dry phlegm catching him full in the face.

Steve wiped his face with his whip hand, glaring down at the Anti.

"Fucking scum!" Dave hollered, preparing to spit again.

"You dirty bastard!" Steve swore. Then with his still free hand, the reins in his other, he struck down at Dave with his whip. The horn end hit him in the face, smashing into his cheek. Steve laughed at his now captured prey, who desperately fought to free himself and ward off any further vicious blows from the stout antler horn hunting whip, knowing he'd receive no mercy.

The second blow of the whip hit Dave on the top of his head and he tried to deflect it with his one free hand, drawing it across his body. Steve's second strike had little strength, his main concentration being on trying to control a distressed Casanova with one hand, whilst hitting the foul Anti with the other.

As the whip swung down towards Dave's head again, with his free hand Dave caught hold of the whip and entwined thong, wrapped around the shaft. With a desperate yank, he pulled the whip free of the Steve's unsteady hand.

In a singular, skilful manoeuvre, Dave flipped the hunting whip around in his free hand, caught the leather-bound shaft and raised it up high, with the sharp horn handled end now poised to strike Steve's body. Dave had the advantage.

He got one blow in, it striking Steve sharply on the thigh, causing Steve to flinch and wince. Then another blow, this time higher, catching him on the bony part of his elbow, causing Steve to curse loudly and sense real danger.

For once, despite the delicate position he found himself in, Dave felt he now had the upper hand in this personal battle. He was still ensnared to the side of the horse and his bitter rival, but this now seemingly acted to his benefit, the tables being turned in an instant. Steve could not escape from the enemy tied at his side and would have to endure further heavy blows from the deadly antler-horn end of the whip, until he released him or fell from his horse.

It was Steve's choice on how to act. Release the Anti or face more pain.

Seeing the Anti raise the whip high, and realising he was in serious danger from another vicious blow, Steve looked through the woods, suddenly spotted something, and focussed upon his target. Pulling tight on both reins, whilst simultaneously kicking Casanova as hard as he could, he set forth.

The big horse responded instantly like a racing car, lunging forward, with all power transferred back onto his strong rear legs. Breaking straight into a canter, Dave's body seemed to lift up off the ground, unbalancing him, his feet flaying in open air as the big black horse, with a smiling Steve atop, now raced through the dead bracken, tearing brambles and low tree branches.

The entrapped passenger, dragged by his arm, could only follow, seemingly now the underdog yet again, as the horse powered on. Dave let out a slight whimper as his legs began to frantically flaying over the woodland floor like a cartoon character. Arm firmly clamped, his body twisted back and forth as he stumbled over the first patch of deep brambles, through which he was dragged. The unyielding thorns tore deep through his jeans, ripping into his flesh like miniature saw blades. Dave regained his footing as the horse cleared the debris and moved onto a clearer patch, but then picked up speed.

Legs spinning around in free space, he desperately tried to keep his feet free of the horses crashing hooves. Turning his head from Steve's smiling, focussed face, Dave turned to look ahead at the woodland spread before him.

Then he saw what Steve was focussed upon.

Now he understood.

A large solitary Beech tree.

"No, No, you mad bastard!" he screamed up at Steve.

Steve glanced down and grinned. Then he winked.

Casanova was set on a course for the large Beech tree directly before him. Steve aimed the big horse slightly to his left; the position tight, but skilfully permitted only just enough room for his knee to pass by. But nothing else.

Dave looked on, flaying legs useless, seemingly propelling him to his own grim fate. Dragged on, the tree loomed before him. All too soon.

The crack, when it came was audible, both to Steve, but more so Dave.

He unfortunately he felt it too. Painfully. In full.

Many within the woods heard the crack. And also some outside.

Along with the scream. That was heard for miles.

The cracking sound both parties heard was not from a tree branch snapping, but Dave's radius and ulna on his free arm. He'd foolishly, yet instinctively, put out his right arm out to stop the tree's impact. Unfortunately, as well as shattering his arm, this action caused his right clavicle to break with the transferred force of the impact from his straightened arm. Three ribs were also broken as he was crushed between the massive horse and equally massive tree, being dragged through a gap between horse and tree too small for both.

As he passed clear of the tree, Steve instantly raised his foot from the stirrup, loosening the strap and permitting the Anti to fall free and away.

Casanova dashed away with Steve atop before he pulled him back, regaining control. He turned in the saddle to see a screaming Dave Pearson, howling in agony, rolling up into a ball at the base of the massive Beech tree.

Free of its unwanted obstruction, Steve managed to pull up Casanova within a few strides and spun him back around. Many witnesses from both sides, both mounted and on foot, looked on in horror at the grim spectacle. All seemed to stop their fighting at that instant, and looked over at the screaming form of Dave rolling about at the base of the tree. He tried to clutch his sides with what only just resembled an arm, the other not moving, as he fought for his breath, the broken ribs making him wheeze and groan violently.

Turning Casanova around, Steve rode towards him in a walk, then paused as he drew level, casually looking down at the annoying Anti for a few seconds, watching him writhing about, fighting for his breath. Steve smiled.

Result. Job done.

Adam Yates, hidden within the woods, watched it all; ensured he recorded the entire incident on his camcorder. Then, pulling out his long-lens camera, he got the money-shot; a close-up shot of Steve's final callous grin. Bingo!

Checking his recording equipment, Adam sadly failed to get a shot of Steve glancing over towards Izzy. It would have said much. And more.

Izzy stood dumb-founded, simply shaking her head in silence.

She always knew Steve had a cold, calculated and wicked side.

He'd now shown it to her in - all its glory.

Izzy shook her head at Steve; expression disgust.

He looked back at her, for once the grin gone.

Chapter 78

What is our aim? It is victory; victory at all costs. Victory in spite of all terror.
Victory, however long and hard the road may be.
For without victory there is no survival.

Winston S. Churchill

Within the rest of the woods and adjoining field, similar pandemonium was breaking out. A group of tail-end riders who'd not made it into the woods to rejoin Steve or form up with the hounds, could hear them being rounded up, so headed in that direction. They soon noticed a group of anti's and foot followers, followed by two police officers, who were charging up the hill and into the woods. Here the sound of screaming and yelling could be heard. The worried and curious group of riders all rapidly headed onto the woods.

Tracey, Julie, Chris and Anna were amongst these and upon riding up to the edge of the wood could see the trouble going on inside. Chris, Tracey and Julie had witnessed various incidents in the past with anti's but they were usually mild. They now looked on in wonder at what seemed to be unfolding.

Anna was confused as to what was going on, but almost accepted it as being part of the normal routine within hunting. Apprehensively she looked at Chris, the yells and screams very aggressive. They noted a number of car followers parked on the road, who'd also witnessed the incident unfold, had now left their vehicles, either entering the woods, or standing on the edge to watch. More joined the group moving over the field, including a familiar face.

Bruce had now decided his vocation in life was to become an Anti, regardless of his views and no knowledge on hunting. He was sure it was a just cause.

He'd noted the other car followers with interest all day and watched jealously from various vantage points as Anna roared about the countryside on her horse, laughing. He'd watched an array of attractive woman, clad in tight riding attire - which he found horny - chase about too, and would loved to have been beside them. It'd always turned him on to see Anna at home in her riding gear, although he never bothered to watch her at any of her events.

However, as Bruce had no equestrian skills, disliked horses and secretly feared the biting, farting, kicking and generally dangerous four-legged beasts, knew he'd never be able to join them. He'd never be a horseman. Nor did he want to. He'd decided all the men were a bunch of ponces. Not real men.

Tight jodhpurs didn't seem right on men, as alluring as they might sometimes appear. It wasn't natural. However, he'd also noted, with growing interest, the anti-hunt campaigners didn't have too bad a time either, and it looked like fun. They seemed to go wherever they wanted, do almost anything, and no one from the hunt or even the police really took any notice of them.

In addition, the attractive anti, with the long blond mane who'd sat in the car before him earlier, was stunning too. She was equally as attractive as some of the horny women he'd seen riding about. Maybe even more so. Tempting.

Bruce had thus decided, upon seeing Izzy's neat backside running across the field, and for the sake of the poor foxes or whatever the bunch of idiots on horseback chased, that today he'd become an Anti. In addition to saving wildlife, and getting to chat up the horny blond, he could also annoy Anna.

Having just seen the group of people running up the field, along with two police officers who'd been following but seemingly done little else all day, Bruce was intrigued what was happening as he watched events from his car.

That was until he spotted Anna and her cousin ride onto the field near the woods, along two other women, and the short guy with the horsebox. Bruce decided this was his calling; his time to join the anti-hunt campaign, and make his indignation at such a brutal sport be known. Also he could to get close to Anna, pester her and her annoying common cousin. In addition, as a bonus, he was determined to get even with the short guy on the white horse.

He was toast. Now was Bruce's moment for glory and revenge.

Leaving his precious Audi, he strolled across the field, along with a group of other people, both Anti and Pro, to see havoc breaking loose in the woods.

Mounted riders were also joining them, seemingly curious to investigate the source of the loud voices and screams coming from within the woods.

Hearing the yells and sensing trouble, something he relished, P.C. Burton raced away from the vehicle, with his colleague Bill labouring behind. As he ran across the field to stand on the edge of the woods and look within he suddenly witnessed a minor pitched battle breaking out, both within the woods; where loud screams could be heard, but also now around him.

Various women with placards, who'd followed from the Market Square, had left their van and began advancing over the field towards where a growing group of the riders milled around the edge of the woods. Knowing there was already trouble in the woods, which looked nasty, and then potential trouble about to break out around him on the field, Burton considered his options, who he should pick to arrest or apprehend first. Such was the varying choice of public order offences being broken; this was his time for real glory.

People scuffling on the ground, mounted riders hitting others with whips, crying children both on and off ponies, and horses moving about everywhere, knocking into people all around. It was total chaos. And Burton loved it.

However, his vision became locked upon one person in particular. A man, quietly riding a white horse. He was doing nothing wrong, but he *was* arguing with someone on the ground, who in turn *was* waving their fist at that rider.

Aggressive behaviour. Burton instinctively recognised the rider and locked his sights on getting him, regardless of what he was doing, or if other more serious incidents going on around him were much worse.

That didn't matter. It was time for justice. P.C. Burton's justice.

Not only was this Burton's day for glory and justice, but also revenge.

He ran across the field, his body armour weighing heavier than he thought, and as he approached the scene he began slowing down, walking a few strides to regain his breath and gain some composure. Now was his moment.

Chris and the small group around him had moved away from an elderly man, who had been berating him, shaking his fist. He turned Cirrus around, only to be greeted by a tall, skinny woman, waving a flimsy placard fixed upon a tomato cane. She began to rant at him, waving the placard inches from Cirrus.

Cirrus was well behaved, considering the woman was only feet away, the placard, almost hitting her, but began to get agitated and shuffle about.

"Don't wave that placard at my horse, you idiot!" Chris called as politely as he could, but with a menacing edge, staring coldly at the tall anti.

Mary, the placard holder, now full of courage, stared at the evil horseman. Anna beside Chris looked in disgust at the skinny woman, with Penny also becoming nervous by the action, as Julie and Tracey pulled in alongside.

Mary was still wearing her beloved hand-knitted, multi-coloured tea-cosy wool hat, which sat on top of her matted, long dread-locked hair; which was almost an ecosystem in itself and could house numerous unknown species.

"Yes, fuck off and get a real hobby," Tracey yelled, joining in, but not quite as polite or distinct a manner as Chris had tried to be to the annoying Anti.

Both Chris and Anna cast Tracey a knowing, but grinning glance.

"Don't you tell me to fuck off, you stuck up cow!" screamed Mary, ignoring Chris, now looking directly at Tracey. She stuck her tongue out at Mary.

"If I want to tell you to fuck off, I will. It's a free country, well almost. Go and eat some meat, you skinny bitch. How about some jugged hare!"

Tracey heartily laughed at her own witty response, as Fred bounced about beneath her. Anna and Chris shook their heads, grinning wildly and trying not to laugh and provoke further trouble, but both were struggling.

Julie didn't care and burst out laughing, jokingly punching Tracey's arm; finding the joke hilarious and almost falling off Bonnie such was her joy.

Mary stormed forward, the placard bashing against Chris's knee, in turn causing Cirrus to scuttle backwards, spinning around. Unseen by horse and rider, she hit a figure that'd rapidly advanced unseen behind them both.

Anna looked warily at Chris, as Cirrus spun backward, just catching sight of a policeman moving in behind, to then be knocked over by the frightened grey.

Chris caught her nervous glance, heard a noise and turned his head, to see a dark figure fall behind Cirrus. A policeman. Worse still, P.C. Burton.

Scrambling up in mud covered trousers, his furious face was scarlet.

"Right, you're nicked! Causing an affray and for assaulting a police officer!"

Chris looked down at the red-faced, huffing policeman he despised.

"You've got to be joking, I've not done anything," Chris hollered, swinging Cirrus fully about to face the policeman. "You came up behind my horse, scared it, and she knocked you over. Piss off! I suggest you arrest my horse!"

Anna grinned at Chris' blunt reply, but with anger boiling inside herself, the tension of the event affecting her too, she yelled at the irate policeman.

"Leave him alone, idiot! He's done nothing wrong. Arrest some of this lot causing all the trouble. This stupid cow with the tea-cosy waved her placard at his horse, which caused her to bump into you. I suggest you arrest her."

Mary looked in horror at the policeman; to think she could have broken any laws, then glared at Anna, instantly disliking the beauty who killed animals.

"Yes indeed," joined in Julie, pushing Bonnie forward, causing Burton to turn and see another horsewoman berating him. "We're not doing any harm here. Bugger off and arrest one of this lot. They're the real trouble makers."

Burton glanced towards the woods where Julie's extended arm pointed.

"You could make a start with that dyke!" Tracey added, moving Fred over.

She then pointed at Mary, who'd moved sideways and approached Tracey.

Burton, now totally confused, wished he had more back-up to join him, than the out-of-breath Bill, who red-faced, was still labouring across the field.

Unseen by the arguing group, Izzy watched from the edge of the woods, her attention switching from the carnage which was Dave and Steve, to then witness the chaos outside starting the woods. She noticed the vulnerable Mary was now surrounded by a group of riders and also now a policeman.

With the mayhem around her, she too was for once unsure how to act.

Help Dave or Mary? Call him an ambulance or stop an arrest or assault?

P.C. Burton was flabbergasted by the melee around him, not helped by rampaging and jostling horses, which he feared. He realised he was out of his depth and looked around for support, which he could see was slowly coming in the huffing form of Bill, whom he hoped had radioed for back-up.

Beside Chris Turner and his girlfriend; the pair he'd happily arrest, but knew in reality he had no cause, so he was unsure really what to do and how to act.

He then looked in amazement as the woman rider, who moments ago had called the tall thin Anti with the placard a 'Dyke' was now flaying a whip at the same woman. She in turn was trying to beat the rider off the horse with her flimsy placard, swinging the sign at both horse and rider. The pair fought like modern-day female gladiators. Burton just watched the pair, unsure what to do. No amount of police training had set him up for this, as all around he could hear loud yells, as well as screams of pain and anger within the woods.

Burton weighed up his odds against all the mad people, what chances he stood, and what he could actually do. Most of those he hoped to arrest were seated upon a horse. 'How would he fit a horse in a patrol car? Difficult.'

He decided he'd better intervene between the battling women, who'd been joined by the other rude rider seated upon a coloured horse. His decisions were instantly changed again when a tall, good-looking and smartly dressed man, looking totally out-of-place, came running up from behind; catching his attention as with a bitter face, he approached Chris Turner and his girlfriend.

"Come on Snooks, I'm getting you out of here. It's too dangerous," Bruce announced boldly to Anna like the all-conquering hero he wasn't.
He reached forward, about to grab at Penny's reins and lead her away.
Anna looked down at Bruce in shock, anger and then disgust. Chris stared.
"Piss off Bruce and leave me alone." Anna said bluntly, turning Penny's head away from Bruce's grasp. He turned, to then stand before her and Chris.
The pair regarded the smug man like bold conquers upon their steeds.
"Piss off! When will you learn to leave her alone?" Chris said with venom.
The pair ignored PC Burton, who stood back and looked on with interest, not wanting to get involved in the incident with the two horse women and the placard bearer, seeing his colleague Bill approach them. He sensed something was about to get heated between the three before him. Then he could act.
He hoped Turner would attack or assault in some form the new man; maybe an ex-boyfriend of the tall beauty, and then he could legally arrest Turner.
"Who the fuck's talking to you pygmy?" Bruce replied, turning to face Chris direct, his face full of hatred and his fear of him now a distant memory.
He'd come to rescue his Anna. He was her hero. And she would follow him.
Bruce reached forward to grab Penny's reins once more, but Anna turned her swiftly, and Bruce lurched slightly towards Chris and Cirrus. Burton waited, wanting any reason to arrest the horseman, who looked down at Bruce.
"Go away. You shouldn't be here," Chris said calmly. "I thought you might have leant your lesson." He smiled a somewhat cheeky, almost wicked grin.
Anna looked puzzled at the comment, as Bruce glared with deep hatred at Chris, understanding and remembering the embarrassing event in Leicester.
Fear and anger mixed together with arrogance, produced a deadly cocktail.
Chris just grinned confidently like a cat. He knew what he was doing.
Bruce erupted. The trick had worked. Perfectly.
"You fucking little shit. I'm going to kill you!" Bruce yelled, as he lurched forward at Chris, his arms flaying wildly, but missing everything.
Chris was too quick and had Cirrus ready. Squeezing his ankles and pulling the reins, the horse leapt forward and sideways, just as Bruce flew past the spot where they'd been standing. Instead, Bruce's wildly flaying fists carried on with momentum, one landing straight toward where PC Burton stood.
"Whoa, hold on a minute sir," said Burton trying to stop Bruce mid-flight, just as the horse moved, but instead he was struck fully in the face by the wild blow intended for Chris. Burton staggered back, nursing his jaw, as Chris pulled back around to the position he'd left seconds previously, to see the policeman trying to grab at Bruce, who was still aimlessly swinging arms.
"You tosser!" PC Burton yelped at Bruce, his new adversary, as another wild blow from Bruce struck his other cheek. "That's fucking it! You're nicked!"
PC Burton, grabbing out, grasping and hanging onto Bruce's arm, pulled him in, and as he drew back his fist, which landed squarely onto Bruce's jaw.
The blow from the policeman's fist was happily witnessed by Anna & Chris.

Bruce took it well, staggered a few feet, and then with a twist of his arm pulled his wrist free of the policeman's grip. Blind with rage, and seeing the policeman as his new target, Bruce charged straight at the policeman, his attention switching to him and away from the smiling horseman and Anna.

"You fucking pig!" Bruce hollered, turning sharply to look at the policeman, as he swung his next blow cleanly. This caught PC Burton fully on his nose, which instantly poured with blood, the intense pain blinding the policeman.

"Anna, lets get out of here!" Chris's said, watching Bruce and Burton about to engage in their own personal, and totally unexpected, private battle.

Anna regarded Bruce with a mix of bitterness, sorrow and amusement, but Chris's command seemed to wake her from the sight of the fight, and with one glance down, the pair turned towards Tracey and Julie and their battle.

"Aargh! I've been bitten!" A cry came from behind Chris and Anna, as they turned to see PC Burton's colleague, Bill, clutching his forearm in evident pain and somewhat shock. The policeman had foolishly tried to grab Bonnie's reins, attempting to pull Julie away from the defeated form of Mary.

The anti's placard shield was smashed and in pieces, and tearfully Mary ran away from the two 'evil horsewomen' and over towards the woods and Izzy's outstretched arms. But worse had happened. Her tea-cosy hat was gone.

The group of four rogue riders rode off, like victors, a red-faced Julie rapidly moving Bonnie away from the policeman she'd swiftly bitten, with a laughing Tracey joining beside her at the trot. Wedged upon Tracey's hunting cap, like some bizarre war trophy, was Mary's tea-cosy hat. It was not a good look.

Anna and Chris trotted over towards the pair of rebellious gladiators, now keen to be clear of any further trouble, all four cantering off to the woods.

"You can't wear that!" Chris commented with a shake of his head and wide grin, smirking at the strange headwear Julie adorned. Anna chuckled.

"Why not?" Tracey enquired quizzically to Chris' comment.

"Because it might have nits!" Chris replied laughing. "You'll get fleas!"

Julie roared with laughter as they all rode off, and even Anna managed a wry smile, then hearty laugh, seeing her cousin's head adornment and the wide smile on her scratched and dirty face. Tracey and Julie smiled, victoriously hitting their whips together in the air like two triumphant musketeers.

Anna turned around once more as they moved off around the corner of the woods, to see Bruce and the policeman still exchanging blows, knowing her former husband, although no fighter, would not give in easily. She looked over to Chris, who was also coldly looking at the two fighting men, but instead of anger, with a mild look of triumphant amusement on his face.

Back at the battleground, the pair of Bruce and Burton faced each other. P.C. Burton, never one to shy from a fight, was now glad to have a real reason to beat someone up and then arrest someone. And maybe give them a pasting. He reached to his belt for his flick-baton, set within the pouch on his waist.

Party time. Now he'd legally batter the shit out this idiot before him.

Bruce noticed the P.C. momentary glance down, about to draw his baton, both hands momentarily tugging at the dangerous implement. He took the opportunity, taking a full swing at Burton, who failed to move in time. The fist connected and caught Burton with full force on his jaw, it knocking him over. Dazzled, but having had worse, he tripped, stumbling over a rut in the ground. Bruce needed no other warning, saw his chance and was off.

He began running back over the field and toward his car. He'd done his good deed for the day, although he wasn't sure for which side. Maybe for both.

"Don't worry Roger, I'll get the bastard," came a familiar voice, as a pair of similarly familiar boots roared past the dazed policeman and across the field.

Burton rose, nursing his stinging face to see the figure of Bill, his usually snoozing colleague, running past and then rugby tackle his assailant. Bruce was unaware of the second policeman, and even more so, that he'd once been a former Flanker for his local rugby team when younger. He'd been good.

With hands firmly clasped about his calves, Bruce fell flat on his face with a crash, his cheek splitting open upon a piece of exposed flint, as the policeman ran, dived, grabbed and then hung onto the falling and defeated Bruce.

Then freeing one hand, seeing his stricken foe move his legs apart, Bill punched Bruce cleanly into the inviting and openly offered testicles.

Bruce's scream was heard above all the commotion in both woods and field, and turned everyone's heads. Crows in the nearby wood flew off in terror.

Drifting around the edge of the woods, Chris looked back at the floored figure of Bruce, Policeman on top, securing hand-cuffs, his face bright red and his body curled up in writhing agony. Chris smiled broadly and chuckled, trying to ensure Anna didn't witness his pleasure, she having already drifted from the view, and now laughing loudly with Tracey and Julie.

Burton sat on the ground smiling, blood pouring down his cut lip and nose, as he saw Bill handcuff the man he'd been fighting. Rolled up in a tight ball, Bruce was reluctant to offer a second hand for Bill to cuff fully, clutching his groin, trying to relocate his testicles, now lost somewhere deep within his lower body. Maybe to be found later; somewhere in his stomach.

As Chris's group rounded the woods and witnessed further fighting, shouting and chaos, with many children in tears and loose horses now being caught, he glanced down towards a man calmly standing on the edge of the woods, seemingly unconcerned by anything, but eagerly watching it all.

The unknown silent man's camcorder followed the triumphant foursome, the operator filming their movements like a true professional. A squeeze of Adam Yates finger zoomed in close on Chris and Anna, the camera soaking up their images, before drifting onto Tracey and Julie, both openly laughing.

Something one of those riders wore especially caught his attention. He'd seen such a repulsive item earlier in the day. The woman, seated atop the large, light-brown horse and laughing loudly to her friend seated upon a coloured horse, had what appeared to be tea-cosy wedged upon on her hat. Funny.

Adam Yates chuckled to himself. He recognised the ghastly hat.
An amusing image, but also poignant. But he also he got the joke.
A photo was taken. A good shot. Maybe a winner.
The photographer knew from where the hat had come.
He smiled too, fully understanding the new hat owner's grin.
Things eased up and the fighting subsided, as the various people, horses and hounds disappeared; many moving back into woods with their red-clad masters, accompanied by the sound of the hunting horn. Others drifted off along the field, over which he'd run moments earlier to find his perfect spot.
The hidden photographer also drifted away as swiftly as he'd magically appeared. He was pleased with the wide range of video footage and the many top quality photos' he'd taken in the few minutes of madness he'd witnessed.
The images would be viewed and edited later, in private, along with all of the other chaotic details recorded that day. A perfect package. A result.
But he now had a lot of work to do. And to a tight deadline.
The presses rolled at midnight.
There was no rest for the wicked. Or for journalists. Maybe the same.
For Adam Yates, award-winning Undercover Investigative Journalist and Private Detective, his Boxing Day had only just begun.
And it'd been a brilliant and perfect day.
All just as planned.
Maybe even better.
Game on!

Chapter 79

In War - Resolution. In Defeat - Defiance.
In Victory - Magnanimity. In Peace - Goodwill.

Winston S. Churchill

"We should check no one's hurt, help find any loose horses or riders, then head back to Steve and re-group," Chris said, once the laughing subsided, and they turned the corner of the woods, seeing the large melee of riders.

"Hopefully Reggie and Martin will collect the hounds, then I imagine we'll all head back the boxes, once Steve has sorted out whatever has gone on in the woods. None of this looks good. I've a feeling the day is over, which is a pity, but we're all going to be making headline news tomorrow. Make sure you buy a copy of the paper. We'll probably be in it. Especially you two!"

They stopped near to what was left of the mounted field, scattered about in the wood, with many having already set off for the boxes, keen to be away and not wanting to be part of any disruptive activity or seen in any bad press.

Martin was grouping the hounds, together with Sharon and Helen, who'd both reappeared with a few loose hounds at foot themselves, just as all the commotion subsided, totally bemused by it all and unaware of everything.

Helen and Sharon were confused as to what had happened, but learnt a red-faced Reggie had vanished, supposedly to look for loose hounds and soon worked it for themselves, upon seeing various people and their new partners.

Mike and Elizabeth stood together at the edge of the woods, hugging each other. Elizabeth's horse stood beside her, the reins in Mike's hands.

Sharon asked Martin what'd happened, but glum stare, dismissive head shake and pursed lips told her it was something for them to discuss later in private, as Sharon guessed, looking at the police officers and various antis covered in blood or skulking about the woods. Helen was also confused, and a shake from Sharon's head silently told her the same and not to ask. The pair knew better as far as Reggie was concerned. Whatever, it didn't look good.

The group slowly began to regain control of the hounds, and regroup riders, including Lady Carter, who returned with the bolted pony and a smiling, mud-covered child who was none the worse and now had a tale to tell. One of the younger girls was being led away with her mother. She'd fallen in the chaos and possibly broken her arm. Several riders were noticeable by their absence and word quickly spread about as to whom and why, with shaking heads and looks of disbelief in response and guarded mouths whispering.

Steve was still in the woods, collecting a few stragglers, but sat proudly upon Casanova as he rode past, looking down at the whimpering form of Dave, lying in heap at the base of the Beech tree. He gazed back up in agony.

Izzy and Mary wandered down the small incline in the woods to where Dave lay, Mary shaking her hat-less head in tears, more so over her stolen hat than the severely battered Dave. She looked away when she saw his battered form, knowing what'd happened, and wondering again why the world was so evil.

But she knew why. Because it was controlled by men. The Devil's spawn.

Izzy squatted down beside Dave, herself not knowing what to do or say, or if she did, seemingly unwilling do so. She knew he would have wanted her to hug or caress him, but to her it'd be like hugging an injured sewer rat. She instead simply informed him an ambulance was coming and he'd be okay.

Steve rode past on Casanova, looking down, shaking her head, face serious.

"You witnessed what he did!" Dave spluttered to Izzy, eyes looking up.

"Yes I did," she responded coldly, glaring at Steve. "Why Steve? Why?"

"Pure accident my sweet!" Steve grinned, then looked harshly at Dave.

"Sorry old chap! Wrong move. You really shouldn't have done that. It spooked my horse and he was away. I had no control. A foolish accident."

Dave Pearson looked back at Steve with bitter venom, wheezing heavily, breathing hard, speaking a luxury. But he wanted to do more than speak.

"Where does it hurt?" Izzy asked, feeling she should, but with no conviction.

"Everywhere." Dave groaned heavily. "My arms. My ribs. Everything!"

PC Burton suddenly appeared beside Dave, and Izzy used the intrusion to step back from her poor stricken comrade. Burton had partially witnessed the horrific scene as he'd run up, briefly seeing through the woods a black horse appear to drag a man into a tree. He certainly recognised the rider, from their previous encounters, and besides, he was the only person clad in red, seated upon a black horse with a man firmly attached to the horse's side. Simple.

That was before the incident with Chris Turner, his girlfriend, and the posh idiot who'd decided to have a fight with everyone, causing further paperwork. He'd now left the temporary eunuch hand-cuffed to Bill, and called for back-up and an ambulance or two, before deciding to see what further chaos lay within the woods. He now looked down at the wheezing form of the Anti, laying at the base of a large tree, gasping for breath, his face a waxy white.

He didn't look good and sounded worse. That said, he realised the battered Anti probably didn't look much better before he'd been dragged into a tree.

Coldly, Burton told him to be quiet and stop screaming like a wimp, then wandered over to a resolute and unconcerned Steve, sitting proudly upon his horse, looking down at the battered man as one would discarded litter.

"What happened here then sir?" Burton asked bluntly, avoiding the horse.

"Accident. Chap ran wildly at me with a big stick, then tried to tip me off my horse. Arm got stuck in my stirrup as my horse bolted. Tree did the rest."

Burton glanced down at Pearson absorbing the response. "Is this true sir?"

"No! The bastard dragged me into the tree. On purpose. He's a Wanker!"

It was all Dave could emit before he gasped for his breath, curling up.

Burton turned to Izzy and Mary, both silently watching, both silent.

"Did you see anything ladies?" Burton was instantly attracted to Izzy, but wondered about her skinny friend, who looked seriously ill and frail.

"I was being set upon by those evil whores! Mary suddenly exclaimed. Satan's Bitches! And they stole my new hat! My hat!" She sobbed, leaning on Izzy.

"I was with her. Outside of the woods," Izzy replied coldly, non-committal, as the policeman looked at her. She glanced at Steve, then down at Dave.

Dave Pearson glared coldly back at Izzy. She looked away.

"Well sir, this looks like a serious case of assault." Burton said at the cool faced hunter. "You'll have to come to the station for questioning sir. Now."

"Not quite my man. I've a hunt to finish," replied Steve, in his calm manner. "Besides, I've done nothing wrong. It was a complete accident. Silly man tried to attack me, his arm slipped in my stirrup leather, and he got it trapped as my frightened horse bolted. Tragic, yet foolish accident. My Barrister will agree."

"I'm afraid you're still going to have to come with me."

"And my horse?" Steve enquired. "He'll have to come too. Will he fit in the back? Or glove box? Maybe you have a horsebox attached to your squad car."

PC Burton remained silent, unsure how to respond, momentarily looking at the massive form of Samson rising up beside him, wondering if the horse would fit in the back seat. No. Too big. And it'd probably shit everywhere.

"Maybe you'd like to ride him back for me sweetheart?" Steve looked at Izzy, a twinkle back in his eye. "Like old days. He misses you on his back. So do I."

Izzy's face went pale, sensing all eyes upon her. They were. She looked away.

"But maybe not. Another time, perhaps." Steve blushed too.

The wheezing figure on the ground coughed as if to draw attention back to him, but no one reacted. Burton flipped his head back and forth from Izzy to Steve, wondering what was going on between them. Something was wrong.

"Okay, then if that is it officer, I'll be off." Steve abruptly broke the dumb silence, looking firmly at Burton. "I'll see you at South Washam police station if you should need statement. With my solicitor. Whenever it suits you. Or you can come to my farm. This beautiful lady beside you has all my details."

Burton looked on in amazement at the horseman's casual reply. Then more so as Steve stood up in his stirrups and yelled out loud through the woods.

"Okay everyone, listen in please," he begun. "This little incident is over. We still have a hunt to finish. If you're all okay and no one is seriously hurt, lets recover. Mount up, catch up with Martin, and carry on hunting. Let's go!"

"You can't just ride off," questioned the Policeman, looking up at Steve, amazed at his ice cool nature, but realised he could and had.

"I can. I'm responsible for all of the horses and riders out with me today. That is the most important thing. Not this. If not, arrest us all. Go on!"

Steve then glanced down at the pale figure of Dave Pearson like he was split garbage, as he saw him, with the sound of fresh sirens wailing in the distance. With that, Steve raised his whip to his hunting cap, nodded politely to the policeman and also to Izzy, but to her with a sad smile. Then he rode off.

Steve's cool nature shocked the policeman and he simply watched as the black horse and arrogant rider rode off, re-joining the other riders, muttering between themselves and examining the array of figures littering the woods.

'Were all of these hunting people a law unto themselves?' Burton mused.

As far as Burton was discovering, it seemed they were. And worse.

"Gavin, are you okay?" Steve called, seeing his trusty Lieutenant with an arm around a battered, but smiling Lady Burlingham. The pair strangely appeared natural together; like a couple who'd been together for years. They had.

"Yes. Thanks Steve. Ginny and I will get back onboard, but think we'll head back alone. We have a few things to discuss." The lovers smiled knowingly.

Steve nodded at them, and smiled warmly at Virginia as he rode out of the woods and joined the rest of the riders, scanning some battered familiar faces.

Elizabeth was getting back on her horse with the aid of Mike. He was talking sweetly to her, but her furtive gaze, looking for Reggie, spoke volumes. She knew he'd be back soon, and no doubt watching intently from somewhere.

"I'll be heading straight back too," Elizabeth spoke warily to Steve. "Lots to sort out, no doubt. I'm sure you understand. Mike will see that I'm okay."

Steve nodded, understanding, smiling at Mike who walked beside Elizabeth as she rode across the field and over to where Mike's Land Rover was parked.

A number of the riders had gone, including Bertie and Dawn, heading away from the trouble, back to Windford to consider their futures. They all had some serious talking to do, and things to sort out when they returned, with relationships ruined. All knew it'd not be good, now the truth was revealed.

The stunning Arab head of Goldie appeared alongside Chris, foam blowing from his mouth, nostrils snorting. Sally was out of breath too. Anna turned, wondering where Sally had been through all the action, only now realising she was missing, as was Carol on Tess, although both always did their own thing.

"Carol is riding back with Bertie," Sally explained between breaths, pulling on the excitable Arab's reins for control, it being clear she'd just ridden back.

"He's not a happy chappy, as I'm sure you can imagine. Very embarrassed. All public." she continued, sadly, liking the nice, if not rather pompous Lord.

"But he's taken it strangely well. Almost as if he knew something was going on. Or maybe he's just plotting to kill her! I hope not. Nasty thing to say, I know. Strangely, I don't think he's totally innocent himself or really cares."

Chris flushed red, as if knowing. Anna looked on curiously, wondering what else he knew about 'Lord B' and the seemingly now soon-to-be 'Ex-Lady B.'

"Carol is consoling him. He seems okay, but god knows what will happen when they all get home. What a mess. Gavin and Lady Burlingham. Wow!"

All heads turned towards Sally, who looked back naively at the grinning faces.

Martin and two Whip's re-grouped the hounds as the field re-formed, to retain some pride, although all knew the day was over. Steve announced they'd take a slow ride back, and obviously expect lots of police and possible trouble when they returned to Windford. And no one was to speak to anyone.

They regrouped outside the woods, from the gaze of the countless antis, who were quizzing the two policeman on how they'd let all of the hunters get away, yet it was the anti's side that seemed to suffer most of the casualties.

Reggie mysteriously appeared from a side wood, silently joining Martin at the front, nodding an acknowledgment to Steve. They all muttered quietly to each other, Sharon and Helen purposefully dropping back. The solemn silence between the riders who all drifted back was clearly noticeable, and the ride back to Windford decidedly downbeat, compared to the joy when they'd left.

Slowly the mood changed and people began chatting about Christmas, rather than the tragic events. Upon seeing her new head adornment Steve regarded Tracey with a quizzical expression and big grin. He said nothing, chuckling at Chris, who shook his head, as did Steve, knowing where he'd seen it before.

Sirens could be heard in the distance, as back-up teams of police belatedly rushed to the now empty scene, along with the two ambulances Burton had requested for the injured, which included at least two antis and child rider.

Chris, Anna, Tracey, Sally and Julie all rode back in a quiet mood, and Chris apologised to Anna for the incident, hoping she'd not been disappointed.

The Boxing Day Meet was supposedly the key meet of the year, and it was Anna's only second proper outing on horseback. They usually expected some minor trouble, but it'd ended early and in violence; bringing danger to her and embarrassment for the hunt in general. But Anna was not at all bothered, and in a way it'd made the day more memorable, even if for the wrong reasons.

She told him he shouldn't apologise and despite it all, she'd had a good day. However, it seemed to cast a shadow upon the whole day they'd hoped for, and took the edge off their relationship, after it had been built up so strongly.

As long as the incident had appeared to take, in reality the whole series of tragic events had taken less than five minutes; from the moment Gavin tried to release the unfortunate hare, to Steve crushing Dave against the tree and the police racing over to intervene. Five minutes of life-changing chaos.

Yet in those few brief minutes, everything seemed to be a separate part of space and time. The events that happened to so many people in such a short space of time all seemed to be in slow motion. Forever etched in people's memories. For a number of people, their world would change completely.

T Junctions in the Road of Life had been reached.

New paths had been taken. Old paths rejected.

There was no looking back. The door behind had been closed shut. Firmly.

Then locked. And bolted. With an extra padlock.

Onward the brave or foolish now strode.

For good or for bad.

What would be their outcome?

Only time and fate would tell.

Chapter 80

Always forgive your enemies; nothing annoys them so much.

Oscar Wilde

Burton wandered over to the whimpering form, which was Dave, who'd hauled himself up and sat leaning against the Beech tree for support. If the Beech could have moved, it would. The gorgeous blond woman Anti and her not-so-attractive skinny friend spoke with him, giving him reassurances. The battered Anti seemed unsure what to do with his arms. One was dislocated, the other smashed; neither working properly and wouldn't for weeks.

Burton curiously wondered how he'd wipe his arse. Major problem.

One thing was certain; it wouldn't be him doing it.

Maybe the skinny dyke would offer. He felt it was beyond the blond, and hoped it was too. She was stunning, and he wondered why she was there. She looked as if she should be on the back of one of the horses and not an Anti.

The policeman talked to Dave, but deep down felt little compassion, realising he'd brought it upon himself; even if the hunters action had been very cold and heartless. He went looking for a fight, but came second. Shit happens.

The large back-up force, which had been requested, ensured the anticipated trouble from any other Anti's didn't happen when the straggling riders arrived back at the car park at Windford. It seemed most of the peacefully and genuine Anti's had gone back home, not wanting to have any further part in the violence, or had vanished. Also that many horse riders simply loaded up their horses and swiftly departed the scene. Two senior Hunt members spoke with officers at Windford and informed him they'd give a full statement the next day. Burton felt they both knew the Chief Constable. Maybe too well.

At Windford it was all quiet and peaceful, as befitting the season of goodwill.

The dark-clad Anti's Burton had briefly seen dashing about the woods, and who it seemed from brief conversations, with those at the scene, had caused the fracas, then seemingly come off worse, had disappeared. None seemed keen to contact the police to press charges, or request medical treatment. Many would have thought it strange, but Burton knew there was more too it.

It was not good press for the Anti's, being battered, or Pro hunters, who'd done the battering. Not a good day. No one had won. But many had lost.

Only two ambulances were sent to the remote location to collect the injured and pick up any who'd not walked or ridden away. Izzy rode in an ambulance with Dave, somewhat reluctantly, for although she strangely felt slightly responsible, she didn't really want to be associated too closely with him.

The other older antis had taken away the still upset Mary in their van. Izzy suggested someone gave her Camomile Tea. Lots of it. Maybe a box full.

Because he had a facial injury; his ripped cheek needing stitches, and because he still couldn't walk; threatening to sue the police officer involved for a permanent injury that might stop him having children, Bruce was also taken away in the same ambulance as Dave, rather than a patrol car. Bruce hoped it was a big facial wound and that maybe it'd produce a scar. That'd look cool.

One of the children had possibly broken her arm in the fall, so went in the other ambulance alone with her mother, the distressed parent not wanting her child to mix with the filthy anti's who'd caused the trouble. Friends would lead their horses back to the boxes to be loaded up as was always the way.

Strangely, the three 'Essex Boys,' as battered as they were, were helped away by a fourth, then whisked away in their car. Battered and bloody, but with a handful of bank notes thrust in their hands by Adam, they simply vanished.

None would be giving any police interviews or statements, and any treatment they may need would be undertaken at another hospital or by themselves.

Adam would see to it all. Also, none would have their photos in the papers.

However, Adam Yates ensured he was at the car park in Windford to record the return of the hunters, bloody and battered, but still resolute. He captured it all, the entire event. Start to finish. Some great shots. A perfect day.

Once he had all the images and footage needed, he set off in his car, back to the comfort of his Norwich hotel room. Adam Yates now had serious work to undertake. And big money to make. His scoop was worth a small fortune.

Back in the ambulance, as painful as the punch to his groin felt, Bruce was determined to make the most of the incident and claim police brutality. Only so he hoped it'd reduce the police's case against him. As Dave drifted in and out of his gas and air induced stupor, Bruce sat crouched on the seat in the ambulance opposite the stunning Anti who sat with him, and began chatting.

Her blue eyes and jaw-dropping looks instantly attracted him. Natural beauty was something he'd always found hard to resist in any woman. So he didn't.

Izzy was immediately charmed by the good looking Northerner, with his confident manner and by the time she'd left the hospital, and Dave was strapped up and in a hospital bed, she had Bruce's mobile telephone number.

He agreed to come out with the Anti's the next time the Shotesham met; if indeed they ever meet again, but if so, he'd help to disrupt their next meet with Izzy. However, all the details would be confirmed after a date at the next opportunity. Maybe in a few days time, over the Christmas break. Izzy happily agreed to the offer and said she'd find a good place for them to dine.

It would be a very good place, as Bruce was paying.

Bruce was glad he'd made the trip down to Norfolk. His over-compassionate company had temporarily transferred him to their Norwich branch. He was claiming compassionate grounds, following his 'painful' forth-coming divorce from Anna. His company in turn were happy to accept his ruthless ways, set to sweep clean the Norwich branch in the New Year. It was also best for the company as well to for him to avoid contact with Lucy. She'd been trouble.

As a senior member of staff, who was well respected within his company, the directors had approved Bruce's transfer for a few months, in order for him to try to repair his marriage, but also get away from Lucy. However, they failed to mention she'd not been seen for several weeks, taking 'Gardening Leave' first and also an extended Christmas break. She too was suffering from stress.
Lucy had strangely stopped pestering him, and he couldn't decide if to be happy or suspicious. He'd never trusted the possessive nymphomaniac, who had a sketchy past he knew nothing off. He wouldn't put it past her to follow him, but he'd deemed she wasn't really that clever. He knew she was dumb and probably didn't even know where Norfolk was. That wasn't too much of a slur on her; as most people in the UK didn't that know either. Norfolk?
'The Big Lump on the Right of England.' Where sugar beet came from. And The Norfolk Broads; whatever they were. Big lakes or summit. That was it.
Now he had an impending date and potential acquaintance of the beautiful Izzy to enjoy. Lucy was gone. Soon would be history. Lucy? Who? No idea.
He was now looking forward to become an Anti, and all it entailed. Especially chasing about with the gorgeous Izzy to assist. Not only could he pester Anna, but also his ultimate goal was now to get at the pygmy on the grey horse, who seemed to have spirited his prized wife away. For now.
That bastard would be history. Chris Turner? Who? Gone. For good.
If this gorgeous Anti could help him achieve that goal, and had a good time with her along the way, then all the better. She'd have served her purpose. And more. But he would have that bastard on the grey horse.
No matter what it took. He'd get his revenge. Bastard. Bitch.
When he'd finished with the horseman, who owed him more than two tyres, he'd be pleading for his life. And more. Then he'd get Anna back to himself.
He'd take her back to Leicester once and for all.
Whatever the cost, and no matter how long.
Then he'd make sure she didn't leave him again. Ever.
And that stupid nag of hers? It'd go. For good.
He'd personally have it put down. Shot.
One day when she was at work. Sweet.
It'd be a nice surprise for when she returned.
Horse dead. Lesson served. Horse gone. Job done.
And he'd have the tail cut off.
But plated into a memorial necklace.
And he'd give it to Anna as a memento.
Of the last horse she'd ever own. Ever.

Chapter 81

Be not afraid of greatness. Some are born great, some achieve greatness, and others have greatness thrust upon them.

Twelfth Night - William Shakespeare

The morning after the Boxing Day Meet, with the light poor and weather as chilly as the cold atmosphere, Anna sat in the tack room. She was joined with Tracey, Sally and a couple of other girls who hadn't been out yesterday, but heard all about it. Several times over. In glorious 'Technicolor' it seemed. Quietly hugging mugs of tea and coffee, they pondered what would happen.

The tackroom door flew open and all heads turned to see a grinning Julie.

"I'm famous! Well almost. But not as famous as you Tracey! Bitch!"

Rushing in, waving a newspaper, Julie's hand held the newsprint extended out towards Tracey, who stared back bemused, then she leapt up, followed by an equally curious Anna, and the other enquiring faces. The small group all leant forward; looking intently at the newspaper Julie had opened with much haste, spreading it out upon the small table, going straight to the centre-pages.

Here, a centre-page, pullout 'Boxing Day Special Feature' showed an image of Julie and Tracey beating a tall anti with their hunting whips. One shot highlighted the pair beating the 'Defenceless Anti,' timidly cowering; shielded by her flimsy placard. A 'Tea-cosy' style hat clearly sat upon her head.

The innocent party was protecting defenceless animals. Yeah, of course!

The next image had Tracey proudly riding off, Julie alongside. The pair were laughing, but importantly, the 'Tea-cosy' hat was visibly upon Tracey's hat.

Tracey's face glowed red as she looked over to her corner of the tackroom, where she kept her tack. There, perched upon her saddle, was that item. The very same Tea-cosy 'trophy hat' proudly atop her black velvet riding hat.

All heads followed Tracey's intent gaze, as a huge roar of laughter broke out.

"Do you think I'll get arrested?" Tracey asked, concerned. "Maybe prison?"

"What, for wearing an offensive hat in a public place!" Julie roared.

Julie laughed at her own joke, followed by deep hearty roars from everyone else within the snug tackroom, the atmosphere changing from frosty to hot.

"Maybe I should burn it. Destroy the evidence," Tracey considered, a finger to her mouth, pondering. "Just in case the Rozzer's raid the tackroom."

"But you'd get prosecuted by the Environment Agency first. Think of the wildlife in that thing you'd burn to death. That hat has it's own Eco-system."

All eyes fell upon the foul hat, considering its fate, mouths sent in big grins.

"Am I in there?" enquired Anna somewhat feebly, peering at the paper.

"Yes, but you're on the front part of the pull-out. Typically looking all posh and glamorous, beside Chris in the market square. We're in the 'scum' bit."

"The posh and glamorous are on the front. Typical. We're in the middle bit." Tracey mockingly sneered at her grinning cousin, who playfully pushed her.
"Looks like they've put all the riff-raff and scum in the centre," Julie joked.
"That's why your dead centre Tracey. Right where the staples go!" The group roared with laughter, all keen to see the various images of familiar faces and discover who was now famous. Or infamous. Or even now liable for arrest.
"But you should see Steve. He takes centre-stage. Actually he's on the back page. He has his own section. 'Well-famous' will Steve be. There's a great series of shots showing him drag the skinny Anti into the tree. Looks nasty, but it's justified. Tosser! Amazing photography, whoever took it. Very good."
The woman's laughter eased as Julie flicked the paper up for all to see.
Set as a series of freeze-frames, the images showed Steve sat upon Casanova. One shot shows Steve hitting the Anti with a whip, the next with him being dragged by the horse. Another of the Anti crashing into the tree. Two others showed a sore, battered, bloody and a pale-faced Dave Pearson lying smashed against the tree. Another of him inside the ambulance, gazing mournfully.
"Oh my god!" Anna exclaimed, looking at the last image. "Look!"
Julie and Tracey glanced at another photo. Looking up; seeing a familiar face.
"Bruce!" Tracey declared. "Oh my God! He had to get in it too. Arsehole!"
"He's in a photo fighting with a copper. It shows the policeman punching him in the knackers! Painful, but justice I'd say. Look at Bruce's face! Sweet!"
Everyone looked at the image, grimacing at the thought; the agony clear.
"Is that the scream I heard when I was riding back around to the woods?" enquired a wincing Sally, recognising the 'hunk' who'd waved in Windford.
"Probably. He won't be covering any mares for a while! Justice! Ha ha!"
Julie roared with laughter at Tracey's crude comment and Anna blushed red, shaking her head, then laughed, punching her cousin, everyone looking on.
The tackroom door then opened, and like naughty girls in a private school, caught peeking at a 'rude' magazine, they all turned red-faced, to stare silently at a bemused Chris. Julie, too late, hid the newspaper behind her back.
With a coy grin on his face, and eyes fixed upon Julie, Chris didn't have to speak. Simply tilting his head towards the newspaper partly hidden behind her back, he extended his hand, flicking his fingers out as encouragement. Then, like encouraging a naughty child caught stealing sweets, she offered the paper.
"It wasn't me Sir, honest!" she joked. "It was Tracey. She made me!"
"Chris, I'm famous!" Tracey roared, uncaring, pointing to her image wearing the Tea-cosy hat. He looked at all of the pictures, read the brief but damning accompanying editorial, then glanced over towards Tracey's tack rack, shaking his head. All went silent. It could be seen Chris was trying to hide a big grin.
"Didn't get my best profile," said a sarcastic Julie looking back at the newspaper opened up in Chris' hands. "Makes me look older than I am."
"Is that possible?" quipped Tracey. Julie thumped her. "Methuselah!"
"Wow, Tracey, where did you find that word, in a cracker!" Tracey replied.

The group all roared with laughter and Anna moved alongside Chris.
"We're in there too. Shows as goodies though. Not like this common rabble. Peasants!" Anna added, with a sly grin to Chris and sideways look to Tracey.
"If I'd have known, I'd have done my nails and put on clean knickers!"
Chris smirked at Anna's dry comments, still absorbing everything.
"Look at that series of shots showing Steve riding that anti into the tree. Good photos. We missed it. Looks very nasty. That'll go to court. Not good."
Chris added more seriously, rubbing his chin, drawing in air, head shaking.
"That's the problem. The press will cause nothing but trouble for us all now. And the police will get involved, questioning everyone. We'll get no doubt get a visit too from that annoying new bastard who keeps coming here. Wanker!"
The seriousness of the incident now ran home again. Everyone blushed.
"Who on earth took all the pictures?" enquired Anna, looking at the whole array of photos. "They're good. It almost looks like it was all arranged."
"I bet it was the guy with the camcorder," replied Chris. "Clever. Did you see him? Seated in the woods. Sly looking bastard. I noticed him as we passed."
"Yes, I remember. He looked over and stared," answered Anna, her mind actively recalling the memory of Adam Yates, although unknown to them.
"I didn't think anything at the time, with so much going on. He must've been a reporter. But how did he know they'd trouble? Some photos are incredible."
"I think it's brilliant!" Tracey said. "Look at that brilliant write-up. Makes it sound like we're a right bunch of mad, evil bastards. Maybe we are!"
Everyone giggled and even Chris chuckled, head shaking, trying to be civil.
"Yes, unfortunately it does. But it isn't going to do the Shoteton any good," answered Chris, a bit more seriously. "I was on the phone earlier to Steve and Reggie. All meets are off for the next week or two until this shit dies down. Apparently the pictures will be on the TV tonight with some of this guy's video footage. The police want copies it seems. The guy who shot everything is a real pro. Good. Possibly set up a lot of it with 'rent-a-mob' yobs. Steve was warned by his solicitors, as the anti rammed into the tree is going to sue."
The group fell silent, now realising exactly how serious it was. Very serious.
"Who was the guy with the camcorder then?" Anna asked calmly.
"Well apparently he's an investigative journalist and sort of private detective. Steve's been making calls. Quite well known for doing various dangerous investigations. Very good at his job. He's put away serious crooks and a gang of paedophiles too, so is not all bad, what he does. But he's a nasty and clever bastard, who'll go to any lengths to get a story." They all looked at Chris.
"We think he latched onto Izzy's anti's and planned all the trouble. Seems it was just bad luck they caught Gavin trying to free a hare that'd been snared and the hounds beat him to it. Sadly, that's what that first picture shows."
All four looked at the image of Gavin taken through the trees; holding up the hare, with a pale hound hanging from it. The heading underneath simply read:
'Barbaric Boxing Day Massacre. Hunters v Protestors. Carnage.'

It wasn't a good advertisement for Hunting. Nor The Shoteton. It was bad.
"Has anyone heard anything of Gavin since?" asked Julie; concern genuine. "I can't believe him and Lady Muck where knocking each other off. If it's true. That's what we heard on the way back. Those two together? Amazing."
"I asked Steve this morning. Spoke with him for ages. He's not a happy chap. Apparently a number of people have been trying to contact Gavin, including Dawn. She's been ringing up everyone all night. Gavin never returned. Seems to have vanished. Also Virginia, along with Elizabeth and Mike. No one has seen or heard from any of them. Bertie's not speaking with anyone it seems. Reggie is putting on a brave face, but must be fuming. What a terrible day."
"What has happened to them all?" asked Julie. "Where have they all gone?"
"I heard we missed the really good action in the woods, when the anti's attacked Gavin and all hell broke loose. Looks like they've all been knocking each other off. Typical horsey people!" said Tracey bluntly, looking at Chris.
"I was surprised it was Gavin. I'd always had you down for knocking off Lady 'not quite a Virginia' Burlingham." It was Julie who made the statement.
Chris blushed, shaking his head, trying not to smile and looked away from the grinning faces and over at Anna, who went crimson. Others in the room chuckled, but knew how close Chris was to Virginia. He recovered with a wry smile to answer Julie's blunt but honest question, knowing all deserved truth.
"Gavin and Ginny had been seeing each other for ages. I had some hints and guessed something was up, but kept it secret. I knew of Ginny's past and that she wasn't as posh as she made. She's clever and a good actress. Apparently they both came from the same council estate, and childhood sweethearts."
"Nothing wrong with council estates," interrupted Tracey. "I came from one and it didn't do me any fucking harm! Unless you want to fight me over it!"
Everyone paused momentarily, silently looked at Tracey, then the tackroom erupted with laughter. Tracey enjoyed the welcome attention as ever.
"I think it's sweet. Really nice and quite romantic," continued Julie, looking quite dreamily. "Sad for Bertie. But he was too old for Virginia. She was just a trophy wife. And Reggie was probably was ready for a change of wife. Again."
"Yes, it's nice Elizabeth is going off with Mike. They look a good couple. I wish them well. Reggie must be fuming. But it's a matter of pride with him."
"Are you going to be applying for the vacancy for next wife?" asked Tracey to Julie, with an exaggerated wide grin. "You might get a free farm. Or two."
"Either that or bumped off when he gets bored. I'll probably be buried alive in a sugar beet field," Julie added. "Not that I'm accusing him! I'll stay single."
"Or maybe he'll get Martin to feed you to the hounds!" Tracey quipped.
Once more all the women laughed, then as it subsided, catching sight of the horse-shaped clock, Sally made her excuses, knowing she had work to do in.
"Anyway, they'll probably all be hiding up, away from their partners and keeping out of the limelight. What a mess. We can only see what happens and if the police get involved with what happened in the field. Let's hope not."

Chris added the final comment with a serious face, all looking in at him.
"I always knew you hunters were a funny bunch," Anna quipped, breaking the silence. "What have I let myself if for? Maybe I'd better leave now!"
They all chuckled and a red-faced smiling Chris grinned warmly at Anna.
All were stopped by Carol dashing wildly into the tackroom. Surprised to see so many; looking like a group of conspirators planning a some secret revolt, she paused, looking confused at all of the silent faces, then spoke excitedly.
"Have you seen the papers? It's terrible. I'm off to see Bertie. I mean Lord Burlingham. He's very upset. This is not good. Not good! I'll turn out Tess then, I've got to dash off to Wroxingham Hall. Bertie needs me. This is bad!"
With that she was gone in a flash, leaving the bemused group sat within the tackroom all staring at each other, now even more confused.
"Interesting," said Julie, hand on chin. "Very interesting."
Chris simply grinned, smile wide, as if he knew what she was thinking.

Chapter 82

There are chance meetings with strangers that interest us from the first moment, before a word is spoken.

Fyodor Dostoevsky

Chantelle and Sarah were back on the streets. It was always surprising that the Christmas holidays didn't stop their customers. If anything, it brought more out. It was often loneliness at a time when everyone was with families and friends that it forced a good number out to find some company, comfort or relief. On the other side, bills had to be paid and habits fed, so Sarah and Chantelle were back out, willingly plying their wares that chilly night.

It was a clear crisp night, with a low moon rising behind a veil of thin cloud, but cold. Their breath began misting, as they stood stamping their high-heeled feet and shuffled about. Not an ideal night for a short skirt and no knickers. But both were hardened and used to worse. Hopefully, they'd soon be warm.

A familiar car, a dark Range Rover, drove past on the opposite side and Sarah raised her head, recognising the vehicle, although not totally sure.

Many customers drove identical vehicles. Other cars drifted past, including a smart estate, the driver behind the darkened glass glancing in the woman's direction, absorbing their images. It slowed down, as if about to visit them for trade, but upon seeing the Range Rover span around and continued on.

The dark Range Rover pulled up, stopping abruptly against the kerb and the side window lowered. Both Chantelle and Sarah eagerly stepped forward.

But it was Sarah who extended an arm out, stopping Chantelle in her tracks.

It was him. Her man from before. Her 'special' customer. Sarah felt a mixed rush of excitement and also a hint of fear upon seeing 'her man.'

This would be her third time and she enjoyed appeasing his unique requests.

"This one's mine. My special guy. Remember?" she winked at Chantelle.

Sarah stepped straight up to the open window, then spoke quietly as before; recognising him, then smiling, opened the door and entered the warm vehicle.

"See you soon," she called, waving a hand, rapidly sealed in as before, as the tinted glass rose up and the dark vehicle moved off, Sarah secured inside.

Sarah had spoken briefly about the man in the 'Dark Rover,' telling Chantelle some brief details and what he demanded. If this was the same man, and Chantelle believed it was, then she was worried; despite how gentle she'd told her he'd been. It still sounded too dangerous for Chantelle. But strangely, it was this sense of danger and mischief that Sarah seemingly enjoyed.

Chantelle sighed, once again left on the streets alone, hoping someone worthwhile would appear to warm her up. And fill her purse with money.

For once her wish was answered. And in more ways than she could dream.

The estate car, from moments earlier, clearly turning around, pulled up.

The driver of the smart modern estate car, which previously had the choice of either the tall blond or the shorter brunette, now had Hobson's choice.

But he would have chosen the tall blond anyway. His type. Very nice.

Unknown to the pair, fate had marked both their cards.

Chantelle sauntered over, red high-heels wiggling and long legs admired from within the vehicle. She noted the estate was the new, sports-type estate.

It meant money and class. But hopefully not in the boot.

The driver wound down his window.

His appearance did not meet that of the stunning car.

Chantelle had had worse, much worse, but the man before him had a slightly chilling appearance, and cold dark eyes. But also something else. Compassion.

"I'm Adam. I don't make a habit of this, believe it or not."

The man spoke politely, which was at least a good start. An amateur.

But Chantelle didn't believe him, nor care. All men lied. Especially clients.

"I'm in a hotel nearby by. I need some company, if you know what I mean? What do you charge for all night? I mean all night. I'll buy you breakfast."

Chantelle's eyes lit up as she considered if the guy was for actually real. But his nervous and naive actions told her he most probably was.

"I'll get out of the cold, and then we can discuss money," Chantelle replied with her professional head on, sliding into the plush passenger seat.

Adam Yates chuckled nervously, but with a grin. His passenger was stunning.

"I like you already," he replied, smiling at the cool blond. "Very much."

Chantelle regarded the man beside her, sensing something strange, but also she felt that there was deep-down a warmth. She actually smiled back at him.

"I'm booked into a local hotel. I've down here on business over Christmas. I'd like some night-time company. If you know what I mean. The bed's cold!"

The man before her flushed, as if embarrassed to ask, then chuckled.

Chantelle admired the way her client politely asked for her services. She also liked the idea of a warm hotel. All night. Mega-deal. If it was all true.

"Did you say all night? As in until dawn?"

Her new companion nodded, as if it was normal.

She discussed her terms, to which he easily agreed.

"Take me to your lair," she joked, as the estate car then moved off.

"And I hope you've got some bubbly on ice." Chantelle joked.

Her companion nodded enthusiastically, much to her surprise.

"Actually, I've got three bottles," Adam replied. "To celebrate."

Chantelle grinned, unsure what he meant, but strangely sensed he was good and she'd found a soul mate. Something about him she genuinely liked.

But she also sensed a darker aspect to him. But she liked that too.

Would her hunch be right?

Time would tell.

Chapter 83

It is absurd to divide people into good or bad.
Wickedness is a myth invented by good people
to account for the curious attractiveness of others.

Oscar Wilde

Meanwhile, for Sarah, the long and silent journey in the Range Rover was the same as twice before. Swiftly out the city and on through the suburbs, then into the country, before heading down the familiar long wooded track, after passing its humorous sign, then pulling up outside the white-painted country house. Once again the man said nothing during the journey and she didn't try to make conversation, unlike she had previously; now knowing him better. She assumed it was part nerves, but also part of the whole experience for him; that of being in total control of the situation, despite his generally mild nature.

As Sarah got out of the vehicle she heard the same background sounds as before, when, on the first occasion, she'd questioned him about horses and dogs and where the location was, being set deep within a woods. But he'd not replied then and now she was no longer bothered, although still curious.

But from the glimpses of photographs she'd seen passing through the house and into the cellar on the two other occasions, she knew he was obviously heavily into riding and possibly hunted, having seem a photo of hunters.

The image on the photo was like the scenes on old paintings in pubs, with a stream of hounds and bright coloured riders, set before a large country house. It all looked very posh, and she knew he must have money to live in such a property. She'd joked to Chantelle about her bondage-loving horseman, and how maybe one day he'd whisk her away, make her his partner, and how she could maybe become the 'Lady of the Manor' and go out riding.

With this dream in mind, and keen to please; as well as enjoying the thrill of the sessions with him, the man once more led her into the warm house and then down into the cellar, just as before. There was no need to lift her down the stairs now, like the first time he'd taken her there. Then she'd been afraid, especially when he began his special tricks and the things that turned him on.

But it had secretly excited her too, and she'd actually orgasmed with the man, such was the experience. A very rare occurrence for her these days. Any grunts and groans, if she had to offer some encouragement, or even bother to show some form of interest to a nervous and slow client, were always faked.

But not this man. He excited her. This was half why she'd been willing to come back and not let him go with Chantelle. Not that she'd have done what she let him do. For a fellow prostitute, Chantelle was a bit of a prude. In a way, Chantelle should have been a model and was too nice for this game.

Her man led the way and Sarah let him guide her, as he seemed to prefer. He was good looking, very fit and clean; which she could not say about most of her customers. And despite what he asked of her, and did, he was actually gentle, very well mannered and showed great class. And he paid well.
Sarah felt Chantelle was jealous, knowing she too wanted a rich guy to keep her long term. It was the dream of all in the trade, and Sarah felt she was a step closer to realising her dream, and getting out of the game with her new man. She thought of Chantelle, possibly jerking off some poor old guy in his car, making a mess of his trousers and the car's upholstery. Or worse, being shagged up a back-alley by an incapable drunk, getting a damp backside.
She knew what to expect this time, so somewhat cheekily, strutted across the cellar floor, adding extra wiggle to her walk, her heels clicking loudly on the stone floor of the cellar. Teasingly she glanced over her shoulder at the man, giving him her best cheeky, coy grin, still sensing his nervous anticipation.
Sarah stood against the beam, and as before, he slowly secured her with the leather straps, this time tantalisingly running his hands softly up and down her legs, enjoying the silkiness of her skin. His fingers to the top and slid teasingly across her shaven gap, with Sarah squirming inside, knowing he wanted more.
And so did she. She loved this, and would have done it for free. Now spread-eagled, secured to the beam, she waited for him to advance towards her.
She knew he'd pull the knife out again. That was what'd initially scared her.
But after the same happened the second time, she knew it was all part of his fantasy. He was so gentle with the razor-sharp blade, sliding it skilfully across her skin; arousing her as much as it did him. Especially when he gently ran the edge along her belly, across her chest, and then with the gentlest of strokes, under her breasts. The sensation and experience; a mix of terror and pleasure, whilst having no control, was almost unknown to her, but totally arousing.
The man advanced towards her once more, completely naked and definitely hard. He'd lit a small hurricane lamp, just as before, it hanging from the wall, switching off the cellar light before advancing toward her. The soft flickering lamplight added to the atmosphere, his shadow appearing deformed against the walls as he slowly moved towards her. The knife appeared massive, almost horrific in the flickering light, as Sarah looked on in excited anticipation.
Then he stood before her; knife and erection long and hard and inches away.
Knife in hand, he slowly began to stroke the blade along her thighs, brushing it dangerously close to her vagina, but careful not to get too close, sensing her wince, enjoying the sensation, and gently responding to suit. The edge of the blade stroked against her skin, stimulating her fully as the sharp blade gliding skilfully up and along her stomach, just missing her pierced belly-button.
He moved in closer, his body touching hers, but still ensured he didn't enter, the control all part of the experience for him. A hand was upon her breast, raising it and gently it entered his mouth, as he drew hard on a firm nipple.

Sarah genuinely moaned as the nipple popped inside and he sucked, caressing her breast with one hand, sliding the blade against her thigh with the other.

His body pressed firmly against hers and she felt his erection, damp and slippery brush against the inside of her legs, as he teasingly moved his hips.

She wanted it inside her now. Hard and deep, as before.

He was growing in confidence, sensing her pleasure, and teased her more, sliding the hard member tantalising close to the damp inviting opening, the tip touching, only to move away, as Sarah slowly gyrated her hips willing it in.

Still the blade glided across her skin, Sarah drawing breath as it slid up high and to her throat. She felt her pulse quicken, the fear and anticipation real, but like a drug and wanting more. He sensed her concern and lowered the blade, then moved his hips firmly against hers and gently slid inside, pushing himself in, hard and deep, moving in deeper until their bellies touched.

Sarah gasped slightly as he entered, then groaned with pleasure as he slowly began to rock his hips back and forth. Soft and gentle, then hard and fast.

Still he held the blade, it's stimulating effect on Sarah adding to her pleasure, it no longer as scary as the first time. Even so he was good, very good. What was more, he was paying her for the pleasure of her having some great sex.

His body was warm and hard, his muscles light but firm, as he began pushing harder against her lean, slender body, pressing her buttocks against the worn, and aged timbers of the beam behind her. His pumping became harder and faster. He gripped a buttock firmly with one hand for increased resistance, one finger slipping momentarily in her anus, slightly increasing the pleasure for her, before exiting. Beads of sweat met at their conjoined waists, as Sarah began to moan gently, deep in the moment and fully enjoying some fine sex.

Sarah was nearing a climax very quickly, a rare thing for her, and one of the reasons she enjoyed this punter. She groaned heavily as his thrusting increased and he bit softly at her breasts, cupping one in his hand, his tongue flicking rapidly over her nipples as he pulled her forward and away from the wall.

The knife skilfully gliding up and down her back and buttocks, the fine edge sliding on damp skin almost too much to endure. This was all Sarah needed and she moaned heavily, her breathing hard and heavy. Her hips forced hard against the man as she came, letting him know with a series of loud cries.

It was all the man needed, and he too let out a deep moan, pushing his body fully against her, entering further and thrusting hard and fast, grunting heavily, biting gently at Sarah's neck, the pair sighing and groaning in sweet unison.

Then the cellar lights came on.

Gone was the soft flickering light of the Hurricane Lantern.

White walls glowed bright. All was clearly revealed.

The sudden brightness startled both parties.

And also one more. More so.

A third person. Watching it all.

They now stood staring in horror from the cellar stairs.

The man was finishing his orgasm; pumping and groaning; aware of a sudden brightness, squinting his eyes, but seemingly lost, ignoring it. Too busy.
Sarah was finished, but enjoying his experience. Uncaring.
He continued to pump away at Sarah's slim hips, his face to the bright wall, moaning loudly, until empty and now satisfied, and hanging tight onto her sweating body, firm fingers gripping her buttocks he became aware.
Sensing her body tense, then fully noticing the light and it's meaning, he relaxed his grip on her hips and swung his head around.
Upon the stairs, the man saw a familiar face.
"Martin! What the hell are you doing?" Sharon yelled.

Chapter 84

Is this a dagger which I see before me, the handle toward my hand?
Come let me clutch thee. I have thee not, and yet I see thee still.

Macbeth - William Shakespeare

The answer was obvious, but difficult to divulge. Instead, silence answered, with no one within the cellar moving. Still firmly conjoined to Sarah, who was firmly conjoined to the woodwork of his cellar wall, Martin froze. His heart began pumping fresh adrenaline, but now for a completely different reason.

He'd been caught out and panic ran through his body.

Eyes wide and staring, still attached to Sarah, he looked over at Sharon.

At the top of the cellar stairs she stared at the pair in horror and disbelief.

Only then did Martin turn back to look at Sarah, who in turn looked over his shoulder towards the untimely intruder. Sarah's face displayed both shock and amusement, it not the first time she'd been caught with someone's partner.

"It's not what you think," Martin began to automatically explain, suddenly realising the stupidity of the comment. He withdrew and pulled himself away from Sarah, turning fully to face Sharon. Her face was ashen, mouth open.

A blob of semen hung from his rapidly drooping penis, to then drip and fall onto the stone floor. Martin watched the blob crash down; seemingly just like his life, whilst then looking at his feet, bare legs and naked sweaty form.

He glanced at Sarah, tied up, half naked, sweating heavily; it blatantly obvious he'd happily been fucking the crucified, scantily clad sexy young woman.

This would take some serious explaining. Or none. It was what it was.

Martin couldn't think of what to say. How do you explain such a thing. More so having a razor sharp knife firmly in your hand to add to the situation.

Sharon stood on the cellar stairs looking silently at him. Then the woman.

Her face was pale and drawn. She shook her head from side to side in a mix of shock, disbelief and amazement. Then tears began to well up in her eyes.

Sharon's focus then dropped down to below Martin's waist height.

Instinctively Martin followed her gaze, knowing it fell upon the knife.

He looked down at the massive blade. That aspect would need explaining.

Sharon erupted and screamed bitter anger. She ran down the cellar stairs and over towards Martin, a whole mixture of emotions running through her mind.

Martin stepped back, and raised his arms, knife still held firm, as Sharon reached him and began to pummel his naked chest with the base of her fist.

"You bastard! You absolute fucking bastard!" she yelled.

Martin winced, stepping back to protect himself from the weak, but firm blows; dodging and weaving his body side to side like a boxer.

"Sorry Sharon," Martin said, shoulder shrugged. "I'm so sorry. I have needs."

"I hate you. You bastard. How could you do this to me?" Sharon sobbed.

Sharon swung her leg up to kick Martin, but he was quick and sidestepped. She threw a wide punch, and again he swerved, her fist brushing past Sarah.

"Oi! Watch what you're doing!" Sarah yelled, still firmly strapped tight.

Her comment drew Sharon's attention to the almost forgotten Third party. She paused her punches, then turned around to look fully at the crucified figure before her, absorbing the woman's image with deep bitterness.

Martin's semen slowly dripped from her wide-open legs and down her thighs. Sharon saw the fluid upon the well-tanned, slender legs, and regarded her fine slim body. She thought of her own body, aging and flabby. Belly fat sagging and her sexual appetite limited and clearly boring. Compared to this trollop.

"You bitch. You fucking stinking bitch!" Sharon yelled at Sarah, then turning to stand directly before her, punched her hard in the stomach.

Sarah wheezed at the blow and instinctively tried to double up, gasping for breath. But she was unable to react naturally, her arms still firmly restrained, as also her legs. She heaved violently, trying to fight for breath, as another blow rained in, this one just below the ribs, taking her breath fully. Sharon followed up, punching hard directly into her firm right breast, then swinging higher, punching her in the face. Sarah yelled out with what breath she could muster, as pain poured through her restrained body and she fought for air, feeling nauseous. Sharon had vented her anger on the woman, and now turned back towards Martin, who still had the knife firmly in his hand.

Instinctively he raised the knife, out of Sharon's bodyline, so he wouldn't accidentally cut her, as she frantically swung blows, her rage overwhelming.

He sidestepped once more, but Sharon made a lunge for the knife, grabbing at his wrist with all of her strength, trying to prise the weapon from his hand.

Martin pulled back, resisting her attempt to grasp the knife, fearful of what she'd do with the lethal blade; either to him or Sarah, such was her anger.

Still Sharon pulled at it his arm, the blade safely pointing behind Martin. He weaved sideward, pulling back with all his might, as Sharon tugged at him with an equal force. Sharon's fingers slid off Martin's sweaty arm and she flew backwards, falling onto the cellar floor. Obeying Newton's Third Law, Martin flew backwards too with equal force, but staggering, maintained his footing.

He hardly felt the contact; such was the speed his hand moved in a sweeping arc, flying through the air behind him, and such the sharpness of the blade.

But it was the sound that attracted him and made him turn.

A sharp intake of breath. And a soft groan. Pain.

Then mixed with a high-pitched wheezing sound.

Sharon stopped fighting, turning to look at the ashen face of the woman still secured to the beams by her wrists and ankles. Spread out, sweat glistening upon her body naked; all bar for her black suede high-heeled shoes. Like hers.

For a split second neither Sharon nor Martin realised what they were looking at until a dark red line appeared stark across the skin of the Sarah's trim belly.

Sarah let out a moan as the thin red line across her white belly became wider, the dark red gap expanding by the second as the cleaved skin separated. As she heaved again, a harsh wheezing cry, the deep red slash across her stomach became broad, the splitting flesh showing a sickly yellow mass beneath.

Martin knew at once what had occurred, and what was about too happen. He moved forward, but too late, as the weight of Sarah's intestines began to force through the fine, but very deep cut Martin's razor-sharp knife had made, cutting straight across her belly; slicing through both flesh and muscle.

As he reached her, with Sharon still standing looking on in terror, the grey and brown intestines began to force their way out of the narrow split. Martin put his hand to the right-hand side, where the intestine was protruding greater and began to push it back into Sarah's stomach cavity. But the force seemed be counter productive, resulting in increased pressure to the split on the other side of the cut, where more intestines now began oozing out instead.

Martin moved his hands, feeling like the little Dutch Boy and the leaking dam. The gap opened wider, splitting in the middle, as Sarah breathed heavily, sucking in air as the first wave of pain hit her and shock began to take over.

She began to shake and judder, her quivering body straining at the leather straps securing all of her limbs as the severe pain and realisation hit her.

"Stop moving you silly cow!" Martin yelled at Sarah. "Keep still!"

Hands pressed to Sarah's belly, he turned to look at the frozen Sharon.

"Sharon, come and help me. Quick! Don't just fucking stand there. Help me push her guts back," he yelled at the silent, on-looking Sharon, in deep shock.

She stared at the horrific sight, unable to move, looking at the image of the crucified naked young woman, who's intestines were now beginning to seep out from the foot long slash in her belly she and Martin had caused.

Martin had handfuls of intestine, which slopped about wet within his hands, slivering out of Sarah's bloody belly like eels fresh from a river. His frantic hands slid over the bloody slit, intestines slipping out a heavily bleeding cut quicker than he could force back into the seemingly ever-increasing gap.

Sharon suddenly reacted and moved forward a few steps, looking as Martin's fingers actually slid inside Sarah's quaking body, roughly pushing a handful of the slopping intestines back in, only for them to slip out from the other side.

Sarah strangely didn't scream, but groaned heavily, such was her shock as she began to pass out. Her legs beginning to slump, adding strain on her arms, the slit thus widening. Martin began to feel despair, as he yelled again at Sharon.

"Put your hand there. Quick woman! Hurry! Stop the flow."

Sharon moved forward and Martin forcibly grabbed her hands, pushing them hard against Sarah's belly. She shuddering at the contact with the warm, sticky flesh, just as a fresh wave of pain hit Sarah and she let out a whimpering cry.

Martin moved his hand over the other side of the gap, as Sharon's hands held the gap temporarily shut. Martin pushed the remaining piece of intestine back into the bloody hole, hoping he'd returned the organs back to their home.

He paused for a second, gazing at the bloody, sticky mess, knowing he had to strap Sarah's wound, but to do so meant releasing the pressure. Dilemma.

Then Sarah slumped, her knees collapsing, and fresh intestine squirmed out of the hole and through Sharon's fingers, like a giant worm. A spurt of bright red blood added some un-needed and unwelcome slimy lubrication.

Sharon screamed, and jumped back, removing her hand completely.

Martin hadn't been firmly holding the gap in Sarah's belly, but merely pushing intestine back inside as Sharon let go. The result was catastrophic.

The intestine, under pressure, and aided by gravity, began to pour out of Sarah's belly in a constant flow. The grey tubing cascaded out of the widening bloody split, slopping down past her thighs, and drooping down to her knees; blood and fluid plopping out onto the hard cellar floor with a gentle splat.

Martin also instinctively jumped back in horror, as Sarah moaned heavily; a cry of deep pain, as both he and Sharon watched the tragic scene unfold.

"No! Oh No!" Martin yelled, as the steady flow of organs slowly eased, but had almost reached the floor, just as Sarah began to convulse violently, her secured arms shaking. Her legs slumped fully, bending at the knees, and dropping Sarah down into a painful suspended squat, still tethered by her outstretched arms, but still strangely standing up in her suede high-heels.

Sarah's eyes rolled backwards in their sockets, as she moaned in deep shock.

Martin bent down and scooped up armfuls of intestine, it slipping out of his hands as soon as he lifted it, to again fall back onto the cold floor. Again he grappled with the sloppy mass, it squirming in his frantic hands as if having a life of its own, before it slipped again, and he dropped it all with a big slop.

Falling onto his knees, looking at the mess, he sobbed openly.

Sharon looked on at the horrific scene in dumb shock. Martin was sobbing, as he knelt amongst a pile of grey-brown, warm, stinking intestines, hanging from the torn, bloody belly of a young naked girl, who remained tied to the old oak beams, her face ash grey and body heavily convulsing.

"Kill her Martin," Sharon said in a low, quiet voice. "Kill her. Do it!"

Martin turned his head and looked up in disbelief, unsure he'd heard her, his sobs easing as the horror of what Sharon suggested hit home.

"You've got to put her out of her misery. Kill her. Please! Now."

Sarah, although in severe shock and semi-conscious, heard the comment and was brought back into a higher state of alertness only absolute fear brings.

"No," Sarah croaked. "Help me. Please help me!"

Martin looked up at Sarah, her stunning face once bring such joy to him. Then down at the gaping hole in her belly, now a wide split of angry dark purple and red. It began to bleed heavily around the torn edge where the force of the intestine had widened the gap, the yellowy fat and muscle layers beyond clearly visible. The mass of hanging intestine dangled from the hole in Sarah's stomach and partially lay against her bare legs, the remainder laying on the cellar floor, pooling around her high heeled, but bloody feet.

Martin turned to look at Sharon, and then down at the offending knife, which lay on the floor where he'd dropped it after their fight. He crawled on his knees towards it, recovered the knife, then raised himself up. Almost like an automaton, unseeing, unfeeling, he knew what he must do.

Sharon looked at him silently, and simply nodded.

Martin looked at Sharon, the tears gone, and nodded back.

He approached Sarah, her eyes open, wide and terror filled, as she knew what was to happen, but dreaded to think it may, and hoped it would not be so.

One could always hope. In vain.

Mouth dry, no words forming, Sarah silently mouthed the words 'No.'

Gently shaking her head, her eyes implored the man she'd grown to like and enjoy over their brief sessions together, and who moments earlier she'd hoped might take her away from her hard life of sin, pain and torment.

He would. But not in the manner she'd sadly dreamed.

Martin approached Sarah slowly, knife raised to her throat.

He gently grabbed hold of her hair, forcing her head back then pressed the large knife hard against her throat. The razor sharp blade lay just below the jawbone and above her Adam's apple. He tilted the blade, levelling it out with her jaw on her right-hand side, before looking at Sharon.

Sharon simply nodded, a tear rolling down her cheek.

Sarah offered no resistance, too weak, and in deep shock.

"Sorry," softly spoken, were the last words she'd hear.

Martin drew the blade hard and deep, cutting in the inch and a half required to hit both the jugular vein and carotid artery together. The first heavy spurt of blood, as both major blood supplies were severed, reached Sharon. The fine red droplets sprayed high in the air, to rain down over her face, causing her to scream, and she clawed at her face to try to remove them. Then she turned and ran away, cowering over in a corner of the cellar, shaking in fear.

By the time Sharon had stopped screaming, the blade had cut deep into Sarah's windpipe, through into the left side of her throat, the jugular on that side being only partly severed, as the blade snagged on the tough cartilage within. Martin drew the knife finally through, pulling it clear of Sarah's now gaping, slit throat, red blood flowing. Blood sprayed over Martin's naked body in decreasing bursts, as Sarah's now dying body continued to pump the blood out, the heart still working. She'd be unconscious within five seconds, due to lack of blood and oxygen to the brain. The wound would prove fatal within twelve seconds, although it would take over a minute for the loss of blood to Sarah's brain flowing out to technically cause her final death.

Sharon watched it all in horror and rose, to blindly run about the cellar in circles, hands waving above her head, screaming in horror and blind panic.

Martin, his bare skin painted red in Sarah's blood, his face and hair covered in red droplets, stood back from Sarah's dead and drooping form. He looked silently on and emotionless, at the piece of meat, regarding his fine craft work.

Martin retuned to the room and the real world he lived in upon hearing and absorbing Sharon's whimpering cries from within the cellar.

He glanced over at her, then feeling a new sensation, down at his waist.

Knife in hand, steady and pointing forward, it was ready and poised. All of his actions were now instinctive. His fresh erection was also as hard as ever.

Turning silently, with no expression, he looked at Sharon.

She stood still, hand on the cellar stair rail and stared at her husband.

She saw the blank, dead look in his eyes.

Then her eyes dropped downwards.

Eyes focussed upon the bloody knife.

Then her focus lowered.

Clearly evident, she couldn't miss his fresh arousal.

Martin stared silently at his wife.

Sharon screamed.

"No Martin, not me. Please!"

Chapter 85

And there went out another horse that was red: and power was given to him that sat thereon to take peace from the earth, and that they should kill one another; and that there was given unto him a great sword.

Revelation 6:4

The woman's feet pounded upon the soft earth, her shoes slipping on the moist ground beneath as she spun around, looking over her shoulder once more. Nothing followed. She continued running along the darkened dirt track, the trees lining the way shielding out most of the moonlight which was slowly rising in the clear and chill night sky. Heavy breaths misted out before her in the crisp air, lungs and legs aching, as she followed the twisting track.

Pausing, she leant forward slightly to gasp for air and gain some composure, and also listen. With only a few hundred metres until the end of the track met the road, she'd soon be out of the woods. Then hopefully away to safety.

The woman reduced her jog to a fast walk, more confident now she was nearing the end of the track and hopefully her ordeal. She wore only a knee length, thin strapped, black cotton dress, cut straight across the chest. More accustom to the summer, than a cold winter's night, it provided no warmth. And her flat-soled black patent leather shoes were not ideal for a muddy track. Not the garments of choice, neither for season, or for the situation she found herself in. But she'd had no choice in selecting the perfect garments for the weather, terrain or purpose. The situation had been imposed upon her, suddenly, with everything happening so unexpected and traumatically.

On she walked, a few more steps towards the end of the wooded track. More cautious, her ears sought out any noise in the gloom, wary of each footfall.

She paused. Something caught her attention. Noise. Movement. Nearby.

Standing in the silence of the night, she cocked her head, listening carefully as the sound continued. Rustling. More movement. Louder. Twigs and sticks cracked from heavy footfall. Behind her. She spun around, her eyes wide, searching the blackness for the source of the rapidly moving footfalls.

It was to her right. Multiple legs. Steadily advancing through the trees. Light, yet powerful. Rustling the undergrowth, but also harshly cracking twigs.

Her pulse raced and instinctively she squatted beside a large Ash tree, its bark smooth but damp. Peering into the gloom she cocked her head to identify the advancing footsteps. They moved swiftly and with ease through the dense undergrowth; seemingly undeterred by the old bracken, nettles and brambles encompassing that area. Steadily the source of the noise moved, all legs in unison, closing in towards her on the edge of the track; the sound like a small group of people moving rapidly together, but all shuffling their feet.

She knew what was creating the unique sound. And who. And why.

Her mind worked rapidly and fresh fear flowed and sprang back upright and began to run down the track on her toes for speed, but also to lessen any give-away sounds of slapping feet. However, the sound of crashing footfalls appeared to be just ahead of her, and moving inwards, towards the track upon which she ran, as if undertaking a pincer motion to cut off her escape.

Her legs moved quicker, sensing the possible ambush. On she ran.

Breathing heavily as she jogged, the exit from the woods, the road and then hopefully safety, were now less than a hundred metres away.

Then she saw it. Moving ahead of her. Out of the shrub and onto the track.

With the milky moon rising, offering a silver glow to the surrounding gloom, the imposing obstacle loomed large before her, filling the track; path blocked.

A chill ran down her spine and she shuddered, her stalling feet sliding on the soft soil, sending her to an immediate and juddering halt.

The large dark horse stood before her on the track.

With a heavy snort, mist drifted from its blowing nostrils.

The dark figure, silhouetted atop, but features obscured by the gloom, peered down the track. Head tilting, unseen eyes stared straight at the woman.

The horse shuffled, then steadied by the rider, advanced before halting. The dark clad rider clearly focussed upon it's target. The woman on the track.

Stepping away from the tree, a wave of valour surged through the woman.

"Why won't you just let me leave?" she hollered bitterly into the dark, at the shadow before her. "Just let me go and be free. It's all I ask. Please."

The only response was the snorting of nostrils and shuffling of hooves from the horse upon the track. Agitated, the horse bounced on its hocks, spinning, sensing danger in the darkness, but was then steadied by the rider. The rider made no reply, nor sound, but tugged on a rein, turning the horse around to face down the track. Reins held in one hand, the other moved across to the rider's side, grasping at the top of an object hanging down from their waist.

The sound of grating steel emanated from the direction of the rider, causing the horse to bounce excitedly upon the spot and the woman sense fear. Her eyes widened upon hearing the familiar sound, then she froze as she saw the dull glint of moonlight reflect off the steel drawn before the horseman's face.

"No!" the woman screamed, turning on her heels, running back down the track up which she had just come. Her feet slipped on the moist ground and she fell heavily onto her knees. Breaking her fall with her hands, the damp soil imbedded itself into her fingernails. Then the sound of hooves hammering on the moist ground behind, rapidly closing in, encouraged her to scramble up.

She rose, and then instinctively threw herself sideways, rolling over to her right-hand side, as the horse cantered past, shoed hoofs glinting past her face.

The sword blade swiped down viciously past the spot where she'd lain, as the horse charged on. The steel tip of the sword flipped up a piece of soil as it was whipped back up in a swift upstroke by the skilled swordsman and rider.

The woman lay in horror, the flash of blade so close to her head chilling.

"Whoa!" the horseman yelled, fighting for control, speaking for the first time as the horse continued on excitedly down the track and into darkness.

This was the break the woman needed. She scrambled back to her feet, turned to her left and threw herself into the dense undergrowth. The thorns of the brambles, which formed the edging to the track, gripped at her dress and tore her skin, but she forced herself through, ignoring as best she could the pain she felt. Behind her on the track, the thud of hooves could be heard, returning to the position she'd stood at moments earlier, eyes now searching.

Suddenly the sound of hooves were directly behind her. Panicking she forced her legs harder, but they didn't move, entwined within a mass of gripping dead cleavers, brambles, nettles and bracken. Legs trapped, the momentum of her body sent her forward, and she fell fully into the mass of undergrowth.

She cried out as the sound of hooves immediately behind shook the ground, then momentarily fell silent. A sudden darkness encompassed her, as though a great black curtain had been thrown over her, but only for a second. Then suddenly, before her outstretched and fumbling hands, appeared the hind legs of the black horse, which had jumped over her and landed into the woods.

Crashing into the decaying debris, the horse frantically ran on out of control, charging off, deeper into the darkness. The bending branches of small trees whipped viciously at the face and body of the unseen rider, before seemingly ensnaring them within a small low tree. The rider fought fiercely to bring the horse back to a standstill and free themselves, the grunts and curses clear.

The woman took the opportunity and fought against the grabbing brambles, pulling herself free. The miniature saw-blades plucked and tore strips off the expensive delicate fabric of the dress, as she freed herself, but she didn't care.

The horse had pulled up, but vanished in the gloom of the woods, now only appearing to the searching eyes of the woman as a dark blurred shape. The sound of snorting, crashing undergrowth and muffled curses denoted the location of the agitated rider, seemingly determined to relocate the woman.

The battle was far from over. The initial attack had only just started.

With a supreme effort the woman tore her legs free from the thorns and scrambled at first on all fours, and then up and onto her feet, running into a clearer part of the woods, but moving away from the exit she desperately sought, drifting deeper on into the woods and away from the cursed track.

The ground inside the woods, where wider spaced more mature trees grew, was carpeted with rotting bracken, fresh fallen leaves and a mix of twigs and other winter debris. Apart from the various saplings and mature trees, with the odd bush, shrub, or clump of brambles, this section of the woods was relatively clear and easy to move within. The ground was firm but soft, and she was able to travel freely and quick, aided by the dull silver light from the now rising moon, offering grey and black colour to shapes and forms.

The sound of the horse could be heard once more crashing close behind. Still running, she frantically peered over her shoulder, to see the dark foreboding shape cantering behind her in the gloom, now only about thirty feet away.

The rider ducked under the low branches with skill and experience, as the horse thundered on, rapidly gaining ground. She looked ahead as a group of closely planted trees approached, then with the sound of the hooves only yards away, swiftly side-stepped between two mature trees, changed direction, to suddenly head deeper into the woods and back into the darkness.

Another more desperate 'Whoa' came from the rider, followed by a cry of pain as the rider's leg smashed against one of the larger tree trunks. The horse had carried on, passing through the horse size only gap, typically oblivious to the cursing rider onboard, who was almost dragged clean out of the saddle.

Proud of her swift action, the woman continued, her pounding legs gaining vital distance between her and the berating horseman, who'd vanished from sight once more. On she ran, as the ground dropped downwards, allowing her to fall out of any direct sightline. She moved deeper into the darkness of the woods, weaving between brambles, shrubs and aged Rhododendron's, where their tendril-like branches reached out like the limbs of a bizarre octopus.

Further into the woods she ran, still not daring to look back. Suddenly, unseen in the gloom, a small ditch appeared, and she fell into it, just up to knee level. Entrapping the her legs, her body continued forward with the momentum built up. She let out a cry, as her face and chest slammed into the soft earth and rotting debris, dirt filling her open mouth. Lights flashed in her head, before she regained her senses and accessed where she was.

She'd fallen flat onto her face, badly wringing both her ankles in the small ditch, which was about two feet deep and filled with damp, rotting leaves and stinking cold mud, which sucked at her shoes. She rolled over in the ditch onto her behind, pulling her legs up to rub the strained ankles, aware her Italian leather loafers were stuck somewhere deep in the cold, sticky mud.

Looking back up the incline, and at the silhouette of trees forming a black spidery backdrop into the night sky, she could no longer see the horseman. She gulped in air, reviewing her dilemma, wondering where he'd gone.

Although fit, her breathing roared and seemed to boom through her head, as she listened intently within the darkness. She could hear no noises, other than her own breath, which she fought to control, along with the thump of the pulse in her neck. Suddenly, the sight of the silhouetted horseman appeared in-between the trees on the moonlit skyline above. It answered her question.

The dark outline loomed above on the brow of the slight incline, some fifty feet away, moving from left to right. It's shape weirdly changing as it passed through the straggly outline of trees, drifting silently along the ridge.

The rider was back out hunting. Doing what it did best.

Searching and listening for any sound of the quarry. Her.

She thought quickly, scanning the ground. Other than the Rhododendron's behind her, a few clumps of brambles and the odd larger tree, she was fairly exposed in this lower section of the older part of the woods. If she remained still and he moved down towards her, he was bound to see or hear her, unless she lay in the ditch and covered herself with leaves, which she had considered. But she needed to get away from the place as quickly as possible and not risk hiding overnight in the cold and wet. She had to get back up the slope, onto the track, then the road. With no mobile phone, nor any hope of getting any other help, she had to make it out the woods and to the safety of the road. However, it was obvious the horseman was patrolling that area, expecting her to head there, knowing it was her only way to escape. She looked behind, to see the ground levelled out, but also appeared to become much denser with closer set trees. Considering her dilemma and any options, her thoughts swiftly returned to the present, with the sound of twigs cracking close by.

She peered over the brambles to see the outline of the horseman now much closer, only thirty feet away, but moving from right to left and drifting away.

She held her breath, worried the light mist that emanated might be seen. The scuffing sound of hooves moved away along the low ridge, but she knew that on his next sweep down, moving even closer, he'd proceed almost directly to where she now lay partially hidden, but she would no doubt be discovered.

Slowly she pulled herself up, and with her ankles aching, in a half squat began to shuffle cautiously away from her cover. As the silhouette of the horseman began to vanish into the gloom, blending in with the levelling ground, she moved, hoping she would be clear away for his next sweep of the woods.

She carefully stepped over the darker shapes of branches littering the floor, placing her bare feet down deliberately and gently, the progress slow.

Sure her hunter would be moving down towards her at any moment on a new fresh sweep, and then catch up with her, she quickened her pace.

The crack rang out through the woods like a pistol shot.

She winced, her body freezing in horror and regret.

Of all the damp, rotting twigs littering the woodland floor, she'd carelessly placed her foot upon the firmest, crispest and driest branch in the woods.

She looked down at the cursed branch and her entire senses re-awoke as a fresh surge of adrenaline washed through her body like hot drain-cleaner.

She knew instantly her pursuer would have heard it too. He was too good.

Now taking no chances, she began running again, dodging between trees and bramble patches, which in the clearer, more open ground, seemed to come at her at lightening speed. The noise she made as crashing through the woods seemed to deafen her, as she ran on almost blindly. But she no longer cared, and knew speed and swift movement were her only chance for escape.

She frantically turned to momentarily look over her shoulder.

What she'd feared to see now loomed eerily behind.

The dark shape of the horseman.

Weaving between the trees in a quick trot, the hunter was following her tracks and already gaining ground; catching her up. The woman forced her legs to move faster upon the energy-sapping, soft ground, scanning the ground and trees ahead, as the thundering sound of hooves behind closed in.

She turned her head around once more, tears flooding down her face and her chest heaving, to see the horseman directly behind her. Turning her sobbing face back around a large darkened shape suddenly loomed directly before her.

She was but too late to stop. Instantly all movement ceased and intense pain shot through her face and chest as her head smashed hard against the trunk of an unseen tree in front of her; the breath knocked from her by the impact.

Her head swam and knees went limp, as dazed, the sound of grating steel was heard only feet away. Thunderous hooves shook the ground behind, as her strength failed and her body slid down the smooth surface of the stout tree.

The sword tip slid through the top of her hair. Thrust firmly into the tree, the tip was directly in the place where her shoulders would have been only a split second earlier. But instead it fully missed the collapsing form of the woman.

The horse continued on, causing the rider, whose hand still grasped the hilt of the sword, to be pulled away sideways from the saddle. Releasing the firmly embedded sword at the last second, the rider had already twisted sideways too far, and was off balance. With a loud yelp, the rider was dragged off the horse and out the saddle, hitting another large tree, landing heavily at its base.

The horse carried on for a few more strides, then sensing no rider, naturally stopped within the gloom. Steam blew from its nose and warm body.

The woman, still stunned from the impact with the tree looked up from her now kneeling position against the tree. Above her the sword bobbed up and down, only a foot from her head. Strands of her hair were impaled between the blade and tree and tugged at her skull as she rose. Blood poured down her face from the smashed nose, the pain burning through her battered face.

Importantly, with a sigh, she realised she was alive. And the horseman down.

A few feet away, lying facedown, the horseman remained still, arms spread out in the soft leaf litter covering the vast woodland flooring. The horse stood a few metres away, partly hidden in the gloom, wary of the silent figure, slowly moving towards it and its now motionless former rider and master.

Shaking her head, the woman composed herself, raising her body. Ensuring she ducked away from the embedded sword, which with the aid of the hilt, she used to steady herself, she rose and looked over at the now gently stirring figure on the ground, groaning and seemingly beginning to recover too.

Her hands frantically gripped upon the sword's hilt, and tugged, trying to pull it free. But it wouldn't move. It was firmly embedded in the tree. Anger now began to take over from the former emotion of fear, but tug and pull as she might, the sword would not release. Her was body exhausted, all energy spent.

The horseman was beginning to push himself up with one hand. Seemingly dazed and confused, he lifted his head, but his body stayed on the ground.

The woman glanced at the man, sensing an advantage and again frantically pulled at the sword. But she was weak, exhausted, and unlike King Arthur's mighty sword, Excalibur, this one was not going to give itself to her. It seemed she too wouldn't be crowned king, nor queen. She sighed, watching the slowly rising horseman, then saw an object that maybe would suffice.

Looking down at her feet she saw a large branch and instinctively picked it up, but stumbled and fell to the ground, as its immense weight overcame her. Undeterred, and seeing the horseman recovering, she scanned the gloom for another. Ten feet from the rising man her hands grasped another branch.

In one continuous movement she grasped at the piece of timber, propelled herself forward and swung the branch with all her force at the figure before her. Half off the ground, and at the last second seeing the woman before him and swinging a branch, the horseman vainly raised an arm to stop its blow.

It caught him fully, then shattered, the remnants of rotting timber crashing into the side of his head. Its momentum threw his body sideways, the branch breaking into chucks and multiple fragments with the impact. The woman fell sideways with the force of swinging the branch, as it dragged her over too.

She released the remaining stump from her hands and looked briefly down at the figure, laying face down. It did not move, nor emit any sound. The horse, jumping at the sound of the blow, ensnared its bridle in a small tree and began to thrash wildly to free itself. The woman momentarily looked at the horse, considering taking it and riding away to safety, but in it's nervous state, decided against it, knowing it'd be almost impossible to mount the panicking horse from the soft ground about her. She took another glance at the still stationary form on the ground, then turning, began to run back up the slope, heading towards the track and safety, this time at a more controlled pace.

The pain ran through her head as she scrambled up the ground, using her hands to steady herself. She slipped and thorns and sharp twigs dug into her bare feet. Several times she looked into the darkness behind her, to ensure that once more her hunter wasn't in pursuit. But nothing followed her this time. Soon she was back level with the edge of the dirt track and wincing, pushed through brambles lining the edge, to again stand back onto the track.

Once back on the track, and with the moonlit arch of the trees showing the exit from the woods and highlighting her exodus, she felt more relaxed.

Despite her breath labouring, and a cold sweat sticking the dress to her back, in a mix of walking and intermittent jogging, she found herself close to the exit of the woods and level with the familiar 'Trespassers Will Be Eaten' sign.

As she walked past the sign, strangely illuminated in the silver glow of the rising moon, the wording seemed even more poignant. She shook her head in disgust as she walked past, but with a chill running through her, but now finally sensed freedom was near, and all going well, only a few moments away.

She began to jog gently the last part of the track, the mix of rotting leaves and stones gently crunching under her bare feet. The exit was yards away.

She again peered over her shoulder, into the pervading gloom and darkness of the woods behind, seeing only darkness and black, but forever sensed with fear that the horseman would appear again on the track at any moment. Nothing but the dark wooded track lay behind her. Sighing, she walked on.

Although glad to finally be onto the minor roadway, the woman knew she was far from anywhere, with no houses for some distance. Despite knowing little traffic ever travelled along the road, she hoped that a car might just pass at some point, stop, help, and take her away from this infernal nightmare.

She stopped jogging along the tarmac road, regaining breath and composure, but still ever vigilant, looked behind. Ahead, the woods on her right began to peel away from the roadside, a raised grass bank and field replacing the dense woodland she was so happy to escape. The wood tapered off gently at first, with low hedging, then it turned sharply at an angle, disappearing into the darkness as a large field then ran off to the right. Across the open field to her right, the world seemed in contrast to the gloom of the woods she'd left, as the silvery wash of the bright moon began to break through the thinning cloud drifting above, lighting up the vast open countryside in a soft glow.

The high hedge on the left also began to reduce in height and thin out in places, leaving clear areas and revealing open fields. The open nature reduced her claustrophobic feeling and provided clear views ahead. Happy to be free of the terror of the woods, he walked at a steady pace, her energy returning.

Now partly illuminated by the silver moonlight, the woman regarded her state, noting numerous tears to the black dress and cuts to her arms and legs. Her feet resembled mud balls and knew her face was smashed. She wanted to cry, the pain in her face throbbing and head hurting, but had to get help.

Jogging on a few strides, then dropping to a walk, tarmac cold and painful to her feet, she keenly listened for either the sound of hooves clattering on the road behind, or the pleasant hum of tyres on tarmac; but she heard nothing.

She wasn't sure what made her look toward the field to her right, but her attention was drawn to an object appearing to race across the silvery grey open field. At first it was a black shape, with no real form, moving steadily and purposefully in a straight line some distance away, seemingly heading for the opposing field headland. In the gloom and silver light, the size and shape were hard to distinguish. Maybe it was a fox, a hare or a deer. But as it seemed to change course, and then head in towards the road, the size of the object rapidly grew. The woman stopped moving and now stationary, looked on.

Mesmerised, her legs went weak as the form of horse and rider closed in.

At two hundred yards she heard the sound of the hooves pounding on the soft unploughed stubble of the field. Still she stood and stared in disbelief.

Within seconds the horse and rider appeared, moving towards her. Then the pair skilfully leapt the bank from the field, and in one bound, jumped at her, landing on the road. With a clatter of hooves her nemesis had returned.

The woman stared in horror at the steaming snorting beast and its rider.

Instinct saved her from being trampled as the horse leapt the hedge to her left, but she felt sure the horse had hit her as her body was involuntarily flung across the road. Straightening herself, she noted the horseman had landed on the road heavily, sparks lighting the dark, being thrown from the road beneath the horses hooves, the iron shoes clattered, as the rider fought for control.

It was as she watched the rider fight with the horse's reins that the woman began to feel the burning in the top off her right arm. Placing her left hand onto that area, she winced, as she felt the skin separate and her fingers slide into the deep, long cut. Black, warm sticky fluid appeared from a gash.

Her head began to swim as the pain and knowledge of how bad and deep, and until then, unknown sword cut was, and began to send her into shock.

However, the sight of the turning horse ahead of her forged fresh strength. Spinning around, she headed straight down the centre of the road at a full sprint, not daring to look back, now yelling with all her gasping breath.

"Help me! Help me! Please!" She screamed loudly, but in vain, with the deafening sound of hooves now clattering on behind.

Suddenly she stopped yelling, stopped running, and instead croaked.

It was as if an unseen hand had knocked the wind clean from her.

An unseen heavy fist, punched into her back. An iron fist. And more.

Her throat began to fill with warm fluid and a choking sound emanated from her mouth. Then, as if in slow motion, she looked in shock at the two feet of dark steel protruding from her stomach. She strangely gripped the blade, but it replied by slicing harshly through her hands as it mysteriously vanished.

The sword, withdrawn from her back by the rider, no longer supported the weight of the woman, and so her legs crumpled. She fell heavily forward onto her knees, cracking open the neat kneecaps, but she felt nothing. Her torso remained upright, head raised, hands held out before her, almost in a begging position. Blood bubbled up in a foaming froth from the silent open mouth.

The horseman manoeuvred the horse to face the woman in the moonlight.

She could see his broad grin. Evil smile. The moonlight turned to pink as she saw the sword rise high above the horseman's head as the black horse raced towards her, white foam blowing from it's lips and hooves clattering.

A whistling sweep of the sword was the last thing she heard.

The razor-sharp blade sliced into the woman's elegant neck.

Swift. Clean. And through.

She heard no more.

With a heavy thud her separated head gently rolled away.

Bouncing irregularly along the tarmac, it came to rest upon its bloody stump.

At the base of the hunter's clattering hooves, sightless eyes gazed up.

Glinting eyes, set within a smiling face, gazed back down.

Chapter 86

The healthy man does not torture others.
Generally it is the tortured who turn into torturers.

Carl Jung

Inside the spacious barn, with bales of straw stacked high in one corner, and an array of white sacks of fertilizer in another, a large moth fluttered around the singular exposed bulb, which dimly lit one section of the barn's interior.

Avoiding a large dusty cobweb, the moth was oblivious to the naked man hanging from the heavy oak beam beside it. The man, suspended from the solid beam by his wrists, with roughly tied rope, hung down. The balls of his feet just touched the cold, concrete slab of the floor, taking some of the strain from his extended arms, and enabling him to breath, just, but causing intense cramp in his taut calf muscles. The naked man flicked his eyes sideways to watch the moth, wondering of its fate and futile fluttering, then reconsidered his own. He heard movement and his focus turned to the man who'd entered the barn, now walking casually through the wide-open doorway, and who had the answer to his current question. What was his fate, and indeed his future.

The entrant's bitter expression toward the hanging man had not eased since their initial fight within the barn. The person he'd planned to meet had not appeared. Instead the last person he'd ever hoped to see had greeted him.

It'd obviously been set up as a trap, the man knowing he was coming to the barn, being ready and waiting. They'd fought viciously, and after being knocked unconscious with a shovel, awoke, not only with a throbbing head and bloody wound, but to find himself striped naked, and suspended by his arms within the barn. This wasn't good. Not at all. But there was always hope.

He'd been in some tough situations throughout his life, but this did not look good. The tape over his mouth didn't help matters, although knowing where he was it made no difference. No one would hear his cries. Or worse.

His antagoniser stood in the soft glow of the bulb, looking with disgust at the suspended naked form a few feet away, glancing at his genitals with a curious expression, then away, as if deep in thought and considering his options.

He looked up toward the singular length of rope, slung over the heavy oak beam, which supported the man, then travelled down, being securely tied off at a metal ring, set firmly years ago in an even heavier, well-aged oak post.

"Did you really think you'd get away with porking my wife, embarrassing me and then walk away and suffer no consequences? Did you? No chance!"

The question or statement hung in the air, like the man.

The suspended man considered the pointless question, unable to answer, due to the tape across his mouth and inability to make any bodily movement.

The man wandered around his victim in a small circle, dust from the barn floor drifting up and over his boots. Then he paused, and leaning forward, reached beside some old paper feed sacks. The clank of metal resounded, catching the suspended man's attention, waiting to see what was revealed.

His eyes widened as the angry man before him pulled out a sword.

A wave of adrenaline surge through the hanging man, as the swordsman stepped forward, the decorative bright-bladed weapon held before him. Tilted at an angle, the clearly sharp tip and edge glinted deadly in the dim light.

The swordsman moved, stopping a few feet from the hanging man. He tried to shuffle backward, but found his feet then had no contact with the ground and he found his body swing slightly. All his weight was taken painfully upon his wrists, the rough rope cutting in deeper. Rocking forward, he regained his footing, steadying the movement, and just in time. The swordsman thrust the weapon forward, pressing the tip against the man's bare belly, the cold steel pressed hard against his exposed and vulnerable white flesh.

He winced, trying to prevent any further movement, his feet almost skipping on the spot to stop any swinging, as the tip of the sword teasingly slid against his soft skin. The swordsman chuckled, enjoying the fear and gently prodded the steel forward an inch, seeing the man wince as the tip pressed into his flesh. It pushed the skin inward, almost at the point of breaking the surface.

The hanging man dropped his vision, to look down at the tip. His eyes fell upon the holder of the weapon, cursing him, but still unsure of his intentions.

Was it simply to humiliate him? To scare him off, and then leave him to fend for himself with nothing? Or worse. Did he really mean to kill him? He could.

The swordsman casually flicked the sword away, the hanging man sighing as the present threat was removed, along with the pain of blade against his skin.

"What is to be done with you? Problems, problems. Nothing but problems."

The questioner muttered, and seemed unsure, which eased the concerns of the hanging man, hoping the longer he hung, the more anger of the swordsman would subside. Then maybe, after a bit of a beating, where his torturer would have vented his anger, he'd let him go free with a warning.

He knew most crimes of hateful passion happened as soon as the affair was discovered, usually with both parties still 'at it' in a matrimonial bed. Intense anger, with a sense of betrayal and the need for revenge were the main cause of harsh, instant action. As sense takes over, and anger subsides, reasoning and thoughts of repercussions of any harsh action taken as a result of an act of violence are then considered by most sensible people. And the anger cools.

The hanging man knew his assailant was no fool. He'd know what he could and couldn't get away with. He was a clever, educated man and not likely to do foolish and rash things. Or so he hoped. For now, hope was all he had.

"Did you enjoy sticking this thing in my wife? Did you?"

The swordsman prodded the hanging man's genitals with the sword tip, the action skilful, lightly touching the sagging member and scrotum with the tip.

The hanging man winced, naturally turning his hips, as fresh fear returned, no matter how he tried to subdue his emotions and retain a cool composure.

The swordsman stepped back, grinning wickedly, moving the sword away with a swift swipe, then almost teasingly swishing the blade back in a reverse swipe, the sharp blade glided only inches away from his bare flesh. He clearly enjoyed the moment of control as he paced about, swishing the sword before him in open air with practised ease, head down, as if thinking up a plan.

A nervous cold sweat began to glisten on the exposed skin of the tormented man, with a few spots of blood upon his chest from the earlier head wound evident. He wanted to speak, apologise and explain, but knew it was pointless, as they'd argued and fought briefly when then first met. He knew he now had to simply await the fate and punishment his tormentor decided to deliver.

He could only hope it would be fair and over swiftly. But not too harsh.

The pair had suffered enough, knowing they'd both lose all they'd previously had with their respective partners. This humiliation was now simply that.

A vent of anger. A need for revenge in some form, then realisation that no more could be done and they'd all have to get on with their new lives.

It was these thoughts of plain reasoning that kept the man calm.

Stepping toward the feed sacks the swordsman reached down and recovered a couple of items, pushing one into the front of his jacket. The other, long and brightly decorated, was the sword's scabbard and black leather belt. The belt was secured around the man's waist, and sword dutifully retuned to its scabbard, the sword hanging down in a position it could be easily reached, but also safely stowed and out of the immediate grasp of its owner.

The man hanging from the beam was observant in life, and likewise took in all the small details, noting the other object thrust hastily into the top of the man's jacket appeared to be a long-bladed, sharp knife. As worrying as this might appear, the man conceived his antagoniser was about to cut the rope from which he hung, and knew the sword would not be sufficient. Knowing he could seek revenge, he assessed that his assailant knew the sword was the perfect weapon to deter any such action, providing a safe distance to separate the pair, should he endeavour to attack his tormentor. This new hope, that his dilemma could swiftly be over, brought him fresh strength.

As bitter as he was about the episode, he sought no revenge, simply freedom. Once he was away from the place, and met back up with the woman he loved, this nightmare would be an event to forget. When in each other's arms, and away from the partners they did not love; but made pretence they did, no one could take away their true love. The man before him clearly knew that too.

The swordsman regarded the soul hanging before him with little emotion, as if the activity no longer entertained him and he'd grown tired with it all.

"Should we end this now?" he enquired, his tone steady, voice calm.

The hanging man nodded, the action rocking his body, causing it to sway.

The swordsman noted the motion, and looked down at the man's bare feet as he tried to steady himself and take some support off his sore, aching arms.

"Have you learnt you lesson?" The swordsman's look was stern.

The man nodded again, but with a gentler, slower lift of the head and chin.

"Are you sorry?" The swordsman was clearly milking the moment.

The affirmative action was repeated, confirming his total repentance.

"Good. Then this finishes now. Forever. It is over."

The hanging man watched the swordsman remove the sheathed knife stowed in his jacket; the long, thin blade like that of a razor sharp filleting knife. He stepped towards the side of the barn where the rope met the wall. Inwardly the hanging man sighed, hoping this event would soon be over and that he'd cut the rope and let him fall onto the floor. Knowing he'd probably be unable to walk when he fell, hands still tethered, naked and bruised from their earlier fight, he knew the swordsman was aware he'd be no opposition to him. He'd be grateful to be cut free, then no doubt pushed into a vehicle and released naked into the cold, dark countryside. He knew his tormentor would find this amusing too. To him, it'd be just punishment, humiliation and duty served.

The hanging man watched him step to the wall, knife clasped firmly in his right hand, sword swinging at his side. The swordsman grasped at the stout, hemp rope, giving it a hearty twang. The vibrations ran through the rope, up to the large metal ring hanging from the beam and then down to the hanging mans wrist. His victim's hands shook. The swordsman smiled, repeating the childish action, watching the vibrations pass on into the man's hands.

Then suddenly the swordsman moved. In a sudden motion, he stepped away from the wall, and in three strides stood straight before the hanging man.

His hate-filled eyes burnt deeply, an evil grin crossing his face.

Reaching forward, in one swift action with his free left hand, the swordsman grasped the man's penis and testicles, and pulled them forward. Then, in an equally swift motion, with the razor sharp knife in his right hand, he cut deep beneath the man's scrotum. Dragging the blade deep and in one steady slice; the edge snagging momentarily upon the urethra tube, with a brutal tug, quick twist, and wiggle of the knife, the hanging man's genitalia were removed.

The action had taken seconds, the hanging man unaware of the action until the sensation of the initial deep blade cut ran through and he felt the pain.

Blood poured down the hanging man's legs as he screamed, both in pain, but horror, knowing what the swordsman had done, feeling the violent tug below.

As if handling a foul piece of meat, the swordsman hurled the manhood of the now hanging eunuch across the barn floor, with no care or regard.

"You won't be needing them anymore," he chuckled, smirking at his victim.

The swordsman watched with a satisfied smile as the small mass of flesh and tubing bounced across the dirty barn floor, settling in a pile of dusty straw.

The hanging man watched too, but in horror and searing pain, feeling the warm sticky blood flow down his legs, onto his feet, and drip off his toes.

Smiling, regarding the eunuch; who had terror etched in his previously calm face, the swordsman watched the blood flowing down the man's white legs, and drip heavily onto the barn floor, such was the steady flow of blood.

Sheathing the razor-sharp filleting knife, he withdrew the sword from the scabbard, then, in a well-practised motion, presented the blade before him. In a swift, forward-stepped lunge, he plunged the sword blade straight into the man's lower belly. The stab was deliberate, aimed to miss all the vital organs, and just pierce the belly and intestines. Thus it caused serious pain and internal injury, but ensured the victim would not die instantly or bleed heavily.

The hung man shook violently as the blade entered and was withdrawn, unable to grasp at either his stomach or groin. The pain was intense, but the need to vent a scream was hindered by his taped mouth. His body vibrated with a mix of shock and pain, dust falling from the old beam above as the rope shook, to be caught drifting in the dim light. The moth had long flown.

The hanging man looked toward the swordsman, as with another well-aimed lunge, he slid the sword into the man's liver, this time pushing hard, ensuring the blade passed fully through causing real injury and pain. Lodging on a back rib, the hanging man's body swayed heavily as the swordsman pulled back.

Trying to withdraw the stuck blade, he raised his leg and pressed it into the dying man's upper thigh to free the long, deadly weapon. Pushing his bloody body away with his raised leg, the man's body moved away, blade sliding free.

Seeing the swinging form of the man before him start to lapse into shock, with two new lines of red pumping in fine flows from him, the swordsman stepped back over towards the wall. The rope now holding the slumping man's body was tight, like taut steel, and creaking. The swordsman ran the filleting knife over the rope where it was secured to the heavy metal wall ring. With three cuts, each severing a strand of the twisted hemp rope, it quickly separated. One strand remained secured to the metal loop, but then it released and the rest of the rope, with man attached, flew through air and back over the beam and ring. The tethered man crashed down onto the barn floor.

He smashed painfully onto his knees, then raised his conjoined arms in an almost praying stance, the rope still tight about his wrists and the loose end falling, to lay over his shoulder. He looked towards the evil man before him, knowing he'd shown him no mercy, but that the end was now close.

The swordsman grinned, then shuffling his feet, positioned himself perfectly before the lying, cheating, deceitful adulterer, who'd openly soiled his wife.

Raising the sword high, in one swiping strike, he cleaved the deadly blade into the neck of the form squatting before him. The blow was not however as swift and powerful as he'd hoped, and the blade partly fouled upon some of the rope, catching around the man's neck. Half the man's neck was severed, the cleaved muscles no longer offering the vital support to carry a heavy head, causing his head to lop to one side. With a second follow-through strike, the sword swept fully through the man's neck, completely removing his head.

Blood sprayed out the roughly severed neck wound, then reduced to a heavy flow as the body collapsed, falling onto its side and the head rolled free, thudding heavily onto the barn floor, rolling briefly, before coming to a halt.

Lifeless eyes gazed at the pile of straw, upon which the swordsman wiped the blade of his sword, returning it into its scabbard, content with his work.

He gazed at the body and then at the head, pondering his next move.

But he had a plan. He always had a plan.

He gazed for a few seconds before casually turning away from head and body and headed out of the barn. He had work to do.

Not so long ago, in that very barn, the owner of the head had made love to the woman to whom he'd lost his heart.

Now he'd lost it all.

His head, heart, love and life.

Chapter 87

Luck is a matter of preparation meeting opportunity.

Lucius Seneca

Whilst Sarah's life had sadly drawn to a tragic and brutal end, in reverse, Chantelle's was strangely about to begin and flourish. But as is typical with Fate, it hides its cards well, and she did not know what plans it had set her.

Awaking to feel a hand on her chest, she frantically looked at the motionless form beside her, trying to recall the previous evenings events.

Who was the life-less man beside her, what had happened and why was she waking in a plush hotel room, rather than her own grubby damp bed-sit?

It flashed back to her in an instance, and in reality there hadn't been anything exciting. They'd gone off together from the cold street to a warm suite, within a rather grand hotel, being a former country house. After a few short minutes of fumbling, grumbling and moaning with her client, she'd then spent most to rest of the evening drinking and talking. Although no 'oil-painting' she was curious about the strange man who'd paid for her 'body' for the whole evening and simply ordered food and drink to be sent up to their room. Not to get her drunk, that wasn't needed, but simply to enable them to relax and enjoy each other's company; which they had, the man interesting in her.

She lifted the paw from her chest and rose, her long slender legs stretching out from the large bed, neat feet crushing the deep piled carpet. It was a different feel to the well-worn threadbare rug she usually trod upon each morning, where split tea-stains blended in to the dubious beige coloured floor covering. It was so thinly worn the lines from the floorboards beneath where etched into the texture, and aged floorboards creaked with each tentative step.

This morning, her skull aching from an excess of at least two bottles of Prosecco, Chantelle tip-toed to the en-suite bathroom and cleaned herself up. She looked long into the mirror, wondering again what she was doing with her life. After a quick rinse of her mouth, she wandered over to the small area within the high-ceiling room where a double sofa, easy chairs and coffee table stood to form the suite. Desperately for a real drink, of tea, she flicked on the kettle, which began to roar noisily as it started to heat the water. She winced at the sound and glanced at the body lying in the bed, where a slightly hairy white leg projected from beneath the duvet. Still the rest of the form snoozed.

Chantelle glanced down at the coffee table, noticing an array of newspapers carefully set out upon the dark walnut top in some order. They'd obviously been there from the previous night, but then she'd been keen on entertaining her client, then eating and drinking. Now she became interested in the pictures and storyline where the papers were opened. All were very similar.

The kettle clicked off, but rather than move over to pour herself a cup of tea, she looked intently at the images in the various newspapers set on the table.

"Do you have an interest in hunting?" a voice suddenly enquired.

Chantelle jumped, looking with wide blue eyes at the bed, where the life-less form had lain. An elbow propped up his body and he looked at her with a smile. The top of the quilt fell down, revealing a long scar across his chest. She'd noticed it last night, but had said nothing, guessing it was a knife slash.

Chantelle strangely blushed, as if ashamed to be caught out looking at a newspaper, let alone reading the small print of the article. But something had drawn her attention. She grinned at the man smiling towards her.

"Are you making tea?" he enquired warmly. "I hope so. I'm parched."

Chantelle looked at him curiously, then nodded with a smile.

"Can you make me a cuppa too? If you don't mind. Please? I like mine strong and white. And hot too. Like my women! But no sugar."

Chantelle saw him grin cheekily. Nodding, she rose with a smile, moving to the kettle, where an assortment of drink making sachets, milk pots and sugar lay. Suddenly she realised she was naked, and the man in the bed was staring intently at her pert backside as she began to prepare two cups of tea.

"Sorry for staring," Adam said, noticing her look his way. "But they are the best set of legs with bum attached I think I've ever seen. Outstanding. Sorry for looking. But, you know! Why aren't you a model? You'd make a fortune."

Chantelle blushed, then smiled, enjoying the compliment. Turning sideward, she provocatively stretched a leg, foot raised, kinking her leg out revealingly.

"No, please don't!" Adam said with a grin and chuckle. "You'll start me off again, and I'm not sure I can cope. Nor you probably. Last night was good."

Chantelle laughed and stirred the tea bag within the white china cup, wary of shattering the delicate porcelain, about to pour in the milk.

"Leave mine in the cup please. I like mine strong. And don't put milk in the cup whilst the bag is brewing. If you do, I'll call the police. It's criminal!"

Adam smiled at a grinning Chantelle, who left the cups and returned to the sofa, looking at the newspapers once more. Sitting down, she curled her long legs beneath her, Adam trying to avoid looking towards the trimmed line of bushy hair and perfect grapefruit-shaped breasts, feeling himself rise.

"Did you say your name was Adam?" Chantelle enquired, glancing back at the papers, reading some detail in the text then looking curiously at Adam.

Adam nodded, smirking. He knew what was coming.

"Did you take all these photos then?" Chantelle asked with genuine interest. "The piece here, with all these photos about a riot at a Boxing Day hunt says, special report and images by Adam Yates. Is that you?"

Adam simply chuckled, but then nodded, blushing slightly.

Chantelle lifted one of the papers, staring closely at one of the photos. Adam watched her curiously from the bed staring intently at several of the images, his interest in her body gone; now more interested in the woman herself.

She lowered the paper and lifted another, staring intently at another image. And then at another in a different paper. She turned to face him.

"I know this man," she announced calmly, to Adam, finger pointing.

Adam stared back, eyes twinkling, watching Chantelle lift the paper to her face, to look at the image more closely, her head nodding positively.

"Yes, it's definitely him. I'd swear to it. This image is best."

"You what?" Adam enquired, pulse racing, rising from the bed. "Who?"

"The posh geezer in the red coat. I know him. Well, sort of. You know!"

Adam leapt from the bed and drew level with her, intently looking over her shoulder and down at the newspaper now held firmly in her hands. His naked skin was close to hers, but all interest now seemed set upon the paper, and the photo at which Chantelle and he stared, rather than her tempting body.

Adam looked at the image of the man in red, to whom Chantelle clearly identified by pointed a deadly red-painted talon; the same nails he recalled he'd enjoyed her running down his back last night.

Adam grinned; chin rubbing, eyes drifting, thinking deep.

"Do you want a job?" Adam asked.

Chantelle turned around, squinting at the man behind her, unsure she'd heard correct, then what on earth he meant, but was curious by the strange offer.

"What do you mean?" She asked.

"A job. Work for me as an employee. Proper job. Real money."

Chantelle looked at him curiously and with suspicion.

"And what would you want me to do?"

"Lots!" Adam chuckled.

Chantelle cocked her head, unsure if this man was serious.

"Are you going to pay me?"

"Yes, of course," Adam replied, as if it was obvious.

"How much?"

"Lots! But first we need to buy you some clothes."

"Why? What's wrong with my clothes?"

"Lots!" Adam chuckled. "We need to visit an army surplus store and get you some combats. Some real clothes."

"Army clothes? Why? Are we going to war?" Chantelle grinned.

"Yes, you could say we are. To war indeed. Now lets drink this tea."

Chapter 88

Nothing is more noble, nothing more venerable, than loyalty.

Marcus Tullius Cicero

Reggie stared at the ringing phone, then answered almost hesitantly. "Yes?"

"Hi Reggie, Bertie here." Lord Burlingham sounded tired.

"Hello Bertie. How are you old chap?" Reggie replied, almost sighing.

"Bearing up, you know, all things being considered," Bertie replied, his voice weary and lacking his usual spirit, as did Reggie's.

"Yes, I know exactly how you feel. Exactly," said Reggie, more of a touch of bitterness in his reply, but also some sympathy. "What can I do for you?"

"Actually it's a bit awkward and rather difficult," replied Bertie, genuine anxiety and concern expressed in his cautious voice.

"No worries. We go back a long way. In many things. Nothing's changed. Loyalty sticks." Reggie replied, sensing caution in the noble Lord's voice.

"Yes Reggie, we've helped each other many times in the past, but this is different. I need a favour. A very big favour. Only you can help me."

Bertie's tone was serious and there was a long pause.

Reggie sensed the serious nature and paused too before replying.

"Bertie, don't worry. Whatever it is, or how serious, I'll help. Do you want to meet in private or can you speak over the phone?" Reggie asked, still happy to help out another member of the same Lodge to which he'd belonged, even if he had lapsed. They were still brothers who looked after each other.

Bertie briefly explained the situation he faced and his serious dilemma.

Reggie listened intently, his rosy cheeks going white and eyebrows rising as he listened to what Bertie told him. This was indeed serious.

But he'd help him out. Willingly.

For he too needed something from Bertie.

An equally big favour.

That was loyalty.

Chapter 89

Every act of creation is first an act of destruction.

Pablo Picasso

The Flesh House is the aptly named part of a Hunt Kennels where carcasses of fallen stock collected by the hunt are stored, then cut up prior to feeding to the hounds. The Shoteton kennels Flesh House was a small, enclosed room, brightly lit with whitewashed walls. It adjoined a boiler house, another small room, where some of the meat, old vegetables and corn or meal were often boiled up in a big copper boiler to mix with fresh meat, all of which was then fed to the ravenous pack of forty plus hounds to provide a balanced diet.

Compared to the heavy cows or sheep he usually butchered, for Martin, the woman's body would be easy to cut up. It wasn't his usual cut of meat.

Once removed from the beams, wrapped in a tarpaulin, then steadily hauled up the cellar stairs - the hardest part - the secluded nature of The Kennels ensured he wasn't seen dragging a lump outside and over to the Flesh House.

Sarah's body now lay in the middle of the floor, her skin pale, waxy and clammy. The gaping slit to her throat was a deep, dark red, turning brown, and the severed carotid tissue resulted in her head flopping back at an unusual angle. Martin disliked this strange angle and tilted her head slightly downward, so it covered most of the fleshy gap. Even dead she had a good body. Great legs. Just a pity they were ruined by the blood splattered all over them.

He'd removed her black suede shoes, which had extenuated her calf muscles so well when she'd been tied to the posts. Taking these from her feet, he'd noticed bright orange nail varnish to her toes and that she had a small heart tattooed on the side of her left foot. He liked her feet; they'd been nice. The former nice black suede shoes, splattered in blood, would sadly be burnt.

He'd hacked off Sarah's intestines in the cellars, slopping them into a large bucket, rather than try to drag Sarah's body out the cellar with her stinking bloody guts dragging everywhere, leaving both a slippery stinking mix of mess to clear up and also any possible DNA clues if the worst happened.

Weighing about seven pounds, the removed guts reduced some of her body weight, and by cutting them free, made moving her corpse easier. Ignoring the gaping slit in her stomach, as he positioned her body on the floor, her legs separated. His eyes were naturally drawn to that location, and glanced again at the opening he'd enjoyed entering. Even now, it still looked welcoming.

He felt himself turned on, but knew he could not and should not do what he felt an urge to perform. A thought flashed through his mind, however, her true beauty was gone and despite his thoughts, knew the lifeless corpse wouldn't respond as she so willingly had when a lively soul had sat within her.

He silently cursed Sharon once more for retuning so earlier and destroying everything. She'd ruined it all. If only. The story of his life it seemed. Martin sighed, ignoring the hard organ beneath his green overalls, knowing the tasks he had to complete, and quickly, regained usual control and composure.

Squatting by Sarah's head, and placing his booted foot on her shoulder, he pulled back her left arm, so it stretched out over her head. Getting his largest butcher's knife, he cut in deep under the armpit, slicing through the flesh and muscle around the arm joint, twisting the pliable limb, which was even now becoming cold and clammy. Martin knew he had to act quickly in cutting up Sarah's body before rigor mortis set in, or it'd be much harder to move or cut up her then rigid body. Rigor mortis would set into her body anything from fifteen minutes to several hours from death, depending on various conditions.

This included glycogen in the muscles, also levels of lactic acid present, and importantly the ambient temperature. Warm environments sped up the onset of rigor, by providing a better environment for the bacteria and processes that cause bodies to decay. However, cooler conditions slow the process. Martin hoped the cold room temperature would reduce the speed of the likely onset.

He hoped the vigorous sex they'd had beforehand would have increased the lactic acid present in her body and muscles, and would thus increase the time period before rigor set in. Her facial muscles, always the first to be affected, had already begun to show the sinister first signs, as she to adopted a strange, almost macabre grin, as though mocking him in death. Maybe she was.

Once rigor mortis had set in he would have to wait around twenty-four hours or more before he could easily handle her body and cut it up, as autolysis would set in and the muscles become relaxed again, as the internal decay began. Hence why he now moved swiftly in cutting Sarah up into much easier to handle parts, and from which the fluids could more easily drained, again reducing rigor. Compared to the bodies of cows and horses he was used to hacking through, Sarah's arms were easily severed from her body. Once all of the meat and tendons had been cut through, the arms released easily from the shoulder joint with a swift pull and twist, breaking the final sinews holding the limb in place. He lifted the first arm and placed it at her feet. He repeated the exercise with the second arm, laying that alongside the other. He noted she had slim wrists and long, almost spidery fingers that he'd not noticed before.

The bright orange varnish on her fingernails, matching that of her neat toes, glistening in the harsh light. He laid the second arm next to the first, typically adjusting the position, so the pair were neatly in line. Unseen, the middle finger bent back as he adjusted the arm, the bright orange fingernail snapping off. It pinged across the floor, wedging, unseen, at the bottom of the wall.

Now fully in his butchering mode, and knowing the task must be completed as quickly as possible, he moved down to her feet and spread open her legs. Leaning forward, and fondly touching the soft opening he'd been inside hours earlier, uncaring, he plunged the blade deep inside, sliding it into the thigh.

Razor sharp, the knife slid around the panty-line, if she ever wore any, slicing through the white flesh, then around to just below the hip, hitting the neck of the femur bone. Flipping over her arm-less torso, her head flopping over, he continued cutting, the long blade running hard and deep, slicing down between Sarah's buttocks and through her anus. Once the line of cut was established, he ran the knife again, cutting deeper around the heavy flesh, hacking hard at the stronger muscle and sinew. A small amount of excreta flowed out onto the floor from the lightly severed bowel, as the blade snagged the organ, but most waste had come out with the intestines, and the smell was nothing new to Martin and something he'd long grown used to in his work.

Once he'd cut through the strong muscles and flesh around the buttock, the leg became loose, attached only by tough sinew. Extra deeper cuts with the knife were needed, slashing through the ligaments and fibres deep within the leg, holding the neck of the femur in place. With some good pulls, and twist of Sarah's slender ankle, the leg separated from Sarah's rapidly reducing body.

With strange care and attention, he carefully placed the limb on the floor, it naturally bending at the knee. Martin adjusted its position, so the leg was straight and the foot pointed out to best accentuated the length of her leg.

He did the same with her remaining leg, gripping the torso firmly, as with very little left to hold it slid about in his grasp. Her smallish breasts rubbed about him as he jostled with her waxy torso, momentarily arousing him, remembering they were a great feature despite being small. He grasped one, squeezing it, fascinated as her dark nipple rose and fell as he applied pressure.

He still had much to do. After further cutting and pulling, with the second leg removed, he placed that beside the other, so her severed arms and legs lay perfectly presented beneath her now limbless trunk, only her head remaining upon the strangely short and now mutilated piece of meat.

He looked at the trunk and more particularly at the head. Sarah's face was almost white, like porcelain, but now with an unattractive grey tint. Regarding the head, partly severed from where he'd slit her throat, Martin carried on, automatically. He moved over to a bench, upon which lay an assortment of tools; some aged, the metal dark and well-worn, with dark smooth timber handles, the other items modern and shining bright. He knew what he needed. Martin lay the heavy knife down and picked up a large meat cleaver and mallet, it possibly being fifty years old or more. Moving back over to Sarah, he shuffled her head around with his booted feet, then placed the cleaver into the gaping slit in Sarah's throat. Raising the mallet high, he struck the back of the cleaver several times. The sharp blade cut through what was left of the trachea and other hard tissue and bone. Another strike, this time harder, severed the spinal column, until the head was joined to the body by only a flap of skin at the back of her slim neck. Returning to the bench, he retrieved the knife again and cut through the skin, finally severing the head.

He looked at it momentarily, but by now any emotion had left him.

It was heavy, something most people don't realise, usually weighing around ten pounds, three pounds of which would be the brain. He cradled the object carefully in both hands, gazing at it, almost like a precious object. Careful not to damage it, as he lay it down sideways, leaning it against Sarah's legs, face down, her nose acting as a natural wedge to prevent it from rolling over.

He stood for a few seconds scratching his head, looking at Sarah's torso. It lay on its back, five dark reddish-brown openings where the four limbs and her head were attached only hours earlier. He looked once more at her breasts, both lying flat against the grey-skinned trunk. 'On or off?'

He deliberated the thought, scratching the back of his neck, then rubbed his chin, considering if he should split open her ribcage or leave it as it was. It was still a large lump of meat to dispose of, and quite heavy, with her main organs still inside. Nodding to himself, decision made, he moved back over to the bench, retrieved a bone saw and bending down, picked up a large bucket.

Five minutes later, with a heavy sweat on his brow, Sarah's main organs lay slopped in the bucket. Her rib-rage was split at the sternum, cracked open at the back, to reveal an empty harsh interior. Martin had removed her breasts, admiring each, and also cut off her buttocks, to ease movement of the split torso and also aid disposal. Sarah's once beautiful and active body, with which Martin had enjoyed moments of pleasure, now resembled a butchered animal.

Glancing at the clock, and his energy sapping, he suddenly realised how blooded he was himself. He'd done all he could for now and the body was in easy to move parts, ready for disposal. It was still late and dark, and he knew he'd best not upset the hounds tonight and still had a lot of cleaning up to do in the cellar. Down there it was a scene of utter carnage and needed cleaning.

At least Sarah's body was in a manageable state, ready for the morning. He covered the severed limbs with an old tarpaulin, locked up the door to the Flesh House and returned to the cellar, where the lights still burnt bright.

The cellar soon became hot and stifling as he worked tirelessly to clean up all traces of the death and destruction that'd taken place only a few hours earlier. With buckets of hot water, detergent and then bleach, after several hours the place looked as it did before the terrible incident. He realised a forensic scientist would soon find traces of blood and DNA if they did a thorough and detailed search, but his plan was the remove all visible traces, so no one would know what'd taken place. Also, he knew the strong bleach used, the fumes pungent as he mopped, destroyed most signs of DNA. Just in case.

Returning to the top of the cellar stairs, he looked over into the corner, then scoured the interior, pleased with his work, before switching off the light, and securely locking the door. Anything else could be sorted out tomorrow.

Tired, he threw off his bloody clothes, tossing them into a large bin outside. The cold of the night prickled his naked skin, as he gazed up at the milky moon, hiding behind drifting cloud. He'd burn the clothes first thing in the morning, a fire now too dangerous, just in case any poacher saw the flames.

The hounds in the adjoining yard nearby, hearing his movements, whimpered and yelped softly, some baying for attention, unsure of the strange, late-night activity, it not part of their usual routine. However, a clunk of the door and the sound of the lock being thrown soon silenced them, as Martin showered fully, then donned fresh clothes. He returned to the living room and lay on the sofa, trying to get some sleep, not wanting to sleep upstairs, the ground floor permitting him to hear any sounds or movements and get away quickly.

But his rest was in intervals. He did not sleep well.

He continuously woke, the image of the dying Sarah fresh in his mind.

Her screams, and groans, as she died.

Blood spraying and intestines falling.

Sharon and all that blood.

All troubled him deeply.

Then the images came.

Real or not, Martin was never sure.

Chapter 90

I became insane, with long intervals of horrible sanity.

Edgar Allan Poe

Martin stood before Sarah, her beautiful smile and neat red lips alluring. He rubbed his body against her smooth warm skin as she lifted her long legs up and around his buttocks, pulling his naked form to her, and Martin slid inside. She groaned as he penetrated her fully and thrust, hard and deep. In and out, pumping hips moving steadily, along with the ever-present knife. Then the shining steel sliced into at her soft tender belly, plunging in and out, matching his thrusts, slits of white flesh turning red, as Sarah's screams roaring loudly. Martin withdrew as Sarah's intestines cascaded out from the tattered opening, and he collapsed, kneeling down to scoop up the life-giving organs and push them back inside. On and on they fell, in an ever-increasing flow, as Martin knelt at Sarah's knees. Her deep moans flooded his mind, as the mass of sticky tubes seemed to consume him. Still the stinking organs fell, rising up around Sarah's legs. They reached Martin's chest, the organs rising, slopping over his face, as he collapsed within the gooey mess. Still the organs fell, pouring from Sarah's belly in a never-ending flow, continuously spilling out. Blood, flesh and hot liquid poured down on Martin, swamping him, covering him in an ever-consuming sticky mass, suffocating in Sarah's spilling organs.

Martin woke with a start, fighting for breath. His hands clawed at invisible intestines that'd covered him, and he rose, his body rising fully erect from the sofa in one lurch. He scanned the lounge to see nothing and no one there.

Glancing towards at ornamental clock, which sat besides hunting photos, he realised how late it was and hurriedly dashed into the kitchen, flicking on the kettle. He moved to the cellar, unlocked the door, flicked on the light and from the top of the stairs glanced toward the corner, to check all was as he'd left it last night. It was. He released a heavy sigh. Light off, cellar door secured and key set back on the dresser, he quickly made a cup of instant coffee. He donned some old work clothes and then pulled out a fresh set of dark green overalls. He had many pairs, which Sharon regularly washed in an old washing machine used only for his bloody work clothes. Door key in hand, he exited the house, the hounds at once breaking into a stream of howls, yelps and whines, knowing it was time for their breakfast and morning exercise.

It was still dark, the early morning light yet to lift, but Martin had over-slept, was running wait, and knew it'd not be long before the sun rose and the usual activity began. And he still had lots to do. Some very important work. He drew in a deep breath, running through his mind his plan and what had to go. The most important part now was to destroy the head. Sarah's head.

Returning to the Flesh House, with some apprehension, he slowly unlocked the door, to begin work on the second phase. His clean up operation.

The most important part. Destroy all evidence. No body, no case.

Head's were notoriously hard to destroy. They had little flesh, being all bone. And they were heavy, cumbersome, and crucially, contained most of the damning identification evidence. Teeth and facial structure were a quick and easy way to identify any body, where often only parts of limbs, without a full DNA match, were difficult to identify. Thus, Sarah's head had to go first.

Carefully, he picked up her head, holding it by her hair, but supporting it by the lower neck section too. Her jaw dropped down in a weird dead grin, as he carried it through into the adjoining room, in which were housed benches, a large copper boiler and a large bottle-gas fired incinerator or furnace.

The incinerator was a large furnace into which all unwanted or uneatable parts of any of the animals recovered by the hunt were burnt and destroyed. Martin routinely burnt piles of intestines, any unwanted flesh or sinew, sharp bones and even animal skulls in the incinerator. It consumed it all. Very well.

However, this was the first time he'd ever undertaken a private cremation. For a person unknown. Well, partly known, but maybe just in mostly body.

He opened up the round door of the incinerator and carefully placed Sarah's head inside, setting it on the heavy metal grill within the centre, upright on the stump of neck. There was space for more, but this was key to his plans.

He looked at the grey-skinned face, which stared back, almost cursing him.

With care, he brushed her blooded and matted hair back, almost attempting to make her image presentable, despite now about to destroy it. Her lifeless face, hideous and deformed, looked back. Sightless, yet seemingly glaring eyes seemed to stare at him, white and cursing. Martin stared back in silence, secretly cursing her for entering his life and then cursing Sharon even more for returning home early and destroying everything else. It was all her fault.

Turning on the large valve to the rear, he fired up the burners, clicked the sparking device and let the gas ignite. A roar of ignited gas flew from the rear of the incinerator and it rapidly began to heat up. Martin looked as the lining glowed an orange and Sarah's hair at once began crackling, as it melted, giving off a sickly acrid stench. He took one last look at the Sarah's face, as the reflection of the flickering flames played upon her pale skin, almost giving it a glowing, youthful expression and strange texture and even signs of life.

Door closed, Sarah was gone. Or at least her head. The memories remained.

Turning the gas on full he heard the roar as the furnace burst fully into life, heat rapidly building, to consume its precious secret. He returned to the main room, pulled back the tarpaulin to look at the of limbs and main torso, which had turned a waxy grey. He knew all traces of Sarah would have to be gone.

The next step would hopefully take less time to undertake, but was possibly the most dangerous, if it didn't work. But he was sure it would. Maybe.

In a way it would be an experiment and the thought alone excited him.

After a cautious check outside, with the first pale light beginning to creep into the darkened sky, looking down the small alley, he saw and heard nothing. Just as it should be and just as he hoped. He was alone. As planned.

Carefully and cautiously he carried each of the remaining parts of Sarah's body the small distance from the Flesh house over towards the feeding area of the Drawing yard. Here he placed each of the major body parts, ready for the next phase. The Drawing yard is a large self-contained and covered part of the main kennels, where, within a certain area, the hounds are fed, it being separate from their main sleeping area or Lodges, as the area is known.

The Drawing Yard is the part of the kennels where hounds are 'drawn out,' to be inspected and checked daily, and also where they are selected prior to a days hunting. Any not required, injured, or deemed unfit, are returned back to the main living areas. The hounds live in compartments, called Lodges, part open with railings set around and part covered. This area is where they spend most of their day, sleeping on raised platforms inside, covered in straw for bedding, yet able to roam outside freely in the open air in the railed yard. With a concrete and brick base floor, any waste material can be washed down and away into the surrounding waste gullies, draining to a main waste tank.

Martin entered the Drawing Yard with the first limb, Sarah's left leg, being the one with the small tattoo on the foot. Through the metal gates, in the adjoining section, a mass of excited and eager eyes watched. The hounds, keen to be fed, observed Martin's every move, leaping about, knowing food was forthcoming. Ignoring the howls and yelps of the pack behind him, many jumping excitedly up the railings separating the two units, Martin hung up the first of Sarah's legs. The area where the hounds were fed had a covered rear section, and from the beams supporting the low roof, hung a series of chains, each ending in a sharp hook. It was from these hooks huge chunks of meat, usually cow, horse and occasionally sheep, would be hung, for the hounds to feed upon. It was a traditional way of feeding the pack, ensured a pecking order was established, and that the hounds retained some natural hunting instinct, by fighting and jostling for their food, rather than it being neatly presented before each one. The hounds were a working pack of hunting dogs, not pets, and thus they lived like a pack and were treated as such.

They were also fed supplements and additives as needed, but this was the traditional way of feeding hounds. Some other feed, such as boiled vegetables, was offered in long communal troughs, where smaller cuts were also tossed.

Carrying Sarah's left leg, supporting the slender ankle in his palm, almost as if carrying the previous owner herself, he carefully raised the limb. Then, with stark contrast, from the care he'd taken in carrying the limb, he brutally pierced one of the deadly sharp hooks clean through the inside of the thigh. Pressing the flesh hard, the tip of the steel hook was forced through, coming out the other side, just below where the main part of Sarah's neat and pert buttock had been. That section of her body would follow later.

As Martin released Sarah's limb, the long piece of greying meat swung, clearly identifiable as a human leg. Sarah's bright orange toenails, stark in the dim light, didn't offer any disguise of the item, and made Martin gaze in horror.

Returning to collect the next part, and ignoring the howls and yelps behind him, he did the same with Sarah's right arm, piercing the hook between the cartilage at the elbow joint, so the limb hung at a strange ninety degree angle.

He then did the same with her torso, this section heavier and bulky. The area where her neat breasts had been, having been hacked off, now bore dark brown fleshy circles. The once trim body, ribcage split, now simply appeared as a hacked piece of meat, almost indistinguishable from something found on a butchers slab. Lifting the heavy section of meat, he thrust a hook through the hole in the top of her neck, where he'd removed her head, and passed the hook out through the clavicle, cracking a rib as he forced it through.

He then simply placed the other arm and her right leg upon the floor, slightly apart and away from the area where the three parts hung. Then, returning with a bucket of random parts, including her breasts and buttocks, he casually tossed each chuck about the yard floor, watching them hit the hard floor with a bloody splat. One breast landed on it bloody base, the nipple clear and standing upright. The buttocks, appeared simply as hacked pieces of unidentifiable flesh, rather than tender parts of a warm body Martin had lovingly run his hands across only hours earlier. This spread of pieces would ensure the pack could between them acquire the taste, and each get a piece.

Martin hoped that between them they'd rapidly reduce Sarah's once beautiful body into tattered pieces of flesh and bone, then slowly chew and gnaw these down, to eventually become hound waste. Martin would collect any excess pieces of bone or flesh not consumed, as he would normally, and incinerate it all later. By tonight, Sarah's once beautiful body, one that he'd enjoyed, would be reduced to a pile of dog shit or ash. A fitting tribute some may say.

Returning to the Flesh house, Martin retuned with two further buckets. From the heavier one, he withdrew a cow's liver, and carried it over towards the main parts of Sarah's body, rubbing the bloody organ across the flesh, before tossing sections of liver about the base of the yard. This mix of bits also included Sarah's liver, kidneys and her lungs, which he'd sliced into chunks and mixed with smaller animal offal. He then emptied a bucket containing a mix of corn meal and vegetables into smaller troughs spread about the yard, as normal, to give the hounds their usual mix of feed. Breakfast was ready.

Stepping back, he moved towards the main gate between the two main yard areas, admiring his work, and prepared to release his children. He looked at the suspended leg, hung from the chains. Swinging gently, it looked strangely grotesque, despite all of the other dead animal parts that had been hung from the chains in the past. The foot hung limp, tattoo clearly visible, and the bright orange nail varnish on the toes looked almost fluorescent in the gloom.

Steadily, heart thumping, he moved toward the hounds gate. Time for action.

"Go on you buggers! Eat it all. Enjoy!" Martin whispered to himself, almost chuckling as he opened the small gate between the yards and watched the mass of hounds eagerly dash through, noses raised, racing about, searching for the food, as Martin quickly exited through the main gate and outside.

Watching intently through the railings, he hoped the ever-ravenous hounds would swiftly make a move onto the body parts and begin the destruction of the evidence. Although they usually hunted with around forty hounds, the kennels housed sixty, as not all hunted at each meet, some injured or resting, if older. Thus, the meat on offer today was slightly limited for the number of mouths, but deliberately sparse, to ensure there would be little flesh wasted.

Dashing through from their lodges, the key hounds ran to the troughs first, and happily scoffed up the corn meal, vegetables and smaller chunks of offal, along with Sarah's key bodily organs. Martin watched on with a smile.

Then turning, drawn naturally by the scent of blood, they began to attack the hunks of cow liver and other pieces strewn about. One hound ran straight up to one of Sarah's breasts and grabbed it. It hung down from its jaws, almost in the natural position, nipple clearly on display; the sight weird. The hound disappeared into a darkened corner to chew on its prized piece of meat. As so many had in the past no doubt, but when the flesh was attached to its owner.

However, the hounds seemed to avoid attacking the main parts of Sarah that hung from the hooks. They sniffed warily at the hanging limbs and were equally cautious of the split torso. Martin quickly guessed the scent was new, and the smell of the flesh clearly too much like their Alpha-keeper.

Martin now began to wish he'd spent more time, and had simply hacked Sarah's body up into smaller sections or pieces of feed, or simply burnt to them all in batches. He looked on, his heart pounding with fresh excitement.

The hounds prowled around the hanging legs, sniffing at Sarah's neat, orange toes. They recognised the smell of the meat, but not as one they would naturally eat, or indeed, should eat. Instead, to them, it was one they should respect and fear. But their hunger and natural instinct seemed to take over and the scent of the cow's liver, and blood spread about, seemingly altered the distinct human scent to some degree. Another hound sniffed at the hanging arm, flicking its tongue out at the cow's blood dripping off a finger. Several others stood on their hind legs, licking at the interior of the split, open torso, sniffing at the freshly hacked ribcage, but wary of the strange flesh on offer.

Martin watched intently, sure they'd overcome the fear of the scent and eat what they knew they shouldn't out of shear hunger and need. Pigs would.

Suddenly the roar of an engine came from the woods. Martin froze.

He couldn't believe his ears, but knew the sound well. His eyes flitted from the hounds to the alley, tipping his head to ensure it was a vehicle coming.

Martin sped sideways from the kennel area, down the small alley separating the two buildings and peeped around the corner of the soft red brickwork.

Gazing up towards the woods his heart stopped. Company. And trouble.

A vehicle was moving at speed; drifting through the woods, bright headlights illuminating the tree line, although first light was now slowly dawning as a patch of grey on the horizon, but inside the woods it was still gloomy.

Martin watched in a mix of horror and intrigue, his mind in two places.

The large vehicle was now clear of the woods, heading swiftly out into the open along the track and quickly began approaching the driveway, clearly heading straight for the kennels, that being its only and final destination.

"Oh shit!" hollered Martin to himself, staring, then moving.

He dashed back along the alley and peered inside the drawing yard.

Inside the main yard area numerous hounds were eagerly sniffing, mingling and chomping at bits of feed in the troughs and scattered on the floor.

Around the dismembered body parts however they were still sniffing.

Standing on their hind legs, they licked and nuzzled the limbs.

The split torso hung, numerous sniffing hounds curious.

But not a bite had been taken, the hounds too wary.

As clear as day hung Sarah's left leg. Untouched.

An elegant leg. Once. Martin recalled licking it.

Orange nail polish and heart tattoo boldly on display.

'Hi - I'm Sarah,' the limbs screamed. 'Murdered by Martin.'

To his side he could hear the rapidly approaching vehicle.

"Oh fuck," he said, running a hand through his hair.

"Eat it you bastard's. Fucking eat it!"

"Eat!!"

Chapter 91

And behold joy and gladness, slaying oxen and killing sheep,
eating flesh and drinking wine.
Let us eat and drink, for tomorrow we shall die.

The Bible - Isaiah 22:13

One hound, aptly named Mayhem, was sniffing at the toes, licking them. The heart tattoo on Sarah's foot stood out clear and damning. But the hound's curiosity was a sure sign he was interested. Another hound nosed in, not wanting to miss out, and began sniffing at the heel. Mayhem, fearing he'd take his food, snapped at the junior hound, then nipped hard at Sarah's middle toe.

Martin looked on eagerly and could see two more hounds now beginning to tug at the arm lying on the floor, starting to fight over who'd get first share.

A third joined them, tugging at the severed armpit flesh, the limb extending.

But still Sarah's leg hung, uneaten, her bright orange toes clearly on view to the world, and worse, Martin's rapidly approaching visitor was upon him.

He leant forward from the kennel section and looked towards the drive.

A dark Range Rover stopped. Reggie's. Martin sighed, wincing.

It couldn't be worse. He had less than a minute before Reggie would be where he stood. Then, no doubt he'd want to go and see the hounds, having a genuine interest in them, and similar feelings as much as Martin. Sarah's leg would be in clear view. And take some explaining. Not the usual leg of lamb.

He stepped back down the alley between the out-building and the kennels, desperately glancing through the railings. The hound's sense of smell was keen and they knew this was no leg of lamb, let alone horse or cow hanging before them. It smelt like their master. Their Alpha-leader. Martin sighed.

Just then Mayhem firmly grabbed at the big toe, pulling hard, the bone audibly cracking as he gnawed with his strong back teeth and tugged hard. As the hound pulled, the hook cut into the top of the thigh where it was pierced, the flesh stretching. Martin gazed on in a mix of horror, fascination and fear.

Maverick, brother of Mayhem, grabbed the heel, his teeth sinking into the softer tendons between ankle and heel bulb. The leg swung on the hook and chain with the hounds tugging violently. Martin glanced about the yard, to see other hounds now sniffing, licking and beginning to chew on other parts of Sarah's body, with two hounds tugging competitively at her swaying torso, a rib cracking under powerful jaws, as they were joined by a third hound.

Attention split between his impending visitor and hounds, Martin noticed Craftsman, an older hound, see the two young hounds on the hanging leg. He decided he'd better get in before the greedy youngsters got everything, and standing on his hind legs grabbed at the calf muscle, pulling hard on the leg.

The hook tore deeper into the flesh of what had been Sarah's thigh, the leg spinning around with all the combined weight. Martin began shaking looking over at the piece of meat so clearly dangling from the chain with three hounds now swinging from it. His hounds were eating a human leg. Shit!

Reggie's Rover engine switch off. Double shit!

Martin clenched his fists, his body swaying; from hounds to alley, alley to hounds. In total confusion he was unsure what to do, knowing Reggie would be there in a matter of seconds and no doubt look in at the hounds.

Currently the hounds were hanging onto and pulling at Sarah's various body parts, and the advancing form of Reggie was walking straight towards him, heading for the alleyway between the Drawing Yard and the Flesh House.

As soon as he joined Martin, Reggie would see his beloved hounds swing from a woman's butchered body. Normal. Nothing out of the usual. Much!

Martin stood dithering, panicking, his mind a whirl. He looked through the railings at the hounds tucking into Sarah, but it still evident as human parts.

Heart pounding Martin glanced at the hounds and the white leg, then at Reggie, now only a few feet away from the start of the alley. He was smiling.

Without thinking any more, he stepped forward. 'Attack is the best form of Defence,' he recalled from his military days, and so moved towards Reggie.

"Good morning sir," said Martin. "Didn't expect to see you this morning."

The first part of the alley between the two areas was walled to both sides, thus not permitting anyone to see directly into the yard. Martin stood in front of Reggie, leaning over on one arm against the wall, clearly blocking any further progress. Reggie paused; looking at Martin somewhat puzzled, himself clearly flustered, seemingly with his own problems and worries to sort out.

"You okay Martin? You don't look too good," questioned Reggie, curious and slightly suspicious of his unusual behaviour; genuinely concerned why his Huntsman was acting out of character and looked so drawn and haggard.

"Me? Oh I'm fine Sir. Well, a little bit under the weather actually. Maybe a chill or bug, but I'm fine otherwise." Martin blushed, not very convincing.

"Good," answered Reggie, not really caring, but wanting his Huntsman well and able to undertake the urgent task he needed performed. "And Sharon?"

Martin froze at the mention of the name, unable to answer the question.

He looked at Reggie, unsure if it was a question or not. 'What did he know?'

Mouth dry, the petrified look in his eyes giving away everything.

"Sharon?" Martin queried, as if he'd never heard the word.

"Yes, Sharon. Your wife. Well at least as of yesterday."

Reggie's comment was both cold and witty; seemingly with no intent.

Martin stared at Reggie, wondering what he knew.

Reggie looked at Martin, wondering what was going on.

"Well I hope she's still your wife," Reggie quipped. "Is everything okay?"

"Sharon? Wife? Oh yeah, of course sir," replied Martin, adding a chuckle and rubbing his head as if recalling her. "Oh her! Yes, I remember her. Sharon!"

Reggie looked at Martin, who glanced sideways into the yard, seeing three hounds ripping into Sarah's torso, dragging it to the floor and away into the rear of the feeding area, tearing away at the ribcage. It split. He smiled.

"Is everything okay?" Reggie asked, concerned, seeing his eye movements.

"Oh yes, sir. Fine. All just fine. Just as planned," Martin replied dumbly.

"As planned?" queried Reggie. He squinted at Martin; very curious.

"You what sir? Oh yes, um no. Sorry, bit tired. Did you need something?" Martin asked, his extended arm still blatantly blocking any further access.

Reggie glared hard at Martin, who missed the look as he glanced sideward, seeing Sarah's suspended leg torn from the chain, as an unknown number of hounds ripped away at her once elegant limb, pulling at toes, calf and thigh.

Reggie looked concerned and was beginning to lose his patience. Removing his tweed cap he ran his hand through his thin hair, staring hard at Martin.

"Are you okay Martin? You look unwell. And where is Sharon?"

"Sharon?" Martin stared a thousand miles. But saw nothing.

"Yes! Sharon. Sharon! Were is she?" Reggie spoke firmly. Too firmly.

Usually Sharon would greet Reggie with a kiss on the cheek, mug of tea, and plate of biscuits. Today Martin was acting strange and Sharon was absent.

"Sharon?" Reggie repeated the word once more for good measure.

"Gone. She's gone," Martin replied, his face drawn. Resigned.

"Gone?" Reggie was confused. "What do you mean?"

"Gone. As in not here. Anymore." Martin spoke, somewhat flustered, then saw Reggie's shocked expression. "Well, just for now. Maybe."

"Where and what?" asked Reggie. "Have you split up?"

Martin thought quick, seeing from his side view the hounds now in full swing, gorging on Sarah's remains. One hound chomped on a breast, nipple and all. The torso was being shredded and limbs chewed. Martin smiled.

"She's gone back home. To her mum's. Whilst we're not hunting. She never gets away over Christmas so I told her to nip back for a few days. Or weeks."

Reggie looked at Martin, not totally convinced. Liar. And he should know.

"Only until we start hunting again, sir," Martin added as some reassurance.

He stared at his boss, as if to reinforce his lie. It worked. Or so he thought.

Reggie glared at the arm, still blocking access to what was technically his property. Martin flushed, saw the harsh look then shrugged his shoulders. Removing his arm, he stepped sideways, but slowly, blocking access and views from the Drawing Yard and hounds, now fully chewing upon Sarah, and instead cleverly pointed towards the Flesh Room, almost guiding Reggie.

"Cup of tea sir?" Martin enquired. "Just about to start. Nice fresh brew."

Reggie, unconsciously encouraged by Martin's guiding arm, automatically entered the Flesh House and naturally wandered over to the large wooden bench where Martin kept most of his cutting tools. He'd clearly been busy.

"Thanks for the offer of a cuppa, but I can't stay. Flying visit. And beside, I need a big favour from you. Can you go straight out to Bertie's, please?"

Martin looked at his boss, trying to listen to the roar of the incinerator in the back room. It sounded quiet. Not good news. Reggie caught the glance and turned, wondering what was wrong with his Huntsman. Clearly not himself.

"Well I'm a bit busy sir," Martin explained. "Can it wait?"

Reggie glared at Martin, his patience worn out and frayed.

"No. I'm afraid it can't One of Bertie's horses is ill. Colic. He needs you to despatch it. He hasn't the heart, not with everything that's gone on later."

Martin sighed, knowing it was his job, and the welfare of the horse touched him too. But he needed an excuse to get out of anything this morning.

"What about the kennels? I've got work to do here. The hounds?"

Martin didn't usually make excuses, and was always totally obedient, but he was playing for as much time as possible to ensure everything was okay.

"It'll only take a few minutes. Can you go?" Reggie was strangely patient. "Now, please Martin. I told him you'd be straight over. I'll lock up here."

Martin was unsure how to act and didn't totally trust Reggie himself. And besides, he had a pack of hungry hounds eating a dead prostitute to attend to.

"Hold on, I just need to check I locked the kennel gates," he lied, stepping swiftly out and across to the Drawing Yard. "Stay there. Just a moment."

Martin dashed to the kennel area, glancing through the railings to see a host of content, bloody-faced hounds, munching happily at bits of meat of no definable origin. In the far corner, Martin could just make out Mayhem, chomping on Sarah's foot, an orange toenail bright in the new light. The hound's teeth began chewing on the side of her foot, the heart tattoo about to disappear down its throat, hopefully with orange painted toes for desert.

Martin sighed, most other body parts not recognisable. He smiled.

"They look happy," Reggie announced. "Well fed!"

Martin leapt. Reggie was standing behind him. Unseen, unheard.

"Whatever you've fed them, they seem to want more."

Heart thumping hard, Martin cringed. He sincerely hoped they wouldn't.

"Okay Martin, you get off to Bertie's. I'll only be a few minutes and then I have to dash. I've got lots to do myself, now that Elizabeth's gone off and left me. It's not really any big secret; not after what happened on Boxing Day."

Martin listened, almost sympathetically, but still tried to block Reggie's view.

"Most people can guess what's happened, but other than a couple of people, no one knows for certain." Martin listened as Reggie continued. "She's gone."

"Gone?" Martin replied, suddenly waking up.

"Gone. She's gone. Elizabeth." Reggie replied, his face drawn.

"Gone?" Martin was confused, mind elsewhere. "What do you mean?"

"Gone. For good." Reggie replied, tone flustered. "Not coming back. Ever."

Martin nodded, as if understanding. But he hoped he didn't.

"Bertie, obviously knows, as Elizabeth ran off with his gamekeeper. Furious about what has happened. Virginia leaving him for that whippersnapper Gavin has left him in a right Bugger's Muddle, you could say." Reggie said.

"Bertie's had a double blow, losing the two people closest to him. Wife and beloved keeper. I'll be honest and tell you Elizabeth leaving me has cut me up more than I thought it would. I deserve it you could say, many would, but that doesn't make it any easier for me to accept." Reggie almost looked sad.

Martin looked at the forlorn figure of Reggie, downtrodden, and no longer quite so brash and arrogant. He even seemed patient and calmer today.

"Hence why this mess with Bertie's horse couldn't come at a worse time. So if you could help him ASAP it'd do us all a big favour. So please, get started."

Martin knew he had no choice. And besides, the main evidence was now consumed. Other than Sarah's head, hopefully now close to being turned to ash, there was little for Reggie to see. Besides, he'd not be staying around.

"I'll get off straight away sir," Martin responded, more like older and more disciplined self. "I'll grab the keys to the truck. The gun is already inside."

Reggie smiled appreciatively. Possibly too much.

"Good man. Thanks. I'll make sure everything is okay and lock up for you," Reggie nodded, his mood also now relaxing. "You go. Please. Good man!"

With a furtive glance around at the kennels and at the now content feasting hounds, Martin grabbed a jacket, set of keys and headed off to his truck.

"I'll call you later," yelled Reggie, following Martin down to the driveway, thankfully ignoring the hounds and then waving as he fired up the truck. As the truck moved slowly down the drive, Martin returned the wave, worried about anything Reggie might find. But he had no choice, or he'd totally blow everything. Glancing in the mirrors, he saw Reggie stand by the boot of his Rover, looking at the slowly vanishing truck. Martin sighed, wondering what he'd find when he returned. Hopefully not the police and a coroners van.

As Martin's truck disappeared into the cover of the woods, Reggie wasted no time. He too had lots to do himself. Important business. Very important.

Raising the split tailgate of the Rover, double-checking no one was about or watching, he looked at the cargo inside.

A large box sat within. Covered by an old jacket.

He grinned, but had no time to mess about.

Pulling the jacket away, he removed the stout box.

It weighed about twenty pounds.

Heaving it from the back with a groan, he held it before him and moved at a fast, waddling pace. He headed down the alley between the kennel buildings then turned into the Flesh House and straight on into the adjoining room.

With a sigh of relief he sat the box down upon a bench.

His eyes fell upon the incinerator.

Smiling, Reggie moved towards the silent, cool furnace.

He had work to do. Urgent and important work.

Better get started, he thought.

He opened the incinerator door.

Chapter 92

The best thinking has been done in solitude.
The worst has been done in turmoil.

Thomas A. Edison

Lord Burlingham was not a good liar. Certainly not as good as Reggie.

But one thing was certain; both were blatant liars. And total bastards!

What Martin didn't know yet, and was curious to learn, was why Reggie had so urgently sent him away from The Kennels and over to Wroxingham Hall.

It was worrying. Very worrying. But whatever the real reason, it certainly wasn't to destroy one of the Lord's horses. Thankfully these were all fine and well and none had any signs of colic. The happy Lord apologised profusely for the wasted trip, saying he'd called Reggie in a panic and misunderstanding.

One of his older horses looked poorly he claimed, thought it might be colic, but was now fine. Maybe a bit of choke. How silly of him!

Worse, and making the deceit more apparent, was the diversionary tactics Lord Burlingham had used to deter Martin from even checking to see if the horse was okay. "No need," he'd insisted, guiding him away as he'd begun to walk towards the stable block. "He's fine. Have some breakfast instead."

After what he'd seen in the last few hours, a full and hearty English breakfast, which Lord Burlingham insisted Martin consume; stating it was the least he could do to compensate, was the last thing he wanted. But he'd relented.

Martin didn't believe his Lordship. Various questions puzzled Martin as he reluctantly munched on toast and marmalade, the forced second course to a 'fry-up' and he listened to Bertie's chatter, feigning smiles and polite laughter.

Strangely not a word had been mentioned of Virginia or Mike Hawthorn, as if neither every existed. They had clearly both gone from the Hall. Martin began sensing a blatant conspiracy between Reggie and Lord Burlingham.

Nothing added up. What was Reggie doing? Why was he at The Kennels?

A pure coincidence, or was he looking for evidence? Did he know what'd happened? If so, then why did he not simply get the police involved or face off Martin. He knew he was no angel. And Reggie was no saint himself. Nor Lord Burlingham for that. All were crooked. A fine bunch. It all felt wrong and he constantly checked his watch, before finally escaping the clutches of Lord Burlingham, who checking the clock, told him had things to do.

All Martin knew, driving away from Wroxingham Hall with an empty truck, but expanded belly, filled with an English breakfast, four rounds of toast, Seville Marmalade and two cups of tea, was that the pair had taken him in.

Hook, line, sinker, rod and boat. And the angler too. Complete with waders.

Martin mulled over the questions with growing nausea, sure he'd be met at The Kennels by a stream of flashing blue lights, armed police, and joined by busy forensics people donned in white overalls, just as he'd seen on the TV.

He'd momentarily considered simply driving off and doing another flit, but this time alone. But he wouldn't get far. The truck had little diesel, his wallet held less cash, and more importantly, something strange niggled at him.

Reggie couldn't have known what happened last night.

No one did. Other than those three people.

And Martin was keeping quiet. And the hounds couldn't speak. As such.

Reggie must have his own reason to remove Martin from The Kennels for an hour or so. But what? And why? And why was Bertie involved? A mystery.

Half out of curiosity, mixed with a hunter's instinct, he drove on, keen to see the awaiting hounds and their own dark secret, hoping they had not let him down. Cautiously he watched the road for signs of police activity, or possible un-marked police vehicles, but noted little traffic, the roads as quiet as ever. As he turned the truck into the woods The 'Trespassers Will Be Eaten' sign stood stark before him. For once its meaning held true horror, and Martin felt himself flush red and nauseous, sensing Lord Burlingham's hearty breakfast might make a quick exit. He tried to address his nerves, and drummed his fingers on the lorries big steering wheel, easing the accelerator and breathed deep as the truck slowly entered the woods. A few breaths, another check in the mirrors and a furtive glance around the familiar woods eased his nerves, as the truck entered the depths of the familiar, seemingly welcoming trees.

Keen eyes checked for police hiding in shrubs or ground cover, but he saw nothing. A pair of ambling male pheasants dashed across the track before the lorry, to disappear behind brambles. A wood pigeon, seeing the truck, flew up from the track, previously rummaging undisturbed. A sure sign no was about.

The darkness of the woods cleared to reveal the driveway and paddocks, just as the first day he'd driven to The Kennels with Sharon. Such happy days.

He felt a lump in his throat but snorted, dismissing the memory.

Times change. Things happen. Shit happens.

As the familiar building loomed, no armed police ran forward waving guns, shouting over-excitable orders to get out of the vehicle and lay on the ground. They'd know he had weapons in the truck. But there was nothing. Nothing.

That included Reggie's Rover. It too had gone. The driveway was empty.

Where was he? What had he done? Was it a trap? Were the police all hiding?

They'd have to be good - very good - but Martin trusted no one.

He eased the truck into its usually place, killed the engine, then with hunters eyes, still seated within the cab, scanned the trees and surrounding buildings.

In the distance a crow sat in a high tree, no doubt watching him. Two wood pigeons flew past, to settle on a nearby tree. Ever aware, he knew pigeons or crows were the first to take flight if danger loomed. For a minute he scanned the familiar landscape, but everything appeared, as it should. Nothing.

He sighed heavily, then exited the truck, to at once be met with a deafening noise. The hounds howled in unison, excitedly knowing from the engine sound their master had returned, possibly with fresh meat. But not this time.

Martin closed the truck door, and with a final glance towards the woods, dashed down the alley and towards the Drawing Yard. What would greet him?

He scanned the yard through the railings, his view being slightly obscured by a group of hounds jumping up, eager to greet him, sniffing and licking his hands through the railings, tails waggling, muzzles clean, bellies hopefully full.

Scattered about the yard lay splintered bones in various stages of destruction and meat of partial consumption. But to the first casual glance, nothing clearly attained the mess inside to formally being the body of a beautiful woman. The orange toenails were no more. The torso had gone from the chain, and a singular fragment of flesh and cartilage from Sarah's collarbone remained hanging. The two chains holding her limbs were empty and only parts of unidentifiable bone could be seen. However, looking in deeper towards the back of the pen, Martin's keen eyes noted something unique and distinct.

Sarah's femurs. The long bones, so characteristic of being human, lay at the back; one discarded, the other beside a hound, still chewing on it. Martin knew he'd have to retrieve them and cut them into chunks and either incinerate the smaller bone parts or feed them back to the hounds.

Cautiously he unbolted the gate, the hounds raising their heads and looking on excitedly, assuming they'd receive more food or be let out for exercise in the paddocks and into the woods as usual. They would later, but first Martin had much more important tasks to undertake. As he entered the enclosed yard, many of the hounds lounged upon the beds beneath the shelter, too full of food or lazy to rise. Others ran towards him as he moved to the back of the feeding area, seeing the first of Sarah's femurs. He bent down and retrieved the tattered bone, as Christmas, ironically the smaller hound who'd started the Boxing Day trouble in the woods, stepped forward. Somewhat cautiously, she sniffed at the bone, still partially flesh-covered, boldly nudging other hounds away. Almost playfully she made a grab for the end, where part of the knee sinew still retained the patella and inner cartilage. She sniffed at this new section, which Martin playfully offered, waving the bone. The hound tugged on the sinew, which separated from the bone, and the hound dashed off into the back with her fresh snack. Martin chuckled at the site of Sarah's kneecap in the mouth of one of his favourite hounds. He was fond of his 'children' and more so today for their excellent work. They'd done him proud.

Stepping forward, he bent down and retrieved the second femur, which lay in a far corner near an older hound. A couple of hounds sniffed at the bone as Martin lifted it, until Martin moved them away. This long bone still retained a lump of flesh around the inner thigh, near the ball joint. Otherwise, it had been almost stripped clean, the lower half of the leg gone, including the foot with bright orange toe-nails and all evidence of the damning tattoo. All gone.

The hounds had done their work, and done it well, as Martin's scanning eyes could see little else left of Sarah. There wasn't much. He'd recheck the yard thoroughly when he let the hounds out to exercise later, and then rinse everything down with Jeyes fluid, both to cleanse the yard, but also remove any possible clues left behind. He knew it destroyed all DNA evidence.

Heading back toward the metal gate with the two long bones, a melee of hounds gathered around, following close. Noses sniffing, half out of curiosity, the others assuming there'd be more to eat, or simply wanting to be released.

As their Alpha-leader, the hounds both respected and feared Martin, who treated the hounds with care, but also ensured they remained a fighting unit, like loyal soldiers. Hunters, keen, alert and trained to do their job, he ensured they had that killing edge, and were always kept slightly hungry. As much as he cared for them, played with them, and attended to their injuries, he knew he had to be a firm leader of the pack and would rebuke them when needed.

He placed the first femur under his armpit, carrying the second. Maverick, one of his favourites and one of the main hounds, came bustling over. Eyes alert, watching Martin's every movements, but more so the bone, he trotted forward, damp nose sniffing the long, partially flesh covered bone.

Martin paused and leant forward, fondly rubbing the hound's head, who in turn sniffed playfully at Martin's hand, then at the bone. He licked the bone and nibbled at a piece of the remaining flesh still attached on Sarah's leg bone.

"Good boy!" Martin cried. "Well done, you clever chap!"

He fondly rubbed the hounds' muzzle, who in turn licked his fingers.

Again Martin praised the hound, rubbing his head. Again Maverick nuzzled.

Then Maverick bit him. Only a nip, but still a definite bite.

Martin whipped away his hand before the hound could make full contact, but the small impression the tooth made to his hand was clearly evident. Glaring at the hound, he raised his hand, instinctively about to strike, but paused.

Over forty hounds heads turned in unison in his direction.

Martin's blood froze. All keen, they stared intently. Those lounging about in their lodges also raised their heads; their attention on Martin and Maverick.

Bright and alert, they seemed ready for their next meal.

Maverick stood proudly before the pack; tail wagging, unaware of his crime, his eyes flicked from bone to Martin. Mayhem, the hound's brother, drew level at his shoulder. Both lead hounds gazed at Martin, their eyes bright; mischief clear in both lead hounds. The rest of the pack shuffled forward.

Martin glared, for the first time afraid of the hounds.

But knowing he must show no fear, cradling both bones under his arms, he slowly turned, opened the gate, exited, and hastily closed it, throwing the bolt firmly home. The keen-eyed hounds watched him walk away, bones and all.

For the first time since he'd met the pack many years ago, he stared warily at the mass of hounds, who all intently gazed back at him. Their eyes glistened.

Alpha-leader or their next meal? Martin was now unsure.

Turning within the tight alley, one of Sarah's femurs fell from his fumbling grasp, the bone clattering upon the slabs with the hollow rattling thud only bones can create. He looked down at the leg he'd had around his back.

What on earth had he done? A wave of horror washed over him as he sighed, already tired from the day. And it was still early. What else could happen?

Retrieving the fallen bone he returned to the Flesh House. He placed the femurs in a tub of bones and meat, where he still had remnants of the cow he'd been feeding to the hounds. Thus, unless someone looked really close, they'd only see a mass of meat and various bones and know no different.

Many people bought such cooked cow long-bones for their pet dogs. Named 'Postman's Legs.' Perhaps he could start a new line called 'Prostitute's Legs.'

He smiled, glad in a way he still had his dark humour. He'd cut the bones into three sections as soon as he'd checked the incinerator. He'd then put the bones back in the yard later, along with more cow parts and mixed feed.

But not until he'd released the hounds for exercise. He sensed they needed a release of energy, along with bodily waste. It'd all naturally pass through the hounds, and by this evening, Sarah would be gone. Problem solved.

Moving into the rear room, he tensed, knowing something was wrong.

The incinerator was off and the low gas warning was bleeping. He'd set the timer before leaving on Reggie's fake errand, so it'd run for sixty minutes.

He estimated, with the secondary burners reducing the larger bone fragments into ash, it'd take forty minutes to completely destroy Sarah's head. Provided it'd burnt for the set time, all the bones, bar her teeth, should be gone. The hard enamel on teeth made them hard to destroy and so he'd sweep Sarah's thirty-two or so teeth from the incinerator and bury them, as he usually did with animal skulls he burnt. But he also knew the furnace had a dodgy valve. It intermittently closed off the burners without warning. However, it wasn't the valve now causing him fresh concerns. It was the soft beeping sound.

He cursed, knowing the gas bottle had run out. But when?

Had Sarah's head been reduced to ash before the gas ran out or partly burnt? Or not at all? Would he find an unburnt head, or a pile of ash and teeth?

He could only hope it'd been destroyed and Reggie hadn't opened the door whilst the incinerator was at full heat. He shouldn't and usually wouldn't.

Martin was sure there'd been more than enough gas in the bottle to complete the job, but noted the bottle dial was showing as completely empty. Why?

Reaching forward, he pulled open the incinerator door.

Physically leaping back, he stared in horror.

The image froze him solid.

Two charred heads. Part burnt.

Two heads. Not one.

Four blackened eye sockets stared back.

Chapter 93

An excellent man. He has no enemies;
and none of his friends like him.

Oscar Wilde

PC Burton had been tied up with many things since his Christmas leave and had almost forgotten about the skid marks. But not completely. Christmas Day at his parents, then the episode on Boxing Day with the hunt, had made him lose track of everything else. Time had been taken up with form filling, much to his annoyance. Now he had to follow up matters, and a legitimate reason to question not only Turner, but also several of the Shoteton Hunt.

Forensics had as good as closed the case concerning the car crash, possibly due to it being the Christmas period and short-staffed. They'd agreed the fire was intense, but by an exploding petrol can, assumed to have ruptured and ignited as the car hit the tree. This after the car had hit the deer. The young lad who'd been thrown clear of the blaze was assumed to have been covered in petrol as the can ruptured, and thus why he'd tragically burnt to death.

There were no other skid marks near the scene, and no other cars were seen in the area that night, nor were there any witnesses to add any such credence.

Thus, the case was likely to be closed off in the early part of the New Year.

A tragic accident. Caused by an inexperienced intoxicated driver, speeding, with both alcohol and cannabis in his system. Sadly one of the many terrible incidents that happen each year with young drivers. When would they learn?

That was the official line and no one was allocating time and effort to pursue anything further. Except Burton. He still had doubts and still had suspects.

He wanted to get into C.I.D. and this could be a great way in. He hoped.

The hunting incident and media coverage was a more pressing topic to be closed down, with a string of potential assault complaints to follow up, and a terse local MP, known to oppose hunting, to keep happy. He'd threatened to raise 'serious concerns' on the behaviour of the local hunt in 'The House.'

However, the Chief Constable claimed there was little real evidence, with few witness statements for them to waste resources on. A few statements were to be taken and then the whole thing would most likely disappear and dropped in the New Year, except for the serious injury claim. But he seemingly had his own agenda, rumours running that he and a couple of those involved with the Hunt, went to the same 'Lodge.' However, to keep the paperwork mill rolling, and make it appear as if the police were actually doing something regarding the 'Windford Boxing Day Incident,' as he was being called - not a riot - he was due to interview the Field Master of the Shoteton. He was the one who'd brutally dragged an anti into a tree. Or at least as claimed by the battered man.

From what he knew and saw, Burton could see it possibly as an accident, for the Anti was as much at fault for getting involved; looking for trouble.

Don't poke a tiger with a stick; you'll get eaten. It seems he did. As such.

However, he still formally had official enquiries to make and paperwork to complete. Besides, he had some of his own questions to ask. He personally wouldn't have gone anywhere near a horse in such chaotic circumstances. Numerous witnesses said the Anti was hitting the horseman with his own whip and that the horse spooked. That sounded like an accident with a mad horse, or at worst, self-defence. The Anti must have been a total idiot.

Having himself nearly been flattened by one of the annoying beasts when he'd tried to speak with the group at the scene, he'd decided horses were big, dumb animals. And their riders were seemingly not much brighter either.

Burton had little sympathy for either party. He'd simply get a statement from the pompous horseman and then let the CPS decide. He had other work.

On the way back from Steve Harrison's he'd check the skid marks outside Chris Turner's farm and call in on him. He'd also been involved in the Boxing Day incident, along with some of his ladies, so he had further questions to ask his little group who were far from innocent. A couple of the woman attacked an Anti. One had submitted an official complaint of assault, and also of theft.

More paperwork to complete, all over some silly hat claimed to have been pulled from her head and stolen, but which she'd probably dropped. He'd spoken with the mad skinny woman. The hat probably blew off her tiny head.

Plus he had a few other witness's names to interview. It was sure to be a busy and totally pointless day or two, and with the New Year only a few days away.

Turning a bend, he approached the tree where the three young men had died. A tragic death just a week before Christmas. Even Burton could feel some sympathy for their families, despite the damning evidence of the accident. As he approached the bend, he noted a collection of flowers at the base of the tree, the scorch marks evident on the ragged bark, as was the disturbed soil on the bank, where the grass had been scuffed away by the speeding car.

Burton slowed down and noticed various cards and messages upon bouquets, placed about the dark, blackened trunk, where a chunk of bark was missing. Curious, he stopped the patrol car, parking on the verge and walked up to the tree, looking at the hand-written notes that had been pinned neatly to the various bunches of flowers. Maybe someone felt guilty. Glancing down, he curiously flicked through the cards of condolences left by those who'd left them and any flowers. A couple of names he recognised as relatives, but also some dubious locals. Also were members of the Shoteton Hunt he was due to question. It seemed strange, but obviously they were a close-knit community, and the boys known to all locally, despite the wide social differences.

He was surprised to see a very large bouquet marked up: 'With Sympathy from Lord and Lady Burlingham. Such a sad accident. R.I.P.'

Posh friends indeed for such simple people, he thought, eyebrows raised.

Burton drove on to where Steve Harrison lived. He was keen to learn more about this member of the hunt whom he'd found out had a dodgy past and who he definitely wanted to question. Checking the map, he noticed two possible ways into the property, with woods shielding the other entrance, with the farmhouse and paddocks centrally placed. Burton decided to use the less popular entrance. Maybe his arrival would be unexpected and he'd catch his victim unawares. He liked things like that. As Burton was about to turn off the road and into the wooded back entrance he abruptly halted the patrol car.

His face lit up, eyes not believing what he saw before him.

Exiting the patrol car, he gazed in awe down at the road.

Skid marks. Clearly defined on the road.

A car. Moving at speed. Exiting the farm. Interesting.

It'd skidded heavily on the road. Leaving tyre marks.

When, why, how and who? Burton wanted to know.

This added another dynamic. He'd seen similar incriminating skid marks outside Chris Turner's. Now he saw equally damning marks outside the property of another dubious person, which could also be linked to the crash.

Burton cautiously peered up and down at the road with a slight grin, just to ensure no tractors or 4 x 4's were coming along to run him over. Again.

With interest, but annoyance, he noted the skid marks here appeared almost identical to those he'd seen outside Turner's. Car tyres; leaving at high speed.

That wasn't good. He'd hoped they might look different. Damn!

Burton paused, kneeling down, touching the road. His fingers ran across the road, as if again the very feel of the black surface would reveal its dark secrets.

Perhaps he'd jumped to conclusions with the horseman.

Maybe he was innocent of any crime after all. Maybe.

Other than two cold-blooded murders. And maybe more. Innocent? No.

Could the 'nasty' Mister Harrison be involved in the death of the three young lads? Did he chase them from his property before crashing their car? Maybe.

This was the same man who'd deliberately ridden an anti hunt protestor into a tree. Coldly crushing him. Putting him in hospital. Accidentally, of course. But, also the man, accordingly to his police file, who had a history of riding over hunt protestors in a similar manner. And getting away with it too. The same man who whipped young girls, after tying them to a bed, and then who'd punched their wife out cold. And no doubt more unknown crimes.

Perhaps Harrison hid other secrets. Pervert. Torturer. Wife-beater. Killer?

Driving into the gloom of the woods and onto a dirt track, he saw the familiar 'Trespasser's Will Be Eaten' sign, now giving it a cursory glance.

How strange, he thought, that all those with such a sign had dubious pasts.

On he drove along a compacted muddy track through the woods, bleak, with brown leaves scattered about the ground, some still on the trees. It was obvious Steve Harrison was not expecting him as the patrol car slowly and eerily rolled out the woods, then along a track running across a rough field.

Before him he could see various mixed barns, a stable block and paddocks surrounding the house, and also a Portacabin office, about which stood an assortment of agricultural vehicles, trailers, lorries and off-road vehicles.

Steve Harrison was clambering out an agricultural forklift, parked up before a rusty corrugated iron covered barn when he saw the patrol car emerge. A large oak tree overhanging nearby partly hid the building from his view.

Realising the vehicle had come from the back wood, Steve appeared uneasy by the policeman's unexpected arrival. He peered from the corner of the barn to see Burton park the solitary vehicle and clamber out of the Land Rover.

Steve furtively glanced back at the forklift, as if to ensure there was nothing incriminating on show, and then to the woods, glancing towards each entry point, to ensure there were no other police vehicles coming, before strolling openly across the yard and towards the policeman. He wandered over from the barn, the pair meeting halfway across the track. Steve winced, hating all police, but more so the man before him. However, fixing his best fake smile, he steadily approached the policeman. Burton smiled back, equally falsely too.

"Good morning. I wasn't expecting you. Are you going to clap me in irons? Perhaps I should call my solicitor?" Steve was already in fine form.

Burton chuckled, but it was clearly false. He scanned Steve's face, wondering what he had to hide. Probably lots. Steve blushed, annoyingly.

"It's a brief chat, to update you on things regarding Boxing Day. But I don't think you'll need your solicitor," Burton replied, trying to sound informal.

"Not unless you have something serious to confess to me sir. Then I'm all ears and my cuffs are always ready!" The policeman joked, grinning sickly.

Steve chuckled, but stared coldly at the policeman, who grinned back, rather cocky, as though he knew some secret. Steve just wanted to punch him.

"Interesting piece of equipment," Burton continued, pointing with his head at the forklift in the barn. Steve followed his stare, hackles rising.

"A teleporter. Agricultural forklift truck," replied Steve calmly. "Used for various jobs. From loading hay and straw, to lifting heavy equipment. Very useful piece of equipment about the farm. Also great for removing cashpoint machines from bank brick walls. Or so I've heard." Steve's smile was wide.

The policeman didn't find the joke funny. He stared back. Coldly.

He didn't understand the complex nature of farming and range of equipment used, nor wanted to. It was all too muddy, smelly and arduous for his way of thinking. He assumed bacon grew on trees and was then handpicked by elves.

The conversation stifled and Steve now stood silently and unsmiling.

"May we could go inside to talk over some points about Boxing Day," suggested Burton, pointing to the house with his head once more.

"Certainly," replied Steve, ignoring the Burton's deliberate gesticulation, but instead turned sideways, blocked his way and with his own guiding arm, led him toward his Portacabin office. A great traditional Salesman's trick.

Without thinking, Burton automatically followed the cue and once inside, Steve offered the policeman a chair. He lifted out a semi-feral tabby cat lying asleep in the chair, tipping out the dust, and offered a cup of coffee.

Burton politely declined the coffee and looked at the offered chair with disgust, watching the mangy cat drift outside, wondering what diseases it had.

Steve poured a fresh coffee for himself from the percolator, touching the lukewarm glass bowl and tutting, trying to recall when it was first brewed. He then sat down in his high-backed, black leather chair. Free of cats and dust.

Placing a mud-covered boot across his leg, he silently looked at the policeman, waiting for him to speak. Burton felt uncomfortable, but regarded the man opposite for a moment, getting a feeling for him. It wasn't good.

Steve regarded the policeman with a mix of distrust and contempt. Whilst he appreciated the good work the police undertook on behalf of the community, he never liked it when he was at the other end of detailed investigative work. Or when being questioned him over attacking antis. Or ex-wives.

Steve stared coldly and impatiently at the piggy-eyed policeman. 'Get on!'

Burton stared back, jealous of the laid-back, good-looking man who owned a farm and no doubt had several horsey women as girlfriends, already knowing about his stunning ex-wife and the pair's well-documented bedroom antics.

The policeman scanned the untidy office, eyes noting all. Steve followed his gaze, wondering what he was looking for and what he wanted. He took a sip of the lukewarm coffee. It tasted like stale cigarettes laced with charcoal, recalling it'd been there since yesterday. Or maybe longer. Worrying.

"Can I sell you a tractor?" Steve enquired, breaking the ice and trying the establish the reason for the unwelcome visit. "Red, green or blue?"

"What?" Burton queried, then got the message. He cleared his throat. "No, thank you. Basically Mister Harrison, I'm here to inform you the details of the Boxing Day will be passed onto the Crown Prosecution Service who will in turn decide if there are sufficient grounds for prosecution. We're still awaiting on some statements, but finding it hard to contact a number of people involved. Especially on the opposing side. Maybe it is the Christmas period."

Steve nodded, the news sounding good. For now. What was the catch?

"Regardless of the CPS and how they feel we should act. It seems unlikely we will be pressing any charges against you regarding the incident on, where Mister David Pearson received serious injuries whilst involved in an accident with a horse ridden by yourself. It's seemingly being considered that there is not enough evidence. We only have his versions of events. No witnesses."

Steve beamed wildly inside, but displayed no emotions and let the policeman continue with his full flow of words. So far it was sounding good. Too good.

"We received a full statement on the day from a Gavin Davis. He explained everything from the start, backed up by several other riders and numerous witnesses on foot. It did seem a rather foolish act by the anti. Unofficially."

Steve nodded, keeping a cool expression, although leaping about inside.

"Also a Lady Carter has made a full witness statement. It seems she saw everything. She is a respected citizen. A former Magistrate it seems. Also she is a good friend with the Chief Constable too. That's rather convenient."

The policeman glared, knowing words had been spoken on high and hence why it was likely there'd be no charges. Steve tried to hide a wide smile.

He knew Lady Carter knew high-level people, and had words with them.

"I've tried to contact Mister Gavin Davis again, but can't get hold of him or his wife. Both seemed to have vanished. I'll try later. Also, I've been trying to speak with a Lady Burlingham. All her husband, Lord Burlingham would say, was that she'd gone to see relatives in Scotland for the New Year and can't be contacted. In the Highlands. Some remote part of the Glens. All convenient."

Steve shrugged his shoulders, unsure why Gavin was suddenly missing, but knew he and Dawn were on dodgy ground. Where Virginia had gone he could only speculate, but wasn't aware of relatives in Scotland. That was worrying. Wroxingham Hall had several deep wells. Steve hoped she wasn't in one.

"Maybe they're all away seeing relatives over Christmas," he offered.

"Any statements from the Antis?" Steve added. "Whom I should state were on private land, and could and should be prosecuted for trespass. Or sued I should say correctly. You can't prosecute for trespass unless criminal damage is undertaken. But I'm sure we could find some. You can however bring a private case and sue that person. Maybe our hosts will consider that option."

Burton looked at Steve, realising he knew the law. He hated smart-arse's.

"No, other than the main defendant, Mister Pearson. All others involved in the incident seemed to have vanished, although one lady Anti wants us to pursue an act of theft. Seems one of your lot stole her new hat. A present."

Burton spoke with fake disgust, glaring at Steve to see if he knew anything.

Theft of a hat. Ten years minimum. After being flogged.

An image of Tracey, riding off with a weird wool hat atop her riding cap flew back into Steve's memory. He grinned, and then straightened his face, lifting the coffee cup once more to cover the ever-growing smirk.

"Strange no other anti's issued statements or want to press charges, don't you think? But we all know why. I assume you saw the press coverage? I think you and your buddy were in the papers. Nice punch by your colleague. Maybe the man with no testicles will be suing for police brutality. But it seems strange none of the main yobs who caused all the trouble have come forward."

Steve's tone was serious, and he looked hard at Burton.

"Why is that then sir," Burton enquired, his tone harsh.

"Because the whole event was rigged. A stunt. Set up by the photographer who sold all the photos to the press. He's supposedly making a documentary on the whole hunting issue and will include our events as part of it. A set up."

Burton had heard comments, but knew he was out of his depth. Political issues and conspiracies were beyond him. As were most things it seemed.

He glared at Steve, but knew he still had his ace card up his sleeve.

"No one else made any statements to back the claim?" Steve enquired, thinking of Izzy, whom he knew saw everything and wondered why she'd not spoken up or made a statement yet. He hoped she wouldn't, but was unsure.

"No. That's the point. We only have Mister Pearson statement, that and also being partly what I witnessed, which honestly was all a bit mad and chaotic."

"Serves him right. Idiot. But what happened was clearly questionable," Steve responded, unsure why Izzy hadn't dropped him in it. She saw everything.

Burton glared at Steve coldly, knowing what he'd seen.

"A rather brutal act. Accident or not. And no sympathy for the victim?"

Steve looked away, face flushing, knowing he'd pushed his luck. He took a sip of the foul brown liquid, simply to break eye contact. But Burton clearly wasn't finished. He hated to see anyone get off the hook, especially someone as smarmy and clearly crooked as the man before him. He shuffled in the seat.

"I understand Mister Pearson might launch a private prosecution against you for damages. It seems he has a brother who has high-flying contacts with some big animal welfare charity. He's a bit of a legal boffin it seems. Takes on big logging companies. That's worrying for you." Burton smiled broadly.

Steve was impassive, but didn't welcome any legal claims. He doubted the skinny anti's brother, if he had one, was any more potent than him. Obviously yet another pathetic Panda Hugging hippy. It was possibly bluff and bluster by the policeman and Pearson, and at best would be a long drawn out affair.

He had legal cover, provided through both the Hunts' own insurance, as well as his own private policy. With few witnesses, Steve wasn't overly concerned.

He'd gotten away with the previous incident. He often joked that he should have small pictures of anti's stuck on the side of Samson.

Like a fighter pilot, recording each kill. Samson had two so far.

Tally-ho! Anti's sun-high! I'm going in hard! Brace! Brace!

He smiled to himself, momentarily lost in the thought.

Suddenly Burton hit him out of the blue.

"Do you know a Mister Peter Jenkins?"

The question brought Steve back down with a startling jolt.

"Sorry, who?" he replied, flushing red. "No, I don't recall the name."

He replied automatically. Maybe too quickly.

"Peter Jenkins," Burton repeated, pausing for dramatic effect it seemed.

"Insurance salesman. Drove a flash silver Merc' coupe. Ring any bells now?"

Steve stared at the policeman stone faced.

'What the hell did he know?'

Chapter 94

Though this be madness, yet there is method in't.

Hamlet - Shakespeare

Steve felt himself glow, pulse rising, wondering what the crafty 'pig bastard' was up to, but remained silent. He shrugged his shoulders as a silent reply, unsure how a verbal response would sound. Probably not convincing.

"Well you had a couple of policies with his company. Made a claim for a horsebox. Seemingly stolen from your farm about twelve months ago. Surely you remember now? That's a big thing to go missing. And you got a pay-out."

Steve eyed the policeman cautiously, thinking quick, before replying.

"Yes, I remember the theft claim and a chap dealing with it, but not his name or what he drove. He could have been anyone. And was. Why do you ask?"

"Simply because he's part of a missing persons enquiry. I note in his diary that he visited your farm again a few months ago," Burton began confidently. "Tried to sell you another policy. Notes in his diary that you were 'rude and offensive' and suggested where he could go or sexually do to himself. Well actually a bit worse than that. But I won't offend you. Why should that be?"

"No idea," Steve replied, possibly too quick, so he added. "Typical salesman. Pushy. Tried to sell me cover I didn't need at a higher premium. A bit too cocky. Never kid a kidder, if you know what I mean. And I'm sure you do."

What Steve didn't admit to the policeman was Pete Jenkins had queried the previous claim, after receiving new information and that it could be classed as fraud pending further investigations. Steve had then caught him snooping around the farm, seemingly looking for the 'missing' horsebox, which he was convinced Steve had hidden, or had moved somewhere else. How dare he!

Steve recalled he'd insinuated the claim was fraudulent and that he would possibly be investigating everything. That would have brought Steve trouble.

"Yes, I think I recall him," Steve said, tilting his head in an exaggerated way. "Bit of a tosser, in my opinion. He simply wanted another sale and was rather pushy, so I probably told him to piss off. But maybe in rather strong terms!" Steve added the final point with a smile, but not convincingly.

"But you said you'd not heard of him?" Burton pursued, sensing an untruth, digging deeper; getting a larger shovel to help open up the already deep hole.

"He was nothing to me. Just a salesman. One of many. I get loads each week. Annoying. A name. I didn't put him on my Christmas card list." Steve smiled.

They looked at each other in silence, then Steve said more.

"You say he's gone missing?" Steve spoke softly. Cocking his head. He didn't want to sound pleased. But he was. As he knew would be many of his friends.

"Yes. A few weeks ago. With his secretary." Burton looked straight at Steve.

Steve simply raised his eyebrows and then grinned widely.

Burton caught the look and had thought the same himself.

"No bank transfers have occurred and his very flash Mercedes has not been picked up by any ANPR cameras or by any of our patrol cars for weeks. It's vanished. You buy and sell vehicles I note. You haven't seen it, have you?"

Burton's lips curled into the sickly smile Steve was beginning to hate.

Steve felt himself flush, eyes instinctively looking out of the Portacabin windows, to gaze out to the yard and beyond up into the far woods.

The policeman's gaze followed, his eyes creasing, obviously thinking, wondering what secrets the man before him held. Many. Too many.

"I mostly deal in agricultural vehicles or equipment. Some horse trailers, horseboxes, four by fours and other horsey or farm equipment. As well as anything to do with horses. Or did do," Steve added, careful of each word, turning to look at the policeman. "Certainly not flash cars. Not my market."

Burton was all ears and kept listening, absorbing it all. Learning.

"If you can't drive it across a field, pull a trailer, put a horse in it or use it on a farm, then it isn't my sort of thing. Anyway, it'd all go through the DVLA."

Burton simply nodded, his eyes scanning the office once more, before giving his final shot, looking straight at Steve. Burton took a long breath.

"Also, could you explain those skid marks outside your property? By your side entrance. I noticed them on the way in. Quite distinct. Fast car."

Steve looked deeply at the PC, unresponsive, but controlled himself this time before answering, as if weighing up his response and thinking up a reply.

"What skid marks are those?" Steve replied coyly.

"The ones outside the wooded entrance to your property. Your second entrance. I noticed them when I came in. Looks like someone left your property in a bit of a hurry. And left a lot of rubber on the road in doing so."

Steve looked at the policeman stone cold, and then gazed down at a heavy glass paperweight in the shape of a hare, which sat upon his desk. It had been a birthday present from Izzy. He convinced himself he only kept it because it was useful and also attractive. He liked hares. That was all. Nothing else.

Steve glanced at the glass hare.

Then he looked at the smarmy copper.

'What a wanker!'

The glass hare was suddenly in his hand. Heavy.

Then smashing hard it into the policeman's head.

Whack! Whack! Whack!

The skull bones cracked and collapsed in.

It felt sweet. Refreshing.

Whack, whack, whack!

Then one more. For good measure. And fun.

Whack! And one more - for luck. Whack!

Down the policeman fell.

Blood sprayed about the office. High velocity spatter. Fine red droplets.
Steve continued to smash the glass hare into the copper's head.
His skull began collapsing, turning to mush. Brains oozing out.
Sweet! A few more whacks.
Just for a bit more fun. And a bit more luck.
Steve stared at the policeman.
The policeman stared back.
Still alive.
Sadly.
Breathing. Staring at Steve.
The glass hare paperweight hadn't moved.
Steve gazed at the copper. A thousand yard stare.
Burton gazed back, his pulse rising, unsure what was going on behind the unmoving horseman's suddenly glazed expression and silent response.
Best he didn't know. He wouldn't approve. Maybe he'd run.
Steve smiled at the policeman. The vision was fresh.
He would enjoy doing that. Teach the bastard a lesson.
Then bury him in the woods.
Easy-peasy. Lemon-squeezy.
But not today.
Steve had other things to do.
More important than burying coppers.
"Yes it was probably me the other day," Steve replied, looking from the paperweight and back at the policeman. He was back in the room. And earth.
"I was late for a meeting and came out the entrance a bit too quick. I doubt I was breaking the speed limit. I'm sure I wasn't. Maybe for a few seconds. Is it a crime to leave rubber on the road? I'll see about getting the road treated and remove the marks. I know a man. Several in fact." Steve smiled.
"No sir, it isn't a crime, although your driving may have been a bit reckless, if you openly admit to leaving such a noticeable tyre mark."
Burton answered formally, his piggy-eyes squinting. He felt powerful.
Steve stared coldly, reconsidering the paperweight option.
But there could be problems.
The copper probably had a thick skull. Very thick it appeared.
Steve didn't want to damage the paperweight. It was sentimental.
Maybe chop him up with a shovel instead. Sweet!
Then drop him down one of Bertie's deep wells. He had many.
Lord Burlingham owed him a big favour. Or two.
The policeman brought him back to the real world.
"We're still investigating the tragic accident just before Christmas. Three youths sadly died. As you know. I just wondered if you knew anything else about it. Some things don't add up and I'm just gaining further information."
Steve looked at him coolly, then answered, equally as calm and collected.

"I heard about it. We all did. Big news. We're a close community. Very close. Tragic accident. Kids messing about in cars and then crashed into a tree. Drunk or on drugs. Sadly hit a deer first. Roe buck I think. That was all I'd heard. Everyone was shocked. I knew their parents. Very sad. I left flowers."

Burton knew he was getting nowhere, but had all he needed for now.

"That will be all for now then sir," he said, his eyes scanning the office, looking at everything. Steve looked at him, the deep-seated hatred he felt for the policeman concealed by a fake smile, wanting him to leave at once.

With that Steve stepped out of the Portacabin and watched the policeman walk steadily across the yard, noticing him regard the various vehicles, trailers and equipment in the yard as he slowly walked off. Clearly taking note.

Steve winced, watching his gaze and hoped he didn't take too much interest in a couple of items. The policeman didn't, seemingly having all he wanted. He stood and watched Burton get back into the Rover. An arm extended out as a polite wave as the policeman drove off, this time going the other way out of Steve's property. Maybe to see what else he could observe. Nosey tosser!

Steve raised a happy hand in response, waving it fondly as the police vehicle moved off, but wanting to raise a finger. Or a gun. Fully loaded.

"Fucking nosy wanker," Steve cursed, watching the police Land Rover drift away up the inclined track and into the other section of woods to then vanish.

He waited until it went out of sight, shaking his head in anger, then wandered back towards the barn where the forklift was standing. He had work to do.

He also had things to hide and serious issues to address.

Just in case the policeman returned. And he knew he would.

He also needed to make a couple of urgent phone calls.

This had been a close call.

As calm as he tried to show, secretly, Steve was worried.

Very worried.

Chapter 95

Expectation is the root of all heartache.

William Shakespeare

P.C. Burton pulled his Land Rover up outside the entrance to Horsewater. He looked down at the tarmac. Before Christmas he'd carefully noted the skid marks that clearly decorated the road. And from memory, and to add further issues, they'd appeared similar to those outside Harrison's property; thus giving him two potential suspects to investigate. Double trouble.

But now he stared hard at the black road, having to look twice before shaking his head in disbelief. He climbed out of the vehicle, checking once more nothing was coming along the road, now aware of country lanes.

Scanning the road and running his hand across the surface for the second time that day, he swore, shaking his head, issuing aloud a serious profanity.

It was fair to say he wasn't happy and stomped back and forth, head down, staring at the road surface, rubbing his chin, cursing and swearing. Thinking.

Fuming, and visibly angry to anyone who may have seen him, which was no one, he returned to the Land Rover. He roared on through the woods and into Chris' property, ignoring the now mundane and boring sign, but intent on his mission. Sensing one of his leads was blown, he was only interested in speaking with the owner of Horsewater and also wanted to question the various women who hung around him, beginning to tire of the respectable, polite and gentle horsey fraternity in the area; longing to return to the drug-crazed yobs of the city. They seemed to be less dangerous and deceitful.

He raced through the woods, dirt spewing from the tyres, trying to contain his anger. As the Land Rover emerged from the woods, Burton had calmed down, but not by much, and eased up as he moved over to the parking area.

There appeared to be a number of vehicles already on the hard standing area, where it seemed everyone parked. Burton joined them, parking his Rover in a free slot, but deliberately didn't park it square, taking up two spaces.

It was good news for him, if the various vehicles were anything to judge. He appeared to have arrived at an opportune moment, when a number of people who kept their horses at Horsewater were present. Most likely one or two of them were the suspects he was looking to question. All going well, he'd take away one or two and charge them. The problem Burton had was he didn't have a clue who they were. Middle-aged women dressed in riding gear.

Worse still, to him all horses looked identical. Four legs. Brown. Usually. Except for the white ones. Or Black ones. Hairy. And so were the horse owners. Food went in one end; shit came out the other. As per the riders.

And they bit and kicked. And again, so did the horses.

His superiors had asked him to check out the riders and horses involved in the troubles, and try to make some arrests, or at least bring someone in for questioning. Some action was needed, or at least something seen to be done.
Burton now had to identify both horses and riders from fleeting glimpses, a vague recall of the day, and from a few press photos he'd been given.
Or find the stolen wool hat. That would be a key result. Crucial evidence.
He knew he was out of his depths, but he would try anyway.
Burton adjusted his trousers and tool belt, moving slowly away from his Rover, feeling like a Western Sheriff leaving his horse, as he scanned the yard area and stables, recalling the layout from previous visits. He noted the owner standing to his left, with the tall attractive woman close beside him.
A woman's head appeared over the tackroom door, glimpsed fleetingly by Burton, before vanishing and ducking back as she saw the policeman. Guilty.
He was about to proceed towards the Tackroom, and find the clearly guilty woman, when he was at once met by Chris Turner. Drifting towards him like mist, he was accompanied by the dangerous looking Doberman and woman walking close by his side. Apart from their heights, they looked like a couple.
Burton froze. He hated dogs. Especially evil looking ones. And their owners.
Chris noted the policeman's glance and so did Max. Chris smiled.
Max stood stock still, ears going back, lips rising. Breakfast.
Anna was beside Chris and he nodded to her. It was the only communication needed. Anna whistled at Max, who swung around to her side and she guided him with a finger towards the house, swiftly following on, letting him into the kitchen via the stable door. Closing the bottom section, Max stood up, front paws resting on the top edge of the door, watching keenly as Anna strolled back to join Chris. She had even impressed herself, suddenly feeling at home with the dog she'd once feared, and the quiet man she was getting to know.
Chris stared silently at the policeman, who in turn watched the woman's casual action with interest. It was clear the two were together or close and silently he was impressed with how they worked together. It was dangerous.
Chris looked at Burton, as did Anna as she stood alongside him.
"Yes?" Chris was as polite, welcoming and blunt as ever.
Anna tried to hide a smirk, now understanding him.
"The skid marks. They've gone!" Burton exclaimed.
Chris looked at the policeman as if he was mad.
"Gone? Skid marks? What are you talking about?"
"Yes! Your skid marks. They've gone," Burton replied.
"That's 'cos I use good washing powder."
"What?" Burton responded, confused. It wasn't too hard.
Anna lifted a hand to her face, instantly getting Chris' joke, even though she didn't understand fully the policeman's comment or apparent rage.
"My skid marks? Gone?" Chris seemed confused, looking at Anna. "I didn't know the police were inspecting people's laundry. That's quite sad, isn't it?"

Anna, a grin set upon her face, tried not to laugh, but a giggle escaped her mouth, followed by a loud chuckle. She clung onto Chris' arm for support.
Burton was now totally confused, angry and shook his head, seriously disliking the pair clearly making fun of him, both about to laugh loudly.
However, he still didn't understand the point of their joke.
"What the hell are you talking about and why the hell are you here? This is private property. Do you have a warrant? What the hell do you want?"
Chris was clearly not happy and went instantly on the attack. He glanced towards the tackroom, knowing who was inside. And it meant trouble.
Burton began to recover his composure and thoughts, his anger controlled.
"Skid marks," Burton repeated. "You recall before Christmas you almost ran me over. There were skid marks by your entrance. I was examining them."
Chris looked at the policeman as if confused. Anna stood silently beside him, genuinely unaware of everything knowing nothing about them. No one did.
"Oh them!" Chris finally remembered, as if the thoughts were miles away.
"Skid marks. So what? Look on the roads, you'll find them everywhere."
"But I thought those were linked to the death of those three local lads."
Anna flushed, suddenly understanding their importance. She turned her head momentarily toward Chris, but noted he remained impassive, simply staring.
"And? I still don't get why you've raced onto my property, uninvited, screaming 'Skid Marks! Gone!' What exactly is your problem?"
Anna was amazed at how rude and blunt Chris was to a figure she'd been told to respect and obey. He seemed to be completely indifferent to a person, supposedly of power, and enjoyed openly baiting them. In a way she also respected him for his hidden strength. Subconsciously she moved closer to him, Burton noting the couple almost standing shoulder to shoulder.
"The tyre marks on the road we spoke about have gone," Burton finally explained in clear English. "Someone's removed them. On purpose."
Chris stared coldly at the policeman. Anna turned her head, looking first at Chris, then the policeman, scanning the two men, waiting for the next move.
"Diesel spillage." Chris announced, without any follow up.
"Diesel spillage?" Burton screwed his piggy face up, wanting more details and information, now even more confused. "What do you mean?"
"Tractor. Over Christmas. Had a fuel tank rupture outside my entrance, so I heard. Spilt diesel everywhere. Messy. The driver cleaned it up, I think."
Burton stared silently, but listened and maybe believed. But didn't want to.
"The guy cleared up what he could, so the tarmac wouldn't rot away with the diesel eating at the surface. As it does. He may have burnt it off or used a detergent. Or both. Probably took away those tyre marks you refer to."
Burton listened to the explanation, it sounding like plausible bullshit. But his evidence was gone. "Who was the tractor driver? Do you know him?"
"No. Something I heard from someone passing by. I was out. I saw nothing. Just something someone else told me. Maybe a contractor. Does it matter?"

Burton stared at the horseman, cursing the clever, cocky bastard. His eyes flitted to the stunning beauty who stood silently at his side. What a dangerous pair those two could be. He was instantly jealous and knew he'd been beaten, for now. But he still had a possible tyre mark lead with Harrison.

He gazed at the odd couple, who silently regarded him, their looks almost angelic. Almost. But he didn't trust them. Maybe the horseman was innocent.

"Okay, we'll leave the skid marks for now. That can be pursued later. I have another line of enquiry and other serious matters to address. Very serious matters you are aware of. Those of assault and theft. Hence why I'm here."

Chris looked impassive, but Anna's face flushed red again, feeling worried.

She instinctively looked towards the tackroom, but wished she hadn't, as the policeman caught her fleeting glance. His face broke into a sickly smile.

He turned his head to look towards the tackroom, still sure his suspect or suspects were possibly inside, maybe hiding. In that fleeting second, as Burton looked away, Chris put a finger to his lips. Anna nodded, trying not to smile, as she began to fully understand Chris and his resolute and tough nature.

Burton turned to face the now expressionless couple, the woman strikingly beautiful, but notably taller than the man beside her, the pair standing silent.

Burton instantly felt unsure, the woman appearing to take on the arrogant and cold aspects of the horseman beside her. They made a chilling couple.

"I was knocked over by your horse, you may recall," Burton begun rather pompously, seeing the pair wait for him to speak. "I fully understand that can be classed as an accident. These things happen and it was chaotic. So I'll not proceed any further with that incident nor look to charge either of you."

Chris almost chuckled, but kept a straight, poker face. Anna copied him, enjoying Chris' cool and calm nature, but also wanted to laugh too.

"However, two woman, who I had noted were in your company, viciously attacked a woman. Then stole her hat. I intend to identify these women, question them, and possibly issue charges. Can you tell me their names?"

Anna froze, knowing he meant Julie and Tracey. Who else?

For the first time Anna's coolness melted and she looked towards Chris for guidance. It wasn't missed by Burton. Chris remained impassive and calm.

"Do you know who they were?" Burton spoke again, turned direct to Anna.

"Sorry, but I don't know your name," he added in an attempt to be polite.

"This is Lady Melrose," Chris instantly replied for her. "Anastasia Melrose."

Anna almost choked, but lifted her hand, feigning a cough, hiding a smirk.

"She is my house guest and I doubt members of the Royal family would appreciate her name being mentioned in public or police enquiries concerning any allegations with no evidence. Neither would your Chief Constable, who knows her family very well. You can call him if you want. But I suggest you keep her out of this, unless you want to cause real trouble. Lets say no more."

Chris stood solid and impassive, Burton scanning his face for any emotion, but noted only disdain and disgust. Lady Melrose simply blushed a bright red.

Burton looked at Anna, wondering who the hell she was, and what circles these horsey people moved in, and why they were seemingly above the law. He did not want to cause trouble with his superiors or any links with royalty. Word around the locker rooms and canteens was that The Chief Constable was not one to be messed with. A pompous Pratt, but well connected.

"However, I recall the women you're enquiring about," Chris continued in a controlling and strong manner. "Very common. Not part of our hunt."

Anna noticed Chris' tone had changed, seemingly growing posher, and he could almost pass off as Lord Melrose, if he wanted. She wished.

Burton listened and squinted, now totally out of his depth and baffled.

"Let me explain," began Chris. "The Boxing Day hunt meet is a long-held traditional, and a lot of people who ride simply turn up on the day to maintain the tradition and enjoy the atmosphere. You were there and I'm sure could appreciate the buzz of the crowd. However, many are not part of any official hunt, especially ours. They pay a 'Cap' fee, and simply to turn up for the day."

Burton listened, still unsure, but already guessing where this was going.

"The two women, of whom I believe you speak, had turned up for the day. We have no idea who they were. Very common and unruly. I think our Field Master had already had words with them. I think they came from Essex. That area is full of common, ignorant people. As I'm sure you are aware."

Chris paused, waiting for the response he knew would come. Anna was dumbstruck and didn't know if to laugh, cry, run away, or wait for the fight to break out. Inwardly she cringed, but was also beginning to understand Chris.

Burton absorbed everything, then realising what he'd said, glared coldly at the horseman, unsure if he'd ever mentioned he came from Essex, although his accent was obvious. He was about to comment that he also came from that fine county, but paused, not wanting to admit such a sin and similarity. He did however want to punch the horseman, but Lady Melrose was watching.

"Unfortunately I've no idea who those disreputable women were. Maybe they came from Suffolk. Even worse than Essex, if that's possible. Those people can barely speak, and simply communicate with grunts. Or so I've heard. The women were very common and one swore like a trooper."

"Yes, I heard her swear too," added Anna, speaking like Lady Melrose would, and enjoying the moment. "Most disgusting language. Common cow!"

Grin stifled, an image of Tracey flashed before her. Chris smirked too.

Burton flicked his head from Chris to Anna then back. 'Was this real?'

"I doubt our Hunt Secretary would know either. Did I mention she's a good friend of your Chief Constable too? Everyone seems to know him. He used to hunt a few years back I recall. Anyway I'm drifting off," Chris muttered.

"Our hunt is half convinced those woman you speak of may have been sent down by the person who organised the trouble. You've heard a lot of it was staged? A set up. Organised by a professional photographer I understand."

Burton took everything in, but still wasn't sure it was all real.

Anna had never heard Chris speak so much, or in such a manner, and stood silently taking in his every word, hoping she, Lady Melrose, wasn't to be asked any questions. Chris seemed to have it sorted. Besides, she was a 'Lady.'

Burton stared at the horseman, totally unsure how to react. Word had gone around the station and at briefings that some of the antis were paid yobs, hired by the person who'd taken the photos, simply to get a special scoop. Steve Harrison had repeated this point a short while ago. Maybe it was true.

Silently Burton was beginning to agree with the horseman and felt his balloon was slowly deflating. But he still had some air left. He pumped it up.

"I fully appreciate what you've said," Burton spoke, looking at the tackroom. "And fully understand your hunt's concerns, but would you mind if I took a look over there? I don't wish to dispute what you've said, but I thought I saw someone hiding over there. Suspicious. I take it you've nothing to hide?"

The comment was a deliberately loaded question and Chris knew the trick and how best to answer. He paused momentarily, before replying.

"The only thing I have to hide from you is the truth, along with that stolen gold bullion. Damn! I've been caught out. Curses! It's a far cop guv'nor!"

Burton paused, taking in the joke, initially unsure how to reply and so simply chuckled, beginning to slowly understand the horseman's dark, cruel humour.

But he also still wanted to punch him. Hard. And repeatedly.

He turned and without another word headed toward the tackroom.

Anna froze, grimacing, glancing towards Chris, watching the policeman walk straight towards the tackroom. She knew who was hiding within.

And there was only one-way in and out.

Other than straight to prison. Or at least first via a Police Station.

The tackroom doorway, to which P.C. Burton advanced towards, would very quickly have a policeman entering. For better or for worse.

Then he'd meet two foul-mouthed aggressive commoners.

Maybe even thieves. Definitely yobs.

Possibly originating from Essex or Suffolk.

Or maybe he'd just meet Julie and Tracey. From Norfolk.

Chapter 96

All hope abandon, ye who enter here.

Inferno - Dante Alighieri

"Aargh!" A woman's screech rang out from the tackroom.

Burton instinctively stepped back from the tackroom door and looked inside, to see a red-faced woman glaring at him and yelling with venom.

"What do you want? I'm changing. Get out you pervert! Call the police!"

Chris, standing a few yards back from the tackroom door, grinned upon seeing Carol shouting at the policeman, slipping on a sweatshirt. Anna looked at him, a puzzled expression upon her face, simply to see Chris smile back.

Burton glanced past the short plump, much-older woman heartedly berating him. He knew instantly she was not one of the women he was looking for; as he recalled from the press photos he'd seen and also his fleeting memory.

Those women were young, slim, and one was quite attractive.

The screaming banshee before him had no such attributes. Definitely not.

"I do apologise madam," Burton announced in his best diplomatic voice. "But I need to look inside here please. If it's okay with yourself? Please dress yourself first. When you're ready. I'll wait here and turn around. I am Sorry."

Chris stood openly grinning, the smirk dropping when Burton turned swiftly around and looked out of the door to see him and Lady Melrose. Anna was not so quick, nor so well controlled, and a titter burst from her grinning face.

Burton blossomed, knowing he was being made to look a fool. Even if he was, he was determined to see who else was inside, sure someone was hiding.

"Can I come inside yet please madam? I'll be quick. Police business. Urgent."

"Okay, if you must! Seeing you're a policeman." Carol tutted loudly, to add effect at her rude interruption and disruption. "I know the Chief Constable, by the way. Dined with him only last week. Do you know him? Nice chap."

Burton sighed, shaking his head. He didn't know him, but felt he might.

"You really should knock or ask before you enter. I could have been naked. Or doing something else. Very rude. Just think of that!" Carol rebuked coldly.

Burton looked at the woman before him, silently agreeing.

The shock of seeing her naked would indeed have been traumatic.

For both parties. Probably more so for Burton.

They'd have had to call out Paramedics to revive him.

It would be a close call. Could even be fatal. Or worse.

Carol huffed and puffed and waddled out the tackroom, muttering inaudible profanities towards Chris and Anna as she wandered past. Burton didn't miss the opportunity to move, and so strode straight inside the dimly lit room.

He was on a mission, feeling like Indiana Jones. Without the whip.

One small multi-framed window provided natural light and ventilation. Or it could have if it would ever open. However, the vent of the window was painted shut, and had been for years. Many. The mass of cobwebs covering the semi-opaque glass and painted bars to the small window helped obscure what poor and limited December light flowed through into the gloomy room.

A couple of un-shaded old-style low wattage light bulbs hung down, partially illuminated the small stuffy room. The first thing that hit Burton was the smell. Maybe that should have been stench. Unbearable. If he had a knife he could probably have cut his way through the heavy maliferous odour.

Burton inhaled, but wished he hadn't, as the disgusting scents entered his nostrils. They appeared to be a combination of coffee, body odour, flatulence, and unknown animal sweat. It seemed obvious the animal stench was from horses, although taking into consideration the woman who'd just left the room, Burton was unsure. He hoped it wasn't all simply from her. Could be.

His piggy, yet well-trained eyes, scanned the interior. As he'd thought, there was only one door in and out of the low-ceiling, wooden, decidedly stuffy and claustrophobic room; which was part of a barn, various old stables or a store. That said, it was surprising large, seemingly drifting off into some darkened recesses at the back, where Burton sensed even brave spiders dare not tread.

Near to the window ran a section of kitchen, comprising of a stainless steel sink, covered in unknown, and best not-known, stains. The couple of old kitchen units, probably dating back thirty years or older, had baler-twine pulls for the drawer handles. Beside it stood a pine table, which wouldn't be out of place in a Sixties drama, set with a number of odd and random rickety chairs.

Upon the aged chairs were various discarded garments, either lying on the seats or hung over the backs. Upon the small table sat a teapot, kept warm by a ghastly woollen tea cosy, and about which sat a number of teacups. Burton stepped forward a stride, noting three cups, all of which were partially filled with some brown liquid. He wasn't brave enough to determine what the foul liquid was, but placed the back of his hand upon one of the mugs. Warm.

He glanced at the tea cosy covered kettle, wondering who would place such a foul looking and disgusting item onto something you prepared drink from. He shuddered at the sight of the filth and reeled at the stench these horsey people all appeared to live in, let alone enjoy. It was almost choking. And they all sat in here and drank tea? From that disgusting thing? He shuddered.

The longer he remained in the oppressive room, the more the heavy stench seemed to envelope him. He felt as if the odour was crawling into the fabric of his clothing and maybe into his skin. The smell was unique. It could not be healthy, the odour distinctly heavy. He felt he should have brought a Geiger Counter or similar device to check the amount of time it was healthy to be exposed to such evil stench. He'd probably already exceed any healthy dose.

The scent of damp leather and wet dog now drifted into his nostrils. Very damp dog. Maybe Werewolf. Wet Werewolf. The smell almost made him gag.

Moving forward, one step at a time, he cautiously headed towards the rear area of the room. Here he could make out a number of saddles, perched upon metal-framed racks, and from which hung beneath bridles and other black and brown leather items. He could only image what they used these items for. But he could see no people. Or Horsey Life-forms. The room was empty.

He scanned deeper, and towards the back he could make a row of what he knew to be horse rugs, hanging down from metal runners, either mounted on the wall or handing from the ceiling. Also scattered about were numerous other rugs, and a mix of large, old-style Steamer Trunks around these were more numerous rugs and brightly coloured boxes, crammed full with loads of varying brushes, of equally dazzling colours. 'Who needs so many brushes?'

The smell in this area was almost unbearable. The stench emitting from the damp rugs hanging in the corner area would probably make cheese curdle. Burton doubted any human being, including those foul Horsey people, could survive in such a harsh environment for long. A bit like Mars. Or worse.

Burton was convinced he could almost see the odour crawl across the floor, like some malevolent spirit creeping towards him; the foul vaporous arms seemingly reaching out to envelope, consume and then slowly devour him.

He'd had enough and swiftly left the tackroom, convinced no one other the short woman had been in the room, and obviously her he'd seen. Where anyone else possibly may be he'd have to ask the obnoxious horseman or posh Lady Melrose. Perhaps the evil smell inside, conditions and prolonged contamination within the tackroom had affected the short woman, stunting growth and the such-like. Maybe The Environment Agency should be called.

Burton emerged from the tackroom like Howard Carter leaving King Tutankhamun's tomb, but without the smile. He just hoped the place didn't contain a curse, although sadly it contained no treasure either. No stolen hat.

"Did you find what you were looking for?" Chris enquired, his tone blunt and non-supportive. Lady Melrose stared in a cold manner, arms folded.

"No, but thank you for letting me look." Burton inhaled deeply, glad to breath oxygen, sure his red blood count level had been drastically effected by the few minutes he'd spent in the tackroom. Maybe he needed to decompress.

"How on earth do you put up with that horrendous smell?" Burton's grim face flicked from the horseman to the rather grand-looking Lady Melrose.

"What smell?" Chris shook his head and turned to Anna. She looked equally confused and shrugged her shoulders, shaking her elegant almost Royal head.

"I think Carol bought a new brand of coffee. Peruvian Yak Droppings, or so I believe. That is quite pungent." Chris began to explain. Anna nodded too.

Burton shook his head, no longer sure what to say or do, but knowing he'd had enough of this pair. He had someone else to speak to, but doubted he'd get much joy from them either, convinced all horsey people and farmers he'd recently met lived within some parallel universe, devoid of all normal human thoughts, emotions, and natural senses. They were like animals. But worse.

"I'll be in touch if the CPS want to proceed matters, but that won't be until the New Year. If you hear anything about those two common, abusive women who attacked the lady and stole her valuable hat, please let me know."

Chris and Lady Melrose both nodded eagerly, looking like well-disciplined lap-dogs, seemingly always keen to help their local police or owner. But not.

Anna was beginning to understand Chris much better, and also sympathise.

"I imagine they're long gone and were all part of the whole set-up, as I've mentioned. Hussy's!" Chris reinforced the point. "They did look common."

"Very common," Lady Melrose added, almost lifting her regal nose in the air. "Especially the one on that awful coloured horse. Like you see in Westerns. She was common too. And the foul-mouthed whore beside was even worse!"

Chris almost lost the plot and wanted to laugh out loud, but held it together.

"We do have two other ladies who are here today, just in case you wondered about all the parked cars. But they've gone out riding. They weren't out on Boxing Day. Vegans. You know the sort. Won't step on an animal's shadow."

Anna shuffled up to Chris, trying not to laugh, loving his dark humour and loyalty to his ladies. She looped her arm through his. Chris didn't move.

Burton stared solemnly at the pair, knew he had nothing to say, his bubble burst. With a nod, he headed away from the stinking pit and the cocky couple.

The pair watched the policeman silently wander back up the yard towards his Land Rover, a figure of dejection and defeat. But neither trusted him, waiting for him to turn around any second like the famous TV detective Colombo, hand to head, cigar in hand and then calmly state: 'Just one more thing.'

But he didn't. Burton was no Colombo. Burton was Burton.

The Land Rover vanished from sight, disappearing from view and consumed by the woods, before the pair turned around to look towards the tackroom. Only then did Anna remove her arm from Chris, somewhat reluctantly.

The pair smiled broadly as after a few moments Julie and Tracey emerged from the tackroom, giggling loudly, being accompanied by a equally chuckling Carol, who'd gone in to tell them the coast was clear. She had a wide grin too.

"Thanks Carol. We owe you! Great acting by the way. An Oscar, maybe." Tracey called, with a thumb's up, smiling widely. "That was such fun!"

"I thought he had us when he walked over towards the rugs," Julie added. "We were hiding under them. I could see his big black boots slowly moving towards us, but he didn't dare come any closer, which was a good thing."

"I think the smell put him off," Tracey added.

"What smell?" Julie asked. "Do you mean Carol's coffee?"

The whole group laughed loudly in the middle of the yard, knowing the firm bond between them had grown even stronger.

Chapter 97

Unbidden guests. Are often welcomest when they are gone.

Henry VI Part 1 - Shakespeare

Standing alone inside the Flesh house, Martin held the glass jam jar up to the light. A glint reflected onto his face as he stared at the contents within.

Teeth. Seventy-two.

He was sure of the number. He'd counted them five times.

Just to be sure.

Seventy-two teeth.

All human. In all shapes and sizes. Four types. The correct mix.

He'd removed them from the incinerator, after re-igniting it, burning to ash what was left of what he'd found inside. Not a good find.

Two heads. Usually better than one. But not on this occasion.

The teeth confirmed the chilling thought. Reggie's visit, and his poor excuse to get him to visit the equally conspiring Lord Burlingham, had become clear. It was fake. Set-up. A foul deed to get him away from The Kennels. Bastard!

It seemed Reggie had his own grim disposal to undertake.

Someone had to disappear. Quickly. And so they had. For good. Almost.

But who?

And was Reggie's brutal task for himself, or was it for his long-term friend and fellow Mason, Bertie? It mattered.

A number of important people were missing.

And missing their heads too it seemed.

So whose heads were they? Martin couldn't tell, but could guess.

All key features had gone; the scorched remains merely hairless heads with dark-brown, charred skin stretched across, like sunburnt ancient leather. All soft tissue and any firm features destroyed. The noses burnt away, revealing only grim darkened cavities. Black, hollow sockets, the melted eyes gone, had momentarily stared at Martin. He'd gazed in terror at the horrific sight, before wasting no time to examine in detail the contents of the incinerator. He'd simply slammed the door shut, reconnected a fresh gas cylinder, turned the valve on and re-ignited the furnace. Set on full. Burn it all. No evidence.

After an hour of intense burning, then allowing time to cool down, with a sense of gloomy apprehension he'd opened the incinerator door. Cautiously, half opening the door, fearing what he might find, he'd peered inside.

The heads had gone. No solid form or shape remained, only tiny bits. He pulled the door open fully, to see only a pile of charred teeth remaining, sitting in the bottom tray of the fireclay interior, along with a pile of fine grey ash, and a few small pieces of scorched bone; possible cheek bones or skull.

Unless a very high temperature is used, the hard enamel on teeth, and some larger fragments of skull bone, often resist full burning. Martin knew what most normal people didn't. When bodies are cremated at modern funeral crematorium, the teeth and other larger bone fragment of bodies are often left behind after the main flesh and soft tissue have long since been incinerated. These harder, and more fire-resistant bodily remains are removed from the cremation chamber once cooled and then placed within a grinding machine called a Cremulator. Here they are ground to a very fine dust, before being returned to the main pile of ashes from the body, to then be placed within a fancy urn, and then returned to the grieving parties to cherish or scatter.

No one wants to be freely scattering Great-Aunt Edna's precious ashes onto the neatly trimmed lawns beside her favourite duck pond, only to be left at the bottom with a handful of charred teeth and an assortment of various burnt bone fragments. The wonderfully named Cremulator solves it all.

Thus, after re-burning Sarah's head, and whoever else had joined her for one final journey to hell in the incinerator, following Reggie's mysterious visit, Martin had scraped out the remains and spread it all onto a large steel tray.

But what he'd found in the ash confused him further. What was going on?

He wished now he'd been less hasty re-igniting the furnace. But he hadn't.

The average adult had twenty-eight teeth, and as maturing, gained up to four wisdom teeth. That made a maximum of thirty-two. But not everyone had wisdom teeth, and most people lost teeth, either through decay, damage or from removal by dentists to create mouth space as they went through life.

So unless Sarah had teeth like a shark, set in rows of three, and which continuously renewed, there was something wrong with what he'd found.

Martin had too many teeth.

Seventy-two.

He'd removed seventy-two teeth from the incinerator.

And they were all human.

He was sure of that, knowing the incinerator was clean beforehand.

If Sarah's head had been joined in the incinerator by just one other, to explain the two part-burnt heads he'd found upon his return, then that would have resulted in around fifty to sixty teeth. But he hadn't.

Martin had too many teeth. Seventy-two.

The number didn't add up. It could only mean one thing.

Three heads. It was the only answer.

'Three heads are better than one.'

Martin almost wanted to smile at the joke. But didn't. This was serious.

Whose heads were the others? And what'd happened to Sarah's?

He'd checked the teeth, and as best as he could, placed them into the four varying teeth types. He had eleven canines and twenty incisors and a mix of molars. Even with a few key teeth missing it definitely pointed to three heads.

Three human heads. Sarah's head. Plus two more. Whose?

Martin was confused, his pulse racing and crazy thoughts in a whirl.

Had Sarah's head burnt completely, and when Reggie had come around he'd quickly put two fresh heads in the 'empty' incinerator whilst he was away at Bertie's, but the gas then ran out?' Martin considered the thought. Seriously.

Hence why when he'd returned from Bertie' he found two partially burnt heads inside the incinerator and empty gas tank. Sarah's was already ash and burnt through and the incinerator timer switched it off. Thus, Reggie would have seen only ash as he'd placed his heads inside, as Sarah's was burnt.

It was some relief for him knowing Reggie probably didn't know about his head, Sarah's head. But the thought that Reggie had tried to burn two heads himself chilled Martin, and he could only guess whose heads had been burnt.

But were the victims linked to Reggie or Bertie? Or maybe both?

The fact Reggie had been so cruel and callous worried Martin. He knew his boss was ruthless; but this displayed him as a blatant killer. If not, he was assisting Bertie to cover up his own evil crime. And thus was equally as evil.

Not good. Potentially two evil killers. That was worse.

But then who was he to judge, knowing what he'd done?

Martin's stressful pondering ceased abruptly upon hearing the sound of a vehicle approach, added by the crunch of gravel outside.

His stress now changed to worry. Not a good swap.

Someone had arrived at The Kennels. Who? Reggie? He hoped not.

What the hell would he say? 'Oh, just to let you know Boss, your heads have been burnt. All done. Would you like the teeth back?'

He cocked his head and realised it wasn't a V8 engine, such as Reggie drove.

Adrenaline flooded as he realised he had visitors.

Unwelcome visitors. But who? And why? Few ever came, other than Reggie.

Jar full of teeth in hand, he weaved about within the small room, dodging from one place to the other, for once unsure what to do, and where to place the damning item. Upon the sound of the small diesel engine dying and door slamming he hurriedly placed the jar upon a shelf, the dull pieces of charred enamel placed beside a used tin of black paint and bag of wire wool.

Brushing down his green overalls, glancing around to check everything was in place, he dashed into the alleyway to warmly great his unexpected guest.

Fake smile ready and perfectly set. Who was it?

Reggie perhaps. Or maybe Bertie. Maybe both. No!

Hopefully not. That wouldn't be good. That'd be bad. Very bad.

Could he become the fourth head? Maybe.

Martin turned to warmly greet his unknown visitor.

A policeman stood before him.

Martin froze, his stressed face draining white.

The huntsman's smile dropped, along with his jaw.

P.C. Burton regarded the startled man, recognising guilt.

Now it was he who smiled. He beamed widely.

The face of the man before him resembled a naughty child. A very naughty child. One who'd been caught with chocolate on lips and fingers covered in crumbs, rapidly dropping the cookie jar. Then pleading: 'Not me! Honest.'

Maybe it was a jam jar. Full of human teeth. Three sets. 'Not me!'

Burton grinned, wondering what crime he'd caught the man before him undertaking. From the man's immediate change of skin tone and furtive eye movements, it was obvious he'd been doing something he shouldn't; rather than the usual shock of seeing a copper most displayed. It was different.

The man's face indicated a mix of horror and guilt. Why?

Inwardly Burton smiled, but maintained a poker-face, as he regarded the man before him, who stood stock still, frozen in time. Gazing past him, with a thousand-yard stare, the man looked as if he was about to flee. But why?

Maybe Martin was contemplating that option. And it was an option.

However, the sudden howling of hounds, mixed with loud barking coming from alongside where Burton stood made him flinch, swiftly turn around and edge sideways along the alley, being overly cautious. His natural dislike of dogs returned and dissolved his cocky police thoughts. He'd suddenly lost his advantage, eyes flicking cautiously towards the sound of the wailing canines.

Martin saw the policeman nervously look towards the hounds, enabling him to regain his composure, knowing his guilt-ridden white face was now flushing red, fully aware the policeman had noticed all of his facial actions.

"Hello, how can I help? I'm a bit busy. Flustered." Martin enquired, trying best to sound genuine, moving toward the now wary policeman. Burton stepped towards him, but turned his head back to the sound of the hounds in the yard beside him, unsure if they were loose and could maybe attack him.

Martin noted the caution and stepped forward, sensing an advantage. He furtively glanced up the alley, pleasantly noting the singular police Land Rover parked outside. No Swat teams seemed poised, about to pour in behind, fully armed and ready to arrest him. Or so Martin hoped. He didn't trust them.

He breathed, now recognising the policeman he'd previously met.

"Hello, I'm P.C. Burton, but we've met before," he announced, looking carefully towards the Drawing Yard, as if a horde of rampaging hounds would attack him. Maybe they would. Maybe they could. Maybe they should.

"I wasn't sure if your dogs were loose. You can't be too careful, you know," he added, as if to cover up his nervousness. "I'm not a dog person. More cats. Normal cats. Not tigers or lions. But hopefully you don't have any of them."

Martin seized the advantage. "Hounds. They're hounds, not dogs."

"Hounds?" Burton looked puzzled, glancing at the large pack of dogs.

"They're Harriers actually, to be totally correct. A small form of Foxhound. They hunt hares. Still a canine that'll happily eat you! Very happily!"

Martin was back on his own turf and stepped toward the policeman, his confidence returning, keen to wash away any signs of guilt from his mind and face and regain his usual composure. Especially when talking about hounds.

Burton watched Martin move towards the metal railings of the yard, seeing the hounds rush over, their barks and howls vanishing, replaced by gentle and subservient whines. Burton followed, curiosity taking over, and confidence growing. He watched a mass of multi-coloured hounds dash across the yard and towards the railings to greet Martin; tails all wagging, noses sniffing.

"They sound bad and look worse than they are. Really they're like kittens. Well, sort of. Unless you're a hare. Then they're not, and they'll eat you!"

Burton looked shocked, but noted Martin's playful nature and smiled, seeing him place his hand through the railings. Martin in turn felt more confident, but still wondered what the policeman wanted by turning up unexpected, instinctively never trusting them, knowing he wanted something. What?

Burton turned to face the array of excitable hounds, suddenly seeing their appeal as they leapt up to the front wall, standing on their hind legs, keen for attention. Burton watched the man beside him put his hand through the railings and rub the heads of the hounds, and so in turn, now confident, placed his hands through the bars, to have his fingers licked. He smiled.

"I'll show you them properly if you like. I think you missed them last time you called. I was excising the pack and passed you as I returned. You spoke with my boss, Mister Hornchurch. I was just coming back as I recall."

Burton nodded, recalling the day, it being one of his many early calls to meet and greet the 'Locals.' He'd then reached the opinion that most 'Locals' were ignorant, awkward, crooked bastards. Those that weren't were even worse.

Burton cautiously waved a hand through the bars and was greeted by a series of damp noses, sniffing and licking his welcoming hand. Martin looked warily out the corner of his eye and across the yard, noticing the two main older hounds, Maverick and Mayhem were watching him intently, eyes meeting.

Silent damning secrets seemingly passed between them. Dark secrets.

His eyes frantically scanned the yard floor, just in case a rogue orange toenail should reappear, or maybe a piece of tattooed foot with neat ankle appear.

Martin felt his face flush and removed his hand. He turned to face the policeman, keen to learn the reason for his visit. Burton caught his look and turned, also removing his hand and wiped it on the side of his black jacket.

"The main reason I've called in today is to see if you have anything to add concerning the incident on Boxing Day. I'm still collating information."

Burton's announcement was both welcome, but also annoying. Inwardly Martin sighed, now understanding the reason for the visit, but still distrusted the policeman. He stood passively and allowed the policeman to continue speaking, his mind drifting, with thoughts of heads reappearing. Three.

Maybe he could add a fourth, he casually considered. It was a big head.

"It seems the person you were alleged to assault with a whip has not come forth. Not unlike many of the other people involved on the Anti side. He's vanished. As have all his mates. That makes a prosecution hard."

The policeman looked at the Huntsman. He saw no emotion.

Martin still did not reply, neither vocally nor with facial expressions. He was too wise to make any comment. Burton noted the cold and silent response.

'This man was cool and was waiting for more. Maybe he was too cool.'

"There were several witnesses, mostly locally based antis. Some claim they saw you attack one of the more vocal hunt saboteurs with a whip, but no one has made a direct claim of assault against you. Thus, there is no real case."

"Possibly because it was a set-up." Martin finally spoke. "It was all rigged."

Burton tilted his head, waiting for more, the reply being a common response he'd heard from many within The Hunt, but was now one he was beginning to believe and understand with the other details he had. Martin continued.

"The main people involved were sent in to stir up trouble. A newspaper reporter. The man with the big camera." Martin paused, awaiting a response.

Burton stood impassive. He'd heard the rumours and seen the photos in the papers, much to the amusement of many at the police station. It was also the same response he'd received from Steve Harrison and from Turner. He was inclined to agree with them all, even if reluctantly. He'd heard various reports and also seen the photographs. Especially the one with him fighting the pompous Anti whom he'd punched in the Knackers. That was a good shot.

One part image, set in a photomontage, and which brought joy to the station; so much so it'd been pinned up, caught Burton being hit by a sign-wielding woman, wearing a ghastly tea cosy style hat. Burton hadn't been amused.

The image sparked something in his head. Tea-cosy Hat. Tea Cosy?

Any thought or image recall was washed from his mind as Martin spoke.

"This yob waded in and started kicking my hounds. They're very precious to me. I merely defended them, as anyone would. To me, all of these hounds are like my children. My family. And so I protect them accordingly. Always will."

Martin paused, glancing at the hounds, noting Maverick and Mayhem now standing proud at the railings. He lovingly rubbed their heads and ears, noting the policeman's attention, hoping the comment had found a home. It had.

"However, whipping someone when seated on a horse is excessive, wouldn't you say? Criminal assault." Burton was on home ground and loved it.

"Perhaps we'd like to counter-claim for animal cruelty. Also, the anti's attacked numerous members of the hunt. We have many more witnesses. I believe you were even attacked yourself. Have you charged that assailant?"

Burton didn't respond, nor would he. He knew the conversation was going nowhere and that the CPS most likely wouldn't push matters any further either and it was all a paperwork exercise. But he still wanted to get a feel for the people he knew he'd be dealing with for some time, not that that thought pleased him. He'd also heard rumours someone key within the hunt knew a circuit judge, who in turn knew the Police Commissioner. That was without the Chief Constable being good friends. Seemingly to everyone. Not good.

Lodges and back scratching. It was all far too corrupt. Even for the police.

"Well, for now, I need to inform you that unless we get more information, it's unlikely we'll proceed further. However, things could change if we get any repeat of such actions in the future or if fresh evidence arises. You could say the incident has been noted for now. A sort of 'Yellow Card' warning."

Martin stood silent, a wave of relief flowing through, although truthfully he wasn't bothered. Reggie had spoken with him after the event and told him what he knew, and also that he'd put out some 'feelers' with a few people he knew in high places. Very high. Reggie had contacts. So did others.

Martin nodded silently, as the only form of thank you or acknowledgement the policeman was going to get. He then turned his attention back to the hounds. Burton also turned, keen to quell his fear and confidently placed his hand back through the railings to rub the heads of the eager hounds.

Maverick and Mayhem now stood before him.

They gazed up fondly at the visitor.

Their damp muzzles rubbed against the policeman's caressing hand.

Wet noses and probing tongues caused Burton to smile.

He stroked the hound's faces, all enjoying the attention.

Burton looked towards Martin, a male bond building.

Then Maverick bit him.

Chapter 98

Dogs never bite me. Just humans.

Marilyn Monroe

Burton swore, rapidly retracting his hand, rapping the knuckles on the rough, black-painted bars of the railings to make things worse. He glanced fleetingly at the hound, his hand, then Martin. His cold cursing glare spoke volumes.

Martin glared at the hound, eyes wide in horror, knowing exactly what had happened. Maverick's look at his owner was nonchalant, almost teasing and devious; if hounds could display such emotions. Martin immediately switched his attention to the policeman, looking down at his hand. A minor nip.

Burton held out the limb, regarding the small cut on the top, as Martin loudly rebuked the hounds, waving a hand at them to get down from the railings, genuine concern in his expression, although he knew the hounds understood.

He looked closer at the policeman's hand, relieved to see only a tiny triangle of flesh standing proud on the back of his hand, but with a small line of red fluid beginning to seep from the small wound. A definite bite. Not good.

Martin's face flushed as red as the policeman's blood, but he hid it well.

"The bastard bit me!" Burton exclaimed, half in surprise and half in anger. He looked towards the hounds, moving back from the railings, his confidence with dogs back to zero. He scanned the almost smiling faces of the multitude of hounds, all looking similar, unable to tell which evil creature had nipped him. The pack scurried about together within the yard following Martin's rebuke; almost like giggling, naughty children, but none admitting any blame.

But Martin knew the culprit and glared at the seemingly proud hound.

"I'm really sorry. They don't usually bite. Maybe just a playful nip. They will sometimes do that. Are you sure you didn't catch your hand on the railings as you pulled back?" Once Martin had made that comment he knew it sounded too defensive and that they both knew what had really happened.

"The bloody thing bit me," Burton repeated, glaring at Martin, waving his hand as evidence, with a small line of red flowing from the open flap of skin. Martin was sure the policeman had suffered worse injuries in his life before.

If he continued to berate any louder, he certainly would. Much worse.

Martin's glowing face spoke volumes as he viewed the small, but obvious puncture wound. Luckily for both parties the cut was minor, and he doubted the policeman would bleed out before him because of the small nick, which would no doubt cease flowing in a few minutes and quickly heal.

"I do apologise if a hound did nip you. Must be over-excitement. They don't usually bite. They're very gentle and even happily greet children. We take them to county shows. The kids love to see and fuss them. No problems."

Martin's genuinely sincere face and apology were enough for Burton, along with the bravado he always tried to display, not wanting to show any fear of the hounds or worries over such a minor wound. He'd had worse, hadn't he? He extended the hand towards Martin again, to show proof of the crime.

A small flap of skin on the top of the policeman's fat hand stood erect, a small blob of blood at the base. It was hardly major arterial bleeding, resulting in the policeman's immanent death within three minutes if not stopped.

But he understood. It was the principle. Hounds didn't bite people.

Usually.

That said, hounds didn't eat people either.

Usually.

But it seemed the Shoteton pack did.

Occasionally.

Quite frequently it now seemed.

Martin swallowed, fearing what the policeman might think, or worse, surmise about the ever-hungry hounds. He leant forward to look at the out-stretched hand and knew he should at least show some concern, even if it was feigned.

Secretly he wanted nothing more welcome, other than for the policeman to leave at once, bleeding to death or not. Maybe letting him bleed to death would have been beneficial to all and given the hounds another hearty meal.

There was clearly a lot of meat on that policeman. Yummy! Tuck in chaps!

"Let me dress the wound," Martin said, deciding to take a less controversial and troublesome option then killing the copper. A missing policeman and Land Rover, with tracking devices, were not quite so easy to make disappear.

"And again I apologise," Martin added. "Follow me and I'll clean it up."

Nodding his head for the direction, the policeman instinctively followed, stepping sideways past the alley and towards the Flesh Room, where a light glowed. Over his shoulder, Martin glanced towards the hounds by the railings. He hoped he was mistaken, but he thought he saw Maverick raise his lips, exposing teeth, as he proudly stood upon two legs, almost regarding Martin from the railings with a cocky Alpha-male defiance. Martin swallowed hard.

With the policeman encouraged on from behind, before he had time for a second glance back, they'd both entered The Flesh Room. Burton scanned the small workroom as he entered. To Martin, it was simply his favourite place of work, and where he spent a lot of his time. But to anyone else, it appeared as if it was a grizzly scene from a Victorian horror movie.

Hung around the whitewashed room were a series of saws, knives, cleavers and instruments used in Martin's daily work to cleave, hack, chop, dismember and cut all forms of dead stock. A veritable butchers shop from hell.

All types of former living creatures were hacked up here.

Including humans.

The images of Sarah's hacked limbs, split torso and the burnt heads flashed before Martin. Her hanging leg. Severed breasts. He felt his face flush.

He breathed in deep, trying to erase the images as he followed the policemen into his parlour; the room of slaughter, wincing internally at the folly of his instinctive action to lead the policeman away from the hounds and instead openly take him inside the room of death, destruction and guilt; simply to treat the policeman's pathetic hand wound. He forgot to add place of murder.

"My god, what do you do in here?" Burton gazed in awe, taking it all in.

"Cut up bodies. Then feed the parts to the hounds."

The policeman looked at Martin, his expression deadpan.

Martin stared, waiting for some reaction. Then he smiled. That was good.

Burton grinned, the wound to his hand seemingly ignored, as he playfully thumped Martin's shoulder. He suddenly liked this strange man. How cool.

"I believe you. Who wouldn't? But I'm not going to be next, I hope!"

"It can be arranged," Martin quipped, but then winced inwardly at the joke.

However, Burton took it well and laughed, naturally scanning the room, looking at the array of equipment, neatly hung about. He gazed at the floor and walls, and the numerous bloodstains and marks, displaying evidence of brutality, despite rigorous cleaning. His head rose, turning to scan the various shelves, eyes absorbing images of long and short knives, assorted saws and shining cleavers, unknown items of dubious usage, all hanging or attached to hooks along the wall. He looked on fascinated, gazing at shelves of cans, bottles and jars of unknown contents. Including what appeared to be teeth.

Martin's gaze followed that of the policeman, silently watching, wondering what he might be looking for, or what he might see. Hopefully no teeth.

The policeman's head stopped, his eyes focussed upon one point. Martin followed his gaze, seemingly towards one of the top shelves. He cocked his head, trying to determine what he was looking at so intently. His pulse rose.

Then something suddenly caught Martin's attention elsewhere. On the floor.

Orange. Bright. Human.

His heart leapt as he gazed down at the object clearly visible on the floor.

Fingernail. Sarah's. Human. Killed. Butchered. Evidence. Prison. Shit!

His eyes bulged as he regarded the rogue fingernail, wondering how he's missed it and how and when it'd come off. Not good. He was getting slack.

Slackness was not normal. It showed poor discipline.

His eyes flitted from fingernail to policeman, then back.

But the policeman seemed oblivious to a key clue to the woman Martin had just hacked up and fed to his hounds, after fucking and then killing her.

The policeman's attention appeared to be focussed upon the shelves.

"He's seen the teeth." A voice spoke to Martin. "The fucking teeth. Idiot!"

A chill, like iced water, rushed through his veins like anaesthetic, and then down his spine. He flicked his head around, wondering who'd spoken.

'Had the copper heard the voice?' Seemingly not. He must have. He had.

Martin's eyes flicked to the small jar, then back to the policeman. Then down at Sarah's fingernail. Still the policeman seemed transfixed. But on what?

The policeman stood before Martin, staring motionless.

"Kill him." The voice spoke. "Now! Kill him!"

Martin looked towards the voice, sure the copper heard.

"Kill the bastard!" The voice repeated. Martin looked about.

No one else was in the room, only the stationary policeman.

"Cut him up. Let the hounds have a feast. Do it!"

Martin looked on, assessing the policeman's weight.

Extra Large. The sides of Martin's lips creased upward.

"The hounds will feed well. Plenty to go around. Tuck in. Do him!"

Martin wondered if the policeman had heard the voice and instructions.

He gazed towards a magnetic strip set upon the wall, from which hung his best knives. Quick and easy to grasp. Sharp and ready. Instant death.

"Do it! Kill him!" The voice screamed. "Cut and slice. Stab and hack!"

Martin gently nodded to confirm compliance.

Lurching sideways, a swift arm reaching out. A long stiletto-bladed filleting knife was in his hand. Sidestep, then forward, and with a long-experienced sword lunge the blade entered welcoming flesh. Deep and hard. Push it in!

Wham! The razor-sharp blade was driven beneath the policeman's stab-vest and pushed upwards. Hard. The sharp point plunged into flesh and organs.

Within a split second the blade was removed. Job done.

Handle firm in Martin's hand, his eyes bright and gleaming.

His smile was wide. He was enjoying the moment.

Wham! Wham!

The blade was repeatedly thrust back into the policeman.

Then to the top of his neck and down.

A killer's strike.

The razor-sharp blade severed key organs and arteries.

Martin swung around, as swift as a cat. Smiling.

Another thrust. Wham!

Deep into the policeman's stomach. But this one was just for fun, forcing his body upward, his toes almost lifted off the floor with the force.

Groans and gasps emitted as the blade cut deep.

In a pool of blood the policeman collapsed.

Martin smiled, enjoying the sight of the dying intruder.

Booted feet kicked out in final death throes.

Good.

The unwelcome guest was no more.

Good.

He shouldn't have been there.

Chapter 99

In the field of observation,
chance favours only the prepared mind.

Louis Pasteur

Chantelle looked good in military fatigues. Then she'd look good in anything. Or nothing. Or so Adam thought. The army surplus combat trousers and matching jacket Adam had thrown at her earlier in the hotel room, formerly belonged to a six-week-wonder; a failed US army recruit looked good.

To Adam she appeared as sexy in them as if tottering in five-inch high heels, wearing no more than a cheeky smile, her neat bottom and long legs alluring.

Maybe the stiletto heels and long legs won out. But only just.

The pair now lay close together on the fringe of a dreary wood, hidden in the gloom by a mix of dying bracken, brambles and scrub. Adam felt at home as he gazed down at a white house in the distance. A hi-power spotting scope, set up on its mini tripod, focussed upon the property, the image clear.

Bizarrely Chantelle seemed to take to the situation like a fish to water and had not complained once. That was despite the cold and damp, along with the long walk across country they'd had to make, before creeping cautiously through a woods, to lie up in their current position. Adam suspected Chantelle thought it all exciting, which it was, and it was part of the reason Adam enjoyed doing what he did. It was also better than working the streets, and if he could help her leave that terrible lifestyle, he would happily assist.

"That's interesting," said Adam, laying beside an oak tree, the view down to the building and occupants clear through his high-power, military binoculars.

Cold and wet, but strangely happy in her new environment, Chantelle pulled up alongside her 'Commanding Officer' and saviour, to see what he'd spotted.

"What can you see?" she asked. "I can see two people beside a Range Rover. Is that who we're following? Have they done something bad? I hope so!"

Adam smiled and simply nodded, glad Chantelle was whispering, although they were too far away for anyone to hear them, but Adam knew how sound travelled. He was also cautious to shield the binoculars, to prevent any lens flash, which he knew would give away their location.

"Take a look through the spotting scope and tell me what you see. Be careful and try not to break the skyline. Cover the front slightly with your hand."

Chantelle, like a keen recruit, did as instructed. Carefully lowering her long body onto the leaf litter, she shuffled forward to gaze through the single eyepiece of the small telescope, moving a long strand of blonde hair from her face and tucking it behind the black beanie hat she wore as she shuffled into position like a well-trained sniper. Adam was impressed. He should know.

Adam grinned at the pleasant sight, eyes flicking to her backside, looking equally appealing in the camouflage. But Adam was working, and was totally disciplined when in such locations and was keen to see her thoughts too.

Chantelle moved her head about, pressing her eye to the scope, taking in the image, before turning to Adam, her face grinning with genuine excitement.

"Wow!" she exclaimed. "It's like looking straight at their faces. That is a great piece of kit. So amazingly clear. I bet it's expensive. It's heavy, so it must be."

Adam smiled and simply nodded, aware that to Chantelle everything seemed to be related to money. Chantelle then looked back into the scope, watching the figures hundreds of yards away; the people she covertly observed totally unaware of the stunningly attractive woman gazing intently at them.

"I know him. I'm sure." The statement was simple, but caused Adam to lower his binoculars and gaze sideways at his new assistant. He was excited.

Adam grinned like a Cheshire Cat, sliding to lie alongside, raising his binoculars, whilst Chantelle gazed at the distant men through the scope.

"Which one?" Adam asked. "Left of right."

"Left," Chantelle replied, head attached to the scope, before she turned to face Adam, his face inches from hers. He was smiling widely.

"Hundred percent. He's one of our customers." Chantelle was pleased.

"Bingo!" Adam's grin stretched from ear to ear. "Well done. Thank you!"

Rolling along on his belly, he reached into a small military rucksack and pulled out a camera with a massive lens. Chantelle had only seen such equipment on the TV where reporters photographed royalty, celebrities and actors, usually from afar. She shuffled out of his way, allowing him to take up a position beside the scope where she'd lain. Adam was impressed.

With deft and ease the camera was to his eye and within seconds the Nikon digital camera clicked, taking multiple long range shots with amazing clarity. Checking the display at the back and happy with what he'd photographed, he returned the camera and extra-long lens back to their black protective case.

"A good days work and thanks to you," he beamed, noting a blob of mud on Chantelle's face, adding to her appeal. "You've certainly earned your salary."

"What now?" Chantelle looked at him curiously.

"That's it. Now we go back to the hotel. Get warm and dried off, then have a good dinner and plan for the next phase. Provided you're still game?"

"I'm game for anything," Chantelle grinned. "As well you should know!"

"Excellent!" Adam gently slapped her backside in a playful manner, as he shuffled back from the edge of the tree line, dragging with him the spotting scope and small rucksack. "Follow me. Onto phase two. Lets go comrade!"

The pair shuffled back, pulling away their equipment, clearing the edge of the woods and skyline before rising up onto cold, aching limbs. It was a cold and rag winter's day, but Adam had known worse. And so had Chantelle.

Once Adam was sure they were clear of being seen by any keen eyes down by the house, he rose fully, Chantelle following suit and brushing off the debris.

Adam stretched a hand forward and gently plucked a brown oak leaf from her hair. She smiled sensing his gentle touch and genuine caring nature. The pair then slowly drifted through the dense woods, Adam cautiously scanning the area, eyes set upon the nearby track, ears keenly listening for movement.

Unlike most women he knew, he was pleased Chantelle remained quiet, and didn't speak, simply following his lead. Her eyes also furtively flitted through the woods, as if she too was aware they could be attacked at any moment.

Once well away from any potential vehicles on the track, and heading on a bearing through the woods back to the small lane where Adam had left his car, he broke the silence, drawing closer to his new and keen recruit.

"Do you have any plans for New Year's Eve?" Adam enquired cautiously, the request seemingly strange and almost business-like rather than a date.

Chantelle regarded Adam with an equally cautious look.

"No, not really. But hopefully I'm not going to be in a back alley or spending it crawling around a cold dark wood. Please don't tell me you are? It wouldn't surprise me if you did. But if it's part of my new work, them I'm game."

"No. Although it wouldn't be the first, or the last time I have on a New Year. Adam chuckled. But I think for now we have enough information. I just wondered if you wanted to go out somewhere for a meal? I'm paying!"

Chantelle looked slightly confused.

Adam wondered if he'd strayed off course too much.

"What, like a date?" Chantelle enquired, unsure.

Adam blushed and chuckled once more. "Yes, like a date."

Chantelle blushed, the smile that crept across her face genuine and adding a sense of humanity to her. To Adam it was welcome and he knew she had it.

"I've nothing planned and would be more than happy to join you," she replied. "Thank you. So long as you're paying of course!"

"Don't worry, I'm paying," Adam grinned sheepishly. "But nothing too fancy or too expensive! How does fish and chips sound?"

"That sounds perfect. I'm looking forward to it already."

"Excellent," exclaimed Adam. "Then we can discuss your future employment with me as well and your next assignment."

Chantelle eyed Adam warily, but with a nervous grin.

"Will it be dangerous?" She had to ask, but smiled.

"Yes." Adam simply replied, smiling fiendishly. "Very dangerous."

Chapter 100

The course of true love never did run smooth.

William Shakespeare

"Do you have any plans for New Year's Eve?" It was an closed question.

As soon as Anna asked the question, as casually as she tried to make it sound, she winced, wishing she hadn't. She scanned Chris' face, sensing the reply.

Chris blushed and seemed lost for an answer without being rude.

Anna knew at once the answer would be a 'No' to whatever she proposed, especially if it involved anything social and didn't involve a horse.

"The girls are going into the city for drinks and to watch the fireworks from the castle at midnight. Nice way to see in the New Year. Be a bit riotous I've no doubts," Anna said, but was flagging. "You can join us. Honorary Girlie."

Chris half smiled, half grimaced, and with a red face gently shook his head. Anna understood. But she'd tried. Poorly. At least she'd asked. Poorly.

"I hate crowds. I'm not a drinker and especially hate the city, as nice as it is. But, no. Sorry to spoil your fun. Honorary Girlie or not, I'd be a bore. I can image what Tracey will be like. God help Norwich and all who sail in her!"

Anna managed a chuckle, but felt deflated, wondering how she'd ever get Chris out alone somewhere, but realised a 'Girlie Piss Up' was not really ideal.

"I'll be riding out on New Year's Day. We'd usually hunt, but it's all on hold. I'd be more than happy for you to join me, if you're awake, capable and want to. Not as exciting as a piss-up in the city with Tracey, but I really hate such things. I dislike crowds. I'm happiest charging about on a horse or standing in a field gazing at birds. Boring, I know. But to make it up, how about we share that bottle of wine you gave one evening once the New Year fuss has died?"

Anna's eyes bulged and her heart paused. She had to think. But not for long.

'Had he just asked her for a date? Just the two of them?'

A wide smile spread across her face and she almost leapt on the spot, such was her excitement, and as clearly and openly displayed.

"Yes and yes," she replied. "To both things I mean!"

It was Chris who chuckled this time, smiling broadly.

"Okay, it's a date. The New Year's Day ride, and in the next week or so, to share your fine bottle of wine. Time, day and venue to be confirmed. Okay?"

Anna couldn't be happier and wanted to reach out and grab Chris, but Carol was walking past where they stood, regarding them somewhat curiously.

Chris grinned, nodding at Carol, who smirked, and did likewise to Anna.

"I'm sorry about New Year's Eve, but it really isn't my thing. So you've been warned! I'm a boring old-fart, who finds enjoyment riding, watching crows fly over a woods, mucking out or simply talking to horses. And Max of course."

Anna smiled even wider and more so now wanted to squeeze and hug him. And kiss him too. But she blushed and smiled, looking him in the face.
"Have you two nothing else better to do? Either snog him, book a hotel, organise a wedding or get on and muck out your horses! Kids! Tut, tut!"
It was Julie who broke the stillness between them, marching across the yard, having just parked up. She cast the pair one of her cheekiest grins.
"Is he coming?" Julie was blunt, but smiled at Chris.
"No I'm not!" Chris answered to save Anna any blushes.
Anna grinned at Chris, who in turn simply smiled at Julie. She'd told her so.
"Thank you all anyway, I'm sure it'll be fun, but I have an appointment that evening anyway. That's the other reason why I'd have to decline."
Anna stared at Chris with an almost blank expression.
Chris took the hint and decided to explain further.
"My uncle will be popping around on New Year's Eve."
"Uncle?" Anna queried, unaware of any relatives. Julie remained quiet.
"Yes my uncle. Family tradition. Always came around to see my parents on New Year's Eve, and has ever since. I haven't seen him this Christmas."
Anna flipped her head from Julie to Chris, then back. She'd assumed he had no relatives, then realised someone must have taken care of him when he was young after his parents had been murdered. She almost winced at the thought, and more so at her selfish attitude, assuming Chris had no other life.
"Will you and Tracey still up for that ride on New Year's Day?"
Chris looked at Julie who winced, the agreed activity seemingly forgotten.
"I doubt Tracey will be joining us. Not unless she has a vodka in hand."
The two women chuckled, knowing Tracey would possibly still arrive for the ride out, sober or still drunk, her drinking abilities seemingly legendary.
"Well I look forward to seeing you on New Year's Day, hopefully sober, although I'll obviously be seeing you both before then." Chris smiled at Anna.
"And make sure you keep that bottle on hold," Anna added, noticing Julie eyeing her coyly. But she remained quiet, guessing something was afoot.
"I'll put it on ice," Chris replied confidently.
"I hope not, it's a lovely red. Room or body temperature." Anna blushed once she'd spoken, knowing she'd opened herself up, seeing Julie's wide grin.
"Maybe Chris can slip the bottle it into his jod's to warm it up." Julie was as quick as ever. "Then you can reach inside, pull it out hard and pop his cork!"
Julie's final comment was enough for Chris, who shook his head and turned away, pretending not to laugh. His grin was wide, face red, as he headed off to the barn. He left the two women almost rolling about in fits of girly giggles.
Carol's curious head rose over Tess' stable door. She'd only heard the last bit. She eyed the two laughing woman, and noted a chuckling, red-faced Chris. Carol shook her head, as if she didn't understand it all. Or maybe she did.

Chapter 101

Curiosity killed the cat,
but satisfaction brought it back.

Proverb - Unknown

As Anna pulled up into the driveway of Pear Tree Cottage, with the fine branches of the overhanging willow standing at the side boundary rustling like fingers on the roof of her car, she cursed. She'd forgotten her bag. Again.

It had her mobile inside, as well as her house keys, so she couldn't get in if she wanted. She'd kept reminding herself to get a spare key cut, so she could place it under the big plant by the timber door, but as usual hadn't done so.

She'd have to drive back to Horsewater, which although wasn't that far, was annoying. It was dark, getting cold and she didn't want to disturb Chris again. She'd been one of the last to leave the yard, after they'd been chatting, and Chris had switched off the main yard lights, waving her a fond farewell, as he and Max withdrew to the farmhouse for a quick tea and loneliness.

She'd returned to Pear Tree Cottage for a double-helping of the same.

It seemed silly. Both clearly liked each other, or so she hoped, with feelings she felt directed to her, and yet they both departed without a hug or a kiss.

The trip back through the dark narrow country lanes was uneventful, with no cars passing for the few miles she had to drive back. Her main annoyance was driving through the main bit of woods, once she'd entered Horsewater.

Even though she drove a small 4 x 4, the track was bumpy and had to drive slowly. Despite having been through the woods many times, and considered herself clear-headed, she still held that primeval fear that there was something evil lurching in the woods, ready to leap out and eat her. Maybe there was.

The woods on this return journey appeared particularly malevolent, even though she'd only just driven through minutes earlier with no thought or care, only what she was going to have on toast for tea tonight. Beans looked likely.

Something dark and unseen now seemed to lurk in the shadows and she felt her foot press a little harder on the accelerator, until she was clear of the main woods and could see the farm, but with everything cast in a silver silhouette.

She'd never seen the yard in such darkness, there usually being a light on, either in the yard or Chris' house. But now it seemed to be in total darkness. Anna was puzzled. It was unusual for Chris to leave the yard, and usually he left a yard light on, or his kitchen or lounge light would spread a soft glow.

But now there was nothing. Simply darkness. Anna felt uneasy. Chris had not said anything about going out, but then why should he? She wasn't his keeper, and he was free to leave and do whatever he wanted, whenever. Maybe he'd simply popped off to get some essentials from a supermarket or local shop.

Either way, as Anna pulled up into the parking area, she knew she'd be quick. Also, she didn't want to upset Max, if he was alone in the house. He usually slept most of the time, despite his chilling appearance, but Anna hoped she'd be in and out in less than a minute, and unheard. Then beans on toast. Again.

Leaving her 4 x 4, she dashed across the yard to the tackroom. She knew a spare key was kept under a flowerpot beside a timber post by the door.

'Why does everyone leave keys under flowerpots?' She mused, then smiled.

Anna pondered the thought as she lifted the pot and removed the spare key.

'You may as well hang the key outside the door on string,' she considered.

When she got her own spare key cut - when - she'd place hers anywhere else other than under a flowerpot. Maybe just hang it outside on a piece of string!

Flicking on the tackroom light, to her relief, but also annoyed frustration sat her canvas bag, with purse, phone and keys safely within. She quickly scanned the room, it looking as messy and as smelly as it ever did, then flicked off the light, returning to the gloom of the yard, her night-vision now slightly ruined.

Pulling the door shut, and fumbling for the lock, Anna secured the tackroom, and repositioned the key under the pot, where no-one would think to look!

Success. She could now return home to enjoy a night alone, gazing lovingly over a plate of beans on toast. Maybe she'd have a glass of Port. Or three.

Looking longingly over towards the farmhouse, which seemed to glow in the darkness, she thought of Chris. She wondered again where he could be and why there had been no lights left on. It was strange. Then she stared harder.

A soft, almost unperceivable light seemed to glow from the kitchen.

Maybe it was the glow from an appliance. But it seemed not.

Ever curious - and in the past her mother had warned her that one day it'd get her into trouble - Anna slowly walked across the yard and towards the dark farmhouse. Then, carefully and silently, wandered up to the house.

The kitchen side wall area had no border or planting, unlike some aspects of the house, where deep bushes of Lavender grew, and where in some areas a small raised wall had bedding plants or dwarf Box. But the kitchen area faced straight onto the yard and parking area. It was a great vantage point for Chris, and he could often be seen peering out the window whenever anyone arrived and parked up to see who was entering the yard from out of the woods.

But seemingly not tonight. One night before New Year's Even and the house was as quiet and empty as a church on a similar date. Or so it seemed.

But maybe Anna was wrong. Very much wrong.

As she crept steadily up to the kitchen window, feeling slightly guilty for her stealth and suspicious manner, she could clearly see a line of light glowing from somewhere deep in the kitchen. It was a fine light, but seemed to cast a glow over a tight area to the room within, mostly spreading over the floor.

Anna moved up to the kitchen window, bobbing down, although she didn't know why, to then place her fingertips upon the stone cill beneath the old, painted window frame. Then she raised her head to look inside the kitchen.

There was a clearly a soft glow of light, more clearly visible now.
Almost in the form of a fine rectangle. Brighter at the base.
Light was seeping through the gaps of a doorframe.
The cellar doorframe.
Someone was in the cellar.
The same cellar Chris had told Anna was disused.
The same cellar she was convinced had freshly oiled hinges.
The same cellar which was obviously usable. And now lit.
And Chris had to be down there.
But doing what?
The ever-curious Anna wanted to know.
She must know. It was in her nature.
Despite her mother's warnings. But what do mothers know?
She eased forward slightly, carefully shuffling her feet.
Keen to make no sound, she pressed her face to the window.
A pair of dark eyes peered back.
Anna froze.
Black, staring eyes.
Anna drew a breath, hands shaking.
Max stared at Anna.
Anna stared at Max.
Max lifted his lips.
Even in the gloom Anna got the warning.
Anna was off, stepping quickly away from the house.
On tiptoes she raced towards her car, her hands shaking.
But not through the cold.
She entered her 4 x 4, amazed Max hadn't barked to raise the alarm.
But then she understood.
Max was a guard dog. A true guard dog.
He'd let you in, but you'd never leave.
Engine fired up, 4 x 4 moving, Anna was now glad to be away.
But driving back through the woods she was wondering
What on earth was Chris doing in his disused cellar?
Maybe he was doing it up. Maybe he wasn't.
Maybe he kept a woman chained up down there.
She grinned at the thought. Then the smile faded.
'Isn't that what John had joked?'
Anna felt her spine shiver as she pressed her foot down harder. Away.
The eerie trees sped past in the darkness as questions raced in her head.
Anna hastily returned to Pear Tree Cottage and a welcoming meal.
But all thoughts of beans on toast had gone.
Suddenly she'd lost her appetite.

Chapter 102

Hide nothing, for time, which sees all and hears all, exposes all.

Sophocles

Izzy was unsure how Bruce had persuaded her to join him for New Year's celebration in Norwich, but he had. Easily. His hand playfully sliding down the front of her jeans, whilst he grinned and she smiled back appreciatively, may have helped convince her he'd ensure a good time, and a great evening, but that wasn't all. She needed to get away from the confusing and conflicting thoughts racing through her mind recently and simply have some real fun.

Going into Norwich wasn't something she usually did. In the past, on New Years Eve, she spent the evening with Steve and other horsey people, either at one of their homes or inviting them to their farm. It would have been a raucous, drunken event, with lots of good food, drink and hearty laughter.

But that was then. Things had changed. Sadly for the worse she admitted.

Last year Dave had asked her to join him at the local pub': to 'have a few ciders and see in the New Year.' But she'd felt it meant more than that, so politely she declined, seeing her parents instead, as boring as it was.

Now she was strolling the chilly streets of Norwich, with a man she barely knew, his arm wrapped around her, and at least helping to keep her warm. Even if she felt no sentiment from the gesture, or to the man attached, he was good company, handsome, clever in a dumb way, and for now, he served a purpose. She also felt his feelings towards her were not totally dissimilar.

Both were seemingly using the other for their own secret and personally reasons and both quietly knew it, but neither spoke about it. Perfect almost.

"The fireworks are set off from the castle mound," Izzy explained, raising a hand to point at the white-stoned castle over-looking much of the old city. "It's usually a good show. That said, it's been years since I've seen them."

Bruce simply nodded, glancing at the edifice, raising his head momentarily to look at the towering white walls. But his eyes scanned the streets, as if looking for someone or something, as he and Izzy strolled arm in arm through the back streets. Behind them, the towering spire of the cathedral, lit up in orange lights, provided an equally stunning backdrop to the historic Medieval city.

"They hung Robert Kett from that wall," Izzy stated proudly, removing her free hand, to point up at the castle again, jabbing a finger to the battlements.

"Who?" Bruce peered up at the castle's illuminated wall, briefly interested.

"Robert Kett. He led a rebellion, way back. Before you were even born," Izzy joked. "But only just. He was a successful leader and took over the city."

"But you said he got hung? He couldn't have been that successful. If not he'd still be in charge of the city." Bruce grinned at Izzy, enjoying his companion.

"It was over five hundred years ago stupid! I think he'd be dead by now. Successful or not." Izzy shook her head, grinning. Bruce chuckled, and then cautiously glanced towards two policemen standing near a shop doorway.

Two pairs of eyes connected. A flash of recognition. Shit!

Then Bruce's eyes connected with someone else. Double-shit!

Bruce flushed upon seeing that person, then furtively turned sharply, almost pushed Izzy into the doorway of a small pub' they were passing alongside.

"Quick. In here. This looks like fine place for another quick drink."

Izzy didn't have time to notice Bruce's nervous reaction, finding herself pushed and almost tripping over the doorway, crashing into a couple exiting.

"Oops! Sorry she apologised," as Bruce bustled in behind, pushing her.

"That copper. From the hunt meet. He was out there!" Bruce began to explain, almost as an apology for the hasty movement. Izzy turning her head briefly, but they were already inside the pub'. They squeezed into the crowded bar area, the sound of laughter and chatter almost deafening. Bruce turned warily to look behind the open doorway, as if expecting to see someone enter.

Izzy turned too, looking past the doorway and beyond, but they were moving deeper within the low-ceiling, former Tudor building, with people all around.

"I didn't want him recognising us," Bruce tried to explain. "You know what coppers are like. We'd both be stuck there answering his questions no doubt."

Izzy hadn't seen the policeman Bruce spoke of, but certainly didn't want to get involved in any more trouble. She knew Dave was trying to take Steve to court, but doubted he'd succeed. Steve was too clever and had access to a good solicitor; as well she knew. The Hunt had lots of 'Fingers in Pies' too.

She'd contacted the hospital to find out Dave had been discharged from hospital and sent him a brief text message, stating she hoped he was making a good recovery, had a good New Year, and that she'd be back in touch in the next week, claiming she was spending New Year Eve with her parents again.

She could only hope he wasn't wandering the streets of Norwich, ribs bandaged and arms in slings. She doubted it. But you never knew with him.

He hadn't text back, which wasn't unusual. But Izzy then thought he possibly couldn't. His arms didn't work.

That was worrying. No arms. How did he go to the loo?

"We'll grab a drink," spoke Bruce, jolting Izzy's thoughts. "Then watch the fireworks from the castle. If you want to after, you can come back with me and set off more fireworks. I've got a large Roman Candle, ready to go off!"

Izzy shook her head, still unsure of the man forcing his way towards the front of the crowded bar, but smiled. Turning her head once more back towards the doorway, she was still unsure if it was the policeman her companion was seemingly avoiding, or possibly someone else.

Bruce seemed to have a lot to hide. Or was hiding from someone?

If he was, then who?

Chapter 103

Wherever there is a man who exercises authority,
there is a man who resists authority.

Oscar Wilde

Norwich was usually quiet and didn't require a big police presence in the evenings, except on the odd occasion, such as for when a 'Local Derby' Football match took place, where trouble between rival teams was often expected. However, it was New Year's Eve, and although any trouble, other than the odd drunk or brawl wasn't expected, the police numbers were increased, the authorities aware some 'merry' people could cause mischief.

For New Year's Eve, any trouble wasn't from people trying to punch the hell out of each other; simply because they came from a rival county, but usually in the form of drunken people staggering about, trying to be 'too nice' to others. Some people didn't appreciate this 'niceness,' in whatever form it might materialise, and acted in a far from 'nicer' manner. For others, it simply meant they'd consumed too much 'nice liquid' and fell over far too easily, laying in busy roads or on pavements, much to others annoyance. Not nice.

Hence additional police support had been drafted in, these being officers who'd usually work in or around the county and not directly with the City Police. It was hoped any potential trouble would be short-lived, and that as soon as the fireworks were set off from the top of the historic castle, dating back to the time of the Norman invasions, most of the crowds would disperse and happily return to their humble abodes. Then collapse onto beds or sofas, maybe after a bit of 'New Year Rumpy-Pumpy.' Then the world could click off another year and carry on just as depressing as it had the day previously.

It was through this hubbub, along one of the popular streets leading toward the castle; where it stood bold and proud upon its motte that a small group of woman drifted. Anna was happy, but realised she was too old for such things. Tracey was very happy and oblivious to everything. Julie was happy, but too coy to reveal much more. The other half-dozen women who formed their group, a mix of work colleagues of both Tracey and Julie, appeared to be a mix of the same emotions. One of Tracey's friends was away with the aliens, where as one of Julie's colleagues repeatedly checked her watch, asking when the fireworks would go off, so she could get her husband to pick her up.

Anna had to admit she felt very much like that woman, and if Chris hadn't snubbed her invite; to do whatever he was really doing, she'd either be cuddled up to him now, or if not, then sound asleep, snug in her own cottage.

However, she was where she was, and trying to look as if she was enjoying herself, which to some degree she was, the drink and company helping.

As they turned a corner, the group swerved to miss a similar bunch of men. Wolf-whistles and calls were made, which made Anna smile, and Tracey forget she was engaged. She ran up to the group; if staggering in five-inch heels like a disabled giraffe can be defined as running, to give one young lad a huge kiss. This was met with a huge cheer from both sides. Tracey then staggered back to her 'girls,' leaving yet another broken heart on the streets.

Anna glanced sideways, and noticed the playful antics were being observed. By a policeman. Anna had to look twice, but at once realised she knew him.

She winced. The policeman stood beside another, his piggy eyes supposedly scanning the crowds for trouble, but seemingly more at home eyeing up the girls who passed by in clothing not suitable for the weather or temperature.

Although thankfully dry, it was chilly, and Anna regretted wearing a short, tight skirt, flimsy top and heels. Tracey's clothing was even more scant, and more fitting for the beachfront in Ibiza. However, the alcohol anti-freeze she seemed to retain in her bloodstream appeared to keep away any touch of cold.

Wincing, Anna spotted the policeman and glanced his way. He glanced back.

'Lady Melrose?' considered P.C. Burton. He looked harder, sure it was, but the stunning woman looked different dressed in 'real' clothes, perfect for a night out. She was baring her elegant long legs, perfectly accentuated in high-heels, and topped off with something sexier other than a sagging fleece.

He noticed her eyes catch his. The look a scowl. It had to be her. 'Posh cow!'

Burton's eyes scanned the group to see if any horseman was in tow, but Lady Melrose appeared to be enjoying the night with girl friends, and obviously keeping her man at home. That's if they were a pair. Burton was still unsure.

He was sure she of one thing; Lady Melrose had a great pair of legs; shown off better in the short tight woollen skirt she wore. Very sexy. Very nice.

But his ever-scanning eyes drifted to one of her friends. The 'Kissing One.' Clearly drunk, she was equally attractive, and after running back from the cheering lads, she now hung onto one of the other woman's arm. Familiar.

Burton stared at the two women, who in turned laughed with Lady Melrose.

The attractive one, clearly drunk, looked slightly similar to Lady Melrose in some way. They must be related. Sister, cousin or something else? Interesting.

He looked on towards the older woman. She was hanging onto the attractive drunk, maybe for support, and laughing loudly with Lady Melrose. Friends.

'Why did those two look familiar?' Burton thought hard; scanning, recalling.

He clearly recognised Lady Melrose, but was sure he'd seen the other two women before, somewhere, but couldn't recall where. The thought bugged him. Maybe they were dressed differently. The gears in his head turned.

However, his police colleague swiftly interrupted the thought. A P.C. from the regular Norwich force, his radio bleeped loudly as he received a call.

Burton half looked at the women, now drifting from view, and half regarded his colleague, realising there could soon be some action. Maybe a punch-up.

"Hang fire," he nodded to Burton. "We may have an incident. Next street."

Burton glanced down at the small cut on his hand, from where the dog had bitten him the day before. Well, maybe. The more he'd thought about the incident, the more he thought he may possibly have cut his own hand on the rusty, sharp railings on the yard that kept the hounds as he pulled it back.

But he wasn't admitting to that. The man, who kept the hounds, although a bit weird, had been overly nice and helpful once he saw the blood. He'd cleaned the small cut, then taped it up, making a huge fuss and apologising.

Burton had appreciated the attention and sympathy, but felt the huntsman was simply trying to cover himself and defend his hounds. He understood.

It was only a nick, and was possible the hounds hadn't caused it, but instead by his own actions, and a natural fear of dogs. But he'd never admit that to a man who walked freely within over forty on a daily basis. Also forty hounds which ate chopped up carcasses. How cool was that? Worrying, but cool.

It both fascinated and impressed Burton, and despite the cut to his hand, and the Huntsman's strange mannerisms, he'd left him almost as new buddies.

He was certainly much nicer and warmer than the other horseman he'd met.

This brought his thoughts back to Lady Melrose, as he waited for his colleague to get more information on the incident just around the corner.

"Fuck me, Cous!" A screech awoke everyone in the street. Burton turned.

It appeared to emanate from the drunken, attractive woman, wearing barely any clothing and ridiculously high heels, who looked a bit like Lady Melrose.

The screech, followed by a laugh caused Burton to turn from his colleague, checking out their call, back to the group of woman, now about to disappear.

It was then he recognised the common one. And frowned. The gears clicked.

'The women on the horses? The Hunt Meet. Assaulting the Anti. Those two.'

Burton strained his fat neck, trying to see more clearly the faces of the two women clinging onto Lady Melrose and staggering equally ungainly in heels

'Cous? Cousin?' Isn't that what she'd said, for all to hear? They're related.

Could the common trollop; attractive with nice legs and gorgeous rear, but clearly common and very drunk, really be Lady Melrose's Cousin?

The posh bitch said she didn't know the two women.

And more to the point, the horseman also said he didn't know them either.

Did Lady Melrose really did know her. Were they family? Liar.

A very posh, horny and attractive liar. But still a liar.

And the other woman. She was there too. On the Western horse.

The Anti-beater and the Thief. The older one, who'd also attacked the skinny anti and the 'Cousin' who'd stole the Anti's hat. Both together.

Now they were staggering about, laughing and joking.

And Lady Melrose claimed she didn't know either of them.

Lying, deceitful, sexy, bitch. But damned attractive. Pity.

And so had the lying, deceitful horseman. Wanker.

The Hat Stealers. Common thieves. Common liars. Bastards!

"Trouble. Around the corner. Punch up. It's action time. Let's go!"

The pert buttocks, clad in tight skirts, sadly drifted from view and thoughts of an immediate arrest of all three was curtailed by a jab from his colleague.

Burton turned his attention from the walking harem back to his enthusiastic police colleague, getting ready to move. A punch up was more up his street, rather than trying to explain to his new City-based P.C. buddy why he wanted to arrest three scantily-clad sexy drunken attractive maidens, who'd more than likely try to kick him in a delicate region with their dangerous high-heels.

With a dash, Burton was off, racing down the street with his new buddy, all worries of the nick in his hand from a day earlier gone, as he happily steamed into a group of drunken youths, who were already attacking another group of lads, who it seems supported a different football team. Nothing had changed.

Unaware of the action on the street they'd just left, Anna's party moved on up towards the castle, aiming to get a good position to see the fireworks.

The pack drifted by a busy bar, where unknown to Anna, Bruce and Izzy had entered moments earlier. But other eyes looked Anna's way. Unseen by her.

Drifting along the paved area, flanked either side by shops, Anna gazed up where the shops separated to reveal the castle upon its mound, boldly highlighted on the skyline. Anna stared, her eyes drifting past the white stone facing of the historic Norman castle, which she recalled visiting as a child, and on up to the dark black sky above. Her eyes focussed upon the stars, bright in the night sky, despite the light pollution from the busy, well-lit city.

Above her glowed Orion. Just rising from the East, it was clearly visible in the sky above the castle. The Hunter. She smiled to herself, oblivious to the banter of Tracey, Julie, their friends, and the hoards of other people around, all waiting for the New Year to be officially announced.

Staring up at Orion, Anna made a wish. She made it silently, and only she knew what it was. If not, and if she told anyone, it wouldn't come true.

And she hoped it would. It involved Chris. And her.

A short while later the boom of the City Hall clock rang, declaring a new year had begun. A huge cheer was let forth, and happy and joyous people leapt about, hugging and kissing each other, as the first of the fireworks erupted.

With a loud crack, and brilliant flash, a rocket exploded high above the castle, cascading bright red flares into the sky, accompanied by loud whoops of joy and happy cheering from the merry crowd below. That rocket was followed by another, then another, and more, as a multitude of fireworks, announced a new year and a new beginning, all brightly erupting into the night sky.

It'd be a Happy New Year. Or so they all hoped.

Many silent wishes were made.

Anna smiled, looking at her newfound cheering and happy friends.

She then stared silently back at Orion.

Anna hoped her silent wish would come true too.

Chapter 104

Observation is an old man's memory.

Jonathan Swift

The various characters all enjoying themselves on the streets of Norwich were not missed by one person. They'd followed them all night.

Watching. Noting. Unseen of course, because they were good - very good.

They knew their trade well; moved in and out of the crowds unseen, like a shadow, and intently watched the target. Or was that targets? Bonus.

Seeing all of their actions, and thus planning the next move. Or moves.

Bungling, chaotic policeman fought with drunken youths.

Neither knew why, other than because they could.

High-heeled sluts, in skimpy clothes, swayed and giggled.

All would have chills or colds in the morning. Idiots.

Newfound lovers, or not, drank themselves senseless.

They'd wake up with a stranger. And possibly more. None welcomed.

Groups of friends sang a Scottish song to which no one knew the words.

Strangers who'd never help another embraced and hugged. Why?

Tomorrow they'd ignore them. Or punch them. Or rob them.

All was seen and watched by the silent observer.

But one group in particular received their keen focus.

They'd been the main centre of attention all night.

From start to finish.

But unseen.

Important information had been collected.

Very soon it'd be utilised.

With deadly affect.

Happy New Year!

Chapter 105

Should auld acquaintance be forgot and never brought to mind?
Should auld acquaintance be forgot and the days of auld lang syne?

Robert Burns

This year, for some, the usual merriment for the New Year Eve was subdued. They had other thoughts and concerns. Very serious concerns.

Reggie had called Steve, asking if he wanted to join him and Bertie at Wroxingham Hall. The idea would be to empty a few bottles of vintage Port. As many as could be consumed in a gentlemanly manner, before falling over. There would also be a large wheel of mature Stilton to help absorb the liquid, as well as other nibbles Bertie's staff would provide. They were still working.

As great as this sounded, and appealed as it was to Steve; knowing that's be quite a few bottles of dusty, well-racked good Vintage Port, and fine cheese, he made his excuses. He informed Reggie he was actually going into Norwich this year, seeing some friends to watch the fireworks. Deepest apologises sent.

Reggie couldn't work out if this was a singular friend; as in an attractive female companion to truly help welcome in the New Year with a bang, or a group of others, probably mostly male, with the odd wanton-hussy thrown in.

Reggie's Field Master wouldn't elaborate. But that wasn't too unusual.

Reggie informed Steve that he'd spoken with Elizabeth. A brief conversation, where both supposedly wished the other a 'Happy New Year' - as highly unlikely as that would be – she finished stating her solicitors would be in touch in January to sort out matters. Happy New Year indeed Reggie added.

Reggie had sounded down, but at least it seemed the couple, although split, were talking. Reggie made no mention of Mike, or where the pair might be.

This was all some relief for Steve. He had wondered where Elizabeth and Mike could be. But things seemed okay if they were speaking to Reggie.

But his lack of concern for the pair, and how they might be, didn't surprise Steve. As far as Reggie was concerned, both Mike and Elizabeth were dead.

And maybe he hoped they were too. It'd save him trouble. And money.

However, Steve knew Reggie had no worries of Elizabeth trying to lay claim to a farm, or a huge chunk of the estate Reggie commanded, as a settlement. That was all tied up in a trust, and Steve knew Reggie had made Elizabeth sign a 'Pre-Nup' before they'd tied the knot, so she could never lay claim to any property already in his ownership. Only a chunk of money. Maybe.

Steve didn't think she actually cared. Nor Mike. Both would find work on their own, and hopefully have a new fresh life together. As much as he liked Reggie as a 'Hunting Buddy,' he wouldn't want to be married to him.

Steve enquired about Martin, who seemed to be keeping a low profile, and had been very quiet since the Boxing Day incident. Steve was aware he too was having problems, it seemed. Reggie had mentioned to him Sharon had 'gone away' seemingly to 'stay with her parents' for a while over Christmas.

For a break, whilst hunting was suspended. Steve knew what that meant.

He'd called Martin and spoke with him, to wish him the best for the New Year, and hoped for his sake, and that of the hunt, that Sharon would return.

Martin had been very quiet and subdued when he called, but thanked Steve for the message. He too told him he'd been invited to Lord Burlingham's with Reggie for a drink or ten, but had declined. He had a cold. Or so he said.

Steve could read between the lines and knew Martin was down. That reason was usually woman orientated, as he well knew. Hopefully Sharon would return in the New Year, and they'd all get back to hunting again.

For Martin, the New Year celebrations were far from his mind. He had too many issues to address, let alone the friendly calls and invites he'd received.

They were nice, polite, but not welcome. He was in no mood to celebrate.

The hounds appeared to have settled down, and although he'd become wary of them after they'd bitten the policeman, they seemed to have relaxed and retuned to their usual cheeky, naughty, but controllable manner, and he could walk amongst them, although he didn't fully trust them. That wasn't good.

If he'd been mad or paranoid, he would have claimed Maverick and Mayhem were plotting against him. But luckily he wasn't mad or paranoid. He hoped.

Reggie had called him, inviting him to Lord Burlingham's, but he'd declined.

Reggie explained he'd spoken with Elizabeth and mentioned divorce.

But the words were lost. He'd also mentioned Bertie felt better, despite his embarrassing loss of Virginia leaving him after 'The 'Incident in the Woods.'

He seemed to believe she was in Scotland. Maybe with Gavin. No one knew.

But Martin knew they were all liars.

In the Flesh Room he had a jar of teeth.

Seventy-two. Three heads worth.

Someone was lying. Telling 'Porkies.' But who?

Maybe Reggie. Maybe Lord Burlingham. Maybe both.

Someone had killed two people and burnt their heads.

But who? And whom? No Happy New Year for them.

And maybe if he discovered the answer, not for him too.

It wouldn't be a late night for him either.

He had nothing to celebrate.

Martin checked the cellar once more, with everything in its place.

Just as it should be. All was fine. For now.

He glanced into the gloom, and into the corner.

'Happy New Year,' he whispered.

Chapter 106

To die, to sleep. To sleep; perchance to dream. Ay, there's the rub. For in that sleep of death what dreams may come.

Hamlet - Shakespeare

Not everyone in Norwich that evening was having such great fun or looking forward to a 'Happy' New Year. For some there wouldn't be one.

For some, tonight would be their last.

Dawn strolled quietly into the bedroom, flicking on the small bedside lamp on her side of the bed and laid down on the chest of drawers a portable CD player, switching it on. The blue digital display lit up bright in the dim light of the room. Dawn hummed quietly, as she put in the Robbie Williams CD.

It was a favourite of hers and Gavin. Well he'd said he liked it. But perhaps he had been lying about that too. Like he'd lied about so much else. Liar. Liar.

But it didn't matter anymore. She knew what was true. She knew it all.

Dawn picked up the bottle of gin she'd brought into the room earlier and refilled her glass with the clear spirit, adding equal tonic water from a small bottle. Humming along to the next track, a tear began to well up in her eye.

She recalled how she and Gavin had made love to the same track.

Only a few weeks earlier. So kind and loving. Yet so false.

Now he was gone. Disappeared. Out of her life.

He'd ridden back in silence after the Boxing Day meet. She had not spoken a word to him, and he none to her. They had unloaded the horses, the usual tasks automatic, and returned home in total silence; he too embarrassed, she too angry. And embarrassed too. The atmosphere was bad and silent.

She simply couldn't understand why he'd want a fling with that stuck-up slut. A whore. Everyone knew she was a flirt. That's all she was. And she'd tempted her sweet Gavin in with that slim body and beautiful face. Why?

Gavin was hers, and always would be. She knew as they drove back in silence that she had to ensure he would never leave her and stray again.

That evening she went upstairs to change and tidy herself up. She quickly showered to come downstairs in a fine, black lace negligee and just a smile.

She knew that'd work, but only found he'd vanished. Gone. Dressed as he was and taking the Rover keys, his wallet, mobile phone and nothing else.

That was five days ago. She'd not seen or heard from him since, despite her constant phoning around everyone, and numerous hourly attempts on his mobile. She'd left countless text messages, all of which were unanswered.

She'd called the police, explained what had happened, but they'd ignored her, telling her to give it a few more days, then call if he didn't return and if she was 'really' concerned. He'd probably turn up, they said. Or not. Wankers!

It didn't matter now. She knew where she stood and it was clear he would not be coming back, for whatever reason. She'd called Lord Burlingham, but he was very vague, stating Virginia had also left, and he didn't want to discuss matters. He thought she might have gone to Scotland. Maybe Gavin had gone with her. He told her he was sorry, understood her worries, but couldn't help. He had his own concerns to address. He sounded like he didn't give a shit.

Wanker. Posh wanker. They were all Wankers! Even the Wankers!

She popped some things into her mouth, rinsing them down with a swig of the G&T and then re-topped the glass back up with gin. She'd lost count of the number of drinks she'd had, but was no longer caring. She fumbled for a couple of small boxes on the side cabinet, dropping one, but sliding the silver-backed blister pack out of another. Out popped several more tablets. Quickly gone, washed down with another swig of G & T. Wow! That was good stuff!

Silly bitch, Dawn thought, as she re-called how the cow at the supermarket checkout would not let her buy all of the boxes of pills she wanted in one go.

"Only two packets per customer. Sorry madam, those are the rules. Sorry."

Silly bitch. What did she know? Fucking stupid cow! Another Wanker!

It didn't matter, 'cos the next supermarket had let her have the same amount. And then she went into another. Two more packets. And the same from the chemist down the road, then she went back into the first supermarket and passed through a different checkout to get two more packets. Ha, Ha! Idiots! They thought they were so clever. Pratt's, all of them, if they all thought they could stop her buying whatever she wanted. They were wrong. She had loads! Who did they think they were? Trying to stop her doing what she wanted. Or even getting what she wanted. No one did that. Wankers! All of them.

She stumbled as she swallowed a couple more, steadying herself on the bed edge as she took another swig of drink to rinse the pills down, the effect now fully taking over as her humming became louder, almost a quiet lullaby, as she joined in with the next track. She liked that one best. She hummed louder.

She'd bathed earlier, taking a G&T in the bath with her. Then she put on a white lace Basque, feeling snug so close to her skin, her small breasts pushed up firmly, giving her some cleavage. She admired them, regretting now she had not worn the sexy outfit before, even though she knew she wanted. She'd carefully pulled up white, lace-topped, silk stockings, clipping them in place with the suspenders, smoothing them down with her hands, feeling the soft texture both against her hands and legs and wishing it was Gavin's hands running down the length of her short legs, then right back up to the top.

Maybe if she had legs like the posh whore Gavin would still be with her.

The lacy white thong, which matched the set, rode up tight between her neat buttocks, her trimmed hairs nestling to the lacy front, so it didn't bristle out.

No doubt the posh cow doesn't have pubes. She's probably clean-shaven. Like a child. Perverted bitch. Dirty Whore! Fucking Bitch! But so smooth.

Another swig of G & T helped. Possibly. And a few more pills.

She wanted to look her best, and stood before the mirror, admiring herself for one last time. She admired the white lingerie. Neat. Sexy. Horny.

She'd show Gavin what he was missing. Idiot!

He'd have some serious regrets. This'd certainly teach him!

It'd show him what he could have had. What he should have had.

She wished she'd worn the underwear long before now. Gavin had bought it for her last Valentine's as a present, slightly embarrassed, but excited that she might enjoy it. But she had refused to wear it. Too sexy for her. She'd told him he should like her as she was, and not looking like some 'cheap tart.'

He'd become quiet and even more introvert from then on. Mistake.

She'd berated him numerous times, and rightly so, asking him if he thought she was a whore dressing up like that. And besides, she'd added, it was too tight. She wouldn't be able to breath in it, let alone do whatever crude activities he obviously expected her to 'perform' in such an exciting outfit.

That'd put him in his place. And rightly so. She had to tell him.

But she'd kept the underwear. Hidden. Secretly she loved it.

It was beautiful and very sexy. But she wasn't. She was drab. Boring.

She knew that one day she would wear them for him. One special day. When she got the courage to do so and dispel her inhibitions; her deep-seated worries, and how she really felt about her body and all it lacked.

She knew she'd wear the sexy underwear one day.

Well that day was now. And Gavin wasn't here. Wanker!

He should be here to see her. She looked stunning.

And she wanted him. She needed him. Why wasn't he there?

She got out her mobile phone and texted him another message.

I'M IN YOUR SEXY WHITE UNDERWEAR. HORNY. CALL ME!

Another swig of G & T then the glass topped up. Fumbling hands struggled to pop out further tablets, dropping several onto the carpet.

"Fuck them!" Dawn hollered, trying to kick the tablets in the deep pile of the carpet, but missing, taking another swig of drink instead.

She checked her phone. The display looked blurred for some reason.

Gavin hadn't called or text her back, yet. Wanker! Or he was busy.

She slid her hands across the tight white silk and lace of the Basque, the texture tempting and teasing. The movement increased, her hands running down her legs, sliding over the silk stockings, fondling the lace tops, before her fingers slid beneath the thong, wishing they were Gavin's. Where was he?

She felt light-headed and probably needed another drink to help matters.

Giggling at the thought, she took a long swig, as she lay down onto the bed, sighing heavily, one hand on the glass, the other with fingers inside her.

She felt something beneath her, and turned on her side, to scoop up the pills she'd laid on the bed earlier; recalling she'd popped them out of the packets.

She'd forgotten about these ones. It saved all that fumbling.

Maybe that's why pills were no longer sold in bottles. Clever bastards!

Dawn giggled at the thought of getting one over the 'pill people' and scooped up a small handful, shovelling them into her mouth, a couple falling out, and another sticking to the red lipstick. She blew the offending pill away.

They began to dry her throat and another good swig of Gin emptied the glass and washed the killer pills down into the rapidly growing bubbling acid pit, which was her stomach. She refilled the glass, but this time with a little less gin and a bit more tonic, as she felt the gin effect was kicking in too quickly.

She didn't want to be too pissed before she'd swallowed the majority of the pills. Where was the fun in that? And besides, Gavin might call. Maybe.

With slightly blurring eyes, she gazed at the discarded boxes and blister packs on the floor. At least half a dozen. Or more. She couldn't recall how many.

It was amazing how quickly you could go through them, she thought.

She felt her breathing becoming heavy and strangely her ears began to ring. Not unlike one time she'd drunk nearly half a bottle of Cherry Brandy with Gavin before setting off at a hunt. A great day. Good memories. Fun.

Gavin? Where the fuck was Gavin? He was late.

Had he texted back? She fumbled for her phone.

No. Wanker! He was possibly busy. Or not. Wanker!

Maybe he was with that whore. The posh bitch. What was her name?

Or he could be at work, Busy. He'd be back soon.

He worked too hard. But he'd be back very soon. He would.

Then he'd find her. He'd rescue her. As usual.

Gavin had always been her hero. Her saviour.

She needed him. She loved him.

Maybe too much.

Her breathing was slowing, she noticed. And her head was starting to sway.

And that ringing in the ears. Wow! Church bells on steroids.

One more quick final message to Gavin:

GAV - I LUV U. GDBYE. D. XXX.

She pressed the send button and it was gone, drifting on an electronic ether, but left forever on her phone as a final record as she lay back on the bed.

She felt so tired. It'd been a busy day. Doing nothing. Tired. Sleep.

Dawn looked at the neat, hand-written envelope placed in the mirror on the dressing table. She noted it wasn't quite level. Pity. She liked things orderly. Tidy and neat. Controlled. She sighed, thinking about getting up to straighten it. It had to be right. Things had to be right with Dawn. She tried to rise.

Fuck it! It'd have to do as it was. Fuck 'em. Wankers!

She giggled as she lay curled up sideways in the foetal position, unable to move as a stomach cramp kicked in, and she clutched her aching belly.

Maybe she needed an Aspirin to ease the stomach pain. She grinned at the thought and reached out for some of the loose tablets laying around, laughing as some pinged across the bed and onto the floor with her fumbling fingers.

Her free index finger flicked the small white pills all around the room.

It amused her, as she moved the small pile and pinged some more, flicking tablets off the bed and around the gently swaying room, seeing what targets she could hit. It'd help if the room wasn't moving. Or was it the bed?
She scooped up some more tablets from the bed, crunching them in one big mouthful and guzzling down more G&T to rinse the chalky paste into her slowly perforating stomach. That's do nicely. That'd ease the pain. Maybe.
The true effects of the aspirin were unknown to her, but were slowly working their secret magic deep within. Dawn's stomach lining was slowly dissolving over the excessive dosage of aspirin she had taken. Soon the fine capillaries of her stomach would then begin to dissolve too. The numbing sensation of the alcohol reduced the pain. Slowly thinning out, until the fine capillaries burst, Dawn's stomach would then begin to suffer irreparable severe gastric erosion, dissolving, causing massive internal bleeding. But this would all happen once Dawn had lost consciousness, and her breathing had stopped. Hopefully.
Leaning across the spinning bed, and grasping at the moving bottle, Dawn refilled the glass with gin, most sloshing out and onto the carpet, followed by the dropped bottle, Dawn giggled, raising a childlike hand to her face.
A bit too much, she thought to her self as she raised the glass of almost neat gin and took a sip, carelessly spilling some over the bed and her stockings.
Pity Gavin wasn't here to suck it off my legs, or higher, she thought.
He'll be here soon. He's got my messages. He'll come. He's busy.
She laid back, breathing slowly, but head spinning and ears ringing.
Was that church bells ringing? Just like at their wedding. Sweet!
Where on earth was Gavin? Was he still at work? He was late. Again.
Dawn gazed up at the ceiling, staring at the crystal lampshade, watching as the room began to rotate, slowly growing faster and faster, but darker.
Whoa! Hold on there. I didn't book this ride. She turned her head sideways, looking at the furniture spin around the room like galloping Carousal horses.
She liked Carousal's. She liked horses. She'd have a horse when she grew up. A nice white one. One day. Gavin would buy her one. Where was Gavin?
Dawn felt her hands grasp at the side of the mattress, holding tight to the bed, lest she should fall off of as it spun like a rodeo horse; it seemingly determined to throw her off and onto the consuming, spinning floor below.
She smiled at the swirling scene, feeling a little nauseous, but happy.
Wow! That was some good gin. Too good. She must get another bottle.
Snuggling her head into the pillow, she focussed on the ceiling. It was more relaxing now and seemed to swirl like clouds on a summer day. Or maybe it was dollops of mashed potato, ready to consume her. Interesting concept.
Being eaten by mashed potato. She smiled at the thought. Funny.
Dawn closed her eyes, now feeling tired. Very tired. Relax. Sleep.
The darkness was warm and welcoming, and seemed to lovingly beckon her into enveloping folds. Like soft warm black velvet, it swallowed her whole body, as she fell deeper and deeper into its dark mysterious depths.

The darkness was nice.
Warm and comforting. Not like life.
Life was cold and hard. Cruel and wicked.
Not welcome.
This darkness was nice.
Welcoming.
Welcomed.
With wide-open arms Dawn embraced the dark.
And the darkness opened its arms. Wide.
'Take me.' Dawn whispered in her mind.
And it did. Willingly.
She smiled as the darkness embraced her.
Wrapping her into its comforting arms, like the wings of a black swan or warm ocean currents on a summer night. Dawn was sucked into its depths.
'Where was Gavin?'
It was Dawn's last thought.
She let the waves of darkness take her away.
They carried her soul off on their peaks.
Like warm comforting hands
Carefully caressing, lapping at her empty body.
The darkness welcomed her.
Then consumed her.

Chapter 107

Pride comes before destruction
and an arrogant spirit before a fall.

Proverbs 16:18 – The Bible

Anna awoke with a start, her alarm bleeping loudly.

An arm lay across her chest.

She froze, her senses numb, but quickly returning. An arm!

Lifting up the quilt, which lay across her face, she stared at the pale arm.

'Who? Where? What? Why?'

At least she was in her own bed. That was a positive start. Wasn't it?

Questions raced through her mind as she scanned the darkened bedroom and glanced at the red digital clock display. She looked again.

'Shit!' She was supposed to be riding out with Chris this morning.

It was New Year's Day. She sighed heavily. What had happened?

Her eyes fell back onto the arm lying heavily across her body.

Flipping back the quilt, the chill air of the room prickled her semi-naked form. She slid her long legs out of the bed and then reaching out with one hand, lifted the arm away and dropped the offending limb onto the floor beside the bed. It landed with a heavy thud upon the bare timber boards.

'Where the hell did that come from?' Thoughts raced through her mind as she tried to recall why she'd gone to bed with a rogue disembodied arm.

Then it all came flooding back. Clearly. In full detail. Unfortunately.

The police incident with the lads. A fight. Broken shop window. Bodies crashing into the front display. Dressed mannequins thrown onto the street. Mannequin body parts. A rogue arm, playfully passed around. Lads running away. Police chasing. The arm thrust at Tracey with a cheeky wink, blown kiss and smile. Tracey grinning and accepting the love token. Police running past.

Then Anna had somehow taken it home. To keep her company.

An arm? A mannequin's arm? She must be desperate.

She winced, looking down at the disembodied arm, wondering what on earth she'd got up to last night. Or technically was it today? It didn't matter.

It was too early to ponder. She knew she'd only had a few hours sleep, and although she hadn't drunk too much, she was tired and far from her best. More especially, not at her best for a ride out with Chris. For that she knew she'd have to be good on a good day. Although today was a day she'd been looking forward to, she now wondered at the sense of arranging a ride out on New Year's Day after a mad night out with Tracey and Julie. That said, if all were as normal, and not suspended, they'd have all been going hunting today.

No wonder many people consider horsey-people as being slightly mad.

Anna shuddered at the thought of rising and could only wonder what state Tracey would be in. Grim to Half-Dead seemed a fitting category. Julie would only be slightly better, but not much. Semi-Grim, if there was such a thing.
With a gentle sweep of her elegant foot, the arm slid across the bare wooden floorboards and Anna moved over to her wardrobe. At the bottom, on the floor where they lived, lay a range of jodhpurs, fleeces and riding clothes. Bleary eyes scanned the varied pile, trying to determine which looked best. She looked in the mirror and wished she hadn't, letting out a heavy sigh.
Why on earth had she agreed to meet Chris today and ride out?
Was she mad? No doubt Tracey would still be in bed, as would Julie.
Snug and cosy until they decided to rise. Like she should be.
But not Anna. She was tired, and felt she looked terrible.
She glanced back into the mirror.
'Hug Me' the lettering on her nightgown read in reverse.
If only someone would. Could it be that hard?
She glanced down at her feet. Too big, she decided.
Why do tall people always have big feet? She questioned.
To stop them falling over, her brain replied instantly.
Well at least she knew that was functioning. But she still disliked her feet.
Too long and spidery. Like witches hands. She shuddered.
With a loud huff, and reluctant slow movement of the too-long lower limbs, she propelled herself into the small bathroom. Ten minutes later, washed, brushed and groomed with the minimal amount of make-up, she was sipping a far-too-hot cup of coffee, hoping it'd finally wake her up. It was almost there, and after adding extra milk to cool it and make it more drinkable, with no patience to wait, she downed the cup, grabbed her keys and a warm fleece. Double-checking she had everything, Anna set off towards Horsewater.
As she drove down into the yard, she was amazed to see lights on. Not only in Chris' house, but also in the yard. To her amazement, shock, and envied disappointment, she saw Julie's Land Rover parked up. She shook her head.
"No," she muttered to herself. "It can't be real? A clone?"
"Good morning! Happy New Year!" Julie called joyfully, her head appearing from Bonnie's empty stable. "How are you?"
"Alive, I think. And you? I thought you'd still be in bed."
"I'm fine. I've put out Bonnie and Fred. Then I'm going back home. I've got family coming around for lunch. Got to get everything prepared."
Anna stared at the woman as she wandered back to the two empty stables, already half done, then heard footsteps from behind and saw Chris and Max.
"Happy New Year!" Chris announced, looking equally as joyful as Julie.
Anna wondered if these people were real, glancing at the fresh faces of Chris and Julie, whilst she felt like she'd been run over by a truck. Several times.
Max, walking steadily at Chris' side, simply stared coldly at Anna. But this morning he didn't run up to her for his usual pat, as if he knew some secret.

He did. And so did Anna. The pair coldly regarded each other.

"Still okay for our ride?" Chris enquired enthusiastically, then saw the curious exchange between Anna and Max before the big dog trotted away to urinate.

"I am, and looking forward to it, but I'm not sure my body is. We'll see."

Chris smiled and strolled to Tirus' stable, clicking at the moody chestnut gelding who approached the door with his ears flat back and usual scowl.

"I'm taking him out today. It'll do him good. There's no rush to get Penny ready as the sun won't think about rising for about half an hour. It's also having a New Year lay in. So get done what you need, have some coffee, and then we'll go off for a charge around the woods to wake us up. Then you can tell me just how naughty your cousin was last night. Very naughty, I'd bet!"

Anna was dumbstruck at how chatty and alive Chris appeared, talking more than she'd known, with a smile, whilst she felt like death warmed up. Twice.

Anna wandered to the tackroom, after checking on Penny and wishing her the best, after she'd whinnied to her over the door, asking for breakfast. The mare seemed oblivious to Anna's internal pains, woes and raging head, just wanting her feed. For her it was simply another day. Which in reality it was.

Anna strolled back with Penny's breakfast, and after a quick pat threw the heavy black rubber feed bucket into the stable, closed the door, then returned to the tackroom, feeling as if her long limbs were made of beaten lead. Flicking on the already warm kettle, she slumped into one of the old chairs.

A heavy sigh was met with Julie's face, peering around the tackroom door.

"Feeling rough?" Julie enquired. "I hope so. You look like shit. Sloppy shit!"

"Oh thank you very much!" Anna exclaimed, but smiled broadly, giggling.

"Yes. Rough. Very rough. Like sandpaper. Or maybe a badger's arse. Although theoretically I don't actually know how rough a badger's arse is. Do you? But, yes, although I don't know why I should. You and Tracey drunk much more than me. How come you're both still alive, yet I feel like death? I'm assuming Tracey is alive and made it safely home and not to a police cell."

"She's okay and will come down later. Her blood is forty percent proof!"

"And Chris?" Anna enquired, still unable to understand why Julie looked so lively, yet she felt so terrible. She'd purposefully drunk less, knowing she was riding out with Chris and wanted to look and feel her best. But she failed.

"I doubt he went out. And besides he doesn't really drink. Too sensible."

Anna managed a smile and gentle chuckle, enjoying Julie's happy and vibrant nature. It seemed to warm her up and enliven her spirits, despite her body and head feeling as if she'd been deprived of oxygen for some period of time.

Julie left to carry on doing whatever she needed to do, and Anna sat sipping her second cup of coffee for the morning, day and the New Year. It seemed to work, and after a short time inhaling the foul tackroom air, which was known to almost kill hardened policemen, she emerged, and headed back over to Penny, who'd almost finished her breakfast. She quietly watched her over the stable door, and then heard movement behind her. It was Chris.

"Did you do anything last night?" Anna enquired, then realised she probably shouldn't have asked. "I remember you said your uncle was coming."

"No. As mentioned, my uncle came around. We chatted and that was about it. I'm not really into piss-ups, punch-ups and fireworks. Mister Boring. I like staring at crows or simply riding horses. Fast." He looked glumly at Anna.

"I wish I'd joined you," she grinned. "I feel like shit, but don't know why. I must be getting too old for going out. What is it with Julie and Tracey?"

Chris simply smiled, shrugging his shoulders for a silent reply, making Anna feel warm inside, but why she didn't know. Strangely he always did.

"I've got the usual rounds to do, but I'm okay, unless you want to help turn out with a few. It'd help, as I'm not sure if Sally will be down. She was going to a family party last night. Once we've thrown these out and I've done the usual chores, we can set out. We can have a dash about and blow all the old cobwebs out. Welcome in a new day and new year in true style."

Anna was impressed by Chris' happy nature, when all she could really think of doing was going back to bed. She did as they said, turning out the liveries, neither really speaking, and before long Chris went to attend to Tirus.

After preparing further mugs of strong coffee, and passing one over to a very grateful Chris, who was mucking out a stable, Anna returned to Penny's stable and began attacking the mare with her brushes and some renewed vigour.

Soon she had Penny pampered and preened; looking as if she was going to a show, and was now looking forward to riding out with Chris. Despite the chill of the early morning and her still muggy head, she now felt warm inside and was genuinely happy to be riding out. Julie had long gone, popping her head over Penny's stable door before she left and wishing Anna well.

Carol appeared as the pair prepared to mount up, grinning as they brought their mounts out into the yard, leaving them both off with a hearty wave.

She'd made a comment about being at Burlingham Hall last night to see in the New Year, to which Chris simply smiled. Anna looked on curious. He'd made no mention or spoken about Virginia. She in turn had thought it wise not to mention her disappearance, knowing how close they were.

That was a hornets nest she didn't want to disturb, but was as curious as any to learn what had become of not only her, but all of the various parties involved in the crazy fracas of only a week ago on Boxing Day.

Anna was amazed Virginia had vanished and Chris seemingly had no idea of where she was. They seemed so close. Maybe she was hiding in his cellar.

It was as if no one dared mention what happened at the Boxing Day Meet, and Anna counted herself into that group. Discretion was best. For now.

Before she knew it the pair were on board their mounts and with no words spoken, only a nod from Chris, they were heading out the yard, down past the ménage and paddocks, and then heading off up into the woods, both silently admiring the grazing horses, snug in their brightly coloured, albeit mud-stained outdoor rugs. Cirrus trotted over to look and Chris gave her a smile.

They were soon riding in the woods and Anna began chattering about general nonsense, then got onto the subject of the evening's events. She mentioned the police incident, fight and broken shop window, but strangely forgot to mention she'd woken up with a rogue arm in her bed. She felt that even Chris wouldn't understand such a thing. To be honest, neither did she.

"Fancy a quick canter?" Chris asked calmly with his usual grin as they approached a long section of wooded track. "Only if you're feeling okay."

Anna knew by now that this meant a charge through the woods, where you had to duck and dive between trees and low branches, hoping you didn't get decapitated or impaled upon a rogue branch, or simply swept off your horse.

Of course she agreed, her keen smile not embraced by her dull mind and aching limbs. Her slow body would have to catch up with her enthusiasm.

With a quick collection of his reins, Chris didn't even have to kick Tirus on, the horse instinctively knowing what his rider wanted and also knowing the tracks and trails within the woods so well as to almost operate on autopilot.

With a swish of chestnut tail, Tirus was off, leaving Anna and Penny to engage brains and limbs, before with a lurch, Penny flew off, to catch her companion. Anna only just managed to collect her reins up as she felt the power surge beneath her and the cool morning air race into her watering eyes.

The pair dodged and weaved along the first main track, one which Anna was beginning to know, and thus aware of where some of the twists and bends would appear. It was only a quick burst, covering just a few hundred yards, to warm them up, rather than a long charge or some test of bravery or stupidity.

It worked, both for horse and rider. As Chris pulled up the frantic chestnut, drawing hard on the reins to stop, and Anna drew up alongside more easily.

"That was a good start," beamed Chris with enthusiasm. "Are you awake now? I hope so. Adrenaline. Better than ten cups of coffee!"

Anna regained her breath, steadying Penny, before replying with a smile.

"It was good, but I think today I'd still prefer a nice strong coffee, along with a hot, jam-filled croissant. Very yummy!" Anna said and could only dream.

"That sounds great too. Good thinking. I've got some indoors. Maybe you'd like one or two when we get back?" Chris replied, his smile beaming.

Anna's eyes widened at the unbelievable sound of a breakfast invite.

Although Chris sounded enthusiastic, Anna noticed he blushed when asking, as if embarrassed to cross a threshold, despite their kiss on Christmas Day.

"It all depends on what type of jam you have," Anna grinned cheekily, looking straight at a blushing Chris. "If not, I'm not coming!"

"I've got a wide selection. All locally produced too. I get them from a woman in the village. Much better than shop rubbish. What do you like?"

"Do you have Raspberry?" Anna enquired sternly.

"Yes," responded Chris positively and with a smile.

"Excellent. You must have Raspberry jam on croissants. It's almost illegal to not. I'm sure you can be arrested for it." Anna smirked. "And plum?"

"Yes, I have plum too. That jam is gorgeous. But I only keep it for best and special people, so I may not let you have any. I'll have to think."

"Oh please do! I love plum jam. Must be really thick. I'll marry you if you let me have some!" Anna grinned wickedly, looking deep into Chris' glowing face, but hoping she hadn't pushed things too far. "And lots of butter too! It must be dripping out the sides, so you have to lick your fingers."

Chris went an even brighter red and looked away, feigning ducking beneath a low branch to break the strong eye contact. Anna blushed too, but liked the slightly risky and humorous banter, knowing it was the only way she'd ever price open his tight armour and win him over. Or so she hoped.

"That sounds like date. Maybe with a cup of strong tea to wash it all down. We just need to get back alive!" Anna added the joking quip to cool things down, but saw from Chris' smirk, knowing that he appreciated the banter.

They rode side by side for a few minutes, neither speaking, but instead quietly enjoying the moment as well as being part of the environment. Anna had quickly learnt Chris loved the woods and natural world around him, and the girls had said that he usually rode out alone quite often to simply enjoy and appreciate what he knew he had and was fortunate enough to own.

The track ahead widened then split, as was common with Chris' woods, with a small glade set to one side and woods to the other. It was one of many Anna knew Chris cut for hay in the summer and about the estate. Despite the maze of woodland tracks, Anna knew they were never that far from the farm.

The woods covered a large area, and bordered onto Lord Burlingham's land and also some of Reggie's. Anna knew the girls in the yard knew most of the areas, but even they didn't seem to know all of the smaller woodland tracks.

The track they now headed down was one Anna hadn't ridden before and was flanked on most side by a mix of coniferous trees. A mix of firs, spruces and larch, this was part of the estate Chris would 'cultivate' at some point in the future and cut down the crop of trees to create a new woodland glade.

Chris glanced at Anna, seemingly enjoying the quiet, with only the soft clop of the horse's hooves breaking the silence, but also her company. He seemed content she was admiring the woodlands too and all the peace they brought.

"Fancy another canter?" Chris' grin meant Anna had no choice. She nodded.

No sooner had she nodded, joined with a genuine excited smile, Chris tapped Tirus into life. The chestnut responded, almost leaping off the track as his legs whirled around, indirectly changing from walk to canter. Chris was off.

Anna felt cheated and had to tighten up her reins to get herself set before she kicked her mount into life. She needn't have worried as Penny was already preparing to go, and just awaiting the 'official okay' or kick from her mum.

She too was off, but Chris had a good head start. The track was narrower and the conifer trees more dense and closely planted than before, with many branches stretching out across the track, the ends whipping into her face and body, causing her to look away from the fast disappearing chestnut.

"Left. Take the left track!" Chris hollered, his head turned, but too late.

Anna saw Chris ahead of her turn his head and look towards her, as he and Tirus peeled away onto another track to the left, but never heard his call.

Penny kept racing down the track before her, Anna's head flicking from track to trees as she realised Chris had peeled away and she was no racing off down a woodland track on a bolting Penny, unaware where she was going.

"Stay there on that rack. I'll" come around and join you!" Anna heard Chris yell, the sound coming through the dense row trees growing along the track and obscuring Chris' image, as all Anna saw was a flash of charging chestnut.

Anna braced her bottom hard into the saddle and began to pull firmly upon the reins, intent on pulling up Penny. But she ignored her.

Tree branches whipped at Anna's face, as she pulled hard on the reins.

Head down, then up, avoiding the branches, Anna sat deep and drew hard, Penny finally responding, as Anna weaved through the trees.

The horse began to slowly ease up, but was still propelling the pair at speed through the dense woods, Penny's legs thundering hard beneath on the track.

Anna regained some control. Penny eased up.

Then something moved on the right.

It was ahead. Set back within the dense trees.

And appeared to be waiting. Poised. Ready to strike.

Anna glanced, approaching fast, suddenly seeing movement.

The dark figure stepped out onto the track.

Anna stared in awe at the strange figure.

It was only metres away.

Then she stared in horror. Eyes transfixed.

The figure moved. Towards her.

A wooden post was held before it.

"Chrissss!" Anna screamed.

The darkened figure sidestepped Anna and Penny.

Horse and rider raced past.

A length of timber was swung at horse and rider.

It hit the rider hard. Very hard.

With a scream, Anna flew out of the saddle.

Chapter 108

In battle there are not more than two methods of attack:
the direct and indirect.

Sun Tzu - Art of War

The hooded figure stepped out, swinging the length of timber, causing Penny to shy sharply into the soft fir trees o the side, crashing into the tree branches, but remaining on the track. However, Anna's momentum carried her forward.
Out of the saddle she flew, feet clearing the stirrups, as she zoomed over Penny's head and on through the air. The ground was swift and keen to greet her, and she hit the firm woodland floor heavily, it knocking out her breath and concussing her, as her head hit the ground and she rolled over to the side.
Face set into hard dirt and pine needles, Anna groaned heavily, wheezing painfully, trying to regain her breath through expelled lungs and bashed ribs.
Instinctively she flipped onto her backside, looked about, wanting to know where Penny was; the action almost instinctive with horse riders, regardless of their own fate or physical condition, the well-being of their horse paramount.
Penny appeared stunned, but upright, standing beside the trees into which she'd crashed, looking at Anna, her reins snagged on one of the tree branches.
Equally stunned, but injured and out-of-breath, Anna slid her legs beneath her, stretching out an arm, about to rise. She began to push her body up, but sensed movement. Turning her head, she was horrified to see a dark figure.
Standing above her, and without warning or comment, the black-clad spectre raised the piece of timber struck it down with full force upon Anna.
Instinctively Anna lifted her arm, the timber crashing painfully into the raised defensive limb. Such was the force, the branch shattered. Anna was unsure if the cracking sound was the snap of wood or her arm breaking. Maybe both.
Anna was thrown sideways by the strike, knocking her back to the ground, the pain in her arm instant, causing her to grimace and grasp at the limb.
Then, shuffling on her backside, aware of the debris from the track beneath her, she saw the strange dark figure step sideways off the track. Anna's keen, but frightened eyes watched the figure's swift movement, totally confused.
The figure returned with a large, half-rotting tree stump. Lifted high above its dark hooded head, the black figure advanced towards Anna on the track.
Anna gazed up in dumb horror at the sky, obscured by the huge tree stump.
Blackened and dirty. Large and heavy. Deadly.
Strangely she noted a rotting section, just as the log was released.
"Chrissss!" Anna hollered. "Hel….!"
Then Anna's world went dark.

Chapter 109

Love sought is good, but given unsought is better.

Twelfth Night - Shakespeare

Anna opened her eyes to see Chris' face. Her head flitted from side to side. Trees. A dirt track. A large chestnut coloured head appeared beside him. Leather bridle attached Tirus to his rider. But no one else.

"Penny?" Anna asked, her voice feeble.

"Safe." It was all Chris needed to say. "Caught in a tree, but safe and unhurt. Unlike you. You look terrible. Worse than when we set off!"

Anna laughed, then cried, as Chris' face turn from playful grin to concern.

"Where are they?" Anna enquired in a soft voice. "Has he gone?"

"Who?" Chris seemed confused. He looked about.

"The Monk?" Anna spat dirt and debris from her mouth. Lip bleeding.

"Monk?" Chris shook his head, confused. He looked about once more.

"The hooded figure. The Monk. The person who attacked me."

Chris spoke, his tone blunt. "Are you hurt? Can you stand?"

Anna heaved heavily, trying to breath, spitting out dirt and timber, wheezing heavily, and then sobbed some more as she collapsed. She felt Chris try to hold her, but was partially restrained by the reins attached to Tirus' bridle.

The usually grumpy chestnut looked down, almost sympathetically. For once.

"I need to get you up and grab Penny. Just in case. Do you think you can stand? Sorry to be so blunt, but you can't stay here. You have to walk."

Anna understood, knowing most horse riders were hard, and when it came to falls, unless dead or they had limbs missing or sticking out at weird angles, most others had little sympathy; only an urgent need to swiftly reunite horse and rider in whatever form possible. She felt Chris lift her up, and her legs wobble slightly beneath her, but then go steady as she rose fully with his aid.

"I think you maybe concussed," Chris announced, looking at the state of her riding hat, which was covered in debris, as well as her general dazed and slightly confused manner. In addition, she had a few minor grazes to her face.

"Do you think you can stand? Just give it a few moments to recover fully. You've taken a heavy fall. Sorry. I shouldn't have dashed off. It's my fault."

Chris looked sad and downtrodden as he held Anna in his arms.

"No Chris. It was okay. It was my fault. I should have been more aware. And besides, it was the person who hit me with a branch. It was their fault. Then they tried to kill me with that big heavy log. The dark monk. It was him."

Chris stared at Anna, a look of concern upon his face.

"Have they gone? Be careful Chris. They may come back." Anna whispered.

Chris looked furtively at Anna, but then around the woods where they stood.

He glanced about the woodland track, where the trees were densely packed in and grew close together, being a 'crop' to be harvested in the future. But all he could see was dense greenery. The track, up and down, was empty, with no signs of footprints, only the scuff of hooves. He looked at the trees once more. Chris could see nothing. Many small branches stretched out across the track and could catch out the unwary rider and pull them off. Quite easily.

"Oh!" Anna winced upon rising. "My bum really hurts. Maybe you could rub it better." She chuckled and Chris was glad to see she still had a sense of humour. Grabbing her left arm she suddenly winced, letting out a loud yelp.

"Aargh! That hurts. Really, really hurts." Anna cradled the arm in her free hand, squinted at the sharp pain. Chris noticed a dark dirty mark running right across the jacket sleeve.

"You may have broken it. Possibly when you fell. Quite a common injury."

Anna stood in silence for a few seconds, and then seemed to recover.

"No," Anna announced in a clear, matter-of-fact manner. "No, I injured it when the monk hit me with the first big stick. I remember hearing the crack."

She moved a step away from Chris, her eyes scanning the track and margins.

"Look Chris. That broken branch. See?" She pointed to a large length of timber that had been broken in two. "It was smashed against my raised arm."

Chris noted the branch Anna indicated, but also noted several dozen other broken branches laying scattered about. He looked at Anna with concern.

Anna's attention drifted and she seemed to scan the track where she'd lain.

"Look! That log. The big old dirty one. The monk lifted that up and smashed it onto my head when I was on the ground. They tried to kill me! Look!"

Chris again could see only a shattered old rotting log. It was big and heavy. Like many. He saw dozens daily as he rode or walked through the woods.

He glanced at the log, and then back at Anna, then her hat and face.

"I agree. It looks like you did smash your head on that log. Probably when you fell. As you can see, it's on the track. You're very lucky it was rotten."

Anna suddenly burst into tears and threw her arms around Chris, whilst he hugged her with one arm, holding multiple reins with the other. Her warm, wet tears rolled onto his cheeks. Welcomed, but not in the circumstances.

"I think we need to get you back to the yard and then checked over. You may have broken your arm and I definitely think you need to see a doctor, just in case you've seriously banged your head. You do seem very confused."

Anna sniffed and removed her head from Chris' shoulder, wiping the tears from her face, only to leave a swipe of mud and blood. Chris lifted his hand and gently wiped her face with his gloved hand. Anna smiled warmly.

"If you can walk, we're only a quarter of a mile from the farm. The woods are like a maze. Hopefully we can quickly get you back to the yard. Okay?"

Anna nodded, whether she understood or not, and hobbled over to where Penny was patiently standing, seemingly unfazed by the whole event, but confused as to why she was no longer racing about, which had been fun.

It took them about fifteen minutes for then to walk clear the dense area of woods and get back onto the main track, which led straight back to the farm.

Anna cradled her left arm with her right and walked slowly before Chris, who led both horses, a set of reins in each hand. Thankfully the horses were calm, having that strange equine knowledge and understanding when they meet young or wary people, to then treat them gently. The pair seemed to sense Anna was injured, and both calmly walked alongside Chris, although Tirus did on occasion try to nibble at Penny's reins. Before long, the familiar sight of the green paddocks, ménage and barns and white house came into sight.

Keen eyes from the yard, in the form of Sally, saw the figures emerge from the woods and out onto the track. She instantly noted an incident, seeing two figures walking and not onboard their mounts. Never a good sight.

Worse still, Anna was trudging wearily ahead alone, seemingly holding her arm, and Chris was walked behind with two slow horses. Very bad.

Sally came running down the track, easing up as she approached and only then saw fully the dirty-faced and dishevelled Anna, who was usually pristine and well-turned out. Chris, leading the horses behind Anna, shook his head.

Sally didn't need to ask what'd happened. A fall. Bad. Chris seemed okay.

"Are you all okay? Anna, you look like a bus hit you. Or maybe a tree. Or maybe both, somehow. Not being rude of course! But you do look shit!"

Anna managed to raise a wry smile, but by now she was simply glad to be back 'home' and looking to putting Penny away, sitting down and resting.

"Go and sit in the tackroom for a few minutes. Me and Sally will put away the horses. Then we can check you over properly, see what's damaged and take things from there." Chris stated as they finally made it into the yard.

All followed Chris' firm order. Anna headed off to the tackroom and Sally took Penny back to her stable. A few minutes later, with horses un-tacked and a few carrots thrown given to briefly appease them, the pair returned to the tackroom to see Anna gently crying. Sally immediately hugged her from behind, making comforting sounds and words and Anna recovered, sniffing and wiping her nose and face on her grubby fleece jacket. Her best one.

"It's not fair," she bubbled. "I won't get to have those croissants now!"

It was all she said, but all she had to say. Chris simply burst out laughing and Sally looked at the pair totally confused, guessing she was missing something.

He moved before Anna and squatted down, holding her finger-tips, looking into her face, smiling, but sympathetically. Sally looked on over her shoulder.

"You can have then another time, you daft old moo!" Chris smiled warmly.

Anna returned the smile, wiping more mud across her damp face.

"But will you still have the raspberry and plum jam?" Anna grinned solemnly. "You'd better, or I'm not coming!"

Chris grinned and went to hug her, but she winced, grasping her arm again.

"I definitely think you need to go to the hospital." He looked over to Sally, clearly concerned, giving her a nod. Sally got the message and nodded back.

"I'll happily run you up there, but the trouble is I can't stay long, as I'll need to get all the horses back in later. It'll be a dump and run, I'm afraid."

Chris looked both concerned and flustered, knowing he wanted to help.

"Well I can get most things done," added Sally, but knew what Chris meant.

"Don't worry Chris. Or you Sally. It's kind, but please just call my mum. She can take me and stay as long as needed. You can do the horses. And Penny."

"Are you sure?" Chris enquired sympathetically, and Sally looked relieved.

"Yes, it's the most sensible thing. She and my dad have nothing to do all day. Well except eat and drink! It'll add some excitement to their new year!"

"I have your mum's number as an emergency contact from when you first came, if you remember. I'll dash off to the house and call her, if you're sure."

With a nod from Anna Chris was off, across the yard and over to the house.

Anna sat silent momentarily, as Sally moved to put the kettle on, looking at Anna to ensure she was really okay. Anna turned, glancing out the tackroom door, almost as if to ensure Chris had gone, before she spoke to Sally.

"This might sound a bit silly, but is this place haunted?" Anna spoke quietly.

"Haunted?" Sally looked puzzled, unsure of Anna. "Do mean right here?"

"Well not the tackroom, or farm, but maybe the woods? Or everywhere."

Sally regarded Anna somewhat warily, as if she was daft, but knew she might be badly concussed and thus confused. She certainly wasn't the bouncy, fun, slightly mad person Sally had grown to know over the past few weeks.

"Not that I'm aware of," Sally replied cautiously. "Nothing I've heard of and I believe in spooks and things. I've never seen anything. Why do you ask?"

Anna went silent, face flushing, then sheepishly smiled, as if embarrassed.

"I think I saw a ghost in the woods. A dark hooded monk."

Sally looked Anna s if she was daft, and tried her best to disguise the emotion displayed. But she failed totally. Anna noticed Sally's baffled look.

"Sorry, I'm being silly. It's the fall. I told Chris a hooded monk stepped out to spook Penny. And then hit me. Worse, it then tried to kill me with a log."

Sally simply stared at Anna. No words were needed. She shuffled uneasily.

Anna fully understood the look. She flushed red and looked down.

"I know it's silly. And I'm being daft saying such a thing. I simply fell off. Bad riding. I must have hit my head on the log. I don't know anymore."

Sally looked at Anna sympathetically, aware of how the mind played tricks when concussed and things were forgotten or imagined in an accident.

"Don't tell Chris I asked about a ghost. "Anna suddenly added. "Or what I just said. He'll think I'm stupid. I know I am." Anna looked long at Sally.

Sally grinned, then reached out and touched Anna's hand, smiling broadly.

"He already thinks you're daft, but in the nicest, mad sort of way. He often speaks about you and asks us questions. That's unusual for him. I know he really likes you. A lot. Mad or not. So don't worry. Just get better. Quickly!"

Chris suddenly appeared in the tackroom doorway, his face red from rushing about too and from the house. Anna and Sally silently smiled at him.

"I've called you mum. She's coming with your dad." Chris declared.
Anna winced at the response, gently shaking her head. Not her dad.
Chris understood the embarrassment and continued.
"Come and sit in the house. It's warmer and god knows what diseases you'll pick up in here. Leprosy probably! Mind you, the germs in here will cure it!"
Anna and Sally giggled at Chris' humour and all were glad to see Anna smile.
The group trudged across the yard and over towards the house, where Chris led her into the kitchen. A big mug of coffee was served, but no croissants.
The cavalry arrived within fifteen minutes. Anna's dad pulled up into the yard in his silver Bentley, making Anna wince, looking out of Chris' kitchen window. In the yard, Sally looked in awe at the massive car with private plate.
If anyone thought Anna might be a 'gold-digger' after Chris and his estate, this dispelled any thoughts. It was obvious her parents had money. Lots of it.
Tracey had often said, seemingly joking, Anna's parents were millionaires.
Maybe Chris was after Anna's inheritance. Sally grinned inwardly.
Anna winced as she saw the big silver car, and the equally big man exit, along with her mum. Chris wandered out and over towards the pair and she winced again, as her dad approached Chris, towering above him, as an arm flew out.
Her dad firmly grasped Chris' hand and seemed to almost break it off as it was shaken so vigorously. He then gave the small horseman a big hug.
"Thank you for rescuing her. Much appreciated. Bloody horses! Dangerous things. She should've done parachuting or bought a motorbike. Much safer!"
Joyce exited the massive car with less pomp, as was her style, simply nodding at Chris and smiling sweetly. He said something and both her parents looked towards the house. Anna couldn't hear what the group were saying, but she imagined Chris would be advising she went to hospital, both to check out her arm, which certainly throbbed, but also her head. It still ached, and she couldn't work out if it was from the fall, last-nights drinking, or a mix of both.
Ignoring the group outside, chatting heartily it seemed, Anna's eyes drifted dreamily about the snug kitchen, then suddenly fixed upon an object. A key.
That key was in the lock of a door.
And that door was the one to the cellar.
This was the cellar Chris had told her wasn't used.
Anna's eyes focussed upon the key. Clean and bright.
The key was new, with light reflecting off the head.
It was an older style key, but certainly not some rusty relic.
The key was well used. Thus, so was the cellar.
Chris had lied. He'd lied about the 'old' cellar. Why?
What did he hide in the cellar? His mistress? Virginia? Or stolen gold.
Anna's mind began to race at the thought of what really lay hidden deep in the cellar Chris had told her wasn't used. She'd seen the lights. And Max.
She rose from the chair, her head turning side to side, her hand gingerly reaching out, as with unsteady steps, she inched towards the cellar door.

Anna rose slightly, glancing sideways out towards the kitchen window, still hearing her parents chatting to Chris outside. Her focus reset upon the door. Shuffling feet drew her slowly close to the dark stained timber. Anna's arm stretched out, and her fingers touched the key. Then they began to turn.

"What the hell are you doing?" A voice boomed out.

Anna jumped, hand retracting, spinning around to the owner of the voice.

"Idiot! I thought you're supposed to stay on horses, not fall off! Come here stupid and let me give you a hug!" Anna's dad stood towering before her.

Anna blushed for a number of reasons. For nearly being caught out trying to open Chris' elusive cellar door, but also because of her doting father; whom she knew loved her much, but still treated her like a child. Which was nice.

"Thank you dad, but I don't think you'd better hug me. You'll probably finally break anything that isn't already broken! Tell him mum!"

The group chuckled as Chris and her mum strolled into Chris' kitchen. He shuffled behind, face red, seemingly embarrassed about the whole incident. Anna suspected he also didn't like 'intruders' in his home. Invited or not.

"Wow!" Exclaimed Anna's dad. "This is great. A lovely place. Really nice and traditional. I love it. What a stunning home. It's a pity about these old timber windows. Drafty, I bet. What you could really do with is some new ones!"

Everyone looked in silence at Anna's dad, who in turn, stone-faced, scanned the faces of his captive audience. Then his face broke into a huge smile, and laughing, he then playfully punched Chris arm, almost knocking him over.

"This place is beautiful. Don't change a thing. Especially the windows!"

Chris' face grew redder with the compliment, and he sheepishly glanced at Anna, whose face was equally as red, embarrassed again by her doting dad.

"Come on then. Let's get you to the hospital and see which bits they can fix and which parts they'll throw away into the bin. Most of you I'd imagine!"

Anna's mother simply shook her head and tutted, whilst her dad and Chris chuckled. Within a minutes Anna was stowed within the rear of the massive Bentley, but left the door open and she spoke to Chris, who looked inside.

"Thank Sally for helping out. And thanks to you for scooping me up. Sorry for the trouble I've caused. I'll call later, or mum will, and a very big thanks for seeing to Penny. And sorry for ruining breakfast. Another day. Definitely.

Chris smiled and stretched out a hand, grasped by Anna and squeezed fondly. Her parents looked at the couple and even her dad blushed. Realising he had an audience, Chris released Anna's hand and her dad stepped forward like a chauffeur, closing the rear door, but shaking Chris' hand once more.

"Me or Joyce will give you a call later. Thanks again mate! I owe you."

He slapped Chris' arm and pair climbed into the front of the big car. The engine roared into life and it trundled out of Horsewater. Turning to see Chris wave, Anna was sad once again her day had been ruined, and another opportunity to spend time with Chris had vanished. The pair seemed doomed to never spend any time together she thought as the car moved into the trees.

As she sat in the comfort of the luxury car and relaxed for the first time in an hour, she began to mull over what'd happened and why she'd fallen off.

Had Penny spooked and deviated at the last moment, and she'd become unseated simply by going too fast? Yes, that much was obvious.

Reckless riding? Maybe. But why had Penny spooked? She was usually good.

The image flashed back into her mind. Clear and crisp. She'd swept it away.

The black figure. Stepping out.

With a stick. Swinging wildly.

She'd dismissed it after mentioning it to Chris when he'd picked her up, feeling foolish; convincing herself it'd not really happened.

But it had. It did happen. Clear and crisp.

As she sat in the big car and relaxed, she remembered it all. Clearly.

A dark hooded stranger had leapt out before her.

Swinging a branch at her. On purpose. No accident.

That was why Penny spooked. It did really happen.

And her arm? It was okay when she fell. She'd used it to raise herself up, so it wasn't injured or broken then. That came after. After being hit!

The dark figure had stood over her. With the stick.

Then forcefully struck it down at her. Hard.

The branch was swung into her arm. With purpose.

The loud crack.

Bone or timber? Maybe both. She'd soon discover.

And then the log. The huge tree stump.

Raised up high over her by the dark figure.

Then smashed down onto her head.

Deliberately.

Had she imagined that too?

No.

That too had really happened.

She didn't hit her head on a log as she fell.

Someone had dropped the log on her head.

On purpose. To try to kill her?

Maybe. But why?

Why would someone do that? And who?

With a heavy sight Anna was unsure once more.

Now her head really ached.

Why would someone attack her?

Now she was confused again.

Maybe she was concussed. Maybe none of this was real.

The dark monk couldn't exist.

It was all in her mind.

Maybe.

Chapter 110

May good luck be your friend in whatever you do,
and may troubles always be a stranger to you.

Irish Quote

A darkened figure watched from the edge of the woods. The Dark Monk.
Through hi-power binoculars, everything was seen. Noted.
All the activity in the yard. People and horses moving about. Cars arriving.
The loving and caring. Sympathy and compassion. All watched. Sickeningly.
Noted and watched with bitter anger. It was pathetic!
Wrong place. Wrong time. She shouldn't have ridden down that track.
And he shouldn't have come to help. What a hero! Not.
Bad timing. But not for him. He'd been lucky.
It'd been a close call. Too close.
Unlucky for some. Yet also lucky for others.
Bitch! She should be dead.
The opportunity had been taken as unexpected as it was.
But her super hero had intervened.
Some were just too lucky. But luck runs out.
Like sand in an hour-glass. Flowing away. Like life.
The Irish Republican Army once famously quoted on the Brighton Bombing, where they failed to kill the British Prime Minister, Lady Margaret Thatcher:
'Today we were unlucky, but remember, we have only to be lucky once. You will have to lucky always.'
That statement had never been so true.
Lucky today. But maybe not lucky tomorrow.
Watch your back. There's a knife coming!
The dark-clad figure, expertly concealed, but with a perfect view, watched from the woods. As binoculars scanned, they pondered the IRA quote.
Today the target had been lucky.
Very lucky.
The assailant had been unlucky.
Very unlucky.
But there would be another day.
Another opportunity to kill.
"Next time you won't be so lucky."
The figure whispered, watching people get into a big car.
"Next time Anna, you will die."

Chapter 111

I have, indeed, no abhorrence of danger,
except in its absolute effect, in terror.

Edgar Allan Poe

Chris received the telephone call later that evening, after he'd rechecked the horses and finally returned inside for the day, to settled down some tea.

Beans on toast. Again. Max got steak. Done just how he liked it.

Alan, Anna's dad, had called. He thanked Chris once more for returning his daughter safely. It was clear she meant the world to him, and god help anyone whoever harmed her. Chris felt a bit guilty, being the one who'd shown-off and indirectly caused the accident. They could have gone out for quiet walk.

The arm wasn't broken, but severely bruised. Similar to a traumatic fracture. Luckily the bone had held, having taken a severe blow from an object. Maybe when she fell. Strong bones, like her 'bone-headed father' Alan had joked to Chris. The doctors believed hit it hard object on the track as she fell, such as a log or stone, as there was a distinct line of hard bruising to her arm.

Anna was relieved it wasn't a break, but the arm had to be treated like one, with ice applied and held in a sling for a few days to be properly rested. She was however furious at being treated as an invalid, with her dad sending her off to bed, and she'd stay at their house for a few days, so they could keep an eye on her. The doctors also believed she may have been concussed.

No CT scan had been taken, as she seemed generally okay at the hospital, despite receiving an obvious blow to the head. It seems she possibly collided with a log on the ground, or tree trunk, when she 'involuntary dismounted.'

Chris was about to explain it was his fault for cantering off down a woodland track, and potentially causing Anna's accident by being reckless, but he was cut off before he could begin. Alan was so full of gratitude and praise to Chris for picking her up off the track and returning her safely that Chris felt he couldn't and shouldn't shatter any elusions or bubbles Alan had of him being the all-saving hero. And so he said nothing. But inwardly Chris felt bad.

It also sadly meant he wouldn't see Anna for a few days.

Alan promised she'd call him tomorrow and that they'd compensate him for anything regarding costs for looking after Penny. He also stated Chris would have to come to theirs again for a formal 'Thank you' once Anna was fully functioning. He also said she'd probably call him tomorrow too, once rested.

Chris was happy Anna was well, and thankful Penny had not been injured. She was munching at her haynet, totally unaware of all the fuss. But Chris winced at the thought of a family meal and a big 'Thank you' for something he'd actually caused. He also imagined that Anna was wincing too. She was.

But something else about the incident troubled him. Anna had mentioned a 'Dark Monk.' 'A Dark Monk attacked me,' she'd initially claimed.

Chris had made light of her comment and Anna had retracted it.

But he shouldn't have.

He knew she was speaking the truth.

As he heard Anna's first scream, he'd looked through the branches of the larches and fir trees. A fleeting glance. But he'd seen movement.

Swift, but clear and distinct. A person had been hiding in the trees.

Someone had been there in the woods. Clad in black.

It was a momentary flash, possibly something imagined Chris had initially thought in the instance he heard Anna's first cry, and then disregarded as he raced Tirus down the tight woodland track and back around. His concerns, upon hearing Anna's second cry were simply the immediate safety of Penny and Anna, as he thundered back along the looped track to help them both.

As he noted Penny seemed okay, and then lifted Anna's prostrate body from the track, fearing the worst, he was swept with relief to hear her groan, and then come around, knowing she was okay, but clearly badly battered.

Then, still in a daze, she'd told him her story.

'Someone dressed all in black. They attacked me.'

Anna's Black Monk.

He'd casually dismissed her claim. Made light of it. He had to.

It was an effect of the fall. Concussion. Confusion. Both. So he told her.

But Chris had to playfully dismiss the comment.

For he knew it was the truth.

There was an attacker hiding in the woods.

Dressed in a black hoodie. And with their face concealed.

As Chris had swung back on the track, which joined the one Anna had ridden down; he'd seen the black-clad, nibble and fast-moving figure.

It had disappeared into the woods. Fast and swift.

Clad in black. Just like a mysterious Ninja. But watching.

His attention however had been drawn to Penny caught in the trees, and then Anna, laying flat out on the track, whom he feared could be dead.

He too had seen the same black figure Anna saw.

But he could never let her know.

Chris had some dark secrets. Very dark.

He had enemies from the past.

And they still sought revenge.

He would have to be more careful than ever.

And also take great care of those he loved.

For they too could now be in great danger.

Chapter 112

I've sometimes thought of marrying -
and then I've thought again.

Noel Coward

All who kept their horses at Horsewater were shocked and concerned upon hearing the news that Anna had taken a 'tumble,' as most called the riding incident. It was a 'Bad Fall.' But she was okay. Tracey came down later in the afternoon to speak with Chris to get a full run down, although Joyce had called her direct when they were at the hospital. Then later to confirm she was fine, but out of action for a few days and asked if she and Chris could help.

Julie was worried too and also offered to look after Penny. Along with all the other various offers provided it meant Penny would be looked after very well.

For Chris is was no big issue as he tended to a variety of absent owners horses, but it highlighted the kindness and generosity of those in the yard, and respect Anna had generated from those at Horsewater in a short time.

From the news Chris received, he hoped Anna would be back down the yard in a few days. He felt it'd be quicker if she could escape the clutches of her doting parents, as he knew she'd miss the company, and especially miss her Penny, whom he knew she worshipped. As is usual with 'horsey people,' their main concern and question asked, when they heard the news and knew Anna was alive, unbroken and complete, was: "How's Penny?"

Usually horse owners are more concerned with the welfare of the horse than the rider. Everyone was relieved Penny was unscathed and Anna came off a poor second best. That was almost insignificant, so long as Penny was okay.

But no one blamed Chris, although he explained to all at how guilty he felt for racing about the woods too fast, when Anna was possibly still hung-over.

Most knew Chris, and how he rode. Fast and mad. They also knew anything concerned with horses was dangerous. Horses were renowned for being fearless when it came to jumping four-foot high hedges with adjoining ditches, having no knowledge of what may be on the other side. But would spook wildly at a 'rogue' wheelie-bin or at a crisp bag blowing in a hedge.

This type of random incident is what often unseats a rider. But it is a risk all horse riders take each time they sit on a horse, knowing it is a dangerous.

'Horse riding: the art of keeping a horse between the rider and the ground.'

A famous and very apt phrase. Sometimes it failed. As Anna had proven.

Chris spoke with Anna several times by telephone over the next couple of days. She seemed well, which brought him some joy, as the New Year faded and everyone sank into the glum and depressed mode January brings once the hype and excitement of the Christmas and the New Year period expires.

For the next two days things carried on as usual at the yard, with the weather luckily assisting, by being mild and grey, but dry, seemingly matching those usually quiet and drab days often found in early January. The gears of life rolled on, and Chris carried on as normal before receiving a call towards the end of the week which brought encouragement and a glimmer of joy.

Steve called; telling him it was unlikely there'd be any charges brought against anyone associated with the hunt, following the 'Boxing Day Incident,' as it was now being discretely called. A person working within such close circles related to the Chief Constable and thus the C.P.S. had carefully called Reggie direct to give him some very welcome news. They'd told him that most likely everything against the Shoteton would be dropped. Due to lack of evidence and difficulty in obtaining any, for what was basically a breach of the peace on private land. Also, and most likely the reason, the police didn't have the resources to waste on a disturbance and scuffle on private land between two rival parties. No one had been hurt, other than the Anti who'd been crushed against a tree, and no one of the other party had lodged complaints, nor could any witnesses be found. The police were possibly looking to bring a case against an Anti for assaulting a police officer, but that was pending too.

It meant the Shoteton would soon be hunting again and rescue the season before it died off in March, as was usual. This was due to hunting rules, crop planting and a real and genuine respect for nature and the Spring mating season, where 'Boxing Hares' would meet up and mate. And fight of course.

As excited and as pleased Chris was upon hearing the news, he also felt glum. He knew Anna most likely wouldn't be able to join them for the next meet, unless her arm had healed sufficiently. That said, she was due to come back to Horsewater that very day to see Penny and give Chris a proper update.

The anticipated arrival of Anna later that day, despite her having only being away from the yard for a few days, was an event for which he strangely felt a tingle of excitement. He liked her. Lots. But he found it hard to tell her.

When Anna arrived mid-morning, with the weak low January sun spreading a subtle purple haze over the woods, Chris felt a pang of emotion. He smiled as he saw Anna park her own 4 x 4 alone and he moved towards her, where she exited the vehicle with one arm clearly held high, but not in a sling.

"Are you okay to drive?" As Chris spoke, he realised the statement sounded condescending, but he realised Anna understood the full meaning and she smiled, waving a free arm, with no sling or cast as she exited the vehicle.

"I can do lots of things with this hand and arm. So you'd better watch out!" Anna grinned as she wandered over to Chris and then pulling him close, openly hugged him, and pecked him on the cheek. Chris blushed and smiled.

After a few pleasantries the pair wandered into the yard, almost hand in hand, where, as if to be expected, Julie's head appeared from Bonnie's stable.

"You're alive!" She yelled, smiling widely. "Chris told us you'd died, and that he'd buried your corpse in the woods," Julie continued with a grin.

Anna walked over to the stable, but swiftly stepped back as Bonnie's head appeared, ears back and teeth on display. However, as Chris wandered over behind her, Bonnie dropped her ears, almost fluttered her long eyelashes, and let him rub her head. As Anna re-approached, the ears went back and her teeth could be heard clattering as she snapped at Anna over the stable door.

"Stop being a bitch, you old trollop!" Julie thumped Bonnie in the chest and forced the grumpy horse back and away from the door. Julie's smiling face replaced that of the emotionally unstable skewbald equine behind her.

"What an old whore! Bitch!" Julie exclaimed, looking at Anna.

"Well that's a nice welcome back!" Anna grinned and raised her eyebrows.

"Not you, but this grumpy old moo! We've just been out for a hack, so you'd think she'd be happy. No chance. Back to the marshes if you don't behave!"

With that Julie exited the stable, leading Bonnie, rug on, ready to turn her out in the paddock for a few hours. Anna and Chris wisely stepped back.

"I've got to dash off, but it's great to see you're looking fine. We'll have to have a chat so you can catch up on the gossip. Are you about tomorrow?"

Anna nodded enthusiastically she would be, her smile beaming wide.

With that Anna and Chris stood side by side, watching the strange pair wander off to the paddocks, where the tall woods towered in the backdrop.

Chris noted Anna's eyes drift from Julie and Bonnie and on to the woods. He wondered what she was thinking, but could guess, though he dare not ask.

Sally appeared from one of the full livery stables and skipped across the yard to hug Anna, with no care of any existing injuries, or of causing any more.

"You're not dead!" Sally's comment was as typically blunt as any horse rider.

"Julie told me you'd died and that she'd cut you up and fed your body in chunks to Bonnie. And I believed her!" Sally smirked wickedly.

The small group chuckled and Chris shook his head, but with a big grin.

Anna playfully scowled, but smiled underneath, getting the dark humour.

"Well, Anna's the best looking corpse I've ever seen," Chris announced without thinking, to suddenly see the two women regard him curiously.

"Please tell me more, Chris," Sally said, looking at Chris, her head tilted.

He blushed, but grinned, realising what he'd said, then joked deeper.

"Well I've had a few corpses in my time! But what happens in Vegas….!"

Anna raised her eyebrows in shock, her jaw dropping in shock, but then the two laughed loudly. Sally playfully punched Chris' arm and shook her head.

"Anyway ladies, enough of corpses, dead or alive," Chris formally addressed, but still grinning. "I may have good news for some, but maybe not others."

He regarded his attentive audience, almost teasing, waiting in anticipation.

"We could be hunting. Very soon. All going well. If you can come or ride."

He saw Sally's face light up and smile, but Anna look down and despondent.

"In just over two weeks time. A week before the Burn's Night Hunt Ball, to which we will all be attending. However, the meet will be at Wroxingham Hall. A private event, held just on his land. Bertie will have some security."

Chris regarded the two women, who were waiting for more, but he could see Anna counting days in her head, calculating if she could ride, then smirked.
"There is nothing definite yet, but pencil it in your diary. I'm looking forward to it, and I'm hoping you'll both be able to join us. Injuries permitting."
Sally stood eagerly nodding. Chris looked direct at Anna, who smiled widely.
"I wouldn't miss it and will ensure I'm there, even if I have to brace my arm with broom handles. You can prop me up like El Cid! Count me in."
Anna saw a twinkle in Chris' eye, but decided to press an outstanding point.
"Sadly, I'm still waiting for a kind Prince to formally invite me to the Ball. It's so sad." Anna put on a pathetic frown, raising a hand to her furrowed brow.
"What can a girl do? Maybe put an ad' in the Local Gazette!"
Chris smiled, glowing red, seeing her tease, but pleased to enjoy her humour once more. Sally laughed loudly. "He'll be taking you, won't you Chris?"
"Hmm? I'll have to see. So many options. And then there're those corpses."
Anna playfully glared, then pulled something out of a bag she'd been holding.
"Maybe these croissants will help you decide? Fresh. Well, were yesterday."
Chris' face glowed brighter, and Sally chuckled, raising a hand to her mouth, her eyes flitting from Anna to Chris. She didn't know, but fully understood.
"Well, it's a good job I'm finished and now off," she added smiling. "Watch where those crumbs get. And all that jam and dripping butter. Very messy!"
Sally said her farewells and the pair watched her move over towards the tackroom to get her stuff, just as Julie strolled back from the paddocks. Her keen eyes saw the bag in Anna's hand, and then noticed Chris' blushing face.
"Breakfast in bed?" Julie joked, her smile wicked. "Or breakfast, then bed?"
Chris went redder than ever and Anna even blushed, but then chuckled.
Julie walked past, ignoring them, and bid them farewell, chuckling away.
"I brought these to say Thank You," Anna blushingly announced as she saw Julie climb into her Rover and Sally wander past, also grinning, simply raising a hand to wave farewell to leave the pair standing in the yard alone.
"We were meant to have some of these a few days ago?"
Chris nodded, clearly recalling the agreement, but then frowned, sighing.
Anna caught the expression. "You're going out, aren't you?"
Chris nodded solemnly. "I've got to see Steve and Reggie. It's to discuss this next hunt meet at Bertie's and something I need to do for Steve too. Sorry!"
Anna sighed heavily, looking at the croissants then at Chris, her plan ruined.
"But I've still got half and hour before I have to go. Will that do?"
Chris offered warmly, appearing to recover, and looked toward the house almost as open encouragement. Anna beamed, her smile clearly evident.
"You wouldn't believe what I can do in half and hour!" Her look was wicked.
Chris chuckled. As the pair turned, he grabbed Anna's fingertips, leading her gently towards the house. She closed in and wrapped an arm around his body.
Chris looked at her. "I thought you had an injured arm?"
Anna chuckled, pulling him even tighter. "What bad arm?"

They made it into the kitchen with wide grins, where Max regarded Anna from beside the Aga. He saw Chris and realised he didn't need to eat her. Anna got the feeling he still might, and hoped their late-night secret was safe.

"Sit your bum down. I'll pop these in the toaster. Tea?"

With a positive nod from Anna, Chris took the croissants from Anna, who sat at the aged timber table. She glanced once more around the kitchen, which was beginning to become more familiar to her. She felt her eyes naturally drift towards the cellar door. No key today she noticed, as Chris busied himself as host, pulling out a slab of proper butter and two jars of jam. Both homemade.

Anna's face lit up, as he placed the items on the table, along with cutlery.

She at once realised he'd remembered and melted inside.

Plum and Raspberry were written in hand on the labels.

Two small side plates were also set upon the table, along with matching cups and saucers, as a kettle boiled. Swiftly the room was filled with the wonderful scent of fresh baking, and even Max lifted his long, black glossy nose to absorb the pleasing aroma, but knew he'd get nothing. Well, maybe one.

Tea was promptly made in cups and Chris placed the six lightly toasted croissants upon a round breadboard, seated centrally about the wooden table. Noting her intent gaze, he gently slid the butter towards Anna. His hand hovered over the two jars of jam, offering a selection.

"Raspberry or Plum?" Chris asked.

"Raspberry. I'll try your plums later!" Anna looked at his unashamed.

Chris almost choked; flushing red, then smirked childlike at Anna.

Anna grabbed a croissant and knife, then promptly slit it open. Smothering butter inside, she then plopped in a generous helping of jam. Chris followed, the crude actions seemingly unashamed, as if relieving some pent-up tension.

The first was consumed and hot tea sipped, and the pair both dived into the second, their hands touching as they went to grab the same pastry. Chris blushed and let Anna take the selected item, and he grabbed another. Butter and jam was generously added once more, and pastries heartily consumed.

Anna looked at Chris, never enjoying such a simple meal in a long time. She stared at Chris, and then smiled. He returned the look, but lowered his gaze.

"You've go butter on your chin," Anna announced.

Chris grinned and wiped his face with a tea towel beside him on the table.

He gazed back at Anna. "You've got jam on your nose."

Anna looked confused, then crossed her eyes to look down and inward.

Chris grinned at the action, then he eased forward and lifted up his knife. Dipping it in the jar, he gently tapped the end of the dinner knife against the tip of Anna's nose, leaving behind a fine trace of Raspberry jam.

"Ugh!" Anna exclaimed, eyes squinting, shuddering, but also laughing.

Chris simply smirked at her from across the table.

Anna fixed her gaze upon Chris. Hard, but also sensual.

"You'd better remove that. Now."

Chris' expression didn't change, but slowly he moved forward, stretching over the table, closing in towards Anna. She remained motionless, her gaze fixed upon his ever closing face, her senses alive and buzzing.

Then, softly, he set his lips upon the tip of her nose.

Anna felt a flutter between her legs as Chris kissed the tip of her nose, then extended the tip of his tongue to lick the sticky jam off the end of her nose.

Anna wanted to squirm, as her heart raced, bodily fluids moved within and her emotions stirred. Her lips curled into to a wide appreciative grin as she felt Chris' mouth move from her nose, knowing they where heading an inch lower. She puckered her lips, willingly ready to meet his and enjoy a deep kiss, when suddenly he spun his head and turned his face away.

Anna awoke, as though from a deep trance to see Chris swirl around in his chair and stare out the window. Then she too heard the sound he'd already noted, as a white Land Rover roared past the house, pulling up in the yard.

Chris rose, his shoulders slumping and he sighed heavily, shaking his head.

"No! What the hell does he want?" Chris stepped over to the side window, Max rising too, along with Anna. The terrible trio. She stepped behind Chris, and lovingly curled an arm around his waist, drawing her body to his. He didn't flinch or move at first, but then spun within her grasp to face her.

"Sorry! What a tosser! I'd better see what he wants. Arsehole!"

With a quick peck on Anna's cheek, he sidestepped the heart-broken maiden and walked out of the kitchen doorway and into the yard to face P.C. Burton.

"Sorry to trouble you Mister Turner," Burton begun, to then pause as he saw Anna promptly step out behind. His eyes focussed upon her, before returning to Chris. "I hope I wasn't disturbing you or anything important."

Chris did not respond, but simply glared in silence. He was. Very important.

It was obvious the grinning policeman clearly wasn't sorry to disturb them.

"Just to let you know there's been a break-in. Woodheath. A holiday cottage. Thought it best to let you know firsthand, so you can be on the look-out."

Anna spun her head around to look at Chris, genuinely concerned. Her cottage was in Woodheath. He regarded her with a similar expression.

"Have you been at your cottage in the last few days?" Chris asked Anna, P.C. Burton catching the comment, guessing Lady Melrose had a house nearby.

"Yes. I popped back this morning before coming here. It all seemed fine."

Burton quickly ascertained the situation between the pair, or thought he did, guessing the 'Lady' had been away from her local country home, and assuming she may have be staying with the Horseman, as his 'House Guest.' But who knew. Maybe she'd been at Sandringham with her Royal friends.

"Someone was seen running from the property by the neighbour. Dressed in black. I don't think they got away with anything. No one knows. Forensics are on the scene and the owner called. Have you seen anyone about here?"

Chris stared back at the policeman, wondering if or what he knew. Then sensed Anna draw close up beside him. He hoped she wouldn't speak.

He turned to face her, face glowing. Anna's cheeks began to glow too, both having their own private secrets. Silently a message passed between them.

Chris shook his head.

Anna shook her head.

But P.C. Burton didn't believe either.

The phone rang in the house and Chris suddenly checked his watch, half turning, unsure which way to head. He looked at Anna, then Burton.

"Shit! I've got to go. I forgot, but I have an appointment. I'm sorry. Thank you. We'll ensure we are extra vigilant." Chris spoke at Burton, then looked back at Anna. "Do you want me to drive back to the cottage with you?"

"Without jumping in," the policeman said, interrupting. "I'm about to head back to Woodheath myself and can escort you back for safety, my Lady."

Anna's face glowed, as did Chris', both from the comment and also the offer.

Burton's face glowed, but for other reasons. He looked at the pair, each of whom seemed slightly confused. The phone inside the house rang once more, and Anna could see Chris was dithering and she knew he had to go, their brief time over. Fate had once more stepped in-between them it seemed.

"You go and see Reggie and all. I'll head to the cottage and at least if there are any issues, I'm sure this big brave policeman will deal with any burglars."

Anna smiled at Burton, her grin slightly exaggerated. Burton beamed back.

"I'll call you later and we can meet up again. And you can let me know what will be happing at Bertie's. I'll be joining you, even if it is with one arm. And we can also finish off those croissants. I want to try out your plum jam!"

Chris shook his head and grinned, as a tittering Anna wandered to her 4 x 4, followed by an eager policeman, who didn't understand the personal joke.

From outside the house doorway Chris raised a hand, as Anna climbed inside her car. She lifted her hand, palm flat, blowing him a cheeky kiss. Chris blushed and chuckled. Burton, standing beside his Land Rover, looked on enviously, the romance he'd assumed there was between the pair being open and clearly evident. Strangely, they seemed like a perfect couple.

That said, he still didn't trust either of them.

More especially, he didn't trust the Horseman.

He'd done his research.

The horseman was bad news.

The people he'd killed all those years ago had relatives.

Some had children. Now grown up.

They were missing their fathers.

And those were the type who never forgot. Ever.

The recent break-ins, and other incidents Burton knew of, but kept private, were enough to ensure he'd keep a close eye on Mister Turner.

And also all those associated with Horsewater. And that included the woman whose small 4 x 4 car he was slowly following back out through the woods.

Stunningly beautiful as she was, Burton did not trust her either.

'Lady Melrose' his arse. He knew who she really was. And her father.
A rich millionaire he might be, but you don't get that much money honestly.
Burton regarded her family as equally low as he did the killer horseman.
But more importantly, hidden deep within him, Burton felt Horsewater, and those who crawled about its murky yard and deep dark woods, were no better than the people he knew were set to seek revenge upon the owner.
The man who'd killed two people. In cold blood.
Over twenty-five years ago.
Revenge went deep. And it held no time.
It'd happen. One day.
Burton had been informed. He knew things. Secrets.
One day they'd come for the horseman.
Revenge and justice would be served.
And in the most unexpected way.

Chapter 113

Give us the tools and we will finish job.

Winston Churchill

Izzy had summoned a War Cabinet. Well, she'd asked a few stalwart Anti's down the pub'. Similar. Well, sort of. The dozen loyal followers had turned up for a quick New Year's catch up, and more so, because Izzy was paying for the first and possibly only round. More importantly, to go with the pint was a free pack of Vegan Pork Scratchings or plain crisps for the true Vegan.

The first thing she noted, other than Dave having what appeared to be one usable arm, was the harsh scowl he gave Bruce, who sat tight and snuggled beside her in the small nook of the pub' the group had retired to for privacy.

If looks could kill, Bruce would be in his coffin already. And buried.

Izzy was beyond such issues, but quietly noted the obvious resentment. She smiled at all, and made them welcome, thanking them for attending.

"A few of you may recall Bruce from Boxing Day," Izzy announced with a smile and what seemed a degree of pride, pointing him out to the blind.

"He's the one who was beaten by the police scum! He'll be suing them."

Mary shook her head in shock and horror and sent a silent sympathetic wish to Bruce in her gentle appreciative and comradeship style nod. Others looked at Bruce slightly bemused, as he did not look like the typical Anti or rebel.

Bruce was dressed in a designer label jacket and shirt, the others assuming he'd missed a Stockbrokers Board Meeting or had come off the Catwalk.

Dave scowled. Hard. Izzy thought she saw some daggers. She ducked.

But Izzy ignored the clear hatred and jealously Dave exuded towards Bruce and so Izzy continued, knowing he needed attention, and thus decided she should make him the focal point, as she knew he silently craved. He was a 'hero' after all. It was just a pity it was Steve who'd made him into one.

"It's good to see Dave making a good recovery, after his brutal, unprovoked assault by a nasty hunt member," Izzy announced, but blushed, knowing she had potentially open a can of worms. And tin of hornets. If that existed.

"Inflicted by your ex-husband," Dave added with venom. "Wanker!"

Izzy curled up side, and wondered why she'd bothered.

Dave saw Izzy glare and a number of the more elderly of the group wince at his harsh, profane language, used to describe a member of the Hunt most knew. That said, most secretly thought Dave was a 'Wanker' too, but dare not say so, and all simply regarded him - the other Wanker - with glazed stares.

"Anyway, moving on from what was not a good day for either side, with no winners, I can let you all now that I've had word, from a secret source, that the Shoteton will be hunting again. Very soon. In about two weeks."

They was a muted gasp and heads turned from side to side, with a few words muttered between the parties, which was the result Izzy had hoped.

Izzy could see Dave was calculating in his head the state of his body by then, and if he'd be fit enough to join them. She hoped he wouldn't, but feared he would, no matter what state his body was in, even if he had to crawl there or secure broom handles to his arms. Maybe he thought he was El Cid.

"Where?" It was Mary who asked the question, but a number of keen faces looked on, also curious for a date and venue. "I want my hat back!"

Izzy stared momentarily at Mary, then at the group of eager faces all looking at her. She was glad of their support, and proud to be seen as their leader, but wondered if Wellington had such a range of weird followers whom they had to lead. Maybe he did. But did Wellington lead his army with a pint of beer and fake Pork Scratchings? She doubted it. Arthur Wellesley wasn't that good.

"Wroxingham Hall." Izzy announced. "Lord Burlingham's stately pile, shared with the young trollop of a wife. Or he did. I've heard she's left him. Good."

"How will we get in?" Dave asked the question blunt and direct, being the ever-keen and masterful military tactician. So he thought. "It's got walls."

"As I recall, we've never been able to get onto their land in the past for any hunts they've held. It's an old-style walled estate, surrounded by acres of thick hedges, gatehouses and tight adjoining woodland. You can't gain access easily without trespassing. Well, not too easily. It's a nightmare to get into or follow. Other than the odd piece they hardly hunt on, which is shit, most of it, including the entrance, is walled off. Plus, I bet he'll have extra security. And the scum police force will be out, no doubt, to offer 'support' to the tosser."

Izzy admired Dave's knowledge of the local hunting areas and estates, which almost rivalled hers of the land upon which the Shoteton usually hunted.

But she did worry too that he knew them all in such detail. Too much detail.

When did he get to see all of the land? Prowling at night? She mused.

Thoughts of Dave's creepy night time extra-curricular activities were put aside from her mind as she regarded her comrades with a playful smile.

"Perhaps you'd like to fill us in. Educate us all, Izzy." Dave asked bluntly.

Dave's comment was cold and harsh, but Izzy understood him. Bruce gave him a hard look, hating the stinking scumbag, wondering why the woman he currently enjoyed sharing a very warm and active bed with, and whom he knew was intelligent, bothered to entertain such a low-life delinquent. He wouldn't toss a coin to if he saw him in the street. Then he wouldn't anyone.

The small nook fell silent and all eyes fell upon Izzy. Waiting.

"I have a cunning plan!" Izzy announced with a wry grin.

For once Dave smiled, getting the joke from a popular historic comedy TV program. Mary looked puzzled. She didn't watch TV. She read poetry.

"Has anyone ever heard of the Wooden Horse of Troy?"

Dave's mouth curled into a cruel grin. Of course he had. All nodded.

And Dave liked the sound of what Izzy was carefully about to announce.

"Bring it on! Fill me in. I want my revenge!" Dave smiled broadly

Izzy breathed heavily, and wondered what she'd done. She breathed in.

A dozen pairs of eyes, some munching Pork Scratchings, others their crisps; some simply staring on in wonder, waited for their leader to speak.

Sir Arthur Wellesley, First Duke of Wellington and Former United Kingdom Prime Minister would have been proud of Izzy. Or so she felt.

Leaning forward over the round beer-stained table, and joined by the host of inquisitive followers, in quiet tones, Izzy began to speak.

In slow and clear detail she informed them of her cunning plan.

Keen faces smiled. Even Dave.

Bruce simply sighed.

He wanted more Pork Scratchings. Real ones.

As Dave listened to Izzy's clever plan, he too was working on his own.

He glanced at Bruce and smiled.

Just as a crocodile does.

Chapter 114

If I had my way, I would remove January from the calendar altogether and have an extra July instead.

Roald Dahl

The following days flew by, as often appears to happen with January, it being a month to seemingly please no one. Other than Gym's and Diet Planners.

Anna's arm was improving each day. Although still bruised, it was now an ugly greeny-yellow, rather than the black and brown it was days after the accident happened. She'd ridden Penny a few times, riding in the school to check out both her and the horse, and was sure, unless Penny bolted, that all well, she'd be able to ride safely at Wroxingham Hall this coming weekend.

When riding in the school, with either Chris, Tracey or Julie watching on, she found herself on many occasions looking across the paddocks and long into the deep woods. She saw Chris catch her wary glance towards the woods once or twice, with a strange look between them both, but neither saying a word.

She felt uneasy about riding in the woods again, but told no one, nor would, hoping she'd get her bravado back one day. However, for now, she was simply pleased to be back in the saddle and couldn't wait to get out hunting again, amongst the rest of the Shoteton and importantly, alongside Chris.

He'd been full of encouragement, and after the event in the kitchen, seemed to have cooled off, and as much as she hoped, hadn't invited her back inside.

The girls in the yard had all been great in helping out over the first few days of her injury, but things had swiftly returned to normal as she then began to look after Penny herself. Chris had helped empty her barrow, and been warm and kind, but after their breakfast had been rudely disturbed, they hadn't managed to find any time alone and no such fun and intimate moment arose.

They passed in the yard, and he spoke with her in Penny's stable, to check she was well, but they'd still not managed to rekindle that momentary sparkle. Both were busy, or nosey people were dashing about the yard, casting curious glances, and wondering if there was any formal relationship between the pair.

Tracey obviously knew the details; as did by default Julie, both sad nothing else had happened, but all were waiting for more juicy news and fresh gossip.

Sadly it was on hold. Chris was his usual busy self, dashing about. The tiny spark of romance they'd found in the kitchen, which was so natural, appeared to be dampened for now, but not extinguished. Or so Anna hoped.

She was equally hoping a day spent alongside him at the next hunt meet could firmly consolidate things, and build their bond stronger and formally. Then there was the Burn's Night Ball to follow, and all it could potentially bring. Fingers crossed. At least she'd look her best and wow in a fine dress.

No arrangements had been made as yet, and in Chris's true 'last minute' and race-about manner, she didn't expect anything until the night before. She was determined to then be formally recognised as his partner, and could only hope things would become serious from there on. She had plans. And hopes.

Anna couldn't put all fault for any hint of romance being dampened solely upon Chris being too busy, as she too had had a number of potential new clients contact her for design work, for which she was excited. It seemed a couple were from contacts within the Hunt, who knew someone, who knew someone, etc. She was thrilled to get a fresh flow of work and knew she could not turn it down. Thus, in-between doing Penny, and trying to ride, she too had been dashing about, working on other projects to build up her business.

Likewise, Chris was as busy as ever with the horses, and had been tied up for a number of days with other members of the Shoteton, helping to organise the next meet at Wroxingham Hall, and ensuring there would be no repeat of the Boxing Day incidents and everything would go well. Hopefully.

Anna had asked Tracey and Julie if they'd heard anything about Virginia and her new man, and what had become of the pair since the punch-up on Boxing Day, where the 'Not-so-Posh' Lady had truly revealed herself and her colours.

No one seemed to know anything, and Carol, who was spending even more time at Wroxingham Hall, 'consoling' the sad Lord Burlingham, was saying little. She would neither confirm nor deny any talks of what was happening, on costly divorces for Lord Burlingham, simply tutting and shaking her head.

Julie had seen a newspaper article, which was backed up by someone she knew in the Hunt, stating Dawn, Gavin's former partner, had killed herself. Anna had been upset upon hearing the terrible news, as had the others, who all sat in the tackroom and reflected on the tragic event. But not for too long.

Tracey, as to be expected, broke the one-minute silence by announcing that she'd never really liked Dawn. She felt she was 'Needy and Clingy' and didn't ever seem to let Gavin out of her sight, or do what he wanted. She said she'd laughed with Gavin once out hunting, and Dawn had almost ripped her head off, thinking she was 'after her man.' She'd clearly gotten the wrong lady.

Hence, she boldly stated, when given the first opportunity, he'd run away with his childhood sweetheart and the 'Emeritus' Lady Burlingham, to be free of Dawn. But possibly without realising the consequences. Or maybe not.

Julie, ever practical and forthright, concluded Dawn was obviously mentally unstable and would've probably taken her own life at some time, no matter what Gavin had done. But she did agree it was sad, and she'd known Dawn from the Hunt for a few years, although never mixed with her.

Although Anna hardly knew Dawn, only just able to recall her from the few meets she'd been on, her death seemed to harden Anna's dislike further for the former 'Whore of Wroxingham Hall,' whom she blamed for Dawn's death; rightly or wrongly. The only positive aspect of the incident was Anna knew she'd been totally wrong about Virginia's intentions towards Chris.

The Boxing Day event now seemed an age away, but in truth was only a few weeks back. But it'd had a huge effect on seemingly everyone linked. Likewise, Reggie and his wife were discussed, but nothing solid was known of their predicament, other than malicious gossip and hearsay, which had come through about what had happened to her and Bertie's former Gamekeeper.

Rumours of an 'Expensive Divorce Settlement' had been whispered in low corners, and high ones, with Julie wondering if or what Elizabeth would get from 'Tight-wad' Reggie. Maybe a bullet she suggested, aware of slander law.

Tracey mentioned she felt Reggie fancied Julie, who in turn boldly declared she would not become Reggie's next wife. Except for a Farm as a Pre-Nup' upon their divorce! No one dared mention to Julie that Reggie wasn't likely to ask for her hand in marriage either. But they let her fantasise anyway.

There had also been rumours spread that Martin was also now free and single. It seemed Sharon had gone to see her parents at Christmas, but hadn't returned. That 'Old Chestnut' someone muttered. Left him more likely.

The gossip-mill again thought she hadn't liked how he'd acted at the Boxing Day event, being too aggressive to the Anti's, and had decided to leave him. The possible cheating activities between the couple were discussed over more cups of coffee and cookies, but they all agreed: 'What went on in people's own homes, stayed in Vegas.' It didn't rhyme, but they knew what it meant.

This aspect, that of Sharon vanishing, was a major cause of concern for the Shoteton, and one of the reasons why Chris had been dashing about for the Hunt, helping to organise matters and having meetings. They were now short of a Whipper-in. Chris had been asked to undertake the role, but declined as politely as possible, hating the thought, as prestigious as it was deemed to be.

He'd openly declared it'd stop him riding out with Anna, and the other girls, he'd been quick to add, and couldn't. It seemed James would take over the role, and much more was being arranged and discussed, with Carol quite willingly spending a great deal of time at the Hall, helping to organise matters.

With Carol being so clearly implicated with Bertie; and it known the pair had been 'old friends' for a long time, Julie asked the chatting group in the tackroom, all hugging half-empty coffee mugs, when they thought Chris would have his next vacancy in the yard. She could foresee Carol and Tess moving onto much fancier stabling, over at Burlingham Hall, very soon.

So, if she left, then who would replace her? An empty stable. At Horsewater.

That was the question she poised, knowing it'd cause much heated debate, as had happened before Anna arrived on the scene. Any empty stable at a Livery Yard was always a point for hearty gossip and potential slander or liable.

Julie teased Anna that a stunning ex-model called Jennifer, who had an equally stunning Palomino horse called Ted, was lined up. She'd almost got the slot Anna had taken, but for Tracey badgering Chris. Anna had won.

Jennifer it seems had known Chris for years. It was well known she had long flowing blond hair, like her equally stunning horse, Ted. The Barbie Twins.

Apparently she'd enquired about a vacancy long before Anna arrived, and previously had her sights set upon Chris. The 'Ex-model' it seems had been very annoyed, hearing 'someone else,' namely an 'Anna' - how common - had taken her possible stable and she and her beloved Ted, had been sidelined.

Anna's face glowed red, and she cast Julie a sideways look, unsure if the crafty woman was winding her up, or genuine. The straight faces of the others in the tackroom, although some had smirks set, were also hard to judge.

Julie teased Anna further, by stating she'd heard Chris had a centre-fold poster of Jennifer stuck on his bedroom wall. And it wasn't for dart practise.

Of course that was also alongside those of his favourite horses too.

Anna's blushing face, and lack of spoken response, left Julie rolling about in laughter in the tackroom, joined by many others. Anna simply threw a rolled up tail-bandage at the woman she'd grown fond of, before everyone laughed hysterically, including Anna, once again happy to be back at Horsewater.

The days ahead would hopefully reveal all and bring some positive changes to her life. Only time and fate would tell.

But for now, Fate was being very quiet.

For now.

Maybe too quiet.

Chapter 115

What harm is there in a kiss?
A kiss may ruin a human life.

A Woman of No Importance - Oscar Wilde

Anna and Chris had both been busy the days prior to the Wroxingham Hall meet. Although they'd seen each other most days at the yard, usually passing like the proverbial ships, they still didn't seem to find any time alone together.

Anna had errands to run, rode Penny alone, or spent a good deal of time at home catching up on her new work. Chris it seemed was hardly about too, either schooling horses for others, teaching privately in the ménage, or out in his lorry, picking up and delivering a number of horses, or whatever he did.

They'd somehow not met to chat in the evenings either, Anna seeing him flit about in the darkness of the yard, casting her a cheeky grin, or simply raising a hand, as he dashed from a stable to the barn and back in the gloom.

They'd spoken briefly on the phone the night before, Chris' unexpected call being a pleasant surprise. It was a quick, business-like chat, more about what was to happen tomorrow, but it pleased Anna, as she was still unsure of Chris and his thoughts towards her. She was so used to the brash, unashamed and openly bold actions of Bruce, that to deal with someone so timid was strange.

Anna wanted to push things, make a bold statement and advance towards him. However, other than the quick kiss on Christmas Day and the cheeky moment in the kitchen with the croissants, the ideal opportunity hadn't arisen; not without it making her appear desperate to get off with him, even if secretly she was. Also, the possible fear of rejection, and thus humiliation and the difficulties she knew it'd bring, instinctively hung in the back of her mind.

So Anna knew she'd have to take things slow and steady. Reluctantly.

But she didn't need to worry for long. The next morning, when everything and everyone seemed to be ready for the meet, and they were just about to load up, things changed. Dramatically. Tracey had nipped off to the toilet, and Anna was waiting in Penny's stable for the call for everyone to load up.

Pointlessly re-brushing Penny's glistening tail, she heard the clink of the stable bolt. Looking sideways over Penny's back, to identify her surprise visitor, she saw it was Chris, who silently approached, smiling gently.

He drew alongside, the pair standing beside Penny, as Anna, half-curious to what he wanted, raised her head, expecting him to speak. Silently, she regarded him with an inquisitive gaze, as he looked deep into her grey eyes.

As she drew close to him, waiting for him to say something, he reached out and took her hand, drawing her fully to him. Then he closed in, their lips met and he kissed her long and hard, taking her breath away. Anna's head swam.

Finally he broke free, kissed her chin, then her nose, and simply turned away, promptly leaving the stable as silently as he'd entered seconds earlier.

As he closed the stable door, Chris grinned broadly over the door at a stunned Anna, whose face was glowing. She was still unsure what'd happened really did happen and licked her lips, tasting Chris. Closing the stable door and vanishing, as if nothing had happened, he stomped back across the yard.

Anna took a huge breath, and then dumbstruck, looked at the departing figure, who'd not spoken a single word from entering the stable up until he kissed and held her. She was shell-shocked, but felt her heart thumping.

"Okay, let's get these horses loaded!" Chris hollered from the yard, as was normal, his voice waking her slightly. But only just. She was still in a dream.

Anna felt her heart skip; shocked by his warm, sensitive, yet unexpected and thrilling action. She realised she'd stopped breathing, so drew a deep breath.

"Wow!" Anna whispered to herself, staring into space. "Wowee!"

She desperately wanted to tell Tracey or Julie what had just happened, and peered over the stable door, to see people bustling about, lost in their own dilemmas, and preparing to load up. Then she felt she shouldn't tell anyone.

It was her own pleasant secret. Special. Very special. Her 'Wow' moment.

Instead she stood beside Penny and gave her best friend, and equally silent witness, a big hug and whispered her joy to her favourite equine and friend.

"Wowee!" Anna repeated, and felt herself bouncing upon her toes.

After returning back to earth, with she steps light and airy for a few seconds, and face like a Cheshire Cat, Anna swiftly composed herself. Breathing in deep, she led Penny out the stable. Luckily all missed her beaming face, all too flustered to notice or care. Chris too was seemingly back to his usual busy and flustered self, deliberately appearing to ignore her, but did cast a sly smile.

Then swiftly, and without fuss, they loaded four horses in the routine military fashion she'd become accustomed to. Inside, all secured within the lorry were The Colonel, Penny, Fred and for a change, Bonnie. All munched on haynets, oblivious to the world outside the flimsy metal box in which they would soon hurtle down a road at speed, it being their only world for a short time.

As Chris had a couple of spare slots in the large lorry, which was capable of transporting five, Julie agreed to travel with them. She'd put Bonnie in last, with an empty partition between her and Fred. Just in case she tried to eat him. Sally was heartbroken she wasn't going out, having to attend to an urgent last minute family issue. Goldie had a day off, but didn't seen to care.

Anna was always curious about Sally. Although technically Chris' groom, she almost seemed to do whatever she wanted, whenever she wanted. She was however so nice and easy-going, in a strange sense; naïve to the world, that Chris didn't seem to care what she did, or didn't. That was Chris. And Sally.

Carol wasn't riding Tess, and like Goldie, she'd had been turned out earlier by Chris. Instead, Carol had sheepishly announced that she'd meet them at 'The Hall,' but being coy, simply said she'd be riding out on 'another' horse.

Seemingly it was one of Bertie's. Everyone wondered if it might be Virginia's horse. Carol's sudden strange behaviour, and links to Lord Burlingham, caused much fresh gossip and curious chatter; it being fuel for a Livery Yard.

Inside the lorry Anna sat next to Chris. Tracey, with a wide grin, blatantly held the door open for her to get in first, then pushed her towards Chris. Anna sat very close to Chris upon the bench seat, their knees touching and hands openly brushing together momentarily at one point. Tracey sat next to Anna, whilst Julie was in the seated area of the groom's area behind the main bench seat. She cast a cruel and wicked grin towards Tracey, who smirked back and forth, the cheeky exchange seemingly missed by the two 'Lovebirds.'

The 'Happy Couple' gazed with thousand yard stares out at the deep woods before them as the lorry trundled away from the yard the short distance to Wroxingham Hall, both seemingly lost in their own private, but happy worlds.

Chris's horsebox was well set out, with seating for about six in the small living area, where Julie now sat, as well as a small kitchen area and even a toilet. The seats could be laid out to make beds as required, only occasionally used if Chris went away to some big shows or events, or had a long journey to make to pick up or collect a horse from a long distance. But that was rare.

As Wroxingham Hall, although a large estate, bordered some points directly onto the back woods of Horsewater, the journey was short. In the olden days riders would often have hacked to a neighbouring meet. But it was easier to transport all the paraphernalia associated with horses, and ensure everyone arrived safely. And so Chris drove the short distance to Wroxingham Hall.

As the lorry approached Wroxingham Hall, and the ornate gateway permitting access to the walled estate loomed ahead, a line of placard waving protestors could be seen either side of the track leading to the entrance.

Bright yellow-jacketed police officers stood before the gateway, clearly prohibiting access. Other people, many clad in tweed, could be seen both inside and outside the perimeter. This was part of Bertie's security party.

To Anna it looked like a foreboding war zone. To Tracey and Julie like fun. To Chris, it was simply routine. Another day and more annoying antis.

"Bloody hell," Julie announced. "Look! Press. And they've got a T.V. crew!"

Julie's arm extended into the cab, pointing to a group of people standing to one side. Anna, eyes wide, cast a nervous sideways look at Chris. But his expression didn't change, his steely gaze set upon the entrance and the bodies seemingly blocking his access point. Julie stretched her head forward.

"Yes! Some real action!" Tracey chuckled loudly, clearly happy. "And TV too. But I haven't had a chance to do my hair. I hope they get my good side."

"You don't have a good side!" Julie prodded Tracey, the pair laughing loudly.

Anna didn't get the humour and gazed worryingly at the throng of bodies set before them, seemingly blocking their path, and growing ever closer, as the lorry advanced onward. She spun a concerned head around, to see a grinning Julie, then sideways, to see a wider grinning Tracey, who was chuckling.

"Don't poop yourself Cous!" Tracey yelled, playfully prodding at Anna. "They won't eat you. Well hopefully not! They're all Vegans. Ha, Ha!"

Anna's didn't care much about her cousin's joke, as her attention returned to the advancing gateway of Wroxingham Hall, wondering what Chris would do next and how he'd get through the chanting crowd. Chris eased up slightly, and then flashed the full-beam and roof lights on the big lorry, to indicate to those concerned he wasn't stopping. And in true fashion, he didn't bother to slow down as he approached the entrance to the estate, but accelerated.

The policemen at the gate, realising the big lorry before them was coming through regardless, managed to move the protesting antis, along with themselves, out the way of the oncoming truck just in time. As Chris drove on through the rapidly opened gates, a torrent of abuse and insults followed behind, along with a whirl of dust and dirt, stinging everyone's eyes, including the cursing police, who wondered why they were doing what they did.

Proudly, the big truck with flashing roof-lights and eager faces set within, was caught by the T.V. crew. They hoped it, along with coverage of a possible punch-up later, would provide good T.V. footage, and justify the tip-off given to them of further possible trouble at a hunt meet of the Shoteton Harriers.

"Woohoo!" Tracey exclaimed with joy, raising a triumphant arm, as the truck moved on into the Wroxingham estate. "We made it. Game on! Yes!"

Anna looked at Tracey, Chris, then Julie in shock and horror.

Chris focussed upon the driveway to the hall. Tracey was beaming insanely.

But it was Julie, face set, who spoke in a slow and deliberate monotone.

"I think we've just entered the Gateway to Hell."

Chapter 116

He who is not courageous enough to take risks,
will accomplish nothing in life.

Muhammad Ali

As the various horseboxes and followers began passing through the main entrance to Wroxingham Hall, the small number of press present were still eagerly waiting at the ornate black iron gates and tall red brick pillars.

Cameras poised and Dictaphones ready, despite the chill of the cold January morning, they hoped upon each arrival for something good and serious to report. They'd been anonymously tipped off about the next hunt meet of the 'notorious' Shoteton Harriers, following the Boxing Day incident, which had become known nationwide. Although a few weeks had passed since the long Christmas break, and events more important in the world had occurred to dull memories of the brief local fracas, the Shoteton hadn't faded from some memories. Thus, a regional TV channel crew and others were in wait, hoping for a 'punch-up' they could happily report. Thus, they, and a few desperate local paparazzi were assembled, with long-lenses ready, hoping they'd catch something as exciting as the events captured by Adam's Yates camera.

Two police patrol cars, set like modern sentinels, were parked on patches of grass either side of the large ornate brick piers, upon which the massive iron gates were hung. They guarded the entrance to the estate. Four officers in all, clad in black, with bright yellow vests, walkie-talkies on the front and black caps proudly set upon their cold heads. They were there to restrict access and ensure order was maintained, as best they could to the sprawling estate, from the group of a dozen anti-hunt protestors camped outside. Clad in a mix of multi-coloured hats and scarves, the Antis stood beside the police, chanting, jeering and waving placards each time another vehicle approached and dared to enter the confines of the hall, from which they were all clearly restricted.

What the four police officers alone really hoped to do if and even larger group did try to enter en-masse, was another matter. It would be carnage.

But for now the Antis were doing as instructed, and most were instinctively, if not reluctantly, obeying the police orders. Obediently they were not passing beyond the defined boundary nor entering onto the private estate, for fear of a private prosecution, or maybe being beaten up. The latter more likely.

For on the opposing side of the boundary, standing either side of the gates, with a bright green and yellow 4 x 4 'Gator' utility vehicle, stood six of Lord Burlingham's best, and most loyal, farm workers and Under-keepers. Smartly clad in a mix of tweeds and moleskin, all with quality green neoprene wellies on their feet, they stood steady and fast, as the inner-perimeter guard.

Checking any unknown hunt members as they came through, but also ensuring the police didn't let any antis sneak past, they'd originally arrived at the entrance gate bearing long-handle pitch-forks. However, the police swiftly persuaded the holders of these 'gardening tools' to place them into the back of the Gator vehicle, rather than parade them openly. The look had not been good. 'Provocative' were the words used. Along with 'Offensive Weapons.'

Suitable for a scene from a post-apocalyptic Zombie nightmare movie, , they were not deemed the sort of thing to be openly carried by the workers, or 'guards', supposedly being there as part of a 'warm and peaceful' welcoming party for Hunt Members entering the large country estate. But did look good.

The main entrance to Wroxingham Hall and estate, which covered hundred of acres of arable farm land, pastures, and mixed woodland, as well as the park gardens surrounding the hall, was mainly through the large ornate iron gateway. Standing fifteen feet high, heavily painted in black with gold points, the steel gates were set upon octagonal brick piers, and joined on either side by a ten foot high brick wall. This wall continued on either side for some distance, before dropping down to a four-foot high boundary wall, and then disappearing much further on, where it become a mix of hedge, fencing and other forms of natural boundary treatment, including ditches and Ha-Ha's.

If anyone wanted to gain access to the estate by foot, and had knowledge of the area, it was fairly easy to undertake, with various other smaller entrances, some with historic gatehouses. But these too had at least one person stationed 'on guard.' Other access points into the estate were simply via tracks leading through the neighbouring woods or the arable land, all eventually leading towards the house in some form. However, the guards to the main gate were really simply a show of force. In reality, someone could simply climb over a wall, push through a hedge, or wander through the woods to gain access.

However, the Antis gathered at the entrance were content to voice their anger and disapproval at the blood-lusting murderous bastards as they arrived at the entrance, and take no further action. They knew the TV crew would be there. The risk of a trespass prosecution, or worse, being dragged off by one of Lord Burlingham's workers for a 'chat' and beating was enough deterrent.

In fact, there was more to it. They'd been told specifically by Izzy and Dave to do little more. The small group positioned at the entrance were instructed exactly what they were to do. In fine detail. Make a big fuss for the cameras.

Also, the meet had been called on in such secrecy by Reggie, that few Antis, other than the local PAACE members, had gained any knowledge of it.

Unfortunately, the Shoteton were not seen as such a high priority hunt to warrant additional support by any of the big nationwide organisations. Also, they did not want to be associated with any direct violence quite yet, so the small group of protestors present would have to manage alone. And they did.

As the meet was on Lord Burlingham's private estate, it'd be much easier for the police to manage, and any Antis easier to spot, wandering about the place.

The police had agreed to keep a good presence and eject anyone found on the estate potentially looking to cause any trouble, or trying to gain access, the obvious entry point being the main gate. The fact the Chief Inspector was a personal friend of Bertie's also helped to arrange the essential police support.

It looked therefore as if hardly any Antis would be causing any real trouble today, and instead focus their protest at the main gate, where they could ensured full publicity, especially with the T.V coverage. Which Izzy organised.

The police guard watched on, the time to the meet as they had been advised, soon approaching. Unseen to them, a member of the Antis noticed the next vehicle approaching. They'd been carefully scanning each vehicle as it headed towards the gate from the small track leading off the road. A woman, clad in a rainbow-coloured, hand-knitted jumper, noticed the next vehicle approach.

The headlights of the vehicle flashed, fleetingly, missed by most, but not so a keenly observant woman. She gave a quick nod to her compatriots and the group moved forward onto the track. The police officers on duty noted the movement, and prepared themselves for some possible trouble, although so far the Anti's had been well-behaved and kept their abuse to simple chants.

Earlier, a bright green horsebox, driven by a single man, had hurtled straight towards the gateway and everyone around it. Clearly not planning to stop for anything, he raced through at speed, tooting his horn, a solitary arm stretched out the driver's window, with a singular finger raised. Cameras clicked away.

As this next 4 x 4 vehicle approached the gate, heading up the section of track from the side road accessing the hall, the policemen on duty recognised the vehicle as being a modern 4 x 4. It most probably belonged to another hunt supporter, not unlike a number of 4 x 4's they'd already checked that morning. Most had been slowed down at the gate by the police, the driver asked some key questions, and then let in. Large horses boxes or 4 x 4's with trailers they'd decided earlier were not to be stopped, with the potential danger of the horses inside becoming distressed if they heard the loud chants, jeering and placard beating outside. However, all single vehicles were checked.

Usually they gave the occupants a quick visual check or polite word to the driver, asking the purpose of their visit to Wroxingham Hall, despite how obvious it was. This was followed up with a nod to the impromptu 'guards' inside the estate, to verify if they knew the occupants of the vehicle. Usually they responded with a swift nod back or a vague shrug, if not known. However, they were always let in; the accent, woollen tweeds or fleece riding jackets usually giving them away at once as being horsey or country-folk.

The next vehicle appeared to be no different, so the officer in charge again stepped forward, ready to slow down this vehicle and check it out, as there appeared to be a large number of occupants crowded inside this 4 x 4 vehicle. As he moved to stand in the middle of the road, in order to stop the vehicle, a large roar of abusive jeers rose from the antis immediately to his side as they too saw the approaching vehicle. Menacingly they began to advance forward.

The policeman noted the aggressive jeers, then regarded his police colleagues opposite with a cautious glance, identifying the evident rise in tension and clear anger towards this specific group of hunt supporters. Clearly unpopular.

The other officers stepped forward, arms outstretched to calm matters down, and to hold back the agitated crowd, who were now stepping onto the track.

It appeared they were determined to stop this on-coming vehicle at all costs, and the anger in their voices was rising. The jeering mob clearly recognised the vehicle's occupants, with obvious dislike of them by the noise, noting they could possibly cause trouble if the vehicle was stopped for any period of time.

One of the policemen nodded toward the inner guard within Wroxingham Hall, who'd noted the tension and noise too as soon as the 4 x 4 approached.

"Let them straight through!" The policeman hollered to the estate workers, the lead man nodding, sensing the danger and obeying the voice of authority.

The occupants of the 4 x 4 vehicle appeared to sense the tension outside too, with furtive glances within the vehicle set towards the police and numerous Antis outside the gate, who angrily waved placards and stepped forward to halt their progress. The astute female driver noted the main policeman nod and wave vigorously at her, and as her 4 x 4 drew level with the screaming mob, with a singular arm, he swiftly waved her on toward the main gateway.

Needing no further encouragement, and hoping none of the flaying placards hit her vehicle, the driver pressed her foot down and the vehicle roared past the jeering crowd, seemingly set out for her blood, or more. Passing between the red brick pillars of Wroxingham Hall, the guard formed by the estate workers stepped aside, to let the bright green 4 x 4 pass through. The five occupants of the vehicle, clad in a mix of bright horsey fleeces and tweeds turned to look back at the wildly jeering mob, now being pushed back by the police, the occupants seemingly relieved they'd made it into the estate safely.

Through the towering pillars and steel gates it passed and onward into the estate it continued from the gateway, the driver of the vehicle lowering the window, her arm rising with 'thumbs up' as a 'thank you' to the kind police.

As the window rose back up, Izzy returned two hands back onto the steering wheel and grinned widely at her loyal compatriots beside her, as her 4 x 4 vehicle headed on into the Wroxingham Hall estate. Then, carefully checking her mirror, and noting all heads were turned back towards the long drive and the mad jeering crowd of antis, she pulled the 4 x 4 off the main driveway.

Knowing the ground well, having spent may happy days in the past riding out at Wroxingham Hall, as well as days in the company of Lord Burlingham and Steve, in 'the good-old-days,' Izzy knew her way around estate. As she headed across an area of grass, she met a dirt track, which she knew led away from the main house and out-buildings, where the members of the hunt would meet up, and no doubt, enjoy some of the finest food and drink available.

Dave Pearson, seated behind her in a borrowed tweed jacket and cap, raised a defiant clenched fist in praise at their success, and courageous victory.

Mary, new 'Tea-cosy' hat held tight on her lap, but wearing one of Izzy's old horsey fleeces and a baseball cap bearing a horse-head logo set upon her head, grinned like a child. Her face flushed at just how 'naughty' she'd just been.

Would the nuns of her former school have forgiven her? Probably not. Did her newly found evil depravity know no depths? She hoped not too. Bad girl!

Bruce just grinned. Seated in the front beside Izzy, his smart attire of tweed jacket and matching cap were what he used to wear out with Anna, if he ever went out. It made him feel like the country-gent he wasn't, nor ever would be. But it gave him the appearance of one of the hunting gentry to the police.

The full impact of the action was seemingly lost on Bruce, who viewed it as a fun, but silly game. Although it was one he enjoyed, along with the strange addictive excitement his newly found compatriots appeared to find in such events, he'd done more exciting things in his life. But it passed the day. Moreover, the activity, and relationship with those seated beside him, served a deeper, more personal purpose. He had plans. But he was telling no one.

Between Mary and Dave sat Jake, a young guy who was fresh and keen, and recently joined them. He was studying law at the local university. Very clever, and from a respectable left-wing leaning family, all heavily into conservation, wildlife and hugging trees. As well as being young, fit and keen to help support 'the cause,' he'd be there for any legal issues or matters likely to arise.

Izzy knew Jake was not likely to start a fight, or cause too much aggressive action, which pleased her, knowing Dave was out for revenge following on from the Boxing Day incident. However, she feared Dave's idea of revenge was far more different to that of Mary's, and his ran much deeper and darker.

Mary just wanted her Christmas hat back. Unfortunately.

Dave wanted blood. And Izzy knew from whom.

But importantly for now, the mission was a success. Part one completed.

They were inside the sacred grounds of Wroxingham Hall and had out-witted both the police and Bertie's private army of beaters, gamekeepers and farm workers enrolled to stop any Anti's from gaining access. Game on!

She'd originally planned to tow a horse trailer behind her 4 x 4 and have half a dozen other Anti's hidden within, complete with banners and placards. That had been her original 'Trojan Horse' plan, which had so much excited Dave.

An old horsey friend of Izzy's had promised her she should could borrow her horse trailer, supposedly for Izzy to move some furniture. But when that friend's horse became ill, and taken to the Vet's, the friend apologised and stated she sadly couldn't lend Izzy the trailer for a while, just in case.

Izzy's grand plan fell apart, but she was determined so get inside 'The Hall'. So instead she devised Plan B, arranging for the less-able-bodied Anti's she'd planned to smuggle inside the horse trailer with placards to instead stand outside the hall and make their noisy verbal protest. In a way, this was what they actually preferred and usually undertook. For them, running across a field in front of galloping horses was too dangerous. As Dave had proven.

The group of Antis waiting patiently at the entrance to Wroxingham Hall, with placards and jeering at the approaching vehicles, was really a ruse, although it was good for the TV cameras. The key anti's had been tipped off to keep an eye out for Izzy's 4 x4. Once seen approaching the driveway down to the gates, they were instructed to storm forward, just as they had, in the hope the police and any security personnel would panic and simply let the approaching vehicle straight through, rather than wait and risk creating a fresh riot or major disturbance. Or worse, having the vehicle smashed up.

That would cause the police far too much paperwork.

And that is what happened.

The revised plan had worked perfectly.

Just as Izzy had planned. And hoped.

Fingers-crossed. And toes too.

And just as Dave knew it would.

All doubts gone.

For now.

Izzy would never let them down. Never.

He hoped too. Fingers crossed. But not his toes.

Now well clear of the gates, the group let out a hearty cheer as their vehicle headed along the small dirt track and away from the hall. Izzy knew the small dirt track led on into a small section of woods, with a mix of ancient trees and historical rhododendrons, along with fresh saplings, some dense brambles, old shrub and bushes. All perfect to provide cover for the group to 'hole up' as they parked up and waited for some action later in the day.

Partly obscured with the limited cover available during the winter months, some half a mile away from the hall, Izzy parked up the 4 x 4.

Those inside released a heavy sigh of relief.

She turned to smile at Bruce. And even Dave. Mary gave Jake an excited hug and looked about the bleak woodland.

Phase one was complete.

Just as planned. Perfectly.

Izzy felt a sense of fulfilment.

Sir Arthur Wellesley would have been proud.

But it would be a long day.

And a memorable one too.

A lot could happen.

And would.

Chapter 117

A perverse person stirs up conflict,
and a gossip separates close friends.

The Bible - Proverbs 16:28

Unaware of the antics of Izzy and her group, soon to be hidden within the grounds of the estate, Chris drove his lorry down the well-worn track that led to the hall. Along with various other lorries, car followers, numerous 4 x 4's and trailers, Chris parked the lorry at the back area of the hall. Surrounded by a mix of period buildings, cart-lodges, aged brick and timber barns along with a traditional stable block, they formed a quadrangle of red brick and pantile outbuildings; the aura was one of stepping back in time to another era.

Years ago, in this same area, faithful horsemen and house servants would harness horses onto gleaming carriages, then, with footmen in attendance, drive them round the front of the hall to await for the then Lord Burlingham, who would then have been driven off in grand splendour. These days, Lord Burlingham simply jumped into a battered old Land Rover, or dark not-so-old Range Rover, parked around the back still, but then driven himself away.

The world had changed. For better or worse? Who knew?

Chris's group climbed out of the warm lorry and stepped into the chill January air to wander nonchalantly around to the stable area, to see what hospitality was on offer. A usual sign was to see where a crowd had gathered or listen for the sound of raucous laughter. In this case there was both.

Anna surveyed the mixed old buildings with a keen and appreciative artists eye, always enjoying good architecture and history, but also never having been to the grand house before. She'd only heard talk of the hall and all the grandeur it held. Chris paused for a few seconds, looking at Anna, wondering.

She caught his look and playfully punched him, as Tracey moved alongside Chris and slipped her arm through his. Not to be out-done, Anna grabbed his other arm and playfully leered at her cousin. Tracey stuck out her tongue.

"That's okay, don't worry about me!" Julie called, as she trudged on behind the group like a true Gooseberry. Chris turned his head and grinned.

"You can sit on my shoulders if you like," he joked. "Maybe not!"

Julie smirked, then jogged a few strides to join the group, slipping her arm through Tracey's, linking up four-a-breast, as they headed towards a barn, which they hoped had food, but from the loud noises, clearly had alcohol.

"People will talk," Tracey said almost seriously looking deep at Julie, and then mockingly kissed Julie on the cheek. "They will now!"

Julie winced but smiled, returning the kiss, as Anna simply shook her head.

Chris felt proud to have three ladies hanging off him and got some looks.

"Ever thought of becoming a Mormon Chris?" Julie asked in a calm, matter-of-fact tone. "I think you should consider it. Think of all that fun!"

Chris went red and a playful scowl from Anna to all sent the group into a fit of childish giggles as the happy group all marched forward.

A small number of bodies dressed in a mix of tweeds and riding attire could be seen in a barn. As they approached, numerous familiar figures, all chatting and laughing, were recognised. However, as they drew closer, they noted the majority of people were inside a lean-to barn, where a number of trestle tables, draped with fine white linen tablecloths, proudly displayed a stunning array of fine food. On a separate group of tables stood various bottles of alcohol and plastic tumblers. Tracey's eyes instantly focussed on this spot.

As ever, Bertie had gone out of his way to put on a fine spread. Or that said, the people who'd undertaken the catering on his behalf had. At no cost. Bertie wasn't one for buttering sandwiches, slicing cold meats, preparing buttered scones, or filling vol-au-vents. He just enjoyed eating them all.

These fine offerings, and much more, lay before the eager eyes and rumbling stomachs of the approaching foursome. Anna gently shook her head in disbelief, still finding it hard to come to terms with it all, but keen to happily enjoy it. Chris and the girls wandered into the lean-to barn, gazed at the array of tempting food, but instinctively approached the drinks table first.

Their group were all smiles at the host, a young catering assistant employed by Bertie for the day, totally in-experienced in dealing with semi-alcoholic hunters, instead of the usual bout of polite corporate hospitality guests.

She naively offered an array of drinks to the smiling foursome. All options were eagerly accepted and then rapidly consumed, to be swiftly replaced by a second. The catering assistant simply giggled and blushed bright red.

It was bitterly cold, but a couple of glasses of cherry brandy and port, or more as was deemed applicable, soon had them warmed up in various ways. Tracey in particular was already being warmed up and then noticed someone across the barn, separated by the many tables of stunning food.

"Look! It's Carol," Tracey announced to all, downing her third Port, her hand automatically hovering for a fourth. A glare from the young girl offering drinks caused Tracey to pause, realising she was being greedy. But with a smile and no conscience she requested two other glasses, indicating with a sideways nod and cold, hard look to the young girl that she was taking these over to her friend across the barn. The young caterer glanced towards a waving Carol, then back at the hard-faced Tracey, who glared at her like steel.

The young girl decided she didn't want her face punched in by the woman before her. She was being paid to simply smile and offer 'a drink or two' to guests as they arrived. Not to end up in hospital, or worse. They had whips.

'Don't be too generous,' she recalled the old 'posh' chap saying. For all she cared, the group before her, who looked as if they belonged in another era, could take all the bottles. She was being paid by the hour, not the bottle.

Two fresh glasses were offered, along with a feigned smile, and with a polite 'Thank You' Tracey headed off across the barn. The other three watched her plough through the crowds of hunters, as Carol happily waved at them all, a glass of port already in her hand, standing boldly alongside Bertie, the pair dressed in full hunting outfits. The girls waved back, then Julie quietly asked the obvious question. "What is Carol doing here with Bertie? She's dressed as though she's riding. I thought you said you didn't think she'd be riding out today. Hence why Tess is in the fields. The crafty bitch!" Julie announced.

Chris simply grinned, and Anna, gazing at him, knew he had prior knowledge or secretly knew something. Anna was beginning to see him in another light.

"You wouldn't happen to know anything, would you sweetheart?" Anna quipped, her laughter-lines creasing as she gazed intently at a red-faced Chris.

"I can't say anything, and to be honest, I don't know," responded Chris. "However, we'd best introduce ourselves to our host, or is that hosts?"

A wry smirk brought grins from Anna and Julie, as the group slowly weaved through the crowd of fellow hunters. Tracey, already beside Carol, was whispering in her ear as the other three approached. Chris nodded politely to various people as he passed, who acknowledged him, hoping he wouldn't get detained today. As per usual, Anna caught several glances and long stares.

"We'll let Tracey do the integrating," Julie whispered to Anna, as they approached. Anna nodded with a grin. "She gives a deadly Chinese Burn!"

Chris approached Bertie from his blind side, but felt the canny Lord had already spotted him and his group upon entry. Bertie didn't miss much, and wasn't as eccentric as many considered. Chris thanked him for his hospitality and then introduced Anna. But as herself, unfortunately not as Lady Melrose.

She noted an appreciative glint in his eye at her appearance, but no more than someone admiring a fine work of art. It relaxed Anna, who stood beside Chris as the pair began chatting. Julie stood to one side, and slightly behind Anna, her attention firmly set on Tracey, who'd moved in on Carol. She was beginning to look nervous, knowing how loud and blunt Tracey could be.

"Hello Carol. We didn't think you were riding today. Why didn't you bring Tess?" Tracey enquired brutally. "The poor Cob is her field weeping!"

Carol looked sideways at Bertie, to see Chris and Anna had his full attention, then shuffled a few steps away, moving towards a nearby trestle table covered with food, randomly grabbing at a sandwich before answering quietly.

"Well actually Bertie asked me if I would like to take out one of his horses," Carol replied in hushed tones, mingling at a sandwich. "I'm actually riding out Virginia's old horse, seeing as she's no longer with Bertie. She left him."

Carol seemed ill at ease for once, and not her usual overly confident self, but continued on, seemingly justifying her presence with the Noble Lord.

"I've known Bertie for years. As you all know. My ex-husband used to shoot on the estate many years ago, so he's simply an old friend really. I'm just giving him a bit of support and TLC at the moment, as he's now all alone."

Carol glanced sideways at the Noble Lord, who was now happily chatting to Anna and Chris. Julie's attention was set firmly upon her and smiled.

She blushed, sensing she was being interrogated by her stable mates, and knew how crafty the pair could be. Very crafty and very cruel. And clever.

Straight for the jugular as ever, Tracey asked the obvious.

"Where's Virginia? Everyone's wondering what the hell he's done with her. Do you know? Has he done her in? Did he throw her down a well?"

Carol went bright red and looked flustered, glancing over at Bertie, hoping he hadn't overheard Tracey's rather loud and slanderous comment. With a sigh, it seems he hadn't, and was still happily chatting to Anna and Chris.

"I'm afraid I don't know. It's not the thing you ask," Carol replied nervously, slipping a finger in her warming collar. "And be quiet, or Bertie might hear!"

"You should be careful," proclaimed Tracey. "He might do you in next!"

Carol glowed redder, choking on the sandwich she'd nibbled, shooting a look at the still oblivious and happily chatting Bertie. Tracey, sensed no wrong.

Carol saw Chris break away from Bertie, making a brief apology as someone drew alongside him, to chat with him and Anna, leaving Bertie alone.

He turned to look back at Carol, noting she was talking to Tracey near to the food tables. He knew of her from many past previous encounters on the hunting field, and had always found her good company, if not somewhat loud and common. But he knew she was a friend of Carol. Bertie smiled warmly, raising his glass. Tracey smiled back, returning the gesture with two glasses.

Bertie chuckled, and at once Carol seemed to sense he was about to step over and join the pair. Danger signs flew. Alarms, sirens and Klaxons blared!

"Sorry for appearing rude Tracey," Carol said, seeing Bertie's glance and his forward body movements, "I've got to get back to Bertie. Don't say a word. I'll explain it all when I'm back at the yard. I hope you all have a nice day."

With that Carol moved swiftly back a stride, grabbed two small pork pies, turned her back on Tracey and then passed a pie over to Bertie, which he happily accepted, nibbling on the crust and chortling to a red-faced Carol.

Tracey could sense the relief in Carol, and stood alone for a few seconds, a smile spreading to her face. She scanned the array of food, and also grabbed a couple of the small pork pies. Feeling dejected, and now standing on her own, she saw Julie looking towards her, and beckoning her over. Tracey moved to join her, and passed one of the pies to Julie as she drew beside her.

"What did you find out," asked Julie. "What's going on? Any big news?"

"She wouldn't spill the beans. But there's something going on," Tracey answered quietly, as Chris chatted to a local farmer, who clearly had his eyes glued on Anna, his head flitting from Chris then back to Anna repeatedly.

"She's being very cagey. Wait until I get the old bag alone back at the yard. I'll pin her down and interrogate her properly. You can help me hold her down. You won't believe what I can do with a hoof pick and a twitch."

The pair laughed loudly, raising a curious look from Anna. And others.

Slightly oblivious to their antics, Anna was aware of their playful giggles and could only hope it didn't mean trouble. She noticed the pair looked towards Carol and Bertie, and Anna also wondered what was really going on between the old, but happy pair. But where was Virginia?

Many were asking the same question Anna silently perused.

Moving back over and drawing alongside Chris and Anna, Tracey and Julie seemed to quieten down, if that was possible, and they all began enjoying the fine hospitality on offer, preparing them for great day of memorable hunting.

Memorable it would certainly be.

Maybe it'd be more.

Historic.

Chapter 118

Absence from those we love is from self to self
- a deadly banishment.

William Shakespeare

The riders, including Chris' party, slowly began to drift away in groups from the barns, and sadly the food and drink. However, as usual, this didn't stop Tracey and Julie grabbing an extra tumbler of cherry brandy, as they dashed past the drinks table. The young hostess had given up caring, having already downed several herself, and eagerly offered then to her favourite customers.

The pack wandered back to the lorries, warmed inside and relaxed by many drinks, and as ever, very good food. Chris strolled alongside Anna, close, their hands gripping the others fingertips, almost teasingly, until Chris moved his hand away, aware of movement behind, but cast a sheepish smile at Anna.

Julie, walking a few strides behind, raised a hand to her mouth to mask a smirk. She had not missed the action. She turned to look towards Tracey, but forever oblivious, she was staring at a smart black Thoroughbred horse tied up to a box nearby, swigging the last contents of her tumbler. Julie sighed.

Back at the boxes everything changed to the routine and almost professional, disciplined system. They unloaded the horses, then quickly, and almost in silence; other than speaking to their various mounts, swiftly mounted up.

It had now become almost a routine for Anna, but one that only a few weeks ago was an unknown and strange event. Chris glanced at Anna ensuring she was okay, confirmed by a nervous smile, warmly returned. He nodded to the group, no words needed to acknowledge they were ready, as girths were tightened further, reins shortened and bums wriggled down into cold saddles.

In silent response they turned their mounts and led by Chris, rode from the paddock down to the side of the hall. Here Anna gazed at the three storeys of the resplendent building, with eight over eight white box-sash windows set within a mix of whitewashed and red brick walls. Ornate gargoyles sat guard, watching on the roof edge, and the building spoke of history and splendour.

The sound of stifled conversations between assembled riders filled the area, drawing her attention. A growing mix of people, horses and riders shuffled in; riders muttering to their horses or companions, trying to remain composed and dignified. Anna counted about thirty riders, as further people joined the ensemble. Polite nods or raised whips were exchanged as quiet greetings, the hearty banter exchanged earlier over food now finished. Now was serious.

Martin had released the hounds. They keenly dashed about, skipping beneath horses bellies with practised ease, sniffing the buildings at the edge of the courtyard, urinating up walls, old farm equipment and metal hurdle gates.

For once Martin seemed to let the hounds roam freely, rather than rebuke and holler for them to stay close, as they wandered about, hopping over sections of dwarf box hedge bordering that side of the hall front garden.

Watching, he sat alone, quiet, curiously scanning the faces of each rider.

He was clearly noting who was in attendance, but more importantly, noting who was not. Thus by default, he could potentially determine who was one of his unknown 'heads,' or 'Owner of the Teeth.' Most evident by her absence was Virginia, who'd normally be astride one of her numerous horses, and usually seated beside Lord Burlingham, whether she wanted to be or not.

So Virginia was his most-likely candidate, as he'd feared. Poor soul.

But also clearly missing was Elizabeth. Reggie had arrived alone, and in a foul mood as usual. Missing too were the twin greys of both Gavin and Dawn, who Martin knew well enough to speak with. He knew Dawn was dead, they'd all heard the news, but where was Gavin? He knew he could be one of the 'missing,' after Virginia publicly pronounced her affections for him.

But Martin was not alone in looking at what prominent faces were missing from the crowd. Also seated unusually quiet and alone was Steve. He too was seemingly scanning the crowds, mounted or on foot. He too was seemingly searching for any unexpected guests. As Martin's keen 'Hunter's Eye' scanned the assembled group, it seemed that almost the entire meet that day, including a eagle-eyed Reggie, were eyeing each other up. Seemingly all eyes were looking to see who wasn't there, or possibly liasing with someone else.

Several horses down from Martin sat Reggie, his mount close to Bertie, their stirrups clunking, as if the pair were almost joined at the hip. A strange aura of companionship seemed to run between them, and they spoke in whispers.

Reggie had only spoken briefly to Martin since his arrival to give instructions. On Bertie's opposite side, a horse's width between them, but clearly evident that she was with him, or at least morally supporting him, sat Carol.

Moving within the group of riders, Chris didn't miss Carol, noting the key position where she sat, and equally important, the horse she was astride.

Julie almost gasped at the sight of Carol seated upon one of Virginia's top hunters, and turned to face an equally shocked Tracey. She simply stared. Carol in turn blushed at the sight of Julie's grin and Tracey's open mouth.

Lord Burlingham's new riding companion in turn smiled sheepishly at Chris, who returned the coy smile, confirming what he had secretly suspected for a long while. He was however surprised to see Carol seated upon one of Virginia's best horses. The 16hh dark bay gelding was a complete change of horse for Carol from Tess, both in size, build and temperament, but still very sensible, Chris having ridden it. Carol has a good rider, but not too brave.

Before any gossip or slanderous whispers could be uttered, and seeming to sense the unease and slight tension, with a kick of his spurs Reggie pushed Samson forward into the centre of the group, the side aspect of the hall a fitting backdrop for him. Pausing, Reggie scanned his attentive audience.

"Good Morning," Reggie hollered, to draw everyone's attention and stop any chatter, which had been minimal. All eyes focussed upon their leader, none wanting to suffer an early rebuke, but also respecting his position. He made a brief announcement, in which he thanked Bertie for holding the meet at short notice in what were 'difficult times' - heavy emphasis seemingly being set upon those two words - and thanked everyone else for attending.

He made a point of warning them all to be extra vigilant for any potential trouble, stating that although they were on an enclosed private estate, had a police presence, and thus hoped for a peaceful meet, they were not to be intimidated by any anti's who might try to access the estate and ruin the meet. Maybe simply to gain some publicity or key press coverage, as could possibly happen. Importantly, he warned the watching crowd, with a strong tone to his voice, for no one to get involved in any trouble, should it sadly arise.

Tracey almost burst out laughing at that point, raising a gloved hand to her mouth. Turning to face her was 'Auntie' Julie, casting her a mocking stern look, reminding her of their bad behaviour at the Boxing Day meet.

Tracey blushed, as did Anna, seated beside Chris. She cast him a glance, noting his attention appeared was focussed on the crowd, seemingly unaware of the three ladies around him. Then he caught Anna's glance and smiled at her, then noticed her silent and almost unperceivable nod towards Carol.

"Don't ask," he whispered with a grin, noting Julie and Tracey glance his way, smirking at the seemingly ever-naive Anna. With a bemused smile, and gentle shake of her head, she re-focussed upon Reggie, who finished his short speech and with a nod, handed control over to Martin.

Sharon was also noted as one of the other obvious absentees from the meet, but with no one appearing to dare to ask where she was; either knowing the truth, that the pair had split, or politely assuming she was poorly. Someone had apparently heard Martin make such a comment to a rider who'd enquired.

With a holler and a few cracks of his whip, to bring the hounds into order, Martin and Reggie trotted off, Martin leading with Reggie alongside, being assisted by James as the single replacement Whipper-in, falling in behind.

As the hounds and lead riders left the courtyard, the mounted field followed on, led as ever by Steve. However, today he appeared to be quiet, and less jovial, speaking little, his usually happy repartee noticeably missing, the whole group seemingly in a quiet, subdued and reflective manner. For now.

Those who knew the truth as to who was missing or banished from the Shoteton pack, and where they were, would remain a secret to them alone.

But time and fate would always play games. It was like that.

Fate had a habit of revealing even the darkest secrets.

And usually at the worst possible time.

It was like that.

Mischievous.

Chapter 119

Fear is excitement without breath.

Robert Heller

With little of the usual chatter and banter, the riders moved away from the rear buildings of the hall, the sound of hooves echoing off the enclosed walls, as they followed on in a tight pack. They proceeded from the rear of the hall in a steady walk, the prestigious building a fitting backdrop, before breaking into a trot as they moved straight onto arable land and headed onto a tramline track, with grass centre. The farm track ran between open fields of drilled winter wheat, the dark soil on either side broken with the fresh early growth of small bright green shoots, but now stifled by the recent cold spell.

The hounds spread out across both fields, Martin letting them get to work and try to pick up a scent on the cold ground. Reggie and James trotted in unison behind, with Steve ahead of the main mounted field some twenty yards behind, as all eyes scanned for signs of movement; hare or human.

The sky was a drab mid-January grey, the wind bracing and blowing from the North. It cut through the riders, chilling everything it touched, reddening exposed cheeks and leaving the ground hard. Many riders quietly asked why they were out in such cold weather, but knew it was because they loved the joy of riding out and the experience of being part of such a unique group.

Within seconds of spreading across the fields the hounds on the left side of the track were onto a hare. Their characteristic howl broke the silence, and raised riders and horses heads, as the front pack on the left side set off after the hare, which skipped easily over the fresh green shoots of the field.

Accelerating, it moved at a blistering pace across the firm, freshly drilled wheat, it's legs almost unseen such the speed. The hounds on the right swiftly followed, running across the track ahead of Martin, to join the pack on the left, streaking across the field in a blurring mass of black, tan and dirty-white.

Reggie and Martin set off at an angle across the field, dark soil flying from the hooves of their mounts, chasing after the hounds, who crossed the field in a triangular pattern, the lead hound Maverick well ahead of the pack.

James raced down the track, in an attempt to cut off any exit for the hare, and draw in any straying hounds, which could be left behind or become lost.

Steve, who'd been quiet, suddenly awoken, broke into voice and hollered to the mounted field close behind to follow along the track, just behind James.

Then a second hare appeared in the top of the left-hand field, rising to seek out the commotion, it then squatted low. White and black tipped ears pressed hard to its sleek and angular head, it both saw and heard the hounds. It pressed its agile body close to the ground, all senses on full alert.

Sensing the impending danger approaching, it sprang up with an energetic leap. In true and unpredictable hare fashion it ran to the right, just before the right-hand section of hounds approached, leading a third of the hounds away from the first hare as they caught sight of the second fleeing creature.

With a few nimble bounds it'd crossed the track, just ahead of James, who saw it flee across his path some twenty yards ahead, only to then race over onto the opposing field of newly appearing wheat, taking hounds with it.

With a curse, James hauled on his reins, and upon seeing a group of 'singing' hounds race on before him, he turned his large and heavy 17hh mount hard into the drilled wheat. Plumes of dark soil flew into the air, as the heavy horse tried to gain its footing and he tried vainly to re-group the split pack of disorganised hounds, now chasing twin hares, racing off in many directions.

Steve approached along the dirt track at speed, with the main mounted field following tight behind, all watching as the hounds chased wildly from side to side across the dark soil, followed by a cursing Reggie, Martin and James.

The soft dark soil was heavy going, slowing the horses of the three lead riders who seem to have lost control of the hounds and now only sought to get them back together as one pack and leave the hares to run free. For now.

The track and adjoining twin fields rose in a slight incline, leading to a wood several hundred yards away. Experience told Steve the chase was almost over before it'd started, but he continued along the firm track at a steady canter, in the hope he might lead the mounted field behind him to a point close to the woods, at the head of the drilled field. Here Martin and Reggie might being able to drive the first hare, or try to re-group in the cover of the woods.

The deafening thunder of hooves behind Steve told him the rest of the field were following close behind, a smile returning to his face as he turned his head to look back. A tight pack of galloping horses followed on, the first wave three abreast, as tight as could safely fit on the track. Outstretched equine heads, nostrils flared and ears set back, were pulled tight by taut reins of serious-faced riders, as they fought to control the horses racing only inches from Casanova's hooves. Steve grinned, then after casting a look back across the field, towards the position of each group of hounds, he turned to focus on the track. He kicked on some more, keen to not have any over-zealous or out-of-control rider from behind crash into Casanova, and potentially bring him and half the riders down. It was an ever present danger with hunting.

Further within the tight pack, now racing hard, were Anna and Chris.

Cirrus and Penny began to flatten out as they increased in speed. Anna was still nervous about racing so fast in such a tight pack, Penny's muzzle only a few feet from the rear of the dark bay galloping ahead of her. Chris had a pair of chestnut's racing in front of him, and he turned to Anna, tears streaming from his red-rimmed eyes due to the cold wind and speed.

"Okay?" he hollered towards Anna, through the roar of wind, and thunder of hooves, but with a grin on his face. "Are you okay!" He repeated.

"I think so!" Anna's reply was not convincing, as she dare not turn, such was her focus on the tight pack of horses racing both ahead and behind. If she'd turned to face him, he'd have seen a wide, but concerned grin from Chris.

Chris turned to look behind, seeing a beaming faced Tracey tight behind on Fred pressing hard. Julie, not as bold or confident, was struggling to keep hold of Bonnie. She was fighting with her head, set on either passing Chris and Anna, or probably seeing an opportunity to bite Penny's rear end.

Any relaxing effects the alcohol consumed moments earlier quickly vanished, as the thirty riders racing down the track focussed on the matter in hand, and tried to remain in a controlled pack, not crash into horses or stumble onto the soft soil of the field, which would fatally bring them and others down.

Anna could hear the snort of a horse behind, which she fearfully assumed was Bonnie, and glanced sideways to see the grey head of Cirrus stretched out, and racing smoothly on. She dared not ease up on the pace, so gently pressed her heels to Penny's sides for encouragement, but also feared getting too much extra speed and crashing into the bay horse ahead.

The hounds to the left stretched further away, followed across the field by Reggie and Martin. James had vanished from everyone's view, trying his best to re-group the small pack of hounds who'd lost sight and scent of the fleeing second hare, but were about to disappear into a small copse to the side.

Steve, a few yards ahead of the main mounted field, noted the woods rapidly approaching and knew the track split either side, with no easy access. Taking the reins tight in one large fist, with tears streaming from the cold biting wind, Steve rose in his stirrups and raised a hand, hollering loudly for the pack behind to ease up, but also hoping the well-trained Casanova beneath him would understand and fully comply, before the track before them ran out and disaster followed, and the mass of horses and riders crashed into the wood.

The mad dash, which only lasted less than a minute, and covered about six hundred yards, seemed to last much longer to the suddenly exhausted riders, and now excited and blowing horses. Steve pulled up and moved Casanova to the right-hand side of the track upon reaching the woods, and with a few bouncing strides began to ease up, whilst ensuring he left space for thirty horses to file in behind or alongside him on the edge of the drilled field, without hopefully creating too much chaos or carnage or damaging the crop.

An array of red-faced riders and snorting horses piled in and around Steve, as most pulled up their mounts up easily, although some shot sideways, in the opposing direction, to avoid crashing into the main group. Steve was back on home ground and beamed wildly at the various riders and they jostled about him. Towards the end of the pack, riding with his new 'Lady Friend' for the day, pulled up Lord Burlingham, his face glowing like freshly split Port.

"Did that wake you up and clear away some cobwebs Sir?" Steve exclaimed to a smiling Bertie, who simply beamed back, nodding, regaining his breath.

With a huge grin, he pulled his mount up alongside Steve, Carol in tow.

"You could have given me time to finish my nibbles and drink," he replied. "I still had a slice of cake in my hand as we set off and I've dropped it!"

"I'll send someone back to find it if you wish," Steve joked. "Maybe it's stuck in a hoof. Let's look. Anyone got a hoof-pick? It'll still be good no doubt."

Lord Burlingham laughed loudly, glad to be out with friends, and glanced over toward the field and to the top corner, where the hounds had run.

"I can't control the hares I'm afraid," said Steve to Bertie, seeing Reggie and Martin regaining control, but with some rogue hounds lost. The hare was gone, disappearing into a neighbouring field or woods. The chase was over.

Steve scanned the array of happy faces grouped together at the top of the track and spread along the edge of the woods, the tall, spindly and leaf-less trees creating a gloomy grey backdrop on the chilly, dull day.

But at least they'd had an early hare, which should at least keep the 'punters' pleased he mused in silence, knowing that as Field Master, not only was he there to guide the Mounted Field safely across the ground and try to keep some control, he was also in a way 'Head of Entertainment' and if the riders had a good day, all returned happy and safe, he felt he'd played his part.

As the group of red-faced riders pulled up together around the edge of the woods, Steve moved Casanova, trying best to keep off the drill, but also permit enough room for the mass of bounding horses still filing in. He was pleased to see nearly all had beaming smiles. Even if out of breath.

Those who didn't were the ones struggling to control their mounts, and their expressions ranged from frustration to fear. Some had a mix of both.

"See Tango is a mad as ever," Steve hollered to one red-faced man, frantically pulling on the reins of his spirited mount, whilst bouncing about.

"Bastard!" The red-faced man uttered through short breathes, but managed a grim smile to Steve as the horse finally stopped. "Not you by the way Steve," the man continued, now getting some control. "Well maybe not!"

Anna pulled up Penny with relative ease, drawing her in alongside Cirrus, her knees and stirrups clattering against Chris'. He grinned, their faces glowing. They were gently buffeted from behind as Fred crashed into them, Tracey smiling wide whilst fighting with Fred's head, but Julie had the good sense to pull Bonnie away to one side, so the irrational mare didn't eat anyone.

"Well that was a great start!" Anna exclaimed. "Mad, frantic, but great!"

"It's cleared all the cobwebs and sobered me up! But I doubt it has you." Chris smirked at Tracey She looked back at him, with mock steely eyes.

"It'll take more than that to sober her up," said Julie. "Maybe a transfusion!"

Steve watched on, enjoying the banter between riders and pleased once more he had a happy field. He also couldn't help but notice the body language between Chris and the beautiful rider alongside him and sensed something.

Reggie and Martin, along with the assistance of the red-faced and out-of-breath James, managed to re-group the hounds and bring the pack together at a point in the field just ahead of the mounted field. They were almost ready.

With a nod from Martin, and tip of the whip from Reggie, Steve watched the pair move the hounds along the top edge of the field, ready to move on and another draw, Steve knowing he was to follow on behind with the field.

"Everyone still alive and happy?" Steve hollered to the group of riders, now chatting, checking girths or even sipping from hipflasks, causing him to grin.

Most simply nodded back, or raised their whips as a positive reply.

He was glad to be back out and it had made him forget his other concerns.

All he could hope was the day continued in such a jovial and great manner, and there was no trouble or any accidents. Then it'd be a great day.

Little did Steve know both lay in wait less than half a mile away.

Nor that it would have a life changing effect on him.

Also for many others involved in the hunt.

That was Fate.

It was Mischievous.

Chapter 120

Affection is a coal that must be cooled;
else, suffered, it will set the heart on fire.

Venus & Adonis - Shakespeare

With Steve at point he quietly led the mounted field on, following some distance from Martin, who sat astride the still magnificent and bold Bert, with Reggie on Samson, now a muddy grey. He was, as ever, berating and cursing the hounds. James rode on a flank, trying his best to keep away from it all.

A lone crow cawed and few away as Steve set off. He watched it fly into the woods, admiring its freedom, but also it's vulnerability. Not unlike himself.

Following Reggie, Martin and the hounds, Steve led the riders onto a new field on the opposite side of the strip wood at which they'd all halted as the hounds were regrouped. They'd passed through the sparse, bare and spindly woods, all leaves long gone, now just a black and brown rotting mulch set upon the soft woodland floor, hiding everything beneath, but with small areas of fresh soil disturbed by wintering animals searching for hidden nuts.

Many generations ago, Bertie's predecessors had set out the grounds and estate of Wroxingham Hall mainly for the purpose of hunting, shooting and fishing, but also with some areas, set up for various aspects of mixed farming, including timber harvesting and agriculture. However, the primary focus of this area of the estate, it being closer to the hall and thus any services it could easily provide, was for entertainment and recreation. That was back in the 'good old days,' when gentlemen of leisure undertook such fine privileges, whilst a busy, hard-working group of staff attended to the estate, surrounding farms, and importantly, to the needs of the estate, the hall and its owners.

Such a relaxed lifestyle was miles from the chaotic world of today, but the landscape remained almost unchanged. Back then, days would be spent out hunting, shooting or entertaining a house full of guests. And their staff too. Most stayed for several days, being transported to and from the estate either on horseback or via fine carriages, drawn by teams of horses. These horses would be stabled and the carriages stored in the large brick carriage houses, where earlier they'd all happily feasted. How times had changed.

However, relatively unchanged, where the woods on the estate, where old harvested trees had been replaced by saplings throughout the years, the estate thus still perfect for hunting, with a mix of small copses, narrow strip woods, and deep areas of native woodland, where mixed areas of dense natural cover grew, for a wide range of wildlife to both freely exist, but also to be hunted.

It was strange and contradictory, with long-term conservation of key aspects of the landscape deliberately created so certain aspects could be destroyed.

This vibrant and stunning mixed landscape was not lost on Anna, who gazed at the surroundings, scanning the areas of woodland set between small arable fields, something not usually seen in farming today. Despite the bleakness of the cold winter day, she could fully appreciate the beauty and wondered what it would look like in high summer, when the trees were in full leaf, or then again in autumn, when she could imagine the mix of brown, orange and red.

She caught Chris glancing her way, looking at her deeply.

"Such a beautiful place," she said dreamily. "I've never been so happy."

Chris smiled back, moving Cirrus alongside, riding close to her, their stirrups clunking; but realised hard on their tails, quite literally, rode Julie and Tracey.

The pair appeared like 'naughty school girls,' both with Cheshire Cat grins.

But Chris fully understood, and never took for granted what he knew he had too; and that Horsewater, an area of deep mixed forest, had at one time been part of the larger Wroxingham Hall estate. That was before gambling debts by Bertie's great-grandfather, in London clubs, had caused him to sell sections of the estate; including Horsewater, that being sold to Chris' great-grandparents, along with a number of the smaller farms, now in Reggie's ownership.

Times were cruel in those harsh days, and people non-forgiving. Debts were debts and were paid. No one accepted Voluntary Liquidation. You settled your debts. However, what was left was still more than ample for the current Lord Burlingham to manage, enjoy, and provide a good income. For now.

Importantly, he wouldn't be selling off any more of the vast estate.

Not even to estranged or now missing wives. He was confident of that.

Led by a still quiet Steve, seemingly happy in his own company, he skilfully watched the hounds milling about a patch of rough unploughed stubble to their left. Martin and Reggie moved them on, over a small tussock headland and into a small field of beet, where the bright green leaves shone in the low light with melted frost. A single track, with two clearly defined wheel marks guided then onwards along the edge of the field, with a bare hawthorn hedge on one side, the field of beet to the other. The hounds drifted across the beet, seemingly oblivious to the soaking wet leaves, noses to the ground, searching for the next scent of hare, but all now relaxed after their first dash.

With James almost disappearing to the far side of the beet field, Martin and Reggie guided the hounds towards the next small strip wood ahead of them.

Riding slowly along the track in pairs, people began chatting, discussing their plans for the forthcoming year in a happy frame, despite the bitter wind making everyone's noses red and the cheeks to their pale winter faces rosy.

Chris and Anna happily rode closely beside each other on the track. Tracey and Julie were tucked in close behind, grinning at each other as the two lovers ahead of them looked longingly at each other, then bashfully giggling in unison. The pair seemed lost in their own world, their own moment, and totally oblivious to the two sniggering troublemakers riding close behind.

Reaching out a gloved hand, Anna took Chris' free hand and held it briefly.

Tracey winked at Julie, then moved forward, forcing Fred in between Penny and Cirrus. Anna was squashed closer towards the hedge and Chris the beet field, although with enough space for the three horses to safely ride on, if not rather inconveniently. Julie chuckled behind, as Tracey heartily apologised to the blushing pair for splitting them, but too profoundly to be genuine.

She turned her head and grinned at Anna and then jokingly grabbed Chris's knee, tweaking it firmly. He let out a loud laugh, then blushed, and in turn playfully tried to push Tracey out of the saddle, as she in turn crashed into Anna and Penny beside her, the former trying to regain control.

Anna then in turn prodded Tracey with the butt of her whip, gently jabbing her in the ribs and pushed her away, noticing a harsh loud chuckle from Julie, riding close behind. Realising she was beaten, and about to fall off, Tracey pulled on Fred's reins and dropped back behind the pair and into the safety of Julie, but not before she'd pulled down the peak of Chris's hat over his eyes. He quickly pushed it back up, and laughed loudly, as he turned around to leer jokingly at the childish pair behind. Julie simply stuck out her tongue.

Anna had first been shocked by the seemingly dangerous and unruly behaviour the riders often undertook whilst hunting. It was something she had seen by various riders, performed upon to each other, and recalled James doing something similar to Steve at a canter once, the pair also seen playfully 'sword fighting' with their whips as they both rode on at speed.

So Anna was surprised when she found herself now beginning to join in the play fighting on horseback, the banter warming, and building a deeper bond with her newfound friends. She turned to see Tracey and Julie looking at her.

Unashamedly, Anna drew tight to Chris, stretched an arm across to his waist, tilted her head and hat, then, as he turned to face her, kissed him on the lips.

Chris happily blushed as the whoops of joy from the raucous pair behind even caused Steve to spin around to see what the fuss was about.

He saw two red-faced, but happy riders, closely followed by two laughing.

Steve turned back, totally unaware of what had happened, but happy the group were enjoying the day. It was what it was all about.

Unbeknown to the happy and playful group, someone was watching them.

Jealously, they were intently gazing upon their actions.

And now they were scheming.

Making a plan.

Another 'Cunning Plan.'

And they were intent on ruining the riders fun.

Once and for all.

Chapter 121

Don't wait to do something.

Mark Bennett (U.S. Masters)

Bruce was bored. He sat in a clump of dry bracken, back against an ancient oak, looking at Izzy, then his watch, then back at Izzy. He wanted to shag her. Right here, right now. The skinny lesbian could watch. She obviously fancied her too, and why not. Izzy was very fit, no matter which way you swung.

Maybe Mary could lick Izzy's pert bottom hole for added pleasure whilst she rose astride Bruce's hard cock, and he could simply lay back, enjoying life and let the two woman do all of the work and pleasure themselves. And him.

Bruce felt himself go hard downstairs, despite the cold, then glanced at Mary.

He winced. Maybe not. Just Izzy. That fucking hat!

Izzy caught Bruce's slightly wicked glance, but tried to ignore him. She was aware of Mary's keen gaze too, as well as Dave's presence nearby. Triple trouble. Dave lay beside a big rotten log. A former bough of the ancient oak, it was home for a multitude of insects and other creepy-crawlies. Also Dave.

However, he was too busy to notice much as he intently scanned the nearby open countryside, whilst listening for the sound of the horn.

"When is something going to happen?" Bruce asked. "This is SO boring."

Izzy placed a finger to her lips for him to be silent. He was pissing her off.

Bruce raised a finger too. A middle one. Then smiled.

"This is just plain boring. What are we waiting for? Christmas, again?"

Mary scowled at the impatient new recruit. Typical man.

"Patience is a virtue," Mary boldly announced, looking smugly at Izzy for confirmation and support. It came in the form of a nod and smile, before she too scowled at Bruce. He looked at Mary as if she'd crawled from underneath the log Dave lay against. He in turn looked disdainfully towards Bruce.

"Seen anything in those binoculars Napoleon?" Bruce smiled, calling to Dave, who threw him a chilling glance. "Is The Iron Duke coming?"

"Bruce, be quiet," Izzy said with calmness, but a degree of authority. Bruce picked up a twig and playfully threw it at her. She responded with a grin, but a headshake, seeing scowls from both Dave and Mary. Jake looked confused.

The area of woods they'd moved into wasn't too far from the track they'd driven down upon arrival. They now lay in wait, hoping the hunt would pass by, as it had on many times in the past when Izzy had hunted here herself.

She hoped the hunt would be going about an hour before they hit the woods, and she was not too far away from her estimation. She noticed Dave shuffle away from his position and beckon Jake to him over to join him. He'd been quietly seated in a hollow a few yards away, scanning the back the woods.

Dave was certain Lord Burlingham would send Gamekeepers to search the area, in case anyone, such as themselves, had infiltrated the estate. Thus, he'd asked Jake to keep an eye on the back area. Just in case. Dave had seen many war movies, and knew you could get caught out from behind if you didn't set up a full perimeter guard. It was essential, as any 'good' commander knew.

The rude idiot with Izzy, Bruce, was as good as useless. Dave wondered why he was there, other than for the obvious reason that he was shagging Izzy.

Although clearly older than him and way out of his class - despite his middle-class upbringing - Jake could see why men were attracted to Izzy. However, he had a girlfriend back at Uni'. He knew he was simply there to help as best he could in preventing the hunters pursue their evil sport, and besides, it all had a hint of 'Boys Own Adventure.' But he did wonder what he was doing.

He caught Dave's muffled call and shuffled to him, moving low across the bed of rotting oak leaves and bracken, crawling up towards Dave's concealed position. He ensured he didn't break the skyline and give away their location.

Dave seemed to appreciate Jake's fieldcraft, nodding keenly as he glanced towards Izzy' who'd noticed the movement and looked at Dave with interest.

"We have movement. Two fields over, heading this way. Hounds and horses. Moving towards us quicker than we thought. Get ready for some action!"

The mounted field was obviously moving fast today, as it was only just after twelve and they could be seen moving into sight from Izzy's vantage point.

Bruce noticed the movement and how Izzy had suddenly responded with excitement, as had Mary. The skinny dyke squealed like baby pig. But Bruce was freezing cold, despite Izzy telling him to wrap up well and put on warm outdoor clothes. Bruce wasn't designed for all the 'outdoor living shit.' He was used to wearing a plush suit, seated in a cosy office, with a cute secretary bringing cups of coffee whenever he demanded them. And a bit more.

He thought of Lucy, momentarily. Then dismissed the scary memory at once, wondering where she was. Far away he hoped. Shacked up with another executive fool. Or down a well. A deep well. Maybe with an executive fool.

Bruce glanced at Izzy again, ogling her perfect rear-end, as she scurried to join Dave and Jake beside the dead log. The small group peered over the top, talking in whispers. Bruce knew something was happening, but was settled.

Izzy seemed a bit offish today, not showing him much attention, and was clearly not as much fun when she was in her hunting frame of mind. She took this 'Anti shit' a bit too seriously. It annoyed Bruce. He couldn't see the point.

It seemed total bullshit. So what if a pack of dogs killed a few rabbits, chased by twats on horseback? It was only a couple of rabbits. Or hares. The same.

Millions of chickens, destined for food, were slaughtered each day across the country. Living for about forty days before being killed, then chopped into pieces to be eaten by oblivious people. But no one seemingly complains or chases the 'cruel and wicked' chicken-factory workers or their rich owners all about the countryside, waving placards and shouting abuse and threats.

No one yelled or burnt down the factories of the 'evil owners' or freed the chicken with deformed feet and non-functioning wings. They didn't matter. The public just happily munched into nuggets, goujons, burgers, or maybe a full Sunday Roast, seemingly without any concern. Because they weren't Posh.

Maybe they thought chickens grew on trees or came out of the ground. Maybe they did. Who knew? Or maybe it was because chicken factory workers didn't drive Range Rovers and speak with distinct Oxbridge accents.

Unless anyone complaining about hunting was an animal-loving one-hundred percent true Vegan, then they were hypocrites. Or at least in Bruce's view.

Bruce's view on the world of animal cruelty was brought back to the here and now as he moved from his position in the hollow, cautiously rising up to see what'd caught the others attention. He lifted his head clear above the edge of the hollow, clearly breaking the skyline - a sin worthy of execution - and gazed across the field. In the distance were a mass of horses and riders, in a mix of colours, moving across the ground. All seemed happily chatting.

Bruce wondered which one was Anna, trying to remember the colour of her horse. He also tried to recall the horse's name too. But he couldn't recall.

He was sure the horse was brown. Or brown-ish. Maybe. Wasn't it? He tried to recall. It was a horse. But not white. Or was it? He paused for a moment, thinking. Then he bitterly recalled the embarrassing incident back in Leicester, with the annoying little arsehole leading the confounded animal into his flash lorry. Wanker! It definitely wasn't white. It was Brown. Brownish. Maybe.

Or similar. Or whatever fancy term they used. Who cared? It was a horse.

He then recalled the name too. Penny. Anna used to bleat on, 'Penny this... Penny that…' All the time. Annoying. Fucking annoying. And selfish.

She thought more of that horse than him. Very selfish. How could she?

His mind returned to the horse, the arsehole horseman, and then to Anna. More importantly his memory recalled him being naked before her, his hands set upon her neat arse as he sank inside her. And Anna had enjoyed it all.

He knew he'd never find such a fun, easy-going, caring, undemanding and beautiful woman in one complete and perfect whole package as Anna. And also, one who'd do anything he asked - both in the bedroom or chasing about the house doing his chores - whilst he did little else, other than moan.

She was special. And he had been a fool. That much he knew.

He certainly knew a good deal when he saw it. But now, lying in a bare woodland hollow, surrounded by dead and decaying undergrowth, and similar people, whilst staring across a bleak field, freezing cold and nose dribbling, he realised he hadn't appreciated what he'd had with Anna. He'd had it all.

But he'd realised that sad fact ever since she'd walked out. It was a pity.

He didn't really love Anna. Not in a romantic, soppy way. How could he?

That just wasn't him. Nor was it the manly way to be. It was all too soppy.

He wasn't sure if he could love anyone. Certainly not any more than himself.

But he cared about her. Well, he missed her. She was fun. And a great shag.

He realised how he'd messed up big-time by going with Lucy; as well as a few unknown others, thus losing Anna. A very silly mistake. He'd been caught.
He'd been a fool. An idiot. More so for getting caught out, especially with that stupid slut Lucy. What a big mistake she'd been.
A nightmare, despite being an incredible shag.
Very good. Better than Anna in some ways.
But now he could see the errors of his ways. He'd been silly. It was simply 'one of those things.' It happened. He was a man after all. A stunning one.
Most women instinctively found him attractive. And they all seemed to tempt him, like wanton succubus. It wasn't really his fault. What was he to do?
The trouble was Lucy. Previous flirtations had been with similar, like-minded women, only out for a quick bit of fun, as was Bruce. Then gone. Forgotten.
The trouble with Lucy was she was deranged. Obsessive.
She had a screw loose. Maybe more than one. All of them. Rattling.
But Bruce had only discovered this when it was too late. Big mistake.
Lucy was insatiable. Amazing in bed, or out of it. She just wanted to shag all the time. She saw to every desire and perversion Bruce could imagine. And then some he never had. She liked to dress up too. Role-play. Wearing various outfits and disguises. Something related to a past job she'd once admitted. But Bruce didn't understand. He simply enjoyed the wild sex sessions.
He'd thought nothing of Anna. But then why should he?
She'd been back at home - cooking dinner. As she should.
However, when things turned sour Lucy had then made sure everyone else knew what they'd been doing, by telling everyone. Then worse, she e-mailed Anna. She told her in full graphic detail what they'd been up to, along with sending some shocking images, detailing in full how 'Nurse Lucy' had been looking after the poor and neglected Bruce, and attending to his every need.
She hoped it'd force them to split up. And it had worked. Perfectly.
However, Bruce knew he didn't ever really want Lucy.
She was too clingy and obsessive. And he'd begun to grow bored with her.
And she wasn't too bright either. He enjoyed the chase. That was the fun. After that he lost interest. Despite the range of wild sexual activities Lucy provided, it soon became repetitive and dull. Once his bolt had been blown, that was it. And also, Lucy was lazy and untidy. She wouldn't do anything.
He wanted Anna back. Knew he would. He knew they'd get back together.
It was so obvious. She'd forgive him. Anna wasn't silly and knew he was the one for her. Anna knew deep down that she wouldn't get anyone better than him. How could she? He was perfect. In fact, better than perfect.
They were clearly meant to be together. And they would.
Bruce had decided it whilst watching the happy group of mounted riders move along the farm track. He was jealous of her and wanted her with him.
And it would happen. Bruce always got what he wanted.
Anna would come straight back to him. He was sure of it.

His attention was drawn back to the group of bodies on the opposite of the hollow, including Izzy, who seemed to take no notice of him, her interest firmly on the riders, along with the others. Izzy didn't care about him. Selfish.

Dave was lying down, hiding behind a large rotting log with a pair of binoculars held in his left hand, which was now slightly usable. He observed the advancing column of horsemen and women, like a military commander about to plan a cunning ambush. In his mind he was. But better.

Next to him laid Jake. As keen as Dave for the cause, and full of youthful exuberance, but not as radical. Nor with any personal scores to settle.

That was a great difference.

Mary kept talking to Izzy, secretly fancying the rebellious blond, but knowing she would never be attracted to her. Mary was happily living with her lesbian lover Rhona, but unsure if she really was the perfect one. If Izzy ever 'turned,' which was unlikely, she'd drop Rhona for Izzy like a tray of fine bone china.

Izzy was wonderful. Mary moved closer, feeling Izzy's long hair blow against her face. Sweet. The hair reminded her of Rhona. But only her hairy legs.

Mary wished Rhona would shave her legs, as she was beginning to look more masculine than most men. Long, black hairs. Like a gorilla on steroids.

Rhona said it was natural and didn't care. Mary thought it looked disgusting, but was too timid to say anything. Rhona was the boss. The dominant one.

Mary bet Izzy had beautiful legs beneath the dark leggings.

Long, slender and silky smooth. Mary could only dream.

She thought momentarily of running her hand along the fine, smooth skin. Then she blushed, wondering what the nuns at her former school would say.

A holler from one of the Huntsmen, drifting across the field in the quiet January air, drew the attention of all in the hollow. Heads turned towards the sound, and all their eyes focussed on the distant hounds milling across a small field of bare stubble, but steadily heading towards them. As the hunters moved clearer into sight Dave looked at Izzy; a darting glance, as if asking permission from a superior officer to launch an attack. She smiled back.

Bruce scurried over to join the group, his attention set on the horses within the middle of the pack. He focussed upon a brown horse and a white one, their two riders close together, and both appearing to be playfully laughing.

Despite all horses looking the same, these horses and riders somehow looked familiar. A slim woman sat upon the brown horse, a smallish man upon the white. Behind them rode a light brown horse, with a female rider. Tracey? It walked alongside a horse that appeared as if it should have Tonto riding it, the horse being a mixed pattern of brown and white. A Cowboy's horse.

The group all looked familiar and Bruce was sure he knew who they were.

But his focus grew upon the woman on the brown horse. Anna.

Although the images were far off and distant, something looked familiar.

As did the rider on the white horse. Wanker.

'Anna and The Wanker.' It could have been a West-end Musical.

"Napoleon," he called direct at Dave. "Pass me the binos. Now. Please. If you don't mind." He glared menacingly, but with a playful leer at Dave, who coldly regarded him as if he was a piece of shit. To Dave he was. Or worse.
Dave glanced at Izzy, who shrugged her shoulders, but nodded an 'okay.'
Almost with some reluctance, Dave passed the binoculars over to Bruce.
The Accountant - now on 'Gardening Leave' - raised the small but powerful field glasses to his eyes. After pale blue sky and magnified treetops whizzed past Bruce's eyes, as he tried to adjust his vision and the lenses through the binoculars, he closed in on a collection of heads skipping about in his vision, until one in particular caught his focus. After readjusting his position, then further fine focusing, he looked at the clear sight before him in dumb silence.
Bruce gazed at the image clearly displayed in the binos.
It was Anna. Proudly seated upon her confounded horse.
He felt a leap of excitement at seeing her smiling face, seemingly so close. Memories and desires flooded back, along with a pang of regret, but swiftly dismissed. Bruce focused in closer on Anna's image, which wobbled up and down through the powerful binoculars, due to the limited field of view.
But Bruce rapidly got the knack of following the subject, slightly adjusting them accordingly, and managed to steady his intent gaze upon Anna's face.
As she rode down the track, Anna was laughing and joking with the three riders about her. Annoyingly for Bruce, she seemed to be enjoying herself.
Too fucking happy, thought Bruce, who scanned the other riders about her, all laughing and joking too it seemed. He recognised her cousin, the annoying common one. She was riding beside a woman seated upon the multi-coloured cowboy horse. The same fucking horse that bit him! Bruce adjusted his gaze back to Anna, as a white horse with a man riding upon it fell into focus. Him.
Bruce felt a sudden weight sink into his stomach as things got worse and he focussed in upon the happy pair. Anna was riding alongside the Pygmy. Close.
Even worse than worse, she was laughing. With the Pygmy!
Anna was not sad and glum, as Bruce had hoped, perhaps pining soulfully for her distant lost love, bitterly regretting her decisions to leave Bruce and move far away. But instead she appeared happy. Very happy. Too happy. Bitch!
Even worse than a double or triple worse, Anna wore a warm radiant glow, sensed even at the distance Bruce gazed sadly at her beautiful, smiling face.
Anna appeared 'starry-eyed;' like someone does when first falling in love.
It was that unmistakable vibrant and happy air lovers have, which can be sensed as soon as the pair walk into a room or are seen walking down a street, and it seems to affect everyone whom they come into contact with or meet.
Anna was too happy. Almost like happiness on steroids.
It was a sight Bruce had not seen from Anna since when they too had first met, and when things had been great. She shouldn't be happy without him.
Bruce felt his blood pressure rise, along with his anger, when Anna playfully punched the man riding beside her on the large white horse.

The pair were openly flirting and clearly at ease with each other's company.
Did she just kiss him? Bruce could only see heads close together. No! Anna couldn't and wouldn't kiss the Horseman. How could she? He was a Pygmy.
"Bastard! Fucking bastard!" Bruce muttered loud enough for Dave to hear.
He sensed something unseen had now rattled the cool and cocky smart-arse.
Dave became interested, sensing an opening. He looked over at Bruce.
Izzy, muttering to Mary beside her, also seemingly sensed Bruce's frustration too, but could not know what exactly it was. Nor did she really care.
She too had grown tired of the attractive, but selfish and self-centred Bruce.
But Dave had suddenly become interested in Bruce.
He noted the figures Bruce was focussing his gaze upon.
Dave knew from Izzy that Bruce's ex-wife had joined the Shoteton.
Within seconds Dave understood the reason for the glowing red-face.
Scanning across the fields, he smiled, as he understood the outrage.
He understood the growing bitterness in the man beside him too.
And he could sympathise. He looked at Izzy. He understood.
With Bruce's eyes still firmly on the bino's Dave smiled.
He had a plan.
A Cunning Plan.

Chapter 122

An evildoer listens to wicked lips,
and a liar gives ear to a mischievous tongue.

Proverbs 17:4 – The Bible

"Bruce, are you okay?" Dave spoke with fake sincerity.

"What?" Bruce snapped back, his eyes still adhered to the binoculars, but focussed upon the pygmy. However, the use of his name by Dave, maybe for the first time, brought him around He lowered the optical instruments.

"You seen somewhat perturbed Bruce," Dave added with an even greater perceived kindness. "Is there a problem?"

Bruce looked hard at Dave, but his thoughts were still elsewhere.

"Wanker!" Bruce cursed, his eyes switched back to the distance fields. Then, sensing Dave calmly staring at him, he turned to face him. "Not you. Him!"

Dave knew the point of Bruce's intent focus and anger. He over-exaggerated the rotation of his head, to gaze wistfully over the edge of the hollow, and focus upon the distant mass of hounds and moving horses, with brightly-clad riders atop towards, to which Dave guessed and knew he meant.

"Wankers is I think the correct definition. Maybe a 'Bunch of Wankers' would be the correct collective noun." Dave grinned.

Bruce momentarily stared in silence, gears clicking, absorbing the clever comment, then likewise his face broke into a grin. He wondered if maybe he'd underestimated the skinny, arse-licking Anti. He had. Totally.

Bruce chuckled at Dave, gently nodding. "I like that. Good description. There is however one wanker in particular I'd like to pick from that bunch."

"Then squash him?" Dave spoke with a dark tone and crafty smirk, like befitting some kind of movie evil genius.

Bruce chuckled more, now liking Dave's line of thinking.

"Yes. Squash the bastard. To pulp! Like a tomato." Bruce added.

Dave gave Bruce his coldest and most evil glare.

"It can be arranged. Quite easily. But she won't be happy."

Bruce understood. The pair glanced at Izzy, who curiously looked at them.

Bruce stared at Dave, then glanced back across at Izzy, aware she could not hear them from where they sat, but was clearly curious.

He smiled at her, one of his cheekiest, then turned back to face Dave.

"Good! Then let's do it. Squash the fucking bastard! Flat!"

For the first time since meeting him, Bruce looked at Dave with a degree of respect, now it seemed Dave wanted some form of revenge and was prepared to take serious action. Maybe Dave wasn't such an arsehole.

"How will we do it?" Bruce enquired in a deep whisper.

"There are ways and means, but it must look like an accident. To all concerned." Dave cast another sly sideways look at Izzy, as if to convey to Bruce he didn't fully trust her. Bruce carefully looked over Dave's shoulder at his current lover, then back at Dave. Then he simply nodded. Understood.

Dave bobbed down from the edge of the hollow, so he did not appear as a silhouette over the skyline, and scurried to the side a few metres, further away from Izzy's group and settled into some deep cover formed by a mass of brown, dead bracken. Bruce instinctively copied his compatriot, wondering what the skinny guy had up his sleeve. Whatever it was, he now seemed set on violent action like himself. Therefore Bruce respected the guy a little bit more and for once was prepared to listen to what he had to say.

"Quick lesson on hares. Hares are territorial animals and live in scrapes within set areas, usually several miles wide. They know their territory very well, and when they are chased away from it, they tend to always run back to where they started out. That's why if you ever watch these mad bastards on horseback, they tend to come back to the same place several times in a day, especially if they get onto a hare. They fully know how they live. The hare usually runs around in huge circles, often several miles in radius, but eventually always return back to where they started, unless they go to ground or unfortunately get caught. It may take hours, but they're in no hurry."

Bruce stared in silence, absorbing the information, but wondering what hares running in circles had to do with him wanting to run across a field and pummel a short man who rode a white horses into pulp, or maybe worse.

Squatting in the hollow, silently listening and wondering what point the scruffy hippy was going to finally get to, Bruce for once remained patient and so let Dave continue, but with half and eye on the distant riders.

"I noted a hare dash off from the edge of this field when we first entered. It was disturbed by us. And I've seem it in the distance slowly circle back. However, it is now moving in the area where the hunters are heading and very soon the hounds will most likely pick up on its scent or see it. My bet is, from looking at how that hare has run, and where the hunt is, they could meet and the whole pack could well come thundering on over to this very spot."

Bruce began to see a clearer picture of how the whole eco-system seemed to work, and also have a greater degree of respect for the hippy before him, who seemed to be able to read fields and wild animals well. To Bruce it was simply a rabbit eating grass or a red-faced farmer's crops. Then killing it.

"So what happens if they come this way? How will I be able to get to the wanker who's shagging my wife? I want to pull the bastard off his horse."

Bruce's volume rose slightly at the last point, and Izzy caught the last few words. She flushed at the hypocrisy of the comment, seeing as to what he'd been doing to her the last few nights, and yet now he was jealous of his ex-partner wanted to simply move on. She also realised what she thought was true, and the real reason Bruce was out in a cold wet field. Revenge.

She looked away, pretending she'd heard nothing, and continued speaking with Mary and Jake, but still wondered what the two new 'best friends' were talking about, other than Bruce's 'Ex' and her new man.

Dave was clearly scheming again, but could only dread as to what.

In hushed tones, having seen Izzy's cold glance, he continued.

"If, as I think may happen, the hare dashes back towards us, followed by the hounds and then the full field of hunters, you can jump out at the appropriate point, scare the horse ridden by the guy you hate, and he'll probably fall off."

Dave leered heavily; grin wide, his eyes almost glowing.

Bruce considered what Dave had said, the gears now rattling in his head.

Wow! What a great idea. Possible injury, but also shame.

How embarrassing, falling off your horse right before your new love.

Bruce absorbed the pleasing thought, but was cautious.

"What about the horse? Won't it stand on me?"

"No," said Dave, his tone re-assuring. "I've done it lots of times. If you remain hidden, leap out at the right moment, the horse will shy sideward and the rider falls off. Horses have very quick reactions. Riders don't."

Bruce smiled. He liked the idea. He liked it a lot.

"And then I can pummel the shit out of him!" Bruce's face was glowing.

"You can pummel as much shit out of him as you want," added Dave with an almost hissing whisper. "But don't let any of the other hunters see you. It has to look like an accident. Maybe a few quick head kicks or a chest stamp."

Bruce's eyes almost lit up at the thought, a wide grin crossing his face.

"Leg. I want to break a leg. Or two. Maybe all three."

Dave grinned even wider. "Whatever, but make it quick."

"The wanker won't then be able to ride, and maybe my ex-missus won't find him quite as attractive. Cripple him. Not permanently. Just for a few months."

Bruce ended his thoughts with a positive nod.

"Cripple him. That sounds like great plan." Dave sounded chilling.

The two new best friends stared at each other in silence.

"What are you two talking about?" Izzy's called casually across the hollow, the two men glancing her way. "Not scheming I hope."

"I'm teaching Bruce all about hares and hunters," Dave replied. Bruce simply nodded, suppressing a smirk. "He's becoming quite interested."

"Best come over here. I thought I saw a hare close by."

"Me too," replied Dave, with a smile. "Me too. Very close."

He began to scurry back across the hollow towards the rest of the 'team.'

Bruce keenly followed his new Commander-in-Chief.

"Let's get ready for some action!" Bruce announced.

Izzy regarded him with a curious, enquiring glance.

For once she was worried about him.

"Time for action. Game on!" Dave smiled.

Chapter 123

Twere to consider too curiously, to consider so.

Hamlet - Shakespeare

"Are we going to draw Blacksmith's Wood?" Martin called over to Reggie.

Reggie appeared to flush red at the question, curiously glancing over towards a small wood ahead and to his right. It was a dense patch of mixed native woodland, mixed with scrub; one of the numerous small woods and copses purposefully created long ago by Lord Burlingham's ancestors as cover and was usually drawn as routine when hunting on the Wroxingham Hall estate. It would often reveal a rogue fox for added sport. Martin glanced towards the small wood, about to steer the hounds over, but waited for a reply.

"No!" Reggie almost barked, and then appeared to ease back, seemingly noting Martin's stunned response to his harsh response.

"Bertie is feeding some late pheasants in that area, I believe for a close to end of season shoot. Out of bounds to us. Sorry. Move on and away."

Martin nodded, but didn't believe the reply, knowing they usually drew the wood, and he'd hardly seen a pheasant in the area all morning. He gave the small wood a curious glance, also knew it was out the way for any shoot.

"We can swing around the back of The Hollow," Reggie added, as if to appease his Huntsman, nodding toward the small sunken copse a field away

Unknown to them, Izzy and her crew lay hidden and were watching them.

"We can go in around the back and see if anything is driven out. Usually gets something moving there. Maybe even a fox, if Bertie's keepers haven't killed them all. Then we can drive it onward. Steve can watch at the front edge."

Martin nodded, and with a heave of the reins steered Bert sideways, whilst cracking the thong of his whip to guide the hounds accordingly. They casually moved across the fields of stubble, sniffing about the legs of the two horses.

Martin's keen eyes scanned the rough ground and the various woods, usually enjoying a meet at Wroxingham Hall. But today the atmosphere seemed tense and toxic. Reggie was more off than normal, and even a number of the riders seemed tense. Steve also appeared to be less of his boisterous, happy self.

"Steve!" Reggie hollered across to his Field Master, trying to get his attention. Seemingly set to contradict Martin's thoughts, he was now laughing with a young lady on a fine Palomino horse, riding at the head of the mounted field.

The rest of the riders were ambling behind at a steady pace along the farm track, most happily chatting, laughing or exchanging various silver flasks filled of alcohol. A few were admiring the scenery, but others were clearly very much enjoying each other's company on a chilly day out on horseback.

Steve turned away from his attractive riding partner and looked towards Reggie, raising his head to hear, apologising to the lady, then realising he had a job to do, he focussed upon Reggie, who was calling to him.

"We'll swing around the back of The Hollow and drive the hounds in from the rear to see what comes out. You head to the front edge. Okay?"

Steve lifted his whip as an acknowledgement, knowing the small sunken copse very well, and the usual routine to drive out a fox or hare. He noted the slight change in direction of Martin and the hounds, then cast a curious glance towards the small but dense wood of Blacksmith's Wood.

He was about to holler over and enquire if they would draw the small wood, but noted Reggie had also turned the large form of Samson around to head about the sideways edge of the hollow, and so disregarded the thought.

They were clearly avoiding Blacksmith's Wood today.

With a sideways glance at the small wood, then at the pair of huntsmen, now drifting away from them towards the hollow in the adjoining field, he resumed his happy banter, now joined by an older man on a spindly dark bay.

But ever vigilant, Steve kept an eye on the hounds, whilst enjoying some fresh banter with the pair by his side, assuming not much would happen.

But it would. And swiftly.

Very shortly, life for many would change forever.

Chapter 124

All is fair in love and war.

John Lyly – Euphues

The hare, previously resting peacefully in the hollow, but disturbed by the human intruders, had eased forward fifty yards onto the adjoining field. There it remained, aware of activity behind, but as yet, it was not threatening.

It's bright eyes continuously observed its surroundings, knowing its own turn of speed would keep it safe if in real trouble, but otherwise, it'd usually remain hidden. Just then, upon hearing noise nearby, the hare flattened, lowering its body and yellow-tipped ears tight down. It's eyes, set high, scanned the field.

Moving across the field before it were two horses; namely Samson and Bert, seemingly drifting over the dark soil upon a swirling carpet of hounds. Atop, clad in red, were their riders. Their focus was primarily upon the hounds.

The multitude of ground sniffing hounds had not picked up any scent, as the light chill wind blew toward the hollow and the hare had not previously been out of its safe, hidden confines. Not until disturbed by five bungling humans.

The swish of the two big horses hooves drew near and the sniffing noses of the hounds moved ever closer. Too close. Beyond this group was more noise.

Gently raising its sleek head a few inches, the hare could see further horses and the human riders always linked to the four-legged creatures. Usually.

Too much activity. And moving ever closer. Danger. The ears of the hare pricked up fully, perched upon a sleek head, raised up on an elegant neck.

Two piercing yellow and black eyes scanned three-hundred and sixty degrees.

Real danger was coming. Hounds & Humans.

The hare was off.

Dashing back across the small section of field, the fleeting hare was instantly spotted by Steve, who hollered loudly, raising his free arm, then pointing.

Martin and Reggie, their attention on the bend in the field around the hollow, turned instantly at Steve's call. At once they noted the hare, now dashing back towards the edge of the hollow and home, but they were moving away.

The hounds, although usually reliant upon scent, heard the sudden call and sensed excitement in the call. Hounds heads rose, and then Martin's toot on the horn brought them fully into life. The rear hounds spotted the rapidly moving wisp of fur as it darted across the field and back towards the small hollow surrounded by trees, from where it'd left earlier. Game on.

The life or death chase was suddenly active.

The scene wasn't missed either from someone inside the hollow.

Dave. Out of sight of it all was Izzy, Mary and Jake.

Bruce was just being Bruce, looking at Izzy and saw nothing.

But Dave had seen it all, even before it happened. He'd worked it all out.
If he'd been a hunter, he'd have been outstanding. Maybe even as a military tactician, he would have been great. That's if his left-wing, anti-rich leanings hadn't biased his thoughts, and bitterness didn't run through his blood.
Dave had seen the hare, knew the tactics of the hunters, seen the location of the mounted field, and guessed what could happen if luck went his way.
And it did. Just as he'd hoped. Maybe as he'd planned.
"Izzy! Game on! They're onto a hare," Dave yelled.
Izzy, Mary and Jake lifted their heads at his cry, ready for action.
"They're coming around the side. Towards the back! Move to the back."
Dave watched the hare heading straight back towards him. Rider following.
All three of Izzy's group looked behind them, suddenly heard the baying of hounds and a blast of hunting horn. Martin's horn.
Izzy's focus was towards the sloping rear area of the shallow hollow, where it joined up with the grassy track, and where she'd parked her 4 x 4 under some sweeping bare branches hours earlier. Izzy assumed the hounds would sweep around the side of the hollow, then pour past where her car lay. Maybe they'd then head back towards the hall. All dependant upon the hare of course.
But she was wrong. As Dave had hoped.
Dave's unseen, yet real and urgent focus was to the front, where the action was really happening. And fast.
"Quick! You three head back and around. Bruce and me will cover anything from here and then swing around to join you. Go!"
Almost instinctively Izzy moved, often taking instructions from Dave. She rose from the damp ground and with a bounce, headed around the opposite edge of the hollow and back to where her 4 x 4 was parked up and hidden.
Mary cast Dave a curious look, before following, also crashing on through the dead bracken. Jake simply followed the neat rear-end of Izzy. Why not?
Dave raised his head over the rim of the hollow, instantly absorbing the rapidly changing scenes everything before him. He already had his plan.
Bruce simply looked confused. He heard the yells within the hollow, saw Izzy move away to the rear area, then heard the hounds, horns and cries out in the field just above him. But he was clueless as to what was going on. Clueless.
"This is your chance Bruce. For sweet revenge. Get ready!"
Bruce heard the deep harsh whisper fed into his ear. 'Revenge.'
"You have to move quick, but you can get revenge on that bastard on the grey horse who's been fucking your wife. Revenge. Sweet revenge!"
Bruce was all ears. He cast a brief glance towards the disappearing form of Izzy and her two loyal followers, then turned his attention onto Dave.
The fool. The words had worked and anger suddenly flowed. Clueless.
Dave lifted his head, but only for a second. The hare was running straight at them both. Only yards away. Behind the Hare ran thirty plus hounds. Behind them, heading toward the edge of the hollow at an angle, the two huntsmen.

And then what came really excited Dave. Following close behind the hounds. The mounted field. Led by their Wanker-in-Chief, Steve Harrison.
"Listen, and act quick." Dave almost spat the words at Bruce. He recoiled. "In a few seconds a multitude of hounds will flow over the hollow, followed by two huntsmen. Stay low and ignore them. Hide low in this dead bracken."
Bruce looked at the dead bracken and grass about them. Still clueless.
"Then the mounted field will follow. All the horses and riders. That wanker on the grey horse is riding right near the front. No, don't look. He's coming!"
Bruce's mind was already working as fast as Dave's lips and could determine what he was about to say before the words were uttered. He could guess.
He smiled, nodding before Dave had almost finished delivering his plan.
Yards away, in the field beyond their line of sight, above the lip of the hollow, they could hear the bay of hounds as they rapidly approached.
Suddenly a brown furry wisp scuttled past. The hare.
Bruce almost jumped as the hare raced down the sloping front edge and then changing into another gear, to race across the shallow basin, then away.
"When I give you the order, leap up from under this pile of bracken, and you'll scare the guy you hate off his horse. Then you can attack him. We both will. We'll both give him a beating. Hard and fast. Hit and run!"
Bruce felt the adrenaline rush through his body, enjoying the new excitement and the thought of revenge. He now understood some of the thrill the Anti's possibly got from freezing to death waiting in the cold wet countryside.
"Hide now!" Dave almost pushed Bruce into a pile of dry bracken, and then scurried to the opposite side of the small section of the hollow where they'd both been hiding . He raised his head slightly, his eyes widening at the sight.
"Hear come the hounds and huntsmen! Don't move!"
He bobbed back down below the edge of the hollow as a stream of hounds raced past, many leaping over the grassy edge to land in the soft yellowy-brown, dying grass of the hollow and other sections of bracken and rotting leaves. A couple crashed through the bracken, one almost landing on top of Bruce as the yelping pack poured through at speed. But Bruce did not flinch, watching in awe, he instead grinned wildly at Dave on the opposite side of the small pathway the pair had left to let the hounds and horses run through.
Then the ground shook and heavy snorting was heard very close by.
Samson, with Reggie on board, raced down the slope of the hollow. Bruce noted the glint of silver spur on the black leather boot as he passed. He winced being so close to a charging horse, but fully enjoyed the new danger.
Bert almost leapt over the edge, as if sensing something nearby, jumping over the hidden form of Dave below the bracken in which he hid. He grinned to Bruce as the first wave had passed their hidden forms. Further away, to the back of the hollow, Dave thought he heard Izzy yell, but he ignored her.
He raised his head once more. Bingo! Game on!
"Bruce! He's coming. He's riding at the front. Get ready!"

Dave saw Bruce shuffle within his bracken hiding place, rotating his body, preparing to leap out. Bruce had seen how close the huntsman had been, and knew to scare the Pygmy off his horse he had to be close, but not too close.

Bruce wasn't totally stupid. Just clueless.

Dave raised his head a tiny amount, then ducked down.

The thunder of hooves could be heard again. Closer.

Dave counted in his head, guessing the distance, the ground feeling as if it was moving, the sound of hooves and snorting horses again very close.

"Now! Bruce. Move. Jump up!!"

Dave's order triggered Bruce's instant movements.

Primed and pumped full of adrenaline Bruce leapt up.

Before him raced a singular Black horse. Not Grey.

Atop it sat a man in a red jacket. Not the Pygmy.

Field Master to the Shoteton. Steve Harrison.

Steve saw the man leap up before him, but too late.

Casanova, in canter, saw the image, but too late.

Bruce glanced sideways and saw Dave.

Dave saw it all. He smiled. Maybe he winked.

Bruce suddenly realised it all. But too late.

Casanova hit Bruce at about twenty miles an hour.

Over half a ton of horse. Heading on a downward slope.

The result was catastrophic to all three creatures involved.

Dave thought he heard the word 'Bastard' but wasn't sure.

Maybe Bruce emitted the sound as the horse hit him. Who cared.

He didn't care. He just smiled. Game on!

The horse ploughed into Bruce, front legs folding beneath the large equine's body, collapsing upon him. Casanova's muzzle dipped and hit the soft grass, his head and neck compacting as the massive horse fell, his front end going down atop Bruce. Flipping over, the bulk of the large black horse catapulted Steve through the air and away into the middle of the hollow.

Casanova lay in a pile upon Bruce.

Steve lay in the grass.

Nothing moved.

Result.

Chapter 125

For there is nothing covered that will not be revealed,
neither anything secret that will not be known.

Luke 12:2 – The Bible

Izzy heard a man scream, but was unsure from where. Or by whom.

Her attention had been to the side and rear, expecting the hounds to flow in a sweep around the trees and bushes edging the side of the hollow. Then as the mass of hounds poured over the lip of the hollow, she turned around. Just in time to see Reggie and Martin leap over the front edge of the hollow too, and run on down towards her. Passing through the hollow, Reggie and Martin cast her and Mary curious and cold glares, surprised to see them hiding on Bertie's land and about to yell at her, but their pace was too fast.

Izzy was surprised to see the field heading directly towards the hollow.

Dave had been wrong. Tragically wrong. Hadn't he?

Things happened too quickly for her to fully comprehend.

Looking back into the hollow, Bruce, for some reason, seemed to be hiding beneath bracken on the front of the hollow. Then he leapt up. Why?

He turned to look at Dave. Did Dave appear to smile? No. Surely not?

Next, Steve appeared in canter at the top of the hollow, stunning as ever in red, seated atop the black form of Casanova. But heading directly at Bruce.

Then disaster. Izzy stood in shock, not believing what she'd seen.

But she then instinctively ran towards the scene of chaos.

She knew moments later a mass of riders would follow Steve. Carnage.

Sprinting up the small incline within the hollow, with Mary and Jake standing behind her looking on in shock, she soon reached Steve's body. As is natural with all horse riders, she glanced down at the unmoving form of her former husband, ignored him, and then raced on towards the horse.

The large form of Casanova lay flat out on the grass. Parts of a human could be seen beneath him. Then Casanova stirred his black head, looking up as if some recognition flowed back. With a heave he lifted his head and blew out his nostrils. He was stunned, winded, but okay. Knowing Bruce was beneath, but also knowing what else could happen, Izzy ran to the top of the hollow.

Before her, only yards away, streamed a mass of riders, in full canter.

Holy shit, she muttered. "Stop!" she then hollered. "Stop! Accident!"

Upon making the call to Martin and Reggie, Steve had raced off a good few yards ahead of the main mounted field, knowing many were still chatting, exchanging hip-flasks or generally relaxed, not expecting another charge. With a hearty holler he'd kicked Casanova on, knowing the mounted field would swiftly pull up their reins, gather themselves and then rapidly follow on.

With a glance back, and a wry smile, he'd jabbed Casanova further, the great black horse responding instantly. Then, like a great leader, he was away, proud to truly lead from the front, knowing the ground well. Steve had a good head start, but was spotted by the ever-vigilant James on a wide flank. He'd kicked on his mount, aiming towards the far edge of the hollow, but was slower due to riding over the soft drilled field. The riders within the main pack awoke at Steve's cry, many completely caught off guard, others more astute, and as ever watching the movements across the fields. This included Chris, who as soon as he saw Steve draw his reins, then call out the hare, he was already warning the girls. They in turn were preparing to race on across the field and bypass a number of the slower riders ahead, still fumbling with open hip-flasks.

Hence, as Steve raced off on his solo charge - worthy of a Victoria Cross if in battle - the main pack of the mounted field were a hundred yards behind. Thus, as the first few raced off after Steve towards the hollow, following their keen leader, they were unaware of his fate and the impending danger ahead.

Izzy's form suddenly appeared from the edge of the hollow before them.

Arms waving, calling loudly, she looked at the charging horses racing on, then back behind her. She saw Casanova recovering, rising up and shaking his body, but no movement from Steve further in the hollow. The condition of Bruce, still lying beneath the winded, rising black horse, was totally unknown.

"Stop! Accident! Steve's fallen. Pull up, now! Stop!!"

"What are you doing?" It was Dave, his tone curious.

Izzy had forgotten about him in the moments of chaos since she'd seen her ex-husband and much-loved horse come crashing down.

She turned to Dave, half-hidden in bracken, his face set like stone.

"Leave the fuckers. Let them pile in on top that wanker! It'll serve them all right. Maybe kill a few more and hopefully finish him!" Dave looked back.

Izzy glanced at the still advancing riders, then at Dave, no longer sure what was going on with him. She glared at him. "What on earth have you done?"

"Killed two birds with one stone." Dave smirked. "Or maybe that should be, killed two wankers with one horse." Dave's look was vacant, but smug.

Izzy stared in disbelief, then flicked her eyes from Dave back over to Steve, then Casanova. Rising fully, a misplaced hoof appearing to stand on one of Bruce's splayed legs. He did not respond. That wasn't a good sign.

"You stupid fucker!" Izzy roared. "Piss off Dave. Now. Go!"

The first few front riders were pulling up, unsure if it was a ruse or genuine, looking down into the hollow, wary if her yelling and arm waving was another annoying prank or if something serious had happened. Mary and Jake arrived.

James was one of the first to arrive at the edge, pulling up his huge Bay, closely followed by Chris, with Anna tight to his side. Tracey roared alongside too, but Fred raced along the top edge of the hollow, Tracey sawing at his mouth, as she fought to control him. Julie drew up on Bonnie and looked on.

"What the hell is going on Izzy? More shit?" James spat out his words.

As more horses arrived at the hollow edge, the riders sensing something was wrong, they began to pull up hard, many riding by at speed out of control.
"It's Steve. He's fallen. Badly. Casanova is hurt and Bruce, one of our lot, is injured too. Looks bad. Very bad. You need to get help. An ambulance."
"Bruce?" A woman's voice rose up above the noise of mutters, snorting horses and general confusion. "My husband? Where? What's happened?"
Izzy at once recognised the woman speaking as Bruce's ex-wife. She simply nodded, grimly pursing her lips. With that Izzy turned around and dashed down into the hollow, to grab the reins of a standing, muddy black horse.
"Steady old chap." She grasped Casanova's reins. He rubbed his head upon her arm, throwing her back, then snorted. Moving the big horse forward, appearing to be okay, she looked at the prone form of Bruce, face down in the ground and unmoving. One leg and an arm stuck out at in strange angles that she believed God hadn't intended the human form to make.
A plethora of horses, thundering hooves, voices and noisy chatter suddenly enveloped around her, as various riders appeared in or around the hollow. Seemingly unaware of the disaster in the hollow, further down the grass track, Martin could be heard blowing up the hounds. Jake and Mary by Izzy's side, looked down at the two bodies and the horse in Izzy's hands.
"Jake, take hold of the Old Codger. Casanova I mean. He's okay."
She thrust the reins of the big black horse into Jake's hands. He looked warily at what he'd been given, having never been so close to one before. He rubbed Casanova's muzzle. The horse responded by blowing snot over him.
Anna seemed to appear from nowhere on foot, having thrown Penny's reins to Chris, to leap off and then rush down the slope and on into the hollow.
The two women, who'd shared the same man, momentarily looked the other in the eye, and a strange feeling passed between them before Izzy spoke.
"He looks bad. Very bad. Can you see to him, but don't touch those limbs. I fear he has some serious breaks. I need to check on Steve, as neither of them has moved. Mary, call for an ambulance please, if no one else has."
"I've already called for one," hollered James, who then rode down the slope, riding past Bruce and Anna and over towards the prone form of Steve. The Field Master lay on his side, with blood flowing from a small cut to his head.
"Steve!" Izzy hollered, bursting into tears and leaning over his prone body, gazing down, then across the hollow. "What has he done to you my love?"
Seemingly unseen by everyone, standing back where he'd hidden himself on the opposite side to Bruce, before being dragged and trampled, stood Dave.
Embers burnt within his eyes as he glared at Izzy gently caressed the cheek of her former husband - her one true love. And his bitterest, most-hated enemy.
Steve was motionless. Gone. Bruce too was motionless. No more.
Dave drifted off through the bushes, a smile on his face.
Truth revealed. Job done. Result. Game on!

Chapter 126

Well, everyone can master a grief but he that has it.

Much Ado About Nothing - Shakespeare

"Izzy my sweet. What are you doing here? Have you got the horses in yet?"

A bleary-eyed, mud and blood-covered face gazed up at the woman caressing his face. A look of confusion crossed Steve's pale face as he gazed at Izzy.

Tears, from a suddenly smiling Izzy, fell upon her ex-husband's face, running in with the blood and mud, wiped away in a smear and followed by a kiss.

"You've fallen, you idiot. Badly. Knocked out. Does anything hurt?"

A look of panic flooded through Steve's face as he now regained his senses, still dazed, but a sense of recognition to his surroundings becoming clearer.

"The Old Codger? Casanova? Where is he? Is he okay?"

"He's fine," Izzy spoke, knowing it was typical of horse people. She glanced across to Jake, who was seemingly enjoying his new role as groom.

"Not as bad as you. Winded, but he's standing. You look like shit! Does anything in particular hurt?" Izzy looked at Steve's arm, clearly broken.

"My arm hurts. Fuck me it hurts. Really hurts." Steve cursed.

"That's because it's broken you idiot. Badly by the look. So don't try to move it at all. At least you can you feel it. Any other pain?" Izzy looked at him.

"Only my heart. Aching for you my dear!" Steve grinned.

Izzy smiled, then shook her head, tears now flowing freely.

"Can you feel your feet? Legs?" She asked between tears of joy.

"My arse hurts. Quite bad. And my head. Is that still there?"

"No. No head I'm afraid. We cut that off," Izzy joked, happy to hear the old banter from days back return, when things were good. Very good.

"What happened? I remember racing towards the hollow, then seeing someone stand up. Some guy. He rose up from the bracken. Then nothing."

Izzy looked up to the rim of the hollow. It was empty of Dave, replaced by numerous riders and horses, some seated upon their mounts, others standing, holding reins of horses. A few faces she recognised, warmed by how their one-time enemies had suddenly become their helpers. Almost like in battle.

Mary wandered over to Izzy, looking down at her and the evil Huntsman she was now caressing. Her heart ached, a sense of bitterness flowing within. But with the natural empathy she held within, Mary strangely understood. She knew Izzy was never to be hers - just a fantasy - but also, she'd always sensed Izzy's attraction for her ex-husband all along. It was obvious too all.

"What can I do? Bruce? Is he…?" Mary dared to ask, but didn't.

"Best check," responded Izzy, seeing a number of dismounted hunters within the hollow. A couple she recognised, including Bruce's Ex-wife.

James wandered over to Izzy, appearing to take control of matters. She noticed Mary was now leaning over Bruce, along with a couple of others.
"I've called for an ambulance or two, and someone is riding over towards Reggie. He and Martin are away. The hounds got onto another hare it seems."
Izzy nodded, wondering why the ranting Reggie wasn't in attendance.
Chris was one of those who walked down into the hollow and towards where Anna leant over the still form of Bruce. He'd passed Cirrus over to Tracey, who now held both their horses. Julie felt helpless, knowing no-one could hold Bonnie and that she'd attack anything else passed to her, so looked on.
She tried to peep into the hollow, morbid curiosity taking over. Tracey, further back, called over. "Is anyone dead? Where's Steve? I hope he's okay."
Bonnie strutted forward a few strides, permitting Julie a glance, before she ran backwards, almost bumping into Tracey and group of scuttling horses.
"Looks bad. Two on the deck. One is Steve. One of the Anti's has Steve's horse. There are a few people looking to help, including Anna and Chris. Also Izzy. I think we had best pull back as James said. It doesn't look too good."
Mary, standing over Bruce, saw a woman rider look up, her face white.
"I'm Mary. Is Bruce breathing? I'm Saint John's trained. How can I help?"
Anna looked at the skinny Anti, suddenly recognising her as the tall one whose hat Tracey and Julie had stolen. For a brief moment she felt a wave of guilt, only a few weeks ago laughed and mocked the unfortunate woman. Now she was squatting down beside her, kind and willing to freely offer help.
"I think so. I heard a grunt a moment ago. But his arm, and that leg…" Anna winced looking at the wrongly pointing limbs. "Shouldn't point out like that."
Mary simply shook her head, then moving forward, put her had upon Bruce's good arm, touching the wrist. "He's got a good pulse," she announced.
"He's always had a good pulse," Anna announced automatically, smiling at her own joke, then she flushed, seeing Chris now standing beside.
He blushed, clearly uncomfortable, knowing he should help, but realistically could do little. Also, he felt as if he was intruding. This was personal.
"Oh Bruce," Anna cried, tears erupting as she looked down at him. "Why do you always have to be such a pratt? Typical. You stupid idiot!"
Chris watched as Anna stroked the face of her former-husband, moving away a clod of soil, which was in imbedded his hair, his face dirty, but unscathed.
She turned to face Chris, tears streaming down her face.
"I'd better stay with him, Chris. You understand, I hope?"
Chris nodded. He did, but didn't want to.
"I'll take Penny back with the girls, and then call you later. Are you going in the ambulance with him and then onto hospital?" Chris enquired.
"I have to, if I'm allowed. He has no one else here. I'll call you."
Anna looked at Chris, then down at Bruce, her emotions a whirl. She felt sympathy for him, just as she would for anyone whom she'd just come across and found injured in the street. However, she felt no real deep emotion.

It felt strange. She was sad for him, as being someone she knew; and in some form cared for, but strangely there was no deep worry or concern. She did not love him, only had natural warmth for someone who needed care, but also someone she knew he'd shared so many aspects of her recent life.

With a red face, Chris turned, to see Anna whispering something to Bruce. The tall skinny Anti, who Chris realised was the same woman whose hat now sat in their tackroom like a hunting trophy, sat beside her. He felt a mix of guilt and cruel amusement. The pair were speaking, the Anti feeling around Bruce's body with great care. As he stepped back and away from the edge of the hollow, he hoped Anna would look back. She did, raising a hand, but her attention was clearly upon her ex-husband and she chatted to Mary.

Chris walked with heavy reluctance out of the hollow and back towards Tracey and Julie, taking the reins of Cirrus and thanking Tracey.

"Is he dead?" Tracey blurted out, then blushed, realising she shouldn't ask.

"No. Not yet." Chris responded, then blushed himself, realising how cold his response had been. Tracey missed it.

Julie rode over to the group, her face a mix of curiosity and concern, as Chris leapt back into the saddle with ease.

"What happened? Was it Bruce? I thought it was. Pratt! Is Steve okay? And Casanova? I do hope he's okay too. Poor horse."

Chris gave a very quick resume of what he'd seen in the few minutes he'd been down in the hollow, and explained Anna would stay with Bruce, along with an Anti, and Izzy it seemed was with Steve, who seemed to be conscious. James was seeing to matters and Lady Carter had gone down to help Izzy with Steve, being the official First-aider for the hunt, but riding at the back.

The small group eased back and away from the hollow, mingling with the other various curious riders, many asking Chris what he'd seen. A number cursed and spoke harshly of the Anti's, shaking heads in disgust, and also amazed Izzy was attending to Steve, seemingly believing she was responsible for the accident, many having seen her waving her arms at the hollow edge.

Turning one-handed, with one last forlorn look towards the hollow, Chris led Cirrus away, Penny in his free hand following. The chatter amongst the riders on the return to the hall was gloomy and despondent. The day over, again.

In the distance the faint sound of sirens could be heard, weaving their way through the country roads leading to the hall. They'd then have to drive over the rough ground before they could even reach their injured parties.

Leaning over across to the Bay mare walking calmly beside him, her reins in his right hand, Chris patted Penny's neck, and sighed heavily. "Home girl."

Chapter 127

In the end, nothing is lost.
Every event, for good or evil, has effects forever.

Will Durant

The hunt meet had been called off for the day. Reggie and Martin looked on glumly, watching as their close friend and colleague was slid into the rear of the ambulance. They'd been called over after the initial chaos and soon learnt what had happened from James, who'd sent a 'runner' and then given a clear account of what happened as best as he knew and who was involved.

Reggie was at first fuming, blaming the Anti's for both injuring Steve, but seemingly worse, for ruining the day. Bertie had been in full discussion with the pair too, and as soon as the serious nature of the event was known to both Steve and the Anti' simply now known as 'Bruce' was made clear, Bertie rallied his own men on quad bikes and set them up at key points along the way to guide in the ambulances and offer assistance as needed. Anti or Pro, Lord Burlingham seemed happy to simply help out as best he could. And did.

One of the police cars previously at the gate had driven bumpily along the track and over to the hollow, breaking a shock absorber in the process. They asked a few questions and wrote down some notes, but otherwise took little interest, simply muttering that it was an accident on private land. Probably too much paperwork. The police car limped back, the wheel grinding on the arch each time it hit another bump, the occupants cursing each time too.

Bertie had at first cursed and moaned to the police officers about trespass and criminal damage by the Anti's, until he became aware of Izzy's attendance to Steve and also learnt from James that she was the one who'd raised the initial alarm and had prevented an even worse disaster from happening.

Secretly he'd always liked Izzy. A pain-in-the-arse, but now a bit of a hero.

But the day was over. Ruined, after all it had promised at the start.

After the various injured parties were entombed in their appropriate ambulances; Steve along with Izzy, hands held, and Bruce with Anna, reluctantly seated beside the now conscious and whimpering battered form; the two vehicles made a slow and careful, if not bumpy exit from the estate.

Lord Burlingham's men, on their quad-bikes, followed alongside; almost like a guard-of-Honour, until the ambulances were able to get onto the firmer main track, then pass on out through the ornate gates, where they sped off.

Casanova had been taken away from Jake, who'd grown to enjoy the placid black horse. He was passed on to another of Lord Burlingham's staff, to be led away to the stable block, where the horse was to be checked over. He seemed okay, and more people asked how Casanova was than the other two.

Izzy had asked Jake to drive her 4 x 4 off the estate, and thanked Mary for her incredible help and promised to call her from the hospital. With a sad face, and childlike wave, she'd climbed in the 4 x 4 alongside Jake. The vehicles was escorted off by a Land Rover belonging to Bertie, driving close behind, with three members of the shoot who usually 'beat' seated inside.

They had clear instructions to ensure the vehicle and occupants left at once, with no shenanigans He doubted they would, both parties realising the day was over and no one had come out as a winner. Both sides had lost.

Dave had vanished. Gone. Melting into the countryside. A loser.

As Steve was being treated by the Paramedics, and about to be loaded into an ambulance, Izzy had scoured the nearby trees and dense woodland. She was sure Dave was watching, gloating in the success of his dastardly deed.

But also, she felt, bitter and angry.

He'd seen how she'd reacted with Steve, thus revealing her true colours.

Whatever his emotions, Izzy knew he'd be planning his next move.

And that worried Izzy. But for now, she had other concerns.

Izzy had spoken to Anna, to ask on Bruce's condition. She got the sense Bruce's ex-wife was only in attendance as a matter of duty. She felt no love for the injured party. She was clearly concerned about her ex-husband, and his well-being, but her loyalties and heart seemed to be elsewhere.

Mary had assured both women that Bruce was breathing, although lapsing in and out of consciousness, probably in shock. That in a way was a good thing, as his body shut down, and so he could not feel the pain of the clearly broken bones. All hoped nothing serious had been injured internally. No one could understand why he'd done what he did. But that was Bruce, thought Anna.

Once the Paramedics arrived and took over, getting details from Mary, she slipped away. However, before she did, to join her fellow Anti, Jake, who was still holding Steve's black charger, Anna touched her hand, warmly thanking her for all she'd done for Bruce and promised to be in touch. The Anti had been genuinely warm and kind, and Anna felt even more guilt over the hat.

She looked down on Bruce with a mix of emotions. Sadness for what had happened to the man she'd once adored, but for whom she now had little true emotion. She hope that he'd be okay and make a full recovery.

But then also there was a tinge of anger. This is what hid any real affection. She'd been enjoying herself and her new life. Then Bruce had to once again interfere and upset matters, as he always did - or so it seemed. He always had to be the focus of attention. Albeit now in a wholly negative manner.

Bruce's actions had destroyed more than the day. She worried Chris may drift away, seeing her with Bruce, who for all she knew, may need constant care.

Momentarily her thoughts flicked to Lucy - the main reason for their separation. Wherever she was, and it could be anywhere, it was highly unlikely she'd want to offer a sick and battered Bruce any after care. All she every wanted from him was his cock and his money. He may end up with neither.

As the first ambulance arrived, and Bruce was strapped to the stretcher, Anna looked over the edge of the hollow. All she could see, drifting off in the distance, were a mix of slowly walking horses with glum-looking riders on board. She looked hard to see a man on a grey leading a bay horse, but could see none. Chris was gone. Just ahead, and passing around a small wood and out of sight, were the hounds. With a heavy sigh, she returned to her old life.

When it was clear the day was over, those attending to the injured parties were left alone, both out of respect, but also aware they could do little to assist whilst mounted upon a horse. The riders thus all drifted away from the hollow, collecting back at the small wood near Blacksmith's where the now long-forgotten hare had arrived and inadvertently started the whole sad event.

Bertie had made a brief statement to the riders remaining; a number having already ridden back to the hall, promising hot tea and fresh cake upon return to cheer up everyone's spirits. Other stronger beverages would be available too for those who needed such matters, as indeed he certainly did.

Carol had been dashing about on Virginia's former hunter, passing on information to various parties, acting as Lord Burlingham's personal runner. Tracey had called to her at one point, as she trundled past, with a red-faced Carol onboard, asking for an update. She could offer little, other than to say all injured parties were okay, or as best as they could be, as was Casanova.

Someone had taken him back to the stable block, with the Vet' already called to give him a check-up, just to be sure. With a hearty smile and tapping her whip on her hat, Carol was off, to re-join her Lord and Master.

Tracey and Julie grinned, but noted a sad and forlorn look upon Chris' face. The pair of ladies tried their best to cheer him, and praised Penny at being such a great trail horse. A few strange looks and muted comments passed between some within the hunt who didn't know Anna, but wondered what connection the owner of the rider-less horse had to the stricken Anti.

Luckily, all kept quiet, but it didn't stop mutters and rumours.

And so the hunt headed back, with Reggie and Martin ahead with the hounds and James close behind. The mounted field, now with less than half of the original riders, was subdued, all the initial happy banter gone.

Reggie, with a glum-faced, and accompanied by an equally scowling Martin by his side, simply wanted to get back to the hall and enjoy a stiff whisky.

He could only hope the ride back to the hall would be uneventful.

Reggie had finished for the day.

But Fate hadn't. It was having a busy day.

And it still had many more hands to play.

Chapter 128

Do not give dogs what is holy; do not throw your pearls before pigs, lest they may trample them underfoot and turn to attack you.

Matthew 7:6 – The Bible

Maverick smelt the deer before he saw any. In comparison to his great sense of smell, which was incredible, his eyesight was poor. He caught the distinct scent of deer. More importantly, them. Plural. Two. A pair of Roe deer. Does. They'd been foraging on the edge of a headland, before cautiously creeping out some bare Blackthorn to explore the spread of bright green shoots before them. Knowing it was dangerous in daylight, but acutely hungry, the freshly drilled winter barley rose as tempting emerald wisps through the dark fertile soil. The fresh growth provided the curious, but cautious and wary deer, with an opportunity to forage on some much welcomed fresh sustenance in the chill of a mid-winter day. Thus, with a wiggle of nose, turn of an elegant head, and flick of two long ears, the deer dared to break cover onto the field edge.

Maverick lifted his head, nostrils hovering inches from the soil, sucking in an array of odours. His quick mind analysed the unseen information, as his head swept from side to side, legs trotting nimbly across the dark soil. To his left ran his brother, Mayhem. He too had scented something unusual, and aware one of the horsemen was close behind, muttering as ever; with cursed whip at hand, Mayhem cast a sideways look, first at his brother, then at the horseman.

But the cautious deer saw the hounds long before the hounds saw them.

With a leap and bound, and panicking somewhat, one foolishly set off across the open ground of the field. The other, wiser, turned back into the woods, crashing through the Blackthorn and towards cover. Both lead hounds heard the noise, and then saw the fleeing deer. With a howl the pair were off.

Maverick, just ahead, and seeing the deer duck back, swiftly turned sideways, to run off into the woods. Whereas Mayhem, who'd spotted the deer charge across the open ground before him, set off with a fine yelp after the fleeting doe. The pair of hounds raced off, with numerous hounds close behind each.

With a split pack once more, each hound heard cursing cries from differing horsemen. But they didn't care. Instinct had taken over, and although all the hounds knew if they disobeyed the man on the horse he'd yell, curse, and possibly whip them, all thoughts of such retribution were gone in seconds, as thousands of years of natural instinct took over. And so the lead hounds split.

Each hound ran with half the loyal pack behind, and each half-pack was joined behind by a screaming horseman. Reggie and Martin. Both fuming.

Mayhem raced across the field in true Harrier style, singing in fine voice at the fleeing deer, enjoying the natural chase for which he'd been created.

Close behind, also singing in tune, noses hovering over the ground, raced half the pack of hounds. Close behind them, but singing to a different tune; one of curses, screams and yells, followed a horseman, resplendent in red.

Maverick heard a similar chorus behind him, both canine and human, as he dashed into the woods; closely followed by a large section of hounds, and also a red-clad horseman. Foul sounds screamed from this horseman's mouth too, but meant little to the hound. He knew what rebukes followed such words, but he'd begun to care less. He'd begun to sense he was the pack leader.

The man who fed and cared for them, led them out, trained and nurtured them, yet also cursed them, and cruelly punished them, was becoming weaker.

He was becoming less powerful. Not so dominant.

The man was not in control. He only thought he was.

Maverick was now in control. Or would be. Very soon.

Onward Maverick ploughed, into the wood, chasing the scent of the deer, more so than its physical body. That had vanished into the dense trees and undergrowth. The well-camouflaged deer dashed through trees, bushes and scrub with nimble and well-practiced ease; seeming to vanish, then re-appear within the dense trees, almost as if translucent. The stream of hounds behind Maverick spread out through the small wood - Blacksmith's Wood - following the scent simply for instinctive pleasure. For the deer it was life or death.

Closely following Maverick, crashing noisily through the hedges and saplings bordering the headland into the wood, was the horseman. Maverick knew his position from the horse, and the noises emitted from the rider's foul mouth.

Harsh and brutal curses flowed freely, the sort usually rewarded to all hounds when they did not undertake actions the horseman wanted. Which was often.

But for the moment Maverick did not care. He was in pursuit of a prey he loved to chase, but restrained from doing by the whole group of horsemen.

It seemed strange to Maverick that he was bred to hunt and kill; which he undertook most successfully, and yet at certain times he was rebuked and stopped from doing so. Kill or not kill? What was he meant to do? Confusing.

To Maverick it was sometimes hard to understand or distinguish what the horsemen wanted. So he simply killed. And he enjoyed it. Naturally.

The gloom of the woods overtook, the deer vanishing, as was its scent, that being overtaken by numerous fresh smells flowing through the trees. He eased up his pursuit, nose hovering, sucking in an array of differing odours and scents, as a new scent flowed heavily into his super-active nostrils.

It was a scent he was familiar with. One he'd long recognised and knew.

But lately it held a different meaning. And this scent was slightly different.

He trotted at a slow pace, nose inches from the ground, hovering over dry, dead pine and larch needles, mixed with other rotting detritus. But just ahead of him his nose detected freshly disturbed soil. The smell of the open earth was strong. It was days or weeks old, but still gave off the strong earthy odour a hound would recognise. But there was something else. Something familiar.

Maverick stood upon the area of freshly disturbed soil. Below, a well-known scent flowed. The soil was neither open nor clear to see by the naked eye; canine or human, being well covered with an array of old and new vegetation. Branches, sticks, leaves and various twigs had tried to disguise the area.

But to Maverick, he saw beyond this feeble veil, this mask or basic covering.

He saw with his nose. He knew what lie beneath the weak and fake facade.

It was a scent linked to something he knew well.

With the sounds of screaming and yelling somewhere back in the woods, a mix of hounds followed him over; some sniffing at the same odour he'd detected, whilst others drifted off aimlessly into the woods, still trying to track the now vanished deer. The voice of the Horseman could be heard within the woods, yelling at any unruly hounds, his whip cracking like gunfire as he tried to gain control and re-group the small split pack. Uncaring of the noises about him, Maverick did another thing that hounds do best. He began to dig.

Within a few seconds of digging he'd removed the light covering of debris and topsoil. A few more frantic scrapes later he'd opened up the surface.

An opening appeared. Widened by more frantic digging.

Soil flew from Maverick's feet to reveal the shallow grave.

Then he found flesh.

A finger was revealed.

Then a hand. Becoming an arm.

The limb had been the last part of the corpse forced into the quickly dug small, shallow grave. The person burying the body was sure, at the time, that no one, or no thing, would ever enter the small, remote section of wood.

Let alone dig and try to uncover the poorly buried body. Wrong.

That person had never understood fate. Or Maverick.

Tempt 'Fate' and she'll slap you in the face. And she had.

And Maverick was that unexpected agent of Doom.

The pale limb, stained with soil, was quickly uncovered.

Maverick stopped digging and sniffed at the arm.

And then he sank his teeth into the semi-rotting flesh.

The flesh was soft and placid, his teeth easily sinking down to bone.

Then Maverick pulled, tugging hard at the limb. Shaking his head, the flaying arm freed itself from the soil. As he'd dug, more curios hounds had gathered.

He was now joined by Christmas, the small pale hound from the Boxing Day incident, who always followed Maverick, knowing he was one of the Alpha hounds. The smaller hound, nuzzling in, bit hard into the exposed limb, her teeth clamping onto the pale hand, and the pair of hounds tugged together at the free limb. Swiftly turning their heads, pulling hard with their muddy feet, the arm rose, a seemingly accusing finger pointing outward as both hounds yanked harshly at the expose limb. The shoulder of the body, still covered by soil, moved, disturbing the loose, poorly packed soil, as both hounds tugged.

Then they heard the horseman. Very close. Too close.

Yelling and cursing, he viciously cracked his whip. The leather tip flew past their heads, cracking violently. Christmas released her grip and fled into the woods. But Maverick remained, pulling hard, partly removing the body from the loose soil, exposing soiled shoulders and a bare upper torso.

And still the hound pulled. The thong of the whip cracked inches above the head of the hound, only missing by bad luck, rather than intent.

Maverick was old and wise enough to know he'd pushed his luck, or maybe pulled at it, as he felt the air snap over his head and heard the deadly cracking sound, knowing it was too close. That whip-end had his name upon it.

As the whip was rapidly re-coiled by the horseman, ready for a second, possibly more accurate crack at the hound, Maverick released his grip of the limb. Dodging sideward, and with a cursing glare at the horseman, he scurried away through the dense woods to rejoin the rest of the mingling pack.

Momentarily, joined at his side was Christmas, the pair of hounds standing in the cover of some bare Rhododendron stems. Sniffing each other's muzzles, a bond was building, and they stared in silent unison at the cursing horseman.

All sound had ceased from his mouth, and he sat upon his steaming horse, staring down at what had been uncovered.

The horseman glanced at the body, and then at the hounds.

Like unashamed naughty children, the pair of hounds moved a step forward, revealing themselves from the gloom of the undergrowth.

In silence, the horseman regarded the hounds.

His eyes met that of Maverick.

The pair connected.

Coldly, horseman and hound stared.

A sound behind the horseman caused him to instinctively turn, breaking eye contact. Turning his horse, he looked back to the edge of the woods.

Another horseman stood proud upon his mount, staring into the woods.

Silhouetted by the backlight of the poor winter sun, both horsemen silently regarded the other, seemingly knowing what each knew.

But had they both seen the same? Who knew?

Maverick did. In the woods, he stared at them both.

He knew each horseman well. Very well.

And he sensed the unseen tension between them.

Then a third horseman appeared, his horse steaming too, the rider also cursing. This horseman was joined by Mayhem, along with the other half of the pack, who scurried on past the three horsemen, racing on into the wood.

The hounds began to reform into the one pack within the small dark wood, but were instantly hurried away by the two horsemen, harried out the woods and back onto the field headland, all spilling out onto the edge of the field.

The third huntsman stared into the woods, curious, looking hard at the freshly disturbed ground. His focus was watched by the two other horsemen.

Each of the two original horsemen wondered what the third had seen.

The third horseman seemed curious at the sudden silence between the other two, lack of hollering or action to disperse the hounds, questionably scanning each horseman. There was an uneasy tension. Even the hounds stood still.

The wood was deathly quiet too. The dead make no sounds.

All three horsemen regarded each other.

Some knew more than others.

The silence did not last long, and a loud yell, followed by a crack of the whip from one, awoke hounds and horsemen alike. Back to work, the hounds drifted onto the field, just as they were conditioned and trained to respond, almost like canine automatons. But some had their own minds.

Only Maverick hesitated, and for that, so did Christmas. She was following the actions of the new leader. Finally, after another cursing yell and softer whip crack, Maverick moved on, along with his new loyal cohort, Christmas.

Within seconds the hounds were back into their usual formation, milling together in the field, the three horsemen exchanging muttered comments.

But one in particular glanced back at the woods.

They alone knew what was buried within.

And they alone knew they would have to return later.

In the dark, that evening, to fix the mess a certain hound had caused.

With a cursing cold stare, the horseman's cold and cursing eyes scanned the milling pack, then spotting that very hound.

The horseman glared at Maverick.

The rebellious hound glared back.

Three horsemen regarded each other.

All unsure what the other really knew or what they had seen, if anything.

But none could take the chance.

Each seemed to know something. But what?

But only one creature knew everything.

Maverick.

Chapter 129

But I say to you, that everyone who looks at a woman with lustful intent, has already committed adultery with her in his heart.

Matthew 5:28 – The Bible

It was late and the yard dark when Anna finally arrived at Horsewater. Telephone calls throughout the afternoon and evening to numerous enquiring people, along with hospital staff asking various questions about Bruce, had left Anna drained. Her mum hadn't helped, repeatedly asking if she wanted to stay at their house for the night, or wait, whilst she collected her 4 x 4 from Chris' yard to drive her back home. But all Anna wanted to do now was see Penny, check all had returned home safely - despite telephone calls from them all to advise all was well - see and speak direct with Chris. Only then would she think about relaxing. It'd been a tiring and long stressful day.

Stepping out from the warmth of her mum's car, into the chill and darkness of the yard, she quickly closed the car door, before Joyce could ask one final time if she was okay. Alone in the gloom, standing beside her own 4 x 4, her mum raised a hand and waved at Anna as she turned her Merc' around in the yard and headed back up into the woods. With a shudder from a chill breeze, despite the warm fleece she wore, Anna was for once pleased to hear nothing.

She watched the sweep of her mum's headlights cut through the darkness of the woods, then vanish, to stand in the shadow of the house in silence.

No beep of cardiac monitors, blips of strange equipment, ring of hospital phones or pagers, or even the squeak of trolley wheels and footwear on sterile grey vinyl flooring. Let alone the chatter of people. Peace. Quiet. Bliss.

She stood in silence, dressed in tight jeans, trainers, a dark T-shirt and thick fleece, changing from her hunting gear at her mum's. She'd spent most of the time waiting at the hospital appearing like she'd been starring in an Edwardian film. Her full hunting attire had caused numerous strange and admiring glances, from both the hospital staff and also visiting patients or relatives.

But she hadn't cared. It was clear to the more intelligent that she was either involved in a riding accident or maybe she had indeed come from a film set.

No one appeared to take any notice of the young man seated in muddy rugby gear, with a bloody head. But to see an 'elegant lady,' dressed in muddy jodhpurs, navy jacket, with shirt, stock, and leather riding boots, seemed to raise eyebrows and some temperatures. Along with whispers and weird looks.

To Anna's relief, Bruce was finally settled for the night, filled up to his eyeballs with pain-killers. Maybe not enough. He was scheduled to have his numerous broken bones fixed in the morning, provided any swelling went down. But Anna didn't care. She was simply pleased to be away from him.

She'd attended to him as he was wheeled into the hospital from the ambulance and straight into the Emergency Treatment area, where she was asked questions, had to fill in many forms, and assumed to be his 'partner.'

Here Bruce regained some form of consciousness, and like a drunk, told her how sorry he was and wanted her back. All much to Anna's annoyance, wishing that at any moment he'd pass out. She was close herself to enabling this to happen, but thought better of any such brutal action; such as a head thumping or strangulation. The hospital staff wouldn't somehow understand.

Bruce howled and whined, but also held out his one good hand to Anna.

He told the hospital staff, in slightly slurred words, how his beautiful wife was so kind and loving, and how lucky he was to have her there be by his side in his moment of real danger and pain. True devotion, he stated to all.

Anna winced, her face reddening even further with each annoying comment.

Bruce, whether dazed or not, seemed to believe in his own world - or in hope - that Anna was beside him because she loved him. The truth was miles off.

But she played the part, as best as her patience would permit, answering the questions from various hospital staff as to who he was, who she was, and what had happened. Anna explained it all as best she could, but was met with confused looks when trying to explain that she was riding with the hunt, and her 'husband' was protesting against it. They did quite understand.

She tried her best to imply that he'd foolishly stepped in front of a horse, but the hospital staff simply wanted technical details of the horse's speed, ground conditions, time of being unconscious and other matters. They weren't interested if the patient was a 'Pratt' or not, even though it was clear he was.

In between, with Bruce being checked over or wheeled away for X-Rays and tests, Anna still had no peace. Her mobile phone was constantly ringing, from Tracey and Chris, all wanting updates, but then from Bruce's parents, whom she'd called as courtesy, to say he'd been hurt in an 'equestrian activity.'

No other real details added. They took the news well and with some sense, having always been calm and collected people, they asked for any updates, as best she could, and enquired where he was. Upon hearing he was in Norfolk, and that Anna was with him, they seemed to assume the pair were re-united and that Bruce had been watching her at some 'horsey' event. That was nice.

Anna tried to explain their situation and the real reason for the accident, but it fell on deaf, ignorant ears. Now all around, from hospital staff to Bruce's parents, seemed to believe Anna and Bruce were back together. Great news!

But it wasn't great news. Being around Bruce once more, then being left alone to wait whilst he underwent the various tests, highlighted to her how far apart the pair had drifted. Miles apart. She felt instinctive sorrow and pity for him, as being someone seriously injured, whom she'd loved and spent so many years of her life with, but realised there was no love or emotion. There hadn't been for years. She merely felt natural empathy to an injured 'friend.'

It was sad in a way it had come to such an ending, but then felt like closure.

The affairs, discrete misdemeanours and other things Anna knew had gone on behind her back for many year, well before Lucy arrived on the scene, had driven the pair so far apart that there was no chance of a reunion in any way.

She'd finally managed to escape the hospital, trying her best to pass on Bruce's parent's details as an emergency contact, before calling her mum and asking her to pick her up. She knew Chris was far too busy with the horses, didn't want to impose upon him or have him leave the yard. She'd already called Chris, and given him an update, telling him she'd change at her mum's, briefly drop in at the yard to see Penny, collect her own car, then go.

They'd enquired after Steve, and all Anna could provide as an update, was that she'd seen James pass by in a corridor not long back. She'd caught his arm and enquired as to how Steve was doing. James recognised Anna and informed her he had a broken arm, but was otherwise amazingly okay and his usual happy self. Her mum had picked her up, took her to theirs, where she'd grabbed a much-needed cup of tea, washed and changed into some 'proper' clothes and then onward welcomed any form of peace and solitude.

Anna now stood in that silence; absorbed the darkness, the chill air, the solitude and calm. But knew it wouldn't last. The yard lights had automatically come on as she'd entered, but now the outside lights to the house lit up too.

She knew Chris would have been aware of her mum's car entering the woods long before anything electronic warned him. That was pure instinct, or whatever other strange sense he seemed to possess. She knew he'd have seen her exit her mum's car, but had the sense to leave her alone for a moment. But then the kitchen light went on and the door opened. Chris framed the doorway and Max sprinted across the yard towards her, as if ready to eat her.

She could do no more than smile as she squatted down to playfully greet the 'savage' guard dog, rubbing his ears and muzzle, before he ran off and promptly urinated up one of the stables. Nothing had changed. She rose to see Chris wander across the yard, his eyes scanning left and right, before focussing upon her with a smile. For Anna she felt as if she was now at home.

"You look terrible," Chris announced. "But in a good way, if possible."

Anna grinned. "It's just so nice to be away from the noise, bright lights and all those busying bodies. It was chaos in the hospital. I just want to breath fresh air and see nothing but darkness. I forgot how wonderful darkness is."

"Well I have plenty of that. And it's free. Absorb. But not too much!"

Anna smiled, missing his simple charm and calm, reserved nature. She looked at him in the gloom, wellies on as ever and still dressed in jods, but with a warming fleece over his old T-shirt. He looked back, the pair separated by a few yards, but each appearing to want to be closer. Neither moved and the conversation was flattering once more, as it always did. Too much tension.

"I was going to see Penny, but now I'm here don't really want to disturb her. They are all probably munching at their hay or relaxing. It's been a long day."

Chris nodded, as if in agreement, but Anna felt some awkwardness.

"Bruce?" He finally spat out the words. "How is he? Okay?"

Anna flushed, feeling herself become awkward, wishing he wouldn't ask, but knew he would. It was natural. He sensed something.

"Okay. He'll live. Unfortunately." Anna flushed, shocked by her reply.

Chris raised his eyebrows, looking equally shocked.

"Sorry. I didn't mean that. Maybe I did. It's been a long day."

Chris remained silent, but Anna sensed a change.

"He's fine," she added. "Well, he isn't really. Broken arm, broken leg, several broken ribs. And soon a broken heart. When the drugs fade away."

Chris looked at her slightly confused, tilting his head.

"He seems to think I'm his saviour. And strangely that we're going to be getting back together." Anna paused. "Just because held his hand."

"And?" Chris moved a step forward, seemingly more confident.

"And we are not. Never. I can't stand him. Bad as I know it sounds."

Anna was becoming emotional, the events of the day catching up. She began to shake her head, then saw Chris move towards her. She stepped to him.

"Oh Chris! It sounds terrible, but seeing Bruce there in the hospital made me realise I have no feelings towards him. I sound like a callous bitch!"

The pair stood inches apart and Anna looked directly at Chris in the gloom.

"Give me a hug. Please!" Anna pressed herself against him, and put her arms about his body, pulling him close to her. Hesitantly at first, Chris simply stood rigid, but then relaxed and fully embraced her slim body, feeling her warmth and then her head nestle against his shoulder. It felt natural for once.

"What a shit day!" Anna stated. "A great fun start with you, then some arsehole had to go and spoil it. An arsehole called Bruce. I hate him!"

Chris held Anna close, simply letting her speak and vent her anger.

"Why does he have to be such a Pratt? I must have been so stupid, for so long. You must think I'm a Pratt too!" She pulled her head back to look.

Chris chuckled, smiling at her face. "No, I don't think you're a Pratt!"

"I want nothing to do with Bruce ever again. He's gone. Understand?"

"I thought you might want to get back with him. See he recovers. Maybe nurse him back to full health. I could fully understand." Chris spoke calmly.

Anna moved her head from Chris' arms and looked at him fully in the face once more, scanning his features in the dim light.

"No Chris. It sounds cold and callous, I know, but I have no feelings for Bruce, other than anger for him ruining my day with you. He's totally selfish and always has been. Everything has to be about him. Even in the hospital."

Anna moved her head and softly pecked Chris on the lips. He instantly responded and kissed her back, then playfully on her nose, a smile spreading across his face. Anna smiled for the first time in hours, warmed inside.

She pressed her face fully to his, kissing him long and deep. She pulled herself tight to him, their mouths opening. Feeling his tongue explore hers, he drew her fully to him, Anna feeling the strength in his small but fit frame.

Anna felt herself stumble slightly and fall back against the corner of the stable block. She righted herself, pulling Chris fully to her body, her hands grapping at his buttocks and pulling his hips tight into her open legs. She felt Chris press his groin to hers, the jeans and jodhpurs preventing anything natural occurring, as each others hands moved across their bodies, exploring.

Chris' hand slid under Anna's T-shirt, his hard, cold hand softly pressing her warm breast. She let out a huge sigh due to the cold, which was in itself thrilling, and slid her hand down to his groin, softly touching him.

His hardness below was evident and she let her hand glide seductively around his crotch. She removed her hand, sliding it under his fleece, feeling his warm bare chest and sensing him tense as her cold hand touched his warm body.

Chris' hand slid around to her rear, gripping her neat buttocks, pressing his hands firmly upon her cheeks, then the gap between, pulling her hard against himself. Anna felt all the stress of the day instantly drain as she felt Chris press hard against her, now simply wanting him deep inside her.

She broke off the kiss, re-gaining much needed air, then kissed Chris again, but this time less frantically, more loving and caring. He responded likewise.

The pair released their lips, both taking in air once more and regaining some form of control and composure. They both blushed and smiled.

"Oh Chris. Can I stay tonight?" Anna looked into his eyes. "Please?"

Chris seemed to hesitate for a moment, as if unsure.

"Well I was going to watch the football…" Then chuckled, simply nodding.

Smiling wide, reaching down, he took her hand. Anna beamed back.

Anna welcomed the warm touch of his strong hand.

"I'll be a good girl. I promise. Or maybe I'll be a bad girl!"

A blushing Chris chuckled, still thinking, and then grinned.

"I'd love nothing better. But please excuse any mess."

He stepped away from the stable, whistling over to Max, as hand in hand he led Anna across the brightly-lit yard. She pulled herself to him, wrapping an arm around his waist, then laid her head upon his shoulder, holding him tight.

She patted Max momentarily, hoping he'd forgiven or forgotten, as he skipped past ahead, moving off into the kitchen, onto the warmth of the Aga.

As they reached the door Chris released his hold and with a sweeping arm, bowed down and ushered Anna inside.

"Please enter My Lady," he joked. "Be my guest."

"Oh, thank-you me Lord," Anna joked in a subservient maid-like manner.

"Treat me nice and gentle-like Sir! But also treat me bad!" Anna grinned.

A beaming faced Chris closed the door behind Anna.

"Don't worry Anna, I'll treat you bad. Very bad!"

Chapter 130

The important thing is not to stop questioning.
Curiosity has its own reason for existing.

Albert Einstien

Anna awoke with a start. Where she lay was silent. Dark. Quiet. Chilly.
An arm lay across her chest.
She froze, her senses numb, but quickly returning.
Lifting up the quilt, which lay across her face, she gazed into the gloom.
Then stared at the arm lying limp across her chest.
'Who? Where? What? Why?'
This wasn't even her bed. That was worrying. Very worrying.
Questions raced in her head as she scanned the darkened room, faint late moonlight glowing silver through old windows.
'Shit!' She was in Chris' bedroom. 'Double shit!'
Then the memories returned.
Sweet memories. She smiled.
She sighed softly, turning her head to see Chris' tranquil face.
It was strange to see his eyes closed and him restful.
Anna grinned, now fully recalling the wonderful moments that had happened within this very bedroom, after their first passionate kiss downstairs.
It was all mad and bad. But good. No, not good. Great.
She recalled the first wild moments in the yard, then the wonderful moments together in this bed, taking time to explore and enjoy each sensual touch.
Chris had been warm and sensual, but also powerful and athletic. She lifted a hand, about to stroke Chris' face, but held off, not wanting to wake him, but instead, enjoy this moment. He seemed so at peace, just for once.
Then she realised she needed to take a pee - badly.
Rising naked from the bed she cautiously tip-toed out the bedroom and into the gloomy, wooden-floored landing. She knew the bathroom was at the end of the landing, but that there was also one downstairs, beside the kitchen.
Then her brain awoke. She had a plan. A cunning plan.
Moving back into the bedroom, she bent down. Now with T-shirt in hands and clutching her knickers and socks, recovered from the floor, she moved back along the landing. Placing feet and legs into corresponding holes, she pulled on her knickers, then threw the T-shirt over her bare breasts, her skin prickling with the chill, now she'd left the warmth of the bed and Chris' body.
She knew the warmest place in the house was the kitchen, where a very wise old dog - namely Max - resided. It was also where it seemed Chris spent most of his life, keen eyes scanning the yard, track from the woods, and beyond.

Carefully stepping down the steep and dark staircase, her bare feet padding softly on the wooden treads, she entered the lounge then walked on towards the kitchen. In the gloom of the kitchen she saw a dark face.

Keen ears already knew she was coming. Dark eyes saw it all.

Anna froze. She looked at Max. He looked back.

Anna feared he may recall a meeting, a few weeks back, separated by glass.

But then he rose, short stump waggling, sleek body wiggling, face happy.

Rubbing his head into her hands he then turned and faced the back door, looking up at the handle eagerly, then back at Anna, desperately.

A few steps forward, a twist on the old metal key, then a heave on the solid wooden door by Anna released the hound into the chill air of the yard.

Max trotted off, sniffing the air and strutting about his empire, urinating up numerous objects, but saving his full load for the corner of the stables.

Anna grinned at the strange but likable dog, then flicked on an under-lighter, the small light illuminating the worktop area, and key items of the kitchen.

Tea and toast. In bed. She smiled at her 'cunning plan.'

No croissants today, sadly, but freshly buttered toast was a good substitute.

A rummage in the bread-bin revealed a proper fresh cut loaf, and then in a cupboard she found some raspberry jam. She knew where Chris kept his tea, so with the kettle flicked on, she was ready. She sighed happily, kettle on and purring away, sitting down at the now familiar kitchen table. Her eyes scanned the room, her gaze nowhere, simply recalling the great night they'd shared.

Suddenly her eyes switched. The allure of the cellar door was before her.

Anna's eyes widened. The key was in the door.

The key. Anna's heart leapt.

In the lock! Bingo.

Softly gurgling, the kettle slowly heated the water within.

The cut bread sat upright within the toaster, slider ready to be depressed.

Jam, butter and knife lay poised and ready.

But not yet. Fate and temptation were calling. Curiosity.

Anna glanced at the ingredients for a fun breakfast in bed.

Then she gazed at the cellar door. Her eyes widened.

Curiosity satisfied first. Then feast? Decisions. So hard. Not.

The key. In the door. So tempting. Just twist and turn. That's all!

She felt the breath of the temptation imp on her shoulder. Do it!

Taking a moment, she glanced towards the lounge, then the back door.

Anna knew Max was on patrol outside, shut out, and wasn't in the room ready to tear her apart, should she make a wrong move. She looked back at the cellar door, her hands rising to her mouth, biting her thumb nail; like a recovering alcoholic staring at a half-filled, open whisky bottle. Tempting.

No one would notice. Take a swig. Go on! Just a nip.

Anna glanced at the darkened lounge.

Then back at the cellar door. And the key.

The click of the kettle switching off made her jump. The boiled water eased off, the bubbling subsiding, returning the kitchen to silence.

A glance at the back door. Then across to the lounge. Silence.

Anna felt herself softly rise, her body drifting; as if guided automatically by an unknown force towards the cellar door, her hand outstretched.

It seemed so natural, as if powered by another force.

She spun her head around; back towards the lounge, and more importantly, the stairs, which ran up from it and then up to the bedrooms.

Silence filled the dark and strange house. A peaceful silence.

She was alone. Chris was still asleep. Max was outside. Urinating.

Just a peek. A quick one. He'd never know. Never.

The Temptation Imp was back. Alone.

Take a swig. Go on! Maybe a glug - or two.

Anna was drinking from the bottle.

Her hand felt the chill old cast-iron handle in her grasp.

Go on; drink the lot, the Imp called. And so she did.

Anna's fingers lay upon the old metal key.

Twist and turn. Click. Unlocked.

The key moved freely. Too freely. Well-used.

Pressing on the lever, the cellar door opened.

The Temptation Imp smiled. Then vanished.

Anna was on her own.

And she took a deep breath.

Chapter 131

A Scout is never taken by surprise; he knows exactly what to do whenever anything unexpected happens.

Robert Baden-Powell

Anna gazed into the cellar doorway. Stooping her head, she looked beyond the small doorway and into the dark space beyond. The paintwork on the wall was clean and fresh, not old and tatty as expected. The stairs were small, of bare natural wood, like the rest of the house, but appeared well worn. Before her the tight winder tread staircase appeared to turn tight and around to the left, the headroom above low. She peered into the gloom, her eyes wide, eager to explore, becoming lost in her world of curiosity. Her hands remained upon the dark-stained wood doorframe, and half upon the small wooden door.

She sniffed the air, it being the typical dank and stale odour of an old cellar.

A bare foot drifted cautiously onto the first tread. The wooden tread cold.

She bobbed down, turning to look at the dark stairwell and gloom beyond.

She glanced backwards over her shoulder. No one. She was alone.

Her left foot moved down onto the second tread, her right, now her trailing foot, was placed upon the third. The door was behind her and so she let go, turning her tall body within the slightly confined stairwell of the cellar.

She was inside. Fully. Like a space walk. A strange thrill leapt through her.

Initial curiosity satisfied. Partially. But like the alcoholic, she wanted more.

Have another swig. A big one. No glug. Take a full glass. A big glass.

Go further down. Go on! Empty the whole fucking bottle!

Anna moved her left foot onto the next tread, her body moving down, as her hands fumbled on the wall, searching for a switch to illuminate the interior.

The small light on in the kitchen provided a soft reflective glow beyond the doorway, her tall body frame now blocking most of the backlight available.

Anna found herself staring down into a black void, her eyes adjusting, still only able to see the next couple of stair treads before her, then darkness.

An empty void. Nothing. She was alone in space.

Then hands grasped tight at her waist.

Anna half screamed, half gasped. Her breath gone.

She felt herself fall. But the strong hands grasped; held her firm.

Unsteady and gasping for breath, she tried to turn.

A body pressed hard against her.

From behind a voice spoke.

"You shouldn't be here!"

Chapter 132

To keep your secret is wisdom;
but to expect others to keep it is folly.

Samuel Johnson

Anna heard Chris' voice, then felt his hands firmly upon her waist.

Seemingly stopping her from falling, but also restraining her, she instinctively fought to free herself, the jolt of surprise making her lose her footing and stumble. But she remained tight in Chris' hands, as he held her.

But her panicked state sent her arms flaying wildly about.

Her hands flayed at the wall. They hit the light switch.

A soft click. The flicker of electric light.

The cellar was illuminated. Bright and clear.

Through blinking eyes, adjusting to the sudden brightness, Anna looked down at the wooden stairs before her. Raising her gaze, surveying the cellar below, she stared in silence. What she saw was like Howard Carter.

Her exclamation was similar, but different.

"Oh my God Chris! What have you done down here?"

Chris was silent, but his grasp still firm.

Anna looked on, taking in everything before her.

Then Chris spoke.

"You shouldn't have come down here. Its my secret."

Anna felt Chris hands still at her waist, preventing any movement.

Her eyes fully absorbing the sight before her.

"Let go of me Chris. Please."

"No. You shouldn't be here."

Standing on the tight cellar staircase, Anna swivelled around.

She stood to stand face to face with Chris.

The man she'd made love to only hours earlier. His face glowed red.

"It's my secret. No one can know."

Anna turned to look once more at the interior of the cellar.

She was amazed. Stunned.

Anna turned back to face her lover.

"Chris let me go. Now! I'm going to call my dad!"

Chapter 133

Three things cannot be long hidden;
the sun, the moon and the truth.

The Buddha

The cavalry soon arrived. Quickly. Too quickly for Chris.

Anna's dad's Bentley raced into the yard, headlights on full beam, halting short of the parking area with a skid. Gravel spewed out from the tyres.

Chris was seated quietly within the kitchen, mug of tea in hand.

His look was almost sadness. A despondent figure.

Anna sat opposite, rising from the table as her dad stormed into the kitchen.

"Where is it?" Alan was short on words and politeness.

"Down there." Anna calmly pointed at the cellar door.

The hulk of a man stepped forward, briefly disappeared into the cellar stairwell, then shortly returned back into the kitchen.

He returned, staring at Chris, head shaking, hand on chin.

"How long have you been doing this?"

A red-faced Chris shrugged, then replied. "Ages. Years."

"What gauge is it?" Alan asked. "Mixed or one type?"

He looked at the big man before him, relaxing slightly.

"A mix of O, HO and OO," responded Chris, setting down his mug.

Alan looked back, nodding, seemingly understanding.

"But we've tried to standardise over the years. Slowly setting up one system."

"We? Is it just yours or someone else's as well?" Alan interrogated.

"It was originally built by my dad and his brother, my uncle. I obviously got involved when I was younger. Helped to build it up to what it is, to a degree, and more, But when dad was killed it was left untouched for some years."

Chris flushed and Anna slid on the chair beside him, putting a comforting arm around him, smiling fondly. She pecked him on the cheek. She smiled.

"Then my uncle inspired me to recondition it, and we've both been building it in dribs and drabs since then, as time permits. It's taken us years."

Chris seemed to relax, but Anna could sense he was still uneasy, and seemed somewhat shell-shocked by it all and what had happened so quickly.

"I can't believe it. It is stunning. One of the best model train set-ups I've ever seen. It is amazing. And I've not really looked at it properly. Would you mind giving me a tour? I can't believe it all." Alan asked enthusiastically.

Chris sighed, and then rose, blushing at Anna as he headed back towards the cellar, ducking down into the doorway. The huge frame of Alan followed, squeezing through the doorway, with a smiling Anna coming along behind.

Once all three were set within the cellar, scanning the miniature railway and detailed world of modelling before them, Alan drew in a deep breath.

"Outstanding. I've seen some set-ups in my days, but this is incredible. The detail is amazing!" Alan stepped sideways towards Chris and almost crushed him with a big hug. Chris went crimson, and Anna chuckled, sliding over towards him and affectionately held his free hand. Chris merely grimaced.

"Dad thought he had the biggest and best model railway in the area. Didn't you dad?" Anna smirked at her father. "But you've beaten him hands down!"

Alan narrowed his eyes in playful spiteful bitterness at his daughter.

"He's built his up over years. It's set up in a huge shed at the bottom of the garden. Mum says she's a model railway widow when dad disappears down there. He's gone for hours, fiddling with his trains and other bits. Big kid!"

Alan grinned widely at his playful daughter. But Chris understood.

"Why on earth did you keep it a big secret?" Alan enquired, stooping down to look at the detail of a quarry area, shaking his head in appreciative disbelief. "People like us love this stuff. You should have sent some photos in to a Mag' or something. You, your uncle and late dad should be proud of this."

Chris shrugged his shoulder, as was his habit, and then responded gently.

"Its not very manly I suppose." He blushed at once, regretting the statement.

Alan spun around, his eyes seemingly wild, and then he grinned.

"Not manly? Look at me. You cheeky sod!" The man towered over Chris.

Chris looked up at Alan, grinned, and merely shrugged his shoulders.

"Well I'm supposed to be mad rider, who enjoys hunting," Chris began to explain honestly, looking at Anna for support. "It doesn't do the cool image any favours telling everyone I still play with toy trains. With due respect!"

Alan pretended to look furious, but nodded, pursing his lips in agreement.

"I fully understand. Hundred percent. The difference is if anyone says I'm a kid who still play with trains, I can simply punch their lights out!"

The small group of new friends laughed heartedly.

Anna hugged Chris and openly kissed him on the cheeks.

"Now then son, whilst Anna goes off and makes us both a fresh brew, and some warm toast, you can show me this amazing set-up. Let's go."

Chapter 134

I must be cruel, only to be kind.
Thus bad begins, and worse remains behind.

Hamlet - Shakespeare

Anna gazed at the 'Pay and Display' parking ticket and shook her head, amazed at the extortionate fee she had to pay to simply leave her car at the hospital car park. "Thieves," she muttered bitterly. "It should be free."

Returning to the hospital was a task she didn't want to undertake, but two days after the incident, and now with his broken limbs set, Bruce had been annoyingly asking the hospital staff repeatedly to get in touch with his 'wife.'

He was pestering them, claiming he needed to speak with her on important personal business. Anna had given them her contact details upon admission - just in case the worst happened - and as a matter of courtesy. But after numerous calls from hospital admin, Anna agreed to see him.

Anna hoped it could be a useful, if brief meeting, for she had important business to discuss. She did also want to ensure he was truly recovering well from his 'incident' as she wasn't totally cruel. But she didn't tell Chris' where she was going, not wanting to involve him; although she knew he would fully understand, but thought it best if she undertook the dreaded task alone.

Returning to the hospital once more brought back a mix of memories. Both of her anger and annoyance with Bruce, and realisation they were finished; but also a smile, when she recalled what had happened in such a short space of time since that fateful hospital trip. So much seemed to have happened in the few days with her and Chris, and life had turned full circle, bringing fresh happiness and joy she had not know for some time whilst being with Bruce.

The visit was important and to be her form of resolution. Closure. She was ready to fully move on and it had to be done, as painful as it might be for Bruce to finally get the message that there was no going back for them. Also, to let him know that he was to no longer call her, or get the hospital to make contact. She felt cold and heartless, but now was a good time, as bad as it seemed, with Bruce unable to coerce her or follow her. He clearly had, or had someone else do it for him. Fumbling in her pocket, she felt a small box. Emotions welling within, she knew she had to be strong and close things off.

Anna crossed the car park, still enraged by the cost of parking to visit sick people, or worse, to have your body healed. She glanced across the array of parked vehicles and then glimpsed a flow of long blond hair. Anna turned, her attention suddenly caught as she looked across at the woman heading towards a small 4 x 4. She looked familiar, but then disappeared from view.

Anna knew the face, but for a moment could not place the attractive woman.

She headed on to the main hospital building, casting a look towards the cars, but could no longer see the blond woman and dismissed the thought, sighing as she looked at the large imposing building she'd left a few days earlier.

Anna entered one of the three main entrance lobbies, the hospital large and daunting, set in three main sections, but with numerous other annexes and smaller buildings spread about the huge site. Anna gazed up at the direction board in the lobby, knowing Bruce was on a ward. She'd originally left him in the A & E area, although she'd moved about with him all over, as he was transferred to various parts of the hospital to undergo X-Rays and other tests.

Anna was uncomfortable in such a place, with lots of people milling about, but soon found a direction in which to head and turned away from the main lobby. She scanned the direction boards above her head and on the walls, it a confusing mass of corridors or self-closing doors, with glazed side panels, leading onto more corridors or rooms, some marked 'Permitted Access Only.'

Proceeding along the clean, Magnolia painted corridors, with grey vinyl floor, she absorbed, with reluctance, the distinct odour. The smell was unique to hospitals. Disinfectant, disease and death. In varying quantities. Not healthy.

Her eyes flitting from overhead signs to walls signs, whilst also trying to avoid walking into people, when suddenly noted a familiar face strolling down the corridor before her. Anna couldn't help but smile as the hobbling person, one arm in a sling and set in a bright pink cast, along with a large on plaster on his forehead, and heavy limp. He looked at her. The recognition was equal.

"Well blow me down and call me Harry!" Steve greeted Anna with his usual enthusiasm. Anna just beamed back and for once blushed, looking at his arm.

"Anna! I recognised your beautiful face, but didn't place you being here. You haven't come to see me I hope, as nice as that'd be. I can't see any flowers, grapes or even a Get Well card in your arms, so it can't be me! Anyway, they've set me free! Parole, I think. Good behaviour, or they just grew tired of me! I've been discharged. That always sounds so disgusting, don't you think?"

Anna simply smiled wider at Steve's happy mood, but chuckled at the joke.

"You look better than when last I saw you," she replied. "Much better."

"I always look good," Steve quipped. "But maybe not on that occasion."

"Chris enquired about you I understand, and said Reggie has seen you too."

"Yes, Reggie's been in. No card, flowers or even grapes though. Tight-arse! Gave me the low-down on what happened. I recall nothing. Idiot Anti. Or antis I should say. There were two, I believe. It's all a bit confusing."

Anna felt herself blush, knowing to whom Steve was referring, but was afraid to admit it. She hoped he wouldn't guess any connection, but sensed he was too discrete to say anything too damning about Bruce, despite the banter.

"Do you need a lift back?" Anna thought to sidetrack him, but being polite. "I won't be long. Just seeing an old friend. A very quick visit. I can drive you back, if needed. Doesn't look like you'll be driving, or riding, for a while."

Anna felt herself wince again, looking at fluorescent pink cast on his arm.

Steve looked down at the damaged limb and shrugged his big shoulders.

"It is what is. Shit happens. Not my first fall. But hopefully it'll be my last. But probably won't. Thanks anyway. I'm being picked up by an old friend."

"Oh, is that James? I spoke with him the day of the fall." Anna added.

Steve unusually blushed and looked down, before replying rather coyly.

"No, he's busy with work. Did offer, as did Reggie, but another old riding friend from way back is picking me up. We met up again just recently."

Anna was immediately curious as to who the mystery person was, and also felt a sense of intrigue and deliberate deception on Steve's part. Maybe it was one of the many 'lady friends' Tracey and Julie had so often told her about. Anna was curious and grinned, wondering, but didn't dare ask or pry further.

"Will I be seeing you at the Burn's Night Ball?" Anna enquired, hoping to move matters on, but also build a bond, always enjoying Steve's fun company.

"Do dogs sniff shit and fish drink? Too right I'll be at the ball, unless this lot stop me. Besides, I've spent ages organising it all. Actually, do fish drink?"

Anna chuckled at the witty comment, then saw Steve raise his head, looking beyond her and distantly down the corridor further on, nodding to someone unseen way behind her. Curious, she turned, but saw only a mass of bodies moving around the Lobby to where Steve was looking. A blond maybe?

She'd hoped to see the person who was collecting Steve. Most likely some mystery woman, but guessed it could also be a male friend. She felt she was intruding, and knew she had her own business to attend, so wished him well.

Steve said his farewells and hobbled down the corridor, seemingly knowing where he was heading and whom to meet. Anna eagerly watched on, looking until he disappeared around the corner into the main lobby area. Mystery.

Onwards she headed, seeing what seemed to be a mix of sick, sad and elderly pass by. No one smiled. Except Steve. He'd been the happiest face she'd seen. Along with the melancholic, dreary and sad public were a plethora of equally miserable nurses, doctors and hospital admin staff. All seemingly downcast in face and manners, but all busy; carrying files, folders or pots of strange 'stuff.'

Perhaps they should employ clowns to wander about and cheer everyone up. Or it'd simply scare them to death. Kill or cure. Maybe an idea to market.

The whole place reminded Anna of an ant colony, with everyone jostling about, focussed upon undertaking their own task, wandering about seemingly aimlessly, but with an unknown common aim or purpose. She hated it.

A sign directed Anna towards the appropriate ward and turning off the main corridor and away from the bustle, she headed down a side corridor, which led onto the ward. She was about to press the green access button; to permit entry, just as the automated double doors opened and a nurse, with dark hair bustled past. The nurse glanced at Anna as she passed through the doors.

Their eyes connected momentarily through the glazed door panels and she glared at Anna. The look was cold and chilling. Then she looked away, turned and moved on. Anna sensed immediate recognition, but could not recall why.

The fleeting unexpected encounter of passing bodies was so quick, Anna couldn't recall the nurse, nor see her fully. Then she had her back to Anna as she moved away down the side corridor. Anna thought she knew the woman, but was at a loss at to where and why, as seemed to be happening today.

Also, the nurse held an orange file close up to her face, as if reading some key notes. Anna curiously stared at the back of the seemingly familiar nurse.

As the nurse turned the corner, to enter the main corridor, Anna caught the nurse swiftly turning her head, to glare down back down at Anna once more, in turn seeing Anna peer out through the long, thin glass door panel.

Anna glared back, unsure who she was. Perhaps she'd met her the other night and for some reason the nurse had an issue with Anna. It was too much for her to worry about another moody nurse who was cast cursing stares.

Hearing a sound behind, Anna turned about, spinning in a half circle, to find directly before her a wheelchair bound patient. Apologising for blocking the doorway, Anna moved aside to let a non-responsive, glum-faced porter press the access button, exit the opening doors and wheel his patient away.

Turning back around, to look through the doors in order to see where the familiar, but strangely unknown nurse had gone, she saw an empty corridor, bar for the wheelchair bound patient and porter. She decided to give it all up.

'What was wrong with her today?' She sighed, seeing the ward area before her at the end of the small section of corridor. She was seeing unknown but familiar faces, becoming paranoid, whilst bumping into wheelchair-bound sick people. Looking ahead and seeing a Nurse's Station and ward beyond, Anna took a deep breath, and prepared herself for more grief, pain and heartache.

"Hullo Missus Bruce!" The cheerful greeting came from a well-formed, but petite, very attractive South-Asian nurse who walked over from a side room.

"I knew it must be you. He say you coming. Your husband told me how beautiful you are, and he did not lie. Cheeky Mister Bruce is a lucky man!"

Anna felt her face go crimson at the warm, genuine welcome from the nurse, who tottered towards her, her warm face beaming with a welcoming smile.

"Mister Bruce is a funny man. He makes us all laugh! And he is so handsome. Even with all of his broken bits. But not the important bits! Ha, ha!"

Anna guessed that Bruce, or 'Mister Bruce' was feeling well, and back to his usual charm, wit and free-flowing bullshit. Nothing had seemingly changed.

She smiled vainly at the nurse, unsure how to respond.

"That'd be Bruce," Anna replied. "Full of himself. Or full of something."

"He is doing very well. He still needs lost of rest, then some TLC, which I'm sure you'll give him. Then he'll be okay. He is a strong, tough man. He has spoken of you lots. Say you oh so beautiful. You are. I take you to see him."

Anna winced, wanting to curl up inside, knowing why she was there. She was tempted to tell the nurse that he was all hers, if she wanted him. Free.

'Take him away as he is. Don't bother gift-wrapping him!'

Anna followed the small nurse, her stomach reeling as she saw Bruce.

"Mister Bruce, you a naughty fun man," the nurse joked, leading Anna over towards her 'husbands' bed, which was in a small private side room, possibly due to his range of injuries it would seem, or simply because he was 'Bruce.'

"I have brought you a stunning woman. She beautiful. You are lucky couple. I leave you now. No hanky-pankie! You naughty man Mister Bruce. Ha ha!"

The small nurse exited the room with a beaming smile. She left Anna with a painfully aching heart, made worse when she saw a smiling Bruce before her.

"Snooks! You came back. I knew you would. I'd told the staff to call you. And they said you'd be coming in today. You're looking great now you're out of that stupid riding kit. Stunning, as ever, even in just jeans. Did you bring me any grapes? Not that I could eat them. You'd have to hand feed them to me. Just like a Roman Emperor. You could put on a sexy Toga too. Ha, ha!"

Anna stared at her ex-husband, wondering if he was on drugs - which clearly he was - or just really believed in his own crap and delusional world, that after the hunting incident, Anna had come running back to him, legs wide open.

She wanted to leave there and then; before she'd said a single word, but knew what sad deed had to be done. Looking solemnly at Bruce, she felt like a Veterinary Surgeon about to end the life a kitten, which was well and healthy, simply no longer wanted by the cold and callous owners. 'Just kill it. Now.'

Anna scanned the array of equipment nearby and noted he still had a cannula taped to his hand. One arm was set in a green fibreglass cast and she could see the bed sheets were raised, knowing one leg was broken and had been set in plaster beneath. His face was remarkably untouched; a few minor bruises, a minor grave to his forehead, but the smug, cocky look was unchanged.

She imaged Bruce would have liked a scar. Just a minor cut, somewhere on his face. As a badge of honour. Nothing disfiguring to damage his stunning looks, but maybe a small cut. A memento almost. He'd then be able to boast about it all, as to where he got it, whenever asked. "Well, funny you ask…"

Anna knew Bruce well. Far too well. Hence her caution at how to proceed.

"How are you feeling?" She needed to break the ice. It was the most obvious thing to ask a sick person, but also the most stupid. But everyone asks it.

"I feel like I've been run over by a fucking great horse!" Bruce grinned widely. "But I'm improving. Broken arm, broken leg and broken heart."

Anna winced internally seeing Bruce wink, then he continued.

"The limbs will take a while to heal, or so the doctors and these very pretty nurses keep telling me, but only you, and you alone, can fix the heart. But I sense that could be healed very quickly. I feel it already healing as we speak."

Bruce looked down at the seat placed close beside his bed, and nodded with a smile, indicating she should sit down. He also noted she had no card or gift.

Anna remained standing, hands in the pockets of her dark navy Hoodie, her fingers fumbling on something within. She glanced down at the chair.

She knew if she sat down it would be fatal. Bruce would pour out all of his old charm and wit, and at the worst, tell her how poorly he as and needed her.

Although her mind had been made up months ago, even before going to Horsewater, the last few weeks, let alone the last few days with Chris, had sealed it. Totally. She couldn't and wouldn't let matters drag on. Now was the time to shut the stable door and firmly bolt it. No escaping horse this time.

"I've just come to see that you're okay Bruce. That is it. Nothing else. It was a nasty accident and I'm glad to see you're looking and feeling much better than when I came in with you. You were a mess. It was very worrying to see you like that. We've spent a long time together and I wanted to check you're okay, as I would any other friend. There's no more to it than that. Friends."

"Friends?" Bruce replied, raising an eyebrow, then smiled as cheekily as ever. "Well at least that's a start if you still like me as a friend. Boyfriend maybe."

Bruce emphasised the word in his usual cheeky manner and grinned, looking down at the chair, moving his good arm, indicating for her to sit. Now.

It was all Anna could take and inwardly fuming, she let rip.

"Sorry Bruce, but I don't really know why I'm here. It's over. Proper. There's no other way of putting it. We are finished. We were months ago really, ever since you chose that stupid little slut Lucy over me. Let alone everything else you've done in the past. And don't lie. There is no going back. Don't hang onto false hopes or stupid dreams. You chose another way of life. Enjoy it."

As soon as Anna paused Bruce was straight in. Sorrow and sympathy.

"Lucy is history. A sad mistake. We all make them. It was a weak point in our relationship. And had work problems you didn't understand. I was weak. She tempted me, and like a fool I was sucked into her trap. I've said I'm sorry."

"But she wasn't the first. There've been countless others. Loads. I even heard by someone, where you got hit by the horse, that you were the attractive blond Anti's 'boyfriend.' How long did you wait to get her into bed? Hours or minutes? You must have only met her on Boxing Day. You're a lying cheat!"

Anna saw Bruce flush, knowing she'd hurt him. Not by her 'vicious words,' but more because he knew she knew things about events over the few weeks since Christmas that he'd preferred she didn't know. At least Anna didn't know about the 'other one.' The one with the itchy crotch. Who was she?

"She was nothing. A fling." Bruce responded. "And she came onto me in the ambulance after her friend got hit by the same rider who hit me it seems."

Anna boiled within, knowing the rumour was really true, now confirmed.

"Well it's a pity she isn't here now to hear you say that about her. 'Nothing.' She could obviously see through you and probably is best done with you too. I don't see her at your bedside with a bunch of grapes. Toga and all."

Anna was on a roll, when an image of the blond Anti sprung something within her memory. They'd only met a couple of times, and each time was frantic, but she recalled the attractive blond Anti. Izzy she recalled being her name. Former wife of Steve. Hadn't she'd just seen her. Minutes ago?

Was it her she'd seen in the car park? And the lobby? Had she just been in to see Bruce? To check he was okay? Why else would she be at the hospital?

Was Bruce lying yet again? He had to be. No doubt the blond anti had just been in to see him. If only she'd have been a minute or two earlier. Damn!

For Anna it was the final straw. She stepped forward, and Bruce raised his head, as if Anna was about to kiss him. But Anna moved slightly, extending out her arm. From her closed hand she carefully placed something on the side unit standing beside Bruce's bed, then she stepped back. And away.

Bruce glanced sideways at the gift and then knew what it was. A ring box.

He flushed brightly, for once having nothing to say. He knew.

Instead Anna spoke, boldly, embracing the moment, her strength full.

"Thank you for some good times. And they were good. Fun too. I can't lie. However, despite what happened before between us, the trust you broke can sadly not be repaired. Ever. Things change, people change. We've changed. Times move on and so am I. Moving onto a new life. What'll happen and where I'll end up, I don't know, but this chapter of my life, in which you were a great part, is over. Thank you for that part, but it now ends. That's it."

The words came out clearer and more freely than she had practised alone in her car all the way to the hospital, glad Bruce hadn't interrupted.

Bruce lay back, his face white, staring blankly. Thinking. Planning.

His eyes flicked sideways to the ring box, then back toward Anna.

Secretly he'd always hoped that so long as she kept her wedding ring he had a way back. Now it seemed that door had been slammed shut. In his face. But he did secretly admire the calm manner Anna had undertaken the cruel task.

She always had class. Bruce pursed his lips. He had nothing to say.

Inside, Anna knew Bruce was aware he'd pushed his luck, and been caught out. She also felt that he probably thought he could get her back anytime.

But not now. Never. And she knew that he knew.

"So long Bruce. I hope you make a full recovery. Do not attempt to contact me, nor ask the hospital too either. I wish you well for the future. Farewell."

She stepped away from the bed, nodded politely, and turned away.

Bruce lay in the bed, watching the tight denim-clad backside of his now official-to-be ex-wife saunter away. 'Neat arse,' he thought gazing at the pert cheeks vanishing from sight. 'At least she hasn't asked for a divorce. Yet.'

Suddenly the cute Filipino nurse walked into the room.

"Has your wife gone Mister Bruce? You lucky man. She is very pretty."

"Yes, but not as pretty as you are my sweet angel. You are so cute. And kind too. Tell me again, where exactly do you come from in the Philippines?"

Walking away, a tear ran down Anna's face, wiped by a tissue.

Snorting hard, head high, she moved onto the main corridor.

She now joined the mass of sad and miserable folk.

But unseen by Anna, the dark-haired nurse observed it all.

Chapter 135

The truth hurts, but silence kills

Mark Twain

Dave Pearson gazed solemnly from the window of his flat. The prostitutes didn't seem as busy as usual he noted, and some of the regulars appeared to have moved on. There was a tall leggy one he'd often noted and secretly fantasised doing obscene acts with, although he wouldn't admit it to himself..

Things were not good. He felt as if a dark cloud of gloom hovered over like a giant Thunderhead; growing high above, ready to cascade down more sorrow.

Overall though the outlook was poor. For now. But Dave had plans. As ever.

Bruce was gone. That was the one glimmer of sunlight peeping from behind the big dark cloud. In a way it was good that he didn't die, as everyone takes pity on the dead and they become heroes. Bruce simply looked like a Pratt.

That's because he was a Pratt. A gullible fool. Idiot.

Who on earth stands up in front of a galloping horse?

Dave managed a wry smile. Then chuckled as he looked out the window.

A dark large 4 x 4 pulled up, beckoning over one of the prostitutes. She was short, with poor legs, not helped by the ridiculously tight mini skirt she wore and clunky high-heeled shoes. Not like the tall, slim one, who strode proudly in her elegant high heels, with legs up to her armpits and beyond. Very nice.

But she'd seemingly disappeared. Not that he kept track of any of the women or ever looked at them through his binos. Not too often. But the tall sexy one had something special about her. Not like the current offering. Very poor.

He watched as the short whore spoke with the owner of the 4 x 4. They clearly had no taste in women. The offer was either very cheap, or he was selecting the whore for his guide-dog to shag. But, for whatever the reason, the short, fat whore disappeared into the big gas-guzzling vehicle. Disgusting.

She was to be whisked away to who knew where, by who knew whom, to perform whatever weird sex acts demanded, for the paid pleasure of someone with more money than sense, who had no care of catching who knows what from who knows who. It was a strange and bewildering world. Who knew it?

No wonder so many whores were killed or vanished. The countryside was probably littered with their corpses. Buried in fields or dumped down wells. Maybe that's where the tall one went. Buried in a field to grow turnips. Sad.

He felt himself go hard below remembering the tall whore, then tried to move his thoughts on and away from such disgusting acts with common sluts, who were not fit to clean dog shit off the streets. He had far more important tasks to attend to this evening. His vital work was far from over.

His real work had only just begun. He had plans.

Izzy returned back into his thoughts, as his eyes caught sight of the old press cutting, still stuck on the wall. He felt his blood begin to boil as he recalled the moment he watched from the safety of the trees in the hollow, as Izzy ran over - almost in tears - to attend to her husband's fallen horse and then him.

That smarmy, annoying, cock-sure bastard. Pure wanker!

And he was still alive too. Hardly injured, except for a broken arm and cracked ribs. Lucky bastard. As ever. He should have been dead.

Then Izzy could have been sad, mourned for a short time, with Dave as the 'Rock' beside her. And then when the tears had died down, she'd see him as the true friend and pillar he was; then fall into his welcoming arms. Forever.

But it wasn't to be. It'd gone wrong. In one way.

Izzy had however revealed her true colours. That was a result.

That in a way was one part of the full plan. The scheme.

Kill off that annoying newcomer, 'Bruce the Cocky Twat' and likewise Steve 'Fucking Wanker' Harrison. Remove them. Two Wankers with one horse.

Then in the process of eliminating the two arse-holes, he'd see where Izzy's true loyalties lay. And she had.

He'd got a true response. A result. In full.

But the result was not as he'd hoped. For now.

However, now he had the answer, he had to move onto the next phase of his plan. Part two of Plan B. He always had plans. Options.

Dave checked his watch. It was just about time to leave and undertake his next mission. He still had lots to do. And so little time.

He'd also heard from his brother, via his mother, that he'd be coming back home soon. But only for a while. A brief visit between jobs, then off again.

He'd been tracking down and filming illegal loggers in the rain forests of Brazil. Undercover. Living off the land. Hiding out in the jungle.

Tough and dangerous work. Very dangerous.

He was good at his job. Very good.

One of the best undercover reporters in that field.

As much as Dave loved and adored his older brother, he was also a wee bit jealous. He too would have loved to get involved, but never got the chance. Plus he hated flying. His mother always ranted about the good work his older brother was doing for the environment and for the whole of humanity.

She never mentioned Dave's contribution.

It was as if what he was doing against the Hunt's didn't matter.

Dave found within his hand his beloved Swiss bayonet.

The neighbouring flat heard two hard thuds against the wall.

Followed by a dull curse. Then silence.

Dave left his flat, leaving behind the bayonet, it being thrust into the wall.

Between its sharp point and blade was a photo.

Chapter 136

Whence is that knocking? How is't with me,
when every noise appalls me?

Macbeth - William Shakespeare

Anna woke with a jolt, as Chris, lying beside her, leapt up from their bed.

She turned in the gloom, her head flicking from side to side, still coming to her senses, looked at the warm space beside her, now empty bar a soft mattress indentation. Seconds earlier Chris was beside her, the pair sleeping soundly after a pleasurable period beforehand, still enjoying new experiences.

Now he was gone. The bed empty.

Before Anna could move, other than her head, Chris was silently moving, like a greased cat, grabbing at a handful of clothes, dressing as he drifted. He reached into one of the old period wardrobes, grabbing at something within.

"What is it?" Anna enquired in hushed tones, her senses returning, watching over the end of the bed, as Chris moved swiftly and did not answer, but in the gloom raised a finger to his mouth. Then cautiously he stepped across the room, a long object in his hands, as he quietly opened the door.

Anna wasn't one to sit about, or even lay about. Now she'd been woken, and with her curiosity as keen as a cat, she stepped out of the warm bed into the chill of the bedroom. Anna shuddered, wishing she'd stayed inside.

Chris had vanished, moving silently out the room and onto the landing. Anna wasn't slack and leapt over towards the door, following close behind Chris, wearing an over-sized white T-shirt. Chris turned to look at her ghostly form.

"You can't come. It's dangerous." His eyes dropped instinctively towards her bare long legs and feet, and in the gloom, grinned. "And besides. You might scare anyone to death! That's without catching your death of cold. Please go back, and stay here. If you must follow me, at least get dressed. Please!"

Anna dashed back over towards the bed and grabbed a set of jogging bottoms, pulled them on, before nipping straight back to the landing.

Looking down the long dark landing she saw Chris was approaching the top of stairs, gun or rifle held before him. Running on the tips of her bare toes, padding lightly along the bare timbers, she caught him up, gripping onto his arm as he was about to enter the long stairwell. He didn't seem pleased.

"What is it? Have you heard an intruder?"

"No," Chris responded in a harsh whisper. "Just a sense, maybe outside in the yard. I had a felling, plus a horse whinnied. Didn't you hear it?"

Anna looked at Chris in amazement. One minute he was sound asleep - or so she assumed - and the next minute he was wide awake, dressed and dashing off with a gun. How could he do that? She'd only woken because he did.

"What's that?" Anna nodded to the long, slender object in his hands, now pointing down the stairs. "Is it a gun? Are you allowed it? Is it real?"

Chris cast Anna a curious glance, almost grinning at her naivety.

"It's only a little gun. No more than a toy. A four-ten. It'll just sting a bit."

To Anna a gun was a gun and they all seemed dangerous. She knew little else and nodded, unsure, but was still worried that he'd picked up a gun so swiftly, and just how easily he carried it; more so as she knew of his past history.

"Why isn't Max barking? I thought he was a guard dog." Anna whispered.

Chris managed a soft chuckle. "Max is not a guard dog. He never barks. He simply sleeps. And shits. And pisses. He looks tough, but as you know, really he's as soft as shit. He's probably asleep now. He's lovely, but useless."

Anna recalled the image of Max staring silently at her through the kitchen window on the night she'd crept back and peered through to the cellar. He'd made no sound back then and simply looked on menacing. He'd scared the hell out of her, but done little else, so Anna understood. That was his job.

"Please either stay here, or if you must follow, as I'm sure you will, be quiet. Speak no more, stay behind me, and do what I say," Chris instructed firmly.

Anna was surprised by his stern manner, but also impressed by his firm demeanour and control of the situation. Sadly, her dad would have been even more impressed with him than he already was. He thought Chris was great.

Anna simply nodded and watched Chris move stealthily down the stairs, gun held out before him, aimed at the base of the stairs with expert ease or from regular practise. She followed on, three steps behind, her eyes darting about the dark stairwell, but focussed upon the gloom of the lounge area at the bottom. Chris entered the lounge, and without hesitation, still in darkness, moved straight through and into the kitchen. Weaving his head about, he looked out the side window, where a subtle orange glow from one of the PIR illuminated yard lights filtered through. Something was out there.

Anna joined Chris in the kitchen, walking on tip-toes, leaning forward in a stoop, her head bobbing about, eyes flicking towards the window too.

Upon hearing footsteps and movement within his domain Max reluctantly lifted his head, looking at both intruders, rising from his deep bed beside the Aga with a stretch and heavy groan. Chris ran a hand over the glossy head and then eased forward, and still with no lights on internally, stepped over to the kitchen door. Slowly he turned the big old key in the ancient lock, the action moving with a heavy clunk. Anna looked on in silence and bemusement, the sudden rush of excitement beginning to fade and a mix of fear and wonder now taking over. She wondered what she'd let herself in for, knowing Bruce would never act so bold or bravely. He'd simply call the police and then hide.

Easing the door slowly open, Chris pushed the barrel of the gun before him, head looking ahead, before marching boldly outside, stepping outside. Anna looked down at the 'vicious guard dog' still standing beside the warm Aga. Max sniffed the air, then Anna, before slowly moving towards the open door.

Only then did he seem to wake up, realising what he should be doing to earn his keep and trotted outside to join his master. Anna eased forward, unsure if to leave the safety of the house, or boldly join Chris and Max outside.

Looking out the doorway, she watched Chris march across the centre of the yard, heading towards the stable block, his eyes scanning in all directions, gun waving to-and-fro, searching for the source that'd set off the PIR yard light.

Max trotted away from the house and over to join him, then seemingly sensing no movement, headed away and urinated up one of the stables. Anna chuckled to herself at his action, then boldly eased forward, stepping out of the door, shivering as the cold air bit at her exposed areas of flesh.

Bare foot, she trotted swiftly across the cold damp ground of the yard, wincing at the odd sharp stone and chilling dampness to her feet, wishing she'd slipped into some wellies like Chris had. Joining Chris in the yard, and standing beside him, now shivering, he looked towards her, and then glanced down at her bare feet, a wry smile crossing his face as he shook his head.

Suddenly Max raised his head, the long black muzzle sniffing the air and ears pricking up. His small black eyes focussed upon some distant point at the far end of the yard, near to where the last stable block ended and adjoined one of the barns used for storing straw and hay, before then leading on down to the ménage, paddocks and then the woods, all of which were in darkness.

Then Max woofed. A singular, deep, heavy woof. Almost a howl.

Chris and Anna both jumped and turned in unison to look at the big black dog, hackles raised, standing four-square and focussed upon the end barn.

"Kill Max! Go and eat them!" Chris called calmly, arm raised, pointing.

Max broke straight into a canter, boldly thundering across the yard, heading straight towards the small barn. Chris moved too, following a few strides behind the quick dog, raising the gun, ready to shoot. Maybe.

Anna stood still in the yard, unmoving, eyes wide in shock, shivering through a mix of cold and fear. She watched the black dog swiftly cover the ground and approach the barn, seeing Chris moving forward too, gun in his shoulder like a soldier, aiming almost at the point towards where Max now headed.

An object suddenly dashed from within the barn. Chris' gun followed.

A PIR light on the far corner illuminated the fleeing body.

Anna stared in surprise to see a small dog-like creature dash past.

Her eyes flicked from the fox to Chris, and then to Max, who paused, simply watching the fox dash away and off towards the ménage, it too much effort to chase. Her eyes flicked back to Chris and the raised gun, awaiting a shot.

But Chris stopped his forward motion, simply lowered the weapon and whistled to Max. He stopped, turned at once and trotted back to join him. He was happy to receive a pat on the head, and now just wanted to return to his warm bed. Surely he'd earned his keep for the week. Maybe even the month.

"A fox, I assume?" Anna called across the yard.

"I think so, but I'll just check," Chris replied.

The brave and valiant Max trotted away from Chris and now sat beside Anna. She winced and swore as he sat straight on top of one of her feet, his sharp toenails scratching the exposed and cold flesh of her feet. Her big feet. Moving her foot from under his huge pads, Anna patted his head, standing in the yard, shivering, but grateful of her noble, somewhat lazy canine guardian. Chris moved quickly, but with stealth, keeping to the centre of the yard as he approached the opening to the barn, before swinging his body around, gun rising, twin narrow barrels pointing within. For a few seconds he stood totally still, senses alert, cocking his head, as if to listen for any movement within. He seemed to sense something and stood stationary. Moving moved.

He glanced up the yard, seeing Anna, who was beginning to shake, now squatting down and hugging Max for some welcomed warmth it seemed. His focus was set firmly upon his Master some yards away, now heading towards the front of the barn, gun poised and ready as he then disappeared within.

Both watched in the cold gloom as Chris boldly vanished into the barn.

Then nothing. Silence, and an empty yard. Wide-eyed, Anna looked at Max.

Moments later Chris reappeared; lowering the gun barrels to the ground and strode straight across the yard to the waiting couple. As he approached, Max trotted forward, then Anna slid an arm around him, hugging onto his waist.

"Nothing?" She enquired, looking into his face, hoping she was correct.

Chris simply shook his head. "False alarm. I hope. Maybe just that fox."

"Brrr!" Anna shivered in the soft orange glow. "Lets get back inside. Please!"

The group wandered back towards the house, Max first in, dashing straight back towards his bed and welcoming Aga. Leading him by his cold free hand, the gun cradled within the other, Anna eagerly guided Chris inside. However, he ensured he took one last look about the yard before locking the door.

The fox watched from the corner of the ménage. It saw all.

But knew it wasn't alone.

Warily, the fox noted the person watching it too.

Also watching the yard. And the people too.

The observer was hidden deep within the small barn. Unseen.

Except for by the fox. But it wasn't telling.

Chapter 137

Cry 'Havoc! And let slip the dogs of war!

Julius Caesar - William Shakespeare

German Wirehaired Pointers seldom bark. Unlike smaller breeds of dogs, especially Terriers, they are not 'yappy' instead preferring to act as trained. Quiet, professional, somewhat reserved, but also very loyal and intelligent.

If surprised, or wanting to raise a warning, they tend to howl, loudly. The call swift and short, but totally effective. Hunt, Point and Retrieve. They are the perfect hunting dogs and Jager was such a well-trained hound and gun dog.

When out in the field with Reggie, seated beside him at a gun peg, or as was his true calling, out rough-shooting and hunting for game - whatever Reggie deemed that to be - he would silently seek out the quarry, then point, or indicate accordingly. When any such quarry was despatched or shot, he'd dash off and retrieve. And all for simply a pat on the head and the odd treat.

But for now he was happy to dream of such days outside, and simply snooze. Warm inside the scullery of The Grange, and lying beside the small warm Aga, slumped on his old lumpy, but seemingly comfortable bed, Jager was uncaring what his master was doing down in the cellar.

Jager knew, but it was a secret.

And he was too loyal to ever say. Or howl.

However, outside, in the cold and darkness, someone else was curious as to what was going on within the closed and locked doors of The Grange.

And maybe within the cellar.

Wary of any PIR lights, the prowler knew where the few were. Unseen, they'd made it down the dark tracks on foot. Then cautiously on through the outer courtyard, to now press themselves tight against the whitewashed walls.

Peering sideways through the large six-over-six window, the interior of the main Sitting Room could clearly be seen.

No one was inside. Empty.

A couple of small shaded table lamps glowing, and a half-drunk glass of wine on a table, indicated someone was at home, but clearly not within that room.

Sliding silently around the wall, the prowler moved onto the next window, this one also revealing another part of the large Sitting room. This area however linked onto the main hall and then onto the kitchen. Within that hall, a bright light could be seen glowing beneath the bottom edge of a small door.

The cellar door. Someone was in the cellar.

They knew who, but doing what?

The prowler had to know.

It was key to the reason they were there tonight.

Moving further along the wall, they slid past a large drain pipe and gully, then up to a slightly smaller window, but still of the small-pane Georgian style.

The prowler peered in through the scullery window.

Cupping their hands to their face, they looked inside.

A large brown nose met their face.

For a second the prowler was confused.

Bright yellow eyes stared back.

The intruder's eyes stared at Jager.

Jager stared back. Unmoving. Silent.

Muzzle pressed firm against the glass. Eyes fixed.

The intruder froze.

Jager howled.

The ear-splitting howl, like that of a wolf rang out.

Heart pounding, the prowler instinctively flew back and away from the window. Stumbling, twisting an ankle as they scurried away, all caution gone, they dashed carelessly across the open inner courtyard. A PIR floodlight, set up high on the house, and designed to light up this area, was activated.

It illuminated the intruder in a wash of bright white light.

Careless and not as planned.

Inside the scullery a red-faced Reggie appeared.

Jager dashed up to him, then over towards the window. Trouble.

He stood back upon the small ottoman set beneath the small window, nose pressed hard to the glass once again. He lifted his right leg, half-cocked.

Hunt. Point. Now to retrieve.

Reggie guessed what'd happened, and that Jager had seen a prowler. He then saw that the inner courtyard had illuminated, and although saw no fleeing prowler, or would-be intruder, he knew enough. Stepping back a stride, and reaching into a small cupboard, he grasped a 'Hush-power' .410 Shotgun.

Small and light, with a single barrel, it was the perfect silent poacher's weapon. Especially when loaded with a totally illegal, home-modified 10mm solid slug. Deadly. One shot, one kill. Guaranteed. Big hole, big mess.

Reggie leapt out the scullery area, through the hall, and past the cellar, where the open doorway cast a bright light. He dashed on towards the kitchen area, which opened out into the inner courtyard. As he raced towards the door, Jager was already ahead of him and leaping up, trying to open the handle, as he often did. Reggie knew he was probably too late. Anyone worth their salt would be well away, but he didn't give up. Almost ripping the door open, half stumbling over the eager dog at his feet, the pair careened out of the door and into the courtyard. Jager disappeared off across the yard, nose in the air.

Reggie paused, listening for sounds rather than detecting a scent, but heard nothing. He assumed the prowler was well away, no doubt by now dashing across the back paddocks, leaving no sound of crushing gravel, only a trail of dew-track footprints in the grass, most likely with sopping-wet feet.

Reggie knew Jager would eagerly track his prey across the fields all night long, if left. However, he didn't want any harm to come to one of his few remaining and truly loyal friends. Pursing his lips he let out a trio of high-pitched whistles altogether. He repeated the recall command as he headed across the courtyard and on through the archway into the paddock area, .410 gun held expertly before him. Once again he blew up, scanning the paddock for either hound or prowler, or maybe both. Then he saw a small cantering form approach, as the bristling grey-brown coat of Jager appeared out of the gloom, slowing to a trot, then to stop perfectly at his feet, automatically moving around sideways, to sit atop Reggie's feet. Just as trained.

But sadly with no prowler hanging from his mouth.

The prowler was probably too big to fit anyway.

"Well done old chap!" Reggie praised, rubbing the wiry old hound's large floppy, velvety-soft brown ears. He smiled at the old faithful dog his steely eyes scanned the immediate area, wondering who had been prowling about and what they wanted. It was lucky for him Jager noticed them. But who?

It could have been anyone. Traveller thieves; looking to steal almost anything. Newspaper reporters; following up on the Boxing Day incident or the more recent accident. Or some other curious snooper.

Or maybe an old enemy. The list was long. Too long.

But Reggie had an idea of who it could be.

He patted Jager once more, scanned the gloom, and then with a shiver, headed back inside. His faithful guardian was close at his feet.

Back inside, Jager - the German Huntsman - was treated to a couple of Rich Tea biscuits, his favourite nibble. Then one more.

Then he settled back down in his old lumpy bed before the Aga. Happy.

Job done. Salary earned - for today.

With a cautious glance once more out of the window, followed by a sweep of his hand to draw the scullery curtain closed, Reggie returned to the cellar.

He had important business to attend to below.

Very important.

Chapter 138

If you must break the law, do it to seize power;
in all other cases observe it.

Julius Caesar

Red-faced, still breathing heavily and with a screen of cold sweat on his damp back, Martin pulled the Range Rover to a halt at The Kennels. He'd had a busy night, and still had lots to do before he could even think about retiring.

Sleep, if it came and was unbroken, would be a blessing.

As he exited the vehicle and glanced at the whitewashed house, the interior set in darkness, he instinctively glanced back up toward the woods through which he'd just driven. He could see only the dark outline of bare trees. Stark and black against the silver sky above, a blanket of thin cloud cast a light-grey hue to form a chilling backdrop. There were no lights within the woods. And with his keen ear he cocked his head to listen for any sounds. None.

He breathed a sigh of relief, for now. Turning away from the Rover, engine gently ticking as it began to cool, he stepped onto the gravel and headed down the alley between the house and kennel block. As if on cue, the sounds of hounds stirring within the walled area of the kennel yard could be heard, followed by the soft pad of multiple feet moving over to see who'd arrived.

But the hounds already knew. The hounds weren't stupid. They were clever.

Soft whimpers and whines were accompanied with keen, harsher howls and then the occasional bark, as Martin proceeded through the small alley that separated the kennel section from the main house and working outbuildings.

Further away, settled in the stable block around the back of the yard, Martin heard a gentle whinny, knowing it was from Bert; obviously disturbed by his return. The soft whinny was a call for attention, requesting further treats or a hay net re-fill. Most likely it was for all, such was Bert.

Martin always gave Bert oat cookies as a 'tit-bit' treat whenever he settled him in for the night. Martin adored Bert, who, despite his 17hh size, was a gentle giant and a true gentleman, despite crushing his toes one day, when he spooked at a fleeing pheasant. But Bert knew all of Martin's secrets, more so than the hounds. Martin spoke with him when he turned him out, chatting about his plans for the day or telling him his worries or concerns. Then, when he rode out alone with him, he could almost hold a conversation with the huge black horse. Bert always listened calmly - for the cost of an oat cookie - and never made comment nor criticised and Martin loved him for that.

Except when Reggie was alongside. He'd think Martin was plain stupid.

As 'Hunt' horses, they were the property of those who had shares in the Hunt: primarily Reggie, Bertie and Steve, along with Lord Burlingham.

Martin had long decided that if he ever had to do another 'moonlight flit,' as he and Sharon had done so from the riding school, that Bert would be going with him, despite not being his to own, or take away. Bert was his only friend.

As ever, Martin looked to his right, stepping toward the metal-railed yard where the hounds lived. A large mass of hounds dashed toward the front iron railing, tails wagging, keen to meet and greet the 'Alpha-male' Master who kindly tended to them. But not all of the hounds dashed forward.

Some hounds it seems were becoming less respectful or appreciative.

They seemingly knew better or had other plans or ideas.

Maybe they thought they were better. Maybe they were. Who knew?

Martin turned to greet a sea of sniffing noses and lapping tongues, all eager to see him and show their appreciation. He pushed his hands through the railings, happy to see and feel his 'children' and enjoy their company, as brief as the moment might be. It helped retain the bond, built their trust and the general pack camaraderie. But he was busy, had lots to do and thus the greeting this evening was to be short and sweet. Again.

"Hullo chaps. I'm a bit busy, but I'll give you all a treat in the morning."

He paused, looking at the hounds before him, multiple eyes and muzzles gazing back, most licking his probing fingers, jostling for the prime spot. But some key hounds were missing from the thong who'd usually be at the front.

Martin looked into the gloom of the yard and towards the hounds that remained back. A number were younger hounds, either wary or aware of the pecking order, and hence they remained back, but their eager bobbing heads and ever-curious eyes could be seen.

However, some older hounds were simply not moving.

In the dark, but back-lit by an old yard light, Martin could make out a couple of hounds who didn't try to move forward, nor appear to be excited to see him. Martin wondered momentarily if perhaps a couple were sick, but as he glanced in, he knew instinctively who these hounds were, despite being little more than silhouettes. Maverick and Mayhem.

Unmoving, they simply stared back at Martin. Cold. Calm.

Martin moved his head, noting the steely glare from the brothers, but then also saw a couple of the smaller, younger hounds also stood between the pair, including Christmas; all unmoving, just staring at their Master.

"Come on chaps. Say hello." Martin called fondly. But none moved.

Martin felt the hairs on the back of his neck bristle.

Still the hounds remained stationary within the middle area of the yard, clearly showing disrespect and independence. Martin felt he should unlock the yard gate, march in, and berate the hounds, ensuring they knew he was their master. Or at least walk up to them to check they were okay.

But he could see they were, and knew they were too. They'd all been okay earlier in the afternoon when he'd exercised them on the paddocks, letting them all run free for half an hour. And when he fed them.

However, now he thought about it, he did recall the three in particular had kept together, slightly away from the pack, mooching about at the paddock.

He regarded the three insolent hounds as a teacher would towards some disruptive and rebellious students, considering the punishment, if any.

But a deep-seated fear seemed to run through his body and for once he did not want to enter the yard. Not now. An image of the policeman who'd stared in fear at the pack of hounds came back to him. Was he now afraid himself?

Suddenly a solitary bark rang out. Not a whimper or howl, but clear instructive bark. It clearly came from either of the two male hounds.

Martin stared, then shuddered when he heard the call again. This time it was acknowledged by the pack of hounds. They all froze and stopped nuzzling.

Martin then watched in dumb amazement.

As a group, almost as trained to obey commands from the horn, the entire pack moved back from the railings, and more worryingly, away from Martin.

Martin felt a chill run through him. The hounds weren't eagerly standing at the rails, as they were before, but now stood back a few feet, as though deliberately distancing themselves. As being instructed. The rest of the entire pack had gone. Sunk back into the depths of the yard, the only evidence being a host of shadows and glistening eyes, all watch intently from the gloom.

Martin moved forward a step and bobbed down, extending a warm and friendly hand towards the railings. "Come on chaps." He called.

Not a hound moved. None.

Not even those hidden in the shadows behind the pack leaders.

Martin had never known anything like it.

He looked on into the gloom; part confused, part fearful.

The three main hounds simply stared. In control.

With a snort Martin stepped back from the railings, turning sideways, his head flicked around swiftly, as if to check no hound was out or moving about.

Did he just see something move in the back of the yard? He looked again.

Did he hear something? Movement? Sound? He cocked his head.

He froze, staring at nothing. Was he becoming paranoid?

Martin stood stock still, head absorbing all.

No movement or sound emanated from the kennel block.

That in itself was more worrying than any paranoia that something was lurking about behind him, waiting to kill him. Man or beast.

From a rush of excitement of howls and barks moments earlier; the hounds had suddenly become deathly quiet. There was clearly something wrong.

Turning his head to look into the yard area, Martin leapt back.

Before him, standing behind the railings were hounds.

Maverick and Mayhem. Slightly set back as a pair, but in-between them, stood the small form of Christmas. All three hounds stared in silence.

Martin locked rigid, unsure what to do or what to say.

He hadn't heard them move. What was happening?

His eyes met those of the now dominant hounds.

Were they in control? Martin shook his head. Unsure. No. They can't be.

Spinning around, not wanting to admit fear, he dashed towards the house, ensuring the gate to the yard at the end of the alley was securely bolted.

As he headed towards the house side door he heard Bert whinny once more.

Martin hesitated, wanting to see his great friend and tell him of his new fears, but also didn't want to go around the back of the kennels and then fully disturb the horses, which included Sharon's. Also he now feared the dark.

He looked in the direction of the stables, but paused, knowing he had too much to do inside. And it was late, cold and dark. Too dark. Bert could wait.

With a hesitant sigh, Martin turned his attention upon the house, casting it a wary and tired eye. But not before he glanced back at the kennel block with wide and worried eyes, ensuring nothing was following him.

There wasn't anything there. Or so he hoped.

Flicking on the utility room light, then the kitchen light, he rapidly drew the curtains and swept through the house. He glanced at the cellar door.

Locking, then bolting the main entrance door, he reached over behind a tea caddy and retrieved a key. An old key.

It was the cellar key. Hidden. For good reasons.

Moving over towards the cellar, he unlocked the door.

Chapter 139

Be wary, then; best safety lies in fear.

Hamlet - Shakespeare

It was no secret Chris and Anna were officially 'An Item.' Although Chris wasn't ever going to scream it from the rooftops, as proud of Anna as he was, it was Anna who clearly made no secret of the fact they were now together.

Even though it'd only been nearly a week, Anna freely walked out the house, usually early in the morning, clearly having risen from Chris' bed, to greet the ever-early Julie. At first it was a surprise for her to see Anna rise from the house early, worryingly assuming something happened to a horse and hence why she'd stayed overnight. But then after two days the 'penny dropped' and she realised what everyone had said would happen, had indeed happened.

Once Julie knew, Tracey knew, and then it might just as well have been a formal announcement made in The Times. Perhaps someone had.

Chris was as usual coy and sheepish, keeping himself to himself, as if nothing had changed, moping about the yard as normal, but clearly with an added skip to his step. Anna though was without doubt 'in love;' floating across the yard, wafted everywhere she walked by a host of unseen winged pink unicorns.

"I assume that you'll be going as a formal couple to the Ball on Saturday evening?" Julie asked with a cheesy grin. "Everyone will know by then. So don't try to pretend otherwise. Maybe I should buy a hat. And a cot."

Anna grinned wickedly, just as Chris wandered over towards her, luckily not catching what had been said, but clearly catching the two cheeky grins.

"Your dad wanted to pop around." Chris blushed. "He called. Again."

Julie looked on curious, totally unaware. Anna grinned even wider.

"He just called on the phone. Some bits to sort out. And some stuff he has."

Julie looked on intrigued. She'd seen Anna's dad in the house a couple of times over the last few days, which was weird, but this got her more curious.

"My dad's doing some work for Chris. In the cellar." Anna lied, poorly.

Chris winced at Anna's explanation, but Julie knew Alan was in the building trade and so possibly doing some work for his new 'Son-in-Law-in-Waiting.'

"But I told him it'll have to be put off. I'm picking up a horse from Newmarket. Joe, for Kerry. The one who had colic bad and then had surgery, remember? I need to take him back to home hers. He seems okay for now."

Anna recalled the conversation. Things had been frantic and she'd forgotten Chris' agenda. Life hadn't changed, just because she woke up in his bed.

"Luckily it seems he's made it through surgery, which is good" Chris added, deep in thought. "Lovely horse and Kerry was lucky we could get him there so quickly. Fingers crossed he'll make a full recovery. Still a long way to go."

Julie looked recalled the incident. Chris and Julie had known Kerry for years, and was at another local yard. He'd received the frantic call two weeks ago, and had dashed the very sick horse to Newmarket for emergency surgery.

Not many horses survive, but Kerry had blind faith and deep pockets.

"I imagine that's going to cost a few bob," Julie said. "A lucky horse."

Chris nodded, not wanting to guess the thousands of pounds the emergency surgery would have cost, with only a fifty-fifty chance of survival, although the odds were getting better. Colic and broken legs were the biggest fear of all horse owners, and all knew the possible chances of recovery. Slim to none in some cases. The group stood silent for a few seconds, before Anna spoke.

"I'm busy on a couple of projects too," Anna added, knowing that despite their budding romance life continued. "I'll phone dad and tell him he'll have to come another day. There's no rush, but I know how keen and impulsive he is to do things. I've never seen his so happy. It's okay for him, he's retired."

Chris nodded, checking his watch, working out what needed to be done.

Julie looked on bemused, the pair before her acting like a long-term married couple, rather than newly found lovers who'd been together for a few days.

At that point a large flock of pink-footed geese flew over, honking noisily to each other, their wings beats a soft swish overhead, as the main group flew swiftly by in an off-set Vee formation, followed by a smaller group of birds.

All three lifted their heads up, staring in silent awe at the big birds.

"I love how they are constantly talking to each other," Anna spoke, as they all looked at the amazing sight of the low-flying geese overhead. Another smaller group followed on from the main pack, trailed by a small family group of four, all honking loudly, racing on to join one of the main groups drifting away above them, before they all vanished over the distant woods.

"I thought geese always travelled in a Vee formation?" Anna declared to all. "That flock were all over the place and in an odd number. Why?" She looked at Chris for an answer, as if he was the oracle when it came to wild birds.

"Simple," Chris replied with a degree of authority. "Geese can't count."

He looked at Anna with a grin. For a second she was unsure, then he added.

"Also, you can tell when they're all first flying into the country, as they have Duty-free bags under one wing. When they fly out, they use both wings."

Anna looked at Chris, then gazed back up at the grey sky, seemingly hoping to see a one-winged goose clutching a bag. Then she heard Julie chuckle.

She looked back to see two grinning faces staring at her.

"Bastards!" She playfully punched Chris, shaking her head.

Julie chuckled and moved back into Bonnie's stable to finish. Anna walked away, knowing Julie had ears like hawks have eyes. Chris followed, the pair moving into the middle of the yard, to where they'd stood the previous night.

"I know you like your privacy, but dad gets excited about, you know what. And wants to know you better. As also do I." Anna playfully fluttered her eyelashes, but saw Chris blush. "He thinks daylight comes from your bum!"

"I have to go into Norwich now and get my dress for the ball," she added. "I don't have anything nice to wear and can't turn up in rags. I've got to look my best if I'm walking into the venue on your arm, sir!" Anna tilted her head.

"I'd be happy to see you turn up in just that baggy T-shirt you wear all the time. Plus those fluffy pink socks of course!" Chris joked, red faced.

"Pervert!" Anna cried, then pecked him on the cheek.

"Oi! I saw that," cried Julie, exiting Bonnie's finished stable with a broom and shutting the door, then smirking at the happy couple. She lifted a hand and wandered towards her Rover, knowing better than to ruin their private moment. The pair raised their hands and watched as the Rover sped off.

"Is it okay for me to stay here again tonight?" Anna asked.

Chris turned to face Anna, his expression uncomfortable.

Anna flushed, wondering what he was about to say, his face was glowing, set on 'serious mode.' Deadly serious. Something was wrong.

That was worrying. Anna felt a knot in her belly.

She remained quiet, waiting for him to speak.

He drew in a breath then began, slowly.

"After the other night, in the yard, with the gun, I have to tell you some facts. You may what to change your thoughts on me and possibly staying her with me overnight. Not that I don't want you to. But I should explain."

Anna look worried, and Chris caught the glance. She let him speak.

"I don't want you to leave, I love your company and you staying here with me. However, you know my background and what happened."

He paused, scanning her face almost for a response. Anna simply nodded.

"I have enemies," Chris began, his tone and manner uncomfortable, it clearly difficult, but it something he had to explain. "From way back. Years ago."

Anna remained silent, looking deep at him, knowing it was a difficult subject and with a nod, and anxious look, she let him continue.

"The people I killed way back had children. But they are no longer children, and they have never forgotten. Never will. Nor have they forgiven, even though I was protecting my home and family. Like the other night. I always would, just as indeed they would have done. But those sort never forgive."

He scanned Anna's face for some kind of understanding, and with another silent nod, she stepped closer, her hands reaching out to touch his fingertips, moving to him. Chris appreciated the touch, looked down, and sighed.

"I don't want to put you in any danger. But if you stay here with me, it could. I have to warn you. Just in case. Do you understand?"

Anna nodded, was worried, but understood very well. She smiled.

"I understand, and I'm a big girl. My dad may look like a big lump, and he is, but in the past he's had people after him, related to business. So I know. I can look after myself, but also I'm happy to be here for you. If you want that?"

"Of course I do. I love having you here and waking you with you. Fluffy pink socks as well! But feel you should be aware of who I am and how I live."

Anna nodded, squeezing his hand, looking at him more warmly.

"I'm a bit tense and wary of everything, as I'm sure you've learnt in the short time we've known each other. Always on edge and alert. Now you know a bit more why I'm like I am." Chris leant forward and pecked Anna on the nose.

Anna winced, but smiled, loving his strange gesture and form of affection.

"Thanks for being honest with me. I really do appreciate it and now you've warned me, I can keep an eye out. But I'm fine about it. Thank you."

Anna pecked Chris on the lips, then gave him a gentle hug, which Chris warmly reciprocated, until the sound of a vehicle caused them to break free.

"Shit! It's Kerry. I'm late." Chris began to move over towards the house.

Anna noted the silver Nissan pick-up truck pull up and a young blond woman get out. She waved at Chris, then looking at Anna, smiled.

"I've got to get my stuff and the truck moving," Chris called back to Anna. "Are you okay with everything here? Sally will be back later to help, but I should be back later this afternoon. I'll call later on. Are you okay?"

Anna nodded and raised a hand, putting a thumb up, then playfully blew a kiss, seeing him blush and smile. He dashed across the yard, Kerry grinning.

Standing alone in the yard Anna gazed at the house, then turned to look behind the stables and at the ménage, paddocks and woods beyond.

She felt such happiness and at peace.

But then she recalled what Chris had said.

She shuddered, as if someone had stepped upon her grave.

She stared at the distant trees of the main wood.

Another knot formed within her belly.

An image flew before her. A recent memory.

Back in the woods. The dark monk.

A killer. Set upon revenge.

But who were they after?

Chapter 140

I don't believe in ghosts,
but they have been chasing me my whole life.

Edgar Allan Poe

The location for the Burns Night Hunt Ball couldn't be more fitting for such a grand occasion, being a place often used by the hunt for formal gatherings.

A late Georgian period house, with sculpted gardens, in rolling countryside, it was originally the residence of some 'big-wig' working in the government of William Pitt the Younger. Ministers come and go, so do family fortunes; thus over years the money became spread amongst numerous wives, children and grandchildren, until the former grand dwelling of a once prestigious family passed away completely onto new money and then disappeared into memory.

When that new money owner became embroiled in fraud and corruption, the property was sold on, moving further along a chain of numerous financially struggling and seemingly cursed owners. A large worldwide hotel chain had most recently swallowed it up; with deep pockets linked back to even deeper oil wells in far off distant countries covered in sand. Times change.

The Hunt held a traditional summer ball, it the main 'Hunt Ball.' However, over time, and since lost in memory why, other than organised by a former Scottish member, The Shoteton also held a mid-winter ball on Burns Night.

The various cars bringing the attendees arrived and either parked up in the spacious parking area to the rear, or the front for the taxis dropping off 'posh' clients, who'd then dash off for another fare. Most had plans to collect them at an agreed time later, hoping when the said party was collected, the former smartly attired, polite, pleasant person wouldn't then suddenly appear as a staggering, dishevelled rude lout, to then throw-up in the back of the car or down the paintwork, as a vomiting head emptied the contents of its stomach.

As each person, pair, or small group entered the main lobby area, a smartly dressed receptionist formally welcomed them. Tickets and names were clearly checked and then the group were ushered over towards a corner of the vast and impressive lobby, being the former entrance hall of the grand house.

Here a man, dressed in period attire, formally announced the newly arriving party to anyone who cared to watch, when a familiar name was announced.

The parties were then ushered to stand before a suit of armour, positioned by the grand staircase, where a professional photographer happily took their photo. Feigned blushes, or more fake shyness abounded, but other than those who were truly reserved, all secretly revelled in the formal announcement, and the hope their photo might appear in a copy of the local events magazine, or if really lucky, in one of the national equestrian or sporting magazines.

The professional photographer was more than happy to take orders for the images taken on the night, at a vast price, as well as take bookings for future weddings and large family gatherings. It was usually a good night for them.

Luckily the flow of people was at a steady pace, and it wasn't raining, so some larger groups were happy to wait their turn for the introduction and formal photo. It all added to the grandeur of the occasion and hence why it was well attended, not just by Hunt members, but by many local dignitaries.

Most then drifted off into the numerous other main rooms that formed the function rooms, dance area and various bars in the now converted country residence, to meet and greet friends and grab a much-needed drink. However, many curious bodies hovered around the lobby, wanting to see who arrived and with whom. And for the ladies, to ensure no 'bitch' dared turn up in an identical dress. Bloodstains, from clawed faces and scratched out eyes, were not a good look for any photo, so all hoped that from the vast array of over three hundred guests, not a single woman would dare wear an identical dress.

Of course for the men there was no issue. A black dinner jacket - or white for those daring or a 'James Bond' fan - along with bow tie, black trousers and smart shoes were all they required. If men ever became jealous over another wearing an identical outfit, it would have been a total blood-bath.

For Chris the choice of footwear had been an issue. He hated formal dress and like most country people, spent his life in wellies or riding boots of some form. However, he knew the rules, and with Anna beside him at Horsewater to ensure he was smart and didn't wear wellies, the pair arrived as required.

Anna dressed at her cottage then drove to Horsewater, knowing - or at least hoping - she'd be staying the night. She'd exited her 4 x 4 wearing trainers, aware of the mud, but had her dress shoes in her hand, along with a handbag and an overnight bag too. Not that she had plans of course. Not much.

She was aware of their height differences, and as much as she would loved to have donned some four-plus inch high heels, she chose a three-inch pair; but they were still smart black suede court shoes, with fine heels. Even then she still stood above Chris, but he didn't seem to mind, and secretly Anna felt he enjoyed her being much taller than him. The three inch heeled shoes matched the long, sleek, figure hugging V-fronted, knee-length black silk and lace dress. Fine straps revealed her slender neck and arms. A gold cocktail watch, an eighteenth birthday present from her dad, set it all off, giving her an elegant, classy, yet still sexy appearance. Chris had warmly complimented her before they'd left together in his Rover, Anna crossing the yard once more in the trainers and only putting on her heels when safely in his Rover.

They drove to the venue in almost silence, but the warmth and tension between them was evident, each casting the other a cheeky glance, smiling in the dark, but other than talk about the horses and the venue, they were quiet.

When formally introduced and then photographed in the lobby beside the suit of armour, Chris had playfully whispered for Anna not to bob down!

She'd gently thumped him, but was proud to be announced with Chris and have their photo taken, although she knew he was uncomfortable with all the fuss and blushed widely. More so as there were many hunt members staring.

The pair wandered off into the main reception room, which had been set out with an array of tables for the various groups and parties, all marked out. Some tables were small, round, designed to seat about half a dozen, others, the 'top tables,' were bigger and designed to seat a larger number or group.

The tables were draped in white linen, then adorned with glassed candles, small Burns Night paper flags on a holder, Highland Tartan place mats and Scottish thistle napkins, along with sprigs of purple and white heather, set out in small silver pots. Chris and Anna were some of the earlier ones to arrive, and as Chris guided Anna towards their table, Anna was much impressed by the layout and the general Scottish theme. Settling down onto her chair, she decided she'd take a small sprig of white heather for luck. Chris grinned, then beneath the table, grabbed at Anna's hand, giving it a gentle squeeze.

The pair were originally to be joined by Carol, Tracey, Julie, Sally and her boyfriend. But Carol had 'jumped ship' and was now seated at the main top table, being a large rectangular table near to the improvised dance floor area.

Reggie and Bertie were already seated there too, with a now blushing Carol seated beside him once she'd seen Chris and Anna. She raised a wine glass in salute to the pair, acknowledged by Chris with a nod and a wide grin.

Four bottles of wine were already set out on the table, two white and two red, and knowing Anna preferred Red, he poured her a glass. He poured himself one too, but as he was driving, knew he'd have very little more. Anna took the glass with a nod and 'thank-you' to Chris, but had already eyed up the impressive buffet food laid out on trestle tables along the sidewalls.

She knew, as soon as permitted, Tracey and Julie would devour the contents, along with the many other hungry mouths, as the room began to fill up.

Tracey and Julie duly arrived shortly after, bustling into the room in giggles. After a quick exchange of pleasantries, and a feigned glare towards Carol on the 'posh table,' upon discovering she wasn't to be at their table, changing to a genuine pleasant smile, Tracey grabbed a wine bottle and glass, promptly pouring herself and Julie a glass of white each, it being quickly downed.

Tracey wore an electric blue dress. Very short, very tight, off-the shoulder and if not careful, easily off her breasts. The piece of stretch fabric, which struggled in reality to be called a dress, defied physics as to how she kept it on her body. Tottering in matching fine ankle strap electric-blue sandals, with five-inch heels, the whole outfit was a potential recipe for disaster, and nudity. But Anna had seen it all before at family events, as had Chris; too many times.

She and Julie had wisely taken a taxi there, both having drunk beforehand. Julie wore a conservative, knee-length velvet dress, in deep burgundy, with matching suede high-heeled shoes. She seemed natural at walking in heels and it was strange to Anna not seeing her in 'yard clothes' or smart hunting attire.

Tracey's partner worked shifts and was typically working that evening. It didn't matter, as he openly hated such flash 'posh' hunting events and hardly attended any with Tracey, much to her pleasure. He was into angling and attended similar club events for his club. Tracey's only interest in fish was if it was battered and served with chips. Usually on a Friday. Bizarrely the pair seemed to totally trust each other and had a great, easy-going relationship, despite neither sharing any interest in the other's main past times or hobby.

Reggie wandered over to do the honourable thing to chat with new guests, and complimenting the ladies on their dresses, much to Anna's pleasure. Then she realised he said it to all the women. He was however clearly struck by Tracey's 'Little Blue Dress;' it being very little and clearly gave him 'Blue' thoughts too. As he drifted off, the women looked around at the various tables or groups milling about, trying to identify unfamiliar faces, but also seeing who was and wasn't at the ball. Clearly noticeable by his absence so far was Steve, who had his own table set aside next to Reggie's, and where a couple of his guests sat alone. Maybe waiting for him? Who knew. This included James, already seated and chatting away to an attractive, although rather plump lady-friend he'd brought. Another couple, older and this rosy-cheeks, sat beside him. But the table looked notably empty with no Steve.

Mutterings could be heard, enquiring if Steve would be coming due to his injury, and Reggie seemed vague when asked by Chris, met with just a shrug.

Martin was seated at the top table too, but at the end, and clearly alone. He appeared to be disinterested in the event, Sharon's absence clearly evident in his mood and general glum look. He did drift around a few of the tables 'meeting and greeting' as seemed to be expected by his position within the Hunt, but clearly there seemed to be some friction between him and Reggie.

Sally arrived with her partner Pete shortly after, and greeted them all, giving Chris a hug, despite having seen him only hours earlier. Sally was wearing a neat cocktail dress in a shimmering gold fabric, cut just above the knees in a Thirties style, with fringes to the hem and breast. On her feet she wore simple gold high-heeled sandals. Anna warmly greeted her and her partner, and then strangely looking down, jealously noticed Sally had delightfully small feet.

Whenever she saw her wandering about the yard, she was stomping about in seemingly over-sized wellies and shabby old clothes. To now see her smartly dressed, in a slim-fitting dress, with her blond hair no longer covered by a dirty baseball cap, and looking very attractive, it made her curious as to why nothing had ever happened between her and Chris. Who knew? The pair were close, very good friends, but almost acted like brother and sister.

The group sat and chattered about the usual horsey stuff, but glances were cast towards Carol, who unashamedly chatted to those around Bertie or who came to greet him and Reggie at the top table. The 'very top table' clearly. It seemed Virginia hadn't been cast out of Wroxingham Hall for more than a few weeks and Carol was already looking to become the next 'First Lady.'

As to where Virginia was, or whatever had happened to her and Gavin, was the topic of wild speculation and gossip amongst the tables; with rumours from being thrown down a well, to the pair now living new lives in Mexico.
Anna had asked Chris if he knew what had happened to her, and also her horses, which he used to train and knew well, especially Marmaduke. His only response was a nonchalant shrug, with no real reply. Other than adding that Bertie still had all of her horses, and they were well, before moving talk on, or remaining silent. It seemed to Anna to be a common trait amongst members of the Shoteton; when asked a difficult question, to which you either didn't know the answer, or simply didn't want to respond, offer a silent shrug.
Numerous people drifted back and forth to the various tables, catching up with people and gossip. A few spoke with Chris, warmly nodding to Anna, seemingly accepting her as being his partner; as well as many recognising her from the various hunt meets she'd attended and ridden out, but unfortunately, and sadly more notoriously, from the recent incident with Bruce.
Suddenly there was a murmuring about the room and number of people dashed off, as someone notable was seemingly arriving in the lobby.
"Introducing Mister Stephen Harrison and Miss Isabelle Harrison."
The voice in the lobby proclaimed loudly and proudly, to be heard by all.
All heads on Chris' table turned towards the lobby doorway, and most others throughout the main room, the murmuring and general chatter of beforehand suddenly paused to a stony silence, so you could have heard a pin drop.
"What the ..." Tracey began to proclaim. "No!"
"Yes! I knew it'd happen!" Julie said, smiling brightly. "Good!"
Tracey glared at Julie, then Anna, and a red-faced Chris.
"I can't believe it. The two-faced cow. What cheek!"
"True love," murmured Chris with a wry smile, glancing at Anna. She smiled back and openly squeezed his hand on top of the table.
Suddenly an image flashed before Anna.
Hospital car park. Pay and display. Blond woman. Lobby too.
Then Steve in the corridor; heading towards the lobby. The blond woman.
Anna smiled too, as it all came back to her and into place.
It'd been Izzy she'd seen crossing the car park and thought she saw in the lobby area. Hence why when she met Steve in the corridor, he'd told her he was being picked up by an old 'Riding Partner.' Indeed he was. In many ways.
Ex-wife more like it! Anna smiled to herself. Clever Steve. The sly fox!
Steve was dressed in a pure white dinner jacket, crisp white shirt with neat black bow tie and gloss black trousers. He did not want people to miss him.
Beside him stood Izzy, clad in a figure-hugging, full-length red satin dress. Matching red satin stiletto heels, just visible below the pencil-thin dress, set her proudly up at an identical height to Steve. The perfect pair. His bad arm was however slung. Izzy's blonde hair; no longer tied in the familiar ponytail, flowed over the fine shoulder straps of her dress like a Palomino's mane.

The pair could have come off the red carpet of a top movie premier in which they'd both had leading roles. They confidently and unashamedly posed for the formal photographs for the event - sure they'd be forwarded onto one of the big country magazines - but also absorbing the jaw-dropping looks from anyone who'd entered the lobby area to just stare in amazement at the couple, who should have always been together, but somehow weren't. Until now.

"Wow!" Julie whispered. "She looks stunning. Wish I could get into a dress like that. Look at that fucking body! I hate the bitch! But not really."

Tracey cast her a sideways glance, her eyes going up and down Julie's body like trained undertake. She looked over at Izzy, then back at Julie.

"You might get into a dress like that, somehow, but you could never have a piss! And you'd need a surgeon to get you out if it afterwards!"

"Cheeky cow!" Julie feigned tipping her drink over Tracey, but knew it'd be wasted, or Tracey would try to drink it. So instead she punched her. Gently.

A number of people without any prejudice, or who simply wanted to greet the couple, drifted over to happily meet them. Many wanted to speak with Steve after his accident, and were also pleased Izzy had 'crossed the floor.'

Others were not so forgiving, including Tracey. She simply spun around; never a fan of Izzy, and after another jealous gloat at the slick red dress, walked away. Julie followed, but did like Izzy. Chris nodded towards Anna for them to follow, but saw Anna staring longingly at the one-time mistress of Bruce; even if only for a few weeks, knowing what he clearly saw in her.

Izzy seemed to sense the stare, despite the mass of people around her and Steve and looked direct at Anna and nodded, whispering a warm 'Hello.'

Anna felt a shiver, but nodded back and smiled, raising her wine glass as a salute, the pair had spent some time together whilst Bruce had been injured in the hollow, so a strange camaraderie flowed between them. Chris followed the gesture acknowledging Izzy, it being spotted by Steve, who gave the pair a big smiling thumbs-up, whilst being swamped by various chatting people.

"Well that spiced the night," announced Tracey once the group were all back together and seated at the table, taking in a drink to recover. "Who knew?"

Sally, who'd remained seated at the table, simply smiled at the group.

"Oh, you mean Izzy? I knew she was coming with Steve. I spoke with her yesterday. Nice dress. I helped her pick it last week. We had coffee."

Tracey stared silently; slowly turning her head to Sally like an automaton, who missed the shocked look. She casually gazed about the room, seemingly oblivious to the events around her, pointing out a gentleman guest to Pete, who promptly rose to speak with him. Anna burst out laughing, becoming more bewildered each moment by the weird company she'd chosen to keep.

Chris, unsure what had amused her, simply took a slug of his wine, looked fondly at Anna and took her hand under the table, giving it a gentle squeeze.

Meanwhile, Tracey was frantically opening the second bottle of wine, Julie almost fighting with her over emptying the contents into glasses and table.

"I think I need to get a couple of extra bottles," Chris announced, and rising from the table, added "And I don't mean just for you two!" He smiled at Tracey and Julie, who, as if twins, simultaneously stuck out their tongues.

Chris wandered to bar with a grin, noting a number of excited people again moving towards the lobby area, as if someone important had just arrived.

If you could hear a pin drop as Steve entered with Izzy; with everyone going silent, to then whisper and mutter before clapping, then the next introduction had the impact of someone dropping a large crate of the finest bone china.

The same tension and noise seemed to rise from the lobby, followed by murmuring of voices, a dash of people, then a deathly silence. A large group of people seemingly hung in the lobby doorway to see the next key arrival.

"Hello, someone else is causing a stir," Anna whispered, gazing to the lobby.

"Who the hell can it be?" Julie asked, glass in hand. "Most people are here."

Chris, arriving back to the table with two fresh bottles of wine and catching the end of the conversation flushed red, looked away, as if he knew already.

A loud and clear voice called out an announcement. A shock announcement.

"Miss Virginia Burlingham and partner Mister Gavin Davis."

The crate of china crashed to the floor. Audible gasps of shock resounded.

Many within the main room; seated at their tables and chatting to friends, or others getting drinks, failed to hear the formal announcement of a pair of late arrivals. But many did. And many still didn't believe what they'd just heard.

After the crash of fine china had subsided, a deathly silence ran through the hall. Mutters followed, along with gasps of astonishment and incredulity.

Numerous bodies rose from their tables, almost in a wave, moving across the main reception room to appear in the lobby doorways. Heads peered around doorframes or shuffled about the edge to look on, checking their ears were not deceiving them. They were not. Stunning, in a tight-fitting black satin and lace dress, stood Lady Virginia; now just 'Virginia Burlingham.'

Head held high, showing herself off to her best and clearly proud of her partner for the night, and maybe life, she had upon her arm a nervous, red-faced and very sheepish Gavin. Smart in his Dinner Jacket and bow-tie, he stood firmly beside his lady, but was clearly reluctant to the publicity Virginia willingly absorbed like a sponge. Her arm was tightly linked through his, and like a pro' moved him over towards the suit of armour, for the photograph. Then kinking out a leg, to reveal a fine leg in black suede heels, she turned her hips at a slight angle, so her best figure was shown. She then turned to peck Gavin on the cheek in an exaggerated 'Movie' style stance, to the wide smile and enjoyment of the photographer, and gasps of excitement, and even a few minor cheers, from the watching crowd and growing blush of Gavin.

"Oh my god! Did you hear that Chris?" Anna exclaimed, looking at him, but already rising up from her seat and turning away, ready to head to the lobby to see what she couldn't quite believe. "Virginia? Did I hear that correct?"

Tracey, about to take a swig of wine, looked at Chris, who simply grinned.

Julie, sipping on her wine too, smiled back at him, and then sank the rest.

"You knew she was coming, didn't you?" Julie stated simply with a smirk. Chris shrugged his shoulders, and blushed as Anna glared down at him.

"I'm going out to have a look," announced Tracey. "See what she's wearing."

"She's not a fucking zoo exhibit!" Julie shook her head. "Give her space."

Julie then she rose too, setting down her wine glass, and smoothing down her dress, tottered across the floor to join Tracey, who adjusted her dress too.

"Wait, I'll join you too." Anna wasn't missing out. "I wonder what Lord Burlingham thinks? He must be livid. I would be. What a cheek. The hussy!"

"He knew she was coming," Chris said, shaking his head at the fuss, and then blushed further, revealing he'd said too much and clearly knew what was going to happen. "He's okay about it and wishes her well. Carol knew too!"

"The bitch!" Tracey scanned the room to look for Carol, but she and Bertie were nowhere to be seen. They'd vanished, either by luck or careful planning.

"Come on. Let's go and gawp!" It was Anna who made the announcement and without any hesitation all three woman dashed off towards the lobby, running almost on tip-toes, hands on dresses, where applicable. All were keen to see that 'The Bitch' was still alive, and importantly, what she was wearing.

Anna arrived first and her mouth could have dropped. It probably did.

She just hoped no one was looking in her direction to see her cold stare. If so, they were in immediate danger of being stabbed via the multitude daggers flying from Anna's green envious eyes. Even though Anna had grey eyes.

The former Lady Sluttington-Whore, now simply 'Virginia Burlingham,' to Anna, wore a long, sleek, figure hugging V-fronted, knee-length black silk and lace dress, with fine shoulder straps revealed her slender neck and arms. A gold cocktail watch sat upon her elegant wrist. An identical outfit to Anna's!

Worse still, she wore identical black suede heels. Same height, same style.

And, to add insult to injury - if it was even possible with such a sinful and condemnable act - the 'Lady' looked better in the identical outfit than Anna.

Or she did in her opinion, which was all that mattered at that exact moment.

Chris suddenly appeared alongside Anna, missing the evil glare, and warmly smiled at Virginia. She stepped away from the staircase and the throng about her, and releasing the red-faced Gavin, headed straight towards Chris.

"Chris! Great to see you. I've missed you. Marmaduke too. He's going to Gavin's yard soon, as you know. A lot has happened since you know what…"

She glanced at Gavin, who, red-faced, drew alongside her. She took his arm. He nodded politely to Chris, then Anna, who'd linked arms with Chris.

"Anna! Delighted to formally meet you. Our paths always seemed to cross. Chris has told me so much about you. Great dress. You look wonderful!"

Anna froze, unable to move, as Virginia stepped forward, placed a gentle hand on each shoulder and air-kissed her. Dumbfounded and totally stunned, she could only smile back, red faced. Anna then turned to glare at Chris, who glowed equally as bright, seeing an awkward situation about to explode.

"It's good to see you Chris," Gavin spoke quietly, shaking his hand. "And thanks for the flowers. So sad. They were appreciated. It was very kind."

Chris nodded, as Anna stared in amazement, wondering what she'd missed and what world she'd been living in since Boxing Day; and more especially since she'd become Chris' partner. She had to admit it'd only been a few days, in comparison to the years he'd known Virginia, and how close they'd always been. But Chris obviously had many secrets. Deep and dark it seemed.

Two other figures joined the mass of curious faces gazing into the lobby.

These faces, in separate doorways, peered unseen over shoulders of others.

Not that Virginia was bothered, for she seemed to soak up the attention, her smile devilish, enjoying the limelight. A blushing Gavin clearly wanted to shrink away from it all, although clearly proud of his beautiful new partner.

One of those drifting out from a side room was Reggie. He glanced across at the couple, a mix of emotions within, but hidden by a nonchalant blank mask.

He didn't appear shocked, unlike some who drifted in to gaze. Reggie just stared at the couple as if they shouldn't be there, although he knew in advance they would be coming. Bertie had told him days ago. It'd all been agreed.

Virginia had asked permission to attend and Bertie had happily agreed. He was a realist and lived for the day. It had been embarrassing, but he moved on

But Reggie hated betrayal and cheating. Except when he did the cheating.

He also had other issues. He scanned the lobby doorways for someone else.

Martin, just leaving the toilets, heard the announcement. He froze, his ears pricking up, unsure he'd heard correctly until the mutterings and murmurings all around, by people at the tables, many now rising, repeated the two names.

Gavin and Virginia. Secret lovers who'd brought shame. They were alive.

White-faced, Martin seemed to drift across the floor, as if drunk, although he wasn't drinking too much. His ears buzzed, the names ringing, all senses locked up, unaware until that point that Virginia and Gavin were still alive.

'You should both be dead. I've seen your heads!' He heard himself speak.

Martin made it to the doorway, half-hidden by some woman commenting on Virginia's dress and fine heels. But as stunningly beautiful as the 'former Lady Burlingham' appeared before him, Martin could only see a charred skull.

Burnt. Disfigured. Dead. Not alive.

'You're dead. And Gavin too. Dead. Burnt. Not alive. But you are?'

Teeth. Those teeth. He still had them all. In a jar. Too many.

But whose? Chillingly he knew.

He now had the answer. In full.

Instinctively he felt as if someone was looking at him.

They were. Intently. With venom.

He scanned the faces, all set upon the couple in the lobby, bar one.

Reggie stared at Martin.

Martin stared at Reggie.

Chapter 141

The only way to get rid of temptation is to yield to it.

Oscar Wilde

Martin was trying his best to pretend he was enjoying the ball, but really he wasn't. This was clear for anyone to see beyond the paper-thin facade he wore when conversing with people. The ignorant, already half-drunk, or mix of both, dumbly asked where Sharon was and why she wasn't by his side. Or they'd spin their heads about, looking to the dance floor for the absent wife, usually fond of dancing, assuming she was in that direction, or another table, drinking with 'The Girls.' Red faced, with the same excuse that she was at her parents, usually saw them off. Those with prior knowledge, some intelligence, or decorum, made no comment and spoke to Martin about 'the season so far,' or of how he was managing with all the trouble the Anti's had caused.

It was all boring hum-drum and annoying. In the past he'd have happily chatted for an age. Not now. Things had changed and there was an unspoken tension with Reggie, who'd been in a foul mood since the Wroxingham meet.

Worse still, he was drinking low-alcohol lager, which tasted of nothing and had none of the desired effects required from drinking real beer, other than refreshment. He'd driven himself to the ball, alone, and would be driving himself back similarly. The last thing he needed was to be pulled over by the police, who knew of the event, and would relish nicking such a prestige scalp.

So he'd suffer a few hours of quietly drinking Yak Piss before disappearing off to The Kennels, when everyone else was too pissed or uncaring to notice.

Subconsciously he'd sensed he was being watched. But he was unsure.

Maybe paranoid. And rightly so. He'd seen a woman flitting about, trying to avoid the advances of many men, but Martin had noticed her because she was stunning, like a model, and hence why so many men, single or uncaring, had tried to make conversation with her. But he didn't recognise her.

Tall, slim, maybe of East European decent, with long dark hair and a neat fringe, she wore an elegant, and expensive, black dress. Pencil thin, both dress and woman, the garment was of a fine figure-hugging material, low-cut to the front into a Vee to her belly-button, with spaghetti-thin shoulder straps. Dropping down to a low-cut back - clearly displaying no bra beneath - it was long enough to be stylish, and yet cut to almost calf length, revealing slim legs beneath. Neat ankles and fine feet sat perched in black patent sling-back high-heels. She wore no jewellery, or importantly, rings. Probably also no knickers.

Not that Martin had taken much notice. Just everything. The woman oozed class, but also wanton and brazen seduction. So much so - as is often the case with such stunning woman - they are sometimes seen to be too beautiful.

Deemed to be out of the league for most mortal men, who looked, dreamt, become aroused and simply wished, they never made any first move, for fear of a blatant rejection. Other than the carefree drunk, or the overly confident millionaire, who can afford such a woman, most men simply dreamed, then imagined the beauty later, alone in the privacy of their own dark room.

Sitting in his dark corner, pleased for a few moments of peace from the annoying people who all seemingly wanted his ear or advice, Martin had clearly noticed the sultry maiden, but tried best to ignore her. Now he supped lager out of the bottle, glad of a few moments. He looked towards the dance floor, seeing a host of happy woman dancing, donned in a variety of dresses.

Some of the women looked repulsive, prancing about in ghastly outfits selected at random in the dark, no doubt by their equally blind guide-dog. Others were clearly attractive and in clothes that fitted and suited them and had been selected by someone with clear vision and a degree of fashion-sense. Some were able to dance, others clearly not. Some already looked drunk, others sober and looking as bored as him. Most he knew from the hunt.

He smiled to himself, momentarily amused by the sight before him.

Then his eyes flicked sideways. Instinctively.

Someone was looking at him. Intently.

His neck hairs prickled.

Staring straight at him, 'The Wanton Hussy.'

The woman sat alone at a small table in the opposing corner, seemingly on purpose. Here she could watch the dance floor and room in general, but also avoid unwanted attention. The table also gave her a good view of Martin.

Martin looked away, momentarily, unsure, and then glanced back.

The hussy, or dark beauty, was still staring. On purpose.

She smiled. A wicked smile. Seductive.

Martin felt a rush in his chest. Unknown to him, he smiled too.

Only after the woman seemingly bashfully lowered her head, then lifted it again, was he aware of what he'd done.

The woman grinned. Martin grinned back.

Lost in the time and space that only seemed to exist between them, being oblivious to the boom of the music from the dance floor, Martin stared in awe at the beauty across the room. He knew it wasn't polite, but didn't care.

But she didn't mind either, it seemed. She stared back, tongue on lips.

Then she rose, straightening her dress, and moved over towards him.

Martin swallowed, eyes on her hands and body. And legs. Wow!

He gazed at her elegant hands, as they smoothed the dress down against her obviously very long legs. He watched as fine feet in stunning heels sent the image of beauty across the room and straight towards him. Him! Shit!

Then he felt his breath release as she stood by his table and leant forward.

His eyes automatically regarding the small, but perfect breasts, seated within the tight fabric of the dress, ready to ooze out. Or given a helping hand.

Martin's mind whirled, as red-faced and caught off guard, totally out of his depth, he gazed in awe at the beauty before him. She gazed at him. He stared.
'Hadn't he seen her before somewhere?' He was puzzled.
"Can I sit here? Beside you?" The beauty spoke in a slightly forced Ox-bridge accent. But she was, at least from appearances, clearly someone of old money. Or at least her parents clearly had it. Old money or new, who cared anymore?
Martin flustered, his mind a whirl, forgetting to respond.
He simply gazed at the beauty, all senses lost in a daze.
"No. I mean yes." Martin flustered, words bumbling, face going red.
"No I meant. No one is sitting here. And yes, you can join me. Please do."
Martin stared at the beauty, who looked back, smiling. Martin's knees melted.
"You don't recognise me do you?" The beauty spoke slowly, as she fluttered spider-like lashes over deep blue eyes. Martin melted all over.
He simply shook his head, unable to speak or respond.
The woman chuckled playfully, moving the chair closer and tight to Martin. She sat down, crossing an elegant leg towards him. Martin could feel her leg rub against him. He could also feel other movement down below too.
"I used to hunt with the Waveley Foxhounds," she added. "Few years ago."
Martin looked at her in silence, memory banks scanning for when they'd had a joint meets with the Waveley; a neighbouring hunt pack with Foxhounds.
He knew he'd remember her if he'd seen her - who wouldn't - but most women looked different in riding hats and hunting jackets, when their elegant figure is covered up. Also, most were usually riding at the back, behind him and the hounds, and other than at the actual meet, he didn't usually mix.
Martin shook his head, face red from embarrassment in not recognising the stunning, clearly beautiful woman, but also from rising blood pressure.
"I fancied you back then!" The woman said with no embarrassment, leaning closer and teasingly whispered the comment in his ear. "You were very hot!"
Martin felt her hand slide across the space and onto his leg. And further.
Downstairs nearly erupted. But Martin kept the cap on his raging volcano and took a deep breath, trying to get control. But he was rapidly failing.
Smiling, looking at her closely, he replied quietly, almost in a whisper.
"Sorry, but I don't recall seeing you. But then I'm usually out at the front and seeing to the hounds. Sorry! I clearly would have!" Martin was totally lost.
"Don't be sorry, be grateful that I remembered you." She purred.
Her hand slid across his thigh and towards his groin, slowly nestling between his legs and pressing softly, kneading the small between. It felt hard.
Martin drew in his breath and frantically looked about the room in panic. But no one was paying him any attention. Luckily. All were enjoying themselves.
A set of fumbling finger had hold of the zipper and began to slide it down.
Martin could feel himself about to pop out of the trousers, so spoke.
"What is your name?" Martin slid his hand down onto his zipper, feeling her hand as it moved inside his trousers, grasped his cock and held it.

"Jasmine. Jasmine Henderson. My family own a couple of farms down in Suffolk. The Henderson's. A few thousand acres. Have you heard of them?"

"Henderson? Oh, yes, I think I recall the name," Martin lied. He hadn't.

"I'm not really from these parts. I'm originally from the West Country."

"I know," the beauty replied. "I've watched you ride out many times, usually leading the hounds. Not only on joint meets. I've fancied you for ages."

Martin blushed at the open and brazen comment, but totally welcomed it.

"Where's your wife. Sharon?" Jasmine's hand was still inside Martin's pants, his hand upon hers, trying to prevent anything from happening prematurely.

She looked about the room, as if searching for the unwanted third party.

Martin knew who Jasmine was looking for and answered her question.

"She's not here. Away. Back at her parents. I'm alone." He lied easily.

The hand was withdrawn from Martin's crotch.

Martin was partly relieved, but wondered what was next.

Jasmine looked Martin straight in the face. She smiled.

Wickedly. Of course. Martin couldn't believe it all. His pulse thumped.

"Good. I'm glad you're alone. Then you can take me home and fuck me."

Martin swallowed hard, his pulse racing even wilder. Had he heard correct?

"Take me back to yours and do bad things to me. Very bad!"

Martin went red, then he smiled. He scanned the room, to see if anyone was watching, knowing to leave wasn't etiquette. But now he didn't care.

Everyone appeared oblivious to him, all engaged in their own worlds, the boom of the disco drowning out sound. Others too pissed to care.

Martin gazed at Jasmine, so tempted, but was naturally wary.

"Well then?" Jasmine whispered into Martin's ear, leaning forward.

The tip of her tongue followed, making Martin squirm inside and almost ejaculate there and then as her tongue entered his ear. The lobe was nibbled.

Releasing, he turned to look at the woman. She was so beautiful.

"Fuck me," she mouthed softly. "Hard! Really fucking hard!"

Martin submitted and rose. He offered out his hand. Like a true Gent.

Jasmine rose. Slender hands smoothed down her dress. Then took his hand.

Martin leant forward, absorbing the French perfume and sensed silky smooth skin beside him. It was too much. Taking her hand, he whispered into her ear.

"I'll take you to mine and treat you bad. Really bad."

The beauty smiled wildly and led Martin away.

Game on!

Chapter 142

No one is immune from suspicion.

Samuel 1 18:6-9 – The Bible

For his own reasons Reggie had been keeping an eye on Martin that evening.

He'd seen him at the lobby when Virginia Burlingham had arrived, sensing then that Martin knew for sure what he'd only before simply suspected.

From then on, he'd noticed his Huntsman drift about aimlessly most of the night, interacting as required, but only as he should, seemingly lost without Sharon. He noted he'd sat alone at a small-darkened corner table, deliberately away from it all, rather than the head table where he'd started the evening.

Martin was clearly pretending to enjoy the occasion, and mingled with the 'Great and the Good' of the local farming world who were also attending.

This was as expected of a Hunt Servant, along with meeting other dignities and key people who's land they hunted, or who's support they may need in local council meetings or even in higher parliament on such occasions.

But he knew Martin hated such bullshit. He was simply a true horseman. A rider. Hunting with horse and hound, that was Martin's arena. Reggie enjoyed being a key part of the social mix; meeting with people and doing deals.

He knew Martin hated such activities and preferred to keep out of the limelight and simply do his job. And he did. And very well too. Until now.

Reggie knew that as the Huntsman, and a key figure in the Hunt, it was hard for anyone with such a profile to have five minutes of privacy and peace to themselves, including himself. As much as Reggie liked to be the centre of attention, even he often simply wanted five minutes of quiet and solitude.

However, with an eye upon Martin, Reggie noticed he'd take a break from the socialising and settled down briefly at a small round table; one of many set to the ends of the large ballroom, purposefully with only two seats around.

The secluded spot by itself, with only one spare chair, was a warning to most people with an ounce of sense of being 'Out of Bounds' to any form of social contact. But that excluded numerous ignorant pompous idiots, the drunks, or those who were keen to have a quiet, 'private word' with any seated alone.

The tables were also ideal for anyone meeting a potential first date too.

Reggie had himself wanted a few minutes alone, being constantly pestered all evening. He'd vowed he'd beat to death the next person who uttered the words: 'Elizabeth not here with you tonight ?Unwell? So sad. If so, I hope she gets better soon. Anyway Reggie, how are you? I just need a word....'

He was being driven nuts himself by such comments, so could understand why Martin was feeling stressed himself and need space, rather than enjoying a key social function in full. But he also knew other things were afoot.

The Hunt Ball was an important social event for not only the hunt, but also for local farmers and businessmen with whom Reggie often did trade, and even the odd Councillor who's favour they might need. That was without all of the genuine people who hunted and supported The Shoteton.

An elderly lady was currently badgering Reggie, someone whom he'd never seen before. Face like cracked concrete, she wanted to recant some tales of 'days long gone by' when she'd hunted with The Shoteton, back when they hunted carted stags. A number on his table half-listened and Reggie feigned interest. Finally he was able to escape, excusing himself for a toilet break.

Steve was on the adjoining table, with Izzy. Reggie boiled within, unable to accept Izzy back onto their side, but politely nodded as he passed, seeing her cold, then almost rueful and cocky smile returned. She knew it'd take time to win everyone over, but knew the likes of Reggie would never change.

Steve, arm in bright pink plaster, was enjoying his moment in the limelight, with numerous people flocking around their table; keen to speak with him, but also secretly wanting to speak with Izzy. Reggie did have to admit she looked stunning. But she always had, even way back when out hunting, before she 'Crossed the Floor' the other way, as Steve had aptly put it earlier in the evening. Now at least she'd strolled back over to their side. The correct side.

Steve always had a way with words, but at least the pair seemed genuinely happy and Reggie could not wish them any bad luck, despite the trouble Izzy had caused in the past. It was part of the game, and at least she'd revealed her true colours after all. Reggie had always doubted her true loyalties; most, like him, thought her becoming an Anti was simply an act, done out of spite.

However, his real attention tonight was on Martin. Reggie had hoped he'd stay on the top table where he could keep a close eye on him, the air between the pair chilling. However, he knew as things progressed through the evening, and people started tucking into the buffet, drinking more, and then took to the dance floor, it'd be harder to keep a close watch on his Huntsman.

And a close eye he'd been keeping on him too. Reggie had winced each time Martin tried to explain where Sharon was. In a way, he'd hoped Martin would be more open and simply state she'd left him. Or he'd killed her. He'd been open about Elizabeth's absence and couldn't see why Martin had to lie.

Reggie had spotted the stunning, unknown beauty that'd quietly drifted in late and then sat alone. Most had. Anyone with any testosterone. She was clearly looking for someone, dismissing advances from old farmers, drunken gentry or suave young 'Whipper-snappers' who dared approach. She seemed clear on what, or who, she was clearly looking or waiting for. A real beauty.

But where had she come from? Who was she? And what did she want?

Reggie was curious and wary. She was too good to be true. Far too good.

With eager eyes he noted her stroll over towards Martin's table, and unashamedly, move her small chair next to his, and talk to him quietly.

Martin looked excited but also scared. Reggie didn't blame him. She was stunning and out of place. And league. Reggie liked to think he knew all the wives and girlfriends of most of the Hunt, and those of the local farmers and other dignitaries who frequented such social gatherings, but she was new.

Many young women, and some not so young, attended the various Hunt Balls in the sole hope of finding a partner. And why not?

It was exactly how he'd met Elizabeth, so many years ago. So it seemed.

A chill ran down his spine thinking of Elizabeth and he drew a breath as he found himself staring at the stunning beauty across the void. In a way he was jealous, but noted Martin looked sheepish, and wary of his new companion.

Reggie's eyes bulged seeing her hand slide under the table. 'Lucky bastard!'

But danger signals began to fire off in Reggie's mind.

Something was wrong and it wasn't all good. All wrong.

He felt danger for the woman, but also maybe for Martin. More so.

This could end badly. Very badly. For both. For everyone.

Reggie had to think and thought best with a Speyside single malt. He walked towards the bar, it being busy and deep with people, but it offered a better view whilst he waited to be served, and time to think and work out a plan.

"Reggie, old chap! I think I owe you half a dozen Malts, let alone one. Care for me to get you one. Or two!" The jovial face of a local farmer obscured Reggie's view of the corner table where Martin sat. Reggie shook the hands of a well-known farmer, who he liked, but the rotund gent now stood straight before him, obscuring his view of Martin and the dark-haired maiden.

The overly excited farmer couldn't thank Reggie enough for advice he'd provided a season ago on increasing barley yields and getting a better deal on his sugar beet. A new Range Rover had been the result of such good fortunes.

Reggie could all but put on a feigned smile, genuinely glad he'd helped out a fellow farmer, but annoyed right now that he'd taken away his moment.

The barman finally approached the pair, where Reggie was presented with a double 12-year-old Aberlour, his favourite malt. For this he was genuinely appreciative, but still annoyed, because he'd lost sight of Martin and his hussy.

Thankfully the farmer's wife, annoyed by the delay in him getting her a fresh G and T, wandered over to bend his ear. She happily greeted Reggie too, but thankfully not long enough to cause any real issues. The farmer's wife dragged away her husband, who raised a fond hand to Reggie. He softly waved back.

Finally, Reggie looked towards the small table where Martin sat. Empty.

Head spinning, he turned his gaze to the bar, then the dance floor, where at past events he knew Sharon would be dancing, Martin always shying away. Numerous bodies in dinner dress and neat gowns pranced and jostled about the floor, but Reggie knew he'd quickly notice if Martin and the tall dark-haired stunner where gyrating. They weren't dancing. They were gone.

He moved a few paces across the room to gain a better view of the main bar area, to see if Martin was buying drinks, but neither of them were there.

Turning sharply, he moved out the main room and into a side room, where the buffet food was laid out. A host of hotel staff busied themselves about, topping up plates, as numerous hunt members were there, piling up dishes once more, happily chatting away, getting food. But no Martin or beauty.
He'd gone. So had she. The pair of them - vanished. But where?
Whilst he knew Martin was entitled to do what he wanted, when he wanted, Reggie had his own interest in Martin. He needed to know his whereabouts.
For the past few days Reggie had held a secret, personal belief that his future, and even maybe his very life, could depend upon knowing Martin's ever action and activity. But now he was gone. Vanished. That was worrying.
Along with the dark-haired beauty. Deeply suspicious.
It was worrying on all accounts. Very worrying.
Dashing into the lobby, rubbing his chin, Reggie glanced at one of the hotel staff at the main desk. Eyes narrowing, he regarded the young man behind a large wooden desk. An array of brass hotel room keys dangled behind.
Reggie smiled, already thinking he had the answer.
"Excuse me please," he spoke, offering his most charming smile.
"I'm looking for one of my group. He may have booked a room, recently. Like in the last few minutes. Good-looking chap. He was possibly with a beautiful, tall woman, in a black dress? Can you help?"
"Certainly sir. Just left. Minutes ago. A fine couple. She was stunning."
Reggie froze in silence, gazing at the main entrance door.
"They've only just left for the car park, sir."
Reggie ran for the door.

Chapter 143

Be patient and calm - for no one can catch fish in anger.

Herbert Hoover

Seated in the comfort of an Audi estate, the man watched the hotel entrance. A flashing red light on a black box beside him told him all he need know.

Just then a couple wandered out the entrance. The man smart in his neat dinner jacket, the woman simply stunning. Tall and slim, the black dress matched her long dark hair and was a perfect fit. Figure hugging, it showed off the wonderful sleek body that lay beneath. She seemed to glide across the car park, despite the fine high-heels she wore.

It seemed years of refinement at a Swiss finishing school, or a few hours in a hotel room, had taught all needed to know to appear the perfect debutante.

The man watching from the car smiled.

He'd taught her well. Very quickly. And bought the dress. A fine dress.

And it'd obviously worked. Just as planned. Or so he'd hoped.

'Attach the maggot, lower the line, wait, then yank hard.'

She'd caught her big fish. Well and truly.

'Now to reel him in, and drop him in the net. Ace!'

Just as planned and rehearsed. Perfect. Fingers-crossed.

The happy couple wandered across the dark car park, the man making a joke. The woman smiled, seductively kinking her head. She shuddered, but seemed to decline the offer of his jacket, instead wrapped her arm around his waist.

Adam watched Chantelle - sorry, Jasmine - walk across the car park, and only momentarily did she glance his way. Adam winced. He'd told her not to, so many times, but the glance was instinctive. No more than a flick of the hair, unnoticed by her new partner and date, who hugged her waist tightly.

Adam smiled with pride, but also felt a pang of concern and also strange jealousy. But for now, this was work. He lost sight of the pair as they walked past some holly bushes and mixed mature trees, to disappear further into the large landscaped car park of the hotel, it being full with a mix of parked cars.

But Adam wasn't worried. He need only to wait for the headlights of the vehicle they'd climb into to illuminate within the car park and move away.

Then he would follow behind via the tracker. Just as planned.

Not that it mattered too much either. Adam already knew the Range Rover she'd be getting into. Besides, inside her handbag she had a small transmitter. Adam could follow discretely at a distance of up to a mile and still find her.

But he already knew where she should be going.

It had all been carefully planned. In full.

There were a few things that could go wrong, but they'd discussed these, and had resolutions and options for any such incidents.

Plans for 'What ifs' and other provisos. Shit happened. Often.

Hopefully the options wouldn't be needed. Fingers crossed.

Adam was a great planner. Usually.

Chantelle was a great pupil.

Jasmine was the perfect bait.

And their prey had fallen for it.

It was all going to plan - so far.

All Adam had to do was follow the pair.

Hopefully they'd travel back to the The Kennels, and then Adam could finalise his action plan against The Shoteton. Just as planned. As such.

Another front-page 'Blockbuster' was on the cards.

Just as they'd planned. Perfectly.

It'd all been worked out in full.

What could possibly go wrong?

Lots.

Chapter 144

Some cause happiness wherever they go;
others whenever they go.

Oscar Wilde

Anna was enjoying herself and Tracey had been instructed to not get too drunk. Whatever she defined that as. So far she was behaving. For now.

Anna was proud to be beside Chris, and their table was near 'the top tables,' being near Steve and his group, which now included his former wife and new 'partner.' Anna had somewhat bashfully smiled at Izzy when they'd taken their places at the neighbouring table, as she glanced her way. The pair now seemed to have a strange invisible bond, despite only ever having exchanged a few words, and always meeting up in strange situations on the hunting field.

The dramatic entrances of first Steve and Izzy, and then Virginia and Gavin had subsided, although was clearly the gossip of the event. Some nodded in the direction of their respective tables; muttering in negative tones, others openly greeted all or one of the couple. It depended on loyalties and depths to which they believed either had been deceitful, corrupt or downright wrong.

But in general the atmosphere was good and there'd been no major issues.

"Are you happy?" Chris asked Anna through the noise of the disco music, smiling, looking her full in the face. He discreetly squeezed her hand.

Anna squeezed his hand tightly and lifted the joined limbs up onto the table, clearly for all to see. Chris blushed, but smiled, then pecked her cheek.

She made him blush further by openly giving him a peck on the lips.

Short and sweet, it was met with joint smiles and grins from many nearby.

"What do you think? Of course I'm happy. Never more so. Thank you!"

The pair scanned the room, happy to watch others. Anna whispered to Chris.

"Hello, Reggie looks like he's forgotten something or is in a hurry to leave."

The pair watched Reggie dash out of the main room and into the lobby area.

"Maybe he needs the loo badly!" Anna giggled. "The buffet food wasn't that bad. Very good in fact. I'm enjoying it." She fed a battered prawn to Chris.

He playfully snapped at it with his teeth, making Anna laugh.

"Or he realised he dropped a pound coin in the car park on the way in!"

Anna grinned at Chris' joke, rapidly learning the ways of the various hunt members and enjoying Chris' dark sense of humour. Happily seated together, they watched as Julie staggered back to the table, another plateful of buffet food in an unsteady hand. She winked at the pair, as she was followed, as expected, by Tracey, wobbling in her five-inch high heels like a newborn giraffe. Her third plate of buffet food was stacked up even higher than Julie's.

Both women crashed into their seats and huffed, sinking a drink in unison.

They contemplated the haggis, which had been blessed earlier in an elaborate ceremony with a traditional Piper. His bagpipes had deafened everyone as he loudly piped in the haggis; the holder walking slowly and ceremonially past their tables, with the poor creature held proudly before him on a silver salver.
Julie informed Tracey that Haggis's were now an endangered species.
Tracey said because of that sad fact she'd become a vegetarian; possibly starting tomorrow, but wanted to know what the Piper wore under his kilt.
If the pair weren't years apart in age, and looked totally different, they could've been twins. Maybe. God help their parents!
Anna looked down at her plate of buffet food, this time picking up a rogue bread stick, which she playfully waved towards Chris like a sword.
He viciously snapped the end off with a lurching bite.
Anna giggled and grabbed at another, stabbing him in the neck.
The happy couple smiled, and Anna kissed Chris' nose.
Tracey shook her head, but with a beaming smile.
"Looks like me and you might need to buy a hat. Or two."
Julie stared calmly, with a wide smirk, like a wise old owl.
"And some baby grows too!"

Chapter 145

Stars, hide your fires. Let not light see my black and deep desires.

Macbeth - William Shakespeare

Reggie dashed out into the dark chilly car park, just in time to see the rear taillights of Martin's Rover heading down the long drive away from the hotel.

"Shit!" Reggie cursed, sliding the cuff of his shirt back to glance at the Rolex on his wrist, squinting to see the time in the gloom, not that it mattered.

Suddenly, another car engine loudly fired-up nearby within the gloom of the car park. He turned to glance at the long dark car, it too heading off towards the driveway, but with no lights on, until it reached the end of the driveway.

He flicked his head back and forth, not recalling anyone else having left the hotel lobby just before hr dashed out or just after him.

Someone was either waiting or had left minutes earlier.

'But why no lights?' Reggie was curious and suspicious.

Then he saw the lights switch on, as the dark estate slowly turned in the same direction as Martin's speeding Rover. The penny dropped with a rattle.

"Shit! Fucking shit!" Reggie cursed loudly. "Bastards!"

He stood in the gloom, watching two cars disappear into the darkness.

Reggie seemed to instinctively know or understand.

He fumbled in his dinner jacket, searching for his keys, cursing as he realised they were in his wool coat inside the hotel. Standing alone in the cold car park he glanced at the hotel entrance and then into the darkness and beyond.

In the distance, cutting into the gloom of the countryside, were two distinct sets of car headlights. One behind the other.

But apart. Purposefully.

The second car was carefully, and clearly, following the first.

Reggie swore loudly.

Chapter 146

If the object of our delight is lust, no good can come from it.

Psalm 37:4 – The Bible

Bruce was bored. Yet again. Life was tiresome stuck in a hospital bed, with various limbs cast, inactive and no action, especially sexual. More so that he was alone in a small side room and had little time to goggle at the passing nurses and fantasise about doing things with them in their sexy outfits.

However, they'd changed and were no longer sexy. Everyone now all wore black trousers, rather than sexy black stockings of the Carry-on films. Boring.

He couldn't see any ward action and there was no one to chat to either, regretting having a small private room. He sighed and then sat up as a nurse entered. He hoped it'd be the petite Filipino nurse who attended to him most of the time and whom he fancied. Sweet and fun, small, perfectly formed, she was far too pretty to be a nurse, doing all those shit jobs. Working as his secretary would be a more befitting role. Or maybe a pole dancer, or stripper.

It was a pity he didn't currently have a job or an employee. Thus, he couldn't take her on as his secretary, or whatever tasks she wanted to undertake. He wouldn't care, so long as it didn't involve wearing boring trousers.

All he had to do was get a new job, once he'd recovered. An executive position - of course - just as before. And he would. Soon. Easily.

Maybe then he might even get Anna back, regardless of what she'd said to him. However, the cute Filipino nurse, called Agila, would do as a stopgap until then. Even if technically 'Out of Bounds' by being a nurse. Stupid rules.

Bruce heard feet enter, sounding like heels. 'Was that her? Talk of the devil!'

"And how is my favourite patient?" A nurse enquired in a sultry tone.

Bruce cocked his head. The voice was familiar, but not. His mind whirled.

He looked intrigued as a dark-haired nurse, dressed in traditional blue dress uniform, with black stockings and high heels, confidently strutted into the room. She softly closed the door, turned and smiled, big eyelashes fluttering.

Bruce felt his heart sink quicker than the Titanic hitting two icebergs. Big ones. With killer whales waiting beneath to consume any passengers.

He looked worryingly at the unwelcome, intruding nurse.

Sadly, very sadly, it was not the small, sweet Filipino nurse Agila he'd hoped or expected would attend to his needs.

It was Lucy. Dressed up as a nurse. A sexy nurse.

Bruce feigned a smile. Or was it a grimace?

"Hi sweetheart. Great to see you." Bruce wasn't convincing, both in tone and in his sudden nervous disposition. He looked at her warily. "How'd you find me? I thought you were miles away. Do you work here now?"

Lucy smiled suspiciously, and didn't reply, but swaggering over to his bed, hitched up her dress to reveal stocking tops, before dropping the hem.

"I'm not feeling too good at the moment," Bruce replied, worried; feeling vulnerable, just as Lucy would like him. She ran a hand along his sheets.

Lucy regarded him with feigned sympathy, then grinned. That wasn't good.

"Well in that case, as you're not well, Nurse Lucy had better make you feel better. Much better. Where does it hurt? Here? Or maybe here?"

Nurse Lucy slid her hand beneath the sheets and fumbled. Bruce flinched, as she grasped firmly at his manhood, which as ever, automatically responded as nature intended. Lucy smiled, feeling it rapidly grow in size, stroking it gently to add extra encouragement, although little was needed.

"Mmm! I see he's pleased to see me again. Even if you're not."

Lucy's head vanished under the sheets, sending Bruce into a mix of pain and pleasure, as Lucy took him in her mouth, then squeezed his testicles. His eyes flicked towards the door, hoping a real nurse would enter. In a few minutes.

Bored with the lack of activity for herself, Lucy removed her head, grabbed at a small plastic chair, then threw back the sheets. Hitching her dress bottom fully up to her waist, revealing tantalising lace-topped black opaque stockings and nothing else, Lucy clambered onto the bed and then straight onto Bruce.

Straddling Bruce backwards, so she faced the door and displayed her rear to him, Lucy slid herself with ease onto him; turning her head, she winked. Sliding herself down fully home, with a sigh and pleasurable wiggle for her, Lucy began to gently rise. Bruce winced in pain, as she sat on his broken leg.

"Reach from behind and grab my titties!" Lucy ordered. "Squeeze them hard and tweak my nipples. Like you used to do. Go on. Do it!"

"I can't. My arm is in a sling. Broken. Remember? It hurts! And my leg!"

Bruce grunted as Lucy squatted harder upon his thighs, slowly rocking and sighing, then increasing the motions and increasing Bruce's pain.

"Aargh!" Bruce cried. "My fucking leg. Get off! Please! Now!"

"Shhh! Be quiet and enjoy your special treatment. Nurse Lucy will heal all your pains. Just relax. Enjoy, but keep it firm. Mmm! Sweet!"

Lucy began rocking harder and faster, pressing down on his legs.

"Aargh! No. Stop it! Get off you bitch. My legs hurt."

"Nurse Lucy likes it when you talk nasty. Ha ha ha!"

Bruce winced in pain; feeling Lucy's weight upon his hips and legs, despite being of slim build. She leant backwards, pressing fully on his body.

"Aargh! No. It hurts. Get off me you stupid cow! Now!"

Lucy ignored his cries, pleasuring herself, then she slid her hands across the front of her tight nurses outfit, squeezing her own breasts as she rocked.

"Get off you me you fucking whore. Leave me alone. I hate you!"

Lucy suddenly ceased her rocking, but remained astride her mount. With Bruce still firm inside and trapped between her squatting legs she turned her slim waist around, her eyes questioning and cursing. Bruce saw fire.

"What did you say?" Lucy asked. "And did you call me a stupid cow?"

Bruce saw the anger in Lucy's eyes, but was in deep pain. He didn't care.

"Yes I did. Get off. Please. It hurts. Bad. No more of this stupid shit. We're finished. As soon as I'm well enough I'm going off to somewhere new. A fresh start. And I'll be taking Anna with me. Not you. Now get off. Please."

Bruce knew at once he'd said the wrong thing, as was the story of his life.

Open mouth, speak or act, and then think. Wrong order.

When recalling things later, he was sure he'd seen flames shoot from Lucy's eyes; but everything happened so quickly. It was all a painful blur.

Bruce recalled Lucy yelling profanities about Anna, along with death threats; screaming words such as 'Frigid Whore' and 'Stuck-up Skinny Slut' as she rose up off his exposed body, brazenly showing the entire world her neat buttocks and shaven vagina. The timing couldn't have been better - or worse - as the 'Sweet Little Filipino Nurse' Agila walked into Bruce's room just then.

She'd wondered as to the source and reason for all of the yelling, screams, commotion and swearing coming from the room by a man and a woman.

As Agila entered the room she saw a semi-naked nurse straddling her patient, clearly having just had sex with him. Then the semi-naked nurse rose up, turned around and violently attacked the patient she'd just been shagging.

For Agila, it was the first time - and she hoped the last time - she ever saw someone re-break an arm set in a cast. The other nurse; dress bottom still hitched up to her waist, everything boldly on display, grabbed at Bruce's arm. Then in one swift motion she violently turned the cast limb fully through ninety degrees, then smashed it hard on the bed frame. Swift and neatly done.

Bruce's high-pitched scream woke half the hospital. And more.

Lucy then proceeded to face Bruce's waist, pulled his bare legs apart and punched him fully in his exposed testicles. Bruce's scream rose even higher.

The small Filipino nurse watched on in frozen horror.

She shouldn't have. She should have moved. Fast. Very fast.

As Bruce lapsed into shock, Lucy stepped forward. With a smile, and singular sweeping arm motion, she grabbed at the hard plastic grey clipboard hanging on the base of Bruce's hospital bed. In a follow-through motion, she chopped the hard edge straight into the nurse's pretty face. She was pretty no more.

The hard plastic clipboard crashed into her cheek, slicing a line clean through, before impacting with her neat nose, smashing it about her face.

Blood erupted in a fountain from Agila's split face, as Lucy sidestepped the now screaming nurse, and with her free hand, punched the nurse clean in the stomach. Just for good measure. And also for fun. Then battered her head.

All screaming ceased from the small nurse, replaced by a painful strained groan, as she slumped to the floor, crashing down onto her knees, collapsing.

The second nurse to arrive witnessed a nurse in stockings, with an exposed and shaven vagina, skirt raised up to her waist, kicking a fellow nurse - her best friend - in the head. It was unusual to say the least. Very unusual.

Like the first nurse, the next entry wasn't trained for such brutal activity. Too slow to react, she looked on in shock at the sight unfolding before her.

Nurse Two got off lightly. Lucy simply punched her clean in the face, the nurse's nose exploding about her face. The impact sent her flying straight out the door, where she fell backwards, crashing into a trolley full of crockery. Hot tea, coffee and various water jugs flew, cascading in a mess across the floor, to the stunned looks of many others and the orderly on the trolley.

Clipboard still in one hand, with her free hand Lucy regained some dignity - not that she had any - by sliding the dress bottom back down from her waist to the official regulation length. At least she now looked to others more like a 'Real' nurse, rather than a horny Porn Star from a low-budget B Movie.

A plethora of hospital staff looked on in shock and amazement, seeing a nurse crash into a refreshments trolley and onto the floor, whilst another appeared to be re-dressing herself, in public, many on the ward catching an eyeful of shaven vagina and black stockings. The bloody carnage within Bruce's room was currently unknown to all, but would soon be discovered.

Lots of bobbing and curious heads looked towards Lucy as she marched away, confidently heading towards the ward door and corridor. An astute doctor, sensing a wrong doing at the mess and screams, hollered loudly.

"You, stop! Someone stop that nurse! Security. Stop her at once!"

The six-foot tall, eighteen-stone security guard was no match for Lucy.

The guard, an over-weight former squaddie, who thought he was 'well hard,' was out of form; but thought he could easily stop the small attractive nurse who strutted his way, to which a screaming doctor asked him to detain.

Lucy smiled as the guard approached her. She had a clipboard in one hand, and a china cup, scooped up from the floor, in the other. The guard smiled.

Stepped forwards and sideways, the security guard raised an arm, with hand and wrist extended, in a traditional stopping gesture. "Stop, please!"

Perfect, thought Lucy, a former Black-belt Third Dan.

With a swish of wrist the china cup shattered onto the security guard's head, cutting his scalp. Then grabbing the security guard's offered wrist with her now free hand, a swift whirl and turn of her arm and body turned the guard's arm and wrist over and around. Within a second the burly 'well hard' security guard was suddenly behind her, screaming, being forced to the floor in agony.

He was soon in greater agony. With a deft lift of her arm, Lucy cleanly snapped his wrist. To finish matters off, and compliment the blood streaking from the china cup cut to his baldhead, she slammed the clipboard straight into his face, flattening his bulbous nose even flatter. A full house of noses.

It was lucky for him Lucy was in a hurry. She left him on the floor screaming and simply marched on and away. Slamming her hand against the green exit button, the double doors automatically swung open to permit her freedom.

Strolling into the main corridor, clipboard in hand, the nurse was intently studying the notes of a former patient. Bruce. Lucy was off. And quickly.

Lucy made it to the main lobby doorway before the alarm was raised and the siren sounded. A multitude of dumb security guards chased about in a blind pursuit, looking for a small female nurse with dark hair. One of a hundred.

Lucy was in the main car park and climbing into her car as the police arrived, all driving blindly past her car and racing onto the main lobby area.

But her exit had been noted on security cameras.

Her car details were noted as she drove calmly away.

Very soon the police would be in pursuit. Car chase.

But Lucy didn't care. For now she was free and away.

And Lucy wasn't finished.

She'd only just started.

She was off on a new mission.

Code Name: Retribution.

Chapter 147

A brave man is a man who dares look the Devil in the face and tell him he is a Devil.

James A. Garfield

Adam had to keep contact with Chantelle - also known as Jasmine - who was seated within the Range Rover he was following. A few hundred yards away, it was currently weaving around the dark country lanes with the skill of a driver who knew the roads well, and was in a hurry to get where he was going.

And Adam couldn't blame him. Chantelle looked stunning.

He could understand why the man who had her within his vehicle couldn't wait to get her alone and explore her fine and stunning body. He'd had carnal knowledge of it himself. But, as cold as he could be, and despite knowing the 'Rules of Engagement' he'd created; in that the current project was a business arrangement, Adam was keen to ensure that no harm came to Chantelle.

But there was more to it than that. He had real feelings too.

A glance in the mirror indicated he was alone and not being followed, the back roads quiet, with no other traffic. This gave him some peace of mind.

His Audi hugged the road well and he had no problem keeping in touch, but didn't want it to appear too obvious he was following the vehicle ahead. Thus he maintained a professional distance. But he also knew cars could easily be lost in country lanes, with high hedges or embankments, and lots of small lanes or tracks which to disappear down. However, he also had a good idea of the final destination for the Rover; or hoped he knew. But, as with anything in life, and bitter experience, he knew nothing could be taken for granted.

And he never did. Hence why he had the substance of a plan, discussed with Chantelle beforehand, along with some 'just-in-case' provisos to cover any change of plan, events or incidents. Chantelle had learnt quickly.

He had to admit that usually his plans succeeded. Usually.

That meant they didn't always. Shit happened.

Things went wrong. Too frequently in his life it seemed.

'Assumption is the Mother of all Fuck-ups,' he'd long since told so many, and tonight he was determined to not fall foul of his own teachings. He may 'think' he knew where the driver of the vehicle containing Chantelle was heading, but also knew he could not be totally certain. Things change.

The driver could decide to 'have his wicked way' with Chantelle in the Rover down a dirt track, or park up in a nearby wood he only knew. As much as this had been anticipated, it was not part of the 'Main Plan' he and Chantelle had devised, based upon information she'd provided Adam with upon recognising the Shoteton Hunt member. That's when the plan was devised.

Their plan, and hope, was the man would take her to his home, and things would hopefully happen from there. Hopefully as Chantelle thought it might. This would get Adam his next front-page and Chantelle a large pay cheque.

Following the vehicle wasn't too hard, as he also had a small transmitter in Chantelle's bag, which sent a signal to the receiver seated alongside in Adam in his car. The bleeping and flashing red LED grew or subsided in intensity, to indicate location. And besides, he could clearly see the bright headlights arc about half a mile ahead in the gloom, with little other traffic to distract him.

That said, he noticed the dark sky light up at intervals, with a car in the distance now heading towards them. Not a problem, or unusual, and in fact Adam was surprised he'd not seen more traffic moving on the country roads.

In the distance too, someway off but within the locality, he also noted the distant flash of blue lights. The blue strobes intermittently illuminated aspects of the darkened horizon, indicating some of the Emergency Services were busy and possibly heading in a similar direction or nearby. But which ones?

He checked the lights of the Rover a long way ahead, going in the direction of travel as hoped, but he also kept an eye on the ever growing bright blue lights in the distance, at a tangent from where the two cars were heading.

He checked his mirror, after passing a small junction and then an entrance to another local farm he knew was also owned by a key hunt member. He knew a great deal about many members of the Shoteton. And their private lives.

The dark country sky slowly became increasingly illuminated, as the distant car, moving at speed, was clearly now rapidly approaching. Clearly heading his way, and not too far off, it was seemingly now moving in a differing direction to the bright blue strobe lights. Where they linked? Maybe a car chase?

Adam noted a strange sudden movement of the Rover's light beams ahead, violently flipping from one side of the road to the other. He assumed the driver of the Rover had swerved to miss an obstacle, but then it became clear it was apparently swerving away from the oncoming speeding vehicle.

It must have just missed the Rover ahead, causing the swerve, and now it rapidly approaching towards Adam, being less than a hundred yards away.

As the speeding car approached, Adam eased up, as the road turned tight, with a raised verge and bank to the right and hedging to the left. The speeding car took the bend wide. Far too wide. The full beam headlights blinded Adam as they probably had to the Rover driver, hence his harsh swerve too.

Adam squinted and eased the Audi tight into the bend, just as the speeding car approached, halfway on his side of the road, the headlights blinding him.

There was enough room on his section of road for just one car, but not two.

At the last second Adam pulled hard. But not hard enough.

Bang! The Audi shook and he felt it spin in the road.

The headlights of the car that'd hit him deviated sharply too and appeared to crash into the hedging behind him and then bounce off the embankment.

Adam cursed loudly, banged his steering wheel and looked into the distance.

In the distance he could see the headlights of the Rover he'd been following racing off into the distance, vanishing as they turned a corner and passed a wood to then disappear from view, as had the blue glow of flashing lights.

Shaking his head to recover, naturally angry, but amazed the airbag hadn't deployed, Adam glanced in the mirror. Steam billowed out from the front of the car that'd hit him; clearly shown in the singular, non-shattered headlight of the crashed car. The rest of it seemed wedged in the embankment.

He looked down for the tracking device. Formally on the seat beside him, it had been thrown into the floor well and disappeared under the passenger seat.

"Damn!" Adam thumped the wheel again. Exiting the car he suddenly saw new headlights appear on the from behind, as another car slowly drove past, the silhouette of the driver obscured. But he was clearly not stopping.

Anyone would've usually stopped to check the occupants of two cars that'd clearly just collided were okay and assist. But not this driver. He drove on.

This person clearly had no intention of stopping for anything or anyone.

Adam watched the headlights of the unknown vehicle disappear in the dark. Knowing he was in the countryside, with an accident to sort and he'd lost contact with Chantelle, he hoped the Audi was drivable. The engine ran and other than bodywork damage, hoped he'd quickly sort matters out and go on.

"You Pratt! Why the hell are you driving like an idiot?" Adam yelled, slowly wandering toward the other car, before he saw the driver exit the vehicle.

The driver's door flew open and a woman fell out the seriously battered car. Staggering into the road, at first on unsteady feet, she rapidly steadied herself; reviewing the damage to the car, then herself, she patted her body down.

Another drunken young woman, Adam thought bitterly as he approached her, having seen her initially stagger in the road as if drunk, but he was also glad she was alive. He then, more warmly, realised she may be concussed and in shock. Even so, she'd been driving fast and erratically, and he was angry.

The woman rose, dusting herself down and gazed at Adam, taking everything in. He curiously noted she looked across the dark fields, as if concerned about something else. He turned his head too and noted the position of the distant blue flashing lights, which now seemed to be heading in a different direction.

The nurse who stood before him straightened herself and her dress down, now seemingly relieved, then looked very closely at Adam.

Adam gazed back at the battered nurse. Shocked.

A flicker of recognition.

Memories returned. For both. The pair stared in silence.

They stood face to face in the gloom, the headlights and interior lights of the cars providing a subtle glow to the scene within the dark countryside, but providing enough light for each party to clearly see the other. And recognise.

The nurse looked at Adam. Then smiled.

Adam looked at the nurse. His mouth dropped.

"Lucy?" Adam had to do a double take. "Is that you?"

Adam stepped closer, looking hard and intently at the face of the battered, but attractive woman before him, as if to check it was really her. It was.

Brushing back her hair, and wiping her face, she grinned - wickedly.

"Lucy?" Adam asked once more in disbelief.

The nurse gently nodded to confirm his question.

"Yes." It was her simple response.

"What the hell are you doing here?" Adam's eyes glared.

Lucy blinked, not responding, still recovering fully from the collision, but also knowing what she had to do. She simply shrugged her shoulders.

Adam simply stared, the gears in his head churning.

Lucy's mind worked quicker. Recovering. Planning.

"Hello Adam. Long time no see."

Lucy smiled at Adam.

Adam did not smile back.

His heart sank with dread.

Chapter 148

No man dies for what he knows to be true. Men die for what they want to be true, for what some terror in their hearts tells them is not true.

Oscar Wilde

Adam stared at the woman before him in horror, then stepped back.

Lucy smiled, looking at Adam, sensing the advantage. She stepped forward.

"Well, well Adam. In all of the places, in the world…"

Adam stared silently at the woman before him; her face a mix of disturbing shadows, illuminated from the glow from their damaged vehicles.

He gazed at her in silence, looking at the nurse's uniform she wore.

Lucy tilted her head to one side, pouting seductively.

"Do you still hold me close to your heart? Do you bare the scars?"

Adam automatically lifted his hand, touching his body where the massive scar run across him belly. He remembered. Too well. Bitch!

"I didn't know you were out. I thought they'd thrown away the key and left you to rot in that hole forever. Should have. How the hell did you get out?"

Adam spoke coldly, genuine bitterness in his tone.

Lucy tilted her head in an exaggerated manner to the opposite direction, tutting loudly, clearly disappointed, but with a wide cynical grin.

"Now, now Adam. There's no need for talk like that. I'm reformed. Fully recovered. The doctors told me. So I must be. Ha, ha!"

"But you tried to kill me. And after all I'd done for you."

"That's the trouble with being trained as good as I was. It came instinctively. You knew that Adam. That's why you liked me. You knew I was dangerous. Trained to do all of the undercover shit you wanted me to do. And more."

"Yes, and as you know I fully appreciated what you did. You were good then. Maybe too good. But you can't attack clients and try to kill them. That's why I had to stop you. Then you tried to kill me too. That's not bad, it's mad."

The bitter memories of his life with a beloved former employee and in addition one-time nymphomaniac lover came flooding back. Too easily.

As did the pain and suffering too. He bore all her scars. Literally.

"And I'm forever grateful Adam. As was that woman at the time. Thank you again for using your body as a shield to protect her. You stopped me from getting life imprisonment. Brave of you to take her blade. Sorry for the scar. As you know, you shouldn't have gotten in the way. Brave, but very silly."

Lucy pursed her lips, as if remembering a sad event. The pout was fake.

Adam scanned Lucy and surroundings, trying to determine his next move. But also, more importantly, hers. There pair were too good and both knew it.

Lucy didn't miss Adam's look, knowing how quick his mind worked.

"Anyway Adam, it's nice to meet again, and I'd love to chat and reminisce on old times, but I'm in a bit of a hurry and rather busy at the moment. I have a meeting to keep, you could say." Lucy momentarily turned her away from Adam, her keen eyes noting the flashing blue hue in the distance getting close.

Adam followed her gaze automatically, realising a number of police or other emergency vehicles were hurtling along the nearby country lanes, their blue strobe lights illuminating the night sky in a strange hue. Now about a mile away, and closing in fast, the vehicles appeared to now be heading their way.

Adam could guess who they were looking for. Lucy.

That same woman now stood before him. A certified 'Nutter.'

As he'd turned, for those brief seconds to gaze across the dark countryside at the growing flashing lights, Adam missed Lucy move. Like a cat.

He should have known better. He trained her.

Schoolboy error. Lucy had moved fast.

She now stood back before him. Poised. Ready.

In her hand she had a wheel wrench.

She smiled at Adam. He winced.

Lucy swung the wheel wrench with full force.

It impacted with Adam's head. Crack!

His body collapsed onto the road. Motionless.

"Oops! Sorry Adam. My hand slipped. Accident!"

Dropping the wrench, she dashed towards his Audi.

Chapter 149

The whole world's a stage,
And all the men and women merely players;...

As You Like It - William Shakespeare

As Martin & Chantelle, or Jasmine, as Martin still believed his beautiful date to be called, travelled to The Kennels, the pair spoke little. Martin was quiet, somewhat timid, back in a controlling mode, as he was in such circumstances. For him it was his usual way of adapting to the tense situation.

Chantelle said little too, simply gazing out into the dark, casting Martin the odd flirtatious glance - to keep up his interests - or making the odd comment about the season. She was wary of blowing her cover too easily. But Adam had coached her well. 'Don't volunteer information,' he'd told her repeatedly. 'Play the role in a cool manner. Don't over-cook it, or people get suspicious. Be confident and seductive, but also slightly nervous, as a 'real' date would.'

Chantelle knew where they should be going. Or hoped. Several times she and Adam had watched the property from the woods beforehand, but knew Martin could give in to undesirable lust and take her in any lane or woods; 'having his wicked way' with such a beauty and releasing his 'pent up desires.'

Chantelle had seen far too many period dramas on TV it seemed.

However, if all the suspicions from Sarah's comments to Chantelle were true - before she'd strangely vanished - all going well, her host would take her back to his country home. Then he'd truly entertain her, just as promised.

Adam only hoped the rumours, which had set him off on this latest mission against the Hunt, were real. That was the plan, and if things went wrong - and Chantelle was old and wise enough to know things went wrong - then at least Adam was close by in his car as back up. Something she'd not had in the past.

Sarah had made murmurings to Chantelle and a couple of the other girls of a tasty country client who kept horses, and had a 'Sex Dungeon' in his posh country house. She'd rumoured he was heavily into Bondage and S & M.

Despite the job she did, Chantelle had been wary, and thus warned Sarah of such clients and the dangers. A few of the other girls thought it amazing; one other claiming she too had an elderly posh client, possibly a Barrister, who had a similar 'Sex Room' too, but he liked to dress up in woman's clothes.

Chantelle knew it took all types, and every man seemed to have some strange sexual need, and her job was simply to relieve this required need. For a fee.

However, after recognising Martin's photo in their hotel from the many Adam had taken at the Boxing Day hunting incident, and then after the pair had done some undercover snooping of a number of properties belonging to key hunt members, she recognised him and his dark Range Rover.

Thus, he was the target. The plan: Chantelle was to entice the Shoteton Harrier's Huntsman. Encourage him to take her back to his home and to his 'Sex Dungeon.' Adam would follow on very close. He'd creep into the property and watch the pair 'at it' - Chantelle preferably being found in the most compromising of all positions. The worse, the better. He'd photograph the 'Pervert Huntsman' in all his glory, clearly with his 'trousers down.' Adam would then 'rescue the distressed lady,' dash to safety with her, and then plaster images all over the tabloid press of the 'Pervert Hunter.' Front page!

The plan sounded a bit vague and more dangerous to Chantelle than Adam, but Adam had advised it should work out okay. All going well. He hoped.

Hence, why he'd issued a few provisos and 'ifs and buts.' Just in case.

At worst, the Huntsman could turn out to be a true gent, who'd only seduce Chantelle with her permission. Nothing out of the ordinary. But better.

The journey from the hotel to The Kennels was not too great and the dark, quiet miles were soon eaten up. As much as Chantelle relished the role, and the activity was nothing knew to her, she was usually 'herself' and did not have to pretend to be a posh farmers daughter gagging for a perverted shag.

She'd noticed Martin cast her a few sideways looks on the odd occasion they made eye contact. It was unnerving, as if he had some doubts it was too good to be true, or as if he truly recognised her. But when she felt a slight unease or suspicion, Chantelle would simply titter, squeeze his thigh and then gaze merrily out the dark window into the darkness and gloom beyond.

She also glanced casually into the side mirrors, just to check. Early on she'd seen headlights far back. She assumed it was Adam tailing at a safe distance. But then, after a speeding car had nearly wiped them off the road, but where Martin skilfully swerved the Rover past the mad woman driver, the headlights seemed to vanish for a moment. Then, a long way back, a few minutes later, she caught sight of headlights yet again, so knew Adam was safely behind.

Her knight in armour was still there to protect her. She hoped. He wasn't.

The journey through the woods brought a fresh tingle of excitement, as Chantelle recalled crawling through the very same woods, totally enjoying the fun experience with Adam. He was a strange man, with mixed morals, but basically good and honest. He'd only treated her well and she respected him.

The Rover stopped at a big white house, and on exiting, Chantelle stood beside the vehicle, scanning the dark wooded surroundings. Provocatively she extended an arm, waiting for her host to take a hand and guide her to his lair.

Suddenly he seemed nervous, but smiling, then gently took her hand.

Chantelle liked this new weakness, knowing, or hoping, she could cajole him to her ways. As he guided her into the house, she nonchalantly glanced back at the dark silhouette of woods, from where they'd recently spied on the very same house and man beside her. But know she saw nothing. That was good.

Was Adam already in place? Or still following on cautiously. Maybe he was creeping about outside of the house. Chantelle was unsure, but had such trust in Adam, that she knew faithfully he'd appear in good time. As planned.

Luckily Chantelle didn't know the truth. It wasn't good. Not good at all.

Adam was unconscious. Lying in a ditch. Close to death.

Chantelle approached the big white house with her guest, holding his hand.

She pulled Martin close. "Inside. Tie me up. Then fuck me. Hard!"

Martin seemed to fluster and stumble at Chantelle's brazen openness as she whispered the chilling request into this ear. With a shudder he led her into the main part of the house, and as they'd entered, Chantelle heard the soft howl, whimper and whine of hounds close by in another part of the property.

But she and Adam had watched her host walk the hounds in the paddocks and even some parts of the woods, when previously they'd spied on him. Adam had even feared once that they may go into the area of the woods from which they were observing and discover them. But luckily any hound excising had been in the lower areas of the woods for the few times they'd watched.

Chantelle admired the surroundings of the typical country house and as they entered the kitchen area, she threw her arms around her host and kissed, which she'd never due to a real client. However, she felt she should act for real, as any date would. Martin nervously returned the kiss, then appeared to relax, kissing her properly. Unrestrained hands pleasurably slid all over her body. His hands slid across her buttocks, waist, and then onto her breasts, the frustration and lust within him clear and desperate, waiting to be released.

"You are so beautiful," Martin sighed, rubbing his crotch hard against her thigh. "Stunning. I need to fuck you. Now. Hard."

"Mmm. My kind of talk," Chantelle replied, biting onto Martin's earlobe and tugging it with her teeth. "Then lets make it something good," she whispered. "I'm a bad girl. Very bad. And I'm not into boring 'Missionary Positions' in silky sheets. I like being … restrained, should I say. Tie me up, bad boy."

Chantelle could feel Martin's excitement and fear within him clearly building. She hoped she'd pushed the correct buttons and not instead scared him off.

"You can whip me too. If you like that. But not too hard. I like it all."

Chantelle slid her hand across Martin's crotch, squeezing for a second, then teasingly removed it, touching his chest, then turned away completely.

Martin paused, stepped back a stride and stared at Chantelle, as if assessing her for someone real. She froze, but then he smiled, taking her hand.

"This way," he spoke softly, his breath already heavy. "I have the just the place. But it's special. Only for very bad girls. Sure you're up for it?"

Chantelle grinned. Stretching her neck out, then with her tongue extended, she slowly licked Martin's face, grabbing his crotch. Hard.

"Let's go big boy. Give me everything. And more. Let's party hard."

Martin led Chantelle through the kitchen area, then and over towards a small door set in the magnolia painted rough-plastered wall. The cellar door.

With a swift, cautious glance, Chantelle looked towards the kitchen windows, which had dark brown drapes drawn across. She hoped she might see faint headlight drifting through the woods, anticipating Adam wasn't far behind.

But she saw nothing. But knew Adam was good. He'd be there, somewhere.

Pressing a light switch on the wall, Martin opened the small wooden door set within an old timber frame. The hinges were black, the door white; all clean, freshly painted and well maintained. He pulled the door open and ducking her head low, she peered into the opening offered by the extended hand to her side. Chantelle felt Martin gently push her from behind and instinctively stepped forward through the door, whereupon her gaze drifted downwards.

Before her were a series of steps leading into what appeared a brightly lit cellar. She hesitated, looking back at Martin, who smiling, silently nodded. He pushed her on. She stepped forward onto the first two steps, the heels of her shoes clattering loudly, echoing into the room below. She faltered, cautious, peering ahead, trying to look into the cellar. An un-shaded bulb blinded her, preventing her from seeing further into the cellar. Martin closed in behind, pulling the door shut as he pressed her forward and deeper into the cellar.

"Keep going. But mind the steps. It's safe. This is where the fun happens."

Chantelle felt a sudden feeling of apprehension. Despite all she'd done in her life; up back alleys, in cars, various dingy hotels and more, she suddenly felt a sense of dread with this man and this chilling cellar. She thought of Sarah.

However, knowing it was part of a plan, for which she was being well-paid, and that Adam would very soon dash in to save her from whatever few minutes of pretence and sexual games she had to endure, it was nothing.

Onward Chantelle proceeded, hoping the tracking device in her bag would work underground. Adam said it should. Or so he thought. He hoped so.

At the bottom Chantelle relaxed, her high heels clattering loudly upon the stone floor of the cellar. The walls were clean, freshly painted and the cellar tidy, with boxes neatly stacked upon numerous benches. The air below was warmer than she'd expected, but there was also a strange smell. Human.

Chantelle scanned the small room, then turned to face Martin. He seemed to sense apprehension from the nervous glance of her head and curious stare.

"You've nothing to worry about. This is going to be great. For us both. It's what you want, isn't it?" Martin enquired. He knew he was pushing things.

Chantelle stepped towards him, wrapping her arms around his neck, and then extending a long leg around his. She slid it up to his backside, pulling him in tight to her slender, agile body. Martin smiled, and relaxed, rotated his body, turning Chantelle with him, spinning on his heels to turn her about fully.

He looked purposefully towards the far wall to which they both faced. Chantelle's eyes followed his intense gaze, to see a series of old wooden beams, seemingly bracing the old building above. Painted black, and stark against the whitewashed wall, they formed a large 'X' shape. Attached to the top and bottom of the 'X' were well-worn soft leather straps. She understood.

There were four leather straps. Two top, two bottom.

Wrists and ankles ties. For restraining someone. Upright.

'Sex dungeon.' Sarah's words rang through her head. Chilling words.

This was it. Chantelle and Adam had the right man. And the right place.

Now to get on with the job in hand. The quicker it was done and over the better. Adam just needs to burst in and take the shaming photos.

Then both get out, whilst the Huntsman's trousers are down. Literally.

Sarah's gossip had not been lies. But where was Sarah? She'd gone.

Chantelle looked boldly at the 'X' beam, turned back at Martin, and then grinned widely, knowing what was expected from such a willing person.

"Mmm. Nice. I like it. But not too tight. I don't want any chafe marks."

With that Chantelle strolled toward the wooden beams, her heels clicking, and neat buttocks swaggering in the tight black dress, which clung to her trim thighs, her slim legs beneath. Even Chantelle enjoyed the provocative walk

Martin watched the beauty before him stroll the few feet across the stone floor of the cellar to the wall, enjoying the sight, wanting her there and then.

Looking at her stunning body, and seductive, teasing kink of her head, his cock felt as if it might explode, but knew he must restrain himself.

His prize for the evening touched the aged timber beams, her hands drifting over the texture of the dark wood, and her confidence growing. Cheekily she slapped the woodwork hard, then turned to grin at Martin.

He remained stationary in the cellar, frozen close to the base of the stairs watching her actions, his mind whirling. He'd seen this all before. Sarah.

Martin's breathing grew stronger. Sarah had slapped the timber too.

Sarah. Poor Sarah. Tragic. He'd seen it all before. All of it.

Then a flicker of memory returned.

Jasmine. The woman before him. He'd seen her before. But where?

Martin stared at the temptress. Memories began to stir. Confused.

Same woman - different hair? Maybe.

And the clothes - more refined now. Not then. Cheap. Common.

Martin nodded to himself. He had it.

He had seen Jasmine before. Somewhere else. The memories clicked.

He recognised the woman. The whore standing before him.

He'd seen her with Sarah. Standing together on the streets.

Both whores. Sarah and this liar - 'Jasmine.'

Martin stared in shock and horror, but kept a poker face.

The woman before him was a prostitute.

A friend of Sarah. Eaten by his hounds.

'But what did she want? What was her plan?'

Martin eyed up Chantelle's long legs. He smiled.

'The hounds will feed well on those.'

Chapter 150

There are only two tragedies in life:
one is not getting what one wants, and the other is getting it.

Oscar Wilde

Chantelle looked at Martin, cheekily extending her tongue. Licking her lips, seductively kinking her head, she saw her host standing motionless. A blank look had now set upon his face. He simply stared. His frozen expression was like that of a shocked rabbit. About to be squashed beneath a car.

Chantelle wondered if he'd suddenly bottled out. Or maybe something else.

Martin stared, absorbing her image, taking in the details of the beautiful face, framed in long dark hair, with her stunning slim body and long legs.

She looked too good to be true. And was. She was not true. A fake. Fraud.

Unsure of his actions, acting automatically, and guided by raw instinct and seemingly unseen hands, Martin moved forward and stood before Chantelle. He smiled, back in control. Wrapping his arms around her, he reached for the neck of the dress. Carefully, and with practised ease, he unfasten it and slid the dress from neck and shoulders, watching it fall to the ground at her feet.

Chantelle lifted each heeled foot away from the fallen dress, revealing long slender legs and a sleek body. As he knew, she wore no bra and displayed her neat, small but firm breasts. Below she wore a tiny black thong, the thin straps extending over her hips, extenuating the long legs. Martin gazed for a few seconds, feeling deep arousal within. He reached down at her heeled feet, lifted up the dress, walked away and gently placed it on a nearby bench.

Turning to survey his victim for the night, and the next meal for his hounds, he gazed at the beauty before him. She was truly stunning. Beautiful.

Better than Sarah. But less meat. Shame to ruin such a body. Ho hum.

Why hadn't he picked her before? Who knew? But now she was all his.

Martin moved back over to Chantelle, who for a split second looked up to the cellar door, wondering when Adam would arrive. Not too soon, but then she hoped he wouldn't be too late. He must be prowling about outside.

Gently the man slid the back of his hand across her flat stomach, skimming over and up towards her breasts, then almost teasingly brushed a nipple.

Chantelle grinned, genuinely excited by his gentle manner, as Martin's hand then drifted down, across her waist and to the thong below. The same gentle hand glided across the silk fabric, before reaching the top of her bare thigh. Slowly his fingers moved up and around, exploring hidden treasures.

Martin's face was inches from Chantelle's, but no emotion was displayed as his hand skimmed over her thong, then between her legs, where probing fingers gently slid softly across the lips of her vagina, but did not enter.

Chantelle felt an internal pleasant squeal of anticipation, almost keen to proceed, enjoying the man's gentle, teasing touch, despite knowing it was a job, and also dangerous. Maybe that was why it was exciting. And maybe that too was why Sarah had secretly enjoyed going off with this man.

But why did she leave? What happened? Where did she go?

And when would Adam arrive? Soon. Very soon. Hurry!

Chantelle was pleased the man was admiring her face and body, as indeed he should if in truth both parties were genuine. She could actually like this guy.

But was he looking too deeply? Did he suspect something?

The fears raced through her mind, whilst she wondered when Adam would appear. Too soon and it'd all be a waste. Too late, once he'd finished, and there'd be nothing to photograph. Nor proof of the Huntsman's 'dirty' habits.

As Martin took away her dress, Chantelle noted an enclosed area beneath the stairs, screened off by a heavy black curtain. She was curious as to what was behind it but took no more notice. Boldly she smiled at her victim.

Stepping forward, Martin reached across, carefully gripped her first wrist, and guided her arm up towards the timber and straps.

"Keep your shoes on," he whispered. "I like them. Sexy!"

Chantelle smiled; glad he was relaxing and proceeding.

Martin gently raised her arm to the first leather strap, quickly fastening her wrist with practised ease. Chantelle offered no resistance, playfully smirking, knowing this was what each expected and importantly too, Adam wanted. Martin repeated the action with the other wrist, it willingly offered.

Then reaching down, he slowly moved her first leg, still with her shoes on, gently gripping her slim ankles. He guided her leg towards the ankle strap, where he fastened the soft, well-oiled leather around her ankle. Moving her own foot voluntarily, legs spreading open, Martin repeated the action for Chantelle's other ankle. Securely strapped to the old wooden 'X' beams, in just her thong and black stilettos, Chantelle felt a mix of fear and arousal.

Martin stepped back, eyes widening and the first signs of any pleasurable enjoyment crossed his face as he absorbed the image. Chantelle pouted seductively, as would be expected. Now firmly secured, with the straps not too tight or painful, she playfully wriggled her hips, hoping he'd proceed.

Again Chantelle's eyes flicked towards the door at the top of the cellar stairs. Any moment the door would open and Adam would appear, camera in hand.

Then her eyes flicked back down to the dark curtained area below.

Did she hear some movement? Was someone under there? Hiding maybe?

Chantelle's attention was drawn back to the man, as slowly he removed his clothes, in no hurry, seemingly it all part of the full experience for him. All his clothes were then placed in a neat pile on the bench and she watched as each layer was removed. He then stood completely naked before her.

She looked down at his waist and raised her eyebrows. Smiling, genuinely impressed with what she saw, Chantelle teasingly flicked her tongue out.

Martin's naked form slowly moved, drawing level with another old wooden bench against the wall. Chantelle watched his movements with apprehension and curiosity, knowing she still had to play her part in the ruse as a sex-mad, kinky, young farmer's daughter with a long-held crush. Some role.

Where the hell was Adam? Now. Come in now. Please!

Whatever happened, she knew she was very vulnerable and had to be careful. Worst case, if he simply screwed her against the woodwork whilst restrained, it was hardly the worst job of her life. She'd had much worse. But there was still something weird about the Huntsman and his actions she didn't trust.

Also, each time her eyes flicked toward the dark curtained area beneath the stairs, the more convinced she was that someone, or something lay there.

Martin glanced at the bench, then looked at Chantelle, his face breaking into a sheepish and coy, cheeky grin. She looked back, both as part of her role, but also partly enjoying the excitement. A mix of fear and sexual anticipation stirring within had naturally brought her alive for once.

She looked at the Martin's manhood and he saw Chantelle's eye movement.

Smiling, pausing beside a bench, his grin broadened.

"Do you want it in you?" Martin teased, almost childlike.

"Oh yes," Chantelle replied, tongue moving over her lips.

"Are you sure?" Martin tittered, his eyes dropping down to his erection, his face a wide, child-like grin. He even blushed.

"Yes! Stick it in me. Hard!" Chantelle almost screamed.

Martin laughed - loudly. Too loud. It was becoming scary.

Chantelle didn't laugh. Something was wrong. Very wrong.

She heard movement within the curtained area once more.

For a split second Martin's attention changed. His eyes flicked towards the curtains, his face flushing, focus gone, cursing inwardly.

'Adam! Where the fuck are you? Come in - now!'

Chantelle thought the words out loudly, as if they may work better.

They didn't. Nor would they. Adam still lay on a country road.

Martin moved forward, one hand behind his back.

Chantelle was too streetwise and aware to miss it.

Martin chuckled, gazing in shear lust as Chantelle.

This wasn't what she wanted. Something was wrong.

Fear had replaced any lust. Any desire turned to terror.

"I know who you really are. Whore!" Martin yelled.

Chantelle knew something was wrong and realised the real danger. Worrying thoughts raced through her quick-thinking mind, but she was keen to keep up her pretence and prepare to call his bluff, trying to kid her way to safety.

"Whore. Am I you're little whore for the night? Cheeky!"

She seductively teased with her tone. "Better not be too rough though, or daddy won't let you hunt his land." Chantelle added the joke threat.

Martin seemed to hesitate, his arm behind his back, but then shook his head.

'Was he calling her a whore as some kind of foreplay he enjoyed, or did he really recognise her from when she was with Sarah?'

The frightening thought entered Chantelle's mind. 'He knows.'

Martin stared at Chantelle, naked, only a few feet away.

'What the hell happened to Sarah. And where was Adam?'

Martin seemed to be preparing to speak, but paused, as he heard movement.

Chantelle heard it too. Beneath the stairs. A shuffling and grunting could be heard, but also it seemed something from the house above. Footsteps.

Chantelle's eyes followed Martin's head movements, as he kinked his head.

She preyed it'd be Adam they'd both heard, possibly entering the house.

Ignoring the sounds, job to be done, Martin stepped closer, and spoke.

"You're my whore for the night, because you are a whore. I recognise you. From the dirty streets in Norwich. I knew your friend." Martin's tone was harsh and his look no longer playful but vile and menacing.

Chantelle swallowed, knowing the game was up. Almost.

"That's rude and you're clearly mistaken. Also, I think it's time you let me go. This has gone far enough. I've had enough. Untie me now and I won't tell anyone. Promise. This is no longer fun." Chantelle decided to call his bluff.

She looked towards the cellar stairs, hoping - no, preying - someone would appear. Adam. God, just anyone. Yes, even you God! Someone. Please!

Suddenly their attention was drawn to distinct noises from beneath the stairs.

Grunting and heavy sighing. Animal-like. Something bashed loudly. Metal.

"And what the hell is under there? Something is moving. Is it an animal?"

Martin flicked his focus from Chantelle fully towards the curtained area.

He seemed to become tense and uneasy, but then moved closer to Chantelle, but hesitantly, his arm still hidden, looking fondly at her naked form.

"What have you got hidden under there? A fucking bear!" Chantelle yelled.

Unresponsive, Martin pulled forward the hidden knife. Deadly.

Chantelle stared in horror, tugging her arms at the straps.

The long blade glinted bright in the white cellar light.

Eyes upon the blade, Martin's expression glazed and became unfocussed.

He was lost in the moment, despite anything else about him.

Chantelle knew. She tried to move a foot and then an arm. She pulled at each limb, then all together, writhing and twisting. But no strap yielded. Standing in her heels, her naked form firmly restrained by leather to solid wood, she was truly trapped, which she'd willingly let the mad man before her undertake.

Fool! And where the hell was her Knight in Rusty Armour? Adam!

Seemingly ignoring the increasing sounds of movement in the area beneath the stairs, and equally blind to the soft whimpering cries beginning to emanate from Chantelle, Martin lifted the knife. Firmly clasping the black wood and brass-pinned handle, he gazed fondly at the blade, admiring the steel, running a cautious finger along its fine edge as if it was his best friend. It was.

Then his gaze turned fully to Chantelle. He grinned, stepping forward.

"We need to cut that thong off," Martin whispered insanely. "Then more."
Tears began to run down Chantelle's face. Real tears. She whimpered.
She shook her head. A plea of 'No' was silently uttered from her fine lips.
Martin smiled, chuckling once more. A deep, dark chuckle.
He drew level with Chantelle, the glinting blade thrust out before him; erect, firm in hand and ready for cutting. Teasingly, Martin drew the blade against Chantelle's belly. Instinctively she pulled in her stomach, retracting the tight muscles as the knife moved across, then slid between flesh and thong.
The sharp blade sliced.
Suddenly the cellar door opened.
A man stood at the top of the stairs.
"Adam! Thank god!" Chantelle called, looking up.
At the top of the stairs stood an old man. Not Adam.
"Adam? No! What? Who the…!"
Firmly secured, Chantelle stared at the unknown intruder.
It wasn't Adam, but may have been God. To her he was.
Martin turned to look up too at the unexpected intruder.
Following Chantelle's glance, knife in his grasp, Martin swung around.
Carelessly, as he turned, the lethal tip cut easily through soft white flesh.
Chantelle winced, feeling the hot slash. She looked down.
A fine red line of blood began to grow across her belly.
"Help me! Help," she screamed. "God, help me!"

Chapter 151

I know them all, though they suppose me mad, and will o-erreach them in their own devices; a pair of hell-hounds and their dam!

Titus Act 5.2 - William Shakespeare

"Reggie!" Martin hollered, looking up at the intruder standing on the stairs.

Chantelle raised her vision to the top of the staircase. So it wasn't God.

"Reggie? Reggie! Who the fuck is Reggie?" She called; ignoring the pain to her stomach, looking up to see an old man gazing down, glad of any help.

"What the hell are you doing here?" Martin looked up, seemingly forgetting he was naked, everything on display, as he turned, unaware of Chantelle's cut.

"Reggie?" Another voice mumbled. Soft. Low. A woman's

Chantelle's head turned towards the dark-curtained area.

Martin's head followed too. He cursed, his face going red.

"Reggie! Is that you? Help!" A woman cried. Louder. Distressed.

The dark curtains began to shake, someone behind them. Metal clanked.

Martin switched his attention from Reggie to the covered area beneath the stairs, which was unseen by Reggie, who stood above on the staircase.

"Shut up Sharon!" Martin called towards the curtains.

"Sharon? Is that you?" It was the old man on the stairs, calling down.

"Sharon? Sharon! Who the fuck is Sharon?" Chantelle hollered, staring in amazement at the curtained area. It began to move and shake, as if grabbed, aware someone or something was clearly hiding behind the heavy black drape.

Suddenly, pulled from within and tugged hard, the black curtain fell free.

A metal cage was exposed beneath the stairs. A dishevelled woman peered out from the metal bars; red, sleepy eyes blinking in the bright light.

"Who the fuck are you?" Chantelle called out, confused looking at her.

The dishevelled woman looked pitifully at Chantelle strapped to the beams.

"Sharon. His wife. Help me. Oh, you can't. Reggie! Help us. Please!"

Chantelle's eyes flicked about the room, now feeling pain to her stomach. Looking down, a fine line of red blood flowed on her firm white flesh.

Martin's gaze became frantic and his actions likewise. His attention switched from Reggie, to the bleeding whore tied to the crossbeams, then to Sharon.

Sharon, now seemingly awake, hollered wildly from the metal cage beneath the stairs, where Martin had kept her securely drugged since murdering Sarah.

Knife in hand, standing naked and exposed to all, Martin's confused and crumbling world was beginning to devastatingly implode all around him.

"Martin! What the hell are you doing?" Reggie stared down at the naked woman tied to the wooden beams in the cellar, now clearly bleeding. He then instantly recognised her as being the stunning hussy from the ball.

"Reggie! Help me, please! It's Sharon," the woman below him called out.

Reggie heard Sharon's cry from beneath the cellar staircase where he stood, and cautiously looked over the handrail. Hidden beneath where he stood he could see nothing, but clearly recognised Sharon's familiar voice.

"Sharon? Is that you? What on earth has happened?" Reggie yelled.

"Martin has gone mad. Mad! He's kept me prisoner down here. Help!"

Reggie's wild eyes returned to glare at his Huntsman. The look was returned.

"Martin! What is going on? What on earth are you doing to that poor girl, and where the hell is Sharon? What have you done? I thought she was dead!"

Reggie hollered at Martin, who stared at his boss, his vacant stare and glazed look a mix of fear and respect, but also deep hated.

Reggie began to stomp down the staircase, his feet heavy in his haste to get to the bottom. Chantelle watched in amazement, unsure what was happening, hoping that at any moment Adam would appear and photograph the lot.

This would now give him a true Front-page blockbuster.

'Fighting Pervert Huntsmen with a Caged Wife.' What an amazing story.

And Adam was missing it! Where the hell was he? He'd let her down.

Reggie reached the bottom of the stairs as Martin moved away, knife held before him, warding off Reggie. But he ignored Martin and instead stepped towards Chantelle, aware of the long bleeding wound to her stomach, and then saw in full the caged area, part-hidden beneath the stairs, where the black drape had fallen down. Here a bedraggled Sharon peered at him through the bars, her hands reaching out at him like some medieval beggar in a gaol.

There was too much for him to comprehend and he regarded Sharon with a sense of shock and horror; mainly because he thought she was dead, but also because of her state and where she'd been kept prisoner.

His attention turned to Martin, shuffling about the cellar floor, away from Reggie, moving around the walls and back to the base of the stairs.

"What the hell is going on Martin? Explain!" He yelled.

Martin looked at his master, then at Sharon, all sense gone from his world.

"Martin, look at that poor girl!" It was Sharon yelling, an arm stretching through the bars, seemingly regaining some awareness, having been asleep or drugged whilst restrained in the blacked-out metal cage to keep her quiet.

"You've cut that poor girl. Look! She's bleeding. Just like the other one you killed. It can't happen again. Help her Martin. Please! Reggie, stop him!"

Martin looked on, for the first time seeing in full the cut to Chantelle's stomach. A fresh wave of panic overwhelmed him upon seeing the blood, as memories of Sarah's horrific death flooded back. He turned his head from Chantelle to Sharon, then wildly back to Reggie, who was stepping forward, closing in on Martin. Only the waving and slashing knife kept him back.

"Keep away from me, or you'll get it Reggie!" He lunged with the knife, raising it up, waving it at Reggie's face in a deadly and vicious slash.

"You're going to die. I know what you did. Killer!" Martin screamed.

Reggie glared at Martin. Sharon gazed on. Chantelle bled. It was a mess.

But the old hunter was quicker than Martin thought. Reggie sidestepped and lunged forward himself, grabbing at Martin's wrist, trying to restrain any movement of the deadly knife, and forced Martin back and his arm down.

Martin let out a sharp curse as the tip of the blade cut deep into the top of his thigh, the impact and pain causing him to fall sideways, crashing against the bars of Sharon's cage. She didn't miss any chance of retribution and leant forward. Martin suddenly felt her teeth sink into a free finger, as Sharon bit deep and hard down to the bone, causing him to swear loudly and scream.

Martin pulled back, now clasping his bitten finger, then saw Reggie approach again. He moved around the cellar wall, stepping back to where Chantelle was tied, Reggie moving forward. Reggie lunged again and Martin crashed against Chantelle's body, only to feel her knee harshly half raise into the back of his knee. It forced him away fully with her flexed torso, her hips and lightly bleeding stomach pushing him away and back into the central cellar area.

Martin's bare flesh was now smeared with blood. The bitten finger dripped heavily. A slow steady flow ran down his leg from the small thigh stab, and upon his backside and legs, Chantelle's warm blood covered his buttock area.

Reggie stepped towards him, clearly set upon grabbing his employee. Then in a manoeuvre any rugby winger would have been proud to pull off, Martin moved forward, did a double dummy sidestep and then leapt forward and straight past Reggie. With an extended arm into his face Reggie, went crashing into the wall, falling at the high-heeled feet of a steadily bleeding Chantelle.

Knife firmly in his hand, Martin frantically dashed up the cellar stairs, aware Reggie would be following close behind him. Grabbing at the cellar door, fumbling for the small handle, the knife slipped. Scrabbling to recover it, the knife fell and Martin bitterly watched as it clattered over the edge of the stairs.

He looked down at the knife, and then at Reggie, who rising, gazed back up. He was seemingly in a mixed mind whether to chase Martin, help the bleeding woman, or go to Sharon's aid. Martin noted his quick furtive glance.

The confusion and delay worked to Martin's benefit. He turned, wrenched open the cellar door, then fled out into the kitchen, to run on and out into the small out-house. Still in a daze, he rushed out into the alley, about to dash out towards where his Rover, and probably Reggie's were both parked. But he cursed, realising he had no keys, and noted Reggie had bolted the alley gate, preventing any easy exit from the main house and away onto the paddocks.

Wasting no more time, and with no plans, the naked form of Martin dashed on, heading into the courtyard ahead, which held the Drawing Yard. The gate to the yard swung open freely. Martin knew it should've been bolted and he shook his head at his or someone's slackness or incompetence, but thought no more as he dashed into the far dark corner of the yard, where some old tarpaulins and crates were kept; thoughts of hiding foremost in his mind.

Controlling his heavy breathing, he stood silent in the dark yard corner.

Hidden from everything in the gloom of the shadows and quiet he began to shiver from the cold and lack of clothing. Ahead of him, somewhere in the yard were the hounds, strangely still and quiet. Martin squatted, his focus on the gate into the yard, waiting for Reggie to come racing in the find him.

Nothing came nor moved. Silence. Martin gazed intently at the gate.

Where was Reggie? What was he doing? He would be there any second.

Martin heard movement. Something damp touched his bare leg.

He heard a rustle. Movement. Small feet.

Another damp muzzle sniffed his buttocks.

He spun around in the darkness, his hands instinctively covering his exposed genitals as he began to feel the cold. Another nose, then small toe nailed feet stood upon his, causing him to flinch backwards and against the damp wall.

'The hounds are loose. Shit!' The worrying thought raced through his mind; concern for them being out and loose initially more than anything else.

Then he smiled. Reggie wouldn't dare enter the yard to find him here.

A perfect diversion. Luck was on his side. Hidden amongst the hounds.

In the pitch black, Martin tried to see how many hounds were loose.

One or two? Clearly a few more. Or the whole pack? No. He hoped not.

He felt another muzzle brush against his hip. He waved his hands towards it, shooing it away. Then one jumped up beside him, harsh nails scratching the bare skin of his leg. He cursed, swinging his hands out, striking the hound.

Then he saw a familiar face. The hound stood before him, only feet away.

Out of the gloom appeared an image he both loved and feared. Maverick.

Martin could make out the dark intelligent eyes. Too intelligent.

Beside Maverick stood the small form of Christmas. Alongside her Mayhem.

Other hounds seemed to mill about behind their three new leaders.

Their new masters. No longer Martin. Martin was worried.

"Hullo," he spoke softly to Maverick, leaning forward, extending his hand in a friendly gesture, as he had many times before. "You have to be quiet boy."

A small muzzle sniffed his backside. Christmas.

She'd cleverly left Maverick and moved in behind him in the dark.

A probing nose sniffed at his blood-covered buttocks.

Her nose drifted down an inch. Martin flinched.

Sharp teeth sank into Martin's scrotum with a crunch.

Martin instinctively screamed and stood upright.

Christmas naturally pulled back, tugging hard, grip tight.

Maverick lunged forward, biting at Martin's penis.

With a hound to his rear and hound to his front Martin screamed and swirled about in pain and confusion, spinning the two attached hounds with him.

Mayhem leapt, jumping at his master, to unbalance Martin, who fell down and sideways, the two hounds attached. Pulling violently, heads twisting, teeth sinking deeper, the hounds ripped delicate flesh away from his flaying body.

An unknown hound moved in. It seized at Martin's throat. A fatal bite.

A natural instinctive strike, the powerful jaws clamped tight, crushing the larynx and silencing any scream, as blood flowed into his throat.
Turning his head in vain, already dying, Martin gazed towards the gate.
There stood the silhouetted image of a man. Reggie.
Martin's mouth opened, but no sound erupted forth.
As more hounds closed in, Martin heard the distinct clunk of the gate being securely shut and fastened. Then locked. Securely.
In the gloom he saw Reggie staring in silence. Watching.
The last sound Martin heard was footsteps. Walking away.
Other hounds piled in, snapping at flaying limbs, grasping fingers, all swiftly chomped off. Legs muscles were bitten and torn free, toes and feet gone. His arms were bitten and flesh torn, as multiple mouths destroyed Martin's body.
The hounds ripped and tore the bare flesh, each removing a preferred chunk.
With their piece of flesh the hounds scurried away to heartedly consume.
The bony sections were left for the younger hounds to pick over.
The head would be burnt later.
Game on! Job done.

Chapter 152

The pale-faced moon looks bloody on the earth.
And lean-looked prophets whisper fearful change.

Richard II - William Shakespeare

It'd been a great night. Anna felt a fresh pang of excitement as Chris drove the Rover back to Horsewater. Passing through the wooded entrance, Anna grinned at the 'Trespassers Will Be Eaten' sign; something only months ago she'd seen with worried eyes, but which now she saw as a dark playful joke.

They passed through the woods, which now felt to her almost like a second home. Exiting into the opening, illuminated by a bright moon, the white house and stables lay before her, with the paddocks and big woods beyond.

She opened the Rover door with a warm heart. Slightly merry from a good few glasses of wine, but not too many for her not to be aware of everything; she was certainly aware of wanting to end a wonderful evening with the man who now stood behind her. Thoughts seemingly attuned, Chris wrapped his arms warmly around her tall, slim frame as they shuffled about the yard.

"Look," he whispered, extending an arm past her body, pointing a finger to the full moon and sky. "Halo around the moon, rain coming soon!"

"You what?" Anna questioned with a chuckle, looking up at the moon.

"There. Look. A halo of light is set around the moon. Ice crystals in the high sky. Cold weather and rain are coming." Chris nodded at his own fact.

Anna gazed at the hazy sky. A distinct fine white ring was clearly set some distance around the moon. She smiled, turning her head and kissing his cheek.

Almost as if contrived, came a soft honking sound, which increased in level. The pair gazed up at the silvery sky, then totally on cue, drifting over from the woods passed a small flock of geese. Flying low overhead and in perfect formation, their gentle honks and soft wing beats enchanted the gazing pair.

Turning around, still in silent awe, they watched the dark silhouetted flock disappear, soon obscured by the back wood. Anna turned to face an equally bewitched and smiling Chris, who turned his head. She kissed him fully, and then felt his arms grip her body, Anna welcoming his warmth and touch.

"That's what I love about you," Anna announced simply, as she broke the embrace. "You never stop amazing me. Simple things, but magical."

She gazed into his face, only to see his attention and focus switch, as he looked over her shoulder and away. Disappointed by the apparent rejection, she realised it wasn't as she felt, as his body became tense, as his attention fixed upon something else down the yard. Anna spun her head around too.

In the darkness the pair stood side by side, the air chilly.

Something moved within the yard area. A small dark figure. Human.

Upon seeing the image, Anna felt her blood turn to ice. An intruder.
But worse. Anna sensed she knew instantly who or what it was.
No PIR lights came on, the yard lit only by the hazy silver moon.
Chris intently watched the form, cautiously waiting for a light to switch on and add depth and size to the dark prowler. But no PIR lights came on.
The prowler had skilfully shot them all out with a silenced air-rifle moments earlier, all the positions known from previous visits. They knew it all.
Boldly, and seemingly unafraid, the darkened shape of the intruder moved away from the small barn, from which it'd exited, and stood proudly within the middle of the yard. Face and eyes unseen, covered by a dark hoodie, it stared menacingly at the couple, and then dashed sideways into darkness.
Chris moved in front of Anna, almost pushing her aside, forcibly behind him.
"Anna, go straight over to the house. Open the door and let out Max. Now. Then stay in the house. Do it. Now. Move!"
Anna held her breath, freezing, unsure and nervous.
Her eyes flitted about the yard then over towards the house.
The big door key, pushed into her hand by Chris, awoke her senses.
Anna's eyes went from the figure to the house. She felt Chris' hand.
She hesitated, her tenses dulled, but also unsure and afraid.
"Go. Now!" Chris issued the order, then nimbly moving to the side of the stable block, in a strategic action, over to an area where brushes, forks and shovels were kept. A long-handled pitchfork was then in his hands.
Anna began to run across the yard, forgetting she was wearing heels, and wrung her ankle. Almost dropping onto the ground, she recovered, flicking the heels off her feet, then rose, to dash barefoot towards the house door on just her toes. Glancing back over to the yard, she could see Chris moving along the front of the stables, the deadly pitchfork poised in his hands.
A number of curious equine heads rose over the stable doors. The grey head of Cirrus appeared, to dash back, the commotion far too scary. The chestnut head and nose of Tirus appeared. He stood bold and brave, watching on.
Anna swiftly made it over to the house, moving up to the door. She fumbled with the big key in the lock, half her attention on the door, the other on the activity in the yard. Then Anna saw the figure appear again in the darkness.
Moving quickly, it seemed to be skirting away from the barn and back over towards the stables, hiding in the shadows. But Chris didn't notice.
"Chris! Careful. Over there!" Anna called, causing him to turn and face her. "Coming towards you! Side of the stables. Look out!"
Glancing back at the door, Anna saw Max's face peering silently through the glass panel, seemingly unaware of the action. She fumbled with the key, trying to put it in the lock, but something seemed to have been jammed inside the lock, preventing the large iron key from sliding securely into place. It had.
A small piece of wood had been forced into the lock. All planned.
No one was going to let the guard dog out in a hurry.

"Chris! I can't get the key in the door. It's jammed. Max is stuck inside."

Anna was unsure if Chris heard her or not. His attention was set upon the person now standing before him in the middle of the yard.

They were set for a fight. Stance firm and solid. Unafraid.

Empty hands hung loosely to each side. Ready for action.

Unseen eyes stared. This person was a trained fighter.

Chris toyed with the pitchfork, adjusting it in his hands.

Like a Western movie, each regarded the other. Game on!

Chris took the initiative and moved on a step, pitchfork held forward, but at a slight angle. The prowler remained stationary; feet set shoulder-width apart, waiting and ready for the first strike. Clearly fearless or mad. Or both

Anna stood shaking by the door as Chris advanced upon the motionless dark figure. Max barked from within as she forlornly gazed with helpless eyes.

With no warning, threats, or chance to escape, Chris turned the pitchfork. The long sharp prongs pointed forward as he approached the intruder, and then he thrust straight at he dark figure. The prowler sidestepped the action, spun and then stood bold, almost like a Bullfighter avoiding the deadly horns.

Anna stared in silent amazement from the house door, hand to her mouth.

Chris readjusted his position and instantly thrust again. The prowler moved with lightening speed, sidestepping, but also moved forward a step just as Chris thrust the deadly tool. Dark-gloved hands skilfully gripped the smooth Ash handle just above the prongs, then, seemingly in a well-trained move, spun around, twisting the shaft and caused Chris to release his grip and trip.

The prowler, firmly grasping the front end of the fork, spun it around in a singular sweeping motion. Then with full force, swung the wooden handle through the air. The top end of the handle was aimed at Chris' head. It hit.

Even standing away over at the house door Anna heard the dull clunk.

Chris' body almost lifted off the ground with the violent impact. Head and neck arching horrifically sideways, his collapsing body following. Pole-axed, his motionless form crumpled onto the cold compacted so of the yard.

Anna screamed, her hero and saviour so easily beaten. In one strike.

Then she watched, as in a simply singular movement, the prowler flipped the pitchfork around and raised the handle, with the deadly prongs poised a few feet above Chris' motionless body, ready to thrust into his prone body.

Anna was off. Anger, bravery or stupidity, she was unsure which - maybe all three - caused her to run barefoot from the house and straight towards Chris.

Help or attack. Who knew? She didn't, but just yelled out and ran. Full pelt.

The prowler paused, seeing and hearing Anna and looked down, sensing no movement from the body beneath them. In a professional manner, they stepped away and carefully lay the pitchfork against the wall of stable block.

As Anna raced across the cold yard surface and rapidly drew closer to the hooded attacker, now clearly seeing Chris' motionless body and the calmness of the prowler, grim realisation of many things brought back to her real fear.

Approaching the attacker, she was unsure what to do. She was no fighter.
But to the prowler a fresh contender stood before them. Or the target.
Anna gazed at the hooded figure, curious of their next action.
'They've pit down the pitchfork. The main weapon. But why?'
The question ran through Anna's mind.
She should have known the answer. Maybe she did.
But she was no street fighter. Naïve. Stupid. Very stupid.
Anna's rapid progress forward now slowed to a stuttered walk.
Then she stopped. Anna now knew she was in real danger.
In the silver glow of the moon she stood before the attacker.
Face unseen, Anna suddenly realised Chris wasn't the target.
He'd simply got in the way. Now he was gone. Job done.
The attacker's real target was now before them. Anna.
She sensed the hidden face smiled. Pleased. Game on!
The prowler stood relaxed, reached behind and withdrew a concealed tactical dagger. Darkened, it did not glint, but even in the silver glow Anna knew its real danger. A long, slender blade, it had a minor area of saw-teeth at the hilt, but the main blade was fine, edged each side, ending at a deadly sharp point.
The prowler raised their hands, grabbing at the sides of the hood, dagger carefully held in one hand as their face was revealed.
Anna shook, from both cold and fear, staring intently.
Inside she knew enough from watching too many scary films.
Whenever an attacker revealed themselves, they usually mean to kill.
This person was clearly going to kill her. She would die. Tonight.
It was the Dark Monk who'd haunted all her dreams.
The figure, in a dramatic fashion, fully lowered their hood.
"Hello Sweetie!" The woman spoke softly.
Face revealed, a wide smile set, Anna knew her killer.
All colour drained from Anna's face and she shook.
Then Anna almost screamed out the name.
"Lucy!"

Chapter 153

Give me the daggers. I'll do it, then.
Saying that the sleeping and the dead are but as pictures ....

Macbeth - William Shakespeare

"Well that is an introduction. Rather dramatic. Are you pleased to see me?"
Lucy fluttered her eyelashes, head tilted in playful manner as she spoke.
Anna looked on in shock, but secretly had thought she'd be in danger from Lucy at some point. Maybe a punch in the face. But this? Extreme.
Anna looked sadly down at Chris. He wasn't moving and from where she stood, could not see if he was breathing. She felt tears begin to well up.
Lucy saw Anna's look down and pitifully shook her head.
"Don't worry about him. He'll either wake up with one-hell-of a headache. Or he won't. Shame. He thought a lot of you, from what I've seen. Even helped stop me killing you a few weeks back in the woods. That would have been better. Discrete. Would have looked more like a real accident. Ho hum."
Anna shook with both fear and anger, now knowing whom she'd seen in the woods and that it wasn't imagined. The Dark Monk was real. It was Lucy.
"What do you want?" Anna could feel her voice quiver.
Lucy simply stared back; either adding to the tension on purpose, or didn't know how to respond. She shrugged her shoulders in a vague, casual manner.
"Haven't you done enough damage?" Anna said. "Stole my husband. Ruined our lives. Now attacked Chris. Why? What have I ever done to you?"
"He still loves you. Bruce. He wants you. Still. Not me. Bastard!"
Lucy's response was cold and direct. Filled with anger.
Anna stared, unsure how to respond hearing the truth.
She felt warmth that Bruce clearly had feelings for her, and had obviously told Lucy, but he was gone. History. Too much had happened.
She looked down at Chris, motionless. Tears formed.
Now the person standing so cold before her had taken away her new love.
Anna felt anger and glared coldly at Lucy, releasing fury.
"Bruce probably hates you 'cos you're a fucking nutter!"
Anna was unsure where the words came from, but she felt bitterness build inside, and her strength grow too. "And I can't blame him. You're mad!"
Lucy chuckled, the dagger held professionally before her.
She caught Anna's eyes flick towards the lethal blade. Lucy smiled.
"Do you like this? It's nice. I like it. Only a five-inch blade, but more than enough to damage all the key organs. If thrust correctly. Razor-sharp edges too. Cuts well. And such a fine point. Slips into skin so easily. It's beautiful."
Lucy spoke so clearly about the weapon, as if selling it on a TV channel.

Anna looked at the knife Lucy lovingly held, regarding the deadly instrument.
"And it sits within a concealed sheath and back harness. Quick and easy to pull out from behind you; but no-one knows its there. A bit like me!"
Anna looked with deepening concern as Lucy gazed at the blade, regained some composure, then grinned at Anna. She shuffled her feet as Lucy moved, dagger poised ahead of her and ready, held out like true knife-fighter.
"And do you know what is best of all about it?" said Lucy.
Anna shook a worried head, not wanting to answer.
"It's great for cutting stuck-up skinny sluts. Like you!"
Lucy strode purposefully towards Anna, who nervously stepped backwards and then turned. Foolishly she found herself trapped with her back against the stables and slid with her back to them. Lucy moved in, then paused, as if relishing the moment, savouring the time before striking the final blow.
Anna wanted to cry. And she also wanted to pee. Badly.
Quivering, Anna felt helpless, but knew that was just her.
Images of her dad, brave and strong, flashed before her.
Lucy sensed her weakness and smiled. An easy kill. Pity.
Playfully she lunged with the knife. No more than a jab.
Anna shuffled swiftly along the stable front, the blade missing her, but she disturbed the horses within. Lucy instantly followed her sideways stride, like a chess piece playing Mate, not permitting any easy escape.
Lucy lunged again, the blade deadly close this time, missing by inches.
Anna knew that any moment it'd be Checkmate.
Lucy laughed, stepping back. The next strike would be it.
A head appeared, rising up, attached to a staggering body.
Chris rose between her and Lucy, forming a human shield.
Lucy looked shocked, not expecting anything to be between her and the intended victim as she made her deadly lethal stab. Her eyes widened, curious as to where the man had suddenly come from, although she knew.
Clearly she'd not hit him hard enough with the fork handle. Mistake.
The firmly thrust blade made contact with flesh and bone. A groan.
With force it cut deep. As intended. But not within Anna. Chris.
Anna winced as she heard the dagger punch easily through Chris' clothing, then into his stomach. She heard his deep groan as Lucy swiftly withdrew the blade, cursing as to his unwelcome interference and stupid heroics. Again.
Then Anna watched in horror as Chris' body collapsed, his knees buckling, to force her own body back against the woodwork of the stables once more.
He fell down, then made no further sound. Collapsing heavily, his body rolled into the yard. Chris' vanishing body revealed another form. Lucy.
She stood again before Anna, close, lit up in the silver hue of the moon.
Her eyes looked hard at Anna; black and mad. She smiled. A deadly smile.
"I was going to let him live. Nice chap. Brave but stupid. How silly. Noble, but a pointless act, as you're going to die. Ho hum. Never mind."

Anna's eyes flicked down at Chris' body, laying just away from her feet. She slid sideways along the stables, feeling the rough wood behind her, passing doorways with horses inside, all shuffling about at the commotion outside.
Lucy moved across in front of her, smiling, dagger poised, ready again.
Anna pressed herself helplessly against another stable door, wincing, wanting to cry, seemingly ready for her own final fate as Lucy lunged forward again.
With a long sweeping strike, Anna sidestepped and ducked simultaneously, but the knife blade made contact, slicing across her face. Anna screamed, feeling the hot blade upon her cheek, plunging into her face and slicing.
She slid along the stable, then stumbled, causing Lucy to trip and fall forward and take her position. Back to the stable door, Lucy smiled in the darkness.
Anna tried to raise herself, but knew it was futile, being in pain and shock. She placed a hand upon her face, blood streaming between her fingers, a wide flap of skin cut open across her cheek. Anna could feel blood flowing into her mouth, knowing the cut was deep and through. She felt sick and dizzy.
Lucy stood boldly with her back to the stable door, gazing down at the stricken Anna only a few feet away, half on the concrete pad, half in the yard.
"Fucking bitch. That'll leave a nice scar. But why settle for that? I'll slice off those lovely lips, then those big ears. Finally that neat little nose. Maybe stab you in the womb. See if Bruce fancies you after some reconstructive surgery!"
Anna felt faint, tried to rise onto her knees, but the trauma of the injury and all that'd happened had taking its toll. She was beaten. Lucy had won. Bitch!
Lucy looked down, adjusting the grip on the knife handle, as if determining how best to strike at the stricken victim. Kill first, or slice pieces off for fun?
In the dark she grinned. Cut her up. Nose or those big ears? Which first?'
A head appeared. But behind Lucy. So it was unseen. And it was swift.
Bonnie lunged with force and bit Lucy straight in the back of the neck.
Lucy howled, partially slumping down, both through the trauma of the hard bite from the unseen horse behind, but also the shock of being attacked by an unknown assailant. She rose, turned, looking into the gloom, ready to strike at whoever had attacked her. But Bonnie was too quick. Teeth bared, she flew again, smashing her teeth fully into Lucy's face, and jaw fully on Lucy's head.
Anna heard the painful crack of horse jaw upon human skull. The force of Bonnie's attack sent Lucy crashing down, dagger dropping from her hand, her head hitting the edge of the concrete pad to finish her off as she collapsed.
Falling with shock and pain, Anna lay in a heap, the cold and damp of the yard seeping through her dress as she glazed at the silver glow of the moon.
Glancing up, Anna gazed lovingly at her saviour, Bonnie. As the aggressive coloured horse looked down at her over the stable door, before she passed out, Anna was sure she saw the grumpy horse smile. Maybe even wink.
High above in the moonlight another formation of geese flew by, their wing beats and soft honks missed by all, as the three bodies lay silent in the yard.

Chapter 154

We are such stuff as dreams are made on;
and our little life is rounded with a sleep.

The Tempest - Shakespeare

Steve was sober, but clearly over the limit, as was Izzy, but neither cared. Steve had booked a taxi a week earlier and the totally reliable local company and driver had arrived at the hotel in good time to collect his awaited fare.

The journey back was quiet, with a contented couple relaxing in the back, snug in each other's arms, the taxi driver quietly looked in the mirror.

Clearly the lovers had only just met. A long-established couple wouldn't be so close, and most likely one or the other, or both, would be bickering or complaining about some aspect of the evening. But this couple were happy.

The driver had picked up Steve and Izzy earlier in the evening, so knew the route back in the dark. Turning into the wooded entrance of the property, he smiled at the sign. 'Trespassers Will Be Eaten'. His kind of humour.

Driving through the dark woodland section of the small farm, he thought his headlights caught the rear reflectors of a small vehicle, parked deep in the woods, just off a small track. He glanced in the mirror at the occupants, about to make a comment, or to see if either of them had noticed it, but seemingly they hadn't, or simply didn't care. The woman had her head nestled in the man's chest and he was playfully prodding at her legs. The taxi driver smiled and turned his attention to the rutted track, knowing he'd soon be finished.

He arrived in a wide-open area, and driving past various bits of farm equipment and Portacabin, pulled up outside the large white house. He admired its size and beauty and dreamed that one day he too might have such a place. Certainly not by driving taxi's he sighed internally.

"We're here chaps. Home sweet home. Off to bed!"

"Thank you so much," Steve responded, the sentiment agreed heartedly by Izzy, who seemed to half stumble out of the taxi with a giggle. Steve chuckled as he passed the driver a bunch of notes. Twice the cost of the fare, it was gratefully received by the driver with many warm and genuine thanks.

A wave from the man and a giggle from the tipsy woman told the taxi driver their night wasn't over. By a long way. For them, it seemed their night was just about to begin. Sometime tomorrow they'd both wake up, most likely with raging headaches, but hopefully no regrets. Who knew?

That was his last fare for the night, and it'd been worth the wait late for the big tip. The taxi trundled back through the woods, the driver interested in getting home. Thoughts of looking for any car parked up in the woods were gone. Besides, it was probably one of the owners. It wasn't his problem or concern. He simply wanted to get home and into his own bed. Quickly.

Thoughts of getting into bed were far from the mind of the person squatting in the woods beside a large Ash tree. They hoped the car wasn't seen.

They smiled, noting the taxi had now disappeared. 'Game on!'

Back in the warmth and comfort of the house, getting into bed was all Steve and Izzy could think about. The fresh air had semi-sobered Izzy, but the chill of the night made her grab at Steve, shuddering for some warmth. And more.

"Brrr! I'm cold!" she shivered. "I hope that bed is warm."

"It soon will be. It'll be red hot!" Steve chuckled loudly.

Izzy laughed as they bundled towards the porch, a security light illuminating brightly as Steve fumbled for the keys. Izzy shook in the long, thin red satin dress, her legs cold, and the red satin shoes on her feet now damp.

"Hurry up! I want to get inside!" Izzy berated.

"So do I. Oh, so do I!" Steve chuckled and grabbed at Izzy.

"Just get me inside; then you can fuck the life out of me!"

Steve delicately kissed Izzy and opened the door.

"To my bedchamber wench!"

Chapter 155

The boundaries which divide life from death are at best shadowy and vague. Who shall say where the one ends and where the other begins?

Edgar Allan Poe

Izzy awoke. Dreamily. Dave Pearson stood before her.

"What do you want Dave? Go away. I'm sleeping."

Her response was automatic. Dreamlike.

But this was no dream.

She opened her eyes wide. Awake.

Or was she? Maybe still part drunk?

"Dave?" She spoke aloud. Dream or nightmare?

A clamping hand silenced her enquiring voice.

Nightmare. A real nightmare. A night terror. Real terror.

She began to writhe and gasp for breath, still unsure in her semi-sleepy state if she was in a weird deep dream or if this was all really happening.

It was. This was no dream. Nightmare.

Her noise and writhing movements awoke Steve.

"What's the matter sweetheart? Dreaming?"

He turned in the bed, partly awake and looked to Izzy.

Then at the man, dressed in black, leaning over her.

One hand was clamped firmly upon her face, the other out of his sight, almost hidden. Then it appeared. Quickly.

A massive steel blade. Bright. Lethal. The Swiss bayonet.

In one swift flowing movement Pearson lunged violently.

The bright steel blade flew down towards its target. Steve.

Arms free of the duvet, Steve raised one to fend off the deadly blow.

But he raised his broken arm. The shining steel blade of the bayonet smashed firmly into the bright pink fibreglass cast. The tip crashed heavily into the hard material, partially penetrated, but instantly becoming stuck; wedged partly in the fibreglass arm cast and partly in Steve's broken arm.

Steve howled in pain; both from the force impacting into his badly damaged broken limb, but also the new pain, as the blade tip penetrated deep.

With Pearson laying over her, now indirectly attached to Steve, Izzy wriggled from the duvet. She threw her right arm hard into the skinny Anti's stomach. He howled at the firm hard punch, and crumpled atop the two bodies.

Steve was already moving and slid from the duvet on his side of the bed and the mass of bodies. Bayonet still stuck in his arm, he pulled himself free of the bed and span around in a mess of limbs, bodies and bedding. As he rose, Izzy wriggled free and bit Pearson's wrist hard, so he lost his grip of the bayonet.

Steve slid free of the bed, his cast arm extended high, with the bayonet weirdly attached. He then found Izzy's hand firmly upon the bayonet handle. With a swift yank, followed by a scream from Steve as the blade withdrew, the bayonet was free and in Izzy's grasp, as she slid off the end of the bed. In a whirling mass of confusion, Pearson, still gasping for breath from the blow, and now with an injured wrist, found he was the only body now on the bed.

Dressed in black he rose up and turned about on the soft bed. Legs entwined in duvet, trying to free and loosened himself, he looked at Izzy.

His beloved bayonet in his beloved's hand. A fine match.

Izzy wasn't sure if Pearson moved onto the blade himself, or she thrust it.

It didn't matter. It happened.

The twelve inches of polished steel slid through his body.

Pearson smiled. Izzy Screamed. Steve yelled.

Steve clambered around the bed to see Izzy thrust the blade into Pearson a second time. Then a third. By the fourth strike Pearson was on the bedroom floor and Steve was once more fighting with his wife. But it didn't take much. No punch to the head this time. He just grasped her wrist and twisted the bayonet free, but not until Izzy had struck for a fifth time.

The bayonet was now in Steve's hand and she simply stood beside him.

In the half-light of the room the pair looked at the dying figure of the Anti each hated. Neither spoke nor moved. Nor helped. Just looked.

The black clothing Pearson wore hid the large dark pools of blood flowing beneath from his heavily wounded body. One of his aortic valves had been punched, and so he had minutes to live, or less. The liver had been sliced, streaming out blood and the third strike had hit him in the stomach.

The fourth was in his back as he fell and then rolled over.

The fifth had only partly struck the back of his neck, as Steve grasped Izzy's hand, but would semi-paralyse most, just as Steve pulled Izzy away.

But the five wounds were enough to kill. Easily. One would do.

Pearson had minutes to live or less. Less. Twenty-two seconds actually.

Steve and Izzy weren't sure if or what Pearson thought as he lay on their bedroom floor, gazing at the pair and rapidly bled out.

Maybe little, dying from shock and organ failure, mixed with loss of blood from multiple stabs wounds. He blacked out and died.

The first strike had technically been enough to kill.

The other two blows could be considered as 'excessive.'

The fourth blow to the back wasn't in any legal way defensive. Aggressive.

The fifth would be legally classed as wholly unnecessary. Very unnecessary.

Unless you knew Dave Pearson.

Then they all counted. Maybe even more.

But to Izzy they were necessary. All of them. And overdue.

Steve wouldn't have disagreed. But he was more clinical in his appraisal of the situation, and could see the true implications, as he began to explain.

An act of self-defence by a frightened couple in their own home, whilst asleep in their own bed. Good reasons to stab an unknown intruder.
By an embittered, deranged person who hated the couple. More so.
All good, clear, and valid legal reasons for them to kill him.
But Steve had history with Pearson. A case was pending.
That wouldn't look good. And Steve was no angel.
And Izzy wasn't an angel either. She had previous. Done time.
Five stabs wounds would be deemed excessive.
Especially the two in the back and neck. Nasty. Not needed.
And a jury may think otherwise with regards to Izzy.
She had a criminal conviction for excessive violence.
The outlook wasn't good for anyone.
Something had to be done.
And quickly.

Chapter 156

In death - no! Even in the grave all is not lost.
Else there is no immortality for man.

Edgar Allan Poe

Steve quickly found Pearson's car in the woods; partially hidden beside a holly bush, down one of the sidetracks. Izzy told Steve that Dave used to park up on various hunt members properties, creep about like a commando and spy on them; his home included no doubt, though he never admitted it to her. Izzy deduced that he wouldn't have walked too far, not in his condition. Thus, a quick drive around the boundaries of the farm, in the two wooded areas and tracks bordering Steve's farm soon revealed his old beat-up car.

The keys were placed on top of the rear wheel, just where Izzy said they'd most likely be, and after which, Steve drove the old car down to the farm.

The pair carried Pearson body down the stairs, out the house door and over to his car. Each had furtively looked for an unexpected visitor to suddenly arrive when his body was outside, but it was the early hours, and no one did.

Pearson's carcass was then unceremoniously dumped in the boot of the car.

Whenever shown on TV, or in movies, it looks so easy. But Steve was strong and Izzy not feeble either. However, moving the lifeless and unyielding body out of the bedroom, down the stairs and through the hall and lobby was not an easy job. Despite being skinny and having no bulk, it was still a heavy and cumbersome load to carry. Not unlike trying to manoeuvre four bags of horse feed, all tied together, but with flaying parts added on to complicate matters.

Once outside, with a huge effort from Steve, Dave's corpse was finally lifted up and dumped into the boot of the old car, his skinny arms and legs carelessly pushed into the boot recesses and head covered by an old feedbag.

Izzy had put the old horse-mix bag over his face, to hide the cold and cursing glare his dead eyes emitted. Boot lid slammed shut, neither bothered to take one last look or say any final consoling words. Dave Pearson was no more.

Like discarding rubbish or unwanted clothing at the tip. Gone.

As the exhausted pair gazed silently at the closed boot, Steve put an arm around Izzy. A breeze blew, the wind seemingly blowing a final lament, but it was the only thing that seemed to care anything for Dave Pearson.

'Bye Dave. You'll be missed.' - But by who? Maybe the rats.

No such words were necessary. No one would miss Dave. No one?

Izzy drove the small car, in which she'd spent many days as an Anti alongside Dave, back up into the woods. It was as she was drove the car, recalling the uneven chug of the small engine and squeaky suspension, that the significance ...t she and Steve had just done began to slowly creep into her mind.

Until then everything had happened at speed; fuelled by adrenaline and an urgent need to simply complete a task both wanted undertaken to save both of their futures. Any morals or legal aspects of the activity seemed to have been totally overlooked or dismissed, the only requirement being to just complete the grim task, it overtaking all other thoughts and concerns.

Now Izzy was alone in the old car, Dave with her once more, but in the boot and very dead. Tears began to roll down her face. Not from the sadness of Pearson's demise, but for the fact it all had to end in such a tragic manner.

It wasn't fair. Why did he still have to ruin their lives?

Steve had already driven the digger, used for various tasks around the farm, up to the woods then down a small track, not far on from where Pearson had actually parked up. The backhoe of the digger had been busy and a large hole was rapidly growing. Steve expertly piled the spoil to the edges of the hole. Rectangular in size, the aperture was only just bigger than the actual car. He'd measured it. Depth would be enough to cover the roof and permit vegetation to take root above and then grow fully in the spring to cover the crime.

A series of old logs, large tree branches and piles of leaves would be placed over the top to fully cover later. Anyone watching the ease with which Steve performed the task would think he'd done such a thing before. Maybe he had.

Watching from the cab, Steve could see the headlights of the small car cut through the darkness as it approached. A tearful Izzy looked at the large roof lights of the big yellow digger, illuminating the spot in the woods where Dave Pearson, along with beloved old wreck of a car, would rest. Forever.

Within an hour the hole was complete; the car raised by webbing slings run underneath and attached to the digger front arm, then lowered into the brown tomb. Standing on the roof of the old car, her footing slipping on the damp metal, Izzy removed the slings and shackles. She jumped over the edge of the small holed and with the front bucket re-attached, the dug soil was replaced.

The car and Dave had vanished. Out of sight, out of mind. Maybe.

The car took up much more space than the displaced soil, but after some landscaping to the area, the soil was as good as level, save for a small rise in the ground. As planned, various logs, branches, and assorted debris was spread over the disturbed area, with digger bucket scoops of dead leaves tipped on top too; spread out by Izzy. In a few days Steve would plant native bulbs, such as aconites and bluebells, along with some daffodils and other native seed mixes, also throwing a wide mix of grass seed over the site.

Anyone looking at the spot the next day would see something had been disturbed. In a week, after some heavy rain, it would need a harder look. In a month, it'd be hard to see anything. In the summer you'd never know.

Dave Pearson and his battered old Ford were no more.

Gone from the lives of everyone who ever knew him.

And who on earth was that? No one.

In a way Izzy felt sad Dave had gone and no one would know or care.

Some might question what had happened to him, or where he'd gone, and think he'd gone off on another valid yet wild cause, but who'd care?

Izzy knew he had a mother - who didn't - but from how he spoke, it seemed to be a slightly distant relationship. She may notice he'd not made contact in a year, or sent a Christmas card, but little else. The Anti's and members of PAACE would ask where he'd gone, note he was missing, but with no more than a shoulder shrug, and no one would question any further. Nor care.

Things would move on. As did life. And death.

As Steve and Izzy spread the last of the loose covering of debris for the night over the dark orange soil, Izzy moved over and wrapped her arms around the man she'd always loved. He kissed her mucky hair, and hugged her tightly.

The pair looked at the ground, all signs of Dave gone.

"You look as if you've done this type of thing before," Izzy joked in a dark manner, needing some kind of break.

Steve simply blushed, looking forlorn, tired and weary.

A simple shrug of his shoulders his only reply.

The Shoteton way.

A tear formed in Izzy's eye, wiped with a mucky hand.

Dropped to her side, it was encompassed by Steve's.

Steve and Izzy were now firmly linked.

Whatever else may happen, they could not go back.

Only forward. Together.

The pair stood in the gloom, the silvery moonlight above broken by the bare tree limbs and branches. They gazed up, hearing a noise and movement.

High above in the moonlight, half-hidden by the trees, a small formation of geese flew by, their wing beats and soft honks soothing.

"Home my love. We've done all we can here."

Steve squeezed her hand.

Izzy nodded.

Job done.

Chapter 157

Your enemies can kill you, but only your friends can hurt you.

Marcus Tullius Cicero

It was P.C. Burton who arrived first at Horsewater and came to the aid of Anna and Chris. It had to be. He also formerly arrested Lucy, after some confusion as to what'd happened. The woman, dressed in black, as though she was about to commit a burglary, had been tied up in a mix of hay-nets and baler twine, and then dragged into an empty stable, with the doors bolted. She was loudly screaming her innocence, stating 'the skinny stuck-up slut' had attacked her, jealous of her being her ex-husband's lover. The irate woman wanted to press charges for false imprisonment and serious assault.

However, the actual seriousness of the situation was clear for all to see, and colleagues who arrived moments after Burton screeched into the yard, soon provided that much-needed assistance. Anna yelled at the police drivers to turn off the sirens and strobes, which were upsetting the horses in the stables as two other noisy cars arrived at speed, sirens wailing in dramatic fashion.

Max, whom she'd released from the house after smashing in the door, also had to be secured for his own safety, due to the concerned looks from Burton and the other officers upon seeing the large, vicious-looking dog.

After numerous police bodies dashed about the yard, they finally understood the situation, helped by Burton, who after speaking with the woman yelling from the stable, fully understood. He realised she wasn't innocent, but the main suspect, and also one who a multitude of his colleagues were chasing.

An emergency call had been made by a woman claiming she and her boyfriend had been violently attacked by a woman know to her. Stab wound to the man. Serious. The caller had also been cut with the knife. Slash to the face. Suspect had been detained and restrained. Urgent medical help required.

Burton was in the area on general patrol that evening, but asked by the main city police to join in the hunt and car chase for an alleged 'nurse.' She was wanted for numerous serious assaults to hospital staff and one patient.

She'd been seen leaving the main local hospital at speed in a vehicle and then chased across the countryside by various patrol cars, before they lost her. It was believed she'd then been involved in a road traffic accident; swapping and steeling the car of the other involved, which she'd hit, before racing off again.

When P.C. Burton got the call for any support in the area, and heard the name of the patient who'd been attacked, it rang a loud bell. He well remembered punching the very same man in the testicles himself at the Boxing Day hunt meet. And it'd been an experience he remembered most fondly. He also knew of his connections with the strange 'Lady Melrose.'

He'd asked for details to be crosschecked, and when confirmed the patient injured was the estranged husband of the woman who'd made the urgent call for police and ambulances at a place called Horsewater, jigsaw pieces all fell into place. Burton, not always the brightest, guessed what may have happened and dashed at great speed to Horsewater. For many reasons. All personal.

Thus Burton was just ahead of the main group of police cars and the following ambulance. He knew how to find the remote woodland farm and where to go; well before his colleagues, some of whom had driven clean past the wooded entrance. Burton knew they'd be only minutes behind him.

Sadly not enough time to do what he really wanted to do. But he was in no hurry. He was patient and could wait some more. No hurry. Just be a hero.

It was moments after the arrest of the mad woman in the stable, who upon realising her fake story was blown, had frantically tried to bite Burton. This was despite being bound up by a variety haynets, seemingly by the tall woman; the one-time Lady Melrose. She'd dragged the mad woman into the stable, whilst unconscious, seemingly from a horse attacking her. It was all confusing. The tall woman held a bloody wadding to her badly bleeding face.

The mad woman in the stable had swore loudly upon seeing the bleeding 'former' beauty with Burton, threatening to finish off what she'd only just started. Seeing the snapping jaws of the mad woman, Burton stepped back from the 'suspect,' issued a quiet, muffled, if unheard warning, then happily tasered her. He pressed the button a couple of extra times for fun, watching the tied up 'nutter' jitter about, much to his wide-eyed pleasure. Sweet!

Burton's colleagues followed swiftly after, with an ambulance moments later.

From the initial call, they were concerned for Mister Turner's welfare.

P.C. Burton wasn't. He hoped he died.

But on second thoughts, he hoped he didn't.

He was in two minds. It was complicated.

In one way he wanted Mister Christopher Turner to live.

But on the other hand, he wanted him to die. Painfully.

When Burton first arrived at Horsewater, just before the main group of patrol cars arrived, he was annoyed. Things were good and bad. Such was life.

He was annoyed he didn't arrive at Horsewater alone. Sooner. That could have been good. It may have worked for him. For he had his own plans.

He was relieved in a way when he found Chris Turner laying in the yard with a head injury, and serious stab wound, that the 'tall skinny stuck-up slut' - as the restrained 'nutter' thankfully tightly bound in the stable constantly called her - had luckily performed some important key First-aid to her lover.

She'd saved his life. He wouldn't die. Which was good. Maybe.

The tall beauty had wrapped the wound with horse bandages and 'Vet-wrap' to [illegible] bleeding, but knew he had internal injuries that could kill him, if [illegible]is lover had done then best she could, whilst also badly injured. [illegible]r would live another day. Sadly.

But in a way, that was also good too.
It was complicated. Messy.
Family issues were always messy and complicated.
If Roger Burton didn't get a good chance to kill, or assist in the death of Christopher Turner, it wouldn't be good.
And so he had to stay alive. For now.
It would've been such a shame if someone else had killed Chris Turner, as the 'nutter' in the stable had nearly done. It was good she didn't.
Annoying. Disappointing. A let down to the family.
That privilege was to be the honour of Roger Burton.
The nephew of a man who recently died. His uncle.
His uncle had a brother. Many years ago.
But he died too. Murdered.
Face blown off by a young child. Chris Turner.
The dying wish of his uncle was for Burton to get revenge on the boy who'd killed his brother. His other uncle.
It was a long time ago. Names and family change.
But not family loyalties. Not for those types of people, with close families.
They look after each other. Always.
They remember and keep promises. As long as it takes.
Roger Burton had been ridiculed, cursed and openly insulted when he'd told everyone in his family group that he was joining the police.
It was unheard off. A traitor they'd called him.
But they stopped laughing when he passed out.
He was a Policeman Constable. Respected. Almost.
Now the family had a copper on the inside. Sweet!
Not so stupid now. The penny had dropped for them.
The family were proud. Sort of. In a different way.
And he'd seek revenge and fulfil his family's wishes.
Chris Turner would die. Time and place decided by him.
There was no rush. Turner had to get better first.
Then Burton would keep the family promise.
Vengeance against Chris Turner.
Kill him.

Chapter 158

Enmity is anger watching the opportunity for revenge.

Marcus Tullius Cicero

Lucy was on remand. She'd initially been sent to a normal prison for a few days, but when identified she clearly had 'problems,' under The Mental Health Act she'd been transferred onto a Mental Hospital. Just as she'd hoped.

She knew it all, and hoped to be detained under a Section 36 remand, then being secured under Section 37, if she was convicted; basically being kept in a secure Mental Hospital, rather than going into Prison if sentenced.

Lucy had it planned. She wanted to go to a 'Looney Bin' rather than a prison.

Anything other than a normal prison.

Although she might be mad, Lucy wasn't stupid. Well, not that stupid.

Just a bit mad. But not totally 'cuckoo.' As such. Not yet.

Mental Hospitals were much easier to either escape from, or to be released from. If the idiots who ran the place thought you were slightly reformed, not completely cuckoo, or no longer a 'real danger' to the l public, or importantly, to the specific person you tried to murder, then they'd happily release you.

So long as it cleared space to lock up yet another raving nutter.

Biting one of the police officers seemingly helped her status, even without planning. He'd been a piggy-eyed, fat cop with an Essex accent, about to untie her, after finding her in the stable. But the 'skinny stuck-up slut' had stopped him. Bitch! She would have been sliced up if that fucking mad horse hadn't attacked her. Both bitches! She'd sue the horse. Maybe, if she could.

Her initial plan, as impromptu as it'd been after she'd unexpectedly met Adam, really hadn't worked. It all happened too fast and not as planned.

'Where the hell had Adam turned up from?' Fate. Or plain bad luck.

It was a pity she'd had to stove in Adam's head, as he was nice. They'd gotten on well in the past. But it was one of those things. Ho hum.

And she hadn't meant to stab the horseman either. But he'd 'played the hero' and stepped in front of that fucking 'Skinny Whore' she was about to cut up.

Idiot. Too bad. But that'd teach him a lesson too. Ho hum. Double Ho hum.

Chewing on items in her cell, then more importantly, on the dock rail whilst being presented before the judge, had helped him think she was totally mad.

He looked concerned, more so as she began drooling, then seemed to go into

stated the defendant clearly had 'mental health issues' and

best health' to remand her to a secure mental hospital until

undertaken. The plan had worked. Great acting.

ssue with 'playing it mad' was sometimes it could take you

actually became mad. Not her. She wasn't mad. Was she?

She knew she wasn't mad. Well not 'hatter' type of 'mad.'
But also knew what cards to play and how 'mad' to appear.
For a mad person she was smart. Too smart. For a loony that is.
Lucy was now working on one of the 'prison officers' in the secure hospital who'd been charged with looking after her. Poor soul.
He was nice. Too nice. Young and naïve. Too young. The fool. Ha ha!
His responsibility was to care for 'loony' prisoners,' such as her.
Those who'd allegedly committed 'terrible' offences; such as she was accused of, but were then awaiting tests before the real trial and sentencing.
That could take some time. Months. Or more. Time to plan.
Lucy knew she was innocent. But wasn't everyone?
Her officer was nice. She'd told him he was.
And she'd told him she was innocent. Who wasn't?
She'd fluttered her eyelashes at him too. So sweet.
He'd blushed. Embarrassed. Enchanted. Taken. The fool!
It wouldn't be long before she'd be in his pants.
And then he'd been inside her. Hook, line, sinker, rod, etc, etc.
His keys would be inside her too. Safely in her hand.
And maybe a shank would be inside him. Sharpened toothbrush.
Then she'd be out. Away. Gone. Freedom.
Once escaped, she'd vanish. Bide her time.
Then she'd seek her revenge. On them all. Bastards!
She wasn't stupid. Just mad! - Mad!!

Chapter 159

The beginning is always today.

Mary Shelley

Adam opened his eyes. A bright white light filled his vision.
Flicking his eyes down he saw the face of an angel.
The angel stared silently at him. Adam smiled. Beautiful.
"You owe me some money." The angel spoke harshly.
Adam blinked; refocusing, head muggy. Not Heaven. Definitely not.
"Anyway it's good to see you're awake. Took your time."
"Thank you Chantelle. It's nice to see you again too." Adam croaked.
He rotated his head, taking in the grey walls of the hospital room, noting the equipment nearby plugged into his body. A gentle bleep repeated in his ear.
"How long have I been here?" Adam enquired, realising where he was, but not how he got there. Then a memory. "And where's Lucy?"
"Lucy? Lucy!" Chantelle queried. "Who the fuck is Lucy?"
Adam shook his head, wishing he hadn't. Lifting a hand he touched a large bandage covering his sore head. A cannula was taped into the other hand.
"What happened to me? How long have I been here? And importantly, how are you? Clearly still alive. That's good. Sorry! How did I get here?"
"Someone hit you on the head. A mad woman. The police arrested her. I'm fine. Still breathing. Three days, the other answer. And you owe me money."
"Three days? Fuck me, it must have been bad. A close call."
"It was. Thought you may not make it. Some coppers found you. The nutter who hit you on the head nicked your Audi. That woman. Went mad in a hospital, then stabbed two other people and attacked the coppers; I heard."
'Lucy.' Adam squinted, wondering what he'd missed. "Good old Lucy!"
"How are you, and how did you get here?" Adam asked.
"In my Range Rover," Chantelle proudly replied. "Smart. Very smart!"
"Range Rover?" Adam was more puzzled. "You what!"
"Yes. It's smart. Dark. Not new, but not too bad. As good as. Cool!"
"How the hell did you get that? Did you steal it? Please say no!"
"No I didn't!" Chantelle responded with some indignity. "It's mine. Legally. It was part of a deal. A very good deal. I look real cool in it too!"
"My he[...]rts, and not through being hit by a nutter."
[...] a breath, and began to explain. Her way.
[...] with the mad huntsman went down, the shit hit big time;
[...]anks to you not turning up. But I understand why now. Any
[...]ame rushing in to save me, as the huntsman cut me, bad."
[...]ence, baffled, trying to take things in. His head did hurt.

"Then the old man, who also hunts, saved me. Along with the huntsman's wife. She'd was caged up under the stairs, like an animal, and I thought she was one, but the old man released her. I thought she was a bear at first, but she wasn't a bear. She was a woman. Then the mad huntsman ran off, naked. Disappeared. Then the old man, and the woman who wasn't a bear, bandaged the cut to my stomach. It was really bad. Just looked bad. Hardly a C Section. Anyway, I told the old man I'd call the Old Bill, but the old guy said he knew I was really a Pro.' A set up. Instead of them feeding me to the hounds - I think it was a sick joke - we agreed a deal for me to keep my mouth shut. That was after they both stopped me from bleeding to death. Well not really, though it was a nasty cut. I'll have a big scar on my belly when I sunbathe."

Adam's head hurt even more than from the blow and he looked on, confused, trying to take in what had spilled out of Chantelle's mouth.

"So what deal did you agree to?" Adam was intrigued. Very intrigued.

"The Rover. Mine to keep as compensation. He said his Huntsman wouldn't need it now he'd gone. Somewhere. I don't know where. They'd argued. Then he ran off. Naked. Bit weird. Must have been cold. However, he also gave me a lead. I think he knew you sent me. It's a bent Chief Constable. Someone I don't think he likes. A freemason. I have full details. Interested?" She smiled.

"I'm lost?" And Adam was, his head now really hurting. But intrigued.

"We agreed I'd say nothing about his huntsman, who he said they'd sacked, if I took the car and shut up. The ex-wife helped me. She's nice. Not a bear."

Chantelle smiled proudly, as if happy with her negotiation.

"I think I need a nurse!" Adam howled. "Help me, now!"

A woman ironically walked in at that moment. She looked at Chantelle for a second, turned her head and then took little interest. Chantelle regarded the intruding woman with a puzzled expression, flicking her head side to side.

The woman stepped over to Adam and kissed his hand fondly.

"Wife?" Chantelle asked bitterly, clear jealousy in her bitter tone and equally envious look. She glared at the woman. "You said you weren't married."

"Wife? Me? Good god no! Please do be serious," the woman exclaimed with indignity. "You'd have to be mad. Mind you, for what I do for him, I am mad and may as well be his wife. I do everything; other than iron his underpants."

"You iron your pants. Really?" Chantelle regarded Adam with deep concern that someone would do such a thing, despite all she'd done.

"That's a bit pervy. I think you may need help. Does he really? Weirdo."

Chantelle looked at the woman, who simply nodded to acknowledge he did.

"Meet Jean," Adam blushed, pointing to the woman, trying to change the subject from his pants, Chantelle's ranting and confusing tall tales.

"Chantelle, this is Jean. Jean, well you know who she is."

Adam looked over towards each of the two women.

Chantelle glared. Jean picked at Adam's uneaten grapes.

"Put her on the books Jean. And pay her. Please! Anything."

"You what?" Chantelle exclaimed. "On the books? What like work for you?"

"Yes. You did good. Very good. Sorry I wasn't there to help you. Genuinely. Things happened. You know. How would you like to work for us. Properly?"

Chantelle looked confused; looked at him then Jean, but smiled. She nodded.

"Yes. Okay. But don't forget you owe me some money."

Adam, sighed, casting her a type of look a parent gives to a child.

"Jean. Take her back to the office. Give her a contract and for god's sake, pay her. She did well. But make sure you get the details of that bent Chief Constable from her first. Before you pay her. Sounds meaty. Good work!"

Chantelle smiled, lent forward also kissing Adam's hand.

"Do you want to see my cut? It was deep. Sore. Big scar."

"Maybe later. When I can actually move." Adam blushed.

"Thank you. What will I have to do?" Chantelle asked.

"Everything. And more." It was Jean who replied with a deep, heavy sigh. "Welcome aboard Chantelle. And God help you!"

Chapter 160

When the gods wish to punish us, they answer our prayers.

Oscar Wilde

Bruce was bored. Again. It'd been a few weeks since he'd been discharged from hospital and he was now back in Leicester. Recovering. Slowly.

But it'd take time. Of course. A lot had happened. He was a wreck.

A long time to heal fully. If ever. Maybe never. Trauma. Compensation.

He had physical injuries from the fresh breaks the 'mad nurse' inflicted upon him, whilst in the safety and care of the hospital. How could that happen? As well as the mental torment he'd suffered; which would be with him forever.

So he boldly stated. On oath. To a solicitor. It all counted towards the huge legal claim he was putting together with his legal team against the hospital.

He had a good case. A very good case.

The compensation could be huge. Hundreds of thousands. Life changing.

As would be their fee. So long as they won. And they would.

The hospital claimed it wasn't directly responsible for Bruce being attacked by some 'Nutter' dressed as one of their nurses; however, the hospital had a duty of care to protect him whilst in their supervision. And they hadn't.

But as well as having a good legal team to settle his claim for compensation, he was in good hands physically too. He'd made sure of that too.

He'd persuaded Agila, the nurse who'd been treating him, to join him back in Leicester. She'd been off sick too since her 'vicious assault' by Lucy.

She'd also put in a huge legal claim, alongside Bruce's. She was also set for a big payout too. Maybe bigger. She hoped. Together they'd make a fortune.

The cut to her face was serious, but some neat and fine stitching by a top plastic surgeon had knitted the cut back together. She'd have a visible scar for life - worth tens of thousands alone - Bruce told her. And that was without the 'Loss of Earnings' claim she'd make for the trauma of the incident; as she would no longer being able to work. A fortune. Easy money!

In reality the scar could be concealed easily with make-up and Agila was more than capable of working. She was fit and clever, and had a great personality. She'd grown up in a poor area of The Philippines and had spent some time previously working for a Relief Agency in Africa. So was hardly squeamish. However, Bruce's charm, along with the opportunity to make a lifetime's worth of money for doing nothing, other than crying openly in court, had convinced her to give up work and move to Leicester with Bruce.

She was now giving him personal 'Physiotherapy' to help his recovery, in many varied forms. Bruce was particularly worried of damage to his testicles and wanted to check they worked and functioned properly, with daily checks.

Agila was quite happy to facilitate this important service for 'Mister Bruce.'

Bruce was also sorting out the legal aspects of his divorce. That had been disappointing, but not unexpected. Anna had sent documents through from her Norwich-based solicitors. She wanted a quick settlement. The house they owned in Leicester was to be sold and split equally. She wanted nothing else from him in any form financially and just wanted to move on. She also wanted no contact with Bruce and had made none. He'd made none too.

It meant Bruce would have to move out of the place, but he wasn't too bothered, had no real care about the place and Agila had discussed moving back to The Philippines with him. With his payment, when he sold the house, as well as the compensation claims, when they came through, the pair would be loaded and could live like royalty. Agila was almost laughing.

For Bruce, living in a tropical paradise for a few years, with a sweet horny nurse, who gave him more than enough sexually, would do. For now. Until he became bored. By then he should have his pay-off and he'd be loaded.

He could then return back to the UK and make contact with Anna again.

By then she'd be bored with her dwarf partner and looking for a real man with loads of money and a proper job. Not some twat who just rode horses.

Anna would take Bruce back. It was only a matter of time.

He just had to hope Lucy was locked up for good. Please!

If Lucy ever escaped, both he and Anna would be toast. Or worse.

Fingers-crossed she'd never be freed. He hoped.

And God help them all if she was.

Chapter 161

Thou calledst me a dog before thou hadst cause.
But since I am a dog, beware my fangs.

The Merchant of Venice - William Shakespeare

Jager had a new master. Or maybe that should be a new mistress.

She was kind and friendly – often rubbing his head and muzzle - which was nice, and she treated him well. 'Spoiling him' as his old master and still other owner would warmly rebuke her for, but to no avail, and usually with a smile.

Reggie had become noticeably warmer and more patient to people he met in the recent months. And also to dogs and horses. Which was strange.

Welcomed, but strange, for Reggie. Many had noticed it, included a number of his workers on the estate. He'd even thanked some of his farm labourers and commented they'd all done a great job. A box of beer had been given to them to share around one day. It was very strange. Reggie had changed.

The workers had been suspicious. Maybe the beer was poisoned or one he'd and which was 'Out of Date.' But seemingly not. All weird. For Reggie.

Maybe it was his new lady. But she was hardly new as such, as most of the farm workers knew her from the hunt. She was well to then all.

That new woman was also new to living with Reggie at The Grange. A challenge for anyone, but Sharon seemed to have mellowed Reggie. For now.

However, time would tell. He was certainly happier and seemed to enjoy Sharon's simple and warm company. Most noted was they almost seemed to share some strange secret, which bonded them together. And for once the bond seemed to be based upon true friendship rather than anything sexual.

Nothing had ever been said or spoken by the pair since they'd left the cellar at The Kennels, other than sorting out their stories and the formalities of what would happen, and what would be said to whom from there on. The pair seemed to form an immediate union and it'd worked well since then.

But time would tell. For now they were happy together.

It rapidly became clear to Reggie that Martin had kept Sharon gagged and chained up in a small cage he'd made beneath the stairs in The Kennels cellar. All she'd told Reggie was that Martin had become 'unstable' and had resorted to drugging her with horse tranquilliser and gin after he'd had a 'breakdown' over some event she couldn't discuss. It was too personal.

Reggie had simply nodded. He knew far too much already.

Sharon never mentioned Sarah and what had happened to her or to cause Martin's breakdown. Or of her involvement. She knew it was in fact her who'd dealt the 'killer' blow with the knife to the poor woman, and that she'd had been party to disposal of her torn body via the hounds. It was horrific.

It was later that day, when it all came home to her what she and Martin had done, that she told Martin to admit it all. If not to the police, then to Reggie. They both knew he was crooked and had done many bad deeds himself, but something happened the following day and Martin totally 'flipped.'

Sharon never knew what or why, but it happened after he'd disposed of the prostitute's body. She was ashamed and disgusted with Martin for what he'd been doing behind her back, and other than the fact the pair had killed the young girl, was unsure how she wanted to proceed with their relationship.

However, Martin had then gone wild, and although caring and sympathetic towards her, from then on kept Sharon as his prisoner, drugging her and tying her up in the 'cell' beneath the stairs. He took care of her. Fed and watered her, like a dog, but didn't permit her to leave the cellar or house and would lock her in the cage whenever he left, to stop her from escaping.

Sharon disclosed to Reggie she'd been drugged up for a lot of the time and was unaware of what was really going on. It was only when she heard the woman's screams in the cellar that it woke her and she realised she had to intervene. Forcing the gag from her mouth, and rising from her cot-bed, she'd pulled down the heavy drape Martin set up over the cage beneath the stairs, which had become her prison. Reggie then knew the rest and set her free, for which she was truly grateful, sure that at some point Martin would have killed her too. Then Reggie set off after Martin, leaving Sharon to attend to the girl.

Martin had run off naked, up the stairs of the cellar to vanish. Sharon never saw him again. What happened she was unsure. She had ideas, but didn't want to explore them. Reggie never mentioned it either. Simply said he was 'gone.'

Sharon had turned her attention to the beautiful young woman who'd been cut along her stomach by her fleeing pervert husband. Fortunately the cut was superficial and not deep or life-threatening, as it had been for the previous girl, she'd known as Sarah from Martin's mumblings as she was slaughtered.

Jasmine or Chantelle's stomach - she was unsure of the woman's name when asked - had bled at lot, but only for a short time. Being a surface cut, in an area of tight flesh, it luckily didn't go deep. Not like the other poor girl.

Sharon had dressed the wound with a mix of first-aid bandages and then a roll of purple horse Vet-Wrap. The young girl had been upset, and rightly so, but seemed hard, starting to protest as she recovered, calling for her boyfriend and abusive about his whereabouts, or lack there-of it seemed.

But when Reggie returned, she became assertive. She was no fool and told him she knew things and had a friend nearby, who in turn knew other key people in the press, and that they'd 'have a field day' if she spoke. Whatever that meant. It clearly meant something to him. He led her away, told Sharon to clean herself up and said he'd deal with the girl. She vanished in Martin's Rover, little more was said and the girl was seen no more by Sharon.

Reggie invited Sharon back to The Grange for a few days to recover, and also she thought, to keep her hidden away. Until they could contrive a story.

But that was all now in the past. Days turned into weeks, seasons changed and strangely the historically rude, gruff and 'nasty' Reggie had mellowed.

He was now 'nice' and treated Sharon well and a few weeks later said she could stay at The Grange as long as she wanted. She wanted, so stayed.

People asked how things were, enquired only once where Martin was, and more importantly it seemed, what was happening to The Shoteton and the next season's hunt. Then Sharon was introduced as Reggie's 'House Guest.'

They were told she was back from her break in the West Country and that Martin had gone away. For good. Back to his parents farm and that he would not be coming back. Dismissed. Gross Misconduct. Too many fights and for bringing the Hunt into 'Disrepute.' Even Steve Harrison seemed to believe it.

Only because it sounded plausible. They were told that things hadn't worked out and he and Sharon were separating. It was no real surprise to any Hunt member and all guessed it was why Sharon had vanished for a few weeks. Martin had been given the Ranger Rover as means of settlement as dismissal payment. Hence why it was missing, despite some saying they'd seen it driven about Norwich by an attractive woman, often with a dubious guy beside her.

Reggie would compensate the Hunt for the financial loss, he explained. And did. The Range Rover he replaced it with, for the new Huntsman – to be appointed - had come from Steve, who he 'knew' with the I.D. changed.

Job done. Everyone happy. Time to move on and get a new Huntsman.

A Huntsman / Kennel Huntsman position had been advertised.

Responses hadn't been too great. Minimal. One actually.

However, at least they'd had an applicant, which was a relief, and soon, all going well, The Shoteton would be appointing a new Huntsman.

Or should that be Huntswoman? Or maybe Huntsperson. Times change.

No one was quite sure. Not until they arrived. But the favoured - in fact only candidate - was as it turned out, a woman. Most definitely a woman.

Jaws had dropped and other body parts risen when 'she' turned up for the interview with the Hunt Committee. Alex turned some heads.

'Alex Adams' - a former member of the Blues and Royals - had been the name of the application letter. Those who took any notice of what'd been written further, and it hadn't been any, everyone too busy, had simply assumed, wrongly, that Alex was an Alexander. A man. Why not?

Not an Alexandra. Alex was a woman. Definitely. Very definitely.

She had boobs. Lady parts too - or so it was assumed. And sadly she was very attractive. Something had to be wrong! That had to be discovered.

A born horsewoman from young, she was good with dogs, upon meeting the hounds, who instantly took to her like a new mum. Also she was great with horses, Bert seemingly as much in love with her as any man who saw her stunning looks. Alex was clearly gorgeous and looked like she should be on the cover of a Men's Magazine. Or the inside centre pages. Maybe she had.

She seemed too good to be true, and probably was. Time would tell.

But Alex was duly appointed as the new Huntsperson for The Shoteton and God would need to help all those who rode with them next season!
But for now, with the quiet summer months about to begin, and the old season finished, life at The Grange began to follow a new, happier set pattern.
Sharon had prepared a wonderful dinner of local Spring Lamb and fresh vegetables, which they'd both happily consumed, and washed down with a fine white wine. Happiness. Bliss. Surely something had to change.
"Will you want me in the cellar Reggie?"
Sharon asked softly, using the correct terminology, which pleased him.
Reggie nodded, with a warm smile.
"Yes please. You know I would. But that's if you're okay with that?"
"Certainly. You know I love it too." Sharon smiled.
She headed towards the small cellar door, the hinges well oiled and set in dark woodwork. Reggie swiftly followed. Almost eagerly.
Jager stood guard, or realistically lay on guard in the utility room.
By the Aga. Warm and snug on his old smelly bed.
His eyes may have been closed, but he was watching. Something.
Watching images of rabbits run about the meadow.
His legs were twitching, running after them in his deep slumber.
And the sound of his heavy snoring was sure to scare away any prowlers.
Below, in the cellar, any strange noises were ignored.
Jager was too busy chasing his dream rabbits.

Chapter 162

Suspicion always haunts the guilty mind.

William Shakespeare

Steve and Izzy sat snug together on the big brown soft sofa. Izzy, long legs curled beneath her slim body, regarded a half-finished glass of Shiraz. She looked hard at the bottle. Much to consider. Steve, beside her, considered a third glass of Cherry Brandy. Problems. Dilemmas. Another drink or not?

"What the hell are we going to do about that horsebox you bought? It's shit. Won't start, chassis' rusty, floor's rotten and water pisses in!"

Izzy sounded concerned. "Apart from that, it's fine. Lovely headlights."

"Yes. Not good. Especially the leaks. Sell it on a sunny day?" Steve grinned. "Remind me again, who said I should buy it to start with?"

Izzy punched his arm, shaking her head and stuck out her tongue.

Nothing had changed in their time apart, or short time back together.

A few months on, with spring all about them and summer arriving soon, the couple were back to their old ways. And loving every moment.

"Well some idiot will buy it. There are plenty about. We did!" Steve winced.

"So long as it doesn't go to anyone we know," Izzy added.

The gravel crunched, with the sound of heavy wheels arriving outside in the main yard. Steve rose to look out the farmhouse window and check out the identity of their unexpected visitor. A new, but dusty red Toyota pick-up truck sat in the yard. Exiting was a tall man, looking directly towards the house, as if he knew where to go. Steve peered out of the window.

"Who's that?" Steve enquired. "Expecting anyone?"

"Not me. I don't live here, remember!" Izzy joked.

The man steadily approached the door, his build slim, but athletic, toned like an Olympic rower. Steve opened the black-painted heavy wooden door. Izzy peered over his shoulder, wine glass in hand, curiosity tugging at her.

Steve looked at the man before him. He sensed trouble.

The man looked back, absorbing their images.

The man's face seemed strangely familiar. Well-tanned, it was tough and rugged; as if the owner had spent many years living outdoors, but kept keep fit and healthy. Army? He had the look of someone who'd been in the military. But not just any unit. Airborne, or more. Maybe a uniform donning insignia with a dagger and wings or a knife with blue waves.

Hardened. Tough. Trained. Disciplined. Trouble.

Steve knew trouble when he saw it; and he'd seen a lot.

Izzy gazed over Steve's shoulder, looking at the face.

The familiar looking face. From the grave.

She felt a shiver run through her. Someone had walked upon her grave.
Maybe they were dancing. With big boots. Hob-nailed.
She took a deep breath and longer swig of Shiraz. Now empty.
Steve gave his best salesman's smile to the man. But it was wasted.
The man stared back like glass. Pleasantly, but unmoved.
"Hi, Sorry to disturb you, but my name is John Pearson."
An all-knowing smile. Intelligent eyes. Too intelligent.
Izzy stared in horror. The eyes familiar. Too familiar.
"I'm looking for my brother. David Pearson. Seen him?"
Steve went white. Izzy's stomach dropped.
The pair stared back at the man, shaking their heads in silent unison.
He clearly did not believe them and simply smiled.
"Izzy?" The words were more a comment than a question.
Izzy stared back, not responding. "You're as stunning as Dave said."
John added with a grin. "He spoke about you. Often. Too much."
"Sorry Steve, I'm not after your wife, just being honest!" And John was.
The pair stared back at the stranger in silence.
'The wanker - John - knows my name,' Steve thought. 'Tosser!'
Izzy blushed. Steve glowed. Both felt ill. John just smiled.
"I'm looking for Dave," John Pearson continued; manner formal, with no emotion, stating simple facts and looking for unseen visual responses.
And he'd seen them. Result. Game on!
"He's been missing for a few months. Just gone. Disappeared. Strange. His mother, my mum, misses him badly. Simply vanished. GPS on his mobile however indicated he'd been in this area. Actually, right here."
Izzy and Steve stared in dumb, worried silence.
"Any idea where he could be?"

Chapter 163

Hold fast to dreams, for if dreams die,
life is a broken-winged bird that cannot fly.

Langston Hughes

The winter had passed as swiftly as winters do. March had come and gone, the Vernal Equinox heralding a noticeable change in the grass colour from a dark brown to a fresh hint of much-welcomed green. Then the clocks sprang forward, changing the whole format of the day, with the extra hour and increased daytime appearing to wake up not only the earth, but also its residents, most of who welcomed the onset of spring. An unusually dry, but chilly April passed by swiftly too and gave way to a glorious and warm May.

In that early warming sunshine, Anna stood in the yard at Horsewater, smiling fondly at two fledgling robins with rubbery mouths and spindly legs, eagerly staring up at her. Bizarrely the more she got to know Chris and learn about him and his strange ways, the more she became attracted to him.

He was strange, but in a nice way, and the past few months at Horsewater had been the best in her life to date. She'd never felt so happy or contented, nor it seems had Chris. Everyone had commented on how 'Mister Misery' was seemingly now 'Mister Happy.' Well, most of the time. He had moments.

Horsewater hadn't become Anna's second home, it was now her home. She still rented the cottage, but even Chris had questioned why, as she only used it for work, the pair spending all of their evenings and parts of the day together.

One aspect of Chris' life she hadn't been aware of until spending time with him, was how important birds were to his life. They added to his eccentric nature. With the birds, she'd discovered how kind he was; not only to dogs and horses, but almost to everything which lived and breathed about him.

Anna soon became aware there were birds everywhere about the yard, realising many were semi-tame. Although at first she thought Chris was a bit mad, she too soon fell into the routine of feeding the multitude of wild birds that visited the yard daily for food or spent time in the paddocks.

Chris had a favourite wood pigeon called Beaky. He explained how he'd helped him, survive as a young pigeon by feeding him peanuts. Beaky had a slightly deformed beak (hence the name) and a deformed and twisted foot. However beaky seemed to be more intelligent than most wood pigeons who visited the yard and soon became quite tame. He'd fly down into the yard, waddle over towards Chris with his twisted foot, where he'd personally feed Beaky in his own 'private area' beneath a spare horse trailer in the yard, which he kept for emergencies or general use. And seemingly, for feeding Beaky.

If Beaky flew into the yard, Chris would stop any chore to feed him.

Anna currently was concentrating upon the fledgling robins before her, their plumage dull brown fluff, rather than the dashing red of their parents. Anna had watched over the last few days as the adults - Rocky or Roberta – (every bird seemingly had a name) both feed the babies. She had no idea, which was which, but Chris claimed he knew them individually. Hmm. She wondered.

The adult robins had gone from constantly pestering Anna for feed on stable doors, wheelbarrow handles, and even fork handles, to take back to the nest, to now watch with twinkling eyes as the adults fed the fledged chicks, who hopped all over the yard. The young would pester the adult with a high-pitch chatter, until a morsel was inserted into the over-sized, pale yellow-rimmed mouth. And then another. And then just one more. But today the parents seem to deliberately ignore their offspring, turning away, forcing them to find their own food, and all too soon it seems, separate from a once doting parent.

Previously, when with Bruce, Anna had taken no notice of baby birds, but now she found herself totally fascinated and knew Chris did too.

As the fledgling robins had seen Anna liberally toss suet pellets to their parents, they thus knew an easy source, and now pestered their potential 'foster' parent, by brazenly hopping into the stable Anna was sweeping out.

She smiled at the dark-eyed chick, which had no signs of it's traditional red plumage, soon-to grow, but merely cream speckles on a brown coat. Anna squatted down as the two fledgling Robins boldly hopped towards her, their dark eyes focussed upon her, awaiting food. But then their gaze drifted off and towards the base of her half-loaded wheelbarrow, filled with bedding.

Something had caught their attention. Anna looked on intently.

The spider, one not large enough to tear your arm off, but a smaller cousin, scurried across the yard and on towards the wheelbarrow for cover. With its multitude of eyes scanning all ways, it became aware of the imminent danger of the robins close by and paused all movement. In the warm sun of the yard the spider froze. Anna watched intently. The two keen-eyed fledging robins in turn had spotted the potentially tasty snack, and hopped forward, almost in unison. The pair gazed down at the arachnid now sheltering under a couple of pieces of barley straw by Anna's wheelbarrow. Anna watched with concern.

The robins looked at Anna, wary of the giant before them, but seemingly not enough, as their attention returned to the spider, and they hopped closer.

Anna, following their gaze, suddenly realised what was about to unfold.

The small black eight-legged object moved towards her. So did the robins.

"Wow! Hold on. You can't eat him!" Anna called softly, bending down.

Cautious not to scare off the robins, but keen to save the spider, Anna leant forward. Shielding the spider with her hand, she ushered it on, encouraging movement by poking it gently with a small piece of straw. The spider moved, dangerously exposing itself to the keen-eyed robins, who watched intently, then both hopped a deadly step closer. Still covered, Anna poked the spider on with a piece of straw, carefully guiding it towards a crack in the concrete.

The spider obligingly moved towards the crevice, disappearing into the deep crack and safety, and importantly, out of sight of the robins keens eyes. Anna smiled, proud at her conservation work, saving the life of the small spider.

Then she looked towards the disappointed robins. They cast her looks of utter disgust, standing in the dusty yard, their gaze set on the space where the spider had been and their singular tasty snack. Anna grinned at the fluff balls.

"Come on little chaps. I'll give you some proper feed."

Anna rose and stepped into the tack room, grabbing her pot of bird feed. She moved to a corner of the yard and lay a handful down, away from the spider. Instantly the two fledgling robins were there, pecking away at the suet pellet morsels, before fluttering away, now satisfied. For a few more minutes.

From across the yard someone else was watching. Hidden. Almost.

Dark, piercing eyes. Seeing it all. Watching closely.

Almost unseen, Anna knew they were there. Knew they were watching.

Anna was becoming wise to the world. Crafty. Chris had taught her well.

She looked over towards where she was being spied on.

Small dark eyes peered out from beneath an old discarded wheelbarrow.

Anna caught their gaze and smiled. With a grin, feed pot in hand, she stepped over towards the wheelbarrow, the owner of the dark eyes disappearing.

A rummage in the food pot sifted out a handful of flaked barley, this was placed in a heap at the base of the barrow. Then Anna moved back towards the tackroom, enjoying the growing warmth of the early May sunlight upon her face. The sky was pure blue and the trees had suddenly burst into life.

Peering around the corner of the doorframe she waited. Watching.

It didn't take long for the owner of the dark eyes to appear from beneath the barrow, to then boldly take a piece of barley in his hands and start nibbling.

An entranced Anna smiled upon seeing the regular visitor.

"Good morning Scrag-end," Anna announced to the half-tailed, one-eared, baby rabbit-sized brown rat. The huge rat appeared to ignore her, but Anna knew it acknowledged her presence and potential danger. He also seemed to strangely respect her, as the rodent took another piece of barley and nibbled, chaff flying out the sides of its long whiskered, yellow-toothed mouth.

Anna gazed on intently with a smile at the rat - vermin to many - both enjoying the sight, but also in disbelief at how she and her life had changed over the last few months. But she'd never been happier. She'd changed.

"I don't believe what's become of me," she muttered to herself with a smirk. "First I'm trying to save a spider, then talking to, and feeding, a mangy rat."

Scrag-end was a huge, battle-scarred Brown rat Chris had noted about the yard and strangely become attached to, and actually fed. Simply because he liked the rat's 'cool' attitude and no-nonsense stance. At first Anna thought Scrag-end was disgusting, but then strangely saw Chris' view and enjoyed the rat's company. Tracey didn't understand, stating she'd throw a brick at it.

Unseen by Anna, more eyes were watching her actions.

Across the yard, and unseen from the house, Chris was dashing about as ever. He saw Anna feeding Scrag-end, the semi-tame rat he'd taken to heart, and grinned to himself. Anna had certainly fitted in well to his lifestyle and he too couldn't have been happier wither presence, as many had openly noted.

The robins weren't the only bird friends Anna had grown to love as part of her new life at Horsewater. There seemed to be a multitude of flying visitors, some permanent, others visiting vagrants, all of whom Chris appeared to have given names and openly welcomed and fed. For someone who 'hunted' he had an amazing attitude towards local wildlife and its preservation.

The more she spent with Chris' the more eccentric, yet lovely she seemed to find him, doting on resident birds and animals as if they his pets.

'Stocky the Stock Dove' helped to prove this. A rare Stock Dove, which until he'd explained it to Anna, looked to her like a cross between a feral pigeon and wood pigeon. 'Stocky' had lived in and around the yard since she'd been at Horsewater, but it took little of Anna's attention, nor she too of the strange 'pigeon.' However, once she noticed Chris almost hand-feeding the bird, she soon realised he too was a key part of life around the yard of Horsewater.

Then one morning in April, an unusually excited Chris spoke, his expression more excited than when she'd seen when he'd won a jumping competition.

"Stocky has a girlfriend!" He announced proudly.

"What?" Anna recalled responding. A headshake added acknowledgement to her confused expression that she had no idea of what he was talking about.

"Stocky. There are two Stocky's now. He's got a mate! Stock Doves are rare about these parts, and he's been alone all winter. Poor soul. But not now."

Anna had grinned, dismissively shaking her head as though he was mad.

"Will the babies be called Stocklets?" Anna asked with a smirk. Chris simply shook his head, tutted and turned, but looked back with a wide grin.

Stocky wasn't the only semi-tame bird seen in the yard. There were loads.

Jack and Doreen were a pair of Jackdaws. Totally wild, but aware of the frequent free lunches placed about the yard for all of the other birds, they'd fly in to poach any food placed out in the various locations, but fly off with a 'caw' as soon as anyone came close, being very clever birds.

Pidge and Widge were other semi-tame wood pigeons who came and went, usually in a flow linked to the free food. But they were almost resident to the yard, sitting on the stable roof, and had also nested inside the eaves of Cirrus' stable and were currently sitting on an egg or guarding a young squab.

There were also a number of ducks who drifted in and out of the yard as food suited them, or whom grazed in the paddocks, and spent a lot of time on the small pond at the rear of the house, but would come about for feeding.

One of these included McQuakety Duck. A very vocal and slightly 'mad' female Mallard duck, she'd had a collection of six ducklings the previous year, before Anna arrived. Chris informed Anna the duck had laid six eggs in the banks of Bonnie's stable, and left alone by Bonnie, they'd all safely fledged

Julie had left them alone and as no one other than Julie would dare enter the mad horse's stable, when she was inside, and thus not disturb the nest either.

McQuakety had then proudly led the fledged ducklings across the yard and guarded them fiercely until they all flew off safely in mid summer. Seemingly mad, McQuakety had returned this early Spring alone, and almost lived in the yard. She'd both annoyed and entertained people as she had a habit of bathing in the horse's water troughs in the fields, to everyone's mix of amusement and annoyance. More so when she left a 'green squiggly present' in the water.

How she came upon her unique name, no one knew, not even Chris, even though he named her. Anna could only chuckle at him.

Of the six ducklings she had, another female, believed to be one of her offspring, had returned that spring. Making a nest in an unknown location, she had just produced a clutch of five ducklings. Less vocal than her mum, this duck and young was simply named Missus Quack and The Quackletts. The group would rush about the yard, or in and around the paddocks or often the ménage, with Missus Quack trying to protect her children from any airborne predators, such as the buzzards who flew high above piping and peeping. The buzzards had a name too. Why not? Buzz and Britney.

Anna enjoyed feeding all the ducklings, and tried to ensure they were safe, although still wild. The ducklings would run to her for food, but Missus Quack was always slightly wary, although happily accepted any feed offered.

A male cock pheasant and his partner were also welcome visitors. Again, returning from last year, the male stunning in his spring plumage was aptly named Mister Majestic by Chris. His hen wife, in a mix of chequerboard pattern browns and beiges, with amazing deep-searching eyes, was named Missus Nutter. The name became apparent when she openly ran up to Anna for food, unafraid, coming within inches to be fed; clearly a former hand-reared bird. Chris explained they'd probably drifted in from Bertie's estate.

A stunning pair, they lit up the yard in the early summer mornings whenever they appeared, the pair boldly strutting about as if they owned it, hence the apt name. There was also Mister Five Toes. Another cock pheasant, to no surprise, he had a toe missing. He'd walk in and help himself to seed also.

There were a family of Carrion Crows who lived in some trees at the back of the house and foraged about the fields, keeping guard to any visiting raptors. A tight family of two adults, with offspring who came and went, including one name 'White Wing' due to having a whit wing. Chris made a point of feeding them every evening. It was almost a religion for him, and he'd go out of his way to feed them, and curse if he'd missed them for any reason.

Anna found this action baffling sometimes, but slowly learnt his ways.

He told her the crows were the 'Guardian's of the Estate' and feeding them each day was an offering to please the 'Bird Gods' whom he said protected the place. He did also smile when he made the bold comment

Anna did wonder. However, she soon found herself feeding the crows.

The crows certainly protected their territory and if 'Buzz' or 'Britney' - often soaring high above the trees of the top wood where the rooks lived - appeared over the yard and their trees, the crow family would valiantly attack these huge raptors and boldly see them off and away, Anna often watching.
The array of birds and Chris' seemingly eccentric ways added to the warmth and pleasure she felt in his company and general well being of her new home.
A small group of semi-tame red-legged partridges would flutter in too, and seemingly had an even fonder place in Chris' ever warm and welcoming heart.
This tale was even more amazing to Anna when she learnt it from Julie.
Chris had found an egg laying in the yard early one June day. Noting it as a partridge egg, left completely alone in the yard, he believed it'd been poached from a nest by a raptor, stoat or rat, or simply left there from God.
He'd been walking with Julie, almost ignored the egg, but she'd encouraged him to pick up, to either blow, or as she suggested to hatch, just for fun.
Knowing partridges usually lay large clutches of eggs, and didn't leave them randomly in the open, upon Julie's fun comment, he was curious to find out if it could possibly be hatched, and thought it worth a chance. He dug out an old incubator, set it up in the tackroom, and for twenty-plus days, regularly turned the egg each day. Eager eyes would look in, before becoming bored.
But Chris persevered. Then, almost at the point of giving up, believing the egg was 'dead' and would never hatch, he suddenly noted cheeping sounds, and realised they were coming from within the singular egg. Then he saw movement, with the shell cracking. Within a few hours, and with everyone at the yard now keen to be involved and watch on, a tiny beak emerged and then with the wonder that is birth, out popped 'Joey.' The named partridge chick.
Suddenly aware he had a singular baby partridge, which he considered unfair, Chris dashed to Wroxingham Hall. He saw Mike Hawthorn - the Keeper of the Estate, before he vanished - and got five newly hatched three-day-old chicks from the hundreds the estate bred and hatched to release and shoot.
Then dashing back to Horsewater, with a newly acquired heater plate and small pen set up in a shed, he now had six partridge chicks to raise. The mad activity and news of a 'birth' at the yard became an exciting event, with everyone interested in 'Joey' and his new family. The chicks rapidly grew from scrawny things to beautiful red-legged partridges, being a popular attraction to those at the yard, with everyone looking in daily to check on their progress.
'Joey' was clearly different to the other five, both in colour and size; being naturally wild, rather than 'factory bred' as the others were, being imported eggs, then raised in the rearing pens. Everyone doted on him, although none were truly tame, Chris clearly stating he didn't want any of then to become tame, as they'd all be naturally released. However, one of the five 'foster' chicks became tame, gaining the name 'Missus Hello.' This was because whenever anyone said 'hello' to the chicks, she'd appear and respond on cue with a 'Pee-wit;' a form of partridge 'Hello' in response, to everyone's joy.

The other partridges were simply known as 'The Bubs,' and all rapidly grew in the few months from being mere tiny chicks. It was Julie who told Anna the story of the partridges when out riding, and said Chris was almost in tears on the day he released them. He set them all free in an area where they could thrive, and not drift into the neighbouring farms where they might be shot.

After being told the heart-warming story, Chris received an unknown extra hug that evening; Anna appreciating fully how caring her strange lover was.

Other feathered visitors would also draw Chris' attention, included a very tame pair of blackbirds named B Two and Missus B. They almost fed out of Chris or Anna's hands when offered food. Mister B had recently brought his two fledglings blackbird chicks into the yard, almost as if to proudly show what their tit-bits had helped them generate, which greatly warmed Anna.

Then they had a pair of tame great tits who visited too, being cheeky and bold, named GT One and GT Two. And why not?

Anna was becoming mad too she realised but understood it all too.

'Wibbly-wobbly Wagtail' was another fledgling Anna had become concerned about, pointing it out to Chris. He was a young fledged pied wagtail who seemed unstable and lame, his wobbly legs making him appear as if he'd been out drinking with Tracey. When jokingly asked if she was to blame for the poor bird's unstable condition, she claimed on oath she'd never seen him before. Honest Judge. But he soon recovered too, after a regular feast of suet pellets, and would then proudly sit on top of the stable block roof, with stable legs, but the characteristic long wagging tail dipping, almost as a thank you.

Harry and Harriett the Herons were the strangest visitors to Horsewater, and would often arrive on the paddocks for a few day, moving about slowly, hunting for mice or frogs, looking very strange and graceful, especially when in flight, as with huge but gentle wing beats, they'd soar across the paddocks.

Anna had never been so happy, had new dreams and aspirations, and was so grateful of life, one she feared she may not have had if Chris hadn't saved her.

Things had changed and moved on since the dramatic Burns Night event.

And further new life at Horsewater, raising more interest than visiting birds.

Chapter 164

I never change, except in my affections.

Oscar Wilde

There were two new additions at Horsewater. Both blonde, both stunningly attractive, but one more intelligent than the other. But neither too intelligent.

Ted was the name of one of the blonde's creating interest, and probably the more intelligent of the pair. Both blonde arrivals had caused bitching tongues wagging, as horsey-people have a tendency towards and keen fondness.

A 16hh Palomino gelding, Ted was only six and just broken in, being a late starter. To say he wasn't intelligent was unfair, and more down to the owner.

She, the other blonde, was Jennifer - 'Jennifer, not Jenny! That's a Donkey!' - as she'd brutally tell anyone who dared to make the mistake of shortening her name, was the second of the stunning blondes. The pair could have come off a film set. She had her hands full breaking in Ted, but he was generally kind, if slightly naïve and young, with the whole world a new experience to him.

But Jennifer was neither naïve, young, nor inexperienced with the world.

She knew that with a few slightly pathetic words, a flick of her fine hair, and flutter of her long eyelashes over her big blue eyes that she could win over most people. A fine pair of breasts, thrust out from a tight top and peach-like rear-end, presented in sleek jodhpurs, seemed to encourage anyone, including Chris, who'd begun to help her develop Ted in the ménage.

He stated he was simply interested in the horse. Honest!

Jennifer would strut about in her skin-tight outfits, making Tracey and Julie wonder how she got the clothes on. And Ted, when in fine form, would strut about in a similar fashion too. Tail up and head held proud, he was a 'looker,' however; he unfortunately didn't have such impressive breasts to display.

Both were stunning, attractive blondes. And both knew it too.

Jennifer and Ted had taken up Tess' stable as the stunning big black Cob was now an official resident at Wroxingham Hall, along with Carol. She'd clearly got her feet under Lord Burlingham's table, and also his bed too it seemed.

Murmurs and whispered comments spread like wildfire around the yard, when it was known they'd be arriving, on how badly Jenny, sorry - Jennifer - and Anna would get on when the two blondes arrived. It was clear to all there would be open jealousy between the pair. People had sworn they had to duck as they saw Commando-style daggers flying freely from Anna's eyes in the direction of Jennifer, and a long scowl sent Chris' way, when she first met her.

Jennifer was someone Chris had known for years around the show jumping circuits. He told Anna he just wanted to see Ted improve and would help Jennifer all he could; as if that was supposed to make her less jealous.

Lessons in the Ménage were to be under Anna's watchful eye. She'd decided, but didn't tell Chris. She was imply interested to watch Ted being schooled.

Julie had enjoyed the action of the new arrivals with a wry smile. Tracey was as brazen about the two newbies as ever, although had fallen in love with Ted, especially his silk-like flowing, blond mane, which never seemed to get dirty.

Gossip ran riot in the tack room, usually over coffee, whenever 'Donkey' - as Jenny, sorry, Jennifer, was cruelly called - but not when she was present.

"Two extremely thick but attractive blondes," Tracey had cruelly commented in the tack room one morning, as the 'Three Musketeers' sat drinking coffee, when Chris and the two 'Blondes' had gone off to the school.

Julie had scowled hard at Tracey. "That's a very mean thing to say Tracey! They are not both dumb. I implore you retract that vicious statement!"

Her look was hard and menacing. As best as it could be. Julie tried to hold it.

Tracey had just grinned, awaiting the punch line. It came. All too soon.

"Ted is not dumb. He is a very intelligent horse."

The threesome fell about laughing, Anna loving the banter, clearly with more to lose than the others. Yet she knew Chris well enough now not to worry, their bond having grown strongly over the last few months together.

But Anna was still naturally jealous of the stunning blond interloper; more so as she now bore a scar across her face, forever to remind her of recent events.

The wound was healing and a light covering of foundation visually hid the deep damage, although psychologically what had happened to them would always be with her. Forever. The highly skilled plastic surgeon that treated Anna's face in hospital had done a good job to close the cut with very fine stitches, being aware of the clearly attractive woman's features, now gone.

Upon returning to Horsewater, when the dressings were removed and she'd first seen the savage gash, still bold and stark, Tracey had look long and hard, She said the scar on Anna's cheek made her look like a pirate.

Anna didn't know if to laugh or cry at the time, but knew it'd been said with a kind and humorous heart. A long warm hug from her cousin helped matters and the pair chuckled with a mix of tears. Tracey said she'd buy her a cutlass.

Julie had been a great friend throughout; sympathetic and kind, helping out as best she could alongside Sally and Tracey. They'd all helped with the horses and kept the yard running normally with Anna, whilst Chris was in hospital for a week and then limited in what he could do upon his return, his injury bad. Everyone was simply happy to have him back, none more so than Anna.

Chris' stomach wound had been deep, but was healing well and it hadn't held him back, although it'd stopped him from riding until quite recently. Now he seemed as happy as ever to be back in the saddle, even if only for light work.

Anna knew she was forever in his debt for what he'd done to save her that night. Some times it seemed a long time ago, but then at other moments, when alone, like only yesterday. More so in the evenings when in the yard, and she swore she could see Lucy's image prowling. Bonnie still stood guard.

If Chris hadn't stepped in front of Lucy that night, she would have either stabbed Anna to death in a mad frenzy, or possibly worse; cut her up as she'd cruelly promised. Lucy knew that disfiguring Anna would possibly be worse than a swift death. And she'd do less time. Lucy was mad and evil. Anna could only hope she was never released, though her trial was months away.

It was this brave and bold action from Chris to save her, along with her own to then save him, which had built a strong bond between them.

Thanks and big hugs had been exchanged when in hospital, along with long looks, each knowing, if unspoken - as was Chris' habit - each owed the other their life and more. A solid partnership had been built, even if unspoken.

Both had gently touched and caressed each other's scars when alone in bed together, after long warm embraces. They were simply glad to be in the arms of the other, knowing what'd happened and what could have been.

Anna had never felt so close to someone before, not even Bruce. She enjoyed the warm, caring horseman, however strange he might be in his own quirky ways. In a way, it made him even more appealing. And to add strength, Anna's dad thought the sun and the moon shone from Chris' bottom.

Luckily Bruce hadn't been in touch, which was a blessing, and Anna had heard only from his solicitors. From others still in touch, she'd heard he was possibly going abroad with the nurse who Lucy also attacked and they were suing the hospital. It was typical of Bruce, and Anna shook her head in wonder that she could have ever worshipped such a man. Life was strange.

Despite all that had happened, things carried as usual in the yard but also moved on and forward. With Tess' stable free, and losing Chris money on liveries, which were always well-desired, the two blondes had arrived.

And another new equine had come to Horsewater too, taking up a small spare stable that had previously been used for storage. Sally had taken in Meg on loan; the small black driving pony who'd originally been stabled at Lord Burlingham's. She'd long wanted to take up driving, and upon hearing from Carol that Bertie was looking to loan her out, Sally jumped at the chance.

Meg was a kind black 11hhWelsh pony mare and an instant hit with those about the yard. Anna had even volunteered to help her out, and was looking forward to some exciting drives around the estate and through the woods.

Bonnie also wasn't forgotten, and Julie had half in jest, set a brass plaque put on the front of her stable with the words 'Hero' boldly engraved in black.

Julie was very proud. Bonnie no different. She still bit anything that moved!

And further to the new equine arrivals, Chris also had another new addition to his life. It was called Riley and he shared Anna and Chris' bed at night. Something she had never expected, but Anna enjoyed the cuddly threesomes.

No one was quite sure what Riley was. A cross between a Yorkshire Terrier and a Jack Russell. Maybe. And a bit more mixed in for sure. Riley had the long, shabby ringlets and curly 'Ginger Dreadlocks' of a Yorkie, but was long and slender, with the face of a slim Jack Russell, but with shortened legs.

Whatever he was, Riley was sweet. Curious and buoyant in nature, Chris had taken him in from a couple moving abroad, and as heartbroken as they were to leave him, they couldn't take him with them. The pair knew Chris well, and that Riley would have no better home than living with Chris at Horsewater.

No one was sure how Max would take to this intruder, but he seemed to welcome him too, and happily let Riley sleep with him in the kitchen.

The rules were simple. Riley could sleep anywhere, but not next to his Aga.

Riley - the 'Ginger Ninja' - was currently seated upon Anna's lap as she sat in the tackroom with Tracey and Julie, as seemed to be their usual past time. Chris was with Jennifer and Ted in the Ménage, working on his trot. As ever, further bitchy comments about Donkey freely flowed, as did the good coffee.

"And I want to know if her grapefruit shaped breasts are real. They just look too perfect. I've got little tits, but they still sag. Hers look like they've been planted on. They can't be real. You should ask her Tracey." Anna bitched.

"You what? I hadn't even noticed. Only you would. Pervert!"

Tracey seemed to have genuinely not noticed the fine perfect breasts.

"I noticed them too," Julie added. "Nice, but too perfect. I wouldn't mind them on myself. Not her tits obviously, I'm not a weirdo. But mine are shit!"

"Maybe you should give them both a squeeze to find out," Anna grinned.

Julie smirked. Tracey chuckled.

"Tell her you're a Lesbo' if she screams." Anna added.

"And if she likes it, and is one?" Tracey enquired nervously. "What then?"

"Then I'll get my video camera out and we'll make a fortune!"

The group fell about laughing; spilling their coffee and once more enjoying the wild and witty banter they loved. Riley ran off. He'd had enough.

The seasons may have changed, life evolved, and things may have moved on, but nothing had really changed. Life was good.

That should have been a worrying sign.

Chapter 165

If you go down in the woods today, you're sure of a big surprise.

John Bratton / Jimmy Kennedy

It was a glorious warm sunny day, the type only mid' May creates; pleasing the soul with visions of the summer to come. The yard was empty, with most off to their daily toil, having been down and ridden, or dashing in to check the horses and then off again. But Anna had some free time, being between clients and projects, and enjoying a less frantic period for a few days. It was a pity the same couldn't be said for Chris. He was busy, as ever, and had a horse to take to Newmarket later in the morning, with various people wanting horse transport for the up-coming summer shows. Nothing had changed.

Anna's dad had been pestering Chris about some aspect of his own railway he wanted Chris to advise on. Anna found this even more humorous; that her dad was asking a respected horseman for advice on building model railways.

Chris found it amusing too, although genuinely seemed to like the attention, the pair getting on well when they met, the strange hobby building a bond.

Max had been about in the yard earlier, before the heat began to build. Staring at Scrag-end, he'd retired inside, the AGA thankfully off. Anna was sure Max and Scrag-end had a secret agreement, as he never chased the rat.

Riley on the other hand had no such agreement, and would chase after him, Beaky, or anything else stupid enough to remain in the yard too long as he raced about. Thankfully Riley was not the best hunter in the world, and would dumbly run straight at the various incumbents in the yard, rather than stalk, only for the intended target to run or fly off, annoyed rather than concerned.

"I'm going for a quick walk in the bluebells," Anna called across the yard to Chris, interrupted at that point by the phone ringing. "I'm taking Riley too."

Chris half caught the comment as he dashed inside, seeing Anna raise a hand as she strolled past the house, parking area and muck trailer, to head on the track up into the woods. He half raised a hand in reply, looking keenly from the kitchen window at Anna as he grasped the interrupting house phone.

The curly-haired ginger form of Riley skipped ahead of her. Nose down.

Max remained with Chris. Loyal as ever, lazy as ever. Sleeping.

It was a stunning morning, with no clouds in the deep blue sky, the heat beginning to build, but cool beneath the fresh green canopy growing above. Anna had decided she'd try to walk more around the estate, and within the woods, having spent most of the time exploring either on horseback with another beside her, or driving on through in her 4 x 4, or alongside Chris.

She'd even gone through seated beside Sally, as she drove Meg through in her small two-wheeler cart, it being a fun experience, if not a bit scary.

But as part of her own recovery from what'd happened to them both on Burns Night, and with the knowledge that it was Lucy who'd previously tried to kill in the woods; when Chris had again saved her the first time, deep down she was still fearful of the woods and being alone in them. So she was keen to develop her personal strength and confidence. Thus, by walking in the woods she'd prove to herself she had nothing to fear, other than fear itself.

Chris had never mentioned anything else about those whom he feared could be after him. Anna had felt she should raise the matter after Lucy's attack, but the moment hadn't arisen, and things had been so good between them since, she didn't want to upset matters by raising such dark demons with him. Chris had saved her numerous times now, so she felt a debt of honour towards him. And besides, she felt she was also becoming more hardened, finding some of Chris' calm and no-nonsense ways of looking at matters were rubbing off on her. Before long, she too would be 'as tough as old boots' too. Maybe.

She smiled at the positive thought, then jumped when she heard rustling in the woods behind her. Spinning around nervously, she saw some movement, then grinned, realising it was Riley. He'd run back behind her, keen nose actively sniffing the ground, but brain operation, highly questionable.

Onward she moved within the woods, the chatter of a loud blackbird breaking the silence, but all the time she tried to dismiss the paranoid feeling she was being followed or watched. She knew Chris held no such fears, nor did most of the other girls, and when on horseback, albeit with someone else, she always felt brave. But she was determined to develop a stronger resolve.

That was easier said than done, as with each fresh crack of a twig, rustle of grass, or movement of bush, Anna would swing her head about, convinced someone was following her, although she knew no one was. Or so she hoped.

She would have much preferred to have Max by her side, rather than Riley, who although cute, energetic, great fun and wonderful company, was as vicious as a fluffy slipper. He was more likely to run up to a stranger and urinate on their feet than tear them to death. Maybe that was worse.

Thus she drifted up along the main track of the woods she'd driven along on many occasions, but never walked through, and only on occasions ridden through in a small part with Chris and Julie. Most woodland riding was in the large back woods, where she'd first ridden with Chris and also where she'd fallen off and was attacked. The thought brought back Lucy's image.

A deep fear of Lucy ran through her and how desperate she'd been to attack her. Her actions were truly evil and devoid of all normal sense.

Pure jealousy. Evil and mad. But also very clever and cunning. Dangerous.

Anna felt her hand rise, touching the scar, which would always be a scar.

Why the hell had Bruce ever become involved with her?

And what would have happened to her and Chris if Bonnie hadn't knocked her out? She dreaded to think, but now fondly held the mad coloured horse in high esteem. Although still couldn't give the horse a 'Thank You' pat.

Lucy's trial was months away, the legal system never quick, more especially it seems for 'Nutters,' who seemingly to manipulate the rules; along with their equally unscrupulous lawyers. Why did they represent such clients? Money rather than choice, she assumed. But Anna could at least take some respite for a while, knowing someone who wanted her dead was securely detained.

At least for now. Anna shuddered. Someone had walked on her grave.

She knew that if ever released, Lucy would be straight after her and Chris. But surely the courts wouldn't set her free unless she was totally reformed. A changed character. Was that even possible for her? And what if she escaped?

A new shudder ran through Anna and she found herself looking about again, checking for the person she felt was following, but knew wasn't really there.

With a deep snort, which drew in vibrant scents from bluebells, and the mass of white and pink hawthorn bushes nearby, Anna boldly strode forward through the woods, turning off the main track and down a smaller one she'd never been along before. 'Embrace the moment,' she told herself, being bold.

The undergrowth around the area of the small track was mixed, with masses of nettles growing in previous barren patches. Brambles spread their prickly limbs wherever they could, with fresh saplings pushing up through well-rotted leaf litter. She turned off at a small fork, the track still just wide enough for a vehicle and noted something had driven along the track within a few months, with hardened wheel ruts partially shown in the now drying ground.

Anna knew Chris worked on the trees within the woods and would bring his teleporter or old tractor into certain areas of the woods. Many areas were still often cordoned off with tape, where trees had fallen or had dangerous loose branches hung, ready to be trimmed back, just as he'd shown her back in the winter when they'd first ridden out. Thus she was wary of entering such areas, not only for safety, but also because she didn't want to upset or annoy Chris.

Riley tottered aimlessly about before her - as Riley's do - nose on ground, with the occasional flick up of the cute ginger head to see where he was actually walking. Anna wandered along the dirt track, conscious of the time and not wanting to go too far, but also keen to explore her new domain.

A large bumblebee, probably a queen, emerged from a hole in the ground. Most likely an old field mouse nest, it buzzed noisily past Riley, tempting fate by flashing a bright orange backside at the head of the terrier. Anna heard the snap of Riley's jaws as he foolishly tried to bite the bee, but which luckily he missed. The cumbersome, colourful bee zoomed off into an array of flowers.

Anna smiled at the bee, glad to find some peace and fun.

Then something rustled in the undergrowth. Movement.

Clear and definite. No paranoia. A body or form was definitely moving.

She spun around, looking intently to where fresh brambles threw out vibrant fresh green leaves, backed by new bracken and surrounded by a mix of bright wild flowers, including Dog's Mercury and Bluebells.

Anna froze, instinctively sure she was being followed.

Turning her head around, she could see only a swirl of vibrant greens, mixed with a wash of blue, yellow and white, where carpets of bluebells mixed with cow parsley and creeping buttercups. But there was nothing about her, other than the buzz of insects and the twitter of birds. The woods were silent.

But then another rustle. Low bushes nearby shook.

Anna felt her heart leap. She'd been right.

There was something out there. Moving.

Riley heard the noise too and sensed the tension.

Cute ginger face, small flopping ears, he now paused too.

Head erect, he scanned the world from eighteen inches.

The pair froze in the vibrant woods. Listening. Searching.

Then it moved. At speed. Running.

Anna jumped, eyes set wide in fear. Riley saw nothing.

Dashing across the track, it turned and ran towards them.

Anna watched on in amazement. Riley still saw nothing.

Suddenly, seeing the intruders standing upon the track, the large doe rabbit froze in her tracks and rose up on two legs. She paused, sensing danger.

Then Riley saw it. Off he ran in pursuit of the big rabbit.

First down the dirt track, then off at a matching tangent. Riley crashed blindly through debris and undergrowth, to set off across a wide mass of mature, native bluebells. The quick rabbit ran on ahead, aware of the dog behind, but also aware it was winning the chase. But Riley wouldn't stop.

Cursing at the ginger dog, Anna raced on behind, first up the track, then turning off. She ran on, ducking beneath branches and weaved around a mix of native mature trees and bushes, even some new mixed conifers. She noted stunning Rhododendrons in vibrant purple and pink flash pass by her vision. Any other time she might revel in the beauty of the large flowering bushes, but her focus now was on retrieving the 'Ginger Ninja;' not embarrassingly telling Chris she'd lost his new dog somewhere deep in the woods. Oops!

She ran down a small foot track, either side of which were masses of bluebells. The flowers reminded her of an area in the main back woods where she and Julie had ridden a few days earlier. Native bluebells grew there in abundance, forming a carpet of vibrant blue and green about the tracks along which she'd cantered past on Penny. Anna had been astounded by the colour impacting her senses, knowing very soon, once summer set in, the stunning bluebells would wither away, to slumber silently for ten months, to rise again next spring in all their fine glory. Anna now hoped she might be there to see them the next year, wondering if losing Riley could cost her such a pleasure.

It was across this similar mass of blue and green flowers Riley skipped, without a brain-cell in his head, nor care in the world, the rabbit now gone. But that didn't matter to Riley. He could still chase something only he thought he could see. Anna huffed on, ducking and dodgy tree branches and brambles. Suddenly she caught sight of the 'Ginger Wanker.' His new name.

Drawing a breath, she sighed, seeing the oblivious, uncaring dog sniffing aimlessly about the small clearing where tree branches lay strewn.

Anna knew she'd crossed some fluttering boundary tape and entered an area of trees cordoned off by Chris. She sighed, looking up for any loose branches or big boughs. Being young, stupid and typically 'Riley,' and also a dog who couldn't read, he'd dumbly entered the dangerous area. Dogs should read.

"Come here you little shit!" Anna cursed under her breath. "Riley. Here please! Come back to Mummy. Riley! Please. Bastard!"

She called louder, noticing him look up fleetingly, then only to turn away, to drift further across the cleared area of woodland; nose on ground and ears closed to sounds linked to Anna. Especially any rude or offensive ones.

"Wanker!" Anna muttered aloud, seeing the little dog ignore her completely, happy in a world of his own, whatever that dumb and vacant world was.

Riley stopped, turned, tongue hanging, catching his breath; seemingly bored with his chase. Or had he seen something?

Standing, he gazed at Anna. Or was it on beyond her?

She in turn returned the gaze, catching her own breath.

With a forced smile, cursing under her breath, she slowly approached the annoying dog, a welcoming hand held out forward, ready to grasp.

Crack! A harsh noise from below.

Riley disappeared.

Darkness. Then pain.

The ground had collapsed beneath Anna.

She winced, coming to rest in a damp but spongy pit.

Then the stench hit her. Sweet. Putrid. Rotting.

Dazed, sensing mild pain in both her legs, arms and one shoulder, she looked about her, trying to take things in. Her senses were in a whirl.

She was in a dark, stinking hole. But more.

'Where the hell am I? What happened?' Thoughts raced.

She looked up to see the bright blue of the May sky above set in treetops.

The view was through a small hole. Rectangular.

It was through this aperture she'd fallen, striking her arms and shoulders upon the edges passing through; hitting her legs on the various hard objects in the base of the hole, causing her to fall heavily onto the items within.

Items such as a steering wheel, gear lever and hand brake.

Car. She'd fallen inside a car. 'Car! What? But how?'

A confused Anna scanned the dingy and smelly interior.

Suddenly the light above her dimmed slightly.

Above her a face appeared. Keen eyes. Looking in.

Ginger. Small blond-tufted ears. Daft, but kind. Riley.

She shook her head at the dog and sighed, then rescanned the interior as Riley's head vanished and he scurried away, seemingly in a hurry.

The smell was suddenly overpowering. A heavy stench.

Anna realised she'd fallen into a car, which had been buried in the ground.

She'd landed precariously and heavily into the driver's seat, bumping legs, arms and shoulders on the sunroof on the way down. But why?

In the gloom, looking around, she noted a large lump or form lying behind her upon the rear seat, dark in colour.

It took a few seconds for Anna to realise the object's true form.

Then a few more to fully comprehend what it was.

Her mind didn't want to acknowledge the answer. But it did.

A body. Dead - clearly. Hopefully. For some time - clearly.

Anna wanted to gag. Confused, unsure of everything.

Instinctive panic set in as she glanced a brief moment at the decaying body lying in a crumpled foetal position. Long dead.

Arms flaying, legs pushing up on the seats below her, she rose up, thrusting her head through the sunroof of the buried car. Soil met her face.

Gasping for air, arms rested on the rim of the sunroof, Anna gazed across the carpet of vibrant fresh bluebells growing around the buried car.

Two faces stared. Silent.

Max and Chris.

Anna stared back.

Chris looked at Anna.

A thousand-yard stare.

Chris spoke. Voice monotone.

"You shouldn't be here."

The End

Maybe

Glossary of Hunting Terms

AMHB – Association of Masters of Harriers and Beagles. Governing body of British hare hunts. Similar to MFHA - Masters of Foxhounds Association.

Anti – Derogatory term for Hunt Saboteur often used by hunting people. 'Sab.'

Blank – Failure to find quarry in hunted area, or all day is termed a Blank Day.

Bowled Over – (Brought to Book / Accounted For / Punished) Hunting euphemism for 'The Kill' or death of the quarry, i.e. Fox or hare, etc.

Brace – A pair of game animals or birds. Typically a 'Brace of Pheasants.' Two.

Cap – Payment made by hunt followers on the day of the hunt, often in addition to their subscription. Usually collected by the Field Secretary or Hunt Secretary.

Cast – Huntsman takes charge of the hounds and encourages them to find a lost scent line. 'Casts' the hounds out onto a new area to pick up a new or lost scent.

Chop – To kill the quarry as soon as it is put up and before it has a chance to run. Not deemed as good or fair sport; either for quarry, hounds or the hunters.

Couple – A pair of hounds. Packs are counted in pairs. 35 hounds = Seventeen and a half couple. Traditionally a young hound was joined / coupled with an older.

Country – The Hunt's general territory, regulated by its relevant governing body. (Hunt Country). Hunts will have a Joint Meet and hunt a neighbouring hunt's land.

Covert – (Pronounced Cover) Woodland, thicket or field where quarry may lie up for shelter. 'Breaking Covert' - termed used when a fox or hare runs into the open.

Cry – (Speak / Music) Sound given by hounds when actively hunting or full pack is speaking to a line. Full Cry when hounds are in pursuit. Also gives 'tongue.'

Cubbing – The period before Opening Meet, usually mid' Sept' to late Oct' to train young hounds. Riders will often wear 'Ratcatcher' tweeds than formal wear.

Drag – Scent left by Fox, Hare or other hunted quarry. Hence term 'Drag Hunt.'

Drag Hunt – Hunt where hounds follow an artificially laid line of scent instead of a hunted animal. Used for most modern UK hunts after Hunting Act 2004.

Draw – The act of encouraging hounds through a covert in search of a quarry.

Field – (The Field) Collective term for the mounted hunt followers (riders) usually led by the Field Master. The Field usually keep behind the Field Master.

Field Master – Person designated by Master and responsible for leading The Field whilst out hunting. Senior Hunt position, usually with good land knowledge.

Form – (Scrape) Small divot scraped out of the ground in which a hare will live. Hares low flat in their form and dash off at high speed only when approached.

Given Best – Quarry is 'given best' when it has evaded the hounds, is allowed to escape, and awarded the 'victory,' possibly to be hunted another day.

Harrier – Small to medium size hound, used for hunting hares, resembling a small Foxhound. Been used since mid' 13th Century. 'A Beagle on Steroids!'

Heel Line – Hounds on the scent line, but wrongly going in the opposite direction to that of the quarry. 'Running Heel' term where hounds are going the wrong way.

Hound – Hunting dogs are always referred to as hounds. Collectively known as a Pack. Most common types are Foxhounds, Harriers, Beagles and Bloodhounds.

Glossary of Hunting Terms

Harrier – Small to medium size hound, used for hunting hares, resembling a small Foxhound. Been used since mid' 13th Century. 'A Beagle on Steroids!'

Heel Line – Hounds on the scent line, but wrongly going in the opposite direction to that of the quarry. 'Running Heel' term where hounds are going the wrong way.

Hound – Hunting dogs are always referred to as hounds. Collectively known as a Pack. Most common types are Foxhounds, Harriers, Beagles and Bloodhounds.

Hunt – Term used to define a group or organisation associated with hunting in a specified area or region of land. Owned by an individual or a group, sometimes with financial interests, often with some property linked; such as Kennels, etc.

Huntsman – Person who hunts hounds and responsible for their care, breeding and training. Also called 'Kennel Huntsman'. Often employed direct by the Hunt.

Jink – Sharp, almost right-handed turn by quarry to throw off its pursuers.

Kennels – Place hounds are kept, usually being a property belonging to the Hunt or a key hunt member, and often linked to a Huntsman's house or dwelling.

Line – The trail or route taken by the quarry or hunted animal, and thus where it leaves its scent. Nominally the 'scent line' hounds follow, rather than by sight.

Master – Person with key responsibility for general daily running of the Hunt and organising the country. Some hunts have Joint Masters or multiple Masters.

Meet – Location where all hunt members, riders and followers collect before a day's hunting. Can be a field, public house, private hall or even a town square.

Point – Location a Whipper-In is sent to watch for a fox or hare to break covert.

Puss – Traditional hunting term for European Brown Hare. Also 'Old Puss' is term often used in Hare Coursing. Doe - Female, Buck - Male, Leveret - Young.

Quarry – The hunted animal in any kind of hunting. Usually fox, hare, or stag.

Rat-catcher – Dress code often worn for Cubbing Meets. Usually Tweed hacking jackets, rather than formal black coats and scarlet jackets, etc. Informal dress.

Riot – Hounds riot when they hunt any animal other than the proper quarry.

Run – Term describing action of hounds finding the scent line of a quarry.

Scarlet – Correct term for red hunting coat. Harrier Hunt's coats are often green with coloured collars. Other hunt's jacket colours vary, including blue and buff.

Stirrup Cup – Drink (usually alcoholic) served to members of The Field at the start of the Meet. Often used as means of a 'toast' or celebration to the host.

Tally-Ho! – Cry, with various additions, to indicate movement of the quarry.

Whipper-In – Staff who assists the Huntsman with hounds, usually riding ahead or on point. Will also often collect stray hounds or holler to guide accordingly.

This list is by no means comprehensive and many hunts across the U.K. and in other parts of the world use different phrases or terminology, but the list is designed to give someone new to Hunting and idea of some of the terms and phrases used by Hunts.

List of the 'Real' Equine Players

The following is a list of horses I've had the pleasure of owning and whose names are used as the equine characters within the plot of Horsewater in some form or variation. All lifelong friends from ownership whose company I've enjoyed and whom I thank for the pleasure of being part of my life. Those who've gone are never forgotten but are sadly missed.

Tirus - St. Swithin - 15hh Chestnut Gelding with quarter trotter.
My first horse. A brilliant showjumper who'd jump anything he was pointed at and who taught me everything. A brilliant horse. My friend.
If ever a horse could read your mind, it was him! We were too alike.
Bold, determined and arrogant. Like me!
A great friend - 'Equine Soul mate' - and forever missed.

Fred - High Flyer - 16hh Light Chestnut Anglo-Arab Gelding.
Amazingly fast! Lovely chap with warm kind temperament who was forever getting his pink nose kissed!
Would come to a whistle and lead the pack home! Sad loss.

Goldie - Berkeley's Fools Gold - 15.3hh Chestnut Anglo-Arab Gelding.
Stunning looks and great character. Playful, kind and gentle.
Show horse, hack, hunter and friend.
He'd follow you around the field like a dog!
My 'Thinking Horse' upon whose back, when out hacking, I came upon many great ideas and plots. Thank you P.J.

Splodgie - Casanova - 15hh Welsh Section D / Cross Black Gelding. Brilliant character, famous for letting himself out from his paddock, walking back down a lane and into his stable. Funny horse with great temperament. Wonderful life until his early thirties. Lovely chap!

Meg - 11.2hh Welsh Black Mare. Great little driving pony whose company was sadly too short-lived. Lost too young through illness, but we tried our best and did all we could. Lovely nature and wonderful character.

Samson - The Colonel - 12.2hh Grey Welsh Section Gelding. Amazing pony. Owned from six months until sad death 27 years later. Gymkhana and show jumping, he did it all. Great character. Best friend & stable mate of Goldie.

Cirrus - Silver Cirrus - 16hh Flea-bitten Grey Mare.
Ex-Steeplechaser, and before joining us, was a mother of four foals! Lovely lady, great jumper and fine ride, with whom I shared many enjoyable years. Died aged 30 years. Forever miss my 'Girlfriend!'

Tess - Contessa - 15hh Black Roan Cob Mare. An amazing horse with stunning looks. 'Head like a Duchess & an arse like a Cook.' The true all-rounder. Winning Show Cob, Hunter, Driving Horse and Hack. In addition to being a wonderful friend and companion. Loved a pat and a cuddle and always received many. Very sadly missed.

Bert - Beezer the Geezer - 17hh Black Irish Draught Cross Gelding. Wonderful horse. Stunning looks and amazing cool temperament. True gentleman and gentle giant, but also with a cheeky fun side. Eventing, Dressage, Showing and former Whipper-In's horse - he did the lot! Loved by everyone and a real pleasure to own. Never forgotten.

Bonnie - The Moo - 15.1hh Skewbald Standardbred Mare. Exactly like the character in Horsewater! Beautiful stunning horse, but only accepts one person (me) to look after her. Amazingly clever character.
Brilliant driving horse, she's truly seen it all. Road-raced with Travellers in her earlier days, spent a year pulling Landau's on the seafront at Great Yarmouth, before joining us. Competed in Driving Trials and used for pleasure driving. You can look, but please don't touch. I bite - hard!

Ted - Lord Chumley - 16hh Palomino Irish Sports Horse. Stunningly beautiful horse and he knows it! Youngster with a warm but slightly naughty and cheeky nature. Funny chap, but clever. Most recent member of the family with lots still to do and learn, but coming along very well.

ABOUT THE AUTHOR

Gary Daynes lives in a village close to the Norfolk Broads in England. A stunning area of open waterways and rivers, famous for being very flat!

Born and bred in Norfolk, he's been a Designer most of his professional life, working in a varied range of creative fields; from mechanical engineering and creative product design, to architectural design and much more in-between.

He has a great imagination and dark sense of humour, having experienced all the good and bad this world has to offer and can throw at him - and more.

Introduced to horses in his late teens, he has since become a lifetime horseman, owning many horses and taking part in most forms of riding. From hacking to hunting, showjumping to showing, and has even ridden in a charity horse race around Fakenham Racecourse in Norfolk.
He shares his world with his family, dogs and horses, still enjoying a wide range of equestrian activities, including carriage driving and schooling.

Spite! was his first novel, a fast-paced, dark thriller, with his second being the even more darker chilling thriller about a serial killer, Luby.
Horsewater is his third, based upon a theme he loves, horse, but there are many more already laying in the nest, just waiting to be hatched!

Boxing Hare Publishing

www.boxingharepublishing.com

Spite!

Gary James Daynes

What would you do out of Spite?

If Mark Davis was vain, he'd have said he was perfect.
But Mark was flawless, so luckily vanity wasn't
a condition from which he suffered.

Mark Davis was a winner - career focussed and destined for the top of the corporate ladder - no matter who or what got in his way. Including down-trodden wife Vicki. And she knew it too. She knew her place in his life. Everything was secondary to Mark; who knew what he wanted and usually got it. The baby Vicki badly wanted could wait. Until he decided it would fit into his plans.

However the 'Gods of Planning and Ambition' had smirks on their faces, with other ideas planned for Mark Davis.
Within a few days his perfectly ordered life begins to rapidly fall apart, with horrific consequences for all.

Paranoid people think someone is out to get them. Mark wasn't paranoid. He knew someone was out to get him.

As Mark's life rapidly goes from bad to worse, in a fast-moving and twisting plot, laced throughout with black humour, grim brutality and non-stop action, he desperately tries to discover who has shattered his once perfect world. And more importantly – why?

Spite! is a fast-paced, dark and twisting psychological thriller, which takes the reader at speed page by page through a range of emotions to finally learn what some people will do simply out of Spite!

Luby

Gary James Daynes

Who's been in your home lately? - Do you really know?

Carl Luby is a clever and witty double-glazing salesman. Whilst charming customers with his slick sales presentations, ensuring his clients get the best deal and he gets the biggest commission, he also hides a dark secret. Unknown to those whose homes he's warmly invited into, Luby is a brutal and vicious woman-hating killer.

Whilst surveying the client's home, he's evaluating the means of entry for when he'll return to attack the selected victim, determining exactly how and where they'll be killed.

The fast-paced, dark and twisting plot is mixed with tension and scenes of extreme violence, with the main protagonist - Luby - being written in the First Person.

Thus the reader experiences the thoughts and emotions of a serial killer as he carefully plans each rape and murder, permitting you to see inside the cruel mind of a serial killer. Then again, as he commits his brutal crimes, and in the aftermath, where he cleverly sets up innocent people for the murders he's committed, destroying multiple lives.

Luby's nemesis is D.I. Paul Munroe, who is investigating a series of horrific murders, where woman are tortured and murdered, but there is no clear link or connection; each woman being murdered in the safety of their own home.

Luby is a cold, chilling, brutal and sexually explicit novel, but laced throughout with aspects of dark humour, as you see inside the cruel and calculating mind of a serial killer.

Be warned - Luby is not one for the children!

Check out the Boxing Hare Publishing website
for these fast-paced, chilling novels
and a wide range of other great publications.

Printed in Great Britain
by Amazon

57369840R00425